THE
MEMOIRS
OF
CLEOPATRA

ALSO BY MARGARET GEORGE

The Autobiography of Henry VIII
Mary Queen of Scotland and the Isles

Margaret George

The Memoirs of Cleopatra

MACMILLAN

First published 1997 by St Martin's Press, Inc.
175 Fifth Avenue, New York, NY 10010, USA

This edition published 1997 by Macmillan
an imprint of Macmillan Publishers Ltd
25 Eccleston Place, London SW1W 9NF
and Basingstoke

Associated companies throughout the world

ISBN 0 333 71547 0 (Hardback)
ISBN 0 333 36719 6 (Trade Paperback)

1 3 5 7 9 8 6 4 2

A CIP catalogue record for this book is available from
the British Library.

Printed and bound in Great Britain by
Mackays of Chatham PLC, Chatham, Kent

MY THANKS TO:

My editor, Hope Dellon, who, with insight and humor, helps fashion the potter's clay of first drafts into finished works; my father, Scott George, who introduced me to the Principle of the Ninety-Nine Soldiers; my sister, Rosemary George, who has Antony's high sense of fun; Lynn Courtenay, who patiently scours obscure references in search of classical tidbits; Bob Feibel, who helped me refight the Battle of Actium; Erik Gray, for his help in the mysteries of Latin usage (any remaining errors are mine); and our old pet snake, Julius, who for sixteen years has taught me the way of serpents.

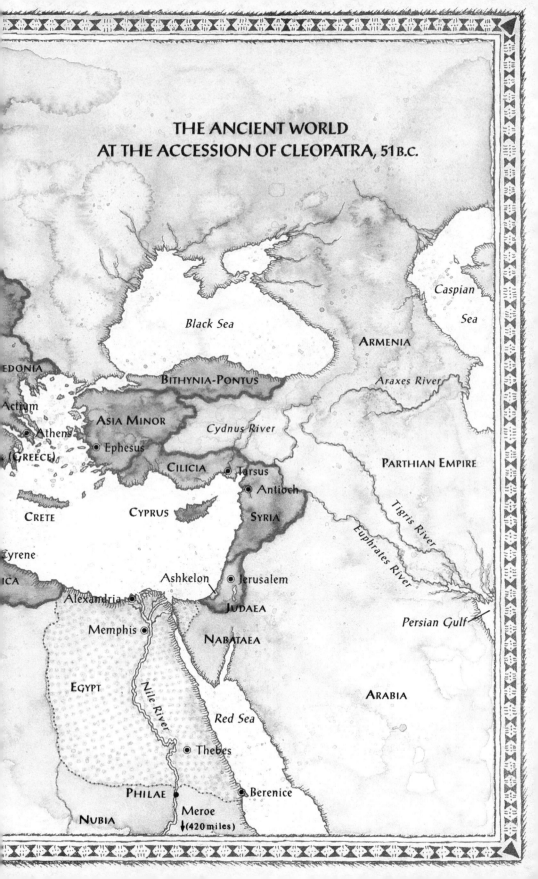

THE ANCIENT WORLD
AT THE ACCESSION OF CLEOPATRA, 51 B.C.

Caspian
Sea

Black Sea

ARMENIA

EDONIA

Araxes River

BITHYNIA-PONTUS

Actium

ASIA MINOR

Cydnus River

PARTHIAN EMPIRE

Athens

Ephesus

(GREECE)

CILICIA   Tarsus

Antioch

Tigris River

CRETE   CYPRUS

SYRIA

Euphrates River

Cyrene

ICA

Ashkelon   Jerusalem

Alexandria

JUDAEA

Persian Gulf

Memphis

NABATAEA

EGYPT   Nile River

ARABIA

Red Sea

Thebes

PHILAE

Berenice

NUBIA   Meroe
↓(420 miles)

To Isis, my mother, my refuge, my compassionate companion and keeper all the days of my life, from their beginning until it pleases you that they come to their end, I commit these writings, a record of my days on earth. You, who granted them to me, will guard and preserve them, and look kindly and with favor upon their author, your daughter. For as you gave me the formless days—and I marked them with my deeds, and thereby am truly their owner—so I have recorded my life that I might offer it entire and without falsehood to you. You must judge all the works of my hand and the worthiness of my heart—both the outer deeds and the inner being.

I submit them to you, praying you to be merciful, saving my accomplishments, and the very memory of them, from the destruction of my enemies.

I am the seventh Cleopatra of the royal house of Ptolemy, the Queen, the Lady of the Two Lands, *Thea Philopator*, the Goddess Who Loves Her Father, *Thea Neotera*, the Younger Goddess; the daughter of Ptolemy *Neos Dionysus*, the New Dionysus.

I am mother to Ptolemy Caesar, Alexander Helios, Cleopatra Selene, and Ptolemy Philadelphos.

I was wife to Gaius Julius Caesar and Marcus Antonius.

Preserve my words, and grant them sanctuary, I beseech you.

THE FIRST SCROLL

1

Warmth. Wind. Dancing blue waters, and the sound of waves. I see, hear, feel them all still. I even taste the sting of the salt against my lips, where the fine, misty spray coats them. And closer even than that, the lulling, drowsy smell of my mother's skin by my nose, where she holds me against her bosom, her hand making a sunshade across my forehead to shield my eyes. The boat is rocking gently, and my mother is rocking me as well, so I sway to a double rhythm. It makes me very sleepy, and the sloshing of the water all around me makes a blanket of sound, wrapping me securely. I am held safely, cradled in love and watchfulness. I remember. I remember . . .

And then . . . the memory is torn apart, upended, overturned, as the boat must have been. My mother gone, and I tumbling through the air, caught by other arms, rough ones that grip so hard around my middle that I can hardly breathe. And the splashing . . . I can still hear the splashing, hear the brief, surprised cries.

They say I could not possibly, that I was not yet three years old when my mother drowned in the harbor, *terrible accident, and on such a calm day, how did it ever happen? was the boat tampered with? did someone push? no, she just tripped and fell in while trying to stand up, and you know she couldn't swim, no, we didn't know that, until it was too late, why then did she go out on the water so often? She liked it, poor soul, poor Queen, liked the sound and the colors . . .*

A bright blue ball seems to envelop all that terror, that thrashing and the arcs of water flying all over, a sweeping circle, and the screams of the ladies on the boat. They say that someone dived over to help and was dragged down, too, and that two died instead of one. They also say that I clawed and kicked and tried to fling myself after my mother, screaming in fear and loss, but my strong-armed nurse, who had caught me, held me fast.

I remember being pushed onto my back and being held flat, staring up at the underside of a canopy where dazzling blue water was reflected, and unable to throw off my captor's hands.

No one comforts me, as one would expect someone to do for a frightened child. They are too concerned with preventing me from escaping. They say I cannot remember that either, but I do. How exposed I feel, how naked on that boat bench, torn from my mother's arms and now forcibly held down, as the boat hurries for shore.

Some days later I am taken to a large, echoing room, where light seems to come in from all sides and wind sweeps through, too. It is a room, but it feels as if it is also outdoors—a special sort of room, the room for someone who is not a person but a god. It is the temple of Isis, and the nurse is leading me to a huge statue—pulling me, rather. I remember digging in my heels and having to be almost dragged across the shiny stone floor.

The base of the statue is enormous. I can barely see over the top of it, to where two white feet seem to be, and a figure standing above it. The face is lost in shadow.

"Put your flowers at her feet," the nurse is saying, tugging at my fist with the flowers I am clutching.

I don't want to let go of them, don't want to put them there.

"This is Isis," the nurse says gently. "Look at her face. She is watching you. She will take care of you. She is your mother now."

Is she? I try to see the face, but it is so high and far away. It does not look like my mother's face.

"Give her the flowers," the nurse prompts.

Slowly I lift my hand and put my little offering on the pedestal at the end of my reach. I look up again, hoping to see the statue smile, and I imagine that I do.

So, Isis, it is thus, and on that day, I became your daughter.

My mother the late Queen's name was Cleopatra, and I was proud to bear her name. But I would have been proud of it in any case, for it is a great name in the history of our family, going all the way back to the sister of Alexander the Great, to whom we Ptolemies are related. It means "Glory to her Ancestry," and all my life and reign I have tried to fulfill that promise. All that I have done, I have done to preserve my heritage and Egypt.

All the women in our line were named Cleopatra, Berenice, or Arsinoe. Those names, too, went all the way back to Macedonia, where our family had its origins. Thus my two older sisters received the names of Cleopatra (yes, there were two of us) and Berenice, and my younger sister the name of Arsinoe.

Younger sister . . . there were others after me. For the King needed to marry again, and soon after the untimely death of his Queen Cleopatra, he took a new wife, and she straightway produced my sister Arsinoe. Later she gave birth to the two little boys to whom I was briefly "married." Then she died, leaving Father a widower again. This time he did not remarry.

I did not care for my father's new wife, nor for my sister Arsinoe, who was only a little more than three years younger than I. From her earliest days she was sly and deceitful, a whiner and complainer. It did not help that she was also quite beautiful—the kind of child that everyone exclaims over, and asks, "And *where* did she come by those eyes?" and not merely out of politeness. It gave her an arrogance from the cradle, as she saw it not as a gift to be appreciated but as a power to be used.

My sister Cleopatra was some ten years older than I, and Berenice eight. Fortunate sisters, to have had our mother for that many years longer than I! Not that they seemed to be grateful for it. The eldest was a dour, drooping sort of creature; I fear I cannot even recall her very well. And Berenice— she was a veritable bull of a woman, big-shouldered, raw-voiced, with wide, flat feet that made even normal walking sound like stamping. There was nothing about her to recall our ancestor, the delicate-featured Berenice II, who had reigned with Ptolemy III two hundred years earlier and passed into legend as a strong-willed beauty to whom court poets dedicated their works. No, the red-faced, snorting Berenice would never inspire such literary out- pourings.

I basked in the knowledge that I was my father's favorite. Do not ask me how children know these things, but they do, no matter how well parents try to hide it. Perhaps it was because I found the other Cleopatra and Berenice to be so peculiar that I could not imagine anyone being partial to them rather than to me. But later, even after Arsinoe with all her beauty came along, I retained the leading place in my father's heart. I know now it was because I was the only one who showed any concern for him in return.

I must admit it, honestly but with reluctance: The rest of the world (including his own children) found Father either comical or pitiful—perhaps both. He was a handsome, slight man, with a diffident and dreamy manner that could turn quickly to nervousness when he felt threatened. People blamed him both for what he himself was—an artist by inclination, a flute player, and a dancer—and for the situation he had inherited. The first was his own doing, but the second was an unfortunate legacy. It was not his fault that by the time he managed to climb onto the throne, it was practically in the jaws of Rome, necessitating any number of undignified postures to retain it. These included groveling, flattering, jettisoning his brother, paying colossal bribes, and entertaining the hated potential conquerors at his very court. It did not make him loved. Nor did it make him secure. Was it any wonder that he sought escape with the wine and music of Dionysus, his patron god? But the more he sought it, the more disdain he reaped.

Father's Magnificent Banquet for Pompey the Great: I was almost seven then, and eager finally to see Romans, *real* Romans, *the* Romans (that is, the dangerous ones, not the harmless merchants or scholars who showed up in Alexandria on personal business). I pestered Father to let me attend, knowing well how to persuade him, since he was susceptible to almost everything I asked, within reason.

"I want to see them," I told him. "The famous Pompey—what does he look like?"

Everyone had trembled about Pompey, since he had just swooped down on our part of the world. First he had put down a major rebellion in Pontus, then he had continued into Syria and taken the remnants of the empire of the Seleucids, turning it into a Roman province.

A Roman province. The whole world was turning into a Roman province, so it seemed. For a long time, Rome—which was located far away, on the other side of the Mediterranean—had confined itself to its own area. Then gradually it had extended its grasp in all directions, like the arms of an octopus. It grabbed Spain to the west, and Carthage to the south, and then Greece to the east, swelling and swelling. And the larger it swelled, the more its appetite grew to feed its bulk.

Little kingdoms were just morsels to it—tidbits like Pergamon and Caria, easily swallowed. The ancient realms of Alexander would be more satisfying, stave off its hunger better.

Once there had been three kingdoms carved out of Alexander's domains, ruled by his three generals and their descendants: Macedonia, Syria, and Egypt. Then two. Then Syria fell and there was only one: Egypt. There were reports that the Romans now felt the time was ripe to annex Egypt as well, and that Pompey himself was particularly keen on it. So Father had decided to do everything in his power to buy Pompey off. He sent cavalry units to help Pompey in crushing his next victim, our nearest neighbor, Judaea.

Yes, it was shameful. I admit it. No wonder his own people hated him. But would they rather have fallen to the Romans? His choices were those of a desperate man, between bad and worse. He chose bad. Would they have preferred worse?

"He's a big, strapping man," Father said. "Not unlike your sister Berenice!" We laughed together at that, conspirators. Then the laughter died. "He's frightening," he added. "Anyone with that much power is frightening, no matter how charming his manners."

"I want to see him," I insisted.

"The banquet will go on for hours—it will be loud, and hot, and boring for you. There's no point to it. Perhaps when you are older—"

"I hope you never have to entertain them again, so this is my only chance," I pointed out to him. "And if they *do* ever come here again, it won't be under pleasant circumstances. No lavish banquets then."

He looked at me oddly. Now I know it was because it was a strange way for a seven-year-old to speak, but then I was just afraid he was displeased with me and was going to refuse me permission.

"Very well," he finally said. "But I expect you to do more than just stare. You must be on your best behavior; we have to convince him that both Egypt and Rome are well served by our remaining on the throne."

"We?" Surely he did not mean . . . or did he? I was only the third child, although at that point I had no brothers.

"We Ptolemies," he clarified. But he had seen the hope that had briefly flared up in me.

My First Banquet: Every royal child should be required to write a rhetorical exercise with that title. For banquets play such an inordinately large part in our lives; they are the stage where we act out our reigns. You start out dazzled by them, as I was then, only to find that after a few years they all run together. But this one will remain forever engraved in my mind.

There was the (soon to become dully routine) act of dressing, the first stage in the ritual. Each princess had her own wardrobe mistress, but mine was actually my old nurse, who knew little about clothes. She outfitted me in the first dress from the stack; her main concern was that it be freshly laundered and ironed, which it was.

"Now you must sit still, so it won't wrinkle," she said, smoothing out the skirt. I remember that it was blue, and rather stiff. "Linen is so easy to wrinkle! None of that romping, none of that acting like a boy that you sometimes do, not tonight! Tonight you must behave like a princess."

"And how is that?" I felt as encased as a mummy in its wrappings, which were also usually of linen. Perhaps going to the banquet was not such a good idea after all.

"With dignity. When someone speaks to you, you turn your head around, *slowly*. Like this." She gave a demonstration, letting her head swivel smoothly around, then lowering her eyelids. "And you look down, modestly." She paused. "And you answer in a sweet, low voice. Do *not* say, '*What?*' Only barbarians do that. The Romans might well do it," she said grimly. "But you must not follow their example!"

She fussed with my collar a little, straightening it. "And should anyone be so rude as to mention an unpleasant subject—like taxes or plague or vermin—you must not reply. It is unfit to discuss such things at a banquet."

"What if I see a scorpion about to sting someone? Suppose, right on Pompey's shoulder, there's a bright red scorpion, its stinger raised—can I tell him?" I must learn all the rules. "Wouldn't it be rude not to? Even though it's an unpleasant subject?"

She looked confused. "Well, I suppose—" She snorted. "There won't *be* a scorpion on Pompey's shoulder! Honestly—you are an exasperating child, always thinking of something like that." But she said it affectionately. "At least we should hope there isn't a scorpion to bother Pompey, or anything else to ruin his good mood."

"Shouldn't I wear a diadem?" I said.

"No," she said. "Where did you get *that* idea? You aren't a queen."

"Aren't there any for princesses? We should be able to wear *something* on our heads. Romans have those laurel wreaths, don't they? And so do athletes."

She cocked her head, as she did when she was thinking hard. "I think the best ornament for a young girl is her hair. And you have such pretty hair. Why spoil it with anything else?"

She was always very attentive to my hair, rinsing it in scented rainwater and combing it with ivory combs. She taught me to be proud of it. But I longed to wear something special tonight. "But there should be something to mark us out as the royal family. My sisters—"

"Your sisters are older, and it is appropriate for them. When you are seventeen, or even fifteen like Berenice, you can wear such things."

"I suppose you are right." I pretended to agree. I let her comb my hair and pull it back with a clasp. Then I said, "Now that my forehead is so bare—not even a fillet?" A small, discreet one, a narrow band—yes, that would be fine with me.

She laughed. "Child, child, child! Why are you not content to let things rest?" But I could see that she was going to relent. "Perhaps a very small gold one. But I want you to use it as a reminder, the whole evening, that you *are* a princess."

"Of course," I promised. "I won't do anything rude, and even if a Roman belches or spills or steals a gold spoon by hiding it in his napkin, I'll pretend I don't see."

"You may well see some spoon-stealing," she admitted. "They are so hungry for gold, they drool at its sight. It's a good thing the artworks in the palace are too big to be tucked into the fold of a toga, or some of them would be missing come morning."

I had been in the banqueting hall before, but only when it was empty. The enormous chamber, which stretched from one side to the other of a palace building (for there were many palace buildings on the royal grounds) and opened onto steps overlooking the inner harbor, had always seemed like a shiny cavern to me. Its polished floors reflected my image when I ran across it, and the rows of pillars showed me passing. High above, the ceiling was lost in shadow.

But tonight . . . the cavern was ablaze with light, so much so that for the first time I could see, far above, the cedar beams overlaid with gold that ran the length of the ceiling. And the noise! The sound of a crowd—which was to become so familiar to me—assaulted my ears like a blow. The whole chamber was packed with people, so many people that I could only stop and stare at them.

We—the royal family—were standing at the top of a small set of steps before entering the room, and I wanted to take my father's hand and ask him if all the thousand guests were here. But he was standing in front of me, the place beside him occupied by my stepmother, and there was no opportunity.

We waited for the trumpets to sound, announcing our entrance. I watched intently, trying to see what Romans looked like. Which ones *were* the Romans? About half the people were wearing the common sort of loose-flowing garments, and some of those men had beards. But the others . . . they were clean-shaven, with short hair, and they were wearing either a voluminous sort of draped cape (which looked like a bedsheet to me), or else military uniforms, made up of breastplates and little skirts of leather strips. Obviously those were Romans. The others must be Egyptians and Greeks from Alexandria.

The trumpets blasted, but from the other end of the hall. Father did not stir, and soon I saw why: The trumpets were heralding the entrance of Pompey and his aides. As they filed toward the center of the chamber, I beheld the full regalia of a Roman general of the highest order, in which the plain breastplate of the soldier was replaced by one of pure gold, decorated with artwork. His cloak, too, was purple, not red, and he wore some sort of special enclosed boots. It was altogether splendid to look upon.

Pompey himself? I was disappointed to see that he was just a man, with a rather bland face. There was nothing about him as dazzling as his uniform. On each side of him were other officers, their faces harder and more set than his, and they served as a frame to set him apart.

Now a second set of trumpets sounded, and it was our turn to descend, so that Father could greet his guests and welcome them officially. All eyes were upon him as he carefully stepped down, his royal robe trailing behind him. I made sure not to trip on it.

The two men stood face-to-face; Father was so much shorter and smaller! Next to the husky Pompey, he looked almost frail.

"You are most welcome to Alexandria, most noble Imperator Gnaeus Pompeius Magnus. We greet you, and salute your victories, and declare that you honor us by your presence here this evening," said Father. He had a pleasant voice, and normally it carried well, but tonight it lacked power. He must be terribly, terribly nervous—and of course that made me nervous, too, and nervous for him as well.

Pompey gave some reply, but his Greek was so accented I could hardly understand him. Perhaps Father did; at least he pretended to. More exchanges followed, many introductions on both sides. I was presented—or was Pompey presented to me? Which was the proper order?—and I smiled and nodded to him. I knew that princesses—let alone kings and queens!—never bowed to anyone else, but I hoped it would not offend him. He probably did not know all these things, being from Rome, where they had no kings.

Instead of his previous response—a tepid smile—he suddenly bent down and stared right into my face, his round blue eyes just level with mine.

"What an enchanting child!" he said, in that odd Greek. "Do the children of kings attend these things from the cradle?" He turned to Father, who looked embarrassed. I could tell he regretted allowing me to come; he did not wish to do anything that might call unflattering attention to us.

"Not until the age of seven," he improvised quickly. I wasn't quite seven yet, but Pompey would never know. "We believe that that age is the portal to understanding. . . ." Tactfully he indicated that the banquet tables were waiting, in the adjoining, almost equally large, chamber, and steered the Roman commander in that direction.

Beside me, my older sisters were smirking; they seemed to find my discomfiture amusing.

" 'What an *enchanting* child,' " Berenice mimicked.

"Look, there's another one," the elder Cleopatra said, indicating a boy who was watching us pass. "The banquet is turning into a children's party!"

I was surprised to see him, and I wondered why he was there. He looked completely out of place. Would Pompey stop and single him out, too? But luckily he seemed more interested in getting to the food in the next room. Everyone said Romans were most fond of eating.

The boy, who was dressed as a Greek and holding the hand of a bearded, Greek-looking man, must be an Alexandrian. He was studying us the way I had studied the Romans. Perhaps we were a curiosity to him. Our family did not make many public appearances in the streets of Alexandria, for fear of riots.

We walked slowly, and—I hoped—majestically past him, and entered the transformed room where we would dine. Some late afternoon rays of sun were stabbing almost horizontally across the chamber, just at the level of the tables, where a forest of gold goblets and dishes was waiting. It seemed like magic to me, lighted up like that, and it must have to the Romans, too, because they were all laughing with delight, and pointing.

Pointing! How rude! But then . . . I had been warned to expect it.

Pompey was not pointing, nor were his companions. He did not even look particularly interested; or if he was, he hid it well.

We took our places; all the adults were to recline, while only the lesser folk would sit on stools—and there were very few lesser folk present. My nurse had told me that in Rome both women and children were relegated to the stools, but neither the Queen nor the older princesses would ever tolerate that here. I tried to figure out how many couches were needed for a thousand people to recline, and knew it was over three hundred—and yet they fitted into this enormous room, with ample room left over for the servers to pass between them easily with their trays and dishes.

Father was motioning me to a stool, while Pompey and his companions spread themselves on the couches clustered for the highest of the high. Was I to be the only one on a stool? I might as well have worn a huge sign calling attention to myself. I watched while my sisters and stepmother settled themselves, daintily twitching their gowns and tucking one foot under the other. How I wished I were only a little older, and could be on a couch!

I felt myself to be so conspicuous that I wondered how I would ever get through the meal. Just then Father ordered the bearded man with the boy to join us; I saw him sending for them. I knew he was doing it to alleviate my embarrassment; he was always very solicitous of others, seeming to sense their distress even if they did not voice it.

"Ah! My dear Meleagros," Father addressed the man. "Why not seat yourself where you can learn what you wish?"

The man nodded, seemingly unperturbed at being assigned to our exalted midst. He must be a philosopher; they were supposed to take all things with equanimity. And of course the beard confirmed it. He propelled his son forward, pushing him before him, and a stool was quickly brought for him. Now there were two of us. I suppose Father thought that would make it easier. Actually, it just drew more attention.

"Meleagros is one of our scholars," explained Father. "He is at—"

"Yes, the Museion," said a square-faced Roman. "That's where you keep the tame scholars and scientists, right?" Without waiting for an answer, he poked his companion in the ribs. "They live there, but then they have to work for the King. Whenever he wants to know something—oh, say, how deep the Nile is near Memphis—he can just summon someone to tell him, even in the middle of the night! Right?"

Meleagros stiffened; he looked as though he wanted to smack the Roman. "Not exactly," he said. "It is true that we are supported by the generosity of the Crown, but our King would never be so thoughtless as to make such outrageous demands on us."

"In fact," said Father, "I have brought him here in order that he might question *you*, Varro. Meleagros is most interested in unusual plants and animals, and I understand that several of you have been observing and collecting near the Caspian Sea—after you ran Mithridates off, that is."

"Yes," the man called Varro admitted. "We were hoping to learn more about a reputed trade route to India by way of the Caspian Sea. But Mithridates was not the only one to be run off—so were we, by deadly snakes. I never saw so many—all different sorts, too. Of course, what can you expect, at the edge of the known world like that—"

"The geography there is puzzling," one of the other men said, a Greek-speaker. Someone addressed him as Theophanes. "It is difficult to map—"

"You have maps?" Meleagros looked interested.

"Newly drawn. But perhaps you would like to see them?"

And so on. The polite conversation continued. The boy by my side was silent, just looking. What *was* he doing here?

The wine flowed, and the talking grew louder, more animated. The Romans forgot to speak Greek and lapsed back into Latin. What an odd, monotonous sound it had if you did not understand it. And I had not studied it. There was little to recommend it; nothing important was written in it, and there were no famous speeches in it. Other languages, such as Hebrew, Syriac, and Aramaic, were much more useful. And lately I had even decided to try to learn Egyptian, so that I could go anywhere in my country and understand the people. But Latin? That could wait.

I watched my sisters, who were hardly bothering to hide their disdain for the Romans; when the conversation fell back into Latin, Berenice and Cleopatra just rolled their eyes. I was worried about it; what if the Romans saw them? I thought we were supposed to be careful about giving offense.

Suddenly trumpets sounded and an array of servers appeared, as if from out of the walls, and snatched the gold vessels away, replacing them with more gold vessels, even more heavily engraved and jeweled than the first set. The Romans just stared—as I supposed they were meant to.

But what was the point? Why was Father so anxious to show off our wealth? Would it not make them want to appropriate it? This confused me. I saw Pompey looking dreamily at the enormous cup before him, as if he were visualizing melting it down.

And then I heard the word *Caesar*, and it was linked with something to do with greed and needing money. I thought Pompey was saying to Father—I strained very hard to overhear—that Caesar (whoever he was) had wanted to take Egypt and make it into a Roman province, since it had been willed to Rome. . . .

"But the will was false," Father was saying, and his voice sounded as high as a eunuch's. "Ptolemy Alexander had no right even to make such a bequest—"

"Ha, ha, ha!" Pompey was saying. "That depends on who is interpreting—"

"So you are intending to be a scientist, too?" Theophanes was speaking to the boy next to me, politely. "Is that why you came with your father?"

Curses! Now I could not hear what Father and Pompey were saying, and it was terribly important. I tried to blank out the voice right beside me, but it was hopeless.

"No," the boy said, his voice drowning out the ones farther away. "Although I am interested in botany and in animals, I am more interested in the most complex animal of all: man. I wish to study him, therefore I will be a physician."

"And what is your name?" asked Theophanes as if he were really interested. "And your age?"

"Olympos," he said, "and I am nine. Ten next summer!"

Oh, be quiet! I ordered him in my mind.

But Theophanes kept asking him questions. Did he live at the Museion, too? Was he interested in any special sort of medicine? What about *pharmakon*, drugs? That was a way to combine knowledge of plants and medicine.

"Well, yes," Olympos was saying. "I was hoping I could ask some of you about the 'mad honey.' That's really why I came tonight. Or persuaded my father to bring me, I should say."

Theophanes lost his smile. "The mad honey—*meli maenomenon*—don't ask Pompey about it. It grieves him still. You see, the area around the Black Sea where Mithridates held sway—it's known for its poisonous honey. Some of his allies put out combs of it near our route—our soldiers helped themselves, and we lost many. Many." He shook his head.

"But why did you eat it, if you knew it was poisonous?"

"We didn't know; we only found out afterward. It seems the bees feed on azaleas there, and there is something in the nectar that poisons the honey. The plant itself is poisonous; people in the area call it 'goat-bane,' 'lamb-kill,' and 'cattle-destroyer.' That's a clue we shouldn't have missed."

"But what about the bees? Does it kill them, too?" Olympos asked.

"And Caesar tried to get a measure passed in the Senate," Pompey was saying, "so that Egypt—"

"You, too, friend!" Father was wagging his finger, as if it was all just too, too funny, and not threatening at all, and Pompey his great and good comrade, instead of a vulture trying to eat us.

Pompey was smiling disarmingly. "True, true, but—"

"No, the bees are immune," said Theophanes.

"The good honey is all mixed up with the bad." Varro had joined the discussion. There was now no way that the faraway conversation could prevail over three close voices; I might as well give up trying to listen. "It seems that only part of the comb can be poisonous."

"But doesn't it look or taste different?" asked Olympos. He sounded so solemn, so professional.

"It can be a little redder, or more runny," said Theophanes. "But not so markedly that it would always warn us."

"Honey made in early spring," added Varro. "And when it strikes—*then* you know! The soldiers were overtaken with tingling numbness, then started seeing whirling lights and tunnels, they swooned, then started vomiting and became delirious—that's what the ones who recovered described later." He paused dramatically. "Their pulses slowed, and they turned blue."

"Oooh." Olympos looked impressed at last. He seemed very difficult to impress, or even ruffle.

"Did you know that Xenophon's troops fell victim to it, too? Four hundred years ago! Thousands collapsed. In the same area. We historians busy ourselves with such data," Varro was saying. "Now that I'm here, I'd like to consult some of the scrolls in the famous Library. Where supposedly all written knowledge resides!" He shouted over at Father. "Isn't it so? Don't you have a half-million volumes in the Library?" he bellowed.

Father broke off his conversation with Pompey—the conversation I was longing to hear, although I did find the "mad honey" interesting. But not as interesting as the will giving Egypt to Rome. Had one of our ancestors actually done that? Isis forbid!

"Eh?" he said, cupping his hand over an ear.

"I said, don't you have half a million scrolls here in the Library?" yelled Varro.

My sisters rolled their eyes again at more Roman boorishness.

"So they say," said Father.

"Yes, it's true," said Olympos's father. "Every manuscript ever written—or that a Ptolemy managed to lay hands on, rather."

"Yes, we kept the originals and sent the owners away with copies!" said Father.

"Ah, the glories of Alexandria," said Pompey, considering them. He smiled.

"Shall we arrange a tour?" asked Father. "Tomorrow, if the most noble Imperator would like?"

Before Pompey could reply, another blare of trumpets sounded, and the gold service was changed yet again, with much ceremonial clanging and clatter. At each round, the implements became more ornate.

The eating proper could begin, and it did, with a profusion of dishes totally unfamiliar to me—certainly they were not the fare even royal children were served. *Sea urchins in mint . . . baked eel in chard . . . Zeus-acorns . . . mushrooms and sweet nettles . . . Phrygian ewe's-milk cheese . . . Rhodian raisins . . . and fat, sweet dessert grapes*—along with honey-cakes. Unfortunate choice! Pompey and all the rest pushed them aside; the sight and smell of honey were not pleasing to them now.

"But this is from Cos!" Father assured them, in vain.

And there was wine, wine, wine, different for each food—Egyptian red and white, the famous apple-scented wine of Thasos, and, the sweetest of all, Pramnian.

"It's made from partially dried grapes," explained Varro, smacking his lips as he downed it. "That concentrates the sweetness, so . . . ummm . . ." More lip-smacking.

Since my wine was so diluted, I could barely tell the difference among all these, but I nodded anyway.

Would that Father's wine had been equally diluted! For, in his nervousness, he drained cup after cup of it, and soon was wearing a strange half-smile and leaning overfamiliarly toward Pompey. And then—I shall never forget it!—he suddenly decided to call for his pipes and play. Yes! To entertain the Romans, as he said. And because he was the King, there was no one to say, No, stop it! You must not!

I longed to jump up and do it, but I was frozen in my place. I had to watch while his steward brought him the pipes, and while he lurched off the couch and made his way unsteadily to an open space where he could perform.

I watched in horror, acute embarrassment, and shame. The Romans were staring, dumbfounded. Father took a deep breath to fill his lungs and then started playing his melodies. Although the sound was not loud, such a deep hush fell over the entire hall that every note quavered on the air.

Olympos turned and gave me a pitying look, but it was kind, not condescending. I wanted to shut my eyes and not have to behold the painful sight of the King performing like a street musician—or a monkey for its master.

It was the wine that had done this! I vowed, in that instant, never to bow to wine or let it overcome me—a vow I believe I have kept, although Dionysus and his grapes have caused me much grief nonetheless.

Suddenly one of the Romans at another couch began guffawing, and that had a ripple effect; soon even Pompey was laughing, and then the whole hall was roaring. Poor Father took it as approval and applause for himself, and even bowed. Then—oh, the shame of it!—he executed a little dance.

What had he said? *You must be on your best behavior; we have to convince him that both Egypt and Rome are well served by our remaining on the throne.* How could he have forgotten his own mission, and Egypt's danger? Was wine that strong?

As my father wove his way back to his place, Pompey patted the cushion, as if the King were a pet.

"The Romans feel dancing is degenerate," Olympos leaned over and whispered in my ear. "They have bad names for people who dance."

Why was he telling me this? To make me feel worse? "I know," I said coldly, although I did not.

We have to convince him that Egypt is well served by our remaining on the throne. We Ptolemies . . .

Berenice and Older Cleopatra were just staring; there was no help from those Ptolemies, either. Why did they not do something, say something, to offset it?

Tonight you must behave as a princess . . . with dignity. . . . What an enchanting child. . . .

Perhaps there was something I could do, something, anything. . . . Pompey had seemed to like me, had singled me out for his attention. . . .

I left the stool and walked over to him. He was leaning on one elbow, and as I came closer I could see that the wine had affected him, too. His eyes were a little unfocused, and he had a fixed smile on his face. A wide gold cuff gleamed on his forearm, and he was running his fingers over it.

"Imperator," I said, willing myself to feel the gold fillet on my forehead and remember that I was royal, "there is much more to Alexandria than a banqueting hall, or music. Tomorrow, in the daylight, let us show you its wonders: the Lighthouse, and Alexander's Tomb, and the Museion and Library. Would you like that?"

One side of his mouth twitched up as he gave a crooked smile. "An enchanting child," he repeated, as if that phrase were stuck in his brain. "Yes, yes, of course . . . and you will guide us?"

"My father will show you the Museion," Olympos suddenly volunteered, leaping to his feet. "And I personally know the Lighthouse master—"

Meleagros joined in, to help. "Yes, Varro was most interested in both the Library and the Museion. I will be honored to conduct you—"

Thus we all rushed in to save the King—and Egypt.

◁ 3 ▷

Alone in my chamber that night, my nurse having prepared me for sleep, all the lamps extinguished save one, I huddled under my covers, praying to you, Isis.

Help me now! I begged. *Tomorrow . . . tomorrow I have to try to erase what was done tonight.* And the truth was I had no idea of how to do it; I did not even know why I had suggested the excursion to begin with. What did it have to do with Pompey, with Father, with Egypt's fate? What could I, a child, hope to do? But I must try; and I enlisted the help of Isis, my mother, she who has all power. . . .

Shivering, I stole out of the bed and watched the glowing top of the Lighthouse, a sight that I had always found comforting. For as long as I could remember, the huge tower had stood, partially filling the view from my western window. I had grown up watching it change color with the day: pearly pink at dawn, stark white at heated midday, red at sunset, blue-purple at dusk, and finally, at night, a dark column with a blazing tip: the fire roaring inside, magnified by the great polished mirror in its lantern. It sat out on the end of its island, the Pharos—although it was an island no longer, since a long breakwater connected it to the mainland.

I had never actually been inside it, though. I was most curious to see how it worked. Its base was square; two-thirds of the way up it changed to octagonal, and beyond that it became circular. At the very top was a statue of Zeus Soter, which turned, following the sun; from just beneath Zeus shone out the marvelous beacon. Its mighty base was surrounded by a colonnade of marble, and to one side was a gracious temple of Isis Pharia.

Alexandria, being on the sea, has a winter. From December to February it is cold, with sea storms blowing in, sweeping the streets with salty spray. Ships do not put out to sea then, and the Lighthouse stands sentinel over empty seas and boats moored safely in our magnificent harbors. In the other seasons it presides over the enormous number of voyages that begin and end here; our two harbors can hold over a thousand ships.

Tomorrow we would try to amuse the Romans, to cajole and please them, the Lighthouse and I.

I awoke surprisingly eager for the venture. Partly that was because it was an opportunity for me to see things I was curious about. Although I was a royal princess, and one might think that I had the entire city of Alexandria open to me, I was kept confined, for the most part, to the grounds of the palace and all its many buildings. Visitors came from all over the world to admire our city, a vision in white marble glinting against the aquamarine of the Mediterranean, but we, the royal children, saw less of it than anyone else. Oh, what we saw from our vantage point was very lovely. Out of my window the first sight I beheld was the Lighthouse, which stood like a pale finger in the early dawn, the waves breaking around its base. Closer to me I saw the eastern harbor, rimmed by flights of broad steps that descended into the beckoning water, where you could wade and gather seashells. And within the palace grounds themselves, there was the small Temple of Isis overlooking the open sea, where the wind blew through its columns and whispered around the statue of Isis in her sanctuary.

Within the grounds, the gardeners brought forth a profusion of blooming flowers—red poppies, blue cornflowers, scarlet roses—which showed dazzlingly against the stark white of the buildings. Everywhere there were pools filled with blue and white lotus, so that the mingled perfume of all these flowers made its own peculiar and indescribable blend. We could call it *Scent of the Ptolemies*. If it could be bottled, it would fetch a high price in the bazaars, for it was both heady and refreshing at the same time: the fresh sea air kept the flower-perfume from growing too cloying.

Having been built over a long period of time, the palace buildings varied a great deal. The grandest of them had floors of onyx or alabaster, with walls of ebony. Inside was a feast of richness like a merchant's display: couches ornamented with jasper and carnelian, tables of carved ivory, footstools of citrus wood. Hangings of Tyrian purple, adorned with gold, hid the ebony walls—richness blotting out richness. The silks of the far east, by way of India, found their way to be draped over our chairs. And in the polished floors were reflected the slaves, who were selected for their physical beauty.

I should have had no need to go beyond these bounds, but when you are brought up around such things, they seem routine. What aroused my curiosity were the dwellings and people outside. We always want what is forbidden, off limits, exotic. To the young Princess Cleopatra, the ordinary was most alluring. Now I would act as a guide to these sites for the Romans, when the truth was, they were also new to me.

An alarmingly large number of Romans had elected to take the tour. It required a company of chariots and most of the horses from the royal stables. Meleagros and Olympos arrived early, clearly nervous; and Father, shamefacedly, made his appearance as well. Meleagros had enlisted some of his Museion colleagues, and the Macedonian Household Guards would guide us—while acting as discreet bodyguards.

I was grateful for Olympos's company; he seemed to know everything about the city, and prompted me as we went along. Of course he had the run of it, being a free Greek citizen, but nonroyal. And he had made the most of his opportunities to explore.

I was beside Pompey in the large ceremonial chariot. Olympos was at my side, and Father clung to the rail, looking a little green. Behind us were all the rest; the captain of the guard drove.

As we left the palace grounds and clattered out into the wide streets, cheers went up. I was relieved to hear that they sounded friendly; in Alexandria, one never knew. Our crowds were volatile, and could quickly turn on you. These people were smiling, seemingly happy to have a glimpse of their rulers. But the sight of so many Romans might turn sour on them at any moment.

Father and I waved at them, and I was gratified when they cried out to us and threw flowers. Then I heard them calling Father by his nickname, Auletes, "the flute-player." But they said it affectionately.

We turned down the broad marble street that led to Alexander's tomb. On both sides it was bordered with wide colonnades, making the street as beautiful as a temple. Where this north-south street crossed the long east-west street, the Canopic Way, stood Alexander's tomb. Our first stop.

Everyone who came to the city did obeisance at Alexander's tomb; it was a sacred site. It was he who had laid out the plan for the city itself, and named it after himself, and thereby conferred some of his magic on it.

Now even the loud, joking Romans fell silent as they approached it. The Invincible himself, lying in his crystal sarcophagus . . . who could not be awed by the sight?

I had been here only once before, and I remembered it as a frightening place, with its descent into a dark hollow surrounded by flickering lamps, and then the mummified body with its gold armor, distorted by the crystal dome around it.

Olympos kept up a low murmur of explanation as we walked along. *Brought here instead of to Siwa . . . preserved in honey . . . the gold sarcophagus melted down when money was scarce . . . the priests at Memphis refusing him burial, saying wherever he lay would never be quiet . . .*

"How do you know so much?" I asked him, in a whisper.

"I don't know nearly as much as I would like to," he said, as if he thought my question very ignorant.

Pompey was staring at the recumbent figure. His round eyes were even rounder. I heard him mutter something in Latin that sounded humble.

"He wants to be the new Alexander," Olympos whispered in my ear. "People have told him he looks like him; and he *does* affect the hairstyle."

That was not good; Alexander had conquered Egypt.

"Well, he *doesn't* look like him!" I said.

"And people keep drawing comparisons," said Olympos. "They harp on his youth, and call him Magnus, the Great . . . the only Roman ever given the title! And at twenty-six, too. But they say," he leaned over and said so softly that I could barely hear him, "that he gave the title to *himself*! And that he forced Sulla to allow him to have a Triumph."

Pompey was still staring worshipfully at his idol.

I stood next to him and said (*Why* did I say it? Did you, Isis, give me the words?), "I share Alexander's blood. We Ptolemies are of his family."

Pompey seemed startled out of his reverie. "Then you are blessed, Princess," he said.

"He will preserve us, and his namesake city, to his eternal glory," I said. "He is our protector."

Behind me, Father was wringing his hands and looking ineffectual.

Pompey looked down gravely at me. "In you he has a noble champion," he finally said.

On to the Museion—so called for the Nine Muses of creative thought— where the Romans were given a detailed tour, being introduced to the leading scholars and shown the reading rooms. Then the Library, the biggest in the world, with its huge inventory of scrolls. Ptolemy II had started the collection, and each succeeding king had avidly added to it.

The head librarian, Apollonius, greeted us. "My most exalted King, and Princess, and honored Roman magistrates," he said, bowing low. I could almost hear the bones in his aged back crackling. "Let me show you this temple to the written word."

He led us through several high-ceilinged rooms, each connected, like links in a chain. Daylight entered through a series of windows running around the perimeter of the room, just beneath the ceiling. Marble tables and benches were arranged around the open floor, and readers of all nationalities were hunched over opened scrolls. I saw the Greek in his tunic, the Arab in his voluminous robe, the Jew in his mantle and hood, the Egyptian, bare-chested with a leather skirt. They all looked up with a jerk as we walked in.

They followed us with their heads as we passed through, turning like sunflowers before drooping back down to their manuscripts. We were ushered into what looked like a private room, but was actually one of the storage rooms for the library. Shelves ran all around the walls, with labels at neatly spaced intervals identifying the scrolls. It looked like a beehive, with the rolled scrolls each making a cell. A wooden name tag dangled from the knob of each scroll.

"So this is how they are organized," Pompey said. He looked at one label, which read "Heraclides of Tarentum."

"Medicine, Imperator," said Apollonius.

Next to that was another label, "Herophilus of Chalcedon."

"The unrivaled master of Alexandrian medicine," said Apollonius proudly.

"Two hundred years ago," said Olympos, under his breath. "There are more recent writings."

"Everything is here." Apollonius gestured proudly. These manuscripts were his children. "The multi-scrolled works are all in these baskets on the floor, with their labels on the basket handles."

Pompey was clearly impressed. "The organization is an inspiration to those of us who have archives and records of our own to manage," he said.

The Romans busied themselves unrolling scrolls; the resulting noise gave me the opportunity to whisper to the all-knowing Olympos, "What is all this business about a will that gives Rome rights to Egypt? I wanted to hear about it last night, but you were talking too much!"

Now let him tell me, if he could.

"Oh." Olympos thought for a moment. Then he whispered back, "Your great uncle Alexander the Tenth made a will that gave Egypt to Rome. So the Romans claim! But no one is sure whether he really did, or, if he did, whether it was legal or not."

"Why can't they just read it and decide?" That seemed the easiest way to find out.

"It seems to have mysteriously disappeared," he said, raising his eyebrows. "How convenient!"

For us, or for them? I wondered.

Suddenly the scroll-noises around us ceased, and so must our conversation.

Leaving the Library, we gave the Romans a quick look at the enormous Gymnasion, where our athletes trained. And finally, to the Lighthouse.

"Welcome!" The master of the Lighthouse was standing in the wide doorway, waiting for us. "King Ptolemy, Princess Cleopatra, come and show the Imperator Pompey what your glorious ancestor, Ptolemy Philadelphos, built over two hundred years ago."

Once inside, he indicated the enormous store of fuel; it looked like a mountain and took up the entire room.

"The light must burn night and day, and to do that it consumes wood, dung, paper, charcoal—anything that will catch fire. We store all our supply here, and then it is hauled up, four hundred feet, in these baskets." He bade us follow him to a central well, where dangling ropes disappeared upward into what seemed the sky itself.

"Stairs go up around the perimeter," he said.

"Can't we ride up in the baskets?" asked Olympos.

"No," said the Lighthouse master. "For you would emerge right next to the fire; and if you did not, still I would not entrust the pride of Egypt and Rome to a fraying rope."

It would be a long trudge to the top. There were windows all along the ascent, and as we wound around and around, I saw the harbor growing smaller and the boats beginning to look like the toy ones children sailed in lotus ponds. The higher we got, the more I could see of flat Alexandria stretching out behind the harbor; finally, near the top, I could see past the Hippodrome on the outskirts of the city and almost all the way east to the pleasure-city of Canopus, where that branch of the Nile ended.

I had aching legs and was short of breath when we finally rounded the last turn of the stairs and emerged at the top.

The beacon-master waited, framed by his fire. It roared behind him, curling up like the snakes in Medusa's hair, and the sound of the sucking fire, combined with the wind outside, made a fearful howl. Behind it I could see something shimmering and wavering, and then a slave, clad in wet leather, appeared. He was turning the polished bronze mirror-shield that slid in a groove around the fire's perimeter, so that it could be reflected and seen far out to sea. The shield would also catch and throw back the sun's rays at the same time, adding to the brightness. It was said that the fire-beacon could be seen as far out as thirty miles, but that from that distance it twinkled like a star and could easily be mistaken for one.

The fire was a monster, hardly to be contained. Only then did I notice that the beacon-master was wearing thick leather armor, and had a helmet tucked under his arm—obviously removed in honor of us—that had an iron mesh veil for the face. He knew his monster, and would dress to protect himself. In spite of the heat, the high wind blowing in would keep him from becoming faint.

"I heard there was a glass lens here," said Olympos.

"How could there be? The heat would melt the glass," said Pompey.

"We tried to make one, once," said the beacon-master. "But we could not cast a piece of glass large enough to serve our purpose. It would be an excellent idea, though. If we could magnify the light we have, we would not need such a large fire. And no, the heat would not melt the glass, unless it was thrust right into the flames."

"It seems to me," said Olympos, "that if we had a lens, we could use sunlight instead of a fire."

"Good enough in the daytime, Olympos," said his father, "but what of the nighttime?"

Everyone laughed, but Olympos persisted. "Ships don't sail at night."

"But they sail in cloudy weather," Meleagros said. "And get caught in storms. Your sun-lens would fail then."

Ships . . . sailing . . . the thought of being on the water was unnerving for me. Just walking across the seawall toward the Lighthouse today had been difficult. I hated the water, because of that stabbing memory of the boat, and my mother. But I was forced to live by water, and look at it every day. I had yet to learn to swim, and I avoided boats whenever possible. Even the little lotus pools in the palace seemed threatening to me. I dreaded being called a coward, should anyone notice how I avoided the water.

"Your city is fair," said Pompey, turning slowly to see the entire panorama. "White . . . fair . . . cool and cultured . . ."

"No one could love it as we do," I said suddenly. I knew they were the right words, exactly the right words. "We will guard it for you, and it will always be waiting for you."

He looked down at me and smiled. "I know you will, Princess," he said. "It is safe in your hands."

Was it then I felt—or discovered—the strange power I have in personal encounters? I do not *do* anything extraordinary, I say no special words, but I seem to have the ability to win people to my side, to disarm them. I do not know how. And it works only in person. In letters I have no special magic. Let me see someone, talk to him—or her—and I have persuasive powers I cannot explain. It must be something granted me by Isis herself, who has ever been my guardian. And she alone knows how I have tried to use her gift to bend the world to my vision and spare Egypt from Roman destruction.

Mercifully, the Romans departed the next day, but not before extracting more money and aid from Father for their campaigns. But they were gone, gone, gone . . . and Egypt had been spared. Pompey and his retinue sailed away, to grapple with politics in Rome. I hoped never to see him, or another Roman, again.

But it seemed our fate was inextricably entwined with that of Rome. Three years later, a visiting Roman accidentally killed a cat—an animal sacred to Egyptians. The population of Alexandria rioted, and tried to murder the Roman. The city was in a tumult; it was all our guards could do to protect him and quell the mob. All we would need was such an incident to invite Roman intervention, which was always a threat.

During those years my two youngest brothers made their appearance. Both were named Ptolemy; if the women in our family have few names to choose from, the men have even fewer. There were eighteen years between Older Cleopatra and Older Ptolemy, and the same number between Berenice and Younger Ptolemy. Were they supposed to marry each other? Strange thought.

As Isis, most Egyptian of gods, married her brother Osiris, so in the process of becoming Egyptian—that is, becoming the ruling house of Egypt, although by lineage we were pure Macedonian Greek—we Ptolemies adopted some ancient Egyptian customs that others found shocking. One was brother-sister marriage, as the Pharaohs had done earlier. Thus my mother and father were actually half-siblings, and I was forced in turn to marry my brothers—although it was a marriage in form only.

Perhaps it was time we searched in other royal houses for our mates. The age difference in this generation was too great for us to continue our former practice.

Then my whole world changed, and again, it was because of the Romans. Father had finally succeeded in getting the questionable will set aside and himself recognized as undisputed King by Rome. It had cost him six thousand talents, or the entire revenue of Egypt for one year. He had had to pay it to the three unofficial, but actual, rulers in Rome—Pompey, Crassus, and Caesar. In exchange, they had acknowledged him as King, and conferred upon Egypt the formal title *Socius Atque Amicus Populi Romani*, Friend and Ally of the Roman People. That meant they recognized us as a sovereign state, one whose boundaries they would respect. The price of this respect was very high. But not paying it was higher still, as my uncle found out.

My father had a brother, also known as Ptolemy (how monotonous), who ruled in Cyprus. Once we had controlled vast areas of land, but we had been losing them steadily for generations. Some thirty years earlier, yet another Ptolemy, a cousin—with less fight in him than we had—had willed the province of Cyrenaica, which included Cyprus as well as the African coastal land, to Rome. After his death, Rome took it, but left Cyprus, part of the territory, still in the hands of our cousins. So my uncle Ptolemy still ruled there, until the Romans decided to annex it anyway. He did not have enough money to dissuade them, and was powerless to stave them off. They offered him the high priesthood in the temple of Artemis at Ephesus—a sort of honorable retirement—but he preferred suicide.

We were greatly saddened by this, but the people of Alexandria turned against Father because of it. They were angry about the huge payments to Rome anyway, and what they saw as my father's lack of support for his brother infuriated them. They seemed to feel that he could have rescued him somehow, although what he could have done is a mystery. Was he supposed to take on the Roman legions? It was hopeless; but perhaps it was touching that the Alexandrians ascribed more power to us than we actually had.

But Father had to flee! His own people drove him from the throne, sending him to Rome, as a beggar. He came to my rooms the night he fled, his eyes wild and his manner distracted.

"At midnight I leave," he said. "I hope to return in two months, with legions to back me up."

How could he leave? Who would govern Egypt? As if he read my mind, he said, "My ministers will oversee the government. And I will not be gone long—just long enough to secure the military aid I need."

"But . . . if the Romans come here with troops, will they ever leave?" By now I had studied enough to know that when the Romans were called in to "help," they stayed.

"I have no choice," he said, miserably. "What else can I do? They are bound to back me up—they have to, if they ever want to collect their bribe money!" Now he laughed bitterly. "They have quite a vested interest in keeping me on the throne."

This was awful, awful. I felt shame flooding me. But was my uncle's suicide preferable? What vicious, degrading choices the Romans forced on us!

"May all the gods go with you," I wished Father. "May they watch over you."

And thus he departed, making his way to Rome to beg for protection and restoration.

4

Alexander the Great became my friend while my father was away. Strange that a mummy can be one's friend, but I was desperate. I was eleven years old, and as the days passed and Father did not return, I began to fear for him and for Egypt.

Day after day I would descend into the crypt beneath the gleaming white marble dome of the Soma, and gaze upon the Conqueror where he lay in his alabaster coffin. Each day it was the same: As I reached the bottom of the stairs and could see him, the flickering candles set all around made this seem, for a moment, like the night sky, turned upside down. And in the midst of the stars, like the sun itself, lay Alexander of Macedon. I would approach slowly, and then when I reached him I would stare long and hard.

He didn't look alive—I must say that straightway. He looked like a painted statue, and his features were rigid. He was wearing a polished breastplate, but no helmet, and his golden hair had not faded. His hands were crossed on his breast.

"O Alexander," I would murmur, "please look down on your earthly descendant and relative. We are the last of your empire to survive, we Ptolemies in Egypt. All the rest have been swallowed up by Rome. And even now my father is there, begging them to keep him on his throne. We have become renters of our own kingdom, our own throne, with Rome as our landlord!

"What must you think of this, Mighty Alexander? Help us! Help us to extricate ourselves! Do not let us go down into those Roman maws!"

Of course he never answered; he just lay there serenely. Still, being in his presence brought me comfort. He had existed, and had faced great problems too, and had overcome them.

Coming back out into the dazzling sunlight always felt strange, the journey from the land of the dead back to the living. The tomb sat at the crossroads of our city where the wide Canopian Way, running the whole length of the city from east to west, intersected the street of the Soma as it ran from the south lake of Mareotis to the sea in the north. Always when I looked down that wide white street, with its marble colonnades stretching as far as the eye could see, I knew it could not be given up—that whatever Father had to do to keep it, that was what he must do.

In his absence, the people continued to cry out against him. How could he stand by and see Cyprus taken away? What sort of weakling was he?

It was all *his* fault—the helpless, pitiful king, the one they called Auletes because he was so fond of flute-playing and music. Once it had been an affectionate name, bestowed with indulgent love; now it became a slur.

The drunken little flute-player . . . filthy weakling . . . effeminate musician, reeling in wine . . . these were all the names I heard as I passed through the streets of Alexandria on my way back and forth to the Soma. Once the people had enjoyed the festivals of Dionysus he provided for them, but now they derided him for the very same. They had drunk his wine readily enough themselves, but their memories were short. Those who say I do not know what the jeering crowd at Rome would be like are wrong. I know jeering crowds.

It was always a relief to be admitted back into the palace grounds. (Would Alexander have felt relief? Would he be ashamed of me that I did?) Inside the Palace, peace and respect were always shown—outwardly, at least. Always, that is, until the day I returned from Alexander's side and found that a revolution had taken place.

Everything looked the same. There was nothing to make me suspect that anything had changed: The gardeners were busy at their tasks, watering and pruning; the servants were washing the marble steps of the main building, the one with the audience chamber and banquet hall, with slow, languid movements. I passed by on my way back to the smaller building where we royal children lived, when suddenly a tall guard yelled "Halt!" at me. His voice was rough and peremptory. He stood blocking the entrance to my quarters, scowling.

I recognized him; he was one whose guarding had always been somewhat careless. Now he glared at me. No one had ever spoken to me like that.

"You may not enter!" he barked.

"What do you mean?" I asked. Was there some danger in there? A fire? Or even an animal on the loose? Perhaps one of my sister's pet panthers had slipped its leash and run away.

"Until your loyalty is ascertained, I have orders to detain you. And where have you been? No one could find you." He made a step toward me. But he dared not actually touch me; no one was allowed to lay hands on a member of the royal family.

"My loyalty? My loyalty to whom? To what?" This was very odd. "I have been at the tomb of Alexander, which I have always been free to visit." Even as I said it, I realized I could not prove it, as I always went alone.

"Your loyalty to the new rulers," he said smartly.

New rulers? Had the Romans seized power, then? Had warships landed? Troops invaded? But there had been no tumult or fighting in the streets, and—I quickly glanced toward the harbor—no foreign ships there.

"I don't understand," I said simply. I did not know what else to say. But I felt a great fear for Father.

"The daughters of the former King have been elevated to sovereignty," he said. "Come and do homage. Their Majesties are waiting."

My sisters! My sisters, taking advantage of Father's absence and his unpopularity, had seized power. Now I also felt fear for myself. They could do away with me, with Arsinoe and the boys, and there was no one to prevent them. It could all be done swiftly, this morning, before word got out in the city. It was an old family custom of the Ptolemies—murder of rivals, siblings, mother, father, children.

"So you refuse!" he said, taking another step toward me, reaching for his sword. He might have been instructed to strike me down if I showed the slightest hesitation. Or perhaps he might just strike me anyway—after all, there were no witnesses. I looked quickly and saw the servants still scrubbing the steps. Whatever they observed, they would keep to themselves. There would be no help from them.

"No—" How long did I stand there, thinking? It seemed many moments, but that was impossible. I prayed quickly to Isis, to help me. "No, no, I do not. I am their obedient sister, now as always."

"Then prove it." He motioned to another guard to take his place while he marched me toward the main building—again, not actually touching me, but walking so close beside me it was even more threatening. I tried not to betray my fear.

I was taken to one of the larger rooms of the palace, a room that my sisters evidently felt befitted their new status, as our father had held his audiences here. I stood before the outer doors, which were ornamented with tortoise-shell from India and studded with emeralds, but today their magnificence was lost on me. Slowly the doors swung open and I was admitted to the chamber, where the ceilings were fretted and inlaid with gold. At the far end sat Cleopatra and Berenice, on chairs encrusted with gems. They were consciously seated in the same pose as Pharaohs in carvings.

To me they did not look at all like queens or Pharaohs, but only my two older sisters, as always.

"Princess Cleopatra," Berenice spoke, "we have been raised to the honor of the throne. We are now to be known as Cleopatra the Sixth and Berenice the Fourth, rulers of Upper and Lower Egypt. We wish you to proclaim yourself our dearest sister and loving subject."

I tried to keep my voice steady, to sound calm. "Of course you are my dearest sisters, and I, your most loyal sister." I would avoid the word *subject* unless I was forced to it. Saying it was treason to my father. Would they notice it missing?

"We accept your allegiance," said Berenice for both of them. "The people have spoken. They have made their wishes known. They do not want our father the King to return; they will not admit him if he does. But there is little chance of that! The Romans will not restore him because it seems that one of their prophecies forbids it; something to the effect that 'under no circumstances must arms be used to restore the Egyptian King to his throne, although he may be received with courtesy.' Well, they have done that: feasted and pampered him. But that's all. Oh, and taken his money. He owes so much to the Roman moneylenders that, were we ever to take him back, our country would be bankrupt."

"Yes, and is that any way to love your country? He called himself Philopator, 'lover of his father'—his fatherland?—but he has sold us to the Romans!" cried Older Cleopatra, her voice full of self-righteousness. "Egypt for the Egyptians! Let us take care of our own affairs! Why pay Rome to give us a king, when we have queens available for nothing?"

"I am to be Queen of certain districts, mainly in Upper Egypt, and Berenice will be Queen of Middle Egypt and the Moeris Oasis," she continued. "We will begin negotiations for marriages."

"We have brothers," I suggested, as if I were trying to be helpful. "Do not we Ptolemies marry within our own family?"

They burst out laughing in unison. "Those little children? One is three and the other an infant! It is a long time until *they'll* father any heirs. We need *men* in our beds," said Berenice.

"To wed a baby—why, it would be like wedding a eunuch!" Cleopatra laughed cruelly. Then she stopped, pointedly. "Oh, I forgot; you *like* eunuchs. Busy yourself with them and your horses, then," she said grandly, waving her arms over the jasper arms of her chair. "Do not meddle in things of state, and you shall do well. Do you still have your horse?"

"Yes," I answered. My horse, a white Arabian, was truly my best friend at that age. My horse took me away from myself and the palace and out into the desert.

"Then keep to them. Ride, hunt, and study. Do not concern yourself with things that do not concern you. Do this and you will prosper. We mean to be gentle with all who are gentle with us."

"Yes, Your Majesties," I said. I inclined my head, but did not bow and did not fall to my knees. And as for calling them majesties, that was no treason. Were not all the King's children recognized as gods? And are not gods majesties? I acted calm as I took my leave.

But once in the safety of my own rooms, I shook with shock and fear. They had turned on their own father, seized the throne. They had committed a most grave sin; it was the curse of the Ptolemies. Their blood was compelling them to it.

For we came from a very murderous and bloody line, with such familial killings as sickened the world. Brother had killed brother, wife, mother . . . it was a hideous legacy. I had prided myself that we, this generation, were made of finer stuff. Now it seemed that I was horribly mistaken.

Father! Father had been deposed by his own daughters. And what would they stop at? Me, Arsinoe, the two boys—would they destroy us all as well?

I had no one to confide in. I was long since too old for a nurse, and no confidant had replaced her. I felt utterly alone.

There was only, as always, Isis.

I was safe, for now. They would allow me to live as long as I kept myself in obscurity, was young enough to be harmless, and did not attempt to build up a following. As if I could have!

And so I contented myself with my "eunuchs and horses," as they had contemptuously described them. There were, in those days, flocks of eunuchs around the royal grounds. Eunuchs were important in nearly every sphere of life; it is impossible to imagine palace life without them. In a world in which dynastic ambition ran riot, the eunuchs alone were exempt from suspicion. They served as tutors to the royal children, as confidants to both kings and queens, as ministers and generals. A man whose earthly fortunes would end with himself was devoted to his master. Curious how much we do for our posterity, and how our behavior would change without descendants. And the popular, sneering prejudice about their condition meant that they could never seize open power, but must always remain hidden, shadow-figures behind their masters. Ideal servants, then, for such as the Ptolemies.

Obviously, one could not come from a long line of eunuchs—no one ever claimed his father and grandfather were eunuchs—but the practice of designating one's children to be eunuchs seemed more prevalent in some families than in others. Only the most promising boys were selected—for what was the point in making that sacrifice if the boy did not have much hope of attaining worldly success? Therefore, when one said "eunuch," one was also implying "talented, clever, and diligent."

Most eunuchs in Alexandria were Greek, or Egyptians who had become quite Greek in their thinking. There were also Cappadocians, Phrygians, Bithynians, and such, likewise Grecophiles. In Egypt there was no forced castration, or any castration of slaves. It was entirely voluntary, which made it a little less guilt-laden for those of us who employed the eunuchs.

Usually the operation was done at a fairly early age. Not in infancy, of course, because it was best to wait until the child had proved healthy. Sometimes, in special circumstances, it was done later, even after a boy had started turning into a man, and then the eunuch was different from the usual kind. His voice would be deeper and he might be easily mistaken for any other man.

I thought little about eunuchs, taking them for granted. It was only after I went to Rome that I discovered what it was like to live in a world without them.

I discovered Mardian not long after I embraced Alexander as my comfort. Whenever I went to the tomb, I hoped to have it to myself. But for several days in a row, a bulky little boy was always there when I went. He would be kneeling before the sarcophagus, motionless—he must have had knees of iron—his head bent reverently. Or he would be bending over the coffin, a mooning sort of look on his round face. Truth to tell, he annoyed me. I wished he would go away. I could have ordered him removed, but I hoped he would go away without having to be asked. Day after day he was there. My patience wore away. I began to think he was deliberately interfering with my time with Alexander. When at night I closed my eyes and tried to think of Alexander, this boy's head would always be sticking up somewhere in the picture. It was not noble or inspiring.

The next day, as I descended into the crypt, I prayed he would not be there. And for a moment I thought he was not. Then I saw—again!—that round form hunched over, guarding the coffin. It was too much.

"Leave!" I cried, running over to him. "Or come some other time! Come in the early morning!" I could never get away in the early morning; that was one of the busiest times in the children's quarters. He could have Alexander all to himself then.

He stood up. "I can't," he said with quiet dignity. He was taller than I was. I had no idea he was a eunuch. It does not become apparent until later.

"Why not?" I demanded.

"This is my only free time."

"Do you know who I am?" I said. Could he not recognize an order from a princess?

"Yes," he answered, again with that strange dignity. "You are Cleopatra the younger. If you were Roman you would be called Cleopatra Minor, which would be wrong. You are no slight personage."

"And who are you?"

"My name is Mardian," he said. "I live in the Royal Quarters, Princess. I am studying, hoping to be of use someday to the King."

"Oh . . . you are a *eunuch*," I said, suddenly understanding.

"Yes," he said, without flinching.

"Why do you come here, day after day?" I could ask him that, whereas he could not ask me.

"Because I wish to be like Alexander."

I burst out laughing at his answer, then felt bad when I saw his face. He had not expected that blow from me. "There is no one like Alexander." I tried to cover it up. "Anyone who attempts it would seem laughable to others. Think of all the pitiful kings who have called themselves Alexander, tried to emulate him, had themselves carved in his poses with his flaring hair, his turned neck. No, we can never be Alexander." I was talking too fast, trying to apologize without actually saying the words.

"So you, too, wish to be Alexander? You said 'we.' "

He had caught me. "Yes," I admitted. "I would like to be like Alexander. I suppose you would say a woman is an even more unlikely Alexander than a eunuch. And you would be right. But I can attempt to be like him in character. And sometimes he seems more alive to me than to the people walking around the palace grounds."

Alexander lay silent and golden in his coffin while our words flew back and forth over his head.

"Yes! To me also!" Mardian said. "He helps me to bear it all. When I'm teased or taunted, I just tell myself, 'Tomorrow you can take it all to Alexander.' " He looked a little embarrassed that he would admit such a thing.

"Tell me where you live in the Royal Quarters," I asked. "Perhaps I can visit you there." I had almost forgotten I had considered him a pest only a few minutes ago.

"I am in the big building directly across from the Temple of Isis, the one that overlooks the eastern sea."

I knew it well: it was a busy place, with a school for scribes as well as the archives for war records.

"Are there others—" I wanted to say "like you," but I hesitated.

"No, I'm the only eunuch in my study group," he answered cheerfully. "There are about fifteen of us. Our mathematics tutor, Demetrius, is a eunuch;

for the rest, we have a grammatician from Athens and a rhetorician from Chios."

"So do we," I said, making a face. "Our rhetorician is named Theodotos, and I hate him! He's sneaky and mean—like a snake."

"Snakes aren't sneaky, and they certainly aren't mean," said Mardian gravely. He looked offended.

"What do you mean?" Everyone knew that snakes had that nature, even if the cobra-goddess Wadjyt protected the Pharaohs and rulers of Egypt, and the royal crown showed her with hood spread.

"I have studied snakes," he said. "They are different from what the snake-charmers want you to think. You should see my animals; I have several pens of them near the stables. And I built a big enclosure for my snakes."

"What other animals do you keep?" My curiosity was stirred.

"I had an ostrich for a while," he said. "It grew too big for me. So now I have only small animals—lizards and tortoises and hedgehogs. I'd like to get a baby crocodile."

"I'd like to see your menagerie, Mardian," I said. And we left Alexander, not having paid much attention to him on this visit.

5

It was not many days before I found myself drawn to where Mardian took his lessons, and found him and his schoolmates with their tutor. My arrival caused much stirring and curiosity, but the lesson—on geometry, an Alexandrian specialty—continued. I waited, watching, from the back. There were mainly boys there, but I saw five or six girls, and then—I recognized Olympos.

He was hunched over his paper, concentrating on it so hard that it seemed it might take fire from his scrutiny. He was bigger now, and he had lost whatever roundness had still been in his limbs and shoulders when I met him at that memorable banquet . . . was it five years ago already? Now his face was very lean, making his riveting eyes even more noticeable. He must be fourteen now, at least.

When the class was over, I waited for Mardian to greet me. But he ignored me and continued talking to one of his companions. Finally I went over to him and said, "Are you ashamed to know me, Mardian?"

He looked terrified. "No, no, Princess!" His companion withdrew as quickly as possible. "I did not wish to presume—to make any claims of knowing you, since it was only by accident that our paths crossed. It would have been impudent—"

"Nonsense!" I said, while knowing that others in my position might well have seen things that way. A chance meeting did not constitute a friendship. "Are we not brothers in Alexander?" Even as I said it, I realized that *brothers* was an odd word to use, when neither of us was male in the physical sense. Still, *brothers* meant more than just the body.

"If you wish us to be, then so do I," he said.

"Good, then that's settled." I put my arm around his shoulders. "I wish you to show me your animals. Then I'll take you to our royal menagerie. And then—"

Mardian turned out to be such a delightful companion that I found myself missing him a little the next day. Our friendship grew as we did our lessons, picked flowers, constructed miniature walled cities out of tiny baked mud bricks. Together we built a chariot that could be pulled by black she-goats, and we felt very grand as we were carried in triumph around the grounds.

The next time I visited the class, the teacher was drilling them on the Ptolemies, and looked truly alarmed when he saw me.

"And the eighth Ptolemy, when he was officially entertaining Scipio Aemilianus from Rome, was forced to walk—" He blanched as I appeared. "That is, his gown—it was—"

"It was transparent," I finished for him. "And the sight was very comical, because he was so immensely fat, and gasped for breath after walking only a few steps." Yes, I knew all the embarrassing stories about my ancestors. I must not flinch from them, or make the teacher change his lesson on my account. The obese glutton was my great-grandfather, nicknamed Physcon—"Fatty"— by the Alexandrians, who love nicknames. "And the haughty Roman said, 'I have given the people of the city a novel sight: their King actually walking and getting some exercise.' "

The students laughed.

All these humiliations at the hands of Rome—they went back a long way. And Physcon was not the only fat man in my family tree; many others were huge. In consequence, I was always careful of what I ate, determined to stay slim, although the women in our family seemed not to be afflicted with obesity.

"Yes, Princess," said the tutor, flustered. I was sorry I had barged into the lessons; it seemed I could never do a normal thing without calling attention to myself. I must not come there again. But to leave now would cause even more disturbance, so I had to remain until the hour was over.

Afterward Mardian came over to me, followed by Olympos.

"I am pleased to see you again," I said. "But have you studied here all these years, and never let me know?" I scolded Olympos. Was being a princess so intimidating that it drove people to flee from us?

"Mostly I am taught at the Museion," said Olympos. "But it is good to escape from the shadow of one's parents—as you doubtless know. My father, with his scholarly reputation, casts a long shadow at the Museion."

"Not as big as the one my fat ancestor casts!" I said, laughing. "It is difficult indeed to move out from under his umbrella."

"You know one another?" Mardian looked surprised.

"We met long ago," I said. "When Pompey came to Alexandria." I paused. "Both of us wanted to go to a banquet that we had no business attending."

"Olympos probably impressed all the adults—he usually does," said Mardian.

"Not any longer," said Olympos. "I am now too old to get by on precocity. It stops working around the age of thirteen."

"Yes," said Mardian. "Everyone likes a witty child, but beyond a certain age they're considered tiresome."

"Well, I certainly wouldn't want to be *that*," said Olympos, raising his eyebrows.

We three began to spend time together; Olympos seemed lonely, although he would never have admitted it. Perhaps his intellect and adult demeanor put others off. His interest in medicine had not waned, and he was preparing to study here in Alexandria, where the medical school was the finest in the world. Mardian was also a lone figure, as he approached the age where his condition would make him visibly different from others. And I? I was the princess whose future was in severe doubt, an object of curiosity and speculation and whispers. People kept their distance.

And then the feared day came, the day I had braced myself for all my life. Olympos announced with pride that he had acquired a little sailboat, and wished to take us out in the harbor. Would it be permissible for him to use the inner, royal harbor to practice on? The water was much calmer there.

"I know all Greeks are supposed to be born with the skill of Odysseus coursing through their blood, but it missed me," he said. "Still, I love the water."

The water: now I would have to confront it at last or admit that I was afraid, and stay on the shore for the rest of my life. Until now it had not mattered. No voyages had beckoned, no friends had issued invitations that involved boats.

"Of course," I said. "Take all the time you like to train yourself there. You can tie the boat up at the foot of the palace stairs, the ones that go right down into the water."

"Thank you," he said. "I will practice as much as possible, so I can take you out soon!"

Unfortunately, I knew he would. By that time I knew him well enough to know he always honored his promises—and his timetable.

High summer, just like . . . *that* day. Sun riding overhead, pouring its warmth out, heating the water in the shallow sandy-bottomed harbor to a lulling temperature. The colors, too, were the same—milky blue-green, gentle waves wearing a rim of white foam.

"Come." Olympos had waded waist-deep in the water, and was holding the bobbing boat. He expected us to wade out, too, and clamber over the sides. I looked at the water lapping at my toes, seeming innocent. But farther out it got deeper and deeper.

I knew sometimes people learned to swim by hanging on to an inflated animal skin. They paddled around and got used to the water that way. Now I wished I had done that. But it was too late now.

"Come on!" Olympos was growing impatient. Out of courtesy, Mardian was waiting for me to go first. I had to do it.

I had worn a tunic that stopped halfway down to my knees, and had no extra material to tangle itself around me. Gingerly I took one step out into the water, deliberately making it a long one. The water came halfway up my calf. I picked up the other foot and walked farther out, so that the water now swirled around my knees.

I could feel the tug of the current, gentle though it was. Under my toes the sand eroded, making me sink a little deeper. The water covered my knees. A wave came, lifting me a little, then subsided, settling me back down. I did not like it; it felt like being in a strong wind.

"Are you trying to be as slow as possible?" Olympos sounded irritated. "I'm tired of holding this boat."

I moved again, and this time the water was growing so deep—up to my waist—that I had to fling both arms out for balance. I hated the feel of it, cooler than it had been on my legs, encircling me. Another step and it was up to my chest. But now the boat was near. All I had to do was move sideways.

Which proved surprisingly difficult. The water felt thick, and the waves— small as they were—pushed against me, seemingly wanting to make me lose my footing. At last—just as a wave sent spray into my face—I grasped the sturdy wooden side of the boat and hauled myself over the side. Behind me, Mardian was wading resolutely through the blue enemy, unsuspecting.

When we were both in, Olympos climbed over the prow, the tie-rope in his hand. "There! I thought you would never get here!" He looked at me sternly. "If I didn't know better, I would think you had never set foot in the water before!" Then he laughed to show how ridiculous that idea was.

Happily he busied himself with the line and sails, settling himself by the steering-oar. The breeze was coming from the west, and the sail caught it, pulling us over to the right side. I clutched onto the side as I felt the boat lurch, and my own stomach plummet. Olympos was laughing, enjoying the sensation. Even Mardian had a broad smile on his face.

To them it was a pleasurable outing. What is one person's diversion may be another's supreme test. And so often we sit beside one another, unknowing.

We were heading out into the harbor, toward the larger boats. I looked down and saw the bottom disappearing beneath us. At first it had been visible, and the sun-dappled spots played on the sandy bottom, where I could also see fish and seaweed. Now the depths were shadowy.

I felt a cold panic rising up in my throat. We were going to retrace that entire journey of long ago, and were on our way to the very spot where the boat had overturned. I shut my eyes and tried to concentrate only on the sensations of the little slaps of water under the boat.

"Whee!" Olympos gave a squeal as we hit some large wave; it felt like running over a barrier, as hard as dirt. Salt spray slapped me across the face, coating my mouth. I licked the crust and swallowed hard.

We sailed around the harbor for what seemed hours, in and out of the wake of the larger ships, and some part of me noted how delighted Olympos was, how his spirits soared. He had ceased paying any attention to me—for which I was grateful. Mardian was absorbed in looking down into the water to try to see squid or sea urchins or even a dolphin. He peered over the side, not minding when waves smacked him full in the face.

There was no canopy here, so there were no reflections. There were no attendants, screaming and jumping about. Those memories were not stirred. But the sounds, the taste of the salt spray, the piercing colors, all assaulted me. This time I was not helpless, not held down, not torn from anyone. I had the strength to hold myself erect, to make sure I was not dislodged from the boat. I was determined to endure this ordeal.

At last—at long last—Olympos turned the boat for the palace dock. The sun was halfway down the sky, and the tide was coming in. I could feel how it bore us to shore. The rocking of the boat was not unappealing; the terror of it had subsided, become manageable.

"Now let's swim!" Olympos suddenly announced, tossing the rope-encircled stone that served as his anchor out into the water. It sank with a gurgle and jerked the boat to the left when it hit bottom.

Not this! I had thought the torture—which had been gradually abating the whole time we were out—was over. But swimming . . . I could not swim.

Olympos dived overboard, cleanly and neatly disappearing into the water. My stomach turned over, even though I knew he would bob up a few feet away. Or rather, I *hoped* that he would. And sure enough, he emerged on the other side of the boat and slapped the water, drenching us with a wall of spray.

With injured dignity, Mardian, already soaked, leapt over the side of the boat, landing like a catapult stone, sending even more water on my head. Then both boys started a water fight, yelling and trying to sink each other. It took them some time to notice that I was still in the boat.

"What are you waiting for?" Olympos shouted. "You act as if you're afraid of it!" Clearly he thought that was the most insulting, as well as unlikely, accusation he could make.

How deep was it? Was it over my head? I peered over the side, trying to see the bottom, but it was all in shadow.

"Just jump in!" called Mardian. "It isn't cold!" He was paddling near me, enjoying himself.

I looked at the blue liquid surrounding me, and felt the purest form of aversion I have ever experienced. It was waiting—no, lurking, lying in wait, ready for me, ready to devour me at last. It would not be balked of its prey.

You escaped me once, it seemed to murmur. *But not forever. Don't you know that water is your destiny?*

An odd sort of insouciance—I cannot call it courage, it was too offhanded and fatalistic for that—stole over me. Yes, it was waiting. The water, my foe. But I would grapple with it, perhaps take it by surprise. It would not expect that.

Without further thinking—which would have stopped me—I flung myself overboard. In the instant when I hung, poised, above that blue surface, I felt both terror and victory. And now the water was rushing up at me, and I struck its unforgiving face with a hard force. My body sliced into it and I plunged into the depths, hurtling down so fast that I struck the bottom and bounced up again. All this time I had not breathed, and then my head was shooting out above the surface again, and I took a great, gasping lungful of air.

I was flailing about, my arms completely ineffectual. I sank again, then somehow got my head out so I could breathe. I could not feel anything solid beneath my feet. Then my swirling arms succeeded in keeping me on the surface, and instantaneously I sensed how to coordinate my legs so they could assist in buoying me up.

"You're about as graceful as a hippo on land," teased Mardian. "Stop thrashing so much! You're going to attract sea monsters!"

"You know there aren't sea monsters!" said Olympos. But I saw his dark eyes watching me carefully.

I was able to paddle around without worry of sinking. The water had been unexpectedly vanquished as an enemy. Now it was just something warm and tidal. I felt lightheaded with relief and surprise. Surprise that the dreaded moment had come at last and I had survived it, and surprise at how easily it had happened.

As the sun was setting, we returned to the dock and tied up the boat. Our wet clothes clung to us, and now I could see the beginning of the differentiation between Mardian and other males. Olympos, at almost fifteen, was more compact and muscled; Mardian had shot up, but his limbs—both arms and legs—seemed disproportionately long. And he did not have the beginning of the musculature that was revealed on Olympos; Mardian's shoulders remained thin and slight.

Olympos returned to his home in the Greek section of the city, thanking us for the outing. Behind us the sun was setting, and Mardian and I sat on the harbor steps.

The sun made a shining red path across the gentle waves, and the ships at anchor were reflected in the flaming reflection.

"You never swam before, did you?" Mardian asked quietly.

"No," I admitted. "But I had meant to learn. It was time." I hugged my knees and rested my head on them. My wet clothes were chilling me a bit, but they would soon dry.

"It is no accident that you did not know how to swim," he persisted. I wished he would stop. "You must have gone out of your way to avoid it."

He saw too much! I merely shrugged. "I had no one to go out with," I said lightly. "My older sisters were too grown up, my younger one too far behind me."

"Oh, I imagine you could have found a way. If you had wanted to." He paused. "It seems that you find a way to do whatever you wish." There was admiration in his voice. "How did you dare just to jump in like that? Weren't you afraid you would sink?"

"Yes," I admitted. "But I had no choice. It was the only way."

"Then you must have wanted to," he insisted. "Because you didn't *have* to. By the way, you did very well. The first time I tried to swim, I sank three times!"

"I wanted to, because I had to," I said. "My mother drowned out here— in this very harbor."

He lost his color. "I knew—she had died. I did not know how. I am sorry."

"I was with her."

He lost still more color. "And you . . . remember?"

"Only colors, tastes, noises. And the loss. And that water caused it."

"Why did you not tell Olympos? He would never have forced—"

"I know that. But the truth is . . . how much longer could I live in Alexandria, a sea-city, unable to venture out onto the water?"

He bowed his head, choosing his words carefully. "May all the gods preserve our city in that glory," he finally said. "In her independence."

"May my father the King return and take command." There—I had said the forbidden words. Was anyone listening? "In the meantime I must keep faith. And tackle all fears, everything that would cripple or compromise me. Fear of the water, for an Alexandrian princess, is a grave handicap."

"So you banished it." He seemed very impressed.

"Not without hesitation," I admitted. No one must ever know how much.

It was good to have friends who lived a safe and uneventful life, because in our children's palace quarters it was anything but that. The four of us were guarded and watched constantly, and doubtless everything suspicious we said or did was reported back to Their False Majesties. I, as the eldest, had the most freedom, but was also the one likely to incur the most criticism. Arsinoe, true to her fretful and spoiled nature, constantly tested the guards and caused trouble in little ways—ways that seemed designed merely to get attention for herself, since they served no other purpose. It struck me as very stupid, for the best way to behave around enemies is unobtrusively.

The two little boys, Ptolemies both, were too young to merit much watching, as they played in their adjoining rooms. There was no treason in them, no plots, just balls and wooden toys.

Age began to work against me, calling attention to my impending adulthood—and potential as a political tool—as nature began to reshape my body. All my life I had been slight, with arms and legs that had little meat on them, and what there was, I ran off with all my activity. My face, too, was long and thin, my features fine as children's always are. But at about the time Father left for Rome, subtle changes started in me. First I stopped growing taller, and as if in response to that, the food that would have gone into added height now filled out my arms and legs, and plumped out my cheeks. I stopped being sticklike and became softer all over. At the same time, my muscles became stronger, so that I could finally wrench things out of sockets that had been too difficult for me, move furniture that I could not before, and throw balls farther.

And my face! My nose, as if it had a will of its own, began to lengthen, and my little lips expanded, until I had a large mouth. The lips were still nicely shaped, curved and fitted together pleasingly, but they were so . . . wide. The face looking back at me from polished silver mirrors was rapidly becoming an adult's. An adult face, which might harbor adult thoughts. Treasonous thoughts?

The changes took me by surprise; I had never watched anyone's looks alter as they matured. I suppose I had always pictured a miniature version of an adult when I thought of someone's childhood. Our unpleasant tutor, Theodotos, would have kept the same looks, in my mind, but shrunk down tiny. Now I would see what I was truly going to look like; I had to watch myself being reconstructed day by day. I was most anxious for the answer, because I had got used to myself one way and now would have to see myself another.

Of course I wanted to be beautiful, because everyone wants to be. Failing that, I wanted to be at least pleasant to look at. But what if it was worse? What if I turned out to be ugly? It seemed so unfair to have started out one way, in one category, and then, at twelve or so, be reassigned to another.

I had overheard a merchant once, talking about his wife's expected child. Someone asked him what he hoped for, and I had assumed he would say that the child be healthy, or that it be clever. Instead—I shall never forget it!—he said, "If it is a girl, I just pray she won't be ugly." I always wondered if it was a girl, and if she was ugly.

So I peered anxiously in mirrors (when I knew no one would catch me), trying to divine the future in my face.

My breasts and waist started changing, too. At first it was just a hint that things were different, but after Father had been away for a year, the changes were unmistakable. I wished my breasts would stop growing, for that was the most telltale sign of all. I had to wear looser and looser clothes, and even took to wearing a tight garment underneath to squash myself down whenever I had to see my queenly sisters; I wanted to look young and innocent as long as possible. But in my own quarters I could not bear to wear the binding garment; it was terribly painful.

I had no "wise woman" to help guide me in all this. If I had had a mother . . . but she might have been too shy to discuss it. What I really needed was a bawdy nurse or attendant. The male guards placed on me by my sisters would definitely not serve the purpose.

Had things been normal, I might have been able to talk to those very same older sisters. But they were Ptolemies first and women and sisters second and third.

And then it came, the great dividing line between childhood and womanhood. I became capable of bearing children, that summer I was twelve and Father away for over a year now. I was prepared for it; I did not think I was dying or any of those things that ignorant girls sometimes do. I knew well enough what had happened, but still it was a momentous change in the way I thought of myself. Never again could I feel there was little essential difference between me and other children, boys and girls alike; that the category "child" applied to us equally and was the most important designation, the most descriptive term, that fitted us all.

Now I would have this element—this fundamental, awesome element— to me for the rest of my foreseeable future. Marriage . . . I could be married, they would say I was ready. I could be sent away from Egypt! I might have to make my home in a foreign court, wife to some prince. Have children . . . worry about them . . . and the cycle so short, myself so recently a child. . . .

The possibility frightened and threatened me as nothing else had—not my sisters' illegal rule, not the Romans, not even the cruel water in the harbor. It was nature that had done this to me, not another person, and nature could not be pleaded with or dissuaded.

Only Isis, my kindly guardian and wise guide, could understand. During the first days after the great change in me, I spent hours in the temple by the sea, looking at her statue.

She was all these mysteries taken together—womanhood, wifehood, motherhood. Little wonder that women adored her; she personified all their aspects. I could only beg her to protect me in this voyage into the unknown, the frightening land of adulthood, of woman, that lay before me.

6

Partly to stave off these thoughts, partly in rebellion against the role nature was assigning me—without my permission!—I determined to form a group composed of people of my own choosing. I would call it the Society of Imhotep, after the legendary physician and master builder of Old Egypt. In order to belong, someone had to be interested in Old Egypt, of what lay far back both in time and distance. They had to wish to study the Egyptian tongue, and learn the old writing; above all, they had to feel the spirits of those long departed, and listen to what they might want to whisper to us.

A surprising number of students from Mardian's class wanted to join, as well as both boys and girls who were the children of various palace officials. I suspected it was because a princess was leading it, but as time went on that was forgotten. No one stayed in the group unless he or she was genuinely interested, because we worked so hard that the fainthearted fell away. We wanted to be able to read the inscriptions on the old monuments by ourselves.

One of the great inducements of belonging, though, was that the group, and its outings, had to be secret. Why? I suppose because children—and I was determined not to relinquish my childhood without a fight—love secrets, and it made us feel important and daring. In a palace rife with spies, we took pride in having our impenetrable secret society. (It never occurred to us that no one considered our doings weighty enough to spy on. Also, time and complacency had made my sisters relax their vigilance toward me.)

So for the next two years, while Father's exile stretched on and on, we sneaked contentedly around Alexandria, studying the ancient language as contained in the scrolls in our great Library, occasionally having a recital of poetry in Egyptian. We also—extremely daringly, we thought—went into the Jewish Quarter and observed their synagogue, the largest in the world. (Was everything in Alexandria the largest in the world? To me, at the time, it seemed so.) So large was it that a man had to be stationed midway down the auditorium to signal with a flag what part of the ceremony was taking place, as those worshipers in the back were too far away to see or hear.

Alexandria had a very sizable Jewish population; some said there were more Jews in Alexandria than in Jerusalem. That always puzzled me, since their great leader Moses had led them out of Egypt long ago, and they were ecstatic to be delivered. Why had they wished to return? In the Greek translation of their holy book—written here in Alexandria—it said that their god had forbidden them to return to Egypt. Why did they disobey?

We went fishing in the papyrus marshes of Mareotis, the great lake that extended all along the back of Alexandria and then many miles to the west. Another time we got permission to visit one of the lesser embalming shops that clustered like flies outside the western walls of the city, near the tombs. Although Egyptians no longer had the elaborate monuments of former days, people who could afford it still preferred to be embalmed. Greeks had traditionally been cremated, but here in Alexandria these customs, like so many others, mixed, and many Greeks sought the embalming table of Anubis. The shops were busy, and on the day we went, the jolly proprietor had three mortal remains to make ready for the journey to the west.

"It should properly take seventy days," he told us. "Forty for the natron-drying, and then there is the wrapping, and—but now we have a quicker service. Everyone is in such a hurry now. Especially the Greeks. The pace of Alexandria extends even to her dead."

He showed us the various styles of coffins; many were covered with hieroglyphics, and I was proud that I could read much of it.

Oh, we did many other things—we collected perfumes and unguents, which Alexandria exported. There was Balm of Gilead, crushed and incorporated into a jelly; a perfume from Mendes called "The Egyptian" that had balanos oil, myrrh, resin, and cassia; one called "Metopion" that had oil of bitter almonds scented with cardamom, sweet rushes from the sea of Gennesareth, and galbanum. Oil of lilies was strong, and combined with other oils and fats to make a popular ointment. We tried to make our own by melting fat and adding crushed roses and a few drops of lotus dew, but it did not smell very strong. The perfumers of Egypt have no equal in the world, and they guarded their secrets well. No shop admitted us to look on as they worked.

All these preliminary activities were leading up to what we really hoped to do: visit the pyramids. They were situated not far from Memphis, where all the branches of the Nile come together and the Delta ends. It was a long journey from Alexandria, some hundred Roman miles down the Canopic branch of the Nile. We should have asked permission, and notified someone. We knew that, even at the time. But such is the nature of children longing for adventure that they would rather die than invoke the safety and protection of an adult. And it gave me such pleasure, for once, to give them the slip.

Of course it was necessary to have an adult along, and Mardian's uncle Nebamun, a low-ranking chamberlain at court, reluctantly agreed to take us, but only because he wished to return to Memphis himself and see his relatives.

We told our attendants that we were to be going away, on a safe, quiet visit to see the Nile as it began its flooding. Living in Alexandria, we were not on the Nile itself, but some fifteen or twenty miles from its westernmost branch. My chamberlain, who was in reality my keeper (the guards having grown more lax as time went on), deemed it proper, and harmless enough, for me to go. Quietly, all over the palace grounds, the other five young, stalwart explorers were saying the same thing, and their attendants were likewise agreeing.

We set out in the early dawn, being driven in three royal chariots down the broad street of the Soma until we reached the docks of Mareotis. The docks were busy; fishing boats had already made a run on Mareotis and were unloading their catch. Other vessels, which plied their way bringing the produce of Egypt, by way of the Nile, were crowding in and awaiting their turn to dock. Wine from the vineyards of Mareotis and the Delta, dates, papyrus, precious woods and spices from the lands of Punt and Somalia, porphyry from the eastern desert, obelisks from Aswan—all converged on the lake docks of Alexandria.

Nebamun had hired a small boat to take us all the way to Memphis. It was large enough that we could sleep on it, for it was several days' journey there. The prevailing wind at this time of year was in our favor, blowing exactly the way we wished to go, south against the current.

We set sail eastward over the lake, just as the sun was rising. He—Re, the glorious sun—was emerging from the papyrus thickets and the rushes that bordered the shore, green and bristly. The early breeze swept across the water and filled our sail. We sailed straight toward Re.

It was late in the afternoon before we reached the far side of the lake, where the canals connect to the Nile. The boatman cast a look at the sky, and indicated that we should drop anchor, sheltering among the reeds and the huge, cup-shaped leaves of the bean plants. It seemed a holiday sort of thing to do, and so we agreed.

I awakened once in the middle of the night, hearing the gurgle of the water gently slapping the sides of the boat, the rustling of the papyrus stalks all around us, and the cry of a night heron somewhere in the thicket. I had never slept so well on my gilded bed in the palace.

With the dawn, mists rose from the swamp as if they were night-spirits fleeing. As soon as Re appeared, they scattered. We were soon on the Nile, or what was called its Canopic branch.

One of our school exercises was to memorize all seven branches of the Nile, and all educated Egyptians can do so: Canopic, Bolbitinic, Sebennytic, Phatnitic, Mendesian, Tanitic, Pelusic. They fan out from the main Nile and (to an ibis flying over them) have the shape of a lotus flower blooming from a stalk.

The Canopic Nile is small. Date palms and vineyards dotted the fields surrounding it, where all was moist and fertile, with the lush greenness that comes only with living things; the malachite in the palace inlays and the emeralds that glowed in bracelets were dull beside this. Green is the most precious color in Egypt, as it is so hard-won against the desert.

The river took on a greenish hue, which I was told is actually called "Nile green," because there is no other shade in the world exactly like it.

"But as the Nile rises, the color changes," said Nebamun. "The life-giving material is brown, and Hapi, the Nile god, brings it from the source of the river far to the south. When it settles on our fields, it mixes with our old soil and rejuvenates it, by a miracle. Soon the rise will begin. It always happens just after the rising of Sirius in the eastern sky."

I smiled. Did he really believe in Hapi, the Nile god, with his pendulous breasts? I knew that one of my ancestors, Ptolemy III, had tried to discover the source of the Nile. Greeks believed in science, not gods, to explain things. Or, rather, they tried science first, and gave credit to the gods only when they could not find out the answers for themselves. Ptolemy III had failed in his quest. So perhaps it was Hapi after all.

I lay back, trailing my hand in the water as we moved gently along, a boat seemingly sailing in green fields. As far as the eye could see, it was flat, and so fertile it looked like paradise. A thousand irrigation canals spread the Nile water everywhere, and the slow turns of the donkeys pulling the water wheels kept bringing the water up.

There were clusters of mud-brick houses here, there, everywhere. The fields were full of people. It was all so different from Alexandria, with its blue sea and white marble; here the colors were green and brown. It was different in another way as well: the people looked all alike. They had the same skin color, the same hair, and wore the same type of clothes, whereas in Alexandria we had so many different nationalities that every street resembled a bazaar.

The river was full of boats of all sizes: little reed ones with curved prows; wide, workaday barges carrying grain and building-stone; fishing boats with tiny sails; and cabin-boats with reed awnings for shelter from the sun. There was a holiday air on the river, as if we were all at the same party.

Suddenly, Nebamun pointed to a trampled area of a vineyard. "Hippopotamus damage. Look!"

A big swath indicated the path of something as big as an oxcart. "How do you know?" asked Mardian.

"Ah, my nephew, I see you are now truly a creature of the court. Had you grown up alongside the Nile, where you began, you'd know a hippo's tracks well enough! Look how it came out of the water, see the path—it headed straight for the fields. Then you can see it doubling back again, turning—it must have been chased. Then, far ahead of us, see where it returns to the water. We'd best be careful. This means it could be waiting for us up ahead. I hate hippos! They make river travel so dangerous!"

"Aren't crocodiles worse?" asked Olympos.

Nebamun looked amused at our ignorance. He pointed to where some brownish green shapes were lying, half invisible, in the reeds by the riverbank. I also saw some eyes looking out above the waterline; whatever was attached to them was well hidden. "Look where they lie, sunning themselves. They are dangerous for swimmers, or for anyone walking along the riverbanks, but not for boats. But the hippos! They lie half submerged, and suddenly rise up and overturn a boat! And when they are disturbed, or perhaps only hungry, they decide to go marauding in the fields! A croc will gobble up a swimmer, but he doesn't invade your territory and wreck your boats and your crops. Give me a crocodile any day."

"If a hippo is so nasty, why then did you Egyptians make a hippo the goddess of childbirth?" asked Olympos, the young scientist-mind.

"Taueret," said Nebamun. "I really don't know. I must admit, I don't think of a hippo, even a pregnant one, as very motherly."

"Then what about the crocodiles?" Olympos persisted. "Isn't there a crocodile god?"

"I think there's even a place where they're kept, and worshiped!" cried Mardian. "Tell us!"

Nebamun had to think. "That's near Memphis, in the Moeris Oasis," he finally said. "I have never been there. I have heard, though, that pilgrims go to make offerings at a lake with sacred crocodiles, where some of the animals wear gold and jewels on their forelegs and head-bumps."

We all began to laugh, uproariously.

"Sobek is the name of the god who is manifested in the sacred crocodiles," said Nebamun. "And the name of the landing where the temples are, and where the sacred creatures are fed, is Crocodilopolis."

Now we began to scream with laughter. A crocodile bedecked in jewels— imagine its crafty eye peeping out from under a golden bauble—its wrinkled, crooked legs wearing bracelets! And living near Crocodilopolis!

"You are teasing us," I finally said. "There is no such thing as a place called Crocodilopolis."

"I swear, by Amun himself, that it is true!" cried Nebamun.

"Then you must promise to take us there!" said Mardian. "Yes, prove it to us!"

"We won't have time," he said.

"You just said it was near Memphis!"

"The place where the Nile has a small branch going to the Moeris Oasis is more than fifty miles upstream, and then one has to go to the far side of the oasis. It would be almost as far as going back to Alexandria. We do not have that much time. People will begin to question our absence."

"But if we do have time?" said Olympos.

"We won't," said Nebamun. "And once you see the pyramids and the Sphinx, you won't care about Crocodilopolis."

At the sound of the name, we burst out into laughter again.

We stopped that evening by the banks of the river, near a waterwheel and a well-trodden pathway leading down to the water. It looked as though it would be safe from crocodiles, for there was too much human activity. The hippo Nebamun had been on the lookout for remained submerged.

Just at sunset, we clambered over the side of the boat to swim. In the past year I had become a respectable swimmer. The water was moving slowly past us as it made its unhurried way to the sea; we floated little reed boats on it and then tried to outswim the current. It was easy enough going downstream, but coming back up took all our strength. We played hiding games in the reeds, and pretended to be Horus attacking the evil Seth in the papyrus marsh, disturbing a large number of ducks and kingfishers in the process. The whir of their wings felt like gigantic fans as they flew away.

Once again we were on our way before dawn, and before the day was over we had come to the place where all the branches of the Nile knitted themselves together and the river became one. The setting sun—Re in his form as Atum, the decrepit old man sinking in the west—bathed the wide bosom of the river in his magic gold, and as we sailed on it I felt a divine stirring.

"We will rest here tonight, and then tomorrow—you will behold the pyramids!" said Nebamun.

"I hope I won't be disappointed," said Olympos, echoing all our thoughts. It would be so unbearable if they were not worth the journey. Something would die in me, and I might never undertake a long journey again for the sake of the unknown.

"Always the Greek," said Nebamun. "Never willing to believe, always holding back, worrying in advance that something will not be what it claims to be."

"Yes, that is our curse *and* our glory," Olympos said.

"The Romans just take things as they are, and figure out a way to use them," I said, thinking out loud.

"Destroy them, you mean," said Mardian.

"I don't think they decide that in advance," I said. "I think their actions are pure that way—not bound by prior decisions."

"Yes, they just decide each time, independently, to destroy. There's no suspense there. Look what they did to Carthage—leveled it and sowed the ground with salt."

"But, Olympos, they didn't destroy Greece."

"No, only in spirit."

I laughed. "As if anything could destroy the Greek spirit! You are hardly spiritless!"

"Something of the Greek spirit survives around the world, and a little may even have seeped into some Romans, but—what was truly Greek has perished. Except in Alexandria, which has more of the Greek spirit than Athens itself now."

"All things pass away," said Nebamun. "Except the pyramids."

Very early, before there was any stirring on the boat, I was awake. Excitement had kept me from sleeping much all through the night; now that I was on the brink of seeing the pyramids and the wonders of Old Egypt, I was seized with trembling expectation. We were famous the world over for our enormous monuments and statues, the size of which made it seem we once must have been a race of giants, to have created them and set them up. They made us seem different from all other people, with a secret knowledge or power.

But when it came down to it, what secrets did we possess? And of what use would they be against Roman power? Whatever knowledge had raised the pyramids that might still reside in Egyptians today—how did that help against Roman legions, Roman siege machines, Roman catapults?

Only the power of the gods could stand against them. I knew that even then, O Isis. Only you, and Amun, and Osiris. And yet *they* had Jupiter, and Hercules. . . .

In the fresh morning gold of sunshine, thin and without heat, we sailed up the Nile, looking to the western bank for our first glimpse of the pyramids. The seemingly endless green of the Delta fields had been replaced by a nar-

42

rower ribbon of green on either side of the river, and just beyond that, as if someone had drawn a line, the desert began. The golden sand lay flat and expressionless, like the face of a god, stretching into eternity beyond our eyesight.

The sun rose higher; the air on the horizon shimmered. Then, from a great distance—their tips caught the light and flashed. Three of them, winking in the sun.

"Look!" cried Mardian. "Look! Look!"

At first they seemed to be supernaturally huge, or we could not have seen them from afar. But as we glided upstream, coming closer, they shrank into just large buildings, like the Lighthouse. As we made for the landing, and the pyramids were framed behind farmers with donkeys and carts, they seemed to shrink still further, becoming almost ordinary.

We hired donkeys to take us the three or so miles to the monuments, and very glad we were to have done so, for as the sun rose higher and there was no shade anywhere, the sands heated to a foot-burning temperature. We were plowing through the golden sea of sand to what looked like piles of exactly the same material, except that the corners were very sharp. There was no wind, just the stillness and the heat.

The pyramids grew until they seemed to fill the sky; and when at last we stood at the base of one and looked up, it seemed entirely possible that the tip touched the sun. I know now that it looked like a mountain; but then I had never seen a mountain, and it staggered me. I knew only flatness, only the horizontal—the smoothness of the ocean, the straight, wide streets of Alexandria, the level fields surrounding the river—and this mound, this vertical thrusting, I could not understand.

The polished stones gleamed, reflecting the sun like an amber mirror. It was hard, vast, impenetrable. Nowhere was there a single ornament, facing, detail, window, ledge—just this sloping, shining ramp of stones, vanishing into the sky. I felt dizzy. The heat, rising from the sand and blazing down from the sun overhead, and the fierce light made my head spin. Suddenly I knew it was dangerous to remain there. The pyramid wanted to do us harm, strike us down.

"Shade!" I said. "Is there no shade anywhere?"

The sun was almost directly overhead, and the giant structures cast no shadows.

Nebamun brought forth parasols. "Only this," he said. I gave thanks that he had thought of them. "There is shelter under the chin of the Sphinx," he said. "We can wait there."

He mounted his donkey and set out toward the Sphinx, its head peering above the sand. We should have felt the same awe and fear in its presence, but it seemed almost friendly in comparison to the pyramids. It offered us shelter, and it looked like a person, and it did not house anything long dead and hostile.

We spread out our blankets on the sand between the creature's paws and kept the parasols over our heads. There was little talking; it was as if the vast silence of the place forbade it. We could see a raised causeway off to one side, and knew it was an abandoned road to a pyramid, perhaps used to push stones along in the building of it. But no one walked it now.

We watched the day pass from under the shadow of the Sphinx. Occasionally a black shape would fly through the deep blue sky—a vulture. Or the sands would move a little, and we would see a small snake burrowing deeper to escape the heat. But other than that, there was no movement. This was a place in the grip of death.

I wondered who lay inside the pyramids, and what was there with them. There must surely be jewelry, food, books, and instruments. Somewhere in that utter darkness and isolation in the heart of the pyramid would be paintings of stars and Nut, goddess of the sky, as if to fool the dead Pharaohs into believing they lay outdoors under the night sky, rather than imprisoned in stone and surrounded by stale, stifling air for eternity.

The pyramids gradually began to change color. At noon they had been almost white, but that softened to a tan and then, as the sun sank lower— Atum again—they took on a warm glow with a rosy tinge. Little creatures— lizards, snakes, mice—began to stir and leave their hiding places all around us. We also emerged from the paws of the Sphinx and walked around the pyramids again. Now great, long shadows stretched on one side, and the slant of the light showed all the irregularities of the surfaces. Here and there the stones were crumbling; time was eating away at their fabric. Even they, the most immortal things anyone knew of, were not proof against the relentless enmity of time.

The setting sun picked out the pebbles and ripples of the sands all around, showing the pyramids to lie not in a featureless frame but in a richly textured one, whose writing is invisible except under certain light conditions.

The sky was pink and purple, a twisted mixture of colors spreading upward from a bright red spot at the horizon. A breeze suddenly sprang up out of nowhere, warm like melted ointment, and as sweet as a long-ago death.

"Come," said Nebamun. "We should leave. It grows dark very quickly, and we should not be here when the light fades." He hopped on his donkey with surprising speed.

What would the pyramids be like at night? Darkness against darkness?

I wanted to stay. But I was young, and must obey.

7

Nothing is ever the same twice. I expected that the journey back would be exactly like the one coming. And for a while it was—the same riverbanks, the same canals, the same clumps of date palms. But as we neared Alexandria and saw the white towers of the city walls blinking in the sun, we saw an unusual amount of movement, and crowds of people. Nebamun called out, "What's the news?" as we approached the dock.

"Cleopatra's dead!"

Although I knew it was not I, it is chilling to hear the death of someone with your name announced so nonchalantly.

"Poisoned!" cried another man on the dock. "I'm sure of it!"

"Where is Berenice?" asked Nebamun.

"In the palace. Where else should she be?"

"She hasn't fled, if that's what you're asking," his companion added. "But she might well have to. One of the other children already has—the younger Cleopatra. They're out looking for her everywhere. The Romans are coming."

"The Romans? What Romans?" I cried.

"The Romans from Rome," said the man with sarcasm. "What other kind are there?"

"Not true," said his companion smugly. "These Romans are coming from Syria—three legions—to try to restore Ptolemy to the throne. He bought them, after all."

"But the prophecy? What of the prophecy?" I asked. By that time we were out of the boat and scrambling out onshore. "Supposedly the Sibylline books forbade any armed help from Rome."

"Money finds a way," said the man. "Clever child, if you know about Sibylline books, you should know that money overrules all prophecies."

"Come!" said Nebamun, herding us toward the street of the Soma. He was alarmed, and realized he should return us to the palace as quickly as possible. As it was, he would probably be lashed as punishment for taking us.

"Nebamun, don't be afraid," I said. "It was my idea to go; I will take the blame and the punishment." My sister would be pleased enough to order mine, that I knew; but whether she would forgo Nebamun's lashing as well was not so certain.

Had she poisoned Cleopatra? Would she destroy me, and Arsinoe as well? I felt weak with fear.

Once back in the palace, I did not wait for her to send for me, but went straight to her quarters. They were filled with professional mourners, weeping and beating on their breasts, and wailing in high, ghostly moans. I begged leave to go directly to the Queen's rooms, and, flinging myself down in sorrow—and trepidation—awaited her. I heard her footsteps come nearer and stop.

"Oh, sister!" I cried. "Is it so? Is Cleopatra dead? And have I added to your grief by being absent? Forgive me!" I did not have to feign my distress.

"Get up; stop sniveling. Yes, our sister is dead. Mushrooms have been her entry into the realm of Osiris. One must be careful with mushrooms. I avoid them entirely."

I looked at her, stolid and seemingly unmoved by the death. No one should be unmoved by death, I thought. Then, as I looked closer, I saw that there was a half-smile on her face, which she was trying hard to keep under control.

"Where have you been?" she shot at me. "How dare you leave the palace and stay away for days without informing me? You are only a child! Who is behind this?"

"It was I who planned it, and forced Nebamun, Mardian's uncle, to take me, and several others. We did it to him, not he to us." Please let her believe me!

"Take you where?"

"To see the pyramids and the Sphinx."

I expected her to be angry, but she burst out laughing. Then I realized why. She had been afraid we were involved in something political, but this was innocent. I felt relief flooding me. She was not going to harm me. Not today.

"I've never seen them myself," she said. "I am a bit embarrassed to admit it."

"They were all I had dreamed of," I said. "They made me proud to be an Egyptian."

"You aren't an Egyptian, you are a Ptolemy—a Greek!" she reminded me.

"The Ptolemies have been here three hundred years; we must be Egyptian by now."

"What a stupid thing to say! Another of your silly ideas! We don't have a drop of Egyptian blood; it doesn't matter how long we've been here!"

"But—" I started to say that we could be Egyptian in spirit if not in blood, but she cut me off.

"If a red piece of granite stands next to a gray piece of granite for a thousand years, does it change?" she bellowed.

"People are not granite," I insisted.

"Sometimes they can be almost that hard."

"Not you," I said. "There is a part of you that is kind." I was trying to flatter her.

The half-smile returned. "I hope my husband may find me so."

"Husband?" I almost choked.

"Yes. I had just married when our sister Cleopatra left us. She turned my house of joy into one of mourning. But such are the accidents of fate."

"Who—who is he?"

"Prince Archelaus of Pontus," she replied, and this time the smile became a full one. He must be handsome, and pleasing to her.

"How much has happened in the few days I was away!" I blurted out.

"And more besides," she said. "We are making ready to defend ourselves against our father's mercenaries! With Roman money—borrowed, of course— he has hired yet other Romans to invade Egypt and try to take back the throne!" Her voice shook with the effrontery of it all.

"But what of the Sibylline prophecy?" I asked, yet again.

"Cicero found a way around it! Yes, the great Roman orator, who prides himself on being so noble, is like any merchant making a deal in the bazaar. The only difference is that he trades in words, not deeds."

"But what words did he use?" Would no one tell me? I knew the prophecy: *If an Egyptian king should come asking for help, do not refuse him friendship; but do not go to his aid with force, for if you do you will meet with dangers and difficulties.* How to get around that?

"Something to the effect that Gabinius, the Roman governor of Syria, should send the King on ahead of him, so that he won't be accompanying him 'with force'—only backing him up!" She snorted. "We shall be ready for them!" she said with certainty.

Father was on his way back! The Romans would restore him to the throne! It was all I could do not to burst into cheers. "I shall stay in my quarters," I assured her. "You need not worry again about my whereabouts. I am grieved that my absence caused you any concern."

She had forgotten about punishing Nebamun; the Roman army had banished all ordinary thoughts from her mind. I would hide in my rooms and hope she forgot about me, too.

Things happened very quickly. It was your wish, O Isis—you who deliver the plotter of evil against other men into the hands of the one he plots against— that my father, Ptolemy XII Philopator Neos Dionysus, should be restored to his throne. It was you who brought the troops of Gabinius to the outskirts of Egypt at Pelusium, who let them overcome the garrison there, and march upon Alexandria. It was you who caused the confusion and overthrow of Berenice's forces and the death of her new bridegroom, Archelaus. It was you who made Gabinius's young cavalry commander show mercy to the defeated Egyptians, and give an honorable burial to Archelaus, and thus win the love of the Alexandrians. His Roman name was Marcus Antonius, and he was twenty-seven years old.

It was you who arranged it all, moved all these events, in only a few days provided my entire future and revealed its form.

Berenice must be publicly executed. Now I was the eldest surviving child, the one who would be Queen.

Queen. I would be Queen. I kept repeating the words to myself, but I was not impatient for it before my time; unlike my sisters, I would let it happen when it was destined to. Their attempts to twist fate had merely given the throne to *me*. That made me smile.

I—Queen. The third child, and a girl. Truly, this was the work of Isis, she who shapes fate.

My joy at seeing Father again was unbounded. I threw my arms around him, realizing that now my eyes were almost level with his. He had been away three long years, years that had wrought many changes in me.

"You are back! Safe!" It seemed impossible, as the answers to prayers often do.

He was looking at me as if he had forgotten what he would see. "You have grown lovely, child," he finally said. "You will be the Queen that Egypt deserves."

"I am fourteen now," I reminded him, in case he had lost track. "I hope I will not be Queen for a long time—may the Pharaoh live for a million years, as the ancients said."

"Your smile is the same," said Father gently. "I carried it with me in my heart the whole time."

Yet this same sentimental man forced us to witness the execution of his other daughter, Berenice. How can we be so many different people, all contained within the same body?

I tried to excuse myself, on the grounds that it was an intrusion; a person should be able to die privately. But Father insisted.

"Just as her treason was public," he said, "so too must her punishment be."

And he insisted that the Romans be present, too. The Romans, who had restored him to power—for a price. Now they must see what their money had bought.

We had to take our places before a barracks that housed the Household Guards; seats of honor had been hastily erected. Before leaving for the grounds, Father had presented the Roman officers to me. Aulus Gabinius was a square, stocky man, a no-nonsense sort, as one would expect of someone who defied a prophecy. And his star cavalry officer, Marcus Antonius . . . I found him a winsome young man, one whose smile was genuine.

And, to be honest, that is all I remember of him from that first meeting.

Berenice was led out before the barracks, her hands bound behind her back. She was not blindfolded, but forced to look at us all, her ghoulish audience.

"You have been found guilty of treason, of usurping the throne in the absence of your rightful King," intoned Pothinus, one of the King's ministers, a young eunuch. His voice had the timbre of a child's but the carrying power of an adult's. "For this you must pay the penalty, and die."

"Have you any words?" asked the King. It was a formality only. Did he truly wish to hear any?

"Slave of the Romans!" she cried. "There they sit!" She jerked her head toward Gabinius and Antonius and Rabirius, the moneylender who had financed the campaign. "There they sit, never to be dislodged from Egypt! Who, then, is the traitor to this country, Father?"

"Enough!" said Pothinus. "This will be your last breath!" He motioned to the soldier who was to strangle her. The man stepped up behind her. His forearms were the size of most men's thighs.

Berenice was standing rigid, waiting. She closed her eyes as he brought his hands around her throat, then clasped them with a jerk. For what seemed a very long time she was obviously holding her breath, but then suddenly her body rebelled and she began twisting, trying to loosen his grip. Her hands were helplessly tied behind her, and there was little she could do. The soldier finally lifted her up by her neck and held her there as the life was snuffed out in her and her body at last stopped twitching. Her feet hung down straight from the ankles; one of her sandals fell off, making a loud plop in the still air. I saw that her face had turned a hideous dark color, and I looked away. Then I heard a noise of tramping feet, and saw her being loaded onto a litter and carried away. One of her feet—the one without a sandal—dragged along the ground; if she had been living it would have distressed her. But now she did not mind.

Father's face had lost its color, although he did not betray any open emotion. Next to him Gabinius had winced, and Antonius had looked away. Soldiers preferred battlefield killing to this formal, ritualized death. On either side of me sat my remaining siblings, taking in this cautionary lesson. Arsinoe had given a sharp gasp when the executioner stepped forward. The two boys—six and four—squirmed in unison. Even they understood that this was not a game, that Berenice would not jump up off the litter. We all saw, and learned, different things that day.

As I watched the hideous ritual, I knew that she had bequeathed something to me, something she had not exactly intended. From her I knew now that a woman could rule alone—a strong woman, that is. The earlier Ptolemaic queens had come to power through their marriages, but Berenice had proved that a woman could seize her own power, and only afterward choose the man. Or choose no man at all, should she prefer that.

Then, I was acutely aware that Roman troops had brought about this restoration, and that Roman troops were for hire for the promise of Ptolemaic money. Their forces, our money: a formidable combination. And last, in spite of the hatred of the Romans as a political fact, individual Romans were not demons. In fact, they could be quite attractive. Gabinius and this Antonius were personable, pleasant, and well mannered. All the pat jokes about Romans being barbarians—I remembered what I had believed about them before the Pompey dinner—were simply not true.

And there was something else, something I had glimpsed in all this: The Romans were divided among themselves. One group was against restoring Father, another for it. One set of rules forbade it, but a clever rewording got around that. Everything in Rome was not set in stone, and perhaps one side could be used to counteract another. . . .

These were ideas, formless at the time, but just beginning to reveal themselves to me. The Romans were not merely a force against which we were helpless, but were torn by factions and rivalries of their own, which could be turned to our advantage. I saw that our adversary had holes in his armor. Father had successfully exploited one—with Egyptian money. One must always have money.

Father made it clear that the Romans were welcome to stay in Alexandria— for a short time. Then they should discreetly remove themselves. But first there was to be a Dionysian festival to celebrate the King's restoration to the throne. He saw himself as the descendant of that mysterious god of wine, of joy and drama and life itself. In the great festivals of Bacchus—the god's Roman name—he sought release and ecstasy and belonging: all the things he could not find in Alexandria in the broad daylight, dazzling though it is in that city of cities.

In readying myself for the formal procession through the streets, I was acutely aware that I would be the object of intense curiosity. I, hitherto the third child and practically unnoticed, was now the heir. Everyone would want to assess me; all eyes would be upon me. I went through anguish in choosing my costume, having my hair dressed. And when it was finished, I knew I would look in the mirror and have the answer that had been so long in coming. Was I beautiful? Pleasing? Special? Would a timely jar of beauty from Persephone open itself for me?

I settled on a hairstyle that hung down around my shoulders. I was still young enough to wear a girl's hairdo, and I knew that my hair was pretty— no sense in hiding it before its time. It was almost black, thick and shiny, with a slight curl to it. And I chose for my dress a thin white linen, knowing that nothing becomes black hair like a white dress. I wanted to wear the tight style of older Egypt, since my shape was slim, but Grecian style fitted the occasion better, with all its floating folds.

At least I no longer had to bind my breasts; the death of Berenice had ended that. I could let my body speak for itself. And my breasts—even in my critical eyes, I could find no fault in them.

As I finished dressing, I saw Arsinoe reflected in the mirror behind me— Arsinoe, who had all the conventional beauty I longed for.

I moved the mirror so her image vanished. And then I studied myself, tried to imagine a stranger seeing me. And I was not displeased.

If I saw her, I thought, I would want to know her better.

I shrugged, and put the mirror down, as I bent to select the appropriate jewelry. Perhaps that was the best verdict anyone could reasonably hope for: *If I saw her, I would want to know her better.*

Now, as we rode at a stately ceremonial pace through Alexandria, I watched the crowd lining both sides of the wide streets. The procession had begun at the palace, then wound its way past Alexander's tomb, past the long, colonnaded Gymnasion, past the Library, the Temple of Serapis, the artificial hill of the park of Pan, the theater—all the monuments of our great city. The vast, excitable crowd today was cheering, climbing on roofs to see us, shinnying up columns, straddling statues. Since we were following in the wake of Dionysus and his wineskins, by the time we came upon them, the people were flushed and merry and forgiving. These were the very same people who had rioted when a Roman soldier accidentally killed a sacred cat—unstable, violent. Today they were our devoted partisans. Tomorrow?

Far behind us, to signify the end of the procession, walked a man costumed as Hesperus, the evening star.

At length we reached our destination: the Stadium, transformed into a pavilion where the festivities would take place. The normal open-air field had been roofed over with a lattice of ivy- and grape-entwined beams, supported by columns shaped like Dionysus's sacred wand. The brilliant afternoon sunlight filtered through the green leaves as we entered the cave of the god, to the rites of drunkenness and ecstasy.

Or, rather, my father entered it. As a devotee of the god, he took it upon himself to seek union with Dionysus by way of wine. While the rest of us sampled the new vintage from the vineyards of the Canopic branch of the Nile, Egypt's finest, Father gulped it. Then, as the dancing began—for actors and musicians were sacred to the god, and inspired by him—Father seemed to go into a trance. He had put on the sacred ivy wreath, and now pulled out his flute and started playing melodies.

"Dance! Dance!" he ordered everyone around him. The Egyptians obeyed, but the Romans looked on, appalled.

"I said dance!" the King demanded. He waved his pipes toward one of the visiting Romans, an army engineer.

"You! There! Demetrius! Dance!"

Demetrius looked as though he had been ordered to jump into a malarial swamp. "I do not dance," he said, and turned his back and walked away.

"Come back here!" The King attempted to catch the fold of his tunic, but tripped instead, and his ivy wreath slipped over one eye. "Oh!"

A group of Gabinius's soldiers was snickering. I felt deep shame for my father. I knew he was merely engaging in the time-honored behavior of the Bacchanalia, but those rites had been banned in dignity-conscious Rome. To the Romans, this was just a comic, drunken spectacle.

"So that's why he's nicknamed *Auletes*—the flute-player," said a voice nearby. I saw it belonged to Marcus Antonius—or Marc Antony, as he was commonly called.

"Yes, but the people of Alexandria gave him the name in affection," I said stiffly. "*They* understand about the rites of Dionysus."

"So I see." He gestured around at the crowd.

Here was another prissy, judgmental Roman—so proper, while imposing themselves on the rest of the world! I glared at him, until I saw that he himself was drinking from a silver goblet. "At least you don't consider your lips too good to touch Egyptian wine," I said. As I spoke, he held out his goblet for a costumed server to refill it.

"Quite passably good," he said, sipping it. "I've a great fondness for wine; I make it my business to test the vintage wherever I go. I've had Chian wine, Rhaetic, the undrinkable Coan and Rhodian, and the incomparable Pramnian." He sounded like a father naming his children.

"Is the Pramnian really all it is said to be?" I asked, as he seemed so happy to be talking about it.

"Indeed. It is honey-sweet; they don't squeeze it from the grapes of Lesbos, they let it ooze out of its own accord."

He really was quite relaxed and unpretentious; I found myself liking this Roman. He was handsome, too, in a bullish sort of way: thick neck, wide face, and a frame bulging with muscles.

"Yes, I understand Dionysus," he said, more to himself than to me. "I also like actors. In Rome I prefer them to the senators!"

He broke off as the King came reeling through the crowd, chased by women dressed as Maenads, pursuing the god, shouting and laughing.

"Dancing is considered immoral in Rome," he said. "That is why Demetrius refused to dance. Please inform the King of that, when he's—not the god any longer, but returns to himself."

How diplomatic of him to avoid saying *when he's sober again*. I did like this young Roman, who seemed so very un-Roman.

But he did not stay in Alexandria long; within a month he and Gabinius had departed, although the three legions were left behind to keep order. The one Roman who should have gone with them stayed—Rabirius, the infamous financier. He was determined to recoup his loan directly from the Egyptians, and forced the King to appoint him finance minister. Then he proceeded to extort huge sums from the populace. The Alexandrians, always with a mind of their own and virtually never subservient, drove him away. Father was lucky that they did not sweep him off the throne again in the process.

In Rome, both Gabinius and Rabirius had to stand trial before the Senate: Gabinius for disregarding the sacred Sibylline oracle and the decree of the Senate, and Rabirius for serving in an administrative post under a foreign king. Gabinius was forced to go into exile, but the crafty Rabirius got off.

Without his commanding officer, the young Marc Antony transferred his allegiance and services to a new general: Julius Caesar.

8

My life now took another of its abrupt turns; from acting younger than I was, and keeping myself hidden, I must now do the opposite. I must take my place alongside Father at all his official appearances—especially as he no longer had a Queen to stand beside him—and look worthy to step into his shoes. My tutors were reassigned to the younger children, and I was given real scholars from the Museion, as well as retired ambassadors to teach me the intricacies of diplomacy. In addition, I was expected to be present at all Father's council meetings.

In some ways I missed my earlier freedom and unimportance; it seems that even unpleasant states have a way of recommending themselves to you after they are over. My days of running about with the Society of Imhotep had ended; and even Mardian and Olympos seemed distant, as if they were unsure how to treat me now. Never had I felt more alone—solitary and elevated.

Yet would I have wished to be other than I was? No.

Learning how to govern, day by day, was a painstaking process. To have command of all the workings of the country, a king had to master a multitude of details. These were covered, tediously, in council meetings. While Father sat at the head of them, I took a place to one side and listened. To have the canals dredged . . . to collect the import taxes more efficiently . . . to ration grain in a poor harvest year . . . yes, the ruler must know, and have wisdom on, these things. He who did not would be at the mercy of his ministers.

And the choosing of ministers—that was an art in itself. You wanted the most talented, the most dedicated, as nothing less was worthy of the country. Yet the more talented, the more dedicated, a man was—the more his loyalty might waver. Seeing all your shortcomings, he might be tempted to turn against you.

But to have fools for ministers was also a recipe for disaster. There were so many pitfalls a ruler could fall into.

During the first year after Father's return, the infamous Rabirius and his debt dominated the council meetings. Father's total debt to Rome was now sixteen thousand talents; Gabinius had demanded ten thousand on top of the six that had already been agreed on. Egypt was reeling under it. Small wonder that certain elements later rebelled.

But at this time, the problem was being tackled straightforwardly.

People were in a benign, welcoming mood, glad that their King had returned. But when they were presented with the bill for restoring him, the murmurs would begin. And maybe grow into a full-fledged revolt.

Father tried to get Rabirius to forgive some of the debt. Other advisors suggested that we increase import taxes to cover it. Still others said we should ask for an extension.

I could not help but think that countries were only groups of people, and that the answer lay in remembering how individuals thought. People are more generous after they have been granted a favor; then they are more likely to grant one in return.

"It seems to me that the people should pay the debt, and it should be paid on time. Otherwise the interest on it will just increase," I said, speaking up from the side of the gathering. "But it might be wise to announce a general amnesty before you announce the debt collection. Forgive bad debts and minor crimes and thereby appear magnanimous."

One of the advisors opened his mouth to disagree, but Father looked impressed. "A good idea," he finally said.

"It would create widespread goodwill," I said.

"Yes, at a loss of our income!" protested one of the financial councillors.

"It is a small loss, to offset such a large collection. There is little likelihood of our collecting those old debts in any case," I said. It seemed so obvious.

"I shall think on it," said Father. And he ended up following my suggestion. I was most pleased.

Father was safe now; his throne was steady, supported by the might of Rome and the borrowed Gabinius legions. He was almost fifty, and purposed to enjoy his reign in peace—or, rather, in ease and comfort. He had his Dionysian revels, of course, his banquets and his poetry readings late at night to occupy him. And once he took us all hunting in the western desert, to emulate both the Pharaohs and the earlier Ptolemies.

He had seen so many pictures of Pharaohs killing lions that he was minded to seek one; he had had so many depictions made of himself smiting enemies on the walls of the temples that he had come to believe it had truly happened. And so we set out in order for the King to slay a lion—two hundred beaters, slaves, kennelmasters, provisioners (for what was the King to eat while waiting to bag his game?). We rode camels—the best beasts for the desert, despite the pictures of kings shooting from chariots. The lions had been driven farther and farther back into the desert wilderness, and we must seek them there.

For a piece we kept along the seashore, but after a bit we turned inland along a ridge where the hunters assured us that lions lurked.

I was swaying along on top of the camel, enjoying the rocking motion, my head protected against the piercing sun by an elaborate headdress. I did not care whether we found a lion or not, but I loved seeing this dangerous and empty land. The terrain stretched out supine in all directions, colored every shade of gold and brown. The wind, still fresh from the sea, came whipping around us, sometimes murmuring, sometimes sighing, sometimes whining.

At night we slept in luxurious tents. The fabric was embroidered with tiny, painstakingly sewn designs, and over our beds were unfurled curtains of lightest silk to keep out any grains of sand or insects. Lanterns flickered on little ivory-inlaid folding tables, and our attendants slept on pallets at our feet. The largest royal tent, where the King was, was large enough that he could gather all his remaining children around him after the evening meal.

As the wind whistled around the tent ropes, we would sit with him, lounging on cushions at his feet. Sometimes we would play a board game, such as draughts or senet. Arsinoe would play the lyre—she was quite talented at it—and the two boys would sometimes be playing a board game of their own. I can see us in my mind right at this moment; I can even smell the light, dry scent of the desert air. Four little Ptolemies, each ambitious, each determined to rule when the benevolent King passed on—the King who would soon begin nodding in his cups.

I watched Arsinoe carefully. By this time she was thirteen to my sixteen, and every year she grew more beautiful. Her alabaster-pale skin had a pearly glow to it, her features were almost perfect, and her eyes were the color of the sea at Alexandria. Her temper was not good, she was demanding and emotional, but beauty has a way of softening all hearts.

My oldest brother Ptolemy, almost eight now and presumably my future husband—what of him? I wished I could like him, I thought, as I watched his dark head bent over his game of dice, but he was a nasty little character, devious and selfish—the sort who moved the mark in games and lied about it when confronted. He was probably using crooked dice even now. He was a coward as well. I had watched him running from the most harmless dogs, and even from cats.

Little Ptolemy should have been born first, so I would have been matched with him instead. The child seemed to have a double portion of the things his brother was lacking: he was forthright, cheerful, and high-spirited. As a couple, I realized, he and Arsinoe would be more appealing than the elder Ptolemy and I.

Isn't that appalling? To be lying at our father's feet, a supposedly happy family relaxing, and to be thinking those thoughts? But that is what it is to be a Ptolemy: all our family affections are subordinated to our own ambitions, which are never at rest. The only thing that distinguishes any of us is whether we will draw the line at nothing to achieve our goals, or whether some acts remain forbidden.

On this particular night, Arsinoe was lounging back against the cushions, plucking at her lyre and murmuring some words. Her voice was not particularly pleasing, I was glad to note. The lanterns were winking, and Father was lifting another cup of wine to his lips, a dreamy expression on his face.

"Give me some," I suddenly said. "Anything that brings such an otherworldly contentment to your face must have been sent from the gods."

When the servant poured me some and I tasted it, it was truly sublime—heavy, sweet, and golden.

"From Cyprus," said the King. "They have long been famous for their wines, which keep a long time and don't turn bitter." A dark look came over his face. "Cyprus. Our lost Cyprus!" He reached for his pipes. He was about to start playing, and then weep.

"Tell me more about Cyprus!" I said. I didn't want to sit through one of his musical performances, followed by a bout of self-pity. I think that was what I liked least about him—the maudlin indulgences, not the wine itself. "What happened with you and Cato there?" On his way to Rome, Father had stopped at Cyprus, where Cato sat, inventorying the last Ptolemy's possessions.

"Cato! What do they call him in Rome? 'The austere, hard-drinking Cato.' How can they go together?" He laughed, a tinkling, drunken laugh. "The Romans took Cyprus from my brother! Just annexed it, and my poor brother had to drink poison." Tears welled up in his eyes.

"But Cato? What did he have to do with it?"

"They sent Cato out to help himself to the treasury there, and to complete the annexation, make it part of the province of Cilicia." He sniffed. "When I arrived, Cato—Cato—! He received me while—while—sitting on a privy!"

I gasped. I knew Father had been insulted, but not to this extent. So we had truly fallen this low? A Roman official received a Ptolemaic king while seated on a privy? I burned with shame, and anger. Did everyone know about this? Had Gabinius and Antony?

"It smelled bad," added the King. "Very bad. So I suppose what he said was true—his bowels were upset, and he dared not move."

"Curse his bowels!" said Arsinoe suddenly. She had not even seemed to be listening.

"I think, from what Father says, they *were* cursed," I said. "I hope they continue to be so."

"He has enemies," said Father. "He is very conservative; he tries to make a case for himself as a noble of the old Roman type, but his day, and the day of others like him, is passing. Caesar will sweep him from the board, as I sweep these draughts." He gave an unsteady swat that knocked a few pieces to the ground.

"The same Julius Caesar who took over Rabirius's debt?" I asked. "When will he come to Egypt to collect it?"

"Never," said Father, "if we are lucky. He is busy conquering Gaul; they say he's the greatest general since Alexander. Of course our patron, Pompey, doesn't think so. Their rivalry grows every day. No, child, only if Pompey is put down by Caesar will Caesar ever come here. And if Pompey is vanquished, the fortunes of Egypt will vanish with him. So pray Caesar never comes here!" He hiccuped gently.

"Caesar must be surrounded by enemies," said Arsinoe. "Cato on the one hand, Pompey on the other."

"He is," said Father. "But he seems to be made of iron; nothing bothers him. He trusts completely to his luck, to his destiny. At the same time, he seems to tempt it." He began laughing—cackling, almost. "He has made Cato's sister his mistress!"

We all screamed with laughter.

"Love as a weapon," said Arsinoe. I knew what she was thinking: *With my looks, it is a weapon open to me.*

"That is one we Ptolemies have never employed," Father said. "Strange, when we've exploited all the others."

"Perhaps none of us were very lovable," I suggested.

"Nonsense!" said Father.

Time passed; Father stayed on his throne; the Romans continued their bickering amongst themselves, which diverted their attention. There were many ceremonial occasions to keep us busy, in addition to the real, behind-the-scenes work.

The Alexandrians wished to dedicate a newly laid-out precinct to us—a park that included plantings, statuary, and pools on the outskirts of the city. We attended in full royal regalia, presented by Father for the occasion, human statues in the midst of the stone ones. I was seventeen then, becoming used to such ceremonies.

But on this day two things were different. The inscription—dictated by Father—carved on the stone called us all "Our Lords and Greatest Gods." So we were all gods now, not just the ruler? He stood proudly as the stone was exhibited and the startling words recited.

"O living gods, and goddesses, we throw ourselves at your blessed feet—" the magistrate was saying. One by one citizens came and bent their heads before us, then knelt. I looked down and saw people shaking, as if they were afraid of inhaling some deadly, divine mist. Who could know how much playacting went into it, or how much they were overtaken by the moment?

And then Father spoke, saying, "Today my children, the gods, assume a new title: Philadelphoi, Brother-and-Sister-Loving. May they be locked together in the love that binds those who share the same blood."

Standing shoulder to shoulder with my siblings, I knew it could never be. But it was touching that Father wished it so.

Afterward we gathered in Father's private dining chamber to seal the ceremony with a meal. Arsinoe was the first to fling off her gold robe: Pronouncing it too heavy to drag around, she let it fall in a crumpled heap.

"Should not the weight of gold sit lightly on a goddess's shoulders?" I teased her. Underneath it she was wearing a thin blue gown that duplicated the blue of her eyes.

She merely shrugged. Either she felt no different, or she had always assumed godhood for herself.

Father took his place at the head of our family. He looked tired, as if he should be the one to find the heavy robes oppressive. It was only then that I saw the weariness in him; suddenly he seemed much older.

He took up an agate cup and stared at it moodily as he motioned for wine. "This cup came from our ancestral homeland," he said. "Macedonia. I wish you to remember that we started out drinking from stone cups, even though we have ended surrounded by gold." He took a sip. Then another.

"Did the ceremony please you?" he asked.

We all nodded dutifully.

"Surprise you?"

"Yes. Why did you bestow the two new titles?" I finally asked, since no one else seemed willing to talk.

"Because I wish you all to be treated as sacrosanct, by each other as well as by outsiders, after I am gone—"

Was he just being foresighted and tidy, or was he aware of a reason to hurry?

"Gone where?" asked the smallest Ptolemy, perched on his stool—it was padded and studded with gems, but it was a stool nonetheless—and leaning on his elbows.

"After he's dead," said his brother, coldly, the nine-year-old realist.

Arsinoe kept chewing languidly on an onion stalk, such was the warmth of our little family. "Oh," she finally said.

"It is kind of you to think so far ahead," I said. "But surely that is not of immediate concern." I meant it as a question. But he chose not to answer it.

"A good ruler must take precautions. Now, I wish to inform you about my will. I have dispatched a copy to Rome, since they have such an . . . interest in our affairs, proclaiming themselves guardians of our welfare. It might give offense if I did not. And there is already a precedent for it." He took several sips of the wine, each one closer to a gulp.

"One copy remains here," he continued. "That, too, is a precaution. Wills can be altered, lost . . . and to offset that, you must hear my provisions from my own mouth."

I noticed that Arsinoe had stopped chewing and was sitting up straighter.

"Surely it will come as no surprise to you that Cleopatra will succeed me," he said. He turned toward me with a smile. "She is the oldest, and has been trained for the station." But his eyes said more; they said, *And she is the child of my heart, the one I choose above all others.*

I did not look at Arsinoe, but I knew that she was sullen.

"With her as co-regent will be her first brother, Ptolemy. In due time they must marry, as is the custom."

Both boys giggled, as if they found it all silly and odious. Well, it was odious, but too serious to be silly.

"Father," I said, "perhaps that custom should be allowed to lapse."

He shook his head, sadly. "Ending it would bring more trouble than observing it. Every fortune hunter of a prince would converge on our shores. It would be like one of the old myths, where suitors hung about, being tested by the father or the gods, having to perform impossible feats—I have other things to do than to preside over contests for your hand."

"I always wondered why the suitors came and risked themselves in the stories," said Arsinoe. "The rejected ones always got killed."

Father laughed. "Princesses exert a deadly lure."

After the meal was over, Father asked me to remain with him. The others did not linger; the scowling Arsinoe picked up her robe and dragged it scornfully behind her as she left, as if to show that she disdained Father's gifts, since he did not offer her the highest one.

"Now, my child," he said, as he took his seat on a cushioned bench beside me, with a fine view of the harbor, "there is something else."

I had sensed that there must be. "Yes?"

"I think it would be wise to associate you in ruling with me now," he said.

"In ceremonies? But we already—"

"No, to elevate you formally to co-regency. To proclaim you Queen."

Queen . . . now? It seemed too wonderful—to taste the joys without having to swallow the sorrow of Father's loss at the same time. "I am touched by the honor you offer me," I finally said.

"There will be another ceremony soon, then," he said. He gave a cough, then another, and I knew then that these arrangements were not premature.

"Father, please don't make me marry my brother!" I must say it now. "He's a whining little tattletale! And he will grow up to be something worse!"

But the King was not to be dissuaded, even by me. He shook his head. "You are fortunate I don't just skip over you and name him as heir. It is unprecedented for the Queen to be first ruler."

"You wouldn't dare." But I said it affectionately, not angrily. I leaned my head on his shoulder, thinking how seldom I touched, or was touched, by anyone. Even normal human contact was shunned in our family.

He sighed, then permitted himself to pat my head. "No, probably not. You are too strong-willed to be pushed aside. That's good."

"I don't like your minister Pothinus," I felt obligated to tell him. "Perhaps you should replace him."

"Ah," he said. "One strong-willed person to keep another in check." He could be as stubborn as I—which is probably where I got it.

"I don't like him," I repeated. "He's untrustworthy." The worst trait I could think of.

"I plan to make him head of the Regency Council."

"I don't need a Regency Council. I am already a grown woman."

"You are seventeen, and your future co-ruler, dear little Ptolemy, is only nine. Should I die tonight, *he* would need a Regency Council."

"Must you make it as disagreeable as he is?"

Father sighed. "You weary me! Be happy! Stop arguing! Learn to like Pothinus!" He paused. "I plan to live so long Ptolemy won't need a Regency Council, but a nurse for his old age!" He coughed again, and I took his hand.

The first time I stood beside Father in robes of state, and heard the fateful words *Queen Cleopatra, Lady of the Two Lands*, I felt not as if a weight were laid on me but a hitherto unknown strength and readiness miraculously conferred. Whatever the task would be, this mysterious power would graciously be granted me to meet it. Nothing I had read or heard had hinted at this transformation, so it came as an unexpected gift.

In the old tales, to question a gift too closely meant the gods could revoke it; it bespoke ingratitude and disbelief. And so I accepted it with all my heart, trustingly.

In the thirtieth year of Ptolemy Auletes which is the first year of Cleopatra . . . So it began, as the gods would have it.

In the late winter of the next year, when the gales had quit lashing the sea and the waves did not dash quite so high against the base of the Lighthouse, I was spending a great deal of time reading poetry—both the old Egyptian poetry and Greek. I had interested myself in learning the Egyptian language, and I told myself that was why I was reading the poetry, but that was not strictly true. I was reading it because it concerned love, and I was nearly eighteen years old.

> *The kisses of my beloved are on the other bank of the river; a branch of the stream floweth between us, a crocodile lurketh on the sandbank. But I step down into the water and plunge into the flood. My courage is great in the waters, the waves are as solid ground under my feet. Love of her lendeth me strength. Ah! She hath given me a spell for the waters.*

I would read the poetry late at night, when my attendants had left me and only the oil lamp kept me company. Then the poetry felt different from the way it did when I went over it with my tutor. In lessons I paid great attention to my translation, and to verb forms. Now, by myself, I could exchange all that and feel the faint, humming thrill of the words themselves.

"Oh! Were I but her slave, following her footsteps. Ah! Then should I joy in seeing the forms of all her limbs."

I ran my hand along my leg, wondering how it would appear to someone else. To a young man. I stroked it with sweet-scented oil, feeling the long muscles under the skin.

"Love to thee fills my utmost being, as wine pervades water, as fragrance pervades resin, as sap mingles itself with liquid. And thou, thou hastenest to see thy beloved as a steed rusheth to the field of battle."

I shivered. Such feelings seemed close to divinity, to madness.

I put away the scroll. There were more poems there, but I would save them for another night.

I was restless. The poems had made me so; I should be ready to lie down, and instead I paced the chamber. The sea outside was loud tonight, and I could hear the long, mournful sounds of the waves dashing against the rocks, then sliding away. Again. And again.

And then, far away, a sound of music, of pipes and voices. It seemed to be coming from the east, but that way lay only the sea. It grew a little louder, and now there was no mistaking it for anything besides human instruments and exquisite voices. Was it in the palace? Now it sounded as if it were coming from under the ground, directly beneath the building. It swelled louder, then passed by, wafted away, faded. I lay down, hearing its last faint strains. I slept.

The next morning, early, they awakened me. The King was dead. He had died during the night. And I knew then what music I had heard. It was the god Dionysus, playing his pipes, come to the palace to take his devotee to himself.

I arose. Father dead! Only yesterday I had seen him, and he had seemed in fine spirits, although his health was obviously delicate. But he had not been ill. Father dead! And I had left him without a word of good-bye. We had bade only an ordinary good-night. We were cheated; we always bid farewell after the simplest supper, and is it right to send those we love off on the greatest journey of all without a special word?

I asked to see him. He was lying on his bed, eyes closed, looking asleep. His parting had not been violent; he had gone gladly with Dionysus.

"He must be prepared for the Monument," I said. There he would sleep surrounded by the kings of his line, near where Alexander lay. O to have to make these heavy plans!

"The orders are already given," said a distinctive voice behind me. Pothinus.

"I am the one who should issue the orders," I said. "I am Queen."

"Co-ruler, along with my charge, the most divine Ptolemy the Thirteenth." He enunciated each word deliberately. "Queens do not attend to ordinary details."

"Queens that do not attend to ordinary details soon find themselves ignorant of the larger ones." I glared at him. So here we were, so soon, crossing swords. "You may attend to the details of the announcement of the King's death and my coronation."

"Your and Ptolemy the Thirteenth's coronation."

This was going to be wearisome. "Yes." I let him win that point. "Please let it be as soon as possible. We will have to address the people from the steps of the Temple of Serapis, and then be crowned according to Ptolemaic rites. Then I would like to be crowned at Memphis as well, according to the ancient custom of the Pharaohs. See to it." Let that keep him busy.

As he walked away, his tall frame swaying, I turned back to where my father lay. He seemed smaller, changed. My heart swelled with grief for him, and for all the hardships he had had to endure to retain his throne.

It will not have been in vain, Father, I promised him. Your sacrifices will bear fruit. We will not end up as a Roman province!

Thirty days later, on a brisk and windy day, Ptolemy and I rode together in the gilded ceremonial chariot at the head of the coronation procession that wound its way through the streets of Alexandria, past thousands of curious citizens. I had just had my eighteenth birthday, and he was ten. He had not grown much yet; he came up only to my chin—and I am not a tall woman. But he stood on tiptoe and waved at the cheering crowds, holding up his spindly arm and nodding his head.

I looked behind us at the chariot carrying Arsinoe and little Ptolemy, followed by the retinue of the Regency Council: Pothinus, of course, and Theodotos the tutor and Achillas, general of the Egyptian troops. Pothinus, with his unusually long legs (which eunuchs often have), towered over the other two. They looked almost gleeful; clearly they saw their future as bright. Behind them rode the ministers of state and, marching in their wake, the Macedonian Household Guards. The turning of the chariot wheels made winks of gold all along the way.

We wound our way out of the royal palace grounds and skirted the harbor, then turned at the Temple of Neptune and traveled through the Forum. Turning west, we passed by the Soma. *Alexander, are you proud of me?* I wanted to call to his tomb as we passed. I could almost believe I heard his reply in my mind: *Not yet, for nothing yet has come to pass.*

Across from the Soma, thousands more spectators were standing in the shade of the porticoes around the Gymnasion and the law courts. Then, a little farther down, more people were thronging over the steps of the Museion, particularly the scholars and their students. I recognized the various schools of philosophy by the styles of beard on the faces of their adherents.

The hill crowned by the great Temple of Serapis began to rear up ahead of us. This hill, the only natural one in all Alexandria, made a fitting site for our city god. His temple was known throughout the civilized world as something to take one's breath away—huge, imposing, framed against the sky, with fast-moving clouds always in the background. Inside the marble building was the statue of the god himself, gilded ivory and, if not as large as the Zeus of Olympia, still a marvel of beauty and construction.

The temple grounds sloped upward, and as we entered the sacred precinct, the crowds had to remain outside. But we were in view of all as we left the chariot and mounted the temple steps slowly, approaching the priests who stood, robed in scarlet.

They draped purple mantles over our shoulders, then led us inside, to the cool, dark, echoing hall of marble. As we walked slowly to the statue of Serapis, the holy flame lit before him flared up.

"A good omen," said one of the priests. "The god welcomes you."

They brought a silver vessel with two carrying handles, and poured some of the water into a gold basin. We were to dip our fingers in the sacred water, and then touch our tongues with a drop of it.

"The god has chosen you to rule," the priests said.

They went to a shrine behind the statue and brought out a little coffer, bound round with iron bands and sealed with a jeweled lock. One of them had the key on a band around his neck; he removed it, fitted it in the lock, and opened the coffer. With trembling hands he removed two plain strips of material: the Macedonian diadem. One priest handed mine to me. "You must fasten it yourself," he said.

I held it, looking down at it in the dim light. It was just a strip of linen, a piece of cloth! Yet the power it conveyed! This was what Alexander had worn, not a crown like other rulers, but this.

I took the cloth, positioned it across my forehead, then tied the ends in a knot at the back of my neck.

"It is done, Your Majesty," the priest said.

The cloth lay wide and heavy across my forehead, like no other cloth I had ever felt.

The ceremony was repeated for Ptolemy.

"Now turn to Serapis and say, 'We accept the state to which you have called us; we pray to be worthy of your favor.'"

Did the god acknowledge us? O Isis, only you know that. Do the gods listen to every word? Or are they careless sometimes, bored, preoccupied?

We were back out on the loggia of the temple, the bright day hurting our eyes, blinding us to the screaming crowds below. The wind lifted our garments a little, as if giving us a blessing as it passed.

I was Queen. I wore the sacred diadem, and the day, the people, the city, and Egypt itself were mine—to cherish and to protect.

"O my people!" I cried. "Let us rejoice together! And let me always be worthy of your love, and be granted the wisdom to preserve Egypt for you!"

Our crowning at Memphis was another thing altogether. For the second time in my life I was taken in a boat down the Nile—how different now! The barge was a royal one, with a gilded lotus flower at its bow, and banks of oars—not a little cabin-boat. The riverbanks were lined with the curious; everyone had left the fields. Only the donkeys remained, tied to their wheels. These people were all smiling, and there was no edge to their voices, only the lilt of delight. Ptolemy and I stood on the deck and waved at them, seeing them slide by behind the reeds and bulrushes.

We passed the pyramids, and I felt as though I were taking possession of them. All Egypt was mine, all the monuments and the sands and the Nile itself. I could barely speak for emotion.

Memphis was not far from the pyramids, and the landing stage was decorated for our arrival, hung with banners and garlands of lotus. Date palms lined the road, their dusty branches meeting overhead to make a canopy for us; people climbed them and shook the branches, making a rustle of welcome. Through their branches I could glimpse the limestone walls surrounding the inner palace and temples that had given Memphis its early title, "City of the White Wall."

Here the Pharaohs had had their coronations, and here Alexander had come to be crowned ruler of Egypt. His successors have done likewise, paying obeisance to the old forms, the old gods.

Before Alexandria, Memphis had been the largest and most important city of Egypt. Here the Pharaoh dwelt, and here was the place where the mysteries of Osiris were enacted, the holy of holies for the Egyptian. Today we were to be initiated into those mysteries by the high priest of Ptah, who was clad in a long linen gown with a panther's skin across his shoulders. The ceremony was in Egyptian, and I was proud that I could understand all of it—the only one of my family ever to have done so.

In the dim light of the inner temple, we received the symbols of a Pharaoh: the golden crook, the flail, the scepter, robes of linen from Lower Egypt, and ceremonial leather garments. Upon our heads were placed the *uraeus* of pure gold, Egypt's guardian serpent.

I grasped the handles of the crook and flail, circling them firmly with my fingers, feeling them almost welded to my hands. I vowed never to release or relinquish them until death made me relax my grip. Until then, they were mine—and I was theirs.

Afterward we had to perform the special rites of a Pharaoh. Dressed in ceremonial robes, we had to yoke the sacred Apis bull and lead him through the streets. This was to show our people that we were physically strong, and could be warriors; at the same time we had to chant a refrain promising never to be cruel to anyone beneath our sway, as the bull was beneath his yoke.

At your temple, O Isis, we took more vows. Do you remember that day? The day I bound myself to you by solemn oaths? We promised the priest that we would not interfere with the calendar, neither adding nor subtracting days, nor changing feast days, but allow the three hundred sixty-five days to complete their round as instituted. We also swore that we would protect the land and the water given to our charge.

Then the Memphis diadems were brought out, and we were crowned Pharaohs of Upper and Lower Egypt. They no longer used the heavy, hatlike double crown of the old kingdom, but had adopted the diadem. The cloth had been woven of flax grown in a field sacred to Ptah.

This was my true wedding day, my wedding to that which, if it lay within my power, would live forever: Egypt. I have saved my diadems from those ceremonies, and the gowns. My four marriages to earthly men have not survived, because nothing that is human can last. But Egypt . . .

The ceremonies over, all the rites observed, I set about taking power. The Regency Council tried to obstruct me, in the name of their protégé, Ptolemy XIII. They insisted I marry him forthwith. I demurred. Too many ceremonies, I said, are confusing. People enjoy ceremonies, but they should be doled out like candies, lest the appetite become cloyed. For now, the lavish public funeral of the King, followed by the coronation procession and citywide banquets, was enough.

We were all in the throne room of the alabaster palace, the one where I had attended on my sisters not so long before; the one with the tortoiseshell doors and gem-encrusted chairs. I was not sitting, but pacing back and forth in front of these men. They were all much bigger than I, and I needed to remember that.

Pothinus was taller than the others; his legs were spindly, but his chest was covered in rolls of fat where muscles should be. With his long nose and sharp, close-set eyes, he reminded me of a sacred ibis, except that he was not in the least sacred.

"Your Majesty," he intoned, with his child's voice, which he had trained to be soothing, "if you believe that, you do not understand people. There is no such thing as a surfeit of festivities."

"And the people are anxious to see you married," added Theodotos, once my tutor, then passed down to Ptolemy, a giggly little man with a large bald spot that he attempted to disguise by growing long curls he could fluff up over it. He had also taken to wearing a fillet, like a Gymnasion director.

"I cannot imagine why," I said. "It is not as if anything would change. Ptolemy is not a foreign prince, bringing an alliance with him. And we could hardly have an heir yet."

"It was your father's express command!" barked Achillas. He was the Egyptian commander of the army, and came from Upper Egypt, where the soldiers are the best fighters. Dark-skinned and lean, he looked like a tomb painting come to life. I always imagined him wearing the pleated kilt shown in the old paintings; but of course he wore the latest military attire, with bronze breastplate and shin protectors. He had taken a Greek name, like many Egyptians who wish to ingratiate themselves with the powers that be. His real name was probably "Beloved of Amun" or some such.

"And I shall honor it," I assured him. "I esteem my father. Have I not added the name Cleopatra Philopator, 'She Who Loves Her Father,' to my other titles?" I looked up at my three enemies, for such they were.

"Obedience is the best way to honor a parent," said Pothinus.

"And the best way to honor your Queen," I reminded them. "You are my subjects as well as Ptolemy's advisors."

I myself had no advisors, no older, wiser councillor I could consult. I was surrounded on all sides by enemies; my friends were all younger or less powerful than I. The trio in front of me seemed to grow larger, their penetrating eyes more feral.

They glared at me. "We of course will obey and honor you," said Achillas, with his flat Egyptian accent. "But you must not neglect your duty to your brother and co-ruler."

"I shall not," I assured him.

Ptolemy XIII was guaranteed a place at court and in history. But what of the others? What were Arsinoe and little Ptolemy to do while we ruled? Just wait in the palace—wait their turn? Circle like vultures? I shivered.

"I have no wish for a civil war!" I blurted out. Best to let them know I knew where they were leaning. "But I will rule in my own court, and in my own land!"

If only they were not so much *bigger* than I! Those who denigrate physical strength and power have never had to tilt their heads back to look an enemy in the eyes, or had to drag a stepstool over to peek out a high window.

"The Romans are, as usual, setting us a bad example," said Achillas with disdain, settling on the first part of my words and ignoring the second. "They are about to embark on another round of civil war, this time between Julius Caesar and Magnus Pompey. If we are very lucky, they will destroy themselves in the process." He sniffed like a greyhound scenting the wind.

"If Pompey sends an appeal to us, we will have to respond," I said. He had been my father's ally and now, if the tables were turned, might require our help. Caesar was responsible for collecting the money Egypt owed to Rome. I hoped he would be defeated. But Egypt would be the poorer even so, because we would have had to help equip Pompey to conquer Caesar. And someone else would just take over Caesar's debt. . . .

"Why? Egypt is a long way from Rome. We can ignore the appeal," said Pothinus.

Was *this* the man who thought himself a wise, sophisticated advisor? I had all I could do not to snort in derision. "Like a child pretending he does not hear his mother calling him to bed? No, Pothinus, that is the way of a coward. And Rome, the city, may be far from Alexandria—some twelve hundred miles—but the might of Rome, and Roman armies, is as near as Jerusalem, only three hundred miles away. Remember how quickly Gabinius and his troops arrived? No, we cannot pretend we do not hear when Rome calls. But we can frame our answer to our best advantage."

"And what might that be?" asked Theodotos. I had almost forgotten he was there, as the presence of the other two overshadowed him.

"That we will comply—later."

"Exactly the answer you have returned to us about the marriage!" snapped Pothinus. "It fools no one!"

"It is not meant to fool anyone," I said, as grandly as possible. "There are true delays and diplomatic delays and obstructionist delays; there are as many types of delays as there are situations. Surely you don't mean to imply that your request that I marry my brother forthwith is the same as a command from the Romans?"

"It is not a *command*—" began Achillas.

"This is a quibbling about words." I cut him off. "You have made a request. I have refused it at present. That is enough. You may leave me now."

Their faces dark with anger, they bent low and backed out of the chamber.

They had forced me to be curt with them. I sensed that the time of niceties was already past.

I also sensed that I must set about finding myself devoted supporters.

There were many small details to attend to, the sort of details that one can easily mistake for true action and important decisions. (Yet a leader must never lose grasp of them. So many things a leader must do, and be. No wonder most fail.) The King's quarters, the most beautiful in the whole palace grounds, stood empty. I had shied away from occupying them, but now I realized that was foolish. Why not honor my father by living there? Who else was entitled to do so? In the alabaster palace, on the entire upper floor, the King's apartments stretched from the northwest tip of the Lochias promontory, looking across the turquoise waters of the harbor to the Lighthouse, to the southeast, looking out over the open ocean. Breezes blew constantly from one open window across to another, keeping the onyx floors deliciously cool, like the flavored ices we ate in summer. Light played about all day, crossing the floor as the sun made his way from one window to the next, turning the entire apartments into one big sundial. At night the moon did the same. The sound of the sea was so satisfying that one hated to call musicians to compete with its distinctive voice. The royal apartments seemed a magic dwelling place in the air.

As I walked through them, considering what to order or change for myself, I was struck by my father's mania for collecting. He had beds made of ebony from Africa and inlaid with ivory from Punt; handworked metal tables from Damascus; embroidered cushions from Syria; woven carpets from India, and silk hangings from the far east. There were painted Greek vases and candelabra of Nubian silver and water clocks from Rome. From Egypt herself he had carvings of the gods, done in basalt and porphyry, and fine vessels of multicolored glass, a specialty of Alexandria. Entering his quarters was like entering a bazaar of the world, one where no ordinary merchants traded, but only artists. The transparent white silk window hangings billowed and flapped in the soft breeze, as if trying to shed different lights on the wares for me to appreciate them fully.

His wardrobe room was as large as a normal palace audience chamber, and crammed full of robes and mantles, sandals and cloaks. I smiled, remembering how he had loved to dress for ceremonial occasions. His wardrobe, however, unlike his water clocks, could not be transferred to me. As I was staring at it, I became aware that someone else was in the room behind me. I whirled around and recognized a familiar face: one of the servants of the inner chamber, a woman.

"I did not see you," I said. "What is your name?"

"Charmian, Your Majesty," she said. She had a very deep, husky voice. "Forgive me. I did not mean to startle you."

"You were keeper of the King's wardrobe?"

"Yes. An enjoyable task." She smiled. She had a very winning smile. I also noticed that she had a distinct Macedonian accent.

"Are you Macedonian?" I asked. She had the coloring for it: tawny hair and smoky gray eyes.

"I am. I was brought here to serve His Majesty after his stay in Athens." There was a discreet pause. We both knew why the King had been in Athens; he was on his way to Rome after being deposed. "It was said that our families are distantly related."

I liked this Charmian, or else I was merely fascinated by her voice and bearing. It would take a little while for me to figure out which. "Would you like to return to Athens, or would you prefer to stay here and serve me as wardrobe mistress?"

I was in sore need of one. My childhood nurse had no knowledge of clothing, beyond knowing that milk removed scorches, and that salt should be sprinkled on red wine stains as soon as possible.

She gave a wide smile. "If you would deem me worthy, I would be happy beyond measure to stay with you."

"Worthy? Anyone who could select and oversee all *this*"—I gestured to the glittering piles of brocade and silks—"certainly can oversee whatever I will have. But what shall be done with it all?"

"I would advise putting all this away until the day when you have a son who will wear them."

"That will be such a long time that they will be quite out of style."

"Things of this quality will not go out of style quickly." That deep, intimate voice . . . it wrapped itself around her words, cradling them.

So now I had the beginning of my staff. I would appoint Mardian to my household as chief scribe and administrator. I had seen little of him in the past year, but whenever we met, our friendship was still strong. And Olympos, who was now studying medicine at the Museion, would serve as my physician. I knew I could trust him not to poison me! But I needed a soldier, a strong, trained military man, to counterbalance Achillas, and I knew no one like that. I had at my disposal the Macedonian Household Troops who guarded the palace grounds, but the three Roman legions—composed mainly of huge barbarians from Gaul and Germany—had a Roman commander, and the Egyptian army was under Achillas's control. Even if the Macedonians proved to be completely on my side, they were outnumbered by the legions and the native Egyptians. I would have to see what fate provided for me.

Long ago, Egypt had been protected by its deserts on the east and west. We had lain in our Nile valley out of reach of the rest of the world. But Bedouins on camels had breached our western frontiers, and armies could march overland, through Syria, to our eastern borders now. We were part of the larger world, and what happened elsewhere affected us directly. Thus the first crisis of my reign came not from something in Egypt, but from the happenings in other countries.

To be brief: the Parthians (O Isis! How I was to learn to hate that word! The Parthians have been the scourge of all my hopes!) had troubled the Roman province of Syria, and the new Roman governor there, Calpurnius Bibulus, wanted the Roman legions back to aid in his revenge attack on the Parthians. He sent his two sons to command the troops and lead them out of Egypt. The soldiers, who had settled down, did not want to leave, and so they set upon the governor's sons and, far from obeying them, killed them.

Like foolish rebels everywhere, who do not think beyond the deed of rebellion itself, the troops were jubilant. The city of Alexandria rejoiced along with them, for any defiance of Rome sent them into fits of excitement. And Pothinus and his henchmen were pleased beyond measure. A blow had been struck against Rome! Never mind that this was the simple murder of helpless envoys.

I called a meeting in the royal council chambers. I was seated in the Queen's chair of honor when the Regency Council filed in, pushing Ptolemy like a hostage.

"My brother may take his seat here, beside me," I said, indicating the other royal chair. Let him separate himself from them, for once! "The rest of you, sit here." There was a bench, albeit a richly gilded one, for all of them, including Mardian.

"You know what I have called this council for," I said. Outside, the day was glorious, brilliant and sparkling. The fleet was bobbing up and down in the harbor. "The Roman governor of Syria has had his sons murdered by the very troops they were sent to command."

"We didn't do it!" crowed Ptolemy. "It was done by Roman troops! It's not our fault!"

Pothinus gave a smug nod.

"Is this how you advise your Prince?" I asked. "His youth excuses him, but if you truly believe that, you are a child yourself and have no business serving on any council, even one to ration donkey dung!" I watched the smile drain from his face. Good.

"The troops do not want to leave Egypt," said Pothinus. "They have settled here, married, have children."

"In other words, they are no longer soldiers but civilians?" I asked. "Then we shall not miss them if they go, for they can no longer serve their purpose.

We hardly want more civilians. We have a million in the city." I looked at all of them. Now was the time to make things clear. "The murderers must be apprehended and turned over to Bibulus."

"No!" cried Theodotos. "That is acknowledging him our master! We are a sovereign state!"

"Sovereign states, *real* ones, not pretend ones, observe civilized laws. It is not a sign of weakness, but of strength, to be able to control our own people and, when mistakes are made, to offer to set them right."

"The truth," sneered Pothinus, "is that you are afraid of the Romans! So you cower before them and degrade yourself."

How dare he speak thus? Degrade myself! "It is you who degrades Egypt by advocating lawless and insulting behavior," I finally said. "I see you have scant love of your country."

"I love Egypt more than you can ever understand!" he insisted.

"Then do as you are ordered," I said. "Discover the murderers. Bring them to me. If you have no appetite for sending them to Bibulus, let me do it." I looked over at my brother. "Have you anything to say?"

He shook his head.

"Good. Then carry out my instructions, Pothinus."

The tall eunuch sat as stiff as a stone statue in a temple.

After the council had departed, I found myself limp. I knew I was doing the honorable thing, but was it politically wise? I would alienate the Alexandrians. Yet to insult the Romans was to court worse danger; they never forgot a slight or a defeat. I had been caught, like a creature exposed on an open field, with no cover.

The murderers—three very ordinary-looking men—were rounded up and sent to Bibulus to answer to him. The Roman magistrate surprised us by acting in strictest legality. Although his sons had been killed, he said, Roman law forbade his dealing with the murderers; it was rightly a matter for the Senate to judge. He himself would not take direct vengeance on them.

O Roman law! If ever I saw the murderers of my children, I would forget all about the law, except the eternal one of vengeance for a dead child—the prerogative of a mother. Laws can go only so far, and at the crucial moment they fail us. They are a poor substitute for justice. The Greek gods know more about that than the Roman law.

The Bibulus affair turned the people against me so certainly that I could almost believe Pothinus had engineered it. (I know this was not true, but, Isis, why did the gods favor him?) There was murmuring about "the lover of the Romans," "the Roman slave," and how I was truly my father's daughter. They had ousted him from the throne for groveling before Rome, and I was the same. Away with her!

It did not help that, shortly after this, the son of Pompey came to Egypt to request troops and provisions for the coming clash with Caesar. We had to yield them, and so the troops ended up serving Rome after all. Sixty ships were dispatched, along with hundreds of soldiers. Pompey and his followers had been ejected from Italy by this Caesar, who had defied the Roman Senate and acted as if he commanded his own destiny. It was said he was lucky above all men; it was also said that his main weapon was speed, for he could appear at a site before his enemies realized he had even started out. They said he covered a hundred miles a day, making lightninglike strikes.

I must here refute a piece of Roman propaganda, heaped on me with all the rest of Octavian's later abuse: that the younger Pompey and I became lovers on his visit to Alexandria. I met him, I entertained him at banquets, and showed him the city with pride, but he never even touched my hand. To do so would have violated every principle of protocol. I was a virgin, and as protective of my chastity as Athena. Besides, he was not very attractive!

The other thing that worked against me at the time was the Nile himself. At the last flooding he had not risen up to the level required, and so a famine was inevitable. Scientists had worked out a table of the exact degree the Nile must rise to guarantee crops, and the levels below that they called "the cubits of death." In that year, the great river's level fell within that death range.

The gods send the waters, or withhold them, but the rulers are blamed. I gave orders for the grain from the previous season's harvest to be rationed, but what happened is what always happens: there was not enough, although profiteers somehow managed to get their own supply. People were starving. In Alexandria, the riots began. In the countryside, there were threats of uprisings. The farther one went up the Nile into Upper Egypt, the greater the disaffection of the people. Being so distant, they had never really been welded to the Ptolemaic state, and now they were starting to pull away.

At about this time the sacred bull of Hermonthis died, and the installation of his successor was to take place. This was an elaborate ceremony in which the new sacred bull must be escorted on the Nile to his holy precinct. Pharaohs had taken part in the water procession in times past, but no Ptolemy had ever done so. Hermonthis was one of the hotbeds of disaffection, a few miles upstream from Thebes. I thought it would be politically wise to partake of the ceremony. It would remove me from the intrigues of the palace for a while, and strengthen my position by allowing me to cultivate support in a dangerous area.

Accordingly I set out in the royal barge. I looked forward to the journey, expected to take about ten days.

I sat in the shelter at the stem of the barge, protected by awnings, and watched my countryside slide by. I saw how low the Nile was as we plied our way upriver, past the pyramids, past Memphis, its white wall gleaming in the noonday sun, past green fields studded with palm trees, banks lined with red-black earth, donkeys and waterwheels and houses of mud brick. The strip of land near the river was always the same; what changed was the background.

The desert was sometimes golden and sandy behind it, other times an ashy white, bleached wilderness, other times rocky cliffs. The size of the ribbon of green waxed and waned, from less than a mile to almost ten, but always it stopped somewhere within eyesight and the desert took over.

When the sun set, a red ball sinking into the diminished Nile and making him run red, light did not linger. Night came swiftly, a black, inky night with a million stars. Silence reigned, brooding over the desert just beyond us. It got cold, even in high summer.

We passed the ruins of a stone city about three days' sail past Memphis, and I asked our captain what it was. "The city of the heretic Pharaoh, may his name be lost forever," he muttered.

Akhenaten! I knew a little about him, about his breaking with the old gods and attempting to found a new religion based on a worship of Aten as the one god. The priests of Amun at Thebes had made short work of him. We were gliding past all that remained of his life and work. I was profoundly thankful that my dynasty had never attempted to quash any religion. No, we threw ourselves into them all with relish! The Ptolemies, and my father in particular, had been avid builders of temples in Upper Egypt in the old style. As a result, our temples were the most beautiful still standing in the land— Edfu, Esna, and Kom Ombo were famous now. A little way past the ill-fated Pharaoh's city we passed the Hatnub alabaster quarries on the eastern bank, where so many of our perfume and ointment jars have their origin.

Two days later we passed the town of Ptolemais. It was founded by the first Ptolemy; almost four hundred miles from Alexandria, it was the last Greek city outpost on the Nile. From here on, the foreign influence faded away.

On the ninth day of our journey, the Nile took a sudden bend and we were sailing due east. Near the very elbow of the bend, at Dendera, we passed the Temple of Hathor, the goddess of love. It was a very recent one, with new sections having been built by my father. I could see it from the water, its carved columns visible above its brown mud-brick guard wall. I wished I had time to stop and visit it.

Directly across, at the exact place where the river turns back west, was the town of Coptos. I was familiar with it because it was an important trade route. At this spot, where the Nile comes closest to the Red Sea, camel caravans set out to the ports, to fetch goods from Punt and Arabia. My father had been very interested in this trade route; he believed that Egypt should be looking farther east, to India, for her trading partners, leaving the Mediterranean to Rome.

The earlier Ptolemies had founded a number of cities up and down the coast of the Red Sea, naming them after their queens: Cleopatris, Arsinoe, Berenice. Berenice, the one farthest south, was the point at which the elephants captured in Africa were ferried. Lately the elephant trade had fallen by the wayside. They were no longer the novelty in warfare that they once had been. Julius Caesar had perfected the technique of routing them, and now they had lost their superior value as a weapon of terror.

Julius Caesar . . . I wondered about him. As a soldier, he seemed formidable and infinitely resourceful. The business with the elephants—why had no one before him exploited their weak points so effectively? The animals are easy to stampede: If they are frightened by a volley of stones and missiles, they turn and run over their own troops. For centuries elephants were coveted as war machines. Yet Caesar had lately rendered them almost obsolete. How could Pompey stand up against him? I wished we had not had to take sides. It boded ill for Egypt.

A day's sail farther took us to Thebes, with its massive temples. This was the stronghold of Old Egypt, and here the priests of the temples of Amun still wielded great power among the people. The fourth Ptolemy had been faced with a rival native dynasty from this area, and so preoccupied was he with putting an end to it that he lost most of Egypt's overseas territory—territory never regained.

The priests and their retinues lined the steps at the waterside, and I could hear their sour, dirgelike holy music as they greeted us in passing. Gigantic temples reared behind them, dwarfing them. The smell of incense wafted over the water.

Across from Thebes itself lay the desolate, baking cliffs and valleys where the royal tombs were sculpted out of living rock. Here Queen Hatshepshut had set up her mortuary temple, a long, horizontal series of terraces and chambers built into the hard, bone-dry cliffs. Now her myrrh trees and fountains had turned to dust. Not far away were the great mortuary temples of Ramses II and Ramses III, as well as the Colossi of Amenophis III, seated statues over sixty feet high. But the priests, paid to perform rites forever in the temple, were as dead as their masters. The rites were forgotten, and only the stones remained. The temples, bones of that belief, lay radiating heat under the desert sun.

A little farther, and Hermonthis, our destination, appeared on the western bank of the Nile. It was a small town, with little there except the Bucheum Temple and its enclosure where the sacred bull, believed to be incarnated by Amun, resided. Under the temple are long catacombs where the mummified bulls were entombed.

The people lined the riverbanks, and the priests, with their shaven heads and white linen robes, stood ready to receive us. There was intent curiosity on all their faces. *Is this really the Queen?* they thought. *May we approach? Is she truly a goddess?*

In that instant I was profoundly glad I had come all this way to be welcomed unequivocally at last. Let my brother stay behind in Alexandria, where we were treated as all too human—and disposable. I felt a soaring joy and release, as if I could breathe for the first time in my life.

"Your Majesty," the oldest priest said, "the sacred bull rejoices that you have come to escort him!"

Even though I disliked bulls, I rejoiced as well.

When the previous Buchis bull died, a search was made all up and down the Nile for his successor. The right one had been found quite nearby, to his owner's delight.

The ceremony consisted of loading the beast—who had to be dun-colored, with white horns and a white tail—onto a specially constructed boat, which docked near the bull's breeding grounds a few miles upriver. He wore a crown of gold and lapis lazuli, and a face net to guard against flies. He was festooned with flower garlands, and his hooves were stained red, I noticed as his keeper led him over the gangplank. He seemed a very gentle bull, as bulls go. I hoped he had a long and uneventful tenure in Hermonthis, with cows to satisfy his every urge. It is not easy, being a holy thing and set apart.

The silver-tipped oars on the boat sparkled as they emerged with each stroke, sending sprays of water high in the air. The bull was going to his destiny, and he rode placidly as the boat rocked on the water.

There was much feasting, as is customary. The priests had prepared public banquets for all the people from the surrounding area, as a new bull's installation is an uncommon occurrence. Most live to be over twenty.

The high priest held a private feast for us, spreading a table with the produce of the area: onions, leeks, garlic, lentils, chickpeas, spinach, lettuce, and carrots. Goat and lamb, and game such as gazelle and ibex, were the meats. Out of deference to the sacred bull, beef was not eaten.

"We will raise a ceremonial tablet to commemorate your being here," said the high priest. "Forever and ever, as long as there are men to read, this deed will live on."

I was served a platter of the vegetables, sprinkled with oil from the *bak* tree, flavored with herbs. "Your harvest seems plentiful enough," I said. "How have you gathered all this food, to feed not just us but the multitude?"

He looked downcast. "I am afraid—I must confess to Your Majesty—that it was most difficult. The harvest was scanty, the Nile stingy in his bounty this year. You saw how high the landing was above the water? Usually the boats ride at a level even with the platform. Now you need a ladder."

"How are the people faring?"

"There is no starvation yet. We pray we can outlast the time of want until the Nile rises once more."

Although we were as yet three days' sail from Nubia, I noticed a number of distinctively Nubian faces among his servants and priests. I asked about it.

"Oh yes, we find the Nubians to be very spiritual. They are attracted to temple service, and faithful. We are always pleased to welcome them."

The woman serving me was a tall Nubian with very graceful movements, as if she had been trained as a dancer.

The host shook his head when I commented on it. "No, it is just her natural way. Nubians are lithe and elegant in all they do, from setting a dish on a table to the way they turn their heads. They are born with a sense of bodily dignity."

"What is your name?" I asked her. Her movements had captivated me.

"Iras, Your Majesty," she said. When I looked puzzled, she said, "It means 'wool,' *eiras*, because of my hair." Her Greek was very good. I wondered where she had learned it. She must come from an educated family, or have received her education in Thebes or Hermonthis. Her hair was indeed woolly, thick, and worn in Nubian style, with the sides short.

"I will do all in my power to help future harvests increase," I promised the high priest. "The irrigation canals need to be deepened, I know that. They have silted up. This will be corrected."

"I will pray daily to Amun that this shall be so," said the priest.

I guessed his unspoken thought: *I will pray daily that you stay on the throne to carry out your promise*.

We rested after the day-and-night-long ceremony in the palace attached to the Bucheum. I had meant to return to Alexandria within two or three days, but at dawn a messenger came. He had traveled at twice our speed by combining rowing with sailing. His news was grim: The Regency Council had seized power in the name of Ptolemy XIII, and I was declared deposed. My absence from Alexandria had been my undoing.

So soon a queen, so soon unqueened! I could hardly believe it. That they would dare—!

"It is true," the man said. "I beg your pardon for bringing you this unwelcome news. But I thought it best your friends told you before you were officially informed, and before the rest of the country knew. So that you can— make your plans."

Yes. Make my plans. For I would not submit meekly. No, never!

"I thank you." Calmly I bade him wait. I asked Iras, who had been assigned to our quarters for our brief stay, to bring him water to wash with, wine to refresh him.

"Gladly," she said, gesturing—in her exquisite way—for him to follow her into another chamber.

Outside, the sun was beginning to penetrate the golden haze that lay over the river at daybreak, gilding the reeds along the bank. The royal barge was tied up, waiting for me. I took several breaths of air, steadying myself on the windowsill.

What should I do? I was here in Upper Egypt, in the place traditionally most hostile to the government of Alexandria. But they seemed to like and support me. Should I attempt to raise an army here? The best soldiers came from this area, and Achillas himself had his origin here.

But how could I pay them? I had no money with me. The usurpers in Alexandria were now in control of the treasury as well as the Macedonian Household Guard and the Egyptian army. I could not equip an army, let alone train one, with my resources here. My popularity with the people, and their obvious love for me, was gratifying but of little military use. If I attempted to stage a counterrevolution from here, all I would achieve would be bloodshed.

These thoughts raced through my mind so quickly I was stunned to realize I had breathed in only once or twice while thinking them. I gripped the windowsill.

"Your Majesty." It was Mardian. I always knew his voice: it was soft and not—thank Hermes!—shrill. When he had passed the age at which the voice normally changes, his had mellowed and grown stronger, but not deeper.

I did not turn. "You know that you may call me Cleopatra in private."

"Cleopatra." He said it in a way that made it very pleasant on the ears. "What will we do?" He paused. "I know we will not give up."

"That much is decided." I turned to him. "I will not even rant about treachery. I was brought up in a sea of treachery and deceit and betrayal. I swam in it like perch in the Nile. I am completely at home in it. I shall not drown."

"But what will we *do*? Practically, I mean. Similes are very poetic, but what specific course of action shall we take?"

"Patience, Mardian! I have only known about the crisis for five minutes. Let me think!"

It was then I prayed to you, Isis, to help me. To clear my head of all vanity and anger and folly, so that I might see clearly how things were and what you, my guide, would have me do. So often our human thoughts do not go far enough. We seize on first this and then the other, misleading ourselves. So I sat quietly, clasping the silver image of you I wear about my neck, and waited.

The moments ticked by. I could feel (although my eyes were shut) the sun begin to enter the chamber as he rose higher. People were stirring out in the courtyard, and chanting priests were making their way to the bull's stall to begin the day's ceremonies. Still I waited.

A sweetness pervaded me. That was when you came to me, and hushed all fears and uncertainties. I was your child, your incarnation on earth, and I was to rule. I was to leave Egypt and go to Ashkelon in Gaza. That city had been freed from Judaea by my grandfather and favored by my father. There I could gather an army. The kingdom of the Nabataean Arabs nearby, and the people of Ashkelon, would lend themselves to my cause. The neighboring province of Syria also looked favorably on me because I had complied with Bibulus's orders. Yes. It was all very clear.

"We will go to Gaza," I told Mardian.

He looked very startled. "Leave Egypt?"

"It has been done before. I am not the first Ptolemy to have to retake my country from abroad. But it is the wisest course. Egypt is in the throes of a famine, and cannot support us. Ashkelon has more resources."

"But—how will we get there?" Practical Mardian.

"We have the royal barge, have we not?"

"Yes—a huge vessel, visible from miles away!"

"They will not come looking for us on the Nile. They are content to hold Alexandria. If we wish to dislodge them, it is from Alexandria that they must be ejected. *We* must attack them."

"You have taken Alexander to heart."

"Of course." I smiled. "We will double our speed on the Nile by adding rowers to help out the downstream current. When we reach the Delta, we will take the easternmost branch of the Nile, then leave the barge and follow the line of the old Necho canal over to the Reed Sea and the Bitter Lakes. We will cross there."

"Avoiding the highway between Egypt and Gaza that passes along the coast."

"Yes. They are sure to have it guarded at the fort of Pelusium. But this way we will slip around behind them."

It would be several days before the official announcement even reached Thebes or Hermonthis. We would set out as soon as possible.

But the high priest surprised us. He appeared at the chamber door, his staff in hand. "During the night I had a dream," he said. "I fear that some evil has come to Egypt. I sought to warn you."

"Your dreams tell you true," I said. "Indeed, a messenger has just arrived." I explained the situation. "Therefore we will depart as soon as is seemly. I do not wish to alarm the people."

"Stay with us another night, then," he said. And we did, glad of an excuse to rest a bit before the task confronting us.

After the evening sacrifices had been made to the new bull and to Amun, the priest blessed me and my entire household. "As a parting gift, I wish to give you a part of us. Take our servant Iras with you. She has become dear to us, and therefore it is a sacrifice to give her up. She will be a living reminder of us. She is also"—he smiled—"more useful to you than a poem or a necklace or a blemish-free goat."

I was very pleased for I was already surprisingly fond of Iras.

As I was being escorted ceremonially to my barge early the next morning, he pressed a paper into my hand. "So you will know," he said. "It begins."

When I unfolded it and read it, I saw that an order had gone out to Upper Egypt from the Regency Council: All grain and foodstuffs that could possibly be spared were to be sent directly to Alexandria. No provisions were to be shipped anywhere else, under pain of death. They meant to starve me out.

I laughed and tore the paper into bits. Too sure of themselves, they had miscalculated. Fools. They could not touch me in Gaza. And when I had ousted them from Alexandria, I would have a feast to end all feasts on the food they had stored. Yes, I and my followers would dine for seven nights running on dates, figs, melons, pancake bread, radishes, cucumbers, ducks, and geese. Simple fare, snatched from the mouth of an enemy, is more satisfying than any feast of dainties.

We were unhindered in our journey downriver. The rowers strained and sweated to keep the boat moving as fast as possible. The current was sluggish because of the low water. Whenever we did have to stop, we found the people friendly and on our side. News had traveled faster than I expected, and people had already heard about the coup in Alexandria. Nonetheless they professed their loyalty to me, and wished me good fortune.

When we neared the sacred site of Heliopolis with its sturdy obelisks, we knew we were approaching the place where the Nile splits. The green was beginning to widen as we entered the fertile area. We steered the boat onto the eastern, Pelusic branch of the Nile, and rowed toward the rising sun.

This was the part of Egypt that was least Egyptian, because foreigners had come in this way for thousands of years. The Israelites had settled here, and the Hyksos had followed them.

We had gone some way when we saw the remains of the old canal on the eastern bank. The stone entranceway, guarding the lock, was still there, but there was no need of gates or watchmen. Everything was overgrown with climbing weeds and reeds. Here we must abandon the barge and set out along the canal's path on camels or donkeys. As we climbed up over the levee, I saw the few stagnant pools of water, choked with lotus, that were all that remained of the waterway. For a moment I felt overwhelmed by the task of keeping a country going: Everything molders, falls into decay; everything needs constant patrolling and repair, and that takes men and money. Upkeep, not conquest or expansion, drains us dry and makes us collapse into our graves as rulers who accomplished nothing memorable. Who wants as his only epitaph, "He kept the canals clean"? Yet they must be kept clean, almost offhandedly, while we pursue greater ends.

The canal had followed a natural canyon, and we made our way along its rim. Once this had been fertile farmland, and I could still see the traces of field boundaries. But when the water vanished, so had the crops. The desert, with its dry scrub and pebbles of a thousand sizes, came right up to the trail.

The canal had been about fifty miles long, connecting the Nile with the Lake of Timsah, one of the Bitter Lakes, which fed into the Red Sea. The port nearest it was Cleopatris, but it was on what was called "the foul gulf" because it was so treacherous with reefs and vegetation.

"That is near where we will be crossing," said the captain of my guard. "The Sea of Reeds will let us wade across, if the winds are right."

"Like that legendary Egyptian who took up with the Israelites?" asked Mardian.

The soldier looked puzzled. "I don't know who you mean," he said. "But this crossing has been known since ancient times. It can be treacherous, so we must watch our footing."

"Moses," said Mardian. "That's who it was. It's in that book of Hebrew legends. Moses is an Egyptian name; it has something to do with Thutmose."

The captain was not interested. "When we get to the banks of the Sea of Reeds, halt and we will test the waters."

"In the Moses story," insisted Mardian, "the waters were so deep, all the army was drowned."

"They can be deep," admitted the captain. "Let us pray today is not one of those times."

Glittering from afar we could see the waters, waiting for us. They were flat and a cruel shade of blue, indicating they were stagnant and filled with bitter salts. The reeds and vegetation in them would be different from those living in fresh water.

As we finally reached the banks, I smelled the foul odor of slime and decay. I could see oily rings around the stalks of the reeds; a dull sheen reflected the sunlight upward. Yet there were birds in the thickets, twittering and flying from stem to stem.

"The water is passable!" announced the captain with elation, as his scouts reported back to him. "The guides will lead us! We will hire reed boats, and have the beasts led across riderless."

And so we did. And I sat in the rocking little boat made of papyrus stalks lashed together, which was buoyant only up to a point, and the foul water seeped in all around me. We had to push through the tough, stringy roots and reeds and blades of the vegetation, which slapped our faces and cut our hands. And the stench! I thought I would vomit from the gases that were stirred up in our passing. When I put my hand into the water to grasp a stalk to steady us, it emerged with a coating of oil and foul salt.

Never had banks of sand looked so pure and clean as when we reached the other side at last! It had been only about two miles, but it was the most unpleasant two miles under the Egyptian sun, of that I was sure.

The rest of the journey was tame. We made our way across the thirty-five miles of sand separating the tip of the lake from the open Mediterranean, until we could see that sea, intense blue that reflected the sky, with its white waves also reflecting the clouds. Then we made sure to keep well away from the well-traveled road that ran alongside the coast.

Gaza, the former land of the Philistines, was easy enough to reach. And in the rich city of Ashkelon I found welcome, supporters who were only too willing to take up arms against the usurpers. The word went out that Queen Cleopatra was raising an army.

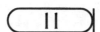

Night; hot, windy night. I lay in my tent unable to sleep. I had my army, and we were camped just outside the borders of Egypt, near where we had passed months ago. I now had almost ten thousand men, some Egyptian and some Nabataean Arabs. They were good fighters.

But my brother—or Achillas, rather—had more troops. He had what was left of the old legions of Gabinius as well as fresh Egyptian soldiers that he had been able to recruit. They were camped just opposite us, occupying Pelusium, the fortress that guarded the eastern borders of Egypt. We could not get past them, nor could we take Alexandria by sea, because they had closed the harbor with underwater chains and guarded it by fleet.

Two months. Two months now we had been facing each other across the sands, and I had been barred from Alexandria for a year before that. I was well supplied from Ashkelon, and they from Egypt. How long would we sit here? Who would strike the first blow?

I tossed on my folding camp bed. The strings underneath creaked. My hair was damp on my forehead, and when I slept, my dreams were vague but disturbing. The hot wind puffing in through the net around the door was like a feverish lover's kiss—or what I imagined a lover's kiss to be. I knew of them only from dreams, from poetry, and from my own imagination. The lantern flickered. On the other side of the tent, on her pallet, Iras moaned and stirred. There was a sighing sound as she rolled over.

It was the middle of the night. Everyone slept. Why could I not? I shut my eyes again. More hot puffs of wind. I felt as though someone were standing at the entrance to the tent, lifting the net, stepping in. I started awake—or was I dreaming? I seemed to see a tall woman, holding a cornucopia. The emblem of our dynasty? She was silent. I could not see her face. Yes, I was dreaming. For in a moment a real visitor came, and the sound as he lifted the tent flap was entirely different.

"Mardian!" I recognized his blocky shape.

"Shhhh!" He bent down and crept over to my bed. "Something terrible has happened," he whispered. His voice was shaking.

I sat up and put my arm around his shoulder, then I murmured, "What? Spare me not."

"Our country is shamed before the world. O Egypt!"

"What?"

"Treachery! O treachery!"

"In the name of Isis, stop lamenting and *tell* me!"

"Ptolemy has slain Pompey!"

"But how?" was all I could say in my shock. Little Ptolemy, with his tiny sapling arms, slay mighty Pompey?

"They set upon him, it was lies—" He broke off suddenly. Iras was awakening.

"It is all right. You may speak in front of her." I had come to trust Iras completely, and to rely on her serene good judgment.

"The defeated Pompey was making his way to Egypt." Mardian decided to begin again.

In all my own troubles, I had forgotten about the Roman ones. But during the time of my exile, Pompey and Caesar had met in full battle at Pharsalus in Greece. Caesar had won, but Pompey had escaped with his life and a handful of men. I had known that, but had not cared. Rome and its woes paled before my own.

"He meant to raise another army. He was coming to Egypt to regroup his forces; as Ptolemy's guardian—for so your father's will named him, he claims—Ptolemy owed him that loyalty, and a base of operations. But they knew he was doomed, and so they wanted to be rid of him."

"Continue," I said. "How did you learn this?"

"A deserter from Ptolemy's camp just arrived. I think he speaks truth. They will bring him to you in the morning, but I wanted to tell you first."

Dear, loyal Mardian. "I thank you."

"This man was watching from the beach. He saw what happened. Pompey was murdered by Achillas and two other men who were rowing him to shore, within sight of his wife on the warship. They stabbed him and cut off his head before her eyes!"

Pompey—who had treated me so kindly as a child, whom I had met and gazed on in wonder—now beheaded! We had talked of Alexandria, and I had promised him, *We will guard it for you, and it will always be waiting for you.*

And when at last he came, my evil brother and his men had given him a hideous welcome; they had given my promise the lie.

"They are beasts," I said. "It is beasts, not men, that I contend with. Then I myself need have no pity for them." I shuddered at the thought of them. Calling them beasts was an insult to animals. Then I had a sudden thought. "What of Caesar?"

"Their killing Pompey was to forestall Caesar coming to this part of the world. But they did not understand the likes of Caesar. Caesar came in hot pursuit of Pompey, following so swiftly that he arrived with very few troops. Our informer heard that Theodotos presented Caesar with the severed head and Pompey's signet ring, thinking to earn his approval. Instead Caesar wept, then raged at them."

"Where is he now?"

"Caesar is in Alexandria, so this fellow says. He has settled himself in the palace. He does not seem eager to move on."

"But what is he *doing* there?" Why was he lingering? Was Ptolemy with him? Caesar was a politician as well as a soldier. Might he become Ptolemy's next "guardian"?

"I do not know," said Mardian.

Iras spoke for the first time. "As long as Caesar is there, Ptolemy does not rule," she said. "That is in your favor."

"It can never be in one's favor to have a strong power occupying one's home. It would be like a lion coming into this tent and deciding he wished to sleep on this bed," I said.

After Mardian had left, and Iras had lain back down, I stared at the ceiling folds of the tent. They were lost in darkness, and the jumping flames of the lantern only served to make the hidden parts of the tent seem blacker. The hot wind was relentless. The desert tribesmen had a name for that wind, for its pressing intensity. It was keeping me from thinking. All I could do was lie still and sweat. I was a prisoner in the oppressive night, shackled to my bed.

Julius Caesar had defeated Pompey. Julius Caesar was master of the Roman world. Julius Caesar was in Alexandria, living in the palace—my palace! He was daily in the presence of my brother. Why? Why was he staying? What was his purpose?

I would have to go there and present my case to him. Iras was right. As long as Caesar was there, Ptolemy and his nefarious Council did not rule. I could appeal to a judge over their heads. But I would have to go quickly. Every day that passed with Ptolemy having Caesar all to himself made them more likely to become allies.

A fly was buzzing inside the tent, bumping from fold to fold. We had not used mosquito nets here, as we were not near swamps. Now I wished we had, for I hated flies. He was coming closer; I heard him approach and then saw, by the dim lanternlight, where he landed. I sat up quickly, grabbed my sandal, and, with one movement so swift the eye could hardly follow it, smashed him.

Was that how Caesar smashed his enemies? They said he moved quickly and took his opponents by surprise. He had never lost a final battle, even when outmanned. And according to Mardian, he had come swiftly to Egypt with only a few troops, relying on surprise to win the day with Pompey. That must mean that he was now in Alexandria without many soldiers to protect him. Again the question: Why was he lingering?

What did I know about Caesar? Precious little. Only that he was generally more popular with the people than with the aristocrats, that he had achieved his military successes relatively late, and that he was constantly involved with women, usually married women. Mardian had once told me that every fashionable divorce in Rome seemed to involve an adultery with Caesar. And his taste was not restricted to women, Mardian said; Caesar had also been involved with the King of Bithynia in his youth. He collected works of art as well, Mardian confided, and prized them above his romantic conquests.

My heart sank. He would probably make off with some of our best artworks, then. He would strip the palace of our Greek statues and our Egyptian furniture and paintings. And that stupid Ptolemy would let him!

Outside there was stirring, the first faint sounds of daybreak. I could tell the hour by a subtle shift in the way the air blew into the tent. Before long they would awaken me, and by the time the sun came over the sands, they would be bringing the informer to me to recount his tale. I was glad I had had time to prepare for his message.

The man was Egyptian, an older warrior who had been in my father's army before the troops of Gabinius had arrived. He looked ashamed, as deserters and spies and informers always do, even if they feel the cause of their erstwhile masters to be wrong or hopeless.

I had prepared myself for him, wearing my most regal robes. After all, he should feel that he had deserted to a queen, not a vagabond. He prostrated himself on the ground, kissing the gravel, then lifted his head. "O great Queen of the east, my soul is yours and my body I lay before you to command."

Yes, as it was for others before me, I thought. Traitors might be useful, but they could never be trusted.

It was as Mardian reported. The black deed was performed by Achillas and a Roman commander, Septimus, one of Pompey's former soldiers. But it was at the urging of Theodotos, who had said, "Dead men don't bite." Loyalty, honor, and debt were all wiped out by that practical advice. And so Pompey was slain on the very shores where he had come to seek sanctuary and had every right to expect a welcome.

His bleeding trunk had been tossed onto the sands and left there for his freedman to attempt to cremate. The poor man had been forced to go up and down the shores hunting for driftwood, and was not able to find quite enough. And so the body—

I stopped him here. "I do not wish to know these details. It is demeaning to Pompey even to allow us to picture them. Tell me what happened when Caesar followed."

"I was not there. I was sickened by what I had already seen. I was watching and waiting for an opportunity to desert. I never saw Caesar. I only heard that he was in Alexandria. Theodotos had taken the . . . the head and ring to present it to him. Caesar punished him instead. I heard Theodotos ranting about Caesar's ingratitude. But that was only a few hours before I left."

"Where is Achillas now? And Ptolemy?"

"Achillas is still at Pelusium, facing your army. Ptolemy goes back and forth between the army and Alexandria. Caesar resides in the palace in Alexandria. The last thing I heard before I was able to escape was that he had angered the people of the city by landing as a Roman magistrate with his insignia and officials, as if he expected obeisance. And Theodotos was muttering that Caesar had claimed he had the right to arbitrate between Your Majesty and Ptolemy."

Could it be true? On what basis could he claim that? "What, to the best of your knowledge, is the state of the city? Is it well guarded?"

"Very well. Achillas has seen to that. Every entrance is bristling with soldiers, and the harbors are blockaded."

"So Caesar is trapped?"

"He does not see it that way, apparently. He does not seem alarmed."

So Caesar was locked in, and I was locked out.

A week passed, then two. Nothing happened. Our armies continued to face each other across the stretch of desert, and neither moved. Then another deserter appeared, and his news was that Ptolemy had gone to Caesar and they were residing together in the palace. (What were *our* deserters telling Achillas? That we were disheartened? Tired of waiting, but with insufficient soldiers to force a battle?)

Day after day we sat by the wells under the shade of the palm trees and waited. The camels dozed with their long-lashed eyelids closed, and the rocks in the direct sun gave off the characteristic smell of overheated stone. A sort of torpor overtook us. It was as if we had always been here and always would be.

And then one day the light seemed dimmed, and the captain of the guard, a man from Gaza, came to my tent and said, "Sandstorm! Prepare yourselves!"

Everything had to be covered several times over, the openings of tents and boxes and bags secured, and we must veil our faces. Soon the wind would come howling, bringing a mist of fine sand particles, and we could breathe only through gauze.

"Hurry, Iras!" I said. "Put the jewel boxes and the money chests on a mantle, lest they sink into the sands. The water jars too. Then cover them over. And come and huddle with me under my cloak, with a blanket spread over that. A tent within a tent."

She did so, and we waited. The wind rose to a howl and we could see the sides of the tent straining. Sand got in through all the tiny spaces in the cloth, seeping in almost as if it were water. The air was hazy with it.

The full force of it went on for hours, and then lasted into the darkness. We dared not stir. I was thankful that it had started during the day so we had seen it coming in time to prepare.

I thought it had abated, but as I was preparing to lift off the covering, I saw the side of the tent bulging and straining. The wind was strong! But then it seemed to be focused on one area only, and feeling its way along. Suddenly hands appeared in the door of the tent, and I saw someone crawl in.

"Here, sir," said the voice of one of my guards.

Another shape followed on its hands and knees. Both figures were completely swathed in cloaks.

"Your Majesty," said the guard. "Are you here?"

I threw off the outer cloak but kept on the veil, and stood up. "Yes," I said. "Whom do you bring to see me? Announce him."

"This is Rufus Cornelius, a messenger from Julius Caesar."

Caesar! I stiffened. "We will receive him. Pray you, stand up and show your faces."

The two men both got to their feet and unwrapped their head coverings. Under the hood of Cornelius I saw the Roman helmet with its decorative brush.

"Welcome," I said. "What has Imperator Caesar to say to Queen Cleopatra?" My heart was pounding.

"My general and commander says he has come to Egypt to rectify the sad situation whereby King Ptolemy's will is not being obeyed. This will, which was entrusted to Rome for execution, declared both Queen Cleopatra and King Ptolemy to rule jointly. Caesar finds, alas, that brother and sister are at war with each other. This grieves him."

And what did he plan to do about it? "It grieves me as well," I said, choosing my words carefully. As I spoke, I could taste fine sand in my mouth. It hung suspended in the air, like lingering smoke. "Treachery is everywhere, preventing justice. Pompey was betrayed, as I have been. And by the same people!"

"Caesar will hear the case, and decide."

"Caesar has not, perchance, already decided? The words of the little King must sound sweet in his ear."

"He wishes to hear your words as well. He suspects they will be sweeter."

I stiffened. What exactly did that mean? Bribes? Ceding part of Egypt to Rome?

"He wishes us to bargain with him? Like merchants in the bazaar?"

Cornelius looked truly insulted. "Caesar is more intelligent than that. And in order to bargain, you must have goods you can withhold. Such is not the case with you and Caesar."

He dared—! But he spoke the truth. Caesar was master of the world and could take what he liked. No need to bargain. But if he could be persuaded . . . that was a different matter, altogether different. . . .

"Caesar requests that you come to Alexandria and meet with him and Ptolemy face-to-face."

"Will he give me safe conduct?" I asked. "I would need to pass through the lines of Achillas's army."

Cornelius looked apologetic. "He has no means of doing that. He has no soldiers to spare."

"They will never let me pass."

"But perhaps if I spoke to them—"

"You may speak, but they will answer no. Or, saying yes, they will take me captive when I attempt to go through."

He looked confused, as though he had not considered this suspension of courtesy.

"This is Egypt," I said, "home to treachery. But return to Caesar, and tell him that I will try to arrange a meeting with him."

We spent the next two days digging out the mess left by the sandstorm. In spite of our efforts, sand had found its way into all the stores of food and into the jars of water and wine. Every article of clothing was dusted with sand, so that the garments were scratchy when we put them on. Our skin was chafed and raw by the end of the day. And then we lay down on mattresses that were just as scratchy.

My mind was constantly working on the problem of how to get to Alexandria. Since I could not enter openly, I would have to be disguised. And I needed to do more than just get into Alexandria proper; 1 also needed to gain entrance to the palace where Caesar was staying. That would be impossible.

I thought of various schemes. Enter by a sewer? That was repulsive and dangerous. Pretend to be a maidservant? Too obvious. Put on a bearskin and amble in with a keeper? What if they set the dogs on me? What if they tried to get me to perform and stand upright? Or could I be smuggled in in a crate of food? But that still would not get me into Caesar's chamber. There would be guards at his door.

And then, as I lay on my bed, looking idly at the large patterned carpet that served as the floor of the tent, the idea came to me.

"Too dangerous," said Iras. "And not fitting for a queen."

"That is why no one will suspect it," I insisted.

"You might suffocate," said Mardian.

"Or be bitten by fleas," said Olympos, as a joke. "That's by far the greatest hazard. And how would Caesar respond to a queen covered with flea bites rolling out of a dusty rug?"

"Perhaps he would kiss the flea bites away," said Iras, raising one eyebrow.

I attempted to smile. But the truth was, that was the most intimidating aspect of the plan to me. "You will give me an ointment to prevent them," I said to Olympos.

"What if Caesar cries out, and his guards rush in and stab you?" asked Mardian.

"He will not. All reports say he always keeps his head in an unexpected situation. He is the least likely of all men to cry out in alarm."

"You deceive yourself. He will assume it is an assassin. It is the most likely thing, after all."

"I will have to trust to the gods, then," I said firmly. "It is all in their hands."

And that was true. There was absolutely nothing I could do to predict Caesar's reaction or to prevent him from acting exactly as he pleased at that moment, even though my fate depended on it.

It was then, Isis, that I knew I trusted you. It is only when our fate hangs in the balance, when our very life depends on something, that we see whether or not we trust that the rope to which we are clinging will support us. If we do not, then we will not let go of the ledge and swing on it with our full weight.

I trusted you, and you made good that trust, Isis. All hail to thee!

It was a simple enough matter to find a willing, brave man to ferry me to Alexandria. He was already at hand—Apollodoros, a merchant of Sicily who had supplied us with rugs and tents. But as to what I might be called on to do once I was there—ah, that was a different thing. It called for an expertise I was entirely lacking.

Caesar had only one weakness, indeed, only one aspect that seemed human in the midst of all his superhuman attributes. The gods are kind: They always leave some gap in us through which we can approach one another as equals. Caesar was partial to love affairs—or, to be more painfully honest, to sex affairs.

The gods can also be cruel, for this was the one area where I could *not* hope to interest him. Had it been horsemanship—Caesar was reputed to be able to ride at a full gallop with his hands behind his back—I could have won his admiration. Had it been languages, I could have stunned him with my knowledge of eight—whereas he had only two, Greek and Latin, at his command. Had it been riches, my personal fortune and the palace treasures would have left him speechless. Had it been ancestry, I came from the oldest royal house in the world, whereas he was of ancient patrician, but still citizen, lineage.

But love! Sex! He had been with men and women of all ages and types, and had acquired an expertise that marked him out even among his peers. Whereas I—I was a virgin, and knew nothing of the refinements or even the fundamentals of lovemaking, beyond what I had read in poetry. My closest friend was a eunuch! I felt helpless at the thought of facing Caesar.

And then the question: Would I even be willing to give myself to him? No one had ever touched me in an intimate way. Could I allow a stranger to do so?

I reminded myself of what was at stake: Alexandria, and Egypt. I pictured the Nile flowing in its flat green ribbon past the palm-lined banks. The granite obelisks reaching toward the sun. The bright, shifting sands under the aching blue sky. The dark, seated statues of ancient Pharaohs. Waiting. Yes. For Egypt I could do anything. Even give myself to Caesar.

I shook my head. Then that was decided. Now I must prepare myself. Prepare myself as I always did for any venture. I almost said "prepare my body," but I knew, instinctively, that in this case it was the mind that needed to be prepared.

It was twilight, and it had been three days since the appearance of Caesar's messenger. There was no time to waste. I sent for Olympos.

When he arrived, I invited him to sit on the cushions and share a supper with me. Thanks to Apollodoros, the royal tent was furnished beyond the usual Spartan camp bed, folding table, and brazier. I had many hassocks covered in embroidery or tooled leather, brightly woven wool carpets, and curtains shot through with silver threads, which divided the areas of living and privacy. Overhead was suspended a fringed movable canopy that served both to cool us and to shoo away insects.

We lounged on the cushions. We were served on brass platters from Damascus. Iras passed us baskets of plump, juicy figs and sweet dates, followed by the puffy round bread of Ashkelon. We sipped wine, and I waited until Olympos had eaten his first platterful before speaking of the matter at hand. I knew that men are always most approachable after their hunger has been appeased.

"Excellent figs," said Olympos, holding one up and inspecting it.

"I remembered how partial you were to figs," I said.

He cocked one eyebrow. "Then you must have a favor to ask me!"

"It is impossible to fool you, Olympos," I said, using one of my foolproof flatteries. In my experience, there are only two things no one will admit to: having no sense of humor, and being susceptible to flattery. "Well, the truth is I need your medical advice. You are my personal physician, are you not?"

"Yes, and honored to be so." He waited.

"If I became Caesar's lover," I said calmly, "what would that mean, medically, I mean?"

He almost spat out the fig he was so contentedly chewing. I was startled; Olympos was usually impossible to shock or even ruffle. "It would—it would mean you would bear him a bastard!"

"But why? His other mistresses did not. Servilia and Mucia and Postumia and Lollia. And his current wife, Calpurnia, has no children. In fact, none of his wives had children but his first. Perhaps he's incapable of fathering them."

"Or has been careful not to, since all those women were married." He shook his head. "Do you mean to go to the bed of that old libertine? The thought is repulsive!" He looked as if he were my guardian uncle, and ready to punish me.

"Why? If he were that repulsive, he would find himself alone in his bed, which, from what I hear, does not happen!"

"Power makes even the unattractive attractive." He looked most severe.

"Women went to his bed before he had power," I insisted.

"He's old!"

"He's fifty-two."

"That's old!"

"He can swim a mile in his armor. That's *not* old. Not many young men can do that. Can you?"

"No," he admitted reluctantly. "So you're determined to do this?"

"I am prepared to do it if necessary. There is a difference."

He sat pouting, almost as if he were a jealous lover.

"I need your advice. I have no desire to conceive a bastard. I have heard there are herbs one can take . . . medicines. . . ."

"Yes," he muttered. "From Cyrene, there's the silphion plant to make Cyrenaic juice. And for emergencies, though it isn't as effective, the pennyroyal, which grows everywhere. I suppose you want me to get you some!"

"Yes, but more than that, I want you to get me something else. We have an army here, and wherever there are armies, there are prostitutes. I wish to speak to the most accomplished of the prostitutes, the queen of the prostitutes, as it were."

"One queen to another?" He could barely get the words out.

"Yes. There are things I need to know."

"Well, then," he finally said, "I think I know exactly the one you seek."

"Why, Olympos," I said, "it sounds as if you have sought her already and can give her a personal recommendation!"

He glared at me. "I will send her to you this very night."

"Caesar will be eternally grateful," I said, lightly.

Olympos grunted. He was dangerously near to having no sense of humor at that moment.

The oil lamps were guttering low when there was a stirring at the door of the tent. I had given up expecting any visitor, and had put on my bedclothes. By the poor light I had been reading Caesar's *Commentaries*, hoping to gain an insight into his mind. But it was written in a very impersonal style, and Caesar even called himself by name, as if he were a bystander. Was he really this self-contained? It boded ill for my venture.

Iras poked her head around the curtain. "Your Majesty, a woman is here for you. She says her name is Jehosheba."

It was obvious to me who Jehosheba was. "Show her in," I said, sitting up, and pulling on a robe. I was barely covered when Jehosheba, majestic in her calling, stepped into my quarters.

First of all, she was beautiful, like a goddess of abundance. Everything about her was more so: She seemed to have twice as much hair as a normal woman, with color that was twice as rich and deep, and curls that were twice as strong and shiny. Her face and its features were exquisite, her teeth glistened like pearls, and were perfectly matched. As to her body—I could tell, by the way the taut skin moved on her well-molded arms, that it was perfect, too.

"Thank you for coming," I said. "I like to behold fine works of nature." And indeed, that was what she seemed to be.

"And I have longed to behold you close-up," she said, with winning simplicity.

Winning simplicity, I thought. Mark that down. Remember that.

"I am in need of your help," I said. "You have had much training in that in which I am but a novice." I paused. "I mean, the art of making love to a man."

"I am pleased that you recognize that it is an art," she said. "Just because anyone may indulge in it does not mean that anyone knows how to. Everyone knows how to walk, but only a few are pleasing to watch while walking."

"Tell me," I said. "Tell me everything."

I cannot recount all she said. Much of it was common sense, of course. Do not take off your clothes in a cold room. Do not allow interruptions. Do not speak of any other matters. Do not, under any circumstances, speak of other women. And never, never ask, *Do you love me?* Second worst is, *Will you come to me again?* Only a fool says those things.

"Each man has a dream image of himself and a woman, and it is your job to answer that dream. Inasmuch as you do, you will satisfy him," she said. "The challenge is that it is not readily apparent which man has which image in his mind. He may not even know himself. It takes a genius to discover it. All great courtesans are geniuses that way. They pull out what is deepest in the other person and give it a face and form. Such is magic. Forget potions and perfumes. The spellbinding comes in summoning forth this deepest desire and dream, and making it live. And in becoming this, you will find yourself changed as well, and you may come to love him. For there is a possibility he may answer your own deepest secret dream. Always that possibility."

"Has this ever happened to you?" I asked this creature of inspiring love.

"No," she admitted. "But there is always the next time!" She threw back her head and laughed, a great, hungry laugh. Even in that, she was beguiling. She indicated my trunks. "Let me see your gowns," she said. "They are your tools!"

After she left, I felt more lost than ever. Before, I had not known what I did not know, imagining it a simple matter of assembly, like building a chair or cooking a stew. Now I knew it was much more than that, and something that was unteachable. I would have to face Caesar with neither knowledge nor experience in this realm, and by the time I acquired any, it would be too late. I felt like a human sacrifice.

(12)

I took special care in selecting the rug. I knew that, as a connoisseur of fine furnishings, Caesar must not disdain my gift. It also allowed me to distract myself by comparing the scarlet thread of Cappadocia to that of Arabia, and other such weighty questions. I took an entire day to decide between my two final choices, which served the purpose of postponing my meeting with Caesar a little longer. But the rug was finally lying in its canvas bag at my feet, and I was sitting forlornly in the fishing boat that Apollodoros was rowing—ah! all too competently—a safe distance from the shore, westward to Alexandria.

I could see the dim glow of the enemy campfires, see the smoke drifting inland. But we soon passed them by, and the sands were empty. He raised the sail. Then, much too soon, the green of the Delta started. We were coming closer.

I did not see the Lighthouse. Long before we came in sight of it, I had crawled into the rug and Apollodoros had fastened it around me. I was imprisoned in the dark, faintly sweet-smelling, threaded prison, and I could feel every shudder and thump as the boat bounced over the waves. I felt us shake as we passed a very rough spot, and I guessed that was the entrance of the harbor, where the waves dashed against the base of the Lighthouse even in good weather. As we bobbed and bucked, and I began to feel sick, I couldn't help a faint smile; all that effort in selecting the rug, and I might end by ruining it!

Now, that would impress Caesar, I told myself. How inviting, how alluring! I bit my lip and willed myself to think of flat horizons. Then, just when I thought I could not stand it another minute, the pitching stopped. We had entered calmer waters. In a muffled way, I began to hear voices. There were other boats nearby.

Of course there would be. The palace still had to be supplied with food, linen, and firewood. Surely one more boat would not be noticed.

I heard Apollodoros shouting good-natured remarks to the other boats. The water under the boat was quiescent now, and we glided along. Soon there was a gentle bump, wood against wood. Then I felt the boat bounce and ride higher in the water as Apollodoros stepped out. He was pulling it along a canal, most likely the main one that led south to the lake and north into the palace area.

What was the hour? It must still be daylight, the normal hour for commercial vessels to be out, but I hoped it was near sunset. The later I got to Caesar's quarters, the more likely he might be alone.

We glided along the waterway and then came to an abrupt stop. This must be the entrance to the palace grounds. I heard, muffled and indistinct, the voices of the guards and of Apollodoros. What was he saying? O Isis, you must have given him the words, because next I heard the sound of the iron grate being lifted so we could float past. Apollodoros gave a cheery call of thanks.

I felt us being tied up. Then nothing. No movement, no voices. I felt as if I were strangling. The tightly rolled rug prevented me from filling my lungs with air, and the lack of movement was disorienting.

I must have either gone to sleep or become unconscious, because I have no memory of what happened until I was jolted awake. The rug was being carried. But was it by Apollodoros, or someone else? I tried to lie so naturally that nothing—except my weight—might betray my presence. I had told Apollodoros to explain the weight by saying there were gold goblets inside as a gift to Caesar.

I lay as straight as I could, hoping that I did not make any suspicious bumps. Yet I mustn't be so rigid that the rug looked as if it held a rod inside; I had to drape as if I had no backbone.

My neck was about to be snapped, and with each footstep my head thumped against the inside of the roll. That, added to the lack of air, began to deprive me of my senses. I saw little shooting stars before my eyes at each jolt.

Now we were stopped again. I heard low voices, then louder ones arguing. Then the creak of a door.

I stiffened; I could not help myself. I heard more voices. Then I felt the rug being placed on the floor, and a tug as the bindings were cut away. Suddenly there was a yank, and the entire rug shot out from around me, propelling me out and onto the slippery onyx floor. I slid several feet before I could free my hands to stop myself. As I looked up, I saw two lean and muscular legs, their feet encased in Roman military boots, right before me.

I sat up, my eyes following quickly up past the leather strips of the general's uniform and then over the cuirass, and then I was looking directly into his face: Caesar's face.

I recognized it from his busts and his portraits. The features were the same. But what none of them had captured was the reserved, deadly power of the man.

"Greetings," he said, and his voice was quiet, almost a whisper. But not the sort of whisper that is afraid of being overheard; it is the whisper of one who knows others will strain to catch his every word, and he need not deign to raise his voice to conversational level.

Still, I caught the shadow of surprise crossing his face; he was unsuccessful at hiding it entirely.

He reached down to take my hand and pull me up. I was struck with his utter assurance; how easily I could have slashed at him with a knife. Instead I merely rose and found myself facing him.

I forgot that I had been frightened, so puzzled was I by this man and by my surroundings. The hours inside the rug had left me dazed and unsteady on my feet. It was dark outside. Oil lamps had been lit in the room. Where had the time gone? How long had we waited in Alexandria? Caesar seemed to be alone. Could this be possible?

"A gift from the Queen of Egypt," Apollodoros was saying, gesturing to the unfurled rug. Caesar stepped on it.

"But it is not Egyptian," he said.

"I am the Egyptian," I said.

He was staring at me. He looked as if he knew well how to smile, but was deliberately withholding it. "You are not Egyptian either," he finally said, with virtually no expression. It was impossible to tell what he thought. Yet his lack of animation was not cold, but strangely teasing and luring.

"My ancestry, as Caesar well knows, is Macedonian, but as Queen of Egypt I have taken the spirit of Egypt for my own."

"Is that so?" Caesar walked around me as though I were a tree, rooted and growing in his—my—chamber. For I now found myself as an intruder in my very own apartments.

"Do you like the tortoiseshell doors in this chamber?" I asked, more boldly than I felt. "I was always most fond of them. Are you my guest, or am I yours?"

Now he laughed, but his face still held that peculiar reserve of power and watchfulness. "We are both one another's. You will have to educate me about these things. I am merely a Roman barbarian." He sat, selecting a hard-backed chair.

I chose not to answer that. "I am here, as you requested." I waited.

He raised one eyebrow. "In good time, too. I am impressed. Most impressed." He nodded.

"I was told you respected speed."

"Above almost all other things."

"And what are the other things you respect?"

"Fortune, and the courage to grasp it." He leaned back and crossed his arms. They were brown, lean, and sinewy.

"I have heard you are a gambler. That you cried, 'Let the dice fly high!' as you crossed the Rubicon."

"You have heard much," he said.

"Your boldness was rewarded," I continued. The truth was, I had not heard much, and had almost come to the end of my knowledge of him.

"As you hope yours will be," he said.

"Yes."

Now, at long last, he almost smiled. "Boldness is its own reward. It belongs to only a select few."

It was as if I were hearing my own thoughts miraculously voiced aloud by another. "No, it *brings* rewards. For many rewards are grasped only by the bold," I answered.

"Enough words," he said, and waved for Apollodoros to depart.

He bowed and withdrew. Then Caesar turned to me.

Now was the moment. He was going to reach out and take me, just as he took Gaul and Rome. I braced myself. I was ready.

"Why did you send supplies to Pompey?" he suddenly asked.

I had had my eyes downcast, waiting. Now I looked up to see him watching me, well aware of what I had been expecting, but not interested in pursuing it. He even looked disgusted, or possibly only amused. It was impossible to tell with him.

"I had to," I said. "Magnus Pompey had been my father the King's patron."

"What about the son, Gnaeus Pompey?"

"What about him?"

"Is he your ally? What did you owe him?"

"Nothing."

"Good. I mean to kill him. And I would not have you be my enemy thereby." He said "I mean to kill him" as casually as a boy says, "I am going fishing." Then I remembered hearing once that Caesar had threatened a Roman tribune with death if he continued pestering him with questions about treasury funds, and that Caesar had then added, "And this, you know, young man, is more disagreeable for me to say than to do." Suddenly the story was absolutely believable.

"Do as you like," I heard myself saying.

"Oh, are you giving me permission?" he said. "Kind of you."

"I am not here to discuss Pompey. I am here because I have been unlawfully deposed from my throne, and because you have the power to set it right. My brother and his advisors are evil—"

He winced. "Please. That word is overused. Suffice it to say I don't care for them or for their manner of operation: inept and without honor. You shall have your throne back, never fear. I shall see to it." He paused. "As you said, boldness brings rewards. And you have proved most bold."

"I thank you," I said. But could I trust his word?

"Now all that is over," he said, smiling at last, "do I have your hand, as my loyal ally?"

I gave it to him. He grasped it in both his. I was surprised to find that he had small hands. "You will find my loyalty to be absolute," I said.

"A rare commodity. And even rarer among Ptolemies."

Now he seemed to have switched into another personality. His brittle demeanor had softened, but his dark brown eyes were still wary. He sat relaxed, and his hand was nowhere near his sword. "I wish to believe you," he said with all sincerity. "I myself always keep my word, but until now I have found no fellow in that."

"You will see," I assured him. And I kept that promise, being loyal to him until long after his dying breath.

"Yes," he said with that same smile, "I remember promising the Cilician pirates who kidnapped me that I would return and kill them. They didn't believe me, because I sang songs with them and kept good company around the campfire. But I kept my word."

I shuddered. "Do you mean you keep your word only about killing? I mean more than that when I give my word."

"I keep my word in all things, good and bad."

"What about your marriage vows?" I blurted out. How could the notorious adulterer claim to always be loyal?

"Well, where marriage is concerned, it is a different matter," he admitted. "In Rome the marriage vows are trampled on. But I was faithful to Cornelia."

"The wife of your youth," I said.

"Yes. I loved her. Perhaps that is a capacity that one loses with age." He said it regretfully, and I almost believed him. "Perhaps all that is left after the age of fifty is loyalty and love for one's fellow soldiers."

"Do not think that way!" I heard myself saying. "That is worse than being defeated in a battle!"

Now he broke out into a true smile, not a half one. "Wait until you are defeated in a battle before you say that. There is *nothing* worse than being defeated in battle."

"Spoken like the conqueror of the world," I said, staring at him. He *was* the conqueror of the world, the new Alexander. Yet here he sat on a chair in my room, and he was not even a particularly large man. "I hope you will utterly defeat my brother and his army!"

"Thus far nothing has happened. I have been sightseeing in your magnificent white city, going to the Museion, taking in lectures, reading in the Library. The Egyptian army is still guarding against *you* on the eastern frontier."

"When they find I have slipped through, they will be here soon enough."

"Then I shall have quite a challenge. I have only four thousand men with me, and thirty-five ships. I understand there are twenty thousand men in the Egyptian army. I am outnumbered five to one." He said it cheerfully.

"We shall defeat them!" I said fiercely.

"But in the meantime I shall send for reinforcements," he said.

"Prudent," I said. Then we both laughed. "Let me show you your quarters, Imperator," I said. "I am familiar with them, as they were mine."

"And can be again," he said. He crossed his lean arms.

"I would appreciate that," I admitted. "I can find you very comfortable quarters in the building adjacent to the temple of Isis."

"No, I meant that you should live here with me."

"With you? To share your couch?" Here it came, as I had expected. The conqueror must take all the spoils.

"Couches are uncomfortable. I prefer a bed. Show it to me."

"Where have you been sleeping?"

"On the couch. I was waiting for you before I used the bed."

"You were waiting for me?" I was disappointed. Had I not surprised him? Was he not astounded with my ingenuity in coming to him through enemy lines?

"I was. I was informed that you were resourceful, clever, and passionate—at least that is what your enemies claimed! That made it a sort of test. I would have tried to find a way to get to Alexandria, were I in your place; I believed that you would, also, although I could not predict what method you would use. And so I waited. Knowing that if you came as I expected you to do, I would salute and admire you for it. And want you. And only then would I wish to use the bed. Show it to me." He stood up, his powerful lithe frame rising instantaneously.

The astonishing thing was, I wanted to. The terrible chore, the awful sacrifice—it was not to be that way. This was entirely unexpected. I could not explain it to myself.

"Come with me," I said. "Follow me wherever I take you." I took his hand, liking the feel of it.

"That is not something I am accustomed to: following."

We were traversing the rooms that lay between the general audience chamber and the innermost one of the royal bedchamber. Abruptly he stopped and pulled my hand.

"I go no step farther until you swear to me that this is of your own volition," he said in a very soft voice. "What I said in the audience chamber, about the bed, was a jest. I am no rapist, no pillager. I will support your claim to the throne regardless. You need not ever have anything to do with me personally." He paused. "I have never touched a woman who did not wish me to."

"It *is* my desire and wish," I assured him. It was true, but I could not understand it. This man was a stranger. I did not even know if he was right- or left-handed. Perhaps that was the thrill of it.

But no, I deceive myself. It was Caesar himself. Just looking at him—at his powerful frame, his straight bearing, his lean and tanned face—made me want to touch him. I had never touched or lingeringly stroked anything besides an animal before—only my horse, my dogs, my cats. Now I wished nothing more than to touch the flesh of this man standing before me. Had I gone mad?

As in a dream, I led him through the rooms. They were in darkness, except for a few corners where standing oil lamps had been lit.

We walked on onyx floors, slippery beneath our feet, with the lamplight reflecting but faintly in them, past pale rooms covered in ivory panels. I could hear the low hiss and murmur of the sea outside the eastern windows. Still I led him on wordlessly, I Orpheus and he Eurydice, until we reached my chamber.

It remained as I had left it months ago. The bed coverlet, steeped in rich Tyrian dye, looked brown, not purple, in the moonlight. A half-moon was setting outside the window, as if it hastened away and would not look.

Now, suddenly, I was at a loss as to what to do. I had brought him here, but this was so formal, so abrupt. It almost seemed like an initiation ceremony, one of the mysteries that were celebrated in secret rites. And it was a secret rite of which I was ignorant. What was I thinking of?

Caesar stood still, like a statue. And then I said—the thought suddenly came from nowhere—"You must wear the robes of Amun." Opening an ebony-inlaid trunk, I took out the ancient robes that the ruler kept in readiness for ceremonies at the temples. This one was shot through with gold thread, heavy with encrusted jewels, and woven with rare glistening colors.

"I am not a god," he said quietly, as I draped the robe over his shoulders. "Yet in Ephesus I was hailed as one." There was a wistfulness in his voice, faint, yet there.

"Tonight you are a god," I said. "You will come to me as Amun."

"And you? Who are you?"

"Isis," I said. My ceremonial robes were also at hand.

"Can we not merely be Julius Caesar and Cleopatra?" I had to strain to hear his voice.

"Tonight we are more than that, and we must embrace it," I said. I was frightened at what I had embarked on; I was not even sure I could complete it. Perhaps the costumes would serve to disguise my confusion.

He stood before me in the robes of the god. In the darkness his face was hidden, but his physical presence filled the robes and did them justice.

He bent down to kiss me, the first time anyone had ever done so. I almost flinched at his touch, it was so foreign to me to let anyone come that close. He touched my hair, bringing both hands up to do so; he embraced me gently, he kissed my neck. Each action was so slow and deliberate that it felt portentous, as if he were unbolting a sacred door or unsealing a shrine. He took my hands in his and guided them to embrace him as well, as if he knew I needed to be taught. And touching him, even just his shoulders, felt as forbidden as his touch on me: unpermitted, shocking, alien. Not only was he a stranger, but now I seemed a stranger to my very self. And yet . . . it was as if I did know him, in some fundamental, reassuring way. My fear evaporated, its place taken by eagerness and excitement.

He reached down and picked me up, more easily than Apollodoros had. I felt his arm bones, and I wanted them to be dedicated to me, to protecting me, to fighting for me. He took only two steps over to the bed.

The robes of Amun were heavy and smothering. Now he must throw them off. But no; he insisted on stripping off his military gear in a ritualistic manner, and lying naked beneath the robes.

I removed my gown in turn, and was glad to do so; once becoming, after the hard journey it was dirty and smelled of the rug and the bottom of the boat. With unsteady hands I drew the Isis robe around my shoulders and over my back.

"Ah." He put out a hand and touched me, as if in wonder. Had I not known better, I would have believed he had never seen a woman's body before. "You are beautiful." And I knew that tonight it was so.

Bolder now, I touched him, feeling his muscled chest, so different from the eunuch Mardian's—the only male I had ever embraced. I ran my hands over his shoulders, exploring like a child in a new room. He seemed amused.

"You must teach me," I whispered into his ear, freely admitting my lack of knowledge. I trusted him absolutely, a curious thing.

"Can Amun teach Isis?" he said. "No. They are both fully knowledgeable. A god and a goddess." Then he pulled gently and unfastened the clasp of my robe. The heavy costume slid off my shoulders. He kissed the place where the robe had lain. His lips made my skin rise in gooseflesh.

He bent his head and kissed my breasts, first the right, then the left. He touched them almost reverently.

"Even Venus is never portrayed with breasts this perfect," he murmured. He held me gently, as if he were still undecided whether to pursue this course of action. After what seemed a long, quiet time, he said, "You are young and offer me a great gift. But I would not rob your husband of it."

"I'm free to offer it as I will," I cried, suddenly afraid he would refuse me. "And fate is unlikely ever to grant me a husband I want!" Certainly not my brother—I had no wish to save anything of my person for him, or even to let him touch me. "You must be my husband!" I insisted. "Yes, Amun to Isis—" Let me hide my unbidden and impolitic desire behind the conventions of the costumes.

"Then, for tonight—" At last he pressed himself against me, and we sank down together on the pillows. He was lying on me, the heavy Amun robes weighing us down. I was yearning for us to join together. Everything was gone from my mind but this desire. I did not remember that I had been afraid, or sought information from the prostitute or Olympos, only that I wanted to be physically possessed by Caesar.

"—I will be your husband."

"So be it," I said, with all my heart.

And I gave myself to him, and our destinies merged. He became my lord and partner, I his queen and wife.

He was gentle and patient with me; it was I who was eager and hungry, as if he had created an appetite in me that had never existed before. I was caught up in it, picked up and transported to another world, as I had heard happened to sages; afterwards they returned to earth babbling about the visions they had had, indescribable, ineffable, transforming. Sometimes these holy men claimed to have been sucked up into the clouds by whirling winds and carried great distances; sometimes they departed only from the utter quiet of their own chambers. Always they were changed when they returned, and so I was, as well. I had touched and been touched by another human being, had allowed someone beyond all my guarded gates of privacy, into my very self, so that there were no boundaries left. What I had dreaded all my life as annihilation I now experienced as completion. My world changed utterly in that instant. I clung to him as if I would never lose him. I wanted that revelation, that moment of transfiguration, never to fade. But it would; it did. So I learned two things that night, and the next day, from him: the perfection of a moment, and the fleeting nature of it.

He slept. His body lay stretched on the bed, a linen sheet draped over his back as if he were just dozing from the baths. The Amun robe lay somewhere on the floor, discarded after it had served its purpose. I could tell from his breathing that he was asleep, his broad back moving slowly up and down, exposed to a dagger should I have one hidden. Pompey had been killed by the treachery of a Ptolemy, and yet here Caesar lay, sleeping peacefully at the mercy of another one. But he had gauged me right; not only would I never harm him, but I would kill anyone who tried to. I sat up for a long time in the bed, just watching him, listening to him breathe and move in his sleep.

I felt profoundly bound to him. The lovemaking over, my heart beating only at a normal pace, the heat of the moment replaced by cool watchfulness, I saw him not as an abstract Roman, or even as the famous conqueror Caesar, but as a lone man, an exile like myself. In the faint lamplight I could make out the lines on his back, the little bumps where his spinal cord lay like a rope under his flesh, even some scars. He had had a hard life the last few years; months of being out in the field, leading half-starving soldiers to attack his once brother-in-law, now his foe. No rest, no safety, betrayed by the very city he had won victories for, having to risk his life just to have his rights recognized . . . he had said that only his troops had kept him from being sacrificed by the Senate, when all was said and done. A weary man, an un-appreciated man . . . an exile, like me. But he had ended my exile. I wished to do the same for him—if there was any way I could.

The enormity of what I had just done began to sink in. I had blithely handed him—the famous seasoned voluptuary!—my virginity. Did he even value it? Why had I done it? I tried to ask myself these questions, as if they mattered. They ought to matter. The "sacrifice" had been unnecessary—he had said he would take my side regardless. My coming to him in the rug had already won him over; it was I who insisted on sealing the bargain further by making him my lover. And now . . . I was supposed to be weeping with shame and loss, but instead I was feeling this unbearable, improbable happiness. It, and he, were so altogether different from what I had imagined.

I remembered the first time I had ever heard his name, in connection with Father's debts and annexing Egypt. He had been Consul then—it was even before he had gone to Gaul. I had imagined him to be coarse, grasping, greedy, red-faced, and loud, growing more so as the years went on, so that by this time he would be almost a swine, in spite of his rapacious appetite for stolen artworks. I thought his bed behavior (one could not call it lovemaking) would be brutish and rough, like the field soldier he was. No one had prepared me for this vital yet oddly courteous and elegant man. And certainly no one had prepared me to find in his words and beliefs an echo of my own values and very self. We were alike, in our deepest substance, even though we were born years apart and on different sides of the sea, and of different peoples. He was much more my brother than were my real brothers.

And no one had prepared me to feel so fiercely loyal to him, so instantly bound to him. And as for the lovemaking . . . I was eager for more of it. I would refuse him nothing; I did not even want to.

I was supremely happy, perhaps the first time in my life I had ever been so. I laid my head down across his back and closed my eyes, letting his breathing lull me into a state where I could float and savor that peaceful happiness.

I must have slept, because when I opened my eyes it was quite light and he was up and looking out the window. He had already put his tunic on, but was still barefoot. I slipped out of bed and came up behind him, putting my arms around him. "You have stolen from my bed," I said.

"Lest I should be chained there by my own desire in the daylight," he said, turning to me. The eastern light showed his face, with lines around the eyes but otherwise taut and healthy.

"Is that wrong?" I asked. I knew already that being together in the daytime would be entirely different.

"It is most un-Roman," he said with a laugh. "Don't you know that such things are done only by the degenerate people of the east? But then, of course, you *are* of the east!"

"How could anything Caesar does be un-Roman?"

"There are those who like to prescribe Roman behavior. One must be careful not to run afoul of them, when their opinion still counts." He gave his half-smile. "But later . . . well, one must admit their standards are questionable. They say adultery is permissible, but only in the dark!"

"Who are these Romans?" I was curious.

"Oh, Cicero, Cato, Brutus . . . but there is no reason for you to be concerned about their murmurings."

"Nor you, while you are here." I took his hand. But I could see his thoughts were already on the business of the day ahead. I dropped it and let him go to the other side of the room, where his clothes lay abandoned. He quickly put them back on. I marveled at how fast a soldier can dress himself.

"I had arranged for your br—" he started to say, when there was a knock at the door. "Enter!" he bellowed.

The doors were flung open, and in stepped Ptolemy and Pothinus. Now I suddenly understood why Caesar was up and dressed, and why I was not. I had nothing on but a sheet that I had wound around myself. That was how he had wanted it.

The visitors gasped. Ptolemy looked as though he were going to cry, and Pothinus, for once, was speechless. He bobbed his ibis-head up and down over his obese body. He stared at me, at the royal bed with its sheets and pillows still in disarray, and then at Caesar, smiling and self-possessed. He understood.

"It isn't fair!" shrieked Ptolemy. "It isn't fair! What's *she* doing here, how did she get here, it isn't fair, it isn't fair!" He turned and ran from the chamber.

"Great Caesar," began Pothinus in a shaky, high voice, "we are most surprised by the presence of—"

"Stop that boy!" barked Caesar to his guards, who had crept up outside the doors during the night. "Stop him before he gets outside."

But my brother knew all the secret passageways in the palace, and before they could even locate him, he had run out into the forecourt and then almost to the fence separating the palace grounds from the rest of the city. A large crowd was always there, and today was no exception. I watched from the chamber window as he rushed toward the people, yanked off his royal coronet, threw it to the ground, and burst into a howl of tears.

"I've been betrayed!" he yelped. "Betrayed, betrayed!" Then followed a paroxysm of weeping.

Two burly Roman soldiers, the sun glinting off the brass on their breastplate straps, ran out of the palace after him, grabbed him from behind, and dragged him back into the palace.

My blood felt chilled. I had just had an unrehearsed—and therefore all the more revealing—demonstration of who held the real power here. Common Roman soldiers had laid hands on the King of Egypt, and treated him like any naughty village boy. I must not lose Caesar's favor, lest they do the same to me.

Behind me, Pothinus was still trying to talk. "Forgive him, he is . . . unpracticed in ruling," he whined. "He cannot hide his feelings."

Caesar was standing, one lean arm resting on the back of a chair. He had not bothered to go over to the window to see what would happen to Ptolemy. He knew what would happen. He just looked at Pothinus, and it appeared that he was not going to bother to answer him.

"Shall I decide to allow him to be your co-regent, most exalted Queen?" he asked, in that deadly quiet public voice I was becoming accustomed to. But it was not the voice he used in the dark of the night.

"I prefer not," I said.

"But your father's will wished it so," Caesar persisted. Was he teasing me? What did he mean to do? "And did you not take as your title 'Cleopatra, the Goddess Who Loves Her Father'? Then, of course, you should honor his wishes. Would you care to proceed with the marriage to Ptolemy?"

The thought of yoking myself to him in any way was politically repellent; yet that was nothing compared to the possibility of his ever touching me as Caesar had. "I could not bear it," I said.

Ptolemy was led in, crying and scowling. The two soldiers supported him by his bony little shoulders.

"Ah! The bridegroom himself!" said Caesar. "Come, dry your tears. It is not fit to weep on your wedding day."

His tears dried up in surprise. "Wh-what?" he sniffled.

"It is my judgment, as executor of the late King's will, that we must abide by the terms of it. You will marry your sister Cleopatra and reign as joint monarchs in time-honored fashion."

He couldn't be doing this! How could I have trusted him, or hoped for justice from him? Had all my impressions of him been wrong? Now it seemed he was as devious and cruel as the rest of his countrymen. I was stunned.

"And then, together, you will raise the money you owe me. As you may recall, I have assumed responsibility for collecting what the late King still owed the Roman Republic." He nodded matter-of-factly.

That man! So he *was* just greedy, after all. "You cannot be both judge and beneficiary," I said coldly. "Choose which way you will be satisfied—either as high judge or as debt collector."

He shot a look at me. His eyes were flat and betrayed not anger but resolution. "I will be satisfied both ways, as it pleases me. So make yourselves ready for your marriage, under whatever form you choose, and then we shall have our reconciliation banquet." He waved his hand at Pothinus. "Prepare for it. It should be a huge fete, held in—what was that hall with the gold rafters and the porphyry columns?—and serving at least two hundred guests. Do all the things you Alexandrians excel in. Dancing girls. Acrobats. Magic tricks. Gold plate. Rose petals on the floor. You know what better than I. Yes, the people must see that we all embrace and love one another."

They stood as if they had been mummified, as stiff and wrapped as Osiris.

"Well?" said Caesar. "I have told you what you must do."

The mummies bent their heads and withdrew.

I whirled around to Caesar. "How could you? I thought we were allies!" I was intelligent enough not to scream, *You even called yourself my husband!* Had he forgotten that? But I knew Caesar did not forget.

I felt angry, betrayed, seething. I had had only hours to bask in the momentous thing that had happened in the night, and already it was gone. And for what? So I could be made a new sort of prisoner?

Sternly I took myself in hand, one part of my mind speaking to the other. You came from Ashkelon, risking your life to gain an audience with Caesar, I reminded myself. And you succeeded. You had a private interview with him, and he agreed to set you back on the throne and enforce his will on your brother and his band of pathetic advisors. They seemed so wily and formidable, but now that Caesar is here, they are swept aside like schoolboys. They are nothing. I have got what I came for—political security. If I wanted more than that after meeting him, then I was a fool.

Caesar was standing, leaning on the handles of the chair, his head bent. I saw that the top of his head was balding. Amun in the daylight was no god. And I no goddess, just a woman who wanted a man in the oldest of all ways, but it was new to me.

"And so we are," he said.

It took me a second to realize what he was answering—my secret cry, as well as my spoken words. "Then make me sole Queen!" I said. "Why must I tolerate *him*?"

"It is not for long," he said. "But for now it must serve."

"Why?" I cried.

He looked at me, a long, searching look. "Cleopatra—how I love the way that name sounds on my tongue!—you know why. And you know that legalities must be followed, if only to be discarded later."

"So there must be this public reconciliation?" I knew I sounded as pouty as Ptolemy, but I could not help it.

"Yes," he said briskly. "You and Ptolemy will be proclaimed joint monarchs, the army can be demobilized, Pothinus can be disposed of—" He stopped as if he had just remembered an insignificant fact. "Did I tell you I banished Theodotos? That was his reward from me."

Banished . . . swept away . . . in the twinkling of an eye. . . . Yes, he did swat people as I had swatted the fly in my tent. And he did not even get a mess on his shoe. Just a wave of his hand and the person disappeared. Forever.

I laughed out loud with joy.

"Now, that's my Cleopatra!" He crossed the room swiftly and took me in his arms. "And no—Ptolemy will never be your true husband. I am he. As I promised." He kissed me, bending down to reach me. "We are alike, you and I," he said in so low a voice I could barely hear the words. "I know it; I can feel it. At last I have found someone who is exactly like me. I do not think I ever want to part from you. We are two halves of a pomegranate, and each section fits perfectly together."

I clung to him. I believed his words, because I wanted to, and thought I understood their true meaning.

The banquet was in readiness. Pothinus had followed Caesar's orders, and had prepared a feast for all the court dignitaries: the chief scribes and librarians, the state treasurer, the priests of Serapis and Isis, the commander of the Household Guard, the envoys and courtiers, the most celebrated court physicians, poets, rhetoricians, scientists, and scholars. The gold-covered rafters indeed gleamed their distinctive mellow sheen in the lamplight, and the floor was covered in rose petals brought by sea from Cyrene, where the best roses grow. Wherever you stepped, the drowsy sweet scent was released in the crushing underfoot.

I had gritted my teeth and allowed an abbreviated wedding ceremony to take place in the upper chambers of the palace, on the roof where the sea wind whips in. Ptolemy and I had gone through some words that officially linked us in marriage, in a formula invented by the palace. We were witnessed by Caesar, Pothinus, Arsinoe, and the younger Ptolemy. I mumbled the words, hoping thereby to make them invalid. As soon as it was over, I hurried away to dress myself for the banquet.

Now Caesar could never accuse me of not doing my part, I thought. The loathsome thing is done.

Charmian was still in the palace, waiting faithfully. I had not realized how much I missed her until I saw her familiar face, and heard her humming as she folded silk mantles and tunics in the room that held my wardrobe.

"Your Majesty!" she cried, a thousand questions on her face.

"Charmian! Oh, Charmian!" I said, rushing toward her.

She continued staring, suppressing a laugh, and then I looked down at the dusty gown I still wore.

"I have had no opportunity to change my escape clothes," I said. "I came by boat yesterday, and gained secret entrance to the palace."

"Everyone knows," she said. "It is said—but oh! how thankful I am that you are here, and safe! The last few months have been dreadful. They have strutted and swaggered all over Alexandria, the happy trio with their puppet, and proclaimed you dead."

"They are no longer a trio, but a duo," I said.

"Caesar has—?" The question hung in the air.

"Banished Theodotos," I said. "He will not trouble us again."

"And you have seen Caesar?" she asked delicately.

"As 'everyone knows,'" I said, quoting her, "I had myself smuggled into his chambers inside a rug."

She burst out laughing. "He must have been shocked!"

"He did not show it," I said. "And now—oh, but it is too long to tell. Later. Now I need to be dressed as a queen, for the banquet that is being staged below. Make me beautiful enough to give a kingdom to."

Make me beautiful enough to love, I meant. But with Caesar, it was always kingdoms and crowns and possessions. Love, if it came at all, must follow only in their wake.

And now I stood at the entrance to the great ceremonial hall, my back against the cool panels of ebony. I was so weighed down with pearls from the Red Sea that I felt enveloped in a glow of moonlight. They were woven skillfully in my hair by Charmian, and draped over my neck, and the largest and most prized of all hung from my ears, swaying whenever I moved my head. I was swathed in Sidonian silk that was almost transparent, and swirled around me like a mist. On my feet were sandals of braided silvered leather. I stood still and breathed deeply, and as I did so I could smell the lotus scent Charmian had rubbed in the bends of my elbows and in the spot on my neck where the vein throbbed. All day long my body had felt different, serving to remind me that what had happened was real—and irreversible.

Musicians, grouped in a corner, gently strummed the strings of their lyres and piped soft melodies on their flutes. The sound echoed against the polished stone walls.

The tramp of boots. Soldiers were coming. The Household Troops, or Caesar's? I watched as uniformed men entered from the entrance on the far side of the hall. I recognized the Roman cloaks and spears.

In the middle of them was Caesar. But he had chosen to wear the costume of a Consul of Rome—a white toga with a broad purple band at the hem—rather than that of a general. He must have just spent time with the barber, for his face was shiny and freshly shaven, and his hair trimmed. To me he was as stunning as Apollo, though I could see he was not young, not large, and weighted down by the world he carried with him.

Let me help you carry it, I thought suddenly. *It is too heavy for one man.*

They approached me, and Caesar stepped forward. I saw him staring at me, and knew that in his eyes I must appear transformed, an altogether different creature from the dispossessed one he had met in secret.

He held out his hand and I took it, wordlessly. Together we walked to the large ceremonial table, made from a section of the trunk of an enormous tree from the Atlas Mountains, and balanced on elephant tusks. He did not look at me all the while, but I could feel his attention. Finally he leaned toward me and whispered, his breath moving one of my earrings, "This has been a very long day, and I feel I have met you over and over again, in guise after guise. Which is real?"

I turned my head, not lowering it but moving it most royally. "And I have seen many Caesars," I said. "Which of those is real?"

"After the banquet you will know," he said. "And then after that, you will know yet more." His keen, dark eyes appraised me. "Child of Venus," he said. "You are fair!"

"Are you not also the child of Venus?" Supposedly Caesar's family was descended from Venus on his mother's side.

"Yes. As I told you, we are alike, both having that goddess's nature." His breath was warm on my ear.

Just then Pothinus approached, walking slowly toward his assigned place, his stiff linen robes refusing to accommodate themselves to his fat body. He looked like an exercise in papyrus folding. He had greased his ringlets and wore enormous, boxy earrings that stretched his earlobes painfully.

Behind him came Ptolemy, dressed as an ancient Pharaoh. And behind them, making a slow and stately entrance from the far end of the hall, came Arsinoe and young Ptolemy.

All heads turned to gaze at Arsinoe, at her graceful, almost undulating walk, and her shimmering silken gown. Her dark hair was swept up on her head, in the old Grecian style, and Helen of Troy could not have been more beautiful.

I watched Caesar staring at her. His eyes had widened, and although he did not move at all, I sensed his alertness. They had been together in the palace, Caesar and eighteen-year-old Arsinoe, for at least two weeks before my arrival. What had happened between them? The fact that neither betrayed any recognition of the other meant nothing. Arsinoe was beautiful in a way that ate at one's insides with either desire or envy, and Caesar . . . I knew his nature now.

She was taking her place on the royal couch, smiling with her smooth, tinted lips. Her bright blue eyes were drinking in Caesar, then fluttering in a most obvious manner, almost a parody of flirting. I hated her.

Caesar gave the welcome after the hall had filled with the hastily invited, and puzzled, guests. I also addressed them, and Ptolemy put in a few high-pitched words. Then Caesar rose again, and cried, "Let us all wear the garlands of gladness and celebration, for now we proclaim that all is peaceful once again in the land! Queen Cleopatra and King Ptolemy have consented to live in harmony and to rule as one!"

He lifted high a garland of lotus, cornflowers, and roses, and draped it around his neck. "Rejoice with them!" I was deeply grateful that he did not proclaim the "marriage." I sensed he would do that only if absolutely pressed to make further concessions.

Servants scurried around the hall, trays piled high with fragrant garlands, passing them to all the guests. The scent of flowers against warm skins soon rose in the room.

Next, Caesar lifted a jeweled cup and filled it from a pitcher of Falernian wine. "Drink!" he ordered them. "Drink and rejoice!"

He put the cup to his lips, but I did not see his throat move in drinking it. He set the cup down, then motioned for the servers to come forward with the crystal bowls and scented water to wash our hands before eating.

Then he abruptly held up his hands. "One thing further! I wish to announce that, as a gesture of friendship, Rome restores Cyprus to the house of Ptolemy. It will be governed by Princess Arsinoe and Prince Ptolemy." He nodded to them, and they slowly rose. The people cheered, astounded, and the recipients of the honor looked just as astonished. So this was one of Caesar's surprise strikes; this was the way he operated, both on and off the battlefield.

He looked over at me, and only in the slight change in his eyes and the lines around his mouth could I read his message: *I told you you would know me better after the banquet.*

"Can Caesar give away Roman territory on his own authority?" I asked coolly.

"Yes," he answered. "Does it please you?"

"Should it? You did not give it to me."

"I gave it *for* you, for your protection. And as a pledge from me."

My heart was beating so fast I dared not continue speaking. It was true; Caesar had made a bold and shocking gesture, one sure to antagonize the Senate of Rome.

The meal commenced. There was course after course, and I could not but admire the ability of our royal cooks to have produced such lavish fare on short notice. In addition to the usual roasted oxen, kid, and duck, we were offered purple shellfish, sea nettles, fish pastries, honey from Attica, and nuts from Pontus.

But Caesar ate little, and drank nothing from his wine goblet, preferring well water flavored with rose petals instead.

"You do not drink," I said, nodding toward his goblet.

"In my youth I drank enough for the rest of my life," he said. "Now I find it incites dizziness and causes strange symptoms in me. So I do not court Bacchus."

"You eat little, as well," I commented. "Does food, too, incite strange symptoms?"

"You seem very interested in watching everything I do," he said. "Have you, perhaps, added something to this food which you are anxious to see me eat?" Only the rising inflection at the end of the sentence assured me he was not serious.

"You are most suspicious," I said, spearing a piece of food off his plate and eating it. "Let me lay your fears to rest." Pothinus frowned at the lack of etiquette, but Caesar laughed—almost.

When the pomegranates were passed around with platters of fruit, Caesar took a large one and slowly cut it in half, pulling it apart while its center ran with bright red, acidic juice.

"You see how all the seeds fit," he said. "But pulling it apart causes it injury." He handed me the other half, watching my face intently.

I took the fruit and looked at its center, at the places where it had been wrenched open. "It should never be split away from itself like this." I indicated my stained hands, and anyone listening would have assumed we spoke only of that particular pomegranate. He smiled.

At the conclusion of the meal, when all the dishes had been removed, the acrobats tumbled into the hall, their oiled bodies flashing and their movements so swift the eye could hardly follow them.

"I have watched snakes strike," Caesar said, "but I never knew human beings could move like that."

Next came Nubian dancers, tall, thin, and muscular, who performed intricate dances to the high, wild beat of drums and hand-clapping.

The sound of their frantic music drowned out all other sounds, and I did not see Caesar motion to his guards. I did see Pothinus look up and suddenly leave his couch. But the loud performance made it impossible for me to ask what had happened. By the time the music had finally ended, Caesar was looking impatient and chewing on a stick of cardamom pastry.

"Where is Pothinus?" I asked.

Arsinoe and Ptolemy were also stirring nervously in their places.

"By this time, beheaded, most like."

"What?"

"Let us step outside!" said Caesar, grabbing my wrist in a grip as powerful as a lion's jaw. He managed to pull me to my feet in a way that made it seem I was rising of my own accord. He guided me toward the small door that opened between two pillars on the balconied side of the hall.

The brisk air outside smacked my face after the overheated, highly scented air of the hall. The wind was rising, whipping up whitecaps in the harbor.

"Around here," said Caesar, pulling me around the corner.

As I rounded it, I saw Pothinus—or what was left of him—lying sprawled across three steps. His head—if he had still had a head—would have been pointing downward. As it was, all the blood from his severed neck streamed in one direction down the white marble steps. Standing over him, holding the oiled, ringletted head with its swinging earrings, was a Roman soldier. His sword, or rather the middle part of it, was covered in globs of blood.

"Pompey, now you are avenged," said Caesar. "Take away this carrion," he ordered the soldier.

I was speechless. I could only stare at the corpse and then back again at Caesar, standing so calmly aside.

"Now I have seen a snake strike," I finally whispered.

"No, now you have seen a snake prevented from striking," said Caesar. "This afternoon my barber told me of Pothinus's plot to have me killed tonight. My trusted barber is one of those timid men with a hundred ears. And so . . ." He shrugged and indicated the bloodstained steps. "The snake has been killed halfway through its coiling."

"Halfway? He was only eating his dinner!" Somehow the thought of being butchered on a full stomach of sea pastry and roast ox was macabre.

"No, he had already performed half of his treachery," said Caesar. "He had sent word to Achillas to bring the army and besiege us here. While he was reconciling you and Ptolemy, bowing and kissing your hand, he was sending for the troops that would put an end to us both."

Now I felt sick. Was my only safety to lie with Caesar, who somehow— so far—managed to think faster, strike quicker, and thrust deadlier than those around him? But even Caesar must rest sometime, must nod and relax. . . .

I burst into tears. It was the only release besides screaming, and I did not want people to come running out from the banquet hall.

He put his arm around me and led me away. "We cannot return to the banquet. Even I cannot pretend that nothing has happened."

We were back in my—our—royal apartments. Caesar ordered a double guard around all entrances, using only his most trusted soldiers. Once in the innermost room, he sank down on a bench. Suddenly he looked much older, and the lines on his face were deeply etched. In the twilight, a gold signet ring on his tanned hand was the only bright thing about him.

"Oh, Caesar," I said, standing beside him and putting my arms around him. "I thought I knew the world, and now I see it is even more merciless than I had imagined."

"When first you realize that," he said wearily, "it changes you forever. But then, in the morning, when the sun comes up, and there is work to do . . ." He sighed. "You surprise yourself by enjoying it."

But he slumped against the wall, worn out by that day's work. I stood behind him, and kissed the top of his balding head. I rubbed his temples and pulled his head back, so the master of the world rested his head against me. He closed his eyes and sat motionless.

I watched as the light outside changed, faded, and finally disappeared. Darkness stole into the room and veiled everything. Still Caesar rested against me, my arms around his neck, rising and falling with each breath he took.

What made him trust me? I wondered. Why me, and not Arsinoe or Pothinus? It would have been so much easier for him to ally himself with them. Now he had enveloped himself in a mantle of troubles by supporting me.

He could have come here, accepted Pompey's head, confirmed Ptolemy on the throne, and gone his way back to Rome. So much simpler for a weary general. But he trusted me, for the same inexplicable reason that I trusted him. We had known each other instantly, recognized ourselves in each other.

He stirred. He had actually slept in my arms. I was deeply touched; no words could have given higher proof of his trust.

"My dear," I said, "let us rest properly. I think we will not be disturbed in our bed tonight. Your guards are strong."

He allowed me to pull him up and lead him to the bed, to unwind his toga and put it with his belongings on a trunk, to untie his sandals and rub his feet.

He watched me with drowsy eyes. "How well you perform all these things," he murmured. "You can be queen or servant, as it pleases you."

I lifted his legs gently onto the mattress, and spread the shining silken coverlet over him. "Rest," I said. "Even Hercules rested after his twelve labors."

He closed his eyes and turned his head to one side, giving a deep sigh— of contentment? exhaustion? relief?

I lay down beside him in the darkness, pulling up the coverlet. Silence pervaded the room, but I knew elsewhere in the palace, in the streets of Alexandria, there was no silence, but tumult. Our silence was the artificial child of the Roman guards outside the doors.

Sometime in the darkest part of night, when the heavens stand suspended, Caesar reached out for me. He was wide awake, and so was I.

"I told you you would know me better after the banquet," he said quietly. Somehow he must have sensed I was awake.

"You knew about Pothinus then? You had already given your soldiers their orders?" I spoke equally quietly, as I turned to him.

"Yes," he said. "Can you love the person you now know me to be?"

"More than ever before," I said. "You did what had to be done, and did not flinch." I admired him, was now in awe of him.

He pressed me to him, to his lean soldier's body, already rested after only this little sleep. He kissed me and it seemed all the hungers he did not allow himself to feel—for food, for sleep, for wine—came together in his desire now, melted together and multiplied.

How intrusive it may seem for me to recount here that Caesar was noted for his thoroughness in war; it was said that any battle he fought was decided so completely that there was never any need to refight it. So he was with me that night; as he possessed me and made love to me, many times through that long night, in many different ways, he captured me forever, body, heart, and strength.

13

The Alexandrian War now commenced—for so Caesar called it when he began writing his commentaries on it. I was scarcely mentioned in the commentaries, but then that was Caesar's way. It was a tricky war, not least because Caesar had not expected a war when he landed, but also because it was the first time he had ever fought with a city as the battleground, which required different tactics and strategy from those used in the open field.

The army of Achillas, which was already on its way during the reconciliation banquet, reached Alexandria in only a few days, twenty thousand strong. Caesar sent out envoys to Achillas, who were killed rather than being answered.

"So," said Caesar in that quiet voice, "he not only kills when it seems a matter of political advantage, as with Pompey, but does not recognize time-honored diplomatic rules. I need have no mercy on him, then."

I marveled at how he seemed to contain his anger, if indeed he felt anger. Perhaps he was past the stage where vile behavior was anything other than expected; perhaps to him it was loyalty and honor that were the rare finds. I also marveled at how he assumed he would beat Achillas and his large army of old Roman legionaries, runaway slaves, pirates, outlaws, and exiles—a motley, desperate bunch.

My own army, abandoned in Gaza, had dissolved for want of action and pay, and could not help. Earlier, Caesar had sent for reinforcements from Syria and Cilicia, but for now he would have to fortify the eastern section of Alexandria and try to make it secure, particularly the part where the palace was located on its peninsula. Safe inside the eastern harbor were his ten Rhodian warships among his others. I could see them from my windows, as they anchored inside the breakwaters. In the western harbor was the Egyptian fleet, which Ptolemy and I commanded: seventy-two warships.

Achillas and his forces, with the help of the excitable citizens, built gigantic triple barricades of stone blocks forty feet high across the streets, so that the magnificent Canopic Way was no longer passable, nor the wide north-south Street of the Soma. They hastily constructed mobile towers ten feet high, which could be pulled by ropes to any location they wished. Arms factories were established in the middle of the city, and the adult slaves were armed, while their veteran cohorts were centrally located, to be rushed to whatever site needed them. They were able to reproduce any arms they captured from our side, so cleverly that it seemed ours were the copies instead.

In the meantime, Caesar turned the banqueting room into his military headquarters, where he spread out his maps and reports on the long marble table and held conferences with his centurions and commanders. I insisted on attending the meetings, as I found myself fascinated to learn how the most disciplined and advanced army in the world operated.

"We must take the offensive," said Caesar, after the first week of fighting.

He tapped the diagram of the city tied up between two of the pillars in the hall.

One of his officers gave a snort. Caesar shot him a look.

"Not the entire city," he said. "But we must capture the island and the Lighthouse so that our reinforcements can reach us from the sea. We are pinned in here, and must keep this sea side open."

Was this the sort of daring for which he was renowned?

"How do we attack?" one of the centurions asked.

"There is only a little stretch of the waterfront between our barricades and theirs that controls the causeway. At the signal, we will rush from our section and storm the waterfront. We will fight our way there and then onto the causeway, then all the way to the Lighthouse."

At midday after this conference, Caesar held his customary meal with me, my siblings, and his officers. The table was set with wooden platters, moldy bread, and cheap, yellowish Taeniotic wine—standing orders from Pothinus.

"See how the King and Queen of Egypt, and the rulers of Cyprus, dine," said Caesar, gesturing to the table. "Soldiers' fare after a long campaign?"

"Pothinus said there was nothing left for us to eat because of the Romans," complained "big" Ptolemy in his whiny voice. "He said it was all devoured by your soldiers! And they melted down all our gold plate!"

"Pothinus will tell no more lies," said Caesar. "And I am pleased to see that you are voluntarily eating such sparse fare, when there are fine foods aplenty in the kitchens. It will build your character. A man shouldn't care overmuch about food. I myself once accidentally poured ointment over a vegetable dish and didn't notice—even after I ate it."

"Barbarian," muttered Arsinoe.

"What's that, my dear?" asked Caesar. "Barbarian? Yes, perhaps so. I came to have great respect for them in the nine years I fought them in Gaul. They have a different mentality from some of the degenerate minds of the east. For example, they do not kill their chiefs."

Arsinoe gave a sour smile that still did nothing to ruin her beauty. Caesar lifted his wine goblet to her and took a sip.

"I do not feel well," she said, putting hers down. "I must return to my quarters to rest."

That night she escaped from the palace, accompanied by her eunuch-tutor Ganymedes, and went to join Achillas and his forces.

I expected Caesar to be angry, now that he could no longer claim the Egyptian troops were simply a treasonous faction in rebellion against the entire royal family, but he was not, even when the troops proclaimed Arsinoe their queen.

"Well, she's lost Cyprus," he said. "And she never even went to visit it. You and I must do that when the war is over. Venus was born on the seafoam and washed ashore there; it would be most fitting for us to be together there." He gave that seemingly lighthearted smile that did not extend to his eyes.

When the war was over . . . how certain he was of victory!

That night, before retiring, he stood a long time on the roof of the palace, looking at the harbor and its configuration. His lined hands gripped the railings, and I could see the muscles pulling in his arms as he clenched and then relaxed his fingers.

"It will not be easy," he conceded. "It is a long way, and the width will not allow very many men on it at any one time."

Behind us the servants were lighting the evening torches, and the sun was sinking, turning what would be tomorrow's battlefield into a basin of red.

"Tonight the sun, tomorrow the blood of men will color it," he said.

"How can you ever get used to it?" I wondered. "How can you accustom yourself to death in advance?"

"Death," he finally said. "Perhaps I am like that king of Pergamon who had a garden of poisonous plants that he enjoyed cultivating. Perhaps I surround myself with death in order to accustom myself to it."

"And does it?"

"I think so," he said. "I can honestly say death holds no terror for me, only sadness—sadness at what I must leave behind." He turned and looked directly in my eyes. Even in the failing light I was riveted by the intense expression on his face. "I would hate to leave you so soon. We have so much to talk about, to see, to explore together. It is just the beginning for us. When I set out for Gaul, I was forty-two. It was a new world, an infinite green expanse— forests, mountains, lakes, rivers, all unknown and waiting for me. What happened to me there in those nine years should be enough for any man. But now I want more, not less. It built fires, it did not quench them." He turned back to look at the harbor, growing blue and dim now. "Down there, tomorrow—it seems unthinkable that a short little piece of polished metal could put out my fire."

I put my arm around him and leaned against him. "Don't you Romans believe there are three immortal sisters who control your span of days? One who spins your thread of life, one who measures it, and one who cuts it? Your life is not measured yet."

"Such is the skill of the sisters that one does not feel the thread being drawn out, or perceive the scissors being opened." Then his tone of voice changed. "This sort of talk is bad luck! Come!" Abruptly he quit the rooftop and went inside.

Such was the oddness of the Alexandrian War that I was able to station myself on the roof to have a commanding view of the action the next day. I did not want to watch it, and yet I had to, for I needed to know what happened, and not from any messenger.

Early in the morning, before the sun's rays had even reached beyond the tops of the temples, and when the streets were still dark, Caesar and his men poured from the palace grounds in full force, taking the enemy by surprise. The streets were quickly theirs, and by the time the sun was shining fully on the waterfront, I could see fierce fighting by the docks. The Romans were easy to spot because of their helmets and their distinctive military attire, in contrast to the forces of Achillas in their varying, pieced-together costumes.

I could see Caesar himself in his purple general's cloak, and although I wished I could look elsewhere, I could not for a second take my eyes from him.

I saw how he led the men into the most thinly guarded and dangerous areas, putting heart into them by his reckless bravery. He did not spare himself, but rushed out into the thick of the fighting. But then the superior numbers of Achillas began to tell, and suddenly the Romans seemed to be swallowed up. I felt a horrible cold fear as Caesar disappeared from view under a swirl of swords and shields. The tumult of metal against metal, of stones being lobbed and smashing against the docks and houses, and the screams of dying men, rose, like the cry of a monster, all the way up to my rooftop.

I saw a trace of fire arcing across the dock; someone had thrown a torch. Others followed, and suddenly one of the warships was on fire. The flames caught in the rigging and quickly spread to the deck.

One of my warships! I gasped. No!

The flames spread so fast it was obvious that tar and pitch on board had caught fire. Men poured from the ship and dived into the water. Then the ship next to that one caught fire. Screams rose as the water filled with escaping sailors. The fighting on the docks continued as furiously as ever.

My ships were aflame! My navy was being destroyed! I watched in horror as the entire fleet caught fire, and my pride and wealth of sea power vanished. But then—the wind carried sparks from the burning ships and set fire to warehouses on the docks. Well I knew what was in the warehouses—grain, oil, but most precious of all, manuscripts for the Library. An entire warehouse of manuscripts was being annihilated! I began to scream in helpless horror, but I went on watching.

The fires distracted the Alexandrians, which gave Caesar and his men their opportunity to make for the causeway. They swarmed down it and out to the Lighthouse, where I soon saw more smoke and fire rising in the midst of hand-to-hand combat.

It was impossible to tell what was happening, who was winning, until after what seemed hours, when the glint of the sun on the returning Roman helmets told the tale: They had subdued the island and were now going to secure the length of the causeway. The men spread out, and now—thanks be to you, Isis, and to all the gods who held him in their care—I saw the flash of Caesar's purple cloak. He was out in front, leading the men back across the causeway and toward the waterfront.

Suddenly, almost out of nowhere, an enemy warship laden with soldiers sailed through the burning hulks of my ships in the western harbor, and made for the middle of the causeway, cutting the Romans in the forefront off from the rest of their troops, stranding them in one section of the causeway. It was Caesar they were after; they meant to hem him in and destroy him. The newly landed soldiers advanced on him, while the ones from the shore closed in on the other side.

The Romans decided to retreat to their ships, but the ships had pulled in their gangplanks and cast anchors to prevent themselves from being boarded by the enemy. The Romans dived into the water and began swimming to the ships; I saw Caesar plunge in and make for the nearest ship, but it was so overladen it was near capsizing, so he was forced to swim to one far distant, all the time dodging a hail of arrows and missiles. His progress was slowed by the fact that he was swimming one-handed, holding up a sheaf of papers—what could be so important, I wondered—and trailing his heavy general's cloak behind him, determined not to yield the enemy that trophy. But at length I saw him throw off the cloak and swim free of it to the ship. The cloak floated back toward the causeway, where it was retrieved by the enemy with jeers and jubilation.

He was safe. He was safe. The sweetness of realizing that he would return from that day's fighting almost overwhelmed me with gratitude.

He sat in our private room, hunched over his charts. His hair was matted, and he was shivering from exhaustion and the cold water. His arms were covered with cuts, and his legs were bruised, and he kept shaking his head.

"Four hundred men lost," he was saying. "Four hundred!"

"But you won," I said. "You won. And you did everything you set out to do. You captured the island and the Lighthouse."

"And burnt a fleet!" He sounded bitter. "Forgive me! But it had to be done. I could see they were going to capture it, and that would have given them a navy, which they do not now have."

"So it was you who threw that brand!" I said. "It was no accident!"

"No, of course not," he said. "It was my decision. And a good one, too. Look at the damage they managed to do with only one ship!" Again he shook his head. "I lost four hundred men," he repeated softly. "And my general's cloak. They got that."

"At least it was not *you* they got," I said. "And why did you persist in trying to protect those papers? What was so important in them that was worth risking your life for?"

"Military plans," he said. "Ciphers. Codes. Those must not be lost by us, or gained by them." He withdrew them from inside his sodden leather jerkin and threw them on the table, heaving a deep sigh of relief. "There."

"Manuscripts were lost that were on the docks, waiting to be transferred to the Library," I said.

"I am sorry," he said. "The burning of the warehouses was a true accident."

"Yes," I said. "An accident of war. I can see that war, once launched, is not very easily controlled. It goes wherever it pleases, like a mad but cunning animal. Even the great Caesar cannot keep it leashed!"

"I am sorry," he repeated, throwing off the last of his soaked, tattered clothing and lying down on the bed.

"You are safe," I said. "That is all that ultimately matters."

And as I watched him slide into sleep, I knew that was true for me. He was safe tonight. But tomorrow, when the fighting commenced again?

The Roman civil wars that had spread to us now seemed to infect everything. It did not take long for the murdered Pompey's ghost to exact his final revenge: Achillas did not outlive Pothinus by many days, because Arsinoe killed him and turned the army over to Ganymedes. The knives that the assassins had used against Pompey had now found their way home into their masters' entrails.

Jubilant with power, Ganymedes launched a direct attack on the palace. Caesar and I were dining in the private apartments a week after the fighting on the island when a burning missile was lobbed right onto our balcony, followed by a rain of arrows with messages attached.

Caesar pulled one out of the wooden sun canopy and held it up for me to see.

Surrender, you Roman dogs! it read.

"How original," I said.

"Here's another," said Caesar, bending down to pick one up.

A gold piece for every soldier who comes over to Arsinoe, it promised.

That was more dangerous.

"They have no money to pay," I said scornfully.

"The common soldier does not know that," said Caesar. "I must go below and rally them." He hastened away.

Within a few days the furious ingenuity of Ganymedes was manifested directly in our water supply. Unable to storm the palace or to dislodge us from our holdings in the city and the island, he resolved to drive us out by thirst.

The cooks had discovered that the water in the conduits had turned salty and brackish, and the soldiers stationed in town reported that all the water in the local households had the same problem, which had mysteriously developed overnight.

"How did they manage to do it?" Caesar marveled. "How did they taint all our water without hurting their own?"

I called in our engineers, and the answer was soon clear. Alexandria's water supply comes from underground tunnels that channel Nile water through the city. Ganymedes had divided the water flow, protecting his own, and pumping seawater into ours.

"This war has not been easy," Caesar admitted. "The enemy is resourceful and clever. They force us to be more so. I will speak to the troops." I thought he sounded tired, and nearer the end of his resources than he would wish to sound.

From the upper balcony of the palace he addressed his officers and men, as they waited in the open space below.

"The cowardly Ganymedes and his put-together army of pirates and slaves and corrupted Romans have the knowledge to construct giant waterwheels to draw seawater up to higher ground," he shouted. "How clever! How impressive! Does he think by this to conquer us? By a boy's toys?"

From the way the men were restlessly moving, I could see how uncomfortable they were. They were thirsty. They had probably drunk all the wine available, and now there was nothing.

"A boy should not go to war! A boy's toys cannot triumph over an experienced man's knowledge, and the determination and courage of his troops! You see, I know where there is water to be found, and easily. There are always veins of fresh water in beaches, and not far below the surface. A few hours' digging will yield us all the water we wish!"

Was this true? Or was he merely hoping?

"And furthermore, even if there is no water there, we hold command of the sea, and it is an easy matter to sail forth in either direction and bring back a supply of water. So fear not, but get out your shovels!"

The men did not give their usual cheers. They craved an orderly retreat, to sail away from this mess.

"Think not of abandoning your posts! If they see us boarding ships, they will rush our barricades. An orderly withdrawal is not possible for us now." He paused. "Nor is it necessary! To the shovels!" He hoisted one up and flourished it. "To the beach!"

Once again, the fair goddess of fortune looked upon her favorite son, and Caesar's conjecture was proved right. Overnight digging yielded several wells, and when the sun came up the next morning the problem was solved. The enemy's days of labor had been thwarted in only a few hours by Caesar's efforts.

News came that some supply ships of the Thirty-seventh Legion, arriving ahead of the overland troops, had overshot Alexandria and were anchored to the west. Caesar took his small fleet and went out to meet them. It looked as if the end of the war was near, but even this simple action turned into a battle, as the enemy attacked the ships and Caesar was hard put to avoid being captured. In the end, the seamanship of the Romans defeated the enemy, and Caesar returned safely.

"Each thing has proved harder than I ever expected," he said wearily. "And this has gone on for much too long. I am very tired." He shook his head. "I was expecting Alexandria to provide me with a rest from all my campaigning. Amusing, isn't it?"

Yes, the war had gone on for a long time. And in the last few days I had finally realized something, something I had decided not to tell Caesar until the war was over. But each time I thought it might be over, it proved to be merely one episode that was over. It seemed to stretch out interminably.

One of my odd ways of thinking is that I find it hard to mix things. I like to take each thing in its turn, one at a time. That was what I had meant to do now. But the war went on and on! And seeing Caesar grow more and more worn and tired, his sleep deeper and his footsteps less springy, my heart took hold of my tongue. I also found it harder and harder to keep anything from him, he seemed so much a part of myself.

"You are a great general," I said slowly. "There is now no one in all the world to challenge you. What is occurring here is almost an accident, as if these men have not heard what everyone else knows. I have heard of isolated troops fighting on long after a war is ended and their commanders have gone home. Such is the situation here. Do not lose heart."

"I haven't lost heart," he said, "so much as patience."

"If you conquered the entire world, it is not too late to found a dynasty," I said.

"Rome does not have monarchs."

"I said the entire world, not just Rome. Egypt joined with Rome is no longer Rome. And this new creation would need a dynasty."

He jerked his head up and looked at me as if I were dangling something dangerous in front of him. A forbidden golden object. A sealed will. An enormous bribe. His eyes narrowed, but not before I had caught the quick leap of curiosity and desire there. "What are you saying?"

"I am saying simply that—if you have an empire to bequeath, then we shall have the child to bequeath it to." It was thus I told him.

"A child." He looked shocked and disbelieving. "I had not thought to have a child."

"I know. It is almost thirty years since your daughter was born, your only child. All the world knew of your sorrow when she died."

He struggled not to show his rising joy. "It is possible?"

"Yes," I said. "It is not only possible, it is a certainty. And it is my gift to you. Not Alexandria, not Egypt—for those you could conquer—but a child, an heir of Caesar."

"A gift from the gods," he said, rising slowly and holding out his arms to me. "A most sublime, and unlooked-for, gift from the gods." He held me differently. And I was filled with joy that I had not waited any longer to tell him.

It was, of course, your gift, Isis: you, the Great Mother, had decided to bestow this fortune on us. It is you who can command barrenness to depart at your will, and you did so for Caesar. It was your purpose that—just as your son Horus could avenge his father, Osiris—when Caesar fell, attacked by evil men, he would have a son to avenge him. I know that now, whereas then I only rejoiced in the fact that I was able to give Caesar something that he wanted so badly, which until now had been withheld from him, when all the rest of the world had been laid at his feet.

I wished for Olympos, for his medical care, but he and Mardian were still retained behind the lines of the rebel army. How he would shake his head, and say, "Where was the silphion when you needed it? Why did you neglect it?" and when I replied, "I am happy with what has happened," he would be perplexed. And Mardian! What would he think? Everything was changed from what we had expected and planned for, back in the tent in the desert sand.

Caesar could not hide his delight. An uncharacteristic smile played over his features at meetings, until his officers asked him if he was pleased that the populace was destroying the buildings of the city in their attempt to replace their navy.

"They are determined to build themselves a fleet," reported one of the centurions.

"With what?" scoffed another.

"They have doubtless remembered the guard ships at all seven mouths of the Nile, stationed to levy customs duties," I said, speaking from the back of the room, where I had been quietly listening. "There are also a number of secret dockyards with old, moldering ships. These they could lay hands on with little difficulty."

Still Caesar did not lose his pleasant expression. "And they will make these seaworthy—in how many months?"

"Days, Caesar," said one of the soldiers to whom the spies reported. "They have already gathered some ships on the lake, and set about preparing them. The shortage of oars and timbers is being met by dismantling public buildings and chopping off the roofs of colonnades for the beams. I have heard that twenty quadriremes are being readied."

"Twenty quadriremes!" Still Caesar did not lose his composure. "An industrious people."

"How much has been destroyed?" I asked. My beautiful city! That they could so wantonly tear her apart! I braced myself to hear the worst.

"They have ripped the roof off the Museion, and even attacked the Temple of Neptune," the man said. "As for the Gymnasion—the long porticoes proved to be too great a temptation. They are taken apart."

I gave a moan of anguish. All that beauty, gone. "The Library? The royal tombs?"

"Those still stand untouched," he said.

"But not for long," another said, "if they wish to equip quinqueremes."

"So, if we are to save your city, Queen Cleopatra," said Caesar, "we will have to distract them, or make it clear there is no further need for naval vessels. The next engagement will be a land one, perforce. After all, we came to rescue Alexandria, not destroy her."

That night, in our apartments, Caesar was pacing up and down the largest of the rooms, where sliding doors opened out onto the terrace. The marble floor was so polished that his legs and the lower part of his military attire—the red tunic and the leather thongs—were reflected in it, although the upper parts of him disappeared, dissolved into the dark.

"What troubles you so, my love?" I asked, coming over to him. "We can rebuild the city, when it is all ours again." In truth, I was not as unconcerned as I made it sound. My heart ached to picture what was being destroyed, and I knew nothing could ever be the same again. Those timbers could not be replaced; the forests in the Atlas Mountains and in Lebanon no longer grew trees of such height. Skill alone cannot restore the vanished.

"The destructiveness of war somehow hurts more now that it is lessening what I will leave behind to—to our child," he said. "But the sailors of the

Thirty-seventh told me that land forces, raised by Mithridates of Pergamon, are already on the march. The war will indeed end soon."

"Forever," I said. Now there would be no more uncertainty about who ruled Egypt, what its status was with Rome, whether it would remain independent, and what its future was. All those questions had been answered, even if blood had been spilled to do it. In the future—in the days of our child—there would be no bloodshed necessary, because his parents had already sacrificed it.

"Mars is a very thirsty god," he said. "He never seems to have his fill of blood." He paused. "But, yes, for the time being . . ." He pulled out a small message scroll that he had been keeping in his belt. "What do you advise?" he asked me.

I read it over quickly. It was from a delegation of Alexandrians serving in the council of the enemy army. They stated that the whole population was turning against Arsinoe and Ganymedes and wanted to follow Ptolemy instead, were he released to them. They would sign a cease-fire and negotiate with Caesar under the leadership of their King.

"This is absurd," I finally answered. "They can come forward and submit to Ptolemy now. There is no need to release him from the palace."

"Exactly. Yet I shall do so," said Caesar. "This could not be more perfect! Now we can rid ourselves of him, and remove the last enemy from our midst."

"No!" I said. "It is a trick!"

He looked at me as if to say, How slow you are! "Yes, of course it is a trick! But we have a greater trick! For we know their forces are doomed to be crushed between ours and the land army bearing down on Egypt even now. So let us send him out to lead his troops—for a little while. Let him put on his crown and wave his sword. Don't you think every child deserves to play for an afternoon?"

I smiled, but his chilling analysis was troubling. How long did it take to become that way, that hardened? How many wars, how many betrayals, how many disappointments? Was that the ultimate outcome of survival? *Count no man happy until he is dead*, a saying went. Perhaps it should really say, *Count no man happy unless he dies young and inexperienced in the ways of men.*

"It is almost over," I said, to reassure myself. "It is almost over."

The next morning, after Caesar had arisen and had his customary cold meal of bread, honey, and cheese, he called for Ptolemy to come to the military room. The little King came striding in, attired in rich golden brocade, wearing his royal fillet. Caesar was seated and did not rise.

"Good morning," he said blandly. "I have what I believe will be welcome news for you."

Ptolemy looked apprehensive. Could any news that was good for Caesar be likewise good for him? "Yes?" He braced himself.

Caesar unrolled the little scroll and read it. "As you can see, your subjects long for your presence. Who am I to stand in your way? Perhaps this will be the heaven-sent opportunity we yearn for to end the war. Go to them!" He gave a theatrical wave of his arm.

Ptolemy was puzzled. "But . . . why should you force me to leave the palace and join them? I have no wish to do so."

"What sort of talk is that for a king? A king must do what is best for his subjects, for his kingdom! Sacrifice, boy, sacrifice!"

At being called "boy," Ptolemy bristled and drew himself up taller. He was thirteen now. "I fear they wish to sacrifice *me*. Arsinoe and Ganymedes will attack me. No, I will not go!"

"And I say you shall," Caesar insisted. I watched his face carefully, and I could tell he was enjoying Ptolemy's discomfort.

"No, please!" Ptolemy's face wrinkled up, and he burst into tears. "Please, please, don't send me away! I wish to remain with you! My loyalty is with my sister and you!"

"Ah." Caesar looked touched. "How this pleases my heart." He solemnly laid his hand over his breast. "But you must have pity on your poor subjects, go to them and help recall them to sanity, persuade them to stop scarring the city with fire and desolation. Thus will you prove your loyalty to me, and to the Roman people. I trust you; why else would I send you directly out to join an enemy under arms against me? I know you will not fail me."

He grabbed Caesar's arm. "Don't send me away! There is no sight so pleasing in my eyes as you! Neither my kingdom nor my people—only you, great Caesar!"

Caesar disengaged Ptolemy's clinging fingers and grasped his arm in a commander's grip. "Courage!" he exhorted him. "Courage!"

Weeping, Ptolemy scurried from the room.

Caesar examined his arm for scratches. "He has a nasty grip, and long nails." He shook his head. "It felt like being grabbed by a monkey."

"So now he's gone," I said. "How long until he comes at us at the head of his troops?"

"Before sunset, no doubt," said Caesar.

He was off by only two or three hours. Indeed, before the day was over, Ptolemy had been received by his troops and, raised up on a royal sedan chair, denounced Caesar and me in such vitriolic language that the spy who reported it had to stammer, " 'The—word unfit for repetition—tyrannical, unprincipled, greedy Julius Caesar and his whore, the—another word unfit for repetition—pleasure-soaked, lustful Cleopatra, must be destroyed, and the evil—yet another word unfit for repetition—gluttonous Romans stopped in their tracks as they seek to devour us,' the King said."

"I see Theodotos installed an extensive vocabulary in his charge," said Caesar. Then he laughed, and the messenger breathed a sigh of relief.

"He makes me sick!" I cried. That heart-wrenching display of loyalty he had put on only that morning—disgusting!

"You can understand why there are those who likewise question your loyalty to me?" said Caesar. "I am afraid that over the ages the Ptolemies have earned their reputation of being deceitful. Your brother is a classic example of his lineage." He leaned over and then whispered into my ear, so low I could barely hear him, "But those who question do not know what I know of you. How could they?" He slid his arm around my back and squeezed the flesh near my hip. I am embarrassed to remember how it excited me, bringing back memories of the long nights with him, making me look forward to the coming one. The sun had already set. Oh, had Ptolemy unknowingly been correct in describing me as pleasure-soaked and lustful?

Caesar's purpose had been fulfilled. Ptolemy would be destroyed, separated from us, who would ultimately prevail. Had he not sent him away, Ptolemy would have been able to stay on the throne with me after the war was over, claiming Caesar's victory as his own. Perhaps Ptolemy had not been altogether untruthful when he begged not to be sent away; he could see what his miserable end would be.

The war now came to its height and closure. Mithridates of Pergamon, Caesar's ally, was even then at the gates of Pelusium, at Egypt's eastern borders. He stormed the city and took it, then began to march through Egypt to join Caesar. But Pelusium is a long way from Alexandria, and Mithridates had to march diagonally across the Delta until he reached the spot near Memphis where the Nile is but a single river, before he could cross it and head for Alexandria. Ptolemy and Arsinoe set out to intercept him to prevent him from reaching Caesar, and hurried toward that spot on the Nile where he would be crossing.

Caesar kept abreast of all this by a constant stream of messengers. I will never forget him standing on the rooftop terrace of the palace and gazing out over the harbor while he formed his plan. His eyes searched the horizon as if he expected a ship, but that was just his way of thinking. Other men's eyes grow clouded and dreamy when they confer within themselves, but Caesar's were focused like an eagle's.

"When the sun sets," he said resolutely, "then I go."

"How?" I asked. I had learned that he always had a plan, and it was one I never could have guessed. "Part of Ptolemy's army is blocking the route from the city. They mean to keep you bottled up here."

"Do we not have ships? Did I not retain sea power, while destroying theirs?" He smiled slowly. "Tonight, at sunset, I will leave the harbor and sail east, in full view of the enemy. They will look for me to land at one of the mouths of the Nile. Then, as darkness falls, I will turn the fleet. We will sail due west, and land to the far side of Alexandria, on the desert. Then we will march south, circling Ptolemy's forces, and join Mithridates." He nodded. It was all so simple—for him.

That was exactly what happened. I heard all the details from my messengers and the soldiers who reported each engagement. Ptolemy had taken his forces by way of his patched-up vessels down the Nile, then set up a fort alongside it on a bit of high ground protruding above the marshes. Caesar approached, to the shock of the Egyptians, and they sent out cavalry to stop him. But the legionaries forded the river by makeshift bridges and chased the rebels back into the fort. The next day Caesar's forces attacked the fort, having ascertained that the highest sector of it was weakly guarded because it was the most naturally secure point. They stormed it, and the Egyptians, in a panic to escape, hurled themselves over the walls, heading for the river. The first wave of them tumbled into the encircling trench and were trampled to death by those behind them, who rushed to the little boats and attempted to paddle away in the reeds and papyrus. The boats were never meant to hold so many, and they sank. Ptolemy was on one; it capsized and he disappeared into the water, vanishing among the reeds.

The rebels surrendered. Arsinoe was brought before Caesar, her hands behind her back, her dress spattered with swamp slime, her shoes gone. She spat at him and cursed him before she was trussed up and led away.

"Find Ptolemy!" ordered Caesar. "Where was he last seen?"

One of his soldiers pointed to a dark, oily-looking area of reeds. Birds were clinging to the swaying stalks.

"Dive for him! Bring me his body!" He knew that a drowning in the Nile was considered sacred to Osiris, and he also knew that a king who mysteriously disappeared had the potential of reappearing years later—in the form of an impostor.

It was a nasty business. The shallow swamp had many fetid, oozing beds, home to snakes and crocodiles. Time and again the men emerged from the water, gasping for breath, covered with black decaying matter, empty-handed. But at last one surfaced, holding the slight body of Ptolemy, his eyes wide open, his mouth streaming dirty water. He was wearing a corselet of pure gold, and its links gleamed through the tangle of weeds entwined in it.

"The weight is what drowned him," Caesar said, staring at the corpse. "The gold sent him to the bottom." He reached out and touched the finely wrought show-armor. "Exhibit this to the troops, and the people. Let them all see with their own eyes: The little King has perished. He will not rise from the Nile to lead them again."

Caesar left the battlefield and, mounting his horse, set out immediately for Alexandria with his cavalry. Darkness had fallen before he reached it; but from the palace I saw streams of people making their way to the city gate to receive him. A thousand tapers flickered as they moved slowly through the streets, dressed in mourning. They had been beaten; for the first time, Alexandria had fallen to a conqueror.

Alexandria, and Egypt, had fallen to Rome: the very fate that I had always seen as the worst misfortune that could befall us, that I had vowed to prevent at all costs. Now I was waiting in the palace, watching, eager to receive the conqueror, with child by the general who was even now approaching the city that lay supine before him. I should have been torn with shame had I been told, in these very sentences, these simple facts a year ago. (Of what purpose are oracles, then, if they veil such major events from our sealed eyes?) But the general, the conqueror, was Julius Caesar, and in those two words, in that name, was the reason why I was waiting, happy, to embrace him. True, he was a Roman, formed of that race, with their habits and way of thinking, but he was so much more. He would not remain only a Roman, but would grow into something incomparably greater, something new.

The people of Alexandria met him on their knees, bowing down, lying prostrate before the Gate of the Sun, placing statues of Anubis, Bastet, Sekmet, and Thoth on the street to submit themselves to his authority. Dressed in blue mourning cloth, unshaven, barefoot, throwing dust on their heads, the city elders wailed in chorus, "Mercy, O Son of Amun! We submit, we bend our necks and back before you, mighty conqueror! Hail, Caesar, descendant of Ares and Aphrodite, God Incarnate, and Savior of Mankind!" I could hear the dirgelike sound of their lamentations, thin, like a eunuch's voice, rising in the night air.

I heard the groaning as the gates were flung open, and Caesar rode past the rows of hunched Alexandrians, past the gilded statues of the gods who silently let him pass through the shattered, torchlit street to the palace.

He strode into the wide, pillared hall where the windows admitted only the perfumed air of the palace garden to fill the space. I was waiting, scarcely able to breathe. I held out my arms and embraced him.

"Egypt is yours," I said.

"You are Egypt," he said. "The most precious conquest I have ever made."

14

Caesar wished to see his new possession, and I wished to show it to him in its entirety: Egypt from Alexandria to Aswan, over six hundred miles up the Nile. We would travel in the state barge of the Ptolemies. I counted on it to take his breath away; this conqueror of forests and wild vales of Gaul would now behold the riches of the east, fabled and ancient.

As large as a warship, dedicated to pleasure and power, the barge rode on the bosom of the Nile. It stretched over three hundred feet from its lotus-flower bow to its curved stern, propelled by many banks of oars, and the decks contained banqueting rooms, colonnaded courts, shrines to the gods, and a garden. The cabins and corridors were of cedar and cypress, with the dazzling colors of carnelian, lapis lazuli, and gold everywhere. Caesar marched on board and then, as I had hoped, he stood stock-still and looked about him, letting his eyes sweep over the room in hungry appreciation.

Suddenly I had an apprehensive thought: What if he decided to annex Egypt after all? It was his by right of arms. He had given no indication that he wished to do so, but every other defeated country had been made into a Roman province. Was it only my person that prevented him from doing so? And might this trip whet his appetite for my country, rather than appeasing it?

"Ah," he finally said, turning his gaze back to me, "Rome suddenly seems mean and squalid, her buildings cramped and dark, even her Forum plain and limited."

Again, that hungry look in his eye. "We have much to learn from you."

When we cast off, and the stately vessel began slowly to make its way under silken sails, Alexandria was gleaming white under the spring sun, as pure as the clouds racing overhead. Most of the buildings had been spared after all: the Museion, the Serapion, the Library, all were visible from the ceremonial deck. But there was much damage in the city, and I knew that it would take years to restore it to its former perfection. The people lining the harbor were dressed as Greeks, and shouting in Greek.

"Now we leave Alexandria for Egypt itself," I said, as the city grew smaller. "You will hear less and less Greek. But never fear, I speak Egyptian."

"Fear?" he gestured toward the four hundred smaller ships following us, loaded with his soldiers. "Not as long as I have my legionaries."

"What, are you naked without your soldiers?" I teased him.

"Any general is," he said, "but particularly a Roman one. I learned that, in spite of my services to the state, they would have rewarded me by killing me after I returned from Gaul, had it not been for my soldiers."

"I am happy you have brought them. Egypt needs to see us both, to be reassured. They need to see the strength of the army that will prevent any further civil wars here."

As we sailed in majesty, slowly, as befitted a procession, I relived the time I had come this very way, on a child's adventure with Mardian and Olympos to the pyramids. Now I would show them to this man I loved, show them with the pride of possession.

The royal bedroom was as large and sumptuous as the one in Alexandria. There was a square bed, covered with leopard skins, and hung around on all sides with the sheerest silk netting to keep out insects. Elsewhere in the chamber were couches inlaid with ivory, gilded ebony footstools, bowls of rose petals, and alabaster oil lamps. Caesar and I retired here soon after the setting sun had stained the broad waterway of the river with its dying. We watched the night mists begin to rise from the reeds on the banks, and then pulled the silk curtain across the square cabin window.

"My world has shrunk down very small, into this crystal of luxury and pleasure," he said, kicking off his sandals and stretching out on the couch.

"Is this not the whole world?" I said, coming over to him, and seating myself on one of the footstools. "For lovers, is not their private room the center of the world?"

"The center of their world," he agreed. "But when the lovers are Caesar and Cleopatra, Queen of Egypt—then their worlds reach far beyond these walls."

"You called me Queen of Egypt, but to yourself you gave no title." I tried to say it lightly, but I knew the omission meant something. "Surely there are many you could choose from. Some you already hold: Consul, general. One you are: master of the Roman world. And Amun."

He threw back his head and laughed. "Amun! Oh yes, I wore his robes once. And a miracle happened." He leaned over and put his hand on my abdomen. "The god must have brought this about."

I covered his hand with my own. "You know he did." I was sure that it must be the divine wish of the gods, for with all his wives and lovers, he had begotten only one other child, and that was over thirty years ago, before I was born. So lavish in their benefices to Caesar in every other way, the gods had withheld from him the gift of offspring. Was that not their way: to make someone master of the world, and then give him no one to leave it to? It had happened with Alexander as well.

"What will we name him?" I asked, not idly. What would the name signify? Would Caesar acknowledge this child as an heir? And what would it mean if he did?

"You may choose," said Caesar, taking his hand back and resting it across his chest.

"By that, do you mean there will be no official Roman recognition of him—or her? No name conferring membership in a family?"

He looked pained. "It can be no other way. You are not my wife, and under Roman law a foreign marriage is not recognized. The children of such a union have no status."

I was incredulous. Was this the conqueror, the man who smashed all the Roman laws, who had delivered the death blow to the Republic with his armies, and revealed the Senate for the impotent thing it was? "Roman law?" I asked in wonder. "What does Roman law mean to you?"

He looked alarmed, and sat bolt upright. He took several deep breaths as if to steady himself. "That is a thought that should not be voiced aloud."

"It is a thought that is in everyone's minds. You have shaken the Roman world to its foundations. Now you can rewrite the laws to please yourself."

He reached out very slowly and took my face in both his hands, and guided it toward his, where he kissed me lingeringly. "Egypt, Egypt, you are very dangerous," he murmured. "If I stay longer, I am lost. I left Rome a general, and I shall return—"

"A king," I whispered. He *should* be a king; all the fates shouted it.

"I was going to say 'Amun,' " he said with a smile.

Like the conquering general he was, he picked me up and carried me to the bed, pushed aside the sheer floating curtains around it, and laid me carefully on the leopard skins. They felt cool and slippery under me, and I made myself comfortable on them, waiting for him to come join me, to hold me close to him. How I had missed his touch in the past weeks, when he had been either absent or absent in mind while the war had produced ever more taxing problems. I realized with sadness that I had come to need him the same way that I needed rest, and fresh air, and the scent of flowers in the wind. His presence was joy itself to me. Just as I could exist without rest, or fresh air, or the perfume of flowers—in a prison—so I could exist without him, but his absence would make it a prison, no matter how sumptuous.

In his lovemaking it always seemed as if he had never touched anyone but me. I knew that was not true, and whenever I let myself imagine it, picture where he had got his learning, it sent stabs of jealous pain through me. I consoled myself with the thought that together we made a perfect whole: he my first love, and I his last. In that way I could bear to remember Pompeia, and Calpurnia, and Servilia, and Mucia, and . . . always Cornelia, his early love.

Now darkness enveloped the room as he extinguished the lamps, and I heard his footsteps coming toward me. Then he was beside me in the still, fragrant night, and when he held me and pressed me close against him, I could only tremble with anticipation of what pleasures he had planned for that night.

For many long moments he did not move, but lay quietly breathing, his chest rising and falling almost in rhythm with the slight movement of the water underneath us. The stillness that he was able to keep within himself was powerful. Where other men would lunge and grab, he held back. I began to wonder—had he gone to sleep? Was he so deep in his own thoughts that once again he was absent? Just when I myself had begun to wander away in my thoughts, I felt him stir and turn to me. One arm reached over to touch my neck, and he turned easily on his side, leaning on his other shoulder.

His hand—not as hard and callused as I would expect a soldier's to be—caressed my neck, my cheek, my ear, lightly. He was running the backs of his fingers across my skin, as if he only needed to feel the slightest contours. I closed my eyes and enjoyed each feather-light touch, finding it very soothing, but arousing at the same time. It made me feel like a precious relic, a carved gem that a collector would touch reverently, in awe. His touch grew firmer as he seemed to be memorizing all the planes and hollows of my face and neck, like a blind person who sees only through his fingers. All the while he said nothing. Finally he rose a little higher and turned and kissed me, a kiss as light as his earlier touches. It caused such a surge of pleasure in me, it was as if he had ravished me; the light, teasing promise of more ignited a fiery impatience of desire within me.

Now he began to touch my shoulders, my breasts, my abdomen—all with that slow deliberateness that was beginning to be torture. Outside the windows I could hear the low gurgling noise of the Nile as it flowed past, liquid and yielding. I felt my own legs begin to loosen, like one of those floating flowers on the Nile, and to twine themselves around his. His legs were long and muscled, and I loved the hard, sleek feel of them.

I had been wearing a silken gown that was the color of the Alexandrian sky at dusk; it was one of my most prized possessions, because the silk had come not from Cos but from somewhere even beyond India, and it was as transparent as early morning fog. Now, pressed against Caesar, it seemed to exist only as a layer of silken mist, almost a sheen on the flesh rather than a covering. I had forgotten it was even there—although no natural flesh is so shiny and perfect—until he deftly untied its laces and peeled it away.

"The serpent's skin must be shed," he said. "Come to me all new."

And I did feel as if I had left off a skin, or a former part of my being. The gown fell to the floor beside the bed, so light it made no sound.of settling.

"The tunic must follow," I insisted. It was already off his shoulders, and his chest was bare. "It is not wanted here." I pulled it off.

Around us the slight breeze was puffing out the filmy bedcurtains.

"The Aurae of the light, playful winds keeps us company," I said.

"The Aurae should depart," he said. "I wish no witnesses to our private hours." He kicked at one of the curtains, deflating it.

"So even the gods obey you," I said. I was longing for him to take me, almost shaking with desire for it.

"Sometimes," he said, taking me in his arms. But he seemed in no particular hurry to do the rest. He slowed when I would have hurried, and to this day I am thankful, because I remember every bit of it, prolonged as it was, and at each stage I was like a thirsty man who got a half-cup of water, so that no water seemed cooler or more delicious. In the end he did not disappoint me.

"Just as winning Gaul conclusively was worth the nine long years it took," he said, "I have learned that there are times that call for speed and others that call for a stretching of the time."

I sighed; I could hardly speak as yet. Finally I said, "Pleasure should always be stretched and pain shortened."

"No matter what they are in life, in memory they always seem to rearrange themselves in the opposite manner. All pleasures are seen as foreshortened and hasty and fleeting, and all pain lingering." He raised himself on one elbow, and I could feel him staring at me in the dark. "But I swear to you, I will never forget these days with you. My memory may shorten them, but it can never erase them."

I felt a deep, shadowy presence passing above us. "How darkly you talk!" I said. "Why, I have made you sad!" Nervously I leapt up from the bed and fumbled for a way to light one of the lamps. "We must have some spiced wine, to make us merry."

I managed to get the lamp lit, and it sputtered feebly into life. I looked back at where he lay, sprawled in the bed linens, one sheet draped over his shoulder. Around him the bedcurtains made a frame.

In the dim, flickering light he looked as bronzed as a statue, and for a moment his solemn expression made me think perhaps he had somehow been transmogrified into one. Then he laughed, and held out his hand for the spiced wine I was pouring from the gem-encrusted gold pitcher into an onyx cup.

The royal barge plied its way up the Nile, and from our shaded pavilion on the upper deck we watched the countryside slide past—bristly-topped palms, flat-roofed mud-brick houses, creaking waterwheels, and fields of glowing green. Our sails billowed and flapped; from every village the people sighted them and hurried down to the banks of the river to stare at us as we passed.

"The richest country on earth," said Caesar, shading his eyes against the sun. "Mile after mile of bright green, producing grain to feed the world." Was it wonder in his voice—or greed? Again, I felt a bit of fear. "Italy looks barren beside this, with its stony hills and little scrubby pines. And Greece—a bare, rocky ground is all Greece is. No wonder Greeks have to leave and live abroad."

"Oh, but Egypt is green only near the Nile. Wait until you see the desert. Egypt is mostly desert," I assured him.

"A long ribbon of fertility," said Caesar, seeming not to hear me. "Six hundred miles of garden."

"We shall be at the pyramids tomorrow," I said. "And I shall show you the Sphinx."

"You have already shown me the Sphinx," he said. "You are the Sphinx."

"I am no riddle! Nor am I unknowable," I protested.

"Does the Sphinx know he is what he is?" he said. "You are more of a riddle than you imagine. I know less of you than of any other person I have spent so many hours with."

"I tell you, I am no mystery!"

"No one is a mystery to himself," said Caesar. "But what you truly want, what you truly are—those things remain veiled to me in regards to you."

It was so simple! How could he say that? I wanted to be with him, to be loved by him, to become a partner with him in a union that was—political? military? matrimonial? O Isis, I realized then that I was not sure what I wanted—or rather, that the thing I wanted might be brand new: a new alliance—a new country—perhaps formed of east and west, the way Alexander had envisioned it. But it was a vision that had died with him, whatever it had been. If it was to be reborn, it would have to be refashioned for our world, three hundred years later.

"You look so solemn!" he said. "Whatever are you thinking?"

"Of Alexander . . ."

"Strange. I think of him, too. It must be this country. Something about Egypt, that calls forth visions of Alexander. Here he went to the oracle, and found out he was the son of Amun."

"Whereas you *are* Amun," I said, laughing.

He laughed, too. "So I am Alexander's father!"

"No—but this child that you are father of, is perhaps—can be—"

He quickly put his finger over my mouth, and stopped me in mid-sentence.

"No! None of that! Do you wish to call down the wrath of envious gods? No!" He looked angry. "I went to Alexander's tomb before we left," he said. "I wished to see him. Long ago, when I was in Spain, and I was only forty, I came across a statue of Alexander. I realized that forty years after his birth, he had already been dead for seven years! He had finished conquering the known world, and had died, and here I was, seven years older, and I had accomplished nothing. That changed me. I left that statue a different person. Now, this time, I approached the man himself, lying there all encased in his golden armor with his shield by his side, stiff with death and angry about it—I could see the rage on his face—and I was able to say, 'I have done all that I wished since that day in Spain, excepting one thing only: to complete your conquests.'" He turned and looked at me, his eyes a little surprised that he had voiced it aloud.

"Yes?" I encouraged him. "Say it. Say what it is you still want."

"To conquer the Parthians. And beyond that, India."

The air was still. The words hung there.

"O Isis!" I breathed.

"It can be," he said. "It is possible."

But . . . *you are fifty-two years old, the remnants of Pompey's army are still at large, Rome is filled with your political enemies, you have little money to finance such a venture . . . Egypt . . .* I thought. The empire of Alexander, revived and enlarged. . . .

"I too have sought solace at the tomb of my ancestor Alexander," I said cautiously. "His blood runs in me. And in *our* child," I reminded him. "But his dreams can be dangerous—desert demons drawing us on to doom."

"No, when Alexander went out into the desert he *found* his dream," said Caesar stubbornly. "And if dreams and doom are intertwined—I could not find it in myself to avoid the dream for fear of the doom."

I shivered, watching the horizon for the appearance of the tips of the pyramids, the only monuments to defy doom. Certainly their builders had not—we have forgotten their stories if not their names, and robbers have made off with their treasures and desecrated their mummies.

It was twilight when we first perceived, like the tiny points of pins, the apexes of the pyramids, far away above the green banks of the Nile. As the sun sank and touched, fleetingly, the stones, they glowed.

"Look!" I said to Caesar. "There they stand!"

He stood up to see them better, and watched a long time at the rail as the day sank down into night.

At the faintest light of dawn we set sail, and as the pale yellow gold crept across the sky, we saw the pyramids loom larger. By the time we docked and they filled a portion of the sky, Caesar had fallen silent. He stood and stared. Then he set out, walking briskly, on the causeway toward them. I followed in my litter. I could not have walked as fast as he in any case, but certainly not now.

My mind conjured up the shades of the old priests who had accompanied the Pharaoh's funeral sledge; they must have swayed, walking slowly, chanting, clouds of incense enveloping them. Now one Roman walked in their stead, his bright cloak snapping in the wind.

At its base I alighted from the litter, and stood beside him. He was still silent. He had to tilt his head far back even to see the top. I put my hand in his, and pressed it.

He stood there so long I felt some spell must have come over him. At length he moved, and began to walk around the base of the pyramid. My bearers quickly brought me the litter and I followed, bouncing over the rough, stony ground. Caesar kept walking out in front, faster than I have ever seen anyone walk without actually running. It was as if he wished to outpace us, and encounter the pyramids alone. I told my bearers to stop, and to take me near the Sphinx instead. I knew he would come there, when he had had his fill of the pyramid. I also knew he would not come before he was ready.

They erected a pavilion to shade me from the sun while I waited. The sun had crept up in the sky, and the marvelous shadows of the Sphinx were disappearing. I stared at the melancholy face of the creature. Had we been here at dawn, we would have seen his face bathed in those first rays that are pink and soft, for he faces east. He has greeted the rising Re for—how many years? No one knows. We believe he is the oldest thing on earth. Who built him? We do not know. Why? We do not know. Is he to guard the pyramids? Were they built to lie under his protection? A mystery. Sand covers his paws, and every few hundred years it is dug away. Then the desert blows it in again, and he settles down in his soft, golden bed. He rests, but does not sleep.

Caesar came around the corner, as suddenly as a thunderclap. He hurried over to my side. He seemed excited; far from tiring him, his hike seemed to have invigorated him. "Come!" He yanked my hand, and I stumbled up out of the folding chair.

The sun was hot, beating down on my head, making me feel faint. I twisted my hand away. "More slowly, I beg you!" I said. "It is too hot for such haste, and the sands here are treacherous!"

Only then did he seem to lose his trance. "Of course," he said. "Forgive me." Together we walked in a more normal pace to the Sphinx. Its earlier tawny color had been changed by the noon sun into hard whiteness, and there was no shadow of pity anywhere on its features.

"The lips," Caesar finally said. "They are longer than a man lying down. The ears—bigger than a tree!"

"He is mighty," I breathed. "He will keep Egypt, as he has since before living memory."

"Yet he was made by men," said Caesar. "We must not forget that. The pyramids were made, block by block, but still made by men."

"Higher up the Nile you will see other wonders," I said. "Temples with columns so thick and high it seems impossible that men could have raised them."

"Yet we know they did," he said. "There are no mysteries, no things intrinsically unknowable, my love, only things that we do not understand yet."

We watched the day swing round the monuments from the shelter of the pavilion. The heat grew intense in midday, and I could feel the sunlight trying to enter between the cracks of the awnings, searching like eager fingers for an opening. Wherever they succeeded in getting through, the sand they struck grew too hot to touch. The pyramids and the Sphinx radiated white heat, dazzling like a mirage in front of the pure blue sky.

Caesar leaned back and watched them, sipping some wine, and allowing one of the staff to fan him with the small, brass-bound military fans. It did not do much to stir the overheated, still air.

"You should use one of mine," I said. My servants were standing by with fans of ostrich feathers, wide half-circles that could wave and send rolls of air in all directions.

"Never," he said. "It even looks decadent. Who would use a fan like that?"

"People who are hot," I said. "As we go farther up the Nile, closer and closer to Africa, and the heat intensifies, I wager you will beg for one of these!"

"You know how fond I am of wagers," he said. "I am a gambler. I accept."

"What will you give me if I win?" I asked.

He thought for a moment. "I will marry you according to Egyptian rites," he finally said. "You will be my wife—everyplace but Rome. Because—"

"Yes, I know. Roman law does not recognize foreign marriages."

But laws are made by men; and the only things built by men that so far have proved immutable are the pyramids.

The heat began to lessen; I could feel it release its grip on us. The colors outside began to change; the stark white was replaced by a honeyed tinge on the limestone, and this gradually faded to a rich golden amber, so sweet a color that it made gold seem gaudy by comparison. Behind the monuments the sky had turned a tender shade of violet-blue, with long fingers of purple clouds stretched out to welcome the setting sun home. The sun would go down behind the pyramids, lighting them from behind for a while.

The smell of heated stone beginning to cool came to me on the evening breeze that had sprung up. Soon darkness would fall; we must make our way back to the boat.

"Come," I said, rising.

"No. I want to stay," said Caesar. "We would not sail at night anyway. The moon is nearly full. Why hurry away?"

Because . . . because the desert changes at night, I thought.

"You are not afraid?" he asked in a low voice.

"No," I had to say. And I was not afraid so much as uneasy. I did not wish to lie so close to the monuments of the dead, to a city of the dead. Traditionally, this side of the Nile was deserted by the living after the sun had gone beneath the earth each night.

They had enlarged the pavilion for us, made it into a proper tent. Now we could lie down and stretch out; now there were cushions and refreshments at hand. But after the servants had arranged all these things, Caesar ordered them to leave. We were to be completely alone.

"Something we have never been," he said. "One gets used to being always in the company of others, but it colors everything."

Caesar all to myself! Caesar alone! How many other people would have paid exorbitant sums to change places with me? They would have had petitions for him, supplications, bribes . . . possibly even poison or a dagger. He must have trusted me completely.

The only thing I wished from him was to let the hours stretch out unbroken between us for a little while.

Darkness falls swiftly on the desert. There is little twilight. One moment the pyramids and Sphinx were rounded, whole, emitting a sort of light of their own, as if they had stored it up during the long day; the next they faded out against the sky.

"But there is a moon rising," Caesar said. "Soon there will be light enough."

A gigantic, swollen moon was struggling on the horizon. Its face was still pale and dreamy-colored. It would throw off the clouds clinging to it, then shrink, yet grow brighter at the same time.

The sands were blue-white and the moon so bright we could see every line in our hands, could see the fibers in the ropes anchoring the tent. The pyramids were sharp-peaked, casting vast shadows on the sands behind them. The eye sockets of the Sphinx were empty black pools.

It had grown surprisingly chilly; we pulled our mantles around us. I could hear, not so far away, a pack of hyenas yowling.

I had thought we would talk, speak at last of all that was within us. Instead, silence reigned. It must have been past midnight before Caesar finally said, "Now I have seen six of the seven wonders of the world."

How many places he had been! And I had gone nowhere, had seen nothing outside Egypt. "Tell me of them," I said.

"There is no need for me to describe the Lighthouse of Alexandria," he said. "But for the others, quickly: the Colossus of Rhodes has fallen, but you can still see the bronze pieces; the great Temple of Artemis in Ephesus is so vast you can get lost in it; and I can never think of Zeus as looking any different from the statue at Olympia. But the one wonder I have never seen is the one I am determined to conquer for myself: the Hanging Gardens of Babylon."

"Are they even real?" I asked. "Has anyone seen them for hundreds of years?"

"Alexander has."

"Always Alexander."

"He died there in Babylon. Perhaps his last sight was of them, outside his window. In any case, I intend to conquer Parthia, and when I take Babylon, my reward will be to visit the sacred place where Alexander died, and to see the Hanging Gardens."

"Can you trust me enough to reveal your intentions? Have you a plan for this conquest, or is it still unformed?"

"Come." He pulled me up from the cushion. "Let us walk outside." He carefully arranged the warm mantle around my shoulders.

I had to squint, so bright was the light. Everything under the moonlight looked different, sharp and cold and hard against the inky sky.

"I have been cut off from the outside world since first I landed in Egypt," he said. "In truth, I should be even now on my way back to Rome. I linger here because"—he shook his head—"I seem to be under some sort of spell." When I laughed, he said, "If you knew me better, you would know how out of character it is for me to dally like this. Work calls. Duty calls. But here I am—on the desert at night with the Queen of Egypt, far from Rome, and going farther and farther toward Africa every day. I shall have to answer for it to my enemies, who will doubtless make the most of it."

"Then you should make the most of it as well," I said. "I hope the monuments are worth it."

I waited for him to say, *It is more than the monuments*, but he only gave a sort of grunt.

I felt him hesitate, then stumble. He pitched forward, and fell stiffly to his knees, before sprawling out, and making a choking sound. It happened so quickly that I had no chance to say a word or react. He lay on the ground, and his limbs thrashed and stiffened as if he were in the most excruciating pain. But he was silent, except for that one first cry.

I fell to my knees beside him, frantic. What had happened? Had someone been lurking behind a rock, and thrown a dagger? Had a serpent struck, darting out from a rock underfoot? Had he been poisoned by a secret enemy who had had access to his food earlier in the day?

With all my strength, I pushed his shoulders and turned him over. He was limp, like a—a dead body. His face was covered with sand where he had fallen facedown. My heart was racing so fast I could hardly think; I was confused; only when I put my hand on his chest could I feel that he was still breathing.

"O gods!" I cried. "Save him, save him, what have you done to him?" I moaned like one of the hyenas. He could not die, he could not, he could not leave me. It was impossible for Caesar to die so easily, so suddenly.

He groaned, and stirred. I felt his flaccid limbs begin to fill with life again. His breathing was rough and strained. I brushed the sand from his lips and nose. It was all I could think of to do—a useless little gesture. I kept brushing it off, getting it off his forehead, blowing it out of his ears.

Finally his lips parted and he murmured, "So now you know."

"Know what?"

"That I have—that I am afflicted with—the falling sickness." He struggled to sit up, but his arms would not quite obey him. "It has struck me . . . just in this last year. I never know when . . . it will come. I see a flash of light, there are sounds—and then weakness and falling."

"Do you—see anything in the flashes of light?"

"Do the gods speak to me, you mean? No. Or if they do, they allow me so little time to hear them before I lose consciousness that when I wake up . . . I know no more than before." He was unable to speak anymore; he had exhausted his little store of strength. He fell immediately into a profound sleep. There was nothing I could do but stay with him out on the bleak, silvery desert while the moon stared down at the fallen general. I took off my cloak and covered him; then, cold myself, I crawled under it and lay shivering beside him.

It was still dark, although the moon was now behind the pyramids, making them huge black triangles, when Caesar stirred and was taken with a violent fit of shivering. He shook himself awake, and frightened me. What was happening? Was this a second, fiercer attack? I flung myself on him, trying to stop the shaking.

"I am freezing," he muttered. "Where am I?" He looked up at the night sky, pierced all over with stars. He rolled over, feeling for the stones that had been cutting into his back.

He remembered nothing! I marveled at it. Yet he seemed himself again.

"You were taken . . . ill," I said. "It was necessary to rest here. Come, can you walk? The tent will have a pallet—more comfortable than this unyielding ground."

Slowly he sat up, then pulled himself to his feet. His legs were quivering. He put one in front of the other and began walking stiffly to the tent.

Once inside, he crawled onto the pallet and once again was immediately asleep. I heard him breathing softly, and each breath seemed like a miracle.

I could see the hard shadows grow longer and longer outside and then fade away as the sky lightened. I had not slept at all.

The sun was up. At any moment, servants would be coming to get us. I dared not wake him until he was ready, yet I did not wish anyone else to see him like this and know what had happened. Stay away! I begged them in my mind. I knew the captain would want to get under sail early.

My thoughts must have had power of their own, for Caesar awoke. He flinched a little at the bright light coming in the tent, and shielded his eyes. He groaned like a man who has had too much to drink—but no more than that.

"I feel dreadful," he said simply. "I am sorry you had to witness this."

"Who better than I?" I said. "But I was frightened—I did not expect it, and I did not know what to do."

"There is nothing to do," he said, and his voice sounded half disgusted and half resigned. "Someday I will hit my head on a stone or a metal statue, and that will be the end of it. Desert sand is more forgiving than marble or bronze. This time I was lucky."

"Has this ever happened during a—a battle?" It was a terrible affliction for a soldier.

"No. Not yet." He shook his head. "I must hide the evidence before someone comes. Is there water here?"

I brought over the pitcher and poured some into a bowl. "Here, you must let me help you." I washed the dirt off his face, revealing the bruises and scratches underneath. "We must pretend we have had a fight," I said lightly.

"Greetings, O mighty rulers!" a cheerful voice announced itself outside the tent.

He was quiet that day, but the only change in him anyone could have observed was that he sat more than usual, watching the journey from a seat under the shaded pavilion, rather than standing at the rail. Once during the day he turned to me and looked at me so searchingly I knew all the memory had returned to him, and that he was grateful for what I had done to help. I was glad he had remembered. Now he would understand my love for him.

It took us twenty days to sail as far upriver as Thebes. All the way, people lined the riverbanks, straining to catch a glimpse of these modern Pharaohs who were sailing in state, followed by a great flotilla of boats. The wind lifted our cloaks, and we gave royal acknowledgment to our onlookers with a wave of our hands. Caesar, now fully recovered, took it all in: the adulation, the yearning of the people for a god. *Isis!* they called to me as we floated past. *Amun!* they saluted him, and he allowed them to do so.

After thirty-five days we reached the first cataract of the Nile, Aswan, the end of our journey. Here it proved impossible to drag the enormous barge overland to avoid the treacherous rocks in the river's channel, and so we had to stop. Caesar had seen Egypt from north to south. But his soldiers were growing restless and uneasy on this journey farther and farther south, along what looked to be a never-ending highway of water, into the heart of Africa. And as it became hotter and hotter, one late afternoon, when the sun's rays were especially burning, Caesar beckoned to an attendant to fan him with the ostrich-feather fan.

"I yield," he said to me with a smile. "I capitulate. Here, in your land, for your climate, I admit that your fans are superior."

Did he remember his wager? Should I remind him? But this should mean more to him than just a wager.

"Show me the Temple of Philae," he said. "Have a priest ready."

So it was that I first entered the temple that came to mean more to me than any other. Your home, O Isis, on that island sanctuary where the most devoted rites are held, and pilgrims from all over Egypt and Nubia come to worship you. I had heard it was beautiful, but I was unprepared for its white, ivorylike purity, its perfect proportions of marble and graceful carvings. Across on its sister island lies the shrine of Osiris, and like a faithful wife, every ten days you, in the form of your statue, make the journey across the waters to visit him. What more fitting place for a wedding than at your very feet? Your statue, all overlaid with gold, watched over us as Caesar took my hand and said the words that constituted marriage under the rites of Isis. He repeated the words after the priest in a whisper, in the Egyptian tongue.

Afterward he said, "I don't have the slightest idea what I just promised."

"You promised to bind yourself to me in marriage, on your honor to Isis."

"Very well," he said with nonchalance. "Caesar always keeps his promises."

I was stabbed with disappointment and hurt; he acted as if he had just purchased a handful of dates in the market, and it was all the same to him whether they should be edible or not. It was just a game to him, or something to satisfy a child. But he had made marriage vows, and there were witnesses to the ceremony.

On our journey back to Alexandria, it was formally announced at Thebes and Memphis: The god Amun, in his incarnation as Julius Caesar, and the goddess Isis, his wife, in the incarnation of Queen Cleopatra, were going to bring forth a royal, divine child. It had to be announced, as my pregnancy was now obvious. At Hermonthis, construction began on a birth-house that would commemorate the royal birth and make clear his parentage. Amun's face bore an exact resemblance to Caesar's.

He seemed amused, pleased, even. But now that he was my "husband," I felt farther from him than before. It was as if the ceremony had separated us rather than uniting us, and made us awkward together. I think it was because neither of us really knew what it meant, and we were each afraid to ask the other. I did not want to hear him say, *I did it for fun, as part of my forfeit*, and he did not want to hear me say, *Now you must announce this at Rome, and divorce Calpurnia*. As long as neither of us mentioned it, we could live as before.

In vain on the return journey I longed for him to tell me he loved me, and considered me in some fashion his wife. He was jolly, entertaining, light-hearted. He was a passionate lover, an attentive listener. But he never alluded to the brief ceremony at Philae, and I did not dare do so, as the boat came closer and closer to Alexandria.

15

We halted at Memphis, and anchored the ships across the waters from the white walls of the city and the groves of sycamores that threw their flat shade on the procession way. As we approached it, and I saw the stepped pyramid of Saqqara rearing its head, I felt oppression overtaking me. We were reentering the world of politics, commerce, wars, and alliances, leaving behind the realm of gods, temples, and mysteries. The only flicker of worldly matters that had interfered with our idyll had been Caesar's interest in Coptos on our homeward journey. He had wished to know more about the India trade routes that passed that way. When he had mentioned India, the covetous look had passed over his face again. But the intrusion had been brief.

Now, however, Memphis sat on the border of the wider world for us, a world that would reclaim Caesar—I knew it. And before we had properly set the anchors and aligned the ship, a smaller vessel full of Romans was paddling furiously out to us.

"Caesar!" cried an officer I recognized, Rufio, whom Caesar had left guarding Alexandria. "Caesar!"

Never one to hide in his cabin or dismiss business, Caesar waved to him enthusiastically. I almost hated him for that; it made him seem the slave of someone else's urgencies. (Since then I have been accused of having the "eastern vice" for not respecting time or messengers. I do—but at my convenience, not theirs.) Rufio was soon on board, and Caesar was greeting him like a long-lost brother.

"How black you are burnt, Caesar!" cried Rufio. "Has the sun turned you into a Nubian?" He cast an eye toward the ostrich-fan bearers in obvious disapproval.

Caesar laughed and said, "I have seen much and gone many miles, but I am still Caesar, under this sunburn." Then the dreaded question. "What news?"

Rufio pulled out a sheaf of papers and waved them at Caesar, who pushed them aside. "No, tell me yourself. It is quicker. Alexandria?"

"Alexandria is quiet. No more fight in them. But in Pontus—King Pharnaces has overrun your general Calvinus, taken the Roman province, and slaughtered or castrated all the Roman merchants and citizens. He assumes he can get away with this because you are too . . . preoccupied."

"Calvinus! He sent his Thirty-seventh Legion to us here—and left himself unprotected." Caesar's good-natured mien faded. "He must be avenged."

"You have a full platter of wrongs to avenge, then." Now Rufio seemed apologetic at having to heap them all up. "The reports we have received from the west of Alexandria is that the remainders of the forces of Pompey, including his sons, are gathering along the shores of North Africa, trafficking with King Juba of Numidia."

"The only question, then, is which one I must address myself to first."

"Precisely." Only then did Rufio take any notice of me, standing near Caesar. "Greetings to you, most exalted Queen."

"I am always pleased to see you, Rufio, but your news is not as welcome as you are." It was true, I had always liked Rufio. He was a freedman's son, with a broad, toadlike face, but pleasant nonetheless. It is a mystery to me what makes one person more inherently appealing company than another.

"Will the world never be a quiet place?" barked Caesar, as if, momentarily, the constant tasks were too much even for him. He sounded worn out, even after six weeks of rest.

"Not much longer, my dearest," I assured him. "In only a little while, when you return to Rome—"

"Rome is a mess," said Rufio bluntly.

Caesar started. "Here, come below to our stateroom," he said. "These are not matters we can discuss in passing on deck." He turned on his heel and expected us to follow.

He made his way down the ebony-trimmed steps and into the great chamber in the midsection of the ship, where he and I had consulted with the captain, studied maps and manuscripts relating to our journey, and held conferences with the accompanying Roman officers every so often. He sat on the edge of a long table of polished cypress wood, one of his legs dangling.

"Now," he said.

I pulled up a gilded chair and indicated that Rufio should do likewise. "There *are* chairs," I said pointedly to Caesar. "Or are you already in a war camp?"

He grabbed one and jerked it up to the table.

"What of Rome?" he asked in that low voice, full of menace and tension. I had almost forgotten it on the trip.

"It is all in disarray," said Rufio. "There have been no leaders there since you passed through it a year and a half ago. Your lieutenant Marc Antony may be a good fighting man, but as a political deputy, he seems in water beyond his depth. There has been fighting in the Forum, Antony's men against Dolabella's mob, with eight hundred killed. There's also a mutiny of your veterans in the Italian countryside. They say they haven't had their promised rewards."

"Anything more?" asked Caesar.

"No." Rufio looked surprised that he would even ask. Wasn't that enough?

"I have been in Egypt eight months now," said Caesar slowly. "I came in pursuit of Pompey and became embroiled in another war. I have lost much valuable time."

"You were so out of touch with Rome that until December they did not even know of your whereabouts," said Rufio, almost scolding. "There were some who assumed you were dead."

"I was not dead," he said. "But in some ways entombed." He looked around at the richly furnished stateroom, and dismissed it with the wave of a hand.

"Egypt is like a gigantic tomb. Everything that stays here long enough becomes mummified. This is a country of dead men surrounded by monuments to death."

I could stand it no longer. "Am I a mummy?" I cried. "Is Alexandria—the foremost city in the world for learning, beauty, and the art of living—a tomb?"

He laughed. "Alexandria, as everyone knows, is not Egypt. But even it seems remote from everyday life—perhaps because it is so opulent, so civilized."

He had finished with us. He was ready to go. He was straining at his tether.

That night, in our sleeping chamber, he seemed thoughtful, almost sad that it had come to an end. He sat staring at his goblet, which he had uncharacteristically filled with wine. He had even drunk a cupful, and it seemed to soften his stern features. He toyed with its base, running his fingers over the raised decorations.

"Long ago I told you I avoided wine because it incited strange symptoms in me. Now, after that night on the desert, you know what they are. But tonight I do not care."

I stood behind him and put my arms around him. "What will you do? When—must you leave?"

"Soon," he said. "In a few days."

"A few days? Can you not stay for the birth of our child? It is only a few weeks from now."

"I cannot wait a few weeks." He sounded so certain that it was pointless for me to object.

"I see." So I would be left alone to bear this child. But there was no arguing with Caesar. I tried my best to keep my voice level and betray no tremor of emotion. It would serve no purpose but to annoy him. *But what about Philae?* my mind cried. *What did it mean to you? Anything?* Would it be announced in any way?

"There is one thing more," he said, still turning the goblet in his hands.

"Yes?" My heart leapt up.

"You should marry little Ptolemy before my departure. You cannot rule alone, and must be nominally married."

"I am married!" I cried. I could not help myself. "It is already announced that this child—"

He laughed indulgently. "That is in the divine, mystical sense. But the Alexandrians are more jaded and skeptical. They will laugh at such a story. And those we laugh at, we lose fear and respect for. Without a husband, foreign princes will come courting you, and that will be tiresome."

"For me or for them?"

"For you and for me," he said. "I am hoping that you would find their attentions tedious, and for myself, I would find them . . . disturbing." He stood up and put down the goblet. At last he took me in his arms. "I find I cannot stand the thought of you with another man. This has never happened to me before. I excused Pompeia's liaison with Clodius, and frankly I wouldn't care if Calpurnia had been rolling around with Cicero himself the entire time of my absence. But you . . . no Syrian princes for you. I could not bear it."

"So I am to wait, preserved, for you—like the mummies you say Egypt is filled with?"

"I will send for you to come to Rome as soon as it is safe."

"Which may be years!" The awfulness of what I was facing suddenly spread itself out before me. To bind myself to Caesar was indeed to make a mummy of myself, with all living forbidden, and no promise of any recognition as anything but his mistress. "The life you are offering is no life at all!"

"Trust me. In just a little while, things may be different." In an ordinary man, his tone would have been close to begging. But could Caesar beg?

"How can they be? The laws of Rome are as they are, and your nature is as it is."

"Trust me," he said, and this time the tone really was begging. "I have never known another person like you, found my counterpart in a woman. You have my spirit, my daring, my gambler's nature, my seeking for adventure. Wait and see what I can bring about."

"Wait and see," I murmured. "What if nothing happens?"

"If it is humanly possible for me to bring about a future for us and our child, I will," he promised. "But I must know you will wait, and that you trust me."

"I have no choice," I finally said. "My heart wishes me to, even though my head warns me not to."

"Because you are very young," he said, "they may be evenly balanced. At my age, it is a wonder that the heart speaks at all."

In two days we were back in Alexandria. From a distance it looked as perfect as ever, but after we had landed and were being transported in litters through the city, I could see the heaps of rubble and the charred timbers that choked the streets. There would be much to repair. The war had been a costly business—but if that was the price for keeping my throne, so be it.

As we alighted and entered the palace, I was aware of more than just welcoming looks. During the journey my pregnancy had advanced to the stage where it was clearly visible. We would have to make the Amun announcement immediately. Or just make no announcement at all? Caesar was right; such a claim would only cause the Alexandrians merriment. My city was known as a place where lovemaking and pleasure blended the sophistication of the Greeks with the sensual indulgences of the east; they would know well enough where this baby had come from. I blushed to realize that even their imaginations might fall short of the actual acts. Who could believe the old Roman soldier, so austere in all his other physical appetites, would be so inventive and vigorous in his amorous behavior? On the other hand, *inventive* and *vigorous* were the two words that best described his prowess on the military field as well.

Much as I hated to leave our private world on the ship, I was delighted to see Mardian and Olympos at the head of the officers waiting to receive us. And when I reentered my chambers, Charmian and Iras were there.

"Oh, my dear Charmian! My Iras!" I held out my arms and embraced them.

"Your Majesty! Welcome! Look! We have all in readiness! Goods are flowing into Egypt again, now that the war is over. There are new silk hangings for the bed; fresh incense from Arabia; the good Caecuban wine; and roses from Cyrene—both red and white." I could smell the distinct rose odor, piercingly sweet. Two bunches of them were in large glass vases. "We are so happy you are here," they said, simply.

"What have you done for Caesar's quarters?" I asked.

"Made ready a working table," Charmian said. "Mountains of documents have come in for him."

I sighed. He would not care about, or notice, the new silks or the roses. Only the documents. "There are undoubtedly documents for me, too," I said.

"Many less," they said. Iras pointed to a table that held a little pyramid of them.

Yes, I did not rule the world, but only one country. And on this journey I had seen many of the concerns of that country with my own eyes. The business in Egypt was the same as it had been for the earliest Pharaohs: crops, harvests, taxes, soldiers. It was Caesar's world that was in flux, not mine.

"He thanks you for your efforts," I said. I felt tired, and sank down on a chair of citrus wood.

"Your . . . your . . . condition . . . ?" They flopped around, searching for words.

"I have had no problems except that now I am growing tired easily. The journey was restful for me," I said.

"And when is—is—?"

If my own dear ladies were so embarrassed about it, how did the rest of Alexandria regard it? "I am not really sure," I said. "I must ask Olympos to do the calculations. I think in a month, or perhaps a bit longer. Caesar cannot stay." I had to say it then, so there would be no mistake about it. But the look on their faces told all. They disapproved. I found myself in the position of having to defend him—to myself and to them.

"There are urgent matters—" I began, but my voice trailed off. It was not convincing. "This is the drawback to loving the master of the world," I finally said. "One tends not to be as important to him as one would wish."

And that was the truth of the matter. I was a queen, descended from an old royal house, and my country was the richest one in the world. But he did not need to remind me that when we met, I had been reduced to living in exile in a tent. Without him I would still be there—or dead. He could have turned Egypt into a Roman province after Alexandria had surrendered, like every other country in the Mediterranean after a defeat: Greece, Syria, Judaea, Spain, Carthage. The fact that he had left me on my throne and had even spent precious weeks on our journey up the Nile spoke of his personal feelings for me. More than that I would not get.

Now we belonged to the world again, and our privacy was gone. Caesar read detailed reports of the insurrection in Pontus, the gathering of malcontents in Africa, the turmoil in Rome, and received a flock of messengers with current information.

He shook his head late one night as he sat in a wide chair and dropped each report on the left side as he finished reading it. Outside, the waves in the inner harbor were dancing in the moonlight. It was a soft night; the breezes barely swayed the flames in the wicks of the lamps. Probably all over the city people were sipping honeyed wine, listening to soft lute music, holding evening *symposia*, reading quietly, or making love. That was what Alexandria was famous for: pleasures of the mind and body. Caesar worked on through the hours, stopping only to shake his head or stretch his arms occasionally.

It was well past midnight when he muttered, "That's all." The pile of papers on his right side had all been transferred to the left.

"Where have you decided to go?" I asked quietly.

"Pontus," he said. "I cannot return to Rome, leaving an enemy at my back. The east must be made secure."

"But you are already in Africa," I said. The Roman rebel forces were much closer.

"I always finish pesky side rebellions before turning to the main task at hand," he said. "That is why I reduced Spain before pursuing Pompey. It looked as if I were going in the wrong direction, but it was by intent. Now I must go to Pontus before returning here. It is almost sixteen hundred miles in the wrong direction." He stood up and made for the open roof terrace. I came and stood beside him, looking at the Lighthouse belching out its fire and smoke. It still had the power to move me with pride every time I looked at it.

"You will sail out of this harbor," I said, voicing the obvious. "When?"

"In a few days," he said. "I have decided to leave behind three legions to protect you, under Rufio. There will not arise another Pothinus."

"But—that will leave you only one legion to take to Pontus!" No, I could not let him endanger himself so. Better I should take my chances here.

"Yes, the Sixth," he said.

"That is not enough!"

"It will have to be," he said.

"No, not again! It happened once in Alexandria that you were undermanned. Do not repeat it!" Then I remembered something else. "The Sixth Legion is not even up to full strength! There are only a thousand men in it—not even a fourth of its full quota!"

"Yes, I know," he said.

"You push your luck too far!" I cried. "I think you mean to force the goddess Fortune into abandoning you! It is insane to take only a thousand men!"

"That is my business!" He was starting to show irritation.

"No, it is my business as well, now!" I resorted to touching my belly.

"My military campaigns are my business," he repeated.

"Why do you tempt fate so?" I begged. "Why do you think you are immune to defeat and misfortune?" I could hear my voice rising, propelled by fear. "I think that fate spares us—spares some of us—for a good long time, to lull us into the trap she means to spring for us. Those she spares the longest, she may have the cruelest ending for."

"In that case, there is little I can do to sidestep it," he said. "Fate will have her way, whether I take one legion or twenty."

"Yes, and no." I knew that if fate wished otherwise, twenty legions would not protect you, but sometimes fate did not care one way or the other, in which case you were better off with your little human preparations.

"You are confused," he said, putting his arm around me. "I think it is fatigue that makes you talk so. Come, let us take some rest." He gently took my shoulders and turned them around.

Lying beside him in the dark, I found it hard to believe that he would soon be gone, away on another battlefield. He made me feel very safe. For that instant.

Just before he fell asleep, he said softly, "I think you must go ahead with the ceremony with Ptolemy."

The priest was waiting in the small chamber just off the banqueting hall, where Caesar and I had arranged for the vows to be exchanged. Ptolemy, only twelve years old, stood obediently ready to cooperate. He was the last of my five brothers and sisters; all the others had met violent deaths trying to take the throne, except for Arsinoe, who survived only in prison. Caesar planned to send her to Rome to be paraded through the streets in his Triumph. At the time I thought little of it. Now . . .

Ptolemy was a pleasant, light-featured boy. He seemed to have none of the guile and viciousness of the others; perhaps it had been scared out of him.

"O most gracious Caesar," he said, "most beloved sister, I am pleased to obey you in all things!" He fingered his carnelian and lapis collar nervously.

"Stand over here," said Caesar, pointing his finger at a floor mosaic of a hippopotamus. Ptolemy fairly flew across the floor to the spot.

"And you here," he said to me, indicating a mosaic crocodile. The entire design was part of a scene of the Nile, which included fish, birds, flowers, and boats. I stood on the crocodile's snout.

Olympos, Mardian, Rufio, Charmian, and Iras stood by as witnesses. The priest of Serapis uttered a few sentences that we repeated, and the deed was done. Ptolemy XIV and Cleopatra VII, Father-Loving and Brother-and-Sister-Loving God and Goddess, were united as rulers of Upper and Lower Egypt. Caesar was beaming, and pronounced a Roman benediction. Then we all turned to the feast tables that were prepared and waiting.

Caesar's last night had come. In the morning he would sail out of the harbor with his ships and his thousand legionaries.

"I leave with great reluctance," he said. "You cannot know with how much."

"Your lingering here has caused great comment everywhere," I admitted. "What stronger proof could there be that you wished to stay?"

"I take with me many ideas to be transplanted to Rome. I see now what a city should be. Thank you for that."

"What do you mean? What would you change at Rome?"

"Rome is a very primitive place," he said. "You will see when you come." He hurried over that, I noticed. "But now that I have seen the wide marble streets, the public buildings, the Library . . . I would like to copy them. And your calendar is far superior to ours. I will certainly change all that when—"

"When the wars are over," I finished for him. "All the more reason not to tempt fate, but to help her."

"I will raise reinforcements once I get to Syria," he said. "You are right."

I watched as the last of the warships sailed out of the harbor and off toward the horizon. They grew smaller and smaller, and disappeared. I felt as if my life were departing. I had known him for such a short time, but in that short interval my world had changed forever—like everything he had touched. Neither Gaul nor Rome nor I would ever be the same as before he came. There was no going back; Caesar had remade the world.

HERE ENDS THE FIRST SCROLL.

He had gone. I looked all around me, as if awakening from a dream. For what seemed the first time since I had left Alexandria to go upriver for the bull ceremony at Hermonthis, I saw the palace and the city as they were, through the eyes of an adult. I had left almost two years ago. At that time I had known little or nothing about ruling, and even less about what lay beyond our borders. Luck had seen me through—Caesar and I seemed to share that luck. But now more than luck would be needed. I had to rule a once-great nation single-handed, and bind up its wounds.

At least, I thought, all my efforts can now be directed toward Egypt, and not be squandered on civil wars and palace intrigues. I am given a free hand, but if I fail, I have nothing else to blame. Rufio and his legions will assure that free hand: Caesar's great gift to me. His greatest, next to the child.

I went out immediately to inspect the royal area, taking Mardian and Charmian with me. During my Nile journey, Mardian had carefully assessed the damage to the grounds and buildings, and now he acted as a guide to the dismal sights.

"Here is where—forgive me, Majesty—the soldiers camped out, destroying all the plantings." He pointed to what had once been a lawn planted with sweet grasses and flowering shrubs.

It stank. "And I see they have left behind enough fertilizer to ensure new plantings," I said. "Even the most delicate plant should find all its needs met for some years to come."

The Temple of Isis, farther out on the peninsula, seemed to have suffered little damage, perhaps because it was out of range of the rocks and missiles lobbed by the townspeople over the walls of the palace grounds. But the nearer we got to the walls, the more destruction I saw. The stables, the storehouses, the baths, the cisterns, all were damaged in some way—either the walls had been cracked and broken, or the roofs burnt. One of my favorite trees, a giant sycamore that I had played in all during my childhood, had been burnt to the ground.

Now, turning to look back at the main palace building, I could see ugly black stains left by firebrands hurled against its sides. My beautiful white palace by the sea! I gave a groan of unhappiness.

"It will be repaired as soon as you give the word," said Mardian.

I was impressed by the inventory he had compiled. Now I would put him in charge of the restorations.

"Dear mistress, I think you are tiring yourself," said Charmian, in her husky-sweet voice. "Save the rest of Alexandria for tomorrow."

"Yes, I shall go into Alexandria tomorrow to pay homage at the large temple to Isis. Providing it is still standing."

"You may rest assured it is," said Mardian. "One or two of the columns damaged, but other than that—fine."

"I must place myself in her hands, for I shall need her help at the hour of childbirth." I felt a bit unsteady on my feet, a little dizzy. I put out my hand and leaned on Charmian. "This evening," I said weakly, "I think I would like to consult with Olympos."

I waited for him in my most private chamber. As I looked around at the marble-inlaid little tables, the three-legged standing lamp holders, and the footstools, I became aware that each object now seemed to bear Caesar's imprint in one way or another. Either he had asked a question about it, sat in it, or used it. It is thus that inanimate objects seem to soak up the essence of living things, and later cause pain or pleasure when we merely look at them.

I was seated in one of the few chairs with a back, and I rested my feet on a stool. I felt very clumsy and tired. Strange, when I was with Caesar I had not paid much attention to the changes in my body, but now I was all too aware of them.

I knew Olympos would scold me. He had that privilege, as a childhood friend and as someone who was totally, blazingly honest. Sure enough, when he came into the room, his lean, hawklike face was almost frowning.

"Greetings," he said. Then, immediately, "Is this all the light there is?" He indicated the floor lamp, which had five wicks in it.

"We can light others," I said. There were several more bronze table lamps, filled with oil, ready to light. "I am not sure what it is you need to see."

"I can see well enough the main thing!" He looked directly at my stomach. "Oh, dear Cleopatra—why did you do it? I taught you how to prevent it! What happened to the silphion? You were supposed to make it up into Cyrenaic juice that would have prevented this."

"I did carry it with me, but I could hardly make it up when I was inside the rug!"

"You must have had time afterward! Surely you did not go right from the rug into his bed." He waited for a denial. When I did not give one, he seemed shocked. It is not easy to shock Olympos, and even when he is shocked he usually hides it better. He gave a groan.

"I cannot expect you to be sympathetic. You did not approve from the beginning," I said.

He snorted. "Even so, probably the first time you . . . after the rug . . . you could have taken the proper measures then! It was not too late! After all, he is not Zeus, so that he only has to visit a mortal woman once for her to conceive!"

I could not help laughing. "I do not expect you to understand my decision. You must know that I am content that this has happened; *happy* is a better word. It was not at all as I had imagined, there in the tent at Gaza. No, it was something completely different, something—"

Olympos gave another snort. "Save me the mush. It makes me sick."

"You just don't like him."

"No, and I never will."

"That is honest."

"I am glad you appreciate that. Now, as to your questions . . . what would you wish to know? It seems to me you have no need of my prescriptions or advice!"

"You have studied with the foremost physicians here in Alexandria, and your training is impeccable. Can you know in advance the day I can expect to give birth?"

"No. Only within a certain span of days. It varies a great deal." He came over and put his hand gently on my abdomen, and felt carefully all around the sides as well. "When did you first feel it stir? Usually it is about a hundred and fifty days after that."

I could remember exactly. It had been when an enormous stone had been catapulted over into the palace grounds, and it made a sickening explosive sound as it hit a well. My stomach had moved, and I had thought it was in response to the noise. But when it came again a few hours later in a quiet time, I realized it was something else. And that had been just before we heard that Mithridates was at the eastern borders of the country.

"Late February," I said.

"Then it will arrive in late Quintilis, next month."

"Quintilis! That is Caesar's own birth month! What a favorable omen!"

Olympos looked disgusted. "No doubt the great general will be honored," he said.

"He *is* honored," I answered. How could Olympos even begin to suspect Caesar's great delight? "So I have another fifty days or so? It seems a long time to prepare. Will you procure knowledgeable midwives for me? I do not want superstitious old hags, but young women who have been trained well."

"What about your own women?"

"They will be there, of course, but I wish others to be present who have had experience. After all, Charmian and Iras are virgins."

He rolled his eyes. "Charmian is hardly very virginal. That voice . . . it would make even Helen of Troy's sound grating in comparison."

Yes, her voice smoldered and promised great knowledge of man-woman things. "That is true, but she is still a virgin."

"Not for long. And not if she follows your example."

"It is nowhere a condition of serving me that a woman must be a virgin. This is not Rome; we have no Vestal Virgins here."

"Yes, we Greeks and easterners are more realistic. Only the Romans would invent Vestal Virgins, but have as their leader someone like Julius Caesar! I love his remark, when divorcing his third wife, Pompeia, that 'Caesar's wife must be above suspicion.' What about his friends' wives, whenever he was in Rome?"

"I think you should stop before you say something you cannot retract."

"So he is to come between us! It is always thus. Rulers say they wish their friends to treat them as always, but sooner or later they turn imperial on you."

"I am not turning imperial, but responding as any woman would to slander about the father of her child. I do not wish to demean him by listening to it, nor myself by considering it, nor you by allowing you to speak in such a manner."

"So you will silence the truth!" His voice was getting pompous.

"I will not silence it. But neither will I belabor it." I looked over at his face, still scowling. "Olympos, I treasure your friendship. As a ruler, I am blessed to have such a friend as you. I know Caesar has . . . been with many women. I do not delude myself about his past. But I see no need to torture myself about it. I look to my future with Caesar, not to his past."

"The past predicts the future," he said stubbornly.

"Not always," I said. "I have a more optimistic view of the world."

The next morning, very early, I made myself ready to visit the Great Shrine of Isis at the Serapion. I wished to go as any other supplicant, for Isis is the protector of all women, and it was as a woman and not as a queen that I sought her blessings and help. I would have to go through childbirth like any other woman; my baby would be born the same way. Like any ordinary woman whose husband was a soldier or a sailor, I loved a man who had gone far away and would be in danger. I came before you, Isis, my Mother, my succor and hope, as the humblest petitioner.

I robed myself in dark blue linen, and made sure I had a cloak to hide my shape. I also had a cowl that I could pull over my head. I wished no one to recognize me. I took up a round stone jar with an offering of goat milk, and drew a veil over my face.

The sun was only just rising as I left my litter at the foot of the hill of the Serapion and mounted the stairs slowly. The climb left me out of breath, with my ever-growing burden, but when I reached the summit of the hill I was rewarded with a glimpse of the sea at daybreak, and all of Alexandria glowing gold in the new light. Behind me, at a discreet distance, came Iras.

I prayed I would not be too late. They had already opened the temple doors with incense—I could smell its pungent sweetness. I stopped to wash my hands and face with the ceremonial water in its bronze vessel at the entrance, to purify myself. As I made my way into the vast, shadowed building, toward the shrine of Isis, I saw that the white-robed priests were only just sprinkling the sacred Nile water at the entrance. Behind them, in a line, were the acolytes, chanting the morning hymn.

"Arise, Mistress of the Two Lands of Egypt, Mistress of Heaven, Mistress of the House of Life. . . . ' "

The deep, sonorous tones of the voices rose and fell like the Nile itself. The shaved heads of the priests and acolytes were like smooth, pale stones in the dim light. Swaying, they walked slowly toward the pedestal where the veiled statue of Isis stood, and then prostrated themselves at its base.

At length the chief priest rose and approached the statue, delicately drawing aside the veil. Reverently he placed necklaces of gold and turquoise around her neck, and a headdress of vulture's feathers.

A statue of you, Isis, can never be mistaken for that of any other goddess. You always hold the timbrel, the sistrum, in one hand and the long-spouted pitcher filled with Nile water in the other. Your gown is always tied with the knot sacred to you, a mystic knot. In this great shrine you also have the cobra headdress, and beneath your feet is a crocodile. And upon your face is the most perfect smile, emblem of that vast love you have for all of us.

For a long time we all knelt in silence. Then a group of women began beating on their breasts, uttering loud wails of the "lamentations of Isis." They poured out their troubles to you—their ill husbands, their ungrateful sons, their rebellious daughters, the ache in their knees, their ovens that would not bake the bread properly, their rat-infested grain supplies. Anything, no matter how important or petty, was presented to you in confidence that you could make it right. One by one they crept forward and left their offerings at your feet—flowers, bread, jars of honey, garlands of flowers. I crawled on my hands and knees to present the milk.

" 'I am all that has been, and is, and shall be,' " intoned the voice of a priestess, speaking for you.

The very words spoke to my heart, and I gazed on your face. You seemed to be younger than I, but I knew you had endured all that any woman ever can. You had finished the journey I was just setting out on. You had been wife, and widow, and mother.

"I am she called God among women." The voice went on.

"I overcome Fate. To me Fate hearkens."

"I am the one of innumerable names."

Your face took on an unutterable beauty to me, and I adored you.

I remained at your altar a long time, asking for help in the coming ordeal of childbirth, and in guidance for Egypt. Gradually the rest of the worshipers departed, and by the time I felt the glory of your presence fading and I began a return to the ordinary, I was almost alone. Only a very few women remained, and two in particular were making their way so slowly to the door,

I wondered if they were crippled. Yet they stood straight enough, and their gait was normal. As I came closer to them, I saw that one was blind, and feeling her way along, while her companion helped her. Then I noticed that she was not blind in the usual way, for she kept rubbing her eyes as if she expected light to flood into them.

"Have you asked Isis to restore your sight, my sister?" I asked.

She quickly turned toward me, as if she could see me. Her companion, I saw now, was a young girl, most likely her daughter.

"Yes, I have asked," she replied. "Every day I come and ask. But the fog remains."

"I pray that Isis, the Great and Compassionate Mother, will help my mother," said the girl. "I will not give up hope."

"I am not used to being blind," the mother said, as if apologizing. "Perhaps if one is born with it, then . . . but to suddenly become someone else, and have half the world taken away from me . . . as well as my work! The skills of a blind person take years to develop. It is not as if I can do what other blind people do! I cannot carve, I cannot play a musical instrument, I cannot serve as a royal food taster."

"What did you do?"

"I worked as one of the silk-looseners."

How unfortunate! That type of handiwork, in which a skilled needle-woman loosened the fabric of silk we received from Arabia to make it stretch farther and be more transparent, needed keen eyesight. Perhaps the job had cost her that sight.

"How did this happen?"

"The war!" she said. "In the fighting, it seems there were fires everywhere. Alexandria is nearly fireproof, the buildings being stone, but there was plenty of loose material to be set afire. When one of those pitch-soaked torches landed right in my textile shop, I threw a rug over it to smother it and dove on it to keep everything from going up in flames. The smoke from it—it's a very nasty kind of thick, oily smoke—got in my eyes. The next day—no more sight."

The war. This one was particularly terrible because it had taken place not on a battlefield, but within city streets and people's homes.

"I will take you to my physician. Perhaps he can help. Are there others you know who were injured, have lost jobs, means of living?"

She drew back. "Why should I go with you to your physician? I have no money to pay! Who are you?" She sounded indignant.

I pulled aside my veil. "I am Cleopatra, your Queen, but also the devotee of Isis. I will help her to help you."

They both looked terror-stricken.

"Is not Isis the champion of women? And I, as her daughter, am also your champion. I wish to help women who have suffered here in Alexandria. Come with me to the palace," I said.

Still with that frightened look, they obeyed.

———

Olympos examined the woman's eyes, but pronounced that the damage might indeed be permanent. He prescribed a twice-daily wash of rainwater mixed with an infusion of an herb he obtained from an Arabian shrub. I told her that she and her daughter could remain in the palace during the treatment, and that if her eyesight did not return, I would find new employment for her.

"Why have you taken this woman into your care?" asked Olympos. "The city must be full of ones exactly like her!"

"Yes. Isis opened my eyes to that. I would like to find a way to help all of them. They suffer as the result of the war—a war fought on my behalf. It is the least I can do."

"You continue to surprise me," he said dryly.

But it was my child who had the biggest surprise for us all. In the middle of the night, not more than twenty days after my conversation with Olympos, I was taken with a violent onset of pain while I was sleeping. It jolted me awake, as if I had been struck by a heavy object. I lay flat on my back, wondering what had happened. Was it a dream? Just as I was drifting off to sleep again, another bolt of pain struck me. I gasped and sat up, panting.

The flames in the lamps I always kept burning in the chamber were steady. All seemed so peaceful, so quiet. Outside I could hear a gentle sound of wind, but on this June night all else was tranquil. It seemed an aberration to be visited with pain at such a time.

Just as I was thinking this, another wave hit me. Trembling, and breaking out into a burst of sweat, I rang the bell for Iras and Charmian, who slept nearby. I had to ring a long time before they heard me; it was, as I said, a night for sweet sleeping.

"I think—my time of childbirth has come," I said, when they arrived. I was startled, and a little frightened, to find how much effort it took me even to speak. "Get the midwives!"

I was taken on a litter—oh, how it bounced!—into a chamber that had been prepared for this. There, on a low chair, hung twisted ropes that I could grip on to; beside it were stacks of linen towels and sheets, and washbasins. They stripped me naked and I was taken with shivering, even on that warm night, until they covered me with a sheet. All the lamps were lit, and I braced myself against the arms of the chair. The midwives stood about, murmuring and attempting to make all this seem very normal. To them, it was. I was profoundly grateful that I had obtained them so far in advance.

The pains increased; Iras and Charmian took turns wiping my face with scented water. I hung on to the ropes and arched my back. I did not want to cry out, no matter how high the pain mounted. I felt hot rushes of water pouring from inside me, and heard one of the midwives say, "The waters have broken!" Then I lost track of time. The pain seemed to be its own world, and it enveloped me and I felt myself always trying to mount it, as I would try to climb up a slippery ball that kept rotating and throwing me off. Finally there was a crest to the pain, and I felt enormous pressure, and then—it stopped.

"A son! A son!" they were shouting.

There was a loud, quavering wail.

"A son!" They held him up, his red legs flailing, his chest heaving with the exertion of crying.

They wiped him off with the warmed, scented water and wrapped him in fresh linen. They placed him on my breast. I could see only the top of his head; it was covered in fine dark hair. His little fingers flexed and uncurled, and he stopped crying. I felt his warmth against me, and I was flooded with joy—and exhaustion. Against my will, I closed my eyes and slept.

It was midmorning before I came to myself again. I saw the reflections of the seawater dancing on the ceiling, moving in little white jumping patterns, and for a moment I just lay and looked at them, stunned. Then I remembered everything.

I struggled to sit up on my elbows, and saw Charmian and Iras and Olympos at the back of the chamber. They were speaking in hushed tones. Outside the sunlight was so bright it hurt my eyes.

"My son!" I said. "Let me see him again!"

Charmian bent down over the royal crib, an elaborately carved box on little feet. She picked up a wrapped bundle and brought it over to me. It looked too small to have a human being inside it. I pulled away the linen near the little red face. He looked like an angry, wizened, sunburnt old man. I laughed.

Olympos hurried over to my bedside. "He is small, but he will live," he pronounced with satisfaction. "Eighth-month babies often do not fare as well."

"Yes, he is a month early," I said. Then I realized that Caesar had barely missed seeing him. I felt a double disappointment that it had been so close. I looked carefully at the little face staring back at me with unfocused, hazy blue eyes. "I think it is impossible to see a likeness in a newborn's face, regardless of what people claim. I have never seen this face before!" I smoothed the fuzzy hair growing on his head. "Nevertheless, I can say, he isn't bald, like his father!"

How pleased Caesar would be when he heard the news! How thrilled I felt to be able to present him with the one thing no one else in the world had been able to give him for so long, and which was unobtainable to him through all his conquests of land. I must get the word to him at once. But I did not even know how to reach him; I had received no message from him since his departure.

"What will you call him, Majesty?" asked Charmian.

"A name to blazen forth both sides of his inheritance," I said. "Ptolemy Caesar."

Olympos looked startled. "Do you dare to bestow the familial name of Caesar without permission of that family?"

"I do not need permission from that family! What have they to do with it? The leading member of that family is the child's father. It is between him and me," I said.

"Did he agree to this?" Iras asked quietly.

"He told me it was entirely up to me what I named him."

"But he probably did not assume you would appropriate his own name," said Olympos. "He probably only meant he didn't care if it was Ptolemy or Troilus."

"Troilus?" I gave a hoot of laughter, but it was so painful I stopped abruptly. "Troilus!"

"A fine name, from the great story of Troy," said Olympos, with a smile. "A fitting heroic name. Or how about Achilles, or Ajax?" We all laughed. But then Olympos continued, "I am not sure you have the legal right to use the name Caesar. There are many rules about it in Rome—"

"I am the Queen of Egypt! Sink Rome and her laws! Gaius Julius Caesar is the father of this child, and it shall bear his name!" I shouted.

"Calm yourself," said Iras. "Calm yourself. Of course it shall bear his name. He would not hear of it otherwise."

"You will force him to recognize the child, then," said Olympos. "You will put him to the test with this name." His voice was full of admiration.

He did not understand. What he said was true enough. But I wanted my son to bear the name of his father. It was as simple as that.

"He will not fail me," I said quietly. "He will not fail *him*." I kissed the top of the baby's head. But Olympos had put fear in my heart. I knew that in Rome, a father must *formally* acknowledge his child. Would Caesar do that?

The next few days were days beyond happiness. That simple word cannot begin to convey the joy, the ecstasy, that filled my being. I felt as light as a feather from the wing of a falcon, and it was not just being delivered of the weight and bulk of the baby, but the exhilaration of being still mysteriously united to him. The baby was entirely himself, but he was always and forever part of me, as well. As I held him, and nursed him, I had the overwhelming conviction that I would never be alone again.

I knew, intellectually, that that was not true. We were not one person, and there is no way another person can keep you from that ultimate aloneness that we all fear. Yet it *felt* that way to me; I felt complete at last.

Olympos did not approve of my nursing him. He said it was demeaning, and I should find a wet nurse. I promised to do so in a little while, but for the first few weeks, while I watched and wondered where Caesar was and what he was doing, I needed to hold my son close to me every few hours.

Every day little Caesar—for the people of Alexandria nicknamed him Caesarion, "little Caesar," thus skipping all the legal niceties and going straight to the heart of the matter—changed. His little face stopped glowing fiery red, the wrinkles smoothed away, and his eyes grew rounded and lost that odd, slitted, stretched look of a newborn. Now the game of looking for likenesses could start in earnest.

My features are strong ones. My nose is long and my lips are very full, as full as any of the lips carved on stone statues of the Pharaohs. (Note that I said the Pharaohs, and not their wives, who had dainty faces.) My face is long and thin, and the full mouth helps to offset it, but by itself it is, truthfully—too large. Caesar's features are the opposite; they are all very fine, for a man. In our child, surprisingly, it was the fine features that triumphed over the more prominent ones. Caesarion favored his father, not me. That gave me great happiness.

I decided there must be some way I could celebrate this birth, some way despite Caesar's absence to salute it in an official way. No parades or public festivals; they were too ephemeral. I wanted something substantial, something lasting. I would issue a coin commemorating it.

"No!" said Mardian, when he heard of it. More and more he was becoming my foremost councillor, in spite of his youth. I trusted him, and he had shown very good judgment in every task I had given him so far; his supervision of the rebuilding of Alexandria had been superlative.

"Why not?" I was reclining on a couch in my favorite large room, the one where the sunlight came in on all four sides, and the breezes met and played within the chamber. Silken curtains billowed like a ship's sails, and scented rushes from Lake Gennesareth rustled in their vases. Caesarion lay on a black panther skin in the middle of the floor, his eyes following the whipping movement of the curtains. I had recovered entirely from childbirth, and was bursting with energy. "Why not?" I asked again.

"Would it not seem to be—well, conceited?" he said. "And it would raise more questions. For example, what about your husband, little Ptolemy? Would he be on the coin?"

Little Ptolemy was like another child of mine. He had accepted Caesarion as his little brother. He never made any demands, other than to be allowed a larger sailboat to sail in the inner harbor. I almost forgot about his existence.

"Of course not," I said.

"No Ptolemaic queen has ever issued coinage in her own right, alone," Mardian reminded me. He spent hours researching just such things, and I took his word for it. "Even your exalted ancestor Cleopatra the Second would never have dared."

I popped a large, chilled grape into my mouth and enjoyed the sensation of bursting its skin against my palate. The thin, tingling juice squirted out. "Then perhaps I should put Caesar on it as well?" I asked innocently.

Mardian just shook his head indulgently. He understood my humor. "Oh yes, try that. That should shake them up in Rome." He paused. Unlike Olympos, he knew better than to oppose me when my mind was made up. "What sort of coinage are you considering?"

"Cyprus. I shall mint a coin in Cyprus."

"Oh, you do tempt Rome!" He could not help chuckling. "Caesar's gift of Cyprus was controversial. He just gave away Roman territory. Not a popular thing to do. Of course he covered it up by saying he was forced to conciliate the Alexandrians, since he was hemmed in by hostile forces at the time. But that excuse no longer holds. After all, he won the Alexandrian War. He should have quietly taken Cyprus back. There has been a lot of grumbling about it in Rome."

I always admired Mardian's astounding ability to collect gossip from far-flung places. It was as if he had an outpost in Rome. How did he do it?

"It is the international brotherhood of eunuchs," he once said, and I half believed him. Nothing else could account for it.

"What else are they saying at Rome?" This was delicious.

"That he lost his reason in Egypt, dillydallied when he should have been going about manly Roman tasks like pursuing the last of Pompey's rebels, indulged himself with the effeminate pleasures of the Nile, and so on. It's done wonders for your reputation and created quite a sensation: a woman whom Caesar actually changed his plans for! His veterans made up verses about it, something to the effect that 'Old Caesar wallowed in the mud with the daughter of the Nile, and swelled her banks' . . . I don't, er, remember the rest."

"Of course not," I agreed. I felt my ears grow warm. I've often been thankful that my face does not blush with embarrassment, but only my ears. And they were invisible beneath my hair today. "Now, about the coin. I think it should be bronze. And it will show me nursing Caesarion."

"Like Isis," he said flatly. He understood the significance.

"Yes," I said. "Like Isis and Horus. And Venus and Cupid. Cyprus was, after all, the birthplace of Venus."

"And Venus is Caesar's ancestress."

"Yes."

"How a simple coin can send so many messages!" he exclaimed, nodding in admiration.

I was posing for the coin. One of our Alexandrian artists had come to make the likeness, and I was seated on a backless chair, holding Caesarion. He kept grabbing at my hair, and I kept gently removing the hands. They were fat, soft little things, as smooth as yogurt. A baby's hands give you immense sensual pleasure just to touch; a miracle that soon fades—like tender new leaves, like the mist of early dawn, like all new things that cannot last, but change into something more prosaic as the day goes inexorably on. Caesarion's hands were still precious.

The artist was making a model in clay, and I would have to approve it. I wished I had more conventional beauty. Although I now knew that my features, taken all together, produced a pleasing effect, they looked best when viewed from the front. A profile showed only the size of my nose and lips, not the harmony of the whole. Nonetheless, coin portraits traditionally showed a profile. Oh, for the profile of Alexander!

"Head higher," murmured the artist, and I lifted my chin.

"You have a regal neck," said the artist. "It has a lovely curve."

A pity that necks are not dwelt upon in poetry, I thought. No one ever mentions necks.

"Your hair should show up well on the coin," he said. "Shall I portray the curls?"

"Certainly," I said. They always portrayed Alexander's tousled curls. My own hair was thick and wavy, not unlike Alexander's. But mine was black, whereas his was fair. The advantage to black hair was that you could rinse it with herbs and oils and make it shine like a raven's wing.

"The eyes. Shall I have you looking straight ahead?"

"As you wish."

It was almost impossible to show life in the eyes from the side. And of course you could never indicate color. I had found it curious that Caesar, the Roman, had had dark eyes while mine were a lighter, amber green. Caesarion's had darkened; they would be like his father's. Had I not borne him, I would wonder what I had contributed to Caesarion's heredity.

I sat for what seemed hours. I had to hand Caesarion over to Iras, because he began to squirm and cry. Just when I thought I could bear it no longer, the artist said, "I believe I am finished. Would you care to look?"

There is always a moment of dread in first looking at one's portrait. It is how another perceives you, and you are sure their view must be truer than yours. I got out of the chair—my legs were almost asleep—and came around to look at what he had created.

It was ugly!

Without thinking, I burst out, "Is this what I look like?"

He looked crestfallen. "I—I—"

"This woman looks like an old Hittite axe!" I cried. Stolid, jaw clenched, the matron glared out across the coin. The infant at her breast—was it an infant or a stone globe? It had no features but an abnormally large, round head.

The ridiculous infant made me feel better. I knew that Caesarion looked nothing like that.

"You have to change it!" I said. "I know I am not as beautiful as Aphrodite, but neither do I look like I am sixty years old. I am not the size of the Apis bull! And my child has eyes!"

"I thought—I thought you wanted to stress the dignity of the throne," the artist said.

"I do," I said. "But age and size do not automatically confer greatness. Look at the rotting old hulks of burnt-out warships! Come to think of it, that is what you have made me look like here!"

"Forgive me, forgive me! But I thought, your being a woman—that it would be better—I mean—"

I knew what he meant. For unknown reasons, if one wished to show that a woman was powerful, or intelligent, the way to signify it was to portray her as being physically unattractive. For a man, however, it was the opposite. Alexander's beauty was not felt to detract from his generalship. Nowhere was it hinted that a handsome man could not be a good ruler, or clever, or strong, or brave. In fact, people longed for a resplendent king. But for a woman . . . I shook my head. It was as if beauty in a woman rendered all other traits suspect.

"I know there is a hidden code in all this, and coins must abide by the code," I said wearily. "A young woman who has any physical charms at all is seen as incompatible with queenship. That is the convention. But this is too much!"

"Gracious Majesty, I will change it," he said. "Please allow me to adjust it to your approval."

Mardian and I were looking at the almost-finished product. A facsimile of the coin had been rendered in bronze by another artist, and then a die would be cut. Assuming, of course, that it met with my approval this time.

"Well," said Mardian, trying to suppress a giggle. He failed.

"Have you ever seen anything so—grim?" I asked. The artist had made little change.

"It serves you right," he said. "It is an antidote to your vanity."

"I am not vain!" I believe this is true. I have never dwelt on myself, but I do try to have an honest appraisal of my traits, that is all.

"It was vain of you to think of the coin at all," he insisted.

"It was a political statement, pure and simple."

"It was a political statement, but not pure and simple." He rotated the coin. "You do look formidable. Rome will tremble." He laughed. "They will also wonder what Caesar saw in you."

I sighed. I was anxious to know what had happened to him, how he was faring. Why had he not written me?

"Mardian," I said, trying not to sound plaintive, "have you had any word about his whereabouts?" If anyone knew, Mardian would.

"I have heard that he landed in Antioch, then made his way to Ephesus. I think he is still there."

"What is the date?"

"He was reported to have reached Ephesus in the latter part of Quintilis."

It was now the last day of Quintilis. He had sailed away in early June. Caesarion had been born on June twenty-third, almost exactly the summer solstice. Why had I not received a single message from him?

"Is he going directly to Pontus, then?"

"That is the assumption," said Mardian. "He wants to strike quickly."

"That is what he always does," I said.

He strikes quickly and then moves on, I added to myself. He moves on and never looks back.

Veni, vidi, vici: I came, I saw, I conquered.

Even today, those words have the power to excite my soul. They were the three laconic words Caesar used to describe what happened when he finally met King Pharnaces of Pontus. After traveling hundreds of miles, Caesar pursued the King into his own territory, and then, on the very day of sighting him, joined battle. It lasted only four hours, and ended in the utter defeat of the braggart King. The forces of Pharnaces were flushed with enough bravado to attempt a chariot charge uphill toward Caesar's stronghold. The result was inevitable. Later Caesar reportedly said that it was no wonder that Pompey had been regarded as an invincible general, if such was the caliber of his enemies.

The battle had taken place on the first day of the Roman month of Sextilis, less than two months since he had left Alexandria with his one-quarter legion. Once again his speed and feat had seemed superhuman.

I wish those words, *veni, vidi, vici,* had been written to me, along with a description of the battle, but they were not. They were in a letter addressed to a certain Gaius Matius in Rome, an old confidant of Caesar's. Of course, spies picked them up and echoed them throughout the world. The same spies, as well as Mardian's "international brotherhood of eunuchs," reported that he returned to Rome in September, after redistributing offices and appointments in the troubled territories.

I made my way almost every day to your shrine, O Isis, to give you thanks for his deliverance. My constant apprehension about his safety was difficult to bear. I felt, even then, that the gods were almost mocking him, as if they were preparing him for a sacrifice. We pamper the bulls and pigeons we have selected for the altar, as if we thereby render them more choice. We deck them with garlands and give them the sweetest grass and corn. We shelter them from the heat of the noonday sun and the chill of night. Nothing can touch them. Nothing but their supposed guardians. But you, Isis, alone of the gods, are compassionate. You have known the sorrow of a wife and the joy of motherhood. I knew that you would not turn a deaf ear to my pleas and prayers.

Almost at the same time as Caesar's victory over Pharnaces, the Nile began its annual rise. At the time I took it as a good omen, meaning that both our fortunes were swelling on a great tide upward. It was the New Year of the Egyptian calendar, and all along the riverbanks the festivals began to welcome the first perceptible rise of the water. At Thebes, the sacred boat of Amun-Re was taken in procession by the priests, with thousands of lanterns swaying in the warm night. At Coptos and Memphis, they flung open the gates of the canals to welcome the water, to let it take possession of the land like a man with a woman. This turned into a great festival of love, nights of feasting and marriages, as young men sang:

> Light my bark upon the water,
> And my head is wreathed with flowers,
> Hastening to the temple portals,
> And to many happy hours.
> Great God Ptah, let my beloved
> Come to me with joy tonight,
> That tomorrow's dawn may see her
> Lovelier still with love's delight.
> Memphis! Full of sound and perfume,
> For the gods a dwelling bright.

And his sweetheart would answer:

> My heart is sick with longing
> Till my lover comes to me.
> I shall see him when the waters
> Hurry through the opened ways,
> Give him wreaths for wreaths of flowers,
> Loose my hair for him to praise,
> Happier than Pharaoh's daughters,
> When I lie in his embrace.

I would hear Iras singing this song, and it filled me with longing for Caesar, as I thought of all the lovemaking and night festivals going on up and down the land, while I, only twenty-two years old, remained in the palace alone in my bed, in a room that suddenly seemed stifling.

As the waters continued to rise, everyone rejoiced. During the first two years of my reign there had been insufficient water, causing famine. Now, on this first flood since I had been restored to the throne, a restoration in nature seemed promised as well.

But then the waters kept rising, and rising. They came up into the very precincts of the sacred temples, lapping at the portals of the inmost sanctuaries. They overwhelmed the dikes and basins and flowed out over the desert sands. The mud-brick houses, which were supposedly set a safe distance away, were overtaken and began to disintegrate back into Nile mud.

My engineers at the First Cataract, where the floodwaters initially appeared, sent frantic dispatches. There the Nilometer, the gauge by which the floodwaters were measured, already had a marking higher than any in living memory. And it was "thin" water, not the deep brown that signified fertility. Something was wrong.

Water. That night I sat staring at a beaker full of freshly drawn Nile water from Upper Egypt. It sat innocently on my table, betraying only the slightest hint of color. It was completely unlike its usual self, which at this time of year should be opaque with the life-giving black substance that came down in the flood. Egypt called itself the Black Land, after the black ribbon of rich soil the Nile left behind on its banks each year. Not to have that gift was not to be Egypt. And after two previous years of too little water!

Was there anything to be done? What caused the black soil to enter the river in the first place, and where did it come from? Surprisingly enough, neither Olympos nor Mardian seemed to have any clear idea, or even an opinion.

"It must gush out wherever the source of the Nile is," said Mardian. "And you know no one has ever found that."

"I thought the Nile god Hapi brought it," said Olympos innocently.

"You, who mock all the gods on Olympus and in Hades, give me a disappointing answer," I said.

"I think someone at the Museion might know," said Mardian. "Let us sound the call rousing those most formidable beasts, scholar-scientists."

A soft breeze, scented with jasmine from a nearby walled garden, blew over us. I sighed. I wished I could just give myself to this delicious night, rather than concerning myself with meetings and scientists.

In a window on the second story of a villa overlooking the colonnaded street, I saw a lamp being extinguished, and the glow of the room faded. Someone, one of my subjects, was doing just that. But I, the Queen, must stay awake so he could sleep in peace.

"Tomorrow we will consult with them," I told Mardian and Olympos. And tonight I will lie awake thinking of what I must learn from them, I thought.

My bed, spread with bleached linen sheets, felt soggy to me. There was moisture everywhere. I remembered being told that engineers set out unfired pottery near the Nile and weighed it after a night to see how much water it had absorbed; in this way they predicted the river's rise. If it was true that the Nile gave off a foggy breath, then his exhalation was full of dew now.

No one can stop the Nile, I told myself. All we can do is to move things out of its reach, dig bigger basins to contain the water, and collect manure to spread on the fields that will not get any silt. As for the vermin and the snakes—I must inquire about those snake-people, the Psylli, they say they have magic powers. . . .

Despite the oppressive air and the tangle of heavy sheets, I slept.

I had sent word that a council of scholars and scientists should be assembled at the Museion to help me plan how to combat the threatened disaster. Have I recounted the history of the Museion? It is an academy devoted to the Muses—hence its name—and attached to the Library; they share a common dining room. But in the years since it was founded, it had grown into a beehive of scholars, who were supported by the Ptolemies. We provided for their every need, gave them perfect working quarters—a magnificent Library with manuscripts at their fingertips, lecture halls of polished marble, works of art brought from sites all over the world to inspire them, and laboratories in which to study the phenomena of nature—while asking only one thing in return: that they should put their monumental knowledge at our disposal. We seldom called on them for it, outside of asking them to be royal tutors, and so they had the better part of the bargain. But now I would require their help.

I met with them in the great rotunda, flanked by my advisors and scribes. Ever optimistic, I hoped there would be a great deal of useful material for the scribes to write down. The engineers, historians, geographers, and naturalists were waiting; they clustered around a large potted plant with thick, sole-like leaves, examining something on its trunk. They snapped to attention when we walked in and abandoned the plant.

I felt relief at seeing so many of them, as a sick patient does in seeing a shelf full of medicine bottles and jars. Surely the remedy must be in one of them!

"Good scholars and scientists of the Museion—famed throughout the world—I come to you today in hopes you can help me save Egypt." I paused to let those blunt words soak in. "The report from Upper Egypt is that the river is cresting higher than it ever has, but that life-giving substances are not in it. So we have a double catastrophe: all the damage of a flood combined with the crisis of a famine. I ask you: Is there any known help from science?"

They stared back at me, silently. I saw them shifting their eyes back and forth, watching to see if anyone would speak. Finally a young man stepped forward.

"I am Ibykos of Priene," he said. He had a thin, wavering voice, completely at odds with his compact, overmuscled frame. His arms, shiny like swelling fruit, bulged out of his upper tunic. "I am an engineer. All I can suggest is that we raise the earth—or else lower it—to contain the river. Build dams or dig enormous reservoir basins. Perhaps both."

"And how could we do this in time?" asked another man. "It would require more workmen than built the pyramids! The Nile is hundreds of miles long!"

"Most villages already have irrigation basins. Perhaps each could enlarge the ones they already have. That would not be so prodigious a task," I said. "But as for building a dam—is that possible?"

Another engineer said, "No. The Nile is too wide. We could not stop it up long enough to dam it, and as for diverting it—again, it is too wide. And the current is too strong." He blinked a few times, as if to emphasize his words.

"Very well, then." I believed that exhausted the subject. There was little we could do to hinder the flood itself. "What happens in a flood? What can we expect? Can anyone here tell me?"

A huge mountain of a man stepped forward. "I am Telesikles," he said. "I come from the Euphrates valley, where we often have floods. Indeed, there is a poem about our great flood, the epic of Gilgamesh. The great Utnapishtim had to build a gigantic boat, six stories high, in order to survive. 'As soon as a gleam of dawn shone in the sky, came a black cloud from the foundation of heaven. Inside it the storm god thundered. His rage reached to the heavens, turning all light to darkness. Six days and nights raged the wind, the flood, the cyclone, and devastated the land,' " he intoned.

We all just looked at him. His flesh was shaking as he recited the poetry, as if the wind were blowing over his limbs.

"And in the Hebrew holy books of Moses, there is also a flood, and an ark is built," said another.

"We are not going to build boats or arks for everyone in Egypt," I said. "After all, the flood is not going to cover all the dry land. I am not interested in poetic descriptions of floods, but in what actually happens as a result of a flood. When Noah stepped out of the ark, everything had been destroyed. What will happen to us?"

" 'And all mankind had turned to clay. The ground was flat like a roof,' " Telesikles recited ominously.

"That is absurd!" another man said in a shrill voice. "The Queen has asked us for details, not a lot of poetry. Everyone will not turn to clay, and the ground in Egypt is *already* flat like a roof. Be quiet, you fool!"

"If I may be permitted—" A hawk-nosed man stepped forward, and I saw that he was fairly young. Although his face was creased, his hair was still dark and fairly thick. "I am Alkaios of Athens, an engineer with an interest in history. I have lived here in Egypt long enough to acquaint myself with what happens in the countryside when too much water descends." He looked around, and saw that no one was going to challenge him. "Dangerously high floods are rare, but memory has recorded them. In the first place, what happens when the tide comes in along the seashore?"

No one answered.

"Come, come. Have you never walked along a beach? Never been in Judaea? What a bunch of parochials! Well, the tide comes in and destroys everything built of sand. All the little houses children construct—they're washed away. Children aren't the only ones who build of sand. What are the Egyptian villages made of? Sun-dried brick. What happens when brick gets wet?" He gestured toward a tub of water that was standing near the mysterious plant, waiting for his demonstration. Then he tossed a mud brick into it, sending a spray of water out onto the floor. "Watch this. In an hour or two it will revert to mud."

The other scholars drew up the hems of their gowns. "Must you be so vehement?" one of them asked.

"I wish to make a point," he said. "Thus the buildings will collapse. No great loss or expense, if in advance new ones are built out of reach of the floodwaters. Unlike the floods of poetry, this one comes gradually. There is time to prepare." He paced a little before whirling around and announcing, "Standing water, however, is quite different from running water."

This fellow was quite a showman, I thought. But what he was saying needed no flourishes.

"It breeds insects, frogs, and scum. It stinks. Diseases rise up out of it. It seeps into things out of its reach as it creeps underground. Stored grain, unless it is kept some distance away, will become wet and moldy. Then mice will multiply like mad. There will be a plague of mice!" His voice rose like a thunderclap.

"Calm yourself," said Olympos. "They are not scurrying beneath your feet."

"And what will come then?" Telesikles continued, ignoring the gibe. "Snakes! A plague of serpents!" He grabbed an old man's arm and pulled him out of the crowd of scholars. "Tell them, Aischines! Tell them about the serpents!"

The old man had skin like ancient papyrus: it was all lined and flaking and seemed brittle. His voice was likewise fragile and brittle. "The snakes! The snakes!" he muttered. "The storehouse of venomous serpents will open and pour forth her treasures!" He blinked and looked around, clearly measuring his audience. It must have been a well-prepared recital. "We live in a part of the world the deadliest of serpents calls home," he whispered. "Is not the asp the symbol of Egypt? The sacred snake, whose spread hood hovers over the brow of every Pharaoh, protecting him? His bite renders the Pharaoh immortal, should he choose that way of death, and gives him the blessing of Amun-Re. The asp!" Now his very voice seemed like the dry sifting of leaves in a sepulcher. "It induces sleep with its concentrated poison. Death is swift. In sudden darkness its victim departs to join the dead, when bitten by this serpent of the Nile."

He suddenly whirled around and stabbed his scrawny finger in another direction. "But the Seps! The horror of its bite! For its poison dissolves the very bones within the body. A person melts! And when the body is burned on a funeral pyre, no bones can be found! Other poisons remove life, but the Seps removes the body as well."

Olympos rolled his eyes in disbelief, but Mardian's were growing large in fascination. I did not know what to think. Was any of this true?

"Then there's the Prester snake," the old man said, now lowering his voice almost to a whisper. Everyone strained forward to hear it. "It causes such extreme swelling that a man will blow up to giant size, so that his features are buried in the shapeless mass. He cannot even be put in a tomb, because the body just keeps growing and growing."

Olympos gave a great hoot of laughter, and so did many others. But the laughter was nervous.

The speaker held up his hand and glared at them. "Do you laugh? But you have never seen a victim. Had you, there would be no laughter, I assure you. I suppose you haven't seen a man bitten by a Haemorrhois, either? It turns a person into one big wound—blood gushes everywhere. His very tears are blood! His sweat is blood! And what about the Dipsas? Its venom drinks up the moisture of the body and turns a man's innards into a scorching desert! It is a thirsty poison! A victim will cut open his own veins to drink his own blood!"

"This is most informative," I said, cutting off his recitation. "But we already know that men die of poisonous snakebites. Not all the snakes that will arise to eat the mice are poisonous. In fact, the snakes do us a favor by eating the mice. It is the mice that cause us to lose our food, not the snakes."

"Yes, snakes are not our enemies," said Mardian, finding his voice at last. "They also seldom attack unless they are threatened. As a boy, I kept snakes and I know their ways. I think we need not worry about the snakes."

"The mice and rats are a different matter," I said. "Still, should the proliferation of the vermin cause villagers to be bitten by a poisonous snake, is there not a group of snake-handlers that can help them?"

"You refer to the Psylli of Marmarica," said the old man, haughtily. He had not appreciated having his speech interrupted, and now he made a show of his hurt feelings. "They are immune to the poison of snakes. I *was* going to tell you that they can render a site harmless by incantation to drive away the serpents, and by a medicated fire that will guard the borders. And if anyone is bitten, their saliva can counteract the poison in the wound, and they can also suck it out. So skilled are they that by the taste alone they can detect which type of serpent bit the victim! I *was* going to tell you where to find the Psylli, but now, since you think you are in no danger from the snakes . . ." He shrugged majestically and stepped back into the group of scientists.

"We would welcome the information," I said, to soothe him. "Pray, you must tell us. But it seems to me that we must first secure our food supply. The grain remaining from last year's harvest must be transported to new storehouses. These must be built hurriedly. How difficult will this be? Can anyone estimate?"

"I have anticipated this question," said a voice from the back. A Nubian stepped forward. "I have already done the calculations."

"Very well. Tell us."

"The storehouses are not even a quarter full at this time of year. Most of the grain has already been consumed or shipped abroad. I estimate there are around a thousand storehouses up and down the Nile. But we would have to build only two hundred fifty full-sized ones to accommodate all the grain left. And they would not have to be well built. Any sort of structure would serve, as long as it is dry and enclosed." He had a deep, sonorous voice that made his figures sound authoritative.

"How long would it take?"

"Not long," he said. "It takes only a few days for mud bricks to dry, and then the building could proceed quickly."

"Is it possible to estimate how far out the floodwaters will spread? We want to build the emergency warehouses at a safe site, but no farther away than necessary. Transporting all that grain will be difficult enough," I said.

"Your Majesty, I am sorry to say I don't think there is very much grain," he said. "Therefore transporting it will not take long."

And should we need to import grain, was there any place to buy it? It was Egypt that fed the world, not vice versa. Some could be procured from Sicily or Numidia. But would it be enough?

"We will have to set up food distribution centers, and appoint overseers," I said. "We must ration the remaining grain. I shall appoint officers to do so in each district. And I will personally visit each of the centers."

Suddenly I felt very tired. The task before me, and all Egypt, was a formidable one. "I thank you all for your help. I appreciate your preparing the information so carefully and thoughtfully," I said. I glanced over at the water tub. "Pray, show us what has happened to the brick," I requested.

With a theatrical gesture, Telesikles stepped forward. "Behold!" he said, dragging an empty tub. He then bent down and picked up the other one, pouring its dark contents out into the waiting receptacle. Once all the water was gone, nothing remained on the bottom but a thick layer of pure brown mud.

"Your dwellings and storehouses!" he said. "See their ruin!"

18

The sun was sinking. I sat waiting by the side of the sacred lake of an Upper Egyptian temple—a lake that tonight would be swallowed up by the Nile, an unwilling offering to the angry god. Perhaps that would appease him.

My legs were tucked up under me as I hunched on the stone bench that overlooked the lake. Water was ankle-deep around the base of it. That meant that no officials, no priests, no servants or advisors were likely to stand there, looking over my shoulder. I was alone—blessedly, wonderfully alone. It felt like purest balm rubbed over my body, massaged into my skin. *Alone. Alone. Alone.*

For the past few weeks I had been surrounded by people at all times. My visitations up and down the river meant that I was always a guest in someone's home, always being officially welcomed with some ceremony or other, always having to make speeches or read reports or confer gifts, and never betraying any weakness, boredom, or fatigue. In its own way, it was worse than war for wearing me down. The truth is, I found it a trial to be pleasant all the time. Perhaps I am not naturally a pleasant person!

No, I think it is more that I need a certain amount of privacy every day—a few minutes completely alone—in the same way I need food or sleep. Just as everyone's need for food and sleep varies, so, apparently, does everyone's need for privacy. I have noticed that some people seem never to have an instant to themselves, and their humor is none the worse for it. I envy those people. But I am not one of them.

Tonight I would swim in a sacred lake. It was something I had always wanted to do, but did not think would ever be possible, for doing so would profane the waters. But tonight the Nile was going to taint it, and before this lake could ever be used again for religious purposes, it would have to be reconsecrated.

The flat, rectangular surface of the lake gave back the fading colors of the sky. It lay tranquil in the twilight, waiting serenely, never suspecting that it was about to be violated. Its waters were supposed to be carried away only by priests in silver buckets, to be used for purifying the temple and the priests themselves, and only a miniature barque of the god was allowed to sail upon it in the mystery plays. Now I would enter it, swim in its forbidden waters.

Along with privacy, I had longed for a bathe during this whole journey. In the palace we had pools exclusively for swimming, but once I left Alexandria there was no such thing to be found. In each district I was usually a guest of the head official. His house was invariably a fine structure of whitewashed mud brick, with an enclosed walled garden and an ornamental fish pond, bordered with palms and acadias. It provided a cool, pleasant place to sit in the evenings, but the fish would have been startled indeed had a person suddenly joined them.

Children swim for fun, but adults generally do not—most likely because of few opportunities. In Rome I was told—and later saw for myself—that going to the baths was an important part of the day. But their type of bath was neither pure sport—as the Greeks would have—nor pure diversion, as children would have. The Romans managed to turn baths, like everything else, into a hotbed of political intrigue and gossip.

But enough about the Romans. Why am I letting them intrude on my memories of that dusk in Upper Egypt? I remember waiting, silently, for the evening star to come out. When I saw it, I rose from the bench and walked over to the edge of the lake. My bare feet made ripples as I waded through the encroaching flood. About ten feet remained before river and lake would meet.

I made my way over to the flight of steps descending into the water, where the priests in their vestments bend to fill their sacramental vessels. I stood and looked down, at the water so dark and unknown. I had no idea how deep the waters were. I assumed they would be well over my head, but I had long since lost my fear of water.

One foot in, then the next. The water was warm, as it soaked up the sun all day long. Now it was hard to tell just where the air ended and the water began, so nearly alike were they in temperature. The hem of my gown floated out around my legs, white and delicate, like the sacred water lily. I took another step down; now the water was at my knees. Ripples spread out over the wide surface of the lake, smoothly reaching for the far corners. They made no sound.

I moved farther down the steps, until the warm waters were lapping at my shoulders, soothing them like the gentle touch of Charmian. How monumentally calm it felt. I closed my eyes and breathed deeply. Tomorrow, tomorrow I would think about the flood and the people and taxation and relief for the oppressed. But now I need think of nothing, nothing, nothing. . . .

I pushed away from the steps and hung suspended in the water. It was deep; I pointed my toes and still could feel nothing beneath them, not even the hint of a bottom. Slowly I began to move my arms, to swim languidly and keep myself afloat. I had no desire to do anything other than float, drift, give myself up to the stillness.

The sky had darkened; one by one the stars were coming out. In a few moments I would not be able to see the edge of the lake, or be able to tell how near I was to the side. I could still see the faint trace of white where my wet gown waved around me, but soon even that would be gone. No one could reach me, no one could see me, and no one would even know I was there.

I should make for safety while I could still see my way, but still I lingered in the warm water, turning slowly, feeling weightless. Weightless, that was what I wanted to be. I was tired of the weight of the kingdom, tired of carrying what felt like the load of ten men. I had thought to help Caesar carry the burden of the world. *It is too much for one man*, I had said to myself. *Let me help you carry it.* What a fool I had been! I could barely carry Egypt, and I offer to help shoulder Caesar's world as well?

But you are only twenty-two, came the voice from inside my head. And Egypt is not just any country, but one of the largest in the world, and still the richest. And the gods have not been kind to Egypt since you came to the throne; they have sent famine and now a flood. And there is the aftermath of war. . . .

Silence, I told that voice. The strong look for more strength, the weak for excuses. The truth is that any country is more difficult to rule than it would first appear. Even a small village has its problems. Nothing is easy.

Inside the nearby temple, I saw a flicker of light. Torches were being lit, and reflections of fire danced on the water. The thick sandstone columns seemed to glow. I saw the outline of black figures moving between columns, and even from this distance could smell the sweet-burnt smell of camphor incense. The priests were preparing the statue of the god in his shiny black stone sanctuary for the night.

I could also hear a faint grunting and wheezing coming from some distance away. The sacred crocodiles! Their pond lay on the far side of the temple, with strong fences around it—if I remembered correctly. But when the Nile rose higher—might not the crocodiles swim free? It would seem a blessing for them, and they would doubtless praise the Nile for his kindness.

I swam silently toward the far corner of the lake, making for the other set of steps. I bumped up against them and sat on one that allowed me to remain nearly all submerged. Now that I had found my way to safety, I had no desire to quit the waters entirely. I could stay there as long as I liked.

It was thoroughly dark by the time I finally climbed the stairs, water streaming from me as from a sea god's daughter. Now the air felt strange to be so light and cold; water had come to seem natural.

Yes, it was cold out here. I shivered as I remembered I had a long walk back to the town, and I had not even brought a mantle. During the day in Upper Egypt it is so hot you cannot believe you will not always be comfortable in the sheerest linen, and so it is easy to forget to bring a covering.

Yet I was glad to feel the cold, to learn what my subjects who cannot afford a mantle must feel. I have been told it is common to share a mantle, one staying at home in bed while the other goes out. What must that be like? And Egypt is the richest country in the world! They say the poor in Rome are indescribable in their misery.

But I'll not think of Rome now, I told myself sternly. No. Not now. It is far away, and it may come about that I shall never see it.

There now remained only a small strip of dry path between the river and the sacred lake; while I had swum, the river had silently risen. I splashed through it, kicking up waves and spray. I felt like a child again, playing in forbidden places, jumping in puddles, not thinking about Rome or diplomatic dispatches.

When I reached the village administrator's house, my idyll came to an end. They were all waiting for me: Senenmut, the secretary; Ipuy, the district official; and even Mereruka, the governor of the bureaucratic jurisdiction. The walled house, the grandest in the village, was nonetheless barely big enough for all of them to sit in the garden comfortably, where they were playing a board game called "snake" by the light of a smoky lamp. They all leapt up when I entered, and Mereruka sputtered, "A covering! A covering for the Queen!" Then he clucked, "What has happened? Did you have an accident in the Nile?" Clearly he was terrified that I might perish within the boundaries of his jurisdiction, and punishment would follow swiftly.

I shook my hair, still wet. "No." Should I tell them? "I have been swimming. It was delightful—I found all my cares were borne away on the water."

"In the dark?" cried Senenmut. "With the crocodiles?"

"Not with the crocodiles," I assured him. "They are still behind their fences, although I heard them thrashing about."

"Where, then?" demanded Mereruka.

"In a secret place," I replied, in my most imperious tone. "Now, my good ministers, what have you been discussing here in the dark?" It was my turn to interrogate them.

"A little of this, a little of that," Ipuy replied.

"In other words, a mixture of gossip and business," I said.

Mereruka smiled. "Is there any business without gossip?" I liked him, this broad-faced man from Upper Egypt. I could not imagine that he would ever be tempted to leave this place of his birth; his family had probably lived here since the time of Ramses II.

"No," I admitted. "Business is just a reflection of a man's personality, and his personality is what lends itself to gossip. We talk about a man's over-fondness for wine, about his fight with his brother, not about the way he keeps his ledger books."

"Speaking of wine . . ." Mereruka nodded to the servant to bring a cup for me. I could make out the blue-green glazed goblet in the jumping light of the torches, and the tall young man holding it.

I reached out and took it. The cup was cool in my hand. There was some lovely workmanship in the pottery of this area. How unusual it was for me to be sitting among what felt like friends, to have someone say, "Speaking of wine . . ." instead of the usual formulas we use at court. They did not know the prescribed phrases and rituals—thanks be to all the gods!

"Tomorrow we must begin the evacuation," I said. I must admit I hated to spoil the carefree mood, as we sat around the garden pool, with the shadows of fish moving in the shallow water. I could smell the lush fragrance of the lotus in the pond, and overhead the palms were rustling tenderly. Yet I could also hear a chorus of frogs, calling to tell us the river was almost here.

"Have all the arrangements been made?"

"Yes," said Ipuy. "And the mud bricks for building the new dwellings and storehouses are all dry now. The livestock has been moved already. We have laid out a road that will serve well enough to pass the goods along. I am afraid that the only safe place to build will be on actual sand."

"As for the granary . . ." Mereruka let his voice trail off. "When it runs out . . ."

"We have, of course, guards to prevent people from stealing it during the transport," said Ipuy quickly. "But even with rationing, it will not last more than three months."

"The crown will procure the necessary supplies," I assured them. I would import it from anywhere I could find it—paying exorbitant prices, no doubt. I would have to take the money from the fifty-percent import tax on olive oil. If that was not enough, then I would have to use the thirty-three-percent tax the government received from figs and wine. That would severely drain the royal treasury. But I could not turn my back on them, saying, "Starve, then. I know you are doing it to get out of paying your grain taxes." Some Pharaohs and Ptolemies might have done that, but I could not.

What would Caesar think of my decision? In Rome they were more accustomed to supporting the poor; thousands of people received free grain.

What matter, what he would think? I must do what I must do.

Upstairs, in what served as the royal bedroom—vacated by Mereruka—I made ready for bed. A coolness pervaded the quarters—a vent on the roof served to capture the north wind and funnel it into the room. The bed was low, and made of woven reeds. I would lie on my back, my neck resting on a carved wooden headrest. Pillows were unknown here; perhaps they became too inviting to vermin in these villages. At least a headrest was clean and cool.

At the beginning of the journey I had wondered if I could ever sleep this way, but now I had become accustomed to them. They even seemed to induce odd dreams, as if spirits could enter more easily into my head as it hung suspended above the flat surface of the bed.

I peeled off my wet gown and draped it over a stubby little peg on the wall. It would dry swiftly during the night. I changed it for a sleeping garment of the sheerest material Egypt afforded—silk that had had its threads stretched. It was like wearing a mist. The blind woman had presented it to me—her finest work, before losing her sight. That sight had not returned, and I had found work for her ears and her good practical sense instead: she settled disagreements among the servants, hearing complaints from both sides. I wished there were more I could have done for her, I thought, marveling at her skill in fashioning the garment.

I lay down and put my neck on the slightly curved headrest, pointing my feet toward the dark corner of the room. I felt as if I were lying on a sacrificial couch, waiting to be received or rejected by . . . what god? An angry monster, like Molech of the Ammonites, or a lover like Cupid? I shivered a little.

Tomorrow this village would begin its move to higher ground, and my ceremonial part in it would be done. Then I would go on to another village, and then another . . . all up and down along the Nile. Then back to Alexandria, to news of the wider world.

Here it is so easy to forget it even exists, I thought. Families like Ipuy's have seen the Pharaohs, the Nubians, the Persians come and go, and it probably made no difference to them who wore the crown of Upper and Lower Egypt. The rest of the world—Assyria, Babylon, Greece—was as meaningless to them as an old woman's tale.

I felt a wave of envy pass over me in imagining it. They had existed in a warm green bosom, protected from any intrusion. There must have been a time when my mother provided a similar enclosed little world for me, where everything flowed placidly and predictably. But the most telling thing was that I had no memory of it. It had not lasted long.

Odd as it sounds for me even to recount, I felt a great longing at that very moment to see her once more, to talk to her, to touch her hands. Why then? I cannot explain it; I can only wonder that the yearning swept over me while I was lying alone in an upper room in the night in a remote village in the heart of Egypt, some nineteen years after I had last been held in her arms.

In the fuzzy golden light of the early morning we saw that the line of sticks that had been planted at the edge of the river was now barely visible; the Nile had widened another five or six feet. It was time to seek higher ground. All was in readiness. The past faded for me in the morning light, and my memories and lost desires dissolved into a haze swallowed up in the needs of the present.

I was upon the river for almost two months. We went as far up as Aswan, in some ways retracing my journey with Caesar. From the deck of my boat I saw the temple where his features had been carved onto the shoulders of Amun; and when we arrived at the First Cataract I could glimpse the Temple of Isis where we had exchanged our vows—of what, I am not sure. But I did not go into the temple. Forgive me, Isis. At that time I had the thought that I would never go into it again, never stand in that place again, without him beside me. I imagined he would be returning to Egypt many times.

Yes, I imagined many things, dreamed many things—which have all been denied me. But then I believed that if you wanted something badly enough, you could will it—if the gods allowed.

Alexandria again. How white she looked from afar! How huge! How populous! How gleaming, set against the aquamarine waves of the Mediterranean—so utterly different from the brown and green of the Nile villages. My Alexandria!

The palace. Or rather, the palace grounds, with all the many palaces and temples and parade fields . . . it seemed an abode of the gods, as if no mere people could live there. I had seen how ordinary people lived, with their whitewashed mud-brick houses, their little walled gardens, their tiny ornamental pools. I suddenly felt like an explorer in a strange realm as I entered into my own palace, my own apartments. The halls, how long and polished . . . the doors, taller than even a giraffe would need to pass through them . . . and then, as always happens, it became familiar again and I could no longer see it through the eyes of a stranger. Why, there was the same old ebony cosmetic chest, with its ivory geese inset near the handle, but in seeing it I was also seeing all the other times I had seen it, and so it was part of myself. . . .

I shook my head to clear it. Home again, that was all it was; home seeming alien for a moment. I wondered how long one would have to be away before it would never seem like home again. Ten years? Twenty?

There was a letter from Caesar, written while he was in Rome. It had taken almost two months to arrive. It was short, and impersonal, like his *Commentaries*. I could expect no love letters from him, nothing on paper to brood over or cherish. "Greetings to the most exalted Majesty Queen Cleopatra of Egypt," it said. "I am pleased to receive news of your son's birth." My son's— not *our* son's! "May he live and prosper and have a reign of blessed memory." Did that mean he assured the continuance of the Egyptian throne? That Rome would guarantee our independence? "May his name be great in the annals of your history." His name! Did Caesar know about his name? This letter had perhaps been written before mine, announcing and explaining it, had reached Rome. "I find myself beset with problems here in Rome to be taken in hand. I allow myself only a few days in order to do so, for I am bound to set sail for Carthage to carry on the last battle against the rebel forces of Pompey. They have gathered in North Africa and I must pursue them." How like him not to reveal any of his strategy. The gods could only guess how many eyes had read these words before they reached mine. "When all is done, I will send for you, and I pray your duties in Egypt will yet permit you to leave for a little while and come to Rome. Your—Gaius Julius Caesar."

My duties! If only he knew how demanding they had been, and were not over yet. He would send for me to come to Rome—"for a little while." Did he say that to reassure me that he would not demand I leave my own duties for him? He recognized that I was not simply a woman free to leave. Or was he warning me that his own life in Rome was so demanding that he had little time to spare, that his behavior in Egypt was never to be repeated? And he had signed it "your" Caesar. Let spies see it and murmur!

I was content. All would be well. It would not have been wise for him to say more, and at this time there was nothing more he could have said. We both had battles yet to fight, and much that needed repair in our homelands.

I stood in one of the great government warehouses on the docks. It was a huge building, almost as big as a temple. Row upon row of amphorae—fat, rounded ones that contained olive oil—lay in their straw beds. They looked like a gathering of especially short, affluent citizens, and that was just what they were. Each jar, imported from Italy, Greece, or Bithynia, swelled the coffers of my financial office. Merchants were required to pay a fifty-percent tax on imported olive oil. Since Egypt did not grow enough olives, that meant much of it was imported. And Egypt ran on olive oil. It was what everyone used to fuel lamps, and what we used in cooking. There were other oils—castor and sesame, croton, linseed, safflower, and oil of bitter apple—but they were of limited use, and none could compare to olive oil.

This collection of amphorae represented enough money to aid in the relief of ten flooded villages. I would have to multiply it by hundreds. But so be it.

"Good Majesty," said the official in charge of the warehouse, "I trust you see how well I have provided for storage. It is always cool in here, thanks to the high roof and the vents, which let the sea breezes circulate at all times. I have never had an amphora turn rancid on me! Unless it was improperly sealed, of course. Never liked the ones with sheep's fat and clay in the stoppers."

"I require your books as to the duties collected on these shipments," I said. "I am most impressed with the order and tidiness here."

"The owner sees to that," he said. "He is most diligent. I think if even one mouse were caught in here . . ." He winced. "That is why we have so many cats." He gestured up toward the sacks of grain stored on the other side. It was only then that I saw all the cats, perched like statues of Bast everywhere.

Mice. Yesterday's dispatch had reported the beginning of a plague of mice in Upper Egypt. Yes, relief would be needed. The tax money must be surrendered.

I dreaded the bookkeeping. I have a good head for mathematics, and enjoy playing with figures—up to a point. But I was in sore need of a minister of finances. Mardian could not serve as both chief minister and financial official.

"Who is the owner?" I asked. He must be a maniac for organization.

"Epaphroditus, of the Delta section of the city," he said.

"The Delta? He is a Jew, then?"

"Yes. His Hebrew name is Hezekiah."

"How is his ability to keep figures and accounts?"

"It is outstanding, Your Majesty. He can straighten out the most tangled records. And I have never known him to make a mistake in his additions and subtractions. He is scrupulously honest. He makes sure his merchants scrub out their scales at the beginning and end of each day. And he issues the weights himself, so there can be no replacements. Once, when he found a shipmaster cheating on his inventory of tin bars, he delivered him right up to the elders for trial. Since their god, Yahweh, says cheating with weights and measures is an abomination to him, you can guess what happened to that shipmaster. There have been no false inventories since."

"If I wished to send for this—Hezekiah—?"

"First, you would not be allowed to address him as Hezekiah. Gentiles must use his Greek name."

I left determined to interview this Epaphroditus. Perhaps his Yahweh would have provided me with just the person I was seeking to fill the post of financial minister. When we are ready, the gods send what we need.

Hezekiah—that is, Epaphroditus—pronounced himself willing to meet with me. He was very busy, he said, but perhaps could spare an hour in midday just before the upcoming celebration of the dying of Adonis.

Was he being facetious? The Jews held all such festivals in either pious horror or sophisticated ridicule, depending on whether they themselves were pious or sophisticated. And his haughty reply indicated that he was one of the Jews who disliked Ptolemaic rule, even though the Jews as a group had helped Caesar in the recent Alexandrian War. I determined to pay this no heed. It was the *man* I was interested in interviewing, not his beliefs and prejudices.

When he arrived—punctually—at the appointed hour, I was shocked to see what was probably the handsomest man I had ever beheld, outside of statues and works of art, stride into the room. What had I expected? I suppose a molelike creature who spent all his hours peering at weights, inspecting measuring pans, and scrutinizing the ledger books. Maybe he did all these things. But he still had riveting blue eyes, as blue as the waters surrounding the harbor rocks, as clear as the purest sunlit shallows. His lionlike mane of hair, black and shiny, framed his face like a classic portrait of Alexander. Ruby-red robes made the entire picture arresting.

I just stared at him. "I thought you would be old!" I blurted out.

"I am forty-five," he replied, his Greek perfect and seemingly from Athens itself. "Perhaps that is old to you, since you are only twenty-two ... most gracious Majesty," he added carelessly.

He did not look forty-five. "Epaphroditus," I said, "is your name? How did you come by it?"

He looked amused. "My mother gave it to me, Your Majesty. I fear she had read too many poems and books. It means 'lovely.' "

I certainly was not going to make the obvious comment. He probably had gone through life enduring it. "And what does Hezekiah mean?" I asked. "You should know that I speak Hebrew," I added.

"Oh, do you prefer to conduct our business in Hebrew?" he asked. I had to look in his eyes to see that he was teasing; his voice had not betrayed it. "Hezekiah means 'strength of God.' "

"No, I do not care to hold our discussion in Hebrew," I said. "Mine is good enough for following diplomatic conversations and set speech formulas, but, as you undoubtedly know, your Greek is perfect."

"They said you knew Hebrew," he said. "I was surprised. Why did you learn it?"

"I like studying languages. I seem to be gifted in them. And, as a queen, I find it a great advantage to be able to forgo translators as much as possible."

"A wise decision. People always interject their own emphasis and select words that may reflect their own leanings." He paused. "For example, if I had said 'betray' their own leanings, rather than 'reflect,' it would give a different shade to the words."

"Just so. Now, Epaphroditus—"

I went on to explain my needs. I would require help right away; before relief measures could be begun, the records would all have to be in order.

"That is a full-time job, Your Majesty," he answered with no hesitation. "I already have one. Several, in fact."

"Could you not take this temporarily? This is an emergency!"

"What, on an hour's notice? Do you have any idea of my responsibilities? The harbor would have to shut down if I suddenly abandoned my post. Then what would happen to your revenues? Find someone else."

"Please! Help us, even just to review the books. I will find someone else to do the rest."

All during this conversation, he had remained standing. His robes fell in straight folds down to his feet, which were clad in expensive gazelle-hide shoes. He was so perfectly contained, so still.

"And no," I continued. "I certainly do not expect you to take it from this hour forward. But I want the best person in the kingdom to direct one of its most important jobs. It never fails to grieve me—I would say 'amuse' if it were not so vital—that subjects want their rulers to be wise, humane, and honest, but then wish the most incompetent and stupid ministers on them! They complain all the time that their ruler surrounds himself with second-rate people, but if a first-rate person is tapped, he hurriedly makes an excuse and runs back to his family business. You have no one but yourselves to blame, if your ruler's ministers are inferior."

"I am not the only man in the kingdom who can run a business effectively," he said stubbornly. "And perhaps an Alexandrian is not the man to oversee affairs for all of Egypt."

"Money is money!" I said. "A drachma is a drachma, whether in Alexandria or Aswan!" The truth was, he did not want to be connected to my government. "It is not that you are an Alexandrian, but that you and your people disapprove of my rule. I know you dislike me!"

For the first time he betrayed an emotion besides detachment. "No, *I* do not dislike you. It is true, some of the Jews feel slighted that they were excluded from special decrees that favored the Greeks. But certainly *Caesar*"—he paused to give the name emphasis—"was generous to those he perceived to be his friends in his hour of need."

"And so was I! And this is another hour of need. Need is not just battles between men, but also battles between men and nature."

"We were pleased to help Caesar."

Why did he keep repeating that? His real question must be, *Who will be our true ruler, you or Caesar?* Obviously they preferred Caesar!

"In helping me, you are showing respect for him."

He shook his head almost imperceptibly. "How so?"

"Because Caesar himself fought a war to keep me on the throne! It was his wish that I be Queen!"

"And you are the mother of his child."

How bold of him to say it so bluntly!

"Yes. And that son will follow me as Egypt's ruler. Of course Caesar will be pleased if you help me . . . and his son."

"Have the books brought to my warehouse," he said abruptly, like a merchant whose price has been met, and who now does not wish to prolong the bargaining in case you change your mind. "I will look at them. I cannot promise to have them back by tomorrow."

I tried to keep my expression from changing. Tomorrow! I was hoping for seven to ten days. No one would have thought tomorrow possible! Except Caesar . . . and this Epaphroditus, beauty-of-Aphrodite-in-a-man . . . I *would* be served by the best, after all. I need not compromise. The only drawback is that such people spoil you for anyone else, anyone whose talents are merely human.

"I thank you," I said. "The books will be there at the hour you request."

As he left the room, his red robe shimmering in the noonday sun, I wondered how he and Mardian would find working together.

Winter came, with its lashing gales of seawater and storms. I celebrated my twenty-third birthday quietly; far more important to me was Caesarion's six-month birthday on the same day. I had missed him so when we were separated; now I let myself watch him as he crept slowly off his mat and onto the marble floor of my apartments. I wondered what was so fascinating about one's own baby that a mother can even watch him sleeping and enjoy the experience—but it is true.

The Nile flood had begun ebbing, but the damage was even greater than we had predicted. Thanks to our preparations, and the organized manner of carrying out our plans, the people had fared as well as could be hoped for. The swollen Canopic branch of the Nile near us had flooded Canopus, and the notorious pleasure gardens and drinking pavilions had floated away, perhaps with their patrons in them. They did not need any help to rebuild their bowers of indulgence; somehow that is always the last place deserted and the first place rebuilt.

All was calm; all was in order.

Then came the report. Mardian had brought it to me, one late winter's morning as I sat watching Caesarion unwinding a large ball of wool, pushing it slowly across the floor, inching after it to examine it solemnly at each roll.

As always, I was pleased to see Mardian. There are some people whose nature has a mysterious effect on one's own, and in their presence you find your mood always bordering on the joyful. Such was Mardian, with his big square face, his ever-ready quips and penetrating comments.

"A report," he said, handing it to me. He then took his seat on a large cushion and made a point of turning his entire attention to Caesarion.

It was exactly what I had longed for, waiting anxiously. My agents in Rome had managed to acquire the news of Caesar's campaign in North Africa, where he still was.

Caesar had crossed over safely, taking only six legions—five of them brand-new recruits—and two thousand horse. Then—evil omens!—he was driven northward by a storm and did not land where he wished, nor with most of his men. And upon reaching the shore, he had stumbled and fallen facedown on the beach.

I heard myself gasp. Mardian looked up with a jerk.

But then, the report went on, he grasped a fistful of sand and cried, "I hold thee, Africa!" He had never been one to heed omens, but he knew others did.

The enemy forces—ten legions strong!—were commanded by Metellus Scipio, and the people had a superstition that a Scipio could never suffer misfortune in Africa, because Scipio Africanus had decisively beaten Hannibal there. Another thing against Caesar. But he had countered it by appointing a Scipio in his own army, an undistinguished fellow of that same family.

All the old partisans of Pompey were gathered together to make their last stand: the two sons of Pompey, Gnaeus and Sextus, as well as the stern, fanatic Republican Cato. Scipio had taken the shocking step of allying himself—actually placing himself under the command of—Juba, the king of Numidia. A Roman serving under a foreign king was considered beyond the pale. Juba contributed war elephants to the contest, as well as cavalry and four legions. The total cavalry at the rebels' command was fifteen thousand.

Because his crossing in winter was unexpected, the enemy had let Caesar make his landing with no interference. But he soon found himself in a position where simply securing enough food was a problem. Despite being so far outnumbered, his instinct was to try to force a battle as soon as possible—

Again I heard my sharp intake of breath, and Mardian looked up at me. Why did he keep staring at me like that, as if waiting for me to get to the horrible part?

"Is he dead?" I burst out. "I cannot bear to sit here and read of all the things leading up to it, and have you waiting to see me read it!"

"No, my lady, he is not dead," Mardian assured me. "Nor even wounded."

"Then, pray, stop looking at me so anxiously!" I returned to the report.

Cato warned the army of Pompey to avoid an immediate battle, since they could only grow stronger in time, having all the food depots and shipping routes under their control. Caesar's horses were already being fed seaweed rinsed in fresh water. Caesar launched a food-foraging expedition that was ambushed by the enemy forces, and only by using a classic military tactic, in which alternate lines of cohorts turned each way so all sides were covered, were they able to escape under cover of darkness back to their camp. The engagement had been a setback—Caesar's first since Dyrrhachium with Pompey.

And there they sat, waiting for Caesar's other legions to join them, dug in at Ruspina, on a plateau overlooking the sea.

"So," I said. "He waits. Nothing has been decided."

"No," said Mardian. "Nothing has been decided."

There were only a few more lines. They said that Caesar had acquired Bocchus and Bogud, the two kings of Mauretania, as African allies to counter Juba. They said he was castigating Scipio publicly for groveling and serving under an African king, Juba, taking orders from him and being fearful of wearing his purple Roman general's cloak in Juba's presence. Scipio had countered by saying that Caesar had gone to bed with Eunoe, Bogud's wife, cuckolding his own ally on the field.

"What?" I cried. Again, Mardian jerked his head up. Now I knew why he had been watching. "Is this true? Is this true about Caesar and Eunoe?" My voice was rising. Control yourself, I told myself.

"I—I—" he stammered.

"I know you can find out! You and your spy system!"

"I—I don't know for certain, but my initial information says that yes, it is true."

Caesarion batted the wool ball just then, and it rolled under a table. He crept after it determinedly. The pain I felt just in looking at him I can never describe.

"Another queen," I finally said. "I see he has acquired a taste for the beds of queens." I could barely get the words out. I could scarcely even breathe. But I did. And I never raised my voice or even let it tremble.

"You may go now, Mardian," I finally said. "I would appreciate your finding out exactly what is going on. I know I can always rely on you." Quickly I stood up and left the room.

I had to be alone. I felt as if I had been hit with a heavy log right in the middle of my stomach. Outside the clouds were racing, chasing one another across the sky, tumbling like demons poured out of a tunnel. If only it were night, so I could close off the curtains and be undisturbed for hours. Curse the daytime, with all its comings and goings and busyness! I walked stiffly into my innermost chamber. Charmian was there. I waved her away, not trusting myself to look at her, for the instant she saw my face or heard me speak, she would know there was something wrong. Then there would have to be talk about it. I did not wish to talk; I wished only to feel.

Here was the room where we had spent so much time. All the furnishings brought back some memory or essence of him. Now each one hurt. So it is when something dies; the very inanimate objects the loved one has touched in passing serve to wound us. What should be a comfort causes us more pain. The very curtains that he had parted when looking out at the harbor—the little table where he had often rested his hand—the mosaic he had admired—the lamp he had lit to study his papers—they all rushed upon me like a gang of thugs, intent on injuring me.

No need to pretend to myself that it was just a rumor. I knew in my heart it was true. He had not changed. Not changed, after all.

It was I who was the fool for hoping he would. Somehow I had thought his time in Egypt had transformed him. But it had not.

Eunoe. What kind of a name was that? It sounded Greek. But she was the wife of a Mauretanian. A Moor? A Berber? Was she old? Young? And what was she even doing with her husband out in the field?

What matter? And what matter even if it is not true? I suddenly asked myself. The sad thing is that I have found it in myself to believe it is true. In that way I have also betrayed him.

I stood beside the windows, watching the tumultuous weather move across the sea. I grabbed handfuls of the curtains and crushed them in my fists. My hands ached for it to be his flesh instead of the filmy curtains. I did not know if I wanted to claw him or caress him. I left the window and sank down on a couch. I was drained. A thick blackness seemed to settle around me like a mantle, cloaking me and weighing me down. I sat very still and closed my eyes. I willed it all to go away. And what may have been minutes or hours went by, but when I opened my eyes again, the knowledge I hated was still there.

In late March a dusty messenger arrived at the palace, announcing that he had traveled all the way from Meroe, beyond the Fifth Cataract in Nubia, to bring urgent news for my ears alone. The palace guards were suspicious of him, and insisted on shackling him with chains before allowing him into my presence. I was sitting at the large marble table that (more memories, but I was used to them now, it had been weeks since I had heard the report from Africa) Caesar had used to spread out his maps. Now I used it whenever I had large numbers of books to consult; this morning I had been looking at the rolls of figures that Epaphroditus had compiled for me. Little by little he had been assuming the duties of a finance minister, protesting all the while that he was utterly uninterested in doing so. Men! How could I believe anything they said?

Briskly I pushed aside the figures. Life had become monotonous, and always in the midst of the monotony, like a sore that would not quite heal, was the fear that bad news would come from the African front, shattering the monotony with tragedy.

Yes, tragedy. For the death or defeat of Caesar would be nothing less than that for me. I still loved him, and always would. I knew that now, and I accepted it, just as I accepted my height or the color of my eyes. It was a given, apparently never to be shaken. A source of joy and immense pain.

"Well, let the man approach the throne and speak his piece," I said, although I was not seated on a throne.

The high doors swung open on their oiled bronze hinges, and a tall Nubian entered the room, straight and with long strides despite the chains weighing him down. He was flanked by a pair of my household guards.

"Most gracious Majesty Queen Cleopatra, I am the emissary of the exalted and mighty Kandake Amanishakheto of the Kingdom of Meroe. Greetings!"

The man's voice boomed out like a warrior's.

"Unchain him!" I commanded. "I would not be pleased to hear that my messengers were bound! Neither will the Kandake."

I knew that *kandake* was their word for queen. Meroitic was similar in some ways to Egyptian, and to Ethiopian, which I spoke. I had always had great curiosity about Meroe, our sister kingdom to the south.

Hastily they bent and unlocked the chains. The messenger stepped out of them and flung them off like a crane flinging water from its back. He seemed to grow even taller.

"I have come, O Majesty, many, many days' journey on the Nile. I have traversed the Five Cataracts, and passed from the land of the ostrich and hippopotamus and lion down to this city of the sea," he said. His Egyptian was heavily accented. It was hard for me to understand all his words. "I bring gifts of gold, ivory, and leopard skins."

"For which your land is renowned," I said.

"The box was taken from me to be searched," he said. "It will be presented when your servants have inspected it. But I have a message which only you may hear. These attendants must leave."

This was not wise. I must not be left alone with this unknown man on such a pretext. "One of the guards must stay," I insisted. "And I will send for my senior minister, Mardian."

"No. The Kandake said no one."

"Then I cannot hear her message. You have come all this way for nothing. My minister is to be trusted. And a guard must always be present."

He stood for a moment, trying to decide what to do. Clearly he revered every word his queen said, and was as obedient thousands of miles away as he was in her presence—the sort of servant I would treasure.

"Speak to me in Ethiopian," I said. "Do you know that tongue? The guard and my minister cannot understand it."

The man's face broadened in a wide smile. He nodded enthusiastically. "Very well, Your Majesty," he said.

I had a little trouble following him, but could understand the main thrust of his speech.

"What is this urgent message?" I asked.

"It is this: A man claiming to be Ptolemy XIII has been captured in Meroe."

I was stunned. "What?" was all I could manage to say.

"He is about seventeen years of age, almost a grown man. He was gathering an army when the Kandake's soldiers captured him. He demanded to be taken for an audience with her, and in her presence he swore he was your brother, the true ruler of Egypt, who had escaped after the battle with Caesar's forces and made his way into Nubia. He was most persuasive. My Kandake wishes to know your instructions. We are holding him in confinement."

An impostor! I had seen my poor dead brother, seen him collapsed in his golden armor, little trickles of swamp water running out his nostrils. He was entombed right here in Alexandria, in the mausoleum of the Ptolemies.

"Execute him!" I said. What other instructions could there be?

"I am afraid we cannot do that, until he has been positively identified."

"Who knows who he is? Does it matter? He is not my brother, of that I am sure. He deserves death for pretending he is."

"Then you must come and look him in the face and say he is a pretender."

"What? Journey to Nubia? Let him make the journey! Send him here and I will deal with him," I said.

"We cannot," he said. "Surely you can see why. It is too dangerous; he might make his escape somewhere along the route. No matter how carefully we had him guarded, there would doubtless be opportunities on the way. The moment the word got out—the moment there was a rumor—supporters would appear. It is always thus. People rally to any cause, just to have something to occupy them. That is why I did not wish anyone in Alexandria to hear of this. The merest whisper must not reach any ears. Are you sure they do not understand Ethiopian?" He looked nervously over at the one remaining guard and at Mardian, who had arrived and was standing at the far end of the table, his eyes fastened on us.

"I swear it," I assured him.

"Will you accompany me back?" he said. "I am prepared to wait. But I urge you to come as soon as possible. The less time between his capture and his . . . settlement . . . the better."

He was right. Every day that passed, with the self-styled Ptolemy XIII talking—to his guards, to his fellow prisoners—the more dangerous he became.

"Very well," I groaned. "I can see that I have no choice. But I must think of a reason why I suddenly must undertake this journey, which no Pharaoh and no Ptolemy ever has. It is not like deciding to visit Canopus!" I realized I had to think of it before this interview ended, so I could pretend it was part of the man's message. Mardian was staring at me, clearly trying to fathom what was happening.

Why would I have to go to Meroe? What possible reason? Think! I told myself. To see something for myself . . . what could it be? The trade routes to India? A lost city? Should I take a scientific expedition? I could take geographers and mathematicians from the Museion, those who were always concocting experiments to measure the earth's curve. But why would I need to go? Surely the scientists could go by themselves. And so could the merchants who might be interested in the trade route. And the elephant and leopard hunters. None of these excuses would serve.

Mardian was watching me as the moments of silence passed. When I spoke, I would have to give the reason for this visit—the public reason. Privately I would be able to tell Mardian the real reason. But now, spies might be in the outer chamber.

"My sister queen, the renowned Kandake Amanishakheto, has extended her hand in friendship to me," I finally said. "I wish to go in person to her fabulous court in Nubia and see what none of my ancestors has ever beheld. On the way I will make treaties and trading agreements with the tribes along the Nile. Let me open a new frontier, in a new direction, for Ptolemaic Egypt. Perhaps our future lies southward, toward Africa, rather than eastward to Asia or westward to Gaul. Rome has taken most of Asia and all of Gaul. Our way is blocked. What my ancestors held in those regions I cannot hope to regain. But other lands, other horizons beckon. Can I do less than see for myself?"

I said this first in Ethiopian, then in Greek. I saw Mardian's expression. I knew it sounded implausible. But what else could I say?

19

The wide highway of water drew me southward, ever southward, past the sites in Egypt that were old friends to me: the pyramids, Thebes with its golden temples, the teeming life alongside the riverbanks. The weighted poles were lined up, dipping and swaying as their buckets hauled water; children ran on the dusty paths; donkeys and camels blinked at us as we swept by, dogs barked, and the village daughters, coming to fill their water jars, paused, looking curiously at my royal vessel with its lotus-bud bow and its fringed sun pavilion as our sails filled with the north wind, sweeping us past.

I could see the water damage, but all that was over now, and the fields were green as the barley and emer and beans grew. Egypt had survived.

Philae again—the Holy Island, with its sacred college of priests. Again I did not go there and visit the little chamber where I had stood with Caesar. My heart felt as if it had no power to beat as we sailed slowly by, seeing the white buildings turning gold in the afterglow of sunset. It had not been holy to Caesar, had it?

"Sail on," I said. "Sail on, and let us anchor out of sight of Philae."

We were approaching the First Cataract. I could hear it—first just a low murmur, like a lover's whisper, then louder, like a whining child. Finally it turned into a roaring bull. And suddenly I could see it ahead. The Nile had widened into a lake, and in the lake a thousand islands gleamed, some sprouting palm trees and others only jagged, naked rocks. The river is glassy there, reflecting the islands and trees, making everything double. I leaned over the side of the boat and saw myself looking down, reached out and touched my own fingertips; only the sudden ripples showed me it was an image. As night fell, the surface turned from bronze to silver, but still it shone like polished metal.

We would anchor here for the night, and then in the morning be hauled up over the cataract by a team of men who, five months out of the year when the river was low and the rocks exposed, made their living doing just that.

The sun burst out of the horizon, rising hot that morning. The labor for the men hauling the boat was intense; they were strung together with long ropes, some guiding and some pulling, all under the direction of the foreman who knew where rocks were positioned to gouge a deadly hole in the bottom of the boat. We were bumped and buffeted, and it took two days until we finally floated free of the vicious rocks.

Beyond the cataract, the river changes as you enter Nubia. On one side are black granite cliffs, and on the other golden sand. There is little life on it; the Nile flows silently past valleys too narrow for cultivation. The dogs, the villages, the fields of Egypt have vanished, and in their place is the quiet of desertion. High in the bright, cloudless sky I could see an occasional hawk, but nothing else moved.

Yet the Pharaohs had been busy here. There was gold to be mined in the wadis and ravines, and forts built to smelt and refine it—massive mud-brick structures at Kuban, which marked the extent of my jurisdiction. We floated past it, on the dreamy surface of the Nile, the fierce sun glinting off the water. I was in alien territory now, under the hospitality of another ruler.

Suddenly the river valley widened, and a huge plantation of date palms beckoned us. They were the famous fields of Derr; we sent ashore for some of their renowned date palm wine.

Sunset, another day. All the days were flowing together on this endless journey, although we were making good time with a steady wind. Abu Simbel in the cliff ahead. From a distance we could see the giant figures, but the darkness had fallen before we reached them. We anchored and sat on the deck, drinking the fiery yellow date palm wine as the figures dissolved into the dark. We lit lanterns and continued to drink the wine; everything seemed to pulsate in a golden glow. What a strange country this was.

That night I noticed for the first time that no coolness ever came. There was no need for any covering, for anything to drape around the shoulders, and in the morning there was no chill. There were only two temperatures now: warm, and hot.

At earliest light we set sail, so that we could see the great monuments at Abu Simbel as the dawn light touched them. The likenesses of Ramses the Great sat in serene contemplation as we passed them by; we watched the rosy light creep down over them. The Pharaoh sat guarding his frontier, drifts of sand up to his massive knees, as he had for thousands of years, still warning the Nubians of his might. He stared at us as if to ask why we were hurrying by, and what we sought. His enigmatic smile seemed to say that it was no use seeking it, that it would do us no good and could not last. Even statues were futile, and would crumble like old bones. One of his heads lay on the ground at his feet, staring up at the empty sky.

We approached the Second Cataract, set like a plug in this land of scorching sun. The bleak, hard terrain showed no pity to living creatures. Several gigantic mud-brick fortresses, built to guard both sides of the Nile, glared down at us from the Semna Gorge.

At this cataract, known as the Great Cataract, we would abandon our vessel; it was too arduous for our boat to withstand. We transferred to another one waiting beyond the sixteen-mile stretch of hundreds of rocks and channels.

Our new boat was a plain, stoutly built vessel of thick timbers that would serve us the rest of the way. Immediately we embarked on the sixty-mile stretch called the "belly of rocks" for its utter inhospitality. The Nile pours through a channel of stone, bordered on each side by rocks, boulders, and sheets of granite. The sun pierces down like a thousand javelins, transfixing you, blinding you. The light screams from the sky, the rocks, the water. No living creature moves, neither are there any clouds. The heat radiates like an oven; the rocks shimmer.

Then the Third Cataract comes, a baby after the others. And all at once the landscape changes, the valley widens, and there are green fields. The river spreads out with a sigh, and embraces the land. I saw livestock and villages, and then we were passing Kerma, once an important city of the Nubian kingdom, now dwindled into a village once again. I could see the ruins of a huge structure off on the horizon—a mud-brick temple? Ramses was right; it does not last. A few chipped and half-buried ram-headed sphinxes were visible from the boat, looking forlornly at us, remnants of a forgotten avenue leading to . . . what?

Now we passed the Dongola Reach, and the scenery stayed friendly— green, palm-studded. The Nile makes a gigantic loop back toward the north as it approaches the Fourth Cataract, the farthest outpost of the Pharaohs. There was the Holy Mountain of Jebel Barkal at Napata, still a site of pilgrimage; strange, steep-sided pyramids were barely visible on the plain.

The Nile continued to go northward, like a son who has lost his way; at last he turned south again, and as he made the curve and the sun was once again in our faces rather than at our backs—although most of the time it was straight overhead—I saw the last trace of direct Egyptian power: a boundary text inscribed by a Pharaoh on a boulder. It had been wishful thinking; Egypt never truly controlled this portion of the Nile valley, although it had laid boastful claim to it.

Again the river narrowed as we rushed toward the Fifth Cataract, were pulled and guided over it, and came to the Nile's first tributary: the Atbara, bringing water from Ethiopia. Then before us loomed our goal: Meroe, the rich city of fabled Kush: that is, Nubia.

It lay on a fertile plain, waving with millet and barley, dotted with cattle. A fresh breeze, smelling of cool green plants, blew across the bow of our boat. Instantly I could understand why the Nubians had retreated to this area and held it. They could not be reached here easily, and this place was a paradise.

Ahead of us I saw an impressive long landing pier, jutting far out into the shallow waters. The palmwood pillars were carved and gilded, with blue and gold pennants flying. A royal welcome indeed.

They had spotted my boat, identified my insignia, and before we arrived the dock was thronged. As we tied up, I saw so many rich robes milling about that it looked like a tumble of jewels.

A tall man, even more ornately dressed than his fellows, approached and addressed us, but I could not understand him; evidently he was speaking Meroitic.

"Can you speak Greek?" I asked.

He shrugged, unable to respond. Someone whispered in his ear, then he shook his head.

"Egyptian, then?"

He smiled. "Yes, Exalted One."

"Or Ethiopian?"

"Yes, that as well. Which do you prefer?"

It seemed selfish to choose Egyptian, but I could speak it much better. "Egyptian, unless you have another tongue you wish to use," I said.

"Egyptian suits me as well as any other," he said. He nodded to the messenger, standing beside me. "Kandake Amanishakheto will reward you for your speed and powers of persuasion." He turned to me. "Come, Exalted One. I will take you to the palace."

As we made our way through the staring throng, immediately I was struck by two things: Some of the people were very tall and almost spindly, while others were like elephants from the waist down, with wide haunches and enormous, treelike legs.

Litters were brought to transport me and my companions to the royal enclosure; the rest would walk. I had brought Iras with me, thinking that she would like to see her homeland again. But as we glided along, borne by six strong men, she leaned over and confided to me, "I have never seen anything like this. My family was from Lower Nubia, near the border with Egypt. This is different . . . so different!" She was wide-eyed.

"Can you understand any of this Meroitic?" I asked.

"No. Only a few words sound familiar, but they speak so fast, and the accent is difficult to follow."

I studied her features: the shining dark skin, the high-bridged nose, the curving lips. Facially she resembled them, but her body was in no way like the two types predominant here.

The city was one of wide streets and circular dwellings made of mud and reeds that looked African; certainly we had nothing like them in Egypt. Then, suddenly, we approached a high stone wall with a massive gateway to the royal enclosure, carved with Pharaonic-looking figures. Guards in kilted uniforms flanked it; they wore silver caps topped with colored plumes. Gigantic bows were slung over their shoulders; Nubia had been known as "the land of the bow" since ancient times, and the Nubians' prowess with the weapon was fearsome. At our approach, they threw back the bolts of the gate; the heavy studded doors swung open with a deep groan, revealing a tender green vista.

Spread before us was a carpet of tiny ground flowers, framed by jewel-toned shrubs; arbors covered with the heavy, twined vines of grapes and climbing roses waved their multitude of pointed leaves and blossoms in the soft breeze and urged us to enter into their scented shade and linger. I saw a movement from the shadows; someone was stretched out on a bench, one hand trailing down in aimless repose. Farther in the distance I saw an orchard of fruit trees, their branches frothy with bloom.

Scattered about these sensual grounds were many buildings: what looked to be temples, palaces, baths, all of golden sandstone.

Pathways paved with wide stones wound throughout the enclosure, and servitors, wearing thin red and green tunics, passed from building to building. Gigantic plane trees and graceful palms sheltered them from the noonday sun.

They set the litters down before a square building with entrance steps of marble. "The guest palace, Exalted One," said our guide. "We have many envoys, merchants, and traders from Arabia, India, Africa, and we treat them as kings. It is not our wish to dishonor you by lodging you in their quarters, but rather to honor them by allowing them to experience royal accommodations." He bowed. "Besides, we find it makes them more amenable to trade agreements," he added.

"Yes, flattery will do that," I said, stepping out of the litter. As ruler of the greatest trading city in the world, I appreciated all the tricks. I would have to see about building a palatial visitors' lodging in Alexandria.

Iras and I were led up a flight of wide steps of gleaming blue-black porphyry to a suite of rooms. The ceilings were of fretted cedar—obviously imported from Lebanon. But how had they managed to get it here? Certainly the fifty-foot timbers could not have survived a trip over the cataracts—let alone all five of them. They must have come by way of the Red Sea. But how did they get *there*? I must ask the Kandake.

I have been accused of being a hard-hearted businesswoman, grasping, greedy, and calculating. (It is primarily Octavian and his mouthpieces who say this.) But all calumnies are built on some leaning or grain of truth, and in standing in the midst of this magnificent chamber and wondering about trade routes, I show myself where this later slander came from. I do think of money and trade; when I see gold I think of mines, and when I see silk I think of India and trade routes, and when—oh, why try to explain it? It is both my strength and my weakness. And I notice that Octavian lusts after my treasure in most unseemly fashion himself. But that is getting ahead of my story.

One of the things I noticed immediately was a service of silver vessels on the table—a tall, gracefully spouted pitcher, slender cups, an oval tray. Silver is rarely used in Egypt because it is actually scarcer than gold; now it caught my eye for that reason.

I picked up the pitcher, liking its feel in my hand, and poured out some brownish liquid into a cup; it proved to be tamarind juice.

"From India, Exalted One," said a voice from the doorway. I set the pitcher down with a jerk.

A wraithlike girl, wearing what appeared to be both an odd and strangely familiar costume, stood in the door. "I am here to serve you," she said, bringing up her cupped hands in a gesture of submission. "My Kandake wished you to have our favorite refreshment, and me to explain about it." She glided across the floor and took the handle of the pitcher and poured, in one gracious, sinuous motion. She handed both Iras and me a cup. "Drink, and welcome."

The tart, tawny liquid stung my lips. At the very hint that it was sour, the girl said, "There is honey for that." She gestured toward a shiny black-lidded jar. Now I saw that Iras's extreme gracefulness was part of her heritage. This girl had the same smooth, liquid movements.

"Large shipments of the tamarind come to us on the winds of the monsoon," she said. "We can tell by the flavor which area of India they come from."

"It is most delicious, and refreshing," I said. The taste was strong, bracing:

a drink for soldiers, sailors, traders—and queens. "You may tell the Kandake I am pleased. And when may I meet with her?"

"In the cool of the evening she would like to receive you, at the pavilion by the water sanctuary."

As she turned to go, I realized what it was about her costume: she was clothed in the style of ancient Egypt, in the sort of clothes we had not worn in a thousand years. I recognized them only from temple wall carvings.

At sunset I was led along the winding path, with its border of flowers, to the water sanctuary. We would have called it a pleasure pool, for it evidently existed to provide a passive sensual indulgence for the ruler. The eyes were pampered by the azure-colored tiles at the bottom of the pool, which tinted the water magically blue; the nose by the scent of the water lilies; the skin by the cool air wafting across the water; the ears by the discreet chorus of tiny frogs cheeping, and the twittering of birds among the lilies. A few butterflies swooped in and out of the water garden's thicket.

I was alone in the falling evening. Servitors lit silver lanterns, and behind me I could hear the low, confiding murmur of a fountain. Then a great, umbrella-covered litter swayed its way into my line of sight, the fringe over its parasol dancing wildly. I saw a bejeweled hand draped over the side.

The curious vehicle, borne by sweating, broad-shouldered men, approached the pavilion. Just before the steps, they set it down and stood back. The curtains parted, pushed aside by another hand just like the first. A head poked out, then a leg draped in voluminous, pleated robes. With a heave, the entire figure burst forth, her enormous shoulders shaking the medals pinned to her sash. It was like an elephant crashing through the underbrush. I expected her skin to be gray and wrinkled. But it was richly black, and smooth as polished metal.

She drew herself up in quiet dignity, and, with a disproportionately small hand, adjusted her wig and vulture-goddess headdress.

"Your Majesty, most honored Kandake Amanishakheto," I said, "I am pleased to behold your most noble face."

She sighed, and the medals on her bosom shimmied. "Queen Cleopatra," she said. "You are as beautiful as they say. Welcome to Meroe. You are also as clever as they say, since you knew the journey was necessary, and as determined as they say, since you have managed to make the trip in less than fifty days. It is indeed a great surprise and pleasure to see something that *is* as it is reputed to be. So few things are."

"I thank you, Your Majesty. From what I have seen, Meroe exceeds the fables. It is an unknown treasure."

"Good. We do not want to be overrun with settlers of the wrong sort. When a place becomes popular, that's the end of its charm—don't you think?" She gestured, and out of the shadows a servitor appeared and began fanning her with an enormous ostrich-feather fan. The feathers, dyed scarlet, gold, and blue, made a rainbow in the air.

"Let us seat ourselves." She walked with slow, deliberate steps over to a stone throne—the only type strong enough to support her weight. I saw the outlines of her legs through the sheer pleated fabric of her gown, and they looked bigger in diameter than the cedars of Lebanon in my chamber ceiling. Her feet—like her hands, strangely small—were shod in golden sandals.

She sank down with a sigh, and all her clothes seemed to sigh around her. Thick tassels, hanging at the ends of silk cords, rustled and swung at her hem like barley in a windstorm.

"I know this boy is not your brother," she said quietly. "But others are all too ready to believe. Why do impostors always attract followers? It is best we deal with him between ourselves. I detest lies and deception, and I especially abhor those who turn their backs on the truth to follow falsehood!" Her eyes—soft, brown, melting ones—flashed as hard and black as obsidian.

"It is part of the human condition, I fear," I said. I did not want to stir her up; she seemed terribly agitated.

Does this mean I was without ideals or honor, as my enemies have said? No. But no one could have grown up in the court I did and held any illusions about what people are capable of. And then there was Caesar. . . . Ever since he had left, Caesar had destroyed what little belief in men had remained to me. It was touching that Amanishakheto had preserved so much of her original trust. Obviously no one but an enemy had ever betrayed her—never a friend or a lover. It is the latter that crush us.

"It should be punished whenever it occurs, then perhaps it won't rear its head so readily!" she said. "Even a born behavior can be whipped out of someone." She nodded emphatically. "Yes, the lash can cure interrupting, pushing, stealing, and fighting."

"But it does not cure hatred or plotting or ingratitude," I said.

"No, it cannot cure the heart, only the hands," she agreed. "But it is the hands that ruin a kingdom. Let people think whatever mischief they like, as long as they keep their hands folded nicely in their laps."

I laughed. She had a point. "I think the people of Meroe are fortunate to have such a wise ruler," I said.

"And the Egyptians are fortunate to have such a resourceful one," she shot back at me. She was quick. "I think perhaps we should consider a partnership."

I looked at her carefully. In the dull twilight it was hard to study her face without being rude. I had not had the opportunity really to look at her, and before I have a serious conversation with someone I like to have taken their measure. I believe I am able to read much in a face.

I turned my full attention to Amanishakheto.

She was giving her equal attention to me, studying me quite frankly. "So young a queen," she said. "And already so many years of governing—not tranquil years, either. Difficult to manage. It excites the imagination—my imagination, at any rate. Do you really have any intention of sharing power with your brother—your *real* brother, that is?" She was smiling serenely, a mountain of solidity.

Such penetrating, deadly questions, asked as if she expected straight answers. "No," I said, obliging her. "No, I plan eventually to share the throne with, and pass it to, my son."

She was nodding in approval. "That is what we do in Meroe. The Kandake's son will reign—we call him the Qore—but his wife becomes the next Kandake. The truth is that it is the Kandake who has power."

"Your son?" Where was he? Was there one?

"Oh yes, my son," she said. "He is a naughty boy, doesn't pay much attention to his duties. But that is typical of men, don't you find?"

"I am confused. Is he a boy or a man?"

"A grown man in years," she said. "I myself am over forty. My Naughty One, Natakamani, is almost twenty. But he has a good wife, Amanitore, who, thank all the gods, will make a good Kandake after me."

"Is there a—the father of Nata—Natakam—?"

She rolled her eyes, then closed them as if in bliss. "Oh, he has gone to his pyramid." She certainly seemed happy that he rested there, and not in the palace.

"May he reside there in peace," I said piously.

"I haven't heard any stirrings," she replied. "No rustling of his *ba*."

I thought we should leave her unnamed consort to molder, and return to the living. While she was talking my eyes had been caught by the wide, intricately worked gold bracelets she wore on both her upper and lower arms. The patterns and design were unlike anything we had in Egypt; the two heavy halves were secured with a thick pin.

"Here." She seemed to read my mind, for suddenly she extended her arm to me. "Look." She undid the bracelet and handed it to me.

It was very heavy; it felt almost like a manacle. But the workmanship on it was delicate: a raised figure of the goddess Mut with four outstretched wings, each feather gleaming with a lapis inlay, guarding a patterned wall of geometric lapis stones.

"Take it. Wear it. It is yours."

I was insulted. "No. I wished only to see it. I was not hinting in any way that I expected it for a gift." I handed it back to her.

She pushed it back into my hands. "Had I thought that, you can be sure I would never have given it. Did I just not finish saying that I hate falsehood? I wished to give you something I could see for myself that you appreciated and fancied, rather than some trinket that my ministers would find suitable. Besides, we have a plenitude of gold here."

That was the usual claim. Even poor countries said that, when presenting a gift. Or hoping to lure someone into an alliance. But Nubia abounded in gold mines.

"I thank you, then." Wearing it would require a very muscular arm. "I noticed a great deal of silver," I said. "Now do not give me any! But it struck my eye because it is rare and seldom used in Egypt. It has a subdued beauty of its own, like moonlight."

"I have always imagined that Isis must love silver," said Amanishakheto.

"Silver seems very like her. I have been to Philae in the moonlight, and if ever she was there, it was then."

Philae. I forced myself to smile. "Yes, Isis seems like a silvery being," I finally said. "Your clothing is shot with silver thread, I see. And it is quite different from ours—either Egyptian or Greek." I waited for her to explain about it—about the tassels and the shawl, and the medals—but she did not. "I noticed when I arrived that your palace servants dress in an ancient manner. The servant who came to my chambers was dressed in the style of some-one from the court of Ramses."

"Ramses once ruled Nubia. We retained what we liked of that reign, and discarded the rest."

"So it is preserved here long after it has vanished in its homeland."

"Such is often the case," she said. "It is the gods who preserve or destroy, by hiding things in odd places." She stirred on her stone throne. "It is time for me to eat again," she said suddenly. "I must keep up my weight."

"I am afraid I do not understand." The darkness had come upon us rapidly and suddenly I could barely see her face. A lively wind was whipping the flames of the torches, and swaying the tassels around the hem of her garment.

"I mean I have to work to be this large! If I let myself become as thin as you, I would be off the throne in an instant! It shows my might to be big, so I can trample my enemies underfoot." She removed one of her sandals and dangled it before my eyes. I could just make out the stylized depictions of enemy peoples on its sole. That meant that with every step she was treading heavily on them. Poor enemies. "Who would tremble before a woman like you? No one here in Meroe, I can tell you!" I could not see her face well enough to see if she was joking.

"Are the men required to be large? What about your son? Or your—the late—?"

"No, of course not! The men are supposed to be tall and bulging with muscles, able to chase their enemies in the desert. But the women are sup-posed to look like elephants, grave, majestic—and unstoppable."

Elephants. I suddenly remembered Juba and his elephants against Caesar. *No, no, I'll not think of Caesar now.* Caesar would take care of the elephants, as he had taken care of everything else—Pompey, Ptolemy, Pothinus, Phar-naces. Unfortunately Juba and Scipio's names did not begin with *P*.

"But I will do anything necessary to be Kandake, even eat ten meals a day," she said cheerfully. "I've come to adore those fatty ostrich patties, and camel milk with a sediment of honey, and pastry made of ground walnuts, rolled in butter, and coated with honey. The fat of lambs' tails . . . oh, it's been an ongoing battle, but I've conquered my aversions, I tell you. I can even relish a platter of fried peacock sausage swimming in olive oil, covered with melted cheese. Umm." She clapped her hands, and out of the growing darkness her litter appeared. "I will have to return to the palace to partake of my mid-evening meal. Tomorrow we will meet in the throne room, and I will have the impostor brought before you. You may give your verdict on him." With the help of two bearers, she heaved herself up off the throne. "I trust your quarters are satisfactory. I have assigned a servant of the chamber to wait on you."

"That is not necessary," I assured her. "I brought my own attendant; in fact, she is Nubian."

"No, I insist you permit this slave to serve you," she said.

"I do not care for slaves. I do not have them in my royal quarters; all my attendants are free men."

"This is a slave unlike any you have had before. Utterly discreet, hard-working, amusing, loyal—and green."

"Green?" Now she was joking.

"Yes, green. Her name is Kasu, and she is an African green monkey. Her only drawback is that she has a tendency to steal. On the other hand, she can fetch things down from high places."

"A monkey! You have monkeys as chamber servants?"

"Indeed," she said, as she made her way majestically—and laboriously—down the steps to her litter. "The King of Punt sent a family of them to me long ago, along with a shipment of other animals destined for Rome. I took a fancy to them and kept them for myself. I suppose I, also, have a tendency to steal. Like master, like servant." She daintily lifted up her foot to enter the litter. "Now they have bred and are everywhere in the palace. Handy creatures. Well, just try Kasu for one night." She gave an airy wave of her hand and disappeared into the dark.

My own litter materialized, but I waved it away so I could walk a bit. My head was spinning. Amanishakheto was no ordinary monarch, and no ordinary woman. Perhaps the two never went together.

The luxury of the suite of rooms I had been given was more noticeable to me upon returning. Perhaps Amanishakheto did have gold to spare, after all. Iras was attempting to read a commemoration—I assumed—that was set in the wall. She shook her head.

"This script means nothing to me."

"Have you been able to understand better the conversations you have heard?"

"No, I have to request that they speak the Lower Nubian dialect. You must remember, my family came from near the border with Egypt and were connected with the priesthood; that is why I was serving in the temple at Hermonthis. In many ways we were Egyptianized. For example, I've never heard of this lion-headed god they have here, Apedemak."

I was very tired, and sank down on the bed. "I have had a most . . . unusual . . . evening with the Kandake." I held up my arm, with its heavy bracelet. "She gives gold as easily as children give away field flowers. And she seems to harbor a great disrespect of men."

Iras laughed.

"I did not say 'dislike,' I said 'disrespect.' That is unusual in a world where they rule and control most everything—except here in Meroe, evidently." I lay down, weariness surrounding all my limbs. Then I remembered. "The monkey! The Kandake said there was a monkey in here to serve us!"

"There has been one, scurrying around," said Iras. "I saw it sitting up on top of one of the chests, then it ran away. I called to have it removed, but I suppose no one could understand me."

"Her name is Kasu," I said. "She is supposed to see to all of our wants."

"Ah, then where is she? Now we are ready to sleep, and no monkey in sight."

"Kasu!" I called. "Come, Kasu! We are ready to retire!"

I never imagined that the creature would appear by the side of the bed like magic; she must have been hiding inside the window curtains. She walked over to us with dignity, bowing her head. She *was* green. Her stiff, brushlike fur, framing her black face, looked as if it had been tinted. The rest of her fur, except the tip of her long tail, had a similar hue. She was about the size of a two-year-old child. But from what I had heard of monkeys and apes, I knew that, proportionate to their size, they are much stronger than a human. Someone at the Museion had once told me that an ape is eight times stronger than a man—how he arrived at this conclusion he did not explain. That would make Kasu a monkey to respect.

"Bed, Kasu," I said, patting it.

The monkey looked disdainful, as if I were insulting her. Obviously she knew what a bed was, and that I wanted to sleep in it, her eyes seemed to say. She ambled over to a chest and took out bed linens and coverlets, and then put them carefully on the bed. She polished the headrest tenderly with her leathery palm, then cocked her head as if to say, *All right, it's ready now, stupid.*

I disrobed and put on my sleeping garments; Kasu quickly gathered up the discarded clothes and carried them off somewhere. She then prepared Iras's bed and took her clothes away, and returned solicitously carrying a small lamp, which she placed by our bedside.

"I hope she did not light it herself!" said Iras.

"It must have been already lit," I said, hoping that was true.

"It looks as if we must go straight to sleep," said Iras. "Our keeper has decided it."

I yawned. "It is just as well. I am exhausted; without this parentlike monkey, we would probably stay up too late."

I watched as Kasu made her way over to a far corner of the room; now I could identify a basket that probably served as her bed. She was going to retire, herself. She flopped down and stretched her arms above her head once. Then she sighed and lay down.

I closed my eyes. What an overwhelming day this had been; what a mythical kingdom I had entered. I removed the bracelet and dropped it on the floor beside me. It landed with a loud *clunk* that sounded more like lead than gold.

———

I slept; I dreamt; I awoke with a start. Moonlight, as silvery as Isis's garment, spread itself across the floor, lying like a carelessly tossed shawl. It was not brilliantly bright, but diffused; it embraced the lower legs of the tables and chairs and left the rest in shadow. I could see the gold cuff on the floor by my bed, its detailed miniature figures coming alive in the peculiar slanting light.

Then I saw the cobra. I thought I was dreaming, or that it was a wooden sculpture that I had somehow overlooked earlier. A dark wooden one, against the far wall. It was motionless. Yes, it was a sculpture. I felt my fear drain away.

Just then it moved. It inched forward and raised its head. My heart stopped.

It was not especially large. But all cobras are poisonous, even the babies; I knew that. I held as still as I could, and tried to remember everything else I had learned about them. Mardian and his snakes had been part of my childhood; he had had one old cobra that he kept in a pen by itself, with very close-fitting bars. He had been fond of it, but certainly had never handled it.

"It's a lie that you can become immune to snakebite," he had said when I asked him about a tribe of men reputed to be so. "Our happy little fellow here has enough poison in him to kill five men with one bite."

Remembering his words, the very tone of his voice, I felt sweat break out all over me. Five men. This snake—the royal cobra of Egypt—could dispatch five men, all in one bite. A good night's work.

"And how long does it take to die of snakebite?" I had asked.

"Some men have succumbed in only a quarter of an hour," he had said. "Others may take an hour or so. It depends on where you are bitten, and whether the snake has bitten someone else first. It does not seem to be especially painful. Prisoners beg to be executed by snakebite. Of course it would be improper, since the cobra is a royal beast, and divine," he had said, in his most official tone.

"Of course," I had echoed him.

The cobra moved again, gliding away from the wall. He came out into the center of the room, but avoided the patch of moonlight. He just remained still and looked at it quizzically. I could see the bead of his eye, with a smaller bead of light reflected in it. His tongue flicked out; he seemed to be testing the air.

Could he smell my fear? Could he sense our living presence? Was he going to glide over to my sleeping couch, spread his hood, lean over me and strike?

I held as still as a statue. I did not dare to speak, or to warn Iras, lest she move suddenly.

He made his way cautiously into the light, moving only a hand's breadth at a time. He was banded, and his light and dark skin was beautiful. He was indeed a divine instrument of death—sleek and slender and delicately colored.

He did not care for the light. He turned his head and slithered to one side, coming still closer to the bed. I gripped the wooden frame, prepared to vault myself in the opposite direction, hoping my arms were strong enough to propel me. Even so, I might not land far enough away; cobras were supposed to be lightning-fast. I had never seen one strike from a distance, as Mardian's old pet had never been given the opportunity.

A movement from the other side of the room. Were there two of them? No, it was the monkey, moving in her sleep. The cobra turned so suddenly and sped off toward her so fast that I did not see his actual path. One instant he was near my bed, the next speeding across the room. A dark shape reared up; his hood was spread. I heard noises, scrambling, a hiss, high, raucous squeals, first of anger and fear, then of shock and pain. Another hiss. Then something falling across the room.

Trembling, I stood up and grabbed the sputtering oil lamp and held it up. Its feeble flame did not reveal much, but I saw the long, dark shape of the cobra disappearing out the open window. At the base was the standing lamp he had overturned. He was gone!

Kasu was howling, grabbing her tail. I rushed over to her, followed by the dazed Iras.

"Light another lamp!" I cried. "A snake has attacked us! We need more light!"

Iras shrieked.

"The snake is gone, there's no need to fear!" I said. "But we need light!"

The monkey was shaking in terror. But had she been bitten? It was hard to tell. I did not see anything at first. But she clutched her tail, and between the fingers I could see a swelling beginning.

"It got her tail," I said. "Oh, please, Kasu, release your grip so I can see!" But such was the strength of the monkey that even now I could not pry her fingers away from the injury.

"A tourniquet," I said. "It's only the tip of the tail. We can tie it off." Hands shaking, I drew off the leather thong that was woven around her basket to hold her blanket in place. I tied it halfway up the tail, making it as tight as I could.

"Call for the guards," I said. "We need someone strong enough to get her fingers loose so we can cut open the wound and suck out the poison, before it spreads further."

Suddenly Kasu went limp; the fear and shock had caused her to faint. Her fingers loosened and fell away, and I could see the wound. There was only one scratch; evidently the snake had missed and hit her only a glancing blow rather than a full puncture.

"Thanks be to Thoth!" I breathed. The baboon-god of wisdom had protected his own, even against the royal cobra.

After such a night, it is little wonder that I found myself nervous as I stood beside Amanishakheto in the throne room and awaited the prisoner. Outside, all was bright and glorious; night had fled with the snake, and they both seemed unreal.

Amanishakheto was dressed in fiery red robes overlaid with a blue beaded sash, and again she was loaded down with gold jewelry. On her head was the Nubian crown, which had a double cobra. The Egyptian one had a single cobra. Just seeing the creature depicted in gold and wrapped around her head made my encounter of the night seem even more nightmarish.

The doors at the far end of the room swung open and a young man, yoked and chained, was brought in. Two enormous guards flanked him.

I was startled by the resemblance to my late brother. He was almost exactly the same height and build, and his features were similar enough to convince anyone who had not seen the true Ptolemy. When he spoke, I could see that he had hoped to win followers by his voice and words. He had obviously studied Ptolemy's manner of speaking, and had mastered his inflections and choice of words. He must have heard him many times; this boy may have been in the royal household as a servant.

He stood, feet in their iron fetters spread apart, head high.

"Greetings, most noble sister," he said.

Oh, he was bold. And clever. I could not help but admire that in him.

"I am not your sister," I said coldly. "You share no blood with me."

"It would be convenient for you to convince others of that. But you and I know the truth. You thought you were rid of me in that battle at the Nile, but I escaped. I let you and Caesar think you had won. But now Caesar is gone, and you are alone."

"Except for my three Roman legions," I said coldly.

"Bah! What is that? Foreign troops. They will flee when you need them. Now you must admit the truth, and restore me to the throne. As Caesar had proclaimed me to be, I am joint ruler with you. As our father wished."

"Enough of this. It is amusing, and I admit you are clever. You have studied the accent and expressions well. But you are a liar. My brother is dead. I saw him; and now he rests with his ancestors in our mausoleum. Now you had best name your true ancestors, so that we can allow you to rest with them."

The color drained from his face. He had expected more of a hearing. But surely he did not expect me to be fooled. Perhaps he had assumed I had spent so little time with my brother that I would have a faded memory of him. But not enough time had passed. It was only a year since Ptolemy's death.

I turned to Amanishakheto. "This person is no kin of mine, not brother, not consort, not joint ruler. He is a common impostor. Let him die the death of a usurper. He who attempts to wear the royal cobra on his brow must be of the blood royal. His is not—although he has courage, that I grant him."

His eyes sought mine out, begging, challenging. *Let me live*, they said. *Let me live.*

Today, tonight, they haunt me. Not because I was wrong in my decision, but because it had to be made. Soon my son, my dear Caesarion, may have to look in Octavian's eyes the same way, make the same silent plea. And Octavian is much harder of heart than I. Thus the boy's eyes haunt me, because they are now my own son's. All our deeds are visited on us from a different vantage point. A cup that tastes sweet when we are sitting may be bitter indeed when we are standing.

"Take him away," said the Kandake. "Prepare the place of execution."

As the young man was being led away, she said to me, "They are taken beyond the city gates and slain there. Unless he reveals his true family, he will be buried in a desert grave."

The boy turned to us with one half-defiant, half-pitiful look, before he was shoved out the door.

"After the heat of the day has faded, I would like to show you my pyramid," she said. "I always enjoy a desert ride." She smiled. "Don't you?"

Shadows were creeping from the rocks and trees when we set out. It was the time of day when the light changed, and the desert began turning from white-hot to mellow red. The sky was still blindingly blue, heat still emanating from the ground. But high on our camels, swaying and dipping, we were protected from the worst of it.

Amanishakheto's saddle had a canopy on it, and she sat happily shaded from the sun as the beast ploughed his way through the sand like a ship.

She had seemed most anxious that I view her pyramid. Did she think I had never seen one? Now I understand, of course, that one is always very proud of one's projected resting place. I am in the process of completing mine; indeed I find it oddly fulfilling to design my own tomb. But then I considered the Kandake peculiar and morbid to want to visit it with a guest.

As we came over the top of a ridge, I suddenly saw a field of pyramids, hundreds of them, like toys. They were smaller than ours, and with much steeper sides. They also did not end in a point, but had a platform on top. Coming closer, I could see that they had portals and small structures attached to their east faces.

"Here!" She pointed to a half-finished one, larger than the rest. She urged her camel forward, and it broke into a run over the glowing sands. At its base she reined it in, and waited for me to catch up.

When I dismounted, she threw her arms out as if to embrace the entire pyramid. "Here is my eternity!" she said proudly.

"Indeed, it is a fine pyramid." What else could one say about it?

"Let us inspect the prayer chapel," she said. "I ordered certain wall carvings—"

After the brilliance of the desert, I felt blind once we were inside. I could see absolutely nothing. It was like being dead, like already lying in the bedrock under the pyramid.

She pulled a piece of reflecting metal out of her voluminous leather pouch, and used it to bounce light onto the walls.

"Tsk, tsk!" She bent forward to examine a carving showing herself—I assume it was she—holding a brace of enemies by the hair, ready to plunge a spear into the backs of their shoulders. "The artist has botched my headdress!"

"I am sure it can be remedied," I said.

"Why do they never get it right?" she fretted.

"Because artists are people, and people make mistakes," I said.

"You do not think you made a mistake this morning, do you?"

I turned to her. "No. Why do you ask?"

"I was only testing you." She turned imperiously and made her slow, deliberate way out of the chapel door. More carvings of herself punishing her enemies were resplendent on either side. "I have a pavilion on the north side," she said. "Let us sit there, and contemplate the pyramid."

A structure of woven reeds sturdy enough to withstand the winds was waiting for us, as were the inevitable, discreet stone seats for her ample majesty. She sank down upon one. I sat close by.

"My dear, you have passed the test," she said. "And now I will ask you to join me on my glorious enterprise. An empire, an alliance of women!" Before I could speak, she went on at breakneck speed. "I can see that you are a woman beyond all other women. Leave behind your alliance with men, with Rome. Let us forge a new one. Together we can make a nation that will look to the south, to Africa, to the east, to Arabia and India. A great nation, turning its back on Rome and its leavings. What do the Romans know of our kind? Of art, and poetry, and the mysteries of Osiris and Isis? They understand nothing but what happens in the sunlight. Of the dawn, the twilight, the dark of the moon, they know not. Yet they wish to destroy it."

"I do not think they care enough about it to destroy it," I finally said.

"They only want to crush it beneath their chariot wheels, their chariot wheels turning in the constant Triumphs they celebrate at Rome. Crush it, and then sweep it away." She leaned over to me. "You are our only hope. You may be the savior predicted by the oracle. The woman who will shear Rome's hair. Who will save the east."

The truth slowly dawned on me. "Why . . . this is why you wanted me to come to Meroe. So we could sit together in private and you could make this proposal. Ptolemy the pretender was just a ruse." She was devious and clever as Odysseus. And a gambler—like Caesar himself.

"You know you don't belong with them," she said, ignoring my question. "They will never understand you, never understand what it is Egypt stands for. To them, it is just a big grain factory, existing to placate the grumbling Roman crowds and soldiers. Separately we will be taken by them. Together, we can resist. And the nation we can create! The glory of Greece, the splendor of Africa, the riches of India! And all ruled by a spirit of sophistication, tolerance, experimentation! The way of life, of joy!"

"You sound like a merchant hawking his wares," I said. "Do not make such extravagant claims for your new nation. It would be made up of men, not gods."

"A nation that will follow in the tradition of the great Alexander. Did he not look to the east? Did not his yearnings draw him there, and would have drawn him still farther into India, if only his fainthearted soldiers had not faltered?"

"We do not have an army like Alexander's," I said.

"No one does. Not even Caesar, since he must expend his energies fighting fellow Romans. But Nubia has a fine army, and the best bowmen in the world. Against anyone but Rome, we would do well."

"But Rome would never just let us alone."

"Ah! Do I detect a serious consideration of my proposal?" She leapt in like a dog scenting blood. "Think of Rome! What can you expect of her? I know of your feelings for Caesar, but he is just one man, and not immortal. What would Rome be to you without him? Its meaning for you would vanish. Our alliance is more natural. It is not based on your person or my person, but on the needs of our countries."

"You say it is not based on our persons, but earlier you stressed that it should be an alliance of women. My son will succeed me; what then?"

She was persuasive; she had many clever reasons for her plan. But in the end it was not sensible. Rome was master of the world. It was best to be on that side, rather than attempting to go it alone. Yet the image of that magical kingdom Amanishakheto beckoned me to was to linger, and linger. . . .

"You will live a long time," she said. "It is you who will put the stamp on what sort of kingdom it will be. Your son will inherit your creation."

Successors sometimes respected traditions and sometimes did not. It was no certain thing. "I will not live a long time if cobras keep coming into my room," I said. "Have you been informed about last night? Poor Kasu took what I fear was meant for me. But I think she will survive. The snake was clumsy."

"Yes. I heard. I fear that this happens more often than I would like to admit. The snake charmers and snake catchers seem to be doing a poor job. I am more thankful than I can ever say that you were unharmed. The gods protected you, and *made* the snake miss. But what of our alliance? Do consider it! Remember how our ancestors, the noble Ptolemy the Fourth and Arqamani, worked together to build the temples at Philae and Dakka. It was the beginning. This is meant to be, I tell you!"

"Not for now," I told her quietly, but as definitely as I could. "You tempt me. I find your proposal intriguing. I will always remember it, and be honored that you asked me. But I do not believe it is possible. And when something is not possible, it is best to let go of it with gentle respect. I thank you for the offer of the alliance, and I trust that, even with no formal agreement, we will always be friends and allies."

Her face fell, but she accepted my answer. "Very well. And when the Romans let you down, know that I will avenge you!" She took a deep breath. "I will not make the offer a second time. Should you ever wish it, the proposal must come from you."

"Very well. I will not be too proud, should the time come. And thank you again. It was worth the journey to obtain such a friend."

As we rode back toward Meroe, I saw a fresh mound of sand, topped by rocks. The setting sun made the rocks cast jagged shadows.

"The grave of the impostor," said the Kandake. "There he lies."

The camels trotted by the heap of stones, and we left it to face the coming desert night and its scavengers. I hoped there were enough rocks on it to protect it.

(20)|

Noon on the Nile, Nubia gliding past. We had taken leave of Meroe at dawn, and now the backs of my rowers were glistening as they manned the oars. To double our speed, we were rowing with the current. The sails were folded away, useless on the return journey. I sat in the shaded deck cabin, Kasu by my feet. She had recovered after a spell of weakness; Iras and I had nursed her in our chamber, which the Meroites found amusing. A queen tending a monkey, they had laughed; an upside-down world. But our care was repaid. Her only scar was the bald tip of her tail; the residue of poison had killed all the fur. And I, who had wished to refuse the gift of her, now found that I did not want to be parted from the creature.

I felt queasy, and touched my stomach gingerly. The ostrich-egg feast Amanishakheto had served as a farewell banquet was not sitting well with me. She had outdone herself in having her cooks prepare ostrich eggs in every normal way, and every outlandish way as well. There were fluffy whipped ostrich eggs flavored with cinnamon, baked ostrich eggs served with toppings of dried lizard tails and salted sea slug, ostrich eggs layered with camel-milk cheese, starfish arms, and baby crocodile snouts (finely chopped, of course), boiled ostrich eggs to be eaten out of their gilded shells and flavored with fermented-fish relish or spiced honey. Boiled ostrich with date sauce was the only meat. Since each ostrich egg must be the equivalent of twenty or thirty duck eggs, the amount of food served was staggering.

The Kandake managed to sample at least three or four of them, as well as several helpings of the boiled ostrich meat. She had decked herself out in so many ostrich plumes, she appeared to float. I could see that she was diligently doing her part to keep up her vast proportions.

But it was all I could do to choke down samples of the food. The fast Nubian dancers and acrobats who had performed during the feast had not aided the task of digestion. The flavors all fought with each other—both last night and now. I would fast today; I *must* fast today.

Iras was standing beside me. As always, she was somewhat quiet. One felt her presence rather than heard it.

"I am pleased you could come with me," I said. "I feel I understand you better now that I have seen your ancestral lands."

"They were a bit foreign to me," she admitted. "But it was good for me to see them, too."

On we went, down the river, leaving the green fields behind, heading into the forbidding, baking desert.

Time seemed to lose its meaning, to dissolve in the days on the river; it appeared that our boat was standing still while the scenery changed around us. Green, brown, gray, golden; trees, crops, waterwheels, cliffs, temples, monuments; glowing sunrises and fiery sunsets that stained the water red; a sandstorm once that flecked the waters of the Nile brown and foamy and veiled the sun, bending the palms on the riverbanks almost double. At one point we entered an area of cliffs on one side and sand on the other that I called the Yellow Vale, for everything there was yellow in all its shades: buff, gold, orange, topaz, amber.

I was deeply glad that I had come; I did not regret the time spent. I found the Kandake and her proposal to me very comforting; in some ways it was the only honorable one I had yet received.

Alexandria, sparkling in the sun, brisk and bracing with its sea breezes. Perfect now in early June; and it felt good to return.

Rebuilding had been going on apace, and much of the war damage had been repaired. Mardian and Epaphroditus had managed things well, although there had been squabbles over—what else?—power. Mardian had resented the intrusion of this newcomer, and Epaphroditus had not liked taking a secondary position. Each of them was waiting to pounce on me and pour out his complaints about the other.

I spoke with Mardian first, and listened patiently to his recital of the aggravations of working with Epaphroditus: his arrogance, his insistence on his own methods, his unavailability at certain times, owing to his other business. I attempted to soothe him. Epaphroditus was there to ease his burden, to free him to take care of higher matters of state.

"Free me!" Mardian had snorted. "How can he free me when he imposes his own schedule on everyone else's?"

I sighed. I knew it would take some time before Ephaphroditus was weaned away from his other concerns, and if Mardian made his life difficult, working at the palace would never be very appealing. "Give him time," I said. "He is a stubborn man."

"I can say he is! I don't know why your heart is so set on him!"

"It is for both our sakes," I insisted. "You should not have to expend more than a quarter of your time on the financial matters." I paused. "You have done wonders in the rebuilding," I said. "I am most impressed. Soon the war will be erased."

"Not completely," he said. "There is always Caesarion to remind us that it happened."

Caesarion. I had returned to find my son about to begin walking. At the end of the month he would be a year old.

I nodded. "Yes. I know that, although sometimes it does seem unreal." I noticed that he was carrying several scrolls. "You have news. News of Caesar." I held out my hands for the letters and reports. Whatever was in them, I could face.

"He won, my lady," said Mardian. "He won."

The story was all in the scrolls, and I read and reread them for hours. This war had taxed Caesar's ingenuity and resourcefulness to the utmost, for one of his best lieutenants of the Gallic Wars, Labienus, was with the rebels. It was he who directed their strategy and tactics; it was he who knew how his former commander thought, and could anticipate his moves. It was he, Labienus, who knew that Caesar liked to strike fast and fight pitched battles. For four months he thwarted Caesar's attempts to do that. Caesar was unable to bring any of the parties to battle, and in the meantime was hard put to feed and supply his men.

At long last, through his own cleverness, Caesar managed to trick the enemy near the city of Thapsus. The city was located on an isthmus, and Caesar proceeded there with his entire army as if he meant to besiege it. He made an easy target for the enemy, who thought they had captured him. Actually it was he who had captured them. They divided their forces, thinking to bottle Caesar up. On his western side, Scipio and his legions and elephants dug in; on the eastern, Juba and Afranius. Like a nugget between them lay Caesar—his army all together in one body. The enemy was on narrow terrain, where the deployment of forces was difficult and cavalry was particularly hampered. It did not seem to occur to them that they were now exposed, divided, and on battleground unsuited for their strengths. Instead they gloated over having fenced Caesar in on a narrow neck of land.

While Scipio was entrenching, and drawing up his lines, Caesar left two legions to guard the city of Thapsus (whose inhabitants were cowering inside the walls) and his rear, with Juba and Afranius, and took the rest to fight Scipio. Against the two wings of elephants he deployed his four best legions, backed up by the Fifth, specially trained in terrorizing elephants and turning them against their masters. Likewise the other legions had been trained not to flinch in an elephant attack.

The troops were even more eager for battle than Caesar was; months of humiliating inactivity and hindrance had made them almost mad. It was all Caesar could do to restrain them; they pressed forward almost before he could give the battle-cry *Felicitas!* and lead the charge. The Fifth Legion, along with the slingers and archers, broke the left wing of elephants, and the animals stampeded back into their own lines; the rest of the army turned and fled. At the sight of Scipio's army collapsing, Juba and Afranius likewise fled. Caesar's angry troops pursued them, and even when they surrendered and begged for mercy, they slew them to a man.

Too many of the enemy soldiers had already been pardoned once by Caesar for fighting against him earlier. His soldiers were finished with clemency, even if their commander was not.

Immediately after the battle, Caesar rushed to Utica, where Cato and his supporters were. This was the gathering place of the wealthy senators and property owners who supported Pompey's cause. Doubtless the defeated generals would flee there; Caesar hoped to catch them, and also to capture Cato, his most relentless foe.

But Cato robbed him of the opportunity to demonstrate his clemency. "I am not willing to be indebted to the tyrant for his illegal actions," he said. "He is acting contrary to the laws when he pardons men as if he were their master, when he has no sovereignty over them." Then followed his stubborn and gory suicide. After a dinner with friends, and a private reading of Plato's dialogue of the soul, he smuggled a sword into his bedroom and, in the middle of the night, stabbed himself. His horrified family and physician discovered him before he could bleed to death. The wound was sutured. Then, before their eyes, he ripped it open with his own hands so his entrails spilled out, and he died on his couch.

The end of the others was equally showy. Juba planned to immolate himself—as well as his family and his subjects—on a giant funeral pyre in his capital city; the citizens did not wish to render their city for the service, so they refused him entrance. Juba and his ally, Petreius, instead held a death banquet in which they dined sumptuously, and then they fought a duel. Juba killed Petreius and then had himself killed by his slave. Scipio fled by sea and, when captured, stabbed himself on the deck of the ship. Mortally wounded, when his captors asked where the Imperator was, he told them, "*Imperator bene se habet*"—"The general is well enough, thank you"—and then he died.

Labienus, Varus, and both Pompey's sons, Gnaeus and Sextus, escaped to Spain—doubtless to fight again. But with the death of Cato, the Republic had expired.

In three weeks—three weeks that were long-sought and long in coming—all of North Africa had fallen into Caesar's hands. He proceeded to turn Juba's kingdom into the Roman province of New Africa, and doled out bits and pieces to reward the Mauretanian kings for their support.

Only Egypt remained free. All the rest was now Roman, won by Caesar.

Other letters contained vignettes of Caesar's behavior. One reported how, in an earlier attack, when all was confusion and Caesar was almost routed, he caught one of his fleeing standard-bearers, took him by the shoulders, turned him around, and said firmly, "*That* is the direction of the enemy."

Upon being told of Cato's suicide, he had said, "Cato, I must begrudge you your death, as you begrudged me the honor of saving your life." I myself rejoiced at Cato's death, as he had caused my uncle's more than ten years earlier in Cyprus. Death chasing death; suicide giving rise to suicide. Now, surely, it must end.

There was also a report that Caesar had loaded Eunoe, wife of the Moorish King Bogud, with presents, and rewarded her husband lavishly for allowing his wife to be his mistress. Nothing more. No details.

I forced myself to read on, though my heart was heavy. I had hoped to find no mention of it, so that I could dismiss it as an earlier rumor and slander put out by Scipio, with no foundation.

In order to hearten his soldiers, he did not belittle the enemy's strength, but rather exaggerated it. When his troops were in a panic over King Juba's advance, he addressed their fears thus: "You may take it from me that the King will be here within a few days, at the head of ten infantry legions, thirty thousand cavalry, a hundred thousand lightly armed troops, and three hundred elephants. This being the case, you may as well stop asking questions and making guesses. I have given you the facts, with which I am familiar." He was complimenting their valor by presenting them boldly with these overwhelming odds, as if they were of no real import to such soldiers as his.

He was liberal about his soldiers' predictable misbehavior, and one of his boasts was, "My soldiers fight just as well when they are stinking of perfume." But he was brutal in punishing desertion or mutiny—soldierly dishonor.

He always addressed his soldiers as "comrades" and gave them expensive equipment—weapons with gold and silver inlays, for example. But this was clever of him, for it made them more determined not to be disarmed in battle. He loved his men dearly, and they loved him. He won the devotion of his army, and their devotion to him made them extraordinarily brave. Private soldiers offered to serve under him without pay or rations, and throughout all the civil wars there were almost no desertions, including during this one.

It was his custom to spare all enemy soldiers captured the first time; only if they were taken a second time did he order their execution.

Other letters concerned the state of affairs in Rome, and Caesar's expected return there in Quintilis. Only it was no longer to be known as Quintilis, but to be renamed *July* in his honor. *July*, the month when Gaius Julius Caesar had been born.

But for all those letters, reports, dispatches, and scrolls about Caesar, there was no word from Caesar himself. He was silent toward me, silent toward Egypt.

More news trickled in. The shattered forces of the followers of Pompey, bedraggled and dazed, were gathering in Spain. Spain seemed to breed one uprising and discontent after another. Caesar would have to go there and end it once and for all. But not yet.

At last it came: a letter from Caesar; and it came from Utica, not Rome. He was still on our coasts. I took it and withdrew onto the most secluded part of my terrace, holding it for a long time before opening it. I had waited so long, and now I was hesitant to end the suspense. But finally I did break the seal and read it.

To the Most Divine and Mighty Queen of Egypt, Cleopatra, Greetings:

The war is finished, and I have been victorious. It was a difficult campaign. I cannot say veni, vidi, vici—*I came, I saw, I conquered—this time. I would have to say, I came, I saw, I waited, I planned, I overcame—the opposite of succinct, both the statement and the war. But it is the final outcome, the* vici, *that matters. Knowing that Egypt was always to the east gave me courage. I knew that I had an utterly reliable ally nearby, a precious thing.*

And now I return to Rome, where the Senate has granted me the right to hold four Triumphs in succession: one to celebrate my victory in Gaul, the next Egypt, the next Pontus, and the last Africa. They will be held in September. Rome will never have seen anything like it. I invite you to come and share my celebration. It is especially important that you be present with me during the Egypt Triumph, to show that it was your enemies I overthrew, and that you are a staunch supporter of Rome. Your sister Arsinoe will be led as a captive.

Please bring as large a retinue as you wish. I will house you all in my private villa across the Tiber, which has extensive gardens. I think you will find the accommodations suitable for a long stay. I greatly look forward to seeing you again, and to seeing your most royal son.

Your assured friend and ally, Gaius Julius Caesar, Imperator

I let my hand, holding the letter, fall to my side. It said so much; it said so little. Every phrase could be interpreted in different ways. "I knew that I had an utterly reliable ally nearby, a precious thing. . . ." Was it the knowing that was precious, or the ally? "I think you will find the accommodations suitable for a long stay. . . ." Was he expecting me to stay indefinitely? Why? And as for the clever way he both asked to see our son and avoided legitimizing his name by writing it—!

No! I would not go! He could not order me to, like a vassal or a client king!

And yet that is what you are, a vassal, a client monarch who holds her throne only because Rome allows her to. You are no different from Bocchus of Mauretania or Ariobarzanes of Cappadocia. The proud kingdom of Ptolemy has been reduced to that. But at least it has not been reduced to a Roman province—New Africa.

There was a threat in his words, and not veiled, either. Be there to show you are not Rome's enemy, or, like a watchman with his dogs, he was saying, I may not be able to control what *they* do. So be there.

He had promised to bring me to Rome. But I had not thought it would be like this—to do obeisance to his conquests.

My anger had passed. I knew I had to go. Never mind what he had meant when he wrote the letter. What mattered was what would happen after I got there.

I would have to learn Latin, that much was certain. If I could not understand what was being spoken all around me, I would be at a terrible disadvantage. I had never learned it because it was not a very important language, and besides, all educated Romans spoke Greek. But in Rome, of course, they would be speaking Latin.

I asked Mardian to find me a good Latin tutor, and also informed him that I would be departing for Rome in only a month and leaving him in complete charge of the government—with the help of Epaphroditus, of course. He looked uneasy.

"It is no different from when I went to Nubia," I assured him. "That did not worry you."

"It *is* different," he said, his broad brow all wrinkled up. "You may stay in Rome indefinitely!"

"That's ridiculous. What would I do there? The Triumphs will last a few weeks, that is all."

"What if Caesar—what if he—wants you to stay there? What if he divorces Calpurnia?"

"What if he does? He's been divorced before."

"Yes, and then he remarried. Are you—is there a possibility—?"

"Even if I married him, I would not live in Rome like a housewife!"

"That is what women do in Rome."

"That is changing. There is, for example, a firebrand named Fulvia, the wife of a politician, who doesn't stay home at all but takes to the streets for her causes. Servilia, Brutus's mother, is influential with the Senate. But that is beside the point. Those are Roman women, with Roman concerns. I have a kingdom to rule, and it is here."

"Roman concerns would quickly become your concerns, I fear. And you would be engulfed in them, like falling into a tar pit."

"Egypt is my first and only concern."

"Does Caesar know that?"

"He should! He saw it firsthand!"

"You may look different to him in Rome, just the right queenly ornament to acquire for his house."

"I have no wish to be his ornament, or to be put in a niche in his house."

"What do you wish, then?"

"I will be his equal as a ruler, or nothing."

I had scant time to prepare. I would have to embark for the voyage in fewer than thirty days. Thirty days to plunge into Latin, to select my entourage, to foresee the problems that might arise during my absence from Egypt, to fit myself out as if for a campaign. For it *was* a campaign—a campaign to secure myself and my country in Rome. It was also my task to take the measure of the infamous Romans on their home ground.

I set about it in methodical fashion. The Latin lessons began at once. I found them daunting. It is a difficult language, because nearly everything is determined by the case or tense of a word; its place in the sentence can be deceiving. *Amicum puer videt* and *puer amicum videt* both mean "the boy sees his friend." So you could throw all the words helter-skelter, like a child tumbling blocks, and wherever they landed you could still reassemble the original thought by the form of the words. This should have been reassuring, but it was not, because it meant you had to memorize enormous numbers of word endings.

At least, my tutor assured me, it meant there were no double meanings in Latin. A word could mean only one thing. Ah, but what that one thing was—a Herculean task to determine!

And so I toiled away twice daily in the thickets of *sum-esse-fui-futurus* and *duco-ducere-duxi-ductum*.

My entourage was relatively easy to select. Not knowing how long I would be gone, I would not remove Olympos from his patients, but take one of his associates; I would leave Mardian and Epaphroditus behind to steer the government; I would leave Iras but take Charmian, whose expertise in wardrobe matters was a necessity. At all times I would be on display, I knew that. Even supposedly alone in my chambers—Caesar's chambers, rather—there would be spies. I must do Egypt proud and make Caesar realize I was someone to be reckoned with, even far from my base of power. And I did not want him to have to defend himself for his taste in taking up with me; that would just lay a heavier burden on me. Of course there was vanity involved as well—why bother to deny it? I wanted all of Rome to gasp when they saw me, to say, *So that is Egypt!* I wanted to erase all memories of my father as an embarrassing, begging representative of Egypt. I wanted to dazzle their eyes with gold and beauty.

But what sort of clothes would achieve this? Charmian, with her exquisite and elegant taste, helped me to choose a variety of costumes, from the near-gaudy—gilded threads and bejeweled in the Persian style—to the most simple Grecian gowns with plain, flowing silk mantles.

"For until you actually set foot there, it is hard to tell what will *feel* appropriate," she said. "What seems perfect here in your high, open chambers in Alexandria may be all wrong in Caesar's villa. They say it is stifling hot there this time of year—that the Romans would sell their souls for a fresh breeze in summer. Then in winter it is very cold—oh, but you will not stay until winter," she said quickly. "No need to worry about that. But for summer, you will need the thinnest fabrics. And for the Triumphs—then you must look a queen indeed. For your headdress: either the double crown of Egypt or the diadem of the Ptolemies. And you must be loaded with jewels, to the point of vulgarity. Let them all look, and lust, and envy Caesar!"

"Shall I wear the Red Sea pearls, all five strands of them?"

"Indeed. And the rope of emeralds, to twine around them."

"I am not beautiful," I said. "What if all these jewels just call attention to it?"

Charmian looked surprised. "Who told you you were not beautiful?"

"When I was small, my sister Arsinoe. And later, my friends never told me I *was* beautiful." *But Caesar did. He said, "Child of Venus, you are fair."* I stamped on the memory quickly.

"Mardian and Olympos wouldn't tell Aphrodite herself, and as for the others, perhaps they assumed you knew it, or that to say it was to sound as if they were flattering a queen. Whether you are classically beautiful or not, this one thing I know: you give the *impression* of being beautiful, which is all one can ask. The jewels become you, they do not belittle you."

I took her hands. "Charmian, you give me courage. Together we will conquer Rome!"

Little Caesarion must also be prepared. As I said, he was walking now—just barely. And although he was able to understand many words, there were few he could say as yet. I tried to teach him to say *Caesar* and *Father*, but they are difficult words to pronounce. He would laugh and blurt out all sorts of other sounds. I watched his face carefully, trying to imagine what it would look like to someone who had never seen it before. But it was an impossible task, because he was so much a part of me now, I could not make that leap of imagination to seeing him strange and anew.

I stood on the quay of the royal harbor. The wind was whipping the traveling cloak that I had draped over my shoulders, and little waves were dancing in the harbor, showing underbellies of white. Clouds raced across the sky; it was a good day to set sail.

The ship—a fast galley—rode the waves, pulling at its ropes like a child impatient to run away. Caesarion was stabbing his finger at the gulls flying overhead, shrieking with excitement. It was time to be off.

I mounted the gangplank and went aboard. All of Alexandria was spread out before me, extending far to the left and right, its white buildings more lovely and precious than any ivory. My city! My nation! I had never felt prouder or more protective of it.

I go to secure you, I thought. Alexandria, I go to make sure you are free forever.

I turned to the captain, who was standing behind me on the deck.

"Cast off," I said. "I am ready. Make for Rome."

HERE ENDS THE SECOND SCROLL.

THE THIRD SCROLL

21

The sea rolled before me, the flat horizon opening toward lands unseen. Behind me I saw, for the first time, what sailors approaching Alexandria beheld: upon the low, featureless coastline, the tall Lighthouse beckoning; and behind it, the gleaming white buildings of the city, spotted here and there with the bright colors of flowering vines climbing over the walls. I had never left that coastline, and now I was seeing it as strangers do.

The color of the open ocean was darker and more solid than that of the harbor or river. I felt a thrill of excitement at the prospect of my voyage, of venturing out over all this deep, heaving water. We were going to follow the same direct route as the large, grain-transporting merchantmen, rather than hugging the coastline like a timid fishing boat. It was much faster, but it was also more hazardous. The route from Alexandria to Rome lay on a gigantic northwest slant of over twelve hundred miles, if you could fly like a stork. If you could not pass through the Strait of Messina—the narrow stretch between Sicily and Italy that at one treacherous point shrinks to about two miles, bounded by tidal currents and rocks and whirlpools—then you were obliged to go the long way around Sicily, making the journey even longer. The fastest time ever made on a journey from the Strait of Messina to Alexandria was six days, but going the other way it was slower, owing to the prevailing winds and currents. I prayed we would not take a great long time to reach our destination; although I was uneasy about what I would find when I arrived in Rome, neither did I wish to postpone it. My courage is highest when I can go to action; inaction saps my resolve.

My ship was an oared galley, not a warship by any means, but armed with a small number of soldiers. It was speed I had wanted for this journey, but also sufficient size to permit sailing on rough or open waters. I had not thought to need the protection of a warship. Pompey, after all, had put down the pirates.

Some twenty years earlier, Pompey had been dispatched by the Roman Senate to clear the Mediterranean of pirates, which were infesting the sea from one end to the other. Many high-ranking people—including Caesar himself—had been taken captive by them, and shipping was unsafe. Pompey had fulfilled his mandate, and swept the seas clear of them, by assembling a full-scale navy against them. Since then the goods had flowed freely and sailors had been unhampered. There were still undoubtedly places where they lurked, for no vermin is ever completely eradicated—rats scurry back to the cleanest-swept pantry. But their numbers were small now, and their favorite haunts, the Cilician and Dalmatian coasts, were far to the east. I did not know then that Sardinia and Sicily were their western playgrounds.

The ship dipped and rose, like a huge sea beast. The long, rolling motion felt good, as if I were striding over all the earth. It was now, as I stood upon the deck, feeling the first slap of salt spray on my cheeks, that I began to think seriously of rebuilding the Egyptian fleet.

It had fallen low since most of it had been lost in the Alexandrian War. Many of the ships had been burnt in the harbor because my brother had had control of them. I would have to import long timbers from Syria, but that should not prove difficult. Syria was a Roman province, and would have to obey Caesar. Yes, it was time for the Egyptian navy to be resurrected.

Now that we were under way, the captain came to stand beside me on the deck. We were headed almost due west, and the going was slow. Our big, square sail was of little use, as the prevailing wind was from the west; the rowers were hard at work, their oars dipping rhythmically in and out of the bright blue water. Overhead the sky was clear, the clouds passing to the east.

"This is the fastest route, is it not?" I asked.

"Yes, it is as straight as a Roman road," he said. "The problem is the winds at this time of year. They blow in exactly the wrong direction. And the expanse of water is so great that there is a natural limitation on the speed of the rowers. This galley has four men to each oar, but they cannot row without rest for days on end."

Because I had decided to enter Rome with little fanfare, and to go quietly to my place of residence, I had selected a modest ship. Now I wondered if that had been a mistake.

"A larger ship is not necessarily faster," said the captain, as if he had read my mind. "Their heavy timbers require much more wind and muscle to move them. That is why the pirates, the best sailors in the world, keep their vessels relatively light and small. No, my lady, this is the best speed we can hope for."

Disappointment and anxiety flooded me. Travel was so slow!

A private cabin had been outfitted for me and my attendants inside the deckhouse where the captain and officers would retire. Although they had painted it in bright colors, I could see by the paint already peeling that it would be a damp journey. They had built a bed bolted to the floor, and a smaller one for Caesarion, with guardrails. Charmian was to sleep on a pallet on the floor, which was rolled up during the day. Our chests of personal belongings were chained to rings on the floor and walls.

Little Ptolemy XIV, my consort, had a separate room of his own. I had brought him along because he had been so curious about Rome, and besides, seeing what had happened to Arsinoe would be a warning to him, although he was a sweet child so far. Also, leaving him behind might prove a temptation to enemies to use him as a figurehead and start another dreary round of civil war—the last thing I needed.

I went in to see what Caesarion was doing; he was playing with a bag filled with lentils, which one of the sailors had given him. While I watched him, his fingers released the bag and he dozed off to sleep.

Poor child! I thought. This will be a long journey.

The next morning I could barely make out a golden smudge on the far horizon; it was the coast of North Africa, the desert that lay to the west of Egypt. Gradually it receded from sight and we were alone in open water, the sea stretching endlessly on all sides.

On the eighth day a squall came up; the skies blackened and released torrents of rain. But in its wake came a gratifying change in the wind's direction: it swung around and turned into an easterly Levanter, blowing us where we wished to go. Up went the sail to harness it.

Now we seemed to be flying—for as long as the wind continued. We reached that point in the sea where we were opposite Crete, then Greece; and then we were swept out into the greatest stretch of open sea on our entire voyage.

Charmian was not faring well on this voyage; for the first few days she had been grievously seasick. Now, pale and shaky, she emerged from the cabin and stood beside me.

"How much longer will we be on this wretched sea?" she moaned.

"I'll put you on a camel for the return journey," I said. "You can go the long way round—by the time you reach Alexandria we shall both be old. Caesarion will have made me a grandmother."

"I don't care to waste my youth on a caravan journey," she said. "But I feel as if this journey has already made me old."

Strange, but it had had the opposite effect on me: I found the sea air invigorating, and the unfamiliar smells and sounds I encountered every day fascinated me. There was, first of all, the pervading sea-salt odor, and the smell of the wind, bringing with it the faintest tang of the land it had blown over. There was the rich smell of the fresh-caught fish—so different from those sold in markets—and the musty dampness of the soaked ropes. The tar and resin found everywhere on board gave off a warm, raisinlike aroma that grew stronger as the sun rose.

As for the sounds, I loved the *slap-slap-slap* of the water against the hull of the ship; it lulled me to sleep. The creaking of the rigging and the *whoosh* of the sail as it filled and deflated was like nothing else. How ordinary the sounds of street and market were by comparison.

Water had lost its terror for me, for which I was deeply grateful. First I had ventured the harbor, then the Nile, now the open sea—I was cured of my fear, thanks be to all the gods!

"You will not even remember the misery as soon as you set foot in Rome," I assured her. "You will recover readily enough in Caesar's villa."

I hoped it was true. I was beginning to lose count of how many days we had been traveling. Every night I moved a bead on a bracelet to keep track. We were sailing even at night, since it was impossible to anchor in these deep waters. For some days the moon had been dark, making it easier to see the stars, but nothing else.

To my disappointment, the captain had decided to take the long way around Sicily.

"If this Levanter keeps blowing, it will be much safer, even if longer," he said. "The Strait of Messina is best approached from the opposite side, with a north wind at your back. That way you encounter the whirlpool and the rock at the outset, when you have the most maneuvering room."

"Scylla and Charybdis," I said. "Are they as fearsome as legend says?"

"Indeed they are," he said. "The rock—Scylla—is almost impossible to avoid if you are trying to escape the whirlpool, Charybdis. Of course the whirlpool is not there all the time, only when violent water boils up at the tide changes, four times a day."

"Have you ever seen her seize a ship?"

"Yes. I watched from land as a fishing boat got pulled down into her maws. The water swirls—a big, oily-looking circle—and anything nearby gets drawn into the circle. Then, once in it—the boat spins faster and faster. I saw it break up, saw its timbers come apart where they had been fastened, and the fisherman was thrown out. He clung to a piece of timber, but he disappeared right into the center of the funnel—it has an indentation that's dark and sucking. The pieces of the boat followed him. At the center they were spinning so fast they were just a blur to my eyes; then they disappeared."

I shuddered.

"Charybdis disgorges things, but not the things she swallows," he said. "The fisherman never returned. But the monster vomited up deformed fish—fish without eyes and with grotesque appendages on their heads. Enormous strands of seaweed erupt from that evil center, like huge sea serpents." He paused. "So we'll go the other way, with your permission."

"My permission? I am no navigator, no sailor."

"Yet you have a feel for the sea, I can tell."

Surprising but true. "I will leave the command of the vessel to you," I assured him.

———

Landfall! The mountains of Sicily became visible, their rugged tops shining like a mirage. We steered for her, and the mountains grew slowly clearer. I felt relief flooding through me. We had reached the other side of the Mediterranean.

Then, as unexpectedly as one of Homer's gods, the wind shifted quickly to the south—a hot, damp wind, oppressive and heavy. At the same time, Sicily suddenly became wreathed in fog. The wind was forcing us toward that shore, and we could see no rocks or other natural features.

"No more sail!" ordered the captain. The deckhands rushed to disengage the now-dangerous sail. "Oars! Oars! Row to the west!"

I was standing, watching all this with bright interest, when I saw the little ships emerging from the foggy shoreline. They were moving at breakneck speed—how could they go that fast? They must be all oarsmen and no cargo.

"Look!" I pointed them out to the captain. I expected him to say "Sicilian fishing boats" or "racing boats," and explain about them.

Instead he went pale and cried, "Pirates! Pirates!"

They were making for us—three boats.

"Hemiolias," he said. "Of the fastest kind."

"I thought Pompey had destroyed the pirates," I cried, as if saying it would make them disappear. I was still so ignorant then—I trusted in so many things.

"Most of them, yes. But some linger on—like lions in the far mountains of Syria." He found his voice, and his courage, again. "Sails again! Sails again!" he yelled. "Come about! Make for the strait!"

The ship spun wildly around as the sail was let out and the fierce wind filled it, dragging the ship northward. We were headed toward the shore, where rocks waited in the mist. Behind us the pirates had swung their ships to follow. They were hoisting their sails now, too.

I could hear the dashing of the waves against the rocks ahead, even though I could not see them through the fog.

"Turn! Turn! Hard astarboard!"

The ship thrust itself to the right, riding on the crest of a wave. Suddenly we were in the channel, the opening of the strait. Was the current flowing north or south—with us or against us?

I was dismayed as I saw the pattern of the waves. The current was coming toward us; the wind and the waves would battle, and we would make little headway. The pirates would catch us easily—if they dared follow us into the strait.

We plunged on, the boat dipping and bucking. The wind was pushing us forward, but the waves were hitting and slapping us in the opposite direction, thudding against our bow and trying to turn us sideways, to drive us onto the rocky shore.

"Port-side oarsmen, row with all your strength!" cried the captain. Only that would keep us from drifting to the side.

The channel narrowed, becoming more dangerous by the minute. In one stretch of relatively calm water, a pirate boat caught up with us, and a grapnel was thrown on board. They tried to board us, but our soldiers hacked off their lines and let them fall into the sea. All the pirates had elected to follow; the other boats were closing in on our wake.

Now the channel narrowed even more, and the sea began to churn. Ahead of us, in the white, clingy mist, I could see only darkness. The channel was veering to the east, rightward.

A dull noise filled my ears, a low undercurrent of sound.

"The whirlpool! It's spinning!" The captain was pointing. "Row as far east as possible! Stay out of its grasp!"

Now, opening up before me, I could see the disturbed water surface, innocent-looking, just a series of large ripples, all curving in the same direction.

"Stay away from those margins!" the captain yelled.

Caesarion was in my arms, and I held him tightly. We would not lose one another to the dangerous waters; no, I would never let him go, as my mother had me. The wind was whipping my face and sending columns of sea spray high over the deck. The noise of the whirlpool was increasing; now it was as noisy as a cart rumbling over a stone road.

Coming up on our left—the whirlpool side—was another of the pirate boats. I saw the men standing on deck, and one of them grasped a line and swung directly onto our deck, dropping down as lithely as a monkey. He straightened himself and looked around, pulling a dagger from his belt. Behind him, with a steady *thump-thump-thump*, came his shipmates, landing softly, one by one.

My soldiers swung around to confront them as the deck rose and fell. Looming closer and closer ahead of us was the whirlpool. All hands were needed to save the ship; only my guards could be spared to fight the pirates.

"Insignia!" one of them cried, a tall, wild-haired man, with the glee of a child who has discovered a pile of toys. "Royal insignia!"

"It's the Queen's ship, all right," one of them cried. He was red-faced and shouting. "We were right. First one to capture her gets half the ransom!" They advanced, bent over. Again I thought of monkeys.

How did they know I was passing this way? The word must have got out quickly, for I had not been gone from Egypt that long.

One of my bodyguards drew his stout sword, and the others around me sprang into action. The fight was on. I clutched Caesarion. They would never get him, even if I had to kill every one of them myself. I was so blinded with rage I wanted to kill, and never doubted that I could.

One of the burly soldiers managed to fling a dark-haired pirate overboard, and he hit the water like a stone, sending up an enormous column of water. He was an excellent swimmer, and soon surfaced. But he had landed on the outer rim of the whirlpool, and I watched in fascinated horror as the mighty force of it lifted him and spun him toward the center, where he disappeared.

One of the pirates on deck, who looked older than the others, gave a bloodcurdling cry and flung himself through the air at me, like a big cat. He knocked me to the ground, but I did not let go of Caesarion.

"You've killed my brother!" he screamed. "Now I have two to avenge!" He slashed with his dagger, but his hand was trembling so much that he missed.

"Fool! Kill our ransom?" Another pirate, landing sickeningly near, pinned his arm down. "Let Caesar pay for her! Like he paid for himself!" He had a loud, commanding voice.

I twisted and rolled away. One of my soldiers attacked the two men, and another joined him.

They knew exactly who I was, and had some grievance with Caesar. This had been carefully planned.

The soldiers had the pirates pinned, and were about to slit their throats.

"Stop!" I screamed. "This is an attack against Caesar. Let him see them, and punish them!"

Disappointed, the soldiers had no choice but to obey. They savagely hit the pirates on the head to knock them unconscious, then threw their bodies down with the rowers.

The hand-to-hand fighting on the deck went on, but the pirates were retreating, demoralized at the capture of their leaders. One of them plunged overboard, diving directly into the center of the whirlpool in a spectacular arching leap of suicide.

Now we were passing just to the side of the monster, and its cry had become a roar. I felt the ship straining as the almost irresistible force of the suction pulled on its timbers; I could smell the foul odor of whatever it was belching up from the deep, perhaps the remains of its digested victims.

"Hold fast! Hold fast!" cried the captain. The ship shuddered and groaned; the whirlpool reached for us; we shot past it.

Ahead of us loomed the ugly, high, jagged rock.

"Quick! Steer to the other side, to the other side!" screamed the captain. The gushing white foam that surrounded the vicious rock like a skirt touched our sides. There was no escape. We were going right for it! We were going to burst open on it!

With a wrench, the boat dashed against a seaweed-bed that had been disgorged from the whirlpool and now matted against some rocks. The boat struck them broadside, but the seaweed cushioned the blow and we escaped gouging. The force of it turned the ship so it changed direction and scudded past the base of the great rock of Scylla. The sea monster, she of the six heads who had devoured six of Odysseus's men, missed her meal with us. The boat emerged on the other side of her, and suddenly we were out of the strait altogether, being blown clear of it by our old companion, the south wind.

Behind us straggled two of the pirate boats. One went down in the whirl-pool, to the ghastly wailing of its crew. The other escaped destruction, but gave up the chase once we had cleared the strait.

I was trembling all over, as if my limbs had incorporated the waves within themselves. I clung to the rail and kept looking behind us to see the dark-toothed rock of Scylla growing smaller, receding behind our wake. The oars-men were still rowing frantically, and in their panic they started to lose the rhythm of their strokes. Oars started hitting oars instead of dipping and leaving the water in perfect timing. The timekeeper, the *keleustes*, calmed them by ordering them to slow down.

In the meantime, the two captured pirates were being chained up before they regained consciousness. They were hauled up from the rowers' benches, where they were hardly wanted, and tied to the mast. They slumped over, their heads lolling to one side.

I studied them carefully. One of them was bald and very muscular; his fellow was a weedy little man. It was the bald one who had tried to stab me, and had yelled about his brother. The skinny one had talked about a ransom from Caesar. They both looked old to be pirates; I guessed them to be around fifty, unless the harsh sun had aged their skins unduly.

"They'll talk soon enough," said the captain. "But why didn't you let them be killed?"

"I wish to make a present of them to Caesar," I said. "It was his name they invoked; this has something to do with him." Although I had brought gifts—a costly Pharaonic statue that I knew Caesar coveted, as well as the usual gold and pearls—I knew the pirates would please him most of all.

More sail was let out, to give the rowers a rest. We were now beginning to slide past the coast of Italy itself—Italy at last! Ahead of us in the sea, like a gigantic natural lighthouse, sat the great volcano of Strongyle, its top emitting steam and clouds.

"How much longer now?" I asked the captain, knowing I sounded like a child.

He looked up at the clouds being pushed along with us.

"If this south wind holds, only another few days," he said. "Another few days until we land."

It was ten days—the wind died down—until we approached the port of Ostia at the mouth of the Tiber, the famous Tiber. I stepped onto the landing and felt the solid earth beneath my feet for the first time in weeks. We had made surprisingly good time, considering the prevailing winds and currents, but it had still taken over forty days.

I looked at the stream before me with astonishment. The Tiber was a small river, nothing like my Nile. It looked so harmless, so utterly negligible, a child's river. What kind of people lived on its banks, in their city that sought to rule the entire world?

22

The sun had set; the sky above remained a rich and tender gold-streaked blue. Slowly I turned around to study my surroundings, this first soil of Italy upon which I found myself. The most immediate thing that struck me was the trees—towering pines with wide parasols of bristled branches. I had never seen anything remotely like them. Their trunks were bare until a certain height, like a palm tree, but their twisted limbs and odd foliage, of a deep, dark green, seemed something from a fanciful traveler's tale. Just then a gentle breeze stirred the tops of the trees, and the most extraordinary aroma came out of them: sweet, piercing, seemingly the very essence of greenness.

Under my feet was a thick carpet of grass, denser than any I had ever seen. There were brittle brown needles in it—dead pine leaves, I assumed—that my shoes crushed, releasing still more pine odor. The grass itself felt moist and strangely springy and resilient; alive, not dead like a flat rug.

We had sent messengers to notify Caesar of our arrival, but before they could possibly have reached him, a contingent of officials approached us. They brought sleek horses and several litters, and were headed by a magistrate riding a white horse. He was clearly looking for us; his head was swiveling from side to side. Behind him rode another official-looking man.

Sighting us, he reined in his horse and, dismounting, walked toward us. I saw that he was a middle-aged man with one of those round faces that are difficult to remember, because they are so ordinary. He was wearing a white tunic with narrow vertical bands, and a light cloak over it. He carried a scroll in one hand.

"Queen Cleopatra?" he asked, before bowing his head. "Welcome to Rome. I am here in Caesar's name to greet you, and escort you to your quarters. I am Gaius Oppius."

So Caesar had not come himself. Of course it would have been improper for him to wait on the ramparts for my arrival and then rush out like a schoolboy. My arrival was not predictable; I could have come at any time. Yet I was disappointed. My sting of disappointment told me how much I wished to see him. I forced myself to smile.

"I thank you, my good friend," I said.

The second man had now dismounted, and was making his way over to us. He was tall, with formidable dark eyebrows. He approached briskly, bowed, and said, "Cornelius Balbus at your service, Your Majesty. In the wars, *praefectus fabrum* of Caesar's army." His Greek had a heavy Spanish accent.

"We are the most trusted agents and secretaries of the glorious Caesar," said Oppius. "It is our honor to serve him day and night." He handed me the scroll. "A message from the Mighty One."

I broke the seal and unrolled it carefully. It was still light enough to read—

most peculiar, for it to remain light so long after sunset—and I was glad; I did not wish a hovering torchbearer to read it over my shoulder.

It was very short, and it would not have mattered if a torchbearer had read it. It also bore no date; obviously he had prepared it ahead of time.

> Welcome to Rome. It is my privilege to be able to repay your kind hospitality to me in Alexandria. I have no palace in which to house you, but I offer my best residence: my villa and gardens across the Tiber. Regard them as if they were yours. I myself will be at my home near the Temple of Vesta in the Forum. I will call upon you, with all respect, as soon as I may. I trust your journey was without incident.
>
> With all honor and regard,
>
> G. Julius Caesar, Consul, Imperator, Dictator of the Roman People

"Dictator?" I wondered out loud.

"For the next ten years. An honor just conferred," said Balbus. "One without precedent." He beamed as if he had engineered it himself.

"What does it mean?" I asked. "I thought a Roman dictator was appointed only for emergencies, and only for six months."

They shrugged. "Caesar makes all things new, rewriting them in his own image." They looked around at my party. "Young King Ptolemy?" They asked in unison. My little brother blushed with pleasure at the attention. "And . . . ?" They leaned over and studied Caesarion.

Now was the time to say it. "This is the son the Dictator Caesar has given me." I held him up so they could see him clearly.

They did not respond, except to say, "The royal litter is for you, and your son. For the rest, we have brought horses and carriages."

It was dark before we reached our destination. I watched from the litter as we proceeded along the Tiber, up toward Rome in the failing light. We passed alongside the city wall, rough-cut stone with torches flaring in their sockets. The creak of the leather straps on the litter, and the angle of it, told me we were climbing up a hill. As we went higher, I could just see the city of Rome on the far side of the river. It looked small and its buildings were dark— mostly of brick, I assumed. There was no glow of white marble, and nothing lofty, reaching toward the sky. Here and there I thought I saw a temple, but I could not be sure.

I heard the rustle of what seemed a forest, and a cool breeze reached inside the litter. Caesarion had fallen asleep against me, only to be awakened as they set the litter down.

"We are here, Your Majesty." Balbus himself drew the curtains and offered me his hand to help me out.

Before me loomed a large dwelling, surrounded by a frame of trees and grounds filled with—from what I could see—hedges, statues, and fountains. The air was more than cool, it was perfumed with light, playful fragrances. The flowers here were evidently more delicate and their perfume more subtle than ours of Egypt. The leaves on a thousand trees were whispering to me in the night.

Servants emerged from the entrance to the building, carrying torches.

"Welcome, welcome," they chorused. At least I could understand that much Latin without difficulty.

I followed them toward the doorway, flanked with statues in niches on either side. Immediately I found myself walking on mosaic, and ahead of me was a large open room, a sort of enclosed courtyard. More doors opened off that; the servants were gliding through one of them, and I followed.

Up a stairway, and then down another hallway, and finally into a large tile-floored room. Even in the dim light I could see that the walls were not white, but a deep green, with painted garlands hung all around.

"Here is Caesar's own room, now yours," said the servant. "He gives it to you."

A table stood, draped with a heavy red cloth, and on it a tray of fruit, breads, and a pitcher of wine. To one side was a large bed, its legs of carved wood, a coverlet of fine wool on it. Several couches, more tables, ornate oil lamp stands, and then—I began to notice how many statues were displayed here. At least now I could know that Caesar would always welcome another one, but I wished he did not already have so many.

The servants lit the many wicks in the standing holder—six or seven lamps swung from its arms. The room grew much lighter. Suddenly I was very tired, and only desired to put them out again and lie down.

I was asleep. I had no idea how long I had been asleep; the odd sensation of walking on firm ground again after so many days at sea, as well as the sudden impact of unfamiliar language, colors, and smells all around me, had confused my sense of time and place. I opened my eyes to see the faint light of a lamp being held up over my head. Someone was standing beside my bed, watching me.

With a start I sat up, but swifter than my movement a hand grasped my shoulder. The other one put the lamp down and embraced me.

"I am here, my dearest, my beloved," said the voice of Caesar, a soft whisper in the darkness.

It still seemed like a dream, but there was no other voice like that in all the world. In the miracle of his physical presence I forgot his long silence, I forgot Eunoe (but if I did, why then do I mention her?), I forgot his stilted, cold, peremptory letters. I flung my arms around him with a cry of gladness.

"Forgive me, I could not meet you, could not ever send a private letter. I knew whatever I wrote would be public knowledge. I rejoice that you came anyway. I prayed you would sense all the things I could not openly say."

He kissed me, and it was as if he had never been parted from me for more than an instant. Yet so much had happened since then; so many battles, so many men killed, so many victories for him and defeats for others. Still, here he sat in the dark, on a bed like any other person, stealing in at night, eager like a lover unsure of himself.

"I did. I do," I assured him. Such simple words, after so long a time. I reached out my hand and touched his face. I thought of all he was, here in Rome.

"My Dictator," I murmured. "Must I obey all your commands?"

"Only Roman citizens are bound to do so," he said. "You are free from my demands. Whatever we choose to do, we need only follow our own private desires."

I leaned over and kissed him, feeling once again his firm, narrow mouth, so often remembered. "So when the Queen of Egypt kisses the Dictator of Rome, it is not political?"

"No," he said. "Whatever my enemies say, I swear to you that this is a private passion, and entirely my own."

"For no other reason?"

"I swear it. In bringing you to Rome, I have given my enemies grist for their mill. It serves no political purpose; a wiser politician than I would never have done it. It will excite the envy of all who are not so fortunate, and give offense to those who are overly moralistic." He shook his head. "But I care not. This repays me—just to see you once again." He kissed me then, so fiercely that I had no desire to continue talking, no wish to resist him. He seemed to have the power to ignite such consuming passion in me that all thought fled before it. It was always his own genius to cause me to suspend all reason, all caution, to give myself up entirely to his secret moment.

I ran my hand over his shoulders, feeling their hard strength beneath the seam of his tunic. He was barely back from the field, and his soldier's life there had clearly burned off any remnants of ease from his body. He seemed entirely an instrument of war, polished and honed like one of his legionaries' swords. In the feel of his arms there was no cushion, no softness. Yet his words were tender, his voice caressing.

Moving my hands over his chest, I found it felt more like the leather cuirass a common soldier wears to protect it than like weak flesh that needs protecting. But I could feel the rise and fall of his chest as he breathed, proving that he was no suit of armor or a bronze statue. His breath was coming faster than if he were merely at rest; it was more as if he had sighted something from the crest of a hill, something he had not expected. He sighed, and a relaxation spread through him.

"You are here, and all is well," he said. He turned slightly on the edge of the bed where he sat, and took my face between his hands. Silently he studied my features in the dull, flickering light for so long I wondered why. Why was he staring at me so intently? His dark eyes seemed to be searching for something in mine, something out of his sight. "Yes, you truly are she," he finally said.

Who? I wanted to ask. *Who is "she"?*

He bent his head to kiss my shoulders, kissing each one in turn like a priest bestowing an honor, then he kissed all along my collar bones, until he reached the hollow of my neck. His lips were light, fluttering against my skin like the brush of a butterfly's wings, making my blood leap up to meet them.

Once, twice, three times, he kissed that hollow, each time more lingeringly, until at last he put the full force of his mouth against it, causing something inside me to turn over with sickening desire. I threw my head back and felt my body beg for more. I wanted him to go on kissing me there forever, but at the same time remaining passive and limp was too much torture for me.

I twisted my head and began to kiss the side of his neck all the way up to his ear, and ran my hands over his back. This tunic! He had to get rid of it, it was standing between my hands and his flesh, his marvelous flesh that I longed to feel directly. I pulled at its sleeves, trying to force it down over his arms. He stopped what he was doing and laughed softly.

"I am happy to oblige," he said. "But I would not wish to have you as my general; clearly you are impatient for battle. Such generals often lead charges before their troops are ready, and lose battles thereby."

"Are you not ready for battle?" I asked. He had embarrassed me. I dropped his sleeve.

He kissed me, this time on the mouth. "But, my sweet child, this is not a battle, O ye gods, nothing of the sort." He moved back a little and very gently untied the shoulders of my gown, letting the silk fall away, down to my waist. Then he bent his head and kissed each of my breasts a long time, until I thought I could stand it no longer. I pulled his head up and clasped him against me, at the same time falling back on the pillows and drawing him with me. A great rough sigh escaped from him. Now I could feel his heart beating faster, and his breath coming in shorter, louder bursts.

He still wore his tunic. "The tunic . . ." I murmured. Its material was making folds all over his back.

He sat up and, with a twist of his arms, flung it off over his head. Then he pulled my gown off; I was eager to have it gone, to have nothing between my body and his.

My blood seemed to be truly on fire, my veins bursting with too much of it. To my disappointment, he did not fall on me and cover my body with his, but crouched over and kissed my breasts and belly with a slow deliberateness that made me want to shriek with madness, especially when he lingered over my navel, treating it with infinite tenderness, more suitable for an infant like Caesarion than for me, a woman with such desire I felt it choking me, felt my throat tightening so much I could hardly breathe. My air was being cut off, and all because of this overwhelming desire. I let out one long, ragged cry of anguish.

Instantly he leaned forward and buried his face against my neck. I could feel his breath against my ear, could barely make out the words. Was he speaking? *Now you are mine . . . now, now. . . .*

At last I felt his body against mine; I rose up to meet him, surging forward to bring us together. I felt as if I would die if it did not happen in that instant; I had waited a year for it. Every particle of me was stinging with desire.

It had been a long time since we had come together, but the body retains its secret and intimate memories. His body fit into mine, making one person. I had forgotten, yet not forgotten, what it felt like to have a part of him become one with me. But all the while I also knew him as separate from myself, a sweet distinction.

Now I felt the long-forgotten urgency of lovemaking, when it seems one's human selves leave, to be replaced by hungry beasts bolting their food. Gone are the civilized beings who talk of manners and journeys and letters; in their places are two bodies straining to give birth to a burst of inhuman pleasure followed by a great, floating nothingness. An explosion of life followed by death—in this we live, and in this we foreshadow our own sweet deaths.

I felt my hands on his back, and I tried not to scratch him, but I knew I was doing so. There must be more we could do, more, more, more—I wanted to drive it higher, ever higher.

Later I lay beside him, panting and coughing. I tried to focus my eyes and look into his face. It was younger than I had ever seen it.

"My dearest," he finally said, "I thought never to feel this way in my lifetime."

We lay in the tangle of sheets, soaked with sweat. They were growing cold, in spite of the warmth of our bodies. So quickly passion becomes something separate, not part of our real selves.

"I love you still," he said wonderingly. "I love you here as well as in Egypt, in this shuttered room in Rome as well as in the open palace in Alexandria."

It was only then that I realized he had thought of me as fixed in time and space, immovable, something to be found, like the pyramids—then left behind. Instead, I had followed.

"I am a real person," I said. "I can live and breathe in different climates, different lands."

"But I must confess, I did not think of you so. I thought of you—like a local goddess."

I laughed. "One of those who inhabit a spring or a rock?"

He looked ashamed. "Just so. When I came to Alexandria—which now seems like a dream—you were a part of it. It is hard to reconcile that memory with you, here. Why"—he laughed at the idea of it—"I shall take you to the Forum! And yes, you shall meet Cicero and Brutus and young Octavian—and I shall prove to myself that you are real."

"You have held me. You know I am real."

"No. All this still seems like a dream." His voice was low. "A darkened room. A surreptitious visit. Lovemaking with one lamp lit, and hushed voices. Tomorrow, in the daylight, I will think it all a dream I had while in camp."

"I will see you in that daylight," I said. "Only a few more hours."

"And I will formally welcome you to Rome," he said. "I shall be dressed in my toga—infernally uncomfortable garment!—and I will doubtless make a stilted speech, and try not to wink at you."

"And I will try to ascertain whether you are excited beneath the toga."

"I won't be," he said matter-of-factly. "My formal self will have taken me over." He paused. "You realize that you are my own personal guest, rather than a guest of the Roman state? It seemed simpler that way. You do not have to make an official entrance, and it prevents the Senate from using you as a surrogate for me—insulting you when they wish to insult me, flattering you when they wish to flatter me. They are a thorn in my side," he said bitterly. "They will use anything against me. I did not wish you to be their pawn."

"Why do you bother with them?" I asked. "They seem to exist only to create stumbling blocks."

He laughed softly. "I 'bother' with them—charmingly said!—because they are the legal rulers of Rome, and have been since the kings were thrown out over five hundred years ago. They are supposedly the watchdogs of our freedom, and they delight in being on the lookout for tyrants like me."

"They are nothing but a nuisance," I said. They hindered Caesar. What good were they?

"Spoken like a true Ptolemy!" He bent over to pick up his tunic, and in the low light I could see the marks I had made on his back. I had not meant to do it.

I licked my finger and traced over them.

He straightened up at the touch of my finger. "Calpurnia will be curious about them," he said.

Calpurnia! Did he—I thought they were separated, or practically so. "I am sorry," I said contritely, and meant it. I assumed she was a tight-lipped, austere old Roman matron.

"Poor Calpurnia," he said, surprising me. "She spends most of her time waiting for me to return home. In the dozen or so years since our marriage, I have been away from Rome eleven."

Was she young? It was possible. And he had been with her so little since then. She must feel herself still a bride. As a woman, I felt pity for her. Then I remembered Eunoe. I felt myself stiffen. "What of the Queen of Mauretania?" I asked tightly.

Deny it! I begged him in my mind. Say it was just slander on the part of Scipio!

"I was lonely," he said simply. "And she set out to comfort me." He sighed, like a man who had bought a bad carriage, one whose wheels did not turn properly. "There was one night, only one—that was enough! If I ever thought that it was being a queen that made you so desirable, that the thought of bedding a queen was what made it magic, then Eunoe taught me better. For that, you should be grateful to her. Then Scipio, eager to wound me, if not on the battlefield, then in the opinion of the world, put it out that it was an ongoing thing. Believe me, it was not. It served only to make me long more for you, the unique, the irreplaceable, the sole keeper of my desire—the one woman I wanted most to keep with me, and could not."

So deep was my love for him that I believed him, knowing all the while that he was a great lover, and that great lovers excel at saying what a woman most needs to hear. Yet, even now, I still believe him. What we had together was extraordinary, more than mortal, and we both felt it.

I kept tracing the lines and circles of the marks on his back. He squirmed a little—from chill, or was I tickling him? He turned to me with a sigh, and kissed me. "I was ready to go, and now—"

He put his arms around me again, and they were tight with desire.

It was growing light before he dressed and made ready to leave.

"It is almost time for me to be back here," he said. He bent over and put on his sandals. It was now light enough that I could see how many straps they had, and discern what shade the leather was.

"You can see him now," I said. "You won't need a lamp." I took his hand and guided him over to the little bed in the adjoining room where Caesarion slept on his back.

I was startled to see a look of pain cross Caesar's face, and his voice give an unguarded groan. He stared down at the boy, then got down on his knees to see him closer. Wordlessly he took my hand and squeezed it. He remained there, on his knees, looking, for a long time. Then he abruptly got up and made for the door. At the doorway he lingered, and looked at me sadly. "It is my very self," he said in a whisper. Then he was gone.

23

I stood in the garden, by a stone fountain, and watched the sunrise. I had waited until I knew he was gone from the grounds, then I stole away from the room and ran outside. I could not bear to be in there any longer, to lie still and pretend to sleep and wait for others to stir. I could hear the sound of the birds, their songs a tangle of cries, a chorus that came before full dawn. It was not too early to join them outside.

The air was fresh, a slight coolness to it. Light mists were twining around the statues, the clipped hedges, the flower beds. Soon the sun would rise and dissipate it, chase away the blurred edges. I felt dazed, my head light. Exhaustion was setting in after the arduous journey, culminating in this glorious long night without sleep. I stood trembling by the fountain and plunged my hands into it, bringing up handfuls of water to splash on my face. I knew I was washing away his kisses, but I could not help it.

I sat on one of the stone benches and drew up my legs, hugging them. I would love never to disturb any relic of that night, never to wash my face or wear anything but this gown—fastened again now, and discreetly covered by a mantle—or move anything in the room. I gave a silent laugh at the idea of the bed remaining forever rumpled, with the sacred sheets undisturbed. It was a ludicrous picture, a ludicrous desire, but for those few moments I had it.

The light was growing stronger now, and the birdsong fading. What was it he had said? *My formal self will have taken me over.* The next time I saw him he would belong to the daytime world, to the world of Roman politics and proprieties. And we would present our gifts to one another, and he would invite me to his Triumph, and we would each entertain one another in turn. One head of state to another.

He returned at midmorning, riding up the steep path to the site of the house, with a large company of attendants. The sun glorified the white of his toga, making me blink. He sat his horse with the commanding posture that was so distinctively his; I had never seen him slump or even lean back. That was part of the reason he always seemed taller than he actually was.

Marching before him were his lictors, carrying those strange bundles of branches with axes that denoted power in Rome. There seemed to be an enormous number of them. Behind them was a company of soldiers—his bodyguard? His staff?

I, in turn, awaited him at the entrance to the house, seated on a small throne. (I had brought it all the way from Egypt, knowing it would be necessary for formal audiences, and also knowing it would not be politically wise to ask the Romans to lend me one!) I had attired myself in my usual audience clothes, nothing too elaborate, as this was ostensibly a personal visit, and besides, it was still morning. I felt that I looked wretched; the exhilaration of the night had worn off, leaving only fatigue and nervousness. I did not wish to see him. Not now; not so soon. Another day, perhaps!

He approached. I gripped the arms of the throne. He came forward from the mass of attendants. I could hear the sound of each of his horse's hooves on the gravel. He sat looking at me. His face betrayed no emotion whatsoever, no recognition. We were on the same plane, he on his horse, I on the throne at the top of the entrance steps. Then he dismounted, moving in one quick motion, and walked slowly up the stairs, never taking his eyes—his dark, impersonal eyes—off me.

This was a stranger, a foreign Roman official, surrounded by bizarre attendants carrying weird symbols of authority. I hated the axes. They all were turned toward me. He was different here, after all. Suddenly I was frightened of him. Why had I come, and put myself at his mercy—and Rome's? The axes gleamed in the sunlight, grinning at me. I was a prisoner here.

"Greetings, Most Exalted Majesty," he said in his elegant Greek. "Queen Cleopatra, you do us great honor to journey to Rome with the express purpose of attending my Triumph. You do me great honor to live as my guest in my garden home."

He stood there, straight, his toga hanging in gracious lines. There was only the slightest hint of a smile on his face, such as he would have given to any visiting dignitary.

"I thank you," I said, loudly enough that others could hear me. "It pleases me to come, and to thank Rome's foremost general for preserving my throne and enforcing my father's will for Egypt when usurpers refused to honor it."

"I have brought a gift that I hope will please you," he said. There was a stirring in the ranks, as they shuffled around to bring the object forward.

"I am pleased to receive it," I said. "But you may speak to me in Latin if you wish. I have studied it for this journey."

Now, for an instant, his face registered surprise. Why had I not told him this last night? he was wondering.

"You outdo yourself, most gracious Queen," he finally said in Latin.

I was grateful that I could at least understand that.

The attendants brought forward a large rectangular wooden box, which they had lifted off a cart. They laid it at my feet, then pried its lid off. Caesar stood by approvingly.

It was a mosaic of the finest sort, the kind called *opus vermiculatum*, made with minute pieces of colored stone, meant to be transported and set in a larger floor within a border. The tiny size of the stones meant that the color variation and shading could depict almost any scene realistically. This showed Venus emerging from the seafoam. The colors of the sea were exactly those of the waters in the palace harbor at Alexandria. It was magnificent. How had he had it made so quickly? Then I realized he hadn't. It had been looted from some site the Romans had taken. It must have been part of his own collection.

"I thank you. It is beautiful," I said. I hoped my Latin did not sound laughable.

He inclined his head. "I am pleased that it pleases you."

"And I have brought you a gift from Egypt," I said, nodding to my attendants. They returned, wheeling a statue of Pharaoh Cheops in matte-black graywacke stone, a treasure that it had hurt me to part with. Every plane on it was perfect, buffed to an impossible smoothness, yet with no shine.

Now, again, just for that instant, his face showed an emotion: surprise and pleasure. His eyes, covetous of all beauty, widened a bit at the sight of it.

"The Queen of Egypt is most generous," he said. "I thank you with all my heart." He paused. "The Dictator of Rome would be most honored and personally gratified if the Queen of Egypt would come to his home for dinner in three days. This will allow me time to prepare. I trust it will not be too humble a dwelling for her to enter. It is in the Forum, near the Regia. As Pontifex Maximus, it is my official residence."

Pontifex Maximus? What was that? It sounded priestly, and he scorned all religion, believing only in the goddess of fortune, who had made him her favorite son.

"The college of sixteen priests, pontiffs," he explained. "A most ancient and sacred order, the state religion."

How had he ever been chosen for that? "I would be pleased," I managed to get out.

He nodded his head. The meeting was over. Suddenly I remembered that I had something else to present to him. "Great Caesar," I said, "I have two other gifts to make to you. Pray, wait a few moments until they are brought out."

Then we had to remain as we were, static, he standing, I sitting, silent. At length—it seemed like forever—my soldiers brought out the two pirates, shackled and bound to a yoke.

"Behold!" I said, and had the pleasure of seeing Caesar finally lose his composure as he recognized one of them.

The heavy bald man shook his chains and began cursing. "May you rot in the ground, may dogs bolt your flesh, you monster! This woman is as bad as you—you're killers both! Had things been but a little different, it would be she in chains and you begging for her life!"

"What is this?" asked Caesar. "How did you get these men?"

"Answer me first," I said. "Who are they? They attacked my ship as I journeyed here, and forced us into the Strait of Messina."

"This one here"—he nodded at the big one—"was one of my captors on the island some thirty years ago, when I was held prisoner by pirates. He managed to escape when I returned for revenge."

"He kept talking about his brother." Without realizing it, I had lapsed back into Greek.

"His brother, the scum, was the ringleader. I slit his throat myself, as he was being crucified. He had always been entertaining and courteous to me, as only villains can be. The crucifixion was too cruel for him, so I ended it early."

"And what about him?" I nodded to the thin one with the burning eyes.

Caesar walked over to him and stared at him, squinting his eyes. "Yes . . . this melts the years away. How are you, Philetas?"

"Free me and you'll find out."

"Free you, so you can kill me? I think not." Caesar sounded amused and kindly. "So, you are still at it. Aren't you a little old still to be a pirate? It's a strenuous profession."

"Aren't you a little old to be a general?" his adversary sneered. "It's a strenuous profession as well. I heard in your last campaign you were showing some wear. And then, all the enemies you make—it must make sleeping difficult, guarding yourself against all those who'd like to put a dagger between your ribs."

"Like you?" He shrugged. "One gets used to it. Now, really, Philetas, I would think you'd be ashamed still to be a pirate! And not even a very successful one. It sounds as if the high point of your career was when you held me prisoner, and when was that—over thirty years ago? Now you're reduced to attacking medium-sized ships around Sicily in—what sort of a boat was it?" he asked me.

"There were three of them, fast hemiolias," I said.

"Leftovers. Outdated," he said, dismissing them. "And all that killing you do, for so little return."

"You're the king of the killers. You've killed thousands and thousands in your campaigns in Gaul—uncountable thousands."

"That was war."

"It was pure ambition," spat the big one.

"Well, then my ambition has been better rewarded than yours." I detected a slight change in his voice; he was shaken by the sudden appearance of the pirates and their accusations. "And now you will have to write an end to your life, tally up your accounts."

"Still playing a part?" yelled the big one. "Now you're a philosopher? You played the jolly companion with us, then came back and killed us."

"Did I not tell you that was what I would do?" he said. "Be reasonable, gentlemen. I merely kept my word."

"Mark you, all of you!" cried Philetas, addressing the entire company. "This man is dangerous! He is not what he pretends to be! If ever you feared anyone, fear him!"

"Take them away," said Caesar. "Take them away." His voice was hard. Then he turned to me with a different one. "Thank you for this unlooked-for presentation. It gives me faith that in some fashion all the threads of one's life are eventually gathered together, and answers are given." He smiled a little uncertainly. "I will expect your company three days from now. Until then, please use this villa and the gardens for your own pleasure, and do not hesitate to send me word if there is anything you lack." He turned and stepped smartly down the steps to his horse.

The lictors turned to precede him, their axes flashing. Soon the whole company had departed, the tramp of their boots dying out in the distance.

When I reentered the room, I saw it had been discreetly tidied, the sheets whisked away and replaced by fresh linens, windows opened, floors swept, and bundles of herbs hung to sweeten the air. All gone. The night had never happened. I wondered if any of the servants had seen Caesar come and go; probably not. He would have made sure of that.

Charmian had dressed Caesarion, who was playing in the middle of the floor with Ptolemy. They all looked well rested and eager to explore.

"What a company of soldiers!" cried Ptolemy. "And what were those things they were carrying? Those funny bundles of sticks with ribbons and axes?"

"I believe they are called fasces. They denote some sort of authority," I said. I realized I badly needed an advisor on Roman customs and history, and I could hardly expect Caesar to take on the task himself. Whom could I find, without embarrassing myself?

"Everything here is so odd!" he cried, happy with the novelty. "The trees are all different, the language sounds ugly, and why do they wear those voluminous togas? Aren't they hot in them?"

Just then two servants entered, bearing trays of food. Ptolemy ran over to one and crowed with excitement.

"What's that? And that?" He stabbed his finger at each foreign-looking dish.

After eating, we wandered through the villa and its grounds. It was peculiar to have complete access to someone's private retreat in his absence. He was there, in every decision that had been made about the furnishings, the plantings, the decorations, the comforts, yet he was not there, so I could stare or linger as openly as I wished. As a child I had always been entranced by the story of Psyche in the palace of the invisible Cupid. I had known it by heart.

> As she walked through the lovely rooms, a voice all sweetness and gentleness spoke to her: "Fair Princess, all that you behold is yours. Command us, we are your servants." Filled with wonder and delight, Psyche looked about in all directions, but saw no one. The voice continued, "Here is your chamber, and your bed of down; here is your bath, and in the adjoining alcove there is food."
>
> Psyche bathed, and put on the lovely garments prepared for her, then seated herself on a chair of carved ivory. At once there floated to its place before her a table covered with golden dishes and the finest food. Although she could see no one, invisible hands served her, and unseen musicians played on lutes and sang to her.
>
> For a long time Psyche did not see the master of the palace. He visited her only in the nighttime, going away before morning dawned. . . .
>
> Psyche begged her husband that her sisters might visit her. At first they were happy to see their young sister and to find her safe, but soon, seeing all the splendor in Psyche's palace, envy sprang up in their hearts. They questioned her rudely concerning her husband.
>
> "Is he not some dreadful monster," they asked, "some dragon, who will at length devour you? Remember what the oracle said!"

I smiled, remembering my favorite tale and marveling that it seemed to have come true. Now I was acting it out myself, except that I knew Caesar and what he looked like.

He is not what he pretends to be! If ever you feared anyone, fear him! Unbidden, the pirate's words sounded in my mind. The hateful man—what did he know?

The story had ended happily, for the unseen husband, Cupid, had loved Psyche dearly and protected her from the envy of his mother, Venus.

Venus—Caesar's ancestress.

Suddenly the villa began to take on an ominous aspect. Stories of men and stories of the gods should be kept separate.

"See this statue?" I said brightly. "I am sure it is a copy of one by Praxiteles. . . ."

The villa and its grounds occupied us all that day, and by nightfall we were ready for a quiet supper and a recuperative night. The twilight was tender and lingering, as if day were loath to depart from Rome. In Egypt, so much farther south, we had little interim between full day and full night.

I lay down, grateful to be able to rest my head. Charmian came in, sat beside my bed on a low stool, and played the flute softly, as she did at home.

"Are you happy to be here?" she asked me.

"I think so," I said. One moment I was, the next I was not sure. I would be relieved when the second and third ship arrived, bringing more of my attendants. At the moment I sorely missed Mardian. But I knew he could not come.

"I wish we could see Rome itself," she said. "I am about to die of curiosity."

"We can," I said. "We can go tomorrow."

"I want to see Rome without being seen," she said. "If you venture out, throngs of curious people will mob you—all eager to see the famous Queen of Egypt. You will spend all your time fending them off, and see nothing at all."

"Then we will have to go as Roman matrons," I said.

"Who do not speak Latin?" She laughed. "I enjoyed seeing Caesar's face today when you told him you spoke it. You exaggerated more than a bit."

"Yes, I know. But by the time we leave, I shall speak it." I was determined to do so. "And I can understand enough that we can get along. After all, all we need to do is ask the most rudimentary questions and make the plainest remarks—'good day,' 'fine wine,' and so on. Oh, let's do it! Let's go out tomorrow—to the Forum! And to the Circus Maximus! That way, when I go there to the dinner, I won't be at such a gawking disadvantage. It is always best to spy out the unknown. You get us some clothes. . . ."

The next morning, a fine bedecked litter set out from the villa with two sedate matrons leaning back against the cushions, their faces veiled. Charmian and I had struggled with the unfamiliar garments—the undertunic, the long, full *stola* with its many folds around the hem, the enormous *palla* that enveloped it all and was draped over our heads, hiding our hair—for an hour.

"It seems to me," she had said, "the purpose of Roman clothes is to obliterate the body."

I giggled. "Yes. The only parts visible are the face, the hands, and the feet."

"Do they hate their bodies?" she wondered.

"Evidently," I said, wondering what sort of society would have invented these garments. They were not only unwieldy, because of their sheer bulk and layering, but unflattering. "Romans are reputed to be very uncomfortable with all the body's natural functions."

Except Caesar, who was so different in so many ways, I thought.

The litter left the villa's grounds, and we were borne along to the river. The Tiber was not wide, but it was a serene, pleasing green. I could see the docks where the commercial ships tied up, with the usual warehouses and emporia alongside them. We had not landed there, and I was glad, for the odor of it was not very alluring. We kept to our side of the river, where there were only open fields, and gazed at the city sprawling on the other side.

It was a cluster, a jumble of buildings of all sorts and sizes. I could see hills rising here and there, and tried to count them. Were there seven? There were supposed to be. I could see five or six. The city was shimmering in the moist heat of the summer day, and its aspect was not particularly inviting.

But that is compared to Alexandria, I reminded myself, and Alexandria is supposedly the most beautiful city in the world. My judgment and senses have been spoiled by my native city.

We continued along the shore, then we approached a bridge spanning the river to an island in its midst. I knew it was Tiber Island, which had a famous hospital dedicated to Asclepius on it. We crossed it and then took the other bridge onto the Roman side.

Immediately it was different. There seemed to be an anthill of people milling and bobbing about in the narrow streets. They were loud and aggressive, shoving and yelling. A cleared space with the foundations of a new structure reared up before us.

"What is that?" I asked one of our bearers, who luckily spoke Greek.

"A theater being built by Caesar," he said. "It's the second stone one to go up. He is trying to outdo Pompey, who built a gigantic one not far away."

We took a sharp turn to the right, and once again everything changed. We were now fighting our way through a flower and fruit market that seemed vast. A loud din hung over the area, as sharp as the mingling odors of roses, field poppies, onions, and garlic. Everyone was gesturing and shouting, so it appeared. I saw a basket of unfamiliar fruit, dark and light green mixed together.

"What are they?" I asked, pointing at them. "I would like some."

The bearers set down the litter. Now I was right in the crowd itself. Instinctively I drew my *palla* closer around my face.

I could understand some of the conversations around me, but not enough. Most of it was the usual: bargaining, complaining, comparing goods. But occasionally I could hear the words *Caesar* and *Cleopatra*. What were the common people saying about us?

The bearer returned with a handful of the fruits. They were olives, but larger and of a different color than I had ever seen.

"We call them black and white olives, Your Majesty," he said. "They grow near here, in the region of Picenum."

"Happy Picenum," I said, "to have such treasures for the palate." I bit into one; it it was running with juice, almost like a grape. The sweet oil had a slightly tangy undertaste.

We finally fought our way free of the market, and were on a wide road winding to the left. I saw that we were at the base of a hill, and that crowning the hill were several temples. Could this be the Capitoline? If so, then the temples were among the most sacred in Rome, housing statues of their ancient protectors. Then, suddenly, we swung into a flat, wide area congested with buildings—and people.

"The Forum Romanum," said the bearer.

So this was it—the heart of Rome. It looked like an ill-planned, crowded mess—like something a child makes when he assembles his blocks on a table too small for them. Everywhere buildings fought with one another for space, aligned at crazy angles to eke out the smallest advantage of site. Temples, covered porticoes, platforms, statues—there was no harmony or beauty to the whole. But then, that was how the world saw Romans themselves—as clumsy, unmannered, trampling on beauty because they had no eye for it.

I suppose they think this is attractive, I thought. Poor Romans!

A platform with steps sat in the middle of a somewhat open area, with the bronze rams of ships, called *rostra*, mounted on its front wall, bristling out like a row of boars' snouts. This must be the famous place, named for those rams, the Rostra, where their politicians shouted speeches, backed up by the reminder of Rome's military might. How subtle!

Off to one side was a tall, square building that looked like a box standing on end. "What is that?" I asked the bearer. He must have been tiring of my questions by now.

"The Curia, my lady," he said. "Where the Senate meets."

So the mighty Senate of Rome met *here*? In this coffin?

"There are special tiers inside for the senators' seats," he said, almost as if he sensed my thoughts. "The doors are of bronze," he said proudly.

And, indeed, they were the only fine thing about it.

"Caesar rebuilt it," he said. "He had to move it to make room for his new Forum."

"What?" I asked. "What Forum?"

"Caesar is building a new one, because he says this one is crowded and ugly. He is paying for the new one entirely out of his own funds. They say it will cost over a million sesterces. But then, he can afford it."

"Let me see it," I said suddenly.

Obediently the litter swung around and we made our way across the paved center of the Forum, over a broad paved roadway, between the Curia and a huge covered building, and found ourselves overlooking a small, perfect rectangle bordered with colonnades. A welcoming green space covered the middle. At the far end was a temple, finely proportioned and gleaming in white marble.

"The temple isn't dedicated yet," said the bearer. "He built it to fulfill a vow he made before the final battle with Pompey. It's to honor his lineage, and the goddess Venus—and incidentally, to show off some of his artwork."

I stared at it. It was lovely, as graceful as any in Greece itself, of that I was sure.

"I hope I shall be here when it is dedicated," I said.

We returned to the old Forum, and continued down its middle, being careful to avoid the pedestals and statues. We passed what I had to admit was an admirable temple, and then came to a cluster of buildings: a large, long one, a round one with columns, and a square, blocky one with another attached.

The patient bearer pointed them out one by one.

"The square building is the Regia, where the College of Pontiffs meet and

232

keep their records. The round temple is the Temple of Vesta, where the sacred flame is kept burning," he said. "The priestesses, the Vestal Virgins, live in that long building beside it, so they can tend the flame, and—"

"The house attached to it is the Pontifex Maximus," I said. "Caesar lives there."

"Yes, my lady."

His home! This was where he resided—right in the middle of the Forum! How did he stand it? My eyes swept up to a cool-looking, wooded hill rising beside the Forum, covered with spacious homes.

"A popular place to live for the rich people," said the bearer, pointing at it. "The Palatine Hill. Cicero has a home there—he bought it from Crassus—and Marc Antony's family home is there as well."

Yes, I would choose the Palatine to live on, were I a Roman. I understood now why Caesar had a villa outside the city. I understood so much more than I had this morning. In that way the disguised visit was a success, even though I had not been able to penetrate any conversations. What the man in the Roman street thought about politics, I still had no inkling. But now at least I had met him face-to-face.

<hr>

24

I awoke on the day of the dinner to a gentle rain. I could hear it falling on the trees outside, hitting the leaves. A moist breath came in the windows. It was a kind of rain I had never encountered before—a summer rain. In Alexandria—the only place in Egypt where it rains at all—there were lashing winter gales, but no sweet, warm rain like this.

I lay in bed and sighed. I had heard nothing more from Caesar. Tonight—who did he plan to have at his table? He had said dinner at his home. Was it to be a banquet? Truthfully, his house did not look grandiose enough to have one. This villa was probably where he usually held large banquets. I assumed Ptolemy was invited; after all, it was Caesar who had insisted we be "married." Since he was my legal husband, he could hardly be omitted.

At midday I availed myself of the baths on the premises, marveling at the engineering genius that allowed the Romans to have hot and cold running water, as well as heated floor tiles. Thus had the Romans conquered most of the world, with their eager corps of engineers attached to each legion, putting up bridges over swirling rivers, laying down roads over bogs, copying the designs of captured ships. Now Roman engineering was providing for creature comforts like these baths, building aqueducts to bring fresh water—and wasting it in fountains and pleasure grottoes—and inventing concrete, a liquid stone, that let them mold buildings, as rich as they liked, to their fancy. Soon there would be nothing left of the famous Roman asceticism. Those who could afford to wallow in comfort and pleasure usually ended by giving themselves up to it.

I thought hard about what to wear to this affair, because it was all symbolic. Should I go in full monarchical regalia? I was, after all, a visiting queen. But this was a small dinner, not an official banquet—I assumed. On the other hand, to go in unadorned clothes might seem insulting. The question was— how did Caesar wish to present me? He had not indicated.

"Charmian, what is your true feeling?" I asked her. "Your sense of these things is usually correct. What must I wear?"

I was standing before my trunks, brimming with clothes of all description. The very variety of them made choosing more difficult.

Charmian said, "My instinct is that you must make yourself as beautiful as possible. However you do that is up to you. Whatever you do, don't be plain! Leave that to the Roman matrons."

"But it may offend them."

"I said beautiful, not vulgar. What is appropriate in the east may seem garish here. So put on only half as much jewelry and cosmetics."

I had a sudden suspicion. "You don't suppose Calpurnia will be there?" Surely he couldn't!

"Unless she is conveniently away, how could she not be?"

My heart sank. "I don't know the Roman custom. Do husbands and wives attend all the same functions?" Maybe they didn't. Maybe they went their separate ways at the table, as they seemed to in bed.

"Probably," she said. "Where else would the women get to plan their assignations with their husbands' friends?"

"Is it that bad?" It sounded so sordid.

"It is always the scandals that reach our ears," she said. "No one ever talks about someone who behaves himself—which most people in Rome probably do."

I pulled out one costume after another. It did not help that they came in three varieties: Egyptian, Greek, and what I thought of as simply Mediterranean. Finally I decided, on an impulse, to wear Egyptian garb.

"It is what people have the most curiosity about," I said. "It is the thing they see least often, and will provide the most diversion." I had a feeling that it would please Caesar, reminding him of those long warm days on the Nile.

I was ready. I stood before the pool in the atrium where I could see my full reflection: a slender column of white with a broad gold collar. I was wearing a close-fitting linen dress with sheer sleeves, tied with a wide sash of red silk. The heavy gold bracelet the Kandake had given me graced one wrist, and on my head was a gold fillet ornamented with the sacred cobra of Egypt in miniature. The effect was regal, exotic, and understated.

234

Ptolemy was similarly attired in Egyptian style, wearing a jeweled collar, pleated linen robes, and gold sandals.

I drew myself up and took a deep breath. The figure in the pool did likewise. I had to admit that she looked most imposing. Now to set out—and calm my pounding heart. I felt as if I were back in the carpet again, ready to be rolled out before a hostile audience.

The litter swayed sensuously from side to side as it descended into the Roman twilight. The rain had stopped, leaving a sweet aftermath. Birds were singing madly, celebrating the end of the rain. In the fading light the Forum was much more appealing; the rain and the dinner hour had driven most people away, so it was almost deserted. Now I could see far down to the area where the Regia lay, and the round building of the Temple of Vesta. Torches were burning outside it, and as we came closer I saw that servants were stationed outside Caesar's house to guide us.

The litter was set down. A servant helped both me and Ptolemy out. Another bowed and then ushered us into the house. From the outside, it was a simple one, although of two stories, and the doors were plain wood studded with iron.

My own attendant, who had followed in a separate litter, announced our entrance when we passed into the atrium. I saw several people gathered at one end of the room, but really I saw only one person: Caesar.

His face broke into a smile when he saw us, and immediately he came to our sides. His gladness was unfeigned, and I felt joy flooding through me. It would be all right. I need not fear the others; they could not touch us.

"Welcome to my home," he said, "Your Majesties." But he did not bow, since he was not our subject. "Allow me to present you. I have gathered together those nearest and dearest to me, whom I most wish you to meet." He was speaking Greek. So that would be the tongue for tonight.

There were some five or six people in a knot at the back of the room.

"I am pleased," I said.

He led us over to them, to all those faces with mixed expressions of curiosity, wariness, and—distaste.

"My wife, Calpurnia."

A tall woman with tightly bound brown hair closed her eyes and lowered her head. "Your Majesties," she said in a low, expressionless voice. She was prettier than I had hoped.

"My great-nephew, Gaius Octavian."

I try now to recall my exact first impression of him, of this boy who was only sixteen years old at the time. To be honest, it was that he was a slight, pale, beautiful statue. His features were delicate, his eyes a cold shade of light blue, his hair dark gold. Even though he was short, his proportions were perfect. He looked like a work of art that Caesar might have carried off from one of his conquests.

"I am honored," he said quietly.

"And his sister, my great-niece, Octavia."

Octavia was more substantial, older, larger, with abundant thick, dark hair. She inclined her head.

"My dear friend Marcus Brutus, and his mother, Servilia."

A middle-aged man with a melancholy expression and straight lips stepped forward, and an older woman with an ample bosom, bound with crisscrossed linen strips around her gown, inclined her head.

"He honors us by returning from his post as governor of Cisalpine Gaul to attend our Triumphs," said Caesar.

Both Brutus and his mother were silent. Finally Servilia smiled and said, "Welcome to Rome, Your Majesties." Her voice was very pleasant. Brutus just made a stabbing nod of the head in concurrence.

"Now, let's see, that's all of us—oh yes, last of all is Marcus Agrippa here." With a sweep of his arm, Caesar indicated a youth standing next to Octavian. He was ruggedly handsome, with plain, blunt features—deep-set eyes, straight eyebrows, thin, well-formed lips. His hair was a close-cropped, dark thatch. "They are inseparable, so that makes Agrippa almost related to me."

Agrippa gave the only full smile I had received so far, besides Caesar's.

"The King and Queen of Egypt have traveled a long way in order to attend the Triumphs," said Caesar. "It was, indeed, in restoring them to the throne that I was forced to fight the Alexandrian War. So it is fitting that they should come and gaze on their vanquished enemies."

"Including their own sister." A man spoke—someone with a low voice.

"Yes, Brutus," said Caesar. "As we know, so sadly, family ties are not always strong enough to prevent treason. That is the agony of civil war—brother against brother. That is why I am so deeply thankful to have ended the civil wars that have torn us Romans apart."

A heavy silence fell over the group. With a beginning like this, I thought, how could we endure an entire evening?

Caesar made a motion with his hand, and from an alcove a lyre and a flute began playing, simple melodies that belied the tension. I had not even glimpsed the musicians when we first entered. Now a maidservant came with her arms brimming with garlands of roses we were to wear as chaplets on our heads. I remembered now that the Romans liked to put on flowers for dinners, twining them in their hair and draping them around their necks. These were white, many-petaled, and very fragrant. Close on her heels came the *cellarius*, the wine steward, with silver cups of *mulsum*, a divine blending of wine and honey. Gratefully I took mine, hoping that the magic of wine would act on the company to make the evening easy.

"The tables await," said Caesar, gesturing toward an adjoining room. We all followed him, marching two by two, with only Agrippa by himself.

The room was surprisingly large, and I saw that beyond the far doors a garden opened. The entire center of the room was taken up with the couches and tables where we would dine—three couches, touching end to end to make a rectangle with one side open. Each couch held three diners, and where one reclined was subject to the strictest protocol. No one needed to be told where to go; everyone knew. I was on the end of the middle couch, in the place of honor, and Caesar, as host, was on my right, at the top of the family couch. On my other side was Octavia, and on her other side was Ptolemy.

There were bolsters for us to lean our left elbows on, and the couches were spread with costly material, not ornamented but luxurious in the fineness of the wool and silk itself. Servants brought footstools for us, and removed our sandals, after first wiping our feet with scented water. The *cellarius* discreetly refilled our wine cups.

Before each couch was a long table, inlaid with silver, a little lower than the couches. There our plates, knives, and spoons rested, along with gigantic napkins made of stuff even more precious than the couch-covers themselves. Nonetheless we took the napkins and spread them out in front of us, protecting one material with its better.

Caesar leaned on his elbow and held out his cup. Even in this awkward position, such was the strength of his arm that he did not tremble; his hand was absolutely steady.

"Welcome, friends and family," he said. "As Aeschylus said, 'What is pleasanter than the tie of host and guest?' "

Everyone made polite low murmurs of assent and smiled.

Now I in turn raised my cup. I must speak. "That is one of the chiefest joys of life. As our own Alexandrian Callimachus wrote, 'You are walking by the tomb of Battiades, who knew well how to write poetry, and enjoy laughter at the right moment, over the wine.' Let us enjoy laughter tonight, over the wine, my friends and companions." I took a sip.

Everyone followed. Dear Dionysus! I thought, as I watched them drink. Don't fail me!

"The Queen and King have had a most perilous journey here," said Caesar. "It seems that I must count my enemies not only on land but on the sea as well. Those I thought long dead have risen up against me. Seeking revenge, a group of pirates, led by two who had held me years ago, attacked their ship and drove them into the Strait of Messina." He paused, while everyone waited to hear the outcome. "The gods were with them—so that in addition to their other gifts, they were able to present me with these enemies as prisoners. A most welcome present!" He gave a hearty laugh. "And so, to celebrate this adventure, tonight, instead of the usual Falernian wine, I serve Mamertine, from Messina." He nodded to the *cellarius*, who now presented a new amphora, then disappeared to transfer the wine into smaller pitchers.

The servers now began to bring the first course, the *gustum*, which would serve to stimulate our appetites. There were platters of mackerel in rue, with slices of egg; olive paste with flat bread from Capea; a roll of asparagus and figpecker; and sliced stalks of leeks, on beds of curly lettuce. Everyone busied himself with the food, and the awkwardness began to subside. I stole a look at Caesar, then at Calpurnia, next to him on the other side. She was gazing at him possessively. Our eyes met for an instant before I looked away.

Calpurnia was somewhere around thirty, I would guess. She must have married young. She was not beautiful enough for Caesar, but still I wished she were plainer. We want our lover to be loved by someone worthy of him, but never to be worthier than ourselves.

"Tell me about this house," I said. "I know it is the official house of the Pontifex Maximus. But what does that mean? What office is this?" I hoped my tone was brightly interested, and that the topic was an innocent one.

"Uncle Julius, may I answer?"

I was startled to hear Octavian, sitting in the lowest position in the room—the third place on the family couch—speak up in a clear voice.

"Certainly," said Caesar, looking pleased. "Now that you yourself are a pontiff in the college, it is fitting."

Octavian leaned forward, his fine-featured face solemn. "It is the oldest and most sacred order of priests in Rome. We go all the way back to the founding of Rome. We guard the shields and spears that foretell victory, and we keep the archives and the city annals." In all his youthful earnestness, he burned pure as a flame before the altar of Mars. "My uncle has been Pontifex Maximus for almost twenty years."

"Yes," said Caesar, "and the Pontiff is going to exercise one of his prerogatives and reform the calendar."

There were sharp intakes of breath all around the tables.

"It is time! Our calendar no longer bears any resemblance to the natural one. We celebrate harvest festivals while it is yet summer, and midsummer when the days are shorter than the nights. The priests who had the duty of regulating it have failed. So I shall revise it. It falls within my purview."

"But, Caesar," said Brutus, "it is not something for an ordinary man, no matter how well intentioned. It requires knowledge of astronomy and mathematics and other calendar systems that have been tried, and failed." I watched his face; it was hard to tell whether he thought Caesar a fool or was just trying to warn him.

"In Alexandria we have a man who excels at that, and is world-renowned among scholars," I said. "Sosigenes. You have heard of him?"

Nodding heads told me they had.

"I will send for him straightway, Caesar," I said. "I place him at your service." Suddenly I remembered what I had heard about a month being named in his honor. "Is it true that the new calendar will bear a newly named month?" I asked.

"There has been mention of perhaps renaming my birth month, Quintilis, in my honor, but—" He shrugged.

"It is just a rumor!" said Brutus, scowling. "The months are properly numbered, or named after gods, not human beings. Rome would not permit such a thing."

"Nonetheless I have heard it spoken of," said Octavian. He looked, unblinking and adoring, at his uncle. Did he wish it to be true? Or would it offend his fierce sense of propriety?

His very intensity made his finely chiseled features seem to take on yet more beauty. I had heard of the characteristic "Julian beauty," had heard that all the faces of that family were known to be delicate, with an exquisite bone structure. Even though Octavian did not look like Caesar, they did share that characteristic. I looked at Octavia. Again, she did not resemble the other two, but her features were likewise elegant and well formed. I noticed she wore a wedding ring on one of her long, graceful hands. I wondered where her husband was.

"He has honors enough," said Brutus. "A thanksgiving of forty days for his victories has been proclaimed, there will be four successive Triumphs, he has been appointed 'Prefect of Morals' and Dictator for ten years, and his Triumphal chariot will be placed on the Capitoline Hill opposite Jupiter's. He has no need of a month of 'Julius.' He has more than a month already, all his!"

"Brutus, do you begrudge me these things?"

That awful silence, only just dispelled, descended again. And I heard in Caesar's voice such sorrow, such pain, that it hurt me to hear it. What was Brutus to him, that his disapproval should rend him so?

"No, of course not." It was not Brutus who spoke but Servilia, his mother.

"Brutus?" Caesar asked again.

"No," he mumbled, looking away and not at Caesar.

"My Caesar has been away from Rome eleven of the past twelve years," said Calpurnia. "If Rome wishes to honor him for what he has done for her, toiling so far afield, why should we object?" She had a pleasing voice, I had to admit. "Since we have been married, thirteen years ago, he has been at my side only a few weeks."

As she spoke, I realized that he had spent more time with me than with her.

I picked at my mackerel and waited for the remark to pass.

"It is difficult, now, to know what is noble in Rome and must be preserved, and what has served its time and must be replaced," said Octavian thoughtfully.

"Young Octavian is a fierce guardian of all things traditional," said Caesar. "If anything passes his scrutiny, it is sure to be proper."

"In Egypt it seems we have nothing but tradition," said Ptolemy suddenly. "We are surrounded by things made so long ago they seem divine. Everywhere there are tombs, statues . . . ghosts."

"But Alexandria is a new city," said Octavia, beside him. "All new, and very beautiful, from what I have heard."

"Yes," I said proudly. "It is the most modern city in the world, and it was planned by the Great Alexander."

Servers began removing the plates of the *gustum* and made ready to bring out the main course, the *mensa prima*. The rattling of the utensils, and the busyness of the attendants, made us pause in the conversation. I looked at Caesar and noticed that he had not touched his wine. Then I remembered he had told me he seldom drank it, lest it provoke his condition. He also had eaten very little.

"Did you enjoy Alexandria?" Calpurnia asked Caesar in a loud voice.

He started, taken by surprise. Clearly such bluntness was out of character for Calpurnia; she must be very angry. He cleared his throat, thinking hard. "I enjoy all battlefields," he finally said. "And Alexandria was a battlefield; it required all my resources to teach myself how to fight in city streets, with a civilian population all around. Especially as any mistakes could cost innocent people dear."

Calpurnia opened her mouth to press further, but lost her nerve.

Just then the new courses were brought out, arranged on silver platters. There was a rich, dark pork stew with apples. I was most curious to try it, as pork is not eaten in Egypt. There was also a kid, prepared Parthian style, and a dish of stuffed thrushes fed with myrtle. Then, to the sighs of the guests, came a platter with a gigantic red roasted mullet on it, accompanied by a pickle sauce.

"Did you go down and bid on the mullet?" asked Agrippa, laughing. It seemed that mullet had become a passion with Romans, and prominent houses bid in auctions for them at the fish market. "How did you ever outbid Marc Antony? He goes down every day, determined to carry off the best."

"What, in person?" Octavian sounded scandalized.

"It's no worse than the other things he does. Carrying on with that retinue of actors and actresses, drinking, living in Pompey's house without paying for it," said Brutus. "But I speak of the man you appointed to take charge of Rome in your absence, Caesar."

"He did not perform well," said Caesar. "I was disappointed. He was dismissed. There's an end to it. What he does with his drink and his actresses concerns me not."

"But is he not related to us? Is he not part of the Julian house?" Octavian sounded distressed.

"Distantly," said Caesar.

"Not distantly enough," said Octavia.

"Why speak any further of him?" said Caesar. "He has his merits, and they have served me well in the past. He failed in this latest task. But he is a great general, nonetheless. He has a deep intuitive sense of tactics. There is no man I would sooner have with me on the battlefield."

"I met Marc Antony once," I said. "It was when he came to Egypt with Gabinius." I remembered the laughing young cavalry officer who had refrained from making fun of my drunken father when the other Romans looked at him askance. He had been kind.

"That was ten years ago or more," said Brutus. "He has changed since then." He speared a large chunk of meat with his knife, and transferred it, dripping, to his platter. Splatters of sauce fell on the napkin.

More dishes followed: boiled cucumber and what Caesar announced was "squash, Alexandrian style." It was something I had never tasted before, but obviously it fit what Romans imagined about us. It was filled with cinnamon and honey.

"This is new to me," I confessed. "There is much we do not know about

240

one another's customs. I have found many things in Rome puzzling. For example, the lictors and the bundles of branches they carry. What do they mean? And the ranks of senators, the *quaestors* and *praetors* and people called *curule aediles*—what responsibilities do they have?"

"You ask questions like a child," said Brutus. "Is this how a queen receives knowledge?"

"It is how all wise people do, Brutus," Caesar reproved him. Then he turned to me. "I see that you need someone to explain things that are foreign to you. Very well—who better than Octavian, that Roman through-and-through?"

Not his nephew! It would be irksome to have this boy trailing around after me, I could tell. Nonetheless I smiled and said, "No, Octavian must not leave his duties at the College of Pontiffs."

"Oh, but this will be good training for him! He can clarify his own thoughts in explaining things to you," said Caesar. "He must venture out in public. He is, after all, to ride in a chariot in my Triumphs."

"Even though he did not join you on the battlefield," said Agrippa. "Well, next time we'll both be there!" He chewed heartily on a piece of kid.

I bent to my plate and enjoyed tasting the pork. It is a robust meat, with a rich flavor. This particular animal had been fed on acorns in Brutus's province, so he said.

"Brutus may soon remarry," said Servilia abruptly. "He may marry my niece Porcia, Cato's daughter."

Caesar put down his knife and looked steadily at Brutus. "Perhaps you will wish to reconsider," he said slowly.

"We have no king in Rome from whom I must ask permission," he answered. "Or does the Prefect of Morals control all the marriages?"

"Of course not," said Caesar lightly. "But marrying within one's own family can get monotonous. One has heard all the same family stories, knows all the jokes and all the same recipes. No novelty."

"Well, we Ptolemies like it that way!" said my brother. "We've practiced brother-sister marriages for generations, just like the Pharaohs! That's because we're divine!"

Everyone stared at him.

"We don't believe in that in Rome," said Servilia quietly.

"In brothers marrying sisters?" Ptolemy asked.

"No. In kings, and in people claiming to be divine. We have a republic here—all citizens are equal."

"What a funny idea!" Ptolemy laughed.

"It is a western idea," I said quickly to him. "People in the east feel differently. In our part of the world, kings are the tradition. And we believe that gods mingle with men on many levels."

"Yes, particularly in bed," said Agrippa. But there was no malice in his voice. "Zeus seems to spend most of his time attacking mortal women in one guise or another—first as a golden shower, then as a swan—and creating hordes of half-divine offspring. Bastards."

"Men do enough of that on their own," said Calpurnia. "They need no help from the gods."

Clearly she was alluding to me and Caesarion. So it was known all over Rome. Now it was up to Caesar to say something. Let him speak!

But he refused to rise to the bait. The moment passed, and the servants began removing the plates and getting ready for our last course, the *mensa secunda*—a selection of rich, sweet treats. We would drink *passum* with them, a heavy raisin wine.

On little trays they brought out honey custard, made with Attic honey, and a preserve of pears. Last they brought a platter heaped high with pomegranates. Caesar took the topmost one off the pile and put it directly on my plate, looking knowingly at me.

At last I have found someone who is exactly like me. We are two halves of a pomegranate, and each section fits perfectly together. I remembered those words he had spoken in Alexandria. Yet here, in Rome, surrounded by his family— was he more like them, or more like me? Which was he, truly?

"What will happen?" I asked, so low that only he could hear it. I saw now that nothing was settled, nothing safe. The master of the world, who had swept aside all the playing pieces in Egypt with one quick brush of his hand, was just a man at a dinner in Rome, surrounded by cold, unfriendly friends. And beyond them lurked—genuine animosity. I sensed it. *We don't believe in that in Rome.* What could be Caesar's ultimate place here?

"I know not," he answered, equally softly.

I had thought the dinner was over, but I was surprised to hear the musicians begin playing new tunes, and Caesar said, "Friends, I wish you to be the first to hear the beginning of a composition on the Alexandrian War. My good friend, the *praetor* Aulus Hirtius, has begun to recount it, and I invited him to join us and bring both his account and his famous mulberries in sapa."

Everyone murmured expectantly, and I later was told that Hirtius was well known for his refined tastes in food. His mulberries, it seemed, would be far superior to regular ones.

A pleasant-looking man strode into the room, a slave following him with a silver serving dish. I could see the deep reddish purple berries inside.

"It is my honor to give my humble recounting of the war before those who lived it," he said. "Your Majesties, I beg you to correct anything I say that is wrong. As you know full well, I was not there." He nodded to us, looked around at the company, then stepped back and began reciting. " 'Bello Alexandrino conflato Caesar Rhodo atque ex Syria Ciliciaque omnem classem arcessit: Creta sagittarios, equites ab rege. . . . ' "

Caesar frowned. He knew Ptolemy and I could not follow it. Yet I wished he would just let Hirtius continue. It gave me an opportunity to look carefully at the others, to study them without the constant necessity of being on my guard and responding to comments and questions.

My wish was not to be granted. Caesar held up his hand. "I pray you, our royal guests are not as practiced in Latin as the rest of the company. I believe they could better enjoy it in Greek."

"Oh yes. Of course." Hirtius shut his eyes and went back to the beginning. " 'When the Alexandrian War flared up, Caesar summoned every fleet from Rhodes and Syria and Cilicia; from Crete he raised archers, and cavalry from . . . ' "

The berries had been ladled out into small, multicolored glass dishes. Multicolored glassware was an Alexandrian specialty. Who had thought of this touch—Caesar or Hirtius? I tasted the berries, finding them tart and pungent.

" 'Highly productive and abundantly supplied as it was, the city furnished equipment of all kinds. The people themselves were clever and very shrewd. . . . ' " Hirtius's voice droned on. I had trouble following him; my mind kept wandering. I felt a slight breeze coming from the open garden opening off the dining room; it was heavy and scented with unknown leaves, dusty and vaguely sweet.

Octavian started coughing, a high-pitched, fretful hacking. It was only then that I realized that his fragile beauty might be the result of illness. He had the transparent look of a consumptive. Hirtius paused until the boy had got control of himself.

Then he continued, " 'Yet, as far as I am concerned, had I now the task of championing the Alexandrians and proving them to be neither deceitful nor foolhardy, it would be a case of many words spent to no purpose: indeed, when one gets to know both the breed and its breeding, there can be no doubt whatever that as a race they are extremely prone to treachery.' "

"I object!" said Ptolemy shrilly. "Why do you say such things?"

"I believe what Hirtius *meant* to say was—" began Caesar.

"No, let Hirtius speak for himself!" Ptolemy insisted.

Hirtius looked around to be rescued. "It is a well-known fact that the mob of Alexandria is volatile, violent, and fickle," he said. "Even in peacetime, they riot! Isn't that true?" He turned to me.

"Yes," I had to admit. "They are difficult to rule. Ever since they more or less deposed"—how I hated that word!—"Ptolemy the Tenth, they have grown ever more strident. When I was a child they rioted because a Roman had inadvertently killed a cat. When I came to the throne, they had got much worse. They drove me from the throne. By the time Caesar fought them in the Alexandrian War, they had become almost ungovernable. Now they have met their master."

"In other words," said Brutus, "Caesar arrived to put down the people, to force something on them they did not wish?"

"You make them sound like heroes," I said. "These same heroic people are the ones who turned on their benefactor Pompey, and slew him when he came seeking refuge on our shores. They are not noble, merely traitors who disregard all moral laws."

"It was not the people who killed Pompey," he insisted, "but a corrupt palace faction."

"Supported by the people," I said stubbornly. One would have to have grown up in Alexandria to understand it. This Brutus had all sorts of misguided ideas about things he had never seen.

"And this corrupt faction embraced some of the royal family; one of them is to pay the price by being led a captive in the Triumph, and the other has paid with his life," said Servilia. As she spoke she moved her head vigorously, and her two enormous pearl earrings swung to and fro.

Caesar's eye was caught by them, and his voice softened. "I see you still enjoy the treasures of Britain," he said.

Brutus looked down at his mulberries and fell abruptly silent.

"Is it true you invaded Britain just to satisfy Servilia's love of pearls?" asked Octavia. Her question was straightforward and seemingly lacking in malice, but it was shocking nonetheless.

"Who started such stupid gossip?" said Caesar. "People will not desist from spreading the most insulting and inane stories about me!"

"I—I did not start it," said Octavia, her low, pleasing voice trembling.

"Then don't repeat it!" he barked. "I would never conduct a military campaign to please anyone's vanity, including my own. My gods! What do you take me for?" He struggled to beat his anger down. "I explored Britain and claimed her for Rome because I was called to do it. For the glory of Rome."

Brutus opened his mouth to say something, then closed it in a hard, straight line.

A hot gust of wind came in, followed by a rumble in the distance. Hirtius's papers rattled. Gamely he tried to continue his reading, but a clap of thunder drowned him out. Suddenly the thunder sounded as if it were right here in the garden.

"My friends," said Caesar, "perhaps we should cease with the recitation and allow you to return home before the storm comes. These summer thunderstorms can be severe."

Everyone rose hastily. Giving Caesar profuse thanks, they did not linger. One by one they said farewell to me as well—Servilia and Octavia kindly, Brutus and Calpurnia curtly. Octavian said he would be pleased to show me about, or to answer any questions, whenever I wished. I assured him I would send for him later, thanking him. He coughed his way out the door, accompanied by Agrippa.

There remained only Ptolemy, Hirtius, and me. Caesar said, "Dear Hirtius, thank you for your recitation. I will send both you and Ptolemy home in the litter; I myself will see to the Queen's safe return."

"But—" began Ptolemy.

"Go with him," I said. "The storm is going to break any moment." Even as I spoke, a gigantic clap of thunder boomed out.

We were alone in the room; Calpurnia must have departed upstairs. A blast of wind, carrying loose leaves, flapped the doors against the wall. They hit so hard they chipped some of the deep blue-green fresco, depicting a seaside, behind them. Outside, bright streaks of lightning appeared, stabbing the air and illuminating the garden, with its statuary, in blue light.

I shivered. There was coldness wrapped in the mantle of the hot gushes of air. I had never seen thunderbolts before, even though our Ptolemaic coins all carried the picture of an eagle with thunderbolts in his talons. I was not prepared for the power of them.

Caesar stood next to me, watching.

"Thank you for the dinner," I said. "It was—"

"Unpleasant," he finished for me. "Yet it was necessary. Now all of you have seen one another; curiosity has been satisfied."

"Why did you invite Brutus? He is not of your family."

"No, in spite of idiotic rumors that he is my son!" He sounded disgusted. "Yet in some ways I feel as if he were . . . as if, had I a grown son, I would wish him to be like Brutus."

"Why?" He had seemed so dour, so lacking in any human vivacity.

"He has a purity about him that's rare. His outside is the same as his inside."

"His outside is so off-putting that one has no desire to get to know his inside," I said.

"He can be charming when he wishes," said Caesar.

"Obviously tonight he did not wish to be," I said. "And what do you mean, people say he is your son?"

"Long ago Servilia was in love with me," he said. "And I was very fond of her."

"So that's why Brutus disapproves of you."

"No, it's more than that. He's so high-minded he would never allow such a base reason to color his behavior. I think it's that—that he cannot forgive my pardoning him for joining Pompey's forces. And he joined Pompey only out of principles having to do with the Republic, because he personally hated Pompey for killing his father."

"What a mixed-up, complex man!" I said. "I would never wish such a son on you. Pray to all the gods that Caesarion is nothing like Brutus."

"I do pray, dear Cleopatra, that our son is nothing like anyone who has yet lived," he said. "I would not have him be a copy of anyone else."

"Yet you said, in watching him, that he was your very self," I said. "What did you mean?"

"I am not sure," he said slowly. "I only know that in seeing him for the first time, I was overcome: a part of myself was sleeping, unawares, while I watched over him. I am afraid—that to have a child is to be a hostage to fate."

"We are all that."

"It is easier to bear for ourselves alone than for others."

25

I would have answered, but a terrific blast of thunder made it impossible to talk. The house shook. We stood and watched the trees bending outside, their heavy limbs whipping up and down, and heard the deluge of water striking the ground like an army of javelins. I had grown up being told that our climate of Egypt was gentle, and that was one of its gifts, but I had never appreciated what that meant until I saw the fury of this Roman thunderstorm.

Caesar put his arm around me, and I leaned against him silently. I had not realized how weary I was until then; the dinner had been a strain. Now we were alone, but not really alone: Calpurnia was upstairs, doubtless straining her ears to hear us. In her place, I would have done so.

At length the rain tapered off, dying in fits and spurts. Parts of the garden were flooded, and the heavy smell of wet earth now swept in through the doors. The thunder rumbled away, trailing lightning from its skirts, and ragged clouds tore across the sky. An almost full moon burst out from its inky confines, and shone with an eerie light over the scattered leaves, soaked benches, and muddy puddles.

"Take a cloak," he said, "and pull it up over your hair. I wish to show you something."

A servant brought him one along with mine, and together we arranged them to cover our heads. He took my hand and guided me outside, to the shadow of the Temple of Vesta.

"Look," he said, pointing down the length of the Forum. It lay in stark black and white, its shadows sharp and deep.

It was almost deserted. The lateness of the hour, and the wildness of the storm, had driven everyone away. Now, devoid of the crowds and noise, it took on the dignity and grandeur it had lacked during the busy afternoon. The temples and covered porticoes, the statues and commemorative columns, bespoke a splendor I had begrudged it earlier.

"This is the Via Sacra," he said, tapping the pavement beneath our feet. "This is where I shall ride my chariot in the Triumphs, on my way up to the Temple of Capitoline Jupiter. And there"—he pointed down to an area before a covered assembly hall—"is where the viewing stands will be set up for the dignitaries and leading citizens. You will be seated in the front seats, along with the rest of my family." He seemed most anxious to point out to me the precise spot. "I am going to have silk awnings to protect you all from the sun—*they* will say it's extravagant—to hell with them—in spite of the largesse that will be distributed, and all the games to entertain them—ungrateful dogs—there's no pleasing them—"

"Stop!" I said. "You are agitating yourself for no reason." His hand, which was holding the lantern, was shaking. I feared he was about to suffer an attack of his illness. "Are you all right?"

"Yes, of course." He sounded annoyed. "I haven't been troubled with—with *that* since just before the battle of Thapsus. It sought to prevent me from fighting, but I overcame it." He paused. "I overcame it by willpower."

I did not see how that could be, but I kept quiet.

"Thousands of people will be in the processions—the magistrates, the senators, captives, and my troops. And the booty! You won't believe it! Wagons and wagons of it, mountains of gold and arms and jewels! And the sacrificial oxen—"

"We have all those things in Egypt," I said. Indeed, it was the Egyptians who had perfected such parades and displays. I had long since grown accustomed to them.

We were walking along the Via Sacra, being careful to avoid the wide puddles everywhere. The moonlight came and went, fast-moving shadows of clouds rolling over the buildings. The Temple of Castor and Pollux, with its tall white columns, looked like a row of unearthly trees, revealed and then eclipsed again by the passing shadows.

"You sound jaded," he said. "But this will impress even you." He paused. "I have waited a long time for recognition for my achievement in Gaul."

"I pray it is all you hope for," I said.

We passed three men who had likewise ventured out for a walk. None of them glanced at us; none of them thought the two in plain cloaks could be anything but fellow citizens. They were speaking about the storm and something to do with a shopping stall: it was the same conversation one could have heard in any city in any country.

"Come," said Caesar, steering me over to the right. We passed near the Curia and by a stout building that was built into the Capitoline Hill. I had not noticed it before—although I would never tell Caesar I had come here earlier to see the Forum for myself.

"What is that?" I asked, pointing to it.

"The Tullianum Prison," he said. "The place where state prisoners are kept."

"Is—is my sister there?" I could not picture proud Arsinoe in a prison.

"Yes, along with all the others to be displayed in the Triumphs. There's the Gallic chieftain Vercingetorix, and little Juba, son of the Numidian king, and Ganymedes, Arsinoe's accomplice."

"What happens to them—afterwards?"

"They are executed," he said. "In the little chamber beneath the prison cell."

"Always?"

"Of course. They led armies against Rome. Now they must pay the price. But they are killed privately. It is not part of the spectacle." He paused. "It is not sad. What's sad is their lack of self-respect. If they'd had any, they would have committed suicide rather than end up like this!"

"Surely the child is innocent of his father's deeds," I said.

"Oh, Juba will not be killed. He will be brought up in a Roman family."

"Arsinoe is a woman. Do you execute women, too?"

"Did she lead an army?" He made it sound so simple. "If she fought like a man, she must die like one."

I had seen my other sister executed by my father's command; I should accept it. Arsinoe had tried to kill both me and Caesar. In my place she would have had me dispatched without a second thought. Still, defeat and exile were a great punishment in themselves.

"You do not sound very merciful," I said, "and yet you are known for your clemency."

"That depends on who I am compared to. But no one spares foreign enemies. Your own countrymen—well, that's a personal matter. I myself believe that if someone wishes to join me, having previously fought against me, he should be welcomed. I burned the papers of Pompey that I found in his tent; I did not wish to know who had corresponded with him."

"That is very magnanimous of you," I said. "But is it not rather foolhardy?"

We were traversing a small street that was completely dark, and I had to take Caesar's hand, since I did not know the way.

"Perhaps," he said. "But I believe that any other way leads to tyranny, and provokes such hatred that you cannot survive."

"But if you pardon your opponents—like Brutus—it seems to me that you must do more, in order to please them and bring them around. Just pardoning them without making any attempt to win them over is purposeless. It achieves nothing."

"They should be grateful to me!"

"Not unless they like you." It seemed so obvious to me. If someone we hate does us a favor, we spurn both the person and the favor.

"I would never fawn and pander to them," he said. "I leave that to Cicero and his like. Cicero wants so badly to be *loved* and *appreciated*, he is like a girl just coming into womanhood who peers in the mirror constantly to check his appearance, and analyzes every remark anyone makes. Feh!"

There was no arguing with him. Perhaps he was right. We stumbled along the dark paved street; where *were* we going?

"The office of Pontifex Maximus—how did you get appointed to it?" I was curious, and it seemed a safe subject.

"I bought the election," he said. "In Rome everything is for sale."

Abruptly we swung around a corner, and I saw before me Caesar's new Forum. The clouds had vanished, and the moonlight shone full and bright on its white perfection.

Even though I had already seen it, in this light it was supremely beautiful, and it took my breath away.

"This is my gift to Rome," he said. "A new Forum."

He strode across the half-paved courtyard, keeping hold of my hand. We mounted the steps on the side of the temple, and then he bent to light his lantern.

"And this is my gift to the goddess Venus Genetrix, who founded the

Julian clan through my ancestor Aeneas—this temple, which I vowed to build, if she would grant me victory at Pharsalus."

His voice was hushed in reverence of his own creation. The portico sheltered a number of paintings—Greek, by the looks of them—and there was a suit of antique armor on one of the walls.

The inner recess of the temple was dark and silent, and it had the smell of new stone, a dusty, sharp smell. It echoed with our movements, and it *felt* cavernous, although I was not sure how I sensed that, since I could see nothing.

Caesar swung the lantern over his head, illuminating a little circle around us. Still the corners and the far end were invisible to me. He walked as silently as a priest to the back. Looming ahead I saw three statues on pedestals—large statues.

"Here is the goddess," he said, holding up the lantern to the face of the middle one. She had an expression of supreme contentment, with a mysterious smile, and her marble breast was laden with pearls.

"Arcesilaus of Greece carved her," he said.

"So you have indeed honored her," I said. "He is among the greatest of the living sculptors."

He swung the lantern to the right, lighting another statue, this one of himself. Then he said, "And this is my gift to you," and moved the lantern to the left, to the remaining statue.

She leapt out of the darkness. She was myself.

"Arcesilaus wants only to see you in person in order to refine the details," said Caesar.

"What have you done?" My voice was trembling. I was stunned.

"I have ordered a statue of you, in the robes of Venus, to put in the temple," he said simply.

"In your family temple," I said. "What can you be thinking of?"

"I wanted to."

"What are you trying to say?" I kept staring at the huge statue; myself wearing the robes of a goddess and flanking his protective goddess and himself. "What will people think? What will Calpurnia think?"

"Aren't you pleased?" He sounded disappointed, like a child. "The affront to public opinion is part of the gift. Anyone can make gestures that earn him credit with the masses, and offer them up to his friends. But to risk displeasure—that's a gift of a higher order."

"What do these statues say?" I asked. "What do you mean them to say?"

"What would they mean to you, if you saw them as an ordinary citizen?"

"They would mean—that you are descended from Venus, that your house is semidivine, and that I, in my incarnation of Venus and Isis, am your consort. What else could I think?"

"Just so," he said. "That is exactly what I mean." He stood and stared at them. "I felt led to do it. I know not what repercussions there will be, but I could not disobey. Now do you believe I love you?"

249

"Yes." Indeed I did. But there was more than love at work here. It seemed mad to court such public disapproval.

"I will dedicate the temple in between Triumphs," he said. "There will be games and banquets."

"Yes." I could think of nothing more to say.

"We must be bold," he said. "We must be who we are, and not shrink from it."

"Do you believe your victories have earned you the right to do as you please?" I asked. "Is that why you do not hold back?"

"I only know I must follow my own instinct," he said. "It has never failed me yet. My goddess of Fortune leads me on; all she asks is that I grasp eagerly what she offers."

"This was not offered by Fortune, but conceived and built by you. You did not stumble on this temple; you created it."

"I created the victories in Gaul, in Alexandria, in Pharsalus, in Africa, as well. Fortune offers you opportunities to create; she does not hand you presents."

I could not answer. There was no answer, or none that would satisfy him. He was bent on this course, as he had been bent on crossing the Rubicon and marching into Italy. But whereas others had given him reason for those actions, in this case no one but he was involved.

"They will blame me," I finally said. "They will say I made you do it."

"I care not what they say."

"Yes, you do. You cannot be that lofty. You are not a god, to disregard the opinions of men."

"To regard them overmuch is to be less than a man, to cower and grovel and—"

"You are describing a beast, not a man. There *is* a middle ground between arrogance and prostration."

He set the lantern down on the shining marble floor, plunging the upper part of the statues into darkness. He took my shoulders gently. "Show me that middle ground," he said. "You tread it so well; but then you have had many more years of practice than I. You were born royal, born to rule, recognized as a goddess from your childhood on. So you mix that element with the human so easily."

"Just be Caesar," I said. "That is enough." Then I added, "And do not wound enemies you do not have the heart to kill."

He stood silently for what seemed a long time. I could hear water dripping off the pediments of the temple outside, splashing onto the pavement: the aftermath of the storm.

He bent down and kissed me, tightening his arms around me. "I would conduct a worship of Venus here," he said softly.

Short shafts of moonlight were lying in bands at the entrance to the temple, and I knew we were alone. The goddess was looking down at us, as well as the idols of ourselves, waiting to see what we would do.

"When the dedication of the temple takes place, we would have already made offering to it," he said. His arms tightened around me, and I felt myself longing for him. The enforced polite distance between us during the dinner had sharpened the ache for closeness.

But there had been too much talk of enemies, of executions, of fate; there had been too much of the company of Brutus, Calpurnia, and Octavian. It was not a promising night to indulge in the pleasures of Venus.

"Those who worship Venus must come to her wholeheartedly," I finally said, pulling back from him a bit. "My mind is clouded with all that has passed this night before we entered her temple."

"Ask the goddess to remove it," he said. His voice was low and persuasive. "She can do so."

I marveled at how he could put aside troubling thoughts and be only here. The echoing space of the pristine temple indeed seemed to be crying out for some warmth, some stirring, to break the spell of incompleteness within it.

I let him guide me back into the utter darkness of the apse, behind the base of the Venus statue. He left the lantern on the floor in front of it, and a soft, diffuse light shone from around the sides.

"Have you not a villa for this?" I protested weakly. "A villa, with a room appointed with couches and coverlets, and windows opening onto a garden that lets in the smells of paradise?"

"You know well I have," he said, "but it is missing one thing all lovers want, and which we have never tasted: privacy. Behold a paradox: the richer you are, the less of it you have. Now we shall have it, by heaven. We shall have it."

His voice was warm in my ear, and I felt myself melting with it. He was right; we were alone as we had rarely been before, and might never be again.

He eased the sleeve of my gown down over my arm and kissed my shoulder lingeringly. I could feel my own bones beneath his lips, and became at once aware of my body; the confusing thoughts of the mind began to take flight.

"I love you," I said. "I would die for you."

"Hush," he said. "No talk of dying. That belongs to poets, not to queens." He kissed me then, strongly, and I returned it, clinging to him in the darkness. We were alone. He was mine, and I was his.

The goddess above us looked down with favor.

Brilliant sun. Piercingly blue sky. A slight breeze on this day, the first Triumph. I sat in the special stand of seats constructed along the Via Sacra to enable exalted guests to observe the last, most important part of the Triumphal parade that wound its way through the Forum and then up to the Temple of Capitoline Jupiter. We would wait a long time in the sun, which

251

is why Caesar had ordered silk canopies to be erected over us. They flapped now, billowing as each breeze passed through them, diluting the light and turning it blue.

Ptolemy was beside me, and in the other places of honor were Calpurnia, Octavia, Caesar's nephew Quintus Pedius, and his great-nephew Lucius Pinarius. He had a very small family.

People had begun waiting long before dawn along the route he would pass: from the Campus Martius and through the Circus Maximus before circling the Palatine Hill and entering the Forum. I could hear the roars and shouts from far away as he appeared at each station, and wondered what they were seeing; I was impatient to behold it.

At midday I saw a slight movement from the far end of the Forum, and soon a company of men appeared. Slowly, very slowly, they wound their way down the Via Sacra, past the Temple of Vesta, past the Temple of Castor and Pollux, past the half-finished porticoes of the Basilica Julia, and then abreast of us. The faint strains of music grew louder, and the leaders of the procession, the musicians with their trumpets and pipes, passed by. Behind them came a company of priests, swaying as they lifted their thuribles of incense high, the sweet perfume burning in the summer air.

Then came a vast company of dignitaries, the officers of the city of Rome, and behind them the senators, walking proudly in their magisterial togas; there must have been more than five hundred of them.

Then a shout went up from the far side of the Forum, and as the elaborately decorated wagons trundled into view, I knew why. It was the spoils, heaped high in carriages built of Gallic timber and inlaid with citruswood. Spears bristled from the wagons, shields rattled, the wagons strained under the weight of the gold and silver. Sometimes a goblet or a platter would fall off, and people would dash out and grab it, like dogs lapping up leavings from a table.

Wagon after wagon groaned past, sagging under its mountain of gold. The wheels of one got stuck between the paving stones, and had to be heaved out. Caesar must have raided every hamlet, stripped every rural altar of its trappings. There must be nothing left in Gaul of value.

A company of men paraded past, holding signs with the names of battles: Alesia, Agedincum, Bibracte, Lugdunum, Gregovia, Avaricum—unfamiliar names for the wild, unknown places where Caesar had conquered.

A decorated wagon with an effigy of the ocean in chains rolled past, with a sign denoting the invasion of Britain.

Then came a company of prisoners, long-haired chieftains, clad in leather and furs. Behind them, walking alone, came a tall figure in chains. It was Vercingetorix, the Gallic chieftain who had led a mighty uprising of the Arverni tribe against Caesar and had finally been defeated at Alesia, where Caesar had emerged victorious against an enemy five times his number. Vercingetorix had lost none of his proud bearing in the six years he had been waiting for his march through the Forum on his way to death, and the crowd, jeering freely at the other prisoners, fell silent as he passed by.

I shuddered. In the next Triumph, Arsinoe would walk in his footsteps, passing before us in defeat. The shame, the unendurable shame of it!

Following Vercingetorix paraded the sacrificial animals bound for the temple, columns of white oxen with gilded horns, garlanded and curried, the thanksgiving offering Caesar would make for his victories.

From the farther end of the Forum a vast shout arose, and I knew that Caesar had finally entered it. Preceding him came the lictors—all seventy-two of them, allowed because Caesar had been dictator three times. They carried those ugly bundles of branches and the gleaming axes, and I liked them no better this time. Their ceremonial red capes made bright spots like blood as they passed by.

Then Caesar himself, high in a golden chariot pulled by four horses. He stood like a god, dressed in purple and gold, looking out at the people. In his left hand he held an ivory scepter surmounted by an eagle, and in his right a laurel branch. Behind him stood a slave, holding the heavy gold crown of Jupiter over his head, a crown too weighty for a mortal brow.

A frenzied shout arose from the throats of all who beheld him. They showered him with flowers, with personal tokens and treasures, with bracelets and earrings.

Behind him, slight and straight, rode Octavian in his own chariot, as the only other adult male in Caesar's family.

The Triumphal chariot passed us by, moving on like the chariot of Phoebus transiting the sky, and I saw wave after wave of people rising to their feet and shouting.

Then, suddenly, the procession stopped. The Triumphal chariot sagged and lurched. I heard a buzz of confusion. Caesar stepped out.

The axle of the chariot had snapped, just as he drew abreast of the Temple of Fortune. He dismounted and stood on the pavement, then immediately walked to the steps leading up the Capitoline Hill to the Temple of Jupiter Optimus Maximus, where he was supposed to ascend to dedicate his wreath and scepter.

He fell to his knees at the first step, and shouted in a ringing voice, "Behold! I will climb to the Temple on my knees, as a sign of my submission to the will of Fate!" And he did so, laboriously making his way up the long incline, his purple toga trailing on the ground behind him.

The people roared their approval; by quick thinking, Caesar had turned a bad omen into an occasion of good grace. But the incident unnerved me. It was very bad.

Behind Caesar came his troops, the men who had made his victories possible. They were happy, shouting Io triumphe!—Hail, God of Triumph!—and singing at the top of their lungs. But I was not so happy when I heard the words of their verses:

> Home we bring our bald whoremonger;
> Romans, lock your wives away.

All the bags of gold you lent him
Went his Gallic tarts to pay.

The crowd roared at that, and cheered. Then followed more verses:

Gaul was brought to shame by Caesar;
By King Nicomedes, he.
Here comes Caesar, wreathed in triumph
For his Gallic victory!
Nicomedes wears no laurels,
Though the greatest of the three.

Nicomedes—that king of Bithynia that his enemies claimed had been Caesar's lover! I had thought it was a lie. Someone had shown me the libel Cicero had written in private letters: "Caesar was led by Nicomedes' attendants to the royal bedchamber, where he lay on a golden couch, dressed in a purple shift. . . . So this descendant of Venus lost his virginity in Bithynia." Evidently the soldiers preferred to keep the lie alive.

Now the crowd screamed with laughter. And there was worse to come.

Caesar tarried in Egypt,
Taking in all the spoils,
The Lighthouse, the Library,
Queen Cleopatra and
Her many-perfumed oils.

More roars of laughter. I watched Calpurnia; she was smiling gamely, and I attempted to do likewise, but I was furious.

More verses followed:

If you do right,
You will be punished,
But if you do wrong,
You will be King.

I stiffened when I heard the word *King*. Why was that word on everyone's lips in connection with Caesar? Why was he suspected of it? I knew his association with me must be part of it. Who keeps company with a queen but a king? And when they saw what he had put in the Temple of Venus Genetrix . . .

A seemingly endless file of the soldiers marched past, following Caesar. At their forefront I heard wild cries of joy, and I was later told they were receiving gifts for their courage and loyalty: ten thousand *denarii* for each centurion, five thousand for each legionary. The crowds were surging; other soldiers had to hold them back. The poor, too, expected to receive largesse.

After the sea of soldiers passed, it was over. The sun had swung around until it was almost shining in our eyes, despite the canopy. I saw a procession of litters coming down the Via Sacra, swaying in rhythm with their bearers. All the honored spectators from this section were to be transported to the Circus Maximus, where the celebratory chariot races would be held, as part of the Triumphal Games. Caesar would open them; as foreign rulers, Ptolemy and I would be seated nearby. But I would not be next to Caesar; Calpurnia and Octavian would have that honor.

Even though it was the long way around, we were taken up to the Capitoline Hill so that we could honor Jupiter by passing his temple. Before it now stood Caesar's chariot, and in the inner recesses of the temple I could see the seated statue of Jupiter, sitting majestically in the dimness. Beside it was a new bronze one of Caesar, his foot upon a representation of the entire world. Later I was told that it had an inscription saying that Caesar was a demigod, and that Caesar had just ordered the inscription removed.

The doomed oxen were placidly awaiting their sacrifice, which would take place as soon as the last of the litters left. Priests were standing by, smiling benignly, even stroking the beasts.

We descended from the hill and made our way through an area crowded with shops, markets, and apartments, and then we were at the Circus Maximus, the enormous racetrack that lay in a valley between the Palatine and the Aventine Hills. Huge walls encircled it like a rim, inside of which tier after tier of seats rose. We were taken in through the entrance arch while soldiers held back an enormous crowd waiting to rush inside once all the dignitaries were seated. I could see that people were already in the special section under its arched roof. There was the purple toga—Caesar was there! We approached slowly, and I watched him, searching to see how he looked, how he behaved.

He seemed very tired, and his eyes kept sweeping the arena as if he expected an ambush. The day had told on him, and now, when he thought himself unobserved for a moment, he had let his guard down. He looked every bit of his fifty-four years; there were harsh lines sculpted between his nose and mouth, and his neck was gaunt. His eyes were wary, not happy, on this day he had so longed for. Respectful, pleasant, he nodded to Calpurnia. Then he caught sight of us approaching, and he instantly altered his expression. Any doubts I had about his feelings for me were swept away: his face truly lit up, and the years lifted from it.

He stood, his purple toga with its gold embroidery glinting like an ancient treasure. He wore the gold laurel wreath, and its leaves encircled his head like a corona.

"Hail, great *Triumphator*!" I said. "The greatest on earth."

"Hail, great Queen of Egypt," he said. "And King of Egypt." He indicated Ptolemy. "Pray, take your seats of honor."

All the members of his family, small as it was, were seated around him. Where his son should have been, sat Octavian, who was only a great-nephew. But Caesar *had* a son, and someday that son would sit beside him—Caesarion.

Ptolemy and I were seated with a number of distinguished foreign visitors and envoys who had traveled for the occasion. The kingdoms of Galatia and Cappadocia, the cities of Lycia, Laodicea, Tarsus, and Xanthus sent ambassadors—the east, that so fascinated and titillated Romans.

The stands filled rapidly as spectators rushed in like a wall of water. Their spirits were high; a wild excitement filled the air, as palpable as the heaviness just before a thunderstorm.

Caesar was talking to Calpurnia and Octavian, leaning over attentively. I saw that he was seated on a special chair; it was gilded and had a carved back. Undoubtedly it signified something; in Rome, everything did.

At last the arena was full. Every last place was taken, and the stands were a sea of color. The trumpeters, a company of at least fifty men, rose from their places and sounded their horns. The notes rang out, both glad and stirring. The noise of the crowd subsided.

A professional caller, a man with the loudest carrying voice I had ever heard, took his place at the railing before Caesar.

"Romans! Noble guests!" he yelled. There were more than a hundred thousand spectators—could all of them hear him? His voice rang and echoed all around us. "We are here to honor our *Triumphator* in the ancient way, inherited from our ancestors, with contests of valor and skill. Here before you the young knights will race their horses, to the glory of Jupiter and Caesar."

A roar went up. He held up his hands for silence to continue. "We will begin with the *ars desultoria*. Accept their offerings!"

Caesar then stood up. He raised his right arm and cried, "Let the games begin!"

Immediately, from the gates at the far end of the Circus, two-horse pairs emerged, trotting nervously. The horses, the finest I had ever seen, gleamed in the afternoon sun. On their backs were young men who waved and bowed to the crowd, before coming to our section and making obeisance.

There were some twenty pairs of them, and the horses seemed to be matched in size and speed. At first they all trotted abreast, once around the track, but then the first pair left the others behind and went into a full gallop, necks straining and feet flying. Their riders were stretched low on their necks, gripping the heaving withers. Suddenly one of them stood up, and leapt onto the back of the neighboring horse, while the other rider did likewise. For an instant they crossed each other in the air, hanging there in sickening immobility, while the horses thundered on. Then they slipped onto the horses' backs, and a cheer from the crowd went up. They turned backward and flipped themselves around, like acrobats, and all the while the horses hurtled forward. Scarves and handkerchiefs had been placed at intervals on the track, and the riders leaned so far down to scoop them up that their heads were right beside the pounding hooves. At each victorious feat, the crowd grew more excited. Behind the first pair there were now several others, all performing dangerous stunts on the galloping, skittish horses.

In attempting to grab a scarf near the sharp turn at one end of the Circus, one of the riders slipped off and his horse ran over him. A groan escaped from the crowd, but it was a groan that had a hungry edge to it. A team of men dashed from the sidelines to carry off the victim in a litter, but they were almost run down by the other horses and had to let the man lie there to be trampled for one more round.

Ptolemy was leaning forward, trembling with fear and excitement. "Is he dead?" he kept asking.

It surely looked as if he was. Before I could answer, another rider fell off; his head exploded in a red spray as his horse's hoof landed right in the middle of it. This one was indeed dead.

The sand was beginning to be streaked with red. I looked around at the Romans surrounding me. Their eyes were fixed on the arena, and they seemed to have little revulsion for what they saw. The noise in the stands was growing steadily, feeding on the violence as a fire feeds on straw.

The teams attempted increasingly more difficult feats, until the winners did two midair somersaults between the galloping horses, landing precariously on the slippery, sweating backs. Caesar awarded them the prize, and the remaining fourteen or fifteen pairs of foam-flecked horses were led off the track.

A company of workers ran out and began raking the sand, getting ready for the next event. A late-afternoon breeze had sprung up; normally this was the part of day reserved for relaxation. But the tension was mounting.

"Why do they want to kill people?" Ptolemy was asking. "Why does anyone want to be one of those riders?"

"Men are ever drawn to dangerous enterprises," I said. "No matter how dangerous a mission, someone will always volunteer for it." That fact had always puzzled me.

Just then there was a stirring in Caesar's section. Octavian had stood up and was making his way over to us.

"The most noble *Triumphator* has asked that I sit with you and explain the proceedings," he said. The ambassador from Tarsus quickly vacated his seat next to me.

"How thoughtful of the *Triumphator*," I said. I nodded to Caesar.

"Did you enjoy the exhibition?" Octavian asked.

"For an exhibition, some men paid a high price—their lives," I said. "But their skill was impressive. What is the next event?"

Octavian smiled. "It is the favorite sport here in Rome—chariot races. Originally they were a religious rite. Today there will be ten four-horse teams, and the winners will come away with big purses of gold."

"Oh, that should be exciting!" said Ptolemy. "And safer."

Octavian shook his fair young head. "Hardly. Someone always gets killed. Sometimes three or four chariots get tangled up and are all destroyed. The sharp turns at each end of the Circus invariably cause some to turn over, even if nothing else goes wrong."

"Is that why everyone likes the races so much?" asked Ptolemy.

"I wouldn't say that," said Octavian.

"Then why don't they make them safer?" Ptolemy persisted.

"That would ruin the sport of it."

A shout rose, and I saw that the chariots were emerging from the entrance arches. Each team burst through the narrow arch, horses pulling at the reins, eager to run. Behind them the light chariots, with their drivers standing on the tiny platforms, wheeled and shone in the golden afternoon sunlight. The horses were as large as possible, while the chariots were small and feather-light—which meant they were unstable and easily bounced and overturned. The helmets of the men glistened, some with spikes, some with feathers, some with colored scarves.

Octavian had stood up, and was shouting. His cheeks were flushed, and his eyes were riveted on one particular chariot driven by a swarthy man and pulled by four bay horses with unusually thin, long legs.

"Those are mine," he said hoarsely. "From the stable of Arrius." I had never suspected he could show such fervor. "You choose one," he said.

There was another team of particularly well-favored horses, cream-colored, with gray manes and tails. I knew full well that a pleasing configuration did not always mean speed or stamina, just as a pleasant demeanor in men did not necessarily denote honesty, but I was still drawn to them. "The team with the small driver," I said.

"From Campania," he said. "They are reputed to be well fed and trained."

"Which is Caesar's favorite?" Ptolemy asked.

"He is partial to the blacks," said Octavian, "because that stable bred his own favorite riding horse. But they are more powerful than speedy."

The teams trotted once around the track, forty horses abreast, sweeping around the turn like a giant wing. The drivers must have had extraordinary skill to keep them all in line in this manner. Finally they halted just in line with us, and waited for the signal to begin.

Caesar rose, and held up a large white cloth. He raised it high above his head, and then, releasing it, let it float down to the arena. When it touched the ground, signalmen lowered their banners, and the horses were let loose.

Two or three of the teams leaped instantly ahead, and began immediately to struggle for the best position on the track. The width of four horses yoked in parallel meant that the competitors could not crowd too close together, but they also needed to make close turns if they were not to fall behind. The inside team risked being dashed against the central axis of the Circus and wrecked; the middle one squeezed into an accident; and the outside one losing his position by having to cover a greater distance.

The leaders were Octavian's bays and two others; on the very first turn, one careened out of control and smashed on the wall of the spectators' stand. Immediately one of the other teams, which had been hovering just behind, moved up into the vacated outside position. Another team hit the wreck of the first one, and was itself wrecked; the chariot seemed to explode and the driver was thrown a long distance, while his horses galloped aimlessly on.

The spectators were standing now, yelling. Beside me Octavian was breathing rapidly, muttering, "Yes! Yes!" as his team kept its lead, and he jumped to his feet. Only Caesar remained sitting, watching intently but calmly.

Another turn, another wrecked chariot; this one tumbled over into the central axis and impaled itself on a statue of Jupiter, who had been presiding over the contest. The horses squealed with fear and pain as they went down in a tangle of harness.

Now Caesar's team unexpectedly began gaining on the others, coming up from the outside in a burst of speed. There were only seven teams left, leaving more room to maneuver. Octavian's charioteer and the other one lashed their horses as, from the corner of their eyes, they saw the intruder catching up. But Caesar's team, fresher than the others because it had conserved its energy, kept pace with them. It was unable to pass them, however, because it had to cover such a greater distance in pacing, using the outside lane.

My team was hanging back at a respectable distance, in a clump of the middle runners. One lone team of horses, all differently colored, brought up the rear.

On the next-to-last turn, the middle chariot of those in the lead seemed to stumble; suddenly it fell back into the knot of the other three. There was no room for it; the chariots on either side were unable to find a safe place for themselves. The three collided, including the former leader, and the grinding wheels and splintering wood were sickening. They were so enveloped in each other, harnesses crossed, yokes rammed together, limbs entangled, that they went down in a mass together, the horses and men crying out in one long, anguished scream. My team skidded around them, saved only by the fact that it had been lagging on the outside.

A roar went up from the crowd, almost a sigh of pleasure at the flying debris, the wheels rolling away, the chariot railings flying through the air, the arms and legs waving from the mess, the screams cut short by the stampeding horses pounding the helpless drivers into the dirt with their deadly hooves.

The lead chariots thundered on, unconcerned, and the hungry crowd had a choice of two equally arousing sights to satisfy them: the speed and flying finish of the front runners, and the carnage of the losers, stirring feebly on the sand behind them. Soon the leaders swept around to that section again, and had to steer wildly to avoid the mess; a gigantic cheer went up.

Octavian's chariot won, followed by Caesar's blacks. Mine finished a distant third, and the last one received an affectionate cheer, probably because by being so comically slow, it had preserved its own life.

"Congratulations," I said to Octavian. "You choose well. How did you know?"

He turned to look at me, and I saw how clear and light his blue eyes were, with a little darker rim around the outside of the irises. He looked utterly detached, but I could not help noticing how ragged his breath still was, as he struggled to get his excitement under control.

"A lucky guess," he said. "I looked at the legs and ignored all the rest."

Caesar was standing, ready to receive the winning charioteer. The young man, trembling and covered with sweat, was led to him. Caesar placed the laurel wreath on his head.

"We triumph together this day," he said.

The charioteer looked at him adoringly. "I will preserve this always," he said, touching the laurel wreath. "I will keep it for my children, and my children's children, and say, 'This I won on the day of great Caesar's Triumph.'"

"If he keeps on racing, he won't have any children," said Ptolemy in my ear. "He'd better retire right now!"

There were several more chariot races, but none as exciting as this first. There were more four-horse races, and several two-horse ones. They went on until it was almost too dark to see, and then riders entered the Circus with torches and announced that it was over. Behind them I could see a parade of elephants, each with a torch mounted on its back. They filed into the arena and walked around once majestically, the circle of fire punctuating the twilight. One elephant, fitted with a huge platform on his back, approached the stand where we sat, and knelt.

"Caesar will now be borne back to his home in the Forum. All loving citizens are welcome to accompany him," the announcer shouted.

Caesar rose and descended to the kneeling beast, then mounted his back. The obedient animal lurched to his feet, and Caesar, his ceremonial toga's gold embroidery winking in the torchlight, turned and lifted his hand to the people. Then he rode slowly away.

The rest of us mounted on other elephants, sharing them. Ptolemy and I were on one, Octavian and Calpurnia on another, the other nephews on a third. Between the line of the rest, the dignitaries walked, then streaming out behind them, as far as the eye could see, came the people. The torchlight threw long, jumping shadows on them, knitting them into one big creature instead of thousands of separate ones. Ahead of us I could see the rain of flowers and tokens being showered on Caesar, could hear the shouts rise wherever he passed, sighing like people let out into the light after a long imprisonment.

Caesar! Caesar! Caesar! they cried. *Our joy, our savior, our life!*

The parade went through the Forum, retracing in jubilation the way of the Triumph, a throng of careless worshipers. They were fed, they were entertained, they were lovingly looked after by Caesar; they wanted for nothing.

They escorted him to his house. He climbed down from the elephant, then stood for a moment in the doorway.

"Good night, my friends all," he said. "I thank you for this day."

Then he turned and went inside. The door shut gently.

I waited a moment, then saw Calpurnia and Octavian enter behind him. I ached to follow, to be with him in this aftermath of his extraordinary day—often the most precious part of all, when it could be savored in private, but when the blood was still coursing with the victory of it.

"Let us return to the villa," I said to the man leading the elephant.

I turned to Ptolemy. "We cannot enter. We do not belong with them tonight," I explained. "It is their moment."

I would pass the night alone, excluded from Caesar's private celebration. But so would his only son.

<hr/>

26

The sun rose in a cloudless sky the next morning, as if Caesar had ordered it to do so. The perfect weather meant that the expansive—and expensive—public exhibitions and celebrations surrounding each successive Triumph could go on unimpeded. Today it was to be theatrical performances in the morning, and Greek-style athletic contests in the afternoon in a temporary theater in the Campus Martius, while simultaneously patrician boys were to enact a mock battle called the Game of Troy elsewhere on the fields.

In the Circus Maximus, hundreds of condemned prisoners and prisoners of war fought in a gigantic gladiatorial contest on the sands where the chariots had raced the day before. I was told that they fought together in companies, horsemen against horsemen, foot soldiers against foot soldiers, with a company of forty elephant-mounted warriors against one another. The sand was soaked with their blood. But I did not see it, nor did I wish to. The Roman appetite for blood bewildered me. All day long I could hear, from the upper windows of my chamber, the shouts and cries of the crowds, drinking in the violence as the sand drank in the blood.

A sea of people had swarmed into Rome to feed on the excitement, the gore, and the free food. A city of tents had sprung up, so that the Rome I beheld from the summit of the hill was twice as big as when I had arrived. People lost their lives in the crush down there; some who had come merely to enjoy the death and violence ended up sharing it, trampled in the crush of bodies. Two senators were killed that way, as well as nameless others.

I dreaded the next Triumph, the one celebrating Caesar's victory in Egypt. I would have to watch as representations of my own country were paraded past me, would have to smile with approval at the subjugation depicted. All eyes would be on me, and I must not flinch. That was the only way to show that my regime was different, the *true* government of Egypt, the one in alliance with Rome. I almost hated Caesar for imposing this on me; I did not know if I could stand it. Yet stand it I must. His political judgment here was correct, however much it hurt to obey it.

<hr/>

The Second Triumph, over *Aegyptus*: cool day, stiff breeze, racing clouds—very un-Egyptian weather. Again we were seated in the stands at the end of the Via Sacra; this time the silken sun-canopy whipped up and down in the wind. I had attired myself, and Ptolemy, in Greek-style clothes for the occasion. Let everyone remember that we were the descendants of Alexander's general! No glittering headdress with cobras rearing on my forehead, no broad collar of Pharaonic jewels, no ostrich feathers. In me, today, there would be nothing exotic or foreign. A simple diadem, low across my forehead, was better than a crown—today.

Again, the shouts as Caesar passed through the different stations of the city on his way to the Forum—then the sounds rising as he approached us. A movement came from the far end of the Forum as the musicians led the way of the procession. First came a company of native Egyptians blowing silver trumpets and beating on long drums, clashing cymbals and waving ivory clappers, followed by a retinue of dancers, oiled and leaping. Behind them walked a company of women wearing the thinnest linen gowns, shaking their sistrums and chanting. A sigh went up from the crowd; this was the mysterious east, brought to them in the Forum itself. Shaven-headed priests of Isis, trailing incense and intoning hymns to the goddess, followed.

In contrast, the magistrates of Rome, bulky in their togas, stepped lively behind them, looking disdainful of the nonsense of Egypt.

The wagons were coming! I braced myself to endure the sight of the treasures of Egypt heaped in them, even though Caesar had not taken them; indeed, I had given them. But who knew that? And they were just as thoroughly gone from Egypt, no matter how they got here. The first of them was heaving into view—an enormous, lumbering thing made of acanthus wood, a precious wood of our region. Inside it were arrayed gilded statues and mummy cases, small obelisks and scarves woven with jewels. The next cart, made with enormously thick wheels, contained the graywacke statue I had just given Caesar! I was thankful, then, that most of our art treasures were so heavy that no conqueror could cart them off. At least the pyramids and Sphinx were safe! And the great temples along the Nile, and the Lighthouse—

But I spoke too soon. For next the Lighthouse itself appeared—a gigantic model of it, on a specially constructed wagon. Its top glowed red, and a light winked out of it. It was followed by a representation of the River Nile, a luxurious bearded reclining man of ample proportions, surrounded by crocodiles and horns of plenty.

Next came the living spoils: animals from Egypt and Africa. There were crocodiles, rumbling along in their wooden cages, then panthers and ostriches, and finally the creature that excited everyone's curiosity: a giraffe. There had never been one in Rome before, and the people were amazed by it. They cried out that it seemed to be half camel and half leopard, and asked how they had ever bred.

Then the first of the prisoners came into view: a wax figure of Pothinus, chillingly accurate, rolled by in his own chariot. I had thought never to see his slick, evil face again. But his head was attached—something that could only happen in art and the imagination.

His follow conspirator, Achillas, made his appearance, leering from a wagon in effigy.

I shuddered. How those men had once held power over me! Now they were reduced to wax dummies before a jeering crowd. I began to understand the need that the Triumphs satisfied.

"Vile eunuch!" People were spitting on Pothinus.

"Killer! Killer! Killer!" A group rushed from the stands toward the effigy of Achillas. They pelted it with dung and offal. "You killed our Pompey!" They were about to wrench the dummy from its cart when soldiers stopped them.

"Nay!" they said. "You must not rob others of the opportunity to spit on him!"

Now the dead were replaced by the living. Dragging by me in chains was Ganymedes. His hair was long and matted, his face pale from his long imprisonment. No trace now of the elegant palace tutor.

He flinched as waves of trash were thrown at him. Luckily he probably did not understand most of the Latin curses and abuse that were shouted at him. His eyes were dull; his spirit had long since been broken.

And then—O ye gods! It was Arsinoe! She walked some fifty feet behind him, bound in silver chains. But her head was held high; it took all her effort not to bend under the weight of the chains, but she stood erect and walked with a sure pace. She was thin; her cheeks were gaunt and I could see the bones of her shoulders. The proud Arsinoe, a captive in a Roman Triumph, being led like a spoil through the Forum and thence to her death.

It could have been I! I lowered my eyelids and let the image dim, and I could see myself, walking in her place, the vanquished. If I had sided against Rome . . . if fate had not favored me . . .

Beside me, Ptolemy was crying. I clutched his hand. "Don't look," I said.

But just then Arsinoe turned and looked at me, a riveting, direct gaze. Her eyes were drawn to mine and would not let me go. Hatred burned there, and anger leapt across the space separating us. I was the captive, held in her stare.

She passed me by, her spirit already elsewhere, so it seemed. The crowd was now watching her, and sighs of sympathy rose in the air like currents. Hostile eyes turned on me. Suddenly I was the villain and she the wronged one.

How could they forget so readily? Arsinoe had fought against Rome. But Romans had a soft spot for the underdog. They saw a beautiful princess in chains, and forgot Caesar. No taunts or rubbish followed her; a hushed, respectful silence descended.

Files of sacrificial oxen followed in her wake, bound for death, and that just excited the crowd further. They moaned with pity. This poor princess, being led like one of the white oxen to her doom!

Now Caesar appeared, resplendent. But he rode into a sullen arena, filled with low murmurs. The sight of his lictors and gold chariot did not stir people as it had the first time. There were a few shouts and cheers, sounding thin in the vast space. Some people threw vials of perfumed oil, and one landed on the rim of his chariot and broke. He seized the broken bottle and held it aloft.

"Well done!" he cried. "I always say that my soldiers fight just as well stinking of perfume!"

That brought the crowd around, changed the mood. They began shouting and stamping.

"Is this Egyptian perfume?" he cried, seizing the moment.

They roared with approval.

"I tell you, the perfumes of Egypt are rich beyond imagining! And I have brought them all to you!" He waved expansively. "I shall distribute them along with your largesse! There's cassia and camphor and oil of lilies!"

Where was he going to get these on such short notice? I knew he had not procured any in Egypt!

Octavian, riding behind him, was also dodging perfume flasks.

"Cleopatra and her many-perfumed oils!" the crowd yelled.

For an instant Caesar froze. Then he turned and presented me to the crowd with his extended arm. They screamed and stamped.

Quickly he rode on. My face burned. I felt the presence of Calpurnia intensely, even though I could not see her. Octavian jerked his head back and kept looking straight ahead.

The tramping of the soldiers' feet drowned out all other sounds. They were shouting and singing in chorus the Cleopatra song again, now joined by the crowds. New verses were added:

> While the Lighthouse blazed
> and the soldiers gazed,
> Caesar spent his nights and days
> In his Cleopatra phase.

I hated this! I hated it! How could Caesar endure it so good-naturedly? It was like being led in the Triumph himself.

> Days and nights were all the same,
> He sported himself until he was lame,
> He always knew how to play that game,
> And now he gives us the Queen to blame!

Enough! I could stand no more of this! Was I supposed to laugh, as Caesar did? They were calling me a whore!

At last the horrible procession passed by, and the Triumph was over. It was over.

The spectacle to follow this Triumph was a naval battle—fought in Rome. Caesar sent a message to tell us that the customary litter would be sent for us, and that our presence was essential. As it had been for the Egyptian Triumph?

This time the litters set out away from the Circus Maximus, and we were transported toward the river; the crowds were thick, and I could see the sites where they camped at night. There were fewer buildings here, but still I saw several small temples abutting on a huge, pillared complex that ended in a theater.

"Why, it's almost as big as one of our temples!" said Ptolemy in a shrill voice.

What could it be? I must ask Caesar.

Oh, if only that building had never existed! I shudder now to recall it; but then, in the sunlight, it seemed innocent enough. And is a building to blame for what evil men do inside it?

"Where is that temple with enemy territory around it?" asked Ptolemy. "The one where the Romans throw blood-tipped spears to start a war?"

I had to confess I did not know what he was talking about. Another thing to ask Caesar.

Abruptly the litters were set down and our attendants helped us out. As we alighted, I thought my eyes were deceived. Before us was a lake, and upon it were true ships—biremes, triremes, and quadriremes, massed in two wings, banners flying. A gigantic crowd surrounded the entire basin of the lake, milling and shouting.

A gallery had been built on stilts on the shore, and I could see Caesar and the knot of his family and attendants already grouped upon it.

We mounted the platform and were shown our seats. From this height, the spectacle was even more miraculous. The artificial lake that had been excavated on the Campus Martius—the Field of Mars—must have been at least half a mile long, and who knew how deep? Obviously deep enough to accommodate warships.

I saw Caesar watching my face, as if he had dug the entire thing just to see my reaction. I was stunned and could not hide it.

I knew he would send Octavian over, and I was right. He made his way to us, his eyes watchful. "Greetings, Your Majesties," he said. "We are pleased you could join us for this Triumph and its celebration."

Was it my imagination, or did he stress the word *this*, and look carefully at us?

"It was necessary for us to behold it," I said, being as honest as I could. "I do not pretend that it was not painful. It brought back many ugly memories."

"Caesar will be distressed to hear it. He is under the impression that you regarded those people as enemies, as did he. And the sight of an enemy in chains is usually an exhilarating one."

"Perhaps when you have actually fought a war, you will understand," I said. He was just a boy and had never seen a battle, and his smugness was unpleasant to me at that moment. Yet I should have disguised my reaction better. "Tell me of this spectacle," I said lightly. "Is there no engineering miracle the Romans cannot perform?"

265

"None that I am aware of," he replied, with that cold, perfect smile.

This entertainment was to feature a naval battle between the fleets of Tyre and Egypt. Two thousand oarsmen and a thousand fighting men from each nation manned their respective ships, and, at the sound of trumpets, cast off from the spots where they rocked on the sparkling water. I assumed it was to be an exhibition only, but as smoke rose from one of the ships and men dived overboard, followed by groans and screams, I suddenly became aware that it was real.

I turned to Octavian accusingly. "What is this? Are these men called upon to mimic fighting, or to fight?"

"In a *naumachia*, great battles are reenacted—reenacted in all their particulars," he said. "We have staged the battle of Salamis, with the Athenians defeating the Persians, and watched the Carthaginian fleet being destroyed again and again from the comfort of our seats."

"If a war is once fought, and an issue decided, is that not final?" I demanded. "What purpose is served in fighting it again? Will history's verdict be reversed?"

The ships were ramming one another; grapnels were hurled and soldiers swarmed onto enemy ships, swords flashing. Firebrands flew through the air, setting rigging aflame. Some of these missiles landed among the spectators, causing screams and panic.

The ships swung around as the men on them struggled for mastery. I saw bodies being flung overboard, and dark stains of blood began to spread out on the water. The first ship sank, and screams rose from it and then drowned in silence.

"Are men to die for our amusement?" I cried. I looked at the others on our platform, who were nodding and watching, smiles on their faces. Two men were conferring about the tactics, and I saw Agrippa arguing about some maneuver. Caesar looked pleasantly entertained.

Blood, blood everywhere! Why did the sun not shine red on Rome, beaming through a haze of blood? Why did it rise an ordinary color?

"Can there not be a chariot race without death, a sailing exhibition without death, a swordplay without death?" I tugged on Octavian's shoulder, where the toga was bunched. "Why must death be a sauce to accompany everything you Romans devour?"

Devour. That was the word for what they did. They devoured everything . . . and they needed a lively spice for their digestion.

"Because without death everything is bland," he said. "Without a final price, everything is make-believe."

Even as he spoke, his voice soft and reasonable against the background cries of wounded men and the shudders of ship timber against timber, I pictured Arsinoe being strangled in the dark, airless stone prison cell. Death in the sunlight and death in the dark—the two kinds of Roman death.

Abruptly I left the "entertainment."

———

I assume the *naumachia* lasted until after sunset. As it got dark, from the top of the highest part of the villa's hill I could see winking torches in the Campus Martius. I also could see what looked like bonfires, but from their sheer size I knew they were the burning hulks of ships. The spectacle had consumed itself.

I felt sick and exhausted. I wished to bathe and then stretch myself out on my bed and purge my mind of the hideous images that were racing through it. But before I could do so, the door of the house flew open and Caesar stamped in. His face was a mask of anger.

"How dare you leave?" he yelled as soon as he saw me—no other greeting was offered. "You shamed me, you insulted me, you have caused every tongue in Rome to natter!"

How had he got away from all the people? Where were his guards, his attendants, the ever-worshipful Octavian?

"I could not stand it anymore," I said. "The killing—"

"So you have a weak stomach for killing? Perhaps you're not a true Ptolemy after all!"

I stared at him. He was ranting, red-faced, like an angry merchant. "I think killing should be reserved for danger, not sport," I finally said. "You devalue death to treat it so casually. It is the great final thing and should not be demeaned."

"Egyptians revere death too much," he grunted.

"Romans revere it too little," I said.

"Yet we both make art out of it. You with your tombs and paintings and mummies, and we with our entertainments." His temper seemed to have cooled, but I was not fooled. He was most angry when he showed it least. "Enough of this death talk. By leaving, you undid all you had done earlier by attending the Triumph."

"It was horrible. But I did not cover my eyes." I paused. "I hated every second of it! I hated seeing Egyptian treasures in the carts, hated the verses they sang about you—and the perfume bottles! Is that what people think of me?"

"Be thankful that's what they think. It's harmless enough."

"Arsinoe. It was dreadful. And the people were stirred in sympathy."

"Yes." He walked toward a bench and sat down on it. His shoulders sagged. "I spared Arsinoe."

My first feeling was a rush of relief. My second was worry. Arsinoe the proud would not retire quietly.

"Where is she to go?"

"She has requested sanctuary at the great Temple of Diana in Ephesus," he said. "And I will grant it, if you agree."

Ephesus! Too close to Egypt! Better send her to Britain! Yet . . . I would gamble, and be merciful. Perhaps I was not enough of a Ptolemy after all. Arsinoe would not have granted it.

"Yes, I will allow it."

"Ganymedes is dead."

Ganymedes had been dead already, the broken creature I had seen in the Forum. There could have been no reprieve for him.

"We must do something to offset the bad impression your leaving gave today," Caesar insisted. "The crowd was in a dangerous mood. You sensed it. The perfume bottles at least allowed us to divert them. But they were not wholehearted in their cheers. And it may be worse in the other two Triumphs to follow, especially the one over Africa, because Cato died in that war. I think, in order to quell any rumors that you harbor any enmity to Rome, you must give a lavish entertainment here to celebrate the Egyptian Triumph. Tomorrow. And it is then that I will formally proclaim you and Ptolemy Friend and Ally of the Roman People. I'll invite all my enemies and shut them up."

"No! I don't want to give a party! All those people hate me!"

"You sound like a child." His voice began to lift, and for the first time I sensed that his anger had gone. "Of course they hate you. It should make you proud. If they hate you, remember that they hated me first. You must get used to being hated if you are to rule successfully. The greatest weakness a ruler can have is the aching need to be loved. That is why Cicero—whom I shall by all means invite!—would be a disaster as a ruler, even though he wants to be one so badly."

"Not Cicero!"

"My dear, if you can withstand the withering gazes and eloquent insults of Cicero, you can withstand anything. Consider it training."

Caesar would take care of everything, this being his gathering—in effect, another of his Triumphal entertainments. Ptolemy and I were to leave the house and amuse ourselves elsewhere. I requested that we be taken out into the countryside, so that we might see what surrounded Rome.

It proved to be a good choice. The ripening fields of grain, green-gold against arched aqueducts bringing water from afar, and the clustered flocks of sheep, were a cool antidote for the fevered insanity of the crowded city. This countryside had a somnolent beauty, drowsy and warm. Even the clouds were rounded and gentle. I found it deeply restorative.

But the sun began to throw slanted shadows as its setting neared, and the day was over all too soon. We must return—to what?

The torches were already lit along the road by the time we reentered the city. The crowds were still swarming; even on this uneventful day there were theatrical performances and athletic contests, as well as gladiatorial contests between upper-class Romans in the Forum, to amuse the populace.

I began to have misgivings as we entered the grounds of the garden and found it transformed into what a man costumed as Osiris announced as "Ca-nopic pleasure gardens." Colored lanterns were strung from tree to tree, and drinking pavilions had been set up under the branches, filled with rowdy "patrons." As we ascended the hill, the landscape grew more and more fan-tastic: we seemed to be wading through a papyrus marsh—complete with statues of hippos and crocodiles—and then approached the house, which had been given a false front to make it look like a temple by the Nile. The river itself had been re-created in the form of a large moat around the entrance. A pyramid, about fifteen feet high, reared itself just beside the entrance steps, where the "Nile" lapped against the stones.

"Welcome to Egypt!" bellowed a huge Nubian, clad only in the scantiest loincloth, stationed at the entrance. Just inside the atrium, a company of musicians sat playing the lyre, flute, and bells. Eerie, light music floated out.

This was some soldier's heated dream of Egypt; it was nothing like Alexandria or the villages along the Nile. It existed only in the fevered imaginations of someone longing for a land of pleasure; it was a product of Roman prurience.

It got worse. Vials of perfume and scented ointment were piled up into pyramids all around the atrium, and there was a fortune-telling Sphinx by the pool. If you knocked on his paws, an echoing voice inside pronounced your fate. Half-naked dancers were writhing and bending to the musicians' tunes.

A gigantic sarcophagus, gilded and festooned, was propped upright against the farthest wall, its lid removed to reveal a wrapped mummy. But the mummy had very alert eyes, and I could see his chest moving up and down. Beside him a masked Anubis was keeping watch, his jackal's ears pointed and upright.

I felt myself grow cold. What madness had taken hold of Caesar to make him create this grotesque setting?

I entered my chamber to find a message from him. True to the spirit of the banquet, he had enclosed it in a miniature obelisk.

> My dearest, forgive me for this travesty modeled on Egypt. Politics oblige us to do many unseemly things. Remember that what one laughs at, one does not fear. If, by a fortune-telling Sphinx and a dancing mummy, Romans forget the riches of Egypt and think it only a country of pleasure gardens, they will be content to let it alone. It will remain yours in perpetuity.
>
> Look beautiful as only you can, so that my enemies can never say my powers of desire are waning.

Caesar was correct in one thing: this certainly made a mockery of Egypt. Well, then, should I complete the masquerade? Should I be the Serpent of the Nile? Why not?

I ransacked my trunks for attire that would serve, combining the most extreme elements of costume. I put on an all-but-transparent gown, fringed with gold and faience beads; I twined serpent bracelets on my upper arms and tinkling anklets on my feet. I draped my neck in a four-tiered gold collar and put on a head-hugging vulture headdress. My feet were encased in jeweled sandals.

Surprisingly, the whole was not ugly, but arrestingly strange. I looked like an idol in the dark sanctuary of a temple. The combination of the heavy gold and the gossamer gown gave me a feeling of unreality. My clothing was as light as a breath, but I was weighted down with metal.

I found similar fantastic garments for Ptolemy, and I ordered the nurse to dress Caesarion. I would achieve my purpose this night; I would force Caesar to it. This night would serve me as well as him.

"Charmian, have you ever seen anything like this in Egypt?" I gestured around me, to the pyramid of perfume and the swaying musicians.

"Never," she said, with a soft laugh. "But should such a land exist—it would have a queen that looks like you tonight."

The guests began arriving. I had no idea how many Caesar had invited. As if the gods had read my wishes, a young woman purporting to be a niece of Caesar's sought me out and said he had asked her to stand by my side all evening and explain who everyone was, lest I grow confused.

"My name is Valeria," she said. "I will try to explain about them as honestly, and as briefly, as possible." She looked at me, clearly taken aback by my costume.

"I do not usually look like this," I assured her, "even in Egypt. *Especially* not in Egypt. This was Caesar's suggestion. He seems determined that this evening will outdo every parody of Egypt."

She laughed outright, a hearty laugh. "He has got his wish. Rest assured, Your Majesty, that my uncle and I have always seen eye-to-eye about people. That is why he chose me to be his spokesman this evening. I hope you will not think me rude when I speak my mind."

"No. No, I will welcome it!"

"He himself foresees that he may be busy, but there were many things he wished you to know."

Guests started pouring in the entrance, their feet wet from wading through the "Nile." I stationed myself at the far end of the atrium, near the mummy.

A group of senators and their wives were the first to be presented, and none of them was important enough to elicit a comment from Valeria. They circled the pyramid of scent and were urged by the dancers, "Help yourself! Take some!"

A knot of people I did not recognize came in with two I did: Brutus and his mother, Servilia. I smiled as they approached. With them were several men, all wearing senatorial togas. One was thin and dark, with a straight, lowering line of eyebrows; another was beefy and red-faced; and a third had an expression that combined worry and self-complacency.

"Gaius Cassius Longinus," muttered the first one, almost spitting out the words. I did not need Valeria to inform me this man did not care for me. How he felt about Caesar I could not know yet.

"Publius Servilius Casca," said the stocky one. He nodded gravely and passed on.

"Marcus Tullius Cicero," said the third, as if he found it amusing he should have to introduce himself.

Cicero! He had the surprising attribute of looking almost exactly like his busts.

"My wife, Publilia," he said, presenting a woman who looked more like his granddaughter. She smirked and bowed.

Cicero lingered by my side. "The spoils of Egypt," he said lightly, indicating the room decorations. His hand circled the periphery and then, ever so casually, included me in its sweep. "How I should love to travel there and behold it."

"You must visit us," I said. "But I have been told you regard leaving Rome as being in exile, even when you were governor of Cilicia."

"It is true that I find myself happiest in Rome. It has all that a human being needs in order to fulfill himself." He sighed like a smitten schoolboy. Truly he was in love with Rome; in that he was sincere.

"I know that wherever the government is to be found, there Cicero calls himself content," I said.

"And the government of the world is in Rome," he said pointedly.

"It is true that Rome has conquered much of the world," I replied, "but she has yet to perfect a means of governing it, especially from Rome. The boundaries of the empire stretch now far to the north and west, as well as to the east."

Cicero stiffened. "The Republic is the best system of government the world has ever created," he said.

"Until now," I insisted. "But the Republic may not lend itself to governing a large area. Rome was a small city, after all, when it was invented."

I expected him to say something witty, but instead he drew his robes around himself as if he had been contaminated, and muttered, "Come," to Publilia. They wandered off into the large banqueting chamber.

"Cicero made a mistake in marrying that girl," said Valeria in my ear. "He wanted her money, but he's got more than he bargained for."

"She's very beautiful," I admitted.

"He should have stuck with his grumbling old former wife," said Valeria. "They were well suited."

I remembered the dark looks of the first man. "Cassius—what about him?" I asked.

"He's one of Pompey's generals who came over to Caesar afterwards. He's related to Brutus by marriage. They glower together."

"So he's one of the ones Caesar forgave. Did he come willingly?" I asked.

"I am not sure. I think the former followers of Pompey gave up after his death. They have shown little interest in supporting his sons."

"But do they support *Caesar*?"

She thought for a moment before answering. "They tolerate him," she finally said.

Octavia arrived, with her husband Gaius Claudius Marcellus, a handsome man.

"He also was in Pompey's party, and pardoned by Caesar," Valeria informed me.

I was beginning to feel that all of Rome had been pardoned by Caesar. That meant he had an enormous number of former enemies at large.

More people swept into the room. They were coming in great waves, the hems of their gowns wet from their crossing of the "Nile." But they were smiling and laughing, so perhaps the ludicrous staging was one of Caesar's ideas of genius. Nothing else would have put his critics in so jolly a mood.

A middle-aged man, accompanied by two women, entered hesitantly, then made a straight path toward us. He appeared thin under the voluminous toga, but then, that was one of the glories of a toga—it hid fat and bones alike, so one could never tell the true dimensions of the wearer underneath.

"Marcus Aemilius Lepidus," he introduced himself. "I have the honor of serving as Consul with Caesar this year." He smiled warmly. "My wife, Junia."

"He is too modest," said his wife. "He served as Caesar's right-hand man as governor of Further Spain while Caesar fought in the east. He held it for him."

Lepidus looked embarrassed. "My wife overpraises me," he said. "No one could be called 'Caesar's right-hand man.' I would say it is enough to serve as his left-hand man, but that sounds threatening." He laughed.

"Caesar has granted him a Triumph for his actions in Spain," his wife persisted.

"Enough, Junia," he said. "No one likes a braggart."

The other woman now spoke up. "I am also Junia, Junia's sister, and the wife of Cassius."

"Then . . . you are also Brutus' sister?" How confusing all these names were! Why did all of a man's daughters share the same name in Rome?

"Indeed," she said.

They passed on into the larger room, and I turned to Valeria.

"At last, a wholehearted supporter of Caesar!" I said.

"Yes. But he is such a broken reed to lean upon." She shook her head. "Lepidus is . . . flaccid."

In what way? I wondered. On the battlefield, or in bed? I watched his wife's back as she disappeared into the throng.

A woman approached us boldly. She was with no man, but carried herself with a soldier's gait. She was rather attractive, with masses of wheat-colored hair bound in at her neck, and a wide jaw.

"Fulvia, Your Majesty," she said, looking directly into my eyes. She waited a moment before saying, "Of the Fulvian family of Tusculum," as if that would enlighten me.

But I had heard of her. . . . What had I heard? Was she not that fiery wife of the insurrectionist Clodius? I remembered hearing her name in connection with the street fights of Rome.

"Welcome," I said, thinking how fierce she looked—like an Amazon.

"Is she not the widow of Clodius?" I asked Valeria a moment later.

Valeria looked surprised. "So her fame has spread even to Alexandria," she said. "Indeed she is. And also of Curio."

"She does not look as if she will need another husband," I said. "He would have to be Hercules."

"They say that is exactly what she has in mind," replied Valeria.

As if this were a staged performance, she had scarcely got the words out when a man dressed as Hercules burst through the doorway.

He was big and muscled like a bear, and with a lionskin knotted around his neck and a club slung over his shoulder, he looked Olympian. Hanging on his arm was a woman so garishly dressed I had to blink at beholding her.

"He didn't!" said Valeria. "He didn't bring *her*!"

The man made his way over to us, striding easily. He stopped and stared at me as if he were seeing a curiosity of nature. He had a wide, well-formed face with intelligent dark eyes, and a thick neck, and a smile that would have blinded a god.

"How the child has changed!" he blurted out. "Princess Cleopatra, do you not remember me? I am Marcus Antonius—Marc Antony. I came to Alexandria with Gabinius. I saved your throne, if you don't mind my saying so."

The young soldier. Yes, I remembered him now. He had changed as much as I. "Yes, of course. But I thought it was Gabinius who saved my father's throne, since he was the only man in the world who dared undertake the task, which all of Rome had forbidden."

"Gabinius needed a cavalry officer," he said. "And it was I who overcame the frontier fortress of Pelusium, the most difficult part of the campaign."

"So you did." I remembered now the recounting of it, how he had bravely and quickly taken the fortress, thought to be unassailable. "So you did."

"Yes, Princess. I did." He said this not particularly proudly, but as a matter of fact.

"I am Queen now," I said likewise matter-of-factly.

"And Caesar's woman," he said. "Fortunate Caesar." He waved his hand high. "Beloved of the gods, to be given you as prize and treasure!" His voice was too loud, and everyone heard him.

"Why are you dressed as Hercules?" I asked, to deflect the curious ears.

"Why, is this not a costume party? Do you mean to tell me you dress this way daily? I came as my ancestor, for I'm descended from Hercules—as everyone knows."

"Yes, as everyone knows," parroted the woman.

"May I present Cytheris, the foremost actress of Rome?" said Antony innocently.

Fulvia glided over and said, "My dear Antony, I have hoped to speak with you—" and guided him off forcibly.

Valeria could not suppress a laugh. "So he brought that actress. Does he have no restraint? It is hardly the way to win back Caesar's favor."

Where was Caesar? I began to long for him. The party was becoming overwhelming, and there was no one to direct it—although Antony and his actress friend would doubtless relish trying.

Octavian approached, boys near his own age on each side. He actually had a smile on his face, and seemed relatively lighthearted.

"Your Majesty," he said. "You remember Agrippa?" Beside him, Agrippa nodded. "And my friends Publius Vergilius Maro and Quintus Horatius Flaccus."

Two pale faces stared at me, as if they were bewildered by the sight.

"I am called Horace," said one, the sturdier one.

"And I am known amongst my friends as Vergil," said the older, slighter one. "I must tell you, Your Majesty, I am greatly enamored of the Alexandrian mode of poetry."

"They have come to Rome to study," said Octavian. "All of us country boys seem to be drawn here. But afterward Horace will go to Athens, to the university there. Perhaps I'll follow him."

I thought to myself that Octavian would probably be best suited to a scholarly life. I assumed he would spend his adult years espousing some field of philosophy or history, and writing manuscripts no one would ever read.

The boys drifted away, and I saw Octavia bringing someone over. He was a tall, impressive man who was actually flattered by the lines of a toga.

"I wish to present to you Vitruvius Pollio," she said, excitedly.

The man bowed low. "Your Majesty, I am honored," he said.

"He is dear to Caesar as an arms expert," Octavia said. "But he is dear to all Rome as an architect and engineer. He understands the mysteries of water, of wood, of stone, and translates them for us."

"I had the honor to serve Caesar in his campaigns in Gaul and Africa."

Africa! So he had been present in that last, grueling war. I was grateful for whatever he had done to bring about its success. Certainly Caesar owed a great deal to his military engineers.

"Caesar is blessed to have men like you at his side," I said.

Another woman was wandering about alone. I saw her as she entered the doorway, but she was searching the crowd for someone. There was something in her bearing that made me curious about her, and I pointed her out to Valeria.

"Ah, that's Clodia," she said. "I thought she was dead!" She shook her head. "Clodia was Catullus's and Caelis's mistress—not at the same time, of course. Now they're both dead, and she's not so young herself. She must be looking for another lover, and what better place to look than a party?"

I was puzzled by the Roman freedom—and lack of it—granted to women. They did not have their own names, but had to take versions of their father's. They were married off callously to make political alliances, and were divorced just as casually. They held no public office, nor could they command troops. Yet they themselves could instigate a divorce, and they could own property. They accompanied their husbands to social gatherings, unlike Greek women, and seemed to have their menfolk well in tow.

Married women also had love affairs, so it seemed—the virtuous, respected Servilia; Mucia, the wife of Pompey—were there others? But the men could carry them on openly, whereas the women could not. And what of women like Cytheris and Clodia? And why must "Caesar's wife be above suspicion," whereas Caesar himself could carry on openly?

And was I, a foreign queen, exempt from these mores?

Trumpets sounded, and a hush fell. Caesar strode into the room.

Even though he was not the tallest or biggest man there, the ranks gave way before him. People backed away to give all the space to him. For an instant complete silence surrounded him, as if he were ringed by stones.

"Welcome, friends! Welcome all!" he said in a ringing voice, and suddenly sound sprung up all around him.

He was alone. Calpurnia was not with him. Was that why he had come so late?

"Egyptian music!" he commanded, and the musicians took up their playing again, the unfamiliar—to the Romans—chords filling the hall.

He turned and stared at me, his face not registering any emotion. Was it a good silence, or a bad one? One never knew with him.

"The Queen of Egypt presides," he announced. "The Queen reigns over this feast." He took his place next to me.

"You look like a whore," he whispered in my ear.

"This villa looks like a brothel," I whispered back. "I took my cue from you."

He laughed. "I think it is your boldness I always love best," he said.

"Why did you choose to depict Egypt in such a fashion?" I demanded.

"I told you in my note," he replied. "What we scorn, we do not desire."

"What about whores?" I asked.

He looked surprised.

"I mean, the highest men seem to consort with them, even if they shun them in public. They are highly scorned, yet highly desired."

Clodia drifted by, giving Caesar a conspiratorial look.

"Such as Clodia," I said. "And Antony has brought an actress whom everyone is leering at."

"Antony would be naked without an actress everyone is leering at." He turned to Valeria. "Thank you for helping. I trust that you enjoyed the task."

She smiled. "Gossip is always a pleasure." She detached herself and disappeared into the crowd.

The feast table was laid, with a lidded crocodile skin serving to hold piles of fruit—cherries, pears, apples, sweet figs and dates, pomegranates. Huge rimmed platters swam with such sea creatures as squid and sea urchins and oysters. Stuffed boars looked at us forlornly, their gilded bristles drooping. People swarmed around the table, stuffing themselves, washing down the food with enormous quantities of wine. The noise rose, casting us adrift in a sea of voices.

At the end of the meal, the sarcophagus was wheeled into the hall by "Anubis."

"In the midst of this feasting, it is good to remember the eternal," he wheezed. "Hear what the dead are telling us!" he stood back and recited. "Follow thy heart's desire while still thou remainest! Pour perfume on thy head; let thy garment be of the finest linen, anointed with the true most wondrous substances among things divine."

He did a little shuffling dance. "Do that which is pleasing to thee more than thou didst aforetime; let not thy heart be weary. Follow thy heart's desire and that which is well pleasing in thine eyes. Arrange thine affairs on earth after the will of thy heart, until to thee cometh that day of lamentation on which that god whose heart standeth still heareth not thy wail."

He leaned over the sarcophagus and spoke to the mummy. "Weeping obtaineth not the heart of a man who dwelleth in the grave. On! Live out a joyful day; rest not therein."

The mummy started to groan and stir; the bandages heaved with breath. People were disturbed, even though they knew perfectly well it was a performance. The sight of the dead stirring is distressing.

"Lo! It hath not been granted to man to take away with him his belongings." Behind him, the mummy threw a stiff leg out over the side of the coffin. Its fellow followed. The mummy lurched upright.

"Lo! There is none who hath gone hence and returned hither." Then Anubis turned and saw the mummy, and let out a howl. He threw up his hands and then yanked on the strip of linen sticking up from the mummy's shoulder. The mummy spun and turned, unwinding himself.

"Free! Free!" he cried joyfully. Then he began turning cartwheels, stiffly. He ran back to the sarcophagus, dug out handfuls of gold coins, and began flinging them to the crowd. "Spend it for me!" he ordered them. "I'm not going back in there!"

Now, with the crowd in a playful mood, Caesar led a group out to the Sphinx.

"Ask of him your deepest concerns!" he said, thumping his rump.

"Will Clodia get another man?" yelled someone into the mouth of the Sphinx.

"I see many sleepless nights for Clodia," said a muffled voice within.

"That's not fair!" said Caesar. "You can ask only for yourself, not someone else."

"Oh, I *am* asking for myself!" the man answered blearily.

Lepidus approached and asked it quietly, "Will I lead troops again?"

"Yes, more than you would wish," was the prompt reply, startling Lepidus.

"Will the Republic be restored?" asked Cicero in ringing tones. A hush fell over the room.

"As Heraclitus says, 'You cannot step twice into the same waters, for other waters are ever flowing over you.' "

"Yes, I know that!" said Cicero irritably. "There will be different men, but what of the institution?"

"Only one question, Cicero," bellowed Antony.

Cicero glared at him and turned his back.

"Now I'll ask one!" roared Antony. "Have my fortunes reached their highest peak?"

"Your fortune is only in the foothills," came the reply. "You have not known your fortune yet."

"Come out and show yourself," I demanded. Who was this man? Was he truly a soothsayer, or just an actor?

Slowly the Sphinx's head was raised, and a dark-skinned man peered out. He was frightening to look at, he was so wizened and sunburnt. "Your Majesty?" he asked. "What question will you put to me?" I knew he was not an actor.

How could I phrase the question whose answer I most longed for? I would not ask it so publicly.

"Will Egypt be blessed by the gods in my lifetime?" I finally asked.

"Yes, by many gods," he said. "By gods in the sky, and by gods standing in this very room."

I felt a violent shaking trying to take hold of me. I dared not let it show. But what gods did he mean? *Standing in this very room. . . .*

Nay, it was a foolish answer, an answer that told nothing. Just as my question had not been direct, neither had its answer. Nothing comes of nothing.

"Now that all are silent," said Caesar, holding up his hands, "I wish to give you my thanks for coming to honor Egypt and myself. Yesterday we celebrated a Triumph over rebel forces in Egypt. Today we honor its Queen and King, Cleopatra and Ptolemy, and here in your presence do solemnly name them and enroll them as Friend and Ally of the Roman People—*Socius Atque Amicus Populi Romani.*"

The company cheered as the gesture, for which this entire evening had been preparation, was enacted.

"Let no one question their loyalty!" cried Caesar. Again, a dutiful cheer went up.

Now was the moment. Now! I nodded to Charmian, who in turn nodded to Caesarion's nurse. She quickly left the room.

Caesar, Ptolemy, and I stood before the people, and in order to hold them there at attention I began a speech—a somewhat rambling one, I am afraid. But soon enough the newly awakened Caesarion was brought to me, dressed in kingly robes, and rubbing his wide eyes.

"This is Egypt's greatest treasure," I said, taking him in my arms. "And I lay him at your feet, Caesar."

I placed the child on the floor before the hem of Caesar's robe. An immense silence fell over the crowd. Well I knew that if Caesar picked him up, he was acknowledging him as his own. But did they know I knew? Or did they just assume I thought I was presenting a vassal prince to Caesar? It was up to Caesar to act. It was his action I cared about, not the people's.

Caesar was deadly quiet. I knew then he was angry, very angry. I had tricked him, and that was unforgivable. But, unlike other men, Caesar was always able to think clearly through his anger. He was able to set it aside if necessary, so that anger was never the basis for his actions.

He stared down at Caesarion, his mouth set in a tight line. "And what do you call this treasure?" he asked in flat, measured words.

"He is named Ptolemy Caesar—*Caesar*," I said loudly.

People murmured, for it sounded as if I were stuttering. The two names were the same, deliberately linked.

Caesar watched while Caesarion reached out and touched his sandal. Then he bent down and picked him up. He held him aloft and slowly moved him from side to side so everyone could see.

"Ptolemy Caesar," he said clearly. "I believe you are known as Caesarion—Little Caesar. Let it be so." He handed him back to me. He did not look at me, but did touch the child's cheek.

"We are grateful, Caesar," I said. "We are yours forever."

"How did you dare to do this?" Caesar's eyes were blazing. We were alone in the empty atrium. Food and trash lay all over the floor.

"I had to," I said. "This was the moment. All were gathered, it was a celebration of Egypt—"

"You tricked me," he said. "You have acted like a slave girl."

"If I did, it was because you treated me as one." When he started to argue, I cut him off. "I am not just some slave girl, to bear bastard sons to her master! I am a queen! You made me your wife in a ceremony at Philae! How dare you ignore our son?"

"Because he has no legal standing in Rome," said Caesar. "Can't you understand that? What was the point of it?"

"There is a place where the legal ends and the moral begins," I said. "By not acknowledging him publicly, you insulted me and him. It has nothing to do with legality. What, do you think I am concerned about his inheriting your property? He, who will inherit all the treasures of the Ptolemies?"

"If I allow him to," he reminded me. "If I allow Egypt to remain independent."

"I hate you!" I screamed.

"You don't hate me. You hate the truth of the situation, which is just as I have described it. Now lower your voice. We cannot help the situation. I cannot give Egypt back her Pharaohs. Nor would I wish to. Things are as they are, and we might not flourish in any other times as we do here."

"And you do flourish," I said. He flourished like a great cedar, towering above all others.

But I was satisfied. Words aside, I had achieved my aim. In front of all Rome, Caesar had acknowledged our son. The trip to Rome had been worth it.

27

A day's respite: then the Pontic Triumph. The crowds had grown, a thing which I had not thought possible. News of the extravagance and spectacle had spread, bringing in spectators from farther afield. At each event, Caesar was expected to outdo his last effort, and people strained to see it.

Again we sat in silk-shaded stands and waited. This day was not particularly fair; rain was threatening. Thunder had rumbled all night, causing people to rush to the statues of Jupiter and see if he manifested any signs. But nothing had happened; no statue had fallen, or turned itself, or been shattered. And the day went forward, with no hindrance from Jupiter.

This time the musicians played Asian instruments—arched harps, rattles, round tambours, zithers, and goblet-shaped drums. A company of sword dancers followed, leaping and bending. Again the Roman magistrates marched, and then the booty wagons lurched into the Forum. These were decorated with tortoiseshell, and exhibited piles of gold platters, small mountains of raw amber, lapis lazuli from the region bordering Pontus, bows and arrows of exquisite workmanship, horse bridles with bells, chariot wheels with scythes gleaming from their axles.

A howl of laughter rose at the far end of the Forum, and soon I saw what was causing it: no effigy of Pharnaces, just a picture of him fleeing, panic-stricken, before the Roman armies. His mouth was open in a cry, and his huge, comically turned eyes made him a caricature of cowardice.

A long pause, an empty space. Then, all by itself, came a wagon with a gigantic sign, the letters emblazoned in scarlet: VENI VIDI VICI. Those three words stood for all of Pontus, as if it did not even deserve a representation of its cities, its terrain, its monuments. It had all been reduced in an instant by Caesar, who had taken only four hours to defeat the enemy.

This banner served as the messenger for Caesar, whose chariot now followed. He was wreathed in amiable good humor, as if that battle had been an afternoon's entertainment for him, as it was for the citizens now. Cheers resounded throughout the Forum, and he basked in them.

The soldiers followed, yelling their bawdy verses, and the crowds roared with delight.

The entertainments given to celebrate this victory were more subdued than at the other Triumphs. The sons of the allies in Bithynia and Pontus gave an exhibition of Pyrrhic sword dances. Magicians and acrobats swallowed fire and leapt through flames. Of course, the theatrical performances and gladiatorial contests continued as usual.

Now must come the last of them, the African Triumph. Because it was the final celebration, people were both impatient and critical, jaded and sated. And it required delicate political posturing, for the African War was part of the Roman civil wars. Victory had been achieved over other Romans, not foreign enemies.

Caesar had elected not to celebrate his victory over Pompey on these very grounds, for to do so would have given offense to the many who had supported Pompey and still respected him. And it was thought unseemly to rejoice in the death of fellow citizens. But in this case, his caution seemed to have deserted him. Perhaps he had reached the end of his patience with the civil war, or perhaps he wished to let this stand as a warning to those who might yet harbor rebellious ideas. He went ahead with the African Triumph, using the defeat of King Juba of Numidia as a disguise, as if the war had been against the foreigner only. In fact, he stressed the shameful fact that Romans had served under the king, when the truth was they had served together.

Riding behind him in the procession, did Octavian that day absorb the idea? For he was to imitate it later, casting me in the role of Juba and declaring that any Roman who fought with me acted in shame—indeed, had ceased to *be* Roman.

The day of the African Triumph was hot, not hot as in Africa, but hot with the characteristic Roman summer heat—a damp, enervating heat. Sweat could not evaporate off the skin; it mingled with perfume and oil to cause the clothes to stick to the body. It caused a peculiar temper in the people—a restless discomfort.

The crowds began gathering before dawn, and by the time the procession got under way they had been milling and waiting for hours. The sun beat down mercilessly, shining through a damp nimbus.

African musicians marched proudly, draped in leopardskins, sounding their trumpets and beating the drums, and the huge carts, decorated with ivory inlays, creaked and bent with the spoils of war. The people gasped at the sight of so many ivory tusks; the gigantic crescents looked like a thousand moons fallen to earth. Caged beasts—panthers, lions, leopards, pythons, hyenas—were rolled in. A file of elephants followed, ridden by Getuli, a nomad people from Mauretania.

Then came Caesar's mistake: huge pictures showing the ignoble ends of his enemies. Cato was shown ripping his wound open, letting his intestines spill out; Scipio was shown stabbing himself; and Juba and Petreius were pictured fighting their gruesome suicide duel.

A moan went up from the people along the Via Sacra. They were deeply offended. Caesar's chariot was greeted with murmurs instead of cheers, and his face showed that, too late, he understood why. He tried to make the best of it, smiling and looking to the left and right, but frowns and head-shaking were all he got in return. Behind him bounced Octavian, taking in every nuance and standing straight as he rode past them.

In the wake of the triumphal chariots came the sole illustrious prisoner: the small son of Juba, also called Juba. At the sight of the four-year-old walking bowed down by chains, the people began to hiss and boo. The little boy looked at them, flashing a winsome smile.

The tough soldiers followed, the fighters of the Ninth and Tenth Legions, and they had the thankless task of facing the unresponsive crowd, just as they had had the thankless task of fighting a nasty, protracted war. Nevertheless they sang loudly in honor of the commander they followed so passionately, knowing that the people of Rome would never fully appreciate what occurred on the battlefield. They held civilians to be stupid, unfeeling creatures, anyway.

In honor of Africa, there was to be a wild beast hunt in the Circus immediately following. Caesar had calculated that this extravagant entertainment would win the disaffected; and certainly the common people, no matter how much they revered Cato, were not about to turn their backs on the promised spectacle. Rumor had been circulating for days that hundreds of animals were to be hunted and matched against one another, and the people were fairly salivating to see it.

We were carried along in our magnificent gilded litter to the Circus, held above the sea of sweating people making their way toward it. I could smell them; they stank like a combination of caged animals and a market spilling over with overripe food. What had happened to all the perfume bottles they had collected?

Once inside the Circus, I could hardly believe my eyes: the entire central section, the *spina*, which had looked so permanent with its statues of Jupiter and its polished turning-stones at each end and its lap-counting devices, had vanished. The expanse was open, with only shadows to mark where the structures had stood. A deep ditch had been dug all around the perimeter, to protect us from the wild beasts.

Caesar and his family were already seated in the places of honor. Sharing the benches were the allies who had helped defeat the enemies: Bocchus and Bogud, the kings of east and west Mauretania. They looked pleased, even if no one else did. Perhaps they understood the dangers of Africa better than others who had never set foot there.

A number of brightly dressed men made their way into the arena. Some were heavily protected in leather and leg shields, and others were more lightly dressed, in tunics. These were the *venatores*, the men who fought beasts.

"Where are the animals?" asked Ptolemy peevishly. Like all the rest of Rome, he had grown weary of the never-ending spectacles, so when his excitement should have reached a fever pitch, instead he was increasingly difficult to impress.

"They are coming," I assured him. "These are the men who must fight them."

"Oh." He stifled a yawn and twisted in his seat. The hot sun was still beating down.

"These beasts are sent by Gaius Sallustius Crispus, the most noble governor of the new province of Africa—the province won by this war—for the glory of Rome and the marvel of her citizens," Caesar announced in his loudest voice.

A cheer went up. Now the people were coming around.

"We shall fight the beasts in two ways," one of the men cried, the one dressed only in a tunic. "I have been trained to fight with a long hunting spear, but I have no protection other than my own quickness. My companion"—he indicated the man protected by the leather—"must come closer to the beasts in order to strike, and so he must be able to withstand a direct assault. And he"—he gestured toward another man who had no weapon at all—"well, you shall see what he can do! You shall see, and be astounded!"

Trumpets sounded, and a parade of cages on wagons were wheeled into the Circus. I could see the dark shapes inside, but could not tell what they were.

A group of attendants, wearing protective helmets and padding, approached the cages. The door of the first one was opened, and out sprang a lion. A cry of excitement rose from the stands.

The lion landed on the sand soundlessly, and shook his mane as he got his bearings. Only one man, the spokesman with the spear, remained nearby. The lion crouched down and eyed him cautiously, sniffing the air. The man advanced toward him, making little whirring noises in his throat to excite the animal. The lion cocked his head and stared for many long minutes.

Then, swiftly, he rose. And almost in the same moment, he sprang.

But the man sidestepped him, and plunged his spear into the animal's shoulders. Quickly he pulled it out again, its tip red with blood, and retreated. If he lost the spear, he would have no weapon at all.

The lion seemed more surprised than hurt. He fell back on his haunches and took several deep breaths. Then he rose and leapt again.

Again the man avoided the flying paws and dripping jaws; again he plunged the spear into the lion, this time into the chest. With a muffled roar, the lion rolled over. The man wrenched the spear out and fled to a safe distance to see if the lion would recover.

The animal roared; he clearly was not mortally wounded, but now he was angry. He chased the man, who turned quickly—he never could have outrun him, and there was not a single rock of safety—and, deftly spinning, speared the lion again. But this time he was unable to extract the spear, and in attempting to, he seemed to pull the lion over to himself. The huge clawed paws raked his shoulders.

Suddenly he had the spear free again, and he fell to his knees and let the animal leap in a great arc toward him, exposing its chest and belly. With superb timing, he sunk the spear into the lion's heart, the shaft sinking deeply.

The lion crumpled in midair and fell awkwardly to one side. He writhed and turned, trying to dislodge the weapon. But the blood was spurting out of his body and draining away his strength, and soon he lay feebly panting on the sand, unable to move.

Delicately the man approached him, and ripped the spear out. Then, as if he wished to spare the beast further shame and pain, he killed him.

An exuberant cry went up from the crowd, as the man turned and showed that he had suffered no injury except his clawed shoulder. A most impressive performance.

The next to be loosed in the arena was a black panther, and the leather-clad man had to wrestle with it several times in order to get close enough to try to stab it with the sword. The animal, its curved teeth white and shiny against its black fur, embraced the man like a pet several times, but the very closeness was what gave rise to the suspense. The panther was not licking him, or cuddling, but trying to devour him.

The fighter got in three cuts, but that was not enough. And then he lost his sword in wrenching it out to try to stab again. It lay tantalizingly out of arm's reach on the sand, beyond his wildly scrabbling hand, when the panther managed to tear off his protective helmet and encircle his head with a hemisphere of sharp teeth. A shriek told us that the man was doomed, and an instant later the panther was shaking his limp body, like a cat with a mouse.

But it was not allowed to savor its kill; there were no Triumphs for victorious animals. Two of the armed guards rushed out; one shot the panther with arrows, while the other finished it off with a javelin. Then the dead bodies of both man and beast were removed.

The third man, seemingly unshaken by the event, now gestured for a cage to be opened. Another lion emerged, landing on the sand and looking for prey. The man deliberately teased it, jumping up and down and making feinting movements. The lion, cautious, stood still. The man threw an apple at it, forcing it to attack. Even so, it was a halfhearted attack, for it was a reaction rather than a true hunting leap. The lion opened its mouth to roar, as the man knew it would.

When its jaws opened, he plunged his arm right into its mouth, ramming it down its throat and choking it. With his other hand he grabbed the lion's tongue and twisted it like a piece of rope.

The heavy beast fell gasping. Still the man—and I saw now that he had leather arm protectors on—did not let go of the tongue, but continued wringing it. The lion was clawing and fighting for air, but already it was losing strength. Its limbs buckled, and we could hear the hideous sound of it trying to suck air past the brave fist of the man. His arm was lodged in the gullet like a stone, and the animal began twitching and jerking. Its eyes glazed and its massive head fell on the sand. The tail quivered and then nothing moved.

"Did you see that?" Ptolemy was wildly excited. "How did he do that? How? How?"

"Through training," I said. "And unbelievable courage." I could not help but be impressed. To kill a lion barehanded had always been a feat reserved for Hercules.

Tumultuous cheers exploded from the stands. The man was carried out of the arena, its new hero.

Now a group of men trotted in, with strange devices: a spherical cage, bundles of reeds, and rollers. One of the men climbed inside the round cage and closed a flap after him, and the others took up their stations. Several bears emerged from cages, and were teased and taunted by the men. The bears rolled the round cage along the ground like a ball, but could not figure out how to get the man inside; others slipped on the rollers, and still others were baffled by the bundles of reeds. The men outsmarted them at every turn, and the spectators were amused. This was for comedy only. In the end the bears were tricked back into their cages and the men took bow after bow.

A few moments' respite led to the next part of the program—matched fights between different types of animals. Bulls fought crocodiles, bears fought pythons, and panthers fought leopards. For variety, the animals might be linked together, so that they had to fight, and could not slink away. The lions were paired against many types of animals, for people loved to see them fight. They took on tigers, bulls, and wild boars. Usually the lion won.

But the dead bodies of the animals, dragged off into piles, were growing into a mountain. The afternoon seemed to go on and on, stretching out in death. The beautiful pelts of the slain beasts gleamed in the sun.

Suddenly enormous numbers of lions were set loose in the arena, to hunt each other even as they were being hunted by armed men. In a melee of roars, screams, and growls, the golden beasts worked themselves into a frenzy.

"I've never seen so many lions," cried Ptolemy, "not even in a dream!"

And indeed, it did seem dreamlike, this huge gathering of lions filling the Circus. Later I was told there were more than four hundred of them. Not one was allowed to survive.

At length the most extravagant hunt of all was staged: Scores of elephants were gored into panic and attack, and they rampaged, trumpeting, all over the arena. Only the depth of the ditch kept them from stampeding into the crowds. I understood now why Caesar had had it dug.

The waste, the waste, the carnage! I could barely stand to watch as the elephants were sacrificed—to what? To entertainment? To Rome? What nation destroys its own wealth? All this killing—of valuable beasts, of men— was crippling to the country, as well as cruel.

And the Romans prided themselves on their rationality, I thought, looking at the corpse-strewn field. This was not rational; this made no sense. It was their own peculiar madness, to kill in enormous numbers, for sport.

I felt myself shivering, even in the oppressive heat.

Twilight fell; the slaughter had to stop. The crowds, on fire with the spectacle, were almost as wild as the maddened elephants. Caesar's massive, city-wide banquet would have people thronging to his tables in high revelry and excitement.

This was to be the closing event in the ten-day celebrations; Caesar invited all of Rome to partake in a feast to be set at twenty-two thousand separate tables throughout the city. Twenty-two thousand—all loaded with such delicacies as sea-eels and Falernian wine. He had in mind a scene in which all the warriors, weary from battle, eat and drink together to celebrate their deliverance. It was a scene straight from mythology; probably he was the only one who believed in it. But the people were willing enough to eat at his expense.

Down in the Forum, the tables were set out where people walked during the day and merchants had their stalls. The most exclusive tables were reserved in the area of the Regia and Caesar's own house, but thousands of others were set up around the half-finished Basilica Julia, around the Temple of Castor and Pollux, the Rostra, and the Curia. The Via Sacra, where the Triumphal wagons had lumbered, was now a thoroughfare of revelers and waiters, dancers and wine-servers. Torches blazed everywhere, and musicians played on the Rostra.

Caesar and his family were dining at one table next to his house. The leading senators and magistrates were at another nearby: Cicero, Lepidus, Brutus, and others I did not recognize. All the formal Friends and Allies of the Roman People were at my table: Bocchus and Bogud, the Moorish kings, as well as the rulers of Galatia and Cappadocia, and the envoys who had come from the cities of Asia. I could not help watching Bogud, a rather handsome man with a hawk nose, as I tried to imagine what his wife, Eunoe, looked like. I wondered why she had not come to Rome. Had Bogud forbidden her to? Or was it Caesar? I burned with curiosity to know.

Throughout the Forum the outdoor party was celebrated raucously; the Falernian was doing its duty. Since the wine was so rare and costly, everyone thought it his duty to drink as much of it as possible. The noise level rose, echoing off the stones. I saw several men get up and dance around the columns of the Temple of Saturn, and another group link arms and form teams to try to knock benches over on the Via Sacra. A bellowing singing contest was held on the steps of the Curia. One man pitched headlong down them and rolled over and over like a barrel, yelling with glee.

Women, too, were joining in—weaving flowers in their hair, climbing over the benches. The heat of the night added to the intensity and fervor. I felt sweat running down my face and back, plastering my gown to my body. The jewelry I wore felt like manacles. It was no night to have metal against the skin.

When the dinner was over but the revelry was reaching its highest pitch, Caesar suddenly stood up. Trumpets blared, and he seized a torch and leapt up on the table.

"Friends! I wish to postpone no longer the dedication of my gifts to the Roman people. Why wait for daylight, when we have the light of a thousand torches here? Why wait for another day, when everyone is gathered here already?" he cried.

At the far end of the Forum, no one even heard him; they were still guzzling, gorging, and dancing. But around us, everyone fell silent and listened.

"I wish Rome to be the most beautiful city in the world. And to that end, I have constructed new buildings for her." Two of his soldiers stepped up beside him, as well as priests, garbed in their striped togas. "Let me show them to you. Come with me!"

He took Calpurnia's hand and obediently the rest of his family followed him; he led them to the steps of the almost-finished Basilica Julia. Now a big throng had gathered, following in his footsteps.

"I give this new covered marketplace and public building to the citizens of Rome," he said. "Our older ones no longer serve our needs; they are neither large nor modern enough. And so I name this the Basilica Julia, in honor of my family line, the Julian clan. It is yours forever!"

A vast—although somewhat bleary—cheer rose from the populace.

Then Caesar turned and began to walk northward between the buildings, leading the people to his gleaming white new Forum and the temple within it. He stood at its entrance and brandished a torch.

"A new Forum for a new day!" he cried. "The city of Rome has need of a new Forum!"

Everyone had watched it being built, but even so, it seemed a surprise when it was actually presented. A new Forum. But the old one was sacred—it contained so many historic sites, all bound up with the history of Rome. Here it was that Jupiter stopped the assault of the Sabines, here it was that Curtius had vanished into the mysterious Curtin Lake. So many stories, all dear to their hearts. A new Forum? What did it mean? It could not be as simple as Caesar made it sound, simply a new place with more clean space to do business. No, Caesar must have other motives, I could almost hear them thinking. They were always so ready to believe the worst of him.

"Come, follow me! Tread on the grass, walk in the porticoes, make it yours!" he urged them. But they hung back, like frightened children.

Caesar walked alone across the grass and mounted the steps of the temple. He stood there for several moments, one foot placed on a higher step than the other, turned sideways. His *Triumphator's* robe looked darker than any wine, splashed against the white of the marble.

"And here I solemnly dedicate the temple that I vowed to Venus of my ancestry, my family's origins, *Venus Genetrix*. I honor the goddess here, in all her manifestations. Come, and see!"

A company of guards holding torches mounted the steps and took up their stations inside, so that suddenly the interior glowed, and a yellow light shone out through the marble. Slowly the people streamed forward, making their way inside the temple.

Was I to follow? For I knew what they would see there. If I did not, the people would think it coyness in me. So I forced myself to enter the temple, there to behold the three statues—Venus herself, Caesar, and me.

People were staring. Calpurnia was still clutching Caesar's hand, but her eyes were downcast. The loud voices had ceased.

Caesar said nothing, but he had forced them to see—to see that he considered me a part of his family, not in an earthly sense, but in a divine one. I was ashamed now that I had not trusted him, and had forced him into the embarrassing recognition of Caesarion.

People were awestruck in front of the statues; they stood like statues themselves. Then they turned and filed silently away. I could not read their faces.

"It is Venus who has favored me as a son, and brought me the victories we celebrated today!" Caesar said. "Venus, I honor you, I give you homage! Bless your descendants, the Julians, each and every one, and let us bring honor and glory to Rome!" The priests bowed and placed offerings before the central statue.

Caesar was surrounded by the knot of his family, as if they would protect him from any ill wishes. They seemed huddled there before the three glowering statues, who did not seem beneficent at all.

Outside, the crowd had fragmented into thousands of parties; the food was being cleared away, and stacks of empty wine amphorae—a veritable mountain—were loaded on sturdy carts. The more respectable citizens were returning to their homes, leaving only the drunken, the young, and the disreputable to carry on.

Calpurnia, Octavian, and Octavia seemed to have vanished; but I was not surprised when Caesar made his way over to Bogud, Bocchus, and me.

"I regret I was unable to greet you until now," he said. "I trust your dinner was enjoyable?"

"Never have I seen anything like it!" exclaimed Bocchus. "It will live in history!"

"I hope so," said Caesar. "Otherwise I have sent a lot of money to vanish into thin air." He laughed. "But I rather think it will live on. The first of a thing always does. Later, others will give bigger feasts, have more extravagant dishes. But the first attempt is what sticks in people's minds." He looked around. "Let us walk the streets, and see how the rest of Rome is celebrating. The air in the Forum was somewhat rarefied."

Together we left the Forum and immediately entered areas where the hot air was not delicate at all, but gross and heavy. The small streets were packed with celebrants, and I could smell the spilled wine, the precious Falernian, trickling between the pavement stones, running like rainwater. Everyone, so it seemed, was drunk, full-bellied, and shouting. So great was the crush, and so poor the light, that it was not necessary for Caesar to cast off his mantle; no one was paying any attention to us, and we might as well have been invisible.

It was an eavesdropper's delight. The comments were flying thick and fast, uncensored.

"He must have robbed the Temple Treasury—again!—to pay for this!"

"So he's put his whore in the temple, you say? A big statue. I'll bet it doesn't show the part that really charms him!"

"I suppose he wants a queen because he aims to be king."

"He sets up all these temples and forums because he saw them in Alexandria. He thinks Rome isn't good enough, that it needs a lot of fancy white marble!"

I could hardly breathe, the crowds were so thick. The heat was radiating from the tight-packed bodies like fumes from a coal fire, and the heavy hand of the night was pressing down on our heads. The words I was overhearing were so alarming I felt my heart pounding.

The people seemed determined to interpret everything in the worst possible manner. Why were they turning on Caesar? He cared more for the lot of the common people than did the well-born, well-fed senators they favored.

One lone voice said plaintively, "I think he's a great man, the greatest general since Alexander."

But his companion sneered, "They say he's even going to change the calendar! Now he thinks he's a god, to alter the days and seasons!"

One man stumbled and dropped his wine goblet, and it glanced off Caesar's shoulder. I grabbed Caesar's hand and said, "Let us not go on. I cannot move, and I do not wish to hear any more of this tripe."

"Tripe?" he said. "So it is. I have heard enough. Now I know well enough what they think."

He gestured, and our little group swung around and he led us back out through the alleys and side streets. How well Caesar knew his way; I was utterly lost.

"I have wasted my money after all," he said, with a hard edge to his voice.

"One man honored you," I reminded him.

"One man," he said. His voice was tired and tinged with bitterness. "But I served two hundred thousand."

28

The next day the sun shone on an army of men cleaning the Forum and the streets of Rome, sweeping the paving stones free of proof of the Triumphs. They had lasted ten days, had provided an eruption of music, soldiers, animals, trophies, combat, food, and largesse. Never had their like been seen in Rome, and they would always be linked with the name of Gaius Julius Caesar, Imperator, Dictator, Consul. But already they were past; the sun had risen on another day. Now bored people could look around and wonder what would come next to mollify and entertain them.

Caesar was eager to push through his reforms, and an obedient Senate endorsed them. He aimed many at remedying abuses in the state. He would grant citizenship to the Cisalpine Gauls—residents of that northern part of Italy that had been Romanized for years. He would outlaw all the religious guilds (in reality, political clubs that promoted insurrection and violence against the elected order) with the exception of the Jews, who stayed aloof from political matters. He would halve the number of people receiving a grain dole, and settle the rest in colonies outside Rome. He gave orders to have the civil law codified, as now it existed in hundreds of different documents. There were also a number of other laws regarding Roman matters which were doubtless very important to the Romans but esoteric to everyone else—as all local laws are. And he had in mind more far-reaching schemes for his country.

"Do you know," he said one evening, when he had come to the villa directly from the Senate, "that I have had my engineers draw up a plan for three projects that will change the world?" Seeing my expression of skepticism, he said, "Well, *one* of them will change the world."

He knelt on the floor and made a tracing there with his dagger. "The Peloponnesus in Greece is almost an island." The metal made an ugly scraping noise against the stone. "It's barely attached to the mainland at the Isthmus of Corinth. Now, if a canal could be cut through, severing it completely—think what that would do for shipping! The seas there are so rough that ships are hauled overland, across the isthmus, rather than risk the waters. But if the Aegean and Ionian Seas could be linked—"

"You cannot cut through that. It is sheer rock, like the rest of Greece," I said.

"Canals have changed Egypt," he persisted. "If there were no canal linking Alexandria with the Nile, think how crippled you would be."

"Egypt is made of sand," I said. "Greece is made of stone. Now, what are your other projects?"

He laughed. "Always your hardheadedness is an astringent to my dreams," he said. "Very well, then, another is that I will have the Pontine Marshes drained to provide more farmland. Now it is a vast, mosquito-ridden swamp."

"And your engineers say this can be done?"

"They are hopeful," he said.

"And the other project?"

"I will cut a new channel for the Tiber—two new channels, actually. One will link it with the Anio River, so boats can navigate all the way to Tarracina. But in Rome itself I will divert the riverbed westward, make it flow onto the Vatican plain. Then all the activities that now take place on the Field of Mars can be transferred to the Vatican, and the Field of Mars can be built up. I wish to dedicate a gigantic temple there to Mars, the god who has been so gracious to Rome. And I wish to make it the biggest temple in Rome—no, in the world!"

His eyes were flashing with excitement, in a way I had not seen since Egypt. He had plans, big and impossible, which brought him to life as mucking about in politics in Rome never could.

Rome was necessary as his home base, the seat of his power, yet, curiously, it drained him of the very energy and strength that made him its master. Whenever he was away from Rome, he flourished; here he seemed to decline.

"Tell me more of your projects," I encouraged him. "I know you must have more, and you are just leading them out one by one, as the animal wagons were rolled out in the Circus."

I could see the expression, almost perfectly concealed, that said, *Do I dare tell her?* But he trusted me, and so he plunged ahead. He was eager to hear himself say the things aloud, to make them more real. He stretched out on the floor and rolled over on his back, putting his head on his arms, as if he were lying out in a meadow somewhere, instead of on the hard stone floor.

"All things are possible in peacetime," he said. "I think the greatest prize of war is what it allows you to do with the peace afterward."

"I know there are those who fear your peace and what you plan to do with it," I said, unable to forget the ugly frowns and sarcastic remarks about him.

"They fear me because they distrust a victorious general," he said. "Always when the battles were past, the victors ripped aside their masks of clemency and went on a rampage of revenge and cruelty. They cannot believe that I will not follow suit. But I will not, and time will prove it."

"What if you are not given time?" Before I could stop them, the words tumbled out—my fears for the future, his future, anyone's future. My weakness.

"No one would assassinate me," he answered, saying the dreaded word. "If I were to be killed, chaos would reign, and they know it. There is no one to follow me, to hold back the deluge of more civil war."

He was right, of course. But are men farsighted? If that were so, everyone would always act wisely, and there would be no ruined men.

"Tell me of your plans," I began again. "I would hear them all."

Lying there on the cold floor, he told me of his ideas for making Rome a grand city: he would build a theater like the one in Athens at the foot of the Tarpeian Rock; he would create a state library containing the whole of Greek and Roman literature; he would construct an enclosed election building on the Field of Mars to keep voters protected from the elements; he would create an extension of the harbor at Ostia to give Rome a shipping port like that of Athens; he would have a new road built across the mountains to the Adriatic; he would refound the ruined cities of Corinth and Carthage.

"Rome's ancient enemies?" I asked. "What about 'Carthage must be destroyed'?"

He laughed. "Carthage *has* been destroyed. But the location is a fine one, and it's time to make it over again as a Roman city."

"Rome in Africa. Rome everywhere," I said.

"I think it is time we had a nation that is more than a nation; a nation that incorporates all nations. It will not be entirely Roman." He paused. "That, at bottom, is what my fight with the aristocracy of Rome is all about. It is a class I was born into, but they cannot see beyond the city itself. They fear the wider world, even though they now possess it. So they try to pretend things are the same as ever, as if those other lands and other people will vanish. I have brought them the world in a basket and laid it at their feet, and they turn aside in fear." He turned and looked directly at me. "That is what they shrink from in you. To them, you are foreign, and all things foreign are a threat." He sighed. "Rome is like a child to me, a child I love and want to help—but she runs away!"

"Perhaps they are just confused," I said, trying to make sense of it. "All of this has happened very fast for them. Less than twenty years ago, there was no Gaul for them to have to worry about. It took Rome hundreds of years to grow to one size, and then it suddenly doubled. And their general made a love alliance with a foreign queen. What are they to think? Be gentle with them."

"I told you, I will be. I am." He began to sound irritated, at me as well as at them. His moods were very changeable these days. He sat up with a grunt. "This floor is too hard. I know what we need here in Rome—a soft place to lie when we wish to relax. We have only beds for sleeping and couches for eating. What about talking and reading?"

"We have such pleasure seats in the east. I'll make a room like that for us here," I said. "It will be another foreign thing you can introduce to Rome!"

He stood up and rubbed his back. "One new invention is about to be unveiled," he said. "Summon Sosigenes to meet with us here tomorrow, and I will reveal it to you."

Sosigenes, my prize astronomer and mathematician from the Museion, had come to Rome at Caesar's insistence. But I had seen little of him during the Triumphs.

"That is because he has been working," said Caesar. "I kept him busy."

"While the rest of the city played? That was schoolmasterish of you." I was suddenly struck with a thought. "These plans you have for Rome—the huge temples, the library, the theater—do you seek to create an Alexandria here on the Tiber?"

"Perhaps. And I will build a marble palace to put you in, an exact reproduction of the one in Alexandria, so that we will not be able to tell where we are. It will be all the same to us, Rome or Alexandria. There will be no limit in time or place for us."

I was as good as my word. I made one of the rooms in the villa over into the essence of lounging pleasure, borrowing freely from many cultures. From desert nomads I took the idea of carpets, and laid many on the floor to create a soft, colorful indoor lawn. Some were silk, some wool, but they all caressed the feet and invited you to stretch out on them, confident that no snakes, scorpions, or insects were hidden in the patterns—unlike true lawns. Tapestry cushions from Parthia were strewn all over the carpets, and Arabian silk curtains were spread across the windows to diffuse and color the direct sunlight, while permitting breezes to enter. Small tables made of carved sandalwood from India gave off a sweet smell, and candles were waiting in colored glass lanterns—Alexandrine lanterns. I even managed to find a steward who could procure snow—brought from the mountains in winter—from a rich merchant's storehouse, so that we could have cooled wine whenever we wished. Everything was the exact opposite of the straight lines and hard pallets the Romans favored.

Sosigenes arrived a few moments early, and I was glad of a chance to talk to him. He came from a family of astronomers and mathematicians who had been at the Museion for generations; such men had had a great deal to do with Alexandria's fame and leadership in science.

"So your work with Caesar is completed," I said, asking a question in a statement.

"As well as I can do it, it is done." Sosigenes gave me a genuine smile. He was in his middle years; I had known him almost since I could remember, and he had had the duty of trying to teach all the royal children something of the stars. "Now it is Caesar's task to introduce it. I think that will be harder than it was to devise it. Well, I shall be on my way home before that is settled."

I felt a stab of homesickness and envy of him. I missed my city, my court, Mardian and Olympos, Epaphroditus and Iras, even my pet monkey. Now would be the finest weather in Alexandria, when the days were blue and brisk and the clouds racing. The Nile would be rising; all reports were that it was normal this year, and there would be no famine or disaster.

Most of all, I missed being a queen in my own country, instead of a foreign guest in another's. In Caesar's dream it would all be the same world. But it was not so now.

Caesar soon arrived, looking harried. But he shrugged it off and gave his immediate, complete attention to Sosigenes, compelling me to do likewise.

"Tell the Queen, Sosigenes," he said proudly—and impatiently. "Tell her what we have created." He gestured toward me. "This will be Alexandria's gift to the world." With a flourish, he unrolled a diagram.

"Tomorrow, two extra months will begin. Yes, we shall have November three times, and extra days besides!" said Sosigenes. He looked amused, knowing how confusing that sounded. "I have redrawn the Roman calendar," he said. "It was based on the moon, and the moon is an unreliable guide. She changes all the time! And twenty-nine and a half days is an unwieldy cycle. The lunar year is only three hundred and fifty-five days long, whereas the real year is ten days longer. Now the Romans are by no means stupid, so they had allowed for an extra month every so often to patch things up. But that made the year a day too long, so every twenty years or so the extra month was supposed to be subtracted. The problem was, there was no fixed time for subtracting it, so people tended to forget during a war or some other distraction. By now the year is sixty-five days ahead of the natural calendar. That's why the Triumphs, held in September, were so hot—because it was really still summer!"

"It was like riding in an oven," said Caesar. "So Sosigenes and I have worked out this new calendar. It is based on the sun—no more moon calendars! Each year will be three hundred sixty-five days long; each fourth year will be three hundred sixty-six days long to correct for a slight discrepancy. And the year will begin on January first, when the Consuls take office, not in March. This year we are adding the extra sixty-five days all at once, so the sun can catch up with our calendar at last."

"With all those extra days, this year will be a very long one," I said. Already it felt very long; I was beginning to wonder if it would ever end.

Now, of course, I am saddened to remember that; for it ended too soon, even if it had had hundreds of extra days added. But then, all things seemed ordinary, as if they would go on forever. What is happening always seems that way. Even my life as I write this.

"Yes, I hope people will use it well," said Sosigenes.

"Will the people accept this? What will you tell them?" I asked. Only those with something unpleasant before them would welcome a postponement. For the rest, they would resent it.

"That it is necessary," said Caesar.

"What will you call the new system?"

"Why, the Julian calendar," he said, as if there were no other name possible.

"Is that wise?" I asked. "Will they not think you are setting it up arbitrarily, as a monument to yourself?"

"If they do, it will sadden me," he said. "But since it is my doing, why should I not receive credit for it? It may last when all the buildings have crumbled, and the Gauls have long since gone free."

Sosigenes left, pleased that his creation would soon be presented to the Romans—and doubtless anxious lest it contain some hidden flaws. Caesar smiled as he watched his slight figure disappearing.

"So much knowledge in such a light frame!" he said. "I have enjoyed working with him; I am almost sorry to see the project at an end."

"Perhaps you'll discover an error and have to call him back," I said, but the expression on Caesar's face told me he did not find this amusing.

"Any mistake in it will be held against me," he said. "Such seems to be the mood of my enemies. They would never credit it to an innocent mathematical miscalculation."

"You seem to feel you have a great many enemies—perhaps too many to merit your policy of clemency. Either win them over completely, by wooing them more than you have been willing to do, or else eliminate them," I said.

"I can do neither," he said. "It is against my nature. They must be true to their nature, and I to mine."

I shook my head. "This is too lofty for me," I said. "I understand and revere one trait above all others: loyalty. All the rest is flimsy stuff, and crumples before it."

"It is more complicated than that," he said condescendingly.

"I am not sure it is," I countered. But, seeing that he refused to listen, I realized that he needed diversion, not a lecture. Perhaps he was too tired to reason very clearly—certainly he had strained himself to the breaking point for months. Was a prolonged rest now possible? "Come," I said, "I have completed my own project. Let me show you."

He shrugged impatiently. "No, I haven't time."

"It does not involve your leaving this villa," I assured him.

Now he looked a little more interested, but still not pleased. "Is it a report?" he asked. "I cannot read it here. But I will take it back—"

"No, it isn't a report! Nor is it poetry that you must read and pretend to like, or maps you must study, or any exercises of the mind," I said. "It is something you professed to wish for."

"I will see it," he said resolutely, a man who knew when to shoulder a burden.

"Come," I said, taking his hand. "Follow me, and close your eyes."

He put his hand in mine, that hand which had been raised so often in battle, and surrendered it into my palm. I led him into the "eastern" chamber, and only when we were standing in its center did I let him open his eyes.

He looked around, blinking. "I—what *is* this?" he finally said.

"You requested a place in Rome where one could lounge and dream day-time dreams," I said. "The requests of the Dictator are law." I sank down on one of the cushions and tugged at his hand. Reluctantly he allowed himself to be drawn down.

"Now, take off this toga," I said. "It is not meant for lounging." I began to unwrap it.

"Stop! That is the office of a servant," he said.

"Why? It is most enjoyable." And I was enjoying unwinding those lengths of cloth that bound him up in awkward propriety. Perhaps when it came off, he would be a freer creature. "No wonder the Romans have no comfortable places to rest or sit; their clothing does not permit it!" With a yank, the last few feet of cloth flapped free. "There!"

He was laughing now, perhaps for the first time that day. "I can remove my own sandals," he said, as I tried to untie them. He set them neatly at the edge of the carpet. He was wearing a plain linen tunic underneath the more finely decorated toga, and it was loosely belted.

I plucked at it like a lyre string. "I have heard that this has been your trademark," I said. "Now, why was that?"

"Who told you that?" he asked, leaning back against one of the cushions and propping his feet up on a Syrian hassock. His face had softened and his dark eyes, tired before, were alert.

"I read it," I confessed. At the time, I had not seen the significance of it. "Supposedly Sulla the Dictator warned people to 'beware of that boy with the loosely belted clothes.' "

He snorted. "Oh. That. It was just one of his attacks. Loosely belted tunics are supposed to denote loose morals. But at the time he said it, I was a model of propriety, almost a virgin. Like dear Cicero, he liked to butcher a man's character by insinuation." But the eastern pleasure room was melting his edge of anger. "Cicero once said almost the opposite about me, harping on my neatness rather than on my slovenliness. He said, 'When I see his hair so carefully arranged, and observe him adjusting it with one finger, I cannot imagine it should enter into such a man's thoughts to subvert the Roman state.' "

"He is obsessed with the Roman state," I said. "But let us leave it behind, so it does not enter here. Cicero, Sulla, the Senate—put them as firmly aside as you have put your sandals. For now."

I touched his shoulders, and finding them strained, I massaged them until the tenseness melted a bit.

"There is no need for you to do these things," he protested. "I have servants at home—"

"Whom you probably never let touch you," I said. "Is that not true?"

"When I have time—"

"You never have time," I said. "But this is a magic hour, set aside from all the rest. Like your extra days to be added to the calendar." I continued to squeeze his shoulders with all the strength in my hands. "Now submit!"

With a great sigh, he flopped down on his stomach, turned his head on the cushion, and let me rub his shoulders. His eyes closed in contentment.

He let me pull his arms free of the tunic so I would not rub the linen against his flesh. With the yellow afternoon light streaming into the room, and he half asleep and not counting the time, for the first time I was able to look at his skin and his broad back and see each line, each sinew, each scar. For a soldier he had surprisingly few scars, although I supposed that the back was the place where a survivor would have the fewest.

I nudged at his shoulder and succeeded in getting him to turn over. He flung one arm over his eyes to shut out the sun, and continued his light sleeping. Now on his chest I could see more scars, some of them perhaps from a boyhood mishap, others perhaps from a deadly battle. They were indistinguishable now; they all looked alike once they had turned white and receded into the flesh. The cut given by a playmate in jest, the slash given by a Gallic foe, reduced to equality by time and scar tissue. I supposed each of them had a history; I had heard of old soldiers comparing wounds.

I loved him so, even his past was precious to me. I found myself kissing each mark, thinking, *I would have had it never happen, I would wish it away*, taking him further and further back to a time when he had known no disappointments, no battles, no wounds, as I erased each one. To make him again like Caesarion. Yet if we take the past away from those we love—even to protect them—do we not steal their very selves?

He stirred, murmured, and slowly pulled his arm away from his eyes. I felt his stomach muscles tighten as he sat up. He took my head in his hands and drew it up.

"No more of that," he said. "I cannot accept such homage. It is not worthy of a queen to bestow it."

I looked long and hard at my reflection in the surface of his dark brown eyes. "I am not doing you homage," I finally said. "If you do not know that, then you are ignorant in the ways of love, in spite of all your women."

"Perhaps I am," he said slowly. "Perhaps I am."

My desire for him seemed unbounded; I felt that no matter what I did, I could never adequately express it or satisfy it. I leaned over and kissed him, touching his face with both my hands, lightly. But at the touch of my mouth on his, he changed from the languid, relaxed creature on the cushions to a hungry man. I felt his hand grip my thigh and close on it. His other arm went around my back and pulled me forward so strongly that I lost my balance and toppled off my knees. Together we fell back against the mound of cushions.

The square of sun on the carpet by our heads was giving off a hot radiance. His skin felt as lusciously, soothingly warm as that square of sunlight. I put my cheek against his shoulder and rubbed it. Skin against skin was both comforting and exciting at the same time.

How long it had been since I had lain against him! Since my arrival in Rome, we had had few private hours. There had been no time, and we did not wish to give scandal. There was scandal enough in my being in Rome at all with Caesarion, living in Caesar's villa.

He rolled over and forced my head back on the carpet, kissing me so deeply and forcefully I could hardly get my breath. Yet I did not care; the dizziness just heightened my desire, making my head spin and loosening all my natural modesty. I seemed to float out into another world as removed from my real self as this room was from everyday life.

But was that not why I had created it—to float free from that ordinary life?

With a soft groan of longing, I pulled off his belt. It was loosely knotted and came untied easily.

"Sulla was right," I whispered. "Loose clothes are causing you to be ravished."

"Of course Sulla was right," he said. "One's enemies often know one better than one's friends." He buried his face in my neck, kissing it as if it were the most delicate, airy pastry, or easily bruised petals. The soft touch of those lips lightly brushing my skin caused stabs of almost unbearable desire in me.

Now I was the unpracticed, impatient child. If I had had my way, I would have ended it within minutes, before the sun had moved very far on that square of carpet. But he, who had made quick striking his most personal characteristic in war, seemed in no hurry to conclude this campaign, the one being fought in the soft cushions, mattresses, and carpets of the east. He pursued me, he teased me, he ambushed me, he brought me often to the brink of engagement, then postponed the final reckoning until he decided the conditions were, at last, perfect for his purpose. Then . . . I cannot describe it, only remember it.

We slept. For me, it was a drowsy sinking into a formlessness that rivaled the pillows; for him, it seemed deeply restorative. I awoke before he did, and I was surprised at how soundly he was still sleeping. The light had moved, elongated, and softened. It must be late in the afternoon.

I closed my eyes and let myself lie there, thinking. We had such little time together, and it was flying by. Yet all I could do now was lie still, my legs curled up under me, my head resting against his, and listen to his breathing.

The light no longer held any geometrical shape at all when he finally awoke, seemingly without any transition. He turned his head on the cushion and looked at my body lying beside him, as if he were seeing an unexpected terrain.

"We are still here," he said in wonder. "I thought it was a dream, and I would awaken on my camp bed."

"No, my love, we are far from any field camp." I raised my head up and rested it on my arm.

"More's the pity," he said. "I think we could be happy there."

"Fighting a war?" I asked, surprised. "Arising every morning, never knowing if it is our last together?"

"It gives a certain heightened sensibility to one's day." He smiled and moved on the cushions, reaching for his tunic. He put it on in one quick movement. "This is how one dresses in the field."

"So quickly that the eye can hardly follow."

I hoped he was not going to leave. Yet I expected it. His time was so short. At least he would be somewhat more rested. It seemed very little for me to be able to give him.

He sat up, cross-legged. But he did not put on his sandals. "To have you here is a great treasure," he finally said.

"I must return to Egypt," I said. The Triumphs were over; Egypt's status as official Ally and Friend of the Roman People had been ratified, and Caesarion had been recognized. There was no reason to stay longer. But I had delayed saying the words. "My place is there."

"I know," he said. "I know. Yet . . . if you could just stay longer." Before I could argue, he raised his voice and hurried on. "It is almost past the sailing season. You would have to leave tomorrow in order to travel safely. And— I have not wanted to admit this, hardly even to myself, but—I will have to leave Rome and fight another campaign."

"What?" I could not believe the words I had just heard. "You have just celebrated four Triumphs."

"Prematurely, as it turns out." His voice was grim. "For several days I have wrestled with the almost certain knowledge that I will have to take the field in person again. This time in Spain—where I fought only four years ago." He shook his head. "It seems to be an open sore that collects and spews every disaffection within the Roman world. Insurrection, mutinous troops, disloyal towns—and now the remnants of the party of Pompey: the wreck of Scipio's army, the traitorous Labienus, my former general, and Pompey's two sons. It is my misfortune that they escaped from Africa. And that they have been able to link themselves with an army mutiny."

"But it isn't necessary that *you* go," I said. "You have other field commanders."

"I sent two already, and they cannot hold the territory. Their forces are too small. Gnaeus Pompey, who managed to crawl ashore, has been welcomed by the mutinous troops, and has raised eleven more legions himself. My governor has been expelled. No one can prevail against Labienus. Only I. After all, I taught him what he knows. He learned well."

"But you could lose everything—even your life. You cannot leave the work in Rome undone! Send someone else. There are many generals; there is only one Caesar with a plan for Rome."

"I have already sent others. Now I must go." He waited an instant before adding, "Please wait here for me. I will return as quickly as I can."

"What if you don't return?" I hated my words, but I feared for him. His luck, his fortune, could not favor him forever.

"I must go," he repeated. "Will you stay here while I am away?"

"For how long? I cannot stay indefinitely."

"If I fight a winter campaign," he said, "by February it could be over."

"Oh, so you have planned it all already!"

"It planned itself. Each war has its own boundaries of time and necessity. Now, will you answer me?"

"I will stay," I said, "until the seas open again in the spring. But more than that is not possible." It was with reluctance that I gave this promise. The thought of staying on in Rome without him was not pleasant. But my word was my word.

"Thank you." He lifted both my hands and kissed them, slowly. "It is difficult for me to ask anything of you."

"You should never be afraid to ask me for anything."

"I said it was difficult, not that I was afraid. It is difficult because I love you, and I know you would hate to refuse me, but you have always the needs of your own country to consider as well as mine." He smiled. "That is what it means to love a queen. If she were not a good queen, I could not love her."

The clouds of sunset were moving across the window, tinted pink and purple. Sunset was an expansive, colorful show in Roman skies.

"The hours of your days are so different here," I said, pointing to the clouds. "We never have sunsets like that."

"I should teach you a little about the history of Rome," he said. "We have a few sacred artifacts that supposedly go back to our founding. In fact, I could show them to you, since they are kept in the Regia. Perhaps then you'd have respect for our ancient ways!"

I laughed. "Ancient ways!"

"Don't scoff," he said. I could not tell whether he was serious or not. "You know Rome was founded by my ancestor, Aeneas, after he escaped from burning Troy. And he brought some objects—"

"Someone should write it all up in verse. You need a Roman Homer to tell your story," I said. "Strange how we feel history does not exist unless it is celebrated in a national poem, or in monumental stone."

"Such is human nature. But if you will come to the Regia tomorrow— around the ninth hour—I will show you our treasures. As Pontifex Maximus, I am their guardian. And then, afterward, I would like to show you the plans my architect has drawn up for the library and the theater and the temple. You can see the beginning of Rome, and its future—you can see the whole of it." His eyes were shining, and I saw once again that eager love he had for his city.

"Certainly I will," I assured him.

He was reaching for his sandals when a tousled head peeked in the door, his fat little fingers clasping the frame.

"Father!" Caesarion squealed with delight, and ran across the carpets, tripping over the hills of cushions. He flung out his arms to Caesar, who picked him up, and lowered his face to his, nose to nose.

Their faces were very alike. At eighteen months, Caesarion's profile was a miniature of Caesar's. No one could doubt whose son he was.

Caesar hugged him and rolled over, encasing him in his arms like a bear. The boy laughed and shrieked.

Then Caesar held him up again at arm's length, letting his plump legs dangle and kick. "Behold," he said, "the new man. The man of the new world that we will create. Rome and Egypt, together. The west and the east, one. One citizen, one birth, one allegiance."

"But not one language," I said in Latin.

"That isn't necessary," he answered in Greek. "We will be able to understand each other well enough using our own languages."

29

I came to the Regia at precisely the time he had indicated. He had had business with the Senate in the morning, and appointments with his secretaries, Balbus and Oppius, in the early afternoon, but he promised to be finished by our meeting time.

As I approached the imposing facade of the Regia, with his house nearby, I found myself hoping Calpurnia was not at home to see me approaching.

Caesar's wife was not mentioned between us. I did not wish to question him, and evidently he did not wish to reveal what their relations were. As long as I did not have to think of her as a real person—a person watching from the windows, a person sorrowing over her barrenness, a person who also dreaded Caesar's departure for another battlefield—I could live with the situation. She was Caesar's wife, not mine.

Go in at the central door, Caesar had told me. I saw a heavy wooden door, decorated with brass bosses, opening directly onto the Via Sacra. I pushed it open and let myself in.

Two chambers opened on either side, and I could see that they both were dimly lit and smelled of recent incense. But the room also opened out onto a paved courtyard, bordered with a wooden portico. Since Caesar was not here yet, I thought it would be more pleasant to pass my time outside. The day was clear and windy, sweeping leaves high into the air and swirling them.

On one side of the courtyard was an abandoned altar. There was also a bench, and I sat down on it, meaning to luxuriate in the sunlight, for it was warm against this wall. I leaned my head back against the stone and closed my eyes.

But as soon as the wind stopped playing with the leaves, which crackled and rustled, I became aware of an unmistakable noise inside.

There were moans and sharp little cries, and excited whispers. Then a lot of thrashing and creaking. I heard something fall on a floor—a floor just on the other side of the wall where I was leaning.

Very slowly, I turned and looked in a corner of the window. There, on the far side of the room, on a low couch, were a man and a woman making heated love. The woman was twisting and moaning, and the man's back was heaving and straining. I could see all the cords of his muscles along his back. He had thin arms, thin pale arms, and—as I caught a glimpse of his face, I almost gasped aloud. It was Octavian!

Crumpled in a heap on the floor was a tangle of clothes, then, oddly, a pair of man's sandals were put tidily aside. I stared at them. There was something strange about them. They were—the soles were unusually thick. They were artificially built up to give extra height.

I turned away, clapping my hand over my mouth in shock. Octavian! The quiet, sanctimonious Octavian! He was having a tryst right in the Pontifex Maximus's precinct. And he wore shoes to increase his height! I did not know which surprised me more.

I peeked in again. Who was his partner? For a moment I couldn't tell, but then I recognized her as—the wife of somebody or other who had come to the Egyptian party. I did not remember his name.

So he was an adulterer as well. People certainly were surprising.

I quickly retreated into one of the rooms opening off the courtyard.

He had better hurry, I thought, or Caesar will catch him. I almost laughed. I knew, somehow, that Caesar would be shocked at the idea of doing such a thing in the vicinity of the sacred artifacts of Roman history—or, rather, he would be shocked that Octavian did not care. There was a difference.

Octavian must have discovered that the Regia offered privacy during odd hours, and put it to good use on a regular basis. After all, he *was* a member of the College of Pontiffs there!

Spread out on the table were several pouches of papers. Perhaps they were Caesar's plans for the Roman buildings. I unrolled one of the scrolls, but quickly saw that they were private letters and reports. My Latin was just good enough for me to decipher that they concerned the movements of Labienus and Gnaeus Pompey. They must be dispatches from Caesar's commanders in Spain. What were they doing here?

As I was putting them back, there was a movement at the door. Octavian stood there, his toga perfectly draped, staring at me. I was astounded to see that there were so few wrinkles in it. How had he managed that? His sandals were not noticeably different from any others, once he was wearing them. He must have a talented cobbler.

"What are you doing here?" he asked. He was as surprised to see me as I had been to see him a few minutes earlier.

"I am meeting Caesar," I said, enjoying watching the expression on his face.

"Now?" He made his way over to the papers and gathered them up, acting as though they were his.

"Actually, he is late," I said. "But he should arrive at any moment."

Octavian looked at me carefully, and I could see him wondering how long I had been there.

"I found it hard to wait inside," I said innocently, "so I have enjoyed the fine autumn day out in the small courtyard."

He wrestled with himself and decided not to gamble. "Don't tell my uncle," he said unhappily. "Please don't tell him!"

"Why, he is hardly in a position to judge you," I said. "He will probably applaud you for imitating him. Nor am I in a position to judge you, for obvious reasons."

"I—I—" He swallowed hard. "It is better that he not know. I—I am sorry."

I laughed. "You need not apologize to *me*. I am not the lady's husband."

"O Apollo!" He groaned. "You know him. You know she is—Don't tell my uncle! Please! Swear it!"

"I hardly think that is necessary. I have promised you I won't tell him."

He snatched up the papers and tucked them under his arm, looking even more furtive. "I—I must go," he muttered, clutching them. He turned back and looked at me with a mixture of worry and anger. Then he was gone.

What was I to think? Had he availed himself of Caesar's private papers as well as the man's wife? He was a sneaky little thing behind his wide blue eyes. Did Caesar realize this? Surely he must.

Caesar arrived a few minutes later, walking in briskly. "So much correspondence!" he said. "I apologize for being late." He looked around. "I hope you have not been bored. This room is quite bare." He indicated the empty table.

"Oh, I have had an opportunity to think," I assured him. I was bursting to tell him about Octavian. But I had given my word.

"Here, in this adjoining room," he said, steering me into it, "is the Sanctuary of Mars. Here is the sacred shield that Numa, the second king of Rome, received from heaven. It foretells Roman victory."

It was dim in the room, despite the bright light outside. An oversized bronze statue of Mars stood on its pedestal, and all around the walls of the room gleamed many shields.

"To keep it from being stolen, Numa had eleven copies made. No one knows which is the true one. And here are the spears, which foretell our doom by vibrating."

"Do you feel them shiver? What do they tell you about Spain?"

He reached out and grasped one. "Nothing. It is quiet."

"So you have these things in your safekeeping?" I asked.

"They are to be guarded by the Pontifex Maximus."

"But they belonged to a king."

"The Regia was the seat of the kings. Rex—Regia. The Pontifex Maximus inherited the priestly power of the kings. It did not die with them."

"Neither, apparently, did the idea of kingship. I have never heard so much talk about kings until I came to Rome." I paused. "So you are descended from kings, and exercise a kingly guardianship. You have little way to go until you are forced to accept the title itself."

He chose not to answer. Instead he said, "It may amuse you to know that I am served by a priesthood of women, the Vestal Virgins. In their shrine is the Palladium, the wooden statue of Pallas that fell from the sky at Troy and was brought here by Aeneas. Would you like to see it?"

"If you would like to show me," I said. I could tell from his tone that he would not take kindly to Octavian's antics in the shadow of Aeneas, as it were. Perhaps there was a glimmer of something sacred that he honored, after all. Octavian had known that, and I had not.

The new calendar was announced, and immediately the extra days were introduced. People "lived" the same day over, which gave rise to some peculiar behavior. Some strove to repeat everything exactly the same way, but do it better; others decided one of the days did not count. Then, the people who had to grumble over everything—like Cicero—made snide remarks. When someone mentioned that the constellation Lyra was due to rise, Cicero sneered, "Yes, by edict."

The new war in Spain was likewise announced, and caused alarm and wonder. Were the civil wars never to end? A mood of despair seemed to seize people, made worse by the earlier sunsets and the growing chill. The blue-skied Triumphs and all they had promised seemed to wilt, killed by this early frost.

Rains fell, dreary days bringing shivering mornings. We had to light braziers in the villa, and close the shutters. I was surprised to find what a downward pull the dullness and drizzle had on my spirits; and at the same time I wondered how much of my usual optimism and energy derived from the bright, bracing climate of Alexandria. I had always thought it natural-born, rather than influenced by the light and air around me.

I saw little of Caesar. He was engrossed in his hurried war preparations, and in pushing his reforms through the Senate; he had so little time. Sometimes, if I were in the Forum, I would glimpse him hurrying from his residence to his new buildings. At a distance, I could always recognize him by his posture. I could also tell when he saw me, by the way he hesitated for just a moment. But he never came over or altered his route.

I dreaded his going; the only good thing would be that once he went, he must soon return—must return—must return—

I wished that I could send him off with news that I was to bear another child. But it was not like Egypt, where we lived together day and night. Here we were so seldom together, and the whole feeling of Rome was different from the bursting fertility of Egypt. I did not conceive, as if the gods of Rome had shut up my womb. They did not care for me—I could feel it.

The hard, stony gods of Rome were not like Isis, Queen of Heaven, she who had both passion *and* compassion. . . .

Caesar would embark at the end of the third November—a speedy preparation, even for him. He would take only his veteran Fifth and Tenth Legions with him, order two other veteran legions to join him, and raise the others later. He had unfortunately disbanded some of his famous legions after the last wars, and they were now busy farming on the land they had been awarded at their retirement.

He announced to Rome that he was taking his great-nephew Octavian to give him firsthand training in warfare. Well, perhaps it would fill out his spindly little arms.

I thought to myself that his surreptitious reading of the war correspondence should stand Octavian in good stead; he would then appear to Caesar to be miraculously well informed on the subject. But such had doubtless been his aim.

I did not think long of Octavian, because Ptolemy fell ill with a cough and fever. The winter was not agreeing with him; he lay in his narrow bed and turned big, sunken eyes upon me whenever I came into the room.

"I want to go back to Egypt," he said plaintively. "I want the sunshine. I want Olympos." He would break off to cough a heaving cough.

"Ptolemy," I would tell him gently, "it is too late to sail now. We must wait until the winter storms are past."

"I'll be dead by then," he muttered, turning his head restlessly.

"There are doctors in Rome," I said. "From what I hear, half of them are Greek. I will get one for you—the best to be had." I rubbed his sweating brow with a scented cloth. "There is also Isis, our own goddess. I will seek out her sanctuary and ask her help. She has never failed me."

Charmian and I set out to find the Isis Temple, which I had heard stood in the Field of Mars. It was a cold and misty morning, when there seemed to be no colors in the world, only shades of gray. The streets, wreathed in fog, were mysterious corridors leading to unseen squares and alleys. I had taught myself enough by this point that I knew which turns to take, and found the place where I believed the temple to be with little difficulty.

But it was a heap of stones. Only the flat marble floor, littered with fallen columns and mounds of scattered rubble, showed where the temple had once stood. Then I saw it—the desecration. A statue of Isis lay forlornly beside a block of stone—her pedestal?—and she was faceless. Someone had chiseled away all her features.

"Oh, Charmian!" I clutched at her arm. The sight of the defaced goddess was chilling.

"It has been deliberately destroyed," she said, looking around warily. "By an enemy of Isis."

An enemy of Isis was also an enemy of mine, as she was the patron goddess of my royal house. "Who would have dared?" I said in a low voice. I bent down to brush the hurt goddess's face, as I had soothed Ptolemy's. "This does little," I apologized to her. "They cannot injure your power, or take away your compassion," I said. "The gods are not weakened by the damage of men."

And that was a comforting thing. What if gods lost their power because we attacked our own images of them? They were not the images, which were merely fashioned with our bare hands.

"Isis, hear me now," I called upon her. "Here I have no sistrum, no sacred Nile water, no pitcher to perform your rites in what was once your holy temple. But you, who are the most loyal wife and devoted mother, touch Ptolemy with your power and make him well. Let him see his homeland again." I watched the featureless face, aching over her disfigurement. Impulsively I took off a necklace I was wearing, and draped it around her neck.

"No, my lady, it will just be stolen," said Charmian, trying to stay my hand.

"Eventually everything is stolen," I said. "Broken, destroyed, stolen." I had a sudden vision of that grim picture. It all ended with toppled columns and things coming apart—the seams of marble plaques, stair steps, the joining of stone arms to stone shoulders. "So I offer it while it is still whole." It lay there on her neck, the lapis the only spot of color apart from the green weeds peeking between the paving stones.

I felt consoled by the offering; I had thrown something into the maw of destruction.

"Come," I said. "Let us leave this place."

We were able to procure a good doctor, a man named Apollos, who was Greek but had become a Roman citizen.

"Thanks to Caesar," he said, "foreign physicians and scholars and artists are given special citizenship. I came here to learn for a little while, but had no thought of staying permanently. It was Caesar who changed the rules." He was bending down and listening to Ptolemy's chest.

"Congestion in there," he pronounced. "We will have to smoke it out. Burn dried fenugreek, and make a poultice of dried figs." He smiled and thumped Ptolemy's hollow little chest. "Make you as good as new. You'll see." To me he nodded, and motioned for me to speak to him privately.

"Do not be alarmed," he said. "He will recover. I suggest wrapping his legs in woolen strips to keep them warm, and give him foods known to produce heat in the belly, such as chickpeas and walnuts."

"This climate does not agree with him," I said. "But I think he is also homesick. In Alexandria we also have rain and storms; it is not all sunny there, as in the rest of Egypt."

"Soon the sun will be out in Rome," he said. "Our winters are short."

"I tried to visit the Temple of Isis to request her help," I said. "What took place there?" Surely he would know.

"It was destroyed by order of the Senate," he said. "First some altars to Isis on the Capitoline hill were broken up by two Consuls, and then the Senate voted to remove the great temple itself. But no one had the courage to touch it, no workmen would obey the order to lay hands on it, until a Consul, Aemilius Paulus, took off his toga and battered down the door with an axe."

"But why?"

"I think it was a shudder of repulsion against anything foreign," he said. "Rome goes through these purges ever so often. I have felt the hostility to foreigners here. Have you not? Forgive me if I speak out of turn."

"Yes. Yes, I have. Well, if they don't want foreigners about them, then they never should have ventured so far from safe little Rome!" Whose fault was it that Rome was involved with so many countries?

"Caesar's view is different," he said. "He seems not to share that prejudice." He laughed. "You and I are proof of that, I suppose."

Caesar came to say good-bye on the yellowish bright morning that began the third November. I saw him come hurriedly up the pathway, his face looking blank, his cloak flying out behind him. I went to greet him, waiting just inside the atrium.

There were servants about; his words were formal.

"I come to take leave of you, on the eve of my departure, and to wish you well in Rome while I am away." The words hung there, silly, slight.

I took his hand and led him into a private chamber. "Do not leave me with this memory," I said. "Your formal words leave much unsaid." I stood on tiptoe and kissed his cheek. "So you go? When? And what of your legions?"

"I depart within a day," he said, taking a seat. "I go overland to Spain—fifteen hundred miles—in a hard-riding carriage. I plan to cover at least fifty miles a day, and take the enemy by surprise. That will put me there around the first of December."

"I know you have fought winter campaigns before," I said, "but this time, will you not be at a disadvantage? The enemy is already encamped there, and has his supplies. What will you do?"

"I must trust to myself to find the solution," he said.

"Would not a little planning be more prudent?"

"I have done all the planning I can, given the circumstances. I must trust that the rest will follow once I am there," he said. He seemed different to me; he was already far away.

"May all the gods protect you," I suddenly said. "May Isis have you in her keeping."

"You know I do not believe in such things," he said gently. "But if I believe *you* have me in your keeping, then—"

I flung my arms around him. "In my keeping, in my remembrance, in all my thoughts!" I kissed him, hard, as if to remember later that he was real, to notice how his lips and teeth felt, how his jaw fitted against mine.

He stepped back and looked at me for what seemed a long time. Then he said, "Farewell, and farewell."

30

The rains continued; the days stretched out, while the city held its breath and waited to hear what would happen in Spain. Would they have a new master, the young Gnaeus Pompey?

Doubtless they would cheer him just as they had cheered Caesar, I thought. O sweet Isis—do not let Caesar lose his life on a bare battlefield far from home. It is not even distinguished as a far frontier, nor is the foe distinguished as a fighter. Grant to him anything but an ignoble end! I prayed.

And waited, like everyone else.

The great winter solstice festival of Saturnalia came, and with it, Rome exploded into celebration. At its close, when the final celebration would be held, Charmian and I took Ptolemy for an outing. I knew whatever detrimental effect the cold would have on him would be offset by the novelty of seeing this most Roman of festivals.

The area around the Forum was jammed with celebrants, all behaving in strange ways—some were masked, others ran about in costumes. I was at a loss to understand what it all meant. It seemed to be an unbridled party, but I could see from the dolls and wrapped food everyone clutched that it had its own rules.

I should have brought someone with me to explain all this! I thought, pulling my cloak up over my head against the chill.

Just then I caught sight of a most disrespectful disguise—someone had a mask on like Octavian's face. Then, as the person came closer, battling his way resolutely through the crowds, I saw that it *was* Octavian.

I motioned to him and drew him over to us. He had to shove and push his way past a boiling surge of people, looking irritated the whole time.

"Your Majesty," he said, bowing. "But no, you cannot be Cleopatra during Saturnalia. You must be someone else—take another name."

"Oh, very well," I said. "I shall be . . . Queen Hatshepshut."

"No, not a queen. Queens cannot be queens. You must become something else altogether."

"Then I shall become—Charmian!" I squeezed her arm. "And she must become me! And Ptolemy—choose someone."

He sighed. "I would choose Socrates."

Octavian made a face. "Oh, not him! You don't want to take hemlock, do you?"

"No. Well, then, Plato."

"What staid longings you have!" said Octavian. "I wish to be Achilles!"

"Why, are you consumed with rage?" I asked him. That Octavian, who was so self-contained, should want to be the ferocious Achilles!

"No, but I wonder what it is to be the greatest warrior in the world."

"Why are you here?" I had thought my eyes mistaken when I had seen him. "Caesar said you were to accompany him to the war."

He looked apologetic. "I got a fever, and could not leave with him. I will join him later. After I am fully recovered." He gave a mournful, hacking cough.

"Have you had any word?" I hated myself for having to ask—for admitting that I had not.

"Yes," said Octavian proudly. "He has reached Spain safely. All is well."

It had taken a month to hear only that he had arrived. Battles had already been fought since then—might be fought even as we stood there, unknowing.

"Thanks be to all the gods!" I paused. "What is the situation there? What did he find?"

A raft of celebrants swept past us, stumbling and laughing. An unintelligible chorus of words tumbled off their lips.

Octavian moved closer to me. "This is a bad place to talk," he said. "I can hardly hear you." Another knot of people, coming like the current of a river, bumped into him, almost knocking him down.

"Come and see us tonight!" one of them said, grabbing his arm. "And wear a costume!"

"Yes! We want a big audience!" said a woman with ivy vines twined in her hair.

"Perhaps," said Octavian. "Thank you."

"Who was that?" asked Ptolemy.

"A bunch of actors," said Octavian sternly. "Ignore them."

"Is there a play tonight?" asked Ptolemy. "Can we go?" He turned to me. "It's so boring just to lie in bed at home!"

"I hardly think their fare would be suitable for you," said Octavian. "Anything Cytheris is in is filthy." As soon as the words were out of his mouth, and I saw the expression on his face, I knew that he remembered, acutely, what I had seen at the Regia.

"Cytheris," I said, trying to smooth out the awkward moment. I had no wish to cause him embarrassment, or to have him associate me with humiliation. "I think I have met her—but where?"

"I saw her at the Egyptian entertainment that you gave," he said.

"That *Caesar* gave," I corrected him. "But why should I remember her?"

"In the first place, because she is beautiful. In the second, because she is scandalous. In the third, because she made a spectacle of herself, hanging on Marc Antony, her lover at the time."

"At the time?"

"Yes, Fulvia has won the battle for him. Some prize! They were married a few weeks ago. Now supposedly Antony has reformed himself. But I suspect he's out in the crowd somewhere with his Hercules costume. People never really change." He sniffed. "It looks as though Cytheris has consoled herself well enough for her broken heart."

"Can we go?" Ptolemy kept asking me.

"Let us see what they are performing first," I said. "Now—about Spain." I was desperate for any news of the situation. I needed to know what Caesar had found there.

Octavian knitted his brows. "It seems that most of southern Spain has gone over to the enemy. As I understand it, the rebels have thirteen legions. Two of those are veteran ones, left over from the original Pompey's forces. Those two prize ones are guarding Corduba, and the rest are spread out over the countryside. Caesar has eight legions—four veteran—and they are better trained than the enemy's. So they may be evenly matched—the superior numbers of one side canceled out by the better training of the other's. One bright spot—Caesar has eight thousand cavalry, supplied by Bogud, against the other's six thousand."

I felt a coldness take hold of me, as if the December temperature could penetrate under my skin. "Evenly matched," I said. "I suppose Labienus will duplicate his tactics in Africa and do everything possible to prolong the war and avoid a pitched battle. *They* are already situated there, after all, under roofs, while Caesar must live in the open field!" I hated Labienus as I despised all disloyal people—in my sight, disloyalty is the most heinous of all crimes.

"Then it will be Caesar's task to duplicate his victory in Africa by drawing them out onto a battlefield," said Octavian. "He may have to trick them."

Southern Spain. The ingrates—the very area where Caesar had served as governor, and was their patron! No ground was safe, nothing permanently secured, then.

"Oh, Cleopatra, dearest sister—can we *please* go to the play?" Ptolemy was smiling at me.

We went. I took the entire household with me, so that we Egyptians could be seen as partaking of Roman drama, rather than as a sister indulging her brother's prurient interests. Actually I was pleased that something had stirred Ptolemy's interest, for the truly sick are not interested in plays. Nor in scandalous actresses.

The Romans had a very divided opinion on drama. They were not an aesthetic people, and the subtleties of Greek tragedies did not appeal to them—did they not understand them? Perhaps not. They preferred the simple butchery of the wild beast hunts and the paired gladiators to the agonizing of Oedipus. The mixed-up bedrooms, the cuckolded husband, the conniving slave—those they understood. So their plays revolved around such themes and characters.

And, yes, the play *was* filthy. Most likely Ptolemy did not understand the worst parts, but some dirty jokes brought a red blush to his cheeks.

Cytheris was indeed beautiful, and I understood how she was received—or semi-received—in the highest circles of Rome. Beauty seems to confer its own *imperium*, although we like to deny this.

When we left the theater, fluffy white specks were descending from the night sky. They swirled into the torches, making little hissing noises as they did so. The paving stones were covered in what looked like a thick frost.

"Snow!" I said. "This must be snow."

We stood out in the open, just looking at it. The flakes that fell all over us were like chopped feathers—light and floating. They caught in folds of our garments and landed, stinging, on our lips.

"Snow," said Ptolemy, in wonder. "I thought never to see it for myself!"

It stuck on our shoes, melted and seeped in with a paralyzing coldness. When our litter bearers took us home, I could see the path their feet made in the white blanket.

Snow. There would be a great deal of snow in Spain, where Caesar had to live under leather tents outdoors.

To occupy my time, I taught myself much about Rome. I saw most of her for myself—I visited her sacred shrines, the tombs of her greatest men, the gardens of Lucullus laid out on the Esquiline, and, most interesting to me, the temple of Asclepius on Tiber Island, along with its hospital. The Greek god of healing had found a home for himself in the midst of the rushing, muddy Tiber.

I never reached a conclusion about Rome. She was so mighty in some ways, so venal in others. Yet I had a premonition that this combination was calculated to appeal most strongly to human nature.

They will crush everything beneath their chariot wheels, the Kandake had warned me. And here, when I saw the chariots clattering past, and witnessed the Roman pragmatism—that most manifested itself in callousness—I knew she was right. They would. Unless, somehow, they could be tempered by association with our older sensibilities.

Octavian left, belatedly, to follow Caesar. He came to bid me farewell one January morning, and to ask if there was any message I wished him to convey.

I thought it polite of him to come, but I had no private message for Caesar I wished to entrust to him.

"Nothing has happened yet," Octavian said. "We have received no news of any battle."

So Caesar had had to endure an idle month in the freezing field.

"I wish you great success," I said.

My wishes evidently counted for little, as Octavian encountered every setback on a nightmarish journey, ending in a shipwreck. He dragged himself onward to reach Caesar nonetheless, long after the crucial engagement of the war.

And thus he recommended himself to Caesar. His very doggedness—his ability, like a mastiff, to sink his teeth into something and not let go—must have impressed Caesar as the very highest virtue. The teeth were thin and precariously anchored, but the courage in hanging on determined Octavian's whole fortune—I know that now. If only he had remained too sickly to follow—as he turned out to be on every major battle afterward. The battle of Philippi, the battle of Naulochus, and finally the battle of Actium, found

309

Octavian lying sick in his tent. Would that he had never gone to Spain—then the others would not have followed. And I—

But quiet, my heart. It is over. And I speak of then, not of now.

Spring came in March. The yellow wildflowers all along the Tiber burst into bloom, and in our own gardens the trees unfurled their tentative green leaves. Ptolemy's cough melted away once the weather became warmer, and as if to make up for it, he grew taller quickly.

But there was still no word of the outcome in Spain. It seemed a mockery to luxuriate in the warm spring breezes and stroll in the twilights when the future of Rome hung in the balance. The Roman festivals of Lupercalia, Anna Perenna, and Liberalia passed, and it was not until the twentieth day of April that the word reached Rome, causing an explosion of celebration in the streets.

Caesar had won. On March seventeenth, he had at last succeeded in drawing the rebel forces into one decisive battle at Munda.

It was a desperate fight, one of the bloodiest in Roman history. When it was over, thirty thousand erstwhile followers of Pompey lay dead on the battlefield, against only a thousand Caesarians. Labienus was dead; so was Gnaeus Pompey. Sextus, the younger Pompey brother, had escaped.

"The thing that turned the battle"—this was recounted in wonder on the streets, and I heard it told many times, ten times for every ten city blocks—"since the sides were almost evenly matched, and it was growing dark, and the Caesarians began to grow disheartened and fall back—was Caesar himself forcing his way into the front lines where the breach was. He ripped off his helmet and shouted, 'Do you mean to deliver your commander into the hands of these boys?' And he began fighting desperately, hand to hand, and at the sight of that his men rallied, and the battle turned."

I must trust to myself to find the solution, he had said. And he had done so, with a foolhardy, wild gamble that had his name, and his alone, written all over it.

I was weak in hearing about it. His courage was something unhuman. And so was his luck.

It was immediately declared that April twenty-first—the day after the news was received in Rome—would be celebrated forever after with chariot races in the Circus. Then the Senate outdid itself in an effort to confer honors on Caesar. Caesar should have the title of Imperator for life, and the title should be made hereditary. He must be Consul for ten years. All the anniversaries of his previous victories should henceforth be celebrated with annual sacrifices. He could wear the laurel wreath at all times and the garb of the *Triumphator* at all official occasions. His statue must be set in the temple of Quirinus, with the inscription "To the Invincible God." At public games an ivory statue of him must be carried in a litter, and a chariot follow with its trappings, in company with the statues of other gods. Another statue of him must be set up beside the statues of the former kings of Rome. A temple dedicated to the liberty Caesar had brought must be built at public expense.

And at his return, a thanksgiving of fifty days should be ordered.

I was hungry to see him. In spite of my earlier contention that I must return to Egypt as soon as the seas opened, good reports from Alexandria now permitted me to stay longer in Rome. How could all the crowds see him return and crown him victor of the world, and Caesarion and I not welcome him home—to his city and to us?

But when was he to return? No one seemed to know. He lingered in Spain, settling administrative problems there, and making appointments. Octavian had joined him in his headquarters. Others rushed to meet him in nearer Gaul, which he would pass through on his way home: Brutus, Antony, Decimus.

At last it came: a personal letter to me. It had been written from Hispalis. I thanked the messenger and gave him some token (doubtless too much), and then waited until I could shut the door of my room and read it in private.

> *It is over, and I am victorious. I know you have heard this already. But what you have not heard I now tell you: I have often fought for victory, but at the battle of Munda I fought for my life.*
>
> *I was spared. I return to you, and to Rome, alive and restored.*
>
> *My love to you and our son.*

I fought for my life. What had I been doing that day? Why had I not felt it? It seemed impossible that it could have been an ordinary day for me. Without meaning to, I crumpled the precious letter by holding it too tightly.

It took him a very long time to return. He was not back at the anniversary of his first Triumph, when the Romans duly paraded out his statue in company with that of Victory, at the Victory games. He did not set foot in the city until the heat had begun to wane; he even retired to his private estate at Lavicum for a week or so beforehand. There he rewrote his will. But no one knew that until long afterward.

There were murmurs that Caesar would celebrate a Triumph. But it seemed unlikely that he would allow this to take place, since his enemies had been other Romans. Triumphs were only to be celebrated over foreign foes.

And then he swept into Rome, bringing the speculation to an end. He had returned. He was victorious. He would order all things anew. The suspension of events would end.

He did not send any messages to me, or invite me to attend any of the private events welcoming him. Yet I knew he was waiting, as was I. All things in time.

The night he came to the villa was a rainy, chilly one—yes, the year was turning again. I heard the crunch of the gravel under his horse's hooves and knew someone was approaching outside. I did not think it was he; I had no specific day I was awaiting him. It was enough that I knew he would come.

I heard his voice, heard him dismissing the servants. Then I heard him taking the stairs two at a time, bounding up them to my door. I flung it open and found myself staring into his face in the dim light.

It seemed forever; it seemed only an instant ago that I had seen him. I was overcome with the impact of it, and buried my face in his shoulder. I had no words for the joy I felt in having him with me.

He touched the back of my neck, gently, and drew my head back so he could look at me. A faint smile was on his face, one I had never seen before. Then he kissed me, a deep kiss that spoke of the pain of our separation.

"Let us get out of the doorway," I finally said. We had remained at the threshold, where anyone could see us. I drew him inside.

He stood, a little changed. He looked thinner. His face had more of the eagle in it—leaner, more acute.

"Thanks be to all the gods," I said. "Fortune has not deserted you."

"No," he said. His voice was softer, more tempered. "The sacrifices just before the battle of Munda foretold disaster. But I ignored them. I said all would be well because I wished it to be."

I shuddered. "Fortune was merciful to her favorite son, after such arrogance."

"Perhaps she likes it." He came over to me and embraced me. "Do you?"

"It is part of you," I said, "and I love everything about you."

"Is that true?" he said. "Then you are different from all others."

The rain spattered outside, the branches of the trees dipped and swayed under the wind, and we huddled together under the coverlet of my couch as if we would shelter from it.

"Was it like this in your tents out in Spain?" I asked him, lying beside him and listening to the cold rain.

"No. This is luxurious. The roof does not leak, and the sheets do not take up groundwater." He took my hand. "You haven't lived until you have experienced a winter campaign."

"You must take me on the next one," I said lightly. When he did not laugh, I said, "Surely you aren't planning another one? There is no one left to fight."

"Except the Parthians."

"Leave the Parthians to themselves," I said. "And they will leave you alone."

"Someday those eagles of Crassus's destroyed legions must be returned."

"Not by you," I said. "Rome is a greater challenge today. Leave Parthia for Caesarion. After all, if you have conquered the entire world, what will be left for him? You have to leave something for the next generation to aspire to."

"I will make a bargain with you," he said in his quiet, mock-serious voice. "I will remain in Rome for a while if you stay as well." He paused. "Will you?" Another pause. "Please?"

Yes, why should we hurry from one another, after such a long parting? I put out my arms to him and held him tightly. I would bind him to me with hoops of iron, keep him away from all harm. No more territory. No more conquests. Let him consolidate what he had already won.

For this one night, he was content with the boundaries of this little room, with me and what I could offer him. And I offered him all of myself.

Against what I held to be all common sense, Caesar was bent on having a Triumph to celebrate his victory. He would claim the war had been a Spanish rebellion, aided by traitorous Romans. This would fool no one, as I pointed out. He said he did not care.

There are those who hold that Caesar, during those days, was not behaving rationally, that his usual clear-sightedness (his sterling trait) was clouded and his judgment suspect. My interpretation is that he was exhausted, increasingly embittered by the failure of his reconciliation policy and the automatic suspicion and hostility of the aristocrats toward his every gesture, and in too great a hurry. He treated the Senate and people of Rome like a pitched battle that must be fought without delay, on the spot. Politics and war are not the same; his genius on the field did not transfer to the byways of the government.

By vanquishing all his foes, and being appointed Dictator, he had been given an unspoken mandate to reorder the government, as Sulla had been. The hope was that he would somehow "restore the Republic"—the pious words on everyone's tongue.

But the truth was that the cherished Republic had grown moribund. Even today, I wonder what could have been done to "restore" it—save going backward in time to an era when it worked. The Republic was a private club, like my Egyptian club—the Society of Imhotep—when I was a child. It answered the needs of only a few aristocrats, while excluding vast numbers of men with equally powerful interests. It was the second group with whom Caesar cast his lot, going over the heads of the old established order. He could not hand the reins of the government back to the rigid old group. And that was what "restoring the Republic" meant.

The Spanish Triumph was held—against my advice, and that of Cicero, Brutus, Cassius, Lepidus, Decimus, and even, some said, Balbus and Oppius. It was an unusually warm day in early October, and once again the streets were swept, garlands were strung on the monuments and buildings, viewing stands were set up. Caesar rode forth in glory, as he had the year before, followed by solemn Octavian in his chariot. But in the midst of all the cheering and adulation, one of the tribunes of the people refused to rise from his bench as the Triumphal Chariot passed by.

I was shocked when, instead of gazing serenely ahead, Caesar pulled his horses to a stop and glared at the offending tribune. In a harsh voice he shouted, "So, Pontius Aquila! Why don't you make me give up the state? After all, you are a tribune!"

Aquila, astounded, just stared back. But he did not rise.

The Triumphal Chariot resumed its journey, but the incident burned its way into common memory.

The banquet afterward was said to have fallen short of Caesar's expectations (or was it the people's?) and so he ordered a second one a few days later.

Then he affronted public opinion further when he allowed his two less-than-competent lieutenant generals, Pedius and Fabius, to celebrate their own Triumphs, even though it was their inability to make headway against the enemy that had called Caesar to Spain to begin with.

At the same time he abruptly resigned his Consulship and appointed Fabius and another man to fill out the last three months of the year.

"Whatever can you be thinking of?" I asked him, one afternoon when he had come to the villa—one rare afternoon when he had a spare moment.

"They keep accusing me of being a tyrant," he said. "Does a tyrant resign his offices?"

"Why must you be so angry?" I asked. "Were you angry at Gnaeus Pompey, or at Vercingetorix? Had you been, could you have defeated them?"

"So now you give me advice—you, whose one experience of war was a stalemate between your forces and your brother's; you, whose one experience of an upheaval in government made you lose your throne and have to flee!" He fairly spat the words.

I refused to rise to this bait. "I admit as much," I said. "But I was only twenty-one years old, and it was my first experience of ruling, or of fighting. You, the most seasoned soldier in the world, should know better."

"And now you are an expert," he said. "How old are you?"

"Twenty-four, as well you know," I said. "And I have had the advantage of being a bystander in this tug-of-war. Bystanders can sometimes see things others closer do not. And what I see is a man acting as if he has been attacked by a pack of wolves—a man striking out in all directions, spitefully. Has it really been necessary for you to say sarcastically at the end of every political promise since the Triumph, 'Providing Aquila allows me to'? It sounds like something a village woman would say at a well about her rival. It is not worthy of you."

He shook his head and sank down on a chair. "I suppose not," he finally said. "It is petty, and petulant." He frowned. "But they drive me past endurance!"

I laughed. "Past endurance? You, who have existed on roots and snow,

314

who have traveled under excruciating conditions. How many miles did you cover a day en route to Spain, in the winter?"

"Over fifty," he said. Then a boyish smile. "And I composed a long poem on the way—I didn't let a minute go to waste. It's called 'The Journey.'"

"Yes, and you have yet to let me read it," I half scolded him. "But as I was saying—how can you now let these political barbs drive you to distraction, when all that nature has thrown against you cannot do it?"

"People are more maddening than cold, starvation, thirst, or heat."

I knelt at his side. Yes, I knelt. I looked up at him as directly as possible. "You have come too far, done too much, to fail now because of human weakness. Repair this weakness! Do not let it gain control of you!" Would he listen to me? "It will bring you down, negate everything you have worked for!"

"Am I not a human being?" he cried, a howl of anguish. "How can I order myself to be a stone? These things rip at me—they tear my very fabric!"

"Mend it, and rest," I said. "Your spirit is wounded, and you must let it heal as you would a cut of any other sort on your body. I fear," I said slowly, "that if you do not, it will become infected. Indeed, it is on the verge of it."

Perhaps he did as I said; he seemed to disappear for several days. But the unrest and the murmurs continued. For a city at peace, and unthreatened by external enemies, Rome seemed singularly nervous.

I was startled when, near the end of the month, Octavian was announced at the villa. I met with him in a chamber opening off the atrium—it was painted in a deep red, with mythic scenes to compensate for its having only one window.

He looked taller, older. (Had he had higher sandals fashioned?) His delicate beauty had been tempered, and the body under the toga seemed more substantial, sturdier. The Spanish campaign had turned him into a man, after all, though he had seen no actual fighting. Just fighting his way there had been enough.

"You have grown imposing," I said. "Your journey must have had a salutary effect upon you." I was surprised at my own warm feelings for him; he had grown on me. And his loyalty to Caesar had been proved. That counted for a great deal.

"I come to bid you farewell," he said. "My uncle has arranged for Agrippa and me to depart for Apollonia across the Adriatic and receive further training—in both rhetoric and warfare."

"I know it is difficult for him to send you away," I said, meaning it.

"We will join him on his next campaign, when we can be of more use to him," said Octavian.

Next campaign? There was to be another? "Parthia?" I asked softly. It had to be Parthia.

"Yes. We will already be halfway there. He will send for us after he has crossed over."

After he has crossed over. . . . When? "Next spring, then?" I said knowingly.

"I believe so," he said.

"I wish you and Agrippa a safe journey," I said. "No more shipwrecks! And I hope your training is everything you desire." I looked at him: at his pure, incandescent features, his wide-set eyes, his light tousled hair. All I thought at the time was, Caesar's family is a handsome one.

"I have benefited from knowing you," I added.

"And I from knowing you," he said, his pleasant smile in place.

And that, I swear, was my last meeting with him, the last words we ever spoke face-to-face. How the gods like to mock us! I sift that meeting time and again, as if some portentous words might flutter out of my memory. But there were none. Nothing but a cordial farewell between two people who loved Caesar well, and would have died for him.

The streets were jammed. My litter could scarcely make any headway. The jostling and pushing meant that the litter rode as roughly as if we had been at sea—and indeed, that was where we were, attempting to tack through a heaving sea of people.

"This is fun!" said Ptolemy, peering out the side. His voice was weak; with the return of the cold weather, his cough and debility had come back.

I wished I had not yielded to Caesar and stayed on so long. Now we were trapped until spring. I longed for the wide streets of Alexandria, where the thoroughfares were never choked like this. We had started out to visit the quarters of the silver- and goldsmiths, because Ptolemy wished to watch them at work. He had a decided artistic bent, especially for design. The arrangements had been made days in advance; they were expecting us at their workshops, and here we were, stuck en route.

What was causing this? I glared out of the litter, as if I could shrivel up the culprit with my gaze. All I saw was the vast throng of heads and shoulders; then I caught sight of an outsized statue lurching along in an open wagon, secured by ropes. Behind it, a little way away, came another. I did not recognize them.

"Look!" cried Ptolemy, pointing. "It's Caesar over there, on those steps!"

I turned to see; indeed, Caesar and some others were standing on the steps of the Theater of Pompey and its attached buildings, bigger than the theater itself.

"That way!" I commanded the bearers, and they turned abruptly and made their way across the road.

What a grandiose building this was, I thought. It looked almost as though it belonged in Alexandria.

Caesar watched us approaching, and came over to us.

"So this draws even you?" he asked, bending down and peering in at us.

"No," I said. "We happen to be here by accident. What is it?"

"Why, it is the day of the restoration of the statues," he said. "Come, and watch." When he saw my reluctance, he said, "Wherever you were going, you cannot get there. You might as well join us." He held out his hand and helped us out. He did not let go of mine as he returned to his spot on the stairs.

"What a day, eh?" said a man I recognized as Lepidus after a moment of memory-searching. "Who would have thought they'd return?"

"Out of storage," said another man—Marc Antony. "Get the cobwebs off them, they'll be as good as new."

"Yes, never throw anything away," said the woman standing beside him; it was Fulvia, his new wife. "That's what I always say."

"It couldn't be about household things," said Lepidus. "For all the world knows you aren't concerned about those."

Fulvia did not look amused. "I manage well enough," she said finally. "I have not heard Antony complaining." She looked to him to agree.

"No, no," he said. "Nothing to complain about." He turned to me. "In Egypt you celebrate the resurrection of the dead," he said. "This is the first time it has happened in Rome. The statues of the vanquished and the forbidden are rising once again on their pedestals."

An extraordinarily large one was approaching, swaying on its cart, steadied by workers. Two tired-looking oxen, their horns down, plodded toward the theater, drawing the load.

"It's Pompey," said Caesar to me. "Do you recognize his moonlike face?"

"Yes," I said, "although it has been many years." Thank the gods I had not seen him, at the end, as Caesar had. I paused. "Why are you bringing his statue back?"

"His *statues*," Caesar corrected me. "All over the city, they are being put back. Along with Sulla's."

"But why?" It seemed very odd to me.

"To show that the upheavals and civil wars of Rome are over," Caesar said. "Now our heroes can be appreciated for their deeds, their bravery or ingenuity, without reference to the particular party they belonged to. All that is past!"

"So you wish," said Fulvia sharply. "But it will take more than just putting old statues back on their bases to make things right!" I looked carefully at her then. She was classically lovely, but her fierceness of expression made me think of Athena with her war helmet on. She looked like a woman, but her words and manner were something else again.

"You just want a lot of other statues to keep yours company," said Antony to Caesar. "So many of yours are going up, you don't want them to be lonely!"

"Oh, honestly, Antony!" Fulvia glared at him. "Sometimes you sound like a fool!"

"Shut up, my love," said Antony lightly. "Let's see—there are to be two on the Rostra and one in each temple in Rome, as well as one in each city in the country and the provinces. It's a good thing they can all be copied from one model, or else you'd get tired of posing, dear Caesar."

"A ruler should never get tired of posing," said Fulvia. "In some countries it's their main occupation. What about Egypt?" She shot the question at me like a challenge.

What was wrong with her? She seemed itching for a fight. But as a queen, I would not give her the satisfaction.

"Perhaps you have not seen the statue of Cleopatra I have put in the temple of my ancestors," said Caesar quietly. "I suggest you do so. It will answer your questions."

Fulvia scowled and walked toward the cart, on the pretext of inspecting the statue of Pompey, which the workmen were wrapping in a sheet and binding to a wooden platform, prior to lifting it out and carrying it into the building.

Lepidus burst into laughter and clapped his hand over his mouth, but Antony roared, as if he cared not if everyone in the vicinity heard him. It was a laugh of pure delight, such as I had seldom heard from an adult. Usually that unbridled happiness dies with our childhood.

"Hush," said Caesar. "The Fierce One will hear you!"

Then all three of the men howled like little boys. Caesar dropped my hand and clutched his sides. He laughed until tears came from the corners of his eyes. "What's so funny?" asked Ptolemy, puzzled. He looked around curiously.

"Something Roman men find amusing," I said. "Wives."

A vendor carrying a basket of sausages and bread was wending his way through the crowd, crying out to advertise his wares.

"Let's buy his whole basket!" said Antony, waving his arms. "Over here, over here!" He jumped up and down.

The man hitched up his tunic and climbed the stairs expectantly. He had a pet monkey perched on his shoulder. "You'll find these are the best," he said. "Sausage from Lucania, bread baked this morning of fine *simila*!"

"We'll take the whole lot of it!" said Antony. "Oh—and your monkey, too!"

The man was taken aback. "But she's not for sale."

Antony looked disappointed. "Then we'll forgo the sale. You see, it's the monkey we really wanted."

"But, sir—she's a favorite of my children . . . however, if . . . perhaps . . ." He looked dismal. "Could you not take the basket instead?"

"No. What use do I have for a basket?" Antony was stern. "It's the monkey or nothing."

"Well . . . very well, if you must . . ." He reached to take her off his shoulder, and very slowly handed her to Antony, who encircled her with one of his muscular forearms.

"Wonderful! Fulvia has long had a recipe for monkey brains," he said gleefully.

The man went white, and Antony could not continue. Gently he handed the monkey back. "It was a jest," he said. "Keep your monkey. I have no need of one." He laughed. "After all, if a man has children, what does he need a monkey for? They look the same, and behave the same, too. But we *will* buy all your sausages, good sir."

After the man had left, clutching his monkey, Lepidus loaded his hands with the bread and sausages, and tasted one.

"Strong!" he said. "Rather much basil, and way too much garlic. I suspect it must be hiding something. Why didn't you at least sample one before buying them all?"

Antony, munching on a sausage, shrugged. "Too much trouble," he said. "Besides, I planned to give most of them away." He yelled out at the crowd standing on the steps. "Here! Free sausage and bread! Help yourselves, courtesy of Marcus Antonius, Consul-elect, bridegroom-suspect—"

Caesar started laughing again. "Hush. Or Fulvia will beat you, and I will cancel the appointment."

"Along with all those other new appointments you have made?" Antony turned toward me, as to a confidant. "Caesar has increased the number of senators from six hundred to nearly nine hundred. Downright barbarians, some of them, imported from Gaul. Sure to cause comment. No one will notice me; I'm much too ordinary."

"These were the men who helped me to victory. If it had been pirates and cutthroats, they too would have their reward," said Caesar. "At least they were my friends, and loyal to me."

"But they wear trousers!" lamented Lepidus. "Trousers instead of togas!" Trousers in the Senate house! The end of the world has come!"

"That's absurd," said Caesar. "Here they will put on togas, regardless of what they wear at home."

The men heaving the statue up the steps were groaning, and I could see the figure sliding slightly on its platform. But they were almost to the top.

"Come," said Antony. "You don't plan to watch it being put on its pedestal? Let's go have some fun. I know a place—"

Caesar gave a mock moan. "No plays. No chariot races."

"I know," said Antony. "Let's go to the athletic field and have a race. As we used to. Do you remember?" He leaned over and put his arm around Caesar's shoulder.

"Yes, I remember," said Caesar. "I wonder if I can still beat you."

"Come and see," said Antony. "Come and see. But I warn you—"

Laughing, they descended the steps together, Caesar walking lightly.

I will always remember that day on the steps; it consoles me when I think the world is a sorrowful place. Joy sticks in the memory, bright and burnished, leaping out across the years. It is a thing pure in itself, joy, and the rarest of traits among men.

It was time for the Saturnalia again, that holiday celebrating license. I understood it a little better now; it seemed to have something to do with Saturn, but why that meant everyone should wear the cap of liberty, and slaves and masters change places, and the toga be forbidden, I did not know. People were permitted to say all sorts of things that would normally be out of order, so those seven days made for lively listening.

Houses were opened to friends, and they streamed in, passing from one dwelling to another, exchanging gifts. Those gifts were curious, often one thing disguised as another—candles that looked like food, food that looked like jewelry, plants painted to look like stone carvings. Some of the larger households appointed a master of ceremonies, a *Saturnalicius princeps*, who ordered people to perform—sing, dance, recite poetry. Caesar held open house, allowing people to circulate freely in and out of his doors, and up on the Palatine, Cicero did likewise, as did Antony in Pompey's former palace nearby, and nearly every other Roman with a hand in politics. It was an opportunity to show those Roman virtues of accessibility and generosity— and a way to please the people that was less bloody than the games.

Because Ptolemy had begged to go—he wanted to dress himself as a eunuch and pretend to be Mardian—I agreed to visit a few homes.

"But not all of them!" I warned him. "I won't go house to house. It is not what queens and kings do."

"But we won't be queens and kings. I'm Mardian!"

"How will anyone know who you are supposed to be? No one here knows Mardian, except Caesar. And how can you dress like a eunuch? They dress like anyone else." I hated to deflate him, but the truth was the truth.

"I'll speak in a high voice," he said.

"But your voice *is* high," I reminded him. "I think the eunuch idea is . . . too far-fetched. Why don't you be something else, like a pirate or a gladiator? Or a chariot racer? There are lots of slave and freedman roles you can play."

"Is my voice really that high? As high as a eunuch's?" He sounded distressed.

"It hasn't changed yet," I said. "Perhaps by this time next year . . ." I sighed. I hoped he was not going to worry about it. There was enough to worry about in his persistent cough. "Now, what can I be? Not a queen . . . I won't be a serving girl, it's too expected. . . . I suppose I could be a gladiator myself . . . that is, unless you want to be."

"Oh, no, *you* be the gladiator," he said quickly. "But are women gladiators?"

"I think I have heard of some," I said. But had I? Perhaps it was my imagination.

"What sort of sword will you carry? Do you want a net and trident?" he asked.

"I don't know," I said. "I think that Decimus, Caesar's favorite general, has a school of gladiators. I'm sure he'll provide me a costume. But I think a net and trident would be awkward in the crowds, don't you?"

"It would be fun to accidentally poke some people—like Cicero! Or that Fulvia!"

"Cicero would likely cry, and then compose an essay about it," I said. "And Fulvia—she probably carries a trident herself at all times, well sharpened. I wouldn't want to give her the excuse of using it."

The short winter's day was already growing dim by the time we entered Caesar's doors. His atrium, his dining room, his garden were packed with people, most with the cap of liberty, denoting freed slaves, perched on their heads. The din was overwhelming.

I clutched Ptolemy's hand in one of mine, and Charmian's in the other. On this holiday the slaves, servants, and masters all mingled together, and the masters had to serve the slaves.

My gladiator's costume was of the type called Samnite, and I had modified it to make it more modest, since true gladiators wore only a sort of loincloth and shin protectors, as well as a magnificent helmet. I had thought it well to cover my upper body with a breastplate, and my upper limbs with leather lappets. But I did love the helmet—it had a heavy curved rim and ornamentation all over the crown, as well as a decorated visor.

When Decimus had brought the costume in person, I had taken the helmet in both hands and lowered it slowly onto my head. As soon as it was in place, I felt different. I knew then, for the first time, what it would feel like to be a warrior, to step out onto the field. I also knew then that I wanted to do so—I wanted to lead troops, or command a ship. True, I had gathered an army against my brother long ago, but I had not seen any actual fighting. This weighty helmet, this sword in my hand, made my blood sing, taking me by surprise.

"It is kind of you to have brought this for me," I told him, removing the helmet.

"It is my pleasure," he said. "I hope you will find it a good fit. I took it from one of my smallest fighters, a man from Malta. For all their small size, the Maltese are fierce."

I liked this man as much for his gentle manner as for the fact that I knew Caesar was fond of him. Decimus had served him well in two sea battles and in Gaul, and Caesar had disclosed to me that he planned to announce Decimus's appointment as governor of Gaul for the coming year.

"You make a most formidable *gladiatrix*," he said. "But you need an opponent. That is why I brought two costumes—Charmian can be your adversary." He handed her the old-fashioned costume of the Thracian fighter. "We don't have much call for this any longer, but I think it will make a good disguise."

At the time I thought, What a sweet, considerate man!

Now Charmian and I, as the two *gladiatrices*, and Ptolemy, as the chariot racer, wearing the green colors of a champion that appealed to him because it was the shade of the Nile, wove our way through the crowd in Caesar's atrium, looking for faces we could recognize in the dim light.

At first I saw no one and wondered why all crowds looked alike. Then, with relief, I glimpsed Lepidus standing against one wall, munching on a stick of pastry. He was not wearing any costume, which was good, as I never would have recognized him otherwise.

"Hail, brave fighter!" He saluted me, and I removed my helmet to talk to him. He looked surprised when he saw who the gladiator was. "Great Queen!" he said. "What battles do you fight?"

I saw him eyeing my arms and legs appreciatively. I thought it best to remind him of Caesar. "Only those who seem to be Caesar's foes."

He swept his hand over the room. "The house is swarming with them. But Caesar has declared an amnesty for those who will not accept an outright pardon, and they have come running back to Rome. Just think, had Cato, his enemy, lived, even he might be here tonight!"

A group of slaves pushed past us, shouting about gambling. "Bets taken! Dicing about to begin!" they yelled.

"This is the one time when slaves are allowed to gamble," said Lepidus. "Openly, that is." He stepped out of their way.

Then a party of men and women dressed like Gauls paraded through the room posing and crying,

> *Caesar led the Gauls in triumph,*
> *Led them uphill, led them down,*
> *To the Senate house he took them,*
> *Once the glory of our town.*
> *"Pull those breeches off," he shouted,*
> *"Change into a purple gown!"*

At the word "breeches," they all pulled them down. Everyone shrieked. Caesar, at the far end of the atrium, laughed and tossed them a purple gown.

"Cover yourselves!" he shouted.

"So he isn't embarrassed by it," said Lepidus. "Interesting. He's so unpredictable. Cato bothers him, and this does not." He looked around. "And I'm surprised there aren't verses about the *libertini* as well." When I did not respond, he explained, "Liberated slaves. Caesar has let their sons into the Senate. It's as if he were appealing to the people, right over the heads of the aristocracy."

The common people, and his legionaries—there lay Caesar's strength. He had harnessed the latter, and now meant to harness the former. A dangerous game.

The heat from the mass of bodies was growing oppressive, the noise level unpleasant. I should seek out Caesar and greet him, but the sight of Calpurnia standing resolutely by his side deterred me. I found myself watching him carefully through the holes of my visor. How did he speak to her? Did she take his hand, or did he take hers first? Why were they still married?

Lepidus bent over and whispered in my ear, "There's to be a motion put before the Senate to allow Caesar to marry more than one wife."

"What?" There was no society that permitted that, to my knowledge. Men had legal concubines, yes; but more than one true, equal wife, no.

"I have heard it from reliable sources," Lepidus said. "It would enable Caesar to beget legal heirs, since Calpurnia is barren. There are several hereditary honors granted to Caesar that he cannot pass on—the title of Imperator, and the office of Pontifex Maximus—owing to his lack of an heir."

"Then let him divorce Calpurnia!" I said. "Everyone seems to be divorcing everyone else in Rome." I had lately heard that Cicero's marriage to the nubile Publilia had ended in divorce—hardly a surprise.

"It seems"—Lepidus hesitated—"he does not wish to."

Yes. Evidently that was the case. Or else he would have. But I would never consent to becoming his second wife while he retained the first. I would be the first, the only, the real wife—or not at all. "Whose idea was this?" If Caesar thought that I would ever consent to such a thing—then he did not know me at all. Or else he truly had begun to think himself exempt from the normal rules of decency.

"I cannot imagine that it would have originated anywhere else but—with Caesar himself," said Lepidus. "No one would dare propose it without his knowledge."

What an insult! Suddenly I hated him, standing there so smugly with his Calpurnia hanging on his arm, surveying all his guests, including the ones he had magnanimously pardoned, whether they would have it or not.

"Come, Charmian!" I said. "Ptolemy! I find that I would prefer the hospitality of Cicero. Yes, even the hospitality of Cicero!" I grabbed their hands.

"But we just got here!" cried Ptolemy.

"It's too crowded," I said. "Cicero's house is grander. Let us go there."

We pushed our way out and into the Forum, where the falling darkness, and the lighted torches, were refreshing after the heat and confusion inside. There were groups of people tramping through, but they were in clumps and much of the pavement was empty.

We turned east and passed by the house of the Vestals, then turned at the site of the Temple of Jupiter Stator and found the road, the Clivus Palatinus, that led in a stately ascent to the Palatine Hill. Torches were planted along the way, and the tall umbrella pines were whispering in the rising breeze. I thought what a soothing place this must be to live, high above the vexations of Rome. The air was delicately perfumed with the pines, and from the winds blowing in from the countryside.

It was not difficult to find Cicero's mansion, which was famous as much for its size and site as for the fact that Cicero's political enemy Clodius had

had it demolished, and Cicero had rebuilt it grander than ever in revenge. Lights shone from every window, and the well-clipped hedges around it seemed as ordered as Cicero's polished writings. The house reflected the man—but then, does it not always?

Show me a man's wife, a man's house, and a man's servants, let me observe them carefully, and I will tell you everything about him, my tutor had once pronounced. I think he was right.

We entered the spacious atrium, with its large *impluvium* pool of collected rainwater in the center. Immediately I could see how tasteful the murals were, with muted green and black backgrounds, setting off scenes of flower garlands and orchards of fruit trees, so lifelike I felt I could pluck one of the apples.

Instead of the close-pressed mob at Caesar's, discreet groups of people stood about talking. I caught sight of Cicero himself bearing a tray of food and serving guests. I approached him, remembering to remove my helmet.

"Welcome, Your Majesty," he said. "Excuse me just a moment." He proferred a basket of fruit to some people nearby. One of them made a show of taking forever to select a fig.

"It is Tiro, my secretary," said Cicero, when he turned back to me. "He greatly enjoys this turnabout." He offered me the basket as well. I declined.

"What? You will not have an apple, or even a pear? These come from my very own estate in Tusculum. Please! You insult my farming prowess!"

I reached in and took one. "Why is it that you Romans must see yourselves as farmers, even when you are statesmen?" I asked. "It is unique to your country."

"Yes, I know," he said. "No one ever pictures Alexander raising pears, or Pericles tending his rows of beans. I depart for my country house in two days, and I am counting the hours."

"If I were to have a country estate in Egypt—nay, I cannot imagine it!"

"You are a creature of the city," said Cicero. "Of course, what a city! Alexandria, dazzling in white marble! I have longed to enter the Library and wander among the scrolls. What treasures there must be, lying unsung in the niches!"

"We are proud to have the finest library in the world," I said. "But Caesar plans to build a similar one here in Rome."

He smiled diffidently. "Yes, but I am already an old man," he said. "I fear I shall never be able to take advantage of it."

Just then I saw a knot of men I recognized well: Brutus, Cassius, and Casca. They hung together as if they were roped. Brutus had a woman with him I had never seen before. It must be his new wife, Porcia. Beside her was Servilia.

I felt a flare of jealousy in looking at Servilia. I suppose Caesar would make her one of his auxiliary wives as well! I thought. After all, he should take a number, or the special privilege would be worth little!

Cicero had been talking, and I had missed most of his words. They ended, ". . . if you might consider it."

"I beg your pardon," I said. "Would you repeat that?"

"I was asking if it might be possible for me to borrow the manuscript you have of the *Iliad*, and I was interested in some of Sappho's poems. I understand there are fragments of her writings found nowhere save in your archives."

His keen eyes, surrounded by wrinkles, were eager. I wished I could oblige him.

"I am sorry," I said, "but it is strictly forbidden to remove any scrolls from the Library."

His expression changed instantly. "Surely you could give the order."

"No. Even I am not permitted to remove any. But I could have copies made."

"So you don't trust me!" he said. "Copies!"

"I told you, it is our rule—"

"Are you not an absolute ruler? Could you not command their removal?"

"It would not be right," I said. "I cannot order it just on a personal whim."

"You would be quick enough to remove them if Caesar asked!" he said coldly.

"A copy should suffice," I said. "That way you could keep it for your own library. With all the shipwrecks, surely you can appreciate that we cannot trust our manuscripts to the high seas."

His smile and genial manner had drained away. "I see."

"Is this a test of some sort? For it makes no sense otherwise," I said. "I have told you I would be pleased to make copies of whatever you request."

"Never mind," he said. "Don't trouble yourself!"

To my amazement, he turned his back on me and walked away.

In all my life, no one had ever done that. But this was Rome, and the Saturnalia was a time of license. Masters served their slaves, and hosts turned their backs on guest queens.

"Come," I said to Ptolemy and Charmian. "I think we should move on."

"But we just got here!" he repeated. "Why do you keep doing this?"

The only other house I knew to seek out was Antony's. It, too, was famous, because he had seized it from Pompey's forfeited estate and lived riotously in it, letting its contents be stripped away by gamblers and freeloaders. They said that slaves had won the purple bedspreads of Pompey, spreading them out on their pallets, and that all the furniture had been carried out on the shoulders of victorious dicers.

It, too, was not difficult to find. It stood, a big jutting mansion, in the area called the Carinae, a short walk from Cicero's. It was not as well situated, being on a spur of land trailing off from the Palatine, but it was still well above the level of the Forum.

The lights were blazing. By this time it was thoroughly dark, and the golden fire of torches was the only illumination in the city.

Loud noise poured out the main entrance. I stood, pushing my helmet down and clutching my shield. Suddenly I was tired. I was doing this for Ptolemy. My first two choices of houses had not offered him much. Surely this one would be better. I squared my shoulders and walked in.

A blast of noise and heat almost knocked me backward. It was like a market day combined with a chariot race. A vast throng milled inside, some dancing, others eating, all drinking.

"Come!" I said. "Let us fight our way in!" I raised my shield and began wielding my sword, brandishing it right and left. I loved the way it felt. People scattered. Oh, the joys of warriorhood! Homer was right.

Behind me, Charmian was doing likewise, and Ptolemy yelled, "Onward, onward!" and cracked his whip. I knew then that I should have provided him with a mock chariot and steeds. It would have made a more imposing entrance, and allowed him to pretend better.

The crowd, blurred with drinking, fell back with good nature. My sword flashed. I planted my feet in fighting stance. All were looking.

At last I was where I felt at ease. These people were not judgmental, they merely wanted entertainment—in some respects, the most demanding request of all. But they cared not who provided it—in their incessant desire for diversion, they were the true democrats. Queen, slave, freedman—can you make us laugh?

I could not see out the side of my helmet. Suddenly Antony was beside me.

"Who goes there?" he asked. "Fierce warriors invade my home."

As with Lepidus, I saw him assessing my limbs and realizing this was no man. I plucked off my helmet and had the gratification of seeing his shock.

"Your Majesty," he stammered. "I—this is an honor!"

"You have a house it is easy to enter," I said. "I mean that as the highest compliment."

"I hope burglars do not feel the same." He laughed. "But then, I have refurnished it once. I can do it again. Only this time, Fulvia may object."

"I meant that one feels at ease here."

"Surely a queen must feel at ease everywhere," he said.

"A queen may go anywhere, it is true," I said. "But feel at ease—or rather, welcome—no."

"Come, let us fill your cups!" He motioned to a server. "My banker tonight must pass trays." Rich wrought-gold goblets were brought forth. "Take one."

I looked at it in marvel. "You allow your guests to use these?"

"Yes, why not?" he said.

"But these are pure gold!"

"Well, what better use for them? Were they not fashioned to hold wine?" He took one and handed it ceremoniously to Ptolemy, and filled it himself.

"This is Caecuban," he said. "Drink as much as you wish!"

Ptolemy turned bright with the implication that he was a full adult.

I looked around. "The costumes are elaborate," I said. Everywhere there were helmets, turbans, shields, capes, high boots. Then I looked carefully at Antony. He was wearing a purple-stained tunic; a wreath of ivy was twined about his dark curls. The tunic, unlike Caesar's, had short sleeves, revealing the muscular bulge of Antony's shoulders and upper arms. "What are you?" I asked.

"Oh, I'm a wine taster," he said. "That's the slave's job that would suit me best."

Suddenly I remembered his knowledge of wine and vineyards long ago, during the festival of Bacchus in Alexandria. "It seems you are a true Dionysus," I said.

"It is merely a hobby," he said. "Despite what my enemies say, it is not my regular occupation."

"And what is that?" I was curious—how did he see himself?

"Why, I am a soldier," he said. "And Caesar's right hand."

"And you have no higher wish?"

He looked genuinely astonished. "What higher wish could there be?"

"To be first in the world, not a lieutenant."

"To be Caesar's lieutenant is to be first in every respect," he said.

<hr>

32

"So you'll have multiple wives?" I said. "Even Jupiter did not! Even though you're to be addressed as 'Julius Jupiter,' that won't be enough! That would limit you to one—Calpurnia, your Juno!"

It was the first time I had been alone with Caesar since the New Year, and I found the proposal to permit him several wives was still causing me to bubble with anger.

"There is no such proposal," he said coldly. "Neither to call me 'Jupiter Julius' nor to allow me more than one wife. O ye gods! My enemies spread the most outlandish lies about me!" He held his arms up toward the heavens, then turned stern eyes upon me. "And that you believed it! That you would think such a thing of me! I can expect little from my enemies, but that you, my—"

"Yes, your what?" Let him answer that!

"My love, my soulmate, my other self."

"But not your wife. You have Calpurnia!"

He turned aside. "This is tiresome."

"For you, perhaps. For me, I would like to know one thing: Why do you stay married to her? Do you love her?"

"To divorce her would give scandal—"

"Scandal has never deterred you. To invite Gauls and *libertini* to the Senate gives scandal."

"How your Latin is improving," he said sarcastically.

"Answer me!"

"I married Calpurnia fourteen years ago," he said. "Her life with me has been one of absences, of separations. Now I am reaping honors. Should she not be allowed to share in them, as a reward for all the privations?"

He sounded so reasonable, so persuasive, as if I were a demanding, selfish shrew.

"You are a queen, with a country bulging with riches. You do not need any of the honors that are coming to me. But she—without me, she is nothing. She has suffered from being my wife, living in the midst of those in Rome who hated me. Is not some reward her due? Would I not seem the most callous of wretches to cast her off now? No one else would ever take her, as she's barren." He was an eloquent pleader. No wonder he was known in Rome as second only to Cicero in his oratory.

"How noble, how self-sacrificing you are," I finally said.

"There is a place for us," he said. "I promise. It is different, grander, more enduring."

"But you never reveal what it is."

"Soon," he said. "Soon. The plan is almost ready."

"And in the meantime, the outsized honors heap up. The Senate spends its hours deliberating what may come next. Let's see—what was it last week? You are to be called *Pater patriae*—father of your country—"

"Yes, your Latin is definitely improving."

"Don't interrupt. Besides that, your image is to be put on coins, and your birth month has finally been renamed Julius—'July.'" I paused. "Oh yes. And you will sit on a gilded chair in the Senate and wear the garb kings formerly wore."

He turned away, as if a little embarrassed.

"Don't be shy!" I taunted him. "There are other honors. Pray tell me! Don't hold back!"

I could see now that I had truly angered him. "I will not be mocked!" he said.

"Nay, tell me." I tried to sound more gentle. "I would know. And I would know what they mean."

"They have proposed that all my decrees, past and present and future, be binding."

"Future? How can they know what they will be?"

"They cannot," he said, "and that is what makes it such a staggering privilege—and responsibility." He paused. "Besides that, my person is to be sacrosanct. When next the Senate meets, they will vow to defend my life. So I will, to show my good faith, dismiss my bodyguards."

"Is that not foolish?"

"They are a nuisance," said Caesar. "This gives me a good pretext for getting rid of them. They have also decided that there must be a college of priests attached to the temple to my Clemency. They will be the *Luperci Julii*."

"All this is grown—monstrous." It seemed alien to the Romans.

Suddenly he laughed. "And I shall appoint Antony my chief priest!"

I was taken aback. "Are you trying to show your disdain for their honors? Will you not insult them and move them to fury?"

"Anger I can stomach," he said. "It is silent hostility and plotting that I cannot counter." He took both my hands in his and looked at me searchingly. "I can answer your anger about Calpurnia," he said. "What I could not endure is your enmity, your grudge." He kissed me tentatively. "I do not have that, do I? I could not live if I did."

He was persuasive; he was compelling; he was overwhelming, as usual. I could not prevail against him in either my anger or my warnings. Would he had not been so compelling; he might have lived.

We had been closeted in his private workroom. His Spanish bodyguards—soon to be dismissed, he had said—were outside and in the main atrium.

"I have an appointment," he said, glancing out the window to see where the sun was. "I must be at the Julian Forum at the ninth hour to meet with some senators." He sounded wary. "They requested it. Come with me."

"I hardly think they would wish me to be present."

"Is not the Forum a public place? *They* are the ones who requested that we meet there, instead of in the Senate house." He grabbed his toga and began putting it on, impatiently. "At least walk there with me. Have you seen your statue since I put the pearl earrings on her?"

"No," I said. "It is always so crowded in there, with so many people looking, that I do not frequent it. Still, I shall walk with you."

"Good." He swung a cloak over his shoulder in case the weather should turn nasty. Together we left the house. A contingent of the guards followed us, marching briskly.

I had to admit that gray skies and leafless trees became the Forum. The travertine stone, the marble, all varying shades of gray or pearly white, seemed enhanced by having a frame of the same color. Even our breaths, as we walked, made little clouds of the same opal white.

The newer stone of the Julian Forum made it seem illuminated, it was so much brighter than anything around it. The building had been completed, and now the mounted statue of Caesar was in place before the temple, as was a fountain—running very slowly now in the cold.

Caesar paced around, waiting, his feet making quick, impatient steps. No one was approaching, and he began to grow cross. Then he saw them—a group of ten or so magistrates, walking slowly toward him, their togas lifting in the wind.

"I will go inside," I said, leaving him. I climbed the steps up to the temple and stood in the shadows of a column, watching.

I saw Caesar sit down and take out a letter and begin to read it, not looking up until they were quite near. Then he seemed to greet them pleasantly enough. There was a great deal of bowing, of flourishes, of speeches, and then, finally, something was presented to him. He took it and unrolled it, then smiled and extended his hand. The men milled about, doing a sort of slow-motion dance around Caesar's bench, but he was still sitting. Why did he not rise?

I could tell by the expressions of the men, and by the way they moved back, that they had heard something they did not like. They fawned some more before taking their leave, walking in single file back across the courtyard and out into the old Forum. Caesar sat watching them go, then he closed his eyes and seemed to be clenching his jaw.

I waited until I was sure the men would not return, then I stole over to Caesar, who was still sitting on the bench, his face drained of color and his whole body rigid. Wordlessly he thrust the scroll into my hand. I unrolled it and read the words: DICTATOR FOR LIFE. The rest, in tiny Latin words, I could not decipher.

"What is this?" I asked.

But he gave no answer, and when I saw his face I understood what had happened.

"Can you walk home?" I asked him. "You can lean on me. We will go slowly."

He had felt an impending attack of his illness, and had been forced to dissemble before the senators.

He stood up stiffly and, under the masking cloak, put his arm around my shoulders. Together we traversed the short distance across the old Forum back to his home; I was thankful that the cold weather meant the usual throng of businessmen, vendors, and shoppers was missing.

As soon as we were back inside his house, he tumbled onto his bed and shut his eyes. "I think it will pass. I do not think it will develop further," he said, through gritted teeth.

I wet the hem of my gown in his washing bowl and used it to wipe his brow. I must confess I felt a certain triumphant relief that Calpurnia was not there.

He remained motionless on the bed for what seemed almost an hour. Then he turned over and sighed. "I think it is safe now. It is going."

"I thought you said you had conquered the illness."

"I have. I do not let it get control." His voice was still weak. "In Spain—it was the same once. Just before a battle. But I never fall anymore."

"No, because you sit down first," I said with a smile.

"You witnessed what it used to be. Sitting down was not a cure." He carefully sat up. "There. The room is still. My limbs obey. And I never lost consciousness." He sounded very relieved.

"The men—what was all that about?"

It was then that he revealed just how ill, momentarily, he had been. He had to reach for the scroll and read it before he could answer.

"The Senate has made me Dictator for life," he said haltingly, each word being led forth like a sacrificial animal. "This is impossible." Obviously he had no clear recollection of exactly what the men had said when they presented it, any restrictions they had mentioned. He shook his head. "A dictator is appointed for a temporary term only. A dictator is an office outside the regular offices of state—Consul, praeter, censor, tribune. It is not a normal part of the government, because the dictator's power supersedes all those other offices. Dictator for life . . . that's another word for 'king.' For what is a king but a dictator for life?" He was thinking out loud. "This cannot be."

"But"—I pointed to the scroll—"there it is, in writing."

"It must be a trick. Was I meant to refuse it? Perhaps that was what it was." He shook his head again. "But I do not remember what I said."

"You did not refuse it, of that I am sure."

"How do you know?"

"The men looked displeased. Perhaps you did not accept it with enough pleasure."

"Pleasure was not what I was feeling—dizziness and stiffness was."

"But *they* do not know that," I reminded him. "Here." I put some pillows behind him so that he could lean back comfortably. "Tomorrow, when you are fully recovered, you will have to attend the Senate. Thank them profusely for the great honor. That is, if you intend to accept it. You always could refuse, you know." I dangled the decision before him. "You could say that you wrestled with your conscience all night and realized, for the good of Rome, you must decline it."

"But the truth is, for the good of Rome, I must accept it." His voice was stronger now, but quiet. "It is for my *own* good that I should refuse it."

"You have never yet refused anything that fate has awarded you," I said. "That is the essence of your character."

The next day all of Rome was buzzing about the unspeakable arrogance and insolence of Caesar in refusing to rise when the senators came to him with this great honor. They castigated him for overweening pride, and since only the truth about his illness would have exonerated him, and he refused to divulge it, he had to bear the full weight of the accusations. One other way lay open to him—to decline the honor. But as I had known, had he been able to do that, he would not have been Caesar.

The next incident happened when he was returning from a ceremony outside the city; a throng of bystanders hailed him as king. (I wondered then, and I still wonder—were they planted there by his enemies, in hopes of deluding Caesar, making him believe there was a popular movement to make him king?) He replied, "I am not king but Caesar." Then all Rome buzzed about that.

It was not long until an invisible hand placed a diadem on Caesar's statue on the Rostra, and one of the tribunes of the people had it removed. Caesar ordered the diadem to be dedicated to Jupiter, Rome's only ruler. Still, Rome buzzed. Under whose orders were these things taking place—Caesar's, his enemies', or were they true indications of popular sentiment?

I had an idea for taking the initiative out of the invisible hands, which I knew were not Caesar's. Let Caesar stage a show of his own to proclaim his intentions. I called a secret meeting at my villa at night to discuss it, and bade not only Caesar but Lepidus and Antony to come. Antony was necessary to the plot, as he was indeed now the priest of the Julian *luperci* as Caesar had joked—or threatened—earlier. And Antony, as Consul, would have a part in a certain ceremony due to be enacted soon. Lepidus was Caesar's Master of the Horse, the second-in-command to a dictator, and I knew he was loyal to Caesar. Beyond Antony and Lepidus, I could not be sure of anyone else.

It had been dark for several hours, and all the lamps refilled once, before Caesar arrived as the first guest. He shook the evening damp from his cloak and handed it to a servant before turning to me and saying, "A clandestine meeting after hours makes me feel like a conspirator."

"That is just what we are," I said. "Conspirators against your conspirators—whoever they may be."

It was a cold night, and the winds managed to find their way in through the windows and doors, rattling the lamp stands, making their suspended lamps sway, throwing wavering shadows on the painted walls. Upstairs I could hear Ptolemy's fitful coughing.

I was wearing closed shoes, and yet the chill of the floor managed to creep through the soles and into my feet. Until this winter in Rome, I had not appreciated just how very cold marble could be.

"Come," I said, leading him into a small chamber that I had already heated with a brazier.

"I have become truly a guest in my own house," he said. "You have lived here so long now, it seems as if it was always yours."

"It does not feel like home," I admitted. "And soon—"

"Yes, yes, I know. We will speak of it later," he said. "I have plans that I think will please you in that regard."

Before he could say anything further, I heard Lepidus arrive. The servants ushered him in. He appeared puzzled. "Greetings, fair Queen. I am about to die of curiosity." He looked at Caesar.

"Nay, it is not my doing," said Caesar. "I am as much in the dark as you."

Lepidus stood over the glowing brazier and rubbed his hands vigorously. "I hope it does not involve spending time outdoors," he said with a smile.

Then Antony arrived, and seemed mildly surprised that he was last. "It was a challenge getting away from Fulvia," he said. "I could not tell her this was anything political, for then she would have insisted on coming. Nor could I pretend it was a pleasure excursion, or she would have barred me from going."

"Has she tamed you that thoroughly, Antony?" asked Lepidus.

"Well, you have got away, no matter how you managed it," I said. "Pray, sit down." The three of them had been standing practically at attention in the center of the room. "I have made sure the couches are comfortable." I managed to look at Caesar; I wanted him to think of the pillows and carpets upstairs.

Obviously cautious, they took their places with care on the couches—wooden-legged ones with extra cushions and pillows to soften their austerity. They all stared at me, blank-faced, waiting.

"Tell me about this upcoming Lupercalia festival," I said, taking a seat on a straight-backed chair across from them.

I could see what they were thinking: Had I invited them, the three most powerful men in Rome, to teach me about folk festivals? Finally Antony said, "It is an ancient ceremony—only the gods know how long it's been celebrated. It has to do with fertility. The priests of the various colleges take strips from the hides of sacrificed animals and run through the streets whipping people with them. It's a boisterous, rowdy festival."

"What he has forgotten to say is that the priests have to run through the streets half-naked, and it's the women who wish to conceive that crave the touch of the strips, which are called *februa*. It's a bloody, messy business," said Lepidus. "Not my favorite holiday."

"If I remember last year, it's wildly popular," I said. "Everyone turns out to see it. And you, Caesar—won't you be on the Rostra observing it? Isn't that your station?"

"Oh yes," said Antony. "He's required to preside over it, sitting in his golden chair, wearing his Triumphal robes."

"Then everyone will be looking at you?" I asked Caesar directly.

"I am not the center of the festival, if that is what you mean," he said, shifting on his elbows.

"But the priests have to run to him; he is their destination," said Antony. "They dash through all the streets of Rome to end up at the Rostra."

"You mean that's what *you* are going to do," said Lepidus. "You are one of the priests now."

"But you are also a Consul," said Caesar, and I heard that note of disapproval in his voice. "The dignity of a Consul may not permit the hijinks of a priest of the Lupercalia."

"It is you who created this conflict," I said to Caesar, startling him, "when you appointed him to two contradictory offices."

He glared at me. I had never chided him in public, and it was clear he did not like it. "What is the point of all this?" he said coldly.

I realized then how odd it must seem to them to be summoned by a woman. Roman women were at home quietly minding their business or else doing what wives were known to do in joke and song: boss, nag, forbid. As a foreign queen I was the only woman who was their equal and had the power to summon them, question them, and advise them on matters other than domestic details. I thought that a pity; there should be others.

"Just this," I said, rising to my feet. "It is time that you made your kingly intentions—or lack of them—absolutely clear, and before a large audience. What better time than the Lupercalia? You will even be on a stage, elevated, where everyone can see you. So seize the initiative and shout your message where everyone can hear."

"What message?" asked Caesar. He swung his feet around and sat up, leaning on his knuckles.

"That is for you to decide," I said. "But I would assume you would wish to reassure the people that you are not trying to become a king." I paused. "Haven't you had enough of these staged slurs—people shouting titles at you, anonymous hands placing crowns on statues, invisible people writing Republican slogans on Brutus's praetor chair?"

He sighed. "Oh, I've had enough of it, all right," he said.

"Then end it! One of you—Antony, or Lepidus—should offer him the crown right on the Rostra at the Lupercal, with all Rome looking on. You should do it as ostentatiously and ceremoniously as possible, and you, Caesar, should resolutely refuse it, just as ostentatiously and ceremoniously. Then you should have it recorded in the Temple of Jupiter on the Capitoline Hill that you have refused it."

They sat silent for a moment, but I could see Caesar's only quarrel with it was that he had not thought of it first.

"Very clever," he finally said. "Yes. It would be an answer to the problem."

"Providing this is the answer you seek," I said. "You should look into your heart and make sure."

His eyes flared, and I knew I had gone too far. I should have asked that question privately. But it needed to be answered now, so that Antony and Lepidus could be assigned their parts.

"Well," he said, "I am sure. I will not be king in Rome, nor would I wish to be."

Was it only I who caught the distinction—*in* Rome rather than *of* Rome? "Then you will agree to the plan? Antony will offer you the crown and you will refuse it? Or Lepidus?"

"I will offer it," said Antony. "I am already known as someone given to playacting and theatrics, whereas you, Lepidus, are less demonstrative."

"Then perhaps I ought to be the one," said Lepidus. "People would take it more seriously."

"No, it would be more believable as a spontaneous action if Antony did it," said Caesar. "He is known for whims and outbursts, whereas you are much more of a planner. We don't want people to think we planned it."

"The people are one thing," said Antony. "But who do you think is in back of the other gestures? They were no more spontaneous than this one will be."

"I don't know," said Caesar slowly. "Of course the diehard aristocrats, those known as the *optimates*, wish to regain all their lost power. But which ones? I have tried to offer them places in the government—I've made both Brutus and Cassius praetors, and other former followers of Pompey I've pardoned are all underfoot and seemingly reconciled—but I cannot read their minds. I sense more than I can prove. Day after day they gather around me, pleasant enough, but when they meet privately, as we are doing, what do they say?"

"We should place spies among them!" said Antony.

"Then I would truly be what they whisper—a tyrant. A ruler with secret police, spies, and suspicion. Nay, I would rather die at their hands than be what they imagine me to be."

"Don't say that!" I said sternly. "A good spy system has saved many a good man."

"How eastern!" said Caesar. "Sometimes I forget where you come from, my little Ptolemy, my child of the Nile. But it doesn't transplant well here."

A servant stole into the room to refill the lamps with olive oil. She stood on tiptoe and poured the gold-green oil, with its pungent scent, into the lamps from a narrow-spouted pitcher. Was this a spy? Had she been listening? How easy it was to become obsessed with suspicion. Perhaps Caesar was right.

We all waited silently until she was finished, then, after she left, burst into nervous laughter.

"Then it is decided?" I finally spoke. "When is Lupercalia?"

"In fourteen days," said Antony. "The fifteenth day of February. Why, the month is named after the whipping strips!" he said, as if just realizing it.

"Not long, then," said Lepidus. "Not long."

After Antony and Lepidus had left, stealing away into the cold darkness, Caesar hesitated. He took a long time to draw on his cloak, and stood in the room studying the murals as if he had never seen them before. There was one, of a deep-green background showing a ship and harbor, with a fantastic rocky promontory. The waves of the harbor were tipped with whitecaps, and the sails billowed.

"Surely this vista is not new to you," I said. "You must have chosen it and seen it many times." I leaned up against him—the first personal gesture I had permitted myself that night.

"Oh yes," he said. "But it looks different tonight. It depicts a world fresh and clean." He allowed himself to put his arm around me. "I am weary of ugly city things—of whispered rumors, feigned emotions, crooked elections, anonymous scribbled slogans. Now I join them with this staged demonstration." Before I could defend my idea, he added, "But I am realistic enough to know it is a good plan. You have more than a touch of political genius, and I am ofttimes in awe of it. You have much to teach me. And you shall have the opportunity. Soon."

"What is it you keep alluding to?" I said. "Pray, disclose it to me."

"Not until after Lupercalia. Then I will tell you the plan in its entirety. First we must enact yours. Sleep well, my queen." Kissing me lightly, he turned to depart.

"You enjoy keeping it from me," I said. "It gives you power over me."

"No," he said. "Not over you, but over my enemies. It is best for now that no one know but me."

With his quick footsteps, he was gone out into the night, swirled into darkness.

After he had gone, I climbed the steps to my chamber, my limbs weary. It was so late; what upside-down hours plotters had to keep! I wondered who else was awake in Rome tonight, meeting in someone's home, whispering? There was a fog in the air, and the waning moon, worn like a detached marble statue's head, was just clearing the tops of the pines. Anyone leaving a dwelling now would have to mask himself against the searching moonlight.

I listened outside Ptolemy's chamber. He had fallen asleep, but I could hear an occasional feeble cough. As soon as the seas were safe for sailing, we would have to leave. Rome was very bad for his health.

I entered my own chamber, where I had left a lamp burning. It threw flickering shadows; it had exhausted its oil and was about to go out. Caesarion still shared the chamber suite with me, and was sleeping serenely in his little bed with its ebony inlays depicting panthers and elephants. I watched his face and felt, as always, that leap of joy and possession, as he was both me and not-me. He was two and half years old now, no longer a baby but a child, running about on sturdy feet and beginning to speak—Latin. It was his first tongue. If we did not return soon, he would know Greek and Egyptian only as foreign languages.

I knelt and brushed his hair, light and feathery. My dear child, I thought. May Isis always have you in her keeping.

I disrobed and changed into my sleeping garments. It was too late to call Charmian to assist me. I slid into place on the narrow couch-bed and pulled the wool blankets up around my shoulders, shivering until the space around me grew warm under the covers.

Cold. Cold. Rome is cold, and one shivers here, I thought. Strange that I have been here so long and it still feels alien. It is not just the climate, but the way of life. So constrained. So watchful. So rehearsed.

Well, I told myself, perhaps that is just in the higher circles of power. Certainly the common people are none of those things, but the opposite: explosive, indulgent, loud, and hungry. All you have to do is watch them in the Forum, in the streets, at the games, to know that.

A sharp pang in my breast, as I thought of the brown banks of the Nile and its palms, told me I was homesick. It was just that simple. I ached to return to Egypt.

I turned on my hard, narrow bed. Why, even our beds in Upper Egypt are more comfortable than this! I thought. Yes, I must leave. I cannot fathom what plan Caesar has for us. Clearly there is no place for me in Rome, where I can never participate in the government or appear publicly by Caesar's side.

There is nothing for us, nothing for us. . . .

I heard Caesarion give a cry as he chased a dream, and then he turned in his bed.

Only this child, I thought, but he can have no place in Rome.

February fifteenth, the day of the Lupercalia, was clear and frosty. It was cold in the villa, but I knew that across the Tiber in the Roman streets the body heat of the crowds would more than offset it. People had been readying themselves for this wild festival for days, and long before dawn they lined the streets, warming their hands before smoking heaps of coals, stuffing their mouths with cheese and goat meat from the food stalls, and singing off tune with the street musicians.

I had no intention of setting out before late morning. I knew that the ceremony of sacrificing the goat and dog, symbols of Pan and Lupercus, would not be over until then, and the priests, with their bloody strips, would not issue forth earlier. But Ptolemy and I were carried into the Forum in good time, and we took our places on the steps of the Temple of Saturn overlooking the Rostra, along with the dignitaries of Rome who were permitted into the temple's precincts—a guarded area because the state treasury was kept there. Out of the corner of my eye I saw some of the very people we had discussed earlier: returned exiled members of Pompey's party, senators that I recognized but could not name, and others I knew, like Brutus and the two Casca brothers and Trebonius and Tillius Cimber. I smiled and nodded at Decimus and his cousin Brutus, standing a little lower down.

Below us the Forum was a knotted sea of bodies. Caesar was sitting calmly on his golden chair on the Rostra, wearing his purple *Triumphator*'s robes, his laurel wreath curling around his head. On each end of the platform stood the two statues of Caesar, as if they were guarding and duplicating him. I thought of our Egyptian *ba* and *ka* depictions in tombs, which are supposed to incorporate the difference essences of the soul, and thought how similar it was.

A shout arose; the *luperci* were on their way, running and prancing. The crowd parted, and wild, half-naked men leapt into view, cracking their bloody strips. They darted about nimbly like Pan himself, as if their feet were hooves and their thighs haunches. The women ducked and shrieked, but some bowed their bare shoulders to receive the blows.

There was Antony among them, clad only in a goatskin loincloth, his shoulders and torso smeared with blood from the sacrifices and the flayed hides. He glistened all over with sweat, but betrayed no other evidence of exertion.

"A Consul of Rome!" I heard the loud, whistling pronouncement of disapproval from someone below me—Decimus? Trebonius?

"O ye gods!" muttered someone else.

But I thought what a splendor there was about Antony that day—not only in his courage in appearing thus in public but also in his very physique itself, glowing with health and strength, unashamed, like a Greek athlete of long ago. It was something the Romans could never fully comprehend, the glory and beauty of it, and so they murmured and condemned. The world of togas could never respect the Greek exaltation of the human body.

Now he was approaching the Rostra, now he detached himself from his fellow *luperci* and leapt, with one graceful bound, onto the platform. In his hand was clutched a royal white diadem. Where had he got it? Had Lepidus, stationed nearby, handed it to him?

"Caesar!" he shouted. "I offer unto you this diadem. The people wish you to take it and be their king!"

His perfect forearm, straight and strong, thrust the diadem toward Caesar. It trembled in the clear air, its whiteness making it shimmer a little.

Caesar looked at it as if he were eyeing a snake, something dangerous that was about to strike.

"Nay," he said, pushing it aside.

A loud cheer went up, almost balanced by a loud groan of disappointment.

Antony stepped closer to Caesar. "Once again the people offer this!" he proclaimed.

Again Caesar put up the palm of his hand and turned it away.

This time the cheers were louder, and the cries of disappointment softer.

Antony held the diadem aloft and brandished it—he turned from one end of the Rostra to the other, passing it before the eyes of the crowd. "Behold!" he said loudly. "For the third time we offer this. Do not refuse the wishes of the people!" He stepped boldly up to Caesar and attempted to remove the laurel wreath and replace it with the diadem. For an instant his hand hovered over Caesar's head.

Then Caesar stood up. "No," he said, seizing Antony's hand, making him release the diadem.

A deafening roar of approval went up from the crowd.

Caesar waved the diadem. "Jupiter alone is King of the Romans!" he said. "Pray, take this and crown the statue of Jupiter in his temple on the Capitoline!"

Wild shouts of approval exploded from the crowd, roaring now with excitement. Caesar took his seat again with deliberate movements; Antony jumped off the Rostra and ran toward the steps leading to Jupiter's temple, bounding up them like a mountain cat, waving the diadem.

Below me, I saw the heads turning among the dignitaries, as they whispered to their neighbors. They had witnessed what we had meant them to; had they believed it?

33

Alone that night, I received a message from Lepidus saying that from what he had observed, the thing (he did not identify it any further) had been well received. I hoped he was right, but only over the next few days would the truth unfold. Still later, near midnight, a message arrived from Caesar, saying simply, *I can do no more. Let it be*.

I folded the letter and tried to imagine what he had meant. Perhaps it was just another way of saying, as he had said long before at the Rubicon, *Let the dice fly high*. Things would have to take their course now; they would be what they must be.

Watching it all had drained me. I had not realized how every muscle had strained, how I had almost held my breath throughout, and how intensely I had focused my mind, willing every onlooker to believe what I desired them to believe. Now I was wrung out, and in solitude I poured myself a portion of sweet wine. It would dull my racing thoughts, I hoped, and soon I lay down on the straight, hard bed and closed my eyes.

One day passed; two, three. In the villa on its hill high above Rome, I was shielded from what was being said in the streets and in the Senate. I remained where I was, waiting, but also beginning to make plans for my departure from Rome. Soon the seas would open again and we could make our way home.

A few brave ships had been able to carry dispatches back and forth, and all was apparently quiet and in order in Egypt—one of the blessings of leaving good ministers in charge. But I was anxious to take the reins in hand myself; it is not good for a ruler to have prolonged absences, as I knew all too well from Father's experience as well as my own.

Walking along the straight paths of the vast garden surrounding the villa, I said farewell in my mind to the statues I had come to know so well, hiding themselves among the green clipped hedges and presiding over still ponds. Here was an Aphrodite shielding herself after bathing, here an athlete, bending, straining to throw the discus, there a fleet-footed Mercury, heels aloft. At the end of one avenue of green-black cypresses, there was even a Hercules, his luxuriant curly hair making a halo around his head, the lionskin deftly knotted so that the animal's paws crossed right over Hercules' breast, the wide club resting jauntily on his shoulder. Now that I knew Antony better, I no longer thought he resembled Hercules that much. Probably that would not please Antony.

I had grown fond of these shady walks; Caesarion had learned to run in this garden, and had a few baby scars from his falls on the rocks here. It had become part of us, and when I returned to Egypt I knew that some nights I would lie in bed and see it all in my mind. I shut my eyes now and breathed in deeply. It smelled like the change of seasons—a sharp sort of dried-mushroom smell.

Odd how quickly the seasons could change; the Lupercalia had been frosty, and now, only a fortnight later, the locked earth seemed to be melting. Persephone had been released from the underworld earlier than usual, and warmth was flooding back into the land.

As I opened my eyes I saw a messenger coming toward me, glistening a little from his exertion coming up the hill. He handed me a note from Caesar and then stood waiting.

Caesar was of a mind to take a long ride about the countryside on horseback. He would be most pleased if I would join him, he said, and he would allow me to select any horse I chose from his stable, where he would await me.

Well! So Caesar could not bear the city any longer, and must escape. It was a perfect day, with the scraps of winter being chased away by high, raking clouds. And I would never refuse an opportunity to see him apart from others; it was very rare, at least during daylight hours.

At the stable I found Caesar already holding the bridle of his horse, an animal of extraordinary size, and smoothing his gleaming hide.

"So this is your famous charger," I said, approaching him. As I came closer, I saw that there were white hairs mixed in with the black; the horse, though in good health, was old.

"Yes," said Caesar. "He is the one who wanted to run today. His war days are over, but who can resist racing on a spring day?"

"Where has he gone with you?"

Caesar laughed. "Where has he not? He was foaled on my private estate almost twenty years ago, and has been with me in Gaul, in Africa, in Spain. There was a prophecy about me, through him—but more of that later." He handed the reins to a stableboy and steered me toward the ring. "Choose any of these," he said, pointing toward a group of alert, well-conformed horses, mainly duns and browns. "They are all fleet of foot, and my horse is not so fast anymore."

I particularly liked a young gelding with trim, firm legs and a large chest. His golden brown hide looked like flecked amber, and his precise, high-stepping movements made me think he would be a challenge to ride. "That one," I said, pointing at him, and Caesar nodded to a stablehand to make him ready.

"What is his name?" I asked.

"Yours is Barricade—because he leaps over them. And mine is Odysseus, for all his battles and travels."

"And is he now retired? Back in Ithaca to stay?"

"As retired as a warrior can ever be," said Caesar.

It did not take long to leave Rome behind. For all its near-million inhabitants, it does not cover a very large area; not all of the seven hills have buildings, and soon after leaving the Capena gate in the city walls, we were in the open countryside. We had left the Via Appia after a very short distance, and gone eastward across the still-sleeping fields. They wore their winter-brown coats, but already farmers were plowing the earth, leaving furrows of blackish soil upturned to the sun. Overhead hawks soared, surveying us as we galloped across the fields, our shadows running under us.

I had heard what a superb horseman Caesar was, but I had never seen him riding fast.

"Hands behind your back," I cried. "I don't believe you can do it." This was a feat for which he was renowned—staying on a galloping horse with no bridle to direct it, no reins to hold, and no arms to balance himself.

With a smile, as if he hated to have to bother, he dropped the reins and folded his arms behind his back, urging Odysseus to run faster by a nudge from his knees. The horse leapt forward—who could have ever suspected he had such reserves?—but Caesar was not even slightly dislodged. He sat straight, his balance perfect, as the animal rose and fell with each long-legged stride. It was as if he were part of the beast himself.

I kicked my own horse after his, but Barricade had trouble catching up. As I held the reins and leaned forward, I made up my mind that someday I would learn Caesar's trick myself.

"Stop!" I cried, as he seemed to disappear into a thicket of trees. Just then a hedge reared up before me, and Barricade excitedly jumped it, almost throwing me off. My face slammed into his mane, and for an instant I could see nothing; then I righted myself and saw that we were passing through a stand of hazels, and that Caesar was already out on the other side, still galloping with his hands behind his back.

Odysseus wanted to run, all right, and so Caesar let him have his way. The enormous spring sky made me think of the boundless ocean, urging us to gallop on and on forever. There were clouds racing in the opposite direction, their tops white and their undersides gray, and the wind blowing my hair was sharp and thin.

I had not ridden like this in years—not since I left my army behind in Ashkelon, and not really since my days west of Alexandria in the desert, when as a desperate child I had sought escape from the palace.

Wordlessly, soundlessly, in a silent world—silent except for the bleating of a few mischievous goats on the hills, and the cawing of crows—we rode on, far apart.

At length I saw what looked like a river, its banks marked by stands of trees, and beyond that, a wooded area with a ruined circular temple halfway up the side of a hill. Caesar had disappeared over the rise, and I followed, emerging over the crest of the hill to find a row of stately poplars lining a brook. Their tall, straight forms were like the caryatids on Greek temples. Caesar had halted beside one and was waiting. He pointedly still had his hands clasped behind his back.

"You can let your hands free now," I said, dismounting. "You have convinced me." There was no need to withhold the admiration he had earned. "You are the best horseman I have ever seen. And I was taught by the desert Arabs, who are practically born on horseback."

He seemed genuinely pleased that I was impressed. "They taught you well," he said. "I would never have believed a woman could ride like a man. You are a very Athena." He patted Barricade's head. "I see you tried to throw her on that hedge," he said. "Better luck on the way home, friend."

"Now, Odysseus, what was that prophecy?" I asked the horse, who looked at me as if he would answer.

"See his divided hooves?" Caesar pointed to them, and indeed, they were oddly cloven. "When he was just a foal, they caught the attention of the augurs, who said that his rider would one day rule the world. Naturally, I made sure I was the first to ride him, and have been the only one so far."

"May I ride him?"

He hesitated a moment, then lifted me up and put me on his back. "Now this alters the prophecy a little," he said.

I rode Odysseus only a little way up and down the riverbanks, but what mattered was that I had ridden him. After all, Persephone had eaten only six seeds.

I dismounted and we tied the horses up. Caesar walked to the side of the little stream, flowing swiftly past. It tumbled and bubbled and laughed in a clear, childish voice. He found a boulder and sat on it, letting his legs hang down. "Come. Sit by me." He held out his hand and pulled me up.

The rock was oddly warm; it must have absorbed the thin sunlight and stored it somehow, magnifying it. I looked up to see Caesar watching me intently.

"I must tell you of my plans," he said. "But I am loath to ruin this clear blue day."

I waited. I knew he would speak.

"I am planning a military venture," he finally said, his eyes straight ahead on the stream, not on me. "I will set out for Parthia, to avenge the defeat of Crassus, to conquer it and add it to our dominions."

I had suspected this. It was the only region yet untouched by Rome, the only area that defied it. It was also valiant and remote, probably unvanquishable. Alexander had taken it. But those were different times.

"When?" was all I said.

"In March. That will allow me the luxury of actually starting a campaign early in the season."

"March!" I cried. March was upon us. "But—it is nearly March now. How can you manage that?"

"I have been planning it for some time," he said. "I already have six legions, with their auxiliaries, ready in Macedonia."

"Where you sent Octavian and Agrippa to wait," I said. "Yes, I was told."

"I will raise another ten legions, and employ a cavalry of ten thousand. This cannot be a makeshift operation; that is what led to our previous defeats there. Crassus had only seven legions and four thousand cavalry."

"I thought it was the Parthian arrows that led to your defeat," I said. Everyone had heard the grisly story of how the Roman legions had been wiped out almost to a man.

"It was the Parthian *supply* of arrows," said Caesar grimly. "Their general,

Surenas, equipped a corps of a thousand camels that carried nothing but replacement arrows for the ten thousand horsemen. Strange no one had ever thought of that before." He gave a bitter laugh. "Did you know that Cassius escaped? He saved himself by deserting and rushing back to Syria, supposedly to defend it."

"The same Cassius who is now praetor?" The fierce Republican who glared whenever he saw us.

"Yes. He is part of the Roman disgrace that must be avenged. The victorious Surenas even staged a hideous parody of a Roman Triumph in the desert, with a mock Crassus dressed in women's clothes. We cannot rest until those eagles from the fallen legions are returned."

"But—now is not the time to leave Rome. There is still so much to be done. Don't leave it in the hands of your enemies!" I could not but question his thinking. "How long do you foresee being gone?"

"I envision three years," he said.

"No! No! I beg you, do not do this!" I gripped his upper arm. The muscles there were still hard and strong, but in three years he would be almost sixty. "It is insane!"

"What is more insane than Rome herself now? Oh, in the years I was away I have outgrown it—outgrown the stifling pettiness, the continual bickering, the lack of any vision or even foresight for the simplest things. The field— out in the field I'll be free again, free to dare, to make decisions, to be obeyed. No one has ever loved me like my soldiers!" he burst out.

"True, if it's love you want, Rome will not grant it," I said. "But must you run away? That makes you just another Cassius!"

He started to say something, then sat silently. From far away I heard the low tinkle of sheep's bells on some hidden hillside.

"What are your military plans?" I finally asked.

"I have to settle a messy business in Macedonia," he said. "And then I will invade Parthia from the north, through Armenia. That route has not been tried; everyone always invades from the west or the south."

He turned to me, took my hand. "You are an essential part of my plan," he said. "While I am in Parthia, you will be in Egypt, my foremost ally. You will be my partner in conquest, for I will rely on Egypt's support and resources for the campaign. Will you agree?" He waited for my answer. "I do not need the support and approval of the Senate and the people of Rome, as long as I have you. Do I have you?"

"Do you have Egypt, do you mean?" Suddenly I was gripped by a horrible suspicion that perhaps he had seen me all along as only an incarnation of Egypt, someone to abet his ambitions and plans. He had not annexed Egypt to Rome because that would have put Egypt at the disposal of the Senate— the last thing he would have wanted. "My country's resources?"

"Yes, of course that is what I mean!" He sounded impatient. "But as my partner." He grasped my hand tighter. "You are a queen; I come before you as your client. If I had a crown and scepter, I would place them at your feet. Please consider my request."

"And what do you foresee for us?"

"A kingdom that you and I can rule together, equally. And that our son can inherit, as sole ruler." Before I could say anything, he continued hurriedly, "You know he can have no inheritance at Rome. But what of it? There are grander things. Let him be King of Egypt and Parthia and all the regions in between. Then I—though not a king myself—will have given rise to kings. That is enough for me."

"You ask an enormous commitment. Egypt is at peace. Parthia has never attacked us. You ask that we spend men and money to chase your dreams."

"Your dreams, too."

"No, that is not my dream."

"Then what *is* your dream?"

"I have achieved it. Egypt at peace, independent, strong. Myself as sole ruler. I have no need of Parthia."

"Have you no need of *me?*" he asked. "For only away from Rome can we have a life together."

"Your price is very high. I must spend heaps of silver and gold, rivers of blood, in order for us to have a life together."

"We cannot reckon in those terms."

"I am afraid it is the only way I can reckon. Oh, I would give anything for you—except Egypt."

He looked at me with subdued respect. "Then you are a better queen than a lover. Your subjects are fortunate."

He climbed down from the rock and walked a little way down the stream. I came and stood beside him.

"I shall be your ally, I will provide a staging area for you, a place to rest, but I do not wish to fight Parthia," I told him. "I shall be the first to rejoice when you have conquered. You may stage the biggest Triumph in the history of the world in Alexandria."

I tried to keep my voice light and happy, when all the while I was seized with the dreadful fear that he would never return. Never, never return from the east, to die like Alexander in the shadow of Babylon. . . . I felt sick.

"Perhaps that is enough," he finally said, hearing only my words and not my thoughts. At length, after many minutes of silence, he reached his hand into the bosom of his tunic and drew out a pouch of leather.

"This is for you," he said, handing it to me.

I opened it slowly and found a silver medallion there, on a small chain. I shook it out into the palm of my hand and turned it over. It had an elephant on one side, and lettering on the other.

"It was my mother's," he said. "The elephant is one of the emblems of the Caesars; an ancestor killed one from the Carthaginian army at a crucial moment. She wore it for my father. I wish you to have it."

I bent my neck while he fastened it.

"She wore it always. I have kept it for years. I loved her dearly; I still miss her every day. She died six years before I came to know you. Please take it. I do not know what else I can give you to show you how precious you are to me, how you alone fill that one place in me left vacant all my life. This is my most guarded, most treasured possession."

As I felt his fingers on my bowed neck, I knew it was an anointing of a kind. Caesar was making me a part of his family in the only way he knew how.

"I am honored," I said, raising my head. I touched the medallion, now hanging near the top of my breasts. It seemed more precious to me than anything of gold, emeralds, lapis. It had protected Caesar's mother, the one woman he had always been true to and respected. Now it passed to me, the mother of his son.

"I told you, you are my very self," he said, and his lips sought mine. They were hungry for me, wishing to unite us. I stood on tiptoe on the banks of the stream and held him tightly.

The horses were standing patiently watching us, not disturbed by the future.

"Will you take Odysseus?" I whispered.

"No, he is too old," said Caesar. "He has earned his rest. And I could not bear to watch him fall in a foreign field."

I feel the same, I thought. Why are you kinder to your horse than I am being to you? Yet I cannot forbid you to go, and withholding Egypt's forces has made no difference to your plans. What else can I do, what other influence bring to bear?

My hands trembled as I stroked his back. Everything about us was open to the air and sky, and it was too early yet for there to be masking leaves on the hedges and branches.

"Come," he said, wading across the stream. "The temple isn't far."

It was the only shelter for miles, and it looked derelict, its path overgrown, its roof partially collapsed. Yet its old marble was a fine white with bluish veins, and its circular shape was graceful.

As we approached it, I saw green lizards darting through the overgrown grass. Whose temple was it, I wondered. We reached the decaying door and looked in; there was a crumbling statue of Venus on a pedestal.

"Venus," he said. "This is extraordinary. Even here, my ancestress provides for my needs."

We stepped inside; it was a sorry sight. Tree roots burrowed in the pavement, causing its black and white marble slabs to buckle, and moss, weeds, and wildflowers sprouted in the chipped wall crevices. The worn goddess tilted on her pedestal and looked at us wistfully. At her feet a brackish pool of water had collected. Light poured in through the broken domed ceiling, making a spot on the far side of the temple.

"Poor goddess," said Caesar slowly. "I hereby vow that when I return from Parthia, I will restore this temple, if only you will grant me victory once more."

The goddess did not indicate that she had heard, and her sightless eyes stared out the door into the open fields.

"It does not look as if anyone comes here," said Caesar. "We are quite alone." He leaned one powerful arm against the wall. Then he turned to me and, putting his head down, began to kiss the hollow of my neck, then to each side of it, and then softly up to my ears.

I turned my head to one side, letting him continue because of the sweet feeling of his mouth on my throat, even in this dispiriting setting. The uneven floor was damp and had lizards and worms crawling on it, and the air was chilly. Yet I moved back and flattened myself against the rough, crumbling wall and let him press himself against me. His lean, hard body against mine made me tremble with expectation. It had been so long since we were together as a man and a woman that I hungered for it, all the more so because I could never predict our times together.

I threw my head back, closing my eyes and giving myself up to the rising sensation of pleasure. He was silent, making no noise at all but the sound of his shoes scuffling a little on the ground. His mouth, hungrier now, was traveling up my cheek and seeking my lips; when he reached them he kissed me so deeply I had trouble breathing.

Then I suddenly knew that this could not be suspended, or even broken off midway, not with my blood galloping faster than my horse had through the fields, pounding in my ears, my throat, my stomach. I gave a groan of fretted longing, and sighed, "This floor is worse than the riverbank."

He took my right leg and lifted it up over his hip, positioned me gently back against the wall and lifted up the other leg, then, putting his arms under my shoulders, whispered into my ear, "I will make sure you never touch the ground." He moved his own body to brace his strong legs and repeated, "No, it is no place for a queen," his voice low and uneven, but then he said no more. He stood and made love to me, looking at my face all the while, and I thought I would die of both the exertion and the pleasure. I longed for the life force of him to infuse me, so thereby I could keep him forever, and while it was happening I felt as if that took place. But all too soon it was over, and we were standing, panting and shaken, in the sad little temple, where the beauty had long since fled.

Our return ride across the fields at sunset was subdued. The sky was streaked with purple—like a *Triumphator*'s robe—and the peculiarly Roman slanted yellow light of late afternoon was splashed everywhere. It glowed with a joyful intensity, bathing Caesar's straight back in gold.

At the gate of the villa there were no farewells. He took the reins of Barricade and said he would return the horses to the stables.

"May you rest well tonight," he said, wheeling away.

But I did not. How could I?

Caesar made his announcement about the Parthian campaign to the Senate, and at the same time revealed that he had filled all the political appointments for three years in advance. For this year, the Consuls were Antony and himself, with himself to be replaced by Dolabella when he departed for the east. For the next year, the Consuls were Hirtius and Pansa; for the year after, Decimus and Pansa. The governors of provinces were to be Decimus for Gaul, to be replaced by Pansa and Brutus thereafter. Trebonius would take Asia and Tillius Cimber, Bithynia. He meant to leave a smooth-running government behind him.

But I wondered whom he meant to employ as his generals? Antony was to be tied down in Rome, Munatius Plancus likewise, and Cassius—a fairly good general in spite of his cowardly record in Parthia—was *praetor peregrinus* in Rome now and could not leave. Surely Caesar did not mean to fight his war with Octavian and Agrippa—those boys! My fears for him mounted.

Yet I continued making ready to leave Rome. At least in Egypt I would be able to help, in a limited fashion. Here I was nothing but a troublesome guest.

His news was not well received. People were horrified that he meant to leave without surrendering his absolute control of the government. For three years decisions would have to be suspended; the ordinary business of life would come to a standstill. All power had been invested in Caesar, and now he was removing himself, with no provisions for a substitute. When he had been away in Egypt, in Africa, the same thing had happened. No one had had the authority to act in his name. Everyone had hated the situation, and that was but a taste of what was now looming. The Dictator for life had Rome by the neck, strangling her, and was preparing to leave her gasping for air, abandoning her for the east.

I saw him not at all. He was furiously busy, fending off his critics, trying to make final arrangements for both his appointees and his army. Then a strange rumor began circulating, circulating so widely that even my servants heard it in the marketplace: The priests had consulted the Sibylline books of prophesy—the same one that had forbade anyone to "restore the king of Egypt with a multitude"—and they said no one could conquer Parthia but a king, or he would be annihilated and Rome humbled. If Rome sent Caesar, or allowed him to go, it would have to be as a king. The moment had come, the moment they assumed he had been aiming at all along.

The rumor said that at last the Senate was going to confer this title, when it met at Pompey's theater for the last time before Parthia, on the Ides of March. He was to depart for Parthia three days later—as a king.

34

The warm winds blew through the garden during the first half of March, gently coaxing the hedges to bloom and the trees to unfurl their tightly rolled, delicate leaves. My preparations for my journey were occupying my thoughts, but not quieting my heart. Parthia . . . why was he going, really? What was driving him there? Egypt's role in his campaign . . . no matter how much I thought about it, my feeling was still the same as my initial outburst. No, I would not involve Egypt in it! And the gift of his mother's jewelry—how could I adequately express the depths of my feelings about it? I promised myself I would never take it off until he returned from Parthia—as if that would make up for having refused him men and arms. I was confused and longed to see him, so that we could have a happy parting. The night before the Senate was to meet, he had planned to come to the villa, but in the late afternoon I received a message that he must dine with Lepidus that night. He would postpone our meeting until the day after. But there were still three days left in Rome, and we would have time to say our farewells.

The weather changed abruptly by the time the messenger brought me that note, and everyone was scurrying inside. Black-bottomed clouds coalesced, blotting out the sun, and a high wind shrieked through the trees. The shutters, drawn tight, rattled like an old woman's teeth.

"Roman weather is so changeable," I complained to Charmian, "just like Roman opinion." I had almost got used to the severe, booming thunderstorms that Jupiter hurled at his chosen city, but I would never like them. And the lightning—everyone had a story to tell about a statue, if not a person, that had been struck by it.

"It's a very nasty night," said Charmian, drawing a woolen shawl about her shoulders. She started as one of the tall lamp stands—a pretty one with a slender pole and clawed feet for its base—was blown over. It rolled, clanking, a little way and then stopped, spilling its oil in a trail.

I was sorry Caesar had to venture out at all, but at least Lepidus's house was conveniently near him, not like this villa across the Tiber.

What did Caesar think about the rumor? Did he believe it? Encourage it? Dismiss it? There were so many things I needed to know.

But I would not know them this night.

I slept almost not at all, for the bright blue lightning flashes and the crashing thunder seemed to invade my very chamber. Perhaps I dreamt, because at one point I thought the shutters had blown open and a tongue of lightning licked at the foot of my bed.

In the morning the ugly aftermath did not dispel. The wake of the storm had left several trees in the garden uprooted, and flooded the plants by the ornamental pool. In addition, the Hercules statue had been overturned, and his club was broken off, although he still stared up at the sky as if he had the situation well in hand.

As I walked through the strewn garden, I heard ugly noises coming from across the Tiber; people must be fighting, or lamenting the storm's damage to their market stalls.

I forced myself to continue with the busywork of packing my clothing, with Charmian helping. I had brought so many beautiful gowns, so much jewelry, ornamented sandals, hairpins and diadems and headdresses. And I had worn most of them, too, and now each one was connected with something in Rome. There was the dress I had worn to Caesar's dinner party, and the Triumph gown, and now my riding costume, which I had worn on our gallop through the fields.

I can remember exactly how I was smoothing out the material of that gown, running my fingers over the sturdy woven linen, when I heard a commotion downstairs. There were cries and shrieks, and then footsteps running lightly up to the door. I looked up and saw a boy I recognized, someone from Caesar's household. He was standing, trembling, panting and gasping.

Then he said those words, those words that struck me down.

"Murder! Murder! Caesar's been murdered!" he cried. He flung himself on me, collapsing in my arms, sobbing. "Caesar's dead!"

In my most terrible, dark dreams I had heard those words—in dreams you cannot even repeat to yourself the next morning, hiding away the horror, lest it truly happen. The unthinkable.

Charmian was staring, her face white, her hands to her mouth.

Caesar was dead. Caesar was dead. No, it was impossible. Caesar could not die. I could not be hearing those words now, not now, not after all the danger was past, the old wars over, the new one not begun, he here in Rome, with his honors. . . . A strange sort of cold gripped me, it had an urgency of its own, and it sucked me into a place I had never imagined—unconnected, beyond time, cold, cold, cold, all the familiar gone. No. It could not be true.

I heard myself asking, "What has happened?" and felt myself stroking the boy's hair, comforting him, as if he were my own child.

He was wrong. He would explain it away. Or . . . if there was anything wrong . . . Caesar was only injured.

"How do you know Caesar was murdered?" I asked him, as gently as I could. I almost whispered, lest speaking it loudly might make it true.

All he did was sob, and I could not stand it any longer, could not give him another instant before refuting the false news. And all the while that awful coldness, encasing me, making a stiff sort of shield around me.

"Tell me!" I lost control—but it was so crucial that I hear it was not true, and even if it was true, perhaps I could reverse it, or someone could, yes, someone could, doctors in Rome, yes. . . .

I shook his shoulders, but all he did was cry louder. "Tell me what you saw!" I cried. "Was Caesar assaulted in his house?"

But the guards would protect him. . . . No, he had dismissed the guards!

"No, not in his house," the boy snuffled.

A silly reassurance came to me, proof that it was false, founded on the idea that *this boy is from the house and this boy didn't see it, and there's nowhere else he would have been attacked. Not at Lepidus's house, and certainly not in the Senate!*

"Did someone try to attack him in the street?" I cried. Robbers? But he could have defended himself there.

And then . . . oh, those words!

"N-no," he whimpered. "They murdered him in the Senate. In front of everyone! They surrounded him and stabbed him to death, there were lots of them, and then he covered his face and died at the foot of Pompey's statue. The one he just—just had put back."

The statue . . . the statue we had watched being carted up the steps . . .

No, it was a mistake. It was someone else. No one would have . . . not someone who knew . . .

"Who are 'they'?" I cried aloud, my voice reaching a hundred miles away, I felt. My throat was stripped raw by it, by the anguished howl.

"A group of senators—I'm not sure, I wasn't inside. Brutus and Cassius were the first ones out of the meeting hall and into the portico, where I was waiting, and they ran out all bloody, waving their daggers and shouting about liberty and the Republic. And all around them, all the senators were fleeing for their lives, holding up their togas and running. Now there's a big riot in the Forum, with the murderers shouting and Cicero trying to make a speech, and an entire company of gladiators loose and looting."

Yes, I had heard the dreadful din of it, even from this far away. But I had not attached any meaning to it. There were always riots in Rome.

"O all you gods—" I think I said. I could not distinguish between what I thought and what I said, because within that cold cage, I was held a prisoner, muffled, the shock wrapping me like a cloak. I wanted to beat my way out of it, but I could not move.

The mob . . . the Roman mob . . . I could hear them so plainly, now that my ears were opened. Would they come for Caesar's son, here at the villa? Now that horror took me captive as well, adding fear to shock and pain. *Everyone knows that Caesar's son is here, his only son, and if they hate Caesar, then they also hate his son. O my child!* Were they even now running toward us, waving their daggers?

"Are they pursuing?" I asked the boy.

"No. They were all running in the opposite direction. No one stayed behind."

But they might remember, at any minute. I must protect my son. And Caesar? O gods and goddesses, where was Caesar? I must go to him.

"Where is Caesar? What has happened to him?" I cried. I could rescue him, save him.

"He—he's still lying at the base of the statue. Everyone ran away and left him, and he's alone in the Senate house, in a pool of—of blood." He burst into tremulous tears again.

Now there was feeling, pain penetrating the cold cloak, as if they had plunged a knife into me as well—driven it deep inside, so mortal was the wound that pierced me all the way through. It was impossible—to have left him like that. Everyone fled?

"Oh, the shame of it!" I wept. "To leave him there! Is everyone afraid of the murderers? Will no one even touch their fallen commander, the man that until this morning they called sacrosanct? Is not his body to be honored?" I cried.

At that, the boy had a horrible remembrance. "They said that they—they were going to throw the body of the tyrant into the Tiber! Yes, that's what I heard them yelling when they ran out of the building!"

I felt sick. It was inhuman, degrading. I hated them with a hatred I did not think it possible to experience.

"Never!" I said. I knew we must go to him. And we must hurry! And when we got there, perhaps . . . perhaps he still lived. If he had been left alone, and no one with him, perhaps he had only been unconscious, and we would revive him. When we got there, yes, it would be all right. "We will go there this instant and convey him to his home," I said. "If anyone attempts to prevent it, they will have to kill me as well! Get some other boys, and bring a litter! Now let us go—directly to Caesar!"

"No, madam!" Charmian grabbed on to my arm and attempted to stay me. "It is dangerous! There's a killing mob there, and Caesar's murderers—"

"Caesar's murderers are the most abject of cowards and men of the utmost dishonor. Think you I will shrink from them? Never!"

At that moment my newborn anger was serving to protect me, forming a shield around even the coldness gripping my heart.

Pompey's theater in the Campus Martius lay closer to the villa than the Forum, and it did not take us long to reach it. The enormous structure, with its Portico of a Hundred Columns, reared up, and I could see that it was deserted. No one was lurking, save a gladiator or two with his hands full of stolen goods, and they slunk off furtively.

The building was empty and dark. "Where?" I asked the boy. There were many rooms branching off the portico, and I could never guess which one had been large enough for the Senate.

He pointed a shaking finger at a doorway far on the other side and walked with me to it, but drew back at the entrance, after he had glanced inside.

"He is still—safe," he said.

Strange use of words, I could not help thinking. But now he would be safe, we would make him safe, we would save him. . . .

At the back wall of the chamber I saw the statue first, more than life-size and standing proudly. And at its feet—a bloodstained bundle, with feet protruding, that looked too small for someone of Caesar's height.

At once the relief: *It isn't him.*

I approached the motionless bundle, holding my breath. There would be someone else there. I knelt down and, with a hand that was shaking so badly I could barely grasp the cloth of the toga, I lifted it and saw Caesar's face.

I screamed when I beheld it, and dropped the cloth. His eyes were closed, but he did not look asleep. He looked different than I had ever seen him, and those who say the dead look asleep are liars. Then, after getting control of myself, I lifted the cloth again, reached out my hand, and stroked his cheek: cold, as if the coldness of the marble floor had crept into him and suffused him while he lay there.

I gazed at him, and all of myself seemed to drain away; my inner being melted, and I felt utterly lost, deserted, abandoned. My life was gone, torn from me, not gently extinguished.

"My love, my friend!" I whispered, touching him again. I held absolutely still, but not as still as he. And all the truth rushed in on me, and I knew the purest form of anguish.

"O Isis!" I wailed, and suddenly the story I had always known about Isis and the death of her husband Osiris, cruelly murdered and then dismembered by his brother, came true. I *was* Isis and here lay my Osiris, attacked by those who had called him "father of his country" and vowed to protect his life with their own. Now I saw the places in his toga—it seemed like hundreds of them—that had been ripped by the daggers. He had been set upon as if by a pack of wolves, killed by those sworn to protect him. He had been without any weapon, for it was against the law to have weapons in the Senate.

I flung myself across him and embraced him, stiff and bloody as he was. I knew I was smeared with blood, but I did not care. I wanted to stay there with him forever—but at the same time I was suddenly anxious for him to be taken from this abominable place.

The boy had come back, bringing two companions and a sturdy canvas litter. They hung back in the doorway and stared. Finally I said, "Come here," and they obeyed, tiptoeing up as if they were afraid Caesar would rise up under the toga.

And, oh! if only he could. I would have given my own life if he could.

"It is time. Convey him to his house. Does—has Calpurnia been told?" There was that to face, as well.

The boy nodded.

"Very well, then. Take him to her. I will follow."

Gingerly they managed to pick him up and place him on the litter. They covered his face again so no one on the way could gaze at him, and hoisted the litter up onto their shoulders. I saw that they had left one arm hanging over the side. It trailed down, swaying with the motion of the bearers, and the hand was limp.

The sight of that hand, now powerless, ripped through me so that I could hardly stand. If only Charmian were here, so I could lean against her. But I must not fall, I must not fail that poor arm, now utterly unable to defend itself.

And I would avenge him, if it took me all the rest of my life. Somehow I would do it, using any weapon, or person, that came to hand.

Ahead of me the arm swayed, the litter bounced.

I am here, Caesar. I will not desert, nor will I leave your enemies unpunished. And what I leave undone, your son, Caesarion, will finish. This I solemnly swear to you.

The boys carried the litter down the steps, the same steps where Antony had bought all the sausages and Caesar had laughed so loudly.

The Forum was filled with milling mobs, but we managed to make our way through as if we were invisible, there was such confusion. I was walking and called no attention to myself by an ornamented litter, and no one suspected the three boys of carrying anything important. Strange how blind and dull a crowd can be, even at its most agitated.

Caesar's house loomed just ahead, and the boys knew which side entrance to go into with their precious burden. We entered and quickly bolted the door behind us.

The same airy atrium, the same central pool, calmly reflecting the dull gray sky, where Caesar had so elegantly received guests, awaited us. The boys set the litter down, and Calpurnia emerged from the shadows, walking stiffly, leaning on two servants.

Her face was changed almost as much as Caesar's—puffy and ravaged at the same time. Weeping, she took each halting step toward the litter, her feet dragging. I turned away and sought the other end of the room, to allow her privacy. I heard loud screams, cries, stormy weeping, and then a dead silence. At last I turned back around and saw her in a heap beside the litter, its covering sheet drawn back.

I went over to her, unsure what to do, but feeling united to her in a terrible way. I bent down and laid my hands on her shaking shoulders. Caesar's face— that face—was turned toward us. I could not bear it, to see it so changed and ugly-still. I pulled the sheet back over it.

"My dear," I said—and she *was* dear to me at that moment, as she had been his, and now everything he had ever touched or been connected to in any way was inestimably precious—"I know you feel the daggers as if they had struck you themselves."

She allowed herself to lean against me a little. "Yes," she whispered. "I could feel them, even as it happened." She turned her face to mine. "I dreamed it all, last night. I saw it, I felt it. The only difference was that in the dream he collapsed and died in my arms—I saw him alive, not like— like this!" She attempted to lift the cloth again, having a need to see him, but her hand fell back limply. "I warned him—I begged him—not to go to the Senate!"

She hunched up on her knees, bending over him. "And he had dreamed that he was carried up in the clouds, and Jupiter reached out for him. Oh, it was all so clear! We *knew!* We *knew!* And yet he went. . . ."

She slumped back down again. Then her voice rose, as she suddenly re-membered. "He had agreed not to go after all! A soothsayer had warned him about the Ides. Yes . . . and the hour had passed, and he had not appeared at the Senate, and then Decimus came and begged him to make an appearance. He explained about my dream and the bad omens—for during the storm the shields of Mars fell down off the walls, a terrible warning!—and said he would not come. And then—then"—it began to come together in her mind—"Decimus laughed and said the Senate might change its mind about the honors if he had to announce that Caesar stayed away on account of his wife's dreams. He made it sound so foolish—but I knew what I had seen in my mind. Oh, we never should have yielded!"

I had a horrible suspicion. "Decimus—what was he to you?"

"Why, he was one of Caesar's most trusted friends," she said.

"And did he escort Caesar to the Senate?"

"I believe so," she said. "They set out together, Caesar in his litter. I watched them. There were crowds all about, and—someone thrust a scroll in Caesar's hand. But then, petitioners do that."

"The litter—the ceremonial one he rode in—where is it?"

"I don't know."

"It's at the theater still," one of the boys said.

"Bring it," I ordered him. "Bring it, so we leave nothing of Caesar's for the mob." Perhaps the scroll was still in it.

Outside I could hear the noise of the crowd. "Observe well who is at large," I told them. "Where have the murderers gone?"

Calpurnia allowed herself to be drawn to her feet. "I am afraid they will come and raid this house!" she said. "There is no one to protect it. Caesar had dismissed his guards."

Lepidus. Lepidus had one legion in the city, as Caesar's military second-in-command. What other forces were there? Decimus had his gladiators. Gladiators! What was it the boy had said? *An entire company of gladiators loose and looting.* Again I had that sickening lurch of feeling. Decimus's gladiators—why had they happened to be there?

Decimus had brought them to Rome and stationed them here. Decimus had brought Caesar to the Senate against his will. *Decimus was one of Caesar's most trusted friends.*

It was a plot, a huge plot. It was not just Brutus and Cassius, it was a widespread, organized body of assassins.

For weeks, Caesar had been surrounded by secret enemies—for if they had Decimus, they had other, unsuspected partisans. What about Antony? Was he one of them? And Lepidus? Were Calpurnia and I his only loyal adherents?

He had eaten with them, laughed with them, planned his Parthian campaign with them, walked through the Forum with them. And they had smiled and fawned and voted more honors to him—I remembered the obsequious magistrates meeting him at the temple—all the while planning to kill him! How they must have gloated over that in their secret conclaves, mocking him.

The boys returned with the litter, and in it were several rolled-up scrolls, all unread. Most of them indeed contained petitions, but one detailed the entire plot and begged Caesar to save himself. It said the conspiracy encompassed some seventy men.

Seventy!

How could they have kept the plot secret?

But then, they had not kept it secret. Caesar was warned in this scroll, only too late.

It said that Cassius wanted to kill Antony as well, but that Brutus had argued against it, saying that the sacrifice of Caesar would not be sacrifice but just plain murder if it took in others. So Trebonius was assigned to detain Antony outside.

Antony was loyal. I felt an immense relief. But where was he? Where had he fled to?

Rising noise outside. I had a ladder brought so I could look out the upper windows without opening the door. I did not know whether to be thankful Caesar's house was right in the midst of the Forum or not.

A huge mob had gathered in a knot near the center of the Forum, and I saw a single file of men coming down from the Capitol, holding their hands up and yelling, "Cicero! Cicero!" But I did not see anyone who looked like Cicero. I saw Dolabella, a wild, unstable man who was an expert at whipping up crowds, stand on a pedestal to address the crowd, then Brutus, then Cassius. I could not hear anything they said, but I knew how to read crowds, and I could see that the people were not responding. The conspirators turned and went back up the hill to the Capitol.

It was growing dark. How sudden! But of course it was not sudden; it was just that time was no longer the normal stretch of minutes but some other monstrous thing. The sun had kept on its journey as if this were any other day.

It should have stopped. It should have sent forth sparks. Anything but this peaceful transit across the sky, and now a twilight like any other.

There was a loud banging on the door, and as the bolts were pulled away, Antony burst in. He looked around wildly, throwing off the hood of his slave's cloak, his disguise.

"Caesar! Caesar! O my lord, my captain!" He rushed to the litter and fell to his knees. Yanking off the covering, he threw back his head and let out a long, mournful wail. His fists were clenched, his arms rigid by his side. Then he brought his hands up to his face and wept.

Calpurnia and I stood back, silently. It was many minutes before his shoulders stopped shaking and he wiped his cheeks and turned and saw us.

"Thanks be to all the gods that you are here," said Calpurnia.

Antony got up, slowly. "And thanks be to all the gods that we are safe," he said, looking around. "And that Caesar is here with us. Now they cannot desecrate him unless they kill us all."

"They are probably willing to do so," I said. "What would stay their hands—the hands that swore to protect the very man they have slain?"

"Only their misguided belief that they are high-minded and not ordinary assassins and murderers," he said. "They believe themselves honorable."

"Honorable?" said Calpurnia.

"They believe that it was honorable to kill Caesar, and equally honorable to let us live," said Antony.

"Well, they shall die for their honor," I said. Anger and sorrow kept fighting within me, and at this moment the anger had its turn.

Antony spun around and stared at me. "When?" he said.

"As soon as we have forces to oppose them," I said.

"The gods themselves will see to the hour and place," said Calpurnia.

"No, Caesar and I will!" I swore, looking at him. I knew his spirit and mine would range over all the world before we would let his murderers live.

"First we must calm Rome," said Antony. "We do not want the city destroyed in senseless riots—the city upon which Caesar has lavished so much care. After the danger is past, we shall pursue the murderers. But all in good time."

"We have a lifetime," I said.

"I am sole Consul," said Antony. "I am now the head of the government, the senior magistrate. I will take control as best I may, but it is tricky. We must disarm the conspirators, both literally and figuratively. I will call a meeting of the Senate for tomorrow."

"As if everything were normal!" I cried.

"We must pretend to them that we think it is," he said. "We must not alarm them, but must wrest control from them." He turned to Calpurnia. "Caesar's will—where is it?"

"With the Vestal Virgins," she said.

"And what of Caesar's papers, and his money?"

"All here," she said. "Here!" She pointed toward a room opening off the atrium.

"They must be transferred to my house," said Antony. "Tonight, under cover of darkness. They must not fall into the conspirators' possession. And once I have control of them, my hand is strengthened." He turned to me. "Return to the villa. Stay there until I send you word it is safe."

"Do we have any soldiers at our command?" I asked. I had my Egyptian guards; I would encircle Caesarion with them tonight.

"Lepidus is with us," he said.

Lepidus. So that question was answered.

"He will bring his legion onto the Campus Martius tonight, to be ready to move into the Forum at daybreak and occupy it. We will seize the state treasury as well, to prevent the conspirators from having any money at their disposal." He put his arm on my shoulder. "Return to the villa now," he said. "Return, and pray that all goes well in the next two days for us."

I glanced back at the litter, lying so quietly by the pool. No stirring, no change in it. The hand still lay exposed. I went over to it, took it in mine, and kissed it.

"Farewell, and farewell," I whispered. That had been his favorite parting, the words he had used when he left for Spain.

I wanted never to leave him, but I could not bear to stay by his still side any longer.

I watched from my window all night. How could I rest? Caesar was dead— the entire world was destroyed. Never for one instant did that terrible vision, the sight of him lying there, fade from my mind; it veiled and shrouded everything, the things seen and the things unseen. I stood, leaning on my shaking elbows at the window, as the stars wheeled in the black sky and slowly faded in the early morning.

What would happen to me? To Caesarion? To Rome? To Egypt? I was only twenty-five. What would another forty years without him hold for me? The universe was empty; he who had blotted out the sky was gone.

In the darkest time of the night, when the tumult in the Forum began to die away, I wept at last. Quietly, because I did not want Caesarion to be disturbed—the poor child, unaware of what he had just lost. I was unable to cry aloud as I needed to, so all the sorrow stayed contained within me. The hot tears did no good; my throat was raw and felt as if it were swelling with the very effort of holding in my cries; my chest was on fire, aching with the unearthly pain that filled it. My sobs were silent heaves that tore at me and seemed to increase my suffering, not assuage it. *Caesar was gone, gone, gone . . . how would I bear it?* Sudden death had torn my dearest and most loving protector away from me a second time.

The following day had the dull feeling of the aftermath of a natural disaster. There was nothing to do but wait, and continue to prepare for my leave-taking. I was drained from my suppressed crying, and moved like a sleepwalker now, or a person underwater, as if afraid that any sudden movement would cause me to feel even more pain. The things I had cared about—was this container waterproof, had I arranged my official correspondence in the correct chronological order so that it could be transferred intact to the archives in Alexandria?—were of no moment, and so what was usually so wrenching and time-consuming was soon done. Later, when I unpacked, I had no memory of any of it.

Antony faithfully sent messengers telling me of events. Brutus had called another meeting on the Capitol to try to generate public support and enthusiasm, but he had failed again. The mood was starting to turn ugly; the praetor Cinna, who had denounced Caesar, was pursued into a nearby house, and the hostile mob would have burned it down if Lepidus's soldiers had not prevented them.

Another night in which I did not sleep. How many sleepless nights can a person endure? The stars blazed again, circled the sky, and died away, and dawn came up, leaving me lightheaded and exhausted beyond mortal weariness. I held my own private communion with grief all through those hours of darkness, but there was no comfort anywhere, and this second night was worse than the first. Each hour seemed to increase my pain and my awareness, not dull or soothe it.

More messages. The Senate had met, and the senators had expressed a wide range of reactions. The most extreme had proposed that the conspirators be given special honors as public benefactors. So much were the "honors" of the Senate worth! The less extreme merely said that amnesty should be granted to all, and Cicero proposed an "act of oblivion."

An act of oblivion—like the one they had dealt Caesar?

Someone else had said Caesar should formally be declared a tyrant and all his acts illegal. Antony had reminded them that if that were done, then every one of them who owed his appointment to Caesar would have to resign it. There would be no praetorships for Brutus and Cassius, no Bithynia for Tillius Cimber, no Asia for Trebonius, no Cisalpine Gaul for Decimus.

There should be torture and hell for Decimus at the hands of his own gladiators!

The conspirators had tried to prevent the reading of Caesar's will, but Calpurnia's father had refused to be bullied by them, had ordered the Vestals to release it, and had announced that Antony would read it from his house. Next they tried to block a public funeral for Caesar, but Antony pointed out that any Consul who had died in office was permitted a public funeral, and Caesar was Consul.

The whole world would pay homage to him. His enemies who had killed him— now let them see how they would be hated.

It grew dark again, and this time I felt sleep coming over me. I knew I would, at last, rest, or what from now on must serve as rest. But at midnight a messenger arrived, with a vehement note from Antony.

The will—I read it out to Caesar's friends and family. It is not what I expected. He has named Octavian his principal heir, and requests him to be adopted as his son! He is to assume the name of Gaius Julius Caesar! And Caesar named Decimus as one of his secondary heirs, should his other great-nephews die early. Oh, the perfidy of Decimus is now made more hideous than ever!

He has given the gardens of the villa—your villa—to the people of Rome, along with three gold pieces a person. Generous indeed. And when the people hear of it, I cannot vouch for the safety of any of the conspirators—or the Liberators, as they now call themselves.

I was forced to have Cassius as my houseguest tonight, in exchange for my own son as a hostage on the Capitol! The food tasted like poison. I asked Cassius if he had a dagger, and he said, "Yes, and a big one, should you try to play the tyrant, too!"

We shall see what awaits him at the hands of the mob!

The funeral tomorrow night. I speak the eulogy, as his nearest male relative here. There will be a funeral pyre in the Campus Martius, but the bier and ceremony will be in the Forum. Should you wish to attend, you and Calpurnia will be safe on the steps of the Temple of Vesta, where Lepidus will station soldiers.

My head whirled. Octavian to be his—son? To take his name? But there was already another who bore the name Caesar—Ptolemy Caesar.

How could there be more than one Caesar?

As if Octavian could ever be Caesar! He was only distantly related, a mere great-nephew. And there was nothing of Caesar about him. His slight frame, his utter lack of athleticism or soldiership or oratory—no, nothing!

Whatever had possessed Caesar to name him? And why had he not warned me?

Perhaps I had known him very little. How much more there would have been to learn, had the gods just granted us time!

Drawn as if by a strong wind, I went to the Forum on the night of Caesar's funeral. I arrived well before dark; my litter had taken me past the enormous waiting funeral pyre in the Campus Martius beside his daughter Julia's tomb. The logs were neatly arranged and decorated. I shuddered. I hated the whole idea of burning someone, but then the Romans hated our custom of embalming. It was all ugly; there was no redeeming death, no matter which method we chose to consume the body.

Calpurnia was already there, on the curving steps of the round Temple of Vesta. She looked almost pleased to see me, her sister in this strange way, her companion in loss.

"They are on their way here," she said. "They took his—they took him away this morning. Look! See where they will lay him!" She pointed to a huge bier, made to look like the Temple of Venus Genetrix. Under its columns an ivory couch, covered with purple and cloth of gold, waited to receive him.

A low sound filled the air, as musicians began to play dirges and solemnly beat their drums around the bier. The people joined in, moaning and swaying.

Torches were lit all around the Forum, ringing it with golden light. I could see the procession now, making its way toward us. A sigh went up from the people.

The decorated litter, borne by ten magistrates, wound its way to the waiting bier. Then it was placed reverently on the ivory couch, and the men stepped back. Antony appeared and mounted the bier, resplendent in his consular robes.

First a herald recited in ringing tones all the decrees passed in Caesar's name by the Senate and people of Rome, including the oath of loyalty they had all sworn. At this the people gave a groan. Then he recited Caesar's wars and battles, the enemies defeated and the treasures sent home, the territories added to Rome, the thanksgivings voted to him.

Antony then stood beside the bier, and began intoning the sonorous funeral chant. The people took it up, moaning and moving back and forth.

The chant finished, Antony then began to speak, with the loud, resonant voice and oratory for which he was famed.

"Caesar, Caesar!" he cried. "Will there ever come another like you to

Rome—you who so tenderly loved it like a son, cherished it like a wife, and honored it like a mother? No, no, never, never, never!"

He looked around at the entire crowd, his head held high. "For the gods, Caesar was appointed high priest; for us, Consul; for the soldiers, Imperator; and for the enemy, Dictator. But why do I enumerate these details, when in one phrase you called him father of his country, not to mention the rest of his titles?"

He turned and gestured toward Caesar, lying on the ivory couch. "Yet this father, this high priest, this inviolable being, this hero and god, is dead, alas! dead not by the violence of some disease, nor wasted by old age, nor wounded abroad somewhere in some war, nor caught up inexplicably by some supernatural force, but no! he who led an army into Britain died right here within the walls of the city as a result of a plot!"

His voice rising, he swept his right arm in an arc, indicting everyone before him. "The man who enlarged its boundaries—ambushed in the city itself! The man who built Rome a new Senate house—murdered in it! The brave warrior—unarmed! The promoter of peace—defenseless! The judge—beside the court of justice! The magistrate—beside the seat of judgment! He whom none of the enemy was able to kill even when he fell into the sea—at the hands of the citizens! He who so often took pity on his comrades—at their hands!"

He turned back to Caesar again and cried out to him, "Of what avail, Caesar, was your humanity, of what avail your inviolability, of what avail the laws? Now, though you enacted many laws that men might not be killed by their personal foes, yet how mercilessly you yourself were slain by your friends! And now, the victim of assassination, you lie dead in the Forum through which you often led the Triumph crowned. Wounded to death, you have been cast down upon the Rostra from which you often addressed the people. Woe for your blood-bespattered head, alas for the rent robe, which you assumed, it seems, only that you might be slain in it!"

His voice broke and tears streamed down his face.

Just then someone near the bier shouted the line from a well-known play by Pacuvius: " 'What, did I save these men that they might slay me?' " And it sounded as if the voice were coming from Caesar himself.

Suddenly, Antony snatched up Caesar's bloody toga and held it aloft on his spear, twirling it around. The torchlight showed the stains—turned black now—and the gaping holes in the garment. "Look there! See! See! See how he was brutally slain—he who loved Rome so that he has left his gardens to you, as well as bequests of money. This was his reward for loving you, the people of Rome!" He waved the toga like a battle flag, and a great cry arose from the crowd.

They rushed forward in a shouting mass, yelling about Caesar. Suddenly, as if by magic, they were hauling furniture toward the bier—benches, stalls, chairs, staves—and turning it into a funeral pyre.

"Here! Here in the Forum!" they screamed, piling up the furniture. Antony hastily jumped down off the platform just as the first torch cartwheeled through the air and landed on the pile. It flickered and caught, and then a rain of other torches followed.

People rushed toward the roaring fire as it reached upward to Caesar. Caesar! My heart stood still as I saw the flames licking up around his couch, and he lying motionless on it. They tore off their clothing and heaved it into the flames. The official mourners, who had worn his four Triumphal robes, tore them to pieces and cast them into the fire. Soldiers ripped off their valuable breastplates and threw them in, and women flung their jewelry, as if they were all sacrificing at some primitive bonfire to the god Caesar.

Thus the people proclaimed him a god long before Octavian did.

People fell on the ground, sobbing, beating their breasts, wailing. The smoke rolled in billowing clouds, blocking out the stars; sparks flew upward in the darkness, each a new star, flaming and dying.

A group of people differently dressed stood by the flames, swaying and chanting. I learned later that these were Jews, who knew Caesar as their partisan and friend. He had obtained many privileges for them, and they were to mourn by the ashes of the funeral pyre for days afterward.

We watched, transfixed, as the great sacrifice was consumed in the night. The gods accepted it. And I relinquished Caesar into their pitiless hands.

HERE ENDS THE THIRD SCROLL.

THE FOURTH SCROLL

35

In the fetid, close cabin of the heaving ship that plowed its way through the high seas, I was torturously reborn. Weak and sick, I lay on the bed that bucked and jumped and afforded no rest day or night. But I did not care; it was impossible to be more miserable than I was, no matter where I lay or what surrounded me. I felt that I could lie forever on that foul bed, entombed in the dark. I was dead, as dead as Caesar.

The tight cabin, the lack of light, the smell and sound of water, all were a hideous repetition of my journey in the carpet to meet Caesar four years—a lifetime—ago. Now I was being borne away from him, knowing that no journey on earth could ever bring me to him again. Then my heart had raced with the gamble of it; now it beat feebly with the blow of defeat it had been dealt. And as day followed day, and the water-seeping, moving cabin held me prisoner, I felt I was enfolded in a birth canal, moving back toward a womb, toward oblivion and nothingness.

I did not eat. I did not wake—or perhaps I never really slept. And I did not think. Above all, I did not think. But the dreams! Oh, the pursuing dreams that curled around me. I kept seeing Caesar, seeing him first as alive and strong, then seeing him engulfed in flames as he had lain on his bier. Then I would scream, or mumble, and Charmian would be beside me, taking my hands, quieting me. And I would turn away, close my eyes again, and be taken back by the dream-demons.

I had not collapsed in Rome. Somehow I had got through those days that now seemed more like a nightmare than the real nightmares besetting me. But I had little memory of them. After the funeral, nothing has a clear edge to it. I left, that is all. I left as soon as I could, without actually running from the Forum directly to a departing ship. Only when I was safely aboard and saw the shoreline of Italy receding in the distance did I go to the cabin, lie down, and die.

Charmian would sit by me, enduring the dreadful cabin day after day, reading to me, trying to interest me in something besides the all-absorbing world in my dreams. She and the cooks prepared dishes to be as tempting as possible under the circumstances—fresh-caught fish stew, boiled peas and lentils, honeyed cakes. They all looked, and smelled, revolting to me, and would make me sick. I would hang my head over the side of the bed and retch, even though I had not tasted them.

"You will waste away," Charmian would chide me, taking one of my wrists and circling it with her own hand. "Is this a royal arm? You could not even lift it if you were wearing the bracelet of the Kandake." She would attempt to joke. "I know your ancestor Ptolemy the Eighth and several others were obese, but must you do penance for it this way? To turn yourself into a skeleton?" She appealed to my pride. "What if Caesar could see you now?"

But that was to no avail. Sometimes I felt that Caesar was nearby, was watching me, and I knew that he—he who had had the weakness of the falling sickness—would understand my state and sympathize with it. Other times I felt that he had vanished entirely, leaving me naked and abandoned in the universe much more thoroughly than if I had never been held close to him at all. Then I knew it did not matter what I looked like. He was gone, and would never behold me anymore.

Days passed; and because I was not dead but alive, and because life—if it is life—eventually stirs, I was gradually reborn, emerging from the weightless, timeless darkness that had held me.

On the deck again, the light seemed too intense, and stung my eyes; the winds too sharp and raking against my skin; the blues of the sea and sky artificially bright and stabbing. I had to shade my eyes and narrow them in order even to endure the sight of the horizon where the two blues met. There was nothing else to be seen—no land, no clouds.

"Where are we?" I asked Charmian, that first day when I leaned against her as she guided me up on deck. My voice sounded shaky and faint.

"In the very middle of the sea—halfway home."

"Oh." On the way to Rome I had followed our route so eagerly, willing the winds to fill the sails and blow us there as fast as possible. Now I had no idea how long we had been at sea, or when we would arrive, nor did I care.

"We have been gone from Rome almost thirty days," she said, trying to spark some interest and sense of time in me.

Thirty days. That meant Caesar had been dead for almost forty-five. That was all any date meant to me—did it come before or after Caesar's death? And how long before or after?

"It is already the beginning of May," said Charmian gently, trying to orient me.

May. This time last year, Caesar had still been away from Rome. He had already fought what turned out to be his last battle, at Munda, in Spain—and almost a year to the day afterward he had fallen to the daggers of the assassins. This time last year, I had been waiting for him in Rome.

But he had not returned to Rome for a long time. Instead, he had gone to his estate at Lavicum and written his will—the will that named Octavian his heir, and failed to mention Caesarion at all.

At the memory of it, I felt an emotion stirring, like the head of a fern breaking the ground after a winter's sleep. It was spindly and pale, but it was alive, and uncurling.

It was grief, regret, and anger all mixed together. It would have taken so little for him to have formally named Caesarion as his son, even if he left absolutely nothing to him; even if he had reminded the executors that under Roman law he could inherit nothing. It was Caesar's name that his son needed, his paternal recognition, not his property. Now, forever after, his enemies had the opportunity to claim that Caesarion was not Caesar's own—after all, the Dictator had not mentioned him in his will! Eyewitnesses to the occasion in Rome when he picked him up and acknowledged him as his own would forget, would grow old, die, while the historical document of the will remained, and lived on and on.

Oh, Caesar, I cried inside, Why did you abandon us, even before you abandoned us?

I remembered how joyous I had been to welcome him back, all the while unknowing of his actions at Lavicum. He had been so sensible, so rational, in giving all his reasons for why he could not formally acknowledge Caesarion. But just a word in the will—a few precious words, that would have cost Caesar nothing, but the lack of them would cost us dear!

Weak and shaky, I returned to the cabin. Enough daylight for one day.

My mind became nimble and restless long before my body. It did not want to be forced to return to the dream world, the nightmare world, but began to feed on more substantial things: wondering what had happened in Rome since I had left, wondering what news had been received in Alexandria. Perhaps, in Egypt, they did not yet even know about the Ides of March.

When I left Italy, messengers were still en route, overland, to notify Octavian. What he would do was anyone's guess. But what could he do, really? He was still a schoolboy in Apollonia, and Caesar's offices were not hereditary. Lawyers could see to the estate. There would be little purpose in his returning to Rome. There was no place for him there. He was too young to assume a seat in the Senate, and he had no military skills, so could not take command of troops. Poor Octavian, I thought. His political future looked bleak.

At least he would be rich. Caesar had left him a fortune. There are worse fates than being a wealthy private citizen, I thought. But I knew he had loved Caesar and would grieve for him.

And Antony—what had happened to Antony? He was attempting to step into Caesar's shoes and take command of the state, steady it, and then unseat the assassins from their cozy perch, so that he could exact revenge. But what had actually happened?

What difference does it make to you now? I told myself. You are finished with Rome. It died for you with Caesar. Had Caesarion been named in his will, then we would still be a part of it. But he did not, and we are not. No more Senate, no more Cicero, no more Forum, no more Antony, no more Octavian. It is gone, over, done with.

I felt immense relief at that thought. I never wanted to set foot again in the city that Caesar had loved, and which had betrayed and murdered him.

I remained weak and thin, seemingly unable to regain any strength. My distaste for food, my lethargy and fatigue, continued to hold me in their grip. The captain and my attendants set up a comfortable folding couch for me on deck, in hopes that the fresh sea air would help me. Bolstered with pillows and sheltered from the sun by a giant canopy, it was all an invalid could wish for. The spray of the passing sea danced around me, flicking me lightly, while I reclined listlessly.

"We are passing between Crete and Cyrene now," the captain told me. "We have passed the halfway mark on our journey."

Cyrene. Where the roses, and the fast horses, came from. Caesar had loved both.

That night, as I made ready to lie down in the all-too-familiar bed, I sighed when Charmian opened the tiny window to admit a little air and drew the coverings over me.

"I am weary of this illness, whatever it may be," I told her. She was still dutifully bringing me food to tempt my appetite, and I was feeling increasingly guilty in turning it away, day after day. I was very thin, and my mirror revealed a face with cheekbones that stood out as never before, and oddly pink-tinted, translucent skin.

" 'Whatever it may be'?" she said. "I think we both know well enough what it is, my lady."

I just stared at her. What did she mean? Was it something that others could see, while I was ignorant of it? Leprosy? Some clouding of the faculties that is obvious to everyone except the victim? "Do you mean I have a disease—an identifiable disease?" I tried to keep my voice calm. Only in thinking I had some fatal malady did I come to realize how much I wanted to live after all.

"Yes, a very common one. Come, stop pretending! It isn't amusing, and I don't know why you have kept it up so long. Making me take care of you, make special dishes for you—really, it's been tiresome."

"I don't know what you mean."

"Please, stop it! Why do you pretend you don't know?"

"What?"

"Stop this game! You know very well you are with child!"

I just stared at her. They were the last words I had ever expected to hear out of her lips. "Why—do you say that?"

"Because it's obvious! You have all the symptoms of it—and remember, I can see your face, and you cannot. Your face looks like it did the first time."

I burst into bitter laughter. How ironic, how cruel! The gods were mocking me, were mocking Caesar and me both. Was it true? Yes, in an instant I realized it was. I bent down my head and wept.

Charmian knelt beside me, stroked my hair. "I am sorry, I did not mean to be harsh. It never occurred to me that you hadn't considered it—but then, your mind has had such a shock that you have been disoriented. And you have lost all sense of time. Forgive me!"

Great sobs burst from me. How could new life survive all that death? It seemed obscene, unnatural.

If only, if only . . . it had happened in the course of things while we were in Rome, how different everything would have been. All Rome would have seen it was his. Now even he would never see it.

Onward the ship ploughed, cutting a great white wake behind it. The sails filled, bearing us eastward, straining the mast as if impatient to arrive. Free of the grip of the waters near Italy, the ship seemed to have grown more buoyant, as if the stern hand of Rome had extended out even into the waters surrounding her, grasping everything that swam or sailed past, holding them immobile.

I even felt my own spirits rising like bubbles bursting forth from deep, sunless water. The surface of things—that was what I sought, what I needed now. Let me have simple, straightforward people, let me have unembellished dishes, let me have constellations in the sky that I already knew—stars that were old friends, standing in their accustomed places, so I knew where to find them.

After her outburst to me, Charmian had been overly contrite, and scurried around pampering me more than ever. But I assured her it was not necessary; I had taken no offense, since what she had said was true. I was sorry that I had been such a difficult mistress for so long, lying like a stranded jellyfish on my bed.

I made an effort to avoid that from then on, but it took an enormous act of will. This pregnancy was very different from the first. I remembered how healthy and energetic I had felt then—dashing out to watch the fighting in the Alexandrian War, providing space and refuge for the military staff, spending the nights with Caesar. In all the tumult of the war, my condition had passed almost unnoticed.

The war . . . thanks to that war, I had an Alexandria to return to. It had been secured for me at great cost; I must not let that cost be in vain.

The captain predicted that we would arrive the following day, as he stood by me one moonless night on the deck. Waves sounded all around us, but were hard to see. Only the stars illuminated the sky. And I saw no Lighthouse.

"We are still too far out to sea," the captain said. "And from a great distance, the Lighthouse lamp looks like another star. But by dawn you should be able to glimpse it."

"This has been a good voyage," I said. "I thank you for bringing us safely across the open water."

"Open water has its own dangers, but coming into Alexandria is always tricky, with the reefs and island. That little narrow channel between the Pharos and the breakwater is difficult to steer past, especially when the prevailing north winds are strong. I don't have much room for error."

Yes, but death could also occur on a flat sea, in a calm harbor, when the water was soft and greenish blue. Water was unpredictable. "I have faith in you," I assured him.

Long before dawn I was up on deck, waiting for my first glimpse of Alexandria, watching for her to emerge from the formless gray of the horizon. And she arose, glimmering pale and white like a mist, floating above the flat land. The Lighthouse looked like a temple, its fire winking.

Home! I had returned! My city awaited me!

Enormous crowds lined the shores of the eastern, palace harbor; the captain had flown the royal banner as we approached, and people came running. On the long voyage, lying in bed, I had imagined the city so many times that seeing it now was no shock. It was the people who were unfamiliar. They were subtly different from Romans, at least as a crowd. Was it the absence of togas? More bright colors? More skin colors and languages?

We descended the gangplank to tumultuous cries of welcome—less thunderous than the shouts at Caesar's Triumphs, but loud enough from a crowd that was tiny by comparison. Sweetest of all are the shouts for oneself—I had not had any of my own for two years now.

"I return to Alexandria with joy!" I cried, holding my arms aloft, reaching toward the sky, thanking Isis for my safe return. "And to you, my people!"

They roared back. In Rome, I had almost forgotten what they sounded like. The shouts for Caesar were not the same.

The gates swung open, the palace grounds beckoned—delicate white temples and pavilions; gardens with sapphire-blue flowers bordering the long water channels. The grass was long but still pale, early green.

How had I left it all for so long? Here was paradise.

"Iras! Mardian! Olympos!"

They were all standing on the palace steps, my dearest ministers. One by one they descended, knelt, and then rose.

"At last!" said Mardian. "You cannot know how I have longed for your return."

"What he means is that he is tired of carrying all the duties of the government," said Olympos. His voice had its familiar sardonic tinge—sorely missed, dear to me now. "He grows as round-shouldered as any scholar in the Museion from the weight of it."

"Then you must go to the Gymnasion and build them up," I said. "I don't intend to let you put the burden down entirely."

I had learned that lesson from watching Caesar: the task of governing was too difficult to be carried by one person alone. I was fortunate that, unlike him, I had ministers I could trust.

"Your Majesty," said Iras, her face shining with a smile. "It has been a very long two years."

Her formality was in such contrast to Charmian. I realized that by coming with me to Rome, Charmian would forever be closer to me than anyone else; she had shared that difficult passage with me, and now would be the only one to share any memories of it.

Standing a little distance behind them was a dark, handsome face. Epaphroditus! I was shocked to see him there, as if his primary business were here now, instead of in a warehouse on the docks.

"Welcome home, Your Majesty," he said, stepping forward.

"I am pleased to see you," I said. And I was; when had he decided that palace business was not beneath him?

Inside the palace, the familiar drained away, and I was seeing it all anew. The many small changes in it, the kind we make in the course of everyday living, rendered it foreign. Was this corridor always so dark? Were there always torch holders here?

Was this how a dead person would feel if he came back to his own home a little while after his death? I felt like my own ghost, walking those corridors again.

Caesar's house . . . the room that had been mine, had been ours . . . would it already be changed, alien to him? This table gone, fresh paint on the west wall, the mosaic moved . . . Cleopatra gone. . . .

Stop, I told myself. Stop, stop. Picture that room no more.

I was standing in my own old room, the filmy curtains stirring with the harbor air, the blue-tinted, diffuse light filling the chamber. It was pristine, as only a place can be where no one lives. Without human beings, things remain untainted and perfect, stretching on into eternity without a wrinkle, until nature puts an end to them with an earthquake or fire. And then it is a clean, blameless end.

I shook my head. What disturbing visions I was having! "Dear Iras," I said, to break the spell, "have you received any letters from me since the winter?" If she had, then that ship had beaten ours, and we had sailed almost as soon as the seas permitted it.

"No, my lady," she said.

"Then you will read it when the news is old. Is not a letter that arrives after its author a peculiar thing?"

"Not as peculiar as a letter that arrives from a dead person."

Caesar! "Have you had word—" I began, then brought myself up short. How absurd. He would not have written me in Alexandria, when I was by his side in Rome. Was I going mad? "—from anyone in that state?" I attempted to make a joke out of it.

"No, my lady," she said gently. From the look in her eyes, I knew she guessed what I had thought. "Perhaps you would like to rest now."

The bed did look inviting. The horror of Rome, the long sea voyage, my pregnancy—all had drained me, until I was in the weakened state that could long for a bed in the daytime. But I must not begin that way; I must not present such a picture of myself at this crucial time. "Of course not!" I said lightly, my limbs aching. "What sort of person would sleep at noon?"

"Any person who needs to," she said pointedly. "But, my lady, what would you have told me in this letter—this letter you have outraced?"

I could not bear to repeat the news over and over. "I will tell it once, and wait until everyone is gathered to hear it," I said. "For I need to know what news has reached Alexandria, as well."

The remainder of the day I spent reacquainting myself with my own palace, lingering over the views from the upper windows opening out onto the sparkling harbor, running my hands over the marble inlays on the walls, standing in my workroom where the shelves were laden with brass-bound boxes containing old correspondence, copies of decrees, inventories of furnishings, and summaries of tax and census rolls. Even though the full archives were elsewhere, a précis of the kingdom's business was here.

My ministers had kept me as well appraised of events in Egypt as was possible, but the long delays in communication meant that I would have to spend several days studying summaries and catching up. I was devoutly thankful that harvests had been good and no catastrophes had happened while I was away.

Perhaps, while I was with him, some of Caesar's luck had accrued to me as well.

I had called a meeting for twilight—hoping I could endure until that hour. This day, beginning with my early rising to see Alexandria, would be extraordinarily long. A bath and a change of costume helped; I was happy to use my deep marble tub again. Floating in the scented water, I looked out on yet more water in the harbor below me. The tub was positioned behind an ivory screen, between the bedchamber and the rooftop garden. Even though it was poised just above the sea, the palace used pure rainwater for its baths and washing, and for this deep tub it was first heated and then cooled slightly, with perfumed oil added to it. I saw the soft sheen of the oil on the surface of the water, making little iridescent ripples, soothing balm for the senses. It seemed preposterous that such comfort, such innocent luxury, could offer itself side by side with a world of violence and death—and still have the power to please us. At bottom, we are appallingly simple creatures.

I was dressed in clothes I had left behind and almost forgotten, which made them new again. I put on gold jewelry in the Greek style, earrings and necklace, but kept on the pendant Caesar had given me. It must learn to be a friend to all my other necklaces, for it would keep company with them from now on.

We met in the room used for private dining; this enabled me to stretch out on a couch. I arranged myself before anyone else arrived, covering my feet with the hem of my gown. There would be no food—I did not wish to call attention to myself by whether I did or did not eat.

First to enter the chamber was Mardian, his ever-more-ample frame draped in a gold-fringed tunic. He smiled and saluted me. "A meeting on the very first day!" He bowed. "I brought all the records—"

"Oh, I don't propose to look at records tonight," I assured him. "That's much too specific. I merely wanted to speak with you about what has happened in both Rome and Egypt since our last communication."

Epaphroditus appeared in the doorway, resplendently dressed, as I had come to expect. He had looked so darkly handsome in crimson; now he looked equally forceful in a deep blue robe.

Others arrived: Allienus, commander of the four legions guarding the city (Caesar had lately added another); the overseer of the tax collectors; the head customs official; the guardian of the state treasury; the chief priest of Serapis; the inspector of canals and irrigation. And, of course, several scribes.

One by one they formally greeted me, going through all the set phrases, but I could tell by their expressions and the tone of their voices that they were genuinely happy I had returned.

"I am blessed to be able to return so safely," I said. "And blessed to find that you have taken such care of the kingdom while I was away, have guarded and nurtured her so well." I looked around at all of them. Time to begin, and to begin with the event that loomed over all others. "You have heard about—what has happened in Rome?"

"Indeed," said Mardian. "The whole world has heard of it. I expect that even the Kandake in faraway Nubia has heard of it—nay, even in India. The tallest cedar has fallen, and the sound has shaken the world."

"I—I was not there," I said, fighting to keep my voice steady. "But I was told immediately afterward, and it was I who conveyed him to his home and gave him into the hands of—of his wife, Calpurnia." I paused. All eyes were fastened on me. I should tell it now, all at once, rather than responding to questions. "I was there at the funeral, when he was—was cremated on the bier. I saw the crowd turn frenzied, and behave as if they wished to elevate Caesar to the state of a god."

And what afterward? I remembered the blazing fire, the wild shouts, the dark night—but after that, nothing, until I found myself on the ship. But they must not know that; it would cause them to doubt my strength and sanity. "As for afterward—what have you heard?"

"That Antony, as Consul, has taken his place as head of the government," said Mardian. "The assassins are very unpopular in Rome, and have failed to keep control. They will probably leave soon, for their own safety."

"And what of Octavian?" I asked. Had he received the news yet?

"The young Caesar—for so he wants to be called now—left Apollonia immediately to claim his inheritance," said Mardian. "He should be in Rome by now."

So he was wading into that nest of confusion and danger! I was surprised; I would have expected him to wait and see what developed first. "The young Caesar?"

"Why, yes, that is now his name—Gaius Julius Caesar. Gaius Julius Caesar Octavianus."

That name! That name could belong to only one person! This was a travesty! Before I could say anything, General Allienus spoke up.

"The legions have hailed him as Caesar," he said. "Not all of them, of course, but a surprising number. There is magic in that name, and they want their old commander back." He paused. "As do we all," he added dutifully.

"Antony had best come to terms with him," said Mardian. "He will have to share the power with him. But we know nothing more than this."

This was unexpected. Shocks kept spreading out from Rome.

"We must look to our own safety," I said. "Egypt had just been recognized as Friend and Ally of the Roman People, which meant that we were guaranteed independence and security. But now—the whole world is unstable."

"My legions remain as Caesar positioned them," said Allienus. "They will protect Egypt from predators."

How farsighted of Caesar to have stationed them here! I was deeply grateful.

"So we will wait together," I said, "and keep Alexandria well. But what of the rest of the country? Perhaps we should raise more troops to strengthen the line of defense up and down the Nile, as well as east to west along the coast."

"If we can afford it," said Mardian.

"What is the present situation of the state treasury?" I asked the guardian of it.

"Recovering, slowly. It will take years to recoup the losses to Rabirius, and repair the war damage to the city. But as long as there are not other extraordinary expenses, we will first survive, then live well, and finally be rich," he said. "And of course, Egypt always has her food, and that in itself makes her rich. She can feed not only herself, but others if need be."

I hoped we would not have to feed anyone but ourselves, or customers who could pay, and pay well.

I turned to the chief official of the waterways. "What of the irrigation canals? And the reservoir basins?"

"They are in reasonable condition," he said. "The Niles of the past two years have been adequate, and that has allowed us to do maintenance work on the irrigation system—water neither too high nor too low. But there has been some silting of late. It needs to be addressed."

"It is all related—the crops cannot grow without adequate irrigation, and without the money from the crops, we cannot dredge to improve irrigation. What of the taxes?"

"Import tax has been collected as usual," said the customs head.

"Profits are up," added Epaphroditus. "Suddenly there seems to be a craze for olive oil. I don't know what people are doing with it—bathing in it?"

"What do we care, as long as they are paying the fifty-percent import tax?" said the tax collector.

"True," said Mardian. "People seem to demand the best nowadays. Earlier they were content with linseed oil; now it must be olive or nothing. Well, why complain?"

"Am I complaining?" said the tax commissioner. "Not I!"

"The great festivals of Serapis and the pilgrimages to Isis have attracted large crowds and many pilgrims during the past two seasons," said the priest, speaking suddenly. He had been so silent I had forgotten he was there. "Perhaps it betokens something."

"People are searching, tired of this present world," said Epaphroditus. "Religion everywhere seems to be attracting converts. The mysteries, the Isis devotions, Mithras—all the eastern rites—seem to be especially popular."

"But not Judaism," said Mardian. "Your laws and rules are too exclusive. You make it too hard to join you."

"That is the idea," said Epaphroditus. "We don't want to become too popular. When things become too big, too successful, then they change into something else."

"Like the Romans?" said the high priest sharply. "When they were just a city, they were supposedly high-minded and self-controlled. Now look at them—now that they own most of the known world!"

"Yes, our God foresaw that pitfall," said Epaphroditus. "He said, 'Beware that thou forget not the Lord thy God—lest when thou hast eaten and art full, and hast built goodly houses, and dwelt therein; and when thy herds and thy flocks multiply, and thy silver and thy gold is multiplied, and all that thou hast is multiplied; then thine heart be lifted up, and thou forget the Lord thy God, and thou say in thine heart, My power and the wealth of mine hand hath gotten me this wealth. And it shall be, if thou do at all forget the Lord thy God, I testify against you this day that ye shall surely perish.' "

"No wonder you don't attract many converts," said the priest of Serapis. "Now *our* god is much more realistic about man's frailties. And of course, Isis is the supreme compassionate one."

"We await a Messiah who will complete our God's intentions," said Epaphroditus.

"Oh, everyone is expecting a deliverer—a golden child," said Mardian breezily. "I made a list of them all, once. There's a whole range of them. Some even think the deliverer will be a woman. And come from the east. I think the truth is, we all know there has to be something better; we are good enough to perceive it, but not good enough to bring it about. So we think, 'If only this mysterious person would come and *help* us . . .' " He shrugged his rounded shoulders, and the tunic fringe swayed. "But in the meantime we must soldier on."

"I think you have soldiered on splendidly in my absence," I said. "All of you are to be commended; no ruler ever was served by better ministers." I would have to see to it that they were given some sort of public award.

Suddenly I was so tired I could hardly hold up my head. Egypt was well; I had found out all I needed to know.

36

The fresh air of the harbor poured into my chamber the next morning, and the reflected light played over the walls. I awoke slowly, feeling as if I were submerged on a sea-bed, as I had been dreaming I was. Long strands of sea-weed had tangled themselves around my legs, and were streaming out behind me; my hair was waving slowly, caught in branches of coral. As I awoke, I ran my hands through my hair to free it, and then wondered why it was not tangled. What a strange, realistic dream it had been.

I stretched. I felt the fine, polished linen sheets—sheerer than anything in Rome—wrapped around me. I felt somewhat better; the night had done its restorative work.

I gave directions to Charmian and Iras to unpack the coffers and trunks, and sent for Olympos. I needed to see him, both for myself and for Ptolemy. Ptolemy had kept his cough, and been sick much of the voyage—the two of us had surely taxed our attendants during that journey. Yesterday Ptolemy had busied himself out in the gardens, but he seemed subdued to me. Perhaps he was just tired. That was what I hoped Olympos would tell me.

But when Olympos stepped into my chamber, after having first spent the morning with Ptolemy, his attempt to smile was unconvincing.

"Dear one," he began, and I knew it was bad.

"What is it?" I asked him. I could not bear to lead up to it. "What is wrong with him?"

"I listened to his chest, and had him cough up some congestion for me, and examined it. I also examined his spine, his joints, and looked carefully at his color. I did not like what I saw."

"What *did* you see?" Let him say it!

"It is the lung rot," he said. "Consumption."

It was Rome that had done it! Rome, with its cold, its frosts, its damp.

"It occurs elsewhere than in Rome," said Olympos, as if he had read my thoughts. "Egypt has many cases of lung rot."

"Rome did not help it."

"Perhaps not. But he is back here now. People come to Egypt for a cure."

"Do you think he can throw it off?"

"I don't know," he said. "If you were any other ruler, and not a childhood friend, and if I were another type of court servant, I would assure you, 'Yes, yes, Your Majesty, I see a full recovery for him.' But you are Cleopatra and I Olympos, and I must tell you honestly—he is in great danger."

"Oh!" I could not lose someone else. Not Ptolemy. "I see."

"There is nothing we can do. Nothing, except make sure he is kept warm, gets plenty of sunshine, lots of rest, and spends time outdoors. Then we must wait. In autumn we may have to send him to Upper Egypt, where it stays warm and sunny."

I bent my head. To send him away again, when he had been so anxious to return home. "So be it," I said. I looked up at him, and saw that he was staring at me intensely. "What is it?"

"You are different," he finally said.

"How so?"

"Thinner," he said. "Something has been burned out of you. If you were gold, I would say you had been refined. It is most becoming. You are finally, truly, beautiful." He attempted a laugh. "A useful attribute in a queen."

"I am with child," I told him.

"I guessed," he said. "But I do not need to be a soothsayer to see that this is very difficult for you. Both in the heart and in the body."

"I do not feel well at all."

"Are you surprised? Why should you? The situation is dreadful. Caesar dead, not just dead but murdered, assassinated; your patron and protector gone; a child with no one to claim him."

"I shall claim him."

"And no story to tell your people. Amun has inconveniently disappeared, at least in his human manifestation."

His words were hard, but it was a relief to have them spoken so boldly.

"I am sorry," he said. "I am sorry about what happened to Caesar."

"I know you didn't like him. You never did, and you were honest about that."

"That has nothing to do with lamenting his end, which he did not deserve. He *was* a great man," he said. "I just never thought he was worthy of *you*. He attained you too easily; and I thought it meant he would not treasure you as you should be treasured."

"I think he came to, in time."

"Well, time ran out for him. And I am sorry."

"I thank you." I paused. "But I also do not feel well, physically. I fear there may be something wrong. Pray, tell me what you think . . ."

He tapped around and listened to my heartbeat, felt my neck and ankles, had me breathe on him, squeezed my ribs and rotated my feet. He listened to my recounting of all the symptoms I could recall. At length he said, "I cannot find anything overtly wrong—nothing that cannot be accounted for by the bad experience you have had. Come, walk with me in my new garden.

Or rather, it is your garden, since I planted it on palace grounds! We will walk, and I will teach you a little about medicine."

Outside, the air was soft and perfumed with the last bloom of ornamental fruit trees, and their spreading new leaves were creating a dapple of sun and shadow on the green lawns beneath them. How different these grounds were from Caesar's villa. Here the lawns were flat and winking with white flowers, and seemed to call out for a rich purple cloth spread out for a picnic. *Come, and enjoy yourself*, the lawn whispered in the breeze.

Ptolemy was kneeling under one of the trees, and we called to him. He looked up sharply and said, "I am watching this bird's nest." He pointed to a neat round nest on a forked branch above his head.

"The mother bird won't return if she sees you," said Olympos. "Come with us. I have something to show you."

I looked over at him while he was talking. He also had changed while I was away. His features had sharpened, and now I would describe him as saturnine. That, and his dark sense of humor, must isolate him from people. I wondered if those traits were reassuring in a physician, or kept people away. And what of his private life? He was near my age—had he plans to marry? Such information never passed in letters.

Ptolemy dragged himself to his feet and then ran over to us. I noted how weak his legs looked, and how out of breath even that little run had made him.

"Olympos has made a garden while we were in Rome," I said.

Ptolemy made a face. "Oh, a garden! That's for women—or invalids. No, thanks."

"This is a garden for murderers and for miracle workers," said Olympos. "I think you'll find it unlike any other."

It lay on a flat expanse not far from the temple of Isis, but facing the harbor rather than the open sea. It was bordered by, first, a low stone wall, then, inside that, a hedge covered with red blossoms. Olympos lifted a heavy-bolted gate to let us in.

A fountain was gurgling in the center, and from it four paths radiated out, neatly quartering the garden. "Behold—death in one corner, life in the other."

All I saw were beds of plants, some blooming, some tall, some short. I looked at him questioningly.

"I came across a manuscript in the Museion that had a list of poisonous plants," said Olympos. "Some of them were quite clearly imaginary—such as a plant that emitted flames and engulfed bystanders. But others—I became curious about them. How did they work? Why did they kill? I thought it would be helpful if someone compiled a treatise on them. After all, some of them are harmless or even beneficial in small doses. And I must admit I was curious to study them—plant equivalents of poisonous snakes."

Ptolemy's eyes had grown round. "Poison!" he said. "Which ones?"

"For one thing, the entire hedge is poisonous." Olympos gestured to it.

"But it is so beautiful!" I said. It was; it shone with deep-green leaves and was studded with flowers.

"Nonetheless, it is violently poisonous. It is called the Jericho rose, and if the flowers are placed in water, they poison it. If the twigs are used for cooking meat, the meat will be poisoned; even the smoke from it is poisonous. Honey made from the flowers is poisonous, and horses and donkeys die from eating its leaves, but here's a mystery—goats are immune!"

"So, if you wanted to kill an enemy, you could serve him the poisoned honey?" asked Ptolemy.

"Yes. I don't know how much it would take to kill him, though. He might have to eat a great deal."

We began walking along the pebbled pathway. On each side lay neat beds of plants.

"I have arranged all the deadly ones to the left," said Olympos. He paused before a clump of plants with lobed, hairy leaves, standing about a foot tall. Buds of flowers were visible, furled on top of the stalks. "Can you guess what that is?" he asked us.

"Just a weed, like what we see in meadows everywhere," I said. "And sometimes I have noticed it growing out of crevices in walls."

"It's henbane," said Olympos, with satisfaction. "It can kill you in only a few minutes. Painfully, too. But in small doses—I have a feeling that it could actually be medicinal. I think it could be used to stop vomiting. But there is no way to control the strength of it. The poison probably varies from plant to plant, and the leaves have different amounts from the roots. It can either make you excited, singing and dancing and talking to imaginary people, or stupefy you, giving you vivid dreams of flying or becoming an animal. Then death. One cannot predict."

"What about just touching it?" I asked.

He smiled. "I always wear gloves." He strolled a little way down the path, then pointed to a patch of white, star-shaped flowers swaying on slender stems. They looked like miniature lilies. "These are called 'dove's dung.' "

"What an ugly name for such a pretty flower," I said.

"All of it is poisonous, but especially the bulbs," said Olympos. "They can be ground up and disguised in flour, to bake a pretty loaf of bread. Of course, it's somewhat bitter, so it would have to be dipped in Jericho rose honey to entice the appetite." He laughed.

"What happens if you eat it?" asked Ptolemy.

"The first thing you'd notice is shortness of breath," said Olympos. "Then gasping. Then—you'd die."

"All in just a few minutes?" he said. "Then that isn't what I've got, even though I have trouble getting my breath."

"No," said Olympos, but I could see him struggle to make a joke of it. "There are no enemies to put a poisoned loaf of bread at your plate."

"Look! What's that?" Ptolemy was enthralled. He pointed to a bushy stand of plants, topped with bunches of delicate white flowers. The stand was almost waist-high.

Olympos stood by them proudly, almost paternally. Yes, it was time he married, and had children to dote over, rather than his plants. "You know how to select the most illustrious. This is none other than hemlock, which ended the life of Socrates."

Hemlock! I stared at it in fascination. The white-topped stalks, with their drooping foliage, looked merry enough. "What happens when you drink it?" I asked.

"Oh, you needn't drink it, although a draught can be made. It has a characteristic odor of mouse urine." He seemed to find this amusing. "You can also use the leaves to make a tasty salad. It takes a little while before the symptoms appear. You would have an opportunity to finish your meal in polite company."

"What does it feel like?" asked Ptolemy.

"Well . . . it has been described as a gradual weakening of the muscles, and a creeping paralysis. The mind remains clear, though."

"Is it painful?" I asked. It did not sound like a bad way to die.

"Unfortunately, yes. As the muscles die, they cry out in pain."

"Tell me, Olympos—is there any relatively painless way to die? Through poison, I mean?" I asked.

He thought a moment. "None that I can think of. The body does not want to die, especially if it was perfectly healthy up until the moment it ingested the poison. So it fights. And many of the poisons have more than one effect, causing multiple symptoms."

"What about the hemlock?" Ptolemy was persistent. "How long does that take?"

"Long enough to make memorable deathbed speeches, as Socrates did. That makes it a good choice for writers, poets, and philosophers." He paused. "But hemlock isn't all bad. A little of it can be used to treat chest pains and asthma. Of course, you have to be brave to try it."

"Or desperate," I said.

"Poison and medicine are closely allied. In fact, in Greek the term *pharmakon* is used for both. And who's to say that when life itself has become a disease, poison may not be the best remedy?"

I thought of the "Roman way" of impaling oneself on a sword. Certainly poison seemed more civilized. And I thought the Romans were a little too eager to commit suicide. It did not take much of a setback before they were reaching for their swords, or opening their veins.

"That is true," I said.

We continued walking down the path, while Olympos pointed here and there. "Deadly nightshade," he said, indicating a spindly-looking shrub with oval leaves on it. "Now that's a lively plant. Everything about it is poisonous. It produces wild symptoms—blurred vision, and heartbeats so loud you can hear them an arm's length away. Very painful." He turned to me. "You wouldn't want to take *that*."

He ambled along. "Here's the dog-button plant," he said. The flowers were gray and fuzzy. "There's something in it that kills with violent convulsions. It leaves a hideous grimace on the victim's face."

"Enough of this!" I said. "Frankly, they are all beginning to sound alike."

"No, I want to hear more. What's that?" Ptolemy pointed to a bush with stalks of white blossoms.

"A most interesting plant," said Olympos. "Spurge laurel. Even the scent of the flowers can make someone unconscious in a closed room, and it stays poisonous long after it is dead and withered. The symptoms are dreadful: unquenchable thirst, excruciating stomach pains, skin all over the body peeling off, burning inside."

Laurel. I was sure it was not the same leaves as the Romans used in their laurel wreaths, but some of the symptoms sounded similar: unquenchable thirst—for glory; burning inside—for power; stomach pains—gut churning from envy and strife.

"Is there no antidote?" I asked, more for my allegorical illness than for the real one.

"Antidote? Only in trying to help the victim vomit up the poison. And often that seems to harm him as well."

So. Once you were afflicted with it—once the laurel wreath went on your head, you were doomed.

"Let us leave these poisons behind," I said. "Show us the other side of the garden, the side that cures."

Ptolemy made a face. "Oh, that's boring!" And he paid little attention to the beds of healing plants—to the wormwood, henna, labdanum, tragacanth, ginger grass, balsam trees, aloe, and spikenard.

"Now here," said Olympos, "is the corner of the garden where the plants have both properties. Like the bitter apple." He waved at a vine on the ground, just finished flowering and budding with baby gourds. "In small amounts, the fruit can be used to kill insects or induce miscarriage. In large amounts, it makes a messy, painful death."

"Please don't use it on us," Ptolemy said.

"And here is the famous, mythical mandrake," said Olympos. He pointed to a plant with fleshy, wrinkled leaves growing in spokes from a central stem. Purple blossoms nestled in the middle. "The love apple. It induces desire in its . . . victim? Or beneficiary?" He laughed. "In addition, it aids in conception. But, in large doses, it causes stupor, purging, and death. Unfortunately, it can't be mixed with wine, so any seducer can offer wine to his partner, but cannot partake himself—lest his love potion turn into a death potion."

"I thought there was something strange about its root," I said.

"Yes, it looks like a—a phallus," said Olympos. "And supposedly it shrieks when it is pulled up from the earth."

"Like a phallus?" I could not help laughing. "I never heard one shriek."

Olympos actually looked embarrassed, and Ptolemy turned bright red. Then they both burst out laughing.

"It would make a good scene in a Greek comedy," Olympos finally said.

With that, we were all ready to quit the garden. I took one last look at the mandrake, lying there on the ground so innocently, and laughed again.

That evening I took a quiet supper in my chambers with Charmian, Iras, Ptolemy, and little Caesarion, who was now learning to eat with manners.

"As King someday, you must endure many banquets," I told him, tucking a napkin into the neck of his tunic. Banquets were not the least onerous duty of a monarch. How many ways could oysters be prepared and presented, and how many cries of delight could one give in a lifetime? "Now you recline thus. . . ."

The light was fading, and oil lamps were lit. I felt a sad listlessness, a letdown. In some ways I did feel like an alien here. Rome had changed my view of the world; what had once seemed entirely sufficient and happily self-contained here now seemed isolated and neglected.

But that is nonsense, I thought. It's not neglected at all—thousands of ships pass through our port, and goods from all over the world converge here before continuing their journey. Silk, glass, papyrus, marble, mosaics, drugs, spices, metalwork, rugs, pottery—all are funneled through Alexandria, the greatest trading center in the world.

But still, it seemed quiet. Perhaps it was only that normal life seemed quiet after the steady progression of intrigues, coups, murders, and revolutions that had begun in my eleventh year.

Isn't it a miracle that you are sitting here now, undisputed Queen of an independent Egypt, eating a serene meal? I lectured myself, like a stern teacher to his students. And being able to tell Ptolemy truthfully there would be no poisoned bread at his table? Your country is pacified, content, prosperous. What ruler could ask for more? And who started life with less chance of achieving it?

". . . mandrake plant."

A conversation had been going on all the time, and I had not heard a word.

"Why are you talking to yourself?" asked Ptolemy. "I see your lips moving. And you aren't listening!"

"My mind was wandering," I admitted. "I am still on board that ship in many ways."

Charmian cast me a sympathetic look. She knew what I meant, and it did not refer to the waves nor being shaky walking on dry land.

"I should think you'd be glad to be off that smelly old thing!" he retorted. "Now tell them about the mandrake—and about that plant with the fuzzy button flowers that makes you contort up, until you look like a Gordian knot!"

"He was quite taken with the poisonous plants in Olympos's garden," I said. "He ignored the healing ones. And you've made up the part about the Gordian knot—Olympos did not say that!"

"Well, he should have." Ptolemy picked at his food. "All this makes me lose my appetite."

"We have to get the tasters back," I said. Our faithful food-tasters had retired—it was a nerve-racking occupation, and no one did it for very long. After they returned to their hometowns, they usually let their food impulses run wild, eating anything that took their fancy, day or night.

"Yes, my lady," said Iras. "There is much to be done, now that you are back for good."

Back for good. Why did the whole world, even my wonderful realm, feel so desolate to me? All these people gathered here looked to me for strength and shelter, of one sort or another. And I would provide it, I would provide it . . . and may they never know how unsheltered their shelterer truly felt.

After supper, I asked Mardian to come to me. I needed to speak to him alone. When he entered the chamber, I was so pleased to see him, I almost laughed. He had grown stout, as I noted earlier, and soon would look like other eunuchs. I hated to see it, but there was nothing to be done. I could hardly forbid him food or order him to restrict himself. And I guessed that dainties of the table were a way of rewarding himself from the strain of having to carry the weight of the government for two years. At least I could rest assured that he wasn't rewarding himself, like so many ministers, by stealing from my treasury.

"Dear Mardian, I am more grateful than I can say to have a minister like you. Very few rulers can have been so blessed."

He smiled, and his big, square-shaped face lit up. "It is an honor to be given the responsibility, and I shouldered it gladly. However"—he took the seat I indicated—"I am relieved to have you back." He settled down, and arranged the folds of his gown, wiggling his feet in bejeweled sandals. "A new style from Syria," he said. "The merchant had to surrender a pair as part of the customs duty." He smiled wickedly.

They were most opulent. I thought of the austere Roman ones, and suddenly Octavian's built-up ones flashed through my mind. I laughed. "They are very becoming," I said. Mardian had no need of extra-thick soles, for he had grown quite tall. Poor Octavian—to be shorter than an Egyptian eunuch! "And your gown—is the fringe a new style as well?" Fashion never stood still here in the east.

"Oh, it became popular last year," he said. "The fringes are actually reputed to come from Parthia. But of course we don't admit it!"

"I have grown quite out of fashion, like an old tune," I said, with wonder. "I will need to have new clothes."

"That should be an enjoyable task."

"More enjoyable than poring over the reports and summaries, and meeting all the new ambassadors."

"That is what makes you a good queen—you have the fortitude to endure it," said Mardian.

"Mardian, I need to know how my absence was looked on here." I trusted him to be honest with me.

"In the palace? Why—"

"No, not in the palace. In Alexandria, and in Egypt herself. I know you always have your ear to the ground, and your family is in Memphis. What did people think?"

"They wondered if you were coming back," he said bluntly. "They thought—they feared—you might remain in Rome, that that would be the price of Egypt's independence."

"What, that Caesar would hold me prisoner?"

He looked horrified. "No, of course not. But that it would take a constant monitoring—and mollifying—of the fickle Senate, which cannot be done from far away."

"And what did they think of my liaison—my marriage—with Caesar?"

He shrugged. "You know Egyptians—Greeks too. They are practical. They were proud that you'd selected a winner, not a loser, in the civil wars."

Yes, it was the Romans who were obsessed with morality. The older peoples of the east had more wisdom. "At least I don't have to contend with that. Mardian, you cannot imagine what it is to live for two years among a people who do nothing but judge, moralize, lecture, and condemn. It's more than the climate that's gray and oppressive there!" Until I had said it, I had not quite realized the weight of that crushing mantle of judgment. Suddenly I felt quite giddy to be out from under it.

"Ugh!" he said, making a face. "Well, now you are back where we understand you. And treasure you. Welcome home!"

Home . . . but why, why, did it feel so odd?

"Thank you, Mardian. I longed for it all the time I was away."

He paused, as if wondering whether to speak further. Finally he did. "I must tell you, though, that now that things have—changed—there are those who will say that your policy was a failure, that your efforts have achieved nothing lasting for Egypt. It all vanished on the Ides of March, and we are back where we were before Caesar even came here. Who can guarantee our independence now?"

"I will guarantee it. I must." But I felt as though I had climbed an enormous mountain range only to find myself not on a fertile plain, but facing another range just as high. A second climb would be almost beyond imagining. And then there was the other thing.

"Mardian, I must tell you of what I discovered on the voyage. I am with child. There will be another 'Caesarion'—a little Caesar."

He raised his eyebrows. "Oh, that will upset the balance of politics once again. How do you manage to affect people, and lands, hundreds of miles away? It's your peculiar magic."

"I doubt that it will change things in Rome. Caesar did not mention Caesarion in his will, and this one will have even less claim."

"Don't be so sure. I would guard Caesarion well. It was all very well to joke with Ptolemy about the poisonous plants, but it's Caesarion whom someone would have a reason to kill."

I felt cold. It was true. Caesar's will or not, the world knew about his son. And my own father had been illegitimate. The royal bastard, perpetual threat, was not only a stock figure in stories and poems, but he often attained the throne.

Was Octavian capable of murder? He seemed too squeamish and law-abiding. But . . .

"By leaving no Roman heir, Caesar left three—now you say four—contenders for his name. The adopted son, Octavian; his cousin, Marc Antony, the natural successor to his military and political legacy; Caesarion, his natural son by a non-Roman; and now another." He paused. "Of course, he has another heir—the mob, the Roman people. It was they to whom he appealed, they to whom he left his villa and gardens. Don't leave them out of any political calculations. It's they who will decide if Caesar is to be a god, not the Roman Senate."

"I cannot wish that my children inherit any of the mess at Rome. I just wish they could have known their father as they grew up. And I wish I had something of his—besides just this pendant." I held it out to show it to Mardian. "It was a piece of family jewelry. But I wish he had given me something for Caesarion, as well."

"Well, all he will have to do is go into any forum or temple throughout the Roman world, and he'll see a statue of him. They'll make a god out of him, mark my words. Then there'll be busts, and little statues and plaques, available from every hawker and merchant from Ecbatana to Gades!"

Dear, irrepressible Mardian! "He can start a collection!" I said, tears of laughter welling up as I pictured a shelf full of Caesar statues, all sizes and shapes. There would be muscular naked Greek Caesars, Syrian Caesars with big eyes and formal robes, desert Caesars mounted on camels, Pharaoh-Caesars, Gallic Caesars clad in wolfskins.

I held my sides and bent over. When I could finally catch my breath, I said, "Oh, Mardian. This is the first time I have truly laughed since—" I shook my head. "Thank you."

He wiped his eyes. "Since everything passes through Alexandria, think of the duty. We shall profit by the fashion!"

37

A high, breezy day in June, when all of Alexandria was an aquamarine set in silver, so bright that I had to shield my eyes.

Today the mosaic Caesar had given me was being installed in the floor of my banqueting hall. My memory had been correct; when I had first seen it I had known it was the exact same colors as the sea at Alexandria, and so it was. The form of Venus rising from the seafoam was rendered so finely that it made all mortal women look crudely executed, disappointing.

I sighed. Was art to inspire us, or depress? Was the fact that no living woman could ever approach such perfection to inspire me to come as close to my own perfection as possible, or did it merely throw all my shortcomings into high relief?

Today, with the glorious light and strong fresh breezes of the morning, I felt inspired by her. Once I had felt this newly created, once I had felt I had just emerged from a sea, eager to stand on the shore and claim my inheritance, my destiny. Would I ever feel that way again?

Her golden hair waved in tendrils over her shoulders, so skillfully depicted that I could see the muscles and delicate roundings in the flesh.

How old are you? I asked her, in my mind. Fifty years? A hundred? You would look very different by now if you were flesh instead of stone. Art cheats truth that way.

"I remember when it was presented." Charmian's husky voice behind me made me jump. The sound of the workmen's chisels had drowned out her footsteps.

"It is magnificent, isn't it?" We both looked at Venus, envying her. "You look more like her than I do," I said. "You have the right hair color."

"No one looks like her," said Charmian. "That's why she has the power she does."

Charmian herself had a Venus-like allure. I had seen how men looked at her, like lovesick schoolboys, even the old scribes.

"Charmian," I said, "I think you should consider marrying. It does not mean you cannot continue in my service. I cannot help but feel sorry for the man who would have been your husband—but you pass him by."

She laughed, that beguiling, low laugh. "I have been thinking of it," she admitted. "But I have found no mortal man yet. You see, just as Venus spoils most women for men, just so Apollo ruins other men for women. I'd like someone like the statues of Apollo, and, well—have you seen any about?"

Yes, I thought: Octavian. But, unlike a statue, he talked, moved, and exhibited unpleasant characteristics. "No, not recently."

"Ever?" She persisted.

"Probably not ever," I assured her, lest she think I was hiding one. "But I will look harder from now on."

A grunting pair of workmen wrenched a stone out of the floor, and shoved it to the side. They were grinning, and I realized they had overheard us. Did they fancy themselves to resemble Apollo?

One had a hairy back, more like Pan than Apollo, and the other was so short, with long forearms, that he looked like an ape.

Barely able to keep from laughing, we hurried from the hall. As we rounded the door, we leaned against the wall and let ourselves laugh silently.

When I said, "That reminds me, where is my monkey, Kasu?" it sent Charmian into hysterics.

"I am serious," I insisted.

"I think—I think—Iras has her in her chambers," gulped Charmian. "She was fond of her."

We were standing on the steps of the palace, which led directly to the private royal harbor. Directly overhead the gulls were flying, white against the sky.

"Let's go for a boat ride," I suddenly said. It was too fine to be indoors today. "No, not sailing, something more—languorous. Where we can lie and look at the colors of the sea and sky." I had all manner of boats to choose from—a pleasure barge, a small sailboat, a shaded raft, a replica of a Pharaonic boat. That I had come to enjoy being on the water was a tribute to my determination of will—perhaps my most characteristic, and valuable, trait. Will can serve when talent, inspiration, and even luck desert us. But when will deserts us, then we are doomed indeed. . . .

Charmian was eager. "I have never been on the Pharaonic boat," she hinted. "The one with the lotus-bud prow."

"Then that is what we shall take."

We descended the wide, gently curving flight of marble steps—like a theater whose rows of seats overlooked waves. On the seabed below I could see the rocks and bright anemones through the clear, clean water. Far out, the ocean was breaking against the base of the Lighthouse, sending up columns of spray, as high and light as an ostrich plume.

I must have a sister-mosaic made for the Venus one, I decided at that moment. It should depict exactly the scene I am looking at now, and the blue of the seas will match. It must show our Alexandria's harbor on a fine day in high summer.

The boats were kept in readiness at all times, so there was no waiting while the captain made adjustments to the Pharaonic one. Charmian mounted the painted gangplank and hopped onto the deck.

"Oh!" She gave a gasp. "Is this real?"

Joining her, I answered. "If you mean is the wood really wood, and the gold really gold, yes."

"I meant only that it is fantastic, in the truest sense of the word."

"It is meant to satisfy a Pharaoh. I have been assured that they really floated about like this." Yes, they had lain on couches in the shaded cedarwood deck pavilion; they had been cooled by long-handled jeweled fans, should the winds not oblige; they had run their hands over gold-leafed rails. "Come." I led her to the pavilion, where we sank down on the cushions.

A servitor, dressed in the kilt, collar-necklace, and headcovering of ancient times, appeared, as in a dream, to bring us cool drinks.

We cast off, the rowers pulling silently with their silver-tipped oars, and rocked gently on the warm water.

The sea, the sea was what made Alexandria great. It brought the riches of the world to our doors, and gave us power. I must rebuild our fleet straight-away. As it was, we were powerless to defend ourselves except with the Roman legions that Caesar had posted here. But should they leave—or turn against us at the bidding of some Roman master, one of the assassins, perhaps . . .

The bright day seemed all the more tantalizingly bright for being so unsecured.

My spirits had soared for the first time that day, but by evening, like birds flocking back to their trees, they swooped and fell again. Was I never to be free of this shaded mantle that descended on me? Just as Caesar's love for me had enveloped me, now its absence, and his loss, provided an equally dark cloak that wrapped itself around me, at any time, but most particularly when the light of day faded into night.

I stood watching the stars come out. Venus had appeared first, of course, but one by one the others became visible, taking their assigned places in the constellations. Just so we had stood watching together, here on the roof garden. Just so he had named Orion, his favorite constellation, and recounted the story. . . .

The sky now seemed hard and empty in spite of all the familiar stars. I turned my back on it and forced myself to go to my work desk in the adjoining room, where a pile of treasury ledgers awaited me. At times the figures blurred before my eyes, and it was not because of the flickering of the oil lamps.

Always, even as my mind became absorbed in the additions and subtractions, there lurked that *other*, that melancholy, just beyond the line of my vision. So I was not unhappy when a servitor announced that Epaphroditus had come to discuss some business. It was a relief to be interrupted.

He was all apologies about the late hour.

"It does not matter," I said, putting down my papers. "As you can see, I was working. Work hours never cease. And the evening is a good time for them."

Out in the warm Alexandrian night, there were people walking the streets, singing, laughing, drinking, while their Queen was shut up in a room with her ledgers.

"Then we are two of a kind." He smiled. "My wife does not appreciate my continual working, but she enjoys the fruits of it."

It was the first time he had ever permitted a personal remark to pass his lips. So he was married. Did he have children? But I would wait for him to tell me.

"I have the final reports about the contents of the three new warehouses, built to replace those destroyed in the fire. We have installed shelves that are narrower, so that no inventory will be hidden. It also makes rat control easier." He handed me the papers proudly.

I waited. It seemed an odd errand for him to come on, at this time of night. He could have sent the papers at any time with a messenger.

"I also wanted to report something I heard from one of the captains who arrived today."

So. I was right. "Yes?"

"This is not official, merely what this man heard. But it seems the assassins have had to leave Rome. Where they will go is anyone's guess. Caesar's heir has come to Rome to claim his inheritance, and has been rebuffed by Antony. It seems Antony treated him with rudeness and tried to scare him away, because he did not want to admit that he—Antony—had spent most of Caesar's money."

The money! Yes, Antony had obtained it from Calpurnia, to keep it safe from the assassins.

"But the young man has not gone away. He has enlisted Cicero on his behalf, and is making a ruckus. Antony will have to come to terms with him. In the meantime, no one seems to be ruling in Rome."

Antony should have known better than to treat Octavian with contempt. The younger and less secure someone is, the more he has to be flattered. "So they are preoccupied with the chaos there?"

"For now," said Epaphroditus. "But will the assassins eventually flee to the east and set themselves up here? That is the danger."

"I wish they would, so we could kill them!" I said.

"With what? The Roman legions here? What if they took command of them themselves?"

"I have thought of that," I said. "What Egypt needs now is a strong navy. I must start to build one up. And I can see that the treasury will permit it."

He smiled, pleased and surprised. "Good."

"I would like to discuss the procurement of the long timbers with you soon," I said. "I know you deal with the Syrians."

"Indeed."

He seemed such an enigma—this cultivated man, immensely resourceful, of limitless energy, with his two names.

"Madam, you seem very dispirited," he observed. "Forgive me if I speak out of turn. May I help?"

I was so startled I could barely keep the surprise off my face. But at the same time I was touched and grateful.

"Not unless you can turn time backward, erase events that have already happened." But I said it gently, wistfully.

"That is beyond man's power," he said. "Only God could do that, and he does not. But he does provide consolation. Our scriptures are full of questions that we put to him, and he answers in verse. Betrayal, and loss—they are all there."

"Teach me," I said, feeling like a child before a particularly erudite tutor.

"In our main book of poetry, there is one that says, 'Mine enemies speak evil of me, When shall he die, and his name perish? All that hate me whisper together against me: against me do they devise my hurt. Yea, mine own familiar friend, in whom I trusted, which did eat of my bread, hath lifted up his heel against me.'"

Yes. That was exactly the way it had been, with Caesar and his "friend."

"'For it was not an enemy that reproached me; then I could have borne it. But it was thou, a man mine equal, my guide, and my familiar friend.'"

The hateful Decimus, his kinsman, named one of Caesar's heirs—who had lured him from his house to the Senate!

"I must acquaint myself with your holy book," I said. "It seems to have much of mankind in it. It can ease sorrow by acknowledging it." Not like the philosophers who wished to deny it, or tried to avoid it by advising anyone embracing his wife to think only that she must die, so that when she did, he would have lost nothing.

"We were sorry to lose Caesar, too," said Epaphroditus. "It will be a long time before the Jews can count such a man among their friends again."

Yes . . . I remembered the sight of the Jews, keeping a faithful mourning by the funeral site for days.

"He confirmed our rights to the free exercise of our religion, including the right to send the yearly Temple tax unmolested from other countries, he gave us back the port of Joppa, which Pompey had taken, he stopped the abominable practice of 'tax-farming,' which bled us dry, and he exempted us from military service, since it would require us to break our dietary laws and work on the Sabbath. Yes, he was our friend. We lost our champion, just as you did."

"Perhaps he was good to you because he sensed you valued it," I said. I knew how unappreciated he felt most of his gestures were. It was comforting to know that others felt deprived and bereft in this horrible aftermath. "What will happen to Judaea now?" I wondered out loud.

"That will depend on who succeeds Caesar in Rome," he said. "And how successful young Herod is in outsmarting his enemies in Judaea. Antony and he are old friends from the campaign with Gabinius to restore your father to the throne; Herod helped him with troops and supplies. Would he help the assassins now, if they came east and demanded it? Hard to know. He's a clever young man, but the politics of survival in that region are going to be tricky." He paused. "Personally I prefer Herod to his rivals, because he is the only one with the sense to see that a zealot-led country is doomed. He divorces his religion from his politics. But the others . . ." He shook his head. "They will not stop until Judaea ends up completely subjugated and smashed."

"How odd, to have religion run a government," I said. I could not imagine the highest contest in the land being Zeus versus Serapis versus Cybele.

"We are different," he agreed. "That always makes it hard to predict what will happen to us, in the short *or* the long run."

The wind was starting to stir the curtains dividing the room from the terrace. Outside, the golden lamps in houses were being extinguished. It was getting late, and people had retired. I should let Epaphroditus return to his home. He had done me a favor by coming to me privately to report the news from Rome, but it was far past business hours. Yet I found that every remark he made aroused my curiosity and led me to ask another question.

"Mardian mentioned, almost offhandedly, that you do attempt to predict what will happen to you—that you have books of prophecy, and expect a deliverer, or a messiah. What is that?"

He looked almost embarrassed. "The sacred writings of one people are apt to provoke ridicule when recited to an unbeliever."

"No, I truly want to know. To what was he referring?"

"Over the ages our beliefs have changed," he said. "We never believed in an afterlife—we had our own version of Hades, *Sheol*, a dark place where shades wander. Nor did we think of the ages as a story, marching forward to some preordained end. But some of our newer writings have begun to see life as continuing after death, of the soul's survival—and the body's, too—and events proceeding to some great change. The agent of this change will be the Messiah."

"But who *is* this Messiah? Is he a king? A priest?"

"It depends on which prophecy you read. Zechariah, one of our prophets, speaks of two messiahs—one a priest, and one a prince from the line of our great King David. Daniel calls him the Son of Man, and says there is only one."

"But what does he *do?*"

"He ushers in the new age, one way or another."

"What new age?" I asked.

"An age of purging, of judgment, followed by a golden age of peace and prosperity."

Peace and prosperity. That was what we had in Egypt now—if Rome would allow us to keep it. "That is what I wish for my people, and my land." I looked at him sharply. "Do you believe these prophecies?"

He smiled. "I do not trouble myself with them. I have found that if you have urgent daily business to take care of, the dreams of what may happen seem to recede. I don't *disbelieve* them, I simply have no need of them. They do not answer any lack in my own life."

"There are also prophecies about a woman savior," I told him.

He grinned at me. "Ah. So now I see. You are wondering if you are she, and unaware of it?"

"No, but I wonder if any of the people see me as that."

He thought for a moment. "It is possible. But you would have to study those writings for yourself. I am not familiar with them."

389

I sighed. "They are scattered writings. I know one is called the Oracle of the Mad Praetor, another the Oracle of Hystaspes, and there's something called the Potter's Oracle. Then there are many uttered by different sibyls. I shall have to have them copied at the Library and study them."

"If you look hard enough, you are sure to see yourself in them," he warned. "That is the way of prophecies. They expand and contract and always fit the situation at hand. Like fortune-tellers and astrologers."

"You don't believe in them either?"

"That they may have some knowledge, yes. That it can be partial, and deliberately mislead you, makes them dangerous. That is why our God has forbidden us to have anything to do with them. Moses told us that God said, 'Do not practice divination or sorcery. Do not turn to mediums or seek out spiritualists, for you will be defiled by them.' "

I thought of all the astrologers and fortune-tellers attached to my court. It was a good thing I was not bound to follow this Moses. Then I had a sudden remembrance. "Is not Moses the one who led you out of Egypt? Someone told me he had absolutely forbidden you to return. So why are all the Jews of Alexandria here? It seems you obey about the astrologers, but not about Egypt."

He laughed. "Now, if I wanted to be difficult, like some of our legalists, I could argue that Alexandria is not 'in Egypt'—she is called *Alexandria ad Aegyptum*: Alexandria-by-Egypt. But I find such arguments tiresome and cloyingly clever. The true answer is that we disobeyed, as we have a habit of doing."

I laughed. "Like all subjects," I said. "I must count myself lucky that my subjects have not been as rebellious as your people."

"Indeed." He bowed. "Your Majesty—"

"Yes, I know. It is late, and I have kept you too long. A poor reward for your diligence in coming to me after hours. Pray, go now."

Clearly relieved, he took his leave. After he was gone, I stood for a long time at the window, gazing out at my sleeping city. *Was* there anything to these prophecies? What did they say?

As I lay down and rested at last, I knew he was right: the idea of them was dangerously seductive . . . both for the ruler and the people. But I still wanted to see them.

38

Day followed day in the splendor of high summer, and I gradually mastered all the accounts, ledgers, and reports that had accumulated awaiting my return. It was the Egyptian month of Epeiph, and the month of Quintilis, now officially called Julius, in the Roman calendar.

From what my informers told me—for by this time I had established a few listening posts in Rome—Brutus was incensed. He was especially infuriated because, while he himself had to stay away from Rome for his own safety, the *Ludi Apollinares*, games that he as praetor was required to sponsor, were going take place right in the middle of this newly named month. The honors would accrue to Caesar, but the cost would be borne by Brutus.

Then I heard that Octavian, as if to snub Brutus's efforts, was holding games right afterward to celebrate Caesar's victories—the *Ludi Victoriae Caesaris*—and he was doing it at his own expense, to show his "father's" love for his people. He was also demonstrating his own loyalty, since the officials in charge of putting them on were too cowardly to dare.

But before any reports came to me about either set of games, I had yet another misfortune. I lost the child I was carrying, the last legacy from Caesar.

In its particulars, it was like the birth of Caesarion, only the child was too small to live—it was only halfway to its time of normal birth. I was forced to lie abed, dosed with pennyroyal and draughts of red wine. It was not my body that needed cosseting, however, but my spirits.

Farewell, and farewell, I thought, holding tightly to the pendant around my neck. Now there will never be a new thing between us; our life together is frozen in the past.

Gone, gone, and gone, I repeated to myself, lying on the bed, and each word was like a hammer on my soul. Gone forever.

Everyone was very kind, hovering around me. Charmian and Iras anticipated my every wish, Mardian came with jokes and riddles, Ptolemy wrote some stories that he insisted on reading to me, and Epaphroditus had some of his scriptures copied out for me. They all dealt with loss and fortitude.

I particularly liked one that went, "Thus saith the Lord, A voice was heard in Ramah, lamentation, and bitter weeping; Rachel, weeping for her children, refused to be comforted for her children, for they were not." *For they were not* . . . sad words, sad thought, true thought.

The nights were hot, my chamber stifling. They moved my bed out onto the terrace, where sea breezes blew and I could see the stars. I would lie and look up at the blue-black bowl that arched over me, thinking of the Egyptian belief that each night the goddess Nut, stretched across the sky from east to west, swallowed the sun, which traversed her body to be reborn each dawn. She was always depicted in gold, lying across a deep, rich, blue sky.

It was artistic fancy. The stars were not gold, they were a cold, fiery white, and the sky was inky. And the nights I lay outside, the moon was dark as well.

Then the anticipated rising of Sirius, the star that had been below the horizon for seventy days, took place. A brilliant spot of light, it signaled the first day of the new year and announced that, far away to the south, the Nile too would begin to rise. The year was cycling, moving relentlessly on.

I could hear, far below me and outside the palace grounds, the shouts of excitement as Sirius was sighted, and the noisy celebrations began. Even to the Alexandrians, the rising of the Nile was life-bringing, as it was necessary to produce the grain the city exported.

How bright the light of the Lighthouse was tonight! They must have stoked it up with extra fuel—how long a trail the flames were making! Then I suddenly saw that it was not the Pharos at all, but something else behind it, something in the sky.

I flung off my light coverlet and went to the edge of the roof, changing my angle of vision. Yes . . . it was a brilliant light, hanging all by itself in the sky, low, so that it was almost even with the top of the Pharos. But it was not a star—it had a long tail.

A comet! There was a comet in the sky!

I had never seen a comet, but I somehow knew that was what it was. It was beautiful, unique. The tail trailed off in little twinkles that looked like glowing sparks; the head hovered protectively like the hood of a divine cobra.

At once a strange sensation passed through me, a jolt of recognition. It was Caesar, taking his place in the heavens, among the gods. And also, at this very time, rising to show me that he would never leave me, would always be with his true wife and fellow divinity, and take my part from heaven. He would not suffer our son to be kept from his inheritance. He would fight for it with me, more powerful now in the heavens than ever he was on earth, where he was hemmed in by little men and his own mortality.

I heard his voice in my ear, softer even than a whisper—or was it merely inside my own head?—saying that all would be well, but I must stop this mourning, I must rise from the sickbed and be the Cleopatra he admired for her strength and ingenuity. That was the true Cleopatra, the Queen of Egypt and wife of Caesar, not this weak creature weeping and lamenting and languishing.

You must bear losses like a soldier, the voice told me, *bravely and without complaint, and just when the day seems lost, grab your shield for another stand, another thrust forward. That is the juncture that separates heroes from the merely strong.*

The comet blazed, commanding my attention, saying, *Take heed!*

And I said, "Yes, I do," and felt joy for the first time since his death—or rather, as I knew it now to be, his departure.

I lay back down and watched the comet, closing my eyes and letting it hang over me all night.

————

392

Far away in Rome, unknown to me at the time, Octavian also saw the comet, which appeared just as he was holding his Caesarean games between July twentieth and thirtieth. It caused a sensation among the populace, who also interpreted it as I had: They knew it was Caesar, being accepted into the panoply of gods.

Octavian at once announced his "father's" divinity, and affixed the supernatural star to the brow of Caesar's statues and declared that henceforth all coins would depict Caesar wearing his celestial star.

And, also unknown to me at the time, Octavian took the comet to be a summons to himself, announcing his destiny and calling on him never to rest until he had avenged Caesar's murder.

Both of us called to arms by Caesar that night—both of us wishing to avenge him and complete his work—both of us needing to destroy the other to do so. Caesar had two sons, but there could be only one heir. Caesar had a vision of his future world empire—but was it to be centered in Rome or Alexandria? Would it be western or eastern in location and spirit? And who would preside over it?

The astrologers were abuzz with excitement about the comet, which remained in the sky for many days, and held nightly gatherings in the Museion to study it. From as far away as Parthia astronomers and astrologers came—they were honored with the title *magi*, or wise men—to meet with their fellow scholars. Once again Alexandria was the center of intellectual excitement, and I took great pride in that. I met with them myself one evening, asking them to draw up some astrological charts for Caesarion and Ptolemy and me.

They were gathered in the circular marble hall of the building, in its very center. Most of them wore Greek dress, but the foreigners wore their long embroidered robes and two Egyptians from Upper Egypt wore the ancient costume of the Nile.

"Gentlemen, I am surprised that you are not outside studying the comet and the heavens directly," I told them. Rolls of charts were spread out on folding tables, along with mathematical books.

"Some of us are," said Hephaestion, our leading astronomer. "The viewing platform on the roof is very crowded. The rest of us are working on the charts down here, amending them."

"Had you predicted this comet?" I asked.

"No," he admitted. "No, it was a complete surprise."

That strengthened the proof that this was no ordinary comet, but a supernatural appearance. "What is your conclusion about it?"

"It is miraculous," he said. "It must portend some event of great importance. The birth of a child, perhaps, who will fulfill one of the many prophecies?"

No, that was not it. Caesarion had already been born, and the next baby lost. Even Octavian—should he fancy the comet was for him—was already eighteen. Could it be interpreted by him—erroneously, of course—as marking his taking Caesar's place in Rome? "No, that cannot be," I said impatiently. "More likely it announces the world upheaval that started with Caesar's death."

He nodded in assent, just to be polite. I looked over at all the scholars pouring over their charts and arguing. "Can you deliver these horoscopes to the palace within three days?" I asked, presenting him with the data. I was most anxious to peek behind the workings of fate and see what was ahead.

Again, he bowed politely.

When the horoscopes were duly presented, I discovered that even though the astrologers had used the most ambiguous and soothing language, the stars were not kind to Ptolemy. As for Caesarion and myself, our destinies were intertwined, taking strength from each other. The fulsome prediction for me was that I would die as I wished, and live eternally. The words shimmered—did it mean "die as I would like to die, in the manner in which I would like to," or did it mean "die because I would wish to"? Astrologers! But as for Ptolemy—I saw now that I would have to take him to Upper Egypt for the winter, if he had any hopes of recovery.

"But I don't *want* to go," he protested, when I told him. "I want to stay here. There is nothing up there—nothing but palm trees, mud huts, and crocodiles!"

Yes, plenty of crocodiles. Reports had just come in that there seemed to be a plague of them. Suddenly the Nile above Thebes was swarming with them, and so many crocodiles were basking on the sandbanks that it looked like a forest of wrinkled logs spread out on each side.

"Upper Egypt is very beautiful," I said, remembering my voyages there. I had found it peaceful and lulling. "I will come with you, help settle you. We will stop at the shrine of Kom Ombo and pray to the crocodile deity there to call back his plague of crocodiles. And you shall see Philae, the most beautiful temple of Egypt, set on an island in the Nile."

He made a face. "I don't care about that! I want to stay here and help design the play-trireme they are making for Caesarion!"

"I will have them wait until you return," I assured him. "Caesarion is too small to go out alone in it yet."

For the first part of our journey, he was sulky. He did not wish to watch as the Nile and the land slid past us, but I paid careful attention to the condition of the irrigation ditches and dikes, especially in the Delta, which depended on irrigation. The waters had not started rising down here yet—it took almost twenty days before the flood reached us from the First Cataract.

In spite of his fierce words, Ptolemy lay listlessly under a canopy, scowling and coughing. He was clearly miserable.

We passed the pyramids, and he scarcely looked up at them. We passed by Memphis, passed the Moeris Oasis, passed Ptolemais, the last Greek outpost on the Nile. The river began to swell with the inundation. We had come to it, rather than waiting for it to come to us in Alexandria.

The river widened into a lake, and still we sailed onward, past Dendera with its Temple of Hathor, then past Thebes with its enormous Temple of Amun and its outsized statues of Ramses seated before his mortuary temple. The bleak hills where the dead Pharaohs held court in their rock-hewn chambers stretched far away from our line of vision.

Suddenly the river began to boil with the shapes of crocodiles. Everywhere I looked, there were the ripples in the water where a scaled back would break the surface; there were churning pockets in the reeds. Along the mudbanks they were lined up, some yawning and exposing gleaming curved teeth. They thrashed their tails slowly, and wiggled in the mud to settle themselves.

"Look!" I said, shaking Ptolemy, who was dozing in the midday heat. "Have you ever seen so many?"

He opened his eyes groggily, but they widened at the sight. "Great Serapis!" he exclaimed. "All the crocodiles in the whole world must be collected here!"

In fascination we watched while a dog came down to drink at a place on the bank that looked deserted. He approached warily, but thirst was his master and he had to drink. Gingerly he lowered his muzzle down to the surface of the empty-seeming water. He had barely touched it when an enormous shape rose up and snatched him, so quickly that my eye could barely follow the motion. A crocodile had been waiting, submerged.

The water frothed and the dog, yelping, shot above it, held in the grip of a crocodile jaw the size of a plow. The crocodile plunged him beneath the water and held him there until he drowned. Then the outsized jaw surfaced, its maw open, gulping down globs of flesh that had been alive only moments before. Blood spread out over the water and a flotilla of crocodiles rushed toward it, attacking the first crocodile and trying to wrench his meal from his jaws. Limbs and scaled tails lashed in the bloody water.

Pieces of the dog, its ears and tail, floated free but were soon snatched by other waiting crocodiles.

I shuddered. No wonder the villagers had sought help from the government; they could scarcely obtain water for themselves. I saw that the lone village water dipper was now enclosed by a high mud-brick wall, barricaded in. No one could dare approach the river to fill water jugs or wash clothes. And as the river flooded beyond its banks, it would wash the crocodiles out into the streets and houses. There would be crocodiles wandering the streets at noon, crocodiles lurking under benches, crocodiles napping in the shade behind buildings.

Ptolemy struggled to sit up and make his way to the rail. He hung over it, fascinated by the beasts.

"Don't stand too close," I warned him. I had seen how far out of the water a crocodile could lunge.

When at last we reached the temple of Kom Ombo, the sun was setting.

I knew we could not make the proper supplications before darkness closed in, and so I gave orders for us to anchor offshore, far from the rustling reeds and from the sandbanks that were covered with the draped forms of crocodiles.

"No sleeping out on deck," I told Ptolemy. The crocodiles would probably be prowling about, watching for a dangling arm. Crossly, he obeyed and came in to his bed in the cabin, flinging himself down. He fell asleep almost immediately.

I lay in the darkness, listening to the lapping of the water against the side of the boat, hearing—or imagining I heard—other sounds as well: of big, muscular animals slapping against the boards, or trying to claw their way up onto the deck. In the early dawn I rose and, drawing a mantle around me, stood and watched the sun rise. It touched the swaying reeds, kissed the golden sandstone of the temple, lighting first its roof and upper columns. Purple clouds still lingered, with a few stars on their fringes behind the temple.

My father had built part of the temple, and very proud of it he had been. On the temples of Upper Egypt he had been—carved in stone, at least—the warrior king he had not been in the flesh. I remembered my excitement when he had brought me here as a child to show me the new pylon and columns, and had kept me up late at night telling me about the caravan trade running from Kom Ombo to the Red Sea, where once the African elephants had been brought north to be trained for the Egyptian army. It had seemed a magical place then, and this morning it still cast a spell.

In the reeds a stirring announced that the crocodiles were beginning their day, and it was time we did, too.

A long gangplank was flung across the mudbank, with protective mesh on each side, and we hurried across it, alerting the crocodiles, which were still sluggish in the early light. We climbed quickly up the little hill where the temple reared itself above a bend in the Nile, looking out over the countryside. The golden pillars, carved with scenes of all the rulers who had helped build the temple, greeted us. There was one of my father being ceremonially cleansed by Horus and Sobek, for this temple was dedicated to both the falcon god and the crocodile god. Sobek, the crocodile god, stood taller than a man, with a man's body, broad shoulders, and kilt, and then the snouted head of a crocodile, wearing a headdress and crown. His shrine and hall were on the right, and we made our way into them, passing through the roofed hall from the honeyed sunlight outside to ever-increasing dimness, and finally to the inner darkness of Sobek's sacred shrine.

We lit candles, and approached the shrine holding the divine statue of the god, carved of dark granite. From inside the shrine the eyes of the god glared back at us, white and rounded, the perfectly rendered scales of his long snout making him look lifelike.

As Queen, and incarnation on earth of Isis herself, I spoke to him face-to-face. "Great Sobek, why do you trouble my land? Why have you sent out legions of crocodiles to infest the waters downriver from the First Cataract? Is there something you lack? Let me provide it, so that you may call your creatures home."

The idol stared back at me, unyielding. The leaping flame of the candle played over his impassive features.

"I will provide what you lack, but I must ask you to desist from your attack on my land."

Beside me, Ptolemy tugged at my gown. "Don't sound so peremptory," he whispered. "You shouldn't talk to him like that."

No, it was fitting. I was Queen, indwelt by Isis, and he was—let us be frank—a minor god, restricted to this little area. Other gods had beaten him back a long time ago, and Horus had even taken over half his temple.

"I leave you gifts here, Sobek, great god of the crocodiles, but in the name of Isis and of the people of Egypt, who are in my care, I insist that you call your creatures back."

Or else Olympos and I would devise a way to poison the waters and kill the crocodiles.

Together, Ptolemy and I intoned a hymn of praise to Sobek and laid our gifts of flowers, wine, and precious ointment before his sacred barque. We stood in silence for a few moments, then departed.

The sun was well up now, and warming the courtyard of the temple. Over to one side stretched the necropolis of mummified crocodiles; on the other, a great rounded well attached to a lower Nilometer. I made my way over to it, and peered over the edge.

I was surprised to find that the water had not risen very high yet. Along the Nilometer's wall the line of the "cubits of death" was clearly marked, below which famine would result. The Nile was still quite a bit below this cutoff point, but the season of flooding should be well advanced by now. I felt a wave of unease.

We hastened back to the boat, rushing over the gangplank serving as a bridge across the crocodiles, who were now eagerly awaiting food. They snapped to attention as our shadows flitted before their eyes; one large fellow opened his mouth, displaying rows of teeth and a fat, healthy tongue, as pink as a flower. Obviously, Sobek was taking good care of his own.

Now may Isis be so kind to us as Sobek is to his creatures! I prayed. We would press on to Philae, lay our concerns before the great goddess, and give Ptolemy up into her care.

It was another day's sail up the gently swelling Nile before we reached the vicinity of the First Cataract. The usual roar of it was muffled, because the water had risen high enough that many of the sharp rocks were submerged, and we could sail—albeit very carefully—through the area that was normally so dangerous. The wide bosom of the water looked lustrous and pearly, reflecting the sky at twilight, where we anchored within sight of Philae.

In the dying light, the tiny island glowed from hundreds of votive candles left by pilgrims. Although the walls of the great Temple of Isis were made of sandstone, tonight they looked like the thinnest alabaster, white and translucent.

I had vowed never to return, after the strange ceremony I had gone through there with Caesar, which afterward seemed a mockery. Now I was not so sure. Perhaps ceremonies—even ones recited in unknown tongues—have a power in and of themselves. Perhaps Caesar had found himself bound by it after all.

One by one the lights flickered out, snuffed by the wind, and the outline of the temple faded. It remained only faintly illuminated by the struggling half moon that hung impaled by the reeds growing everywhere.

I lay on my bed, feeling the warm wind caressing me, feeling protected by Isis, hovering over her holy island.

We went ashore at first light, before the throng of pilgrims would arrive. We wanted time alone with the goddess. Ptolemy seemed especially listless, and had trouble walking the short distance from the landing area to the gateway of the temple.

"Look!" I said, pointing to the first pylon, where our father was depicted in full glory, armored, smiting enemies.

"Yes, yes, I see," he said wearily.

A white-robed priest of Isis met us, bowing low. "Your Majesties," he said, his voice low and melodious. "In the name of Isis, we welcome you to the shrine."

"We have come to petition the goddess for healing," I said.

"Ah yes," he replied, moving his head to indicate all the offerings left in the courtyard. "Many hundreds come here—tribes of Nubians from the south, Greeks, Arabs, even Romans. This is the premier site of healing, the fountain of it, so near the source of the Nile. And the burial place of Osiris. It is truly holy ground." He looked at Ptolemy kindly, and would have reached out to touch him, but it was forbidden.

I put my arm around Ptolemy's shoulder. "May we approach the sanctuary?" I asked. "Our gift-bearers follow." I indicated the four menservants, dressed in the requisite new unbleached linen, carrying gold caskets with myrrh, gold, cinnamon, and sacred white sweet wine from Mareotis.

The priest turned and, walking in the slow, measured steps of ceremony, led us through the portals of the first pylon into the smaller court, and then through the second doorway that led into the darkened interior, where sacred chapels flanked the inmost holy of holies.

No natural light entered here; the stones were fitted together so closely that no seam was visible, keeping out the prying sun. In the left chapel, intricate candle stands flanked a life-size gold statue of Isis standing on a pedestal, throwing a soft yellow light upon her.

She was beautiful, serene, all-compassionate, all-wise. Gazing on her, I felt a tranquillity, a peace that I had seldom felt, and then only fleetingly.

O great goddess! I murmured to myself. How could I ever forget your face?

I bowed, feeling supremely blessed and yet supremely humble that I was chosen of all women on earth to be her mortal representative.

The priest flung incense into the thurible at her feet, and a piercingly sweet scent filled the air. He began to pray, reciting a hymn of praise to her:

> Isis, giver of life, residing in the Sacred Mound,
> She is the one who pours out the Inundation
> That makes all people live and green plants grow,
> Who provides divine offerings for the gods,
> And invocation-offerings for the Transfigured Ones.
>
> Because she is the Lady of Heaven,
> Her man is Lord of the Netherworld,
> Her son is Lord of the Land;
> Her man is the pure water, rejuvenating himself at Biggeh at his time.
>
> Indeed, she is the Lady of Heaven, Earth, and the Netherworld,
> Having brought them into existence through what
> Her heart conceived and her hands created,
> She is the Bai that is in every city,
> Watching over her son Horus and her brother Osiris.

I stepped forward and, laying down my gifts, said, "Daughter of Re, I, Cleopatra, have come before you, O Isis, giver of life, that I may see your beautiful face; give me all the lands in obeisance, forever." I inclined my head.

The goddess was silent. Now I must sing her a hymn, and I would sing my favorite, the joyful one I had not spoken since the ceremony with Caesar.

> O Isis the Great, God's mother, Lady of Philae,
> God's Wife, God's Adorer, and God's Hand,
> God's mother and Great Royal Spouse,
> Adornment and Lady of the Ornaments of the Palace.
>
> Lady and desire of the green fields,
> Nursling who fills the palace with her beauty,
> Fragrance of the palace, mistress of joy,
> Who completes her course in the Divine Place.
>
> Raincloud that makes green the fields when it descends,
> Maiden, sweet of love, Lady of Upper and Lower
>   Egypt,
> Who issues orders among the divine Ennead,
> According to whose command one rules.

Princess, great of praise, lady of charm,
Whose face enjoys the trickling of fresh myrrh.

From a hollow behind the goddess, a high-voiced priest answered in her name, "How beautiful is this which you have done for me, my daughter, Isis, my beloved, Lady of Diadems, Cleopatra; I have given you this land, joy to your spirit forever." There was the dry, silvery rattle of a sistrum, and the disembodied voice continued, "I instill fear of you throughout the land; I have given you all the lands in peace; I instill the fear of you in foreign countries."

Fear of you in foreign countries . . . to what destiny was she calling me? The Ptolemies had not had any foreign possessions in generations, and it was Rome who inspired fear in foreign countries now.

I bowed to show that I accepted her benefactions and gifts.

Beside me, Ptolemy was standing stick-straight, trembling.

"You must speak to her now," I said. "She awaits."

Still he stood silent, as if he were afraid to utter a sound.

"I will leave you in private," I said. Perhaps that was better.

Coming out of the dark, smoke-filled sanctuary into the bright morning sunlight made me dizzy. The courtyard was still empty; the guards were holding the people back until we departed. I was alone there, except for a swaying priest or two, walking in the shaded colonnade, chanting private prayers.

Off to one side was the birth-house, a symbolic depiction of the birth of Horus to Isis and Osiris. The legend of Isis and her husband, in its many forms, was celebrated and reenacted here. Is there any child today who does not know it? Osiris was killed by his evil brother Seth, was searched for and found by the grieving, faithful Isis; miraculously she conceived her child Horus by the dead Osiris, and gave birth to him in a papyrus marsh in Lower Egypt. Then the evil Seth killed Osiris again, dismembering him and scattering all the parts up and down Egypt. Once again the faithful wife gathered all the parts and reassembled them, bringing Osiris back to life in the Underworld, where he reigns as King of the Dead, "he who is continually happy." In the meantime, Horus grew to manhood and avenged his father by killing his uncle Seth. Together Osiris, Isis, and Horus live as the holy family, a blessed three. The birth-chapel commemorated the miraculous birth of the child. Across the water from Philae, on the neighboring island of Biggeh, part of Osiris lay buried, and every ten days a golden statue of Isis was ferried over in a sacred barque to visit her divine spouse, reenacting the old tale. I gazed at its rocky shore through one of the openings of the colonnade.

It was so close to the truth in my own life that I was shaken. I was Isis, Caesar Osiris, Caesarion Horus . . . Caesar, killed by evil men, now a god . . . I left behind to grieve and avenge him, and raise his son to carry on his name and heritage. Like Isis, I felt that great loneliness in roaming through all the land, looking for bits and pieces of him.

Suddenly resolute, I made my way to the small chapel where we had recited those mysterious vows so long ago. Bits and pieces of him . . . and here was one.

I entered the little square room, its walls carved with low reliefs showing Pharaohs making offerings to Isis, watched by the winged vulture of Upper Egypt. Just here we had stood. I saw the very paving stones where his sandaled feet had rested, and the places where the hem of his cloak had brushed. I placed my feet where mine had been and reached out my hand to clasp— empty air.

Yet I was not alone. Only the thinnest of barriers, an invisible but immensely guarded one, separated us—time and death. I no longer felt mocked, or bereft, but oddly comforted. The ceremony still held across that barrier, uniting us.

Outside in the sunlight, I walked and waited for Ptolemy to appear. The gentle lapping of the water against the banks of the island was soothing, calming my racing heart. I remembered that there was a Nilometer here, too, in the form of steps leading right into the water. I descended them and realized I walked down a great many before I came to the water. The mark for a minimal rise was still five steps above where the water ended. My heart started racing again.

That there had been some rise was obvious; had we not floated over the Cataract? But it looked meager. I searched for the carving I knew was on one wall depicting Hapi, the god of the Nile, in his cave of Cataracts. What was Hapi doing to us? I said several prayers to him.

I did not notice how long I was there, but I looked up to see a weak, coughing Ptolemy being led from the temple, leaning on two priests.

"He is quite overcome by his encounter with the goddess," said one of the priests, fanning him. Ptolemy continued to cough. I suspected it was not the goddess's presence but the smoky incense that had overcome him. Doubtless Olympos would agree; he thought incense was a poison to the lungs.

"We wish to leave him under your care in the healing-shrine," I said. "Do you not have a home where priests and priestesses tend the ill who have come to Isis?"

"Yes, and it is a private one. That is, it is not open to all pilgrims—or it would have to be enormous. This is a small home, where the patients can live in a healthy manner," the priest assured me.

I was well pleased with all I saw. The paved courtyard was swept immaculate; flowers bloomed around the well in the center, and no dogs or cats prowled the quarters. Attendants, gentle women who felt they were serving Isis in her guise as a healer like Asclepius, tended the invalids, walking them in the sunshine, reading to them, bringing them food. It seemed to offer Ptolemy the best care possible.

When he did not protest at being put there, I began to be alarmed. It meant he did not have the strength to struggle.

Smoothing his brow as he was put to bed, I assured him, "The goddess will heal you, and you will be back in Alexandria this time next year, with this just a memory."

He nodded docilely, and squeezed my hand.

I decided not to depart for several days, but I did not tell him that, lest he bolt and try to come back with me. I asked the priest to report to me each morning and evening.

For the first four days, all the reports were good. Ptolemy had slept well; his color was improving; he was even eating soup and bread. But on the fifth day the priest came rushing to me before sundown.

"Your Majesty, the King, he—he choked on his food, and went into a coughing fit, and then fainted. We fanned him, and propped him up in bed, and then he started spitting up blood."

"I had best come back with you." Together we hurried out the door and rushed to the sick-house.

I found Ptolemy slumped over his pillows, his arms limp like cut willow branches. His face had a deathly pallor, with red spots dotting his cheeks. He was utterly changed from my last sight of him.

"Ptolemy!" I spoke softly to him, kneeling beside him.

He opened his eyes with great effort, and focused them on me. "Oh . . . I thought you had gone."

"No, I am still here. I am here as long as you need me."

"Oh." He reached out a feeble hand and fumbled for mine. I took it; it was hot and dry, like a locust husk lying in the sun.

He gave a great sigh, filling his lungs with air. When he breathed out, frothy red foam appeared in his nostrils.

He closed his eyes, and did not open them again.

I felt his hot little hand tremble and contract a little, and then grow limp. He died, quietly, effortlessly, with a sigh for all he was leaving behind.

I said nothing, but remained holding his poor little hand. Time enough to talk when the priest returned.

Down the Nile, our boat now a funeral barque. The priests at Philae had prepared Ptolemy, readying him for his journey into eternity. That took many days, and all the while a transport-coffin was being prepared. I waited, suspended between the world of the living and the dead.

Day after day I watched the Nile making faint efforts to rise, and not succeeding. Trouble after trouble seemed to be raining upon me; would I now have to face a famine in the land, in addition to the loss of my husband, my unborn child, and my brother?

How strong do you think I am? I implored Isis. I cannot bear any more!

Yes you can, and you will, the waters seemed to murmur back, unmoved.

The boat was draped in funeral hangings, and the oarsmen wore mourning. People lined the banks—as closely as they could and still avoid the crocodiles—and watched silently as we floated past. The journey seemed interminable, and when we passed Kom Ombo and I remembered Ptolemy's fascination with the crocodile god, I wept. So many things had delighted him. The world would be a grayer place without his laughter and boyish curiosity.

He was on his way back to Alexandria. I remembered my promise: *This time next year you will be in Alexandria, and all this will be just a memory.* The goddess had fulfilled my words, but not in the way I had intended.

39

Merciless, pristine-clear sun poured over the funeral cortege like water from a jar. The wagon bearing the sarcophagus of Ptolemy wound its way through the streets of Alexandria, following the route of all official processions before ending at the Soma, the royal mausoleum at the place where the two great thoroughfares crossed.

All my ancestors lay there, entombed in elaborate chambers, in ornamented stone sarcophagi. To walk past them was to see the changing taste in burial fashions—from the plain, square container of Ptolemy I to the overly decorated one of Ptolemy VIII, so festooned with carved vegetation that it looked like a grape arbor. It was a ghastly parade of the dead. I shivered as I walked past my father's tomb, and then the unembellished—for we had punished him in death—one of my other brother Ptolemy, the traitor. This Ptolemy would have a solid one of pink granite, polished to a high gloss, carved with boats and horses. I had tried to think of what he loved best and would want to keep with him, but there were so many things he enjoyed.

Flaring torches lighted the underground passage, making a brief day. But it was soon over, the gates were clanged shut and locked, and we emerged out into true daylight.

Two funerals, each horrible in its own special way: Caesar burnt to ashes, his bones gathered later to be put in his family tomb; Ptolemy preserved to the best of the embalmer's art and laid in a dark box, stiff and cold. Death was grotesque.

All Alexandria had to observe mourning along with the palace for seven days. Business was suspended and ambassadors waited, boats rode at anchor with their cargoes, bills went unpaid.

It was now October, and the Nile had clearly failed. The water barely touched the demarcation line of the "cubits of death" at all Nilometers. Here in Lower Egypt the water had spread out in little puddles, barely filling the reservoirs. Now it was already receding, a month ahead of time. There would be famine.

At least the low Nile meant that the crocodiles suffered. Unable to catch enough food, many of them disappeared into the mud, to sleep and wait for better times. Others waddled up on land and found themselves stranded, or at the mercy of villagers who could corner them and spear them. Others apparently withdrew to the waters beyond the cataract. Sobek had obeyed me—or, rather, Isis-in-me.

When the time of mourning was officially over, I consulted with both Mardian and Epaphroditus about the expected crisis in the harvest.

"Yes, there will be a shortfall," said Mardian. "I have already had the figures drawn up."

"How bad a shortfall?" I asked.

"As bad as ever we've seen," he answered. He shook his head. "It is indeed fortunate that the past two years have been good ones."

When I was away, I thought. Perhaps, in the best interests of Egypt, I should live elsewhere! I said so.

Mardian raised his eyebrows. "Now really, where would you like to live? What other place could compare to Alexandria?"

"Oh, I would consider Ephesus, or Athens." I was curious to see them, and their two wonders—the Great Temple of Artemis, and the Parthenon.

"Bah! Too filled with Greeks," said Epaphroditus. "Who would want to live with *Greeks?*"

"He has a point," said Mardian. "They argue too much. Almost as much as the Jews! That's why Alexandria is so riotous and quarrelsome—the Greeks and Jews keep at each other, in a continual stew."

"Not like you placid Egyptians," said Epaphroditus. "I think you would bore yourselves to death."

"Now, gentlemen," I said. "Let us not start a riot in here. My ministers should be above these national characteristics." I was only half joking. "If we must institute relief measures for the famine, how stands the treasury? Can I afford to start rebuilding my fleet anyway?"

Mardian looked alarmed. "Dearest lady, that would cost a fortune!"

"A fortune to save a fortune," I said. "I know the eyes of Rome will turn to the east again. The last contest, between Caesar and Pompey, was settled in Greece. The assassins are coming east, I know it. I feel it. And when they do, we must be prepared. Prepared to defend ourselves, or to lend aid to the party of Caesar."

Mardian crossed and uncrossed his legs—a habit of his when he was thinking. "What of the four legions already here?" he finally said.

"They owe allegiance to Rome," I said. "We need a force that answers only to us. A sea force."

It was well known that the Romans were weak at sea. Their legions were seemingly unbeatable on land, but little of that love of battle carried over to their navy.

"Yes, I agree," said Epaphroditus. "And I think the treasury can stand it. It will take most of what we have, though. We will be left with no reserves."

No matter. They had filled again fast enough, and we needed this navy.

"I think we will need at least two hundred ships," I said. Both men's faces registered surprise. "Anything less will not be much of a navy," I insisted. "Half measures are of no use at all, but just a waste of money."

"Yes, Your Majesty," said Epaphroditus. "Shall I see to procuring the timbers and shipwrights? How do you propose to compose this navy? Mainly of warships, quadriremes and up, or of lighter, Liburnian-type vessels? It will make a difference in the size timbers I order."

"I would have it half and half," I said. I had done a great deal of reading, studying naval warfare, and it seemed wise to be covered on both fronts. Battles had been lost by overreliance on one type of ship. "And I myself will learn to captain a warship," I said. Now they both looked shocked.

"Your Majesty," said Epaphroditus, "surely you can trust admirals to command the fleet."

"I shall have admirals," I assured him. "But they shall be subordinate to *me*."

Mardian rolled his eyes. "Oh my," he sighed. "Oh dear."

I ignored him. "When the famine gets severe, by March or April, we shall have to open the granaries of Alexandria to the people. We will announce this now."

The grains of Egypt—wheat and barley—were housed in enormous granaries in Alexandria, where they awaited shipment or distribution. Guarding them was a serious duty; I employed a double detachment of soldiers around them.

"Now?" Mardian frowned. "They will come forward much earlier, then, than they need to."

"Perhaps. But it will also serve to keep worry—and insurrection—at bay."

He sighed again. Mardian preferred to wait for a trouble to come, rather than meet it halfway.

"This is an age-old problem in Egypt," said Epaphroditus. "You might be interested in knowing that in our scriptures, there is a story of just such a famine. It has some interesting aspects. I will send you a copy."

"It seems there is nothing that does not appear in your scriptures," I said. "But I would be most interested in reading it."

That night was duly delivered a manuscript, from the Greek version of his people's story, about a Pharaoh—mythical, of course—who had dreamed of the famine in time to save his people. I thought Caesarion would enjoy the story, and so I asked his servants to prepare him for bed and then bring him to me.

He now had his own quarters, filled with furniture, toys, pets, balls, games, and all the things a little boy would want. There was also a bust of Caesar, before which daily offerings were placed. I wanted his father to be ever before him.

He was now three years and six months old, a serious child who seemed to keep his own counsel, as if he had already seen too much, and it weighed on him. He was going to be tall, and as his face grew less rounded and babyish, his resemblance to Caesar became more pronounced. He spoke like an older child.

"Come and sit by me," I said, patting a cushioned hassock. Outside, the sky was a tender gray of twilight—a good time of day, when it slid into night. Obediently he came and settled himself, nestling against me. "Our good friend Epaphroditus has sent me a story about a Pharaoh of long ago, and a clever minister. I thought you would like it."

"Let me hear it," he said solemnly.

"It tells how the Jews first came to Egypt," I said. "There was a slave who knew how to read dreams, and it seems that the Pharaoh had a terrible nightmare. He dreamed that seven heads of good sweet grain bloomed, but they were eaten up by seven ugly, withered heads. Then he dreamed that seven fat cows came to drink at the Nile, but seven starved cows emerged from the river and devoured them."

Caesarion shivered. "But how can a cow eat a cow?" he asked, seriously.

"It was just a dream," I said. "Things happen in dreams that cannot happen in real life. Anyway, that is what puzzled the Pharaoh. When he awoke, he could not forget the dreams. He asked all his wise men what they meant, and nobody knew."

"No wonder. It didn't make any sense." He nodded wisely.

"Let me read you what happened," I said. "One of Pharaoh's servants remembered a Hebrew prisoner, named Joseph, who had the gift of interpreting dreams. 'Then Pharaoh sent and called Joseph, and they brought him hastily out of the dungeon: and he shaved himself and changed his raiment, and came in unto Pharaoh. And Pharaoh said unto Joseph, I have dreamed a dream, and there is none that can interpret it: and I have heard say of thee, that thou canst understand a dream to interpret it.'

" 'And Joseph answered Pharaoh, saying, "It is not in me: God shall give Pharaoh an answer of peace."

" 'And Pharaoh said unto Joseph, "In my dream, behold, I stood upon the bank of the river. And, behold, there came up out of the river seven kine, fat-fleshed and well favored; and they fed in a meadow. And behold, seven other kine came up after them, poor and very ill favored and lean-fleshed, such as I never saw in all the land of Egypt for badness." ' "

Caesarion giggled.

" ' "And the lean and the ill-favored kine did eat up the seven fat kine. And when they had eaten them up, it could not be known that they had eaten them; but they were still ill-favored, as at the beginning. So I awoke.

" ' "And I saw in my dream, and behold, seven ears came up in one stalk, full and good. And behold, seven ears, withered, thin, and blasted with the east wind, sprung up after them. And the thin ears devoured the seven good ears. And I told this to the magicians, but there was none that could declare it to me." ' "

Caesarion knitted his brow. "It must have to do with food, and eating. Grain and cows."

"Wise boy," I said. "Now listen. 'And Joseph said unto Pharaoh, "The dream of Pharaoh is one. God hath showed Pharaoh what he is about to do. The seven good kine are seven years; and the seven good ears are seven years: the dream is one. And the seven thin and ill-favored kine that came up after them are seven years; and the seven empty ears blasted with the east wind shall be seven years of famine. This is the thing which I have spoken unto Pharaoh: What God is about to do he showeth unto Pharaoh. Behold, there come seven years of great plenty throughout the land of Egypt; and there shall arise after them seven years of famine. And all the plenty shall be forgotten in the land of Egypt, and the famine shall consume the land. And the dream was doubled unto Pharaoh twice, because the thing is established by God, and God will shortly bring it to pass.

"'"Now therefore let Pharaoh look out a man discreet and wise, and set him over the land of Egypt. Let him appoint officers over the land, and take up the fifth part of the land of Egypt in the seven plenteous years. And let them lay up corn under the hand of Pharaoh, and let them keep food in the cities. And that food shall be for store to the land against the seven years of famine, which shall be in the land of Egypt, that the land not perish through the famine."

"'And the thing was good in the eyes of Pharaoh, and in the eyes of his servants. And Pharaoh said unto his servants, "Can we find such a one as this is, a man in whom the Spirit of God is?" And Pharaoh said unto Joseph, "Forasmuch as God hath showed thee all this, there is none so discreet and wise as thou art. Thou shalt be over my house, and according unto thy word shall all my people be ruled: only in the throne will I be greater than thou." And Pharaoh said to Joseph, "See, I have set thee over all the land of Egypt." '"

Caesarion wiggled. "What trust the Pharaoh had in him! What if Joseph had read the dreams wrong?"

I hugged him. "The greatest gift a ruler can have is to read those who come to him to serve him," I said. "Now listen: 'And Joseph was thirty years old when he stood before Pharaoh, king of Egypt. And Joseph went out from the presence of Pharaoh, and went throughout all the land of Egypt. And in the seven plenteous years the earth brought forth by handfuls. And he gathered up all the good of the seven years, which were in the land of Egypt, and laid up the food in the cities. The food of the fields, which was round about every city, laid he up in the same. And Joseph gathered corn as the sand of the sea, very much, until he left numbering, for it was without number.' "

"Oh!" said Caesarion. "I should like to see that grain, all heaped up!"

"'And the seven years of dearth began to come, according as Joseph had said: and the dearth was in all the lands, but in all the land of Egypt there was bread. And Joseph opened all the storehouses, and sold unto the Egyptians. And all countries came to Egypt to buy corn, because the famine was so sore in all lands.' "

I closed the scroll. "And so you see, Egypt saved all the world from starvation."

"Do you think that's a true story? Did it really happen?"

"Do you mean was there a real Joseph? I don't know. But I know that we do have granaries now where we store up our crops to protect us from famine. And we know how to predict a famine—by how high the Nile rises. But we can only do it for one year at a time. We already know there is not going to be enough food this year. And so, just like Joseph, when the time comes we will open our storehouses and distribute food."

"To the whole world?"

"Egypt already feeds the whole world," I said. "We export grain to Rome, to Greece, to Asia—we are a very rich country." I ruffled his hair, which was turning darker now. "When we open the storehouses, do you want to see?"

"Oh yes!" he said. "I want to see those heaps and heaps of grain! Are they like mountains?"

"Yes," I said, "golden mountains."

"Do you trust Epaphroditus and Mardian as the Pharaoh trusted Joseph?" he asked suddenly.

I did not have to hesitate. "Indeed I do. I am blessed to have such trustworthy ministers."

"How can you tell whether to trust someone or not?" he asked.

"As I said, it is a gift. And, of course, you should always watch what they do." But as I spoke, I knew that it was not a foolproof gift. Intelligent and discerning rulers had been betrayed. Perhaps the most successful betrayer is one who is loyal until the last minute. No one can detect him; he himself does not realize he is about to swerve.

Caesarion put his arms around my neck. "Good night, Mother. Please don't dream of cows!" And then he padded happily back to his own chamber, hand-in-hand with his nurse.

No, I would not dream of cows. But I did dream of my fleet, my wonderful fleet that I would build with stout timbers from Syria, and I dreamed of a sea battle, a great battle in which I hoisted my sails and shot through a barricade onto the high seas. . . . I awoke hearing the pounding of the sea outside, one of the first storms of autumn.

The fleet began to take shape, and dockyards throughout the Delta, as well as in Alexandria, worked overtime. Through daring seamanship (for which the Syrians were well paid, and for which they were willing to risk much), enough long timbers were brought across the sea that the skeletons of the largest warships could be laid, and allowed to season. The fittings of the ships—oars, sails, steering, lines, and rams—were assembled separately and proceeded apace. I had decided to divide the fleet in two, and station half with my governor at Cyprus, for more flexible deployment. While I was studying all the particulars of the designs for the ships, I made sure that a shipwright here in Alexandria was busy making the miniature trireme that I had promised to Caesarion. He was delighted with it, and we made many trips down the palace steps to the royal harbor for him to see it. It was to be about twenty feet long, small enough for two adult rowers to power it; the other oars were for show only, and were bolted down.

"And am I to be the captain?" he asked, parading around the half-finished vessel, peering up over the railings and onto its deck.

"Yes, but until you are seven you must always have an adult under-captain with you," I said. And this adult would be an expert. There must be no more accidents at sea for my family.

"What shall I name the boat?" he wondered.

"Something wonderful," I said. "But it is for you to decide."

He got that perplexed look again, which made him seem so old. "Oh, that is so difficult!" he moaned.

With the coming of the Roman New Year, the first of the conspirators met his doom. Trebonius—who, although he had not actually stabbed Caesar, had played a key part by detaining Antony to prevent him from interfering on the Ides—had calmly gone to the province of Asia to assume his governorship. Evidently his conscience was not troubled by proceeding to the province Caesar had so kindly allotted to him. But Dolabella, one of the Caesarian party, pursued him to Asia, fought with him there, and wrenched the province away from him. He killed Trebonius and hacked off his head, first flinging it before a statue of Caesar, then tossing it into the streets of Smyrna, where boys kicked it about like a ball.

So it began: the retribution. I rejoiced when I heard it. I only wished I could have stood over the bloody head and kicked it myself, kicked it and ground its eyes into the cinders and smashed the skull in.

In Rome, Octavian and Antony were becoming open enemies, mainly as a result of Cicero's whipping up the Senate against Antony. The orator thought to run Rome himself, to be wise mentor and guide to the young, impressionable, obedient lad. At last he, Cicero, would come into his own, statesman and savior of his country. How little he knew Octavian! It was Cicero who was the fool and the dupe.

But the vain old man wrote and delivered a series of speeches against Antony, and this ended with the Senate declaring war against him. They were filled with the most vicious lies and distortions, but, like most calumny, they were entertaining. There was no one alive who could smear a character better, with clever words and innuendo, than Cicero. He paid for it with his life, but not before he almost cost Antony his.

My prediction came true: After spending some time in Athens, Brutus made his way over to Macedonia, and Cassius came to Asia. They would unite and make their stand in the east. There would be a war.

Cassius set about unseating Dolabella from his governorship, and Dolabella appealed for help to me, asking for the Roman legions. Again, it was as I had foreseen. I had no choice but to yield them, because if they were not sent to Dolabella, Cassius would demand them. But before they could reach Dolabella, they were captured by Cassius.

My legions were in the hands of the enemy—Caesar's assassin! And then he pursued Dolabella over Syria, surrounding him at last in the city of

Laodicea. Knowing he was beaten, Dolabella committed suicide. Cassius was victor, and now commanded all of Asia Minor, as well as Syria, and had fourteen legions, eight of which were contributed by the governors of Syria and Bithynia, Allienus's four captured en route from Egypt, and the two from the defeated Dolabella. Fourteen legions! And then the hardest blow of all— he persuaded Serapion, my governor in Cyprus, to surrender all the ships of my new fleet stationed there to him. They sailed off to Asia, joining Cassius.

The perfidy of it! The assassins were not only making their stand, but they were appropriating my forces!

Cassius next turned his eyes toward Egypt, and announced that he planned to invade and capture us, since we had sent the legions to aid Dolabella. It was time, he said, for us to be punished, and to yield our resources to them— the Liberators, as they called themselves.

Plague was raging; it had followed hard on the heels of the famine. The heavens seemed to be hurling thunderbolts at my kingdom, as if determined to topple it. I fought back, to the utmost of my strength.

More meetings with my ministers—Mardian, Epaphroditus, and Olympos got very little rest during those weeks. Every morning there were mounds of people who had died during the night. They couldn't be embalmed, for no one wanted to touch them; instead they were burned like trash.

One morning after a particularly bad night, Olympos brought me a manuscript and said I should read it; the author had written a brilliant description of the disease.

"What good is a description?" I asked. "Who cannot describe it? Fever, thirst, eruption of boils, black swellings that burst open, quick death. But how can it be stopped? That's the question."

"Please, do read this. He has ideas about how it spreads." Olympos thrust it into my hand.

"Very well. I am ready to do anything to halt the disease." I looked at Epaphroditus. "I suppose there is something about this in your scriptures!"

He grinned. "How did you know?"

"What *isn't* in there? Well, what cured it?"

"Nothing cured it," he admitted. "There was a succession of plagues—of frogs, of gnats, of flies, of locusts, of boils—but they were sent to make a point. They weren't natural."

"What point is *this* plague making? I cannot believe that the gods are aiding our enemies! Am I now to expect plagues of flies, frogs, and locusts as well?"

We were almost bankrupted by the combination of the plague, the famine, and the loss of half the fleet. Work continued on the other half, based in Alexandria. Let Cassius come and get it, and die trying!

A messenger rode all the way from Syria on the bidding of his master, Cassius, who was now attacking Rhodes to get money and ships. I received the man in my audience hall, seated on my elevated throne, in my most formal attire.

He marched into the hall, his Roman soldier's uniform bringing old memories sharply into focus. It was like seeing a shell of Caesar—the breastplate that I had loved, the leather lappets that made a slapping noise when he strode forward, the cloak slung over his shoulder. It seemed a travesty for this runty little man to be wearing the same clothes.

He barely bowed. But he had to wait for me to acknowledge him before he could speak.

"What do you wish?" I asked coldly.

"I come in the name of Gaius Cassius Longinus," he said. "My commander requests that you send the remainder of your navy to him in Syria. Immediately."

As much as I hated and despised the assassins, I knew that craft and dissemblance, delays and prevarication are weapons as powerful as outright defiance. The man who cannot control his face and words before an enemy is soon overthrown. So I put a false smile on my face and spread my hands helplessly.

"I would comply willingly," I said, the words sounding abominable in my own ears, "but my country is devastated by plague. The fleet is not finished yet, and I can get no workmen to continue, let alone sailors to man it. We are in dire straits. In fact, you are a very brave man to have come within our borders—risking your own life!"

He shifted a little on his feet. I noticed that he was bandy-legged. "Indeed?" His voice was gruff.

"Yes. The plague attacks where it will. And one of our physicians has recently written a paper in which he puts forward a theory that it travels through the air." I rolled my eyes about the room. "That would explain its mysterious ability to attack from nowhere. No one is safe. Especially not foreigners, who seem especially susceptible."

"I feel well enough," he said truculently.

"Mars be praised!" I said. "May it continue!"

"We'll send our own men to man the ships," he said. "They must be yielded to us immediately."

"Of course," I said. "But there is no need to send them while the plague rages and the fleet is yet unfinished. They cannot sail ships without keels or masts. We shall complete the fleet as soon as possible, and deliver them to you."

"We will brook no delays!" he said. "Do not toy with us!"

I nodded to one of my attendants, who nodded to two men standing just outside the hall. They marched in, carrying a litter with a corpse on it, and laid it down at the man's feet. He recoiled from the sight of the swollen, stench-ridden body, and leapt to one side.

"Is this toying with you? Is this victim joking?"

The man covered his nostrils and turned his head away. I indicated that the litter should be removed.

"You seem to have a strong enough stomach," the messenger finally said, breathing again. "Do not think to put us off with such dramatic, repulsive displays!"

"Why, how could I? You see worse at the Roman games," I said. "No real *man* would be bothered by the sight of a flyblown corpse. Yes, you shall have the fleet, as soon as you may."

"My commander will be seeing you soon enough in person, when he marches to Egypt. Do not flatter yourself that he can be put off with such tricks." I hated the way he kept rolling his shoulders. I wanted to tell him it made him look like a juggler. Now he squared them. "You should know what has happened to Marc Antony, that Caesarian dog. He attempted to wrest the province of Near Gaul away from Decimus—"

Decimus, the vile traitor! Decimus, who, like the evil Trebonius, had helped himself to the province Caesar had entrusted him with! It was too much to be borne!

"—in defiance of the Senate, which declared him a public enemy—"

The Senate! What had Cicero done to them?

"—and besieged him at Mutina. But Decimus and an army sent by the Senate routed him, and he had to flee across the Alps with his legions. He is struggling there now, starving, we have heard, stranded in shoulder-high snow and reduced to eating roots. That's the end of *him*." He nodded, his chin making stabbing motions of satisfaction.

I felt a sickening, swooping sensation, as if my throne had dipped and plunged. Antony stranded in the snow, starving, freezing! It could not be. Only then did I realize how much confidence I had had in him to prevail, to set the times right again. *I am Caesar's right hand*, he had said. Was Caesar's right hand now to be stilled?

And . . . the only remaining Roman I had liked and respected would disappear, plunging the world into true chaos, where one could choose only between one villain and another, with no honorable men anywhere. Antony had failings, but they were failings of the flesh, not of the spirit—unlike his enemies, who were the opposite.

The man was watching my face. Had my thoughts been visible? "What has happened to Decimus?" I asked calmly.

He scowled. "Decimus had to flee," he conceded. "Octavian could not see his way clear to—cooperating with him."

Hardly. Octavian would never ally himself with Caesar's murderer.

"Where has he gone?"

"He—he tried to go to Greece, to join Brutus, but Octavian's army blocked his way, so he had to flee to Gaul, where he wandered as a fugitive. It seems that a chieftain there has slain him."

Joy surged through me. Another assassin dead, killed!

"They say the chieftain was an agent of Antony's," the man admitted.

O glory! O praise to Antony!

"But Antony will not live to know it," he said. "Undoubtedly he is dead now, a frozen corpse, eaten by wolves."

No. I refused to let myself picture it. "All that is in the hands of the gods," I finally said. "What dreadful things were set in motion by the Ides of March, we cannot know until they run their course."

"The deed itself was noble," he insisted, "and the Liberators acted from the highest motives."

"The gods will judge," I said. Even my iron will could not steel itself to make a polite answer, when I longed to strangle the man. And all I had to do was signal my guards to kill him. But why give Cassius the satisfaction, the excuse to revenge himself on me? I meant to win the battle of wills, and if fate was kind to me, to stab Cassius myself, using his own dagger, the one that had taken my love away from me. I needed to get close enough to him to do it. I would embrace him, only to kill him. Thus I must lull his natural caution, let him think it was safe to approach. Yes. Let him come to Alexandria! And such a feast I would give him, such a welcome . . . wine, song, food, and his own dagger, buried up to its hilt in his lean belly.

I approached the shrine of Isis daily, pouring her sacred water before her as an offering, and begged for the life of Antony with a passion I thought I had lost. I had not thought consciously about him until Cassius's envoy had delivered that devastating message about his fate. His absence from the world would diminish it in a way I was hard put to explain to myself. Only it seemed that with Antony's disappearance, the sun would slip below the horizon for good and true night come, never to depart. Was it only because he shone with the reflected light of Caesar? Was it because all the other Romans were so despicable? As I said, I could not explain it, I only knew that I beseeched Isis to help him, ready to promise her anything in return for his life.

And once again, as she had done so long ago, she hearkened to me. Word came that he had survived the ordeal of the retreat across the Alps, and had emerged a hero.

The report came from a letter intercepted on its way to Brutus in Greece, copied secretly, resealed, and then the copy sent on to me.

I had retired into my most private chamber to read it. The words leapt out at me, written as they were for someone else's eyes.

> *Antony was defeated, and both the Consuls were slain. Antony, in his flight, was overtaken by distresses of every kind, and the worst of them was famine. But it is his character in calamities to be better than at any other time. Antony, in misfortune, is most nearly a virtuous man. It is common enough for people, when they fall into great disasters, to discern what is right, and what they ought to do; there are but few who in such extremities have the strength to obey their judgment, either in doing what it approves or avoiding what it condemns. And a good many are so weak as to give way to their habits all the more, and are incapable of using their minds.*

Yes, that was true. But enough of the lecture. What had *happened?*

Antony, on this occasion, was a most wonderful example to his soldiers. He, who had just quitted so much luxury and sumptuous living, made no difficulty now of drinking foul water and living on wild fruits and roots. Nay, it is related they ate the very bark of trees, and, in passing over the Alps, lived upon creatures that no one before had ever been willing to touch.

A flash of excitement and admiration went through me. Yes, I could picture the struggling troops, and Antony willingly abasing himself to survive and fight again. . . .

The design was to join the army on the other side of the Alps, commanded by Lepidus, whom he imagined would stand his friend, he having done him many good offices with Caesar. On coming up and encamping near at hand, finding he had no sort of encouragement offered him, he resolved to push his fortune and venture all. His hair was long and disordered, nor had he shaved his beard since his defeat; in this guise, and with a dark-colored cloak flung over him, he came into the trenches of Lepidus, and began to address the army. . . .

It was the very spirit of Caesar, such as I had not thought to see again. I was much moved.

The rest of the letter described his pact with Lepidus. Together they now had seventeen legions and a magnificent cavalry of ten thousand horse, and were marching on Rome. They were on their way to a pact with Octavian, to join forces and pursue the assassins.

They would pursue them from the west, and if fate granted me the opportunity, I would slay them from the east. I still meant to stab Cassius by any means possible. Nothing less would satisfy me than turning the dagger upon him with my own hand.

Where it had hung unmoving before, time now seemed to speed up. The year rushed forward. The plague abated, the granaries kept starvation at bay, and Egypt survived.

On the first day of the Roman New Year, the Senate formally declared Caesar a god. So those who would not have him as their leader would now have him for their god! The irony could not fail to amuse Caesar as he looked down upon all this. But events at Rome were even more surprising. Having used Cicero's sponsorship and prestige to the utmost to build himself up to Antony's height, Octavian—or *divi filius*, son of the god, as he now called himself—coldly discarded him, and sacrificed the gray old head to a grisly end.

Octavian joined forces with Lepidus and Antony, and together they proclaimed themselves the Triumvirate that would rule Rome for the next five years—discarding the Senate as easily as Cicero. Next they announced that the assassins were traitors and must be hunted down and punished.

Both sides desperately needed money. The assassins were plundering the east—Cassius and Brutus attacked Rhodes, Xanthus, Lycia, Patara, and Tarsus—and the Triumvirs launched a program of proscriptions, whereby all enemies must yield up their persons and their treasures. They said they would not make Caesar's mistake of clemency; they would not set out for the east leaving enemies behind their backs in Rome.

They bargained lives and swapped names—my uncle for your tutor—and Octavian yielded up Cicero without a murmur. The man he had flattered and called "father" was turned over to the executioners. They tracked him to his country villa, where he was attempting to flee. But his slaves set down the litter, and Cicero, like one of the sacrificial oxen I had seen at the Triumphs, stuck out his neck for the blow.

They say it was Fulvia, Antony's wife, who demanded that the right hand be cut off as well, the one that wrote the speeches against Antony—that it was she who set the head at their table and stuck pins through the tongue, until Antony had it taken away to be set on the Rostra. It must have been then that Antony developed his revulsion against her, for he was never bloodthirsty. To triumph over a foe is one thing, to bathe in his blood another. When defecting soldiers were executed, it was Fulvia who stood near enough, laughing, that the blood splashed on her gown.

Such fierce, primitive bloodlust is alarming enough. But what Octavian had, and was, I realized with a sudden insight that left me shaken. I could see what had been veiled, unclear, before.

I had been reading dispatches describing the rapid changes in Rome, when suddenly I remembered bits and snatches of impressions of Octavian, and they floated together to make a portrait of his true face, behind the innocent beauty.

Why, Cicero had even spun some tale about him—what was it? Yes, that he had dreamed of seeing the sons of senators passing before the Temple of Jupiter on the Capitol, for Jupiter to select one to be the chief ruler of Rome. In the dream, lines of youths had passed by the god, until he had stretched his hand out to one. Then he had declared, "O ye Romans, this young man, when he shall be lord of Rome, shall put an end to all your civil wars." Cicero had seen the face clearly, but did not know the boy. The next day, as he saw boys returning from exercising in the Campus Martius, he recognized the very boy in his dream. When he inquired who it was, he was told it was Octavian, whose parents had no special eminence.

Was this true? Had Cicero seen it? Or was it a tale Octavian himself had circulated? Octavian . . . he fooled Cicero, who declared that he had easily controlled the boy "until now." He fooled Caesar, the gods only know how! Now he was attempting to fool Lepidus and Antony.

He would use Antony and Lepidus, then discard them as soon as they had served their purpose. And as for Caesarion—only one "son of the god" could be permitted. He knew that. And so did I.

I leaned against the marble frame of the window, pressing my forehead against it to stave off the sweat that had suddenly sprung up on my brow. I saw it all so clearly—why did not anyone else? Why did I alone feel threatened, and by this boy, six years younger than I?

Because he is cold, calculating, and ruthless. Because he does not make mistakes. And because his very youth is in his favor—he has such a long time to accomplish his aims. All the time in the world . . .

O Caesar—if you were truly a god, or gifted by the gods, why could you not discern the truth about Octavian? I cried inside, clenching my fists.

What was it Octavian had said, talking of Achilles that night at the Saturnalia? "I wonder what it is to be the greatest warrior in the world." Until now, no one could take over a throne unless he was a commander, a warrior. But Octavian would find a way, since it was clear he was no soldier. He would find a new way. . . . He had already got himself named Consul, eleven years before he was even eligible for the office.

I felt as cold as I had during the snow that Saturnalia.

Antony, Lepidus, beware! I whispered.

Cicero had written to Brutus that Octavian must be "praised, honored, and then got rid of." He had thought to use him. But Octavian had remarked that he would know how to stop himself being got rid of. And it was Cicero's head that was struck off, on Octavian's orders.

Octavian had come to Rome with nothing but Caesar's legacy—no troops, no money, no experience. Now he was one of the three rulers of Rome. It had taken him only a year and a half. He had just turned twenty.

He had achieved in twenty months what it had taken Caesar, the great Caesar, twenty years to achieve.

40

The wind stood fair for sailing, and I walked in measured, stately paces, reviewing my fleet, readied now at last for the voyage to join the Triumvirs at Brundisium where they awaited me. Cassius had continued to demand the ships, and I had put him off with fair words while they were abuilding and I was in secret communication with Antony. Cassius's threatened invasion of Egypt had not yet taken place; Brutus had reminded him that their enemies were the Triumvirs and not Egypt. As if to show his scorn of me, Cassius recognized Arsinoe as the true Queen of Egypt, and hailed her as such at Ephesus.

Arsinoe! Another of Caesar's misguided clemencies now turned against me! He had spared her after the Triumph, his heart touched by her. Now she emerged from sanctuary, decked out as Queen of Egypt. It did not take long for the truth to reveal itself: It was she who had persuaded Serapion to turn over the fleet at Cyprus. Doubtless she had promised him a high office in Egypt—the Egypt she planned to rule soon, with the help of the assassins.

To think that Caesar had had his knife at all their throats as they knelt in submission—Cassius, Brutus, Arsinoe—and spared them! Well, we would not. Here Octavian's ruthlessness would stand us in good stead.

Yes, I was allied with Octavian. For now we had the same purpose: to avenge Caesar's death. And after that?

The fleet was magnificent. I had altogether some hundred vessels—not enough for a full navy, but enough to be of great help to the Triumvirs. My flagship, a "six"—two men on each oar at three levels—was named the *Isis*. I had elected not to have any ships larger than a "six," abandoning the earlier Ptolemaic mania for enormous ships, which had proved to be more a liability than an effective offense weapon. A six, equipped with a ram, could do damage enough. I had five other "sixes," ten "fives"—quinqueremes—and thirty "fours," quadriremes—the backbone of the navy, which could prove surprisingly fleet and agile, as well as powerful enough to sink larger ships. The tried-and-true triremes would be the workhorses, the jacks-of-all-trades, and I had twenty-five of them. The rest were light galleys, Liburnians, and supply transports.

It was a great gift to lay at the feet of the Triumvirs. But it had not come without cost. My price for all this had been that Antony pronounce Caesarion Caesar's undoubted and natural son before the Senate, and that all three Triumvirs recognize him as my co-ruler: Ptolemy XVI Caesar. They had agreed. They wanted these ships very badly.

And what ships they were! I found my heart racing as I looked at them, trim and sleek, smelling of pitch and wood and fresh canvas and rope. Going aboard the *Isis*, I took my place beside Phidias, the Rhodian captain, on the main deck. I meant to learn all I could about commanding a ship, although of course I would leave the moment-by-moment sailing decisions to the experience of the captain.

"Here," he said solemnly, presenting me with a helmet. "You must wear the outward sign of a commander." I took it and lowered it over my head, slowly, feeling its weight encasing me. The feathers on its crest waved in the wind.

"I thank you," I said. I was eager to begin the voyage, to be the first woman since Artemisia of Halicarnassus to set out with her own fleet. And forgive my pride, but Artemisia had commanded only five ships in accompanying Xerxes, although she fought bravely and escaped pursuit by sinking an enemy ship.

We were to sail straight west across the Mediterranean for some six hundred miles, then steer north for another five hundred or so, sailing between Italy and Greece until we reached Brundisium. There, where the gap between Italy and Greece was narrow, the Triumvirs planned to ferry troops across. I knew that the assassins had stationed a fleet of their own on the southernmost point of Greece to intercept me—should I "stray" from the right direction. But I would fight them—that was what sixes, fives, fours, and threes were for. And I prayed that the gods would give me as good victory as they had given Artemisia.

We cast off from Alexandria, proceeding slowly out of the harbor, a straight line making its way through the narrow channel between the Pharos and the breakwater. Once in the open sea, we formed a closer gathering of vessels.

How sweet the wind, how blue and beckoning the sea! The waters grew steadily darker, shading from the greenish turquoise of the shore into deeper blue where the bottom could no longer be seen. The wind slapped the water, chiding it playfully, making whitecaps that glittered as they broke. The bow of the ship dipped and rode the waves like a horse running free. Dolphins dove alongside us.

"A cloudless sky," said the captain, squinting toward the horizon. "If this east wind keeps blowing, our voyage should be smooth and effortless." The sail was filled, creaking as the lines strained, pulling for Italy.

We were skirting the coast of Africa, passing places that had always been just names to me: the desert west of Alexandria, where the sands were as white as alabaster, sparkling like salt; the little town of Taposiris, a miniature Alexandria with a temple of Osiris and a lighthouse one-tenth the size of its Alexandrian sister. I could see the pylons of the temple, and perceive the winking of the flame of the lighthouse. A series of these lighthouses served as signal posts all along the coast, as far as Cyrene.

The wind whipped my cloak and tore at the feathers of my helmet. I was thankful to be wearing it, for it offered protection and shaded my eyes. I might have to adopt other clothing than a gown and cloak; clearly they were unsuited for standing on a deck in high winds. Should I wear the trousers of the barbarians, then?

It made me laugh, picturing myself in breeches. But doubtless they would serve well on a ship. Or perhaps I would prefer the loincloths of the rowers? They had their advantages too. I smiled. No, not a loincloth!

Soon I would be with the Triumvirs, joining forces with them. I could hardly believe that I was becoming part of a Roman army. But I owed it to Caesar to do whatever was necessary to avenge him.

Did I want to see any of them again? I had thought to be done with them. When I had sailed away from Rome—so heartsick, so weakened—I had comforted myself with saying, *No more Antony, no more Octavian, no more Cicero, no more Rome*. Well, there was no more Cicero, but what of Antony and Octavian?

Antony . . . Antony I wanted to see. Lepidus, yes, I would be happy to see Lepidus. Octavian . . . I had seen all I needed of Octavian.

For two nights I slept well in the built-in bed they had fashioned for me in the cabin. There were shelves with netting to hold my goods safe, and trunks bolted to the floor served as storage. So well secured was it that nothing rattled or broke loose as the wind rose during the third night, then turned into a howling monster.

I slept unknowing until the ship lurched and I sat upright, grasping the rails of the bed. The floor was bucking and jerking, and a cascade of water burst in through the closed window, drenching me. I staggered up out of bed, hanging on to the bolted furniture to keep my footing. Grabbing a heavy waterproof cloak, unable to see in the darkness, I felt my way along the passageway to the deck, crawling up the steps.

Now I could see well enough. A storm had caught us in full fury, and wave after wave was breaking across the deck, rolling in like breakers on a beach. The sailors were struggling to take down the sail, and the captain was shouting orders, barely audible above the roar of the wind. I grasped him by the shoulders, and he turned as best he could.

"It pounced on us as suddenly as a lion," he shouted. "The wind changed to the northwest; we're being blown back against the coast."

"No, no, we have to keep out to sea!" I cried. How far were we from shore? It had been visible at sunset, but I had no way of knowing what had happened in the hours since.

"We will do everything in our power," he said. "But our ships are toys against the force of the wind and waves." He broke off to rush across the deck and secure a line that was lashing like a whip, knocking sailors off their feet. While I watched, a man was washed overboard. I crawled to the mast and clung to it. My clothes were soaked, as heavy as metal.

I looked toward shore—or, rather, away from the wind. I could see the faint pinprick of a light—it must be one of the signal lighthouses. If I could see it, that was bad indeed. It meant we were close to the coastline.

The captain made his way back to the mast. "We've dropped anchor, and will try to ride it out," he cried. "The rowers will row against the wind, to hold us in place. But I fear the anchor will rip out anyway."

And we would be borne relentlessly back onto the shore, there to break into pieces.

The moon made a quick appearance between gaps in black, racing clouds. It showed a sea wrinkled, dark, and covered with sharp, peaked mountains of water—enormous waves. Seeing the size of them made my heart feel as if it stopped. They were higher than the mast of the ship. They paralyzed you with their sheer size—what could prevail against them? The ship was like a leaf blown into the troughs between waves. The helpless oars were lifted high, out of the water, where they rowed frantically against air, and the anchor line stretched, straining with a fearful whine, and snapped.

I felt the jerk and shudder of the whole ship as it broke free and, suddenly freed from the weight of the anchor, spun like a top, slammed from all sides. Then the inexorable drifting, shoved by the wind, back, back toward the shore.

The moon came out again, and in all the surrounding waters I saw the bobbing forms of the rest of the fleet. None of them could escape; we had been sailing close enough together that the storm encompassed us all.

The ship listed to leeward, almost on its side. Water poured in through the oar ports. Now our only hope of survival would be to reach the shore before we sank. Suddenly the shore, too close before, looked impossibly far away. The ship lurched as it filled with water belowdecks, and the rowers struggled out from the hold, gasping and coughing. They staggered about on deck, dazed.

Still clinging to the mast, I had to climb on it as the deck tilted, hugging it like a log. I heard a loud crash and realized that two ships nearby had collided, blown against each other. The splintering of wood and the agonized cries of the sailors rose above the wind. Pieces of masts and oars floated by, whirling, disappearing in the foam, then popping up again. Sometimes a man would be hanging on one, riding it like a raft.

Ahead of us I saw the winking light. We would hit the shore—but would we sink first? If only the sinking was staved off until we were within swimming distance—and that meant very close indeed, for normal swimming was impossible in these high seas.

A gigantic shudder, and the ship stuck on something. Then it wrenched free—or, rather, was torn free by the waves, lifted off and sent scudding along on its side again. The force of the momentary grounding tore the mast from its mooring, and I was thrown off, rolling across the sloping deck, until I hit the railing. There I stuck, almost in the sea. My face dipped down into the cold waves, and I pulled my head up, dripping with salt water. I had taken some into my lungs, and I coughed and gasped.

Another shudder. The ship slammed against a sandbar, shaking. I heard a frightful sound, and I recognized it—the gods only know how, for I had never heard it before. But it was the unmistakable sound of the ship breaking up.

It clove in half, and the two halves separated cleanly, flinging us into the heaving sea. I hit the water with such force I lost my breath, and the cold was a shock. But my head told me the water must be shallow here, or the ship would not have caught and shattered. And I swam in the direction of the lighthouse, pushed by the waves. When they sucked out, I found my feet could touch the bottom; only a little farther in, I could walk to shore.

Another huge wave engulfed me, knocking me off my feet, but when it receded, I felt the firmness of the beach once more, and used those few seconds to walk closer to shore. The next wave knocked me over, too, but by the next one, I had reached the safety of waist-deep water, and I struggled to shore, exhausted, and collapsed on the beach.

There I lay, gasping, and watched as others waded ashore, chased by timbers and fittings of the doomed fleet. One by one they reached the shore, falling limp on the sand. And there we lay, waiting for the light and the dreadful and certain knowledge of what had happened in the dark.

The sun showed its rim above the horizon, in the direction of Alexandria. I had lain shivering under my heavy, waterlogged cloak for hours, hearing the moaning of those around me. The dawn showed a sea strewn with debris, half-hulks of ships still floating, other ships that seemed almost undamaged resting on the sands. Hundreds of sailors were hunched, shivering, up and down the beach.

I was thankful to be alive, thankful that so many had survived. Some of the ships even looked—at first glance—to be repairable. But the losses were great, and I would be unable to aid the Triumvirs in their campaign. My magnificent fleet had not got very far.

I could not see it as an omen. Shipwrecks were common, a fact of life. Octavian had been shipwrecked on his way to Spain; Caesar had twice lost his ships in Britain. There was nothing for it but to start over.

But there was no way a fresh navy could be readied in time to help in the coming contest. I would have to be a passive spectator—something that sat ill with my nature.

Where were we? The snowy sands held no landmarks. How far west had we got?

I saw the captain, lurching along, dragging one leg. He had been injured, but was alive. "Phidias!" I called, waving to him. I pulled myself to my feet and ran to him.

"You are safe!" he cried. "Thanks be to all the gods!" He nervously patted his dagger at his belt.

"I hope you weren't thinking of behaving like a Roman," I said. "No matter what had happened to me."

His expression told me that was just what he had considered. A captain who drowned his sovereign had lost his honor and should kill himself. But he was enough of a practical Greek that he wanted to ascertain exactly what had happened before jumping to conclusions. "The fleet is lost," he said. "I did my best."

"I know. You could not control the heavens. And so many have been saved, it seems a miracle in itself."

"The fleet—the beautiful fleet—a shambles!" He shook his head.

"We will build another." I grieved for my lost fleet, my pride, my hopes. And under it, the disappointment that I would let Antony down, that I could not keep my word, although it was the gods who had prevented me, not men. Antony had made it across the Alps in winter, and I could not seem to escape from Egypt.

"I think we are near Paraetonium," he said.

The western border of Egypt, a lonely, sunbaked outpost.

"I suppose I was overdue to see it," I said, attempting to lighten his spirits. "I should see my kingdom from west to east, as well as north to south."

"There is not much to see here, unless you like scorpions," he grunted.

The journey back was a sad one. Merchant ships had to come and fetch the survivors and gather up the debris. Some of the ships could be patched and sail slowly back to Alexandria later. But it was a quiet, sober party of survivors who disembarked on the quay of the capital.

And it was with agitated regret that I had to write Antony and tell him the devastating news—not to expect our help.

The summer came, a time that should have been happy with planting, harvesting, and laden cargo ships plying the seas. But in Alexandria we were tense with waiting. We were defenseless now, stripped of our legions, our fleet destroyed. I began rebuilding it, beginning with an "eight," so that the flagship at least might be afloat before we were invaded. There was nothing standing between Egypt and the assassins now; they could march straight through Judaea and down to our borders. I also began raising my own army; it had been foolish to rely on the Roman troops. But that, too, was a slow business. Men are not turned into soldiers overnight.

The story can be told quickly. Lepidus remained behind to guard Italy with three legions, and Antony and Octavian took twenty-eight to face Cassius and Brutus with their almost equal number. The site chosen by fate for the battle was near Philippi, in Greece. Octavian fell ill, as usual, in the midst of the preparations, and had to linger behind while Antony marched the legions and set up camp. The tactics of the assassins were to hold back and refuse to give battle, knowing that the Triumvirs were weak in supply lines and would run out of food as the weather worsened. Antony, realizing this, tricked them into battle as Caesar would have done, by building a causeway across a marsh to pierce their defense barriers. This lured Cassius from camp to counterattack, allowing Antony to charge into the camp and plunder it. In the meantime, Brutus's troops had attacked Octavian's camp and overrun it.

The gods entered this battle as surely as they had the war in Troy. Caesar visited both camps with signs and spectral appearances. In Octavian's, a dream warned him to rise from his sickbed and not remain in his tent on the battle day, and so he obeyed and hid in a marsh. Caesar appeared to Brutus the night before the final battle and foretold his end. I imagine that the Caesar Brutus saw was robust and healthy, not slain, and by that Brutus knew he had failed in his deed: that Caesar lived on, stronger than ever.

When Brutus overran Octavian's tent and tried to capture him, the bed was empty. Cassius, meanwhile, had been routed by Antony. As a relief force from Brutus followed him, Cassius mistook them for the enemy—the gods blinded him. Assuming that Brutus had already been captured or killed, he did not wait, but killed himself immediately.

What a victory for the Triumvirs, for Cassius was a better general than Brutus. The assassins had lost their best man.

Brutus retired, brooding, to his tent, and Octavian emerged from the marsh. Brutus would have waited for winter to do his work for him, starving out his opponents, but he had little control over his troops. Brutus never knew how to lead men, and now the restless soldiers forced a battle on him the morning after Caesar appeared to him. Antony and Octavian won, greatly helped by the lack of morale in Cassius's soldiers, who had been broken by their commander's loss. Brutus killed himself, and the characters of Antony and Octavian were clearly distinguished by how they treated his remains. Antony covered the body reverently with his purple general's cloak, but Octavian yanked it off, then cut off Brutus's head and sent it back to Rome to lay at the feet of Caesar's statue.

In the end, Brutus and Cassius had driven their cursed daggers into their own entrails, as was fitting.

Thus were Mars Ultor—Mars the Avenger—and Caesar himself satisfied on the field of Philippi.

$$\boxed{41}$$

The world outside us had been rearranged, but for Alexandria, life continued protected and isolated, and for the rest of Egypt, even more so. Only we in the palace were connected with the tides of the times.

After my long, soaking exposure to seawater, compounded with the wind and scorching sun, Iras pronounced my skin ruined.

"The salt has injured it, and then the sunburn has made it like leather—that is, where it is not peeling off," she said, shaking her head. Olympos concurred, saying I looked like a fortune-teller from the Moeris Oasis.

"Tell us our future," he said, cocking his dark head. "Who will control the entire world, and how long will it take?"

"I am no fortune-teller," I said. "At least about politics."

"What about personal things, my Circe? Can you tell if I will marry Phoebe?"

Olympos had fallen in love, a startling thing, given his sarcastic personality. Like most skeptics, once he had capitulated to love, he was acting the fool.

"If you ask her," I said. So far he had not, relying on her to read his mind.

"That would be going too far," he said, laughing.

"You will never marry, my lady, if you don't repair your complexion," said Iras. "Now, in Nubia, where the sun is even crueler than in Egypt, we use the milk of asses to bathe in and save our skin."

"I would recommend oil of almonds," said Olympos. "Easier to come by."

"How many asses have to be milked to provide enough?" I asked. "Surely we have enough!" The idea was oddly appealing to me. Olympos raised his eyebrows.

"I promise to try the almonds next," I assured him. But my mood was darkened, because of Iras's comment in passing. To marry . . . Mardian had been strongly urging it.

I lay in my shallow marble tub and soaked in the asses' milk, rubbing it into my arms and legs and patting my face with it. My toes looked odd, sticking up out of the white liquid. A sandalwood screen veiled me from the view of Mardian, who was pacing about the room. I found baths boring, so I had kept myself entertained by having others, disembodied voices, to talk to.

"My dear madam," he was saying, his voice higher than usual, because he was frustrated. "Your subjects are most anxious about it!"

"I have already provided them with an heir," I said stubbornly. "There is now a co-ruler with me. Even the Romans have recognized Caesarion." I had just issued a new series of coins with our reign emblazoned on them.

"Caesarion is only five years old," said Mardian. He was standing as close to the screen as permissible. "Life is uncertain—for all of us. If he does not attain maturity, the line will end with him. And do you plan to mate with him? It would seem so!"

I cupped some of the milk in my hands and let it run down over my arms and shoulders. "Don't be vulgar," I said.

"But, don't you see—there *must* be more heirs, and you Ptolemies mate only with each other, so—what other conclusion can the world come to?"

"I do not care!" I said angrily.

"Yes, you do. You must. You must face this problem!"

"Not now." I lowered my face into the milk, shutting my eyes.

"Yes, now. You are already twenty-seven years old. Soon to be twenty-eight," he reminded me portentously. "The Ptolemies have on occasion taken up with foreigners. Was not your grandmother a Syrian?"

"Yes," I said. However, my grandfather had not seen fit to marry her. "But whom do you suggest I marry?"

"Well, Octavian is unmarried, and—"

"Octavian!" I cried. "Octavian! What an unappetizing suggestion!" I stood up and called for Iras. I wanted to get out of this bath and look Mardian straight in the eye. Iras came quickly, bringing towels and gowns. Swathed, I stepped out and glared at him. He looked genuinely puzzled.

"I only suggested a Roman because you clearly aren't prejudiced against them as so many others are."

"Caesar was different." Caesar defied categories; his true category was more than mortal.

"Octavian is handsome," he said lamely. "And powerful."

I recoiled at the thought of him; then the memory of what I had seen through the window at the Regia came back to me. Clearly he had a lascivious side to his nature, as out of place in the rest of him as a butterfly in winter. "Oh yes. I grant you that."

"Well, what else does a woman want?"

I laughed. "I admit they are good basics. But I would like a heart to go along with them, a sense of life and joy."

"Then I take back what I said. You will have to look for a non-Roman."

Iras brought out a jar of almond oil. "If you will just lie down here . . ." She indicated a couch draped with thick towels.

"Later." I needed to finish talking to Mardian. "I know you have a good point. But . . ." How could I tell him how little interest I had in it, how even my dreams were curiously dry and sterile? He, as a lifelong eunuch, could never understand the fluctuations of passion—how it could be a madness in one stage of life and then disappear, evaporate, like a dry streambed, in another. I remembered my times with Caesar, but my nature then seemed a curiosity to me now.

"Perhaps you should consider a prince from Bithynia or Pontus," he went on, oblivious. "Someone younger, who would worship you and do whatever you wished. Never make any demands on you, but exist just to . . . to satisfy you." He blushed.

"You make me sound sixty, not twenty-seven," I said. I tried to imagine it, and found *myself* blushing.

"Kings take pretty concubines, so why should you not?"

"Little boys don't appeal to me."

"I didn't mean *that* young, I only meant manageable." He paused. "I have heard that Prince Archelaus of Comana is a brave soldier and well educated."

"How old is he?"

"I don't know. I can find out!" he said brightly.

"You do that." I decided to humor him. "And one other thing—forgive me for changing the subject—is it true about Lepidus?"

After the battle of Philippi, it seemed that the official Triumvirate was turning into an unofficial Duovirate. The world was to be divided like a cake, but only between Octavian and Antony.

"Yes, a new report came in just this morning. I left it on your worktable, with your secretary."

"Just tell me." I drew the silk robe, made of many colored scarves, closer around me.

"They suspect—or *claim* to suspect, which is different—Lepidus of going behind their backs and being untrustworthy. Therefore, when they divided the Roman empire between them—and let us call it that, for it is an empire by any measure—they have ignored him."

"Who got what?" I asked.

"Antony is hero of the day; his prestige stands highest in all the world," Mardian said. "He has taken the best parts—all of Gaul, as well as the entire east. He will be master of our part of the world, and presumably carry out Caesar's plan to subdue Parthia."

"And Octavian?" How had Octavian allowed that? But the man lying sick in his tent or being carried about in a litter could not dictate terms to the soldier-hero.

"He has only Spain and Africa, and two onerous duties to fulfill: He must settle the veterans in Italy, finding land and money for them, and he must pursue Sextus, the pirate son of Pompey. Thankless tasks."

Thankless, but demanding. They should tie Octavian's hands for a long time. I smiled. This was not what he had bargained for.

After he had gone, I allowed myself to stretch out on the couch while Iras massaged the sweet oil into my skin. I closed my eyes and gave myself up to the scent and the sensation.

"Madam, do you think to follow his suggestion?" Iras whispered. "Your skin must be restored to its perfection before you meet any princes!"

"I only said it to please him," I murmured. The perfumed oil and the rubbing were making me drowsy. "It would take more than a pretty prince to . . . to . . ." My voice trailed off.

To awaken that part of me that slept a winter sleep, I thought. Perhaps it had slept so long it had died quietly, without a murmur of protest.

Mardian enjoyed himself thoroughly, searching the world over for suitable candidates for my hand. He came up with Idumaeans, Greeks, Paphlagonians, Nubians—including the Kandake's own son—Galatians, and Armenians. Just to vex him, I had made a list of essential characteristics. I figured that the chances of someone meeting them all was remote. He must be at least twenty, he must be a head taller than I, athletic, good at mathematics, speak a minimum of three languages, have lived abroad, play a musical instrument well, know Greek literature, know the sea and sailing, and be descended of a great royal house. Those were my minimum requirements, I said. Poor Mardian!

The harvest was good, and we began to make up our losses for the year before. I was able to commission sixty new ships, as well as order the most decrepit of the dikes and reservoir basins to be repaired, and I now had twenty thousand soldiers under arms. Neither the army nor the navy was up to full strength—the Romans would laugh at them—but it was a beginning, and we surely had made progress from our low point when the fleet was wrecked.

To my consternation, Mardian's prime candidate, Archelaus of Comana, was not disqualified from the "competition." Mardian prevailed on me to invite him for a ceremonial visit.

"For even if it is a sham," he said, "it will please your people. They will feel that you are at least *trying* to remedy the problem."

Kasu, the monkey, padded forward and offered Mardian a platter of dates. She was so well trained by now, she could almost function as a servant. Mardian pursed his lips and took a long time to select the plumpest one he could. "Umm," he said. "These must be from Derr."

He had the true palate of a connoisseur. "Your tongue tells you true," I said. Kasu scampered back to me, and jumped up in the chair beside me. "I forgot to add one other requirement: He should like animals, especially monkeys. He should not mind a monkey perched at the foot of the bed."

Mardian shrugged, licking off his fingers. "Too late now," he said. "I am sure that Archelaus will pretend to like her."

"When is he coming?" My spirits sank at the thought of it. I never should have gone along with it this long.

"As soon as he and his family have finished paying court to Antony," he said. "Everyone in the region, all the client kings, have to report to him, offer up their crowns, and wait for his approval and reappointment."

I took one of the dates myself, and nibbled on it. They were sweet—almost too sweet, artificially so. "All the client kingdoms—there are a great many of them," I said. "And each one will have to be reviewed separately. Some were wholeheartedly for the assassins, others were forced to support them. Now they will *all* claim to have been coerced. And they were stripped of money, too."

"Antony knows that. He, of course, has to extract money as well. But at least he listens to people. The orator Hybreas of Mylasa said that if he expected them to provide ten years' taxes in one year, he could doubtless provide them with two summers instead of the usual one. And Antony relented."

"Where is he now?" I wondered. He had started out in Athens, that I knew.

"Ephesus. He has been holding a riotous court there for weeks, being hailed as Dionysus and even being called a god."

"He must like that," I said. "It's better than Octavian, who is only *son* of a god. But the Ephesians call everybody who is anybody a god—I hope he realizes that."

Mardian laughed. "I don't think he cares. He's too busy with Glaphyra, Archelaus's mother. She seems to be—er, putting her claims before him."

For some odd reason I was shocked. It seemed so—unfair. I pictured all the male rulers milling about, waiting their turn, while Glaphyra went to the head of the line.

"So you see, as soon as his mother has been satisfied, Archelaus will be free to leave."

No, what he meant was that as soon as *Antony* had been satisfied, the mother could depart. I shook my head. "That may be some time yet," I said. I should be thankful: As long as Glaphyra held Antony's attention, I would be spared her son's.

The court of Dionysus continued for months, with parades of a crowned Antony pulled in a grape-laden chariot, accompanied by women dressed as bacchantes and men as satyrs and Pans, wreathed in ivy and carrying thyrsi, playing zithers and flutes, crying out welcome for "the bringer of joy," Dionysus-Antony. The shouts reverberated over all the east. He must be enjoying himself, I thought. I wondered what Octavian would have done at Ephesus?

He would probably have righteously forgone the exotic trappings and indulged himself with the women secretly, after hours. He liked his pleasures to be furtive. Perhaps he liked them *only* if they were furtive.

Some six months later, a Roman appeared at my court, sent by Antony. It was Quintus Dellius, a man famed for his ability to change horses in midstream, like one of those dexterous circus riders. He had been Dolabella's man, then Cassius's, now he was Antony's. I disliked him before I even saw him, therefore I kept him waiting as long as possible before admitting him to an audience.

Unfortunately the hapless Archelaus had arrived at almost the same time, traveling eagerly over land and sea to come to my court. I felt sorry for him, and that predisposed me to like him—the opposite of Dellius. But he would have to wait until I had dealt with Dellius.

At length Dellius stood before me, his eyes level with mine, as I was seated on an elevated throne. He had very dark eyes and a pitted complexion that made him look hard. Although he was standing, legs apart, and I seated, he gave the impression that it was he conducting the audience.

"Greetings, most exalted Queen of Egypt, from Lord Antony," he said laconically. "I am come from his lordship to order you to appear before his court to answer certain charges."

Surely I had not heard him right. "Would you repeat that?" I said in a level tone.

"I said, Lord Antony requests that you report to him to defend yourself against certain accusations—accusations which are spelled out in this letter." He handed me a scroll, then stepped back smartly. He was almost smirking.

"Requests me," I said, considering the word. "For a moment I thought you said he 'ordered' me."

"Lord Antony would be most pleased if you would come to him in person to explain certain things."

"Now he would be 'most pleased,' and I am only to 'explain' matters, not defend myself or answer charges," I said coaxingly. "Things are softening by the moment." I clutched the scroll. I would read it later—not in front of this haughty, hostile man. "And where am I to come?"

"To Tarsus, where he will move shortly," Dellius said.

"You may tell Lord Antony that the Queen of Egypt does not respond to rude requests, nor obey a Roman magistrate, nor have to defend herself. I am disappointed that my ally, once my friend, would see fit to approach me in such a manner. Unless you have misrepresented him?" I gave him the opportunity to clear Antony.

"So that is your answer?" he asked, bypassing it. "You will not come?"

"No," I said. "Let him come here if he wishes to speak to me. He knows the way. He was here fourteen years ago. He will not have forgotten."

Alone in my chamber later, I read the scroll and found its charges ridiculous: that I had helped Cassius and Brutus! That I had sent the four Roman legions to them! He must know that they had been sent to Dolabella, and captured by Cassius. And it was the traitorous Serapion who had turned the fleet stationed at Cyprus over to them. I had lost a fortune in trying to bring my fleet to Brundisium for the Triumvirs. How could he have forgotten that? I was deeply insulted.

But later I could not help wondering if others had whispered these suggestions to Antony—Glaphyra, or Octavian himself? Especially Octavian, who would be happy to discredit the mother of Caesarion, and sever his tie to Rome.

Archelaus had been waiting for several days, and after Dellius had been packed off, I braced myself to see him. Before I betook myself to the audience hall to welcome him formally (Mardian had done so in my stead already, but now it must be repeated), I let Iras do what she longed to: apply cosmetics to my face and dress my hair. In the meantime, Charmian was to select the costume.

Why did I do this? Did I hope to frighten him off if I looked too artificially colorful, too over-costumed? Although I was the richest, most powerful woman in the world—how lightly that phrase falls, here!—I knew well enough how to put someone at his ease by being approachably human. I also knew how to keep people at a distance. It was all in the manner: the tilt of the head, the tone of voice, the look in the eyes.

I seated myself on a bench where the north light would fall on my upturned face and said, "Very well, Iras, perform your magic." I shut my eyes and waited.

Her deft fingers patted the skin on my cheeks and traced the line of my jaw. "The treatment has worked," she said. "The ill effects of all that salt are gone."

A pity, I thought. It should have lasted a bit longer—at least until this suitor went home.

She spread a creamy lotion all over my face, rubbing it in with circular strokes.

It had a delicious aroma.

"Oil and cyperus grass, my lady," she said. "Now I will remove it with the mixed juices of sycamore and cucumber." She applied linen pads soaked with the juices and rubbed my face. It began to tingle.

"This will make the skin look as fine as polished marble," she said. "Although it does not need much improvement. Now, I will cool your eyes with a wash of ground celery and hemp. Keep them closed."

She laid two cool bandages on my eyes and said, "Rest and think of a cool mountain."

The weight on my eyelids seemed to alter my thoughts, and I drifted away to someplace I had never seen—a wooded hillside with tall cypress trees and sheep grazing, where light breezes played.

"Now," said Iras, removing the pads, bringing me back to the room. Where had I been? "For lining the eyes, do you prefer black kohl today, or the green malachite?"

"The malachite," I said. "Kohl is for every day, and this is not an everyday occurrence—meeting a candidate for my hand." If it were just for holding my hand, I would not be so defensive.

She took a cosmetic stick and drew fine lines all around my eyes, over the lids and beyond the corners. "Now open." She held a mirror up. "See how the green deepens the natural green of your eyes."

Yes, it did. Caesar had loved the color of my eyes—he said they were the shade of the Nile in shadow. But since then, I had not worn the green; I let the kohl make my eyes darker. I nodded, surprised at how bright they looked.

She dipped her finger in a small pot of ram's fat mixed with red ochre, and dabbed it on my mouth, reddening it. "There!" she sighed. "You hide your lips and their shape when you leave them uncolored."

I was beginning to look—not like a stranger, but like a very enhanced version of myself.

"Your hair is gleaming from the juniper juice and oil we rinsed it in last night. Now all I must do is comb it and braid it with gold ornaments."

"That is good," said Charmian, behind me. "For I had selected the green gown with gold embroidery." I turned to see the gown she was holding; it was in the Phoenician fashion, with gathered shoulders and a panel to float from the back.

"I think you are readying me for Mount Olympus, to be received by the gods," I said. "It will be a letdown to walk into my own audience hall."

"For you, perhaps, but not for *him*," Charmian said. "He has traveled a long way, after all, just to see this."

I sighed. Poor man—poor boy—whichever he was. Mardian had been vague about that. "Yes, yes," I said, standing still while Charmian lowered the gown over my head. Another servant brought gold-braided sandals and put them on my feet—feet that had also been rubbed with fragrant oil. Now Iras set to work on my hair, and Charmian brought out a jewel box and selected an emerald necklace and gold and pearl earrings. She also presented a bracelet shaped like a cobra.

"It is his gift, my lady," she said. "Archelaus brought it, and wished you to wear it."

"I see." I took it and examined it. It was exquisitely fashioned, each scale of the snake rendered realistically, and the eyes were ruby. Against my will, I was touched. How could he have known my partiality to snakes? I put it on.

I entered the hall ceremonially, passing a knot of people on one side without looking at them, until I mounted the steps of my throne-platform. Then I turned and welcomed them, bidding Prince Archelaus of Comana to come forward.

From out of the group of courtiers, envoys, and scribes a tall young man detached himself and made his way to me. He carried himself like a prince, neither obsequious nor haughty, I thought, and I was surprised to see how comely and pleasing he looked.

"Welcome, Prince Archelaus," I said. "We are pleased to receive you at Alexandria."

He smiled. "And I, most exalted Queen Cleopatra of Egypt, am honored to be here."

I wanted to find his words or manner unappealing, but they were winsome.

I extended my arm. "I thank you for your gift. It is most beautiful."

"The artisans in Comana are skilled," he said. "It was my pleasure to commission it."

After more of these public pleasantries, I invited him to join me in the pavilion on the palace grounds and dine in the open air. I also pointedly dismissed all the attendants and spying servants. Together we descended the wide steps of the palace and walked across the green lawn to the white, shaded pavilion, where a table and couches were already waiting. He walked very gracefully, and took long strides. He was also quite a bit taller than the one head I had specified.

We settled ourselves on the couches, reclining as custom dictated. He propped himself up on one elbow and looked at me. Suddenly we both burst out laughing, as if we were conspirators together. I had just undone all the careful, formal costuming of myself.

"Forgive me," I finally said. "I am not laughing at *you*."

"I know that." And I knew he did. "Nor am I laughing at you. I suppose I am laughing in relief. I almost did not come, and a hundred times on the journey I asked myself why I *did* come. I felt a fool."

"You were brave," I said. "I appreciate that." I looked carefully at him. He seemed about my own age, with dark, straight hair and a mouth like that of Apollo. I wondered if his mother was likewise attractive, compelling Antony's interest.

"It was worth the journey, just to see you," he said.

"Please. Do not resort to timeworn formulas."

He smiled. "The trouble with timeworn formulas is that once in a while they are true, and then no one believes you."

"Tell me about your kingdom," I said, shying away from the personal. "I have never traveled anywhere except Rome and Nubia." I was becoming more curious about the rest of the world.

He explained that it was a region of Cappadocia, but not as mountainous, and had maintained its independence—just barely. "The Roman eagle is pecking away at us, but so far has not carried us off to her nest."

"Yes, I know all about that."

He looked surprised. "It should not be such a worry to you," he said. "Egypt is a large morsel, hard to digest."

"I think Rome has a big enough stomach."

I could see him thinking, debating whether to launch into the question of my liaison with Caesar. He decided not to. "Comana is safe enough for the moment," he said.

Now I debated whether to say *Thanks to your mother's charms*, but likewise thought better of it. Instead I said, "What do you think of your new overlord?"

A servant appeared, bringing the first course—lettuce, rolled cucumbers stuffed with sea bass, spiced quail eggs. Archelaus took a long time making his selection.

He speared a quail egg before responding. "We are thankful it was Marc Antony rather than Octavian. After the battle of Philippi, the vanquished lined up to surrender to Antony first. No one wanted to fall into Octavian's hands; they knew he would be unforgiving. Some of the prisoners, due for execution, begged Octavian for assurances of honorable burial. He just sneered, 'You will have to take that up with the carrion crows.' " His appetite dampened, he chewed the egg slowly.

Yes, I could picture that. And I could imagine him smiling his perfect smile as he said it.

"It could have gone to no one but Antony," I said. "Along with the territory comes the task of invading Parthia, and only Antony could carry it out. Besides, he has served in the east before, and knows its ways." I took a sip of the white wine, diluted with mountain water. It still had a slightly astringent flavor. "Has he been—terribly busy?"

"Day and night," said Archelaus. "Especially night."

Seeing the look on my face, he reached for more words.

"But he has been diligent in attending to business," he assured me. "Interviewing people day after day in headquarters, making decisions that seem fair and well considered. Ephesus is a fine city, situated on the sea as it is, with its marble buildings and streets—but of course you are used to that in Alexandria. But one thing it has that Alexandria doesn't—a countryside well suited for riding. Lord Antony took me out several times for riding and hunting. I got to know him as a private man."

The second course arrived, roasted kid, smoked peacock, and sliced ox meat. There were three sauces to accompany them: pepper and honey, cream of cucumber, and chopped mint in vinegar. He looked at them and finally took two.

"And what is he like—as a private man?" From Dellius's summons, I suspected that the sudden elevation to power had changed him, corrupting his sweet nature.

I was surprised when he answered, "A prince among men." He paused. "A man among men, a soldier with the common soldier."

"Oh, you mean he changes his manner to suit the occasion! He colors to suit the coloration around him." A human chameleon, that most slippery of creatures.

"No, I mean the opposite," he said. "I mean that he is always himself, no matter the company. He is at base a plain man, an honest man—and what is more noble and princely than that?"

"Unfortunately it is not often found among nobles and princes," I said.

"I believe he deceives others as little as possible, and himself not at all. If people are deceived in him, it is because they have deceived themselves, seeing what is not there."

"Has he seen my sister?" I asked. What had he done about Arsinoe?

"No," he said. "Arsinoe is still in sanctuary at the Temple of Artemis. Antony does not frequent the temple. Enough of his men have been availing themselves of the unofficial prostitutes there, the ladies who . . . er . . . purport to serve the goddess with their earthly skills."

Now we both broke out laughing again. I was glad Antony did not go there; it would be demeaning. But what business was it of mine?

Archelaus was telling a story about his court. I listened, but paid more attention to my own reactions to him. I was watching them as closely as a child staring at a butterfly's cocoon, waiting for it to open.

I had enjoyed the afternoon, and I found Archelaus appealing. But only as I found many other things, and people, appealing: the priest of Serapis who came to me whenever I wished to celebrate an anniversary or make a special offering; the woman who tended the lotuses in the palace pool, and fashioned delicate necklaces from them. The head charioteer, well-favored and strapping. They were all attractive human beings, who warmed my heart with their wit, skill, or kindness. They made daily life a delight.

But they did nothing to awaken that part of me that had gone to sleep, or—worse—been murdered along with Caesar. And neither did Archelaus. I could not imagine him with no clothes on, and most telling, I had no wish to. Nor could I imagine myself in such a state with him.

That night, as I lay in bed and felt the hot air of summer fill the room, I wondered what induced such feelings in me, and why thinking *about* them was not the same as the immediacy of actually *thinking* them.

Wishing for things could sometimes call them forth. Wishing to study could incite a desire to do so, stimulate an interest. Reading about a region could pique interest in it, make you want to travel there and experience it. But passion could not be piped forth, could not be lured from its den by any known device or trick. It seemed to have a stubborn, independent life of its own, slumbering when it would be convenient for it to dance, springing forth when there was no reason for it, nowhere for it to spend itself.

I wished I could will myself to feel desire for Archelaus, but I could not, it seemed, command my own will. Nothing stirred within me, no hint of heat rose from my inmost being. I was as still as the sacred lake of Isis, where I had swum so long ago, parting the waters in silence at night.

42

The winds blew across the Mediterranean, bringing ships and news. I was apprised of everything that was happening on all fronts—from Octavian's near-fatal illness on his return voyage to Antony's rollicking progress across Asia. Once in Italy, still weak, Octavian encountered difficulty after difficulty, from veterans demanding to be paid, for whom he had no money, to the predations of Sextus on the Roman food routes. The fortunes of the two men were diverging, Antony climbing and Octavian declining.

For a while Antony continued to send messengers to "invite" me to attend him. Finally they ceased, and I had no more word from him. Good. I had made up my mind to go, when it suited me, and in a manner that suited me, when he had stopped expecting me.

It was necessary that I have some understanding with Rome. In spite of my harsh words and disparaging thoughts about it, the truth—which I finally had to admit to myself—was that when I bore a son who was half Roman, and the child of Julius Caesar, I had tied myself to Rome forever. What happened in Rome mattered to my son, as well as to Egypt.

Fate had blessed me in sending Antony east, instead of Octavian. I could deal with Antony, and I meant to bend him to the best bargain I could in regard to both Caesarion and Egypt. He had spoken for Caesarion's paternity in the Senate, and I needed him to continue to back those claims. And he must be made to know that Egypt would be a valuable ally but a troubling enemy. We were too large to be treated as a vassal state; we were no Comana. He would have to approach with respect and ask, not command, if he wanted to free his hands to confront Parthia. I wondered exactly how Dellius had described my refusal to answer. In any case, Antony had given up. I had won that round—the first one. Now for the next.

It took two months to ready the ship for its peculiar mission. I selected a "six" and had it completely refurbished inside and out, so that there was none other like it in existence. The stern was gilded in gold leaf. Belowdecks there was an enormous banquet room to accommodate twelve dining couches, as well as musicians and acrobats. I built cupboards to store enough gold plate to furnish the table three times over, and the hold of the ship was turned into stables to carry thirty horses—and as shipwrights know, one horse takes as much room as four men. In addition, I had my artisans design lamps that could hold many lights, and could be suspended in the ship's rigging and altered to shape circles, squares, or triangles. When they were raised or lowered, it looked like the night sky, but brighter and more magical.

As for my own quarters, they were to be in the aft part of the ship, and contained a large bed, tables and chairs, and many mirrors, as well as lamps affixed to the walls.

Yes, I had my plan, and the money invested in the ship would be well worth it.

But as for myself, I was uncertain about the best way to arrive at Tarsus. Should I be dressed as a stern warrior, helmet—ceremonial, of course—and shield girding me? Should I be dressed as Caesar's widow, in drab and severe costume? Should I be a remote queen? This was a state visit—what image did I wish to convey? Should I be warlike Athena, or grieving Demeter, or regal Hera, or . . .

My eye happened to fall on the mosaic set in the banqueting hall floor just as these thoughts were turning idly through my mind, and I saw Venus rising in her splendor from the sea. *Venus . . . Aphrodite . . . We would be passing her island, the island of Cyprus, on our way to Tarsus . . . where she might arise and come on board. . . .*

Antony. Antony was Dionysus. . . . So who should pay a state visit to Dionysus but Aphrodite?

Yes, and Caesar had called me Venus, had put the statue of me as Venus in his family temple. . . . Antony, too, as a Julian, was descended of Venus. . . . It was altogether fitting that it should be Venus, Aphrodite, who came to Tarsus and met Dionysus. We would thus be changed from ourselves, and it would lend a striking aspect to the meeting, one that would command attention, transport it into another realm altogether. . . .

"Charmian!" I called, leaving my chair. "Charmian, call the costume master!"

The sails filled, hesitant at first, then proudly and boldly. The waters clove and we shot ahead, six hundred miles toward the coast of Cilicia, toward Tarsus.

On board the ship were all the provisions to hold court and entertain the Romans and the citizens of Tarsus. I need be beholden to no one there, need not be anyone's guest. It was I who would do the inviting, it was I who would hold court.

The other rulers—who were they? Not one of them could meet Antony as an equal, nor could they present themselves in any guise other than their own selves. The Ptolemaic empire might have dwindled and almost sputtered out, but I would make my ancestors proud of me now. I would go as a queen and as Aphrodite herself, and let them all gasp and gape.

My costume was, I knew, unprecedented. It was neither ceremonial nor conventional nor proper. I was going as a woman, but one who must not be touched.

We had fair weather; this time the winds seemed to conspire with me to transport me exactly where I wished to go. We passed Cyprus on the lee side, skirting the beautiful island, called "of eternal spring," and as we passed I threw offerings to the goddess for the waves to toss at her feet.

Aphrodite, I prayed, *be with your daughter now!* And the flowers and candles rode the water and floated away to seek her.

It had been more than half a year since Antony first summoned me. I had made him wait long enough, and he would have resigned himself to my not coming. But he would not be angry; he was a forgiving man, that I remembered. Forgiving and easy to please.

But I must do more than please him. Those who are easy to please are the hardest to win. Because everything pleases them, more or less—snatches of a song they overhear someone singing over the next wall, bread that is somewhat flat but still tasty, indifferent wine on a very hot day—nothing pleases them to the exclusion of everything else. And it is only in pleasing someone to that extent that one triumphs.

I walked the decks, enveloped in a strange, dreamy world.

I remembered Antony as I had known him in Rome, and then the picture of him at the Lupercalia flashed into my mind. I had kept it vividly intact, stored in a secret recess of my memory, for—truth be told—it had excited me. It was not only his bodily perfection—although let us not slight that!— but his sheer exuberance, his energy and power, that day, that made him close to a god in form and movement.

Yes, I remembered Antony . . . and reminded myself that that was almost four years ago. Now he was forty-one, not thirty-seven: much could happen in four years, much could fall away. But that joy in living, that boyish vitality . . . could he have lost that, entirely? And he had loved playacting—could that have been lost as well?

No, I doubted that. That was his very essence; it would endure.

So I was going to Antony. By my very manner of arrival, I would salute and honor those aspects of him; I would echo and magnify them. Together we would make a resounding noise.

The coast of Cilicia emerged on the horizon. This was the flat, fertile part of Cilicia, where the mountains retreated and left a seaside plain. Once the Ptolemies had owned it, along with Cyprus. Its sister region, "rough" Cilicia, to the west, was a wild area of harbors and tall timbers, where the pirates had had their strongholds, now held by Rome.

The city of Tarsus was located twelve miles inland from the coast, on the Cyndus River. It could be very cold; Alexander had swum in it and taken a bad chill, for the melting snows fed it in spring.

"Anchor!" I commanded the captain as we approached the coast. We would wait here until the next day, when we would proceed upriver. There was much to be done in preparation. And I knew the ship would be sighted, and Antony alerted in Tarsus. I had given no warning of my coming, no message.

That night we rode gently at anchor, and I dreamed strange dreams. At last I had begun to explore the lost world of my ancestors, and see for myself what we had once been. And waiting for me was a Roman, in the trappings of the east. Had he, then, left his toga behind? I would see an Antony who was unknown and unfamiliar. And he would see me as Caesar had, also in my eastern aspect. We would be new to one another.

In the dawn we fitted the special sails—purple, and steeped in the essence of cyprus-tree oil. Winds blowing through them would carry the smell of the forest. But in this lily-choked waterway, sheltered, there would not be much wind. Rowers would be needed, and now the special silver-tipped oars were brought from the hold and replaced the regular ones of pine. The musicians, who would pipe the time of the strokes of the oars, took their places on deck and belowdecks with flutes, fifes, and harps. For this short journey, the wind-burnt sailors were replaced by women dressed as sea nymphs, who stood by tending the lines and the rudder. Others held smoking censers of perfume from which rolled heady clouds of frankincense and myrrh, seeking the shore.

Charmian costumed me, draping me in the folds of the gown of Venus. The thin tissue of the gown was gold, almost transparent, and it fell in clouds of shimmering glory from my shoulders. Up on the deck, the attendants were readying a canopy of cloth of gold, to look like a divine pavilion, and draping the couch with leopardskins. Before we cast off, I took my place there, reclining, while handsome young boys, costumed as Cupid, stood on either side of me, gently raising and lowering feathered fans. It was as near as I could come to translating a painting I had seen of Venus into real life.

Slowly, ponderously, the ship plied its way through the waterlilies and made its way upstream, I holding my pose all the while. I could see, on either side of the river, crowds gathering, people lining the banks, gaping. Charmian and Iras, dressed as mermaids, stood at the helm, tossing flowers to the onlookers.

The river widened out to a lake; I told the Cupids to summon the captain, and when he came to my pavilion, I said he must anchor in the middle of the lake, and not dock at the quays.

"We will not go ashore," I said. "We will not set one foot in Tarsus until first we have been honored here on board."

From where I lay, I saw a mass of people congregating on the docks. Someone launched a small boat, and it rowed frantically out to us. It was filled with Roman officers. One of them stood up and started gesturing.

"See what they want," I said to my steward. He went to the railing and bent over to talk to them.

The little boat was almost swamped by the men straining to see what was on deck. One after another they stood up and craned their necks, rocking the boat dangerously.

The steward returned and said, "Lord Antony's staff officer asks what, and who, has approached."

I thought for a moment. "You may tell him that Aphrodite has come to revel with Dionysus for the good of Asia." His face registered surprise. "And try not to laugh when you say it. Say it in all solemn seriousness."

He obediently did so, and I saw the incredulous Romans searching for words to reply. Finally my steward returned.

"He says that his most noble lord Antony invites you to dine with him tonight, at a welcoming banquet."

"Tell him that I do not wish to come ashore at Tarsus, and that the most noble Antony and his men, and the leading citizens of the city, should be my guests tonight instead, aboard the ship."

More exchanges ensued. The steward came back to say that Antony was holding court today at the tribunal in the city square, and that he expected me to come and pay respects.

I laughed. "He must be sitting on the platform alone," I said. "The entire city is down at the docks." I paused. "Repeat my message: He must come here first."

The message was conveyed, and the boat rowed away, heading for the quay.

"Now, my dear friend," I said, "ready the banquet!"

While the food was cooking, and the banquet chamber was being prepared, the ship slowly made its way across the lake. By the time we reached the dock, twilight had fallen and a deep blue-purple haze enveloped us, deepened by the mist of the smoking incense. Torches were lit, and the unreality of the day gave way to the further unreality of the night.

It was full dark before a commotion on the waterfront told me the guests were on their way. A procession wound toward us, with someone striding in front, accompanied by torch-bearers and singers. A long trail of companions streamed out behind him, and the crowds on either side were milling in excitement. I did not rise, so as not to spoil my careful arrangement under the canopy, but I was eager to know who was coming.

They mounted the decorated gangplank; I heard the heavy tread of their boots, detected the wood groaning from the weight. Then the first of them stepped on board, a Roman legate, followed by another staff officer, then an aide. They filed on, staring every which way at the lights in the rigging and the costumed attendants, the mermaids, nymphs, and Cupids gesturing to them in welcome. More officers stepped on deck behind them.

Where was he? Had Antony elected to stay ashore, to make a point? Caesar would have—or would he?

Just then he strode on deck and stood stock-still, staring at me. He even blinked once, before throwing his cloak over one shoulder and approaching.

He stopped in front of me and looked down, where I was lying on the couch.

For a moment neither of us said a word. He stared, expressionless, and I looked back.

I wore a necklace of enormous pearls, and hidden under their strands lay the pendant, which I never took off. Two of the largest pearls ever brought up by divers were dangling from my ears, and my hair curled in tendrils over my shoulders. My feet, in emerald-studded sandals, were tucked up under my gown, as I lay aslant, leaning on one elbow. His eyes went from the pearls to the hair to the hem of the gown before coming back to my face.

" 'Deathless Aphrodite, on your rich-wrought throne,' " he finally said.

So he knew Sappho! Very well, then, I would quote Euripides. " 'I am Dionysus. I am Bacchus. I came to Greece, to Thebes, the first Greek city I have caused to shriek in ecstasy for me, the first whose women I've clothed in fawnskin and in whose hands I've placed my ivy spear, the thyrsus.' Welcome, Dionysus."

He looked about, holding out his hands. "I seem to have forgotten my thyrsus," he said, with a laugh. "Gaius, go back to headquarters and get it for me!"

"You won't need it tonight," I said. I held out my hand, and he reached down and took it and pulled me up to my feet. "Welcome, Marc Antony."

"It is I who should be welcoming you." He shook his head and looked up at the rigging. The constellations of lights, lowered on silk lines, floated like magic above him. "You have all the zodiac at once," he said, in wonder. He seemed a bit dazed.

"You know our Alexandrian astronomers," I said. "We feel at home with the stars."

"Yes, doubtless," he said. "You know many fabled things." Then he gestured toward his men. "Welcome to Egypt," he said.

"That is for me to say," I told him.

"Then say it."

I gestured to my musicians and had them play a tune of welcome. "We greet you, and welcome you," I said to all the company. Servers began to pass gold goblets of wine around. Antony took one and tasted its contents appreciatively. His square fingers caressed the jeweled surface of the cup.

"I am most happy to see you," I said. "It has been a long time."

"Three years, five months, and some ten days," he said.

I was taken aback. He must have had his scribe figure it out, when he grew angry at my refusal to come. "Truly?" I did not remember the date of our last meeting; I was barely aware of the exact date of my departure from Rome.

"Or my secretary cannot count," he said. He ran his hand through his hair. "I also seem to be without my ivy crown," he noted. "I feel downright naked without it!" His smile faded. "I am pleased that you are here. You look well. The years have been kind to you."

If he only knew! I gave a wistful laugh.

"No, I mean it," he said.

And how did he look? The demands that had been placed on him had changed him, made him seem tougher and more commanding. Yet his good looks remained untouched, if anything, heightened. "For that I thank you." I was finding it surprisingly difficult to talk to him. The old banter had died between us. "I did not help Cassius," I said, as we seemed mired in seriousness. "You must know that he appropriated the legions that I was sending to Dolabella."

"Yes, I am aware of that."

"And you also know I did all within my power to bring ships to you. It cost me a fortune, I might add!"

"Yes, I know."

Why did he keep saying that? "Then why did you charge me with acting against you?"

"Things were confusing, the reports conflicting. I wanted you to explain what had actually happened. After all, you remained in the east, in a privileged vantage point, and you have a better idea of what went on than we do."

"That is not what your letter said."

He threw up his hands, and just then an obliging server removed his empty cup and replaced it with a full one. Antony took a long swallow before answering. "Forgive me," he said disarmingly. "It was wrong of me."

This was too simple. "I do." I smiled. "I could not believe the tone. I thought we were friends."

"Friends, yes, friends," he repeated. He took another drink, draining the cup. It got replaced immediately.

"Come, friend," I said. "Let us seat ourselves at the banquet."

We descended to the banqueting chamber, where twelve couches were waiting, tables before them, ready for the feasters. Antony would face me, on the adjoining couch, in the place of honor.

A server crowned him with flowers. "Here is your crown for tonight," I said. It made him look very unsoldierly.

"Ah," he said. "Now I wear a crown as well."

"Would you like to?"

He smiled. "I will not fall into that trap," he said. "Words have a way of returning at inopportune times."

So he would, then. Well, there was no one alive who would spurn a crown, if offered. Except a few Republicans—but with the death of Brutus, they had lost their leader.

"The battle of Philippi—I have offered innumerable thanks for it to the gods. Now I must offer my thanks directly to you, who brought it about. My eternal gratitude, Antony. I can never repay you."

At once his manner changed, and I realized it was the first kind, personal thing I had said to him this night.

"It was in the hands of the gods," he finally said. "But the outcome was entirely right. Our Caesar is repaid now."

The first course of the meal was starting, and the company of Romans and Tarsians was murmuring in wonder at the dishes, at the smoked Libyan desert hare, the oysters dressed in seaweed, the white cakes of Egypt's finest flour, the quivering jellies flavored with the juice of pomegranate and made sweet with honey and Derr dates. Their voices rose, and as the noise increased, it was easier to speak privately to Antony.

"Our Caesar," he said. "We wept for his misfortune, now we can rejoice in his vindication."

"It was you who turned the tide at the funeral. I can never forget that night."

"Nor I." He began to eat, washing the food down with draughts of wine. "But now we must go forward. I am pledged to carry out his Parthian venture, which he was forced to abandon on its eve. I will use the very spears and shields he had already set aside. They were still in Macedonia, where he kept them in readiness."

"But that is not for this season," I said. It was a question.

"No, it must wait. There is still much that needs to be settled here in the east."

The banquet proceeded, with dish after dish issuing from the kitchen, and singers and dancers providing entertainment for the sated guests. At length it was time for them to depart. Antony stood up first.

"Tomorrow night you must join me," he said. "I cannot hope to rival this, but"—he laughed—"you must allow me to try to repay you." He gestured to his men. "Come, it is time," he said.

"Wait," I said. "I wish to make a gift of all the couches you have lain on tonight, and every man may take away the gold plate with which he has dined."

The entire company stared, shocked.

"Yes, a token of my regard for you," I said carelessly. "Your company has been most pleasing."

They greedily gathered up the utensils and plate, trying to seem nonchalant.

"You needn't worry about carrying them," I said. "My servants will accompany you home, with torches, and bear the gifts."

Antony was staring.

"You as well," I said. "But you need more than that, as guest of honor and supreme commander of Asia. Here." I unhooked the gigantic pearl necklace and handed it to him. "Pray take it, as token of the Queen of Egypt's esteem for you."

His hands closed over it, the pearls brimming out on either side.

Now, as I sat in my cabin, it seemed unearthly quiet after the revelry. The evening had been an absolute success. News about it would go out over all the land, and our myth-ship would be described in many tongues. And as for Antony, he could count the pearls and be amazed.

I removed the two earrings and laid them in a box, and took off the heavy gold bracelets. My feet, barefoot now, stretched in weariness. I felt drained by the entire proceeding; I could hardly believe that it was finally over. It had taken weeks to plan, and had cost as much as a small palace. The frankincense alone . . . I shook my head. I had had it poured out like coal smoke, all to add up, with everything else, to one overwhelming impression of luxury, wealth, and power. I needed to make a statement to all Asia: Egypt is mighty.

There was a commotion outside, a hesitant knock on my door. "Open," I said.

"Your Majesty." A soldier bowed, and opened the door. "A visitor." The soldier stepped back, disappearing. Someone else appeared.

I could scarcely believe my eyes: It was Antony standing in the doorway. I stared at him, bracing himself against the doorframe with both arms. Was he ill? Drunk? Yet he had seemed well enough when the retinue took its leave.

I stood up. "What is it?" I asked, searching his face. It gave me no answers.

"I see I have waited too late to return," he said. "I will see you another time." He moved, took a step backward, and now I could see that he was—not drunk, but changed by the wine.

I went over to him. "No, do not go." I was not undressed, merely devoid of my ornaments. "Stay and tell me why you are here." I motioned him into the room. He hung back for a moment, then followed. I shut the door behind him.

I could see, now, that he was clutching papers of some sort. "I thought we should talk in private," he said. "And we are less likely to be overheard here than in my headquarters."

"Very well." I waited to hear what he had to say. Why could it not have kept until morning? Why had he rushed back to his rooms to get the papers and return? Why did he seem so strained? Casually—for I did not want to give the impression that I was ill at ease, although I found this visit very odd—I reached down and picked up a shawl to drape over myself, almost to shield myself.

"Caesar's papers—the ones in his house—do you remember?" He waved the sheaf of papers in his hand, as if they could talk.

"What of them?" All that had been so long ago, and so confusing. And what matter about them, anyway? The only one that truly counted, the will, had hurt me dreadfully by ignoring Caesarion and adopting Octavian.

"I altered them," he admitted. "I wanted to tell you, explain . . ." He looked sheepish. "I want you to see the originals."

This seemed very tiresome. I did not want to open myself up to the pain of seeing Caesar's handwriting, not now, not late at night like this, when I was tired, my defenses down. "But the light is so poor," I objected. The truth was, I did not want to look at them now, I did not want to entertain Antony now, I did not want to be disturbed now, or to undo my diplomatic triumph by anything I might say or do in an unguarded moment now.

"Oh, it will serve," he said airily, and without my permission he seated himself at my desk and spread out the first of the papers. He bent his head over them and started pointing at something there. "Yes, you see, here, where he appointed this magistrate to oversee the games—"

Wearily I went over and stood behind him, looking over his shoulder to see what he was so adamant about. In the dim light I could barely make out the words; Antony's head was so close to them I saw that he was having trouble, too.

"Why should we care, now, who presided over the games?" I asked. I had to bend way over in order to speak to him, and there was no other way but to lean right into him, pressing against his shoulders and back.

"I changed so many things," he confessed. "This is just one of them. See. The handwriting—can you see how it is slightly different?"

I had to lean still farther over; now I was pressed up against him in earnest. Suddenly I was acutely aware of nothing else.

"Yes," I allowed.

"I have always felt guilty about doing that to him, and using his seal afterward, to secure positions that would benefit me, strengthen my hand—"

I am Caesar's right hand, he had once said. "At least you used that hand in his defense!" I said. "It was not a misuse of your position, but a good use of it." I paused. "And why are you telling me?"

He sighed, and his shoulders moved; I moved with them. "I suppose because you are the only one who has the power—at least in my own mind—to absolve me of the liberties I took in his name. You can say, 'I forgive you in the name of Caesar.' You understand what the conditions were, and why some falsehoods were imperative at the time."

"Yes. I do. I told you I can never repay you for what you have done to avenge him. If rules had to be bent, and documents altered on the way, then—" I started to move back. There was really nothing else to see on this paper, and my eyes were tired of straining.

But as I moved to straighten up, so did he; and it made my cheek brush against his, lightly. I froze—there is no other word for it—as that forbidden touch seemed at once to demolish the barricade between us, so properly guarded and hedged with manners.

He moved again, and once again we touched, and in what felt like a long, slow, dreamlike motion—but what surely was not, what surely happened almost instantly—he turned his head and kissed me full on the lips. Without a censoring thought I returned the kiss, opening my mouth to his, and felt him turn halfway and rise from the chair, pulling me up with him. And now we were standing, face to face, kissing, and unbidden, unable to do anything else, I put my arms around him and held him against me.

His kisses were deep and passionate; there was no intermediate kiss between that first hesitant one and the hungry ones that followed. And I was hungry for them—for him, too—that was the shock and surprise of it. Touching him opened that secret door within me that had remained resolutely shut for so long. Its sudden, opening onrush made me weak.

There had to be some way to halt this; I could not just act in madness. I tried to break out of his arms. But he did not let me go easily; it was as if he was afraid to.

"I've always wanted you," he said quietly, his mouth by my ear, his left hand clutching my head, holding me tightly against him. Was he apologizing? Offering an excuse? As if that made it all right to barge into my quarters at midnight on a flimsy errand?

"I suppose you will tell me it started when you first came to Egypt, and I was still a girl," I said, wanting to sound light and bantering, and all the while trying to calm myself, stop my banging heart. It sounded so loud I could almost believe he would hear it, where it pounded through my temples and his head was pressed against mine.

"I don't know—but I never forgot you. And when I saw you again in Rome, always holding court in some fashion, an ornament of Caesar's . . . oh yes, I longed for you then, like a boy seeing fine candies in a store, but having no money. You were Caesar's, and it was disloyal even to imagine—anything." He paused. "At least when I was awake." I could feel his embarrassed smile, although I could not see it. It made me smile, too.

Now an awkwardness descended. We were caught between two kinds of behaviors; were we to go forward into the unknown or retreat into the safe and the practiced? I attempted the latter.

"My soldier," I said, trying to joke. "My general." Again I tried to extricate myself, to step back. But somehow it did not happen.

"Not *your* general, just *a* general," he said. "Unless you would like to employ me." He started kissing the side of my neck, near my ear.

"I thought that was what this meeting was all about," I said. "Future alliances—political ones."

"No," he said, "*this* is what this meeting is all about." He was still kissing me, and fooling with my gown, loosening the straps of it, letting it fall off my shoulders. Why did I not stop him? But my skin was tingling, charged with excitement. It craved his touch, as if it had a mind and needs of its own.

There were guards on deck, guards who would come running and spear him, if necessary. And the soldier just outside the door. I could call them, and end this. They would evict him and save me from my own runaway body with its unexpected desires. *Call them!* I ordered myself. But my insurrection against myself continued. I stood there mute, and let him keep kissing me, caressing my shoulders and touching my hair.

"I wanted to see you, I must have been half mad to want to see you so much, but I did," he was explaining, in a mumbled rush. I could barely make out the words. "It had been so long—and I had no reasonable excuse ever to see you. Ever. Do you realize that? I could only legally go as far as Syria. I waited for you to invite me to Egypt, but you didn't. Month after month went by, and you didn't. So I had to think of a reason to summon you. I'm afraid . . . it wasn't a very good reason. It angered you." He bent his head and started to kiss the top of my breasts.

Ripples of excitement were washing over me, making it hard for me to reply. "If I had known the real reason, I would not have been angry."

"You should have known. You should have guessed." He paused, and then continued kissing me, moving farther down.

Again I was ashamed of myself, ashamed of the desire he was evoking in me. What was he? Another married Roman! I would have to be mad to travel that road again! I pushed him away.

Leave! I tried to say. You have dishonored yourself, coming here like this! The wine may make you forget, but I can never forget! But the words did not come, because I knew he would, shamefacedly, obey, and leave. And I did not want him to leave.

He was looking at me in the dim light, desire all over his face. He was trembling with it. And I found that I, too, was shaking. I reached up to his shoulders and pulled him down, falling with him on the bed just behind us. We rolled over in each other's arms, tumbling like children. I ran my hands through his thick hair, loving the feel of it. He lowered his face and kissed me, this time gently, as a man who had all the time in the world. It stoked my excitement as even the first heated kisses had not.

"I am not a wild beast, nor will I do anything you do not desire as much as I." He released me and watched me solemnly, waiting for an indication, a signal.

I tried to think, to collect myself, but all I could think was, Tonight is mine, the first night to be mine in years, a night I own myself. Tonight I am no one's widow, bound to no one, only a woman, a free woman.

I ran my hands over his shoulders. They were broad and strong—and young. He was just at the prime of life. "My soldier," I repeated, but this time I said it differently, possessively. "My general."

He twined his hand in my hair and brought my face back to his, where he kissed me so deeply that I forgot everything that was not in this room. My body ached to join itself to his, banishing all other considerations.

Dionysus was the dark god of ecstatic release, and he was Antony that night. I need have no fears that any memories would come flooding back, displacing the here and now, for he was completely different from anything I had known. He took me with no ado or talk, making me forget all else but him.

Ah! my secret self cried, surrendering as I had the first time I closed my eyes and plunged into the water in the harbor, the water that was deep and warm and full of unknown currents. And dangerous.

There were many hours left until dawn, and over and over again in the darkness he roused himself and made love to me, until I thought I would die of it.

Later, as we gradually awakened and felt the approach of the new day, there were drowsy, murmured exchanges. His head was resting on my neck, and he reached out and took the Caesar pendant in his fingers. "You will have to stop wearing this now," he said. "He's a god now, he shouldn't want mortals. He should leave mortals to other mortals."

"Like you?" I asked. "But aren't you a god, too? At least in Ephesus?"

"Umm," he said, sighing. "But I haven't got used to it yet." He turned to look at me, barely visible in what little light there was in the cabin. "And I will never get used to you—like this."

"Then you can never take it for granted." And more of such silly, lovely talk, the words all lovers use afterward, at least in the beginning.

When the sky began to show a hint of light, he said, "I must leave, before it is broad daylight."

"But people know you are here," I said. "They saw you come aboard. You had to pass the guards. Doubtless you gave them some high-sounding excuse."

He shook his head. "I'm afraid it was rather transparent. Most state business does not need to be transacted at midnight."

"Everyone will know," I said. "You need not sneak away like a guilty schoolboy. I think we should be quite unapologetic about it." I felt reborn, bold, and would not disown the night. "I think you should issue forth like the sun rising."

He laughed. "You are very poetic. But that is one of the things I have loved about you—for a very long time."

"You couldn't have known that about me."

"I know a great many things about you," he said. "I was hungry to learn them."

"I can see you know me better than I know you," I said, "for I wouldn't have guessed that about you."

"I told you, I have wanted you for a great long time."

For the first time, I believed him. He was not just mouthing conventions. "Now you have had me."

"It is not that simple," he said. "One night does not deliver you into my hands. It is just a beginning."

I shivered. I wanted it to be that simple. An overwhelming longing, a desire, a desire satisfied. The end. Where could it go? Another married Roman. *That*, at least, was simple.

I shook my head. Why had I done this? But the memory of the past few hours answered that, and quickly.

"Don't steal away," I said. "We have nothing to be ashamed of."

"You mean because we answer to no earthly superiors?"

"No, I mean exactly what I said—that we have nothing to be ashamed of. Do not act as if we do."

43

Antony made his way across the deck as the sun was rising, striking his dark hair, making it shine. I walked with him, and saw the startled stares of the sailors. On the gangplank he turned and saluted me.

"Tonight we will repeat . . . the dinner," he said, laughing. "I will try to match last night—with all my resources."

"Until then," I said. I watched him descend and walk away across the quay. He had a rolling sort of gait.

I spun around and shut my eyes, leaning against the railing. My body was exhausted, but my thoughts were racing and jumbled, running with excitement. I almost did not want to rein them in, and so I breathed slowly to try to come back to the everyday world of wooden decks and coiled ropes and mist rising off the lake. The sun seemed to be probing my eyes, forcing them open.

Across the water I saw the slopes of Mount Taurus, wooded and green. Tarsus was beautifully situated. It was a superlative setting in which to have—to have—

I shook my head, hurrying back to my cabin. I rushed in and closed the door, then sat immobile for a long time in the chair I had been in when the knock on the door had come. I was back exactly where I had started, many hours ago.

The room looked the same. Nothing had been moved. Only myself—I was changed.

Years ago I had sailed west, disguised in a rug, and rolled out and into Caesar's bed—as Olympos had scoldingly put it. Now I had sailed east, disguised as Venus, and Antony had jumped into *my* bed. Two sea voyages, one result. Doubtless Olympos would have equally disapproving words about this.

I realized now I had always noticed Antony, had been unusually aware of him in a way I was not of others. The attraction had lurked beneath the surface, a shadow that swam here and there, darting swiftly, too swiftly to be caught . . . here, there, gone.

What was I to do next? One time can be a surprise, a mistake, a venture. But after that . . . it becomes a deliberate decision. I could never pretend to myself to be taken unawares again by Antony.

What was the point in continuing? He was married to the fearsome Fulvia, and had two sons by her. He was passing through the eastern provinces—he would not stay. And I would never go to Rome again as anyone's mistress. We would have this meeting for the next few days, and then part. Well, what of it? Perhaps it was better that way. It could serve no purpose but a brief flare of passion. I meant to enjoy that, however; I felt I deserved it as some sort of a reward . . . for what, I was not sure.

Antony . . . specific memories of the hours in the dark beset me, making me bite my lips, as if to tame the hot thoughts. I was doing this when Charmian appeared in the mirror behind me, embarrassing me.

"Dear mistress—Your Majesty—I—" She looked flustered and shaken.

"What is it?" I am afraid I was sharp with her.

"Is it true what the men are saying? That the lord Antony has been here all night? In here?" She looked at the rumpled bed.

"Yes, it's true," I said. "And I enjoyed it immensely!" I flung the words out defiantly, as if practicing them.

"Madam," she said, a look of pain crossing her face.

"Don't say it!" I said. "I will hear nothing against it! We answer to no one." I echoed Antony's sentence.

"What about to your own heart? What about to the court of Egypt? And the public opinion in Rome?"

"I am used to flouting public opinion in Rome. As for the court of Egypt, I have done nothing to harm it. But for my own heart . . . ah . . . it is drawn to him."

"Better it were not!" she said. "Better it were only your body that was drawn to him."

I laughed. "It is primarily my body," I said. "In truth, I know little about him beyond that." Still . . . that was enough for now.

She looked relieved.

The day passed. I conferred with the cooks and the entire staff of the boat, praising them for the successful evening. They attempted to mask their smiles and giggles and rib-punching. I ordered them to procure several cartloads of rose petals for tomorrow evening. There. That should keep them busy.

Now for Antony's dinner. This time I would go as Cleopatra, not as Venus. Once was a novelty, twice was predictable. As I watched myself being dressed, I could not help wondering if any of the incandescence I felt inside was translated on the outside, excitement made visible.

I would be carried in a litter, accompanied by four torch-bearers in the falling dusk. From my height, I could see the pleasing buildings and clean streets of Tarsus. This city had been solidly Caesarian, and had been savagely treated by Cassius. Now, in recognition of their sufferings and loyalty, Antony had rewarded them by exempting them from taxes and gifting them with a magnificent new gymnasion.

He had set up headquarters in the center of town, and it was there that the litter was set down and I emerged. I found myself standing on broad steps leading up to a great covered hall. Soldiers were stationed on either side, and an armed escort appeared to guide us into the hall.

The ceiling was flat and high, and rows of pillars divided the hall into three aisles. This was a merchant building, cleared for the occasion. There were brave attempts to make it luxurious—Syrian embroidered hangings draped the rough walls, and lamp stands were set up every few feet. Musicians were playing, seated on a platform near the entrance. But it felt like a market—and smelled faintly like one, too, in spite of the perfumed incense permeating the air. Soldiers, in uniform, were stationed about the room, and the company seemed to consist primarily of men, although there were a few women present—probably the wives of the city magistrates.

While the center of the hall held the traditional dining couches and tables, the rest of the company were to eat at long tables, like a soldiers' mess. I saw Dellius up near the couches, wearing what was evidently his formal attire—a plain tunic and sturdy sandals. The only festive note was a wide gold bracelet on his left arm. He was surrounded by a group of other soldiers, all drinking and laughing too loudly. They must have been drinking steadily since the early afternoon.

Just then, Antony burst into the room with two other staff officers. Seeing him gave me a start—it felt odd to see him publicly again, surrounded by all these drinking companions.

He was somewhat better dressed than Dellius, but not much. Over his tunic he wore a light cloak, held with a bronze clasp, and he was wearing boots instead of sandals, but his hair was wild and his color high. He, too, must have been drinking all afternoon.

He saw me and nodded. Then, abruptly, he raised his arms and shouted, "Welcome, welcome, good friends all!" The noise abated slightly, but some of the men kept on laughing and talking. He had to grab his dagger and bang it against a metal plate to silence them.

"We are here to honor the Queen of Egypt, who has journeyed far to see us," he shouted. He had a very commanding voice, even when it was touched by wine.

All the company shouted. I winced. Had I joined a legion?

"Welcome to our humble dining hall," he said, and the words were not the usual polite disclaimers. "I have tried to make it royal for you."

Still, all the time he was speaking, he was not looking at me, but at his men.

Of course, they did not know. They had been ashore all night, and thought Antony had been, too.

"Sit! Sit!" he boomed. The entire company obeyed, making a racket as they did.

Now I was to take my place at his side on the dining couches. I found him still avoiding looking at me, joking and making endless talk with his men. Finally he sank down on the couch in order for the meal to begin.

I leaned on my elbow, putting my head close to his.

"You have been busy," I said.

Instead of looking at me, he just lowered his head. Finally he said, "I warned you it would not equal yours."

"It is different," I said. "Remember, I have never been entertained anywhere but Rome, Alexandria, and Meroe. I have no idea what a provincial capital is like."

It felt odd, too, to be carrying on this stilted talk about dining halls, after . . . and why would he not turn his head? I longed to take it between my hands and turn it firmly in my direction. Maybe even kiss him. Yes, that would entertain the soldiers.

"Look at me!" I chided him.

He turned, and I saw the veiled desire on his face—or was it just my own, reflected on his? My imagination was so strong it could paint itself on neutral things. The broad forehead, the dark eyes, the fleshy, curvaceous mouth—I could associate them only with one thing.

"A command I gladly obey," he said. Then Dellius caught his attention.

"How early does the winter come here?" he was asking. "We have to clear out before then."

One of the Tarsus magistrates answered. "We have a long autumn, and the mountain shields us from the north winds for some time. Where do you go after this?"

"On to Syria," said Antony. "And then to Judaea. I need to meet with Herod."

"And then?" I asked.

"Back to Rome," he said.

A company of clowns poured into the room, dressed in imitation Roman uniforms. They began running up and down the room, shouting riddles.

"What is it that rises at sundown and only goes down at sunrise?"

I was sure they did not have the full moon in mind.

"What is it that itches more than wool next to that most delicate skin?" and so on. There were also political barbs, although here they had to tread softly. The company clearly adored these "entertainments," and stamped their feet in pleasure.

Well, you were bored with the usual proper Roman dinners, I told myself. Some of the remarks are wickedly clever—admit it.

"I always wanted to be a soldier," I told Antony, laying my hand on his arm.

To my surprise, he edged it away, reaching quickly for a handful of olives.

"Invade Parthia with me, then," he said heartily.

I was unlikely to supply for him what I had denied to Caesar. He would have to bankroll this venture out of his own resources. "As your guest, perhaps," I said.

By the time the banquet was over, I felt I had been on a campaign. In truth, I had enjoyed the respite from expected conversations and ritual phrases. It was as great a novelty to me as the Venus-ship had been to him.

I grew tired, and as the evening was lengthening into a plain old drinking bout, I decided to take my leave.

For the first time, Antony looked disappointed. "No, I want you to stay."

"What, and drink with the men? I think they would be freer to enjoy themselves once I have gone. I have kept them waiting long enough to cut loose."

"Come to my apartments," he said. "I will not be long."

I laughed. "Like a camp follower? No, thank you."

"But I prepared it for us!"

"I suppose you replaced the field bed with a real one? That is not the problem. I would shame myself to parade up there and wait for the great general. And in front of his officers!" Suddenly I was angry with him. "Is that what you were aiming at all along? An opportunity to show off?" I indicated the vast company. "Impress them?"

I had to get out of there. I felt betrayed.

"No, wait, I did not—" But he did not extend a hand to stay me.

"*You* must come to *me*," I said. "That is the only way." I brushed past him and entered my litter quickly.

As I sat looking out the curtains of the swaying litter, I was angry with myself for inviting him at all. If he came to the ship, I was not sure I was in the mood to see him. I did not feel very amorous anymore. He had avoided me all during the evening, acting distant and evasive, and then he thought I would wait for him afterward! Clearly he had been spoiled to death by women. And even last night—it was the act of a man very sure of himself to appear like that. Suddenly I *did* feel level with a common camp follower. I had behaved like one.

It was late by the time I had boarded my own ship and entered my quarters. This time last night, I had just begun to relax after the banquet . . . no wonder I was exhausted. Even without Antony's sudden appearance, the voyage itself and the preparations had been draining. Now I felt the last bit of energy seeping from me.

I could barely sit up, and I no longer had the wherewithal to think about Antony or his soldiers' dinner. Without calling Charmian, I pulled off my clothes and literally crawled into bed, collapsing into a deep sleep. It was the dreamless kind, a black, stuporous envelope.

Then, suddenly, something was in the room. I came instantly and completely awake, and sat bolt upright.

Antony was standing there, holding a dim lamp over his head, throwing a faint circle of light around him.

"I came as soon as I could," he said. "Charmian let me in."

I clutched a covering to myself, and stared at him. Never had I felt so disadvantaged—unclothed, sleep-confused, taken by surprise again, while he stood impassively looking down at me, properly gowned and cloaked.

Charmian would have assumed I wanted him there, that I had been waiting for him. No wonder she had let him in.

Before I could say anything—for my wits were slow in returning—he sat down on the bed and embraced me, his encircling hands touching my bare back. They were cold from the night air, and I shivered. He responded by holding me tighter.

"The men went on and on, drinking and singing," he said quietly. "It got so late, but I could not leave. Ordinarily I would have out-indulged them all, but all I could think of was getting away and following you."

As he spoke, I realized he was cold sober; he had stood aloof from the rest of them. If he was here now, it was not on a whim or impulse. He had had hours to think about it, clearheaded hours.

"At last they left, and I was free."

"And no one saw you leave?" So he had stolen away in secret, leaving his quarters empty.

"I fear whatever I do cannot please you," he said. "First you told me to be bold about it, that it should not be hidden. Then, when I asked you to come to my quarters publicly, you accused me of trying to impress my men. You even said it would shame you—something I would never do. That is why I betrayed nothing during the dinner. It was up to you to reveal whatever you wished. Obviously you chose not to let the company know." All the time he spoke, he merely held me, and made no attempt even to kiss me.

"I was confused," I said. "I admit I said one thing in the morning and another at night. It was easier to be daring on my own ship, among my own people, than before strangers. Here my people know well enough that no man besides you has been admitted to my chambers, whereas your men are used to the parade of women. I had no wish to be another Glaphyra."

"There is no one like you in all the world, and certainly not Glaphyra."

He sounded so earnest that I had to laugh. "Oh, Antony, you are too easy to forgive," I said. "I was angry with you about the raucous invitation, and angry that you stole into this room, and even angry that you caught me like this."

"Like this?" he said, kissing my shoulder where the covering had slipped off. "It is much more effective than the Venus costume. The most beautiful Venus statues are nude." But there was nothing insistent about his action; gone were the feverish embraces of the night before.

His calm speech, his very hesitation, was soothing and oddly erotic. There was a sort of languor to him, a slow passivity. I was drawn into it. The more still he was, the more awake and aroused I became.

"You may stay," I said, finally moving my own arms up his own, over and across his shoulders. "Sir, I grant you permission." Only then did I lean forward and kiss his lips. It was a kiss that lasted a long time, that left me charged with excitement, since it seemed to exist just for itself, suspended, not leading from or to anything. I had never had a kiss like that, divorced from everything but itself. I felt I could live in it for eternity.

For a timeless time I was content with only that—an endless kiss while I held, and was held by, this man who seemed to know how to make me feel both erotic and cherished at the same time.

Eventually, lying beside him, stretched out together in the close darkness, I wished that could go on forever, too. Caesar had loved me, but always he was Caesar. I had never been adored before, never worshiped by the body. It was like beholding an entirely new color, bathing in it.

I had not thought I could ever love anyone physically different from the lean and elegantly proportioned Caesar—even my ideas of what love was had been bound up in *his* body, inseparable from it. Now that had been cast aside, and I must learn anew.

When I lay facedown, fully contented, he took infinite care in untangling my hair, drawing it out and smoothing it across my back. It came halfway down, well below my shoulder blades.

"I always wanted to touch your hair," he said. "But first of all, it was forbidden, and second, it was always braided up or twisted full of jewels. It had such a dark gleam to it."

I thought of all the times when I was just growing into womanhood, how I would rinse my hair in scented oils, brush it, take handfuls of it and try to imagine whether it would please someone. And now it had. I laughed, not a jarring laugh, but one of pleasure. "It is yours to do with as you will."

"Then perhaps I shall cut it all off," he said playfully. "Yes, and keep it for myself, leaving you to hide your shorn-sheep look under a headdress. I am curious what you would look like without that extraordinary hair. But I think it would not matter. Not to me."

"A woman with short hair—how odd that would be!" I said. "I would feel like an athlete—a boy runner."

"I do not think, somehow, that you would look like one."

"Actually, I can run rather fast."

"But you would have to compete naked," he said. "And no one but I should see you that way."

"You are neither my husband nor my brother nor my father, so you have no right to make such pronouncements."

"Yes, I do, the oldest one of all. I am jealous and won't permit it."

"Won't permit it! Listen to you—Fulvia's husband." As soon as I said the word, I regretted it. None of that had any place here, right now. "I am sorry," I said instantly. "That was wrong of me."

"No, it was honest of you. But Fulvia is in Rome, and that is far away."

"Antony, come back to Alexandria with me." I could not bear to say good-bye after only three days, when we were due to sail. Even memories needed more than three days to take permanent form, solidify.

He was silent a long time, stroking my hair. "I do not know that I can," he finally said.

"Come as my guest. You would do it for anyone else! Do not do less for me."

"Because you *are* you, I must do less."

"Then you punish me for being Cleopatra, and not Cytheris or Glaphyra."

"I did not follow them to their cities, for all the world to see."

"The world! Always the world!"

"You care enough about it in the daylight, outside, my lady. You would not even reveal our liaison in front of my men—soldiers, who are a pretty forgiving lot."

"Now, I will." Now I knew it was more than just that one fever-charged burst of pent-up lust. My desire seemed to grow with the very feeding of it, rather than becoming sated or fading. "Come with me to Alexandria. I will show us to all the world. I will present you without shame."

"I am not an idol or a doll to be displayed," he said. "If I came, I would come as a private citizen, a foreign dignitary making a courtesy call."

I noted, silently, that he was sketching the conditions of it—of this visit that he would not make.

But the night still had some hours left in it, and I did not want to spend them talking. I reached out and took his hand, twining my fingers in his. "If you do not come to Alexandria, then you certainly have to use our few remaining hours to the fullest," I whispered, kissing the soft part of his ear. He did not argue.

44

Twilight had spread its tender, soft mantle over the sky, and once again the special lights were lit and glowing in the rigging of the ship. This time the guests would walk not on the wooden deck, but on a carpet of rose petals that would have been knee-deep had they not been held down by a net. No one could sink into them, but instead must tread on their surface, each step crushing the delicate petals and releasing a cloud of fragrance. It would rise like the mist of dawn, a fog of sensual delight.

The perfume of a hundred thousand roses for the nose, the glitter of gold cups and winking lights for the eyes, the sleek feel of silken couch covers for the skin, pure voices and silver lutes making music for the ears, and the finest food I could serve to both caress and tease the tongue—I meant my farewell banquet in Tarsus to linger forever in all five of their senses, imprinted there for a lifetime.

As for myself, it was only fitting I should be arrayed as Egypt's queen, in a gown of gold and blue, wearing a crown of gold and lapis serpents. As Iras braided my hair, pulling it back from my face, I could not help smiling, remembering Antony's comment about it. It was true; most ceremonial hair-styles were stiff and not to be touched. Iras looked into the reflection of my eyes in the mirror, rather than directly at them. Her face held a thousand questions, but she dared not ask them. And tonight I would not answer them. Not until the end of the evening.

A massive collar of gold, carnelian, and lapis beads was fastened around my neck, and wide carved-gold armlets were slid onto my upper arms.

Iras unstoppered a slender alabaster bottle and shook a few drops of per-fume out onto her palms, then touched me lightly under my chin, on my elbows and forearms, and on my forehead. "The scent of roses must also come from you," she said. "And this fragrance, from white roses, smells just slightly different from the red roses covering all the decks and floors."

The same company as before was to come aboard, thirty-six guests to lie on the twelve couches. Antony had expressed little curiosity about it, assum-ing it would be like most of those he had attended for years. I had made him leave before dawn; he took it to be my modesty, but I had not wanted him to glimpse the cargo waiting on the dock, although he must have smelled the cartloads of rose petals as he passed. Let him be as astounded as everyone else.

"My last dinner here," I had said. "And, should you not come to Alexandria, our last night together."

He was still insisting he could not come. Well, I had also insisted I would not come to Tarsus.

The gangplank, draped with rich Tyrian purple and transformed into a triumphal bridge, welcomed the guests aboard. One by one the Romans stepped off it, and onto the carpet of rose petals, their boots sinking, their bodies bouncing on the springy cushion. I watched their faces as they were taken by surprise, these Roman soldiers and citizens of Tarsus. But it was Antony I most wanted to astonish and please; I took the reaction of the others for granted.

He stopped at the top of the gangplank, leaning on the railing, his eyes taking in the entire setting in one glance: the crimson of the roses, the purple drapings, the artificial constellations in the rigging, and then me, as gilded and ornamented as a statue. It was a spectacle of theater, not one natural thing about it. It is a privilege and challenge to outdo nature on occasion.

"O rare ship!" Antony said. "Let us cut the cables and drift away—to whatever magic land you came from!" Then he took a high leap and landed as hard as he could, losing his balance as the roses squashed under his weight. He rolled over and lay on his back, arms spread, feet apart. "Ah!" he cried. "I will suffocate, drugged by elixir of roses. Help me, help me, for I faint."

He made a show of struggling to his knees and then dragging himself over to me, bowing at my feet, clasping my sandals. "I am quite overcome," he said. The company roared with laughter.

I reached down and took his hand, drawing him up. "Revive yourself, Lord Antony," I said, motioning to a servant to bring him a cup of wine. It was a large one, bumpy with inset coral and pearls, filled with the wine of Chios.

He took a deep drink of it, and then shook his head. "Wine has never yet banished magic," he said. "It merely increases its effect."

"Welcome, all," I said. "Pray, drink with us." At once a company of servants appeared, cups in hand. "I wish my last evening with you to be worthy of long memories."

Already they had that half-uncomfortable, half-excited, dazed look on their faces that betokened uneasy enchantment. They were all mine for the evening, to do with as I wished. Even Dellius was wide-eyed. Ah, the persuasion of props and accoutrements—how mighty they are! What power they give us, properly used!

"Is this the same ship I left this morning?" Antony asked, his voice low.

"The very same," I said.

"What have you done to the cabin below?"

"You must wait to find out," I said. "Unless you prefer to go now?"

He looked around, laughing, a little nervously. "I believe you would be bold enough to do even that," he finally said.

I merely smiled. Let him wonder.

Dellius was talking loudly—too loudly—about the Parthians and how, by Zeus, they had gone too far. He then proceeded to abuse Cassius in such blistering terms that one of the Tarsians—who hardly had any reason to defend their tormenter—tried to change the subject.

"Dellius," I said, gliding over to him, "doubtless when you march into Parthia with Lord Antony you will have ample opportunity to smite a few Parthians. But forget Cassius—he has paid the price. A man can die only once."

"No, that's not true—he can die twice. Once the body, next the reputation. Kill the latter, and it's a crueler death than the first." He said it so fiercely that I could almost forget that he had once served Cassius, and come to Antony only after Philippi.

"There's a third death as well, then, and that's to be abandoned by one's former friends," I said.

He smiled his nasty smile. I turned away. I hoped Antony had more than this reed to lean upon for his fortunes in war.

The chief magistrate of Tarsus was explaining to Antony his choice of man to fill the post of gymnasiarch for the city. He was a plump little man, who would probably spend little time on the exercise field himself but would enjoy the baths and the lectures given in the new gymnasion.

"Yes, yes," Antony was saying, clearly not caring whom he appointed. He was attempting to extricate himself, but the mayor grabbed on to the shoulder of his tunic and kept on talking, buzzing like a bee. In fact he was shaped like one—round and wide.

His wife stood nearby, wearing the most nondescript clothes I had ever seen. Why is it that respectability always seems to drape itself in such proper dreariness? Why do we equate beauty with lack of seriousness? I welcomed her and told her how impressed I was with her city, and how fortunate they were to have the mountains to shelter under, and groves of trees nearby.

What I did not say was that once the Ptolemies had owned all this—we had had not only the sea and sand and Nile of Egypt, but these very mountain slopes and forests. Seeing them had awakened a desire to regain as much as possible of this lost empire. Caesar had given Cyprus back to Arsinoe; perhaps Antony . . .

She was speaking, her low, modest voice as mouselike as the rest of her. I tried to turn my attention to her words. But they were as forgettable as her face.

When we descended to the banquet chamber, the company shuffled, walking carefully on the mattress of rose petals, and did not look up until they stood at the very entrance. Torches flamed and flared, and the couches—far more sumptuous than the ones they had dined on the first night—were surrounded by marble tables with gold legs, and rubies on the borders. The red of the roses, the scarlet wall hangings, the rubies, and the crimson couches all blurred together to make even the air of the chamber seem dyed fiery red.

Antony and I took our places, and I gave the signal for the banquet to begin. The food itself was nothing unusual—how could it be? A ship's kitchen cannot rival one on land, and I had to rely on mostly local fare like scarus-fish, purple shellfish, peacocks, and kid. From Egypt I had brought smoked duck, geese, and Nile perch. Toasted papyrus stems, gilded, would serve as a novelty. It was eaten—ungilded, of course—by the common people at home, but would amuse the Romans and Tarsians. I had brought many amphorae of the best Chian wine with me, and I meant for them to finish most of it this evening. When I sailed for Egypt, the ship must be much lighter.

The musicians—also clothed in red—played their instruments softly, and could barely be heard above the rising voices. Everyone was talking, their tongues loosened at last.

"You are extravagant," said Antony, his eyes roving from one thing to another.

"Hardly," I said. "This is modest. I know how to spend ten times this much on one dinner."

"Impossible. That is, without increasing the number of guests."

"I could do so this very instant," I said. "With these very guests, and keeping almost the same menu." An idea had come to me, and I meant to use it. "If I can do so, will you relent and come to Alexandria?"

He thought long before answering. "Yes. But you must keep to the rules. No additional guests, no expensive presents suddenly added. Just this banquet, with these guests, and this food."

"Agreed." I motioned to one of my servers. "Fill a goblet with strong vinegar," I said, "and bring it to me."

Antony frowned. "Vinegar is hardly very expensive."

I ignored him. "Dear guests," I said loudly, "Lord Antony and I have a wager. I have bet him that I can make this banquet cost over a million sesterces. He says it is impossible for any banquet to cost that much, and particularly one with only thirty-six guests. Ah." I reached out and took the vinegar-filled goblet. "Thank you."

Antony was leaning forward on his elbows, watching me intently. His dark eyes were riveting.

"Now," I said, removing one of my pearl earrings and dropping it into the goblet, where it landed with a plunk and then sank to the bottom. I swirled the goblet, and they could all hear the pearl rolling inside. "It will dissolve and I will drink it—the most expensive wine in history." I held the goblet up in both hands, gently shaking it.

Everyone was staring, and Antony looked shocked. I kept shaking the goblet until I felt it was time, then I brought it to my lips, tilted it up and drank it. There was a collective gasp.

"Bitter!" I said. "Vinegar, even flavored with pearl, is still rough. Another goblet, please! All of you must partake!"

My servant quickly brought a second one, and I started to unfasten the other pearl, but Dellius cried out, "No, stop! It is unnecessary! Do not sacrifice the second one!" and Antony reached out and stayed my hand.

"You win," he said quietly. "No need to repeat it."

I returned the goblet to the servant's hands.

"You are . . . there is no word to describe you. 'Extravagant' fades beside all this," Antony said.

I looked at him, and knew that I had won more than the wager.

As the banquet proceeded, and the dishes were brought out and set daintily before us, I found that the chamber was suddenly charged with erotic splendor for me, it fairly shimmered with it. Had my wager excited me, transforming me from calm host to a bedazzled guest of my own self? I found myself watching Antony's arm as he held his cup, leaning on his elbow. It was thick, muscled and tan, and I stared at it, lascivious thoughts racing through my mind. Even his feet, tucked partially under the couch cushion, seemed objects of desire. I had swallowed the pearl, and it seemed to have acted as a magic potion, surrounding him with an aureole of desirability for me, literally from head to toe.

Suddenly I could hardly stand another minute of this banquet. Let it be over, so we could descend below. . . .

When, at long last, it ended, there was still a part for me to enact. I rose, and gestured toward the couches. "All this is yours," I said. "And the vessels and plates you have used, as before."

Since these were finer work and made of more precious material, everyone's mouth fell open.

"As before, do not worry about how to transport them. My servants will do that. But in addition, I wish to present you all with horses which I brought, along with their trappings embellished with silver and gold. These boys from Ethiopia"—I nodded to a company of them filing into the chamber, each taking one of the torches from its stand—"will escort you home, leading the horses."

The banquet was now over, and the guests could take their leave. But there was one more thing to do before they departed. I took Antony's hand in mine, and he stood up with me.

"I bid you good night, and farewell. Lord Antony and I will now take our leave." I turned and left the chamber, still holding Antony's hand, and went directly to my private quarters, leaving the rest of the company to emerge on deck and realize that Antony had vanished, and would not be going ashore with them. And there was only one place he could be, since no one actually has the power to vanish.

Inside the private cabin, I leaned against the door and shut my eyes. It was over. And I had played my part well. One never knows in advance.

Antony was standing in the middle of the room, looking wary, as if he expected something else to happen—a serpent to glide out from under the bed, invisible hands to proffer cups of wine, a ghostly chorus to start wailing.

I went over to him and put my arms around him. "I have waited all night for this," I said. And it was true.

"Then you must take off all these things," he said, reaching down to remove the crown. "Hard, glittering things that are cold." Gently he unfastened the collar of gems and laid it on a table. "And the braids. Take them down."

I unpinned the clip holding them back, and slowly unbraided them, feeling my scalp tingle as the blood rushed back into it. It took a long time; Iras had made a great many of them. At length, all my hair was free, and he put his hands in it and combed through it with his fingers. It made me weak with desire.

"Now you are human again," he said, kissing me. I realized he was as excited as I, that this whole evening had had the same effect on him.

Unable to control ourselves, we had to give in and make fast, unrefined love just to take the edge off our fever and reduce our desire to a normal, if still overheated, level.

Lying beside me in the dark, he said, "I see you decided to tell the world after all." He was still trying to catch his breath.

"Yes," I said, laying my head on his chest. My words were probably muffled. "It could be hidden no longer, nor had I any wish to."

He kissed the top of my head, gently. "Then the fat is in the fire, as the common saying goes."

"It isn't the fat that is in the fire, it is us." And it was true. This fire in the blood . . . when would it be banked, die down?

"Yes, much fire." He sounded as if he did not, at this moment, much care. "Fire in Rome, at least. They do not like changes there, new factors, new contestants. I myself did not like it when Octavian arrived to claim his inheritance."

"And set aside my son's." I paused. "For Caesar had a true son, not this adopted interloper."

"Still, it was Caesar's own will that named him," said Antony. "I think he left you out of it from love, or as a tribute. He knew you could fight your own battles, with no help from him."

My own battles. Yes. There was one more matter to be settled before I set sail. "Antony . . ." I hated to interject politics, but I must. "You must do something for me. My sister Arsinoe, in Ephesus, helped the assassins. You should have summoned her to answer charges, not me. They recognized her as Queen of Egypt, and it was she who persuaded Serapion, the governor of Cyprus, to yield my fleet to them. I have even received reports that in my absence she has been testing the political waters to see if there is any support remaining for her in Alexandria. And then there is a new pretender to be Ptolemy XIII, whom Caesar himself defeated, and who is as dead as it is possible to be. All these threaten my throne's stability."

"And?" he asked, his voice soft, still drowsy with amorousness.

"Destroy them."

"Yes, my love." He was caressing my shoulders.

I had to get his promise before he lost himself again. "Promise me. Execute them all."

"Yes, my love. And I will restore Cyprus to you as well." He knotted his hands in my hair and gently pulled my head toward his. I opened my mouth for his kiss.

That night, of all nights, will never fade from my memory. How often we made love, and how we made it, provide details that I can bring out in private to relive whenever I feel bereft, or sad, or even wish to divert my mind from pain. It was a gift from the gods, given rarely and seldom repeated. But it sealed my belief that, philosophers notwithstanding, the joy of the body can equal that of the mind and spirit.

When he took his leave, I was not sad. This time was over; it could not be prolonged and retain its perfection. There would be other times, in other places, and they too would be perfect in their own, different, way.

"Farewell, my general," I said, kissing him on deck as the sun peeped above the horizon, painting the ship red-gold. The lamps in the rigging were burnt out, and the dawn revealed them as ordinary clay pots—not magic.

"Farewell, my queen." He embraced me a moment, holding me close against his purple cloak. "I will follow as soon as I may."

"A day is too long," I said. "Would that you were waiting for me when I arrived."

"Only if I could fly would that be possible," he said. "And that power is not given to man." He broke away, and stood for a moment apart from me. The rising sun gilded him, touching all the folds of his garment.

"Farewell," I said, reaching out to touch him good-bye.

Alone in my cabin, I sank down in the bed to sleep at last. There had certainly been none during the night. I pulled the covers over my shoulders and closed my eyes, shutting out the sunlight streaming into the room.

I smiled. The banquet, with its costly gifts, had been an enormous expense, but as an investment, it was worth it. As Mardian and Epaphroditus were both fond of saying, it was part of the cost of doing business. But it had not cost a million sesterces, as the company believed. Vinegar cannot dissolve pearls. As an apt pupil in Alexandria, that fount of science, I knew that. Anything strong enough to dissolve a pearl would dissolve my stomach as well. No, the pearl was safe inside me, and could be recovered easily enough.

But for those who were not fortunate enough to have been educated in science in our Museion, well—they had believed it.

Statesmanship means being master of many areas, even unlikely ones. As I drifted off to sleep, I knew I had learned that from Caesar, and that he would be proud of me. Was proud of me. Perhaps Antony was right. He had known I could fight my own battles.

HERE ENDS THE FOURTH SCROLL.

THE FIFTH SCROLL

45

"First Caesar and now Antony!" exclaimed Mardian. He raised his eyebrows. "Do you have some medical condition that makes you go into heat whenever a Roman comes over the horizon?"

"And only high-ranking ones," put in Olympos dryly.

"No, they have to be more than high-ranking, they have to be absolute top dog—the rulers," said Mardian. He looked at me, shaking his head and his finger.

"I think you're cruel!" I said, only half annoyed. I had never minded teasing.

"No, we're your friends. We're only saying exactly what the Romans will say." Olympos laughed. "To give you practice in defending yourself."

We were sitting by one of the windows overlooking the harbor. It was winter, and a storm was approaching across the sea from the west. I could see its line of demarcation, dark and ragged, making its determined way toward us. I drew my wool stole around me, snuggling into its soft depths.

"Archelaus was a prince, but you wouldn't have him," sniffed Mardian. "So I think you're right, Olympos, about their position. It's the power aspect. Archelaus was royal but not powerful, and these Romans are powerful, but not royal. Yes, my dear, it's power that excites you."

"Well, what of it?" I bristled.

Olympos shrugged. "I suppose you wouldn't be a Ptolemy if you didn't lust after power."

"On the other hand, maybe it's married men," ventured Mardian. "After all, Archelaus—"

"Oh, stop about Archelaus! I liked him, he was a fine man, but—"

"He wasn't a married man, and he didn't rule the world. Small failings! You've admitted the power attraction, now what about the married aspect?" said Olympos.

"The challenge, of course," answered Mardian. He looked pained.

"You are awfully free in interpreting my motives," I said, beginning to feel put upon.

"It's our hobby," said Mardian. "We had to do something to amuse ourselves while you were away."

"Antony is coming to Alexandria, and I don't want to hear anything about it out of you two!" I said. I meant it.

"Not us," said Olympos with a straight face. "Not us. We won't say a word." Then they both collapsed in laughter.

After they had left, still laughing, to go to the stables, I sat and stared out at the darkening sky and harbor. What they had said was true enough. I was hard put to explain it even to myself. The political aspects of the situation made sense enough. I would be much more secure on my throne, and Egypt safer, with Caesar's successor our guaranteed friend. But that could easily have been arranged through diplomatic channels. It wasn't necessary to go to bed with him.

I could almost curse the joy of it. How much better—better?—it would have been had he turned out to be lackluster, rough, boring, dull, unsavory, even disgusting as a lover. Then I would have left with a shudder and no backward glance, reassured that a life of celibacy was preferable to disappointing amours.

But I was eager to continue it, I had to admit. In the beginning, I could have called the guards. Certainly the next night, and the next, I didn't have to have anything to do with him. Now I had got myself in an awkward situation, to say the least.

A cold, spray-laden gust of wind whipped through the window. I moved away and went over to the brazier, which was giving off a feeble bit of heat, and warmed my hands over it.

Isis direct me! I thought. This must lead wherever it must lead; the only wrong lies in trying to hinder what must be and will be. The future is veiled from me; I see only what lies directly before me, that Antony will come to Alexandria, and soon.

Outside the storm was rising. There would be no sailing for weeks. But Antony would come by land.

" 'Tis done, my lady," said Mardian, standing before me with a report, which he dutifully presented. "Arsinoe is dead."

His voice was flat. I broke the seal on the message and read its details: how Arsinoe had been dragged from the high altar at the Temple of Artemis, where she had claimed asylum, and killed, by Antony's orders.

"Slain on the steps of the temple," said Mardian primly.

I shivered. So his promise, made lightly in the dark, had been carried out. Caesar had never made such promises, nor would he have allowed himself to be persuaded so easily. In that instant I realized the power I had stumbled onto, in Antony's most willing nature.

"She had no business claiming sanctuary," I said. "Caesar had pardoned her once; she could not expect a second reprieve." People had always taken advantage of that famous clemency. But even Caesar had punished second offenders.

"They have buried her beside the main street of Ephesus, in a tomb shaped like the Lighthouse of Alexandria," said Mardian.

"She can be as Alexandrian as she wishes now," I said. I went on reading. The pretender Ptolemy had also been killed, and the governor Serapion had fled to Tyre, but it had availed him nothing. He, too, was executed. Antony had done as he promised on all three counts.

Reports came about Antony's activities in Syria, where Decidius Saxa was appointed governor. Next he was in Tyre, and then in Judaea, where he made his friend and ally Herod a prince. He was working his way southward, toward Egypt. Next he was in Ashkelon, then came word that he had set out, with his personal praetorian guard, across the desert of Sinai to Pelusium. It was there that, fourteen years earlier, he had led the cavalry charge that took the city for my father—and spared the Egyptian troops inside that my father had wanted to execute for treason. For that, the Egyptians had been fond of him.

He arrived in Alexandria on a clear, cold day. Messengers had come riding to announce his arrival, and I had ordered the eastern Gate of the Sun hung with garlands, the wide Canopic Way swept and decorated. Along the way I posted guards who would direct him to the palace, and ordered that the gates be flung open upon his arrival. Trumpeters would blow as he approached.

A great deal of time seemed to pass between the first trumpet blast at the eastern gate and the final one at the palace entrance. He had been welcomed warmly by the Alexandrians, and his march had been interrupted by crowds swarming around to greet him.

"Antony, keep your tragic Roman face for Rome!" I heard them shouting. "Bring your comic one here!"

And then he was coming up the wide stairs of the palace, taking long steps, hurrying toward me. His stride was sure and easy, his back straight, his curly-haired head high; he fairly glowed with strength and exuberance. There was no laurel wreath on his head, no helmet, no decorations, not even a soldier's uniform. He stepped out in only his own pride and animal spirits, wearing everyday clothes. He could have been anyone, any common citizen, graced with the beauty of an athlete and a glorious future. My heart rose at the sight of him.

He stopped halfway up the stairs when he saw me, and a radiant smile spread over his face. He held out his arms in a gesture of joy and greeting; his cloak swirled around him. "My most gracious Queen!" he said. Then he slowly walked up the few remaining steps.

"My most welcome guest," I said, extending my hand. He took it and pressed it to his lips, and I loved the feel of them.

"You return at last to the city that loves you," I said, bringing him to stand beside me. From the high vantage point we could see much of Alexandria— the long, flat porticoes of the Gymnasion, the massive sprawl of the Museion, the solid Temple of Serapis, far away to the south. Beyond that, the waters of Lake Mareotis gleamed. "Do you remember?"

"I remember it all," he said.

Everyone but Olympos was lined up to meet him: Mardian, Epaphroditus, the commander of my Macedonian Household Troops, the chief gymnasiarch, the director of the Museion, the chief priests of Isis and Serapis. And separate from them all, waiting in a chair of state, sat Caesarion, wearing his diadem.

Antony made his way over to him, and Caesarion said, "Welcome, cousin Antony"—for they were indeed distant cousins, in the fourth degree. How like Caesarion to have known that.

Antony bent his knee to him. "Thank you, cousin the King," he said. Then he reached into the folds of his tunic and swiftly brought out something. I saw the guards flanking Caesarion stiffen, and tighten their grips on their swords.

"A lizard that haunted my headquarters in Tyre, Your Majesty," he said, presenting a green, bumpy creature with rotating eyes. "I thought perhaps he would be a novelty in Alexandria."

Caesarion smiled and stepped down to take the animal. As he moved, I saw Antony's face register surprise. Then he masked it. "I hope you and he grow to be great friends," said Antony. "Or she. I must confess I cannot tell the difference."

Caesarion laughed like any six-year-old. "Neither can I," he admitted. "But I will learn!"

"I am sure the lizards have no trouble," said Antony. "Ask them."

Later, all the welcoming done, the long speeches, the presentation of gifts, the settling of the personal guards, we sat alone in my large chamber. I had assigned him his own apartments in another of the palace buildings, so that he could have privacy and a place to conduct the inevitable business that would follow at his heels. But for now he was at leisure; dinner was over and it was yet too early to retire. The last vestiges of sunset were still staining the sky, but lamps had already been lit in all the chambers.

"I have dreamed of returning to Alexandria for a long time," he said, looking out the window.

"Then why was it so difficult to persuade you?" I asked.

"Because Alexandria is no longer just a city; she is you. And everyone will know that I came not to see the Museion, or to visit the Lighthouse, but to see the Queen."

"I was only teasing," I said. "I know well enough what it means." I remembered his exchange with Caesarion. "What do you think of my son? A strange look came over your face—it was fleeting, but I saw it."

He shook his head. "The resemblance to Caesar is unsettling—especially when he moves. His gait is exactly the same. I thought—I thought never to see it again."

"Yes, it is both a comfort and a source of pain."

"No one could see him and fail to recognize him as Caesar's son."

"Not even Octavian?" I asked.

"Especially not Octavian," said Antony.

"Antony, what am I to do?" The words tumbled out. "I cannot just stand by and see Caesar's son shunted aside and neglected. I know there are no legal claims, but—you saw him move. You know."

"Yes, I know." He paused. "Truth is a strong lady. I know the day will come—"

"We must make it come!" I said fiercely. "Don't you realize that fate holds only one set of keys, and that desire and determination hold the others? Destiny is not writ in stone, but waits to see how badly we wish an outcome."

He looked startled. "I also know that the gates of fate cannot be forced." He paused. "Caesar should have taught us that. All his genius, all his strength—felled by accident, chance, little men." He took my hand, covered it with both of his. "I will do my best to see Caesarion succeed as Caesar's heir. But for now he is King of Egypt, and your son. Not a bad lot."

I smiled. He was right, of course. And what mother would wish her child to venture out in the dangerous, turbulent waters of Roman politics—lethal waters in some cases. Egypt was much safer. "You are tired," I said. "I should not have bothered you with political questions." I took his hand. "Come. You need to lie down."

"I fear that, in your presence, that is not very restful." He did look tired.

"But restorative," I said.

And I led him into my bedchamber, which I had thought sealed forever to any man after Caesar. It was as much a way of freeing myself from the past as of easing Antony's travel-stained weariness.

I took him in my arms, rolled across the wide bed with him, savoring the feel of our bodies turning against each other, and came to rest with his face next to mine on the pillow. And I saw, reflected in his dark eyes, all of me—as I was, had been, would be. He was my fate, as I was his, but we must struggle to shape it as we would. It was not necessarily obedient or benign.

I gave myself up to pure pleasure, pure sensation, thinking at its height that he who has known only this has not got a bad bargain in life. The meanest of my subjects might taste pleasure this keen—and probably did. The gods were kind that way.

Alexandria belonged to Antony. From the first moments, they fell in love with one another. The people loved the way he came to the city, as a private citizen, a guest, rather than storming ashore in full Roman regalia and authority, like Caesar. They were taken with his affable manner, his adoption of Greek dress—something Caesar would never have done—his attendance at lectures and plays, his approachability.

The admiration was mutual, for Antony seemed captivated with the city, and in a way I was jealous, as if he loved her better than me, more unreservedly. He laid aside his Roman persona, folded up his togas, dismissed his guards. He ate Egyptian and Greek food, wandered through the temples, roamed the streets, kept most un-Roman hours. He seemed, truly, to have been longing for Alexandria for a long time. It answered something in his nature.

"Beware," said Olympos sourly, "of the man who adopts a foreign culture with abandon. It ruins him."

Olympos had avoided Antony, seeing him only from afar, and deflected all my attempts to introduce them, claiming that he had many patients to attend, and no time.

"Perhaps you should meet him," I said. "It seems very odd to me that my physician, and one of my best friends, keeps his distance."

"I don't need to meet him," said Olympos. "I can study him better if he does not know me."

"And?" I asked.

"Well, he is a fine physical specimen. He does resemble Hercules. Doesn't he claim Hercules as an ancestor?"

"An evasive answer," I said. "What of the man himself, if you know so much?"

"I can see why you find him attractive."

"Tell me something I don't already know."

"Don't trust him," he blurted out. "He isn't reliable."

I was surprised. I had not expected this. "In what way? What do you mean?"

"Oh, I think he's a good man. I must admit that." He sounded cross to say it. "But he has that nature that's—" He stopped. "He doesn't really want to be ruler of the world, he just wants to take the easy way. The strongest nature that's nearest him will always lead him, rule him. Now it's you. When he gets in the vicinity of Octavian, it will be him."

Again, I was surprised. "You've never seen Octavian. How can you speak knowledgeably about his nature?"

"I just know," said Olympos stubbornly.

"I may have to send you to Rome to observe firsthand," I said lightly, not liking his remarks about Antony. But worse was the feeling that he and I both, separately, sensed something hard, intransigent, and formidable in Octavian. Until now I had thought it was just my own impression, probably colored by personal motives.

The day of my twenty-ninth birthday came, but I did not celebrate it or even tell Antony about it. I was afraid he would stage some gigantic festivity to honor me, and the very thought was unappealing. The spectacle at Tarsus had quite satisfied me in that regard for the foreseeable future. Mardian gave me a new writing set, with seals carved of amethyst, and Caesarion had taught his lizard to pull a miniature cart as a trick for me, but that was all. Olympos brought me an enormous jar of the choicest silphion from Cyrenaica, with a note saying, "Here! A present you can really use!" I was so embarrassed I shoved it into a box and hid it. Why was he so obsessed with that subject? It really was time he married and diverted his attention to his own bed.

But I knew Antony would want to celebrate his own birthday in some lavish manner, and so I suggested that we reserve the entire Gymnasion for him and his guests.

"We can have our own Ptolemaieia," I said one evening. "It isn't scheduled for another three years, but does it matter?" The biggest athletic games and contests outside of Olympia were held every four years in Alexandria, with horseracing, field sports, gymnastics, and tragedies and comedies in the theater.

"What will you call it, the Antonieia?" He laughed dismissively. I knew then that he meant to have it.

"I'll call it *Natalicia Nobilissimi Antoni*," I said. "The Birthday Celebration of the Most Noble Antony."

He raised his eyebrows. "You know more Latin than you let on."

I always enjoyed surprising him. "And of course you will have to compete in everything, so it will be a smaller affair than the regular games," I continued. "After all, you are not a charioteer, nor do you perform acrobatics—do you?" I hoped not. The races were notoriously expensive to put on.

"No," he said. "But you must remember what birthday it will be for me—my forty-second. Perhaps it isn't a good idea to compete, unless I should make a present to myself of losing."

"Nonsense!" I said. "You should compete against your own men and officers, not runners and wrestlers who do nothing besides train. It would be unfair otherwise." And it would give some structure to his days, training for it. He was too proud just to walk out on the field with no practice. As it was now, he stayed up far too late and slept half the morning away, on a perpetual holiday.

"These will be Greek games and athletics," I warned him. "None of that killing you Romans love so much."

"When with Greeks, do as the Greeks do," he said. "It is generally much more civilized."

"Spoken like a convert," I said. "Now if you would just embrace the Greek harmony of a balanced life—"

"Bah!" He laughed. "Dionysus *is* excess—that's what he's all about. Drunken soberness, artistic license, freedom of the senses—"

"But Hercules has to keep himself fit in order to perform all his labors and turn into a god. The two sides of you will have to take turns."

"They do," he said. "They do. Don't you know that yet?"

In truth, Antony had a deep and abiding interest in the theater; he loved plays, and took his patronage of the Dionysian guild of actors seriously. There was that in him that loved costume and playacting, and even in Rome he had had actors and actresses as his friends in his retinue, much to Cicero's disgust. In Alexandria he attended not only the theater, but lectures and demonstrations at the Museion, while I accompanied him in his late-night revels. We were both doing things out of character, seeking to please the other.

January fourteenth, *Ludi et Natalicia Nobilissimi Antoni*, the Games and Birthday Celebration of the Most Noble Antony, was a still, blue-skied day. I was surprised at how enthusiastic all the guests had been about the entertainment. Women were eager to be invited to sit in the stone grandstand and ogle the oiled male bodies, while the men, even the older ones, were unexpectedly willing to strip off most of their clothes and compete. One man of sixty-five—a supply officer from Antony's guard—sought permission to enter the contests. A champion runner from a Ptolemaieia of twenty years ago also asked if he could compete. But the other contestants were personal friends of mine or Antony's, and that was what gave it such curiosity value. We knew these people in other capacities, and suddenly they would appear, flinging off their tunics, imitating famous athletes. Perhaps they had always had a secret desire to do so.

Since there was nothing official about this—it was just a private celebration—we decided that absolute nakedness was not required.

"Unless you'd like to!" I remarked to Antony. After all, he had appeared almost that way at the Lupercalia. But that was long ago, when he'd held a lesser position.

"No, I can restrain myself," he said. "I wouldn't want to be the only one on the field like that, and I don't think the rest would do it."

He was right about that. The only people who ever felt comfortable with nudity were the Greeks; Romans and Egyptians and—horrors!—barbarians avoided it. As for the Jews, they found the whole idea repugnant and did not like even to pass by a gymnasion.

There would be a pentathlon, the test of an all-round athlete—footrace, jumping, discus, javelin, and wrestling. Then there would be military exercises like swordfighting and a race with armor, only for Antony and his soldiers.

"Is Hercules ready?" I said, as we prepared to depart for the Gymnasion. A great group of guests would accompany us, drawn in all the litters and chariots I had been able to summon from the royal stables.

468

"Yes," he said, oddly subdued.

"What is it?" Had he suddenly got cold feet? What a time to do it!

"I was just thinking—I am almost exactly twice Octavian's age. For every year he's lived, I've lived two. I don't know which is the advantage—my experience, or all those years he has yet tucked away in reserve."

"Now that's a Roman Antony, a brooding Antony, that I seldom see." This dark mood would not help his celebration. I must chase it away. "Octavian is so sickly that he'll never reach the age of forty-two. He's not strong like you; not only would he never have made it across the Alps, he can barely make it from his house to the Roman Forum."

Antony laughed. "Now that's an exaggeration, my love."

"Well, isn't it true he's always getting sick—at crucial moments? He was sick at the battle of Philippi, and you did all the fighting. He was so sick at Brundisium, on his way back to Rome, that he wasn't expected to live. He was too sick to accompany Caesar to Spain. He's always sick!"

"Yes, but, as you said, only at crucial moments. Maybe it's his nerves that are sickly, not his body." He laughed. "Here, my little warrior. Why don't you take my sword, the one I used at Philippi? Wear it tonight; it will go with the mood of this whole silly thing for you to dress like me." He unbuckled it and handed it to me.

I took it, almost fearfully. It was a most important sword, the avenging sword. "Won't you use it in the exercises?"

"No. I can never use it for games. But still, I want it there. You take it." He fitted its belt and hilt around me, crushing the gown I was wearing. "Come now!" His mood seemed light enough now. "Take my helmet, too." He lowered it onto my head. "There! A right fearsome soldier!"

"I can kill if I have to," I said slowly. He should know that.

"Now who has a dark mood? Banish it." He laughed. "Lead on to wherever you will take me, my Queen."

"Today it is to the Gymnasion," I said. "Nothing sinister about that."

The trumpets had blown, announcing the beginning of the contests. Almost fifty men were on the field, in various costumes. Some wore only loincloths, others short, barbarian-style pants that stopped above their knees, some kilts, and others tunics. All of them had been oiled in the special room for that purpose, the *eliothesium*, and now they gleamed. Oh, how they gleamed—every muscle and tendon highlighted.

"I adore olive oil on a male body," whispered Charmian. "It's even more arousing than sweat."

"I like both of them," said the wife of the under-treasurer, startling me. I had always assumed she was most excited by ledger books.

Looking at them, I was struck by how well proportioned Antony was for his heavy muscles. He truly was one of those men who looked best with the least clothing, as regular clothes made him appear stocky. There was no sign that age had made any inroads into him; he was blessed with a physique that could maintain itself with little help. Certainly his Dionysian progress through the eastern provinces would have done in a frailer body.

Participating in the games were a number of Romans from Antony's praetorian guard, elite soldiers; the Egyptian head charioteer and several archers; some Greek officials from the treasury; some of the company of Dionysiac artists; a tutor Antony had picked up in Syria, named Nicolaus of Damascus; my favorite Museion philosopher, Philostratos; and perhaps most surprising of all, old Athenagoras, a physician who headed a mummy-preservation society. Oiled up, he looked like a mummy himself, stringy and dessicated. But he trotted by surprisingly swiftly, chortling and calling, "Watch me in the footrace! They call me the Natron Flash!" He was met with a shower of flowers and cheers from the women.

I noticed that Charmian's eyes seldom left one of the Roman guards who stayed near Antony, a tall, light-haired man who knew Antony's comings and goings—and kept them to himself. "I see you find someone interesting," I remarked, and Charmian nodded.

"You will have to give him the victor's laurel—if he wins it," I said.

The contestants were warming up in a series of movements that looked almost comical—jumping up and down, beating their chests, sprinting forward and then stopping abruptly. Then they lined up at the marble starting line, digging their toes into the cleft in the stone, and were off at the cry *Apite!*—go!—for the six-hundred-foot race. At first it looked like a shiny clump of bodies trying to keep together, but soon they separated and one tall Egyptian took the lead, followed by a Greek and then, surprisingly, by Antony. I had not expected that he could move so swiftly, as usually men with heavy muscles are not fleet of foot. But perhaps the thick legs supplied the extra power that propelled him forward.

The Natron Flash lagged two lengths behind the rest, his kilt flapping wildly. But he received the biggest ovation, and yelled as he passed, "What do you expect for a sixty-two-year-old? Hermes?"

The former champion from the Ptolemaieia—who was still only in his forties—finished fourth.

Next came discus throwing, an event that needed both strength and grace. The way a thrower rotated and moved his body was of utmost importance, and no one was allowed to turn and turn and wind himself up like a top. Statues celebrating the pose of a discus thrower were very popular, and as the men practiced, most of the women looked on appreciatively.

"It's like watching all the statues moving," said Charmian. Her favorite was also going to compete in this event. Not everyone would enter all contests; only poor Antony.

Only about fifteen men grasped the discus and, turning their torsos far to the right, stretched out in a graceful arc and flung it far from them. Charmian's man won by a hand's breadth, followed by the Egyptian head charioteer, and, once again third—by Antony. His upper-body strength had made the discus soar as it left his hand.

A great cheer went up for all the contestants, in this most aesthetically appealing of all events.

Next was the javelin throw, a favorite of the soldiers. Of all the athletic events, this was the one most rooted in actual warfare. But these javelins were made of elderwood, a lighter type than the military ones of yew. Besides being of lighter wood, the ones used for contests had leather thongs wound around the middle of the shaft to make them fly steady, and the ends were sharpened to stick into the ground, to measure distance. Each man was allowed three throws.

War is ugly, and no good ruler would wish it on his people. But even the most vehement critic of war would be forced to admit that many of the actions of soldiers are in themselves glorious, almost works of art, and the javelin throw is one such event. Just watching a man as he stood poised and ready to throw, running up to the mark, pulling the spear behind his head, then extending his other arm for balance before stopping and letting fly— such beauty! The gods forgive me for the joy I took in watching it.

Again, oddly, it was Antony who was third, and the other two winners were members of the Guard and Household Troops.

When the long jump was announced, a different group of men swarmed down to compete. At last the lad Nicolaus of Damascus and the philosopher Philostratos came forward. Philostratos made a show of squatting and jumping up and down. I heard him saying, "Oh, I have neglected you, my faithful body! The mind has held you captive! Body, revenge yourself now!" There was small chance of that—he had ignored it for too long, expecting it to exist on the vapors of his mind—but he was laughing about it, at least. His baggy drawers sagged around his sunken waist, and his pale, thin legs protruded forlornly.

The men were to jump forward from a standstill, weights in each hand swinging to hurl them forward. They would land in a long sand pit. As expected, Philostratos managed only a feeble jump; it was a good thing he went last, so he would not have the embarrassment of seeing all the others fly over his mark. This was considered one of the most difficult of all events, because only a clean impression on the sand counted. Anyone who fell backward or forward was disqualified. Hence timing and balance were as necessary as speed and strength. Pipes were always played to help establish a rhythm.

The men were getting tired now. It could be seen in the way they grimaced and grunted, standing still when it was not their turn; no more nervous milling and joking.

Antony did not look noticeably weary; I saw him laughing and stretching, curling the weights in his arms, extending them slowly, drawing them back. He must have extraordinary stamina, and it was beginning to show, in contrast to the others.

Young Nicolaus did admirably, his slight young body going a good distance. The sixty-five-year-old supply officer flew past him—he had clearly been practicing. Charmian's man surpassed him, and Charmian sighed. Then a tall Gaul, one of Antony's guards, set the farthest mark. Last came Antony.

He approached the starting line slowly, moving the weights back and forth, getting his feel of them for the last time. He bent over as if to loosen all his muscles, then crouched, gathering some enormous ball of energy, and exploded forward, hurtled over the sand, and landed just behind the mark set by the Gaul. Wild cheers rang out, for the very force of his effort had been visible. And he had landed perfectly, not losing his balance. He slowly rose to his feet and stepped away from the sand.

"He's truly remarkable!" said Charmian, as if she had only now noticed. Perhaps she had.

I shifted on my seat, and the heavy sword that hung by my side clanked. Odd that he had wanted me to wear it—but I felt it was somehow imparting strength to him. The helmet rested by my feet. His achievement at Philippi was enough in itself, as far as history was concerned.

The last of the pentathlon events was the wrestling. Each contestant now had to call his bodyservant to dust his sweaty and oily body with powder, so that the opponents could grip one another. They would practice upright wrestling, in which they would grapple and attempt to throw their opponents to the ground. Three falls were necessary to win, and just touching the sand with the back, shoulders, or hip counted as a fall—telltale grains of sand sticking there would be proof. They were allowed to trip, but not to gouge.

Antony, like several others, was putting on a tight leather cap to prevent his opponent from grabbing his hair. It gave him an entirely different appearance—much more menacing. His thick crown of hair usually disguised his great strength with a semblance of boyishness. But that was gone now.

The contestants drew lots to see who would wrestle whom, and Antony ended up with a great ox of a man facing him. Bending low, they circled each other, arms spread, looking for a way to grasp and unbalance the other. The man's legs looked like knotted tree trunks, and his shoulders were as wide as an ox yoke. He made Antony seem lithe and slender in comparison. To my surprise, Antony succeeded in tripping him; next he caught him off guard, and the third time, straining against his braced legs, the opponents clasping each other like lovers, Antony bent him over until he lost his footing. Wild shouts exploded from the stands, and from the other contestants. They had seemed so unevenly matched.

None of the other pairs had such a clear-cut victory, and thus it was that Antony was declared the winner not only of the wrestling but of the entire pentathlon, for only he had placed in all five events. The pentathlon was designed to test the all-around athlete, and it required great powers of endurance—Antony's strong points. I almost wished it had not been he, lest people think it was fixed, but I knew it had been fairly won, and my heart was proud to bursting. I was delighted I had thought of this contest, for what better present could I have given him?

There was still the semicomical race in armor—the *hoplitodromos*—to be held. Men were to load themselves up with helmets, shields, greaves, and body armor, and run twice the footrace distance. It made a fitting finale, for all that clanking and awkwardness helped to ease the smart of any earlier loss. Even the fleetest warrior looked a bit tortoiselike as he struggled under the weight, and some—unable to see very well to the side because of their helmets—collided with one another. Then they had trouble getting up, they were so ungainly.

I was to award Antony his birthday garland, but there were prizes for many others, including one for the oldest contestant and the youngest, the lightest and the heaviest, and the man who had got the biggest bruise.

"Thank you, friends all!" shouted Antony, raising his hands high. "I shall never forget this birthday! And now, to Canopus and the pleasure gardens! To the canal, where we'll float on to our rewards!"

Canopus. It had been years since I had been there, and then only with my father, and in the daylight. How did he know about it?

The party streamed out of the Gymnasion, down the white marble steps, and into the waiting chariots and litters. Antony made me ride standing beside him in a chariot; he wrapped me in his cloak with one hand while he drove with the other. He was still heated from the games, and had the smell of victory on him, of exultant exertion. It was a magic smell—of strength, joy, and desire. His cloak flew out behind him as he drove crazily through the streets, his victor's wreath tilting over one eye, yelling gleefully at people lining the sides.

"You drive like Pluto!" I said, grabbing one of the chariot rails as he bounced along. "Are you heading for Hades?"

"No, for the Elysian Fields! Isn't that the name of that place outside the city walls, where all the pleasure houses are? Where the canal floats through?"

"It's called Eleusis," I said, shouting to be heard over the clattering wheels. "The better class of people avoids it."

"Good!" he said, urging the horses on.

We floated toward Canopus in a fleet of pleasure boats, their lecherous ferrymen used to conveying merrymakers along the canal that ran parallel to the sea all the way between Alexandria and the town sitting at the mouth of the Canopic branch of the Nile. A great Temple of Serapis and Isis stood there, but it was infamous for the goings-on in the Temple vicinity. Every imaginable human vice—and some unimaginable ones—flourished there. Along the way there were pretty groves of palms, white sand beaches, and in Eleusis, grand houses with ocean views and decadent inhabitants. They waved at us as we passed, the lanterns on our boats signaling them in the twilight.

"Enjoy yourselves!" they called, and one house sent a boy to pipe raucous melodies to us, his companion bellowing out the bawdy lyrics.

"How do you know about Canopus?" I asked.

"I was a young soldier here all those years ago," he reminded me. "And my own men have been pestering me to take them."

"Not with me and my women," I said. "I can't imagine they would want us along."

"They can always return by themselves some other time," he said. "They're old enough!" He laughed, and pulled me over against him. "This will give all your highborn women a chance to make a safe, escorted visit to the den of iniquity there. Haven't you all been curious to see it? Be honest, now!"

"Well—yes," I admitted.

"Your secret—as well as your august person—is safe with us. We will protect your virtue!"

"From the rogues there, while robbing us of it yourselves!"

"Surely your women will be able to fend off a few well-bred Roman soldiers. They can report any misbehavior to me, and I, as commanding officer, will punish anyone so vile as to take liberties. You have my word of honor." He saluted mockingly.

"I am sure they will be relieved to hear it. They might be happier if you just warned the men in advance."

A look of disbelief passed over his face. "You sound like a palace tutor, determined to guard the virtue of a ten-year-old pupil. Are we not all grown men and women? I don't see Caesarion here." He made a show of looking around. "Your concern for their sensibility is touching—and out of place, as well as insulting. In short, my sweet Queen, my most mysterious and Egyptian Queen—mind your own business." He leaned back on the cushions in the boat and wagged a finger in admonition.

I laughed. He had that effect on me.

In the boats, his men and our guests were singing, calling from one vessel to another, drinking Mareotic wine from wineskins some had brought along. We floated onward, toward Canopus.

There was no missing it: lights blazed from the shore, and all the buildings seemed bathed in that lurid red glow. The streets were full of people, unlike most towns after dark. The boats passed a marshy area, low-lying, where the westernmost mouth of the Nile emptied out into the sea. Flocks of startled birds flew upward as the noise and lights of the boats slipped past.

The bow of the boat bumped against the docks, and soon we were all clambering out. The group fanned out, some going to one tavern and some to another, for there was none large enough to hold us all, although they all beckoned.

"We'll take turns!" said Antony. "Then at the end we'll compare them all!" He turned to me, thrusting a mantle at me. "Here, wrap up! The night will grow cold, and it would be better if no one knew the Queen was among them."

It was against my nature to disguise myself. Always I was the Queen, I could be no one else. But I yielded to Antony tonight, not wishing to cross him on his birthday. With him I had learned to set aside my normal behavior and embrace the foreign. I drew on the mantle and pulled its hood over my head.

The first tavern was dark and smoky with the poor oil they used for fuel; the wine was on a par with the light. "Blehh!" said Antony, swirling it around in his mouth. "Tastes like a brew my mother used to sprinkle on clothes to kill moths."

"Why, did you drink it?"

"No, but I smelled it." He raised his hand. "Here, here, something better, please!"

The owner waddled over, a smile stretching over his flat face, straining his cheeks. "Sir?" he asked. "You wish our finest?" He looked carefully to see if he thought we could afford it. Antony threw down a gold piece and it spun on the table.

The man snatched it up eagerly. "Yes, yes!" He motioned to his servers and they came with a jug of wine only slightly better.

"This is an improvement," said Antony, and the man smiled and bowed. "Why, it's almost up to the standard of army rations."

He downed the rest of it and then gestured to his company. "Come, come, let's go elsewhere!" He put his arm around me and all but lifted me out the door.

The night air felt good after the stale smells in the tavern. Even this air was not pure, however, but filled with the perfume of the harlots who were beginning to emerge from their houses and walk the streets. Their thin, transparent cheap silks—with the threads loosened to let in more light—revealed their bodies almost more clearly than if they had been naked. The light of the dockside torches glazed their floating gowns and painted their lips even redder than they already were.

Tinkling music wafted out from hidden houses, dreary when it was trying to sound so wanton. Squatting men beguiled baskets where snakes were to be coaxed out—for a coin or two.

"Tell your fortune!" A clawlike hand grabbed my mantle and I turned to see a wizened face with bright monkey eyes looking at me. But it was not an old face, it was a very young one—perhaps only nine or ten years old. "I can tell the future!" I hurried on, my hand in Antony's, the sword bumping against my side, heavy and cold. "I can tell you everything!"

So can I, my child, I thought. I can tell *your* fortune—poverty and despair. My heart ached for these people. I did not find them enticing or tempting, merely sad.

"Give him one of your coins," I told Antony, making him stop. He gave him one of his gold ones, carelessly; to him it was nothing.

"Your fortune! Your fortune!" The child scampered after us, trying to earn his wage.

"I would rather not know," I assured him. We hurried on down the waterfront, leaving him behind, staring at the gold coin.

The next place had a large clientele, who had clearly been drinking since sundown. It was as hot as the noon sun at the First Cataract, and I longed to take off the mantle. But it afforded some protection from the press of strange bodies.

A dancing girl, scantily clad, was amusing a group of customers, swaying and shaking and gyrating to the bleat of a reed pipe that sounded like a rutting goat in an agony of lust. Our company, cups in hand, shouldered its way into the circle and watched. I saw the flushed faces of the onlookers; even our group had begun to take on that look of mixed yearning and dissipation.

The wine began to affect me, too. I felt my reserve and standoffishness start to dissolve. Gradually the tavern did not seem tatty and rude, but excitingly wicked. I even felt my arms start to trace out the dancer's movements under my cloak. Suddenly I wanted to move, spin, dance—make love.

"More, more!" The patrons were clapping and demanding another dance. The girl, sweat running down her body, obliged, and the mixed smell of perspiration and perfume was as intoxicating as the fumes of the cheap wine.

"Let's get some food!" cried Antony suddenly, to his companions. En masse they headed for the door, in spite of the owner's attempts to convince them that he served food as well.

"No, we have to try them all!" said Antony. "All the places!"

We selected an eating place at random—since no one knew any particular establishment. Antony had followed his nose, smelling something roasting. It turned out to be the remnants of an ox, and our party ordered it all cut off the spit and served. It was surprisingly good.

"I think—I think we should form a society!" said Antony suddenly, his mouth half full of crisp pieces of ox, chewing furiously. "Yes, and we'd have meals, roasted ox every day if we pleased—we'd have excursions, we'd take our pleasures and try to outdo ourselves each day. Who wants to join?"

"All of us!" cried the birthday guests.

"And what would you call this—this club?" I asked.

"Why, the *Amimetobioi*—the Society of the Incomparable Livers!" he said quickly.

He must have already planned such a club, I thought, for the name was too ready on his tongue.

"I see," I said.

"I want to become a legend of extravagant indulgence!" he said, kissing my cheek. "Just like you with the pearl."

"I thought you wanted to complete Caesar's task and conquer Parthia," I said. "I do not think that goes with extravagant indulgence."

"Oh, Alexander had his bouts of wild drinking, and he conquered the entire world! Who says they are incompatible?"

"Perhaps not for Alexander, but—he did not live very long."

"But gloriously, gloriously!" He raised his cup and drank it all in one swallow.

"Stop shouting," I said. His voice hurt my ear.

He pressed another cup into my hand and I sipped it slowly. I had no wish to get any drunker than I already was.

Stuffed with food and wine, we reeled out into the street again. We passed a knot of people, also from our party, and the groups mingled and then broke away, searching in different directions for more amusements. I saw Charmian and the tall Roman in the other group, but they did not notice me. Nicolaus was also there, and even the old supply officer, celebrating his victory. They drifted away, and we wound our way back into the streets off the waterfront. It was quieter there, but somehow more vicious: it was as if the vice did not even try to drape itself in false gaiety, but just went about its grim business with no imagination at all. Women hung out of the windows, their thin arms beckoning, their dark eyes following us as we trailed down the streets.

Through one of the alleys I saw something big, on high ground. It must be the Temple of Serapis. I tugged on Antony's arm. "Let's go there," I said. I was anxious to leave this quarter.

"Lead on," he said obediently.

We wound our way toward it, and as we approached, the press of people suddenly reappeared. Hundreds of torches were burning, giving off clouds of smoke and the smell of resin, as well as flickering light. The entire area around the rising ground of the temple was filled with booths—booths selling incense, offerings, lamps, garlands. Also, the temple prostitutes plied their trade, lounging in doorways, spilling out onto doorsills. There were also houses with rooms to rent by the hour for anyone who wished to indulge, no questions asked, before or after worshiping.

This had once been a sacred shrine. My ancestor Ptolemy III had built it and dedicated it to the gods, and it had been a place of healing where invalids came to spend the night and be cured. From this it had fallen to a place where evil consorted with superstition and lust. Baths nearby drew off the sated worshipers, where they could frolic naked in heated water, splashing and squealing.

I wished I had not come. Before I could turn and leave, however, an old woman approached us. "Love potions!" she whispered, hawking her wares. "Love potions!" She thrust a vial of green liquid into Antony's hand.

He held it up and looked at it.

"It's powerful, sir," she said, holding out her hand for money. He gave it, and impulsively took a swallow of the brew.

"Don't!" I said. "It may be poisonous—or dangerous."

"No, it's nothing of the sort," he said, wiping his mouth. "Take some." He gave it to me. "You have to join me in drinking it."

Every fiber in me warned against it, but something compelled me to do it. A sip revealed it as sticky-sweet, with an aftertaste of raisins.

"Come, let's visit the shrine." We made our way over the uneven ground and then climbed the steps into the temple. In the forest of columns, the light faded and I could barely see the place where my ancestor Berenice had made her famous offering of hair—an offering accepted by the gods and taken up to heaven, where it was turned into a constellation.

Slowly some odd feeling of both urgency and lethargy stole through me. I felt my arm around Antony's waist, felt the flesh through the tunic, and my limbs were heavy. I wanted to lie down, but at the same time felt inhibitions melting away—the sense of time, of propriety, of order. My head spun. We stumbled back down the steps. He was as affected as I.

A doorway beckoned. A proprietress waited. We went in. Payment was made.

We were in a large, high-ceilinged room with two little windows and a frame bed with leather thongs for a mattress. My mantle was lifted off, falling heavily to my feet. The sword came off. I clung to Antony, feeling odd and transported. I knew I was drugged, but I did not care. I floated. He had had more of it than I, and was even more affected.

His movements seemed slow, suspended. Or was that merely my strange perception?

I held him, and the world spun. There seemed to be only this man, this place, this moment. The world stopped spinning and narrowed down to just this room. I had no past, no future, only this very present.

We were on the bare bed, its crisscross of thongs making patterns in our flesh. Outside I could hear, drifting in from some remote place, the sounds of the revelers and customers below. But in this chamber, empty, barren, I clasped Antony to me, as the only solid thing in this melting, shifting sphere I was swimming in.

He was kissing me, turning me over and over, his breath—almost the only reality I felt—hot on my shoulders, my neck, my breasts. Was he speaking? I could not hear. My ears were stopped. All my senses, except that of touch, had fled. I felt every sensation on my skin, but did not hear, smell, taste, see. My flesh was alive, every particle of it, inside and out.

I know he made love to me, and I to him, for hours through that long, foreign night, but such were the effects of the drug that it all subsumes into one superb blending of our persons, sublime and protracted. I cannot tease out one singular instance, but only grasp, fleetingly, in dreams, the remembrance of the whole.

How we left that chamber, and how we returned to Alexandria, will forever be lost to me, but somehow we did. And I awoke the next morning—or perhaps it was the morning after that—in my own bed in my own chamber, the bright morning light from the harbor dancing on the walls, and Charmian bending anxiously over me.

46

"At last!" she said as I opened my eyes. The light hurt them.

"Here." She laid a compress of cucumber juice on my eyelids; the fresh, astringent smell of it was like a miracle after the artificial, heavy odors of Canopus.

"What did you drink? A sleeping potion?"

The green, heavy liquid—I remembered its glint of emerald coloring, its oversweet taste. "It had that effect," I said. Actually that was the least of its effects. I would have blushed about the behavior it had induced in the rented room—if I could remember the details. I sighed. "I made the mistake of drinking something offered off the streets." Antony had had more than I. "What of Lord Antony? Where is he?"

"No one has seen him." She laid her hands on mine. "But he is back in his quarters, never fear. His guards saw him enter."

I hoped he was not too miserable. I raised one corner of the compress and looked at Charmian. "I saw you with—with—"

"Flavius," she finished.

"Was he as—personable as you hoped?" She had looked happy enough when I passed her.

"Yes," she said quietly. I wondered what had happened, whether this would lead anywhere. He was not exactly Apollo, as she had said she was looking for, but he would do as an earthly substitute.

After a few minutes I got up, swinging my feet over the side of the bed and touching the cool, washed marble floor. In spite of everything, I felt oddly rested.

Outside, the sea was beating against the breakwaters and smashing the base of the Lighthouse. It was mid-January, and the seas were closed to shipping. Very little could enter the port, and almost nothing could leave it, save by land. The caravans were still coming from the east with their luxury goods, but letters, grain, oil, and wine did not move. It was the time Epaphroditus and his assistants spent in inventories and compilations, girding themselves for another year.

I sent for Caesarion, who came as soon as he had finished that morning's lessons. He had an old tutor from the Museion, the same one I had had, Apollonius. He had been dull but thorough, and I thought he would make a gentle start in learning for Caesarion. He never raised his voice, which had the sometimes unfortunate effect of putting you to sleep.

"I thought perhaps we might eat together, and you can tell me what you are studying," I said. "And how your lizard is."

His face lit up. "Oh, the lizard is fine! He's learned a new trick since the one pulling the cart. Today he hid in my boot. I almost squashed him when I put them on!" He burst into high, pealing laughter.

"And your studies?" I asked. Charmian was setting bread and fig paste out for us, as well as goat cheese and olives. Caesarion reached for them eagerly.

"Oh—" His face fell. "I was memorizing the list of Pharaohs, but there are so many of them. . . ." He bit off a big piece of bread and kept talking. "And it was all so long ago . . . and I wish they were more than just names, I wish I knew what they looked like and if they had big feet . . . and if they ever had lizards in their shoes."

"What of your grammar?"

He looked puzzled.

"Doesn't Apollonius teach you grammar?"

"No, just the list of the Pharaohs," he said. "And other lists of battles. And sometimes he makes me memorize a speech. Listen: 'Teach him what has been said in the past; then he will set a good example to the children of the magistrates, and judgment and all exactitude shall enter into him. Speak to him, for none is born wise.' "

"Hmm. What does it mean?"

"I don't know. But it's from the Maxims of Ptahhotpe!" he said brightly. "Here's another. 'Do not be arrogant because of your knowledge, but confer with the ignorant man as with the learned. Good speech is more hidden than malachite, yet it is found in the possession of women slaves at the millstones.' "

According to that, the proprietress in Canopus might have had gems of wisdom to impart. Perhaps she had. But obviously I must replace Apollonius. He was too old, and his teaching was not right for a child. I spread some of the fig paste on my bread. "Very good. We must follow that advice," I said solemnly.

Just then there was a commotion, and I heard Charmian saying, "Yes, they are here, but—" and before she could announce him, Antony walked into the room.

He looked perfectly normal, no trace of even a headache. I stared at him, amazed.

"Greetings, Your Majesty," he said, addressing Caesarion directly. He nodded toward me, winking. "I thought perhaps you might be bored on a cold, windy day like this. It has been a long time since you could sail in the harbor or even ride, hasn't it?"

How well he knew little boys. Of course, that was because in some ways he was still one himself.

"Oh yes, it's tiring," he agreed. "And my lessons are so boring!"

"How would you like to try some different lessons?" Antony asked, whisking out a small shield and sword. "Some soldiering lessons?"

Caesarion looked greedily at the gear. "Oh yes," he said.

"I had them made just for you," Antony said. "The blade is dull, you won't have to worry about cutting anyone's head off." He laughed.

Only then did I see that someone had trailed in behind Antony. It was Nicolaus of Damascus. He just stood quietly in the shadows.

"And for when you're not fighting, I have someone who loves to tell stories to entertain boys," he said. "He knows ones you could never guess." He motioned for Nicolaus to come in. "He'll tell you all about the Persian fire devils."

Obviously something more appealing than the list of Pharaohs.

"Oh yes!" said Caesarion, forgetting all about his food. "When can we go practice with the sword? Can we go now? Can we?"

"Whenever your mother says." He cocked his head at me. "I will take him this afternoon. I think he has the makings of a soldier. It would be surprising if he didn't, with Caesar for a father and such a fierce warrior queen for a mother."

"Perhaps you should teach me, too. I cannot handle a sword very well."

"You handled it well enough the other night."

I still had it, and realized he was asking for it back. "It is safe. Charmian, bring it to me." I took it and handed it back to Antony. "Keep wearing it with honor," I said.

When they returned at dusk, Caesarion was flushed and excited. He was wearing a little set of body armor and a helmet, and he flashed his sword up and down and made stabbing motions. He rushed at the curtains and poked a hole in them.

Antony said, "We'll do this often. He takes to it, and I think he needs it. Too much time indoors in the palace won't make a man of him. When he's older, he can come with me on campaigns—oh, not to fight, but just to see what it's like to be out in the field."

I felt hot tears pushing to spill out of my eyes. All the things Caesar would have done for him! Thank the gods that Antony had come, a man who understood boys and could do for him what I could not. Growing up among women and eunuchs was not enough for a son of Caesar, who would be called upon to do great things, as a man among men.

"Thank you," I said, unable to say more.

The days spun on. Looking back, they seem a multicolored blend, like the scarves of a whirling dancer. With the idleness of winter, there was no guilt in pausing from the business of the world. The *Amimetobioi*—the Incomparables—met often and outdid one another in dicing, drinking, banqueting. At the palace there were always several oxen roasting, in different stages of doneness, so that no matter what the hour or the number of guests, we could be fed on a moment's notice. Another member kept geese always turning on the spit, another a continual profusion of honey cakes, each flavored with different honey—precious ones like Attic and Rhodian and Carian and Hymettan, and obscure ones from Spain and Cappadocia. Wines gushed, from the sticky-sweet, precious Pramnian, to the apple-scented wine of the island of Thasos, to that of Byblos, and the Chian, poured from its sphinx-stamped amphorae. There were hunting and elephant rides and chariot races with tame panthers trotting alongside, down the wide streets of the city and out beyond the walls to the sandy ridges.

Alone, at night Antony and I would roam the streets of Alexandria, disguised, as he liked to do, wandering past the monumental buildings and private homes, listening to conversations, overhearing the songs and quarrels of common people; in our chambers we traded clothes and I became a man while he was a richly appareled courtesan. It was all a dizzy round of pretending, of playacting; we were playing as surely as Caesarion with his sword and shield. In this way I had at last the childhood I had skipped—mine had been too serious and dangerous to have afforded such lighthearted silliness, such lack of concern for safety.

Late at night, together in our darkened room, it felt as if the entire world were concentrated in that one chamber; the rest had vanished, had receded into the night, and would not encroach upon us.

"I wonder what I did before I loved you," he said once, idly, his fingers tracing patterns on my back.

"I don't think you were lonely," I said. But for some reason I was not jealous of who had come before. It could not have been like this.

"No, not lonely." He laughed softly. "But it was all just a rehearsal. Everyone now seems only an early dream of you."

I sighed, and turned my head. It was resting on his shoulder, happy in its home there. "Dreams," I said. "This seems like a dream. This room, this bed, seems a magic kingdom."

"Where we are both King and Queen and the only citizens," he said, tracing the line of my nose, my lips. "An unusual kingdom."

"Oh, Antony, I love you," I said, the words tumbling out. "You have freed me."

"How can a queen be freed?" he asked.

"You have set me free in a garden—a garden of earthly delights, which bloom without any effort." Yes, since he had come I felt I was walking through such a garden—filled with exotic, many-petaled flowers that opened their perfumed throats just for my pleasure whenever I passed by. The shade was always waiting, and there were cool mists and hidden bowers around every corner.

"I would call them *unearthly* delights," he said. "For nothing happens on earth without our efforts, my love." He turned his head to mine and kissed me, a long, lingering kiss. "Even this." And it did take an effort for me to raise my head.

Gradually the winter relaxed its grip on the sea, and our isolation ended. I could feel it ebbing in the increased warmth of the sun and the steady decline in the ferocity of the waves and storms. Always before I had longed for the end of winter; now I dreaded it. I did not want my magic kingdom breached. I wanted to live in it forever, or until I was so sated with love and pleasure that I finally cried, "Hold! Enough!"

I was not at that stage when the first ships arrived, plying the path between Italy and Egypt, Syria and Egypt. Messengers rushed ashore, official ones with the insignia of the Roman army, and sought Antony out. Their news was grim.

"It's all gone to hell," he said, shaking his head, when I found him. At his feet were the curled letters from Tyre and Rome, lying forlornly.

"What is it?" I bent down to pick them up, but waited for him to tell me.

"War in Italy," he said. "My wife . . ." he paused.

Yes, the magic kingdom had been breached. The world was back with us.

"My wife, Fulvia, and my brother, Lucius, seem to have gone to war against Octavian."

"What?" I started to read the letter, but it was very long.

"It's complicated. But it seems they felt that Octavian was taking advantage of his position to settle his own veterans, giving them all the best land, and taking credit even for what he gave mine. So they have launched a campaign against him—and are even now being besieged in the mountain city of Perusia." He ran his hands through his hair. "All my legions are hovering, but without a signal from me, they have not moved. And a good thing, too."

"Why is that a good thing?" I asked. It was never good to be beaten.

"Why, because it would violate my compact with Octavian." He looked surprised that I would even ask. "We are partners, remember? The civil wars are over."

"It would seem they are not." I paused. "Not if he is trying to discredit you."

Antony frowned. "He's not trying to discredit me, he just—he just—"

"Then why have Fulvia and Lucius gone to war against him?"

"It seems they are too anxious for my rights."

It seemed that the anxiety was on Antony's part—to protect Octavian. "Is it not possible that Octavian acted wrongly?"

"Well, he—" Antony paused. "I need more information before coming to a conclusion." He leaned down and picked up the other letter. "Nothing ambiguous about this." He handed it to me.

I skimmed it. It was terrible. The Parthians had overrun Syria, killed Saxa, Antony's governor there, and even taken Jerusalem. Everything was gone but Tyre. The two legions in Syria, along with their eagles, now belonged to Parthia. They had got more for their collection, to add to those of Crassus.

"Oh, the legions!" cried Antony. "The shame of it!"

His client kings, the ones who had so obsequiously paid court to him last autumn, had not proved very stalwart. Perhaps it was time they were replaced.

"Only Herod showed any initiative," said Antony. "He got away, and held out at Masada."

"Good for him," I said. At least someone had.

"A war on two fronts," he said, shaking his head. "I am involved in a war on two fronts."

The war in Italy was a nasty little war. Octavian even descended to having his slingers fire stones engraved with such sentiments as "Give it to Fulvia!" into the enemy camp. He also let loose with an obscene epigram to the effect that:

> Glaphyra's fucked by Antony. Fulvia claims
> A balancing fuck from me. I hate such games.
> Manius begs me: must I bugger him?
> No, if I'm wise, no humoring his whim.
> Fuck or else fight! she cries. But still I've found
> Dearer than life my prick. Let trumpets sound.

He must be desperate—to reveal his true colors. Antony seemed to find the verses amusing.

"Octavian has divorced Claudia," said Antony, out of nowhere. "He must have truly turned against me."

"What are you talking about?" I asked. This was several days after the first letter. More had come in in the meantime. Once the seas opened, we were pelted with them.

"He likes to cement treaties with personal ties. He asked to marry into my family, when we became Triumvirs together. The best I could come up with was Claudia, Fulvia's daughter, since all we had was sons—young ones at that. And so he married her."

Octavian, married. How odd that seemed! "I didn't know," I said.

"But he's divorced her, sent her back to Fulvia. He said she was 'intact'—still a virgin. Married three years, and he didn't touch her!"

"He must have planned this all along," I said. His self-control and long-range planning were almost unhuman. "He always thinks ahead."

Antony shook his head. "It is so—coldblooded."

"Yes. He is a formidable enemy." My measures of him, no matter how extreme they seemed at the time, always fell short. He was beyond anything I had ever encountered—resolute, implacable, unshakable in the pursuit of his goal. I remembered his struggle to reach Caesar in Spain after his shipwreck. Always there was Octavian, crawling out of some wreckage or other, wet, weak, injured—and still coming. I shivered.

"He isn't my enemy," said Antony firmly. "I wish you would stop saying that."

More news poured in. A slave insurrection had started in Campania, but Octavian had stamped it out, and scores of people of all ranks fled to the protection of the rebel pirate-king Sextus Pompey, who all but ruled Sardinia and Sicily. Even Antony's own mother had joined them.

"My mother, forced to flee for her safety!" he lamented. "A disgrace upon me!"

"Oh, stop it!" I said. "Punish Octavian, and set things right!"

"But it isn't Octavian who's at fault—it's Fulvia. She has even raised legions against him, and issued her own coins!"

Yes, I could imagine the fiery Fulvia doing that. "She is only doing it on your behalf."

"That's what you think!" He turned on me. "The real reason she has done this is to lure me from Egypt. She's angry about you."

"So she will raise an army and jeopardize your interests to pry you away from me? Strange sort of loyalty."

"You don't know her."

"I think I do." I remembered the stories of her bloodthirstiness, her vengeance.

"Better that you never learn more, or come closer to her."

"Divorce her," I said suddenly.

He stared at me, shocked. "What?" he finally said.

"She is harming you," I said. I was thinking out loud now. "She is ambitious for you, and has her eyes set on the highest prize. She understands—as you do not seem to—the danger in Octavian. But she is a liability. She cannot really help you to achieve what should be yours. I can."

He tried to joke. "Is this a proposal?"

"Join your forces with mine," I said. "Let me show you what I can offer you. Not a legion here or there, hastily raised, but enough to buy fifty legions, a whole fleet of ships, an army as big as you wish." I grasped his arm, his thick-muscled arm. "Soar as high as you are meant to."

"I repeat my question: Is this a proposal?" He smiled, treating it as mere love-play.

"Yes," I said. "Marry me, join our forces, and I shall never betray or desert you. All you want, I can deliver into your hands."

"All I want?" he said. "I have no desire for more than I already have."

"Which you seem in peril of losing," I said. "To retain what you have, you will have to reach for more."

"I am no Caesar," he finally said. "What made his heart leap up does not tempt me. If you think to have found a second Caesar, I must disappoint you."

"It isn't a second Caesar I want, but an Antony who attains the stature that he deserves. Do not settle for less than your destiny."

"Ah, you make it sound so grand. Destiny. Stature. Very noble. Makes the blood sing. But I must look at what it really means."

"Is an alliance with me so repugnant?"

He laughed. "How can you say that?"

"Because you seem to shrink from it. But I know that you are actually drawn to it." I paused. "Be careful, or I may take up with Octavian! He would not hesitate—he's greedy for glory, no matter what path he must tread to get it."

"I hope you are joking." Antony looked alarmed.

"I could never make a marriage with Octavian," I assured him. "Unless I was guaranteed he would treat me as he did Claudia."

"No chance of that. I know he has a lust for you."

That was unexpected. "How do you know that?"

"I could feel it," said Antony. "And I would rather slay you than let him satisfy his curiosity."

His outburst took me by surprise—both his assertion about Octavian and his possessiveness.

"Then take me for yourself. Legally," I added.

"But such a marriage would not be recognized in Rome," he said.

Yes, I had heard that before. But if he only had one wife, it would have to be honored.

"So I have offered, and you have refused." I stood up and made ready to leave the room. "I must say, the rejection stings." I tried to make it sound light.

"I am not rejecting you, but politically—"

"I know. Our magic kingdom ends where politics begins."

I paced my room that night, until Charmian inquired anxiously if I wished a sleep potion. But I wanted the opposite: something to sharpen my wits, to unlock ideas. I needed to think, think more clearly than I ever had before.

Antony was being offered an opportunity that comes only once in the lifetime of a man, and not to all men, but only to a very few. For all the talk about the Fortune of Caesar, had he not been bold enough to snatch at it as it passed, he would have remained sitting by the side of the road. But he did grab it, wrestled with it, and a new world order was born. We could not turn back.

Rome had taken over the west, and part of the east. It was easier to take over such primitive and virgin lands as Gaul than to take realms that were old past imagining: Babylon, and Syria, and Arabia. And Egypt, oldest and strongest of all. What was Rome to do with them? They could never be Roman, speak Latin, think like Romans. Yet that is what Rome would try to make them do, I knew it. In would come the administrators, the census takers, the tax farmers, the road and aqueduct builders, running roughshod over all the ways that had stood since the beginning of time, obliterating all the wisdom they sorely needed for the new age.

Alexander had known better; he had tried to forge a new race from the old, losing nothing, keeping all intact. Caesar had known better, and his wider views had been part of what killed him. Octavian was parochial, local, entirely focused on the country of Rome and Italy. Should his vision prevail, the east would wither and die, ground under the hobnail boots of the Roman soldiers occupying it.

And Antony? In many ways he had Caesar's wider outlook. He was not prejudiced against something merely because it was not Roman. His Dionysus guise was treated with contempt in Rome, but appreciated by his eastern subjects. He was sensitive to their outlook and beliefs; he was the one Roman willing to shed his toga. Even Caesar had not gone that far.

Outside, I could see the beacon of the Lighthouse winking. There was so much here, so much glorious history—the collective intellect and spirit of the Greek world. Surely its star could not be setting already. Should Octavian prevail, that was what would happen.

No empire can be ruled by two men. One must always, ultimately, make a bid for supreme power. That Octavian would do so, I had no doubt. But he would need time, time to grow in strength. If the contest were held today, he would lose.

Antony was better suited to follow Caesar, with me as his partner. What I said about two people did not apply to husband and wife. They could rule jointly: I would speak for the eastern peoples, and Antony for the western. And our children would inherit all, heralding a new race of international citizens.

Our children . . . for there was to be a child, I had just realized. A child that should wear the mantle of both worlds, but be bound by neither.

Antony stood highest in all the civilized world now—the avenger of Caesar, the victor of Philippi, the senior partner of Octavian. It was all his for the taking. It was *necessary*, for the well-being of all the realms under his protection, that he take over. I would be his faithful partner, the balance to the Roman weight on the other side of the scales. Why could I not make him understand that?

I sank down on my bed, rocking back and forth. He was too modest a man, too fixed on his obligations to Octavian, to the Triumvirate, which was due to expire in only three years. Three years in which Octavian would consolidate his gains, grow stronger. Then what? Strength is always obtained at someone else's expense. Octavian could not grow greater unless Antony grew less.

Oh, Antony, I thought, awake! Take what fortune is offering you. She never offers twice.

47

"Come with me," I told Antony two mornings later. He had come at my summons, and now stood looking at me expectantly. I hoped to convince him of what he must do by showing him the secret workings of my country.

"I don't understand," he said, as we rode in a chariot to the docks and dismounted before the large warehouse owned by Epaphroditus and his company. They were expecting us.

"I want you to suspend all judgment until this morning is over," I told him. "Then, tonight, you must think about it—think of all it entails. Of all it can mean."

We entered the cavernous warehouse, warm after the blustery winds sweeping over the harbor. Enough windows were set in the walls to allow us to see quite well. Epaphroditus came to us immediately, his graceful bearing sweeping all before him. I still thought he was the handsomest man I had ever beheld—in the flesh. Statues did not count, being only a sculptor's wish.

Antony was rocking back and forth impatiently. He looked around the warehouse, seeing the rows of amphorae and sacks of wool, and rolled his eyes.

"This is my trusted finance minister, my *dioiketes*, Epaphroditus," I said. "He has a Hebrew name as well, but I am not allowed to use it." I thought to lighten the meeting by the remark.

Epaphroditus bowed and said, "It is indeed an honor to meet one of the three pillars of the world." He bowed again.

"A triple arch," I said. "But the other two are outflankings. This arch could stand alone; the other two could not."

Epaphroditus raised his eyebrows. "To be the support of others can be draining. Only the strong can sustain it. Welcome, Lord Antony. I have long wished to speak personally with you. I trust you are enjoying our city?"

"Yes, indeed . . ." And so the pleasantries ran on for a few moments.

Finally I knew it could be politely ended. "I wish Lord Antony to be apprised of the financial structure of Egypt," I told Epaphroditus. "And I wish him to be shown the actual holdings—the royal granaries for wheat and produce, the oil factories, the merchant fleet, the warehouses of papyrus, wool, salt, natron, the spices. And the books to go with them."

Epaphroditus looked perplexed. "Your Majesty, that would take many days. Has the most noble lord Antony the time?"

"I have the time, if it is something I should see," Antony said quickly.

"Just a short tour of the receiving stations in Alexandria, then," I assured Epaphroditus.

"Very well." He cleared his throat. "I came into this office only a few years ago, but I find it is even more extensive than I had imagined. In one way it is simple: the Queen owns everything. She owns the entire country—all the land, all the produce of the land, all that labor produces. There is no private property—it is all the Queen's." He waited for a response from Antony. When none was forthcoming, he went on, "It was the way of the Pharaohs, and when the Ptolemies came, the system continued. Of course the Queen does not literally own everything, but everything comes under her jurisdiction. A river of grain, almost as mighty as the Nile itself, flows from the entire country into the royal granary of Alexandria. There are royal receiving granaries for other produce, too—the beans, gourds, onions, olives, dates, figs, almonds. The yearly tax on wheat, paid in kind, is twenty million bushels a year."

Antony stared at him. "What?" he said.

"Twenty million bushels a year is received here, laid at the feet—figuratively, of course—of Queen Cleopatra."

"Ye gods!" said Antony. It sunk in what this meant—Rome was always having to import wheat, and lately Sextus had disrupted the supply route, so that food riots had broken out in Rome. "Twenty million bushels a year . . ." He shook his head.

"We will visit the granary," I assured him. I wanted him to see that mountain of food.

"But there is also the royal monopoly on wool," said Epaphroditus. "We have been quite successful in breeding sheep from Arabia and Miletus, and produce so much wool that we export it. Of course the wool mills come under our control."

"Oh, did I tell you I have my own wool mill?" I said innocently to Antony. "It sports my royal seal, and the rugs are in great demand. People somehow connect me with rugs—I suppose because of Caesar." I laughed. "So everyone wants to own one."

"She has made a tidy bundle from it," said Epaphroditus. "But the profits go to help the needy."

"Yes, and I have an idea of diverting some to Canopus this year," I told him. Something had to be done about their state of despair.

"And the oil," I prompted Epaphroditus.

"Oh yes, the oil. It is the great royal monopoly, and each year we tell the farmers exactly how much land should be planted for the required yield. Then the oil is pressed in state factories by the peasants, and sent here. Let me show you." He gestured to us to follow him to the adjoining warehouse. We passed row after row of wine amphorae until we entered the oil warehouse, where the shapes quickly changed—these amphorae were squat and round. They stretched on and on, lined up like an army, a silent army.

"Here are the containers of sesame oil, the highest quality," Epaphroditus was saying. There must have been a thousand of them. "And here the croton oil"—another thousand. "And the linseed oil"—another mass of them. "And safflower, and colocynth."

"All yours?" said Antony faintly.

"All mine," I said. "Or rather, the profits of them are. I certainly cannot use it all myself—even to feed the Incomparables."

"These are distributed through merchants at a fixed price. We regulate foreign oils by levying a fifty-percent import tax," said Epaphroditus.

"And if that is not enough, we also impose a two-percent harbor tax, and if the goods go up the Nile, another twelve percent. That assures us that no one will bring in any foreign oil—except a very rich man, for his own use, and in limited amounts," I told him.

"You seem to have thought of everything," said Antony.

"We have had generations to do so," I said. "Epaphroditus, do you think we should also include the papyrus warehouse on the tour? It is a royal monopoly as well."

"Ah, what is more Egyptian than papyrus? Of course." Epaphroditus smiled.

"Perhaps, before we depart, we should allow him to see a little of our tax books," I said. "As for the cattle, the royal prerogative gives us many large herds, and we have leather factories. We also have a quarter share in all fisheries and honey."

Antony was shaking his head. "Is anything exempt?" he asked.

"No, not really. We have our own merchant fleet on the Nile. We also have control of the mines, the quarries, the saltworks, and the natron pits," I assured him. "No one can fish or keep bees or brew beer without a license from us. And we receive one-sixth of the produce of vineyards, taken in kind. To keep our wines competitive, we charge a one-third import duty on fine Greek wines."

"But I notice you drink them," said Antony. "There always seems to be Greek wine flowing."

"Well, of course," I said. "We use the profits from everything else to indulge our taste for Greek wine. We don't like to be deprived."

"Of course not." He walked up and down the corridors of amphorae, looking at them attentively.

"Now let's take a look at the wine," said Epaphroditus, returning to the first warehouse. He gestured to one wall. "These are our best, wine from the Delta. Of course, it can't compare with that of Lesbos or Chios, but"—he walked on, toward another grouping—"this is Mareotic, it's quite good, white and sweet. They use a special seal on the amphorae." We kept walking past the jars, Antony seeming dazed. "Here's Taeniotic—usually pale yellow, with an oily quality. It has to be mixed with pure water."

"What is most impressive of all this you can't see. It is our organization," I told Antony. "After all, any ruler can decree that he is owed taxes—but collecting them is another matter. As well you know."

"Ah yes," he sighed. "I have had my troubles there." In fact, his primary mission in coming east was to collect taxes to pay for the last-fought war. "If you have the secret—"

"The secret lies in taking a census on a regular basis," I said. "We try to conduct one every year, or, at the worst, every other year."

"Ye gods!" Antony repeated. "How can you manage that?"

"For one thing, we are not always at war. Peace is needed for such close administration."

"A good point," Antony said. "And so it is a good thing that the civil wars of Rome are over."

That was not the point I wished to make. "If indeed they are," I said. Time enough for that discussion later, and in private. "Come, I think it is time we toured the granaries."

Outside, our chariot was waiting, and Epaphroditus ordered his brought around. He led the way, wheeling around and skirting the wharves, making for the part of the city bordering the canal-fed inner harbor. Most of the produce of the land arrived through Lake Mareotis and the Nile canal, and the ships unloaded there, transferring their cargo onto the canal that ran through the city. The granaries lay there, our own version of a line of pyramids.

He pulled up his horses in front of the largest one, built of limestone and fastened with heavy iron doors. It was locked and bolted from the inside, and two guards stood by, heavily armed. They gave the signal for the master of the granary to open it for us. After the sound of the bolt sliding out, the doors swung open slowly.

A golden haze lay in the air inside, and the sunlight—coming from high windows—broke into shafts and turned into a cloud. It hit the dust from the wheat, which, even after winnowing, hung in the air and gave a dry, sweet smell to the place.

There was a pathway down the center of the building, but on both sides were thick plank half-walls holding back the grain—what looked like an ocean of wheat stretching back and back to the periphery. I pictured the wood straining and breaking, and a wave of grain gushing out and drowning us.

Antony kept turning his head, looking on both sides, but he said little.

"There are similar granaries for barley and millet," I said. "And figs, dates, and almonds have their own warehouses. Would you like to visit them?"

"No," said Antony. "I am sure they are all the same, only the color and smell inside is different."

"Oh, but you must see my favorite—the spice warehouse!" I insisted. "When I was little, I used to make my father take me there. The smells were like airborne jewels." I saw he was getting restless, so I begged, "Please. If ever you want to know what delights me—"

"I would make it my task to learn everything that delights you," he said.

Epaphroditus looked down at his shoes, embarrassed. "Well, then . . ." He led the way out of the granary, and soon we were entering the square stone building that served as the repository for the precious imported spices. There was a ten-man guard set over the doors and around the ventilation vents, for spices were tempting to thieves, being so light and so expensive. Three sets of locks had to be undone before we could enter.

Inside, the mingled smells were overpowering. High above, I could see the latticed air vents, but they let out only the excess heat. It was dim, for the light had to come a long way to reach the floor. It took a few moments for our eyes to adjust, and all the while we were assaulted with the smells. It was as if our noses had ambushed our eyes and left us dependent on smell alone to orient ourselves. I breathed deeply, plunging into the aromatic cloud.

"These are the spices that come from the east from the caravan routes," said Epaphroditus. "We just double the prices we have paid before distributing them to the rest of the world. Of course, not everything comes to Alexandria—some of the caravans go on to the Black Sea and others to Damascus—but we have most of the market. That is because we are a seaport and can export easily, which Damascus can't."

"You seem to have world trade by the throat," said Antony. "Poor Rome does not even have a harbor; we have to use Puteoli, but that's almost a hundred miles away."

"There are many advantages to being based in Alexandria," I said pointedly. I hoped he was paying attention. "Now let's do what I always loved doing—walking past the stores and guessing what they are by smell. Lead us, Epaphroditus." As part of the game, I covered my eyes with one hand and gave the other to Epaphroditus, and led Antony.

"Now this is easy," I said, at the first stop. "It's cardamom. Am I right?"

"Indeed you are," said Epaphroditus. "Here are the wooden boxes holding them, but nothing can imprison the pungent smell." Reaching almost to the ceiling were stacks of boxes, worth huge amounts of money.

We shuffled down the aisles of the rest of the warehouse, passing cinnamon—which was easy to identify—and cassia and pepper, which were not. There were also sacks of saffron stacked in one corner.

"Whole sacks!" said Antony. "I had never imagined such quantity."

"Yes, it takes almost two hundred flowers to produce a pinch of it," I said.

"No wonder it's guarded so heavily," said Antony.

There were bags, sacks, and jars of lesser spices—cumin, turmeric, aniseed, coriander—in the far corner of the building. By that time our noses had become so numbed we could smell nothing.

"All the baths of Rome would not be able to wash these flavors and smells off my skin," said Antony. "I feel they have penetrated down to my bones." Laughing, he flapped his tunic about, like a crane spreading its wings.

When we stepped outside, the air seemed weirdly thin, characterless. "What about the papyrus?" I asked Antony.

"Yes, that would be interesting," he said. And so we went there, touring the warehouse where natron lay in regular piles to absorb any moisture that might cause mold or mildew on the precious scrolls—scrolls that were lying on miles of shelving, ready for distribution.

"Blank scrolls," he said. "I wonder what nonsense will fill them up?"

"They are like newborn babies," I said, plucking one off the shelf. This was the very highest grade. "It depends into whose hands they fall what they will grow into. This one here—it might be used for figures, or poetry of the highest order, or perhaps only household records."

"They wouldn't buy this high-grade papyrus for lowly household records," said Epaphroditus. "They would take grade three or four." There were seven gradations, with the worst used only for school exercises. "We stack those over here." He led us to them. They looked darker, yellower, and thicker.

"I think you should deliver one of our tax records to my chambers in the palace," I told Epaphroditus. "One should do." I turned to Antony. "Unless you want to review them all?"

"No, I've no need. I am not the—what was the word for the finance minister?"

"Dioiketes," I said. "Come, then. Let us depart." I took one of the blank rolls for Caesarion to practice on—one of the best, of course.

As we left, I turned to Epaphroditus. "I almost forgot!" I said. "The gold mines on the border of Nubia. Of course all that comes to me. Antony, would you like to see the gold?"

Surprisingly, he shook his head. "No. I know what it looks like."

"But have you ever seen it not in bracelets, or ornaments, or coins, but in heaps? In huge piles?" I persisted.

"No," he said. "But I do not need to."

He was a most unusual man, I thought. Perhaps this would be harder than I thought.

The afternoon shadows were slanting across the palace grounds by the time we returned. I was not through with him yet, for I still had to show him what I hoped would be the convincing finale to this whole demonstration. I could tell his interest was flagging; prolonged concentration was not his strong point. He was obviously longing to soak in a bath and indulge himself in a feast of some sort, probably with the Incomparables. But there would be no Incomparables tonight; I wanted Antony entirely to myself, for one of the most important pleas I would ever make.

I took his hand and suggested we stroll on the green lawn surrounding the various palace buildings. "I want to show you a special building I am having constructed," I said, leading him toward it.

"Oh, no more buildings!" he groaned, pulling back.

"Please!" I said. "This one is different!"

"Why?" He did not even look curious.

"Because it's my tomb. My mausoleum. It is connected to the temple of Isis, the one overlooking the sea—"

"How morbid! You are only twenty-nine, and building your tomb!" He looked horrified.

"This is Egypt, remember? Tombs are fashionable." I had started building it upon my return to Egypt, when after Caesar's death, I knew too well my own mortality.

I led him on, pulling him along over the cool green grass, starting to sprout early wildflowers. We reached the magnificent marble building, with its high steps and its polished entrance of red porphyry, flanked by sphinxes. It was only half finished, though, and had no second story or roof as yet.

"It will have special doors that can never be reopened," I said. "They will slide down a groove in the frame and, once set in place, will be immovable."

"Why are you showing me this?" he said with distaste.

"Because I wanted you to see where I will be sealed for eternity, along with my personal treasure—unless it is spent elsewhere. That is for you to decide. Either it is used for a good purpose, or it will abide here, locked away, forever."

"I have nothing to do with it."

"Yes, you do," I assured him. "Yes, you do."

It was night, a cool, moonless night. We had eaten a long, languorous meal with all his favorite foods, in privacy. There had been the special grilled fish of Alexandria, with its sauce of stoned damsons, lovage, wine mixed with honey, and vinegar, which he loved. There were plump grapes, kept moist all winter by soaking in rainwater in sealed jars, eggs cooked over embers of applewood, honey custard, and of course enough Chian wine to fill a small swimming pool. We were served in the portion of my apartments that I used for private dinners, with inlaid crescents of tortoiseshell on its walls. He was stretched out on one of the dining couches, looking supremely content. Now. Now was the time.

I got up from my couch and went over to his, sitting beside him and twining my hand in his. I touched his hair with my other hand, more for myself than for him, for I loved the feel of his thick hair. "I have something to show you," I told him, keeping my voice low, although there was no one else to hear.

"Oh, not more things," he protested. "I've seen enough for one day."

But I slipped off the couch and brought over an inlaid box, which was fastened with a bronze lock. Opening it, I flung off the top and let him see the mound of jewels inside—pearls, emeralds, coral.

"Put your hand in it," I said, taking it and plunging it in. The smooth stones slipped around his fingers, and as he withdrew them, some gems bounced onto the floor. I did not pick them up.

"I have many more like this," I told him. "And there are storerooms of rare woods, ivory, silver, and gold. They will go with me into my tomb."

"Unless?" he said. "For you are not parading this out if you have truly decided, once and for all, to hide it away."

"Unless I can put all these resources to a better purpose," I said.

"Like what?" He sounded only vaguely curious.

"Let me buy us the world instead."

He laughed. "I told you already, I don't want the world. And if I did, you couldn't buy it."

"I can buy armies, and armies can buy a world." I let that statement lie there for him to ponder. "Just think, no more constraints. No haggling with Octavian about this legion or that, or who gets such-and-such ship. It can all be yours."

"And your price? For I am sure you do not offer this gratis."

Now he was beginning to sound like a merchant, although he seemed strangely ungreedy to grasp what I was dangling before him.

"I wish to change places with Octavian," I finally said.

He roared with laughter. "And wear his sun hats and chest flannels? The summer sun is too hot for him, and the winter chill too cruel, so he has to protect himself before venturing out. He is quite a sight."

"And is such a man suited to rule the whole world? A little man who cannot face the sun or wind?" And wore built-up sandals, I remembered. "He imagines himself to be Caesar's heir, but he is no such thing! Yet if you allow him to, he will grow and grow, like a mushroom spreading out in the dark. And you'll awake to find yourself uprooted, toppled, while he flourishes." I paused. Antony was listening attentively. "Pull him out while you still can. For it is certain that he means to do the same to you."

Was I making any sense to him? I had to continue. "The world is already under the sway of Rome. Make the transition easy. Form a partnership with me as your wife. I can administer the east, while you shepherd the west. Alexandria is ideally situated to rule the entire Mediterranean. And we have the resources, as you saw today."

"So that was what that little show was all about?" he said. "I knew it was not just sightseeing." His voice had an ugly edge to it. "I could almost suspect you of planning all this from the beginning—maybe your trip to Tarsus and bringing me back here was just another show."

This was not going as I wished. "No—that isn't true!" I said. "I admit I was proud of Egypt and wanted to show you my country. And I wanted to be with you a little longer. But I did not plan what would happen once you were here."

"You lured me here, after driving me mad with your devices—your costumes and perfumes and lights and other tricks. You made a fool of me, and you loved it," he snapped. "It made you feel powerful. You would probably have responded exactly the same if it had been Octavian instead of me. You just like to ensnare men—and you don't care how you do it."

How dare he imply that I would take just anybody? Octavian!

"At Tarsus, you said it wasn't the dinner on the ship; it went a long way back," I countered.

"Yes, because you always made it your business to make men want you."

I could not help laughing. "Then the desire arose from within yourself. When I was in Rome, I was entirely Caesar's, and when you first came to Alexandria, I was only fourteen and more concerned with survival than anything else. I was not on the lookout for men."

"Maybe you can't help it, but that's the effect you have!"

Now I understood. He was jealous and wanted reassurance. How fragile men were! Only Caesar had been exempt from this weakness.

I reached out to touch his face, but he swatted my hand away, and sat pouting on the couch.

"Now you try to entice me into betraying my word. I have sworn an oath to uphold the Triumvirate," he insisted. "A man is only as good as his word."

"No, I have offered you my life, and all of Egypt. Is this to be scorned? I *am* Egypt—all its riches are mine, every palm tree and ripple in the Nile. What you saw today is the last unplundered treasure of the east. I offer it to you—something that has never been offered to anyone else in history. Many generals have come and tried to take it. I offer it to you, free. Instead you insult me and cry, 'O Octavian! O the Triumvirate!' Well, you are right about one thing—if I ever *did* make such an offer to Octavian, he wouldn't be such a fool as to turn his back on it. Your precious Triumvirate wouldn't last an eyeblink with him in the balance." I paused to catch my breath. "So you *are* a fool—not for coming here, but for turning away from this offer."

He seized on the word *fool*. "So I'm a fool? That's what you think of me! Well, I've sense enough to steer clear of this trap you've set, this trap that betrays every sense of honor. No, I won't be your partner; no, I won't go back on my word."

At that moment I debated with myself, because I still withheld one vital piece of information from him: the fact that I now knew for a certainty that I was with child. If I told him, he might reconsider.

But I looked into his eyes, full of scorn and turmoil, and I knew I would not tell him. He had spurned my offer, insulted my honor, flung hurtful accusations at me. Now would I say, "Oh, by the way—" No, never!

It was the worst decision I ever made, for it brought much sorrow upon us. But for women, too, a momentary pride can be the strongest of all pulls. And so I clamped my lips shut and turned away from him. I bent down and retrieved the jewel box, and with all the self-control at my command, walked straight-backed out of the room.

Of course, later that night he came to my chamber, penitent. He knocked on the door and begged to be admitted. He embraced me and put his head in my lap and almost wept, saying he had not meant it. But he must have meant some of it, or the words would not have sprung so readily to his lips. He had revealed himself as a cauldron of jealousy and confusion, as well as a quaint sort of honor—he had no compunction about betraying his wife, but shrank with horror from betraying Octavian.

"Forgive me, forgive me," he cried, clasping me, burrowing his head against my thighs and stomach. "I just—I just—"

I smoothed his hair, feeling oddly detached. He had hurt me badly by his accusations. That he would think those things of me, even in one corner of his mind, stung. "There, there," I heard myself saying, mechanically. "It doesn't matter."

"Yes, yes, it does!" His voice sounded tormented. "Something came over me, I don't know, I didn't mean it—you know I love you!"

"Yes, of course." I still felt remote. It was important to calm him. "Don't think of it."

"You must believe me!"

"Yes, yes, of course. Of course I believe you." This was awful; I wished he would leave.

He rose up and kissed me, but I found I didn't want him even to touch me. Still, I did not push him away. That would just have made it worse, excited his suspicions further.

"Show me that you do," he was saying. I knew what he wanted. There was no escape—I would have to bear it.

"Yes, of course," I said, taking his hand, and leading him to his favorite place, my bed.

He was a frantic lover, driven almost mad, it seemed, by his own torment and guilt and jealousy. Ordinarily it would have been supremely satisfying, but I kept out of it, so to speak. I did not allow myself to take any enjoyment from it, because my hurt was too deep to be plastered over by a few kisses and caresses.

When he finally left, I rolled over and watched his retreating back, thinking, *Tonight you have thrown away the world.*

48

On the surface, things continued as usual. The bedroom visit seemed to have satisfied Antony, and he went back to his bluff self, laughing, drinking, playing with the Incomparables. He assumed I was likewise soothed and happy. The evening, and the things we had said, were never mentioned.

Bulletins from the outside world kept coming in, and he was forced to acknowledge them. Late at night, returning from his days of pleasure, he would stay up reading them, alone and in the silence of his room. I would see the lights burning, and know that he was troubled with the news. Sometimes he would come and spend the rest of the night with me, never alluding to the contents of the letters. But I had my own sources of information, and I knew well enough that the Roman world was in turmoil. Perusia had fallen, and Octavian was merciless in punishing those who had rebelled against "the authority of the Triumvirate." Scores of people were executed, and the ancient town was burned to ashes. Lucius had been captured, but Fulvia had escaped, along with Antony's general Munatius Plancus. Where they were going, no one knew.

In the meantime, Antony kept practicing at arms—a good sign—and sending out letters.

Although I was determined not to speak of the night we had quarreled so bitterly, the words clung in my mind. I kept going over them, brooding on them. But I kept it to myself.

One afternoon I happened to be present when a letter arrived for him, and it would have been so awkward to refuse to open it that Antony went ahead. Then politeness decreed that he let me read it. He was clearly reluctant to do so, but made the best of it.

It was an overture from Sextus Pompey, seeking to make an alliance with Antony against Octavian.

"I offer protection for all those fleeing from the tyrant," he wrote. "Your most noble mother Julia, Tiberius Nero, his wife Livia, and their little son Tiberius have had to seek safety with me, along with many of the oldest names in Rome. They do not wish to bend the knee to that boy—that boy who styles himself ruler, calls himself Caesar's son. In your absence he has done many illegal things. Join with me, throw your lot in with mine, and together we can rid Rome of this menace."

I knew better than to concur. I merely handed the letter back to Antony. "It seems that the entire world seeks to ally itself with you," I said lightly.

"And not only he, but Lepidus has approached me as well," he admitted.

"A noble Triumvir, sounding out one of his fellows?" I am afraid the mockery crept into my voice. "What can have possessed him?"

Antony shrugged. "He has ever been unreliable. He says one thing one day, another the next." He stood up. "Come, the sun is shining. I think the winter is truly past. Let's go fishing on Lake Mareotis. You promised we would—you said there was fine fishing, and boat parties go out among the reeds and papyrus, and there's beer and singing in the villages—"

I sighed. "I suppose you want to invite a party?"

"Well, isn't that what such a day is meant for?"

Three houseboats filled with merrymakers bumped along in the shallow water of the great freshwater lake that stretched behind Alexandria. It was a strangely shaped lake, with its main body south of Alexandria, while a long, thin arm reached westward almost fifty miles. Vineyards lined the south banks, producing some of Egypt's finest wines. Other crops covered the shores: olives, figs, dates, apple orchards. At the very water's edge, papyrus plantations extended out some way. This was the source of our finest grade of papyrus. There were also bean plantations, with the huge stalks growing ten feet high and the cup-shaped leaves providing shelter for boat parties and lovers.

It was March, the Egyptian month of Tybi, and the vegetation was in bloom: The beans had opened their creamy flowers, the white and blue lotus were rising out of the water, and the pale petals of the almonds on the shore were already scattering on the wind. The sun felt warm on our shoulders, and Antony was in high spirits.

Time and again he cast his line out into the open water, baited with plump small fish; time and again he hauled in his hook, empty. The company we had with us—Charmian and Flavius, some of his guard, their women—began to taunt him.

"Good Imperator," they singsang, "how pitiful is this!"

Antony, growing ever more exasperated, threw out his line repeatedly. He attempted to joke about it, and called for us to go ashore and eat and drink in one of the little villages lining the shore of the lake.

A number of them, all friendly and inviting, lay stretched out in the sun, sloping back from the lakeshore. We piled ashore, tying up at one of the rickety docks. I was just another woman at the tavern—gods forbid they should know I was the Queen.

But there was no mistaking Antony. He was as different from his fellows as gold from gold paint. When he seated himself, it was with a certain careless nobility that caused eyes to light on him; in spite of his fisherman's costume, everyone in the establishment became aware that this was no ordinary man. Then their attention turned to his companion, me. But I kept my peasant's hat low and said little. No ordinary person can appreciate what a gift it is for those of us in power to venture out as one of them. Liberty! For we are imprisoned by our very selves all the days of our lives. Here, too, Antony had freed me from my former restrictions.

"Wine for all!" ordered Antony. "Unless you are known for your beer?"

The proprietor bowed. "Indeed, this is a renowned brewing district."

"Then bring us your specialty, in jugs! And perhaps some roasted duck, and fish. I suppose the fish are biting well in this season?"

"Oh yes," said the tavern owner. "Our catches have been phenomenal in the past few days."

I reached out and touched Antony's arm. "You must be using the wrong bait," I said.

"Surely so," he said, shaking his head.

A heap of fish arrived on a platter, and pieces of duck. Already the beer pitchers had been filled to overflowing. "To my catch!" said Antony, raising his glass.

The food was delicious. I wondered how many palace banquets would pale beside what a waterside tavern like this could provide. The white-fleshed fish was moist and delicately flavored, and the duck had a rich, smoky taste, boosted by the plum gravy served with it. Antony wolfed his, washing it down with draughts of beer.

I looked at him from under my broad-brimmed hat. What I saw was an eager, yearning face, younger than its years, with bright, dark eyes. I reached out and laid my hand on his arm, wishing there were some way I could hold him at this stage in his life forever. My anger at him faded in the sunlight of this, his glorious day.

The meal ended, and we returned to our boats. The vessels made their way uncertainly through the thickets of papyrus and tall bean plants, poled by our mariners under the green umbrella of leaves and buzzing insects into the open water.

"Well, now!" said Antony, standing at the rail and flinging out his line. "We shall see what we land!"

There was a rustling of motion on the boat, and I saw some of the younger boat-boys diving off the side when they thought no one was looking. The waters parted silently and they slipped away.

"Oh, what is this?" cried Antony with mock surprise. And he hauled in a perfect fish—a big mullet. He unhooked it and quickly threw out his line again.

"It bites again!" he cried. He yanked on the line and a fat perch flew through the air. It looked suspiciously like the ones I had just seen for sale at the harbor market.

"My lord Antony is most fortunate," I said. "He can acquire fish beyond the measure of ordinary fishermen."

Flavius and the others started cheering, saying now Antony would have to treat them all to more beer, as the winner of the fishing contest. Again and again he threw out his line, and the fish appeared so quickly one could suspect they were all fighting below the waterline to grab Antony's hook.

Soon a pile of prize fish of amazingly many species lay at Antony's feet, a glistening mound. Odd how none of them flapped or gasped when they were hoisted in. And just at the time his luck ceased, the boys hauled themselves on board the ship again.

"I am in awe of your luck," I sighed. "Let us see if it holds tomorrow, for we must venture out again."

"In the meantime, head for that jetty!" one of the soldiers said. "It's time for Antony's treat!"

When we returned home, there were several letters for Antony. He took them and disappeared into his private quarters. He did not come to me that night; they must have been weighty, and depressing. I longed to know what was in them.

The next morning we set out again. The strengthening sun was on us, and as we embarked on our boats from the very foot of the Street of the Soma, where the lake harbor water lapped against the steps of Portus Mareotis, I kept very silent. I had brought along my own divers this time, with their own sacks, and I meant to make a point to Antony.

We rowed out into the middle of the lake, watching the rising sun. It gilded the water, and already I could feel its heat along my arm. The sun would rise higher, achieve the zenith in its season and time; and where would Antony be? In its light or in its shadow?

We sailed and paddled out across the open water, then headed for the marshy borders that were so rich with fish and birds. Some of our party had brought bows and arrows in hopes of shooting wild fowl.

Antony cast his line again. He made reference to his fantastic luck the day before. "Oh, would that such another day would come to me!" The line bobbed and sank. Then at once there was a pulling. Something had bitten. Eagerly he hauled it in. He looked genuinely pleased—this time he had truly caught something!

The line came up, dripping. On it was a large salted fish—produce of Pontus. It all but shouted, "False catch! False catch!" With a solemn face, he removed it. It had clearly been dead for an entire season. Obviously it had been artificially hooked, like his catch of the day before.

He held it up by its tail, for all to see, and then laughed uproariously. "This truly is a miraculous catch! I confess, I confess!"

"Dear Antony," I said, sweetly. "Great Antony, noble Imperator! I pray you, leave fishing to us, the poor denizens of Alexandria, Canopus, and Mareotis. This is beneath you. Your catch should be kingdoms, cities, provinces."

His laughter faded. "You never give up, do you?" He flung the fish down and retired to the cabin.

Back at the palace, Antony stamped away to his quarters, and I waited in mine. Had I been wrong to ridicule him in front of others that way? Show him I recognized his playacting? I thought he would find it amusing, but take the point to heart.

Why were all our words at such cross-purposes? He was under an enormous strain, and seemed unable to take any action at all—besides fishing, boating, exercising, and carousing. It was as if he wanted all the events to resolve themselves in his absence, so that he would not have to make any decisions, as if he were saying, "Wake me when it's all over." This was so far from what Caesar would have done that I felt near despair.

Waiting for him to appear—for I did not dare to go to bed early anymore, in case he came crashing in on impulse—I could see the lights of his quarters in the nearby building. Was he going over papers? Looking at maps? Writing letters? Making a decision of some sort?—O Isis, let him take some action!

I walked outside on my terrace, where two torches were burning, their flames whipping in the sea breeze. This is what happens when you love a normal man, with all the flaws and weaknesses of any mortal man, I told myself. Perhaps the hardest thing I have ever had to do is teach myself to love a flawed man—after Caesar. He was the abnormal one, but he spoiled me for anyone else.

I had my own faults and weaknesses and quirks, but I had grown to expect that my partner would be free of them. Caesar had bequeathed a great burden of expectations to me. It was more than his family pendant that he had asked me to wear for the rest of my life. It was his image as the resolute, the strong, the man who never made mistakes. It made it impossible for his successor—indeed, it made it almost impossible for there to be a successor at all.

My heart went out to the man sitting under those lights in Antony's window. True, he was a flawed man, but at least he did not begrudge others their flaws. I never felt that I had disappointed him or failed to live up to some standard, and was not that in itself a great gift? Caesar had so often made me feel lacking, unable to keep up.

The lights were dimming. He must be preparing for bed. It was late. Now I could sleep. But then I saw a figure leaving the building, and from his gait I knew it was Antony. I stood at the edge of my terrace and waved a long scarf to catch his eye.

He was on his way over to my building, but stopped when he saw the scarf. I motioned to him that I would come down. Wrapping the scarf around my shoulders, I descended and met him on the darkened lawn, the night wind flowing across the grounds.

I embraced him, glad to be with him privately. We seemed always to be surrounded by large numbers of people, now that the world had reached Alexandria again. "You work late," I said.

"You watch late," he replied.

"I feel your distress," I said. "I will watch with you until you can rest."

He sighed. "There can be no rest until I admit what I must do—tear myself away from this place." It was hard to hear his words over the noise of the sea not far away, and the rising wind. "I do not want to go."

"Yes, I know." I remembered how Caesar had grabbed up his armor and rushed away, not even staying for the birth of Caesarion. Yes, they were entirely different men. *I am no second Caesar*, Antony had said. He was giving notice. And while it was admirable that nothing stayed Caesar from his duty, it was more touching that someone wanted to stay. "Nor do I want you to."

He took my face in his hands. "Is it even so? Such doubts have assailed me—ever since—"

"It was but a lovers' quarrel," I said quickly. "And you must know that I am your lover, your most ardent partisan." Let it rest with that; no need to mention any of the rest of it—Octavian, Fulvia, armies, and Sextus. Nor a child. "I would keep you here forever, if we were just private citizens, a man and a woman. But it seems the roof of the world is caving in, and you must go and shore it up."

We had been walking, without really noticing, toward the mausoleum. As we found ourselves approaching it, Antony groaned. "Oh, not that tomb!"

"We can sit on the steps," I said. "Come, they won't hurt you."

"I refuse to enter a tomb! I fear it would be a bad omen."

"We needn't go inside." And indeed, I would not have wanted to—it lay in deep darkness. "We can just sit here." I sank down and patted the place beside me on the step. I noticed a strange coldness emanating from the inside of the building.

We sat, side by side, primly, and he took my hand, like an awkward schoolboy, turning it over and over, as if he had a ring to put on it. "I must away," he said quietly, as if he had finally accepted it. "The events of the wider world call me. As you so glaringly pointed out."

The fishing incident. "I thought I was more subtle."

"How subtle could a salted fish be?" He laughed softly. "As subtle as the pyramids, as subtle as the Lighthouse. What more could I expect from you, my Egyptian? My crocodile of Old Nile. But the crocodile is a most noble creature, king of his realm, living eternally."

"I am as mortal as you," I said, gesturing to the yawning blackness behind us. "Or I would not need a mausoleum."

"Perhaps you won't need it," he said lightly.

"You have a very silly streak in you," I said. "But tell me, if you have decided—what you will do. And when."

"I will go to Tyre and see firsthand what has happened with the Parthians," he said. "And after that—I don't know. It will depend on what I find out. But this one thing I do know: I will come back to you. I could not leave, if I thought it was good-bye."

Pretty words. But in what way could he come back? There was no reason for him to return to Egypt. We were neither rebels nor enemies, or situated near rebels or enemies to serve as a base of operations. And next time Fulvia would most likely travel with him.

"If there is some way for us, I will find it," he was saying. "Do not ever think I leave out of a surfeit of you, for that is impossible." He paused. "Nor because I search for anyone else."

Then why didn't he divorce Fulvia? Perhaps because he was afraid to—because then he would have no excuse not to behave differently. As it was, she could act in his name, staging rebellions, and he could watch enigmatically. Divorcing her and taking up with me would end all ambiguity in the eyes of the world. Perhaps ambiguity was what suited him best. It gave him freedom of choice. Marcus Antonius was a man who disliked making final decisions.

"Then let's have one last private night together," I said, rising.

For the first time since our fight, I desired him again. I took his hand as we walked slowly across the lawn to my chambers. I forgave him for being human, and I think in doing so I became human myself.

The chamber was waiting, delicately perfumed from discreetly smoking burners on tables. The wind swept through from one window to another, and the whispering of the sea far below sounded like ancient music.

"There is only one memory you need to take with you," I said. I stretched out on my couch, pulling him over against me. He felt solid and glorious. Oh, why is this not a permanent answer to all our anguish and aloneness? It is our highest moment on earth. The pity of it is, it is only a moment.

Everything we did was colored by knowing it was farewell. I held him and rejoiced in all the lovemaking, which seemed like a memory even as it was happening . . . hazy and tinged with sadness.

It was good that he would go now. Soon my body would start to change, and he would notice. And I would lose my own freedom to decide what to tell and what not, what to do or not. Perhaps I liked ambiguity as well as he. Caesar would not have approved, but Caesar was gone. I realized with surprise that perhaps I was more like Antony in that regard than I was like Caesar.

49

Once he had decided, Antony moved fast to put everything in order for his leave-taking. He would sail with his small contingent of personal guards directly for Tyre; he sent word ahead that his newly built fleet of two hundred ships should make themselves ready—for what, he was not yet sure. An air of briskness as stirring as the strong spring winds rushed through the palace. There were swirls of mantles, spears, messages, sails, and all the noises of weapons being gathered up.

He stood before me to take his leave. He was flanked by his guard, waiting in the middle of the great audience hall. It was very public, and he was, suddenly, very Roman.

I faced him, Caesarion by my side. I knew this departure would be hard on my son, who had come to depend on Antony as a constant source of amusement and guidance. I put my arm around his little shoulders, which already came up to the middle of my ribs. This summer he would be seven.

"I come to say farewell," Antony said. "It would be impossible for me ever to repay your hospitality, but I thank you more than I can express."

"May all the gods go with you, and grant you a safe journey," I said, mouthing the tired old formula, when what I wanted to say was, *I love you because your honor makes you go, and therefore you will go, but remember my words and my warnings.*

He bowed, then said impulsively, "Come, look out over the harbor with me. Look upon my ships." He held out his hand, shattering the formal leave-taking, and I took it. Together we walked across the wide expanse of the hall and out onto the portico, where the brightness of the sea and sky hurt my eyes. The rest of the party trailed along behind us.

For an instant we were by ourselves; he leaned close and whispered into my ear, "This is not farewell, but just a brief separation." His breath was warm, sparking off a thousand memories and their attendant desire.

"Duty is the stern daughter of the gods," I said. "And now we must do homage to her." I dropped his hand, lest I try to hold on to it and pull him back.

The ships sailed away, their sails as white as the waves on the sea, growing smaller and smaller until they disappeared on the eastern horizon. I stood watching from my window as they rounded the Lighthouse and made out for the open sea; Caesarion watched with me.

"Now they are around the Lighthouse . . . now they must be almost to Canopus . . . now they are gone." His voice sounded faint and sad. The game of watching had sustained him for a little while, but now the last of the Antony-games had finished.

He sighed and made his way back inside, to slump down at the table where an abandoned board game waited. "When will he come back?" he asked.

"I don't know," I answered. *Never,* I thought. "He has a war to prepare for, and after that, we cannot know what will happen."

Odd how he had filled the palace, had filled all of Alexandria, or so it seemed, and now it almost echoed and cried out for him. It had existed long before he came, of course, but now it seemed peculiarly his, as if he had stamped an insignia on it. He had not actually lived in my rooms, but they—and I— ached for him, diminished without him.

I allowed myself to roam around my depleted quarters and touch each place of deficiency, then put it away in my mind, folding it as neatly and resolutely as any Roman soldier ever folded his tent when morning came. That was over. Antony had gone, after rejecting my offer of both a personal and a political alliance, gone to fight his own battles on a different stage, and they were now his battles, not mine.

Of course it was not entirely over. There was that legacy of the meeting at Tarsus, the long winter nights, gaudy and flaming, in Alexandria. Charmian knew, or guessed, even though she was fighting her own unhappiness at the departure of Flavius. One quiet night, after she had brushed my hair and folded my gown, she said simply, "So he left anyway."

"He didn't know." It was a relief to be able to talk about it to someone, to give voice at last to this most important fact. I didn't even ask, *How did you know?*

"You didn't tell him?" She sounded incredulous. "Was that fair to him?"

"I thought it was. It seemed that telling him would be unfair."

"Why is the truth unfair?" she asked. "What were you protecting him from?"

"I don't know," I said. "I felt more as if I was protecting myself."

She shook her head. "No, you've done just the opposite. You've injured yourself. They'll say—oh, I can't bear to think of what they'll say about you!"

"I don't care," I answered, but that was not strictly true. I could not bear ridicule or pity, particularly the latter. "And which 'they' do you mean? My subjects? The Romans? Fulvia?" There, I had said *Fulvia.*

"Oh, all of them—any of them! Judging, clucking, stoning—"

"That is in Judaea. Greeks and Egyptians don't stone," I reminded her. "Besides, perhaps it will convince people that Antony is more Caesar-like than Octavian, since he has followed in his footsteps." The humor of it struck me.

Charmian laughed, her deep, husky laugh. "I don't think it was Caesar's *footsteps* where he followed."

Now we both laughed. Finally Charmian said, seriously, "I don't suppose it would hurt Antony to have a son who was half brother to Caesar's."

No, not if Antony would exploit it, I thought. But he was unlikely to. That was both his honor and his weakness.

In a few days I felt obligated to tell Olympos; perhaps I felt it made up for not telling Antony, to tell another man. His reaction was even more vehement than I had expected.

"Have you no sense at all?" he cried. "What about—"

I opened the box where I had stored his opportune birthday gift, and handed the jar back to him, wordlessly.

"Untouched, I see," he said, peering down inside. He sounded utterly exasperated, like a parent with a wayward child. He set it down on the floor and crossed his arms, as if he expected me to confess. "Well?" he said, tapping his foot.

"You and Mardian were always at me to provide more heirs to the throne, so I have merely tried to comply." I tried to smile at him, but he was having none of it.

"Oh, my dear, my dear Queen and friend," he lamented. "This is terrible, terrible! The world looked the other way the first time, with all that mumbo-jumbo about Isis and Amun, and the gods know Caesar always got away with whatever he did, but this is different. Antony is no Caesar—"

As Antony himself had pointed out. "Olympos—" I was touched that he was so deeply affected; it was comforting that someone was.

"—Antony is no Caesar, and the world is harsh on him. Besides, he has many other children, unlike Caesar. This is not a special gift you bring him, something no one else has offered, but—how many children does he have, anyway?"

I had to stop and count. There was at least one from his marriage to his cousin Antonia, and he and Fulvia had two sons. "Three that I know of," I admitted.

"You see? What is a fourth? Besides, as soon as he sees Fulvia again, there'll be another one."

The thought was painful—especially since it was probably true. I could not think of any reasonable answer.

"Sit down here," said Olympos, ignoring the fact that he had no right to order me to do anything. I was his Queen first, his friend second, his patient third, but now the last took precedence. He then took a seat opposite me, and sat staring at me, his long, dark face drawn with worry. "Who else knows about this?"

"Only Charmian," I said. "And only because she guessed. You are the only one I have told."

"Not Antony?" he said quickly.

"No, not Antony."

"He doesn't suspect?"

"No."

"Good. Then it's still early enough, or else he would have known. Now listen. You have to rid yourself of it. There is still time—thank all the gods."

"But I—"

"At least listen to my argument, and then think over my words tonight. I have an elixir that works if used in the early days. It won't hurt you. No one would have to know. It can be gone, just like Antony himself."

His choice of words hurt, again, because they were true.

"Think about it. Ask yourself why you want to punish yourself by going through with it, when you don't have to. Isn't it painful enough to have been left like this, without having a bastard as well?"

He stood up, again without leave. I just sat looking at him.

"I will come back after dinner. Prepare for bed early. Send Charmian on some errand, say you want to be alone."

"You sound like a lover," I said, faintly.

"No, I am the person who has to undo what the lover has done. I clean up other people's messes."

Like a sleepwalker, I did what he said. It was oddly comforting to be ordered around, to be told exactly what to do. No thinking, just obedience. I was worn out from the burden of making decisions, of orchestrating events, of leading, amusing, cajoling Antony. How soothing to be led, to be relieved of any responsibility.

I waited in my chamber, dressed in a plain sleeping gown with a coat over it. Charmian had brushed my hair, rubbed my hands with almond cream, massaged my feet with mint water. She had lit three small lamps in the chamber, and opened my favorite window onto the palace grounds. Then she had stolen away to what she assumed would be a sweet night of rest for me.

Olympos appeared a little while later, a silent visitor who was suddenly there. He was holding something all wrapped in cloth. Reverently he unwrapped it and handed it to me.

It was a tall, thin glass bottle. Through the sea-green glass I could see that the contents were also green. I tilted it and watched as the heavy liquid rolled to one side.

"This is your friend," he said. "Your friend that opens the door of your prison and lets you walk out free."

"What must I do?" I asked. It seemed impossible that this small amount of medicine could be so powerful.

"After I leave, drink it down—all of it. Cover your bed with these cloths." He thrust a basket out at me; inside I could see folded material. "Lie down. Wait. It won't be painful—just wait. Then gather up the cloths and hide them. I'll come to you as soon after daylight as possible, and take them away, before Charmian or Iras even comes in."

I took the basket and walked over to my bed with it.

"Just remember," he said. "Tomorrow night all this will be only a memory. It will be past. Don't lose your courage." He took my hand. "Your hand is cold. Is this so very difficult for you?"

I swallowed, and nodded. My hand felt like ice in his warm one.

"Most people never have a chance to undo mistakes," he said. "Most of our misjudgments stay with us, and we must pay the consequences. There will be those in plenty—for us both. But this need not be one of them." He squeezed my hand and said, "Please don't be afraid." He paused. "I will be back in only a few hours. I promise." Again, he hesitated. "It is not an easy thing for me, to break my oath as a physician and give you this. It is no light matter for either of us. But it must be done."

After he left, as silently as he came, I stood stupidly by the side of the bed. Why could he not stay with me? But of course he couldn't, if the event was to be erased completely. It must come and go with no witnesses.

I spread the thick cloths out over the bed, and then held out the vial of medicine. My hands still felt so cold that they did not warm the glass. I put the bottle down and rubbed my hands together as hard as I could, snow against snow. Even my nose felt cold. I touched its tip and touched stone in winter. All the blood was fleeing from my extremities, as if I had taken the elixir already.

I held it up before the lamp. Why were all drugs green? I remembered the potion we had drunk in Canopus. Maybe it had caused the condition that now called for this antidote—one green potion requiring another. I shivered.

Don't take it, I told myself, and day will follow day, and you will get bigger and bigger and the whole world will know that Antony came to Alexandria, enjoyed himself, and left a bastard—a bastard that will cause amused laughter in Rome and sneering remarks from Octavian. Another discarded mistress like Cytheris and Glaphyra, they'll say.

And it will even reflect badly on Caesar, I realized with a sinking feeling. *Antony used Caesar's widow for his pleasure, but then cast her aside. What was good enough for Caesar was trifling to Antony.* What did that say about Caesar? I would have dishonored his memory—I, who had promised above all things to revere it. Antony had usurped his place, then trampled on it. And I had allowed it. So they would say.

I reached for the bottle, pried off its lid. *This is the least I can do to make amends,* I thought wildly. *Caesar, forgive me! It is not as the world would think. You know that, but no one else will. There is only one way to stop this dishonor. I will not fail you a second time.*

As I raised the bottle to my mouth and felt the smooth glass rim with my lips, I sensed a presence of something, or someone, nearby. It was enough to make me hesitate. I jerked the bottle away, trembling, and set it down. What was I thinking of? It sat there, gleaming, like the snake's eyes in Meroe, and just as poisonous.

I backed away from it. Why had I not even thought of any counterarguments before starting to down it? It was as if my mind were paralyzed, dumbly obedient to Olympos's suggestions—all rational, all persuasive.

Except . . . they ignored the main fact. Regardless of anything else—Antony's other children, Fulvia, Rome, Octavian, Caesar, bastardy, ridicule—the gods, and Isis, the great mother-goddess, had given me a child. I was its mother, and all the other facts were unimportant beside that one great fact. As Caesarion had brought me joy, so would this one. What happened to their fathers was almost beside the point, or rather, it was a completely different point. One could not cancel out the other.

I fell weeping on the bed, afraid of how near I had come to making what would have been the one mistake—the only mistake—in all this. And it could never have been undone, Olympos's words notwithstanding.

Perhaps it was Isis herself who had come to me.

I jerked off the covering cloths and lay down on the bed. My hands were warm again, and I fell asleep, with deep relief.

I awoke to find Olympos bending over me. He was pointing to the gathered cloth, and stuffed it into his basket. He touched me tenderly and proudly. Then he saw the full bottle on the table. His face changed.

"I see you didn't go through with it," he said sadly.

"I couldn't," I whispered. "I didn't want to."

"You shouldn't have been afraid. I told you—"

"I wasn't afraid," I assured him. "But you see—as hard as it is to explain—I love this child—even though I don't yet know its face or name."

He shook his head. "You are right. You are not able to explain it. Not coherently, anyway." Defeated, he took up the bottle, the basket, and disappeared. It was not yet dawn, and by the time Iras came in and said cheerily, "Good morning!" the whole night seemed a dream.

Perhaps it had been Caesar who had come to me, saying, *Don't protect me at your own cost. I won't allow it.* Or perhaps it was the child itself, calling out to me. Or perhaps it was simply my own good sense. I would never know.

I just lay in bed, feeling weak. Iras was chattering away, talking about the weather and whether it would be warm enough to eat outside on the terrace.

"Iras," I finally said, "I am still tired. I think I will rest a bit longer." I pulled the covers up over my head, shutting out the light.

Days passed. I had no desire to call Olympos back or send for his potion; instead, I felt a great sense of deliverance. I kept imagining how I would have felt, had I taken it. *Tomorrow night all this will be only a memory. It will be past.* I was thankful that what I still had was not a memory, but something still in my future, coming toward me.

There were bits and pieces of news. Antony had reached Tyre. From there he sailed on to Rhodes, then to Ephesus—the Parthians had been stopped east of that. Everything else they held, including Tarsus, so lately Antony's playground. I wondered what had happened to the new gymnasion there, the proud symbol of Greek life. Such odd concerns come to us in the midst of larger ones.

From Ephesus, Antony had sailed on to Athens, where he planned to gather the legions from Macedonia. But they were engaged in fighting off attacks to the north, and so he knew he would have to call on his legions stationed in faraway Gaul, and bring them east. That would take months.

Waiting for Antony in Athens were his general Munatius Plancus, and his other general, his wife Fulvia. I tried to picture the reunion, and failed—probably because I did not wish to see it in my mind. But a long letter arrived from one of Mardian's informants, and he hurried in to show it to me.

"Here, here's news from Athens," he said, thrusting it out at me. "You can trust the writer; he was one of my fellow students here at the palace school, and quite a storyteller."

I took the letter, half reluctantly, and read it. Now that it was here, did I wish to know?

"My most esteemed Mardian, greetings—" and so on; I skipped the personal items.

> The arrival of the Triumvir Antonius has caused a stir here, because all the world waits to see what he will do. We already knew what he has only just now learned: that his fellow Triumvir Octavianus has taken over the legions in Gaul, upon the opportune death of their commander, and Antonius's friend, Calenus. So he has just lost eleven legions, and not to the Parthians. The general Plancus and Fulvia hoped for a better reward for all their efforts on Antonius's behalf. Not only has he not commended them, but he seems (from what we hear) to have blamed them for his troubles.

I put the letter down for a moment. "But it is Octavian who is the cause of his troubles!" I said aloud. Mardian merely raised his eyebrows.

> Sextus has sent representatives, including his own father-in-law, to negotiate with Antonius, offering him an alliance, and lately Antonius's mother has arrived as well, arguing in favor of Sextus. She had taken refuge with him in the latest fighting, which caused much disruption and discontent in Italy.
>
> Antonius refused to consider making the alliance with Sextus, and instead set out for Italy. He had harsh words with his wife, who attempted to upbraid him on account of the scandal he was causing by his liaison with your sovereign mistress, Cleopatra. (And here I must say, Mardian, that it has caused a scandal; there was talk of little else all winter here! The tales we heard of revels night and day, oxen roasting twelve at a time, drinking orgies, some sort of Club of Excess. . . . Your duties must be interesting ones! I should have stayed in Alexandria and made a palace career for myself there; it certainly would have proved more rewarding than what I do now, being librarian for our gymnasiarch.)

I felt my face growing tight, realizing how I furnished a topic of conversation to while away the hours of bored people. A Club of Excess!

Fulvia fell ill on the way to the ships, and the impatient Antonius has left her
behind at Sicyon and gone on with Plancus. Gone where? Sailed west, is all
we know. The problem is that Domitius Ahenobarbus, the lone Republican
admiral, is patrolling the waters between here and Italy. Antonius is heading
right into the teeth of his fleet.

I lowered the paper. That was all there was concerning Antony; the rest
was all personal and local.

"Thank you," I told Mardian. "This is much more informative than official
correspondence." I paused. "So I have caused a scandal?"

"You always do," he said shyly, shrugging. "Even in the days of the Egyptian
Club, remember? That time we ran away . . ." He laughed. "Scandals are just
the earmark of an extraordinary person. What you do is unexpected, and
noteworthy."

"That is a flattering way of putting it, but I shall not argue." And wait
until the next item became apparent, I thought. More for the Athenians to
talk about next winter.

But after he left, gloom settled on me. Antony's situation was grim. How
many legions lost? His own eastern territory had been seized, and now he
was being shut out of the west by the machinations of Octavian.

Egypt should also prepare, in case the Parthians turned their eyes in our
direction. Thanks to the recent good harvest, we had the resources to arm
ourselves, and my new navy was almost ready. Certainly we would put up a
strong resistance; we would not be easily overcome.

Outside, the sun was sparkling on the water. High summer was here, the
time when things happened in the world. Ships sailed, armies marched, messengers galloped where they would. And events gathered force like a coming
storm.

At long last a letter came from Antony himself. It had been sent from Athens,
before he departed, and so the news in it was old. Where was he now? What
had happened since?

My own soul,
Since we parted my thoughts have flown to be with you every day,
but they are deaf and dumb. They cannot speak to you, nor I hear what
they overhear you say. Hence they do little good, except that they are
able to be where I wish to be. O lucky thoughts! How like the drear
time of year it has been to me without you, although all the world would
say it is summer. Perhaps to others it is.
As for what I have found: the Parthians victorious as far west as
Stratonicea. But their advance has been stopped. It is necessary that I
go to Rome, where things are unsettled. I have told Sextus that only if
my solemn pact with Octavian and Lepidus has been irretrievably bro-
ken will I negotiate with him separately. Thus it must be.

I shook my head. He was so stubborn. Even with Octavian taking his legions away, he refused to think ill of him. Or rather, refused to act on what he must sense.

My friend and client Herod has slipped away from Masada and sought out the Nabataeans in Petra for support against the Parthians. He expects to travel to Egypt; please welcome him, and in my name provide him with a ship to come to Rome. He must be restored to the throne of Judaea.

A thousand kisses on your hand, your throat, your lips.

M.A.

I could almost feel them. Smiling, I put the letter into a strongbox for private correspondence. I noted that he had not mentioned Fulvia.

Several weeks passed, with no further news—at least from the outside world. I had taken to swathing myself in voluminous gowns of layers of the lightest silk, proclaiming it a new fashion. I took care to order the gowns and begin wearing them very early, when there was as yet nothing to excite attention. Thus I hoped to keep my condition a secret as long as possible. I made Charmian and Iras wear similar gowns, and soon everyone at court was imitating us. The palace was filled with fluttering human butterflies, long, swirling clouds of color against the white marble. I must say, it was one of the loveliest seasons we had ever had.

Mardian had even let himself try an adaptation of the fashion, using lighter colors and a looser fit in his clothes than usual, and pronounced them very comfortable. As his girth was steadily increasing, this did not surprise me. Tight belts and fitted shoulders must have been torture to him, yet as my head minister he had to dress formally much of the time. Thus he benefited from my condition.

One hot day he came padding into my quarters, his eyes excited. I noted that he had a new type of sandal to go with his clothes—they had a special strap circling the big toe, and another for the rest of the toes. Around the soles, gilded lotuses were painted directly on the leather.

He was waving a letter. "This has just arrived!" he said.

I took it. "It must be good news, from the look on your face," I said. "Pray, pour yourself some of this cool juice; it is a mixture of cherries and tamarind, and quite good." I indicated the pitcher on my table, surrounded with goblets.

He did so, sipping a sample, then refilling his goblet. "Most refreshing," he agreed, nodding. He seated himself expectantly, arranging his gown precisely.

The letter was from the Egyptian envoy at Apollonia, on the west coast of Greece, where the great main road, the Via Egnatia, began. Situated on a narrow strait of the Adriatric, directly across from Italy, it was an excellent listening post for both Greece and Italy.

Most dread and powerful Queen, greetings! Such a sight as we have seen with our own eyes shall never be forgotten, and I shall try to make you see it as well. The fleet, some hundred ships strong, of Ahenobarbus were cruising in our waters. They always excited terror, because they have attacked Brundisium recently, and so we all lined the cliffs watching them with apprehension. From the south we saw other ships approaching, and were told they were those of the Triumvir Antony. Leaving the bulk of his fleet behind, Antony sailed boldly out to meet Ahenobarbus with only five ships, putting himself completely at his mercy if the information he had—namely, that Antony's general Asinius Pollio had negotiated an agreement with Ahenobarbus—was false.

Closer and closer they approached, and Ahenobarbus looked threatening. Only within close range—far too late for Antony to save himself had it been otherwise—did Ahenobarbus turn the rams of his ships away, making the sign of peace. The two fleets united, and sailed off toward Italy together.

What is most remarkable is what the sailors themselves reported: that the general Plancus tried to persuade the Triumvir not to put himself into Ahenobarbus's hands on blind trust, but that Antony replied, "I would rather die by breach of faith than save myself by cowardice."

I stopped reading and tried to picture it. The ships on the sea, making toward one another, with those on land watching . . . the warships turning aside only at the last minute, and Antony doubtless standing on the deck, unflinching.

"How very like him," I said.

"What?" asked Mardian.

"That statement about preferring to die by breach of faith—someone else's breach, that is, not his. Never his." It was both his glory and his folly. Someday it would be his undoing. In that he was like Caesar, only with this difference: Caesar never had any belief in other people's good faith, but only in his own. "And so we are left watching him, still on his way to Italy," I said to Mardian. "The tale is still to tell!" I felt the waiting was killing me.

The next news that came was shocking, even to me, and I prided myself on anticipating the worst behavior to which someone could sink. Octavian, in order to win Sextus to his side, had married Sextus's aunt! She was named Scribonia, was a notorious shrew, and was many years older than Octavian.

I sank down on a stool and began to laugh and cry at the same time. While Antony would give only the strictest, proper response to Sextus's overtures, Octavian was ready to make off with the aunt to disarm Sextus.

"They say she's very tall and bony," said Mardian, shaking his head.

"Well, just because Octavian marries someone does not mean he actually performs his marriage duty," I said, remembering Claudia. "So now he's been married to a child, and to an old lady—for political reasons."

The situation was funny, but his ruthlessness was anything but.

50

Summer continued, the most glorious summer in recent memory; the sea wind was as deliciously cool as alabaster inside a shaded temple, and the sun as beneficent as the gods could make it. Many evenings I invited Olympos's scholar friends from the Museion to come to the palace and—if this is not too inappropriate a word—entertain us. Caesarion was becoming interested in mathematics, and I hoped this would serve as a pleasant way of learning for him. They all were kind to him, never seeming to tire of explaining things. But he was especially taken with the leading astronomer, a young man named Diodorus, who seemed equally at home with older scholars and a seven-year-old boy.

In the evening, near twilight, we would gather in a part of the palace that had rooms especially suitable for our group; its wide windows opened onto the harbor, and the wall paintings repeated the scene, so it looked as if we were surrounded on all sides by open air. The soft breezes entering the room further enhanced that illusion.

At these gatherings we ate very little, but there was plenty of fine wine to be passed around. Olympos accused me of trying to hold a Greek *symposium*, but I pointed out that this did not follow a dinner, that I did not want everyone to get drunk, and that women were present, unlike a true *symposium*.

"You ought to make them drink more deeply," he said. "They would start quarreling over the theories of the circumference of the earth, and whether the equinoxes are precessing, and you would see how petty academics really are. The men you would expect to be the most enlightened are capable of the nastiest fights—worse than gladiators! Men have died defending their theory of the armillary sphere." He laughed lightly.

"Now you are revealing your own deep-seated cynicism," I told him. "Besides, since Antony left, Alexandria has become quite sober." Or at least I had.

"That's because the city is in mourning for his departure," he said. "He and Alexandria made a very good fit."

Antony . . . Alexandria . . . These evenings served to take my mind off the ever-present concern about what was happening in Italy, as well as my own condition. The floating gowns were still an effective disguise, but I had not yet addressed the practical problems awaiting me.

Diodorus announced that he had a demonstration for all of us, but particularly for Caesarion, and it would have to be fully dark to work. "I will show how the earth and the moon both make shadows, cast by the sun, and thereby enable us to measure the size of the earth itself. And I will also show how eclipses happen."

The older men made disparaging noises, but Diodorus held up his hands. "I realize you know all the theories, but can you devise a model to illustrate them? That is what I wish to exhibit." He was a thin little man, who reminded me of a grasshopper—he seemed to jump from place to place, and no sooner land than jump again. He bent down to address Caesarion directly. "I want you to watch carefully," he said.

Then he rushed away to prepare a flare, backed by a sheet of polished metal to serve as a giant mirror, and had servants lower spheres on lines from the ceiling, or suspend them between columns.

"In the meantime, drink, drink, drink!" he said. "It will make it easier to believe the demonstration! You won't notice the flaws, or see the strings."

"Not you," I said to Caesarion, saying no to the wine. "Nor I."

While we were waiting for it to grow fully dark, Diodorus asked me what I was planning for the upcoming solar eclipse.

"I did not know one was coming," I admitted.

"Well!" His chirping voice sounded truly surprised. "You *have* been preoccupied, if you didn't know about the eclipse. It's the most important event in the sky this year."

Yes, preoccupied. What a superficial way to describe what I had been, and still was. "I suppose so," I said. "When is it to come? I have never seen one."

"In fifteen days," he said. "And of course you haven't seen one. There has not been one of this magnitude for fifty years. Oh, it will be an event! The scientists will be standing by to study it. The sky darkens, and the animals think it's night. A hush comes . . . the temperature falls. It's quite dramatic!"

"But how dark does it get?"

"Like night!" he said. Then he admitted, "Of course I have never seen one either, so I have to go by what has been written about it. I can hardly wait to see it!"

An eclipse. What could it mean? I would have to consult the royal astrologers. And doubtless foreign astrologers would make the journey here as well.

He bolted off to light the fire and begin his demonstration.

"Now pretend this fire is the sun, pouring forth its light and heat . . ."

He went on to point out the earth—a wooden ball hanging between two posts—and the moon, and pulled strings to make them pass each other so that one at a time their shadows fell across each other. When the "moon" passed between the "earth" and "sun," it caused a "solar" eclipse, and when the "earth" passed between the "sun" and "moon," its shadow caused a "lunar" eclipse.

"And do you see how the shadow is curved?" His voice rose in excitement. "That is the curvature of the sphere of the earth. Now, by measuring it and figuring out how far away the moon is, we can calculate the size of the earth itself. Do you understand?" He turned suddenly to Caesarion, who was watching all this intently.

"Yes, of course," he said with great dignity. "But the problem would be in calculating exactly how far away the moon is."

Diodorus was surprised at the clear, concise answer. And so was I.

———

That night, as he said good night, Caesarion said, "Perhaps I should be an astronomer. Or a mathematician."

Both of them safe occupations, posing no threat to anyone. "Perhaps," I said. "It depends on what fate calls you to." Certainly he could be King of Egypt as well as a mathematician. No conflict there.

Now that I was alerted, I looked forward eagerly to the day of the eclipse. Each night I watched as the moon grew smaller, waning away like a melting lump of pale wax. A solar eclipse would occur only when the moon was completely dark.

Diodorus had built it up so much that Caesarion could barely sleep, awaiting the great event. Several times he came to my chamber in the middle of the night, saying, "I can't sleep!" Once he said, "Tell me again the story about Artemis and the moon, and how she guides it across the sky! When there's a solar eclipse, does that mean she and Apollo and his chariot of the sun have run into each other? Have they had a crash?" And he would laugh.

I put my arm around him and wrapped a light blanket over his shoulders. "You know that Artemis and Apollo and the sun chariot are just a story," I said. "It's how the poets describe something as beautiful and mysterious as the moon and sun." Since he understood the mathematics of it, he would have to relinquish his belief in the old tales.

"But isn't there really an Apollo?" His voice sounded very small.

"Well, yes . . . but he doesn't actually ride a chariot across the sky with four horses pulling it. He has more to do with creativity—with music and all the bright things of life—of which the sun is only one."

"Oh." He leaned against me, putting his arms around me. "Why have you gotten so fat?" he asked innocently. "I don't see you eating much."

He was the only person allowed to wrap his arms around my waist, and there were no puffy, air-filled gowns to divert his attention. I was taken by surprise, especially since it was the middle of the night. So all I could say was, "Because there's a baby in there."

"There *is?*" His voice rose to a squeak. "Is it a boy or a girl?"

"I don't know," I said. "We will just have to wait to find out."

"When? When?"

"Oh, sometime in the autumn. Are you pleased?"

"Oh yes! Everyone else has a brother or sister. I've always wanted one."

How simple it was for him.

The great eclipse day arrived, and we had a gathering on the highest palace terrace, out in the open, affording the widest view of the horizon. As if to challenge the very idea of any vulnerability, the sun rose hot and yellow, pouring out ferocious light and heat on the sea and land. It burned my arms and made me retire under a canopy. Everyone put on a wide-brimmed hat and had to squint, the light was so fierce. We all felt a little foolish, since we had no proof—besides mathematical calculations—that anything at all would happen. Several astrologers were standing by, ready to interpret the occurrence, consulting with each other, arguing.

"I tell you, the moon is female, and the sun male," said one. "So when the moon blots out the sun, it means a woman is going to rule, or destroy, a man."

"But *what* man, and *what* woman? Is it a prediction for some shoemaker with an overbearing wife? Or does it mean something political?"

"Something political, of course!" the first man snorted. "The heavens do not concern themselves with the events of the lives of common people."

"But everyone has a horoscope," a third astrologer protested. "So the heavens rule everyone's lives."

"But an event of this magnitude—it's to warn us of greater things than a shoemaker and his domestic troubles. The heavens may guide lesser happenings, but they do not trouble themselves to advertise them."

"Well, there are prophecies about a woman of the east ruling Rome," said the middle astrologer.

"Perhaps this confirms it," the third said.

"Or perhaps it's all just a lot of nonsense," said Olympos, speaking directly into my ear.

I turned to him. "Is there anything you believe in?" I asked. I had heard of the prophecies, too, and meant to have them copied out and brought to me. But I would not admit that to him.

"You know well enough what I believe in," he said. "I believe in the strength of the human body, and in its ability to heal itself, given half a chance. I believe in a good night's rest, and the importance of a bath. Oh, and I believe that hot peppers upset the digestion. And I especially believe that listening to all those prophecies is very bad for a person's health. It is apt to lead him astray."

"I don't know," I said. "Think of all the people who have risen higher than they ever would have, because they believed in a prophecy about themselves."

"Doubtless repeated to them every night by their adoring mothers," he said. "Just who are these people? And no cheating with gods and goddesses."

I had to think. "Well, what about Alexander and the oracle at Siwa?"

"He was already a king, already a conqueror. What difference did the oracle make?"

"You are such a scoffer!"

He shook his head and indicated the arguing astrologers. "Someone has to be."

The calculated moment approached, and then passed. It seemed as if nothing had happened. But gradually we perceived a dimming of the light—no, not a dimming. Rather, a peculiar sort of dilution of the light, as if it grew thinner and thinner without actually growing dark. As I looked out on the white stones of the Lighthouse, and to the boats, it was as if I were looking through a veil, but it was so subtle it did not distort the colors. It was the oddest light I had ever seen.

There were still shadows, but although the contrast was sharp, that attenuated light almost seemed to suck away the air we needed to breathe, rarefying everything.

It was not like night, no, nothing like it. And whoever had predicted that had not thought the matter through. The sun continues to light the sky for a while after it descends below the horizon, and it did so all the more now, since it was almost at its zenith. The sky around it stayed blue. It is true that the birds stopped flying, puzzled by the change in light. But the eclipse did not last long enough to let animals creep off to dens and go to sleep.

As gradually as it had crept across the sun, the eclipse passed away. And we were left standing, blinking, in the renewed sunlight, which seemed oddly thick and meaty, robust and yellow.

A few nights later I secreted myself in a private corner, dismissed Charmian and Iras, and pored over the prophecies, which I had obtained quietly. Regardless of Olympos's mockery, I felt that the eclipse was telling me something, if I only had eyes to see. High events of state were taking place now in Rome, there had not been such an eclipse in years—what could be plainer? And it was not an eclipse of the moon, when the earth cast a shadow, but the moon blotting out the sun—of course it pertained to a woman, as the astrologers had stated.

One prophecy, a long prediction from the *Sibylline Leaves*, a collection of eastern verses, might refer to her—to *me*. Especially two of its verses:

> The wealth that Rome as tribute from Asia has taken away,
> Asia shall thrice as much get back from Rome on a future day.
> Insolent Rome shall be judged, Rome to the full shall pay.
> How many Asian folk as slaves in Italy stay.
> There yet shall toil in Asia twenty times as many
> Italians, a host rejected, cast without a penny.

> O Rome, luxurious Rome of gold, you Latin child,
> Virgin drunken with lust in many beds you've run wild,
> but you'll be married without due rites, a slave-slut of despair,
> while still the Queen crops off your delicate head of hair
> and uttering judgments will hurl you to earth from the sky,
> then take up from the earth and set you on high again.

Another of the *Leaves* seemed even more specific:

> And while Rome will be hesitating over
> the conquest of Egypt, then the mighty Queen
> of the Immortal King will appear among men.
> And then the implacable Wrath of the Latin men.
> Three will subdue Rome with a pitiful fate.

Three—the Triumvirate! It seemed glaringly obvious. Egypt, the mighty Queen—me. And the Immortal King must be Caesar, the deified Caesar.

And yet another verse:

> And then the whole wide world under a Woman's hand
> ruled and obeying everywhere shall stand,
> and when the Widow shall queen the whole wide world . . .

The Widow must be me, as Caesar's true widow. Still another went:

> All the confronting stars fall into the sea,
> many new stars arise in turn, and the star
> of radiance named by men the Comet, a sign
> of emerging troubles, of war and of disaster.
> But when the Tenth Generation goes down to Hades,
> there comes a Woman's great power. By her will God
> multiply fine things, when royal dignity
> and crown she takes. A whole year then will be
>   prospering eternity.
> Common for all then is life, and all property.
> Earth will be free for all, unwalled, unfenced,
> and bringing forth more fruits than ever before
> it will yield springs of sweet wine, white milk, and honey.

I felt shaken to read these lines. The Comet . . . Caesar . . . more war and disaster, then a woman ruling. . . .

There were other prophecies, too, one by an oracle called Hystaspes, predicting the violent transfer of power from Rome to a leader of the east. No wonder this was forbidden, upon pain of death, to circulate in Rome! There was a Prophecy of the Mad Praetor, which foretold a mighty Asian army and the enslavement of Rome; a Potter's Oracle, and other sibylline verses.

But the most unmistakable were the verses about the Widow, and the Comet, and the Three, the Triumvirate. The eclipse had given notice: the woman, the widow, was soon to be called to her destiny. My hour had almost come. I had to be ready.

The heavens are kind; they seek to prepare us, if we just hear their messages.

Now another sentence called itself to my attention. As the mighty age is fulfilled, "You shall no longer be the Widow, you shall mate with the lion."

Antony's Hercules, symbol of the lion—Hercules statues always show him draped in a lionskin—was what was meant. The heavens decreed that we be as we had been, and would be again.

Now, as I sit in the state I am in, I wonder why the gods give us a little glimpse of our destiny, if they do not mean to tell it all. Half-truths can be crueler than outright lies. Olympos was right—they lead you astray.

News floated to us in tantalizing pieces, like driftwood coming across the seas. Antony and Ahenobarbus had reached Brundisium, which had closed its gates against them, fortified with one of Octavian's garrisons. Antony cut the town off by constructing walls and ditches, and Octavian began moving troops down to counter him. Antony led a brilliant cavalry maneuver and captured an entire regiment and a half. Octavian called for help from Agrippa, asking him to mobilize the veterans and bring them south. Each saw the other acting as an enemy, and reacted accordingly.

It looked as if all-out war would soon erupt. That was good—good for Antony. The sooner they could grapple and fight, the better. For, as I had told him, Octavian would only grow stronger, unless Antony stopped him.

Then—silence.

Word was brought to me that Herod had arrived on my eastern frontier, at Pelusium. My commander there allowed him to transfer to a ship, and he sailed into my harbor in a ratty old vessel that looked near to sinking.

In preparation for his visit, I had consulted with Epaphroditus, and been reprimanded for my ignorance. I had thought to have a welcome banquet, but Epaphroditus said, "He cannot eat with you, nor can I—as you know."

Yes, I knew that he preferred not to, citing his religion. But I had never pursued the reason why. "I won't serve pork, if that's what you mean!" I said defensively. I knew Jews did not eat pork; neither did Egyptians, for that matter.

Epaphroditus smiled. Over the years he had finally lost his stiff manner around me. "Oh, that's the least of it," he said. "If it were only just pork— or oysters! No, he cannot even sit with you to eat, because of all the regulations about how the vessels must have been cleaned, and what can touch each other, and what foods can be served together."

"What am I to do? Never eat the entire time he is here?" This presented a diplomatic dilemma. I was supposed to honor him, as Antony's friend, but how?

"I can send someone to help plan the menu, but I am afraid you will have to buy all new tableware and have your kitchens purified—er, ritually, I mean." Then he had a thought. "On the other hand, maybe he won't care. He isn't a *real* Jew, you know."

"What do you mean?" This was becoming more and more puzzling.

"His forebears were Idumaeans, and his mother was an—an Arab!" He looked disdainful. "Of course he calls himself a Jew, but I wonder how deep it goes. Politically, he *has* to—I mean, what other constituency does he have? But perhaps it's something he sheds the moment he leaves the country."

"But I won't know that in advance." I sighed. "I have to go on the assumption that he takes it seriously. And change my kitchen!"

"I will sound him out," said Epaphroditus. "Believe me, I can tell. And in the meantime—well, I shall enjoy my first banquet in the palace, after how many years? About seven, I think. High time!"

"Then, dear friend, it is worth it!"

Herod was announced by his aide-de-camp, and assigned to his quarters. I wondered—too late—whether there were also ritual things that should have been done to his apartments to render them suitable. He would present himself in the late afternoon, his aide said.

I was awaiting him on what I always thought of as my "informal" throne; it was a throne, but plain and not much elevated. I wore a gold brocaded coat, the workmanship of his own country, partly out of flattery, and partly because it was stiff and heavy, standing far out from the body and disguising what lay beneath.

Late-afternoon shadows, thrown by the columns, were slanting across the floor when Herod walked in, his white and gold robes shining. He walked beautifully, and there was a smile of such genuineness on his face that no one could disbelieve it.

"Hail, renowned Queen of Egypt." He looked at me, as if he were seeing a blinding sight. "All reports of your beauty fall far short. I am—I am speechless."

And such was his expression, the tone of his voice, that you believed he was absolutely sincere.

"We greet you, Herod of Judaea, and welcome you," I said.

"And the voice to go with the face!" He paused. "Forgive me for my boldness, Majesty."

I already knew I had a pleasing voice; so again, it did not seem like blatant flattery. "Such boldness is easily forgiven," I said. "I am pleased that you have arrived safely. You must tell me of the state of affairs in your country." I stood up and descended from the throne. "Let us walk about the porticoes; you should see the harbor at sunset."

It was possible to walk around the entire periphery of the main palace building, sheltered by colonnaded walks, and see the harbor from all vantage points. As we swept out of the room together—a flock of attendants keeping a discreet distance—I was aware of what a commanding figure he was. Tall, graceful, with the confidence and bearing of the born soldier and ruler. Out of the corner of my eye I assessed his face: he had the Arab beauty of features, the golden skin, dark melting eyes, thin lips, high nose, and thick eyelashes.

"So you are on your way to Rome?" I asked. "You have a long way yet to go."

"It is imperative that I reach the Triumvirs. I escaped from Judaea by the skin of my teeth. I know Antony plans to make war against the Parthians who have overrun my country! I will do anything to help him."

I could not help liking him. "You might perhaps do more good by staying here. I am in need of a good commander of my troops; I too am on alert and arming against the Parthians."

He shook his head, but his demurral was more charming than someone else's assent. "Antony will need me," he said.

"You helped him—and me—once before," I said. "When Gabinius restored my father to the throne."

"Indeed. That is when I first met Antony; I was only sixteen."

"And already commanding troops."

"One comes of age early in Judaea," he said self-effacingly. "But Antony was older then, and I remember how struck he was by you at the time. He commented many times on it."

Now he was beginning to invent freely, I feared. But . . . could it have been true? Antony had alluded to it himself. That is the real power of people who know the tricks of ingratiating themselves; they mix the truth with what serves them best, and they make us *want* to believe it—we do their work for them. We urge them on, asking for more.

"Ah, well, that was long ago." I stopped as we reached the outside, and pointed out the harbor spreading out before us. My pride swelled, as it always did, when I surveyed my jewel, my possession: Alexandria.

"What a sight!" he said.

The sun was burnishing a path across the tossing sea and the calmer, flat waters within the harbor. The sails of the multitude of ships were painted golden red as they rocked at anchor.

"The greatest harbor in the world," he said. "What I would not give for such a harbor in Judaea. All we have is miserable little Joppa. Still," he hastened to say, "it is better than nothing. At least we have an outlet to the sea."

"Every inch of land there is so contested," I observed, more to myself than to him. "How many lives have been lost fighting over Jerusalem? Yet it is not special in terms of architecture, or location, or works of art."

"I will make it so!" he said fiercely. "Provided I am given the chance. The chance that only Antony can grant."

Only Antony. We waited to see what he would do. Herod and I, for different reasons.

"First you must reach Italy. I will provide you with a ship. He is not in Rome, though, but in Brundisium. My news is old, but the last I heard, he and Octavian were facing each other there. By now they are most likely at war."

He groaned. "I flee war in Judaea only to find it in Italy."

"We are not at war here," I reminded him. "Perhaps it would be wiser to wait, stay in Egypt. Command my troops, and when Antony comes east again—"

"No, I must go now. They must not reach any agreement without me!"

As well he knew, his presence could be very persuasive.

Thanks to Epaphroditus, my welcoming banquet was a complete success. The menu omitted all the things hateful to a practitioner of the Jewish religion, and the table was set with newly acquired brightly patterned plates from Rhosus, in Syria—unsullied by forbidden foods.

Herod had changed clothes—for a near-refugee he seemed to have brought an extensive wardrobe—and was now in royal purple, with a diadem. He was a prince, and wanted that made clear. He and his loyal companions were placed in the appropriate places indicating their rank, and acquitted themselves well. They were delightful dinner companions, conversant with all the fashions in poetry and art, dining and entertainment. Politics, being an embarrassment, was not discussed. But Epaphroditus relentlessly attempted to pin him down.

"And so Judaea is still in the grip of the Parthians," he said, shaking his head. "May it soon be liberated." He paused. "And when it is, you must immediately cleanse and restore the Temple!"

Herod turned those liquid eyes on him. "Oh, I plan to do more than that," he said quietly. "It is time that the Temple of Jerusalem be rebuilt in accordance with its importance."

"Its importance?" asked Mardian, frowning. "Forgive me, I don't understand."

"The Temple is holy," said Herod.

"So are all temples," said Mardian, with a forbearing smile. "Our temple to Serapis, for example—"

"The god Serapis did not give explicit instructions for the construction of his temple here," said Herod, his mask of pleasingness starting to slip. "Ours did."

Mardian laughed. "Gods have their ways."

"We believe there is only one god," said Herod. "And he gave us instructions."

"But ours—" an Egyptian started to say, but I stopped him with a look.

"The day after tomorrow is the Sabbath," said Epaphroditus. "Surely you will wish to come with me to the worship at our synagogue—the largest synagogue in the world—since you are so devout."

Herod smiled, and nodded.

"What is a synagogue?" someone farther down the table asked.

Herod stayed in Alexandria for twenty days, fending off Epaphroditus's attempts to force him to take a stand one way or another—to declare himself a true Jew or not. I sensed in him the conflict between a person who is born, or called to, a particular allegiance, only to find it blocking his ambition. There is nothing more wrenching. Only a very few find glory in being martyrs—Cato for the Republic, Spartacus for slaves, the Israelite prophets for their god. All others long to fulfill their talents, their destinies; they do not easily sacrifice them on an altar, slaying them like a placid white bull. In that, Herod was only human.

In the end, he sailed away in a ship I provided, tracking westward into the setting sun, seeking Italy. What he would find there we could not guess. And

I was back to waiting, waiting, waiting, for the outcome, which affected me as much as Herod.

"I don't want to be cruel, but you are simply *enormous!*" Olympos blurted out when he came to see me about a month after Herod's departure. His face, usually so guarded, registered dismay and bafflement.

"Dear old Olympos," I said. "Always so tactful! So diplomatic! So thoughtful!" His words were wounding. I *knew* I was big. The gowns, and even the brocade coat, no longer served.

"Are you absolutely sure about the—the timing?" he asked cautiously.

"Well, I know a date it could not be before," I said. "And that is the one I chose."

He shook his head. "Please—may I?" He reached out his hand toward my belly.

"Oh, go ahead," I said. "And you might as well feel it directly. Be my physician today instead of my companion."

He poked and jabbed with both hands, right on my bare flesh, after discreetly unfastening the front panel—lately added—of my gown. He frowned as he did so, until gradually enlightenment came to him.

"Ah," he said, finally. He took his hands away.

"Well, what?" I demanded.

"Medically this is a relief," he began. "But—"

"Just tell me!" I barked.

"I think there are two of them in there," he said.

"What?"

"Twins," he said. "Two. You know, like Apollo and Artemis."

"I know who Apollo and Artemis are, you fool!"

He grinned. "Yes, of course. But are you prepared to be Latona?"

"To wander about, forsaken and persecuted?"

"You won't have to wander, and you won't be persecuted, but forsaken—I must reserve judgment on that."

"Sometimes I hate you!" I said.

"Yes, when I say things you don't want to hear," he said lightly. "I'd be thinking about two names, if I were you." He got up, his eyes dancing. "Ah, what a man is Marc Antony!"

"Go away!" I hurled a pot of ointment at him.

He dodged it and ran out, laughing.

After he left, I put my hands carefully on the great bulge in my front. There did seem to be an inordinate amount of movement in there—more likely from eight hands and feet than only four.

Two. The names were the least of my problems.

51

"Marc Antony is married," said the sailor, who had been hustled into the palace by Mardian. He stood before me smiling, his cap in hand.

"Yes, I know he is married," I said patiently. What was this? "What news is this? I want true news—of the war."

The man kept smiling. "Then, what I meant is—forgive me, Majesty—he is remarried. And there is no war."

"What are you talking about?" Why could he not speak clearly? Mardian was leaning up against the wall, his arms crossed, frowning.

"I mean to say that the Triumvir was briefly a widower. Fulvia died, and then—"

Fulvia. Died? He had been freed from her?

"—he has married Octavia. In Rome."

"What?"

"The Triumvir Octavian's sister. They have married. There was much rejoicing, as war was averted. Vergil has written a masterful poem celebrating it—saluting a new golden age of peace. Would you like to hear it?" he asked brightly. He started digging in his purse for a copy of it.

"He has married Octavia? He was free to marry, and he chose her?"

"Yes, Your Majesty." He quit looking for the poem.

"When did Fulvia die?" I asked stupidly. It seemed very important to establish that fact.

"After he left her behind in Greece."

"I see." The room seemed to spin, to change into something else, but still I stood there staring at him. Then I asked, but more to fill up the space than anything else, for I knew I would not remember, but have to be told again later, "Why no war?"

"The truth is, the veterans would not allow it. The two armies had fought side by side at Philippi only eighteen months ago, and had no wish to be enemies. They are weary of war—the whole world is weary of war. That is why Vergil wrote about the golden age. All Rome has gone mad with the celebrations! Our ship could barely sail, we had so much trouble moving the cargo to the docks through all the crowds. The agreement was sealed by the marriage, so that now Antony and Octavian are brothers!"

"When did you leave Rome?" I asked. Again, it seemed very important to establish this.

"Less than half a month ago. We had very favorable winds. All of nature is basking in the accord."

Doubtless, I thought. All of nature—all the spheres of heaven—must celebrate this union. "Here," I said, nodding to Mardian. "He will give you something to help you join this jubilation. Oh, and leave the poem here. We would like to read it at our leisure."

The man succeeded in finding it, crumpled and stained, and handed it to Mardian, who escorted him out.

Where could I go, to be alone? Everywhere I looked, there was someone who loved me and knew too much. And as Queen, I could not lose myself in nameless crowds. I was trapped where my grief and humiliation must be seen by others.

Mardian reentered the room, and found me still standing, staring almost sightlessly out toward the harbor. There was no place to hide from the scrutiny of his eyes and his unspoken dismay and pity.

"I am sorry," he said quietly. "When I heard a ship had arrived from Rome, I thought only that you would wish to be informed about the war. I did not know."

"Oh, Mardian." I closed my eyes and rested my head on his shoulder. "Why does it hurt so much?" I asked, stupidly puzzled. I thought I was past ever being able to be wounded deeply again, down to my very core. I thought the funeral pyre in the Forum had burned away all of that in me, leaving me protected from such sudden turns of fate.

He was wise enough not to answer, just to embrace me.

He sent away all the attendants and let me be alone in my chambers. I lay down for a long time, just staring blindly, my thoughts mercifully paralyzed. Far below I could hear the sound of the waves, beating rhythmically against the seawalls. Back and forth, back and forth . . .

Then, little by little, the thoughts crept back in, gathering speed, starting to race to catch up with the turbulent feelings.

There was no war. They had laid down their arms and reconciled, and Octavian had presented his sister Octavia as a peace bond.

He likes to cement treaties by personal ties. He asked to marry into my family, when we became Triumvirs together.

And Octavian, having just married himself off elsewhere, was no longer available. Therefore it had to be Antony.

And here's my sister, in good faith, he probably said.

And why, Antony, did you not say no? What matter what Octavian had said, as long as you had the word *no* at your command?

He was free, unmarried, and he chose to marry Octavia.

What did she even look like? I tried to recall, from my few meetings with her in Rome. She was older than Octavian, but not by much. I thought she was married. What had happened to her husband? Not that that was much of a problem in Rome. She had probably obediently divorced him in order to please Octavian. As Antony might well have done to Fulvia, to please Octavian—rather than to please me. How convenient that she had died instead.

What was Octavia like? My memories of her were hazy. Ironically, she could not have been as fair of face as her brother, or I would remember. What had she said, how had she behaved at the dinners? I had been so preoccupied with Caesar and the other strong presences there, like Brutus and even Calpurnia, that I had paid her scant attention. Had she been unpleasant or ugly, I would have remembered that, too. I had to conclude that she was in between, neither memorable nor outstanding.

And now she was to be his wife. . . . No, she *was* his wife!

Mardian had left the poem lying on a table. I forced myself to read it. Evidently copies of it had been circulated around Rome and this sailor had pocketed one. Oh yes, it was to be a public rejoicing!

> Now the last age of Cumae's prophecy has come;
> The great succession of centuries is born afresh.
> Now too returns the Virgin; Saturn's rule returns;
> A new begetting now descends from heaven's height.
> O chaste Lucina, look with blessing on the boy
> Whose birth will end the iron race at last and raise
> A golden through the world: now your Apollo rules.

I felt strong, refreshing anger start to pour through me. A stupid prophesy!

> But first, as little gifts for you, child, Earth untilled
> Will pour the straying ivy rife, and baccaris,
> And colocasia mixing with acanthus' smile.
> She-goats unshepherded will bring home udders plumped—

What an insipid bunch of tripe! What about the *real* prophesy, the one about the Widow and Rome? That one had some bite in it! What was this imitation thing that Vergil had made up?

> Begin, small boy, to know your mother with a smile
> (Ten lunar months have brought your mother long discomfort)
> Begin, small boy: he who for parent has not smiled
> No god invites to table nor goddess to bed.

Well, I knew all about ten lunar months of discomfort! To hell with Vergil and his prophesy! I cursed it. It would never come true, never! Let her be barren, or bring forth only girls! Isis was stronger than Vergil.

But that night, as I slept, the most horrible image came to me, so real that I felt I had flown to Rome and beheld it myself.

There was a cavernous room—no, it was a temple of some sort, all the walls and floors of black polished marble. Two bronze lamp stands flanked an altar that was elevated on a podium of some five or six steps. The altar was black marble, too, and on it lay—Octavia.

Now I could see her clearly, all the features that had eluded me earlier coming into sharp focus. She had rich brown hair, luminous dark eyes, a pleasing but bland face. The flickering of the two tall lamps lit her nose, her cheeks, the long hair, the white gown, and reflected off all the polished stone.

She was waiting there, still, barely breathing, her bare feet exposed, her ankles tied.

Then I saw Antony, but only from the back. He was ascending the steps of the altar, slowly and ritualistically, like a priest, wearing some sort of religious tunic, carrying a knife.

He reached down and cut the bindings of her ankles, freeing her legs, and then I saw that her wrists had been bound also, and he cut those ties as well.

Then he was standing over the altar, bending over it, then—again in a slow, ritualistic way—he climbed on it, climbed on top of her. I could see her pale limbs raised on each side of him, see his shoulders straining. . . .

And thus they became man and wife.

A new begetting now descends from heaven's height.

I woke up drenched in sweat, my heart pounding. I felt sick at my stomach. It was only a dream, only a dream. . . . Over and over I repeated that, until the ghastly details began to fade a little. It wasn't like that at all. It couldn't have been.

Well, what do you think it was like, then? I couldn't keep the thought away. I remembered so well what he was like. Now she would have all those things—his kisses, his hands on her face, even the heavy weight of him upon her.

Oh, let me forget! Why did I have to picture things so vividly? It was a curse, to have such an imagination. Let it die, along with my love for him.

My worse-than-sleepless night left me shaken and exhausted, the worst possible combination with which to face what now rushed upon me. Without the restoration of a normal night's rest, by late the next night I was in full, hard labor.

It had no gentle onset, but hit me as unexpectedly as the sailor's news. The servants rushed about to prepare the birth room and fetch the midwives, but everyone was darting about in confusion.

The pain was crippling. I could barely stand up to be guided into the room where the birth was to take place. I remember leaning on two midwives and almost dragging them down. My legs would not obey, and each movement of them sent spirals of pain shooting down to my feet. They put me on the special stool that was used only for this purpose, with a sturdy back and very low legs; the entire thing was draped in sheets. I reclined on it, gripping the sides, almost blinded by the pains that kept coming at such a fast rate they were all blurring into one.

In times like that, each instant seems like forever, and hours can be condensed into minutes. I have no idea how long I remained like that, but I heard one of the midwives saying, "Her color is bad, and besides—"

Someone else said something I could not hear, and then, "Send for Olympos! Now!"

The room seemed to grow dark, and I heard Olympos's voice saying, "Has she taken anything?" and then, "If not—"

I was being lifted, transferred to someplace hard where I lay flat on my back. They brought my arms out to my sides and held them firmly. I felt hands pressing on my abdomen, pushing down on it, and heard someone cry, "Blood! Blood!" with panic in her voice.

"Pull!" someone said.

"I can't." Another voice. "It is turned the wrong way."

"Then twist it around!" That was Olympos. "Twist it!"

Now I could feel something warm and sticky spreading out underneath me, under my back. Blood. I turned my head to see it dripping off the table and forming a pool underneath. It looked very thick and very red. It smelled metallic and ugly.

The room was turning very slowly, revolving around some axis. I could feel the black edges of unconsciousness lapping around me.

"O ye gods!" There was a horrifying wrench, and I felt as if my insides were being dragged out. "There it is!"

There was a thin, coughing cry, and I heard someone say, "A girl."

The pain did not cease then, but intensified. More gushes of the hot, sticky blood, soaking even the back of my head now. And shrieks from the attendants, wails.

"It's stuck. The second one, it's stuck."

"In the name of the gods, do something!"

"I can't—"

There was a flutter of voices, faces hovering over me. But I could hardly see. The blackness was growing.

Yanks and pulls, and frantic beating on my belly, which shook my grip on consciousness still further.

"We're losing her!" I heard the words, faintly, and looked up to see Olympos watching me, his face twisted, openly weeping.

"Stop the bleeding! Stop it, in the name of all the gods!" someone cried.

"I can't!" Another voice, a woman's.

"Then pull it hard, now!" Olympos shouted. "Or, here—"

"But how—" a faint voice at my feet asked.

I pulled in one ragged breath after another, gasping.

"Grab it! Turn it!" Olympos said savagely. "Like this!" There was a ripping, and torrents of blood gushed out, surging like a sea wave, engulfing me, even wetting my ears where I lay on my back.

"Got him." Those were the last words I heard.

When I awoke, I was so bandaged and aching I could not move. Every muscle, every sliver of me, was bruised and torn—or so it felt.

The sunlight was pouring in. Obviously it was the next day. Or the next. Or maybe even the next. I felt the throbbing in my breasts; they were all swollen with milk. It must have been two or three days, then.

For a few moments I kept my eyes half shut, watching to see who was there. Two midwives were sitting by a table, and one of them was holding a baby. I felt a cold jolt of fear. Where was the other one?

"She's awake!" One of the women noticed me and was instantly at my side.

I attempted to smile. "And alive, too," I said. My voice sounded very weak and small.

"Here's your daughter." The other attendant brought the baby over to me, placed her in my arms. It hurt to hold her.

Her little face slept serenely. Clearly the experience had not disturbed her much.

"And the other?" I asked.

"We'll bring him," she said. "Tell them the Queen is awake."

In only a moment someone appeared, bearing a second bundle, and placed him in my other arm. That hurt, too.

He was awake, and staring at me with bright blue eyes. Miracle of miracles, he was unharmed, too.

"Thanks be to Isis," I murmured, touching his mouth.

Olympos came hurrying in on the heels of the attendant. I was touched; he had obviously been waiting in the next room for however long it had been. He looked dreadful, as if he had been through the ordeal too. "Thanks to all the gods!" he murmured, taking my hand. "I will never ask them for anything again."

"Now don't be too hasty," I said, but it took all my strength to do so. "You are too young yet never to need the help of the gods again."

"I thought you were going to die," he said simply.

"I know," I said. "I heard you." And saw you cry, too, I remembered.

"If you had, I would have gone personally to Marc Antony and killed him," he said, and I knew he meant it. Then, embarrassed, he hurried on, "The babies were born a little early; they were small. And a good thing, too, for had they been any bigger, none of you would be here."

I winced. "Bigger I don't want to think about," I said, attempting to laugh. That hurt, too. "Will I ever recover?" I asked. I felt I never would be free of pain again.

"Oh, in a year or two," he said, lightly, the old Olympus trying to cover up the one that had revealed himself briefly just now, and in the birth room.

In addition to the battering I had taken, I was weak from the loss of blood. When I first saw myself in a mirror, I was astonished at how white I looked. Olympos plied me with red wine, which he swore built up the blood again, along with an infusion of steeped chervil. He also said I should nurse the babies myself instead of employing a wet nurse, as it helped in recovery, and since there were two of them, I would recover twice as fast. And the babies would grow faster, making up for their small size at birth.

I did not need any urging, for I loved holding the babies, and this meant hours when I could do only that. I was still too debilitated to take on arduous public appearances, and I was not anxious to conduct outside business, so it did not interfere with my duties.

They were both, of course, beautiful babies—as any mother always feels. Both of them had light hair, and the boy kept his blue eyes, whereas the girl's turned a greenish brown. Day after day I watched their faces, their delicate puckered mouths and uncurling fingers, watched them fall asleep in contentment as I held them. Day after day I felt them grow heavier.

What was I to name them? This time there would be no Roman heritage in their names; I refused to include Antony in them—Antony, who had rejected marriage with me as a non-Roman, while rushing into one he considered appropriate as soon as his feet touched Roman soil! Well, now he could do without his children, at least legally. I was eastern, too eastern for him? Then so would my children be. I named the boy Alexander Helios. Alexander after the obvious patron, and Helios after the sun god. First, because Alexander had been associated with the sun god, and his statues often depicted him as resembling Helios; second, because he was born in the year of the solar eclipse; and last, because he was a twin, like Apollo the sun god, and also to remind Vergil and his like that they did not own Apollo, however much Octavian liked to claim him as his patron deity. Perhaps *my* son would be the Apollo they predicted for their golden age.

And my daughter? Cleopatra Selene. Cleopatra after not only me but the many other Cleopatras in my lineage, going all the way back to the great Alexander, whose sister had been named Cleopatra. And further back even than that, there was a Cleopatra in the *Iliad*. Greek connotations—Greek, not Roman! And Selene, meaning "moon." Again, for the eclipse, and also for the twin Artemis.

And so I watched my baby Sun and Moon and asked Isis to make them the bringers of the golden age, or the children of destiny we had in our own, older, *genuine* prophecies, as opposed to that trumped-up mockery of Vergil's!

I was still holding them after a feeding, when a messenger was announced. I thought it of little account, and did not even hand the babies to their nurses, but just gave orders that he should be admitted right away.

I was taken aback when an official Roman courier stepped into the chamber, in full regalia, his breastplate gleaming, the brush on his helmet stiff and thick.

"I bring greetings from Rome, most imperial Majesty," he said in a booming voice. Or maybe it wasn't really booming, but only sounded that way after the cloistered life I had been leading in the nursery.

I just stared at him and nodded. "Welcome," I finally said.

"I bring a letter from Marcus Antonius, Triumvir," he said, thrusting it out. It was encased in a metal and leather cylinder. Very fine; oh, very fine indeed.

I took it, opened it, and read.

So. I held it in my hand, Antony's account of Brundisium, his proud recounting of the agreements—agreements, I could see instantly, that increased Octavian's power at the expense of Antony's. So he had handed over the Gallic legions! Lost the west entirely, without even a fight! And the offhanded announcement of the wedding, couched in official language, referring to himself almost as if he were another person! And calling Octavian "Caesar"—to me! I was trembling with rage.

The Roman was standing, smiling, waiting for me to utter some bland inanity. One of the babies squirmed in the crook of my elbow.

"I thank you for your speedy voyage to bring me these tidings," I said. Undoubtedly Antony had ordered the swiftest ship to announce his doings. But he had reckoned without the chance arrival of another messenger first. So it often happens.

"You may tell the Triumvir Marcus Antonius that I have received his news, and that I congratulate him on his marriage. You may also tell him that I have just borne him two children—a son and a daughter." I spread my arms and held them out for him to see.

The man simply blinked in shock. There was no official protocol for responding to such an announcement. Finally he said, "Have you no—no letter you wish to send? I can wait, as long as you would wish."

I drew myself up. "No. No letter. Merely the two sentences, which surely you can remember. They are not too taxing."

The seas would soon be closing for winter; already the waves were rising and storms had started. But just before they did, another ship arrived from Rome, having set sail at the last safe moment. It brought a letter from Antony, and this time I read it in private. It was wild and all but tear-stained. I could picture him sitting up late at night, indulging in wine and memories while he wrote it, then sending it off without rereading it.

> *My dearest, my love, how can you have done this to me? The messenger told me—he saw you—that we have children. How could you have kept it from me, let me go without knowing? If only I had known— then I could never have made this marriage I was forced into, I would have had an excuse to refuse—you have undone me! Why have you betrayed me? If you loved me at all, it would not have been possible—*
>
> *I have been in hell ever since I left—I can trust no one, now, not even you. They say peace has come because of the pact. Achieved at such a cost—so high.*
>
> *I spend the winter here in Rome. There have been food riots here, and Octavian has been attacked and would have been killed by a mob at the races, had I not intervened. Much remains to be done.*
>
> *What have you named them? Teach them about me, their father.*
>
> *Do not forget me—pray for me, hold me in your heart, as I hold you.*
>
> —I send this posthaste.

It almost made me feel sorry for him—as he meant it to. But what kind of a man was he, that he needed an "excuse" to refuse Octavia, and marry me! He shouldn't need an excuse, and if he did, a pregnancy was not a proper one for the Triumvir—perhaps for some shepherd or schoolmaster, but not for the lord of half the world! And what did he mean, I had betrayed *him*? He was the one who had chosen Octavian, and Octavia, over me. What a pity he couldn't trust anyone! How sad! Well, I had told him that, and told him to beware of Octavian! And yet he continued to rescue him. Why didn't he let the mob put an end to him once and for all?

And as for the children—I didn't know what I would teach them about Antony. It was much easier for Caesarion, his father being dead, and declared a god. The living Antony was a delicate matter. And anyway, the children were a long way away from being taught anything. First they would have to learn to talk.

52

During those weeks when we were cut off from the rest of the world, I had many long hours to think—to think, and to recuperate. Gradually I grew thin while the babies grew big, as if a very source of being were transferred from me to them. My strength returned; even my pain disappeared.

"Youth is a marvelous healer," said Olympos after he pronounced me completely recovered.

"No, I think it was your skill," I said. "After all, plenty of young people die." It occurred to me that the two people who know you best in the world are your physician—who knows all the particulars of your body—and your financial advisor, who knows all the secrets of your bank account. Between them, they have the whole picture.

"Luck played a part in it," he said. "And your basic strength. You are a tough warrior crocodile."

Antony had called me that, too. How strange. "Antony called me a crocodile as well," I said. "I don't think it's a compliment."

He frowned, as he always did, at least in passing, when Antony was mentioned. Which was too bad, since I had a mission for him that involved Antony. "The crocodile has many admirable qualities—I meant it that way. It's very hard to conquer a crocodile, and they can live under conditions that would kill most other animals. An enviable trait," insisted Olympos.

"Indeed." I waited a moment to broach the main subject. This was not going to be easy. "Olympos, your knowledge of wounds and healing is remarkable—for a Greek."

Now his eyebrows shot up. He looked wary, like a gazelle that suspects a lion might be nearby. "For a Greek?"

"Of course the medical training here at the Museion is still foremost in the world," I said. "You are the heirs of the great Herophilus and his anatomy studies; and the operations for stones and abscesses were great advances in their day. The theories, the theories were ingenious! Praxagoras and his hypothesis about the blood vessels! Dioscorides' idea about the plague—intriguing! But—"

"But what?" Now he looked truly on guard.

"But those ideas are just theories. I think, now that I have recovered, you should go to Rome to study," I said.

"I knew it!" He shook his head. "And why, pray tell, should I go to Rome? Other than to spy on Antony?"

I ignored the last question. "Because I prize your talent for healing. But time has marched on; there are new techniques in the world of medicine—"

"Of which you are well apprised, being a physician yourself," he said with a snort.

"I know that the Romans have learned a great deal about treating wounds and lacerations—they have practical knowledge, not just theories. That's because they've fought so many wars in the past hundred years—they've had a lot of soldiers to practice on! Oh, Olympos, don't be such a snob. Greeks *can* learn some things from Romans."

"As you have?"

I let that barb pass. "I have heard they know how to operate on eyes to remove cataracts, and that they can sew up wounds so they won't fester. And that they have invented instruments that clamp blood vessels, and others that hold wounds open so that arrows can be extracted—"

"Of course I know that," he snapped. "Do you think I don't keep up?"

"But wouldn't you like to go and learn about them firsthand? Or is your prejudice against the Romans so strong that it even compromises your work?"

Now he looked embarrassed. "It would take too long—I have duties here—"

"You have some very able assistants and students. And you needn't be gone longer than half a year. When the seas open again in March, you could go. Stay until autumn. You can learn a lot in six months! And I won't get into trouble while you're gone—nothing that your assistant can't manage."

"I know you," he said. "You can get into a lot of trouble in six months."

"Well, I promise I won't."

He looked halfway pleased. Perhaps he really needed a change; and his innate curiosity would enjoy the challenge of a new discipline.

Now that I had his cooperation, it was time for the next part. "And, yes, there is some personal business I'd like—"

"No, I won't go to Antony. You know I hate the man."

His flat statement took me by surprise. I did not know what to say—certainly I couldn't defend Antony to him. After all, there were times when I hated him myself. Finally I said, "I don't expect you to meet with him. But I want you to take along one of my astrologers—someone Antony has never seen, who will find a way to attach himself to Antony's entourage."

Olympos groaned. "So I am to accompany a spy of yours to Rome? You want to put eyes and ears in Antony's household?"

"No," I said. "I don't care about his eyes and ears. What I want to use is his mouth. I want him to advise Antony to get out of Rome."

"Why? Why should he leave Rome? So he can come back here?"

"No. I don't expect him to come back here. I don't want him to come back here." Not as Octavia's husband and Octavian's obedient servant, I thought.

"I find that hard to believe."

"Nevertheless, it's true. But he should get out of Octavian's shadow. He cannot even think clearly around him—it's as if Octavian corrupts and disables his very mind!"

"I told you long ago, he takes on the strongest nature that's nearest him. That's why he's unreliable. I warned you."

"You were right—he does. And that's why he must put distance between himself and Octavian."

"Again, why?"

"I want him to stand clear, on his own!"

"You haven't answered my question." Olympos was relentless. "Why should it matter to you?"

He was determined to make me say, *Because I love him. Because I don't want him to go down to ruin.* But I only said, "Because Antony's task is to administer the east and conquer the Parthians. If he dallies too long in Rome, he will lose his chance. And that would be bad for all of us in the east."

Olympos grunted. "And I suppose you want me to write you long reports about Rome and the gossip there," he said.

"Yes, of course," I answered. "It has been five years since I left. Many things will have changed. I am curious. Indulge me. After all, I will pay for your journey and lodgings—and I hope you will avail yourself of the best."

I knew that was irresistible bait for him. He was one of those thrifty people with secret longings to be profligate. Doing it at someone else's expense should satisfy both needs.

My dear friend and Queen:

After a ghastly ocean voyage, and an equally unpleasant stint up the Tiber on a smaller boat, and then being almost choked to death by the foul odors on the docks, I can attest that we are indeed in Rome. Never have I appreciated Alexandria more, now that I have seen Rome!

I have acquired quite luxurious quarters—remember, you told me to—but one of the horrors of Rome is that poor and rich dwell side by side, so just next door to me is a squalid apartment building filled with the most unsavory inhabitants. Undoubtedly there would be an opportunity to practice a great deal of unusual medicine there, but no, thanks! *I am not interested in contracting skin lesions and lice in the process.*

Through inquiries at the hospital of Asclepius on Tiber Island, I have been introduced to a retired army surgeon who is the grand master of the new science—everyone who is anyone in that discipline seems to have trained under him. He has been most gracious in taking me on, and translates Latin into Greek with nary a complaint. So I must thank you for urging me to come—even if I was merely an appendage to your plots and plans.

And as for that, I can report that Hunefer has departed into Antony's household to do your bidding. It all came about very naturally, as the Egyptians in the city congregate near the vegetable market and exchange information about positions in Roman households. As an Alexandrian-trained astrologer he had no difficulty in insinuating himself into Antony's. There he will disseminate your advice into Antony's ear.

I have been here long enough to have learned that Antony's fathering of your children has caused him great embarrassment in Rome, and that Octavian is said to be positively apoplectic about it. Perhaps to make up for it, Octavia is reported to be pregnant.

Farewell for now, and do not neglect your chervil drink. Keep building up your blood.

—Your servant and friend, Olympos

Octavia pregnant! That horrible dream—there must have been truth in it! I felt anger start to course through my veins, anger that was not even rational. I had *known* they were married; I knew what married people did; I was almost angry at myself for being angry.

I put the letter down. So Olympos had arrived, and was putting the time to good use. What more did I want?

And our children had caused Antony awkward moments in Rome? Good. Let Octavian stew on that—let him think on it, just as I was tormented by the dream.

My nature was at least as strong as Octavian's. May the best man win.

My Queenly patron:
Greetings from one who is becoming expert at everything from sewing small eyelid wounds using women's hair, to the other end of the scale, tying off blood vessels of amputated limbs. I am also learning a method of repairing a large gap in the skin, like that caused by an ulcer, by cutting two flaps on either side, then drawing them together overhead. But I will not trouble you with the descriptions of these wounds, as they are generally repulsive. I know you prefer to dwell on more alluring aspects of the senses.

The great stir here is that Octavian and Antony have made peace with Sextus, concluding a treaty with him at Misenum. I doubt that it can last. They have only just finished edging Lepidus to the verge of retirement, and are unlikely to want him replaced in the share of power. But for now the grain is flowing back into Rome again, and this eases the discontent with Octavian. People's memories are very short—as short as their last meal, for the most part.

Octavian and Antony have been busy seeing to their marital obligations. It is true about Octavia's pregnancy, and now it seems Scribonia is expecting as well—at about the same time. Ah, what a fervid night it must have been in Rome a little while ago. The same constellations must have been hovering over the bedrooms, giving the offspring the same horoscope. The future should be interesting.

Speaking of horoscopes, Hunefer reports that Antony consults him regularly. It seems that whenever Antony rolls dice or bets against his dear brother-in-law, Octavian always wins. Hunefer has used this opportunity to tell him that his noble spirit will always be vanquished by Octavian's superior luck, and therefore he should keep far away from him. So the poison—pardon me, the suggestion—is being poured into

Antony's ear. Look for him in our part of the world again soon. Antony has already dispatched general Bassus into Syria to give the Parthians a preliminary thrashing.

Pat the babies on the head for me, and give Mardian a cuff if he persists in eating the custards I warned him of. He has gotten entirely too fat, and you can tell him so from me. I told him myself before I left.

Keep yourself well, and do not let your thoughts be troubled.

—Your entirely loyal Olympos

I was keeping myself well, but as for not letting my thoughts be troubled—that was not so easy. I was restless and discontented, unreconciled to the present state of things with no clear view of what I preferred instead. I was envious of Antony—envious because he had everything. He could have as much lovemaking as he liked, and all with the world's approval—it was even for the greater good of Rome! He had lands to conquer, a campaign to conduct in Parthia.

I should have been happy to be spared all that, I should have rejoiced in the peace my country enjoyed, its prosperity, my healthy children, my own quiet life. I did. But there was that in me that would almost have preferred the problems facing Antony. I did not like sitting still; at heart I was a warrior, too.

Dearest Queen Cleopatra,

Forgive me if I write just this short letter, but I feel you must know what Antony is saying, since it concerns you. As I told you earlier, Octavian was offended about the children you bore Antony—now his beloved brother-in-law—and made no secret about it. Evidently lately, at a banquet where the two men were feasting envoys from Cyprus and Crete—and with their pregnant wives at their sides—Octavian made a remark about it, to the effect that it was disgraceful that Antony should have been so careless and allowed such a thing. Then (so my informants told me, as I assure you I was not present) Antony put down his goblet and said in a ringing voice, "The way to spread noble blood through the world is to beget everywhere a new line of kings. My own ancestor was got by Hercules in this manner. Hercules didn't limit his hopes of progeny to a single womb. He didn't fear any Solonian laws against fornication and adultery. He didn't fear the audits of his copulations. He freely let nature have its way and founded as many families as he could."

I was ashamed for you when I heard it. I knew I must tell you immediately. When I think what you suffered as a result of his Herculean imitation—! No one who had witnessed what I did would have spoken thus. It is good I was not there, or—by Zeus—he would not still be walking this earth. I may not be as good a swordsman as he, but there are many other ways to die. You remember my garden.

Was this the same Antony who had sworn eternal love, and written the distraught letter? There he was, trying to please Octavian again. *He takes on the strongest nature that's nearest him.* His words dismissed me as nothing but a breeder, a field to be sown by his Dionysian seed. Of course, that was to please the two Octs—Octavian and Octavia.

I had never answered the letter from Antony. Was this his revenge?

But I knew Antony was not a vengeful man. If anything, he was the opposite.

He had to part from Octavian soon! His wits and judgment were being subverted. But of course, wherever he went he would take along a piece of Octavian. I had planted an astrologer in his household, but Octavian had done better than that; he had put a partisan in his very bed—Octavian's loyal and obedient sister.

Octavian. The world was not large enough to encompass us both. Nor could we share Antony.

My eyes strayed to the corner of the chamber, where a spear and a helmet of Antony's leaned against the wall. They were articles we had exchanged when we dressed in fantasy. He had forgotten them, left them behind when he sailed off for Tyre. They had served as a visible reminder of him, and I thought to present them to Alexander someday as a legacy from his father, just as I would give Caesarion the pendant from his.

Now they just looked dusty and forsaken. He had not missed them; or if he had, he was too proud to ask for them to be returned. I walked over to them and touched them. Is there anything more out of place than the trappings of battle in a peacetime chamber? I should put them away.

Oh, Antony. I would rather be the one to go than the one to stay behind—like these castoff weapons, I thought.

I would rule alone. It was my allotted fate. With one hand I touched again the spear, with the other I touched the pendant, which I had put back on again: remnants of the men who had given me my heirs.

Dearest Queen,

Let me be the one to announce to you that Octavia's child has been born, and it is a daughter. So much for the Golden Age son, the Roman messiah. That for Vergil.

Scribonia will follow suit shortly. But they say Octavian means to divorce her. That can mean only one thing: he is ready to launch his war against Sextus, in spite of the treaty. Of course I never doubted it. Treaties serve Octavian only as a means of delay while he prepares himself to break them.

Oh, and Herod has arrived in Rome. He was warmly welcomed by both men, and elevated to King of Judaea, promoted from merely governor of Galilee. Now remains the small matter of clearing the Parthians out of Herod's kingdom for him, so he can ascend his throne.

To continue—twenty days later:

Scribonia has presented Octavian with a daughter. (You see, I told you they would have the same horoscope.) And the very next day he divorced her! Such a kind, thoughtful man! And now he is marrying again—whom? Prepare yourself. She herself is married, and her obliging husband is divorcing her and giving her away, although she has yet to deliver their child. I find this monstrous. I really cannot stomach Rome much longer. Antony is transferring his headquarters to Athens shortly, and I will make the journey on the same ship. I have long wanted to spend time in Athens, and from there I can cross back to Egypt easily.

I meant to tell more of Octavian's bride. He has reportedly fallen madly in love, but I find this hard to believe. The fact that the bride comes from one of the very oldest aristocratic families of Rome, and that that faction is the one where Octavian needs most to win partisans, makes me suspect his sudden passion. She is Livia, the daughter of the ardent Republican Livius Drusus, who committed suicide after the battle of Philippi. She is also the wife of Tiberius Claudius Nero, a political enemy of Octavian's, only just reconciled with him after the treaty of Misenum. What a coup for him. One by one, and bit by bit, his enemies are tranquilized, neutralized, pulverized. Soon there will be none left. And he will reign supreme in all the world, straddling it on his spindly legs.

Athens, I come! Enough of Rome! I have done my best for you here, but with Antony's departure my task is over. The city stinks, and not just because the Cloaca Maxima needs a good cleaning.

To the most exalted Queen Cleopatra—

What a relief to have landed in Athens! How clear and fine it seems after the sinkhole of Rome. How the acropolis gleams in the golden sunlight! Truly, all that's best in either day or night becomes itself here. I feel I can breathe again! The city retains its ancient beauty, and the dark columns of the cypress trees against the fluted columns everywhere give even my cynical soul a touch of peace.

Athens seems fond of Antony, and it has restored the better side of him. Perhaps you were right—he definitely improves, the farther he gets from Octavian. Someday I may even come to understand what you saw in him. But that is still a long way off. He has been feted, and both he and his wife proclaimed gods. He went through some gibberish of a marriage ceremony to Athena. He has taken up Greek dress. (Yes, again he takes on that which is nearest him.) When he finally recovers from this round of meaningless but colorful ceremonies, it is said he intends to get to work reorganizing some of the eastern territories and preparing for war.

As for myself, I find Athens interesting as a version of Alexandria.

It is our mother-city, even if eclipsed by her young offspring. One should always show respect for one's mother.

I trust your children follow this maxim!

Your servant and friend, Olympos

I had always wanted to visit Athens. Now I was once again envious of Antony to be stationed there, far from Octavian's yapping and the Roman mobs, free to do what he liked in such a great city. From what Olympos said, it would appear that Antony found it congenial, and the Athenians appreciated him as well.

Now that he was closer, and in the Greek sphere, I found that my thoughts were pulled to him often. His absence was not like that of Caesar's, whose void seemed to fill all the earth, as well as my own life. And the absence caused by death is so absolute, so remorseless, that I was forced to turn away from it toward the living. Antony's absence was the lack of a fillip to life, a collapsing of an added dimension. Real life went on unharmed, with no gaps, but curiously flat. In my hunger, I reminded myself that no one ever died from lack of seasoning, and that bland food was just as nourishing for the body as spiced.

"Olympos is returning!" I told Caesarion. "Have you written your verses yet?"

He had promised to compose some welcoming verses. I told him if he could manage both to write them in Greek and translate them into Egyptian, I would order an image of him as a grown Pharaoh to be carved on the Temple of Dendera, far up the Nile.

"Yes, but I'm not pleased with them," he said. He showed me the paper where he had written them. "The words are so *ordinary!* I want to use special ones!"

I looked over his composition, finding it very well done for an eight-year-old. "You would do well to remember what your father said about that. His writings were renowned for their clarity and style. He said, 'Avoid the rare and unusual word like a helmsman the rocks.' In other words, steer clear of it. I think he would approve of this verse." I handed it back to him. "I know Olympos will appreciate it. He has been gone a long time—over six months. Studying medicine." And spying, I thought.

"What's he learned? Can he sew heads back on if they're cut off?"

I laughed. "I don't think anyone can do that." Otherwise someone would have stuck Cicero's back on, and he would still be fulminating about the Republic.

Just then the twins came in. They were walking now, not very steadily, but every day they improved. Caesarion did not look pleased. "Oh, it's *them.*"

He snatched his paper and held it up over his head, lest they try to grab it. He stood on tiptoe and whispered into my ear, "When I asked for a brother or sister, I didn't think they would be so *boring*. They don't *do* anything, except cry and tear things up."

"Give them time," I said. "Someday you will be friends. They will catch up to you."

"Never." He sidestepped as one of them reached out chubby fingers to tug on his tunic. Selene fell flat on her face and started wailing. "You see?" He looked disdainful and left the room. "What a nuisance!"

Olympos would be surprised at how they had changed since he left. They had grown fast, and were no longer smaller than others their age. They both had golden curls that made them look angelic, but that was misleading. Children, especially pretty ones, can be tyrants.

Olympos was back, looking rested and yet happy to return. He had lingered in Athens almost to the danger-point for travel, but said he was so beguiled by the mellow sunshine in the city it was hard to realize winter was coming.

In our private chambers, Caesarion recited his memorized welcome verses, then read them off in halting Egyptian. The twins excited themselves so much they went into a frenzy of jumping and yelling, and even Kasu the monkey started climbing on the curtains and leaping from chair to chair.

"Pandemonium!" said Olympos. "Where is the classical ideal of restraint and order? This is positively Dionysian." He leaned forward to kiss my cheek, then applauded Caesarion's literary efforts. Finally he bent down to look carefully at the twins.

"They seem to be thriving," he said. "They must be eating ambrosia, the food of the gods, to shoot up so. If Antony saw them, he would be proud." *But of course he won't*, I could almost read his thoughts in the tight line of his lips. *Your parting must be final, after his insults.*

"You are too protective of me," I said, answering his thoughts rather than his words. But that is how it is between old friends. "I can fend for myself." I drew him aside, when I could divert the children. "What was the last news you heard before you set sail?"

"No real news," he said. "Antony and Octavia will spend the winter in Athens, while he organizes the east for his ventures. All is quiet. It is not known when he plans to launch the massive attack on Parthia. It would seem difficult to ready everything by next spring, since an enormous army has to be equipped. Oh, and I brought you this. I thought you would want to see it." He took my hand and slowly and deliberately pressed a coin into it. "A new issue."

I opened my palm and stared at its bright beauty. It was an aureus, a gold coin, with the heads of Antony and Octavia. So he was minting money with his wife's head on it! It made me angry, as Olympos meant it to.

As if to cover up his blatant provocation, he then produced another coin. "I thought you might find this amusing." He held it between his thumb and forefinger, turning it around.

"Well, give it to me." I took it and saw that it was a denarius showing Sextus's father Pompey with a dolphin and trident on one side, and a war galley under sail on the other.

"What does this mean?" I asked. It seemed silly.

"Sextus is now claiming that he's the son of Neptune; he's blurring his real father, with his sea command, into the divine one. He takes it seriously enough, and so do the mobs in Rome. They cheered like crazy when a statue of Neptune was carted around at the races, in company with the other gods; Antony and Octavian had it removed, and they almost rioted. Sextus has even started costuming himself in a blue cloak in honor of his 'father.' "

"He sounds like a clown," I said. How could anyone pay attention to this?

"Oh yes, everyone is a god these days—or the son of one. I wonder who I should claim?"

"Asclepius, of course," I said.

"He isn't grand enough—he started life as a mortal."

"Well, you have to start somewhere," I said, wishing to end this. I was happy to have Olympos back, but I wanted to be alone to glower at the coins.

After he was gone, I stared at the profiles. Pompey's was certainly a recognizable likeness, but I thought Antony's face looked stretched and flat, as if he had been ill and lost weight. As for Octavia—her profile was behind his, and all it showed was a straight nose and well-formed lips. I thought it looked vaguely familiar, but it might not have really looked like her, if the likeness of Antony was any guide.

So he was proceeding as if this were the only life he had ever wanted, as if he was born to be all the things he now was: Octavia's husband, Octavian's brother-in-law, an exemplary citizen of the patrician intellectual offerings of Athens. Olympos said he had settled into a round of attending lectures, readings, council meetings, and the like, all with his seemly wife in tow. Had his spirits really been extinguished under all that domestic propriety? It would be as sad as the majestic, exotic wild beasts I had seen—tigers, panthers, pythons—turned into broken amusements in cages.

I put the coin into a box, where it would be safe, and where I wouldn't see it.

53

The farther south we went, the warmer it got, so that by the time we reached Dendera, even though it was only February, it was basking-hot at noon. I had kept my word to Caesarion, and was taking him to see the temple where he was represented as a full-grown Pharaoh. It had taken eighteen months for the carving to be completed, and it had taken almost that long for him to become proficient in Egyptian. The bargain on both sides had been fulfilled.

Now, as I stood beside him at the railing of the boat, I thought that it was a good idea for us to have come away together. It was also good that he see something of Egypt beyond Alexandria. He had been as enthralled by it as I had been when I first escaped up the Nile. In only a few months he would be ten; it was time for him to explore a new world. He had watched the land sliding past, green-fringed palm trees bristling by the riverbanks, oxen in the fields, the long stretch between the pyramids and Dendera, the first of the temples the Ptolemies built.

"I can see it from here," he said, pointing toward a massive sandstone structure, a bright golden color against the endless dun sands and soil.

I remembered the voyage when my father had taken me to other temples, which he had helped build and embellish. Now I was aware of repeating the cycle. It was supposed to make me feel old, to see a son growing tall and being trained to follow in my footsteps, but instead it felt entirely right and natural. His coming adulthood did not threaten me. I was thankful that I had an heir, with two more children behind him.

He all but bounced off the boat, running down the gangplank, rushing past the dignitaries lining the banks. He wanted to see himself, an artistic version of himself, up on the walls.

"Look! Look!" he cried, dragging me by the hand, while he hunted for the carving. The entire outer wall of the temple was filled with representations of divine processions and earthly figures carrying offerings in them. "Where is it? Where is it?"

I pulled him to a halt. "You are going in the wrong direction," I said. "It is on the southwestern corner." We turned that way, passing gigantic gods and goddesses on the walls high above us. I stopped at the corner and pointed up. "There we are."

Looming over us were two outlined figures, in ancient Egyptian costume, holding incense and offerings in their outstretched arms. They were at least twenty feet high; standing directly beneath them as we were, we could not see their heads clearly.

"We must step back," I said, and we went quite a ways across the hard-packed earth to a vantage point.

"That doesn't look like me!" was the first thing he said.

"No, of course not. It's just a representation—all Pharaohs are made to look the same."

He studied my profile. "And she doesn't look like you, either."

"No. It's a standard queen. You see, there's a certain way a queen of Egypt is always supposed to look, and so she's depicted that way on statues and paintings. So everyone knows exactly who it is."

"And you don't wear clothes like that, either. And I certainly never wear a transparent kilt!" He laughed. "I think the double crown is so big it would snap my head off."

"Yes, crowns can be very heavy. At least that kind can be. So we only wear them ceremonially. When you are crowned at Memphis, you'll have one if you wish. But by that time you'll have a very strong, heavy neck, because I intend to live a long time." I cocked my head. "This is the wrong time of day to see the carvings—not enough shadow. We should come back at sunset."

"They've made me as tall as you," he said proudly.

"Well, you almost are. You are tall, like your father." And he had kept the resemblance, with the same broad face and keen, deep-set eyes.

"My father," he said quietly. "It makes me sad that I can never see him."

"Yes, it makes me sad too."

"Well, at least you *have* seen him, and can remember. He died before I was old enough to have memories. Did he really look like the bust in my room?"

I nodded. "Yes. Roman art is quite realistic. It is a very good likeness. But, you know, if you learned Latin, you could read his works. His writing was famous. In that way you could come to know him; people can speak to us through what they write."

"But it's just about battles and marches; it isn't about *him*."

"His battles *are* him."

"Oh, you know what I mean! He didn't write essays or speeches, like Cicero. That's easier to see someone in."

"I think he did write them, but I don't know if they were published. They may have been among his papers after he died. If so, then perhaps Antony still has them—or knows where they are. He took charge of everything in the house . . . afterward."

"He probably left them back in Rome, and Mardian says he'll never go back to Rome again, that Octavian has shut him out and won't *allow* him back."

"That's a lie! He can return whenever he wishes. But why would he wish to, before he's defeated the Parthians? After that, he can go to Rome as ruler, and shut *Octavian* out."

Caesarion shrugged. "Mardian said that Octavian called him back to Italy and then refused to meet with him. Mardian says that it set Antony's Parthian campaign back by a whole year. Mardian says that's probably what he wanted—Octavian, I mean—"

"Mardian does like to talk," I said lightly. "It's true that Octavian begged Antony to come and bring ships to Italy to help in the war with Sextus, and then changed his mind. But it has not cost Antony any time in Parthia. His general Bassus has beaten the Parthians out of Syria and back over the Euphrates again. Now the real campaign can begin."

"Good. I think he must be ready to fight at last."

"Did Mardian also tell you that Octavian has been beaten time and again by Sextus? He all but drowned in trying to fight him; half his fleet was wrecked in the Strait of Messina. Scylla on her rock almost devoured Octavian himself; he barely managed to wash ashore and crawl to safety." But he somehow *always* managed to crawl to safety, I thought—crawl, rest up, and gather his forces.

"No, he didn't," Caesarion admitted.

"Octavian's losing is getting to be a joke," I said. "The Romans made up a verse about him: 'He's lost his fleet, and lost the battle, twice. Someday he'll win; why else keep throwing dice?' "

"You seem to know a great deal about him," said Caesarion.

"I make it my business to know," I said.

Someday he'll win; why else keep throwing dice? I shivered, even in the warm sun.

"Come," I said, steering him in the direction of the anxious, hovering chief priest. They wished to honor us by a meal, held under a shaded trellis.

I saw him watching the temple from his seat, his gaze always going back to the carving of himself in that strange garb. He struggled with Egyptian, trying hard not to lapse back into Greek, and the priest seemed flattered.

The drowsy noontime seemed to lay calming hands on our heads. Here, almost four hundred miles upriver, all the things I was so preoccupied with in Alexandria faded to unimportance. Here we were hidden, protected, given sanctuary. This was the true Egypt, the motherland, where Rome could not reach us. If all else failed, my children could rule here unmolested.

If all else failed . . . but I must not think of failure. It would be failure indeed if Caesar's true heir, and the children of a Triumvir, had to content themselves with less than their due inheritance. And that inheritance, for better or worse, was part of the Roman world.

But, ah! How delightful it was to recline beneath the arbor, luxuriating in the dry heat, seeing the white butterflies dancing overhead. Everything here was either brown or green or white.

"Tell me about Hathor," Caesarion was saying. "The goddess who presides over this temple."

The priest's eyes lit up. "She is our ancient goddess of beauty, joy, and music."

"Like Isis?" he asked.

"Yes, only older. Although we believe they may just be manifestations of each other. And once the Greeks came, they thought she was also Aphrodite."

How different this Egyptian-style temple, with its solid walls, its carvings, its darkened sanctuary, was from the Roman one Caesar had likewise built to honor the goddess of beauty. Both saluted her in appropriate ways. Beauty . . . we all worship her, we all stand in awe of beauty. It is the one god we all seem to agree upon.

"You have been most generous, Majesty, in providing for the temple," the priest was saying. "As were your ancestors."

"As heirs of the Pharaohs, we are honored to do so," I said. We Ptolemies had tried to keep Egyptian religion, art, and architecture intact; Greek influence was confined to only a few cities. Some had accused us of becoming more Egyptian than the Egyptians, by taking up brother-sister marriage, decking out the temples, honoring the sacred bulls of Apis, and being crowned at Memphis. Others said it was just political guile. Perhaps it was for some, but in my own life I felt a pull toward the ancient Egyptian ways, and the old stones and gods spoke to me.

As the sun sank low in the sky, we stood once more looking at the figures on the temple. Now the lines were etched dark by shadows, and the Queen and King stood majestically tall, their elaborate headdresses towering above them, every detail of their wigs and jewelry sharp and clear.

"Here you will be Pharaoh for eternity," I said to Caesarion. "You will always be young and handsome, always be offering gladsome gifts to the gods."

Art allows us to do that, while life hurries us on to our crumbling ends.

We had several events to celebrate. First, there was Caesarion's tenth birthday. Then there was the sudden marriage of Olympos to a quiet, even-tempered woman with a bent for scholarly study. There was the welcome news from Epaphroditus that our harvests had exceeded expectations—owing to a combination of a good Nile and freshly dredged canals—and our exports of glass and papyrus were booming. My rebuilt navy was almost complete, with two hundred new ships. Ambassadors from all over the east were flocking to us, courting us. I had even been able to issue new coinage with increased silver content. I had a pile of them on the table, as a proud display. Egypt was not only surviving, she was thriving.

Mardian picked one up and looked at it appreciatively. "There is no weight so pleasing as a heavy silver coin—unless it's a heavy gold one!" He was finely arrayed in a reworked silk robe, and thick gold armlets gleamed on his forearms.

"Perhaps you'd like to contribute your armlets to be melted down," I said, eyeing them.

He laughed and crossed his arms to shield them. "Never!"

Epaphroditus took one of the coins and examined it. "We must be the envy of the Romans," he said. "Lately they have had to debase their coinage, since the menace of Sextus so threatens their food supply—indeed, while he ranges unchecked, their whole economy trembles in the balance."

"Even Antony has felt the pinch," said Mardian. "Far away from Rome, he too has had to debase his coinage."

So Octavia's face would beam out from a coin that was more copper than silver? Pity.

I put my hands over my own coins possessively. If Egypt was strong and prosperous, it was because of my policies and the good ministers I had.

"Ah! The bridegroom!" I saluted Olympos as he arrived. "We all congratulate you."

It seemed odd to me that he was now married, the first of my inner attendants to be so. Certainly I had urged it on him for years, yet now that it had happened I found myself wondering if his wife would be worthy of him, would understand him. I hoped she was not as lost in her manuscripts as some women were in the kitchen. One extreme was as bad as the other. I remembered Olympos saying once, "There is only one thing more tedious than a stupid person, and that is a pedantic one."

"Yes, I have entered the blessed realm," he said. As a joke? "Come, give me some wine!"

"Because marriage is such thirsty work?" asked Mardian archly.

"You said it, not I," said Olympos, taking a cup and draining it. It occurred to me that although Olympos knew an unseemly amount about that side of my own life, I would never know about his. He would never share it with me, as I was forced to share mine with him: a strange privilege of physicians. That did not stop my curiosity, though.

"Is Dorcas to join us today?" I asked. I had yet to see her.

"No, she is at the Library. Besides, you didn't invite her."

"That's her imagination. Of course the invitation was for both of you."

"I will tell her. Later."

I wondered if he had not wanted to bring her. But all that would become apparent in time. Everything does.

"I am happy to be surrounded with all that a queen could want," I said loudly, to get their attention. "In this I am rich. I have the best and most loyal ministers in the world, and a son of whom any mother would be proud, any queen wish to succeed her." Caesarion first beamed, then blushed. "Pray, let us rejoice with one another." I nodded for the servers to bring around the pitchers of wine and platters of delicacies.

At the first opportunity, Mardian whispered to me, "Some Parthians have come, asking for an alliance."

"Are they official ambassadors, or private citizens?" I asked.

"Citizens," said Mardian. "They say they were sent to take a reading, and if the answer is favorable, ambassadors will follow with a formal offer."

"Parthia!" I said. "How puzzling! Do you think they have come to spy, because they mean to attack us next?" They were too far away to bother with alliances, I thought, but not too far away to harbor ideas of conquest.

"No, I think they are on the defensive against the expected Roman attack, and are scratching around for help. Perhaps they see it as black and white: Rome, the west, against the east. Many people do. Are they wrong?"

"Perhaps not." Perhaps it was really that simple. Romans, the west, would keep expanding eastward until they dashed themselves against some stone—the Parthians? the Indians? How far would they roll, like ocean breakers, until they finally hit a barrier?

"Do you want to grant them an audience? Or shall I send them on their way?" he asked.

I was tempted. In certain moments I had toyed with the idea of an eastern alliance. The Kandake had offered one. It had an allure to it. We could band together with Nubia, with Arabia, with Parthia, Media, perhaps even Hindu Kush, and make a stand against the Romans.

But in the cold light of reason, it did not hold up. Egypt was too far west herself, cut off from those other lands by a ring of Roman provinces: by Syria, Asia, Pontus, and all the half-digested client kingdoms, like Judaea and Armenia. We were isolated, forced to deal directly with the Romans, make accommodation with them.

"Send them on their way," I said. "Hear their proposals first. Ascertain their chances against the Romans. Find out their military situation. *Then* send them back to Phraaspa or Ecbatana or Susa or whichever city they came from."

"Ecbatana, I believe." He adjusted his left armlet. "This is the wisest course. Keep aloof. Make no alliances. Make no promises."

"How easily you seem to have forgotten," I said. "We are already in an alliance. We are Friend and Ally of the Roman People."

He shrugged, as if it were of no moment.

"I keep my word," I said. "If it is to be broken, it must be broken by the other side." It was a point of honor with me—quaint, perhaps foolish, but it was my own personal code. Why, then, did I deride Antony for his loyalty to the Triumvirate?

Because, I answered myself, you cannot keep faith with a faithless person, and Octavian is faithless. Except to his own ambition.

When Octavian had first returned to Rome, he had declared his intentions openly: "May I succeed in attaining the honors and position of my father, to which I am entitled." People laughed, or ignored it. How blind!

Yes, I would keep my alliance with Rome, but with both eyes open. And it was really an alliance with Caesar and with Antony with which I kept faith.

"Tell your tale." Mardian prodded the men forward. He had brought them into my audience hall, where they cowered in a group.

Hesitantly they inched toward me.

"Come, come, closer. Do not be afraid," Mardian urged them.

"Now, what is it you wish to tell me?" I asked.

"We—your dockmaster said you would wish to be informed personally," one man said.

"About what?"

"I am—I was—captain of one of the grain transports. We carry a thousand tons of wheat to Rome this time of year. We were attacked just outside Sicily—despoiled of not only our cargo, but our ship as well! I must tell you, such an act of piracy, upon such a huge ship, is unprecedented! Sextus rules the sea. Nothing is safe between here and Rome."

"Your ship is gone?"

"Yes, taken from me. There was nothing I could do to prevent it."

"Did you not have soldiers aboard?"

"Yes, a few, but grain transports cannot provide quarters for many men." He sighed. "All that investment—my family's entire estate—gone."

"I will repay you," I assured him. "But give me more information. From what you say, Rome will be starved out."

"It looks likely. When Sextus—for I beheld him face-to-face—let me free, he told me that Octavian had sent for help from Antony. 'But there's no help against me. I smashed him once and I'll smash him again, no matter how many ships he gets from Antony. The noose will tighten around his neck until he'll beg for mercy.' That's what he said, Your Majesty. The very words."

"He has sent for help to Antony?"

"So Sextus said. He laughed about it, saying that it would harm both of them. Antony would have to postpone his attack on Parthia, and Octavian would only reveal his weakness, making the Romans more discontented with him."

"It is hard to see what Sextus wants—other than to spoil the fortunes of others." He seemed to have no greater goal or calling. What a sad destiny for the last son of Pompey the Great.

"We were able to beg transport home on another merchant vessel, in exchange for seamen's duties," said another man. "And the captain of this ship told us that Agrippa has taken charge of the war against Sextus, and is engaged in secret preparations. He did not know anything about them, beyond the fact that they involved some vast engineering feat."

Agrippa—Octavian's boyhood friend, now his favorite general. I wondered what "secret" measures he could be invoking against Sextus.

"Well," I finally said, "I grieve with you for your losses, and will try to make them good. We are not at war, and there is no reason why you should suffer the pains of war."

After they left, I could not keep a small smile off my face. Octavian was floundering; he had been forced to call upon Antony for help.

———

It took several months for all the pieces of the mosaic to fall into place. Here I arrange them to form the picture of what happened next. A short sketch will suffice.

Antony, obedient to the call, set out for Tarentum, whence Octavian had summoned him in a panic. He brought three hundred ships. To his surprise, Octavian did not meet him. It seems the would-be Caesar had had second thoughts, echoing the first ones of Sextus: namely, that to call for outside help revealed his own weakness. He preferred to bank on Agrippa and his secret plans; he did not wish to share any glory with Antony.

Antony, furious with Octavian, was ready to break with him at last, but in the end Octavia acted as a mediator between them. She wept and cajoled, saying she would be the most miserable of women, should there be a falling-out between the two people dearest to her: her brother and her husband. The two men met reluctantly, and yet another treaty was forged: the Treaty of Tarentum. It renewed the Triumvirate—which had technically expired—for another five years. Antony was to yield two squadrons—one hundred twenty ships—for the war against Sextus. At some vague later date, Octavian would repay him with twenty thousand men for the war against the Parthians. Antony sailed away, leaving the ships behind, but with no promised soldiers. The rendezvous with Octavian had eaten up the better part of the summer, costing him another year's setback in launching the Parthian attack. Thus this treaty, like all the others with Octavian, lessened Antony's power. He took his leave, fuming.

It was very late. I was reading well past my usual time to sleep. I lay on my couch, a bolster under my head, my feet covered with a light blanket. The lamps guttered in the breeze coming through the window, beginning to gather force for the coming autumn. It was a night for ghosts, a night when the sea below seemed to moan and whisper.

At first I was not sure I heard a knock. It was too late for a knock. But it sounded again. I rose and said, "Enter."

Mardian stepped in, his bulk draped in a shawl. "Forgive me," he said. "But I thought you would want to hear this news immediately. Antony has sent Octavia back to Rome. On his voyage back east, he got as far as the island of Corcyra, when he suddenly said she belonged back in Rome. And he sent her packing on the next ship."

"He must have had some colorable reason," I said.

"Well, she is pregnant," said Mardian. "But he knew that before he set sail with her. He could have left her in Italy to begin with. Evidently he changed his mind on the voyage." He stood there looking at me for what seemed a very long time, his eyes holding mine. "You know he will send for you. What will you do?"

Had I been less than honest to myself and to Mardian, I would have given a proud, noncommittal answer. Instead I just told the truth. "I don't know."

I had no illusions about what would happen if I saw him. I did not even bother to deny it to myself. I was very weak where he was concerned—weak as regards my person, not my country's interests.

Still, Mardian did not turn his gaze away.

I asked, "Do you hate him, as Olympos does?"

"Not if you love him. Do you?"

"I—I *did* love him. But much has happened to us since those days. I fear neither of us is what we were then—we are scarred, both of us, and older. He has made decisions that I deplore; doubtless I have done likewise. What changes people, changes love."

Mardian rocked on his heels a bit. "A properly Alexandrian answer—convoluted, artificial, clever."

"I am afraid to say either yes or no, for either of them would be unwelcome to me," I said.

"Then I leave you, dearest Queen, to your own thoughts for the rest of the night." Bowing, he opened the doors and glided away, moving very gracefully.

My thoughts for the rest of the night! I did not look forward to having hours alone to dwell on Mardian's news. I knew that any hope of sleep was gone, yet I really did not wish to substitute soul-searching for it.

I made ready for bed, as if I expected it to be a normal night, hoping to trick Morpheus, the god of sleep, luring him to my bed. I would attire myself in the sheerest night dress, rub my temples with oil of lily, which had both a beguiling and soporific odor—beguiling for Morpheus, soporific for me. I brushed my hair, pretending that I was Iras—whom I would not call, as I did not wish to talk—feeling it and touching it as a foreign thing. I made sure that fresh air was blowing into the chamber, and kept one oil lamp burning. Then I lay down, and waited.

I stretched my feet out, covering my legs with a light blanket, forbidding myself to think on any one thing in particular. I would force myself to picture the harbor, count the masts of the ships tied up there. That was usually effective.

But tonight, of course, the thought of ships made me think of Antony sending Octavia back on a ship. She must even now be only halfway back to Rome; I knew of her dismissal before Octavian would. But what did it mean, really? If Antony was preparing for his Parthian war, perhaps he reasoned that since he would be away for months, it was best for her to return to Rome to be with their passel of children and stepchildren—Antony's three and Octavia's three, plus their own. In fact, she might well have been the one to say she preferred to return to their children, even if he asked her to wait in Athens.

I sighed and turned over. My feet tangled in the blanket and I threw it off. What was it that Mardian had said? *He suddenly said she belonged back in*

Rome. And he sent her packing on the next ship. But doubtless that was his interpretation. There could be perfectly respectable reasons why Octavia had left his side. Although she never had in the three years they had been together. . . . Antony had got away—why did I insist on using that term?— only once, when he besieged Samasota with Bassus. The rest of the time they had been tethered to each other's company.

Now my side was uncomfortable and I twisted onto my stomach. Oh, let me sleep! It was I who was tethered—to the bed, shackled, unable to find a position that suited me, unable to sleep, unable to get up and do anything else—unable, above all, to stop thinking.

The cool air flowed over my back, which was sweaty. I had worked myself up into a state of agitation. The truth was I did not want my world disturbed, dry and ordered as it was. I ran it well, and it repaid me handsomely. Nights like tonight—restive, hungry, questioning—came to me only rarely, and were a small price to pay for my lack of an intimate companion. Nights could be like this, but the days were mine entirely. I deferred to no one, never had to compromise my plans or accommodate anyone's quirks or demands. I had quite got used to it, and would be loath to give it up.

I turned over again. Was there no way to find rest? The bed, and the bedding, felt like an instrument of torture. I had wrinkled and twisted the covers as badly as a spinning crocodile caught in them.

You know he will send for you. What will you do?

HERE ENDS THE FIFTH SCROLL.

THE SIXTH SCROLL

54

I stood on the very edge of the shaded terrace of my quarters in the palace at Antioch, looking out over the river Orontes, which flowed directly beneath. Before me stretched a wide, flat, fertile plain to the distant seashore. The capital of the Seleucid dynasty, the once-great rival of the Ptolemies: It was not so fine as Alexandria, but then nothing was.

The Seleucids had gone now, vanquished by the Romans, their land turned into a province by Pompey—an object lesson for me. But they had never had my opportunities to hand: no Roman leaders with amorous proclivities passing through, no queens of the right age and temperament. We use what we have, and I had been blessed indeed by what fate had sent my way.

We Ptolemies had held this city briefly; my ancestor Ptolemy III had conquered this territory, all the way up to the Euphrates, and almost to India. Now I might be able to regain by personal influence what they had failed to keep by war.

A cool breeze from the sea was sweeping across the plain; Antioch was renowned for its pleasant setting. On the other side of the city glowered the tall peak of Mount Silpius, and in early morning its ragged shadow lay across the streets. I could see the villas of the wealthy built into the side of the mountain, spots of white against the deep green of the forested slopes. Yes, a supremely agreeable spot.

I was in the old palace of the Seleucids—a huge building on an island in the fast-running Orontes. I had demanded, and received, my own quarters here.

For Antony had indeed "sent for me," but unlike his earlier summons, this one was couched entirely in personal terms.

"Come to me. I do not order you as an ally, I beg as one who wants you. Bring our children—I pray you, let me see them," he wrote.

This letter had come in short order after Octavia had left—indeed, she might well have still been traveling when Antony wrote it. He had betaken himself to Antioch and settled in to prepare for the Parthian venture; he would winter there and in the spring set out with his legions.

I would go to Antioch, but this time not in costume. I would go with a long list of demands, which he would agree to, or lose any hope of having Egypt for an ally. I knew he would not want to turn his attention to actual military action to secure us; that would further delay his main venture, not to mention wasting precious time and money. He needed us, and he needed us to be quiet; he could not afford to turn his back on a potential enemy while fighting a real one.

I did not bring the children. If he wanted to see them, there was only one way: he would marry me. And publicly, not like Caesar in a secret rite at Philae. He would take me as his wife, in the east—who cared about Rome?— and acknowledge our children as legitimate. There would be no more nonsense about whether it was legal in Rome. I had heard enough of that excuse from both Caesar and Antony.

And he would cede lost ancestral territories to Egypt—yes, he would bestow Roman holdings on me as a wedding gift. I had no need of jewelry or such as a token; territory would do nicely.

And if he did not agree to *all* these demands, then I would leave forthwith, without spending any time alone with him. Thus I had decreed to myself, which made it acceptable for me to go to him.

As for my own feelings—I prayed morning and evening to Isis to give me the strength not to let them sway me. *When I see him again*, I asked, *let me not disgrace myself. Let me see him only as someone with whom I must deal politically. Let me not give way to any emotion unless he agrees to my demands.*

I had not yet met him. I had been at the palace for two days, while each of us waited for the other's summons. I had no intention of calling for him, even if I had to spend a month there without seeing him. In fact, tomorrow I would go sightseeing by myself in this famous city; it was high time.

The shadows were lengthening, reaching to the palace gates. Beyond the horizon, the sunset stained the sky red; birds winged their way home.

I was about to withdraw into my apartments when a servant approached, handing me a note. At last. I unfolded it and read it in the fast-falling light.

"I would be honored if you would dine with me in my apartments tonight," was all it said.

The boy was waiting, his head cocked.

"You may tell Lord Antony that the Queen accepts," I said.

Now I stood still for just an instant before the tall cedar and bronze-studded doors to Antony's chamber. The Seleucids had certainly liked ostentatious decoration, I thought—not that we Ptolemies should talk. But we had better taste. It was hard to associate Antony with a door like that one, but perhaps it was best that I meet him again in a place that held no memories. It would help to keep me firmly in the present, help me to remember what I must do.

The door swung open, revealing a huge chamber, its ceiling so high it was lost in gloom. Gigantic beams of ornamented wood, gleaming with the same decorative bronze studs as the door, held up the ceiling. Far at one end, on a carved chair, sat a figure who, large as he was, was dwarfed by the monumental size of his surroundings.

It had been almost four years since I had seen him—the same amount of time that had passed after Caesar's death before I went to Tarsus. What if I had suddenly seen Caesar again at that time? The impact, a meeting after long parting, was much more overwhelming than I had expected. And at the same time it was much less, for it was just a man, after all, sitting in a chair.

He rose. His cloak fell in graceful folds behind him. He extended his arm in welcome. "Greetings, my most beloved Queen," he said in the voice that swept all else away for me.

"Greetings, most noble Triumvir Antonius," I replied. I stepped forward and let him take my hand. He kissed it, but awkwardly. There were too few people for this vast chamber, and yet there were still too many.

"Go now." He waved the few attendants away. "I will call when we are ready to dine."

As they padded away, I knew that only made it worse. We were two tiny figures in this empty space that seemed designed to hold an army—an army mounted on elephants. It magnified everything; I fancied that our voices echoed.

Part of me looked at him as if at a stranger, while the other part found him so familiar that it was pretentious to behave formally to him. It was so odd I found myself at a loss as to what to say.

"Here. Sit," he said roughly, shoving a chair toward me. He must be feeling exactly the same. He settled himself back into his chair, then put his hands on his knees and stared at me.

He looked older. In the first few minutes that we see someone after a long absence, we can detect all the changes in their faces; after that it fades, blending into our memories of how they *did* look. His hair was not as dark; it showed streaks of gray in spots, although it was still thick. His face was not smooth as before, but had added lines at the corners of the eyes and along the cheeks. The changes did not detract from his appearance, but made him look more of a commander.

"You are more beautiful than ever," he finally said, and I almost laughed. He must have been going through the same recital of my changes in his mind, and to negate them had blurted out the opposite.

"You must have forgotten how I looked before," I said.

"No. Never!" He looked so earnest as he said it that this time I did laugh. "I swear—"

"No need for that," I said quickly. "Never swear to something you cannot prove." I knew I must look different, too, but my mirror assured me the long slide had not yet begun. "You sent for me. I am here," I said, shifting back to the formal. I must not forget my purpose in coming, get caught up in a reunion.

"And the children? When may I see them?" He was diffident, polite.

"I did not bring them." I watched the disappointment cross his face. "Perhaps you can see them in Alexandria. And how are your other children? Am I to see *them?*"

"No, I—no, they are in Rome."

"Even the one not yet born?"

"On its way to Rome." He could not keep from smiling, and then broke into a laugh.

I tried not to join him, but couldn't help it, and started laughing myself. "Is it—and its mother—to stay in Rome?" I finally asked.

"Yes. Forever," he said.

"And you?" To come to this point, and so quickly! I had not meant to.

"I stay here."

"Forever?"

"That depends."

"On Parthia?"

"Partly. And partly on what happens elsewhere," he said.

"You cannot stay away from Rome forever," I said, "for that would abdicate all power to Octavian."

"Please refrain from offering me political advice in the first few minutes," he said testily.

"Yes, I know, you've done without it for four years now. And seen your authority and power eroded. You have less now than you did when you sailed away to Tyre."

"I'll not quarrel!" he said, his voice rising. "Not tonight! I won't!"

"Tomorrow, then?" I could not help baiting him.

"No, not tomorrow either! Stop it!" he bellowed, holding his hands against his temples.

At the sound, one of the servitors poked his head in a side door, but Antony waved him away. "Not yet!" he yelled.

"But you haven't even asked me if I am hungry. Perhaps I do not wish to delay the dinner," I said. "We can certainly talk while we eat."

"Oh, yes, I am sorry—" He seemed so pliant and eager to accommodate. Perhaps while he was in this mood was the best time to strike.

But not yet, part of me thought. I am not ready. What I really meant was, I am not ready to part if the answer is no. I would like a day or so first—having come all this way. A day or so to reacquaint myself with this man, the father of my children, after all.

The dinner was served straightway, a flock of attendants bringing an absurd number of dishes and courses for only two people. This region was rich in agriculture, and bulging stuffed vegetables, honey-sweet grapes, and aromatic roasted nuts turned the seasoned fish and delicate oysters into a feast worthy of the gods. Fine white wine from nearby Laodicea-on-the-Sea swirled in our chased silver goblets. Antony, stretched out on his couch, ate heartily but silently.

Finally he leaned over and said, "You said we could talk while we ate, but you have said nothing."

"Forgive me," I said. "I seem to have no thoughts worthy of repeating."

He smiled and took a long drink from his goblet, his tanned throat moving as he swallowed. I quickly looked away, down at the dark marble floor. "That I find hard to believe. Come, you are celebrated for your conversation. Speak."

What I had to say he would not find so amusing. But later. "Tell me of your preparations for the war. . . ."

And he talked on gladly about the plans, pieced together from Caesar's, to invade Parthia from the north, through Armenia, avoiding the disastrous open plains that had been Crassus's undoing. He talked about his lieutenants, in whom he had high confidence, including the recently acquired, fiery Ahenobarbus. As he spoke, his face grew flushed with excitement. He wanted this venture very badly, was longing to get started. All the better for me.

Like all soldiers, he seemed to have no fears that he would lose—or, worse yet, die. Would he have been so eager to go if he thought this time next year he might be in a grave? Would he hurry it on so? Yet a very wise man had once explained to me the Principle of the Ninety-nine Soldiers. It went thus: If a hundred soldiers were preparing for battle the next day and a seer told them that without fail ninety-nine were slated to die, each man would say to himself, "Too bad about those other ninety-nine men." I knew that he was right—nothing else could explain soldiers. Now Antony was illustrating it.

The meal over, he casually escorted me back to his private chambers—as I knew he would. He did not invite, or put it into words, he just drifted there in a natural manner, talking all the while about his troops and equipment. Once inside, he adroitly dismissed his servants, without making a point of it, and then we were alone, the door closed.

He flung off his cloak eagerly and came over to me, putting his hands on my shoulders. He bent down and attempted to kiss me, saying, "I have waited for this moment for four years, always—"

But I twisted away, keeping his lips from mine. I could not let him kiss me, or I would be lost. My resolution would dissolve at his touch. I pushed his hands off and stepped back.

"And what have you waited for, for four years?" I asked. "To resume our old life? But we cannot resume it. Two great changes have occurred: I have borne you children. And you have become the husband of Octavian's sister; your political partner is now your brother-in-law. You chose her when you were free to choose elsewhere."

"I don't understand—"

"Then you are stupid, and I know you are not stupid. You are spoiled, always getting your own way like some pampered prince of a minor kingdom, acting without thinking, and always being saved. You ran riot in Rome, but Caesar came back in time and saved the situation. You let Fulvia make a ruinous war for you, but she died in time to save you from retribution. You let Octavian best you time and again—and who will save you this time?"

"What has that to do with us?" He seemed to hesitate between being confused and frustrated.

"Just this. We can resume a life together"—his face lightened—"under these conditions. You will marry me. Publicly. You will divorce Octavia. You will recognize our children as legitimate. You will award certain territories to me, to Egypt."

"And what, pray tell, might those be?" His voice was cold.

"My lost ancestral territory of Phoenicia, Judaea, parts of Syria—and Cyprus, which the assassins appropriated and has not yet been returned as you promised."

I expected him to laugh and say no. Instead he thought for a moment and said, "Judaea I cannot grant. Herod is my friend, going back even before you. He is a valuable and loyal ally; I would not turn him into an enemy."

"Would you rather have me as an enemy?"

"You could never be my enemy."

"If you do not grant me these things, I swear I will be. Egypt will cause you trouble if you attempt a war in the east, unless—"

Now he did laugh. He crossed his arms over his chest and said, "Don't you know I could swat you like a fly if I wanted to? All I have to do is raise my arm and you are dethroned, and Egypt becomes a Roman province the next day. I have twenty-four legions—how many do you have?"

"Enough to delay your start for Parthia. And a respectable navy—two hundred ships." But of course what he said was true. I glared back at him.

"Ships cannot come out on land. And I don't need the sea to transport my troops. They are already here, at your doorstep. They can starve out your navy."

"It would be an expensive undertaking for you."

"I would be amply repaid by capturing the fabled treasury of Egypt. In fact, it would be a worthwhile venture in any case. Any strategist would recommend it at this point."

"Try, and you will find it harder than you think. And it would certainly delay your Parthian campaign by a year, if not longer."

He laughed. "I admire your courage, especially when you know you are outflanked. Come, come. I only said it to show you that what I do, I do willingly."

This sudden turn took me by surprise.

"Yes," he continued. "You will find that I have already acceded to your demands, had thought of them even before you. I will prove it."

He went over to a corner of the chamber and picked up a stout lockbox, circled with iron bands. Unlocking it, he took out another box, this one decorated with delicate designs of ivory. He handed it to me. "Open it."

I raised the lid and saw inside an explosion of gold. It was an elaborate necklace of fine gold leaves, twined to look like a vine, covered with emerald flowers. There was also a matching diadem. It was one of the most exquisite pieces of jewelry I had ever seen, and it must have cost him a year's tribute from a wealthy city.

"It is beautiful." I drew it out; it was heavy, but the edges of the leaves were so polished that, although they were thin, they would not catch on silk or skin. "But what has that to do with—"

"I brought it as a wedding gift."

Why was a necklace proof of that?

"I meant it to go with this." He pulled out another box, a much smaller one, and handed it to me as well.

Inside was a gold ring with his signet and ancestor, Hercules. It was a very small ring.

"I had it made to fit you. As a wedding ring." And indeed, it was not just a ring of his he was pressing into service. It was shiny, new, and too small for a man. "Now you've spoiled my proposal," he said, only half-jokingly.

"You wished to marry me?"

"Yes. Why would you find that so unbelievable?"

"Because when you were free, you did not. Now, when you are married—"

"Ah. Perhaps that helped in the decision!" He was laughing.

"Don't joke!"

His smile faded. "I do not mean to make light of it. The gods know it was no easy decision. But I came here, the decision already made. If you would accept me."

How odd this was. I had never expected this. "Yes. Yes, I accept."

He took the necklace and fastened it around my neck. "Then wear this." The cool, slippery weight of the metal settled like a collar around me. He bent and kissed my throat just above the top of the necklace. His hands took mine and started to put the ring on as well.

"No," I said. "Not yet. It is bad luck. Not before—"

He put his arms around me, running them up and down my back. I shivered, caught my breath—then put my hands on his chest and pushed myself away.

"No," I said. "We do not resume this part of our lives together until after we are married." It was one of the hardest things I have ever brought myself to do. I turned away and put a distance between us. My heart was beating so fast I could almost feel it thumping, even as high up as the necklace.

He stared as if I were crazy. It was true, he was spoiled. No one ever said no to him. But tonight I would.

"Let it be soon, then," he muttered.

"As soon as you can arrange it," I said. "And before the ceremony, you will have the papers ready, granting me the territories we discussed. And the divorce request for Octavia."

"No." He balked. "I cannot serve her with papers of divorce while she is carrying my child. It is—unkind. And insulting."

Antony. Always tenderhearted and noble. But he was right. And it would be unlike him to be deliberately cruel to anyone.

"Very well," I said. "But soon afterward, you must."

"What sort of ceremony do you wish?"

"Not Roman," I said. He had been married in too many Roman ceremonies, and none of them seemed to take. Besides, it would not be legal there in any case.

"We could go to the shrine of Apollo near here," he said. "It is reputed to be very beautiful, and it is ancient. I know you have a fondness for ancient things—"

"No, not Apollo! How can you have forgotten? Apollo is Octavian's patron god!"

"Oh yes. Well, what about—"

"I know. The Temple of Isis. There is bound to be one here. And it is fitting, since she is my goddess, and your god is Dionysus. We will make an offering there, take vows before the priest, but have our festivities within the palace. I wish all your Roman officers to help us celebrate. *All* of them." I wanted hundreds of witnesses.

"Yes, of course." He threw up his hands. "You don't seem to understand," he said. "I wish all the world to see! When I came here, I shook the dust of Rome from my boots. I leave all that behind, and am not ashamed to stand up before the world itself with you."

I knew that this extraordinary man meant it—once again he was doing what he pleased, without thinking. But this time it pleased *me* that he did so.

"Yes," I said. Now let him make it good; let him prove it. "Let us hold the ceremony tomorrow. And now I leave you. We have much to arrange in the next few hours."

He did not flinch. "You will find it all done, and done well."

Back in my own, unfamiliar apartments, I wandered in like a ghost. I was stunned. Although I had rehearsed my "demands," I had not expected this to happen so fast. Tomorrow! To marry a man tomorrow whom I had not seen in four years! It was crazy, as crazy as something the god Dionysus would indulge in. I felt I must be drunk to do it.

Iras leapt up, surprised to see me return so early. Her eyes fastened on the necklace, and she stared.

I touched it lightly. "Do you like it?" I said. Indeed, I did feel drunk. None of this was real. "It is my wedding present. Yes, I am to marry. Tomorrow."

She just sputtered, unable to find words.

"You and Charmian will have to make me ready. I hope the ceremonial gown I brought will be suitable." I had had a special one made, but even to myself I had not used the words *wedding gown*. "You had best get it out and air it. Call Charmian."

Iras rushed off to do so. I looked dreamily around the chamber.

Married. I was to be married—in public. In only a few hours.

"Madam, what is this?" Charmian came running in. "Married?"

"Yes. Tomorrow." I did not have to identify the man. "Well, isn't it about time?" I laughed. "After all, our children are three years old!"

"But—"

"Charmian, Iras, your task is to make me beautiful tomorrow. Nothing else."

"That we can do," said Charmian. "But I must ask—you must ask yourself—and answer before tomorrow—I know you wish to marry Antony, but do you wish to wed Rome as well? Will you yield Egypt up like this?"

"It is a fair question," I said. "But by doing this, I hope to preserve Egypt."

I lay in the darkness, the hours passing in this strange city, under this strange sky. Nothing was as I had pictured it, adding to the unreality. Thus, whatever happened tomorrow would be fitting.

Charmian's question . . . how to answer it to myself? Because my position was unique, I could not expect to be like any other bride. But I felt I was marrying a man, not marrying Rome. He, like Caesar, was an unusual son of Rome, one who seemed to understand that there were other peoples in the world, and was willing to share the stage with them—or at least grant them some dignity and liberty under the Roman eagle.

The wedding would take place in the late afternoon. Basins of water from the famous springs of Antioch were brought in to fill a tub for me to bathe in. I declined to add any perfume or oil to them, since they had been tasted by Alexander on his way to Egypt, and he had pronounced them like his mother's milk. If anything, milk should have been added. Charmian and Iras washed me, one rubbing each arm, and washed my hair. Afterwards they combed it out, drying it before a brazier, brushing it smooth until it gleamed. Then they took a pair of shears and cut a lock of it to be dedicated to Isis before the ceremony.

My gown, a Grecian-style one of pale blue silk, hung airing in the breeze before the open window. On a separate cord hung my veil of matching silk. I would wear it covering my face, in accordance with Greek custom.

Each of them tended to my hands, rubbing them with almond oil, buffing the nails with ground pearls.

I was oddly calm. I knew it was a momentous step, and because it was of such great consequence, I could not dwell on it. I must go forward, trusting my own leading, committing myself to fate. It did not feel unkindly.

The procession to the Temple of Isis, and the ceremony itself, would be witnessed by only a dozen people. Antony would take me in a carriage, with his chief officer, Canidius Crassus, on my other side. Others would follow, including Iras and Charmian and more staff officers.

He came to my chamber early, looking solemn. But whatever his thoughts, he stood there manfully and extended his hand to take mine. Silently we descended to the waiting carriage. Through the gauze of the veil I could see the other man waiting, a man with a long, thin face. He nodded to me and slid far to one side to give us room. Still no one spoke, as the horses clattered along the street. I peered out as best I could. The buildings were handsome ones, the streets swept and clean. There were no crowds, as none of this was expected or announced.

As we swung down another street, I glimpsed the famous statue of Tyche, Antioch's goddess of fortune, staring enigmatically at us, clutching her sheath of wheat. We rattled past her.

At the Temple of Isis the priest was waiting, holding the pail of sacred water. He wore the customary white linen robe, and his head was shaved. Behind him rose a beautiful statue of Isis, carved in the whitest marble I had ever seen. My lock of hair lay at her feet, a dark, shining offering.

Antony and I stood before him, the others from the following carriages grouped around us. He prayed to Isis, she who had instituted marriage, asking her to unite us, bless us, preserve us. He asked us if we came willingly to this marriage, and we each said yes—Antony loudly, I much quieter. I found it hard to speak. He asked us to vow fidelity to one another, to live as man and wife, to care for each other the rest of our lives—not fleeing before adversity, he said, or relying on prosperity, but standing side by side in all conditions until death, faced together.

A ring was not necessary, but Antony produced it and put it on my finger, announcing that in so doing he took me as his true wife.

The statue of Isis was anointed with sacred water, more prayers were said, the hair dedicated, incense lit. Hymns were intoned in the priest's high, singsong voice.

It was over. We were married. Antony took the corner of my veil and tried to lift it. "May I see my wife's face?" he asked.

But I stopped him. "No. Not until much later." That, too, was the Greek custom.

We returned to the carriages, but the way back was much slower. As twilight fell, a torchlight procession walked ahead of us, singing wedding hymns. In the carriage, a still-silent Antony took my hand—the one with the ring—and held it. The gold necklace lay heavy on my neck.

In the palace, the wedding feast awaited—heaps of food, hastily prepared but nonetheless succulent. There were roasted boar, smoked bass, oysters, eels, and lobsters, salt fish from Byzantium, Jericho dates, melons, mounds of cake dripping with Hymettan honey, and more of the famous Laodicean wine.

I met the officers who were to play such an important part in the coming campaign: Marcus Titius, dark, lean, almost satyrlike; Ahenobarbus, balding but with a bushy beard, sharp eyes, and (I had been told) an even sharper tongue. He held it tonight, offering only his congratulations. There was also Munatius Plancus, a broad-beamed man with a thatch of straight, light hair, and again, Canidius Crassus. He had not only a long face but a long body as well, and was exceptionally tall, towering over others. He had a mournful look on his face, but later Antony told me he always looked like that. Certainly he seemed polite enough to me; I did not detect any hostility in his manner.

Last there was Ventidius Bassus, the general who had driven the Parthians back across the Euphrates, and, as Antony put it, "made it possible for us to be here in Antioch tonight."

Bassus bowed stiffly. Older than the others, he was actually of Caesar's generation.

"Bassus is departing for Rome for a well-earned Triumph," said Antony proudly. "And you will be sure to tell everyone in Rome about today's ceremony, will you not?"

Bassus looked surprised. "Why, yes, if you . . . want me to, Lord Antony." Obviously he had imagined Antony wanted it kept quiet, not announced in Rome.

"Yes. Yes, indeed I do. In fact, make sure you don't forget."

"No, sir."

"Here, here, is my wedding gift!" Antony cried loudly. He unrolled a scroll and read off to all the company, "To Queen Cleopatra, I hereby give the following lands: Cyprus, west Cilicia, the coasts and seaports of Phoenicia and Judaea—excepting only Tyre and Sidon—central Syria, Arabia, and the groves of balsam in Jericho and the bitumen rights to the Dead Sea."

Now all conversation ceased, and I could sense the shock and anger in the room. Antony rolled the scroll up and placed it in my hands, then folded them over it. "It is yours. All is yours."

I realized that he had given me not only Roman territory but other rights that were technically not his, such as the ones in Jericho and the Dead Sea, and Arabia. He had gone beyond even what I had asked.

"I thank you," I said, and now at last I felt hostility around me.

It was time to depart for our chamber. We were conducted there by a large company, then escorted inside. The doors were closed, but just outside them the last part of the ceremony must be enacted. A chorus sang the bridal song, and we stood and listened.

> *Happy groom, the wedding took place*
> *and the woman you prayed for is yours.*
>
> *Now her charming face is warm with love.*
>
> *My bride, your body is a joy,*
> *Your eyes as soft as honey,*
> *And love pours its light*
> *on your perfect features.*
> *Using all her skill, Aphrodite*
> *honored you.*
> *No woman who ever was,*
> *O groom, was like her.*

The voices faded away, and I could hear the footsteps departing. We were truly alone.

Now Antony lifted off the veil, freeing my face.

"Yes, it is true," he said, "No woman who ever was, is like you." He finally kissed me, and I let him.

Later, standing before the bed, I spoke. "I am scarred. I am not what I was." The birth of the twins had left its mark on me. He would find me changed.

He took my face in his wide hands. "You earned them for me, and they are precious to me."

I thought I would have forgotten his body, but I had not. The body has a memory of its own and mine remembered his, every aspect of it.

How had I passed those four years without it?

Time and again all night, in between our times together, I would get up and look out at the dark plain stretching beyond the palace, at the starry sky, its constellations moved ever so slightly from Alexandria. That night sky of Antioch, as it holds itself in late autumn, will always be a consecrated memory for me. I cannot separate it from the joy of my reunion with Antony, and of our daring to do what we did.

55

For the first few days I found myself walking about in a peculiar state of mind, bringing myself up short and saying in disbelief, *I am married.* It was hard to fathom the subtle change it entailed. I was almost thirty-three, and had been alone—fiercely alone—all my life. Living with Caesar in Alexandria with the palace under fire, living with Antony when he came on holiday, was not the same. And altogether those had only added up to a year—one year out of thirty-three. I had borne children and raised them alone, had governed alone, using Mardian and Epaphroditus for advice and guidance only, but having no conflict between their wishes and mine.

Now I had a partner, politically and personally, and it felt as odd and cumbersome as the gold wedding necklace on my neck. It was beautiful, it was valuable, it was enviable—but it felt unnatural.

Not that Antony was difficult to live with. I knew already how accommodating he was, how his high spirits could turn any ordinary day into a celebration. That was part of his charm. But now our plans must meld, our aims must be the same; there was no way we could extricate ourselves from each other, no way to say, *You do this; it is of no consequence to me.* We were now of immense consequence to each other.

It was what I wanted, had thought I wanted. And his magic always was that when I was actually with him, these doubts and reservations vanished.

Winter closed in on Antioch. What was a delightful summer spot was dismal in winter—fogs and chilling, torrential rains. I wished to return to Alexandria, but Antony needed to stay where he was to ready his army. Reluctant to leave him so soon, I stayed. There were, of course, the usual festivities that abound wherever soldiers gather, especially in the winter.

And there were the nights we spent together—some of them placid, with Antony reading reports and maps, planning battle strategies, while I allowed myself the luxury of reading poetry and philosophical essays—and others passionate, fueled by our long separation, both past and future, heightened by the wonder that we actually possessed one another.

And, inevitably, there were quarrels. A letter came from Octavia, written before the news of our marriage could have reached her. Antony read it aloud, making it sound almost comically dull.

" ' . . . and you would certainly have enjoyed the reading by Horace, which he presented at the gathering at the home of Maecenas.' Oh yes, I'm devastated to have missed it—I wonder what we were doing then?" he mused. "Horace always bored my toga off."

"Oh, is that what got it off? No wonder Octavia staged Horace readings regularly."

He shrugged. "I should have kept it on. Making love to Octavia was like— was like—"

"I don't want to hear what it was like." Whatever it was like, I had been sleeping alone. It must have been more satisfactory than that.

"It was like—nothing at all."

"Oh, not nothing. Surely." The whole subject made me angry.

"As near to nothing as possible."

"Well, you must have done this nothing often enough to bring forth two children. Strange that you would keep at it so doggedly."

"She was my wife! She expected—"

"I don't want to hear about that, either! I suppose you were about to say Octavian was patrolling underneath the windows to make sure you were performing your duty."

He just laughed, finding it amusing. "No, it was more like having Octavian right there in the room already."

"How appetizing."

"Why do you keep talking about it?"

"*You* brought it up! Reading that letter—" I pointed to it, still hanging limply from Antony's hand. He had been about to drop it into a basket of correspondence.

"Then I won't anymore! I thought if I *didn't* read it, you would take it amiss." He waved it up and down. "I don't care about it! Forget it! Why does it bother you so?"

"Why does Caesar bother *you* so?" The sight of the pendant sent him into fits, so I had reluctantly stopped wearing it. I would save it for Caesarion.

"Because he—because he was Caesar! Who wants to follow Caesar? But Octavia—there's nothing extraordinary about her." He kneaded his forearms. "You are right. It's equally foolish. Anyone who poisons the present with the past is a fool." He got off the bench and came over to me, an intent look on his face. "Let us enjoy this honeyed present which the gods have granted us." He put his hands in my hair and pulled my face toward his.

"Not now!" I said, alarmed. "The envoys from Cappadocia expect to have an audience any moment." It never failed to surprise me how Antony could become aroused at the most inconvenient times.

"They will have to amuse themselves while we amuse ourselves," he said, picking me up and carrying me off into the bedchamber. "This is a wedding custom in Rome—the man has to carry the woman across the threshold. It's bad luck if I stumble. Oops." He dropped to one knee just outside the door, swooping down. "Just missed it." He stepped over the sill and put me down on the bed. "There. Bad luck averted." He leaned over me, lowering his face to mine as he bent his arms. He kissed me, first on my eyelids, then gently on both cheeks, before finally seeking my mouth.

"Now I can pretend that you are war booty," he murmured. "Captured in your palace, tied up and brought here as a captive."

"Why do you make everything into a game?" I whispered. Now he had got me aroused, too.

"Isn't Dionysus the god of actors?" he said, his mouth traveling down to my neck, the hollow of my throat. He moved over closer against me, his strong shoulder taking most of his weight. It bore down on me, pushing me into the mattress. I did feel like a captive, but had no desire to escape. I brought my arms around him, running my hands down his shoulders and over his back. The very feel of the muscles and flesh drove everything else out of my mind. His mouth on me made something inside draw together and then expand. An edge of a shudder ran through me.

"Lord, the envoys—" I heard a forlorn voice in the outer chamber dying away.

"The envoys . . . let them wait . . . a little." I could barely hear his words, they were so muffled against my flesh.

This sudden onslaught of desire did not leave him time to take off most of his clothes, so he had little to do later to ready himself to meet the envoys, besides smoothing down his hair, which he did as he rushed out the door. I lay there, dazed, as if I had just been assaulted by a force of nature, which is what Antony in full vigor was like.

I looked at a cloud formation that had been moving across the sky. It had not gone very far. Antony was right; he did not keep the envoys waiting very long. He had not exceeded the bounds of politeness.

Like an earth tremor, Antony's forthcoming campaign made the ground tingle all over the east, sending out alarm signals. It had been almost twenty years since the catastrophic Roman defeat at Carrhae, and yet the Romans were known always to avenge defeats. Ten years later Caesar was departing to do so when he was felled; now once again an army was being readied for the mission. Vengeance had been delayed but it would be certain.

Rumors about the size and scope of the army went before it like trumpeters, magnifying what was already an enormous host. There were a half a million men, an Armenian merchant reported hearing; no, a million, a trader from the Black Sea had been told by reliable sources. The equipment was secret, made by Egyptian black arts combined with Roman engineering: siege towers that were fireproof, arrows that had a range of a mile and could be accurately aimed at night, catapult stones that exploded, and food supplies that were imperishable and lightweight, so soldiers could live in the field for months at a time.

Antony told me about these marvels as he lay back one night after dinner, almost lost in the forest of pillows he had arranged for himself. I remembered, fleetingly, the time I had amused Caesar with the eastern den of pillows, but that had been downright austere compared to this.

"Yes," he said dreamily, his hands behind his head, "it seems that I command a supernatural force. Rations that never grow stale!" His voice rose in wonder. "An army that can carry all its own supplies, and not have to live off the land. Now that would be a miracle. Ah, well, such rumors may help turn my enemies to jelly before I ever arrive, may do half my work for me."

I looked down at him, where he lay in pure contentment. It was time he went back into the field; it had been five years since Philippi. Five years was a long time for a soldier to sit feasting and dreaming and relaxing. Had Caesar ever taken five years off?

Stop comparing him with Caesar, I told myself.

But the whole world is comparing him with Caesar. This campaign is meant to compare him with Caesar, to carry out Caesar's design, to show who is Caesar's true military heir and successor. That was the truth of it.

Yes, five years was a long time for anything to lie fallow. He must bestir himself.

"Unfortunately, you and I know it is just a myth. This war will have to be fought and won the old-fashioned way," I said. "What is your tally for the troops so far?"

"When Canidius brings his legions back from Armenia, where he has been wintering, our strength will stand at sixteen legions—sixteen somewhat under-strength legions. But they're good soldiers, good seasoned Roman legionaries, of the sort—the sort that will be in short supply for me from now on."

The last thought caused him pain.

"Because Octavian prevents you from recruiting any more in Italy, in spite

of his agreements!" I snapped. "And where are the twenty thousand he promised you, in exchange for the ships he borrowed from you last year? You need
not answer, we know well enough!" It had been this, finally, that had opened
Antony's eyes to his devious colleague.

"Under his command, never to be released," Antony said grimly. "But
after Parthia, I—"

"After Parthia is *won*," I corrected him.

"After Parthia is won, I will have no need of favors from him," said Antony. "As I was saying, I take sixty thousand Roman legionaries into the field,
aided by thirty thousand auxiliaries. Half of those auxiliaries are under the
kings of Armenia and Pontus."

"Can you trust them?" I asked.

"If I were to trust no foreign allies, how could I trust you?" He smiled.

"You are not married to King Artavasdes of Armenia, nor to Polemo of
Pontus."

Now he laughed. "By Hercules, no!"

"Armenia is Parthian by culture and sympathy," I said. "How can you trust
them to support Rome? It seems very risky to march into Parthia and leave
them unguarded at your back."

He sighed. "You are a wise general. We should have garrisoned Armenia
after Canidius's victories there, but we cannot spare the troops. The King
seems honest in his support, and he is contributing a small army to our cause,
commanding it in person."

"I like it not," I said.

"You have trained yourself to be suspicious of everyone and everybody,"
he said.

"If I had not, I would not be alive now to be sitting beside you." All my
siblings were dead, and none—except little Ptolemy—by natural causes.

He reached out and touched my hair. "For which I am profoundly grateful,"
he said. "But stop sitting, and lie here beside me. You look down upon me
too sternly from those heights."

"I cannot think clearly when I am lying down amidst a field of pillows,
especially with you beside me. Tell me—where are the papers of Caesar's
from which you have planned this campaign? I would like to see them."

"Do you not believe me?"

"Yes, of course I do." But I also knew he had altered and outright forged
many papers that he claimed to have "found" in Caesar's house—papers
relating to appointments and legacies. He had confessed it to me himself.
That was forgivable, since it wielded him a counterpower to the assassins,
and even brought them to him, hats in hand. But this was different. I was
deeply worried because Antony had never planned a campaign of this scope;
his successes as a general had been achieved in much smaller arenas. This
venture required not only a vision of the entire campaign, but a genius for
long-range planning and details that even Caesar would have been taxed to
provide.

"I will show them to you later this evening," he said. "They are in another part of the palace. For now, I want to lie here and enjoy digesting my food. I want to feel the heat from this well-placed brazier"—he indicated the ornate, footed brass brazier emitting welcome warmth—"and be thankful I am not outside."

It was nasty that night, with a driving, cold rain that seemed to penetrate the walls.

"If the gods look upon me with favor, this time next year I will be wintering near Babylon. It will be warm enough there to sleep out under the stars."

"Unlike Armenia, with its snows and mountains. Or even Media. Yes, you must be in Babylon by winter," I agreed.

It would take at least two years to carry out such a campaign, I knew. Caesar had allowed for three, assuming—on the basis of his experiences in Gaul—that everything always took longer than expected. But it would be hard to part with Antony again, so soon, and for such a long time. That it might be forever—I refused to let myself dwell on that. Isis would not be so cruel.

"The very name of Babylon has a magic," he said. "In truth, I never thought I might be the one to conquer it—the first westerner since Alexander himself. Fate is capricious, is she not? Why should she grant to me what she denied to Caesar?"

"You have answered your own question—because she is capricious. And deaf to entreaties and questions. And I sometimes think she enjoys offering her prizes to those who seem reluctant to seek them. Perhaps Caesar sought too hard." I had given much thought to this. Did that mean one should never seek? It was confusing.

He propped himself up on one elbow. "When my father died in my eleventh year, he left me a tarnished name, an empty purse, and an unstable family. It was not a promising start. And now, thirty-five years later, I call a queen my wife and will lead the largest and finest Roman army of the age— perhaps of any age—into the east. Fate *has* been a strange partner to me all these years."

"I have heard snatches of your scandalous youth, cavorting with Curio and his gang in Rome—again, not a promising start."

"True. But I wearied of it—just about the time the debt collectors were breathing uncomfortably close to me. I managed to get far away—betook myself to Greece to study oratory. Speechmaking ran in my family, and it made a reasonable excuse for escaping Rome. On his way to Syria, the new governor, Gabinius, spotted me during some military exercises and persuaded me to come with him as commander of his cavalry."

"The first of your good fortune," I said. What if Gabinius had come to the exercise grounds on a different day?

"Yes," Antony acknowledged. "And of course the second stroke of good fortune was leading the cavalry to Egypt when Gabinius agreed to restore your father to the throne. That led me to Alexandria, where I first saw you."

It had seemed so unremarkable at the time—a pleasant young Roman who had been kindly tolerant of my father's weakness. I had been grateful to him for that, and surprised that a Roman could be so likable, but it did not seem a fateful event. "Which did not seem anything out of the ordinary at the time, I am sure," I said.

"Oh no, you are wrong!" he protested, sitting bolt upright. "I was very taken with you!"

I could not help laughing. It was a conventional thing for lovers to plead, but his memory was playing tricks on him. "You said that once before, but I cannot imagine why," I said. At the time I had been barely fourteen years old, badly shaken by the dethronement of my father and the fine line I had had to walk to mollify my sisters and stay alive. I could recall the fear very vividly, even now. Too vividly.

"Because of the way you stood," he said. "Anyone could see you were a princess." When he saw my questioning look, he hurried on to explain himself. "That you could hold yourself like that after all you had endured, all the uncertainty, the loss of your father—it was very affecting. I knew you were no ordinary person."

"So it was my posture that struck you!"

"It was what the posture *meant*."

I had not even been aware of my posture, in my youthful focus on other things—my hair, my height, my skin. "You saw things in me that I did not," I said. "I must thank you for those eyes." I paused. "But Gabinius paid dearly for helping my father—he was sent back to Rome in disgrace. How did you escape that?"

"Luckily—that word again—I was so clearly just a subordinate, taking orders, that I could not be blamed for Gabinius's defiance of the Senate. Still, I thought it best to give Rome a wide berth, and so I went to Gaul to serve as a legate to Caesar. And that was my third stroke of fortune, for all else followed from that. Caesar noticed me, gave me responsibilities, trusted me . . . and in the reckoning with Pompey, when I burst through Pompey's sea blockade in the dead of night, risking all on that venture, I won Caesar's heart as a gambler like himself. In the final battle I commanded the left wing of his army, fighting outnumbered. Caesar won the battle and I shared the victory."

He had a mighty legacy. Truly, Fate had been leading him, step by step, toward something very large.

I, too, had been led past many dangers and reversals, to find myself here. Now, on the eve of the greatest leap of all, let not our guardian fates desert us.

"If I think on it too much, I tremble," I had to admit.

"Then do not think on it, do not look down as you skirt the narrow ledge, lest you lose heart, lose balance, and fall," he said.

"Yet if you lead an army, you must prepare," I said. "I think—I think I would like to see those papers now, hear your plans." Now, before I lost stomach for the details.

He groaned. "So you will force me to spread them out?" He rose to his feet, then held out his hands for mine. "I warn you, they are numbing in their sheer numbers!"

Yet from those numbers and charts our chances would be revealed. "It is early yet, and I am not tired," I assured him.

Down the seemingly endless hallways—oh, how the Seleucids had liked vastness!—unheated, unlighted, he took me to the apartments where he kept all the war records and documents. A sleepy guard—scarcely more than a boy—jumped to attention and scurried to light a fire and additional lamps to banish the bone-chilling damp and dreariness.

Antony flung open a trunk and gathered up an armful of scrolls, then dumped them down on a large table. "The best maps we have," he said. Two of them rolled off the table and lay at his feet. He spread out the biggest one on the table, securing it with a heavy oil lamp.

"There—that's the entire region, from Syria to Parthia and beyond," he said.

I was impressed with its detail. "Where did you get this?" I asked.

"I drew it myself," he said. "I put together all the intelligence about the area. Look—"

He pointed out various features. "It just stretches east, and east," he said. "We are used to the Tigris River marking the easternmost part of the world. To a Parthian, that is far west."

"A world beyond the edge of ours," I said. "I know the Parthians came from even farther east—some other desert region. They still fight like desert peoples, using horses and bows. If the Greeks are of the sea, and the Romans of the earth, then the Parthians come closest to being of the air."

Antony grunted, leaning on his elbows and staring at the map. "Yes, their arrows whistle through the air, with their front and back archers using two different trajectories, so that our shields cannot guard against all of them. But in this war I will force them to fight using Roman methods. And I have trained slingers with lead pellets that carry farther than Parthian arrows and can pierce armor, to show them they do *not* control the air."

Still, they were expert riders and had given the term "Parthian shot" to the world: When they appeared to be retreating, they would turn and shoot over their shoulders with deadly accuracy. And they had invented special bows shortened below the grip for use in the saddle, and a camel corps that carried unlimited replacement arrows. They fought exclusively with long-range weapons, never face-to-face.

"I plan to meet Canidius here"—he stabbed a finger down in Armenia—"and join our armies. Then we will march south, traversing the mountains and making for Phraaspa, where the national treasure is kept. We will attack the city and force them to fight for it in Roman fashion—after all, the city is not mobile and cannot ride away." He laughed. "They will have to stand like men and defend themselves, not flee." He seemed optimistic. "Since the countryside has little useful timber, I will be bringing my own battering rams and siege equipment."

"You will transport them all that way? How arduous and time-consuming!"

"True, but without them I cannot force the cities to yield."

"What were Caesar's exact plans for the campaign?" I asked quietly.

"He also planned to attack from the north, avoiding the west, where Crassus met his doom. He also had sixteen legions, and wished to gain experience in Parthian methods of fighting before actually engaging in full battle with them; his men would get their practice in skirmishes along the way."

"May I see the papers?"

He frowned, reluctant to bring them out. Why? Had Caesar different plans, ones that Antony had abandoned? Was he just using the magic name of Caesar to color his own strategy? "Very well," he finally said, making his way over to a small locked casket on another table. He opened it and pulled out a sheaf of papers, not the neatly folded papers of a man who had had the opportunity to store them, but the papers of a man caught by death unawares and in mid-action—messy and jumbled.

"This is exactly as I found them," he said, handing them to me. "I swear."

I was half afraid to spread them out. I did not want my suspicions confirmed. I did not want to let the force of Caesar loose in the room.

But I did, smoothing them out and holding down their corners with more oil lamps. The familiar writing—but with new, unknown thoughts—rose up and hit me.

How cherished was the writing itself to me—the ink, the very letters. How miraculous that they would tell me something novel, contain a message from him that was brand new.

There were sketches, hasty maps, labels. From the paths traced out in the fading ink, I could see that it was as Antony had said: This was the route he had meant to take. Relief flooded me, as if that guaranteed success. I felt ashamed to have doubted Antony, so to have mistrusted his judgment should it have differed from Caesar's.

I looked up to see Antony studying me intently. He had watched my expression as I read the notes, trying to penetrate my thoughts. I hoped they had not been transparent.

"You see?" he said defensively. "It is as I said."

"Of course it is," I said. "But I gather he planned to garrison Armenia, whereas you—"

"I told you I cannot spare the manpower! The Armenian king is our ally, and contributing—"

"Yes, yes, you did. I only meant—"

"Crassus took only eight legions. I must have adequate troops."

"And it looks as though Caesar meant to take Ecbatana and thereby cut Babylon off from Parthia proper."

"So shall I. But first Ecbatana must be reached, and before that Phraaspa must be taken."

"Of course." Carefully I folded up the papers. I hated to close them so soon, but they had told me what I wished to know, whispering of old memories and future conquests. "Here." I handed them back.

He returned them to their place, like a priest before a shrine. Perhaps that was what he was. In Rome he served as a priest to the cult of Julius Caesar, but here on the borders of the Roman world he was serving in an infinitely more demanding capacity, as the heir of Caesar and the executor of his last wishes—and what could be a higher act of respect and worship than that?

Snapping the lid shut on the box, he said fiercely, "The Parthians knew of his plans, and rejoiced in his murder. They sent a small contingent to help the assassins in their last stand at Philippi. In doing so they have marked themselves for retribution. We cannot let that pass unpunished."

"No. We cannot." We must pursue them to the very heart of their stronghold, as relentlessly as Caesar himself, and in his name.

Outside I could hear the rain beating. In the dark night, in winter's grip, it seemed impossible that warm weather would return, and that Antony would actually set out for Parthia. It was a long journey—over three hundred miles to the spot where he and Canidius would meet and review their troops, and another four hundred, through mountain passes and trails, to Phraaspa. Ecbatana, his target, lay another hundred and fifty to the south: a total that approached a thousand Roman miles, and over difficult terrain, infested with enemies. A land march of a thousand miles for a fully equipped army was a staggering undertaking. It would be a miracle if he reached Ecbatana by winter. The mountains were the sticking point in the plans—he could not cross them until winter was over, but that delayed the starting time a great deal.

"Everything takes so long!" I burst out.

He turned around and came back to the table. "Yes," he said. "And it seems to have taken a long time already, because year after year I have had to postpone the campaign. I think that soured me on Octavian more than anything else—attending to his needs, rushing back to Italy at his beck and call, only to be kept waiting and ignored!" His voice grew angry, an unusual thing to hear. "He has put stumbling blocks in my way, done everything to keep me from this campaign!"

"Yes, and we know why," I said. "Because he would not have you attain the position that fate has reserved for you. Thanks be to Isis that your eyes have finally seen his maneuvering! Now let Sextus sink him in their next sea battle. When you return from Parthia, may you find nothing left of Octavian but an empty ship lying in shallow waters, its mast gone, its hull smashed."

He began rolling up the maps. "Have you seen what you wished?" he asked politely.

"Yes." I had seen the magnitude of the task that lay before him. "I will come with you, at least to Armenia," I said. "Perhaps farther."

He looked startled. "You are welcome, of course, but—"

"After all, am I not supporting the campaign with Egyptian money?" I had invested three hundred talents, enough to support six legions for a year. Antony had had difficulty raising funds in the east, which was wrung dry by

Cassius and then the Parthians. Our allies had little left to give. "I will not distract you." I could not resist teasing him.

"I would insist that you turn back before we cross the mountains," he said. "One of us must survive the war."

I put my arms around his waist and rested my head on his chest. I thought of the Ninety-nine Soldiers. "Yes. I know."

"Before we set out," he said, "please send for our children. I wish to see them, in case—in case—"

In case I am one of the Ninety-nine, and not the Hundredth.

"Yes. Of course."

I wondered if Octavian was even now saying to Livia that the Parthians would take care of Antony for him—just as I had said Sextus would take care of Octavian for us.

56

Surrounded by a hundred shades of green—the deep mourning-green of cypresses, the exuberant bright green of spring meadow grass, the silvery green of old olive leaves, and far away on the flat plain, the many hues of just-sown crops, and beyond even that, the dancing blue-green of shallow waters in the Gulf of Alexandretta—I felt as though I were in a painting on the wall of a Roman villa. Behind us, Mount Silpius was thrusting up into the sky, and we stretched out on its flanks, eating our picnic in the warm sunshine.

From where I lay I could hear the soft clanking sound of goat-bells from herds higher up on the mountain, and fancied they were those of Pan himself, and that if I strained my ears harder I could hear his pipes.

"Here." Antony leaned over and placed a crown of wildflowers on my head. Their delicate leaves and petals felt cool on my forehead, and the soft smell of the violets and marigolds was lulling. Idly I pulled it off my head and looked at the bands of intertwined flowers.

"What is this?" I asked, seeing an unfamiliar pinkish flower with twisted, curly leaves.

"A wild orchid," he said.

I was amazed that he would know.

"I have spent a great many days in the field," he said, as if he had read my thoughts. "Sometimes I have had to survive on what I found there." He motioned to the children, romping farther down the hill, holding up two smaller crowns for them.

"Crowns for my wife, crowns for my children—crowns for all those with royal blood." He laughed, seeming not to mind excluding himself.

"You will earn yours," I assured him. "When you conquer Parthia—"

"No talk of that," he said quickly. "I would not think of anything today but the blue skies and the racing clouds. And spring on the hillside with you, and them."

Alexander and Selene came stumbling over the stones that studded the mountainside. They were three and a half years old now, as eager to play in the open air as any colt or kid.

"For you, Your Majesty," Antony said solemnly, placing the coronet on Alexander's head, where it was all but lost in his thick curls. "And you." He had one for Selene, this one with more poppies. She accepted regally.

"Well done," he said. "You see, that queenly gesture comes from you," he said to me. "It's inherited, not learned."

I put my arms around their shoulders. Antony seemed inordinately proud of them, as if they were the only children he had ever had. Seeing them together, the resemblance between Alexander and him was quite marked—Alexander had the same husky frame and wide face—but the true similarity was in their rambling, exuberant personalities. Alexander never brooded, or minded taking a tumble.

Selene was a bit of a mystery, as befitted a child named for the moon. She was not really like either of us, and with her pale coloring she looked as though she came from far to the north. She was quiet, but unusually self-possessed, and seldom cried or betrayed her feelings, either of joy or sorrow.

As promised, I had sent for them, and they had been with us for almost a month now. Mardian had accompanied them, wishing to confer with me about matters of state, as well as to ascertain my plans for the next few months. He had found Antioch and Antiochenes quite congenial to his tastes, enjoying their frivolity and overlooking their renowned tendency toward luxury and quarrelsomeness.

"Alexandrians can be described the same way," he had said.

"Antiochenes are less intellectual than Alexandrians," I had said, defending my city.

"When a mob forms in Alexandria, it is not particularly intellectual," he said. "You know how volatile they are."

"Well, here in Antioch they are too lazy to get up out of their scented baths to *form* a mob," I said.

"Good," said Mardian. "That makes the streets safer."

Alexander and Selene had betrayed great curiosity about their father. Until now, they had assumed that he was dead, like Caesarion's father. In fact, it seemed the normal state for a father, to have retired to the heavens. Now that he was with them, they kept staring at him and saying, "Are you *truly* our father? Will you stay?"

"Yes," Antony had said the first time, hugging them both at the same time. "And yes, I will stay, although I will be gone from time to time. But I will always come back."

Now he lay back down on the blanket covering the rough ground, and closed his eyes. "I will give you a hundred counts to hide," he said. "And if I cannot find you in another hundred counts, you may name a prize for yourself." He opened one eye and stared at them. "Ready?"

With a squeal, they scampered off. "One—two—" When he got up to ten, he stopped. "That should busy them for a while," he said, sitting up and kissing me.

"You are cheating," I said. "Those poor children—"

"They will welcome a few extra minutes to hide," he assured me.

Behind us the tinkle of the goat-bells grew louder, and the olive trees shading us rustled in the soft breeze. I had never been so content. Just as the vista of Antioch and the plain spread out below me as far as I could see in all directions, so the future lay, fair and promising. I loved, I was loved; I was surrounded by my children; my country was prosperous, and the ugly past, fraught with dangers and defeats, was receding like a distant shore. Antony and I saw eye-to-eye in everything; now that he had cast off Octavian, our aims had truly become one. The joy of it was dizzying.

It is almost impossible to describe happiness, because at the time it feels entirely natural, as if all the rest of your life has been the aberration; only in retrospect does it swim into focus as the rare and precious thing it is. When it is present, it seems to be eternal, abiding forever, and there is no need to examine it or clutch it. Later, when it has evaporated, you stare in dismay at your empty palm, where only a little of the perfume lingers to prove that once it was there, and now is flown.

So those days in Antioch with Antony. The world lay before him, waiting for his invading footstep. Anticipation quickened every day, but reality still was far enough off to float on the mist of possibilities, seductive and soothing, just out of reach.

We danced in a haze of joy like two butterflies, flying from one hedge to another, caught up in a divine drunkenness of the spirit. I was young, sometimes feeling younger even than the children; I was entirely adult, believing myself endowed with mature wisdom, having no trouble making even the most difficult decisions—all answers seemed given to me. *Everything* seemed given to me. If I forgot to thank you, Isis—forgive me. I do so now, belatedly.

Mardian was leaving, taking the children back to Alexandria with him.

"Duty calls," he said pointedly.

"I will return by summer," I promised him. "If I did not have such trustworthy ministers, I could not be away so long."

"Oh, so I am to blame for your absence?" he said. "Am I to be punished for being competent?"

I laughed. "Most ministers would not consider being left in charge to be punishment," I reminded him.

"Perhaps most ministers do not like the kings and generals they serve," he said. "We must be the exception. Well, do not linger too long. How do you plan to return? When shall I send a ship?"

I had been thinking of that. A brilliant idea had come to me. All my ideas during those weeks seemed brilliant. "I won't need a ship," I said. "I plan to accompany Antony as far as Armenia, and that leaves me a long way from the sea. So I have decided to retrace my steps and journey through Judaea. I will pay Herod a diplomatic visit."

He raised his eyebrows. "You're a trusting soul," he said. "Putting yourself in his hands! He has little cause to protect you, and much cause to see that an 'accident' befalls you."

"He wouldn't dare," I said. I knew Herod and I were antagonists now, since I had asked for—and been granted—large portions of his kingdom. He was said to be boiling about the loss of the lucrative date palm and balsam groves in Jericho, and his seaports as far south as Gaza.

"I repeat, you *are* a trusting soul," said Mardian. "There is no limit to what someone will dare when he sees his country's existence threatened."

Now those words return to me; someone continually pours them into Octavian's ear about me.

"It is in my interest to placate him, then," I said.

"Unless you plan to restore his property to him, I fail to see what you can offer."

"My friendship rather than my enmity."

"It is his place to offer that. Naturally, *you* would want to offer friendship, since you are the gainer; it is up to the loser to put aside enmity, and you cannot force that."

"True," I said. "But no harm can come of meeting with him."

"Don't be too sure," said Mardian.

It was hard for me to tell whether he was entirely serious. He raised one of his eyebrows and stretched, breaking the tension.

"You have not shown me Daphne yet, and how can I return to Alexandria without seeing the famous laurel tree? Olympos will be disappointed."

Yes, Olympos had an academic interest in the sites where supernatural transformations had taken place. He had visited the weeping rock that had once been Niobe, had inspected an oak tree said to contain a nymph, and had dissected sunflowers to see if their stems were different from those of regular flowers, since they were supposed to originate from a maiden named Clytie who was hopelessly in love with Apollo. Seeing no difference, he published a paper refuting the story.

"As if anyone had believed it anyway," Mardian said. "Why does he waste his time like that?"

Now I agreed that Mardian and I must inspect one of the most famous "transformation" trees, the one where Daphne had taken root and sprouted leaves to escape the predations of Apollo.

"Apollo seems to have an adverse effect on women," I said. "Clytie had to turn into a sunflower to put an end to her unrequited love, and Daphne decided she would rather be a tree than yield to his embraces. How sad they could not change places!"

"That's how legends are," said Mardian. "Everyone wants what he cannot have, and gets punished. But tell me—if Apollo was so attractive, why did that nymph run away? I ask you, as a woman, to explain it."

"Perhaps she ran away from him because he *was* so attractive," I said.

"That makes no sense," argued Mardian.

It did not, but I knew it happened. After all, I had resisted meeting with Antony.

"Sometimes we run away just to thwart fate," I finally said. "Come, let us go out to Daphne."

We clattered along in our carriage, leaving the palace island, passing the old agora, and then traveling the wide paved street toward the elaborate fountain built over the original sweet springs of Antioch. Crowds of people were gathered idly around it, dressed in outlandish garb. They waved at us and shouted in high-pitched voices. A peculiar oily smell drifted toward us.

"Faster!" Mardian ordered the driver. "That smell—how can they call it perfume?" He held his nose.

"I think it is many perfumes fighting," I said.

"Well, it makes a stink!" Mardian looked disdainful. "And did you see the makeup? As garish as a mummy-carton! On both sexes!"

"Mardian, I do believe you are turning into a prude," I said. "Who would ever have expected it of an Alexandrian eunuch?"

"Don't tell me you *like* these people!" His initial enthusiasm for the Antiochenes had waned.

"I have no prejudices against any particular people. I take them as individuals, you should know that." I would have to, if Antony and I were to rule over many lands and peoples. But I had always felt that way.

"This city seems to have adopted all the bad fashions of Alexandria."

"And much of the good," I insisted. "It is the third city in the world now, after Alexandria and Rome. If it does not quite measure up to them—that is why it is third. But there is much to like here." Could the place where I had married ever be less than dear to me?

Soon we passed the famous Antioch statue, the goddess of Fortune wearing city walls for her crown, resting on Mount Silpius, the Orontes River swimming beneath her feet. How placid, how uninvolved Fortune looked, as she blandly oversaw men's fates. Her indifference was chilling.

Some little distance from the city lay the sacred precinct of Daphne, where Seleucus I had been commanded by Apollo to plant an extensive grove of cypresses. They surrounded the ancient laurel tree; and of course there was the inevitable Temple of Apollo nestled nearby.

We alighted from the carriage and followed a path through the shadowy grove. The long fingers of the cypresses, like a hall of columns, made us feel we were passing through a natural temple.

The laurel, twisted and thick, lay in the very center of the grove. It stood with a forsaken dignity, as if long-suffering. It had long ago lost its slender form, becoming gnarled with age, and any nymph residing within was imprisoned in an ugly citadel—a sad fate for something once lovely and young. She had paid a high price for resisting Apollo.

Mardian ran his fingers over the rough bark. "Are you in there, Daphne?" he called lightly.

Overhead the leaves, still delicate and healthy, rustled slightly, like a sigh.

Final preparations for the army were in hand, as melting snows from the mountains gushed down the slopes, opening the passes. Soon Antony would embark: the long-postponed venture was at hand. His generals—all except Canidius—were gathered at headquarters. Titius, the lean-faced nephew of Plancus, was to serve as *quaestor*, and Ahenobarbus would command several legions. Dellius, the man who had so rudely summoned me to Tarsus all those years ago, would also be entrusted with legions and the task of writing the history of the campaign, as Antony never wrote accounts of his wars. The excitement of the coming campaign hung in the air, like a smell of metal and fire.

Ahenobarbus, who had visited Rome to settle some family business, asked to speak to Antony privately; Antony took that to include me as well. I could see by Ahenobarbus's face that he wished to be alone with Antony. His little eyes focused on me, and his forced smile and flat voice made that clear. But Antony ignored it, and merely urged him to speak his mind.

"And how have you left Rome?" Antony asked, handing him a cup of wine, which Ahenobarbus ostentatiously declined. Antony shrugged and took it himself.

"Behind," Ahenobarbus said. "And faring well enough, although there is a severe shortage of bread. So all the talk is about this season's attack on Sextus."

"It will be a repeat of the last," said Antony. "They are helpless against the self-styled Son of Neptune."

"I think not," said Ahenobarbus. His voice was sharp. "Agrippa created a naval training station near Misenum, and he has been training crack oarsmen all winter. They will meet Sextus as equals. He has also built a fleet of huge ships, so large that Sextus cannot attack them. And as if that were not enough, he has invented a device that allows him to shoot a grappling hook over great distances from the safety of his floating forts. He will haul in Sextus's boats like little silver fish."

"Ah well, I wish him luck," said Antony, and he meant it. "Did you speak to Octavian about our venture?"

"Oh yes. He invited me to a most delicious dinner." Ahenobarbus paused for dramatic effect. "He was curious about your preparations—although he seemed well apprised of all the details I recounted. The man has spies everywhere."

Are you one? I wondered. He sounded like it.

"Aside from Octavian, how do Romans look upon it?" Antony asked.

"They do not seem to pay it much mind," said Ahenobarbus. "They are much more concerned with their bellies and bread than with foreign conquests. We have had so many foreign conquests at the hands of Caesar that perhaps interest has worn thin." His smile was equally thin. He spread his hands as if to say, *What remedy?*

"Did Octavian—how did he receive the news of my marriage with the Queen?" Antony took my hand proudly.

We had had no word from Rome; our announcement was met with a silence that seemed to grow louder with each passing day.

"If he has received it, he does not acknowledge it," said Ahenobarbus. "He spoke of granting you the right to dine at the Temple of Concord with your wife and daughters, when you return to Rome. A great honor."

"Another daughter?" Antony had had no word from Octavia since she had gone back to Rome.

"Why, yes," said Ahenobarbus. "You were not told?" He seemed genuinely surprised.

"No," Antony admitted. "No, I have not been informed." He finished his cup of wine and set it down. I could see that he was taken aback; he might have shaken the dust of Rome from his feet, but he had never considered they might have done the same to him. Ignoring his campaign and our marriage was a signal insult.

"That was rude of them," said Ahenobarbus, half jokingly. "Well, after we give the Parthians a thrashing, they'll mind their manners better in Rome." He paused. "Now, as for the campaign—if you have not lost your touch of splendid nonchalance on the field, we shall soon have a new Roman province."

After he left, I wheeled around on Antony. "How dare Octavian ignore our marriage?"

Antony looked tired, as he sank down on a couch. He ran his hands through his hair and rubbed his temples. "He is not ignoring it, believe me, regardless of what he wants us to think."

"Send Octavia her papers of divorce," I said. "He cannot ignore that." If she had had her child, then there was no reason to hold back. "It is time."

"No," he said stubbornly. "There is no point in fighting a war on two fronts. If he ignores you, then let me ignore Octavia. Sometimes ignoring someone is a stronger statement than taking action. Let Octavian see how it feels."

"You keep giving reasons for not divorcing her."

"Let them *ask* me to," he said. "Let them acknowledge that they have failed to force the marriage upon me, and are hurting only themselves. I have no wish to harm Octavia," he said quickly. "Surely Octavian will see that she is the one who suffers most in this, since she cannot marry anyone else until she is free."

"I don't think he cares how much she suffers, as long as he has a hold over *you*," I said.

That night had the feeling of a farewell, although there would be a few more days before we actually left Antioch. But the chamber, its packed trunks and coffers already taken away, seemed empty and echoing—as if our belongings had embarked on the next stage, leaving us behind.

Lying together in the high bed, its mosquito net making a gauzy tent around us, I said sleepily, "This is like a play-tent." I rested my head on his shoulder, feeling supremely contented after a prolonged session of lovemaking. "There would not be time for this in a real tent, on a real battlefield."

"No." He sounded wide awake. "I will miss you very keenly. Now even a war tent seems lacking without you, so completely do you fill every aspect of my life."

"You make me sound like a faithful hound," I said, with a drowsy laugh.

Now that the moment had come, the venture that carried so much weight sat lightly upon him. Perhaps that was the only way to bear it.

Sometime in the middle of the night a ferocious spring storm broke, with fearsome lightning flashes and sonorous rolls of thunder. Asleep at last, Antony barely stirred, except to burrow his shaggy head deeper against my neck. But I lay listening, hearing the rain washing down from the roof, cleansing the world.

By dawn the storm was over, and only roiling gray clouds remained. The soaked earth, black and deep-plowed, released a thick, rich, fertile-smelling cloud. Everywhere branches drooped with the aftermath of the pelting rain, each end a shimmering knob of water, each leaf and blossom gleaming. Huge puddles lay scattered on the paving stones; a few brave birds were already singing.

"Come." I circled Antony's waist as we stood looking out at the new-washed garden outside our doors, bordering the wide flagstone terrace. "Let us go outside and walk in it."

Barefoot, we emerged onto the terrace, where the cold stones and water made our feet tingle. The hems of our gowns dragged, becoming rimmed with water. Out in the garden itself, the slippery grass, chilled and as sleek as an animal's fur, gave off a piercingly sweet aroma as we crushed it under our toes. A gust of wind would shake the laden boughs of trees far overhead, sending down showers on us, soaking our shoulders.

Everywhere there was the gentle sound of dripping. The Persian lilacs, weighed down with their heavy clusters of flowers, bent gracefully, like a row of courtiers. We walked between them, letting the flowers slap us, sending scented spray into our faces.

After the rain, there is a magic that evaporates when the sun comes out.

I stopped and shut my eyes, feeling only the slight chill, smelling the lilacs and damp earth, hearing the water drops fall from boughs. The perfume seemed intensified by the moisture, and when I looked down at the ground, at all the little plants brimming with water in their cups, the colors seemed magnified as well, the greens sharp and dazzling. The purple of the violets, the blue of the irises were like jewels.

I seemed to be in paradise, for that is what a garden is after the rain, in spring.

After the rain . . . I tightened my arm around Antony, to prove to myself this was no dream, to feel his solid flesh.

Far to the east, behind Mount Silpius and the sunrise, lay Parthia, waiting.

57

Early May, and we were in Armenia, being feasted by Antony's new-won ally, King Artavasdes, in his drafty palace overlooking the valley of the Araxes River. It was an elaborate structure, and as I looked around the dim chamber I became aware that the long arm of Greek architecture, style, and furnishings did not reach here. We had left the west behind, and from here on all would be foreign to us: foreign manners, foreign protocol, foreign motives. Octavian has been pleased to call me eastern and exotic, but that is not so—Egypt and Greece are not foreign, even to Rome.

The hall was many-domed, like a bazaar, or a series of tents. Intricate patterns of gold and lapis covered the span, and were echoed in bright tiles underfoot. More color ran down the walls in heavy gold-embroidered silk, and the tables were draped in what looked more like rugs than cloths. The Armenians did not eat reclining, but sat straight on backless chairs. The vessels on the table were gold, massive, and as encrusted with gems as warts on a toad.

Artavasdes himself was slender and dark, with enormous, soulful eyes and a drooping mustache. He turned mournful eyes on me when he spoke, and although he was polite, his stare was invasive. Over his oiled ringlets he wore a tiara with a veil in back, and his costume was entirely Persian: baggy trousers, voluminous cape, fringed tunic. He had a ring—sometimes several—on each finger, including his thumbs. Mardian would have been scandalized, since he had found even the Antiochenes repulsive in their overdone finery.

Artavasdes was seated between Antony and me, and stretching out on either side were the Roman officers: Canidius, who had brought his legions here to join forces with the bulk of the army, and Titius, Dellius, Plancus, and Ahenobarbus. They wore their plain Roman uniforms—bronze cuirasses and purple cloaks, sturdy nailed sandals, and military decorations, either crowns or symbolic silver spearheads. They looked very workmanlike and unembellished next to the Armenians.

As a child I had studied Median, and it pleased me to speak a bit to Artavasdes, if only to let him know that we could understand his asides to his nobles. Antony was more impressed than he, whispering in my ear, "How many languages do you know?" and then adding, "I suppose you speak Parthian as well!"

In truth, I had also studied it briefly, but only recently had begun trying to relearn it. I hoped I would have need of it, and soon.

"I know a little," I admitted.

When I saw how surprised Antony was, I said, "You must learn it as well. If you are to be master of all the east, you cannot depend on translators; you must not be at another man's mercy that way."

He merely grunted; like all Romans, he expected the entire world to switch to Latin to accommodate him.

Artavasdes was gesturing, rolling his hands in intricate circles to punctuate his words. "My brother King Polemo and I will slay hundreds of the Parthians," he promised.

At the sound of his name, King Polemo of Pontus nodded at us from his end of the table. Antony had made him king recently, and he was enjoying the title as only an elevated commoner can. Together he and Artavasdes would contribute six thousand fine cavalry and seven thousand foot soldiers to Antony's army.

I looked down the table at all the men's profiles—Antony's still firm, no hint of a sagging chin or flaccid cheeks, but with lines at the corners of his eyes that had not been there in Rome, and scattered gray in his otherwise dark hair. Canidius, being older, looked it, his skin more like tanned hide than a youth's. Dellius would have had a perfect profile, but his looks were spoiled by his pitted complexion and his habit of slicking his hair back. Plancus, like Antony, was not young but still in his soldier's prime, as was Ahenobarbus, with his hawk's nose and red beard only a little lightened by gray. Plancus's nephew alone, the dark and caustic Titius, was of the next generation, a youth in search of glory. The rest were wary, less intent on performing astounding feats of arms than on annihilating the enemy in any way possible and returning safely. There was little of Alexander in them, little yearning for wider horizons or conquests; they fought for advancement in the courts of Rome.

"No, make that thousands," Artavasdes corrected himself, with typical

Asiatic exaggeration. Everything was in thousands and tens of thousands. "Tomorrow we will present a demonstration of falconry," he said.

"Tomorrow we must review the troops and prepare to move," said Antony. "The season is late enough already." Indeed, it was quite late to begin, and time was precious.

"But, Imperator, can I help it that the snows refused to melt?" He twirled his ringed hands.

Entertainers filed into the hall, playing unfamiliar instruments: pottery rattles, bull-headed lyres, silver pipes. They had a tame lion that they led about by a silken leash; I wondered if they had removed his teeth, just in case.

Artavasdes had provided us with sumptuous quarters in his palace—an entire set of apartments, hung with tapestries and staffed with what seemed an army. But I found the quarters gloomy and oppressive, smelling of mold, and I did not wish to spend my last night with Antony in them.

"Tell your staff to set up your tent," I suddenly said to Antony.

"What?"

"Your commander's tent—the one you will use in the campaign," I said. "I want to sleep in it with you."

"Set up a tent on the palace grounds?"

"No, down by the river, where the army waits."

Antony laughed. "Decline the king's hospitality and tell him we prefer to sleep in a tent?"

"Put some other coloration on it. Say I wish to experience it, and this is the only opportunity I will ever have. That is true."

"He will take it as an insult."

"Tell him you must do it to humor me, as I am expecting a baby and have odd whims. Or say that you have a personal custom of spending the night before embarking with your men—that the gods commanded it and you dare not break the custom now, lest it jinx the expedition. Or tell him both stories."

"Oh, very well. To be honest, I prefer my tent to this." He looked around distastefully at the dank apartments. Then he turned back to me, suddenly. "Are you? Is it true?"

"Yes," I said. "I had meant to tell you tonight, at a better time."

"Then you absolutely must turn back. You cannot come any farther on this campaign. But—it seems that once again I will miss the birth." He came over to me and put his arms around me, resting his chin on the top of my head.

It seemed fated that the fathers of my children would never be there when I gave birth. I would always bear them alone, with no one to show them to but Olympos.

"It is not your fault," I assured him. Any more than it was Caesar's fault that he had to be at war at the time. It was the price I paid for choosing soldiers for my children's fathers. "I cannot ask you to cut the campaign short to hurry back to Alexandria by early winter. If I did, I would be aiding the Parthians."

He held me to him tightly. "Always politics," he lamented. "Even our most private and precious moments are governed by politics."

"I was born to it," I assured him. "I am used to it."

Down by the Araxes, the tent was duly erected a little way from the common soldiers' tents, who normally slept eight men to a tent. The troops greeted Antony with heartiness and affection, flattered that he wanted to be with them, and their genuine response made a glaring contrast to Artavasdes' oiled flattery. In the falling light, enormous, fair-haired men crowded around him, calling out, "Imperator! Imperator!" These were the soldiers of the Fifth Legion, recruited by Caesar from native Gauls. They had served faithfully with him, even withstanding charging elephants in the battle of Thapsus; he had rewarded them with an emblem of the beasts for their ensign. There was also the famous Sixth Legion, the Ironclad, that had served Caesar in the fateful Alexandrian War, and gone on to revenge him at Philippi under Antony. They were as hardened as their nickname, leathery and sunburnt.

Around the campfire they raised their cups high, toasting us. They were ready to fight, eager to set out, straining like racehorses to be let loose. They had not fought since Philippi, and were starved for action and battle. As the flames bathed them in a bronze glow, almost turning them into statues, I felt the excitement of war, which stirs men's hearts and obliterates thoughts of death. Defeat is never more unthinkable than on the eve of a campaign, drinking with one's comrades before the campfire, polishing the spears.

And how they loved Antony! How they teased and toasted him, as if he were one of them. He seemed to know them all personally, asking after their friends, children, love affairs, injuries. Such things cannot be falsified.

We retired to the tent—a large goatskin one, stretched over an oak frame. Inside there were two folding camp beds, stools, a ground covering, and two lanterns, plus the water pitchers and basins. Antony gestured around, saying, "I hope this is austere enough for you."

"So this is where you will live for months and months," I said wonderingly. That he, who so enjoyed luxury, could switch to this.

"I will hardly notice it," he said. "My mind will be on other things."

We sat down together on one of the narrow beds. The lanterns gave off only a feeble light around us. "I will bring you victory, lay it at your feet," he promised.

"And I will lay our new child at your returning feet," I also promised. My task would be easier than his; my body would form the child, day after day, with no effort on my part.

Suddenly he took me in his arms, burying his face in my hair. He said nothing, but the tight grip of his fingers spoke for him. His silence was more telling than all his usual talk.

Together we lay back on the bed, its light frame creaking under the weight of two people. Still, neither of us spoke. There were so many words I had stored up to use—words of farewell, of good cheer, of love, of encouragement. Now not one of them would come. All I could do was run my hands through his hair, wondering if I would ever do so again, fearing that in our last embrace I was struck mute. But if it was our last embrace, what difference did it make what words I spoke, or failed to speak? It was too momentous; no words would serve.

With Caesar I had not known it was our last time together; this was worse. Better to be ignorant. Damn all leave-taking, curse all staged good-byes! With a cry I held him against me, my heart aching.

I took his head in my hands, and covered his face with kisses, as if I would map it all with my lips, trace it with my tongue. I wanted to remember the imprint of his body on mine, make it permanent; I could not hold him close enough. But I tried, until at last he broke the spell of silence, saying, "I love you," under his breath, sliding his arms underneath me, clasping me to him so tightly I could hardly breathe.

With the amber-colored light of the lanterns sending out faint pulses of illumination, we twined our arms and legs about each other, twisting and turning on the suspended bed, straining to either banish or elevate the moment. I entered him as much as he entered me, and all our unspoken farewells surged through our bodies.

It was a short night. It seemed that dawn came up at midnight. But that was because I would have had the night never end, would have prolonged it until noon. By the time the first finger of light probed its way into our tent, the soldiers outside had already begun their day. Antony stuck his head out the tent flap and was greeted with choruses of teasing, and, indeed, it was embarrassing for him. He hastily pulled on his clothes, kissing me lightly and saying, "By midmorning I will inspect the legions and present them. I especially want to show you the siege machinery before it is loaded."

I stretched. "Yes. I will be ready." As soon as he had left, I got up off the flimsy bed and washed in the cold water that had been provided, then dressed in my traveling clothes. I looked around the tent once more, wondering what it was like to make this one's quarters in heat and cold. I knew the Romans insisted on making ordered, fortified camp at the end of each day's march, which added two or three hours to their day. No wonder they slept well at night—not only from the security of their guarded camps but from sheer exhaustion.

I left the tent and found that the entire army was milling around the riverbanks. It was huge—I had not appreciated just how many men a hundred thousand were, and how much equipment was needed: rolled tents, mules, wagons, stakes, food supplies, engineering tools. Each soldier had to carry on his person three days' worth of food in a bronze box, as well as a kettle and a hand mill. He also had to carry his entrenching tools: a pickax, a chain, a saw, a hook, palisade stakes, and even a wicker basket for moving earth—all of that in addition to his javelin, his sword, his dagger, and his shield, and the heavy bronze helmet he wore. As I watched these sturdy men, thus laden down, I had to marvel that they could cover fifteen miles a day, day after day, and twenty-five on forced marches.

As Antony had told me, there were sixteen legions setting out for Parthia under his command. Some of them were seasoned veterans like the Fifth and Sixth; others were newer. Since each legion was considered a living entity, with its own history and often its own distinguishing emblem, when men were lost they were not replaced with new recruits. Thus a venerable, battle-tried legion might be considerably undermanned, with less than the usual five thousand soldiers. Antony's now were about at three-quarters strength. New recruits were assigned to new legions.

This was the finest Roman army to set out in our times—perhaps in any time. Even Caesar had not had an army like this.

I saw Antony riding through the crowd, making slow progress because it seemed each man had a personal message for him. If he was impatient or his thoughts were elsewhere, he did not show it. How splendid he looked, there among his men; how easy it was to forget the hundreds of miles lying ahead of them, to be painfully and laboriously covered before the actual fighting could begin. Today, with the new-risen sun sparkling off the river, all the preparations seemed merely invigorating.

Antony saw me and waved, then trotted over. "I'll bring another horse for you, and we'll see the siege and field artillery," he said. His spirits were high, and I could tell he thought no more of the night in the tent, but only of the challenge before him.

Together we rode to the far end of the staging field, where the road led off to the south, upon which the wagons would soon trundle and the troops march.

Before me lay what looked like a city—piles of logs cut into sections, thousands of stakes, and massive wheeled machines on thick frames. And, lying on a train of flat wagons, an enormous ram, its iron head gleaming gray in the sunlight.

"How can this ever be transported?" I asked, in wonder. The sheer length of the ram would make it difficult to carry on twisting trails.

"The individual wagons are flexible," said Antony. "They can bend to fit around curves."

"But the ram itself is not," I pointed out. "And its very length—it would breach the gates of heaven. What do you anticipate using it on?"

"It is eighty feet long," he said proudly. "In the open country where we are going, there is no timber. We have to bring our own siege works."

I felt apprehensive looking at all this. It seemed a chain of iron to tie them down, rather than equipment necessary to win. "Curses that they must be located on a flat, treeless plain! And guarded by mountains." An ominous combination.

"I will have to divide the army," he said. "Naturally the foot soldiers will move more quickly than the heavy equipment. But others have done this successfully; it should cause us no hardship."

"And these?" I pointed to the clumsy wheeled machines lying placidly in the field.

"The biggest one is the 'wild ass'—called that because of its kick." It looked like a gigantic grasshopper to me. "It can hurl a boulder over into the forest there—about a quarter of a mile. We use it to break down city walls, or to crush men and horses. There are smaller catapults, of course, that throw lighter stones for shorter distances to give covering fire for the troops as they advance on the enemy."

There were so many of these machines in the field they looked like a herd of animals grazing. Again, my heart sank. How was all this to climb over the mountains?

A blare of trumpets announced the arrival of Artavasdes and his cavalry, trotting proudly toward the parade grounds. The jingle of their bronze bridle ornaments made music in the air. Following behind were the brightly costumed foot soldiers, so much more conspicuous than the Romans. The army was assembling; it was almost time to depart.

By noon they had left, the commanders with their guards riding past the stand where I and my people were watching, followed by the troops marching in columns, the trumpeters, the medical detachment, the artillery and food stores, and the endless baggage wagons and laden mules. It took almost two hours for the entire force to pass by, and another hour before it disappeared from view along the riverbed.

I had wanted to see the departure, but I dreaded the long campaign ahead of them. I wondered why Caesar had been so eager to embark on it, and whether even he had realized what an undertaking it would have been. I had cut short an audience with a self-styled pundit on Roman affairs who had remarked that perhaps the very best of Caesar's famous luck had come to him on the Ides of March. By dying then, he had saved himself from two very possible ignominious ends to a glorious career: either to be King of Rome and not be able to manage his subjects, or to be cut down in Parthia. Perhaps the man had spoken truer than I had admitted. Certainly even Caesar would not have found the Parthians an easy conquest. Their very location, so difficult to reach, served as protective insulation; a Roman army would exhaust itself before ever encountering them.

I sighed and finally turned my gaze from the empty road. We would have to spend the night here, and this time there was no avoiding Artavasdes' palace. Its dreariness exactly fitted my mood.

The curious lack of words had stayed with us to the end. Antony merely saluted me from horseback, and I raised my hand to him, silently.

Tomorrow I must begin my own long journey, traveling down the banks of the Euphrates, ice-green and flat, until I reached Syria. Then I would go due south and enter Judaea, where I had told Herod I would meet him in Jerusalem. I had little heart for it; if I could have waved my hand and been back in Egypt, that is what I would have chosen to do. I felt drained, mainly from seeing Antony off with his army, but also from the early stages of my pregnancy. Another child, and I was no longer so young—I would be almost thirty-four by the time it was born. I wondered idly if I would name it something to do with Parthia, commemorating a victory there? But it would be too early to know the outcome by then.

Antony was my partner in all things, and together we dreamed of ruling over a world empire, stretching from Spain in the west to Parthia in the east, from Britain in the north to Nubia in the south. I knew he loved me deeply, enough to alienate his family and jeopardize his standing in Rome for my sake. I had three children, all heirs to a rich future, assuring us of our dynasty. But I felt curiously alone, and very tired. At the same time I wished I could change my mind and gallop after Antony, surprising him in his tent late that night. I imagined it in vivid detail for a moment; yes, if I rode away now . . . But no. It was too late. The sun was already touching the tops of the trees to the west.

58

My journey southward was uneventful, but all the time my mind was with Antony's army as it marched farther and farther away. For the first few days I knew I could still ride fast and overtake them—should I need to— but after that the distance was too great, and we were gyres widening in opposite directions. I had to commend him into the hands of the gods, of his own patrons Dionysus and Hercules, and pray for their goodwill toward him.

I forced myself to turn my attention to the lands lying before me, lands that had just been returned to Ptolemaic possession after two hundred years— thanks to Antony. I traveled through Damascus—mine!—and down the Via Maris to pass through my seaports of Ptolemais Ace, once the center of Ptolemy Philadelphos's rule of Phoenicia, and Joppa and Ashdod. The flat coastline showed what poor material the Phoenicians and Israelites had for seaports; there was no natural harbor the whole length of the land. The beaches stretched down to the water, allowing for no anchorage and no protection against the wind. At Joppa, men had constructed a facsimile of a harbor, but it was a poor thing compared to Alexandria's. Nonetheless, I found the country appealing; its climate was more temperate than Egypt's, and it actually had rainfall, making for flowers and green meadows, and trees other than palms.

I was deeply grateful that this land had been restored to my family. How my ancestor Ptolemy Philadelphos would smile. Perhaps . . . yes, perhaps it would be fitting to name this new baby after him, to mark the restoration of our ancient kingdom.

A deputation of Herod's—mounted on fine chargers, richly dressed—met us outside Joppa.

"In the name of Herod, King of the Jews, we welcome you to Judaea," said one.

"And will conduct you to Jerusalem, where our lord awaits you," said another. They smiled as though Herod's sole desire were to see me.

As we made our way to the city, the hills, covered in pines and aromatic shrubs, gave way to steeper ground with chalky white rocks rising from the soil. The air grew cooler, the air seemingly finer. I was anxious to see the famous Jerusalem, about which so many claims were made. Like Athens, it was more than a city, it was magic, history, a rarefied site. Men who were more than men had walked, written, and died here. But since the Jews did not believe in demigods, these heroes had a unique, though limited, aura. In any other culture, David would have ascended to godhood, Solomon reigned eternally, and Moses hovered beneficently forever. Yet the Jews stated firmly, "He was gathered to his fathers"; their bones were in the earth.

Just as the horses were becoming fatigued from the climb, Jerusalem opened out before us. Spread out on its mountaintop, it was not a large city, but it was glorious. A bank of gray clouds parted overhead to let beams of sunlight hit the yellow-gold walls and buildings, making them glow.

The recently rebuilt walls of the city were broken only by strongly fortified gates, through which we were escorted with due ceremony. More ceremony on the other side, and then we were sped to Herod's palace, where he awaited us.

In the four years since I had seen him, even more had happened to him than to me. While Antony and Octavian had granted him the title of king, they had left him to secure the land for himself. The Parthians had overrun his country and taken Jerusalem; Herod and two Roman legions had fought bitterly to evict them. He was left the victor of a war-damaged city and an empty treasury. But he was a king, and he had been right to refuse my offer to command Egyptian forces. Knowing he would never be satisfied with less than he now grasped, he was a wise man, albeit a tired one.

"My dearest Queen, most exalted Cleopatra," he said, coming toward me, hands outstretched. A radiant smile lit his face, and one would never guess that I had just stripped large portions of his kingdom from him. He dared not alienate Antony—or Antony's wife. A complaint from me, and Antony would investigate. A word from Antony, and he was dethroned. And so—

"My dearest Queen!"

"Herod, my friend," I said, extending my hand to him—the one with the wedding ring, and Antony's seal. "It is my pleasure to see you here, in your rightful kingdom."

His smile slackened a little. His kingdom would have been bigger, but for me. "It has been a long four years," he admitted. "But the struggle was worth it."

"Where territory is concerned, it always is," I agreed.

"Come, come," he said, leading the way to his rooftop, where chairs, couches, awnings and potted plants made a shaded garden of retreat.

The hills spread out on all sides, and I found myself looking out over the roofs of the city. It was a fetching sight, as Jerusalem lay on many different levels. On the highest ground was a flat plateau, embellished buildings rising in its center.

"Our temple," he said, pointing to it. "I am afraid the grounds were damaged in the fighting, but at least it was not desecrated." He paused. "When Pompey came here, the year Octavian was born, he actually entered the Holy of Holies. An unbeliever! Although he didn't touch anything, the few minutes he spent in there meant it was desecrated." Herod sounded more annoyed than offended. "It was expensive to get it cleansed and restored! Ah well." He nodded to his servitor, who brought a tray of goblets for us.

I tasted the sweet yellow liquid; its fiery strength burned my lips. Watching me, Herod gave a soft chuckle.

"This is the famous wine made from your new palm grove in Jericho," he said. "They call them 'hangover palms' because of the strength of the brew. Now you understand why people pay so dearly for it." Again, no trace of any resentment; he might have been talking about a bouquet of flowers or a handkerchief, rather than a considerable source of income lost to him.

"Its sweet taste disguises its power," I said. "It ought to be called 'the scorpion' for its sting."

"Of course you will want to inspect the palm and balsam plantations," he said, "as well as your bitumen site on the Dead Sea. So I have made arrangements for an excursion tomorrow. We will have to depart before dawn, as it is so beastly hot this time of year."

I was indeed curious to see them, and particularly the Dead Sea, that unique body of water that was more mineral than anything else. They said the waters were so heavy that a man could not sink in them, and so bitter that if you breathed them in, your lungs would never recover. Bits of asphalt bitumen rose to the surface at the southern end of the sea, and were skimmed off to be used in various ways: for mummification, for protection against pests in vineyards, for medicine, and for mortar. Again, a lucrative holding for Egypt.

"I have had an idea," he said casually, as if it was of no moment. "Why concern yourself with the management of these things? What a nuisance for you—having to station Egyptian officials in Jericho and on the ungodly shores of the Dead Sea. Who would want to be exiled there?"

"I thought Jericho was considered a pleasant place," I said. "Is it not an oasis? I have even heard rumors that you plan to build yourself a palace there." I smiled sweetly at him; let him know I was no fool, and made it my business to know what went on everywhere.

"You have heard much," he replied. "But where you can have heard that— why, I have scarcely the money to rebuild the damaged walls of Jerusalem! In order to present my Imperator Antony with a worthy wedding gift, I was forced to melt down my plate."

Yes, I remembered the gold platter he had sent. "It was very beautiful," I told him.

He nodded. "Thank you. I hope Antony was pleased. Now, as to my pro-posal—I would be honored if you would allow me to rent the balsam and palm groves from you, for their true worth. That way you would receive the income, but be spared the bother of having to manage them. And"—he acted as though he had just now thought of this—"I will undertake to collect your fees from the Arabs across the Dead Sea who extract the bitumen. What do you think of this idea?"

I thought that it meant he wished to keep my agents out of his country—an understandable desire. Jericho was too close to Jerusalem, and he did not want an Egyptian listening post in his neighborhood.

"I think it has merit," I said. No need to acquiesce just yet; let him wonder.

"Think on it," he said. "Now let me show you the very spot where our King David looked out and saw Bathsheba on her rooftop—"

Even in midsummer, dawn was cool in Jerusalem. I had to pull two covers over me during the night, and when I was awakened to dress, I needed a wool wrap. But as soon as the sun struck the desert just beyond the city gates, the air heated rapidly.

Never have I seen a quicker change of climate and terrain than that which lies between Jerusalem and Jericho. For a little way the road skirts the city, high on its mountaintop, then abruptly it descends into a reddish wilderness of rock and sand. The road is notorious for bandits, and it is easy to see why: there is nothing on either side but cliffs and gulleys, good hiding places for thieves but offering no mercy for travelers.

The sun beat down on us, and I was glad to pull a covering over my head. After a long, winding way, I saw the plain open up before us, shimmering in the haze and sunlight. A bright green spot marked where Jericho stood, and the flat blue surface of the Dead Sea stretched far away on the right. I was surprised at how piercingly, pleasingly blue the waters looked. I could even make out ripples on the surface, puffed by the winds. Somehow I had expected it to be dull, flat, and metallic—to look unlike water.

Jericho was a city of palms; they were everywhere, their arching fronds beckoning welcome. Flat-topped houses clustered in their shade, and the entire city exhaled an air of pleasure and leisure. Despite his disclaimers, Herod had a sizable dwelling there. He ushered our party inside, where we were met with plates of melon, diluted goblets of the palm wine, and platters of the famous dates. They were enormous, plump, and tangy.

594

"And here, the balm." A servant proffered a flask of balm of Gilead, one of the costliest ointments in the world. It came from the small groves in Jericho; the bush that yielded it was reputed to grow nowhere else in the world. I held out my hands while the servant poured a few drops into my palms, then massaged them into my skin. They were absorbed as if by magic, leaving no greasy stain behind, but only a delightful aroma.

"When the heat abates, in the cool of the twilight, we shall inspect the groves," Herod said. "I know you will wish to see them."

The shadows were lengthening when we saw, from horseback, the small grove of balsam bushes. They were planted in neat rows, with irrigation ditches between them, and numerous guards stationed at the fence.

"The resin is collected from the stems," said Herod. "It oozes out by itself, but if it is slow in coming, the keepers wound the tree and collect it."

"I see it must be guarded," I said.

"Yes," he said. "It is as precious as gold. After all, it is used in holy oil, to heal wounds, and to make costly perfume. Now, as to my offer—"

"I appreciate it," I said. "And I think I will agree." He smiled. "But only on condition that your gardeners make cuttings for me while we are at the Dead Sea tomorrow. I wish to try to grow them in Egypt." His smile faded.

The cliffs on the western side of the Dead Sea were pockmarked with caves and ledges, and radiated heat. We passed them, umbrellas shielding us from the glare that glanced off the sea and the landscape. The sea stretched far away, and it did not look dead. There were waves on its surface, and birds flew over it. But a strange haze lay upon it, a cloud and yet not a cloud; and Herod pointed out that not a single plant grew by its shore.

"It is a lake with no life at all—no seaweed, no fish, no crabs, no slime, no shells. There is no odor of anything but brine, and a corpse placed in it would not be eaten or rot, but float, preserved, on its surface."

On closer inspection, it did look different, and soon crusts and eruptions of white salt reared up in its shallows. We were nearing the area where the bitumen also arose. I could smell sulfur and other foul odors.

"Put your hand in it," said Herod, when we had dismounted near the station where the bitumen was extracted. I walked over the rocky shore and dipped my finger in, bringing a few drops to my mouth. They were horribly bitter and sour. In an instant the water dried on my hand, making a dull white crust.

"You are turning into a pillar of salt, like Lot's wife," he said. He motioned for a jar of sweet water to be poured over my hand, rinsing it.

I would not wish my officials to be stationed here, unless they deserved punishment. Let natives deal with this hellish place.

I looked at Herod. I was sorry we must be adversaries over territory and Antony's patronage. He was a likable man, and clearly a resourceful one. But we had our separate wants, desires, and ambitions. It was nothing personal.

We could be polite, and observe all the pleasantries. That was the civilized way, and we were children of ancient civilizations.

Leaving Herod, I made my way slowly down the Mediterranean coast, stopping in Ashkelon, still a free city, and Gaza, then traversing the waterless desert strip until we reached the Pelusic branch of the Nile. We transferred to a ship and sailed toward Memphis; on the way I ordered my balsam shrub cuttings to be planted at Heliopolis, a site sacred to the Pharaohs that seemed to offer good conditions for the bushes to thrive. If they did, I would have done the next best thing to finding new gold mines in my land. I was determined to increase my country's wealth any way I could.

We sailed into Alexandria from the lake side, and I saw the white city reflected in the waters and framed by reeds. I had left a lifetime ago, so it seemed; in truth, it was only half a year. The changes wrought in my situation were so profound that I was on guard as we landed; I did not know what to expect from the Alexandrians. How did they feel about my marriage and partnership with a Roman?

A crowd was gathered, and I could not read their faces. They had not been asked or consulted about my decision; it was the fate of subjects, but now I faced them uneasily. They watched silently as the ship docked and the royal trumpeters announced my arrival. Wearing my silver robes, I stepped out and hailed them, and a great burst of shouts erupted—welcoming cries. Relief flooded me; I need not have worried. I smiled and greeted them, genuinely happy to be surrounded by my own people once again.

"The bride! The bride!" they cried. "Isis! Where is Dionysus?"

"In his grape arbor!" they answered themselves.

"We wish you joy, happiness, love—"

"And fertility!" yelled one group.

"Prosperity for Egypt!" cried another. "Peace with Rome!"

"All this you shall have," I promised them, and then, on impulse, tore off my silver-threaded veil and tossed it out to them. They scrambled for it, and then my shaded litter was waiting to whisk me through the streets and back to the palace.

The children came racing across the marble floor: Alexander and Selene sliding and jumping, Caesarion—who had grown so much!—walking with controlled dignity as fast as he could. Mardian beamed, and Olympos affected his unexcited look. The rest of the staff were delighted to see Iras and Charmian, whom they had missed sorely.

"Married at last?" said Olympos, kissing my cheek. "So you have staved off spinsterhood?" He laughed at his own joke. "I know you did it only to copy me."

"Indeed, that is the only reason," I assured him. I was wearing the wedding necklace, and I let everyone feast their eyes on it.

"Antony has departed for Parthia?" asked Mardian. I could tell that something worried him.

"Yes, I saw him off from the Araxes River," I said. "The army was splendid, and terrible in its weapons. And the war machines . . ." I shook my head. "But plenty of time for this news later. Let us pull off our traveling clothes, wash our feet, and take refreshment."

Everything was changed, but nothing was changed—the furniture all stood in the exact same places, the curtains ballooned and billowed from the puffs of sea wind, just as I remembered, even making the same patterns as before, and shoes I had left behind were waiting, silent and polished, for me in my wardrobe. But now I, and Alexandria, were tied to something outside; I felt as though a walled garden had been breached. It was a retreat no longer, nor was it self-contained, as Egypt had always been. Now Rome was here, in the person of Antony and his fortunes, in this very room.

"Your face is sad," said Charmian. "Is there something amiss in your chambers?"

"No. No, of course not. It is just that, for a moment, it seemed unfamiliar." I shook my head. What melancholy thoughts! The alliance with Antony would protect Egypt, would preserve it, not compromise it.

The twins came running in. "Where's our father? Where is he? Where's he hiding?"

Their squeals told me how excited they were to have discovered that they *had* a father, let alone one who liked to play.

"He's gone to do his job," I told them. "He's a soldier, and soldiers have to go with their armies."

"Oh." Alexander looked up brightly. "I have some toy soldiers. Want to see them? Now?"

I let myself be dragged into their rooms, but not before I had motioned to a servant to bring along Antony's old spear and helmet. "These are for you," I told Alexander. "They are what a grown-up soldier wears, and your father left them for you to wear someday."

It was something Antony *would* have done.

Selene was hanging on me, and I quickly pulled off a silver bracelet with ram's heads that had been presented to me by Artavasdes, and featured the fine workmanship of his country. "This is for you," I assured her, putting it on.

"And nothing for me?" The ever-taller Caesarion was standing in the doorway, feeling left out. I had to think of something. He was too old for toys and too intelligent to be fobbed off with a makeshift present.

"Of course there is something for you. One thing for you to play with, and another for you to keep. I have brought back a jar of the most extraordinary water, from the Dead Sea in Judaea. I thought you might like to taste it and test it to see how heavy it is. And when you are finished with it, you can evaporate it and compare it with seawater. It must have three times as much salt in it. Just don't make any pets drink it—although I don't think you could. And the other present—it's a beautiful Arab horse, small and as fast as the wind." The bitumen extractors had presented it to me, in relief that they could continue their business unmolested. It was time Caesarion perfected his horsemanship, and I knew he needed a special horse, one that he loved, to do it.

"Oh!" His eyes grew large. "What color is it?"

"He is white, with a gray mane and tail." I had been quite taken with him.

"His name?"

"He had a Nabataean one that meant 'Leader,' but you may call him anything you please."

Thus my presents were redistributed to eager recipients.

Mid-July, and I was pacing up and down in my workroom. Antony had been gone two months. What was happening to him? I longed for news. But instead I was forced to hear about the wretched Octavian—Mardian had just received a dispatch.

"So, what of him?" I hated hearing what Octavian was doing, but braced myself. Let him be sunk on a shoal.

"His campaign is finally launched," said Mardian, reading as he spoke. "Or, I should say, Agrippa's campaign."

"Ha!" I cried. "Yes, he is completely dependent on Agrippa for both the brains and the brawn of any military action." The puny Octavian and his robust friend: a happy combination, for them.

"At least he *has* someone he can depend on," said Mardian pointedly.

Antony fought alone, basically. It would be a comfort to have a reliable partner; yes, it would.

"He is fortunate in his friends," I admitted. "What plans have they settled on?" I had to know.

"You know about Agrippa's strategy," said Mardian. "We had reports all winter."

"Yes, yes!" I barked. "I know all about his naval training station and his twenty thousand oarsmen."

"He has mobilized all the forces at his command against Sextus, as his very political survival depends on defeating him," said Mardian, his eyes darting across the paper. "The battle will be fought in Sicily, on both land and sea. The Consul Taurus is sailing from Italy with the two squadrons Antony donated, and Lepidus is bringing up his twelve legions, plus a fleet from Africa. Agrippa has determined that he will leave nothing to chance. Therefore, against the swift ships and superior seamanship of Sextus he has built such massive ships that they cannot be sunk, but must crush the enemy by weight alone. Last year he struggled under three disadvantages: his ships were no better than Sextus's, his oarsmen were worse, and he had no secure harbor. He has now solved all these problems."

If only we had such an industrious, clever lieutenant! Agrippa had indeed grown into impressive manhood.

"Oh, and he has invented a device called 'the snatcher'—it is a catapult that fires a grappling hook, so that the little boats of Sextus can be hauled against Agrippa's, and a land battle on decks commence."

"They will cut the ropes of 'the snatcher,' " I said. That seemed obvious.

"He has encased them in long tubes of iron, so they cannot."

Damn his cleverness! Marcus Vipsanius Agrippa, that polite boy at Caesar's dinner—who could have predicted his military acumen?

"They expect naval action at any day," said Mardian. "And it will come just in time to rescue Octavian from his growing unpopularity with the Roman mobs. They will not tolerate him or Sextus much longer. One has to go."

The blue seas around Alexandria were innocent and calm, belying the action elsewhere. We waited, day after day, for news, which seemed so slow in coming. Ships limped in with reports. Octavian's fleet had been wrecked, again. Thirty-two ships of the line and many more light Liburnian galleys were destroyed in a storm. Octavian thought seriously of postponing the campaign for another year. Our spirits soared. That would give Antony the lead he needed.

Octavian thought likewise. He dared not let another season pass, allowing Antony a great victory while he suffered from unpopularity at Rome yet another winter. And he feared that Sextus would find a way to destroy his fleet at anchor. So, with his customary determination and thoroughness, he pressed on grimly. "I will triumph even over the will of Neptune," he vowed.

"There is even a report that he almost committed suicide," said Mardian. "He was so discouraged when his fleet was lost, but—"

"With the morning light he thought better of it," I said. I knew his thinking. Octavian would always wait for the morning light.

More reports came in on the next stage of the campaign. The action had narrowed to the wicked Strait of Messina, which Sextus guarded and Octavian's forces needed to cross. Agrippa fought Sextus, and his heavier ships proved the worth of his strategy, crushing Sextus's vessels. But Sextus withdrew and decided to attack Octavian instead as he ferried his troops across; Octavian escaped, but the ships Antony had lent him were ruined, unable to withstand Sextus.

"A lesson for us in that!" I said. "No more small ships!"

"Time had run out for Octavian," said Mardian, with delight, reading the dispatch. "He had to send Maecenas back to Rome to quiet things down. Oh—but then Agrippa—Agrippa—"

"Agrippa *what?*" I grabbed the letter from him. Was Agrippa some kind of god, always able to deliver his friend?

Agrippa had seized a port on Sicily that allowed him to land his and Octavian's land forces—a total of twenty-one legions and auxiliaries. They caged in Sextus, who then decided to stake all on a sea battle.

"And what happened?" I waved the letter. It had ended there.

The battle was long over, but we must wait to know the outcome.

We finally learned: On the third of September, the great battle was fought at last, and Sextus utterly defeated. Sextus's men and ships fought spectacularly and bravely, knowing they could expect no mercy. But Agrippa's big ships won the day, holding Sextus's ships captive, hooking them, boarding them, sinking them. Twenty-eight of Sextus's ships were sunk, against only three of Agrippa's. Only seventeen escaped, and Sextus fled with them.

"How many ships out of three hundred?" I could not believe it.

"Seventeen."

"The victory is decisive, then." Octavian had prevailed.

"Sextus has fled to Antony," Mardian read in disbelief. "He will throw himself on his mercy."

"O Isis!" I said. "What will Antony do with him?"

There was more yet. Lepidus made his move against Octavian and Agrippa. It seemed that he had resented being the neglected member of the Triumvirate all these years; swelled with pride in the twenty-two legions he had acquired—reckoning that neither side had had as many at Philippi—he tried to overthrow Octavian and Agrippa. But the troops were having none of it; they were weary of civil war and unimpressed with Lepidus.

"Lepidus was forced to throw himself on Octavian's mercy," read Mardian. "To kiss his sandals!"

I shuddered. Then I remarked, "His built-up sandals." The ultimate humiliation.

"Octavian made a great show of mercy, but he has deprived him of his office as Triumvir, his legions, and his power. Lepidus has departed for an enforced retirement."

"Octavian is master of the west," I said slowly. "Sextus and Lepidus gone. He rules all, as far as Greece."

"Yes," said Mardian. "He has forty-five legions under his command. Some are undermanned, but they still number at least a hundred and twenty thousand soldiers."

"Whatever will he do with them?" I asked softly. "For they must either be paid and dismissed, or used, and he has no funds to pay them."

Work must be found for those soldiers, then. Octavian could, of course, transfer some to Antony. But I knew he would not. He would keep them busy and in training . . . and find some plunder for them, some untouched treasure trove into which they could dip their hands and pay themselves. Egypt? Or what Antony won in Parthia?

59

The late summer, one of the clearest and windiest in years, cried out for enjoyment, but I was in the grip of dreadful waiting. As days passed with no word from the east, I grew more and more agitated. It seemed as though Antony and his huge army had disappeared over the horizon without a trace. Ships coming from Cilicia, from Rhodes, from Tarsus—I had their captains whisked ashore to be interrogated, but no one had heard anything from the interior.

Five hundred years ago an entire army of fifty thousand Persians had vanished in the sands of Egypt on their way to the Siwa Oasis—every schoolchild shuddered at the story of the sands opening and taking them, one and all. The Siwa Oasis was not as isolated and vast as the plains of Parthia. . . . O gods! Why did he go? Why did we not hear any news?

I tried to play with my children, to continue learning Parthian—although I came to hate it, as daily it seemed more and more hostile—to read all the news coming from the rest of the world, to ready my heart and mind for the new baby. These were distractions, though, while I waited for the answer to the great question: Would Antony truly wear Caesar's mantle and take his place beside him and Alexander in military greatness? Or fail and be accorded a place—where? Or live at all?

The Queen in me yearned for his victory, and prayed for that; the wife feared he would not return alive, and begged Isis only for his life. I was both the Spartan wife, saying, "Return with your shield or on it," and the Egyptian wife, saying, "Only return—even without the shield."

The storms of autumn started, and still no word. But my own body, oblivious of anything else, kept nature's timetable, and in mid-November I gave birth to my new baby—a son. It was an easy birth.

"You are becoming practiced at last," said Olympos dryly.

I held the little boy in my arms and looked down at him. He was possessed of rosy cheeks and a thick head of dark hair. As always, I was astounded at the beauty of a newborn, and that I could have produced him. At the same time, I somehow knew he would be my last. For that I cherished him more than I could say.

"What will you name him?" he asked, dabbing at the baby's matted hair.

Nothing had come to me since I had first thought of Ptolemy Philadelphos. I wished it could have been Ptolemy Antonius Parthicus, in honor of his father's victory over Parthia. Dear Isis, let me not have the right to bestow Antonius Postumus on a son of Antony! Best to retreat into the past, into the height of Ptolemaic glory.

"Ptolemy Philadelphos," I said.

"That's a mouthful," said Olympos, gently wiping the baby's eyes. "You will have to find something shorter for everyday use."

"It will come," I said. "He will name himself."

Despite the easy birth, I did not seem to recover as I should. My limbs felt heavy and swollen, and my energy did not return. Long after I should have been back in the council chamber, or in the customs depot, or inspecting the progress of my shipbuilding station, I found I tired so easily that spending more than a morning or an afternoon away from my couch was a challenge. I also had no appetite.

"You must eat," said Olympos sternly, "or your milk will be too thin." After he had seen how feeding the twins myself had helped my recovery, he had turned against the idea of wet nurses and now had it firmly in his mind that all women, even queens, should nurse their own children.

"Yes, yes," I said. "But octopus stew is not appealing." I pushed away the bowl.

"There is nothing better than octopus! The suckers give strength—"

"To an octopus, yes." The smell was awful. "Please, no more of this!"

"You try my patience!" He sat down beside me, on a footstool, and took my hand, looking searchingly in my face. I knew him well enough to know his frown hid his worry. "The baby is well," he said cautiously.

"Olympos, what is wrong with me?" I burst out.

"I don't know," he admitted. "The whole process of producing a child is a complicated mystery. There are so many ways for something to be—difficult. Oh, you are in no danger. You will slowly get your strength back. But perhaps you should not—should not—"

"Have more children," I finished for him.

"Exactly what I was about to say. But then, the men you take up with seem bent on producing as many as possible!"

"I am a married woman now," I said with imperious dignity. "So you needn't talk about 'the men I take up with'—like one of the temple prostitutes at Canopus!"

"Well, your new . . . er . . . husband . . . sometimes behaves as if he were a devotee of such precincts—" Olympos still did not like him, that was obvious. But he had not seen him, except at a distance in Rome, for almost five years. He would change his mind when Antony returned. When Antony returned . . .

"You insult my father the late King when you insult the rites of Dionysus!" I said. It was a religion, for all that the Romans thought the grape arbors and ecstatic dancing were obscene. They also thought dancing itself was obscene, and did not understand actors or the theater or—Thank the gods Antony was different!

"Forgive me," he said. "Obviously I cannot penetrate the sublime mysteries of Dionysus with my little, scientific, argumentative mind. But from the viewpoint of an ordinary man, it just looks like plain, old-fashioned drunkenness elevated to an elite club!"

I laughed. "I am pleased to have a man with a questioning mind as my physician. It means common sense will never be abandoned as a remedy. Now tell me—is there not something growing in that garden of yours that would help me?"

"Perhaps," he said.

"Does your wife—does Dorcas—have an interest in medicine?" I wondered about her. He had not brought her to many gatherings, and I had yet to have a real conversation with her.

He looked as though his privacy had been attacked. So it was all very well for him to invade my marriage, my motives, and my habits—even in bed—but I must keep a respectful distance from his. Physicians!

"No," he said shortly. "No, she—she is most concerned with literature. Homer and such. Comparing different versions." He looked acutely embarrassed by it.

"So you have married an intellectual!" I said. "What an odd yoking—the scientist and the literary scholar."

"No more odd than the cleverest woman in the world with a simple warrior, whose interests revolve around the battlefield and the drinking-board. In some ways he's like one of those northern barbarians, with their yelling and singing and fighting and drinking . . . and bonfires. . . ."

"You really don't know him at all," I said stiffly.

"Can you honestly say my description is wrong?" he asked, rising to his feet. "Yet I know he makes you happy, and so I pray for his safe return." On his way toward the door, he paused and turned. "I will send you some medicine from my garden. And you will take it!" he ordered.

All the strength and force of nature seemed concentrated on the sea; none of it flowed into me. Day after day as I dutifully rested in my room and drank Olympos's foul-tasting potion—made of a pinch of ground mandrake dissolved in the juice of cabbage leaves—I watched the storms breaking against the base of the Lighthouse, and the ships tossing against their anchor lines, saw the naked power of nature. I longed for the emblematic Ptolemaic thunderbolt to descend and charge me anew with fiery life. In the meantime there were the usual winter pastimes—games and music—and bored children to keep me company and hang on the arms of my chair. My pet monkey finally had the opportunity to scamper all over me and ply me with tidbits, to pull the covers up over me until I thought I would slap her thin, nervous fingers plucking continually at my blanket. But then, that is what monkeys do, and I could hardly punish her for being a monkey.

And all the while, nothing . . . from Antony, from the east.

Yet the news from Rome kept coming in. Octavian formally declared that with the defeat of Sextus the civil wars had at last ended, and put a notice up about his achievement—completing Caesar's work—in the Forum. Unable to have a Triumph because he had not beaten a foreign foe, he had to settle for what was called an Ovation, in which he was lauded—in a restrained manner. He was also granted the right to wear the laurel wreath at all times, like Caesar before him.

The medicine that Olympos made me take often either robbed me of sleep or sent me vivid, disturbing dreams. One night, when little Philadelphos was almost forty days old, I had a dreadful vision—it seemed more a vision than a dream—of Antony surrounded by dead bodies, grotesque, blackened things, stiffening and drying on a field of stones. He was crawling over them, almost rolling over them as if they were a strewn pile of logs—like the ones I had seen stacked in the fields of Armenia to use against Parthia, but these were rotted and burnt remnants. He was alone on the field, which stretched on and on under a colorless sky.

I woke up, my heart pounding, the sight still before my eyes. Antony's face . . . it looked as though he were being tortured.

In the corner of the room, the lamp still burned before the statue of Isis, flickering reassuringly. I flung off my sweat-soaked covers and knelt at her feet. I did not know what else to do. *Banish that evil dream!* I implored her, as the twins did with me when they had nightmares and rushed into my room. But she did nothing, and I knew that meant it was real.

Now I went back to bed and waited. I had seen what was happening in Parthia. Antony was alive, but surrounded by death. I clutched the covers around me and ordered the night to pass quickly. When the morning came, so would the news.

And thus I was expecting Eros, Antony's personal servant and freedman, who was brought into the palace at dawn, shivering and shaken. Yes, it was Eros and not one of the commanders—not Canidius or Dellius or Plancus, but this youth, scarcely more than a boy, who came from his master.

I insisted on speaking to him alone, in spite of Mardian's devouring curiosity to hear all. Time enough for that later. For now, I had to hear privately.

I did not bother with thrones or audience clothes, but took him directly into my most private chamber. How many times had Eros been the last to attend Antony and me before leaving us alone for the night? I could not see his face without remembering how eager we usually were for him to depart—and now he held the dreadful knowledge of what had happened since the splendid army, shining like a new coin, had set out on its mission.

I took his rough hands. "He is well? lord Antony lives?" After all, it was hours since the dream.

Eros nodded. "He is safe."

I looked carefully at him. His face was sunburnt, wind-scorched, and his nails were torn. Then my eyes strayed to his feet and legs—bruised, scabbed, and filthy with the kind of dirt no amount of normal scrubbing will remove.

"Where is he?"

"He awaits you at Leuce Come, in Syria."

Leuce Come? Where was that? What was he doing there? "Where?"

"A small fishing village in Syria," he said. "He was—we were afraid to go to Tyre or Sidon, for fear that the Parthians would already be there, waiting, having followed up their . . . great victory." He bent his head down, unable to look me in the eyes.

I reached out and took his chin, as if he were my own child. "I know there was a victory," I told him gently. "But it is enough for me that Antony lives. You must tell me what happened."

"How did you know?" He allowed me to raise his head.

"It was sent me by the gods," I said. "Now tell me the details. The gods send pictures, not details."

"I shall tell you quickly, and then you may question me as you wish," he said. His voice was thin, uncertain. "The winding mountain passes were slow to negotiate, and the baggage train was acting as a brake to the rest of the army. So Lord Antony left it behind, under the guard of King Artavasdes and King Polemo and two Roman legions—"

Not enough! Not enough guards! Only two legions! Oh, Antony—guarded by twenty-three thousand men, but only ten thousand of them Romans!

"And the Parthians, seeming to have advance knowledge of this, fell on them, and—slaughtered them." Eros seemed close to tears. I should halt his story and allow him to compose himself, but I found I could not.

"They annihilated twenty thousand men?" That seemed unbelievable.

"No—only the Roman legions. And took King Polemo prisoner. Then King Artavasdes galloped away with his thirteen thousand men, back to Armenia."

It was prearranged. I knew it. He was always in league with the Parthians! The lying traitor!

Yet he who trusts without foundation—what is the word for him? I had warned Antony about him. As I had warned him about Octavian. Why can a noble nature never foresee treachery? Does it make him blind? Rob him of sense?

"We did not know about this until too late. When Antony heard about it, he immediately sent back a relief force, but nothing was left. The two legion eagles were captured, and the siege machinery was set on fire and destroyed."

Without it, there could be no conquest. Antony could do nothing, trapped in the midst of Parthia. He could not besiege cities or force their surrender. And unless his legionaries could make the Parthians stand and fight, he had traveled hundreds of miles for nothing.

"And how did Lord Antony take this intelligence?" I asked.

"I saw his sorrow, but he did not show it to his men," said Eros. "He attempted to make the best of the bad situation, to force Phraaspa to fight him, but it was useless. We were stranded there and he knew it—that was the bitter part. The Parthians had no incentive to make concessions or even return the eagles from either Crassus or the latest loss. Then October came and the weather changed. We would have to retreat."

Retreat. That most abject of all maneuvers to be managed by a general! And after nothing at all!

605

"Thus far we had lost only a few men from the main army, since we had fought no actual battles. But that changed. I can tell you, my Queen, that altogether a third of the army has been lost—thirty-two thousand of the best legionaries, more than even Crassus lost!"

Now he did lower his head and weep. I let him cry as long as he wished, leaving him alone in that corner of the room. I stood trembling before the window, seeing—but not seeing—the nasty seas outside. I must control myself. I must hear it all.

The thirty-two thousand legionaries—they were the blackened and drying bodies I had seen in my vision, with Antony crawling over them. On that great, open, stony field . . .

He was wiping his eyes. "A native of that area told us that we must not retreat the same way we had come, in spite of the Parthians' assurances of safe withdrawal. He said they meant to set upon us in the plains and finish us off." He paused. "We did not know whether to trust him or not. Perhaps he was sent merely to mislead us. But in the end Lord Antony did."

Yes, he always trusted.

"And it proved to be our salvation."

Sometimes trust was rewarded. But seldom. "How could it be your salvation? You said you lost a third of the army—not counting those ten thousand killed with the baggage train! Forty-two thousand altogether! Almost half, then!" I cried.

"Had it not been for the mountainous path of our retreat, and the bravery and strength of the lord Antony, we would have lost the entire army," he said. "We were attacked and harried all the way; we fought eighteen defensive battles to get out. It is difficult to keep an orderly retreat from turning into a rout. Antony did that, although we had no food, little water, and winter was closing in. It took us twenty-seven days to reach the border of Armenia, to cross the Araxes. We had to march under the most extreme conditions, and discipline barely held. Antony brought a starving army in rags across the border. And do you know what the Parthians did when we crossed the river?"

"No, I am sure I do not." The gods had not granted me that picture.

"They cheered and applauded our bravery."

Bravery . . . yes, it was godlike. But it could not confer political power. Antony had failed. He had failed, where Octavian had succeeded. Now the scales must tip, inexorably and irrecoverably.

Anger and grief overcame me. I cried aloud to the gods. Then I saw Eros staring at me, unnerved. I must not add to his burdens.

"Pray continue," I said, struggling to make my voice level.

"I would not grieve you further," he said.

Both of us, striving to spare each other.

"No, please speak. I must hear."

"I must tell it—tell of the worst moment of the entire campaign." He straightened himself, squaring his little shoulders. "There was a point when it seemed we were doomed—overcome. The lord—my Antony believed that the Parthians were upon us. He—he ordered me to kill him, run him through with his sword—" He shook with the memory, and I felt all strength draining from me.

"And—" I whispered. How could he have wanted that? How could he have left me like that? I knew it was a sentiment unsuited to the battlefield, where all the rules are different, but had he not thought, even for a moment, of his other life? Was he that ready to throw it away? There can be satisfactions in the life of a private citizen; they should not be scorned.

"I took the sword, and it felt a hundred times heavier than it ever had before. I started to lift it. But when he said, 'And cut off my head, and bury it so the Parthians cannot capture it,' I could not. I ran away."

I gripped the back of the chair nearest me. He had actually commanded that? I felt myself about to vomit. I looked around for some vessel, some container, but found none, and rushed to the window. It was so revolting, so unspeakable—I retched over the side of the window, sour vomit splashing on the marble tiles of the terrace. His head! That dearest head!

Eros looked green as well. I could see his throat constricting. "He remembered what they had done to Crassus's head, using it in a mock Roman Triumph, tossing it about, making sport with it—he had to prevent that."

Still I went on being sick. That this very person in the room would have had to saw it off! There was nothing left in my stomach, but I clung to the windowsill and coughed. I could not even be ashamed. There could be no reserves left between us.

"It was unnecessary," he finally said, softly. "It was a false alarm."

That he could have died for a false report—but for Eros! "Thanks be to all the gods that you loved him enough to refuse."

"There are those who would say that for me to have refused and run away was a lack of love. Certainly a lack of obedience."

"I don't care!" I said. "Sometimes one must submit to a higher obedience! To refuse to kill when you feel there is still hope—" I shook my head, and sought for a napkin to wipe my mouth. This was worse than the nightmare, worse than any dream.

"Once across the border into Armenia, we had no choice but to treat King Artavasdes as a friend, pretending that we believed his excuses for leaving the army. But for our safety we could not winter there. We had to continue our retreat through the mountains of Armenia, where we lost another eight thousand men to disease and exposure."

He was coming to the end of his tale. I braced myself for it.

"Now Canidius is bringing the rest of the army after Antony, who awaits you at Leuce Come."

"He awaits me?"

"Yes. He needs money, and clothes for his nearly naked men. You are his only hope."

O ye gods! To have come to this!

"Here. He has written you." Eros extended a tattered letter in his grimy hand.

I took it and slowly opened it. My first words from him since our parting, a lifetime hence.

> My dearest—Eros will tell you all. It is too long, and painful, to re-count here, and a wound I received on my hand makes writing diffi-cult. Pray come to me as soon as you possibly can. Eros will tell you, and the ship captains, the exact location. I have eighteen thousand men, all of whom need clothing. And money to buy food. I desire only to see you.
>
> —M.A.

Eighteen thousand men! He had started with sixty thousand crack legion-aries! Where now were the other thirty thousand auxiliaries who were sup-posed to support him? Fled like the cowards and traitors they were.

I saw Eros looking at me.

"Eighteen thousand men?" I said. "He wishes food and clothing for all those soldiers?" I looked out at the sea, churning and dark. It was the height of winter, when ships dared not sail. "He mentioned ships. He expects us to sail?"

Eros nodded. "He said you would not fail him."

Did he credit me with miraculous powers? Or had he so far lost his reason that he gave no thought to the considerable risk that I would go to the bottom of the sea?

I had recently been so weak that I could scarcely leave the palace grounds. Now I was to sail to Syria on stormy seas?

"I will go to him," I said. Or die trying.

60

I stood on the deck of a trireme rolling at anchor in the harbor. It had taken some searching, and a hefty payment, to find a captain brave enough—or foolhardy enough—to venture out in the tossing seas. As Queen, I could have ordered one of my warships and its captain to carry me, but I preferred to persuade rather than command, at least for such as this.

Beside me on the heaving deck stood Olympos, wrapped in a heavy cloak, and cursing softly. No one had wanted me to go, and Mardian and Olympos had tried to forbid me—Mardian citing the danger in travel and Olympos warning of the threat to my health.

"You can't even endure a morning of audiences with ambassadors, and now you want to rush off to Syria to comfort Antony," he had lectured. "Send your soldiers and your own ambassadors—what else are they for?"

But it was not in my nature. If I failed him, all his faith in honor would be destroyed. Not going was the sort of thing Octavian would do. And I needed to see him for my own sake. That dream—and then the picture in my mind of his orders to Eros—the remembrance, and the jerking ship, made me start to feel sick again. I clutched on to Olympos's arm.

"This is insane!" he said, turning to me. "We should get off. Now."

Olympos had finally announced that only if he could accompany me would he allow me to go—and he had forthwith abandoned his other patients, his students at the Museion, and Dorcas. He toted along an extremely bulky box of medicines, with mixing implements and empty bottles waiting to be filled. One thing he had not had to urge on me was his beloved silphion. At last I was more than willing to use it—I could not allow myself to become pregnant; I needed all my strength now for other things. I loved my children and I had even enjoyed my pregnancies, but now I must allow no other claims on my mind and body.

"At least let us sit down!" Olympos fussed. I smiled faintly. On a deck there are not many such places, but the captain—newly enriched by my payment—was most gracious in finding one. His ship was crammed with blankets, tunics, shoes, and cloaks to cover the eighteen thousand soldiers, and two other transports would follow with grain.

On this ship, too, was all the money I felt safe transporting by winter sea. The rest would have to wait until later—not that transporting money is ever safe, by land or by sea. Bandits, pirates, accidents attack the waves and the footpath equally. And gold is very heavy; a talent of gold weighs as much as a big child, two talents as much as a woman, and three as much as a well-muscled man. It does not get from place to place easily. I was bringing about three hundred talents on the ship.

The crossing should take around seven days, and Eros had already instructed the captain exactly where Leuce Come lay.

"It's north of Sidon," he said. "I know it. No good harbor, though. Might have to anchor far from shore if I can't get inside the seawall."

I didn't care. Just let us get that near! I would gladly swim ashore, if I had to.

I shivered and pulled my cloak tighter around me.

You will have to improve a great deal in seven days in order to plunge into *these* icy waters, I told myself. Are you expecting a miracle?

As we left the relatively calm harbor of Alexandria to be buffeted on the open seas, I watched the waves rise higher, making jagged crests.

The churning, bucking, jerking sea voyage . . . my fate was always decided by water. From Ashkelon to Alexandria to meet Caesar for the first time; from Alexandria to Tarsus to meet with Antony in costume; from Alexandria to Antioch to meet with Antony again, this time on my terms. And now to

Syria, where yet a different Antony awaited me. An Antony who had staked his reputation and his future on a great battlefield, and been utterly defeated.

With each passing day in the cold mist, my strength came stealing back, sneaking in while I slept. Each morning I arose feeling more restored, my legs less shaky, my muscles firmer. Olympos attributed it to the broth he made me drink five times a day, as well as the herbs he plied me with; but finally he said with a grunt, "I suppose the closer you get to *him*, the faster you revive."

I must grow stronger if he had grown weaker; if we two were one, then as one waned so must the other wax, to preserve the strength of the whole. That I knew. So I merely smiled at Olympos and said nothing.

The harbor—small, low, and desolate—was sighted over the gray-blue sea. Behind it clustered the houses of the village, also small, low, and desolate. There was no color anywhere, no sign of life. As we approached, large waves swept us broadside and threatened to dash us into the seawall, but the captain managed to bring us safely out of the fury of the wind.

"He's worthy of Sextus's fleet," said Olympos.

Sextus. For a moment I wondered where he was, whether Antony had joined forces with him. But all other thoughts fled when I beheld Antony standing—a forlorn, muffled figure—on the shore.

He was staring out to sea like a statue, rooted to the ground. As we approached, he had been a little dot, unmoving. Only when we actually came into the harbor did he break his stillness and start running toward us.

From the railing of the ship I gestured with wide arm-sweeps, wild with excitement. His mantle was flapping, flying out from his outstretched arms, giving him the wingspread of a huge bird.

"Antony!" I cried. "Most noble Imperator!"

He wheeled around and saw me at once, then rushed over to the place where the ship would dock. The folds of the mantle swirled once and then settled as he pulled back his hood. I saw that his face was thinner and much more lined. He was looking up at me.

As soon as the gangplank was down, I hurried ashore and into his arms. He enveloped me in the rough mantle, and in the crush I felt his face against mine and his kisses on my cheek, heard him saying, "You are come, you are come. . . ." I was so close I could only feel and hear him, not see him.

How long it had been since I had touched him—eight months! I dug my fingers into his shoulder and felt the bones nearer the skin now than before, the warm flesh burned off him. I remembered the dried-up men I had seen in my dream, and knew it had almost come true for Antony.

He was pressing me against him, our entire lengths touching, when he suddenly stepped back a little.

"The baby! It is born? Yes, of course it is!" He had left me thin, and now I was thin again.

"Yes, in November," I said. "A son. Healthy and strong."

"November," he said, shaking his head. "In November we were still struggling out of Parthia. But it was near the end."

"Do not think on it now," I said. "You can tell me every detail later."

"I have been watching the horizon every day, waiting for your ship," he said. "You can never know how hard I watched." His voice was strained, and indeed, he looked worse than I felt.

We sat in the mean, dark chamber of his wooden quarters, a sputtering rush lamp throwing deep shadows on the walls. Antony was hunched over, his big hands dangling over his knees. Without his mantle, his tunic revealed how thin and battered he was; in comparison, his head and hands now appeared unusually large.

We had eaten, drunk, and been left alone in the cold room. His bantering, for the benefits of the servitors, faded as soon as they had exited.

"One has to keep up the spirits of those around one," he had said. "If word got out that the commander himself had fallen into despair . . ." His voice trailed off. "And I am not in despair, just . . . tired."

Yes. Tired. That were we both. If only rest were possible!

I reached out and touched his cheek, tracing the new hollows beneath the cheekbones. Then I gently touched his neck, that neck which was still thick and well muscled. As I touched it, I could not help following the line where it would have been severed, right above the collarbone. A nasty, deep-cold fear seeped through me. My hand stopped moving.

"What is it?" he asked.

I would not tell him I knew. He would not have wanted Eros to reveal it. "Nothing." I caressed the line. "I have always been very fond of your neck." I leaned forward and kissed it, just at its hollow.

I saw him close his eyes, heard him sigh as I kissed all around the circle of his neck. He was more than tired; he was bone-weary. As yet he had not told me his true feelings about the defeat, nor his plans for his next move. Instead he seemed almost bewildered, paralyzed by his change of fortune.

He let his head slump down, resting it against my shoulder. It was uncomfortable for me, and I wriggled a little to settle it better. As it slid lower, pulling the strap of my gown down, exposing my breast, it set off that tingling which signaled the rush of milk. The warmth, the touch of skin against skin had set it off; I had not had time to wean the baby completely before setting out. Embarrassed, I pulled away and tried to cover my breast again, but it was too late. The milk oozed out and fell in drops, wetting his cheeks. He seemed amused by it, and reached out a curious finger to catch it and taste it.

"I could not bring the baby," I said, "and I had to rush away as soon—I came as soon as you sent for me." I felt discomfited, as if he had caught me at something unseemly.

He took away all my shyness by saying, "I wish you had brought him. I missed seeing you with the twins when they were babies, and now I must miss this one as well."

"He will still be a baby for some time," I assured him. But unspoken was the question: When do you propose to return to Alexandria? What are your plans?

He sighed and heaved himself up, shaking his head as if he would shake off sleep, and ran his left hand through his hair. I saw then that his right one was swollen, with an ugly, unhealed gash.

"Tomorrow I will show you the troops," he said. "The poor men! And you have brought clothing, you say?"

"Yes," I said. "As many cloaks, shoes, and mantles as I could gather, with the material to make more."

"And the—gold?" He tried not to look too eager.

"I brought three hundred talents," I said.

"Three hundred! But—that is not nearly enough!"

"How much could I carry? Be reasonable! More will follow. But on these seas—I had to divide it, divide the risk. Two more ships are bringing grain. They should arrive within four or five days."

"Three hundred talents!"

I grew angry at him. He had demanded I come immediately, trusting both my person and the gold to the winter seas. And had he forgotten that I would barely have recovered from childbirth? As it happened, I had not—but I had come anyway. "You are unrealistic," I said. "It is a miracle that I have arrived safely—that I was able to come at all!"

He shook his head. "Yes, yes, forgive me." He was rubbing his hand—was it bothering him? He had mentioned a wound that made writing difficult.

"What is wrong with your hand?" Before he could snatch it away, I took it.

There was a diagonal cut across it; it was puffy and an angry shade of red. The area around it felt abnormally hot. It looked ready to fester.

"It is nothing," he said carelessly. But I saw his mouth tighten when I touched the sore place.

"You should let my physician treat it," I said.

"When you see the state of the other soldiers, you will forget this scratch," he said.

Later, alone together in the dark, I caressed his shoulders, seeking to comfort him. Even in his present state, my heart rejoiced to be with him again. But his soul was so burdened that he merely sighed and said, "Forgive me. The spirits of my lost men are with me in this very room, and I would be shamed to forget them so soon." His hunger for me seemed to have been destroyed by what he had endured on the plains of Parthia. We slept chastely that night, embracing like two children.

With the clear, cold dawn, Antony groaned and sat up. He shook his head to clear it before swinging his legs over the side of the bed and walking stiff-legged across the room to the washbasin. He lowered his head over the basin and splashed water over his face; I saw how he winced when the injured hand got wet.

I rose and imitated him, knowing the day began early in camp. We moved silently, unable to form words. Methodically he went about his business, combing his hair and pulling his tunic over his shoulders, then winding the wool strips around his legs before strapping on his boots. It was so dreary and damp-cold that feet turned numb without such protection.

Still we did not speak, as if what we did was too solemn for words. What I witnessed was the opposite of the joyous going-forth of a warrior—it was the retreat, the counting of losses, the licking of wounds after a battle. One was the singing of the blood, the peak of anticipation, prideful organization, the other the messy aftermath of defeat.

"All the commanders returned unhurt?" I finally asked.

"Yes, except for Flavius Gallus," Antony said. "In the fifth day of our re- treat, he pursued the harassing Parthians too far from our column. I sent orders for him to turn back, but he refused to give up. It was a trick to lure him; we lost three thousand men through his stubbornness. Titius wrenched the eagles from his standard-bearers to try to force them back, but it was no use. By the time Gallus realized he was surrounded, it was too late. And the other commanders—like Canidius, who should have known better—kept sending small parties to aid him, and they were cut down also. I had to leave the vanguard of the army and lead the entire Third Le- gion into direct confrontation with the enemy before they were driven off." As he spoke, color came back into his drawn face. "Gallus was shot with four separate arrows and died; and besides the three thousand killed, we had five thousand wounded." He shook his head. "They had to be transported on our mules, which meant we had to abandon much of our field equipment, the tents and cooking utensils. From then on—oh, those twenty-seven days!"

"If Artavasdes had not deserted you, his cavalry could have protected you on that twenty-seven-day retreat," I said bitterly. "He is responsible for those losses as well as for the ten thousand slain with the baggage train!"

"Yes," Antony agreed. "And—"

"He must pay the price of his perfidy!" I insisted. "You must punish him! I suppose he pretended to be innocent?"

"Oh yes." Antony smiled a ghost of his old merry smile. "And I pretended to believe him. After all, by the time we finally reached Armenia, we could not have fought an army composed of stray cats and geese. But neither could we linger in his realm. So I pushed for us to return to Roman territory, even though the snows were deep in the mountains."

"You must return and take revenge," I urged him.

"All things in time," he said.

When someone says that, you know nothing will happen. I remembered once telling my old tutor, "We must wait and see what happens," and he had replied, "Princess, things do not happen, we must make them happen."

I let it go. He must grieve before he could move forward. "You have heard the news of Octavian's victory—or more correctly, Agrippa's?" I asked.

He nodded. "Yes. So the last of the Republicans is snuffed out—or rather, the last of the *sons* of the Republic. Sextus did not stand for anything besides himself."

"And what do you stand for? What does Octavian stand for?" The question must be asked. "Now you have no cause to pursue together. The assassins are killed, Sextus eliminated. What is your mission now?" He would have to decide, or have nothing with which to rally others under his banner.

"I do not know," he said, and it was clear that at that moment he did not care.

"Octavian will find one," I warned him. "He will reinvent himself to keep gathering followers." But Antony was not interested in Octavian just now.

"Oh, perhaps he'll die," he said lightly. "His health is still wretched. He'll cough his way into Caesar's divine company."

There was a knocking on the door, and Eros stuck his head in. "Good sir—I see I am come too late."

"No, you are just in time. Bring us something to break our fast; then we will visit the men and distribute the clothing." He turned to me. "When will the grain arrive?"

"The transport ships were following our galley, but we outdistanced them," I said. "Nonetheless, they should be docking within three or four days."

"Alert the millers, so we can get the grain ground quickly," Antony told Eros. "Bread! We need bread, a mountain of loaves!"

Rows and rows of sick men lay on the ground or on threadbare blankets in the fields behind the town—wilting like plants after a long drought. Some of them were so gray and shriveled it was hard to recognize them as men in the prime of life, and again I was haunted by my dream of the dried, blackened figures.

They stirred as we approached—Antony in his purple cloak, so they could know him from a distance—and called feebly. I saw them struggling painfully to sit up. Awnings had been stretched over the sickest to keep the worst of the weather off them, but the rest had to make do with the open air.

"Imperator," they were whispering, or crying out. "Imperator!"

Antony stopped at the side of one man wearing a ragged bandage on his head that covered one eye. He stooped down to speak to him.

"Where did you receive this wound?" he asked.

"With Gallus," he said. "I was beside him when the full hail of arrows hit us."

"Poor, unfortunate Gallus!" said Antony.

"He got hit four times, and I only once." The man seemed determined to keep defending his fallen commander. "It was worse for him."

"Yes, and later he died," said Antony. "But tell me—where are you from? How long have you served?"

The man—with a surprising show of strength—raised himself up to a sitting position. "I am from Campania—not far from Rome."

"Ah. The best soldiers come from the homeland," said Antony. "Their loss hits the hardest of all."

The man looked pleased, but went on to answer plainly, "I have served ten years—two under Caesar himself. I have another ten before retirement—and, Imperator, I want my piece of land in Italy. The traditional place, not those new colonies in Africa or Greece. No, Italy is my home. I didn't serve this long to be exiled in my old age!"

"There will be a place for you where you wish," Antony assured him. But I knew it was not that easy. Italians were weary of being deprived of their land to make room for army veterans. *Settle them abroad* was the sentiment.

When Antony knelt beside another man whose leg—purple, swollen, and torn—was propped up on a rock, the man grabbed his forearm and almost jerked him onto the mat. "Noble Antonius!" the man said. "I was there! I was there!"

Antony attempted to pull his hand away. "And where was that, good soldier?"

"When you spoke to rally the army on the retreat! Ah, how you stirred us! And then you addressed the gods themselves! Yes, lady, he did!" He turned his fierce eyes on me. "He lifted up his hands to heaven and prayed that if the gods were now minded to exchange his former victories with bitter adversity, to let it fall on him alone, sparing his men."

It was obvious the gods had denied his petition.

"They did not spare you, my friend," Antony said. "Would that I could change places with you."

No. No. Let them deny that as well.

"No, Imperator," said the soldier. "This is better."

"The Queen has brought clothing and cover," said Antony, handing him a blanket. "Food is coming."

Up and down we went, Antony speaking personally to many of the soldiers, bending down, listening patiently, his attention riveted on each man. They were in a pitiful state, and I wondered how many could survive. There were many arrow wounds—some still with the arrowheads in them—as well as cuts, broken limbs, punctured eyes, torn hands. But most were suffering the ravages of exposure, starvation, and dysentery rather than Parthian arrows.

"And here," said Antony, "are the survivors of the poison root—if you can call them survivors." He led me to one of the shelters, where some dozen forms were stretched out.

Lean, with vague eyes, they looked at us with mild interest as we approached.

"Poison root?" I asked. "What do you mean?"

Antony felt in his pouch and withdrew a dessicated, twisted piece of vegetation. "This is what I mean," he said. "This evil plant!" He turned it around so I could see its stringy roots. "I told you how near we were to starvation, and had to forage, eat bark, and dig roots. We knew not what half the things were, and this one was poison. But a most peculiar poison—before it killed, it made men lose their wits, and become obsessed with moving rocks." When he saw my expression, he laughed bitterly. "Yes, what a sight it was! The camp was filled with men moving rocks! Then they would suddenly vomit, and die. Only these survived. That is, their bodies survived—their minds perished."

Several men were moving scrabbling fingers over the dirt, as if they were still searching for the rocks. They were dribbling spittle from their mouths.

"Was there no help?"

"Only wine," said Antony. "If they drank large draughts of wine, it cured them. O happy cure! But we had little wine; our stores had been left behind when we had to abandon our food so we could carry injured men on the mules. And so the men perished—for want of wine."

"My physician studies poisons," I said. "I would like him to examine this root. Perhaps he knows what it is, and of a cure besides wine."

Antony had stooped down and was attempting to soothe the agitated men. But it was no use.

That night we dined with the other commanders. Unlike Antony, they seemed their usual boisterous, bluff selves. Plancus, who talked while he chewed and looked like a camel, was pleased to be appointed governor of Syria. He would depart for Antioch shortly to take up residence.

Dellius, his pitted face now craggier than ever, asked me politely if I had read his account of the war, which he had presented to Antony.

"It's this long"—Antony stretched out his arms—"and then some. I promise to read it first. I trust you have told the *whole* truth—of the bravery of the men as well as the losses."

He smiled, but I always thought his smile was closer to a smirk. "I tried, Imperator."

Young Titius, his long, dark face only slightly thinner than it was before, leaned across his couch and said, "Sextus has sent more offers. We must decide."

Sextus. "Where is Sextus, and what decision must be made?" I asked.

"Sextus has raised three legions since landing on our shores, and he has fallen so low that he is now offering them—and himself—as mercenaries to the highest bidder. He has even trafficked with the Parthians," Titius said.

"Then he can no longer call himself a Roman," said Antony. But his voice was sad rather than angry, as if he was saying, *There is no trust, no faith anywhere. That the son of Pompey would ally himself with the Parthians* . . . He shook his head, slowly.

Antony was being worn away by the perfidy around him; in his old-fashioned loyalty he was continually shocked to discover its absence in others. The murder of Caesar was not a single event, but a reflection of the loss of honesty repeated in lesser betrayals: Octavian's deceptions, Lepidus's attempted coup, Labienus's defections, and now Sextus's cynical prostitution of himself.

"So we are to refuse his offer?" asked Titius.

Antony looked surprised that he would even ask. "Yes. It is over for Sextus." He paused so long I thought he had finished speaking. "And he cannot be allowed to go to the Parthians."

Titius nodded gravely. "No, he must not."

Ahenobarbus waved his hand, showing a coin between his thumb and forefinger. "This has already come into my hands!" he said angrily. "The captured treasure from our wagons—the Parthians are striking over your image, Imperator, and replacing it with their own." He passed the coin to Antony, who examined it carefully. Not only was the outline of his own face flattened out and overlaid with that of the Parthian king, but mine—shown on the reverse side, in tribute to our marriage—had been restamped with the image of a Parthian horse with a quiver slung from the saddle!

"This must not be borne!" said Ahenobarbus.

"No, nor will it be," said Antony. But his voice lacked fervor.

As for myself, seeing my portrait effaced made me feel violated. But sometimes one must let an insult go, if it is in one's interest to do so. That is why politicians are different creatures from heroes. A ruler cannot always afford to be a hero, if the needs of his countrymen cry out for a politician instead.

Eros had worked hard to make Antony's quarters more comfortable while we were out. He had procured carpets, more lamp stands, and even a caged raven that he claimed could talk. But the cage was covered, and we would have to wait until morning to hear him.

"It is just as well," said Antony. "I am weary of talk. Well, you heard them—the officers. They seem undaunted by the defeat."

"So did you, in public." I began to unwind my hair; my neck was aching from the weight of the gold pins used to fasten it, plus the jeweled diadem. I placed the gold circlet carelessly on his folding camp chest, where it gleamed dully. I reached back to unclasp the heavy gold necklace, but Antony stood behind me and undid it. He was very possessive of the necklace, proud of it.

With all that gold removed, I felt younger and lighter. Gold has its own command over the spirit.

I had felt disheartened and too weary for further discussion, but suddenly I knew I must not let it drop. "Antony," I said, "I have now seen the extent of the loss—from the festering wounds of the soldiers to the insult of the coins. But it is over now. What will we do?"

He sank onto the bed and half lay on it, one leg dangling over the side. "I do not know," he finally said. "I do not know which way to move."

"We have suffered a military defeat, but we are no worse off in terms of territory than we ever were. The only battle it is crucial not to lose is a defensive one, when your home territory is attacked. So we have lost Parthia? We never had it. Is it worth expending more money and men to 'revenge' ourselves? Let us think carefully."

I was finished with Parthia. At least Antony was alive, and his commanders intact. A new army could be raised, and directed elsewhere, to where the *real* enemy was.

"Artavasdes must be punished," he said.

"Agreed, but after that?"

"What will they say in Rome about my defeat?" He threw his head back on the pillow and stared up at the ceiling moodily.

"Don't tell them it was a defeat," I said. "Announce your victory."

He sat up. "Lie?"

"It's done all the time—or haven't you noticed? Octavian 'put an end to the civil wars.' Even Caesar claimed to have conquered Britain, when all he did was explore it, and lose two fleets in doing so. Say you have won a victory in Parthia. You weren't annihilated—that's a victory in itself."

"But—no cities were captured, no standards or prisoners were returned. In fact, more standards and prisoners were taken!"

"What good does it do you in Rome to announce this?" I said. "All it does is weaken your position. Wait until you have won another war, then you can announce it. But by then people won't care, because they care only about the latest war. Parthia is so far away from Rome, they have no way of knowing what really happened."

"Even you! Even you!" He sounded stunned. "You are like all the rest."

"No," I said. "But I understand them. I can play their game better than they themselves." I came over and sat beside him, and took the sleeves of his garment in my hands. "If I could not, where would I be now? Who was I? A girl who was driven from her throne by third-rate counselors—"

"Who managed to kill Pompey nonetheless," said Antony.

"—with no army, no resources, no allies, nothing but my own brain. In order to get what you want, you must think like your enemies. Stop being Antony and start being Octavian—when you make your plans, that is. No other time." I twisted my fingers in the sleeves, and leaned forward and kissed him. "I would not want Octavian in my bed."

I felt his arm tighten around my back. "Nor would I," he said.

"Tell Rome you have prevailed," I whispered near his ear. "Rebuild your shattered army. Then you will be ready to direct it wherever you please—eastward or westward."

"Where would you lead me, my Egyptian?" he said. "What would you have me do?" But the gaze in his eyes in the dull lamplight showed that he was all too willing to be led.

"I will show you," I said, tumbling forward across his chest. I kissed his throat, his jaw, the side of his face, his ears. I had not known how hungry I was for his body until I touched him. Just now I did not care about the Parthians or even Octavian; all I wanted was to lose myself in him, throw the hours of night away with him, make his bed a tent of pleasure.

"I am waiting," he said, and the leap of strength in his arms around me told me he had not been vanquished by his defeat. The old Antony still lived—and wanted.

———

In the half-light of dawn I groped drowsily and pulled the cover off the raven's cage. He cocked his big head back and forth and rasped, "Naked Imperator! Naked Imperator!" I quickly threw the cover back on. Who had taught him that? I laughed and reached for Antony once more. There was still a little bit of night left, just its tatters—but it would serve us well enough.

61

When I whisked the cover off the birdcage in the full light of morning, the raven began cawing about the naked Imperator again—clearly someone's idea of a joke. I wondered how long it would take for the rest of his vocabulary to emerge.

Eros appeared, entering the room shyly.

"Your industry in making my quarters more . . . er . . . amusing is impressive," Antony said.

Eros blushed, and bustled around, laying out clothes for Antony and bringing in heated water. I watched carefully as Antony raised his arms for the tunic; the right hand had gotten worse.

"Olympos has to treat it," I insisted. That Olympos would finally have to meet Antony and treat him like a human being might be hard for him, but he would have to endure it. It was time. I would not have Antony lose his sword hand to spare Olympos's feelings.

I am Caesar's right hand, he had once said. Was that right hand now to fail?

Olympos was supposed to meet with me later in the morning; he had spent the previous day visiting the soldiers himself and conferring with the army physicians. His stay in Rome had left him with an abiding interest in treating war wounds.

He met me in the outer chamber of the headquarters, his color up and his eyes dancing. "I've never seen so many arrow wounds," he said. "I've been practicing with the spoon of Diokles—the arrow extractor. It really works!" He sounded elated—and surprised.

"It is a clever instrument," I said. "Of course, since it is Greek!" I had read about them, but never seen one.

"Would you like a demonstration?" he asked. "This afternoon—"

I shook my head, and he stopped chattering and looked at me.

"Well, I must say, you look better! No more drooping! I suppose I needn't ask the cure!" He sounded annoyed, as if he begrudged me any pleasure with Antony.

"I feel much better, but I am not fully restored," I said, to placate him.

"But I have two medical problems—not mine—I hope you can solve. One is this root." I handed him the dried stem and explained about its effect on the soldiers.

He shook his head. "I have never heard of it—unless it could be something called wolfsbane that grows in colder climates—yes, perhaps. But I need the manuscripts at the Museion to check it. Curses—travel makes everything so difficult!" He looked frustrated. "What's the other?"

"Antony's hand—it won't heal. The wound looks angry."

He drew back in a way only I could have sensed, knowing him as well as I did. "A simple wound—I have no magic to cure that. There are no secrets to that."

"He has had it for a long time—he mentioned it in a letter. I can see that it is getting worse, but he ignores it. Please at least look at it."

"A simple wound is a simple wound," he repeated stubbornly. "It either heals or it doesn't. I assume it's already been treated with wine and honey?"

"I don't know. It looks as if it hasn't been treated at all."

He snorted. "Well, when he has tried the usual remedies, and they don't work, call me." He paused. "It isn't bandaged?"

"No. That's how I saw it."

"Hmm. It's good that it isn't bandaged. But—" I could see him thinking.

"He won't bite you," I assured him. "He won't taint you. Touching his hand won't compromise your standards. In fact, *not* treating him would compromise your oath, I would think." There, let him digest that!

"Why are you doing this? You know my feelings. Are you determined to force me to accept him?"

"If you think all this is a plot on my part, you flatter yourself!" Suddenly I was disgusted with him and his high "principles." "It was you who insisted on coming with me. I didn't ask you to leave Alexandria! I want the best physician I know—you—to treat the hand of the best commander in the Roman empire. Is that so nefarious?"

He grunted. "Very well. I'll look at it. But I told you, I have no magic to cure wounds. They can baffle our best attempts."

I had an equally hard time persuading Antony. He voiced the usual disclaimers—*it's nothing, doesn't hurt, doesn't matter, let it alone*—but I prevailed. That night, in the fading light of dusk, he proffered his hand and let Olympos examine it. Only after several minutes of silence, waiting for a word from the taciturn physician, did Antony say, "So I meet the famous Olympos at last."

Olympos gave a noncommittal grunt, and I could have kicked him. He could be so aloof it crossed over into rudeness. It was amusing sometimes, but not now; Antony did not deserve the treatment Olympos usually meted out to bad carriage drivers or overeager merchants.

"You are supposed to be so skilled you can bring back the dead," said Antony, in his friendly, open manner.

More silence. Olympos was turning over the hand and sniffing it.

"But the most wonderful thing you ever did was to bring my children safely into the world, when it seemed they were doomed, along with the Queen herself."

I had told Antony of the debt we owed to Olympos for the lives of the twins.

Finally, Olympos looked up at him, and I saw the faintest trace of a smile on his lips—or rather, a softening of the dour expression. He nodded slightly. "How long have you had this?" he asked.

"In the last skirmish with the Parthians, just before we crossed over the boundary into Armenia . . . about twenty or thirty days, I suppose. I didn't notice it at first."

"Yes, that's the way these things develop," said Olympos, poking at it. "I suppose this hurts?"

Antony attempted to laugh, but it was a thin one. "Oh, a bit—it feels like a mild torture." He jumped a little.

"Hot, I see." Olympos was laying a finger along it.

"Well?" said Antony.

"Untreated, it might cure itself," said Olympos, straightening up. "Of course, it would leave a large scar, and the hand would always be stiff."

"And treated?" Antony was clenching his fist, then stretching out the fingers, like someone trying on a glove.

"It would be very painful," said Olympos in his haughtiest voice. *You certainly don't want that,* his tone implied. "I would have to cut away all the darkened flesh. It is dying—my nostrils told me that. I would have to scrape it down to the raw flesh and let it start healing from there. And perhaps—depending on the size of it—it may need an old device, so old no one uses it anymore—a tin pipe so it can drain—"

"Then do it," said Antony simply.

Olympos looked surprised; he had been hoping Antony would demur and spare him any further involvement.

"I can't do it now!" he said quickly. "I need daylight so I can see. And time to prepare the drain—and I will need other things as well."

"What are they?" I asked. "I will see that all is ready by tomorrow."

"Red wine that is between six and nine years old," he said. "That has the strongest effect on fresh wounds."

Antony laughed. "Wounds have expensive tastes! Order enough that we can drink some ourselves. Afterward, that is."

"I think you ought to drink yours beforehand," said Olympos. "It will dull the pain—which will be considerable." He emphasized the last word, hoping to scare him.

"I will follow your prescription, wise one," said Antony, and Olympos smiled in spite of himself.

"I will need myrrh as well," he said, turning to me. "If you can get it for me by tonight, I can make a medicated stick for tomorrow."

"You don't ask for much!" I scoffed. "Myrrh at sundown!" But I would find some.

———

The next day Olympos and Antony disappeared into a field station set up to admit light without the glare of the sun. They were gone so long I found myself pacing back and forth, even talking to the raven, who alternated cawing with rasping, "Hail! Farewell! Kiss, kiss!"

When Olympos finally returned, he was drained; his medicine case, slung over his shoulder, looked ransacked.

"Well, I've done my best," he said. "But it's nasty. I had to take so much flesh out that he'll always have an indentation there—assuming it heals over."

"Is that why it took so long?" Babies had been born in less time.

"How long did it take?" He sank down on a bench. "I lost track. But with the wine, and the myrrh, it has a good chance. And the drainage tube—I'm quite proud of it. Hippocrates used them, but no one does now. This will be interesting."

"So, did you drink the wine?"

"Not me," said Olympos. "And Antony—he passed the time and distracted himself by asking the oddest questions."

"Well, what?"

"He wanted to know what we did as children—when I first met you, and all that. What you were like."

"I hope you didn't tell him!" Yet I was touched that he would be curious.

"Only the respectable parts," said Olympos. "I did tell him about some of our adventures—like the time we went to the embalmer's, and you lay down on the table like a mummy. And the time we hid in the marsh and overturned the little fishing boat, pretending to be crocodiles."

"Now that I know more," I said, "it's a miracle we didn't encounter a real crocodile ourselves."

He laughed. "Those were happy days," he said.

But I knew better. They had been dangerous days, and my danger had come not from crocodiles but from the court, where my sisters seized the crown. Yet such is the stoutheartedness of childhood that we were able to put that out of our minds for an afternoon and paddle around in the marshes, making memories that lasted a lifetime.

"Yes, I am surprised that he would ask," said Olympos. But he was pleased, I could tell. Antony had begun to win him over. Although it would be a long time before he capitulated completely, at least he would no longer think of him as a demon.

That night Antony waved the bandaged hand, so bulky it looked like a bear's paw. A little tin straw protruded from it, allowing liquid to run out. The entire hand, bandage and all, was to be plunged into a bucket—a bucket—of eight-year-old Falernian every hour or so.

"Does it hurt?" I ventured to ask.

"Like hell," he said jovially.

"If it works, then it will be worth it," I said.

"That's easy for you to say—you didn't have to sit still while he carved you up," he reminded me.

The hand responded, and after several days, and multiple inspections and bandage changes, Olympos seemed elated. The red puffiness of the original wound had subsided, and the edges were clean. Olympos kept dousing it with the wine and sprinkling ground myrrh on it. His stitches looked as neat as Syrian embroidery, and I told him so.

"Next time I must employ gold thread," he said, "and make it truly decorative."

Decision time was at hand—the seas had opened and a message must go to Rome. But what was it to be? At length Antony told me that after much deliberation, he had decided to downplay the losses in Parthia, but not claim outright victory.

"It will not be dishonorable to be vague about the particulars," he said.

"But misleading." I had to say it.

"I prefer 'vague,' " he repeated stubbornly. "It is no dishonor—"

How concerned he was about that word! He would do anything to avoid it.

"—to refuse to dwell on the past, and look to the future. I will emphasize the coming campaign in Armenia."

At least that would buy us some time to recoup our losses. "With Octavian away from Rome, that will serve us well," I said.

"If he has not left already, he will soon." The word was out that Octavian had found a task for his legions—he would employ them on the frontier of Illyria.

"Is he really going to command his own troops?" I asked.

"So they say. He is desperate to prove himself a military leader. Even getting himself injured would be helpful," said Antony. "It has become so glaring that without Agrippa to fight for him, he is totally ineffectual." But then a look of pain passed over his face. It was not Octavian who had lost forty-two thousand legionaries. The irony, of course, was that Octavian never would have attempted such a campaign in the first place.

"If he is gone, it would serve me well to go to Rome myself," Antony said, thinking out loud. "I could renew my ties there."

With Octavia? Quickly I said, "If you were to return in person, you would be questioned closely about Parthia. There would be no hiding it. Don't return in weakness!"

"I have been gone so long, I fear I may be losing my hold there—politically and in the memories of the people. It may be necessary to make a return visit."

"If you go when Octavian is gone, it will appear you are afraid of him!" I said quickly. "As if you are sneaking into the city behind his back, too timid to face him." Of course, I knew well enough that that was the time to go—

when he could have Rome to himself. But if he went, he might drift back into the wake of Octavian.

The strongest nature that's nearest him will always lead him, rule him. I could not risk that. I must keep him away from Rome.

"Then I'll go and call him to a meeting," said Antony.

"No, no!" I said. "Let him stay in Illyria. Let him be beaten there—let the Illyrians do your work for you. Otherwise he'll be looking for an excuse to leave and turn the fighting over to Agrippa, who'll earn him more glory!"

"I suppose that makes sense," said Antony. But I could tell he was far from convinced. "I will go later. After I can present the Armenian king in chains in a Triumphal procession."

"Yes. That will dazzle the Romans. They love Triumphs. And so far Octavian has not been able to claim one." Now I must change the subject, and quickly. "I am needed in Egypt. I must return soon."

"Yes."

"What are your plans? Will you come, or stay here with the troops?"

"If I could only rebuild my legions, I would mount the attack on Armenia as soon as possible. But it is already March, and there is no way I could be ready to campaign this season—it's such a short one in the mountains. And then there's Sextus on the loose, roaming here with his three renegade legions. I dare not march east and leave my back unprotected."

"So you must lose another year," I said. "Another year canceled out by other people." First Octavian's dallying, now Sextus's. How maddening it is to be caught in the grip of faraway events, when you cannot either surmount them or ignore them!

"Sextus must be dealt with," Antony insisted.

He was right, of course. And the truth was that Antony needed to regroup after last year, to revive both his army and his spirits.

"So you will remain here?"

"For a few more weeks," he said. "Then I will probably be able to oversee my responsibilities from Alexandria."

"Hurry," I said. "Your city has missed you."

"Alexandria is wherever you are," he said, taking my face in his hands—one still bandaged and the other normal—and looking at me.

My preparations for departure were almost complete, and I would leave in deep gratitude that Isis and the two gods of medicine—Asclepius and Imhotep—had returned Antony's hand to him. It had healed nicely, the tube and stitches long gone.

Then it came, the letter from Rome, announcing that Octavia was on her way to bring help to Antony: cattle, food, the ships left over from those he had lent Octavian, and two thousand of the best Roman soldiers, handpicked from Octavian's prize guard.

A pleasant messenger—Niger, a friend of Antony's—had brought the letter. I was forced to entertain him and ask polite questions about the journey,

624

trying to find out exactly where Octavia was now. The answer was, almost to Athens with her cargo. There she would await instructions from Antony.

"And what will those instructions be?" I asked Antony as we prepared for bed. "I am sure she will obediently do whatever you ask!" Oh, why had he not divorced her already? Why had I not insisted on it? My mistake!

"I could use the soldiers—"

"This is comical," I said. "Your two wives both sailing to you with aid and comfort. It's a miracle we didn't collide on the high seas."

"She isn't my wife," he said lamely.

"Why? Have you divorced her? And I remember that Rome ignored our marriage announcement completely. I don't exist as your wife—not in their eyes."

"Oh, I am tired of this!" said Antony, flopping back on the bed.

"Then end it!" I said. I wanted to add, *As you should have done long ago.* But I must not nag. Not now. "Send her back." That would convey a loud message.

"But the men—"

"The men are an insult! He owes you four legions, and what does he do but send this little token as a bait—or as a means of bringing you to heel! They are attached to Octavia, hooked to her, so you are supposed to swallow the entire thing, like a fish. 'Be good, Antony, and perhaps I shall let you have more'—that's what he's saying! Is that what you want—to be his subordinate, dance to his tunes? I tell you, it's an insolent challenge! Two thousand men when he owes you twenty thousand, and only in a package with his sister—the extension of himself." I glared at him. "You said it was like having Octavian himself in your bed!"

"Yes, yes." He was staring up at the ceiling.

"Well, do as you like," I said, and I meant it. He must decide for himself. "I am returning to Alexandria. You must board a ship for either Athens or Alexandria. They lie in opposite directions."

I turned on my side and pulled the covers over my shoulders. My heart was beating fast, but it was only because, like all irrevocable choices, this had descended fast and unlooked for. Yet it was welcome, in some mysterious way. Now it must happen; at last he must sail either north or south.

It was unlike me, but I would say nothing further to sway him either way. It must be entirely his own decision, originate in his own heart. Otherwise it would mean nothing.

The next morning a cheery letter came from Octavia, announcing her arrival in Athens, and signing herself, "Your devoted wife." The day after that, Olympos and I boarded a ship for Alexandria.

As he had when we arrived, Antony stood on the shore alone, watching us.

I waited, although of course I told myself I was not waiting. I busied myself with all the work that had accumulated in Egypt in my absence, especially since the seas had reopened. Already trade that had been repressed by Sextus had sprung back full force and healthy.

"There is no doubt that Octavian did the world a favor by getting rid of him," said Mardian. He held a report in his hands detailing the amphorae of oil dispatched in April. "Every time someone dips his bread in oil, he can give thanks to Octavian—for both the bread and the oil. It matters not whether he is in Greece, Cyprus, or Italy."

I glumly had to concur. Even we in Alexandria were reaping the benefits; our merchants' ships could go wherever they liked now.

"Here's proof of the expanded trade," Mardian said, lifting something out of a box. Flailing legs and a wrinkled neck strained and struggled. "Two tortoises from Armenia. The King sent them. He said he knew we had a zoo, and hoped we did not already have some of these." He rotated the creature in his hand. "He said their blood does not freeze and they can sleep in the snow with no ill effects."

"Unlike Antony's men!" So the King sought to avert punishment by such paltry presents. He was truly stupid.

Mardian was stroking the turtle's head, and it seemed to enjoy it; at least it stopped struggling. "A tragedy," he agreed. "And now the . . . situation with Octavia."

"Yes. She sits in Athens, surrounded by her bait. Octavian sent her; it could not be her doing." Of that I was sure.

"How do you know that?" Mardian frowned.

"Even if she wished to, he never would have permitted it unless it furthered his own aims. Besides, she has no thoughts, desires, or plans of her own!"

The weak creature was content to be married how and where her brother decreed, to be ordered about like a slave. What good was all her scholarship, then, and her vaunted lofty character?

"Everyone in Rome praises her," said Mardian cautiously. "And they say she is . . . beautiful."

"I've seen her. She isn't," I said. "People say the most ridiculous things! That's because it makes the story better, and the competition sharper between us. I and my eastern wiles against the virtuous beauty of Rome." I knew that was how it was perceived, and there was no remedy for it. As I said, people like dramatic stories and elemental conflicts.

"Antony will have to decide," I said. "And I will do nothing to help him make up his mind."

"My dear, if you have not done enough already, then it will never be enough," said Mardian.

———

I had spoken bravely to Mardian in the daylight, but at night I lay awake and felt much less sure. The truth was that common sense said Antony should return to the fold of Rome. His eastern venture had failed; he ought to put it behind him as a lost cause. He possessed that unusual, chameleonlike quality of fitting in anywhere. In his purple general's cloak and helmet he was pure warrior, in his toga he was a Roman magistrate, in a Greek robe he was a gymnasiarch, in lionskin and tunic he was Hercules, and in vine leaves he was Dionysus, an eastern god. Unlike me, he could be all things to all people—it was his gift and his charm.

Now he could easily resume the Roman mantle, take the hand of his Roman wife, and sail back to Rome. The east had not answered his dreams; very well, there were others for him elsewhere. Octavian would welcome him back, his errant past forgiven. They would never mention me, as a mutual embarrassment.

The west was sure for Antony. All I could offer was a struggle to build a wide eastern alliance and eventually an equal partnership with Rome. That, and myself.

Yet I wondered about a woman like Octavia. If I had been deserted, my husband publicly marrying someone else, bestowing lands on her and putting her head on coins, I never would want him back—or at least I would never take him back, no matter how much I wanted him. And to chase after him—I would be ashamed even to think of it!

Bending the knee to Octavian entailed great humiliation—even for his "cherished" sister. How much more for his fellow Triumvir?

And as day after day went by, I grew used to the waiting. It became part of me.

Mardian even set himself the challenge of finding literary references to "waiting" and "patience," seeking help from the librarian of the Museion.

"Homer says in the *Iliad*, 'The fates have given mankind a patient soul,'" he ventured one day.

"That is so general as to mean nothing," I said. Indeed it was; plenty of men had no patience at all.

"'Patience is the best remedy for every trouble,' wrote Plautus," he offered another day.

"Another generality!" I scoffed.

"Here's an obscure one, then," he said. "Archilochos wrote, 'The gods give us the harsh medicine of endurance.'"

"Why should it be from the gods?" I felt argumentative. "Sappho understands it better. She says, 'The moon and Pleiades are set. Midnight, and time spins away. I lie in bed, alone.'"

"Ahem," Mardian demurred. "Why do you want to torture yourself by reading Sappho?"

"Poetry consoles me at the same time it inflames me," I said.

"You should know better," he sniffed. "It's poison for the soul!"

Another day he presented a paper from Epaphroditus, who had found a quote from the scriptures of his religion. "He quotes from a scroll called Lamentations, and it says, 'The Lord is good unto them that wait for him, for the soul that seeketh him.' "

I laughed. "It isn't the Lord I'm waiting for."

"My dear, I give up. Inflame yourself with Sappho—or whomever you like. But it isn't helping!" He looked very stern.

I read poetry only late at night, when Charmian and Iras had retired, when the curtains in my room were gently stirring. The night stretched out before me, and the words from people centuries dead seemed to carry an authority that the words of the living never did. They did console; they whispered; they made me feel thankful that—whatever the pain of it—I was alive, while they, poor wretches, were dead.

> Later we will have a long time to lie dead,
> yet the few years we have now we live badly.

That was what they told me: that was what they warned me of.

It was during the day that I expected to receive the news. That was when ships docked and unloaded, when land messengers arrived. So late at night, as I half-lay, half-sat, on a couch on my roof terrace, watching the moonlight sliding on the harbor waves, indulging myself in poetry and Arabian candied melons, I barely looked up as one of my lowliest chamber attendants brought me a letter.

"Leave it here," I said, waving my hand toward a mother-of-pearl bowl that I used for unimportant trinkets. I was too involved in the delicious verses of Catullus to stop; they were as high-flavored and (I suspected) as unhealthy as the candies. I was thankful I had learned Latin after all, the better to partake of his agonies and yearnings.

> Odi et amo: quare id faciam, fortasse requiris.
> nescio, sed fieri sentio et excrucior.

> I hate and love.
> And if you ask me why,
> I have no answer, but I discern,
> can feel, my senses rooted in eternal torture.

How un-Roman! That, in addition to his "inflammatory" ideas, made him even more forbidden.

Only when I grew sated on the excess of emotion—I actually felt wrung out by the time I set him aside—did I idly pick up the letter and open it.

"My dearest and only wife, I am coming to you.—M. A." was all it said.

The plain and simple words were the most eloquent I had ever read, and belittled all the literary raptures I had so admired.

My dearest and only wife, I am coming to you.

Antony himself was already here, and had sent the letter from the harbor below. I had so delayed reading it that he stood on the threshold of my chamber by the time I had finished.

I heard the door being opened, heard footsteps. What now? I thought, annoyed at the intrusion. I wanted to reread the letter, ponder it. I stood up and looked inside, into the darkness of the room.

"Charmian?" I said. No one else would dare to enter at midnight.

There was no answer. Drawing my robe around me, I stepped inside.

Someone was standing there, face hidden by a voluminous hood.

"Who are you?" I demanded. How did he get past the guards? From the size, I knew it was a man.

Still the hooded figure was silent.

"Who are you?" I repeated. If there was no answer this time, I would call the guards.

"Don't you know me?" said Antony's voice, as he pulled back the hood. Swiftly he crossed the floor and caught me up in his arms, holding me tightly.

I could not speak, first because no words would come, and then because he was kissing me so fiercely.

"I will never leave your side again," he was saying, between kisses. "I vow it with all my soul."

I was able to pull my arm free and reach out and touch his face. He was really there; he was not an apparition brought on by the swimming of my senses in dreams and desires.

I took his hand and led him over to the bed, where we sat quietly. I pushed the cloak from his shoulders and let it fall. It had been five years almost to the day since he had been here, in my Alexandrian bed. I had been alone in it a long time.

"Nor will I let you," I whispered. "You have had your chance to escape. Now you must stay forever."

"There is no other reality for me than here," he said.

And I welcomed him back into my heart, my bed, and my life.

Iacta alea est: The die is cast. As Caesar had crossed the Rubicon into forbidden territory, now Antony had sailed down the eastern end of the Mediterranean to Egypt, his embraced destination, his future, his fate.

62

By morning the word was out not only in the palace but all over Alexandria: Marcus Antonius had taken up residence here. But in what guise had he come? Was he the Roman Triumvir, or the Queen's husband, or the King of Egypt? How were they to treat him? Luckily, Antony himself seemed to have no concerns about it; it was enough for him to be here and let others worry about what to call him or what his official status was.

"How very eastern," I told him that morning as he dismissed the stammering valet with an airy "Call me what you will, so long as it isn't fool." "You know we like to leave things ambiguous."

"Yes, that is why the Romans perceive you as so slippery," he said. He padded over to the window and looked out at the beckoning harbor, the green of the water shading slowly into the blue of the sky. Where they touched, a glorious soft blend of colors was produced. He looked content, a man well pleased with where he was. He raised his arms above his head and stretched. "When my clothes are sent up from the ship, I'll get dressed." He had left everything on board. "In the meantime I suppose I could wear that robe of your father's—if you still have it."

As if I would have ever discarded it, having kept it so long. It was the robe he had worn in his own quarters, and I had memories of it draping him as we played board games or he read quietly. Even so, it was jeweled and had patterned sleeves; a Ptolemy is never unadorned.

As soon as he had it on, he asked for the children. "And there's one I've never even seen," he reminded me.

The twins came running in; Alexander jumped on him and tried climbing up on him, like a monkey, and Selene hugged his knees, her eyes closed.

"Did you bring back lots of the enemy?" asked Alexander. "Are they in cages?"

"Well—not with me," Antony admitted.

"But you did get lots, didn't you?" Alexander said. "What are you going to do with them?"

"I haven't made up my mind yet," Antony said. "Sometimes that is the hardest part."

"Maybe we can eat them!" He shrieked with laughter. "Make a stew!"

"You are a bloodthirsty little devil," Antony said. "Now, who could you have got that from? I don't think they would make a very good stew—they are too lean and stringy." He turned to Selene. "You don't want Parthian stew, do you?"

She shook her head slowly, and made a face. "Taste bad," she said.

"Right you are. I'm sure it would taste very nasty." He looked up as the nurse brought in the baby, propped in the crook of her arm.

Little Ptolemy Philadelphos had hair standing up at full attention on top of his head, and bright, dark eyes. He was just perfecting his grin and practiced it on everyone, but Antony imagined it was just for him.

He looked down at him. "What a child!" There was no hiding the pride in his voice. "But his name—can't we find something more—personal?"

I took the baby; he was six months old now and noticed everything around him. He tugged on my hair with his fat hands. "I tried, but it was no use. Roman names are so unimaginative; you only have about twenty first names, and since they run in families, that really means you have only about five you are allowed to choose from. What were your brothers' names—Lucius and Gaius? So ordinary."

"Well, Ptolemy Philadelphos is anything but ordinary. But it sounds like a monument."

I put him down and watched him start to inch across the polished floor; creeping was a new art with him. "I hope a nickname will present itself," I said. "He has such shiny eyes . . . perhaps something there. . . ."

"Or if you *must* have a monument, then Monumentum," said Antony, with a laugh. "And he has hair like quills—too bad we can't call him Erinaceus, 'Hedgehog.' "

"I can see all the obligatory Antonias and Marcuses stifled your imagination. But I won't allow my son to be called Hedgehog!"

"Perhaps the Alexandrians will name him, as they did Caesarion," he said. "And where is Caesarion?"

"Most likely riding. He has fallen in love with his horse," I said. "It is the age for that."

In the flat reaches beyond the eastern city walls lay the Hippodrome—the horse-racing arena—and the pastures and training grounds connected with the royal stables. I had guessed right in thinking that Caesarion would be there, as I had guessed right in presenting him with a wonderful horse. He had named him Cyllarus, after a horse tamed by a Greek hero, and had almost deserted the palace for the stables ever since.

He was riding briskly along near the fence, his long legs gripping the flanks of the horse firmly, guiding him that way rather than by the bridle. Cyllarus responded, finely in tune, turning this way and that with only a nudge of Caesarion's knee. Then, still not aware of our presence, he leaned forward and, by this shift in his posture, signaled that it was time for speed. The horse immediately broke into a gallop, and Caesarion leaned along his neck, out of the wind, seeming almost part of the animal, absorbing his motion as he ran.

I saw it at the same time as Antony: It was Caesar himself, exactly the way he rode. As he had ridden that last day we were together. . . .

The memory, so sharp it actually hurt inside my chest—the antidote, the sweet rush of pride in seeing his son create him anew. . . .

"Caesarion!" I waved to catch his attention. Then, turning to Antony, I saw the look of astonishment on his face.

"I thought never to behold this again," he said quietly. He seemed shaken. "The shades stir to life once more."

Far down the field, Caesarion slowed Cyllarus by gradually shifting his own balance, then guided him in our direction. He sat up straight now, looking curiously over the horse's ears, watching us. As he approached, the uncanny resemblance to Caesar faded a bit, dissolving in the very youth of Caesarion's face. The deepset eyes were neither wary nor weary, nor were they surrounded by lines. The firm mouth cut across a smooth, untried face.

"Mother," he said, nodding, as he slid off the horse. "Triumvir." He acknowledged Antony. Clearly he did not know how to address him, or even whether to smile at him.

"You are a born cavalryman," said Antony, in genuine admiration.

Now Caesarion smiled. "Do you think so?" He tried not to look too pleased.

"Indeed. If you were three or four years older, I would speak to General Titius or Plancus about you. How old are you—fourteen?" He knew very well the boy was only twelve, but he knew equally well what twelve-year-old boys like to hear.

"No, I am—I will be twelve next month." He drew himself up.

"Ah," said Antony. "You have long outgrown the lizard. Remember him?"

"Remember him? He only died last year!" More and more of the boy was peeking out.

"We've brought a raven that talks," said Antony. "But I don't always like what he says."

"Why?"

"It's either nonsense or insulting."

Caesarion giggled. Then a silence descended, a silence that grew quickly.

Sensing the moment, and galloping into it as he dashed into the field, Antony took my hand. "Your mother was good enough to marry me, although I am just an ordinary man—not royal, nor godlike like Caesar. But I have long memories of him, going back years before he ever came to Egypt, and perhaps I can tell you whatever you wish to know about him. I know things about him even your mother doesn't! And I'll teach you what he taught me about soldiering, in the forests of Gaul and on the field of Pharsalus. I think he'd like that. In fact, that's the only reason I married the Queen—to come back to you, and Alexandria." He turned to me with a laugh.

"Yes, that's probably true," I said. "That, and wanting Egyptian ships."

Caesarion smiled. "I am happy to have you back. I have missed you," he said quietly.

Yes, that had been part of the heartache for me—knowing Caesarion had become attached to him, only to lose him.

"And I have missed you," said Antony. "I have a son near your age—oh, not quite so old!—only *ten* or so. Just as you are 'little Caesar,' he's 'little Antony'—Antyllus. Perhaps he'll visit sometime, and you two can gang up on me."

Antyllus was his son by Fulvia, and until that moment he had not spoken of him to me. He made it easy for me to forget that there were people he cared about still in Rome, and whom he had little likelihood of seeing now. I had been so wrapped up in my rivalry with Octavian and Octavia that I had overlooked the rest of his ties and family there. No wonder he wanted to return for a visit.

But he mustn't—no, he mustn't!

"Why, we shall have to invite him," I said quickly. "Yes, let him come to us in Alexandria!"

We were lounging on couches in our private dining room—exactly nine of us for the nine places. Protocol was ignored, joyously. All three children were crowded together on one couch, where they could spill and kick each other; Antony and I faced each other across the couches we shared with Iras, Charmian, Mardian, and Olympos. Mardian discreetly took the middle place between Antony and Olympos, his ample proportions pushing them apart.

This was my family—these were the people who would give their lives for me, and I for them. With all their faults, weaknesses, shortcomings, they still were my only armor and refuge against the ills that fate could harbor.

Olympos was observing Antony's hand, watching how he used it in eating—did he bend it easily? Did it function well? The gods help him if he would do something so direct as to ask!

"You did a good job, Olympos," I said, startling him. "The Triumvir's hand has mended nicely."

Olympos scowled at me. Only in families are we allowed to embarrass one another by reading each other's thoughts—and revealing them. "So I can see for myself," he said.

"You saved my hand, you miracle worker!" said Antony. He waved it about, not bothering to put down the bread he was holding. "Yes, it was about to fall off!" he told a wide-eyed Alexander. "So Olympos put a magic drain in it, and all the poison ran out."

"Oh, *really*," said Caesarion.

"No, that's true," I said. "It was a device from ancient medicine that Olympos rediscovered."

"I learned a great deal about wounds from treating your battered army," Olympos admitted. "I got more practice there than many physicians do in a lifetime. I wish—it might be interesting to—" He quickly stopped himself, and began to nibble hungrily on a crisp piece of honeyed lamb.

"To do what?" I was curious to know what had caught his interest.

"To study a little further in Rome," he said. "That capital of the world of war wounds."

"Why, Olympos, you insisted that Rome had nothing to teach Greece in medicine," I reminded him. I had had such a time in persuading him—if that is the word—to go to Rome.

"Wounds aren't medicine," he said stubbornly. "The treatment is different. Greeks study disease; war wounds are accidents."

"Well, why don't you go to Rome?" said Antony quickly. "We promise not to get ill while you are gone. Or go to war."

Olympos shrugged. "Oh, it was just a thought. I am not an army surgeon. Here in Alexandria, our emergencies are of a different sort. It was a foolish idea," he insisted.

"I think you should go to Rome," said Caesarion in a loud, clear voice. "And take me with you."

I turned to look at him, reclining on his elbow, his plain tunic making him look like any youth in the land. "What?" I said.

"I want to go to Rome," he said. "I want to see it. I've been studying Latin for three years now. My father was Roman, and you keep talking about my legacy from him, which Octavian has stolen, but I've never seen it. I can't even picture it—or Rome, or Romans!"

"You've certainly seen plenty of Romans," said Olympos, jumping into the breach. "They are all over the world. You can't avoid them." He put down his cup and looked sternly at the boy. "So there's no reason to go to Rome, just to see Romans."

"I didn't say I wanted to see *Romans*, I said I wanted to see *Rome*," said Caesarion with that same quiet, stubborn force his father had displayed in conversation. O Isis, how like him he was! "I want to see the Forum; I want to see the Senate house; I want to see the Tiber, and yes—I want to see the Temple of the Divine Julius! I want to see my father's temple!" His voice was rising, becoming more whiny and childlike. "I do! I do! It isn't fair that I can't!" He turned to me. "How can you expect me to care about it, or my inheritance, if I've never seen it? I can't ransack your mind for your memories; I have to make my own. Nothing is precious if you haven't seen it for yourself!"

"Now that is a point for philosophers to debate," said Mardian soothingly. "They say that which is unseen can be more real than—"

"That's a lie," said Caesarion coldly. "And don't change the subject." He dismissed the eunuch imperiously. Where had the child vanished? "Sooner or later I must go. Why not now?"

"Why must you go, sooner or later?" I asked.

"Because if I am to claim my Roman half, it cannot be as a stranger to myself—or to them."

Go to Rome! I felt betrayed; he wanted to go to Rome, to that nest of enemies, which had never been anything but grief to me. But, although he seemed so entirely mine, so completely Ptolemaic, I knew that he spoke the truth—half his blood was *theirs*. My own child, part foreign.

"Yes, I can see that," I said slowly. "But why now?"

"Why wait longer? I want to see it now. And besides, no one notices a child; no one will know I am there. I want to see them, I do not want them to see me. Let Olympos take me with him. Olympos can pass as an ordinary man, and I can be his assistant. We will be invisible."

"You cannot go without a guard," I said. "Don't you understand what a public figure you are? If someone—"

"The boy is right," said Antony suddenly. "He would be safer traveling as nobody without a guard than as Caesarion with one."

Antony! Antony was siding with them! "It is too dangerous," I said. "I cannot send him away like that—"

"There comes a time when a boy—when a young man—has to leave his mother's side," said Antony. "He comes of age on that day—on the day he first desires it and acts upon it. It comes earlier for some than for others."

It was too early. I shook my head. It was asking too much.

"I will guard him with my life," said Olympos. "And I think it would be good for both of us. We would both learn much—to help us in our life's work."

So now he was willing to go! Would to the gods he had never mentioned it in the first place! Yet Caesarion would have found another opportunity, and perhaps a worse one. . . .

"Let me go!" Caesarion was pleading. "I want to go. . . ."

"So," I said to Antony, late that night when we were alone, "you will send my child in your place!"

He shook his head. "No. The boy wishes to go."

"And so do you!"

"I do not deny it," he said. "There are political reasons for going, as well as—well, Rome is home. I have been away for—"

"Not as long as Caesar was, and he returned in power."

Antony sank down on one of the cushioned benches in the chamber. The night seemed to be growing hotter, and two servants were standing by with ostrich-feather fans, moving them up and down slowly. They appeared not to be listening, but I knew they were. I dismissed them. Now the hot air settled on us like a blanket.

Antony looked up at me, his expression not that of a husband or a lover, but of an advisor. "Some say—and I cannot wholly deny it—that the reason Caesar was slain was that he was out of touch with Rome, and what Romans were thinking. That his long absence made him a foreigner to them—that otherwise he would have been able to detect the current of dissatisfaction swirling all around him—"

"Of course he was aware of it!" I remembered the anguish it had caused him; that was one of the tortures of intelligence.

"If he had truly understood, he would have known the people would not tolerate his abandoning them yet again for three years in Parthia, and ruling from a distance. They had had enough of the faraway . . . king."

I had to think for a moment. What he said had weight to it. But what was the remedy? "I am afraid to let Caesarion go," I finally said. Was I afraid he would never come back, be swept into the vortex of Rome?

"He needs to see it for himself," said Antony. "Only that way will its power over his imagination be loosened."

———

As I lay sleepless that night, staring up at the lights playing across the ceiling from the flickering oil lamp—its stores almost burnt out—I kept thinking about Rome. Antony still had many partisans there, many senators who supported him, many of the old Republicans and aristocracy. His inheritance—a grandfather who was Consul and a famous orator, a father who was the first Roman to be given an unlimited military command, a mother from the revered Julian clan—still shone bright in the Roman panoply. But for how long? Things unseen diminish in memory's strength, and Octavian was there, ever before them, to help obliterate Antony's image. The longer it went on, the more complete the process would be.

Yet he could not go there, not now—not after the Parthian humiliation, and his sending Octavia away. Everything I had said against it to Antony was true. But it was also true that his power was eroding in the west, and that was dangerous.

Lepidus gone . . . Sextus beaten . . . Octavia dismissed . . . all the bridges and brakes between Antony and Octavian were down. They were already at war. When would Antony realize it?

Because I am above all a realist, and I face what *is*, not what should be, might be, could be, I knew I must let Caesarion go with Olympos. When beaten, one should give in gracefully, and make the most of whatever opportunities remain to be salvaged in the situation. Caesarion would go to Rome; very well, I must prepare him.

"It is not on the sea," I said.

"I know *that*," he said proudly. "I have studied maps of it."

"What that means is that there are no sea breezes there, and in summer it will be very hot—much hotter than Alexandria. Besides that, the buildings are low and made of brick, the streets narrow and winding—it feels very dark and cramped."

"But there are gardens—"

"Yes, in the old villa that Caesar had across the Tiber, where you lived as a baby. They are public now, and give the Romans a chance to gasp some fresh air."

The orderly, tranquil gardens—were they now filled with foul-breathed, sweating crowds?

"I will visit them, and visit all the places where you walked," he said solemnly. This was a true pilgrimage for him.

"You can see me in Rome," I told him. "Go to the Temple of Venus Genetrix—the family temple of the Julians—it's in the new Forum. There's a statue of me inside—your father put it there and caused a great scandal at the time."

And he made love to me in the empty temple, in the shadows of the statues, I almost added. But he was too young for that. I almost blushed to remember it myself. How young *I* had been at the time, how shocked, how hesitant! But Caesar had always done what he pleased, where he pleased.

Had his son inherited that? I didn't think so.

"Be careful," I said. "Keep your eyes wide open, and see everything. And then return."

Return home, I wanted to say. But eventually Rome might turn out to be his home. Where did he belong, this son of Caesar's and mine?

"Here," I said, handing him the pendant I had kept for him. "It is time you took this. It is yours—from Caesar himself."

63

To the most glorious Queen, Cleopatra—from a student in Rome, reporting on Egyptian medicines:

Hail, Queen of all beauty, dark-haired as moonless midnight, slender as the Nile before flood time, graceful as the serpent that guards your ancestral crown:

I kiss your feet in their jeweled sandals. I console myself that everyone throughout the known world wishes they could do so. I pledge my soul to your health, and will climb crumbling desert cliffs to procure herbs to soften your skin; will dive into the cold depths of water off Rhodes to bring up the daintiest sponges to dab your eyes; will milk a panther to whiten your hands. I will—

Now that I am past the first turn of the scroll, I can stop this nonsense. I will have lost any spying reader back in that welter of groveling. But you probably enjoyed it. Come now, admit it. Did you suspect it was from me? Or did you think it was Antony? He probably talks like that to you—if only in private.

At least that is what they are saying here in Rome. Oh, I have heard a great deal, without even trying. Sometimes it is all I can do to keep my mouth shut, not to shout, "No, Antony does not wear bedclothes to audiences! No, he does not use a golden chamber pot"—I swear, that tale is being told of him, with the proviso "a thing of which even Cleopatra would be ashamed." He is being painted as debauched, corrupted, un-Roman, and all under the unmanly influence of the Queen of Egypt. We don't need to ask who has put these rumors into circulation, but they are thriving. They make such a colorful story! And people would always rather have color than earth-toned truth.

Octavian, in contrast, paints himself wan and white—a virtuous ghost of old Roman piety. The ghost part comes from Caesar, whom he invokes regularly as "son of the divine Julius." He is in the process of making Rome white. Now that the civil wars are over—so he stresses—it is time that Rome was clad in marble. The rivalry with Alexandria could not be more obvious. He wants a Rome as white as our glorious city, so he has hinted to his loyal followers, and they are obediently paying for public works out of their own purses. New temples are rising everywhere, basilicas, monuments, libraries, amphitheaters, and there is even talk that Octavian is contemplating a huge mausoleum for himself, to rise on the banks of the Tiber.

Even the stink has subsided, as Agrippa had the Cloaca Maxima cleaned out, and has built a new aqueduct to bring in more water. And (doubtless at his master's bidding) he has dangled free services before the people—shaves, admission to the baths, theater, food and clothing tokens, open admission to the Circus. He wants them to see him—Octavian—as the great Roman benefactor.

Why, even as I write this, I am using one of the free oil lamps distributed throughout the city—by them. I must bring it back to you. It commemorates the battle of Naulochus with a row of silver dolphins, reminding everyone of the naval victory against Sextus. Who am I to pass up a free lamp? So I use it. So do hundreds of others. They are very clever, this Octavian and his Agrippa.

It occurs to me that perhaps if Agrippa's own ambition could be fired a bit, so he extricated himself from his master . . . perhaps his loyalty would wane as his pride rose. But alas, he seems wholly devoted to the Son of the Divine Julius.

I just reread this—and am horrified. I sound like a newly hatched politician. The atmosphere in Rome must have invaded my brain. The very air is politics.

As for my studies, they are already proving most profitable. Should we fight another war, I will be able to perform miracles, even sewing back severed heads. (I cannot do that yet. But next month . . .)

Your son is happy, and blends in here all too well. He has proved invisible, as he predicted. In three days it is the Divine Julius's birthday, and Rome is readying itself for public observance. It is fortunate Caesarion is here at this time to see it for himself.

I should close. There is a ship leaving this evening. I stop here to allow your son to add his own message, before the boat leaves.

All those fulsome phrases—part of me means them. I pray this finds you well, until my return. Your Olympos.

To my mother, most exalted Queen:

We arrived here after only twenty days—a miracle at this time of year! I know it bodes well for us; it means the gods themselves helped us to get here quickly. All along I knew it was right, but this confirms it.

How sad you were for me to go. I hope you have gotten over it by *now. You promised to ride Cyllarus for me, so he won't be lonely and miss me too much. I would have told Antony to, but I think he weighs too much, and my dear horse wouldn't like it.*

We are all settled in a part of Rome they say is disreputable—the Subura! That way no one will ever think to look for us, or suspect anything. The Subura is east of the Forum, and it's very crowded and noisy. They live in things called insula—islands—that are apartments stacked one on top of another, some of them five or six apartments high. There isn't much light down on the street, so you can't see the garbage you are stepping in. People eat all their meals on the street, buying from little shops. It's great fun—everything feels so naughty, like being on a holiday. Nothing is settled and normal.

Olympos spends a lot of time on the island in the middle of the Tiber, where there's a hospital for poor people and wounded veterans. That leaves me free to amuse myself. Just walking the streets here is an adventure. I will tell you more in a later letter. I can't rush describing things that are important to me. Tell Alexander and Selene that there are a lot of cats here—more than I've ever seen. They are lurking on every corner and in every window. But there are no crocodiles in the Tiber.

> *Your loving son, P. Caesar.*

P.S. The Ludi Apollinares are being celebrated—many days of chariot races and games, in honor of Apollo. Why don't we have anything like that?

I put the letter down, feeling curiously heavy. Outside, beyond my shaded balcony, the sea lay flat and motionless. The weather was uncharacteristically hot and oppressive—the way I had described Rome. Now it was as if my words had returned to mock me.

The perfume I had put on could not escape my skin; the air imprisoned it. I felt mummified, bound by cloth and aromatic smears of ointment.

I should be pleased to hear they had arrived safely. Olympos was doing useful work. Caesarion seemed fascinated with Rome. As I expected, he would find the good in it and compare it to Alexandria—that was what children did. It did not escape me that he signed himself "P. Caesar."

But I did not like the news. I did not like it that Agrippa and Octavian were doing public works; and even the building of the mausoleum seemed suspect. Octavian was only twenty-seven years old—why was he building a mausoleum? Was it supposed to be a national shrine? And what was all this talk about Antony and golden chamber pots—when the talk should be about his victory in Parthia?

I would have to show the letters to Antony, but I did not expect any helpful response from him. He was sunk in gloom because his lieutenant Titius had executed Sextus once he brought him to Miletus, without waiting for Antony's orders. Now that Sextus was dead, a chorus of voices bewailed

him: *the last son of the Republic . . . the son of Neptune . . . the pirate-king . . .*
noble Roman, the last of his kind. . . .

It disgusted me. Sextus was nothing but a renegade, a brilliant admiral who did not have the sense to follow up any victory, make alliances, or provide his followers any cause to rally for. But then his father, Pompey, had had the same problem. After Pharsalus Caesar had said that if Pompey had known how to follow up a victory, he—Caesar—would have been beaten then and there. "The war would have been won today if the enemy had a man who knew how to conquer," was how he put it. Now Pompey's line ended, condemned by that same trait in his son.

But Antony was reaping all the opprobrium about it. He was blamed for not being "merciful" like Octavian in sparing Lepidus; he was painted as a cruel executioner. Once again I knew who was putting out these stories.

The stories . . . they were powerful, and might do the work of armies, in time. In any case, Antony was taking it hard, and I did not want to bring up the subject of Rome just now. I put the letters aside, and waited for the next.

> *Dearest Mother:*
>
> *The past few days have been so exciting I hardly know where to begin in telling you about them! I have been all over Rome—up on all the seven hills, and to the Circus to see the free races, and even out into the countryside . . . it's so different from Egypt! But you have seen all those things, and don't need me to describe them. What I can tell you that no one else ever can is how it feels to discover that my father is real. I know you have done everything possible to make him so for me. You put the bust of him in my room, and told me things he had said— little things, that no one else would know—and made me learn Latin so I could read his reports. But he was still not real to me, he was more like a pretend game you and I played. Or like the imaginary playmates the twins tell me about.*
>
> *But now I come here and everyone is part of the game, everyone pretends to know him or believe in him. There are statues of him everywhere, and in all different poses, so I can see him sitting or standing or smiling or frowning. People talk about him as if he were here; his Forum is a popular place, with the fountain splashing, and the statue of him on horseback.*
>
> *I went inside the temple, and just as you said—there was your statue! I like to imagine Caesar showing it to you, and all the Romans being shocked by it. And the one of him on the other side—well, it's nice to see you together, if only in marble.*
>
> *I went up to the villa, the one Caesar gave to the people in his will, and walked along the paths, and tried to see if I remembered anything. But I felt as though I had never seen it before. The house is used by the groundskeepers now, and I was not allowed in.*
>
> *But the best thing was seeing his temple, the Temple of the Divine*

Julius, in the Forum. There's a finely carved statue of him, wearing his star of godhood like a diadem, and I just stood very quietly and communed with him. Yes, I felt as if he were talking to me, that he sensed I was there, and he was pleased with me and . . . loved me. How odd I feel, writing this down! The feeling was so overwhelming at the time, but now it seems silly, written down. I listened carefully to what people said when they came, bringing flowers or candles or offerings to place at his feet. They were talking to him, too.

"Caesar," one woman said, "have pity on my son, who is serving with the army in Illyria. Protect him. . . ."

And a boy about my own age asked, "Caesar, let me grow up to be a brave warrior like you. . . ."

And a man: "Here is an offering to give thanks for your birth sixty-five years ago tomorrow." Then he placed a wreath at the base of the statue.

And I said silently, "Please, Father, look with favor on your son, your namesake." And I felt his hand on my hair . . . I know it was real.

There will be special festivities at the shrine tomorrow, and all over the city the statues will be garlanded. Thank you for letting me come. Thank you for teaching me enough about him that I wanted to come.

         Your loving son, P. Caesar

P.S. And there is a whole month named after him, so every day for thirty days people have to say and write his name!!!

I smiled. So his dream had come true; he could immerse himself in the presence of Caesar. The assassins had failed after all; Caesar was still alive in Rome.

To the Queen, my mistress:

I mean that in the sovereign sense, of course. All is well. I write here to describe the events at the Temple of the Divine Julius, because I knew you would be curious about them.

On the twelfth day of the former month of Quintilis, now Julius, the great, the near-great, and the not-so-great gathered to honor the deified Caesar on his birthday. Since the miraculous comet was seen in the sky at this time nine years ago, it has grown into a major holiday. Well before dawn, a stream of devotees came to lay down their offerings, but it was not until midmorning that the formal observances got under way.

Poems were read. Vergil—your favorite poet, after his celebration of Antony and Octavia's wedding!—made the following offering. He stepped forward, unrolled a scroll, and recited: "Daphnis, in radiant beauty, marvels at Heaven's unfamiliar threshold, and beneath his feet beholds the clouds and the stars. 'A god is he, a god, Menalcas!' Be kind and gracious to thine own!" Then he unrolled another one and read, "Who dare say the sun is false? Nay, he oft warns us that dark uprisings threaten, that treachery and hidden wars are upswelling. Nay, he had pity for Rome when, after Caesar sank from sight, he veiled his shining face in dusky gloom, and a godless age feared everlasting night.''

He then looked around with those dark eyes to see what effect his words had, before launching into his true speech. When he saw how raptly everyone was listening, he suddenly read, "Never from a cloudless sky fell more lightnings; never so oft blazed fearful comets. Gods of my country, heroes of the land, thou Romulus, and thou Vesta, our mother, that guard Tuscan Tiber and the Palatine of Rome, at least stay not this young prince from aiding a world uptorn!''

And I swear, I thought he was talking about Caesarion, that he had magically known we were present and would turn his eyes to us. But no, it soon became plain whom he meant.

"Enough has our life's blood long atoned for Laomedon's perjury at Troy; enough have Heaven's courts long grudged thee, O Caesar, to us, murmuring that you pay heed to earthly triumphs. . . .''

It was Octavian he meant; it was Octavian who was the "young prince," and whenever the name Caesar is invoked, it is hard to know which one they want. The "young prince" has crept into the name, occupying it so thoroughly that the identities are now blended. I was a fool not to have seen it immediately.

No one calls him Octavian any longer; I was met with frowns when I did so, as if people had to think even to recall that was how he had started out. He is CAESAR now, sometimes "the young Caesar" to distinguish him from the real one. But even that distinction is fading.

He finished up with "Daphnis, why are you gazing at the old constellations rising? See! the star of Caesar, seed of Dione, has gone forth—the star to make the fields glad with corn, and the grape deepen its hue on the sunny hills." He then reverently touched the silver star on the statue's forehead.

Another poet, a little younger, stepped forward—that Horace—you know, the one who fought alongside Brutus. He, too, unrolled a scroll, and started reading. "Merciful gift of a relenting god," he addressed the statue. "Home of the homeless, preordained for you. Last vestige of the age of gold; last refuge of the good and bold; From stars malign, from plague and tempests free, far 'mid the western waves a secret sanctuary.'' Blast me if I know what it meant, but everyone murmured approvingly.

After that there were processions with the priests of the order, hymns, and of course the inevitable gifts of oil and meat in the name of the god Caesar. I watched Caesarion fingering the pendant that he has worn since leaving Alexandria. I was afraid he was going to obey some impulse and present it to the statue, but thanks be to Isis—or perhaps Caesar himself—he didn't. (I would have had to sneak back and retrieve it. I know from experience that such dramatic gestures of sacrifice are bitterly *repented afterward, when it is too late. Would that some kindly person had undone some of mine. But it was unnecessary.)*

I am tired. I will end this letter. God-watching is very draining. It is early to bed for me tonight.

Your devoted friend and servant, Olympos

I felt tired, reading it. All these ceremonies grown up around Caesar and his shrine—it made my head ache thinking of it. Or perhaps it was the continuing flat, heavy heat that made my head ache. The god of the winds had shut them all up in a bag as surely as he had for Odysseus. Nothing stirred, no ships could sail. Only the straining muscles of oarsmen could move vessels, and although their skins shone with sweat, it did not cool them.

In the blazing heat of midday, livestock died—cattle dropped over, swine collapsed, and inside the royal stables I had rows of servants on duty to fan continually. Cyllarus had to survive to welcome Caesarion home, as well as the fine horses that were the pride of the palace.

Antony was drooping as he went about his business listlessly. He was trying to ascertain exactly what had happened to Sextus, and how his orders had become so confused. He had sent word for Titius to report to us at Alexandria, and meanwhile was planning his delayed punitive invasion of Armenia. "But it will have to wait until next year," he admitted. "It is too late now." He acted as if he did not care.

Just then Iras appeared in the doorway, bringing an Indian boy who served in one of the chambers. Several years ago the ship he had come with—along with silks, ivory, and sandalwood—had left without him, stranding him. He had since been employed at tending the silks and embroideries in the royal wardrobe, knowing, as he did, how to clean them and rid them of wrinkles.

"Vimala has a suggestion for cooling our chambers," said Iras, urging him forward. "He says it works well in his city."

"Yes, madam," he said, bowing up and down so fast he looked like a bobbing chicken. "And most gracious sir." He turned to Antony and repeated the performance.

"Well, what is it?" It looked as if this bowing would go on all morning, and he himself drop over from exertion.

"This open doorway," he said, crossing over to the entrance onto the rooftop terrace—now radiating heat like a kiln as the sun beat down on it. "Does air blow in here?"

"Yes, normally, off the sea."

"Ah. Then we can try this. In India we hang weighted, beaded strings across doorways and pour water onto the 'mother' strip. It drips down all the 'daughter' strips and as the wind blows across it, the air is cooled."

It sounded too simple to be effective.

"It can make this chamber cool, my lady, even when it is blistering hot outside. In India, it is hotter than this every day in summer."

"Very well—I am willing to try!" I told him. Anything to free my body and mind from this oppression. My arms felt as though gossamer linens, soaked in hot water, had been placed on them. And as for touching Antony—the thought of more warm skin on mine was unbearable.

As the boy departed, I said to Iras, "Perhaps deliverance is at hand. I thank you."

I handed the letter to Antony. He read it silently, then finally said, "So Octavian is no longer Octavian—he has escaped from his pedestrian past."

"Is that all you have to say?" Surely he understood the implications!

"What do you want me to say? It's his business what he calls himself. He's legally entitled to the 'Caesar'—it's Caesar himself who adopted him."

"I've always thought it suspicious that the adoption was a secret from Octavian. If Caesar wanted to adopt him, why not tell him?"

"What difference does it make now?"

"I'm just trying to understand it!"

"No, you are trying to prove it was a forgery. Well, it wasn't. It was in that will. I saw it."

"I wonder if there wasn't another will—a later one—one that named Caesarion—"

"If there was, it's gone. Please stop this. Caesarion will have to wrest any inheritance he gets away from Octavian. There cannot be two Caesars."

"Yes, I know." I knew it deeply. "At least this journey to Rome has shown him what he has been deprived of. You were right to say he must go."

Antony frowned. "That is not why I said he must go. I thought he must go for personal reasons, not political ones."

"I think when you are a Ptolemy and a Caesar, they cannot exist separately."

To the most gracious and wise Queen of Egypt, dispenser of justice:

Hail. I salute you, and I salute me, for I have been working very hard, actually creating false noses on men who have lost theirs in battle—of course they are not perfect, but better than a gaping hole—and I have been listening very hard to all the news. Of an evening I stroll up the Palatine hill, at twilight when the breezes rise and rustle in the odd, flat pines they have here, and I pass Antony's house nearby, where I look long and observe. First, it is in good condition, nicely trimmed and clean—I know you will be relieved to hear—and the gardens are thriving. A bevy of servants is always about, lending an air of bustle to the place. Octavia presides over it like a proper Roman matron, and once I glimpsed her strolling between some cypresses on the sloped hill garden. The word—which I hear around the public fountains—is that her brother has ordered her to leave your house, Imperator, but that she doggedly stays, maintaining that that is her home as your wife. I could almost suspect that Octavian wishes her to stay, because she is ruining your reputation by being the martyr, faithful to a faithless man, and so on—selflessly dedicating herself to raising your children, even Antyllus and Iullus by her predecessor, and entertaining your senatorial friends at home. If he had wanted to blacken your character, Imperator, he scarcely could have found a better vessel.

They also say—again around the fountains, many of them installed by the generosity of Agrippa—that Octavian and his party are helping to improve the lives of ordinary Romans, whereas his feckless Triumviral partner squanders his money in the east, with the golden chamber pots. (That detail has certainly caught people's imaginations. Do you have one? I don't recall.) They also talk about jewel-encrusted writing tablets, thrones, and eunuchs. They gossip about the Queen as a man-hungry enchantress, whose only mission in life is snaring noble Romans. They make you sound like a spider, sitting in a web of jeweled allure, trapping any Roman general foolhardy enough to venture into the east. Nothing is said about a marriage, legal or otherwise. Nothing at all is said about Parthia or Armenia, either.

I am happy to report that Caesarion's Latin has become quite proficient; I hear him chattering away at the food vendors' and ironmongers' and sandalmakers'. He has also grown in the past few weeks, and needs new clothes—which he enjoys wearing. He is quite well disguised in his Roman garb. It amuses me to watch him.

I will describe the nose-restoration surgery when I see you. It is quite ingenious.

May you never need it!

Your devoted, and busy, Olympos

The words hit me heavier than the still-sultry air in the palace. Octavia again! Yes, Olympos was right—what a perfect weapon she was, in the right hands! The more virtuous she was, the worse Antony appeared for failing to appreciate this paragon of womanhood.

I threw the letter down in disgust. What could I do? Nothing!

I retired to the "cooled" room. Vimala's invention worked quite well; as faint breezes passed through the soaked strings, like a lyre dripping with water, a damp coolness pervaded the air. It had been a relief to be able to retreat here, and I had ordered similar devices installed in other chambers as well.

I poured some perfume out into a handkerchief and wiped my forehead. The scent—a compound of black hyacinth and violet—helped to clear my head. Should I even show Antony the letter? What good would it do, except to make him want to run back to Rome? No, there was no point. I put it away, where he would not see it.

To the Queen:

My hand is still trembling and I can barely write this. But I have to; only by writing it can I calm myself and put it in its proper place. Shall I tell it from the ending backward, or in order? Order, I think. To restore order, one must impose order.

Well, then. It was a fine summer evening, of the sort we enjoy every night. The crowds for the Ludi Apollinares and the birthday of Divus

Julius had departed, letting the city return to normal. There is always a feeling of relief after a festival is over, and the shopkeepers and ordinary people seemed in high spirits. There was the usual sauntering in the streets, the loitering at taverns, the strolling toward the riverbanks or public gardens. As Caesarion and I climbed the steps up to our third-floor apartment, I could not help feeling a pang of deprivation for all the amusements beckoning at street level. But I had promised to keep your precious son out of mischief! And so we dutifully trudged upstairs, where nothing awaited us but some middling-quality wine, overripe fruit, and boring books. Although it was still fairly light outside, the rooms were getting dark. I lighted three oil lamps—including the Sextus one, strange how one remembers such details—and prepared for a quiet evening. There were some medical writings I needed to check, and Caesarion would practice his Latin declensions. It promised all the excitement of keeping watch at a cemetery—even less, truth to tell, because there were no ghosts.

And as we sat there, in the dim light, I heard a knock and carelessly said, "Come in." One gets to know one's neighbors in these close quarters, and I was well acquainted with Gaius the butcher and Marcus the baker, and Zeus knows how many others. I almost turned to stone when I looked up and saw Octavian step in.

I knew it was he—who else could look so like all the statues? Or, I should say, a version of the statues. The statues look like the handsomest man in creation, and he is not—although he is handsome enough, that I grant you. And I must give the statues credit for preserving his individual features—his little ears that are set low down on his head, and his triangular face. That was how I recognized him.

I could barely speak—and you know that is unusual for me.

"Good evening, Olympos," he said, further robbing me of speech. Then he turned toward Caesarion, who was staring at him, and just nodded, without calling him anything. He looked around the room, disdainfully, as if to say, Is this your disguise? But he conveyed it all wordlessly, his eyes sending the message.

And those eyes . . . . clear, grayish blue, utterly emotionless. I have never seen another creature's eyes like that; even dead soldiers' do not have that flatness to them, a flatness with life yet behind it, watching.

"Good evening, Triumvir," I heard myself saying. "Fine night, isn't it? What brings you here? I thought you were busy in Illyria." Did that sound controlled enough? I hoped to match him and ruffle his calmness. Let him think I had expected him. "Did you have trouble finding us?"

"None." He gave an imitation of a smile.

"Well, they say your spy system is good. I suppose you need it—so many enemies."

Caesarion had risen to his feet. I am pleased to report he was almost the same height as the Son of the God. But then, he is also the Son of the God. All that celestial company!

Octavian turned to him, that false smile still spread across his face. "Welcome to Rome, Your Majesty," he said. "It has been a long time—some nine or ten years, I believe—since I have seen you. You should have notified me, so I could receive you officially."

"We did not wish to trouble you, Triumvir, since you were away fighting the enemies of Rome," said Caesarion. I was impressed by his quick response. "It would have been an imposition."

"Nonsense!" said Octavian. "You insult me by thinking so."

"No insult was intended, Triumvir," said Caesarion.

Both of them stared at one another, curiosity gripping them.

Finally, Octavian broke the silence. "But you do insult me by sneaking into my city, by using my family name, and by claiming to be the son of my father." He was staring intently at the pendant with the Caesarean emblem on it, which was too clearly visible around the boy's neck.

"The city of Rome is not your city, Caesar himself allowed me to use his name, and furthermore, he is not your father—he is your great-uncle," countered Caesarion.

"Great-uncle by birth, father by adoption," said Octavian. "At least I share his blood, which you do not. Everyone knows—it is common knowledge—that you are a bastard with an unknown father. If the Queen has told you otherwise, she has done you a great wrong."

"Now you insult my mother!" said Caesarion fiercely. "She would never lie."

"She lied to Caesar, pretending to carry his child, when all the world knew he was incapable of fathering children."

"I beg your pardon, Triumvir," I broke in, "but as a physician I must disagree with you. He had a daughter, Julia."

"Yes, born thirty years before this—boy."

"What does that prove? Perhaps his wives weren't fertile."

"All three of them?"

"Cornelia had Julia, and as for the other two—Pompeia was divorced for her suspected affairs, and Calpurnia spent barely any time with him. The case is hardly conclusive." I certainly knew more about this sort of thing than Octavian did! "And Caesar was not a fool; he could not have been deceived so easily. After all, he knew where he had been, and when. . . ." I hated to have to say these things in front of the boy!

Octavian snorted. His fine nostrils flared slightly. "I command you to stop using the name of Caesar!" he said coldly. "You have no legal right to it."

"Then why did you recognize me as co-ruler with my mother, under that name, eight years ago?" Caesarion was quick to seize on this legality.

Octavian was thrown off his stride for an instant. "It was not I who did it, but the Triumvirs Antony and Lepidus who insisted on it as a concession to the Queen of Egypt, to prevent her sending ships and aid to the assassins in Asia."

"Now you do truly insult my mother the Queen! As if she would ever send aid to Cassius and Brutus! No, you recognized me under that name because you knew it was true. It is only now that you seek to rescind it and usurp my legacy!"

Octavian seemed to grow calmer as Caesarion grew more heated. "So now you admit it—you intend to grasp your fancied Roman inheritance, and overturn Roman law! There are words for such as you—pretenders, bastards, and insurrectionists. By Roman law I am Caesar's son, and inherit his name and estate. Only by conquering Rome and destroying her Senate and judges can you unseat me."

I fancied he meant to say "depose," and only just stopped himself in time.

"It is you who twist the law and deprive me of what is rightfully mine," insisted Caesarion. I was proud of the way he refused to back off.

"Enough!" Octavian barely raised his voice. "Return to Egypt. Tell the Queen to give up her dreams of conquest of Rome, and to release the Triumvir Antony from his bondage. She is mad with the dreams of empire. But she shall not rule here! And you are not Caesar's son! Tell her all this, and warn her to stay away from my country. Never insult me by coming here like this again!" He looked around, his eyes narrowing. "What a pitiful masquerade!"

"Is this your country?" asked Caesarion. "I thought the Triumvir Antony could also claim it for his home."

"When he is ready to quit the east, with his concubines and eunuchs and drunken orgies, then let him return, a Roman once more."

"I am afraid you have fallen victim to your own stories, Triumvir," I said. "It is you who have concocted the concubines, eunuchs, and orgies. Come and visit us, and see for yourself what life he leads."

"Never!" He looked as if he had been invited to a serpent's den.

"Are you afraid the eastern Queen will bewitch you?" I could not help teasing him, although it was no laughing matter. His stories had gained deadly currency.

"She could not," he said. "It would be impossible. Now get you gone! I must return to Illyria, and I will not leave you behind here."

"So you have done us the honor to travel all the way from the frontier for this informal visit?" I asked. "Such a long journey, and for such a short time!"

"It was long enough to say what needed to be said, and for me to see what I needed to see," he said, turning to go.

"And our journey, which was even longer, has also answered these questions," said Caesarion.

"Vale," said Octavian. "Farewell. I do not look to see you again."

He seemed to vanish, so quickly did he step over the threshold of the apartment. I went to the door after him, but all I saw was the gloom of the hallway.

"O ye gods!" said Caesarion, and he was as pale as a ghost. "Was this a vision?"

"You acquitted yourself well, to deal with such an apparition," I said. "Caesar himself could not have done better. You have proved yourself his most worthy son."

And there it is, exactly as it happened, not an hour ago.

Your loyal, almost speechless, and shaken physician, Olympos

I received this letter not long after it was written; luck had speeded it to me. Alexandria still lay in its stupor of heat and debilitation, barely moving. But the letter jolted me like a blast of winter air hitting a naked man. At once I was pacing the room—where I had just been lying languidly on a couch, pronouncing myself too enervated to stir. Octavian! Octavian had swooped down on my son like a bird of prey! He must have been watching—or have spies in every house, on every corner. And even so, how would they have known who Caesarion and Olympos were? Rome had nearly a million people, most of them poor and crowded into places like the Subura. How could two individuals come to Octavian's attention like that?

And the way he appeared and disappeared . . . it was almost supernatural. How had his ship traveled so fast on the windless seas, how had he entered Rome secretly?

And for such a man, a stealthy killing would be easy. Was Caesarion's very life in danger? I reread the letter, with the ominous lines, "I must return to Illyria, and I will not leave you behind here." If Olympos and Caesarion did not comply immediately, would he dispatch his agents to dispatch *them*?

"Antony!" I hurried to his quarters, clutching the letter. I expected to find him at his workdesk, hunched over papers. Instead the table, cluttered with scrolls, ledgers, and reports, stood unattended. I found him in one of the smaller connected chambers, dozing on a couch. One foot dangled off the end, and the other was propped up on a pillow. A bored attendant was fanning him, and his light breathing kept time with the puffs of heated air.

"Wake up!" I shook his shoulders. I could not bear to wait to tell him this horrible development. "Go away!" I ordered the attendant, who gladly put down the long-handled fan and left.

"Uh . . ." Antony slowly opened his eyes and tried to orient himself. He had been in that particularly deep sleep that sometimes falls upon us in the daytime.

Hurry up, hurry up, I thought, *I need you!*

I needed him to read the letter, to convince me, in his unexcited way, that it was somehow not as it seemed, or not as bad, or—I often grew exasperated by his underreaction to what I considered vital, or obvious, but now I welcomed that very trait.

"What is it?" he finally mumbled. His words were thick, his eyes still unfocused. He rubbed them.

"I—a letter has come. A dreadful letter!" I pushed it into his hands, before he had struggled to sit up. He just looked at it, bewildered.

"Well, read it!" I cried.

He lurched up from his supine position, and swung his feet down onto the floor. Groggily he held the letter and read it. I watched his face carefully. It showed nothing.

His eyes went back to the beginning and he reread it, awake now. Now there was an expression on his face—a heavy resignation, something between distaste and bracing himself.

"I am sorry," was all he said, laying it down on the couch. And in the tone of those three words he managed to convey both sorrow and deep understanding of what we faced.

I found myself in his arms, my face buried against his shoulder, thankful for the solid feel of him, wondering why that could comfort when words could not. I also found myself weeping, like a child, while he held me. Sobs tore my chest, and I clung to him, marveling at what, perhaps, at base, marriage really is: someone to cling to when all else fails, someone whose very touch can bring surcease of pain. At moments when we revert to childhood, crying and fighting nightmares, that person stands by as an adult to dry our tears.

I had soaked the shoulder of his tunic, and only when my sobs died away did I pluck at it apologetically. "I've ruined it," I said, feeling foolish. The gold threads were all twisted and broken where I had squeezed them, and the salt in my tears had made the dye run into the white.

"Never mind," he said. "It served a good purpose." He pulled my hair back from my neck and throat, where it stuck to the skin, matted and wet from the crying. "There." He smoothed it down. It was like something I did for the children. Next he would ask me if I wanted a sweet.

"Here," he said, reaching out for a plate of figs, and I laughed.

"No, thank you," I said. He pulled his arm back and put it around my shoulder.

"I don't think I've ever seen you cry," he said, more to himself than to me.

"I try never to," I said. "At least not in front of anyone. It is considered unqueenly."

"Then you must, at last, trust me," he said.

Yes, I supposed it must mean that. Somewhere, sometime, I had let down my guard to Antony as I never had to another person. Now there was no raising it again.

"Yes, I have learned to trust you," I admitted.

"You are like a wild animal that has taken a long time to eat from my hand," he said. "And still you are always poised for flight in case I make a wrong move."

"Not any longer," I said, wiping my face with my fingertips. And it was

650

true—flight was out of the question. We were together, and it was not conditional.

"That gladdens my heart," he said, tightening his arm around me. "Now, my dearest, about the letter—it is alarming. But in some ways it is liberating."

"How so?"

"Because Octavian has finally been forced to make a move," said Antony. "He has revealed himself—revealed his naked ambition to *be* Caesar, and his determination to brook no rivals. And revealed whom he considers his rival. Not me. Not you. But Caesarion."

I supposed that was a victory of sorts. Like a creature that hid under the shadow of a rock, Octavian liked to keep his goals obscure. He shunned the sunlight that would illuminate his movements. But this time he had been flushed out into the open.

But it was scant comfort, when I feared for Caesarion's safety.

Disguises . . . Caesarion's had forced Octavian to abandon his.

HERE ENDS THE SIXTH SCROLL.

THE SEVENTH SCROLL

64

I could scarcely believe that I was once more in Antioch, and in winter, too. I had done everything backward: remained in baking Alexandria for the summer, and then transferred to Antioch for the dreary, rain-swept winter. Once again Antony was spending a winter preparing for an eastern campaign; once more he was gathering his generals around him, readying his troops. This time it was not Parthia he was aiming at, but Armenia.

The drafty, overdecorated rooms were still the same, their cavernous corridors and gaping stairs like empty eye sockets. I should not have returned; it would have been better to remember the palace when it reverberated with the first joy of my marriage. Then the rooms were more than rooms, the windows enchanted vistas. Now it had shrunk back into the ordinary, and I felt the loss keenly. The magic had flown, taken wing to its own secret places.

Antony was too busy to notice. Once he had made up his mind to launch his long-delayed retributive campaign, his days were a succession of embassies and conferences. First he had called Marcus Titius to report to us, to explain the Sextus debacle.

I say "us" because I insisted on being present. If Egyptian money was being spent, if Egyptian resources were being used, Egypt should be privy to all. Besides, Antony and I were now openly co-rulers of an eastern empire. . . . But more about that later.

Titius was commander of the forces in Syria, and had only to journey a little way to report to us. I had always liked him, perhaps because his lean, dark looks appealed to me, and he was younger than the other generals. And he took great care to flatter me. At the same time I sensed that he harbored some faint disdain for Antony. Do not ask me how I knew; I can sense these things acutely. When I said this to Antony, he just snorted and said, "You'll have to have something more definite than that for me to go on."

Titius had been among those who had taken refuge with Sextus when the proscriptions were raging; later he had joined his uncle Plancus under Antony's banner. The two of them made an odd pair: Titius swarthy, long-faced, sardonic; Plancus blond, ruddy, and laughing.

Titus reported to us in the enormous audience chamber. I had wanted us to be seated on thrones, but Antony would not hear of it.

"Here I am the general, not Autocrator," he said. *Autocrator* was a Greek word he used to describe his status as lord and ruler of the east, although not a king.

"Well, what am I?" I asked. "I am still a queen."

"You are the admiral," he said. "Which is fitting, since my navy is mostly made up of your ships. So seat yourself as an admiral, in a comfortable chair, but not a throne."

Titius strode in, looking edgy and defensive. After the usual formal greetings, and his brief summary of what had happened, Titius awaited Antony's response.

"Who gave you the orders to execute him? That's what I want to know," said Antony.

"I was given to understand they were *your* orders," he said. "Sextus was trying to flee, and was apprehended as he ran toward the Parthians. He meant to put himself under their protection. He was a traitor, sir."

"A traitor to whom? He had never sworn allegiance to me."

"A traitor to Rome. A traitor to his ancestors—a blot on their name, a shame to them!"

"So you felt called upon to punish him?"

"You killed Cicero, to punish *him*! And how many others during the proscriptions—of which I was almost a victim?"

"That is the shame of it," said Antony. "Sextus gave you protection and spared your life when you sheltered under his wing. Then, in your turn, you killed him."

Titius bristled. "With all respect, Imperator, Sextus did not flee to me— he was fleeing *from* me. I am a soldier, in the service of Rome. Are you suggesting that I should be traitor to my vow of allegiance to Rome, should spare her enemies, because of a personal softness? A strange sort of honor! Something more fitted for a woman, I think."

I resented that. "If you think that women spare their enemies, General Titius, then you do not know your history. We can be as hard as men—and we have longer memories," I said.

"Be that as it may, Queen Cleopatra, I do not think *you* would have spared Sextus, either." He nodded toward me, smiling. "No one with any sense of self-preservation would. I had the reprobate in my hands, and I squeezed him—thus." He made a choking motion with his hands. "I stopped his breath, so that Rome and Alexandria could draw theirs easier."

"Enough," said Antony. "I will expect you to obey orders in the future, and when you have no orders, to wait for them."

"Can you honestly say they would have been different from what I did?" Titius was bold.

"After the fact, one can never know." Antony sighed, and shifted in his chair. "Now, during the campaign to Armenia, I shall rely on you to secure my back. Syria must be held tightly. I have received overtures from the Medians—they have changed sides for the thousandth time, and want to help us against, as they suppose, the Parthians. They shall not find Syria unguarded. I entrust its security to you, and your three legions."

"You will find me worthy of the trust, sir," he said.

After he left, I said, "I hope you have not made an enemy."

"Nonsense. He expected a dressing-down. He's lucky I allowed him to retain his command."

"I don't think you had much choice," I reminded him.

"Certainly I could have replaced him," he said. "He is not the only young Roman general to hand."

"Isn't he? Since Octavian has cut you off from Rome, and recruiting there, where will replacements come from?"

"Is the east devoid of talent?"

"Choosing a non-Roman would just fuel fears about the Asiatic hordes massing to overrun Rome," I said. "You know that. It's the one thing Rome dreads. They know the prophecies."

"Yes, and that they are to be led by a woman . . . my admiral." He leaned over and touched my hand, lightly.

The Median ambassador assured us that his master was so eager to have us as allies he was willing to betroth his only daughter Iotape to our son Alexander, and to make Alexander heir to his throne.

"My most gracious King reaches out to embrace you," was how he put it. "And to surrender his precious jewel, his only child and daughter, into your keeping."

I felt my heart grow heavy. Not my Alexander—not betrothed at only five years old! I remembered my own childhood, free from the shadow of forced marriage, because of the upheavals at court. Once I was a queen and not a princess, I had been free to select my own men. My children would not be so lucky.

Of course I had not been entirely free; there were the dictated formal marriages to my two brothers. But I had ignored them, and taken the men I pleased.

My children were all safe in Alexandria. Caesarion had returned from Rome, escaping whatever vague malevolence Octavian had planned for him. And I would not surrender them to the world so soon. But sometimes there is no choice for princes.

The Median king had even released King Polemo of Pontus, that poor man who had been captured along with the siege train, and he made his way to us in Antioch, carrying the captured Roman eagles from the two slain legions.

All that remained to redeem Roman honor was to take revenge on Arta-vasdes himself.

"All hail for the birthdays of their most exalted persons, Imperator Marcus Antonius and Queen Cleopatra!" bellowed the chief steward. Antony and I stood at the entrance to the vast hall, decorated with boughs of evergreen and imitation flowers made of dried, colored reeds. So many candles and torches were blazing, it looked like a temple, and filling the chamber were our generals and their officers, military tribunes, and Syrian nobles and merchants. We posed, holding hands, smiling, never betraying our quarrel about what titles we should use.

In truth, it was a delicate matter. Antony was both more and less than a king; as Autocrator—absolute personal ruler—he made and unmade kings. But the title of king was repugnant to Romans. And the title Triumvir—the Triumvirate was due to expire in two years, so it was best not to stress that. In Rome, Octavian's person had lately been declared sacrosanct, and he was using "Triumvir" less and less. "Imperator," meaning "commander-general," was a good, neutral title, and Antony insisted on it for now.

Our birthdays fell close enough together to be celebrated at the same time, early in the new year. Antony was now forty-eight, and I thirty-five. With a heaviness in my heart, I realized my once-youthful, exuberant lord was approaching the age Caesar had been when I first met him. Where had the years flown? A trite though, but they seemed to have winged past, as I recalled flickering images of Antony—the cavalryman in his late twenties, the oiled and leaping priest of Lupercal in the masterful prime years of his thirties. And now, to be almost fifty . . .

Slow yourself, god of time, I begged. *Halt your wagon, let us rest and look about, give us a moment free of changes.* . . . But I knew the cruel god would never grant the request. He was more merciless to those in his grip than Titius.

I turned to look at Antony's proud profile, still beautiful to me, still commanding, still saying to fate, I'll meet you in single combat. . . .

Lifting my arm high, I was ready to descend.

Strange how I did not grieve for my own lost years; I was incapable of seeing them through other eyes. We always think *we* have halted time in his flight, that there still remain many paths for us, unexplored, and of course we shall explore them; yes, we will. . . .

A loud shout of salute greeted us. The Incomparables were long gone, and it had been years since we had celebrated in such a raucous fashion, but it fitted our mood that winter night.

Canidius Crassus, his face more weather-worn than ever, bent stiffly from his waist, then straightened up and slapped Antony's forearm. "To the field once more, Imperator!" he said.

"Jupiter himself grant us victory!" Plancus raised his arm in salute.

King Polemo of Pontus—a soft-voiced and mannered man—presented us with a box of emeralds, and expressed his birthday wishes. "Aristotle says in his *Rhetoric* that the body is at its best between the ages of thirty and thirty-five, and the mind at its best about the age of forty-nine," he said. "That means you both are in the enviable position of being at the best ages!"

"I think it means together we make a perfect whole," said Antony. "My mind in concert with her body."

Dellius sidled up to us, raising his eyebrows as if picturing something lascivious. I had never cared for his manner. "You are not the oldest general to take to the field," he assured Antony, as if it were a matter of concern.

"I have not thought of it," said Antony. "The retreat from Parthia under those inhuman conditions proved me young enough."

"True, true." Dellius was appraising him as if unconvinced.

"And in any case, I am sending you to Armenia before the winter ends, so you—being younger—can test yourself in the snows." Dellius looked alarmed. "I wish you to approach Artavasdes with an offer of . . . alliance. A marriage treaty between our children. He will refuse it, of course, and then we will have an excuse to attack. I have heard, from reliable sources, that he is trafficking with Octavian. Neither of them wishes me well. They are two of a kind."

I was shocked at his harsh public appraisal of Octavian—lumping him together with his betrayer Artavasdes!

"Yes, sir," said Dellius, looking about for an escape before Antony could assign him another unpalatable task. He scuttled—for his movement was sideways, like a beach crab—into the mass of guests.

The torches burned bright; the walls resounded with glad high spirits. Plancus led the officers in a round praising Antony, calling him "Conquering Hercules" and "Beneficent Dionysus." Their shouts seemed like a platform raising him high, lifting him up to the rafters. He had won their admiring loyalty in the courage and toughness of the retreat from Parthia, which he had borne and led so manfully.

Even the piercing-eyed—and piercing-tongued—Ahenobarbus was gentle that night, and presented Antony with a gift of a new sword of Chalybean tempered iron. "A new sword for a new conquest," he said, the light of coming battle in his eyes. "Yet you must keep your old fighting style—coolness in the heat of battle, a splendid daring."

"Now you can give your old faithful one to Alexander, for his heritage," I said.

Antony took the new sword, and ran his thumb appreciatively along its finely honed blade.

"I thank you," he said to Ahenobarbus, "my friend."

Five braziers, fired so hot they almost glowed, kept the cold at bay in our sleeping chamber. The festivities over, we had piled our booty—the tribute from our captive guests—on a table and gratefully exchanged our stiff, constricting clothes for Syrian chamber-robes. We sat on thronelike chairs decorated with mother-of-pearl patterns, and sighed with relief.

"That was tiring," Antony admitted. He yawned.

"It was nothing compared with the old days in Alexandria," I reminded him. "Our evenings with the Incomparables . . . remember?"

"I was younger then," he said, without thinking. Then he realized how it sounded. "Perhaps I've just grown bored with it," he suggested. "Same old people, same old songs."

"Not the same old wine, though," I said. In this area, we drank Laodicean, not Falernian. I poured out a cup from the pitcher left for our pleasure, and handed it to him.

"Wine never lets you down," he said, sipping it.

I disagreed, but did not say anything. Wine was a betrayer, and lately I felt it was betraying Antony. He was drinking too much of it, imagining it did not affect him, but it did. He sat silent for a few minutes, savoring the distinctive taste of this particular wine. Finally he said, "Tonight was the unveiling of our new empire."

"What do you mean?" His statement, coming out of nowhere, was puzzling.

"It is useless to pretend any longer—or rather, for *me* to pretend any longer. Step by step I have been led into a strange role: ruler of a vast eastern empire, with an empress by my side. By Hercules, I did not mean it to happen!" His voice was touched with anguish, and he set the cup down. He ran both his hands through his hair, as if somehow that would straighten out his thoughts. "Tonight we played the roles well, standing side by side in all our eastern finery, accepting obeisance from our subjects—oh, what have you done to me?" He jumped up from the chair and started pulling at the gown, tearing it off. "Away! Get off!"

Was he drunk? I looked at the cup, but it was only half-empty.

"Off! Off!" He flung the gown away in disgust. "I have been transformed!" He looked down at himself, holding out his thick arms and staring at his hands. "All these rings!" He pulled them off and started throwing them on top of the crumpled gown. Then he kicked off his silk-embroidered sandals. They cartwheeled through the air, and one landed in the brazier and caught on fire.

Antony burst into laughter at the sight of the smoking shoe. But he calmed down. "It is you who have done this," he finally said. "Transformed me from a Roman magistrate into an eastern potentate."

"So Octavian has conquered even you," I said, "with his lies and distortions."

"Behind his statements lies enough truth to be considered." He began to shiver in the cold room, and grabbed a blanket from the bed rather than put on the offensive decorated gown.

So now we must have this talk—and I had not prepared myself for it. I gave a quick prayer to Isis to help me keep my thoughts clear. "You look like a fool, huddled there in that blanket," I said. "Almost as much of a fool as you sound."

658

He just looked at me, a picture of distress. "The truth pains me," he finally said. "I do not think I can bear it." He looked so miserable, my heart went out to him. I had never been torn between two worlds as he now was. Life had spared me that particular torture.

I went over to him, where he had sunk down into the chair again. I stood behind him, putting my head near his and encircling his shoulders with my arms, like the statues of Horus protecting a Pharaoh. Now I was the strong one. Let me help him, dear Isis!

"If you have been drawn into it step by step, it is because that was your fate," I finally said. "And no one can repulse his fate. To refuse it is hopeless, and just makes its burden heavier. And each man's fate is tailored to him, like a shirt. There is no second Alexander, no second Moses, no second Antony. You are the first and only to walk this earth. So you have to be the finest version of Antony possible."

I felt his head move from side to side, slowly.

"It does no good to say you would rather be someone else, or covet his lot in life. You have been assigned your own portion. Because you are the foremost living general, it was natural that the rich eastern part of the Roman holdings would fall to you. That being so, it was natural that you would become a part of it. You have a rare sympathy with your subjects—"

"Subjects! I have no subjects! I am not a king!" he cried out.

"Very well, then, your . . . client kingdoms, your provinces." I sighed. What difference did the name make? "You understand them, that is why you belong here. And it is true, the western half of Rome is yoked strangely with the eastern. They do not pull well together. Eventually they will break apart—that is, if they are both ruled by a western-thinking Roman. Only someone like you—a Roman bred and born, who can understand the east as well—can hold them together."

He was sitting as immobile as any Pharaoh's statue. Was he even hearing my words—my raw, unrehearsed words? Were they helping at all?

"It is you who are called to preserve Rome," I said. "And it is not only because you have become partly eastern. As if anything could erase your glorious family history, your long years of service to Rome! No, that will endure. All you have done is to add another dimension, a new understanding on top of the old. It is what will make you the ruler Rome has earned, and deserves."

"I am not a ruler!"

"I meant leader," I assured him. "And when we lead, what a new dawn! The world is much richer than the narrow vision of the Roman patriot, who eats his plain porridge, straps on his sturdy sandals, and scurries past the altars of foreign gods, looking neither to the left nor the right."

Antony laughed, faintly. This encouraged me to continue.

"You know the sort. Wearing his rough homespun, speaking only Latin, feeling threatened by Greek poetry, plum sauce, and the sound of sistrums. What would be the fate of all your . . . client kingdoms . . . to be ruled by such a man?"

"A rather austere one," he said.

"If your fate is here, then embrace it! Rejoice in it! Give thanks to the gods that they made you the master of these people you understand so well, and cherish so dearly! It does not make you any less a Roman to be a citizen of the world as well—no matter what Octavian says! It makes you greater!" Was he listening? "And I tell you this—you will be their salvation. If Octavian becomes their ruler—and he will not demur to call himself that, I assure you—they will suffer. Oh, how they will suffer!"

A long silence hung in the air. Finally he said, "You understand the east well, but I do not think you understand Rome. You reduce her to the same caricatures that you so resent Romans doing to easterners. The ignorant, barbaric Roman eating his porridge is just as false as the wily, effeminate easterner."

"You see! You have just proved my point! You have the wisdom and understanding to see both sides! It is you, and only you, destined to rule—lead—the entire Roman world."

"I do see the merits of both," he admitted.

"As did Caesar. He understood, as do you, that all citizens of Rome must be equal, and each side respect the other. Do not shirk your responsibility!"

"And how will they ever accept you, by my side, in Rome?" he asked sadly. "They are not as broad-minded as your idealized world citizens."

"They are being taught to hate me," I said. "But when they see me, in person, when they realize they have nothing to fear from me . . . Anyway, that is a long time coming. First you must remove Octavian!" I repeated the words slowly, directly in his ear. "You . . . must . . . remove . . . Octavian."

"Under what color?"

"First oust him from the seat of Caesar. Declare him a pretender, and prove it, and you have removed his basis of power."

"His basis, yes, but not the power itself. That resides in all his legions. And in his stranglehold on Italy."

"First the basis, then the power itself. Announce the rights of Caesarion, and challenge Octavian. Then be bold, and proclaim the eastern empire as an entity. Provoke him. The sooner the fight is held, the surer your chances of victory. Day by day he grows stronger."

"Perhaps fate will do my work for me," he said. "If you believe in fate, then fate will give Rome the ruler she deserves, with no help from us. Octavian is still fighting in Illyria. Perhaps he'll die there. I hear he has injured his knee—"

"Caesar always said if luck did not go our way, then we had to give luck a helping hand," I said.

"I am no second Caesar, as you pointed out."

"I know I am right! Please follow my plan!"

He sighed. "After Armenia—"

"Yes, of course, after Armenia. That gives you time to perfect your plans."

"Yes, my love." At last he turned around and buried his head against my shoulder. "We will make our empire together . . . my empress." He rose and took my hand. "Come to bed, and celebrate our multitudinous kingdoms. Let us make love in all their fashions. They are as varied as their clothes and cooking. . . . Shall we introduce them to Rome? Enrich their lives?" He laughed, my old Antony restored. "Or shall we imitate Octavian's way tonight? I am sure it is unimaginative, but thoroughly and officially Roman."

"No," I said. "Let Livia enjoy it."

"I understand," said Antony, "that Livia is not the only one to sample his practices, whatever they may be. He is busy in the beds of other men's wives."

Then he had not changed much. I would not have such a husband for all the gold in the Temple of Saturn!

"Dear husband," I said, "let us get busy in our own."

65

It was spring, and I was parted from Antony once more, as he pursued his campaign in Armenia. He had mobilized sixteen legions—sixteen, enough to crush Nebuchadnezzar!—and set out to punish his foe. This time there was no suspense, and I had no worries; my face was turned toward what we would do *after* Artavasdes was duly chastised.

I was restless. The fresh breezes blowing across the city made me feel like dancing, enveloping myself in the new light silks that had reached us from far to the east, beyond even India. They were so thin they floated about the body like a mist. Just such garments the Aurae, breeze nymphs, must have worn—I had seen sculptures of them, the streaming gowns curling about the outlines of their graceful limbs as they leapt and flew. Their bodies were as visible beneath as if the material had been wet. Now I felt like one of them, ready to fly high over the city, over the Delta, out over the desert.

Flying being out of the question, I decided to sail to Heliopolis, there to inspect my balsam plantings. It had now been two years since I had brought cuttings back from Jericho, and they had been watered and tended as lovingly as a royal baby. I was eager to see them. If they truly thrived here, the possibility of enormous riches hovered like a mirage.

Heliopolis, the ancient City of the Sun, stood near the place where all the branches of the Nile united to make that long stalk that reaches all the way to Nubia. It had been sacred since long before the pyramids were built; no one really knew how old it was. When my dynasty, the Ptolemies, came to Egypt, they asked Manetho, also a priest of Heliopolis—who presumably had access to old records—to write a history of Egypt. He did so, and provided the only list we have of all the Pharaohs. Knowledge of the past was fading even then; its roots were still vigorous in the ancient holy cities, but its branches elsewhere were nearly bare. Fewer and fewer people could read the sacred writings; fewer and fewer people cared; ancient Egypt was already receding into a mist of the fabulous, the make-believe. The last native Pharaoh had surrendered his throne to Persians over three hundred years ago.

But the past was too strong to evaporate; instead, it dyed the new conquerors in its colors. First the Persian rulers, then the Greeks, became Pharaohs once they were on Egyptian soil. I was a Pharaoh, the beloved daughter of Re, as all Pharaohs were. My father had been a Pharaoh, too. That was why we were crowned at Memphis in the old rites.

Did we feel like Pharaohs? That is hard to say. When I was in Alexandria, no. There was so little that was Egyptian there, or old. It was a brand-new city—a Greek head on an Egyptian body, as someone had once described it. But away from Alexandria—ah, that was different. I had found myself drawn to the "real" Egypt in a way my predecessors had not. I was the only one to learn to speak its language, and the only one to travel up and down the Nile so often, visiting so many towns. Perhaps that was why I had been willing to do so much to keep Egypt from being swallowed up.

On days like the one on which my barge approached the landing-stage of the canal to Heliopolis, gliding on the bosom of the Nile, past the tall papyrus stalks vibrantly green against the blazing blue sky, I felt I would be willing to do even more—that no price was too high to keep Egypt for Egyptians.

Awaiting me was Nakht, the high priest of Heliopolis, who presided over the Temple of the Sun. He was a portly man wrapped in a white linen robe, his shaven head gleaming. He had a bevy of priests under him, young assistants, acolytes, scribes, and musicians. Here, in this bastion of Re, he reigned supreme, guarding it as I guarded larger Egypt.

"We salute and welcome you, Queen Cleopatra, Netjeret-Merites, Goddess, Beloved of Her Father." He bowed low, and a file of others behind him did likewise.

I wished Caesarion had accompanied me, so he could see this—after seeing Rome. Here he was Ptolemy Iwapanetjer Entynehem Setepenptah Irmaatenre Sekhemankhamun: Heir of the God that Saves, Chosen of Ptah, Carrying out the Rule of Re, Living Image of Amun. Here he was the heir that would—that must!—preserve Egypt and carry the burden of her past. Even in a larger empire, Egypt would still be uniquely herself. That was the vision Antony and I could offer, rather than the Roman idea of transforming the rest of the world into another Rome.

"You have missed the morning stars washing the face of Re, and bringing him breakfast," said Nakht. "And you have missed the blessed Re descending in the form of a bird to touch the sacred Benben obelisk at dawn."

Was he scolding me? But no, he just sounded disappointed. "For that I am sorry," I said.

"Stay with us through the night, so you can witness these events," he said. "You, Goddess, the daughter of Re, should behold them."

I had not planned to stay. I thought of all the state business waiting in

Alexandria. Then I looked up the row of obelisks lining the gentle slope to the great pylon of the temple, and I felt a strong urge to linger here.

"Depending on the hour, perhaps it will be possible," I said.

The entire company of priests bowed and made a pathway for me to follow through them, while Nakht led me toward the enormous temple, its stone fiercely golden in the intense noonday sun—Re burning down directly overhead. The stone would have looked like solid sand somehow rearing itself high, had it not been for the bright flowers, winged discs of Re, and colored designs decorating it.

Tall, slender palms kept watch behind the obelisks, repeating their lines except in their crowns of bristly fronds.

In the old religion, this hill was believed to be the first piece of land to emerge from the formless waters of Creation, and it was thereby sacred. From here the origins of the world and the gods were studied; a vast school of astronomy had grown up on the grounds. Here the stories of the gods, of Nun, of Geb and Nut, of Osiris, of Isis, had been discovered, and written down in holy texts. But more than anything else, the nature of Re, the sun god, had been understood here. Re in all his forms—the young Khepri of the morning, the strong Re of midday, and the tottering, weak Atum of sunset. They had even divined what Re did after he vanished beneath the western horizon, and how he traveled in his Mesektet-boat, his night barque, accompanied by "those who never grow weary"—men who had been transformed into stars. There at night Re passed through great dangers in order to emerge once more at dawn, where he descended to touch the gold-clad obelisk at Heliopolis in the center of the temple.

Beside me, Nakht kept slow, measured footsteps. We passed the first pylon, coming into the forecourt. Beyond this point, which no ordinary person could pass, the secular world fell away. We were now in the realm of the gods—or rather, the abode prepared for them on earth by mortals. A vast forecourt, open in the center but ringed with pillars and dark, shaded colonnades, spread out on each side. Before us beckoned the deep recesses of the temple.

"Come." He made his way toward the second division between the secular and the sacred, the first roofed hall. We passed through the doorway and were surrounded by a forest of massive pillars, their tops carved to look like lotus buds, supporting a roof that cut off all sunlight, except for the small windows running near the seam where the walls met the roof. There Re sent probes of bright, glaring light.

The party of priests stood respectfully back as we, and we alone, proceeded beyond this point. Behind the next set of doors was the inner hall, much smaller. Here the light was even dimmer.

Gradually my eyes had become accustomed to the gloom, and I could see the pillars standing like sentries in the cool dimness. But the roof was lost in darkness.

Nakht had stopped. I stood still, too. Utter silence and stillness surrounded us. It was hard to believe that outside Re was still beating down above us, so completely was the normal world excluded.

I do not know how long I stood there, but after a passage of time Nakht began to move on, and I followed him. Deeper and deeper into the temple we penetrated, and since there were no torches or candles, I had to pause to accustom myself to what little light there was before proceeding farther.

Eventually we reached the sanctuary, that place of utter darkness, surrounded by polished black stone. Here the Majet-boat, "barque of millions of years," rested on its pedestal—the barque that Re rode, symbolically, during the day.

How odd it was, I thought, for the sun to be worshiped in a place of black nothingness. But the sacred seemed to demand the exclusion of everything of sensation—as if all sensations were too tainted with earthly feelings.

Around the sanctuary lay the sacred chambers—little rooms opening off the corridor. In them the various ceremonies were performed, essential to the life of the temple. Here, Re had his face washed by the stars—the priests acting on their behalf—and here his statue was clothed afresh each day with cloth woven on temple looms.

"And here, Goddess—" Nakht stepped aside to show me the altar dedicated to my father, me, and Caesarion, as gods who worked in concert with the other gods to preserve Egypt. Our statues stood unseeing on carved pedestals, and we wore the garb of ancient Egypt. Offerings were placed here each day.

I examined them critically. The likeness of Father was good enough. Mine did not look like me at all. And Caesarion—no, nothing like him.

"Exalted one," said Nakht, "you see here yourself as Isis. Since you are daughter of Re and Isis is also the daughter of Re, and she is your protective goddess, we thought this representation fitting."

Isis had a snake coiled around one of her arms. She seemed unalarmed by this.

"The sacred cobras are kept here as well," said Nakht. "As you know, they are the embodiment of the burning eye of Atum—the sun in his destructive element. Yet the sacred cobra, the goddess Wadjyt, protects Egypt. She encircles the crown of Lower Egypt, ready to strike. She kills ordinary men, but if she bites a son or daughter of the gods, it is a gift to them. It confers immortality."

"The bite of an asp can take us directly to the gods?"

"Yes, Goddess. For us it is so. For others—no. That is reserved for those already divine, or in the service of the divine."

"You have sacred cobras here?"

"Indeed. I will show them to you later in the day."

We next entered the most sacred place in the temple. All temples had dark sanctuaries with a barque of the god, but only Heliopolis had the obelisk, covered in shimmering beaten gold; this was the Benben stone, touched by Re at the beginning of time, and again each morning. It stood in a roofless room.

Overhead the sky was the color of brilliant blue faience. My eyes hurt at the intensity of it after the dark temple. The obelisk was dazzling, the gold glittering, reflecting Re in his heavens.

"Here is the center of the world," Nakht breathed, and it was easy to believe him.

As the heat of the day grew more intense, Nakht ushered me into a private chamber in his own quarters.

"We will wait for the shadows to grow," he said. "Then you may see your incense shrubs, and the rest of our holy site."

I took my rest on a beautiful carved bed, its head and feet that of a lion, with a long tail trailing from the back. I lowered my head onto the curved headrest and watched the bars of light from the slitted windows move across the walls.

It was good to lie here. Not that I would sleep, of course. Not that I would sleep. . . .

But the heavy, drugged air and the slow afternoon overwhelmed me. I was looking at the walls, thinking how far removed this was from my world at Alexandria, wondering if these rituals and these halls were really unchanged from centuries ago, until it all gradually merged into a dream.

The ancient gods—were they angry at the new gods now set up in Egypt? How did they feel about Serapis, the Ptolemaic god? Did they resent Dionysus crowding in on Osiris? And what about Aphrodite, and Mars, and Zeus? Here the novel, foreign gods seemed so loud, so unsubtle, so intrusive. Our goddess Hathor incorporated love, and joy, and music, whereas their Aphrodite was so one-sided.

I sighed. *Their* gods, *our* gods . . . who was I, really? Which gods were mine? I was not born of Egyptian blood, yet I was Queen of Egypt.

I stirred. I felt sticky from the heat and from sleeping at this unnatural time of day. I saw that the sunlight had slipped far down on the walls, and the edges were no longer sharp. It must be near sunset.

I stood up, arranged my clothes and hair. In the adjoining chamber, Nakht was waiting, as I knew he would be.

"The Goddess has rested?" he asked.

"Indeed," I assured him.

"Now, as Re has turned into Atum—poor weakling!—it is safe to venture outside. He will bathe the landscape in the softest tones, as he lovingly bids farewell."

He was right. Outside the colors had completely changed. Where at noon the sand had been bright gold-white, now it had a tawny tinge. The walls of the temple were rich with color, and the stones now gave back the heat they had received earlier. There was even a slight afternoon breeze, which was at its strongest here on the hilltop.

"The incense grove is here, beside our fields of flax, where we grow the linen for our robes," he said. We left the walled temple precinct, and walked to neat rows of tended bushes stretching toward the orchard.

I was delighted. The bushes were almost knee high, and their leaves looked green and healthy. "Why, they are thriving!" I said.

"They struggled that first year," he said. "We lost a few of them. 'Tis said they will grow nowhere but near Jericho. Perhaps they were mourning their removal, their exile. But then they took root and shot up, and now I think we can assume they will attain maturity. Just think—for the first time they will flourish outside their native land."

"Yes." And they would enrich us tremendously. The small area in Jericho where they grew was the richest spot on earth. Each hand-length of ground yielded a fortune. I sighed. Another means of security for Egypt. As if there could ever be enough! "I am pleased."

I looked around. The pleasant vista spreading itself out around me—the fields and orchards, the mellow radiating stone of the temple—persuaded me to stay. "I will indeed remain here tonight," I said, "if I may witness the arrival of Re tomorrow, and see him attended by the priests."

He smiled, looking as though I had passed a test. "And you will see more than that," he assured me.

After dinner I was taken to a small house nestled near the first pylon, still within the temple grounds. I had barely noticed it at my first entrance; now I wondered why. It was not unobtrusive.

The moment we crossed the threshold, Nakht's manner changed. He became deferential, as if he were entering the presence of one greater than himself. He had not acted so with me. Who was this, to invoke such reverence?

"Goddess," he said, "here is the wisest man in Egypt, he who presides over the sacred texts of the gods. He knows all their movements, knows how they began in ancient times, and where they are going."

At first I saw nothing. The room seemed to be empty. It was neat and clean, with little chests stacked one on top of another, and pots holding scrolls lined up on the floor. Then there was a shuffling. Something moved in the far corner.

I felt the hair on the back of my neck stirring. The sound was of dried stalks stirring, and a faint odor of dust and storage rose. A man, the color of old wrappings, lurched off a stool.

"Ipuwer, this is our Queen, Cleopatra, the Goddess Beloved of Her Father, come to us."

The man seemed to grow taller and taller. I saw then that it was his skin itself that looked like wrappings. He was so old it hung like draperies, and it was a dull brownish yellow.

"Ipuwer is directly descended from the first high priest of Heliopolis," said Nakht. "In my youth he was high priest, but he retired some thirty years ago to devote himself to the study of the origins of the gods. He was the keenest stargazer. Then his eyesight went."

"And I turned to the inner lives of the gods. No longer able to see them in the heavens, I find them within us, around us. I hear them whisper." His own voice was a whisper, rustling, out of practice after long disuse.

"Wise one, do they answer when you ask questions?" I asked. "Or must you wait for them to decide to speak?"

"Usually I wait," he conceded. "As you can see, I have spent many years at it." He spread his thin arms, and I could see that the flesh had withered and hung in folds.

"He knows the secrets of Re," said Nakht. "And he understands the burning eye, the sacred cobras. He keeps them."

"What, here?" I had not seen cages. Surely he did not mean *here*, in this room!

"Yes, they are here," he answered my spoken question. "But not in cages." As well as my unspoken. "Do not move, and they will come to you."

No wonder Nakht had been so guarded and respectful! Snakes! Loose in the room! I remembered Mardian's pet snakes, and I had always taken their part, claiming I liked them, but they had been in wicker cages. This was different.

I looked down at my feet. I saw nothing.

"Stand still, and wait, my daughter," Ipuwer said. "And you, Nakht, may depart. The Goddess must be alone with her own."

Don't leave! I wanted to say. But I could not. Nakht bowed and backed out of the room. I heard the fall of the curtain as he left.

"Yes, we must wait," Ipuwer repeated. "And while we wait, sit down beside me on this bench. Would you like to see the oldest scroll of all?"

He bent down and extracted a thick one from a jar of its own. Carefully he laid it on the little table, then delicately opened it a little way. I could hear it cracking.

"This tells the story of Re," he said. "When the first priests discovered the truth, they wrote it here."

Could it really be that old? I stared at the curling paper, wondering if it could have survived that long, even though it was brittle and faded. He was spreading it out tenderly when a smile of transport suddenly took hold of him.

"Ahh," he said. "She is here." He looked as if something wonderful had happened to him—the way another man would look if his wife had just had a wished-for son. Slowly he raised his arm and I saw, clinging to it, a big dark snake.

"Edjo," he said, his dry old voice a caress. "Protective goddess. You know who has come, do you not? Your own."

The snake seemingly paid him no heed, but twined around his arm like ivy around a tree.

"Is there no question you have to ask, my child?" he said to me gently. "I think I could answer it. The gods reveal much to me."

"I—I—" My throat was stuck fast. Yet I knew he spoke the truth. Did I dare ask? And would they part the curtain of the future and divulge what lay behind it? "I would ask the gods . . . I would know . . . if they will look with favor on Egypt, on the east?"

The man closed his eyes, while the snake crept up his arm and onto his shoulder. It then draped itself across his neck. Just then Ipuwer spoke; I almost closed my eyes, unable to look at the snake, which surely would strike him, annoyed at the movement of his throat.

"The gods grant that Egypt will endure, even to the end of time," he finally said.

"As it is now? Free? And what of the west, what of Rome?"

Now he waited an even longer time.

"As for Rome, the gods of Egypt are silent," he finally said. "And they have indicated that although Egypt will endure, they themselves will be silent after a certain time. They will speak no more."

"Will they still *be*, or does their silence mean they are not?" I had to know. How could Egypt endure without her gods? She would not be Egypt if her gods did not survive.

"I do not know," he said. "They do not say."

The snake had coiled around his neck, and now its head was burrowing down under his robe. I saw another movement: a second snake was on his lap.

"You must not fear them," he said. "They are creatures of Isis, dear to her. And they confer immortality on her chosen ones. I see them as my friends."

"Friends?" I felt a faint stirring near my foot. Isis, I prayed, please keep your creatures from my person. I knew I could not move suddenly or try to push them away or they might strike.

"Death comes to us all, but the sacred asp brings it in a beautiful guise," he said. He stroked the first snake's back. "The hood spreads, the little teeth bite, and death steals over us quickly, painlessly."

"Painlessly?"

"Indeed. Of all poisons it is the gentlest, the kindest. It takes you quickly, and leaves you looking asleep. No blood, no bloating, no writhing. Just a little sweat, a falling asleep, a serenity . . . I have seen it myself."

Yes, Mardian had mentioned the bite of the asp as a pleasant poison.

"How many have you here?" Were there baskets and baskets of them?

"I have never counted," he said. "A great many." He removed one and put it on the floor. "There." He smiled. "I told you they are my friends. But for you, for the Pharaoh, they can be more than that. Their bite can be the instrument of death decreed by Anubis at the appointed hour. They are manifestations of the Lady of Power, the goddess Isis, wearing the crown of Lower Egypt."

My fear was ebbing away in the calm, droning voice explaining all this. He seemed to exert some spell whereby I felt safe, even among the snakes, against all common sense.

"It was long ago revealed to me, by the stars I have studied, that my life would last until I beheld the Pharaoh who is also Isis. Now I have. It is today. Now I can—indeed, must—depart."

Before I could realize what his words meant, he grabbed one of the asps and clasped it to his neck. The creature did not like the rough handling, and spread its hood immediately. Instead of releasing it, he pushed it harder. A hideous hissing ensued.

I dared not move. I could not grab it. All I could do was watch while it sank its teeth into his neck, wriggling and trying to free the other part of its body. He had closed his eyes as if receiving great pleasure. Finally he released the snake and let it drop onto his lap.

I felt one of the snakes moving over my foot. I held as still as possible. But I whispered, "Good sir, what have you done? I must call a physician!" But I knew I was trapped in the room with the snakes; any hurried movement toward the door would make them strike me, too.

"No. Do not keep me from my god," he said. "Do not move."

I was forced to sit absolutely still while he dreamily described the feeling of numbness creeping up his neck, the coldness, the paralysis. Then his words stopped. I could see the sheen of sweat that lay on his face.

I had no way of knowing when he actually died; it was very subtle. And he was right, it had been gentle. He looked happy, and as if he were alive.

How long was I to be a prisoner in here with a dead man and snakes? Surely not all night! Surely Nakht would return!

The time stretched out like a thin wire. I had the opportunity to review my entire life, to pray and compose myself for death, but I could do nothing but strain for deliverance. I wanted to live, and I was not concerned with the particulars, with my mistakes or future plans beyond the instant I would escape from this fetid chamber.

The curtain rose. A young priest peered in, and immediately sensed what had happened. "So he has departed," was all he said. "Our revered father, who—"

"Get the snakes away!" I said. "Get them away!"

"Oh. Yes." He acted as if it were a peculiar request. He dropped the curtain and disappeared, then returned with a cage of mice, which he released on the floor. The snakes all rushed in that direction, almost tying themselves up in knots.

I made my escape, and dashed from the room. "Isis!" was all I could gasp out. My heart was hammering like a rowing-master beating out an attack speed. "O dear Isis!"

The young priest stood in the courtyard and raised a high, quavering wail; other priests streamed toward him, seeming to understand exactly what had happened. At length Nakht strode toward Ipuwer's doorway, stopped and led the others in prayer. The litany droned and rose in a dull surge of voices.

Then he summoned two priests, who stepped forward and entered the chamber, seeming not to feel any danger. I was still stunned, unable to believe what I had just witnessed. The old, mummylike man . . . the snakes . . . the suicide . . .

They emerged carrying the limp body of Ipuwer. His sticklike legs swung to and fro, with surprisingly large feet dangling from them, encased in sandals that looked too heavy for him to lift. His even more withered arms barely gave the men anything to grasp. On his face the same peaceful smile remained that I had seen spread across it when he first felt the snakes.

"Our holy one has departed," said Nakht. "He must be prepared for the journey to eternity."

By that I assumed he must be sent to the embalmer's. Only after the priests with their burden, followed by the other priests, left the courtyard, did Nakht turn to me.

"You have granted him the desire of his heart," he said.

"So you knew he was going to do this? And you subjected me to it, and to danger?" I could not forgive him.

He looked hurt. "No, indeed, Goddess, how could I? I did not know when Anubis would summon him! I only knew he had wished to live until the woman Pharaoh, the daughter of Isis, would rule. He spoke of it, how she would crown the line of Pharaohs, and e—glorify them."

He had meant to say "end them." Was that what they foresaw? Was I to be the last Pharaoh? "I have ruled now for sixteen years," I said. "There is nothing new in that. You must be honest. He meant until he *met* the woman Pharaoh, the last Pharaoh. Is that not what he meant?"

"I do not know, Goddess," he said. "I do not know what he meant. But it was easy to foretell that he would perish by snakebite. After all, he lived surrounded by them. They say anyone who handles snakes eventually gets bitten."

What a prosaic interpretation! Yet true.

"How old was he?"

"Over ninety," Nakht said. "I believe I heard him say once that he had lived as priest, studying the holy mysteries, through the reigns of six Pharaohs—counting yourself."

"Six Pharaohs . . . our reigns must have seemed like the passage of the stars through the sky, quickly rising and quickly setting."

"Yes, to one stationary in the world, that is how it must have appeared. Come, the night barque of Re has set out beneath the earth. It is time to rest."

There were no longer any shadows; the sun had set and the first stars were emerging. The air, warm and scented from the flax fields and wildflowers, stirred against our skin, touching it tenderly. In the villages, people would be walking, meeting by the river, savoring this last sweetness of day as it extinguished itself. But here in the temple, which followed the movements of the sun, it was time to lie down in silence and darkness.

Now I wished I had not agreed to stay. But it was too late.

The chamber I was taken to was large, immaculately clean, bare. It was reserved for guests of the highest order; therefore it sometimes stood empty for years. A bed, itself unremarkable except that it was called the Bed of Dreams, waited to share my night hours. In one corner a very old statue of

Isis stood on a pedestal, keeping watch over the chamber. A snake curled around each of her arms, spiraling upward like bracelets.

Two small lights flickered at her feet. I was alone in the chamber, with no one to undress or attend me. I could not remember the last time I had been alone; although I often longed for it, tonight I felt abandoned. The cold, hard bed waited, and I steeled myself to lie down on it.

Utter silence surrounded me. I was accustomed to sound during the night: the sea itself moving in the harbor below the palace, the faint voices of people in the city streets, sandaled feet passing outside my door, distant music from other quarters. Here, nothing. I felt as though I were Re, making my passage through the twelve hours of night under the earth. Indeed, the long, narrow bed felt like a barque.

Here there were no distractions, no lute-player to flavor the hours delicately with music, no Iras or Charmian to come help me pass sleepless hours, no letters to read or reports to digest. Here there was only myself, watched over by Isis as the night deepened.

What I had witnessed today . . . what I had heard . . . I did not know which was more disturbing: the old priest killing himself with the asps, or what he had *said*—about the gods of Egypt falling silent, and then seeing the last of the Pharaohs. Could he be believed? Or was he just a mad old man, dwelling too long in the temple, becoming as enfeebled as the wobbly setting sun he worshiped? In the sacred stories, Isis had tricked the weak sun into revealing his name, Re. It was Isis who had outsmarted him, challenged him. And it was Isis who had resurrected Osiris through her own determination. Isis did not accept defeat; no matter how hopeless the circumstances, she fought with all her skill and might, and triumphed.

The statue of the goddess seemed to waver in the light. I turned my head and looked at her. I wish to be like you, I thought. I must be strong as well as compassionate. You never accepted fate as something immutable, but you remade your own fate against all odds.

All my life that was what I had tried to do. If the old priest had glimpsed the end of the line of Pharaohs—why, it was but a glimpse, it was not something already written. It was only a warning. I could change that. I *would* change that.

I slept; or, rather, darkness fell around me and entered my head. And then the Bed of Dreams lived up to its frightful name. I was visited, through all the night hours, with my own fearful glimpses of the past, the present, and the future. I saw the beginnings of Egypt, shadows riding in old costumes, driving old chariots; I recognized in human form some of the Pharaohs I knew only by statues (and was surprised at how small they had been in life). I saw my own self as a child, dressed in Greek clothes and living in my Greek palace, white stone instead of native brown and gold, saw Antony come to Egypt, and Caesar too, and then saw a swarm of other Romans, descending like locusts, blotting out the land. And other costumes, too, odder ones, followed them, surrounding the pyramids like a flooded Nile, lapping at their bases. Then the Nile subsided, and did not rise again, neither did it shrink.

And I saw Heliopolis itself a ruin and a sandy mound, only the obelisks remaining to mark the center of the world.

"Awaken, Exalted One." A soft voice spoke in my ear.

I did not wake up so much as I was delivered from these apparitions. Nakht stood by my bedside, lamp in hand.

"Khepri nears the eastern horizon," he said. "Soon he will emerge from behind the persea tree, and we must greet him there."

I felt so disoriented, so transported from my familiar world, that it seemed of utmost importance to greet the rising sun—I who allowed him to arrive unheralded each morning in Alexandria. Indeed, there were times when he was already high in the sky, sending beams into the middle of the room, before I even noticed him.

"Yes, of course." I rose. The lamps were still bright in the gloom. Isis stood watching.

Outside there was no hint that dawn was coming except that the birds had awakened. Somehow they sensed the passage of time, the minute change in the intensity of the dark, in a way we could not. Walking down the avenue of obelisks, the palms behind them still invisible, we passed into the orchard, then to a mound where a circle of priests was waiting, their white robes swimming like mist out of the gloom. In the center stood the sacred persea tree, its bushy branches making the tree appear rounded. No one spoke, and we took our places silently in the circle.

Gradually the sky lightened, and—never has anything seemed more solemn, deliberate, and majestic—a gray bed was prepared for the sun by the clouds on the eastern rim of the earth. Finally a wink of sunlight was seen, strong and true, putting the night to flight. It gleamed through the branches of the tree, painting each of the leaves so they shone, hundreds of little mirrors.

The priests burst into song, rejoicing. Then, as the sun climbed above the horizon, they turned and walked swiftly back to the temple, passing into the open room with the gold-clad obelisk, standing before it in reverence.

The shining surface of the obelisk, its beaten gold giving back wavering reflections, waited. A spark seemed to touch its pointed apex; a star grew there. It hurt my eyes to behold it.

"Ahh," the priests exhaled.

"The sun is reborn," they intoned. The burning spot at the apex intensified; then it faded. Along the ridge of the obelisk a flame seemed to appear, spreading up and down its length. The sun was growing in strength, climbing into the sky. Overhead it was no longer black, nor deepest blue, but a clear, jubilant, bursting azure. The day was here. The sun, the life, had returned.

"Thanks be to Re," they sang joyfully, celebrating their deliverance.

As long as the sun rose each day, as long as they could behold it, their life was secure.

It was their task to live each day as something contained unto itself, whereas I . . . I must try to anticipate the future, manage the present. How much easier just to celebrate the supreme achievement of another night passed. . . .

Now the priests turned and walked toward the ceremonial chamber, where the statue of Re must be ritually washed with purified water, and celestial food offered him by priests wearing the masks of stars. I watched as they lovingly wiped the face of the statue, as they had for more years than could be counted, and attended his imagined needs.

Stars . . . how lovely to be attended by stars.

Alexandria, Rome, Octavian, Antony—how far away they seemed, how small against the Egyptian gods.

66

In my strange life, I played many parts. I was Isis, I was daughter of Re, I was a Ptolemy—most scheming of ruling houses—I was Queen of Egypt, I was mother of the next Pharaoh, I was wife of a Roman Triumvir, I was Caesar's widow, and Octavian's implacable enemy. How fate had cast me in so many parts, I could not understand. How I could play them all, and keep them separate—if indeed I did—I understood even less.

Antony had returned from Armenia some months after I had returned from Heliopolis. Of our two ventures, I think I was more changed by mine, although I had set out on it in all innocence, thinking only to inspect my balsam bushes—a mere business trip. He, who had high matters of state on his mind, had ended by conducting a campaign whose outcome was predictable. The might of all the east turned against Armenia. How else could it end, but with Artavasdes in chains, a royal prisoner?

That he was in silver chains—that was the only novelty in it all. That, and Antony's sudden, fierce desire to celebrate his victory in Alexandria. Rome had been silent toward him, despite the proud announcement of his conquest that he had sent posthaste to Rome. No feasts or celebrations were held, no days of thanksgiving decreed in the capital in his honor.

"It is as if . . . as if they no longer look upon me as a Roman," he had said. I could not tell, from his tone, whether he was insulted or shaken: perhaps a little of both.

"I am sure your supporters in the Senate are trumpeting it," I assured him.

"No, my enemies are muffling it," he fumed.

"It cannot stay muffled."

"They should invite me for a Triumph," he said. "I have earned it! How dare they not?"

"As long as Octavian can counter it, he will."

"Octavian is still in Illyria," said Antony stubbornly. "I want a Triumph. I have earned it!"

He had never celebrated a Triumph, although his grandfather had, in the days when they were not easily awarded. But Triumphs were meant to mark victories over foreign foes, and Antony's successes had been primarily in the civil wars. He had been hailed as Imperator three times, but those had been for actions against Pompey, against Cassius and Brutus, only finally against the Parthians. He and his general Bassus had been granted Triumphs for their success against the Parthians who had earlier invaded the Roman territory in Syria; Bassus had returned to Rome to celebrate his, but Antony had postponed it.

"Yes, I know." For a Roman general of his stature never to have celebrated a Triumph was a great void. He was aching to fill it; he wanted recognition. He wanted to ride in a chariot, be acclaimed, have prisoners of war march behind him, hear the shouts.

"I shall grant one to myself!" he suddenly said.

O Isis! And go to Rome? I felt my heart slow in its beating. He was due two of them: one that he shared with Bassus, and now the one against the Armenians.

"I shall hold one here, in Alexandria!" he continued. "What is magical about Rome? To whom do I wish to present my spoils? Is it not you, my Queen? I fought in spite of Rome, in spite of their cutting off my recruitments, with my own eastern soldiers and the remnants of my old legions. Why not here?"

He wanted it so badly. But a Triumph was not a Triumph outside Rome. It was connected with Rome, granted by the Senate, and its spoils were to be laid at the feet of the Roman god, Jupiter Maximus, in his temple on the Capitoline hill.

"You can celebrate your victory here," I said. "Although it cannot be a true Triumph. That can only be granted by the Roman Senate. But certainly, Alexandria would make a fine setting for a victory parade. . . ."

I sat on a golden throne, raised high on a silver platform, on the steps of the Temple of Serapis. I had granted Antony his wish, and ordered Alexandria scrubbed and prepared for his celebration. My heart ached for him, a man passed over in his native land. He was truly a son of Rome, but they had cast him out. Well, the day would come when they would welcome him—nay, not only welcome him, but bow low in homage. Yes, that day would come! And sooner than they thought!

His procession had started out from the palace at an early hour, and it was still winding its way through the streets, past the harbor and the Temple of Neptune, out the broad white street of Canopus, so all the cheering crowds could see, then back again past the hill of Pan, where it would turn west. It would pass the solemn intersection of the Street of the Soma and the Canopic Way, paying homage to the tomb where the body of Alexander lay, and the

Mausoleum of the Ptolemies, then the Gymnasion and law courts, where, on both sides, the masses would be packed between the colonnades. The windows and steps of the Museion would be crowded with scholars and their students, as eager to catch a glimpse as anyone else. And then, last of all, Antony would process here, to me, at the Serapion. Here I awaited him, with all my court spread out on the steps of the great building.

I could hear the distant shouts as he approached. Each section of the city rose and cheered as the troops, the prisoners, the chariots, the spoils of war, passed by. I watched my children, arrayed on both sides of me like wings, sitting straight and straining their eyes for the moment when the procession would first come into view. It was a sight the children of Rome were well acquainted with; I remembered the hordes at Caesar's. In his Roman tunic and cloak, Caesarion looked every bit the son of Caesar—if only Octavian could see him now! Alexander and Selene were dressed in Greek clothing, and the restless Alexander was thumping his sandaled feet against the silver rungs of his chair of state. I myself was dressed, as befitted a ceremony at the Serapion and the Shrine of Isis, in the costume of the goddess. To all the people gathered here today, I was the visual reminder of her, the earthly representative of Isis. The silver-threaded gown, with its pleats covering my shoulders and breasts like ripples of water, had a prominent knot of the thin, precious material between my breasts—the emblematic knot of Isis. I wore a heavy wig, one that had long braids adorned with silver ornaments that twinkled in the sun.

From our vantage point on the hill, I could see the throngs of people spread out on all sides like a carpet. Each dot of black hair, each red tunic, each yellow cloak, helped to make a pattern that was more intricate than any woven textile that came from Arabia. And far behind them, in the distance, the piercing blue of the sea made a border.

My carpet! My people! My Alexandria—city like no other on earth, a variegated, magnificent whole, a new heaven, a new kingdom. The first of the vision Antony and I had for our empire—or, rather, that I had and that Antony understood.

Now we saw them; a murmur ran through the air. The shields of the soldiers were glinting, catching the sun, as if they were signaling. The drums and flutes kept rhythm with their marching, the sound of their hobnailed sandals ringing on the paved street.

First came the Macedonian Household Troops, my own traditional bodyguard. They, and they alone, had the letter C on their shields, as they always had. The two Roman legions marching after them had no such thing—regardless of the lies told later! They carried only their usual round, leather-covered shields that said nothing whatever on them.

Behind them followed Antony in a gold chariot drawn by four white horses, as in a Roman Triumph. But instead of the purple general's cloak, the laurel wreath, and the scepter, Antony's head was entwined with the ivy, he wore a golden robe—blinding to look upon—and carried the wand of Dionysus. It was as Dionysus that he presented his spoils to Isis.

His face was shining, tanned, and he was grinning as he acknowledged the shouts rising on all sides of him. I knew how thirsty he was for them, what balm they were to him. He had always been a loyal lieutenant, carrying out missions for others with courage and flair, but the cheers had never been bestowed on him alone. Now they were, and I wished I could magnify them until all the buildings rang like a bell, deafening us.

Marching behind Antony's chariot, straight and proud in spite of the heavy chains, swayed King Artavasdes and his queen, as well as several of his children. They were covered with dust, hot and weary from the long walk amid the jeers and hostility. That man! His scented ringlets were no longer dressed and curled, but dull and drooping. And where were his rings now? His only jewelry were the silver manacles that adorned his wrists and ankles. And all the oily compliments and poetry that had greased his treachery!

I glared at him. Because of him, forty-two thousand men had lost their lives. Even if he were butchered, cut into forty-two thousand pieces himself, it could not repay them. One death could never balance all the deaths he had caused.

He stood at the foot of the steps, waiting, while the rest of the lengthy procession continued, then took their places in the open ground around the temple. A host of wretched Armenian prisoners were paraded past, common people and slaves who had been captured. Next came a long train of carts laden with booty. Armenia was—had been!—wealthy in gold. No more. It was all on the wagons.

The wagons. How many of them were there? Twenty? Thirty? But how many wagons had been in the Roman baggage train? Three hundred? Even thirty wagons loaded with gold could not compensate for the loss of those crucial support wagons. After the fact, nothing ever seems to compensate. Killing the assassins was necessary, but it did not undo Caesar's murder. Nor did this undo the devastation caused by the despicable Artavasdes.

The client kings had all sent representatives, along with golden crowns for the victor—so Cappadocia, Pontus, Lycia, Galatia, Paphlagonia, Thrace, Mauretania, Judaea, Commagene, all were there, wearing their distinctive national dress.

Another Roman legion, Gallic cavalry, then an Egyptian contingent, mounted bowmen from Media, light cavalry from Pontus, along with the musicians, brought up the rear and halted.

Antony dismounted, his golden cloak swirling out behind him. He walked slowly over to Artavasdes, then past him, and began ascending the steps of the temple to those of us waiting for him. Roman soldiers prodded Artavasdes to follow, and he began heaving his feet up the steps, dragging the chains.

The sun glinted off Antony's head, showing the thick, still-dark hair curling around the ivy wreath, healthy brown against the green. He was smiling, clearly enjoying every moment of this day.

"Queen of Egypt, Daughter of Isis, Friend and Ally of Rome," he shouted, his voice—so famed for outdoor oratory—ringing out and filling the entire area, as rich to the ears as his gold cloak was to the eyes. "I present to you today this most noble prisoner, a king who now regrets his treachery and wishes to salute you."

The soldiers nudged Artavasdes forward with their spears, and he moved one step upward. His liquid dark eyes met mine.

He was supposed to fall on his knees and do obeisance—or, at the very least, greet me by all my titles, then beg forgiveness for his offense. Instead he clamped his mouth shut.

"Salute the Queen, Her Most Noble Majesty, Pharaoh of Egypt and all its lands and territories."

His mouth remained closed, his head up, his shoulders squared.

"King Artavasdes," said Antony, "you must acknowledge the Queen, who owns your very life at this point, as do I." His voice had hardened.

Still the Armenian monarch stood there, mute by defiance.

"Speak!" commanded Antony.

The soldiers withdrew their short daggers and held them under Artavasdes' ribs. I could see the indentation in his tunic. One move from him and the dagger points would pierce the fabric. Even his breathing was going to leave a prick-mark.

"Greetings, Cleopatra," he said loudly.

There was a communal gasp. To call me by my personal name, no title, in a public ceremony—he, an enemy! Truly, the man was insolent—proud and foolish—past reason. It was fitting he was off his throne; Armenia deserved better.

"Greetings, Cleopatra," he repeated, even louder. He managed to draw out the syllables until the word sounded as long as the doomed baggage train.

"Greetings, conquered traitor," I answered. I would go him one better and not even use his name; reduce him to a *thing*.

I nodded, and Antony signaled for him to be taken away. The two soldiers complied, lifting him up by the shoulders and carrying him, his legs stiff, down the steps.

Did he think, since prisoners were traditionally executed immediately following a Triumph, that these would be remembered as his last words? Make him famous?

Antony now turned to enter the temple and make sacrifice to Serapis. The priests surrounding us on the steps, and the priestesses, shook their sistrums, and the hissing rattles filled the air. Antony disappeared into the dark recesses of the temple, his gold cloak swallowed up in the gloom that filled the temple even on a bright day.

Afterward followed feasts for the people of Alexandria; as in Rome, tables were set up all over the city, and the public invited to help themselves to meat, cakes, and endless wine, all at the palace's expense. Antony went out among his soldiers and presided over the tables of legionaries, then betook himself to roaming throughout the city, dropping in on celebrants, joining in their revelry. Would Dionysus have done less?

But I remained in the palace, enjoying the feast-tables set up on our grounds. All my household servants, officers, and friends were wandering under the lighted trees, drinking, singing—albeit more decorously than the songs filling the streets of Alexandria.

It was growing light before Antony returned, not tired or staggering but exhilarated. His cloak was gone and his fine tunic wrinkled and sweat-stained; around his neck were garlands of flowers and grass necklaces. He had been hailed, saluted, feasted, and adored, and he was glowing with it, as rosy as the color coming up in the east. He ran across the grass and swept me up in his arms like the young cavalry officer that he still was inside, swung me around, my feet flying off the ground. It made me dizzy, but he roared with laughter.

"Come!" He took my hand and made me run up the steps to the Temple of Isis, which stood near the open sea. "Let us watch the dawn come up from here. This day is not over until the sun rises anew."

Six days later I was again on a gold throne, raised high on a silver platform, again dressed as Isis, for another ceremony. Again my children were nearby, and again, Antony presided. But, oh! how different in intent and ritual. For this ceremony was the declaration, the inauguration, of our eastern empire.

We had put the final touches on it late at night some three days after the Triumph. Workers were still sweeping the streets clean, carts were still trundling out of the city piled high with the debris from the feasting; I did not want dogs and crows scavenging. Together we had decided not to put Artavasdes to death, but keep him imprisoned. Let this Triumph—or Dionysian revel—proclaim its difference from its Roman counterpart in this way. Our regime would not be so cruel.

"Although it was different, and not, strictly speaking, a Triumph, it will anger the Romans," I pointed out to Antony. "Just as soon as they hear of it."

"I care not," he had shrugged, leaning back on his couch. His hand groped for a bolster for his shoulder.

"I think you do," I said. "It is not in your nature to anger people on purpose." I paused. "How clever of you to make it just different enough from a Roman Triumph that if you wish, you can say that was never your intention. 'After all, I dressed as Dionysus, not a Roman general, so how could anyone *possibly* think I meant . . . ?'"

"It was not that deliberate," he said. "It is just that . . . here I am Dionysus to your Aphrodite, to the Greeks at least. To the Egyptians I am Osiris to your Isis. All that is unknown at Rome. It seemed more fitting . . ." His voice trailed off.

Slowly Antony had allowed himself to "become" a god here in the east. It had started when he was hailed that way at Ephesus after Philippi. Then he had played Dionysus at Tarsus. Next, in Athens, he and Octavia had been dubbed "Gods of Good Works" and Antony called "the New Dionysus." To commemorate that, he had issued coins picturing himself as Dionysus. Next he allowed himself to be proclaimed Dionysus in all the cities of the east. The final step, after our marriage, was being worshiped throughout Egypt as a god, Dionysus-Osiris with Aphrodite-Isis.

"You have outstripped Octavian," I had teased him. "After all, he is only the *son* of a god!"

As always when Octavian's name was mentioned, even in fun, Antony's face clouded. "I have no intention of competing with him for titles of divinity!" he said haughtily—as haughtily as any god.

"Now that you have embraced your godhood, I think you must have a temple," I said.

"Don't be ridiculous," he countered.

"I am serious. Caesar has one, and so should you. Octavian is building a temple to his new 'patron,' Apollo, right next to his house—how blatant. It is all the rage. You must have one, too."

"Nonsense."

"I will have a building overlooking the harbor put up in your honor. I will call it the Antoneum. Or perhaps the Basilica of the Divine Antony—*Divus Antonius*."

He laughed. "Do as you will," he said. But I could tell he was pleased. It is a rare human being who does not get a warm glow from an honor, especially something as tangible as a statue—or a building!

"Here in the east, any authority is given divine honors—even city magistrates. Of course, that is not the same as divinity. Pompey was hailed as a god, his client Theophanes as 'savior and benefactor.' "

"But these subtle differences—we cannot expect them to be understood in Rome. And in Rome, Dionysus carries a different image from our eastern one. Here he is a rich, benevolent god; he brings fertility, joy, expansion. He is seen as patron of artists and creativity, of civilization itself. There he's reduced to revelry, drunkenness, Pans and satyrs. It makes it easy for my Roman enemies to attack me."

I was struck by one thing. "Artists, creativity—it seems that Apollo has usurped these attributes in Rome. And Octavian has lately embraced Apollo, as if both of you are fighting over who can lead the world most creatively."

"The creativity of Dionysus springs from inner, unnameable forces," said Antony. "It is that which leaps up, unbidden, unexpected, that makes original connections, surprising even the artist himself, because he does not know where it came from and cannot predict its arrival. That is what makes it seem divine, even to its holder." He got up from the couch and stood over a small mosaic I had installed in our chamber. It showed a scene from the Nile: tall papyrus reeds, hippopotamuses, boats, and birds. "Who ever first thought of arranging little stones to make a picture? And this picture—it existed inside the artist's head before a single stone was laid. Or perhaps it grew out of the first stone, uncurling like a fern stalk!" He was growing more and more excited. "And the ideas come and go as they will; they can depart suddenly and without notice. Of all men, I think the artist feels most under the dominance and caprice of the god Dionysus."

I was struck by his personal knowledge of this. "I think you must have been visited this way yourself," I said.

"Well, I have never wanted to paint," he said quickly. "But, it is true . . . even a battle strategy can suddenly present itself out of nowhere, like an inspiration. . . ." He shook his head, as if to scare away any hovering visitations. "But Apollo is the god of rationality, of ordered thinking. That is the exact opposite of the nameless passion of creation."

"One needs both, I think. The empire needs both. We need officials who can think calmly and logically, but not be entirely bound by rules." As I spoke, I knew I was dreaming.

"Such an empire, staffed by such paragons, cannot exist on this earth. We must make do with faulty men and chance." He was still studying the mosaic. "Egypt has a mighty past."

"And a strong present," I said. "But what of the future? What is the future of Egypt?" The prediction of old Ipuwer concerning the silence of the gods troubled me.

"I will tell you," he said quietly, turning from the mosaic. "It is time I made provision for our children. Shortly I will write my will to dispose of my Roman obligations."

A will! *Dispose of* . . . it sounded so ominous. I hated the finality of a will. Yet only a fool does not have one; if you do not provide one, your enemies will attack your heirs.

"I hope you plan to deposit it in a safe place!" was all I said. I was convinced Caesar had had a later will than the one left with the Vestal Virgins, but not safeguarded—a curious sloppiness for one of Caesar's foresight. If he had, then perhaps Octavian would still be studying in Apollonia, a little-known distant relative of Caesar's, like his other nephews who had vanished into obscurity. But enough of that, I told myself.

"Yes, it will be delivered into the safekeeping of the Vestal Virgins in Rome," he said. "There it will remain inviolate until my death. But its contents will not be a secret from you. You shall be present when I dictate it, and Plancus and Titius will serve as witnesses. But we will discuss that later. It chiefly concerns my Roman family. But what of ours? What is their future?"

This was a strange conversation. The only child whose future was a mystery was Caesarion, because of his unique position. "You have already settled Alexander's," I said. "He will marry the Median princess and inherit Media. As for Selene, she will marry—someone. The baby, Philadelphos—or the Hedgehog, as you insist on calling him—the throne of Egypt will likely fall to him, as the one Ptolemy remaining behind."

He stood before me and put his hands on my shoulders. "Such limited dreams, for such an imperial mother," he said. "You continue to surprise me."

"They will all have a kingdom. They will all thrive. The brother-and-sister killings that have stained the name of Ptolemy—not to mention hands and daggers—will cease with this generation. What greater achievement could a mother—a Ptolemaic mother, that is—claim?"

He was looking at me with a depth of surprised approval I had never seen in his eyes before. "And you are thought to be wildly, greedily ambitious," he finally said.

"Because of my goal of reclaiming my ancestral lands? I would call that limited—downright Apollo-like—wishing to regain only lost territory. My house had fallen on such hard times that we had to buy back our throne, and borrow the money to do it! To reverse all that seemed a hard enough task to set myself."

"Yet now you have achieved it," he said. "And because success is rewarded by unsought further success, I will tell you: your dreams are too small."

I laughed, and turned away. No one had ever accused me of that before!

"All the east lies in my hand. I am its ultimate master, both by appointment from Rome as Triumvir and by right of arms as Imperator. I can bestow it where and how I will." How matter-of-factly he said it. "I think 'Queen of Egypt' is too small for you. I think you should be Queen of Kings and of Her Sons Who are Kings. And I think your sons should be kings. Alexander Helios will rule over parts of Armenia, Media, and Parthia, as befits the heir of Alexander himself. Cleopatra Selene, a queen, will be granted Cyrenaica and Crete. Why rely on a husband to grant her a kingdom? And little Hedgehog, Philadelphos—why, he shall also be a king, and rule northern Syria and Cilicia."

"You are announcing a dynasty," I said. "A Roman magistrate, you are founding a royal eastern dynasty." This was odd, unbelievable. What was he thinking?

"No, I am not *founding* it. The house of Ptolemy has existed for three hundred years! I am merely . . . expanding its scope."

"And its claims and ambitions," I said. "You are giving them Roman territory, as well as territory not under your control. Like Parthia!" I could not resist this.

His plan was impulsive, daring. Was that what he meant by Dionysian inspiration? It was not rational; Apollo had certainly not given rise to it.

"I am giving them an idea to pursue," he said. "Should I not manage to take Parthia, it will be left for them to do." He paused. "But I plan to. Next year, now that Armenia and Media are secure. I am proud of having won a new Roman province!"

"Have you?" He had never stated this decision about the status of his conquest.

"Yes. Armenia will be converted directly into a province. I have garrisoned it securely this time, under Canidius. I will present this plan to Rome, to be read out and confirmed in the Senate, at the same time as my territorial assignments to you and the children. They will take them all together!" He laughed. "Not that there is any question about it. All my acts here in the east have been approved in advance. It is courtesy only."

"Are the children not too young for this?" It seemed premature.

"The earlier someone knows his destiny, the better he can follow it. It will forestall all the plots and machinations, and foster peace."

It seemed a pronouncement of great and unknown consequence. But I have learned that things are seldom offered twice; we have to grasp them when they pass, even if the timing feels wrong. "Very well," I said. "I am stunned by your elevation of these children to such high positions. After all, you have others. . . ."

"Antyllus, as my eldest son, will be my Roman heir. His brother Iullus—oh, those are all Roman details, of no concern to you now. But my eldest daughter, Antonia, will soon be in our sphere of the world. I am marrying her to Pythodorus of Tralles. He's as wealthy as a king, and widely respected throughout the east."

"A Greek from Asia! What will they say in Rome? They won't consider her legally married." No Roman would recognize it.

"What they will say is, he must believe in his own foreign marriage, if he allows it for his daughter as well. As you know, we often do things ourselves that we would not approve or wish for our dear ones. I can send no stronger message to Rome. Besides," he said, grinning, "she will have so much money I don't think she'll feel uncompensated!"

So now I sat, awaiting the public pronouncement of the honors we had discussed so lightly in our private chambers. There was another matter, which was not so lightly spoken of or decided, but—of that, later.

As I said, I was dressed as Isis again, and again sat on a golden throne. The silver platform had been erected in front of the Gymnasion, so that spectators could fill the steps along the six-hundred-foot-long side of the building, shaded by the roofed columns. But it was a larger platform than the Triumph's, and it was constructed with different levels. Antony and I were on the topmost. Just a little lower sat Caesarion, on his own throne. Below him were another three thrones, for the younger children. They were sitting, costumed, staring out at the crowd.

Antony, stately in his Roman toga, rose and addressed the people in his official capacity as Triumvir. He had put aside his other roles, the general, the Autocrator, the New Dionysus, the eastern ruler. He, like me, played many parts. Today he was the civilian Roman magistrate, appointed to govern Rome's vast territories in the east as its overlord.

"My good people, I stand here before you to make you witnesses of the gifts I bestow today upon the faithful House of Ptolemy—loyal supporters of Rome. And also to honor the great god, Julius Caesar. For your Queen, who has long reigned over you, let her be known henceforth as Queen of Kings, and of Her Sons Who are Kings." He turned and took my hand, drawing me up to stand beside him. The glare of the sun's reflection off the silver platform dazzled me, making it hard to see.

"And I further declare," he said, so loudly that even the farthest bystander could not fail to hear the words, "that she is the widow of Julius Caesar, having been his true and legal wife by contracting a marriage after the eastern rite." A hush fell on the crowd, as severe as if a giant hand had pushed itself down on their heads. I felt his hand tremble. He had not spoken of this to me, had not warned me. Perhaps he had wanted to ensure my blank stare.

"And I hereby swear that their son, Ptolemy Caesar, seated here, is the true and legitimate son of the great Caesar, and his only heir."

I had not thought it possible that the silence could deepen, but it did. Antony's hand was grasping mine so hard it began to ache. At the same time it grew slippery with sweat.

"Stand, young Caesar," commanded Antony. "Stand, and let your people see you and acknowledge you."

Slowly Caesarion stood up. He had grown tall; he was over thirteen now, and his head was almost level with Antony's. Antony had insisted he wear his best Roman attire today, without saying why.

Shyly he smiled at the people, and made a gesture to them. They cheered warmly.

"As son of Caesar, he is due honors from Rome. But as a Ptolemy and eldest son of Queen Cleopatra, he rules as co-ruler of the land of Egypt and Cyprus and reigns as King of Kings, and overlord of the other territories to be henceforth bestowed."

Again that hush. King of Kings was an ancient, honorific eastern title, borne by the Persians. So Caesarion was to be both eastern and western ruler; he was to bind the two worlds together after Antony and I had left the stage of life.

"Next," he said, "I declare that Alexander Helios is King of Armenia, overlord of Media and of all territory east of the Euphrates as far as India."

King of Armenia? How could there be a king of a Roman province? Antony had not explained this. Was it only a portion of Armenia? But now was not the time to ask.

"Rise, King Alexander," said Antony.

The boy rose, wearing the costume carefully crafted for him: that of a Persian king. There was a high royal tiara—the Persian crown—swathed in a white turban, decorated with a peacock feather. He wore baggy trousers and a jeweled cloak, which glittered in the sun, intensified by the beaten silver of the platform, acting as a gigantic mirror.

Now the Armenian bodyguards, also costumed, stepped up to make a frame around him. The crowd cheered.

"And Queen Cleopatra Selene," said Antony, stepping over to where our daughter sat on her little throne, waiting. "You rule Cyrenaica and Crete. Rise, please." She stood solemnly, her silver gown hanging to the floor, making her one with it, a slender silver flower growing out of the silver ground. Her bodyguard, dressed in Grecian soldiers' attire, carried silver shields.

"And King Ptolemy Philadelphos." Antony made his way to the tiny throne of the two-year-old boy, who sat looking apprehensive. He had never seen so many people, or been made to sit by himself for so long. "You are to rule the middle Syrian territories, and Cilicia, and be overlord of Pontus, Galatia, and Cappadocia, westward from the Euphrates as far as the Hellespont." Antony bent down and took his chubby hand. "Rise." He gently pulled the child up, so that everyone could see—as he stood there on wobbly feet—that he wore a royal Macedonian costume of purple cloak, diademed hat, and Macedonian high boots. To complete the picture, he had a Macedonian bodyguard to serve him.

"Now, all good citizens of Alexandria, Rome, and Egypt—let us rejoice in this happy day! I have issued today a new coin marking the occasion. It honors Queen Cleopatra, with the legend 'Queen of Kings and of Her Sons Who are Kings,' and me, with the legend 'Armenia Conquered.' May it serve to remind us of those achievements when we behold it with our eyes, and may it serve to enrich us when it is in our purses!" With that, he hurled a handful of the shiny silver *denarii* out into the crowd, who roared and scrambled for them.

When he saw how that at last released the crowd—which had been subdued and confused—he quickly motioned for more bags of money to be opened and thrown to the people. Now the shouts and cheering rose.

"Always money," he said, as he returned to my side, standing straight. "I think it is the great joy-giver, more than wine."

"Everyone loves money, while not everyone cares for wine," I said. I was as confused as the rest of the crowd. It was all I could think of to say.

There was, of course, a banquet and celebration in the palace immediately following. While the rest of the populace dispersed, those of our party were to be entertained extravagantly—as befitted a family of kings, kings of kings, queens, and . . . what was Antony? Obviously, if he had the power to create and appoint kings of kings, he must be above them, but . . . It was all very ill-defined. Did "Autocrator" adequately describe this overarching authority?

In the huge hall, its red porphyry pillars twined with garlands, a light sprinkling of rose petals underfoot, long swaths of blue silk were strung between columns. They billowed and fluttered in the wind rising from the harbor below, the scent of crushed rose petals perfuming the air. I put my arms proudly around the shoulders of Selene and Alexander.

"You looked impressive today," I told them. I wondered how it felt to be proclaimed special so early, to have your kingdom handed to you? I hoped it would not stifle them, make it so easy that in later life they could not face difficulties. The ceremonial bodyguards were still surrounding them, and I gave them a look. Time to melt away; the play was over.

"I suppose I'll like Cyrene," said Selene. "Because it's right next to Egypt. And I can stay there, and let the men come to *me*—as you did."

I laughed. Selene seemed at times very grown up; she saw things clearly.

"Yes, it's convenient to have a kingdom of your own," I said.

The silver dress became her, but Alexander was about to trip over his baggy Persian trousers. He slid about awkwardly.

Antony was carrying Philadelphos, letting the child peer over his shoulder. The cap and diadem were too big, and kept falling over one eye. Antony was turning around and around, and Philadelphos was squealing with delight.

Antony's cloak flapped and flew out. Suddenly he grasped its fastening, unhooked it, and threw it out over the crowd. It flew a little way, like a purple bat.

Plancus caught it, and came over to me, clutching it like a holy relic. "Although I would keep this myself—to treasure it as belonging to the Imperator on this glorious day—yet I must return it. I am no thief!" His broad, tanned face radiated sincerity.

"No, keep it," I said. "He who discards something valuable cannot expect to recover it. It must go where it was thrown. In this case, how fortunate that it fell into friendly hands!"

He looked as though I had bestowed a kingdom on *him*. It struck me as odd even then.

Marcus Titius and Domitius Ahenobarbus, who had traveled here for the ceremony, joined us. Plancus was holding up the cloak like a trophy, and they purported to feel slighted.

"This is a day for prizes for everyone," I said. "I cannot give you kingdoms, but what of a city? Would you like a city named for you?"

They looked taken aback, Ahenobarbus especially. As an old-style Republican, it was far from proper for him. But I could see that the flattery of it appealed even to him. Titius, of course, was always ready to help himself to honors.

"I shall rename two cities in Cilicia, calling them Titiopolis and Domitiopolis," I said.

They both gave up trying to suppress grins.

"Your Majesty," said Titius, "what can I say—besides offering my undying gratitude?" His handsome lean face grew even handsomer. He bent and kissed my hand, letting his warm lips linger there a little overlong.

"Madam"—a ticklish matter of names; Republican Ahenobarbus never called me by my royal title—"you are most generous." He bowed stiffly.

The wine was flowing; I had ordered dozens of amphorae of the best Chian to be poured unstintingly. As for the banquet itself, it was worthy of the imagination of Octavian and his loyal, bought poets. Every delicacy from land, air, and sea was presented. There were sea creatures, shellfish, boar, beef, even hippopotamus and crocodile; crane, quail, thrush, peacock, flamingo; sweet melons, cucumbers, grapes, figs, dates; honey cakes, custard, and juices of pomegranate, mulberries, and cherries cooled with Thracian snow. I was most proud of the last; it was not easy to have a mound of snow preserved hundreds of miles from its home, and in hot Egypt.

At the presentation of each new course, the murmurs of approval rose, until they reached a continual high hum, penetrated now and then by the sound of the lyres, lutes, and flutes from the musicians in the back of the hall. The cooled juices, carried in on platters and embedded in the snow, elicited an uproar.

Caesarion was lounging next to the Roman generals on their dining couches; the children—the Kings and Queen—nearby. How well Caesarion seemed to fit in with them! How poised he was. How . . . Roman. I watched the faces of the generals and caught them scrutinizing him when they thought they were unobserved.

"Entertainment! Entertainment!" Some of the more inebriated guests began demanding the next stage. I had planned for dancers, as well as acrobats and something seldom seen—trained monkeys to perform on the pillars. The dancers, lithe young women who moved with skill and grace, were too tame for them today. The acrobats were boring to this sophisticated—and drunken—audience. The monkeys amused them briefly, but their loud yelling frightened the creatures off. I had only one more thing in reserve: a troupe of Dionysian actors who were to enact a drama about Pluto and Persephone. People always liked that, because it had entertaining elements like Hades (with smoke and fire), Cerberus (with his three heads; it was always impressive if they could each emit a bark), the boatman of the Styx, and of course the violence of Persephone's abduction. There could also be decorations like flowers, chariots, falling leaves, and so on.

If this failed to amuse or quiet them . . .

For a few minutes all went well, but then the noise and stirring started again. Suddenly, Plancus lurched to his feet and ran out of the hall. He must have eaten so much he was sick. Romans did that, much to the disdain of Greeks and more sophisticated peoples.

Then he reappeared—naked and painted blue. Wearing a crown of reeds, he brandished a trident and wove his way over to the astonished actors. "Glaucus, the man of the sea, is here!" he yelled. He got down on his hands and knees and I saw, with astonishment, that he had fastened a fishtail on himself, and now he proceeded to wiggle it at the audience.

Utter silence reigned; then the company and guests burst into laughter. This was evidently their idea of high humor. I looked at Antony, who was also roaring with laughter, and of course the children found it just to their level of taste. But that a Roman general, the governor of a province, should behave so . . .

I would never understand Romans. Antony was right.

I looked at Plancus with distaste. And this was what thought itself fit to rule the world!

Late that night, the guests gone, the rose petals mangled, the silk banners tattered and torn from the antics of the frightened monkeys, Antony and I stood in the echoing empty hall. The children had long since been sent to bed, even Caesarion, and we stood surveying the mess, our arms around each other.

"Alexandria will never forget it," he said. "Such a day comes but once in everyone's lifetime."

"Thanks be to Isis!" I did not think I could live through another one.

"I think the honors were well received," he said cautiously.

"Here, yes. How Octavian will receive them is another matter."

"The east is mine to dispose of how I will. Rome appointed me its overlord."

"I meant in proclaiming Caesarion the true heir of Caesar," I said. "It is nothing less than a declaration of war. That was your intention?"

"I—it is not necessarily so," he said. "But it is true, and men must not be allowed to forget it."

"Why did you not warn me of this? Or did you only do it on impulse?" It seemed to me that every important action of his life had been undertaken on a whim. His funeral speech for Caesar; his coming to my cabin at Tarsus; his marriage to Octavia, and his sending her away; now this. Things that decided his fate, chosen offhandedly.

"No. It was not an impulse. It was the right thing to do. It *is* true." He was stubbornly going to keep repeating that. "Surely I haven't displeased you? Isn't it time someone finally took up Caesarion's cause? It seems that is the last duty I can render my fallen chief." He looked so dedicated, so determined.

"No, of course I am not displeased." I would just have liked to be consulted.

"Come!" he said, tugging on my arm. "Everyone has received honors today but you. Did you think you were forgotten?"

"I already have so much—what more can I be given?" Not that I would mind his making a present of Herod's entire country to me.

"You'll see. You must come to my apartments tonight. We will sleep there."

Arm in arm we traversed the corridors of the palace. A brisk wind was sweeping through the windows and porticoes, as if to bear away the stale odors of the riotous banquet. A number of Romans had indeed been sick, and the servants were scrubbing the steps and floors.

Antony's quarters were on the other side of the palace, overlooking the open sea and away from the Lighthouse. I knew he liked watching the ocean, and I knew he also needed a retreat from the rest of the palace, as if he had a private residence. This had met the requirements very nicely.

"Enter." Antony twisted open the doors and ushered me in, as if he were my private attendant.

I always liked coming here. He had furnished the rooms with tables, chairs, and chests from his estates in Rome. Much of it was old-fashioned, having been in his family a long time, but perhaps it made him feel less in exile. Part of him must feel that way, regardless of his affinity for life here. One would have expected him to have created a showcase of oriental luxury, with mother-of-pearl screens, brocaded cushions, pillowed couches, beaded curtains. Instead he lived in Republican propriety. He was a complex man.

He led me into an adjoining room. It, too, was austerely furnished. A large scroll lay on a table, another piece of paper under it. A single lamp had been left burning.

"The gift must be suited to the person," he said quietly. "I know many of the things you hold precious. It is my good fortune to be able to find them and give them to you—nay, to lay them at your feet." With that, he took the scroll and, going on one knee, indeed placed it at my feet.

I felt embarrassed. "There is no need for this," I said. But he remained kneeling.

"It is myself I lay at your feet. But you know that; you have known it for a long time. These are just tokens." He picked up the scroll and handed it to me.

I unrolled it. On the smooth parchment was a deed giving me the entire library of Pergamon. Pergamon, our rival, both in books and in paper.

"Pergamon!" I said. "The entire library?"

"Yes, all two hundred thousand volumes," he said. "They are to be transported here immediately."

"The finest in the world, outside of Alexandria . . ." I was dazed. "And now we will have it all!"

"I know a warehouse of books was destroyed in the fire on the docks when Caesar was here," he said. "I hope this can make up for the loss."

This was extravagant, like all his gestures. It took the breath away with its daring and generosity. "I . . . I thank you," I finally said. The Pergamon library, in its entirety!

"That was for your head," he said, rising and taking up the second piece of paper. What else could there be? "This is for your heart—or your eyes." He handed it to me like a child presenting a wilted bouquet of wildflowers.

It was a drawing of Hercules, beautifully executed, based on the famous statue by Myron.

"I know how you love sculpture, the capturing of the human form in bronze or stone, so that it remains forever held in its perfection. This, after all, is over four hundred years old—but his muscles are not withered, his belly does not sag, his legs are not weak."

Yes, only art could preserve youth and strength. Perhaps that is why we treasure it so. Already I was older than the Venus statue in Rome; it remained, I aged. How would I feel, seeing it now?

"I thank you," I said. How cherished he made me feel, knowing my heart's desires and trying to fill them.

"It should arrive within forty days," he said.

I looked at the paper. "But—" I already held it.

"This is not the gift!" He laughed. "No, the gift is the statue itself. The original. By Myron."

"What? But it is in the Temple of Hera on Samos!"

He shrugged. "I told you everything lies within my gift. I had it removed."

He had robbed the temple of its famous statue!

"It is being packed now, and—"

I threw my arms around him, almost knocking him off his feet. "You are a madman!" I cried. The Myron Hercules—to be brought here! "Oh, a madman!" I grabbed his head and pulled him down toward me. I kissed him joyfully. Then I let my hands go down his neck and embrace his shoulders, his magnificent wide shoulders. Even the Myron statue could not have better shoulders.

His arms tightened around me. I felt the same desire and eagerness that being held next to him could always evoke in me. It seemed a long time since we had embraced privately. We were so surrounded by people, so hemmed in by duties and official schedules, as well as our children, that we were seldom alone. Since he had returned from Armenia it had been one ceremony, meeting, or public appearance or obligation after another.

"Now, my Queen," he said, "let us give ourselves the best gift of all. Privacy, and time."

The quiet, empty, plain chamber seemed wildly exciting to me. No one would come in. No herald would announce a meeting. No Iras or Charmian or Mardian. Even Eros was nowhere to be seen.

"Come." He led me into his bedroom, which was surely as simple as anything of Cato's. We stood in the middle of the floor, kissing, running our arms up and down each other's back, thighs, shoulders. I rejoiced in the very feel of his body, in everything about it. There was not a single thing I would change. Marble might be eternal, but perishable flesh was warm.

His mouth on mine tasted better than all the delicacies of the banquet. His lips were a feast, and I drew out every morsel of pleasure from them. But unlike food, the more I took, the more I wanted.

I felt that I must possess him—must possess all that manly beauty, all that strength. But how? Simple possession is all very well for scrolls and statues, but for another person—how can we fully possess that? We have an instant in lovemaking when we feel we have achieved it, but it is not achievable . . . and so we fall away, separate and still wanting.

We fell on the bed, as hard as a camp bed set up in a common soldier's tent. Was it thus to remind him of who he was? We pulled at one another's clothes, as fevered as any simple infantryman and his local woman. I pushed at the stubborn tunic guarding his shoulders—why was it so sturdy, so tight? His sandals had been flung on the floor, and his strong bare legs twined about mine, pushing, straining. My sandals were gone also, and my feet traced patterns up and down his legs, lightly, teasingly.

I kissed the scars on his arms, his shoulders, leaning over to kiss his back where there were still more. I held out his right hand, touching the scar that marked the bad cut Olympos had treated. That precious hand, strong again now, that had almost been lost. I felt myself close to tears.

"O dear gods, it has been so long. . . ." I heard his faint words, spoken more to himself than to me.

The tunic was gone at last, and my gown, crumpled and discarded, was no longer between us. The delicious feel of flesh against flesh spread warmly over me. The weight of his body, the muscled heaviness of it, pressed against me. I rejoiced in it; he was still a lion, his power not spent, regardless of what his enemies hinted.

"I swear, by all the gods," he murmured, his mouth right beside my ear, "this is all I want, in all the world."

I could not think of anything else; the world had perished for me. I only wanted him—only him, to be possessed by me. To be part of me.

"My dearest," I said. I touched his hair, traced his face under my fingers. I could feel the bones underneath, could outline his eye sockets, his cheekbones. Every part of him was dear, even the parts I would never see and could only touch through the medium of its covering flesh.

"Keep me," he said. "For whatever you treasure and protect will endure."

Odd saying, odd request. But I barely heard it, for my yearning to possess him, even in the limited way flesh can, was so strong it was singing in my ears.

"Yes," I said. "Yes, of course . . ."

I felt him move on me, start the act that must always end, but at the time seems eternal, above all else.

"Ahh." He gave a cry of great happiness, asking nothing more than that moment which still lay before us.

67

"Be seated, my friends," said Antony, freshly barbered, bathed, and wearing a toga so new and white it looked bleached. He indicated the chairs drawn up around his worktable that gloomy day.

Plancus and Titius complied. They, too, were scrubbed and shaved, and wore their official clothing—the attire a governor assumed when he gave audiences and heard petitions in Syria and Asia.

Two scribes were hovering, and of course there were refreshments to hand, as if the work was going to be arduous. Outside a dismal rain was falling. It was winter in Alexandria. But that was preferable to winter in Antioch. At least it did not snow here.

Antony put on a long face. "In every man's life, there comes a time when . . . he must think of . . ." He turned his head toward the small mausoleum outside, adjoining the temple of Isis.

Plancus and Titius shifted on their seats, bracing themselves for Antony to announce his mortal illness. They looked at one another.

"Of late I have realized something . . . something I would rather not admit . . . but face it I must. . . ."

Now the two men listened alertly. Of what was he dying?

Antony hesitated so long it seemed as if he were struggling mightily with himself to divulge a shameful secret. "I do not have a will," he said flippantly. "And I need one."

Was it disappointment that crossed the faces of Plancus and Titius? I do not think so, as such, but there is a little corner in us that relishes morbid news—concerning others, that is.

"Oh," said Plancus.

"And since you hold my signet ring and are empowered to answer my official correspondence, I thought you and your nephew would make excellent witnesses. Are you willing to serve as such?"

"Yes . . . yes, of course." Titius gave a hearty assent.

"Now," said Antony, "I have already made a list, here, of my wishes, but of course they have to be translated into legal language." He waved a piece of paper, scribbled all over. "The scribes will do so, and you will hear my depositions from my own mouth." He looked at them. "Wine?" His hand hesitated over the pitcher.

"Not *now*," said Plancus, with high dignity, as if he had never worn the blue paint.

"Then let us proceed." Antony's eyes ran down the paper. "First, it is my wish that my eldest son Marcus Antonius shall inherit half my estate. . . ." He went on with the list of bequests to his minor children by Fulvia and Octavia. Why had he insisted on my being present? Of what concern was it to me? I did not begrudge his Roman children their Roman property.

"I furthermore desire that my sons Alexander Helios and Ptolemy Philadelphos shall each inherit one of my estates in Campania, and that my daughter Cleopatra Selene shall inherit my house on the Esquiline."

Now Plancus frowned. "Good sir," he said. The scribe stopped writing. "How can you will Roman property to these children? You know in Roman law—"

"Am I not the sole owner of it? Why may I not distribute it as I please? If I wished to burn it up and destroy it, I am within my rights to do so. Therefore, by extension, I should be able to dispose of it however I wish in any other fashion."

"But the law—"

"The law is outmoded and needs to be changed," said Antony airily. "Perhaps this will prove a stimulus for just that." He nodded to the scribe and repeated the bequests. "And now write this: that I affirm that Ptolemy Caesar is the true and legitimate son of the late Julius Caesar and thereby entitled to all his estate. The grandnephew Gaius Octavius should surrender said estate and restore it to its rightful owner, cease using the name of Caesar, and revert to his birth name of Gaius Octavius Thurinus."

Titius lurched forward. "This does not belong in your will! You have no right to dictate what property of others goes where."

"Do you object to my claim?" Antony was staring at him.

"That is just it, it is not *your* claim, it is a claim on someone else's behalf."

"He is my stepson, under my protection. I am his kinsman and Roman guardian, in the place of his fallen father. Who else should make it?"

"But it does not belong in a will!" Plancus sounded alarmed.

"Leave it be!" commanded Antony. "It is for the record only. After all— my will will not be read for many, many years." He smiled. "I intend to live as long as Varro."

Varro, the old historian, was already eighty-two and still writing, although he claimed it was "time to gather his baggage for the last journey." It would be quite a load of baggage, requiring a train of mules; he owned an extensive library.

"Then, sir, I suggest you retire from politics, as did he," said Plancus coldly. "Public life and long life seldom go hand in hand."

Antony stared at him. "Thank you, Plancus," he finally said. He took up his paper again. "Now, one last thing. At my death, after the customary funeral procession through the Forum, I wish to be brought to Alexandria, there to lie next to my wife. We will share a tomb."

Everyone was shocked into utter stillness, including me.

"Yes, sir," muttered Plancus finally.

"You have heard all these provisions," said Antony. "Now witness my seal and signature on the papers."

Obediently they watched as he made them official.

"I will deposit a copy of this with the Vestal Virgins for safekeeping. I want to ensure that what happened to Caesar does not happen to me; I want there to be no question about my wishes."

"Yes, sir."

"But in the meantime I must swear you to absolute secrecy."

"Yes, sir."

They left as soon as he released them.

When they were gone, I turned to Antony. I was shaken. "Why have you done this?" I asked.

"What, don't you want me buried beside you?" He put on a mock look of hurt.

"I mean—why did you announce all this to Plancus and Titius? They will never keep it to themselves."

"I don't mean them to. Let Octavian know we challenge him. Of course the will cannot be read publicly; the Vestals cannot release it. But just the rumors should cause him worry enough."

"Do you . . . do you really mean to be buried here? Abandon your family tomb in Rome?"

"You cannot be buried in it. You must be here, with your royal ancestors. And I would not be separated from you. I like it little enough in life. I will not have it in death."

I leaned against him. Outside, the cold rain was dripping. It was a tomblike day.

"I am touched," was all I could say.

"In three months I will be departing for Armenia, and from thence back to Parthia, this time to finish what I started last year. I would not leave or go into battle again without this—settled."

Another battle. More deaths. I was weary of it, and more apprehensive than ever. How much longer would Antony be guarded from harm?

"I have been attacked," said Antony, in wonder. He was holding a thick letter, direct from Rome. "Octavian has publicly attacked me!" He seemed stunned.

"What of it?" I said. I wiggled my fingers to be handed the letter, but Antony just kept clutching it.

"In public! In the Senate! He—you know he was to be Consul this year, as I was last year. But, just as I could not go to Rome to serve my term, and only 'served' one day, January first, so he has done the same. He is hurrying back to Illyria. But during that one day of office, he stood up in the Senate and—oh, here, read it yourself!"

He thrust the letter at me—at last. It was from Marcus Aemilius Scaurus, one of Antony's party in Rome, and a senator.

To the Triumvir Marcus Antonius, Imperator:

Greetings, and may this find you in good health. Most noble Antonius, I must report what happened yesterday during the one-day term of office of your colleague, G. Julius Caesar Octavianus. Back from Illyria, and limping from a war wound in his knee—which he kept displaying by coyly sticking his bandaged leg out of the fold of his toga—he took the floor and addressed us on "the state of the Republic." He was red-faced and seemed exceedingly angry: a sight I have never witnessed in the young man. Of course, it may have been an act.

He made sure to wear the laurel wreath, which the Senate had granted him the right to wear at all times, like Caesar, and kept touching it. (He has fine hands.) He launched an attack on you personally and on your actions. He accused you of giving away Roman territory, which is absolutely forbidden. He denounced your "Donations of Alexandria," as he termed them, and said:

"He has appointed his own children over Roman lands, not because of their abilities or loyalty to Rome—how could they be able or loyal, as they are only six years old?—and made them kings. Yes, he has made his children kings! And what does that make him—an over-king? It does not make him a Roman Consul! Roman Consuls and generals do not have kings and queens for children! Has he gone mad?" he said. "He must answer to these effronteries!"

Then he made a show of stepping down and resigning his Consulship, so that he could return to the frontiers and punish the enemies of Rome. Look for a letter from him soon.

I must warn you, that although you have much support here, people are indeed puzzled by your actions.

Your loyal friend, M. Aemilius Scaurus

I put it down. "So. Let us wait for this letter from Octavian."

Antony looked morose.

"Do not trouble yourself about it," I said. "It is all staged."

In due time two letters arrived, one official, one personal. In the official one, Octavian complained in lofty language about Antony's appointments in the east, and criticized his judgment. The personal one adopted a sneering tone.

> My dear brother-in-law,
>
> If you can rouse yourself from your bacchanals in the palace of Alexandria, your wife and children would certainly appreciate a letter from you—a novelty indeed. Or have you entirely forgotten your family and your duties in the arms of that Egyptian Queen? I seriously question your ability to shoulder your half of the world, judging from your recent behavior. Perhaps you should think of retiring and appointing a younger man to carry your burdens, before you stumble completely.
>
> I hope this finds you in good bodily health. Mentally I am afraid you may be in sore need of restorative rest—in the west. You will be most welcome at home, whenever you can find it in yourself to make the journey.
>
> > Your brother, and fellow Triumvir,
> > Imperator J. Caesar, Divi Filius
>
> P.S. Cease championing the claims of that bastard son of the Queen's. It is unworthy of you.

"The nerve!" yelled Antony. "Implying I am crazy!" He smacked the letter. "How dare he?"

"Stop yelling," I said, "or you *will* sound crazy."

"And what about the way he calls you 'that Egyptian Queen'—as if you didn't have a name!"

"He knows my name well enough," I said. "Just as he knows Caesarion's." I thought the attack was a good sign. It meant that we had touched a raw nerve, and he felt threatened by our claims.

"I'll answer right now!" shouted Antony.

"No, not now!" I said.

"Yes, now!" He grabbed a pitcher of wine and poured himself an enormous cup. "And in my own hand!" He rifled through his writing-box and extracted all the materials, then started writing furiously. Finally he thrust the letter at me.

> What's come over you? I suppose you're irked because I sleep with the Queen? Well, what of it? She is my wife. And anyway, what's new about it? Hasn't it been going on for nine years now? And, say, what about you? Is Livia your only bed partner? My congratulations to you if, when you receive this letter, you haven't been having it off with Tertulla or Terentilla or Rufilla or Salvia Titisenia, or

maybe the whole lot of them all together! Does it really matter to you where or with whom you have sex? Evidently not!

I burst out laughing. "What a picture—all of them at once. He must have a wall-to-wall pallet."

"He does. He likes a large gathering." Antony drained his cup, and poured another one.

"It's very funny, but it doesn't really answer the accusations."

"I don't care! Let him know I know the truth about his pious act. I will answer the political charges in a separate letter." He paused. "He doesn't even *mention* Armenia! Can it be so unimportant that I won a new province for Rome? What has *he* ever done that's comparable?"

Later, in a sober letter, he duly set out his complaints about Octavian, taking his stand on solemn promises and on strict legality. His fellow Triumvir had shown ill faith toward him, in refusing to send him the four legions he was owed under the terms of the treaty of Tarentum, in not allowing him to recruit new soldiers in Italy, in giving his veterans inferior land grants, and in unilaterally deposing Lepidus from office and appropriating all of Lepidus's territories and legions, rather than dividing them. All these failed to honor the terms of their alliance. As for Caesarion and Cleopatra—the Queen was his wife, and had been Caesar's, and Ptolemy Caesar was their legitimate son. But that was a different matter altogether from the legal misbehavior of Octavian in their partnership.

He sent it off, then left Alexandria to join Canidius with his legions in Armenia, preparatory to making another attempt on Parthia in concert with the Median king.

The shaky edifice of the Triumvirate was still—legally—standing, restraining both men from overt hostilities. However, the Triumvirate would expire in only another nine months. What would happen after that? The Republic was dead, in spite of sentimental talk about it. It had monumentally failed to resurrect itself after Caesar's death. Rome had been ruled by a dictator, then by three dictators—the Triumvirs—and now by two dictators. It was obviously reverting to one-man rule again. The only question was, which man would it be?

And the answer was the old, simple one: the man with the best army. Thus it had always been.

So I set about to strengthen the Egyptian fleet while Antony was away. The profits from the balsam groves would finance it nicely. We already had a respectable navy of some hundred ships, built primarily from the timbers of Cilicia. Now I must procure better ones from the mountains of Lebanon—

huge cypresses and cedars. I needed those longer timbers to build the larger ships. Agrippa had built a first-rate fleet with heavy ships. We must have equal-sized vessels; we must not paddle around in light boats like Sextus and get swamped and crushed.

I was convinced the fleet would be of key importance in any war. Agrippa had a mighty navy, and one always uses the weapons to hand. He was unlikely to let his ships sit idle in a conflict.

I visited the dockyards every few days, finding great satisfaction in seeing these wooden sea creatures taking shape on the shore. The walls of the largest, the "ten," rose high above me like a fort. The oars were fashioned from the trunks of the tallest pines to be had. The socket where the bronze ram would go was as big as an elephant.

"Majesty, just casting the ram is an art," the shipwright assured me. "To fashion a bronze beak of that size—it's hard to keep the metal from cracking. Cooling it is tricky."

It would take days before the success of any casting was known. Fitting the timbers, seasoning them, treating them with asphalt and binding the wood with sheets of lead to keep out worms—what a lengthy, expensive process!

Epaphroditus had warned me not to go overboard. "Forgive the pun," he had said. "But it is easy to go wild in shipbuilding. Sometimes I think ships are nothing but a funnel to send money directly to the bottom of the sea."

"I know," I said. "But we must have a first-rate navy!"

"First-rate means extravagant. Personally, I think you get more for your money with the army. Just the upkeep of ships is ruinous, and finding oarsmen—well, most men prefer the land. So the navy is a second-choice service."

"What about using slaves?"

He laughed. "If you want to bankrupt Egypt in one season. Slaves are much too expensive. Every time a ship sinks, think of the cost! No, it's far cheaper to pay oarsmen. Besides, slaves must be supported for life, whereas you need only hire the oarsmen as you go along, and for short periods."

"You are a hard-hearted wretch," I said.

"A finance minister has to be," he countered. "Let the chief of the physicians enjoy the luxury of a tender heart. But your generals and your finance minister—that's another matter." He laughed. "Can you imagine a general who flinched from battle?"

"Yes," I said. "Octavian."

"He can't be as cowardly as you make out. Are you sure of that?"

"Antony says at the battle of Naulochus, he lay belowdecks in a stupor of fear and had to be roused," I insisted.

"Are you sure he wasn't just seasick? Many normal men are. It is no disgrace."

"Why are you taking up for him?"

"I am not," he said. "I only want to point out that Antony was not there at Naulochus, let alone belowdecks on Octavian's ship, any more than Oc-

696

tavian is present in Alexandria at your banquets. We must be careful of believing what we have not seen for ourselves."

"Ah! You always act as my schoolmaster." Yet it was comforting to hear the viewpoint of someone who lived outside the palace.

As we strolled through the dockyard, under the shadows of the great ships, Epaphroditus pointed to the two just ahead of us. "It is possible that a war can be won by other means, and these powerful ships may be sunk with words. Gossip, lies, innuendo may do more harm than actual weapons, if they unman the opponent. The important thing is not to fall victim to your own manu-factured gossip." He paused. "For example, you must, by all means, put it about that Octavian is utterly contemptible as a man and a fighter. But never believe it. He would not be where he is, were he that negligible. Nor would you need these ships."

Epaphroditus was right, of course. The war of words and reputations, which swayed men's hearts, was an insidious one, and well worth winning. Already in Rome, I heard that various "meetings" were held to "discuss" Antony and the "African problem."

It was Mardian who was first alerted to these, and he came hurrying in to tell me.

"They are, of course, set up by Octavian's agents to appear spontaneous," he said, his wide brow furrowed. "That way he can claim to be responding to the wishes of the people."

"Well, what particularly are they saying?"

"Let the man speak for himself." He then dragged an unwilling youth in by the elbow. The slender reed of a man had to follow in Mardian's wake. "He is just off a ship from Ostia. But before that, he had a stand in the Forum, selling vegetables. He *claims* he came here to make a deal with our leek and fig merchants."

The youth jerked his arm away from Mardian's. "What, have I committed a crime? Is it against the law to walk the docks of Alexandria and try to arrange for a food shipment? Well, pardon *me!*" He brushed himself off. "Get this fat fellow off me!"

"Tell us what you know, and you shall have a free cargo of all the leeks and figs you want. We'll even throw in some Derr dates. Now, what about these public meetings in Rome? Have you attended any?"

"Oh, they're announced in the Forum. I get *invited* to all of them. But I've only been to one."

"Who announces them? Who invites you?"

He looked puzzled. "I don't know. Just—men. Respectably dressed men." "Senators?"

"How do I know? They aren't famous, if that's what you mean."

"And what do they discuss at these meetings?"

"I told you, I've only gone to one. In that one, people were talking about Antony and how he had deserted Rome, forgotten his duty, had turned into an eastern king. . . . I remember they claimed it was Carthage rearing its head once again."

"Carthage?" This was absurd.

"You know, Hannibal and all that . . . Africans attacking Rome."

I burst out laughing.

"It isn't funny," Mardian cautioned. "Don't forget the Dido and Aeneas story—the noble Roman seduced by a foreign queen. It's a favorite in Rome."

"Yes, because he rejects Dido and leaves her to die of a broken heart. I suppose that's what they'd like Antony to do to me!"

"Undoubtedly," said Mardian.

"So what else do they say?" I asked.

"That you are . . . uh . . . not virtuous."

"You mean they call her a harlot?" Mardian's usually silky voice was hard.

"Well, yes." He looked down at his feet. "They also say she's bewitched Antony, using eastern drugs. Made him her slave. As Hercules was unmanned by Omphale. Suddenly there are drinking vessels with the Omphale legend everywhere. Someone is circulating them. They show Omphale, the Queen of Lydia, wearing Hercules' clothes, and carrying his club, while the effeminate Hercules, dressed in a gown, walks beside her chariot under the shade of a parasol, carrying a spindle. He has been ruined, enslaved by the Queen, who plays the part of a man." He blushed. "The drinking vessels are finely made—from Arretium."

Arretium! Those vessels were expensive. Someone was paying dearly for it.

"What else?"

"Nothing. I don't know. I didn't pay all that much attention."

"Didn't you find it entertaining?" Mardian asked.

"Somewhat," he admitted. "But it gets repetitious after a while."

"Well, return to Rome and keep your ears open. We will see to it that some different and equally amusing gossip is soon bandied about."

Antony still had a large following in Rome, and there were plenty of agents willing to spread damaging stories about Octavian. Mardian and I compiled a list of them. I was glad Antony was not here; he would have objected. Now we could say what we wished without censure.

We put it out that Octavian was both cowardly and incompetent, relying on Antony (at Philippi) and Agrippa (at Naulochus) to do his fighting for him, while he cowered safely away from danger. He had broken every pledge. He was addicted to gambling, and so rapacious that he had condemned men to death just so he could get his hands on their fine furniture and Corinthian vessels, for which he had a special fondness.

As for his personal morality—it was unspeakable. First, he had sold his favors to Caesar in exchange for being named his heir, and then passed himself around to Caesar's friend Aulus Hirtius for another three hundred thousand sesterces. Then he had seduced the wife of Claudius Nero and married her scandalously when she was still pregnant with Claudius's child—

or was it Octavian's? And even that did not satisfy him. Nowadays he sent his agents out into the streets to procure women for him, stripping them naked and inspecting them like slaves. Sometimes even at dinner parties he could not control himself, but dragged a guest's wife off into his bedroom right before her astonished husband's eyes.

But what could you expect from a man whose father was a money-changer and whose mother ran a perfume and ointment shop? And whose great-grandfather was a *slave*?

And as for the charges about Antony and his Dionysus revels, at least he wasn't disrespectful to the gods—like Octavian at his Banquet of the Twelve Gods, where he dressed as Apollo and then led a riotous orgy. An insult, a monstrous affront to the gods!

I had balked at the charges about Caesar.

"He despised those lies!" I told Mardian. "His enemies trotted them out whenever it suited them! How can I perpetrate them?"

"Caesar believed in using the best weapon for the job," said Mardian. "If this can help you and Caesarion, well—it would be a worthwhile sacrifice."

Still, I hated it. But every bit of mud I could sling at Octavian must be used. "All right," I agreed reluctantly.

Soon Rome was buzzing with these allegations, while Octavian was off in Illyria, busying himself with his troops. It cost us a lot of money, but what is money for?

Both men were absorbed in military pursuits abroad while Rome boiled with their rivalry in blackening one another's names. In Alexandria, the perfect days passed, unmindful of what was happening in the rest of the empire. But my agents kept me well informed, and I was aware of every nuance in the capital: of Oppius (who well knew the truth! miserable traitor to Caesar) writing a pamphlet "proving" that Caesarion was not Caesar's; of people calling Octavian's patron not Apollo the Benefactor but *Apollo Tortor*, the Torturer; of others accusing Antony of perfidy in executing Sextus; of the snickering about Octavian using hot walnut shells to soften the hair on his legs. Octavian's men accused Antony's style of speaking and writing as being beset with "the stink of far-fetched phrases" in a most un-Roman manner; Antony's agents ridiculed Octavian for wearing built-up sandals to make himself taller. (I contributed that.)

Then, suddenly, Agrippa banished all the fortune-tellers and magicians from Rome. "We want none such here!" he had decreed. "Away with as-trologers and their false prophecies! Let them go back to the east, to keep the company they fancy, with those who worship beast-gods and other abom-inations!" Placards were circulated showing Antony and me with Anubis and Hathor crouched over us—Anubis with his jackal head and Hathor with her cow's ears. My agents managed to secure one for me, and I saw it for myself.

There were also poems about my being a Queen served by "wrinkled eu-nuchs" as "foul" as myself. It seemed I led a parade of perverted creatures—evil eunuchs, whores, beast-worshipers, soothsayers, and necromancers—in obscene rites. All the while I bedecked myself in jewels and perfumes and the kingdoms I had demanded of my drunken Roman general as the price of my favors—I, the *fatale monstrum*, fatal monster, of the east.

At first I found them amusing, if only for an exercise in imaginative writing. I was embarrassed about the eunuch remarks and took care to hide them from Mardian. But as time went on, the sheer venom in them became disturbing. Such a volume of hatred being released—were these the same people who had paid court to me in Rome when I was with Caesar? They had seen me with their own eyes, eaten with me, talked with me. Was it possible they could now believe these charges and hate me past all reason?

Weeks dragged by, and there was no word from Antony. Had he launched his attack on Parthia? Where was he now?

Finally the strain became almost unbearable, and I told my household that I was going to the mineral springs to bathe and rest. The new-style Roman baths were gaining favor everywhere, with their hot- and cold-water rooms, but they seemed too artificial for me. I preferred the ancient, natural springs.

"I suppose the Romans would say I am just returning to my primitive, bestial origins," I said. "Or perhaps I go to indulge in sensual orgies. And I must not forget my jewels."

"You must not wear your silver into the water!" said Mardian. "It will tarnish."

I laughed. "Not you, too! I was only joking. I have no intention of taking to the waters with jewelry on."

I would take Charmian and Iras with me. They had little pleasure of late, and would benefit from the health-giving waters.

Now, looking back, I know it was the last time I was ever to sport and play in Egypt, a free creature, with no one watching. It had been so when I was a child, but less so lately. The court in Alexandria was not private, and was always a stage. But the waters were always waiting, patiently, and if I did not seek them it was my own fault. Later I would be unable to seek them, long for them as I may.

The thick stone columns of the grotto soared to the roof of the cave where the waters bubbled out. Inside it was hushed and solemn, and the sunlight, diffused and gentled with blue, washed over the walls. The warm water spilled out into a wider basin, and from it, over a lip into a still lower pool. Where it originated inside the cave it was hot, but in flowing out, and then into lower pools, it cooled to the same temperature as the body. So, when I submerged myself in it, I had no sense of my arms or legs ending and the water beginning; it was all one. I was floating and moving in a pillow that was myself.

How restorative it was!—although not at once. My nerves were so jangled that when I first lay in the water and began to move slowly through it, I was impatient to get to the other side. Reaching it, I clung to the rim of the pool, letting the gurgle of the outflow wash over me. What an odd smell it had; how smooth it made the skin feel. Back I went a second time, then a third. By the fourth or fifth time I felt calm, as if whatever suffused the water had penetrated below my skin, subtly soothing me. The water was tinged a blue-green, different from the ocean, different from the Nile. Whatever magic mineral was within it must impart that tint.

Back and forth, back and forth . . . the rhythm of it lulled my thoughts, letting them uncoil like a serpent coaxed from his basket.

Serpents . . . the temple of Re, and old Ipuwer . . . had the snakes been caged now? Or did they still play freely on his floor? And his prediction, about Egypt and its gods . . . long ago, the Kandake and the cobra. Her promise to stand by Egypt against Rome, her warnings about Rome . . . what would she think of Antony? Could there be a good Roman in her opinion, or were they all bad? Would she join us against Octavian, or just remain aloof?

Rome. Why could we not just secede from the empire? Why could the eastern half not just drift away on its own? Were we in the first stage of that? Perhaps, when all the smoke of talk and shield-thumping was done, that was just what would happen; the east and the west would float in opposite directions, just as Charmian and I passed one another in the cloudy water, lazily.

I would be just as happy to let it develop so, but Antony's roots were Roman. And Caesar's son—how could he ignore Rome? Still, it would be better to turn their faces away and forget it.

But birth and obligations would not permit it.

I sighed. Under the bright Egyptian sun, held in the loving waters, it all seemed very simple.

I lay on a shelf of warm rock beside the pool, and let myself be rubbed with thick towels, down to my fingertips and toes. Each muscle was kneaded, pressed, caressed. A lotion, as thin as milk and smelling of crushed lilies, was dribbled onto my back and then smoothed around my flanks and shoulders. I felt it was transforming me into ivory, whitening my skin and making it sleek. I sighed, and pillowed my face on my forearms. The delicious scent, the warmth, the relaxed tingle of my skin—all made me sleepy and suspended my thoughts.

When I awoke, it was twilight. The hours had disappeared, and I was restored.

There was only one thing missing from the mineral spring, and I vowed to supply it. We needed sunken columns in the water, so we could swim around them and rest there, like mermaids or sea nymphs.

In Alexandria my world had changed in only the few days I had been away. A letter had come from Antony: Octavian had replied to his charges, refuting them all. It was a stinging rebuke and an open challenge.

Dearest Wife:

I was on the banks of the Araxes—remember that river, and my tent?—ready to launch my troops, combined with those of the Median king, and make good my promise to invade Parthia, when the messenger came from Rome. Octavian has thrown it all back in my face. He no longer cares to keep the appearance of amity between us. Here is what he says:

In answer to my overall charge that he has broken our agreements, he is silent. In particular, I said Lepidus had been deposed without due consultation, his legions, revenues, and territories appropriated by Octavian; he replies that Lepidus was justly deprived of office. I said I was entitled to a half share in Sicily and Africa, and he said I could have it when I gave him half of Armenia. I said he refused my veterans their allotted land in Italy; he replies that they shouldn't need it, because "their rewards lie in Media and Parthia which they have won by their gallant campaigns under their commander."

My hopes for an eastern campaign are dashed. I cannot fight a war on two fronts. I must abandon my dream and mobilize to counter Octavian. I have ordered Canidius to withdraw the sixteen legions and follow me to Ephesus. There, with my officers and fleet, I will have to prepare for the coming clash.

My dream! My goal! My debt to Caesar, to carry out his plans! All shelved, perhaps forever. I feel tricked by fortune.

Gather the Egyptian fleet and send it to me at Ephesus. Only then can I take stock of what resources we have.

O cruel, teasing Tyche!

Will you come as well, my dearest? But if business in Egypt precludes, so be it.

My love, M. Antonius

I stared at the letter, blinking. So. It had begun. Octavian moved swiftly, decisively, once he made up his mind. He was casting Antony and the mask of the Triumvirate aside; he was strong enough now not to need them to hide behind.

How fortuitous that I had already built the extra hundred ships!

68

Blue, blue, blue—as brilliant and deep in color as sapphires, the sea around Ephesus gleamed in the sun. And on it rode my fleet, its tall masts reflecting brokenly in the waves, its gilded sterns and bronze rams coating the water in reflected metal. Like an army, which ranged from generals to foot soldiers, the ships under my command went from the heights of my flagship, the *Antonia* (what else?), to low Liburnian galleys whose oarports barely cleared the water. I had left no gaps in the fleet, no size or type unrepresented. It must prevail; I could leave nothing to chance.

The sea, and ships—once again they loomed very large in my life. Once again they carried more than my person on them, they carried my fate.

There were two hundred of them, and Antony was rounding up more from everywhere: the remnants of the old fleet of Sextus, the seventy ships returned by Octavian, the ships of Rhodes, Crete, and the Roman squadrons stationed at Cyprus.

"It will be the largest fleet ever assembled!" Antony said in wonder, as he shaded his eyes and, standing at the harbor of Ephesus, saw the ships riding at anchor, awaiting his inspection.

"Should we use it to take the offensive and attack Rome while Octavian is away?" It seemed a perfect opportunity. Rome was unguarded, its would-be master far away in Illyria, the people still undecided about him. Antony had many supporters there. If we sailed, and landed with a large army . . .

"No," said Antony decisively. "The sailing season is past."

"Yet ships sail even in winter—sail, and reach their goals, too. For such a prize, it might be worth the risk." Rome was there, a luscious red apple, hanging heavy on its bough, awaiting a hand bold enough to snatch it.

"What is my justification?" he asked. "War has not been declared."

"Who shall decide when it is declared? You—or Octavian?"

"My troops have not yet arrived," he said. "Canidius has not come with the sixteen legions, and I am awaiting another seven from Macedonia. The client kings are only just now on their way here. All I have is a small force."

"Could you not get a message to Canidius to hurry? Or to send the best legions on ahead?"

"The effort would be too patched together. All the ships are not even here."

"You must move with speed. Strike swiftly with a small force, and they will count as many times their size with the element of surprise."

I felt in my bones that now was the moment, uniquely presented to us almost as a gift. Genius was knowing when to grab.

But Antony shook his head. "I cannot invade Italy with foreign ships and soldiers. The whole land would unite against us."

"What you mean is that you cannot invade Italy with me at your side."

"Yes. That is precisely what I mean. It would not be tolerated—no, never. Unless you would consent to stay behind—"

"Impossible. I would have to be there from the beginning, else I would always be seen as a usurper." What I could not say was that if he left me behind, it would be too easy for Octavian to offer him glowing terms if only he would disavow me. It had happened before. I hated myself for not trusting him, but he had such an innate desire to please people, and Octavian was so devious and persuasive.

"You will always be seen as that," he said unhappily.

"After the fact, people may find me more palatable," I said. "The truth is, they liked me well enough when I lived in Rome! No name-calling then; no talk about my being foreign. They knew I was more civilized and cultured than they were. Even Horace and Vergil came calling. They will do so again. But first the battle must be won!"

"It will be," he insisted. "But I must wait for Octavian to come to me. He must be the aggressor. We will draw him away, far from his base of supplies. The farther, the weaker he will be. His vulnerability lies in his poverty. He cannot afford to pay his troops; his very army may collapse soon. He is desperate for money; he will have to disband his Illyria legions and make provision for them out of an empty treasury. Fighting a faraway war is the most expensive venture he can undertake. Just transporting the troops and providing for them in the field may be beyond him. They will mutiny, and at home there will be unrest."

It was sound, and reasonable. But Octavian had a way of coming up with inspired, short-term solutions that bought him time.

"How far away do you plan to lure him? I won't have him in Egypt!"

"Greece," said Antony. "Greece is just over the line that divides our jurisdiction. He will have to cross the line to attack us, and that will make him clearly the aggressor."

"Who cares about the legality? Everyone knows this is a civil war. What difference does it make who is labeled the aggressor? And who is to do the labeling?"

"The Senate," he said. "I want to be seen as the innocent party."

"After the battle is won or lost, the spineless Senate will say and do whatever the victor orders it to. It will declare Agrippa to be Helen of Troy if it's told to. Forget the Senate, and concentrate on the battle!" Why could he not see the Senate for the powerless thing it was?

"We won't attack," he said stubbornly. "We will wait to be attacked. We will use our huge fleet to prevent Octavian from ferrying his troops across, and cut off supplies to the few survivors who manage to get here."

"You surprise me," I said. "You are a land general—the finest one living. To rely on the fleet is—unexpected. Agrippa is on the sea what you are on land; he may not tamely submit to the scene you have written for him."

"He won't have any choice," said Antony. "He cannot change geography. The fact is that Italy is west of here, and he will have to cross the wide Ionian Sea to get within striking distance of us. And we will be waiting, fresh and fit. We can afford to wait, and let the damaged and demoralized enemy come to us."

Waiting was not my favorite mode of action, or Antony's. In some ways waiting was much more demanding than a quick strike, since it involved keeping an army motivated and in good condition through months of inactivity. And Antony's army was now made up heavily of non-Romans, as a result of Octavian's blocking his recruiting privileges in Italy. How loyal would they be to a Roman general? How fervently would they follow him? I did not like it. But I was overruled. I tried to tell myself that he had more experience in the field than anyone else, and that had to outweigh my misgivings.

At first he had been morose about Octavian, with the peculiar sadness that comes in feeling betrayed. The sudden personal attack had left him stunned. My arrival in Ephesus found him sunk in agitated gloom.

The beautiful city was lost on him. I found it to be most pleasing, with its formal harbor reception gates and broad street leading from the docks toward Mount Pion, where the city wrapped itself around the base. Lovely houses climbed up the slopes, and the section of the city that lay on the flat ground near the harbor had an impressive commercial agora near the theater, while the administrative center of the city was located higher up the mountain. Best of all were the fields surrounding it, uneven with craggy rocks and hollows, pierced with tall cypresses, their dark green almost a living black punctuating the landscape. And always there was the shining sea, shining with that glowing sunlight that reflects and diffuses here as in no other spot on earth. Islands and peninsulas swam in the magic water.

I would persuade him to go beyond the city walls with me and sit on the hillside, warmed by the moss on the rocks, and watch the clouds racing in the enormous sky, recorded in shadows on the changing sea.

Then he would forget his melancholy, losing himself in the hypnotic passage of patterns in the sky, soothed by the stillness unbroken except for the bells of goats foraging in the crags.

"Ah," he said, taking my hand, "sometimes I think I would be happy in banishment—if I were in a place like this, with you beside me."

We did not take enough time to look up at the sky as we went through our days. It is a common enough failing, but I wondered why. Why do we so persistently look down at our feet?

"I would not care to be banished," I said. "Banishment means never to touch foot on your home shores again."

"Perhaps we are too attached to home," he said. "Perhaps it would be pleasing to rove forever."

I was not happy to have left all the children behind for—how long? Banishment was not for me. I was too rooted in Egypt. Yet as I looked over at him, I knew he spoke the truth for himself. He was at heart an ordinary man who had been called to an extraordinary position, and sitting in the fields, looking at the sea and sky contented him well enough. Perhaps at base he simply did not desire to rule Rome—or desire it enough to make it come about.

To rule, to prevail, you had to want it above all else, to know that nothing less would satisfy. It was very bad when your rival felt that way and you did not.

"To rove happily, you must never look back on what you have left behind," I finally said.

Ephesus was where his personal journey to power had started, when he came there after Philippi, flushed with success, being hailed as Dionysus for the first time. Now it had all come round again, and another beginning was beckoning. But for now he sat on the hill with the herds of goats and watched the clouds pass overhead.

One morning in Ephesus I had seen it: the imposing, eight-sided tomb that reared up beside the most heavily traveled street. Shoppers from the lower agora brushed by it, hugging their baskets to themselves, as did officials from the upper town, striding purposefully past. It seemed to partake of all the life around it: women rested on the steps circling its base, children played around it, and old men leaned their bent backs against its sides. "Meet me at the Octagon," was a popular saying.

"What is this?" I had asked the magistrate showing me his city, but in some dreadful way I already knew. Its shape was too familiar—the octagon, with its round tower supported by columns and its crowning figure. I had seen it all my life, every day: the Lighthouse of Alexandria.

"It is a tomb, Most Exalted One," my host said, smiling nervously.

I broke away from him and examined the carvings around its base. Mourning scenes: a young woman surrounded by friends, who were clearly grieved at her passing. In the background was a huge temple.

"And what is that?" I pointed at it, letting my fingers brush over the raised surface. Recently carved, too. The edges were still sharp.

"Why, it is the great Temple of Artemis, the magnificent, the wonder of the world! Have you not seen it? Oh, Majesty, I must take you there! And to think you have not gazed on it yet! Yes, we must—" He chattered on like a gushing fountain.

"Who is buried here?" Would he tell me the truth, or attempt to cover it up?

"It is—it is—a young woman," he said, trying to sound vague.

"And a rich one, too, I see," I said. "Perhaps her father was a magistrate? Or a wealthy merchant?"

"Uh . . . yes, that he was." His head bobbed up and down.

"I suppose a king could be described as a magistrate, and a wealthy merchant," I said. "For this is the daughter of Ptolemy, is it not? The princess Arsinoe? And this tomb recalls the Lighthouse of her native city." My sister, sent to this tomb by my request.

Yes, one must want power, and want it above all else, in order to prevail.

706

One must not quail at sending a sister to the executioner, if she has proved to be treacherously aiming for one's throne. Antony was not capable of such ruthlessness—although he had done it at my bidding. It was he who had ordered her taken from the asylum at the temple and put to death—at my request.

Now, looking at her tomb, knowing that she lay inside it, imprisoned there in death, I felt both relief (in recognizing that she would unhesitatingly have done the same to me), and sorrow at what I had proved myself capable of doing. There was also regret for any life that is so short. She had been twenty-five.

"Yes, Majesty." He hung his head, as if somehow it had been his doing.

"She was popular here?"

"We—yes, she was popular here." He had given up trying to put another face on it.

"Beauty wins many friends," I said lightly. People warmed to a pleasing face; they preferred a dishonest beauty to a trustworthy plain person. You can see it even in taverns; a comely hostess serving mediocre food has many customers. Especially if she is personable as well.

I trailed my hand along the polished stone. *Arsinoe was in there.* "Hail, and farewell, sister," I said, so softly only the dead could have heard it.

That night, in the fine house we had been given on the slope leading up to the state agora, I was quiet. I tried to pass it off to Antony as weariness, and indeed I was very tired. I had had little time to put all the kingdom's affairs in order and make provision for my absence after Antony's summons came. Then the sea voyage, in late autumn, had been trying. The fact that Antony, with his perennial optimism, was standing on the brink of war against Octavian was a startling relief, but it had happened so suddenly. I felt I had to hurry to him and bolster his resolve before he changed his mind or talked himself out of it, making excuses for Octavian again. But it had left me exhausted.

"What is it, my love?" Antony had asked, glancing up from his papers to see me staring uncharacteristically out into space.

"I am tired," I said. "I think I will go to bed early."

"Yes, I am sure you are tired. Such a journey, at this time of year! I told you, you need not come. . . ."

"As if I would have stayed away." I reached up and brushed away the hair falling over my forehead. Even that seemed a vast effort.

My feet were propped up on a footstool, and Antony came over to me and took off my sandals. He started rubbing my feet.

"Sometimes this will wake you up," he said. "It sends the blood back into your head."

At that very moment, Titius appeared in the room. Antony looked up at him, but kept holding my feet.

"Yes?" he said.

"Imperator, I have received the promise of King Amyntas of Galatia to contribute at least two thousand cavalry to our . . . effort," he said smartly. But I saw his eyes fasten themselves on my feet, although he did not move his head.

"Good," said Antony. "They are the finest in the east." He let go of my feet and stood up. "I trust the others will commit themselves soon, in terms of numbers." He nodded proudly toward me. "The Queen has arrived."

"I am pleased to see you, Your Majesty," he said. His smile was smooth and charming.

He and Antony drew aside and discussed army details.

I continued sitting there, thinking about Arsinoe. She had given me no choice. Had she been content with her lot in life—as princess, not queen—she would be living still, not shut up in that tomb. But it is rare to be satisfied to stand on the platform next to the highest position. I knew Antony would be happy enough with half the world. But Octavian would have all or none, and would not leave him in peace. It was just as well. I was like Octavian myself—as Arsinoe's tomb silently attested. Now we could grapple, with the whole world as a prize, and Antony could not demur.

We argued at the Great Temple of Artemis, letting all that beauty witness our quarrel. We had started out happily enough, pretending to be ordinary sightseers on the sacred way that wound around the mountain to the temple over a mile away. I was surprisingly excited to be seeing it. I say "surprisingly" because there are those who assume that nothing has the power to stir an Alexandrian, as we are sophisticated, jaded, and sated with the wonders of our own city.

There were, of course, throngs of visitors, since the temple was renowned all over the world. The westerners came to see the architecture, to behold the white marble columns as high as cedars and as dense as a real forest, to marvel at the artistry that had conceived it, and at the engineering that had translated dreams into stone. The easterners came to do homage to the great Artemis, the mother who in this manifestation was a mighty and demanding earth goddess, allied with Cybele Magna Mater, who brought fertility but at the same time demanded that her priests be castrated. She was nothing like the Greek Artemis, the virginal huntress, but was more tuned to the dark rhythms of women and their moon-cycles.

There had been a temple at this site as long as men could remember; an earlier one built by King Croesus had burnt down on the night Alexander the Great was born. When the power of the goddess was questioned—how could she have permitted her temple to be destroyed, if she was so mighty?—the story was told that Artemis had been away that night, attending the birth of Alexander. Be that as it may, when Alexander himself came here, he offered to help rebuild the temple. But his offer was refused, on the grounds that it was not fitting for one god to build a temple to another.

Now, as we rounded a curve in the road, the temple appeared before us, enormous, looming, dazzling. Coming upon it suddenly seemed to magnify it. The clear Aegean sunlight intensified the white until it exploded like a fiery moon upon our eyes. Everyone halted in wonder.

"It is all men say," I murmured. I took Antony's hand; somehow when we gaze on high beauty we want to touch another person, to ground ourselves.

As we approached, the temple grew until it seemed to fill the sky. I had read that the slender columns, more than a hundred of them, were sixty feet high. I knew the temple measured as long and wide as our gigantic Gymnasion. But knowing and seeing—ah, how different!

A fleeting thought as we drew closer, and the atmosphere of the temple enveloped us: How stern and beguiling a mistress is the love of beauty; what sacrifices she demands of her adherents. Yet we seek beauty in order to possess and serve it with the same fervor we seek food and territory. It was the beauty of Helen that had called forth the Trojan War. Helen herself said very little— as little as the statue in the temple we now approached. Beauty is entire of itself; it does not need to add speech.

The temple was elevated on three platforms that served as steps; the first platform itself was taller than a man. The longest side of the temple was as long as the side of the pyramid of Cheops; the sheer weight of the building must be almost unmeasurable.

"And to think this was built on a swamp," said Antony. "And that the temple has not sunk into it—not yet."

Yes, I knew that Theodoros, who had solved a similar problem with the Temple of Hera in Samos, had laid down alternating layers of hides and coal in the bog to serve as a foundation. But how that could support such weight?

Like many lovely things, we found as we came near it, the temple had an unworthy setting. True, the sea nearby made a fitting frame, but the people swarming on the grounds were a motley sort. The temple and its environs offered asylum, and all manner of men took advantage of it. Along with runaway slaves, political troublemakers and thieves betook themselves here, where they could live for years, begging and making pests of themselves. They were bold, knowing they could not be touched. They called to us as we passed, shoving themselves forward and demanding money.

"I'll show you the goddess!" one cried, tugging at my gown. "I know all about her! She is old, very old!"

"For this I should pay you?" said Antony, with a laugh. "Tell me something I don't know."

"Yes, sir, that I can—" He reached into the folds of his mantle and drew out a silver statuette. "Here, the likeness of the goddess, pure silver, that I swear—touch it, see for yourself—"

Antony brushed him aside, only to be met with another, springing up like the warriors sown from the dragon's teeth.

"Very good, sir, this Artemis is pure silver, fashioned by my son, studied in Rhodes, yes—"

"Go away," said Antony. To me he observed, "And to think once the legendary Amazons took refuge here, and the philosopher Heracleitus, and later the citizens of Ephesus stretched a rope from here to their acropolis to extend the sanctuary—making the entire city an asylum. Then these vermin were multiplied a hundredfold!"

Nearer the temple they were joined by hordes of castrated priests who served the goddess, as well as other orders of priests selling pieces of the sacrificial meat, and the famous prostitutes who claimed to help men worship the goddess carnally. The official virgin priestesses ignored them, weaving through them as though they did not exist.

Here was where Arsinoe had taken asylum, hiding behind the robes and office of the chief priest. But she had been dragged out on Antony's orders. I wondered if the sight of Roman soldiers penetrating the sanctuary had caused the others to tremble—or had they tried to sell them Artemis statuettes, too?

But Antony was not the only one to violate the sanctuary; the great Alexander had, too, making three criminals face their deaths.

We passed through the closely packed columns in the front of the temple. They looked like the ones in Thebes, where they clustered so thickly there was no sense of being in a hall. It was said they had to be so close in order to support the heavy stone beams serving as a roof, and that the weight of the lintel was so great that the architect had been overcome by the task of raising it—that he had thought of suicide. But Artemis (of course!) had raised it for him. Around the base of the columns were exquisite carvings of heroes, nymphs, and animals.

Inside the temple, a profound coolness and hush. There was a courtyard open to the sky in the middle, and then the goddess herself reigned in the back recesses of the temple. Here she was surrounded by winking lamps and offerings of flowers.

She was not gigantic as I would have expected from the scale of the building, although she was more than life-size. But she was utterly unlike our Grecian idea of movement and fluidity; she was closer to the deep stillness of the Egyptian god statues. Her body was not that of any normal woman, but stiff and straight like a mummy case, and covered with dozens of breasts, which festooned her chest like swollen bags. On her lower body—or rather, the garment covering that blocky body—were griffins and lions. Her face, impassive and strong, looked straight ahead, and there was no hint of love or softness about her—strange for a mother. On her head a temple-headdress reared up, looking like a tower. She looked mysterious, ancient, and disturbing.

I felt, suddenly, the power of the east that was so threatening to Rome. It was not the present-day armies they were fearful of, but the primitive gods and peoples behind them—shadowy forces that had yet to be entirely tamed. This statue, with its unhuman body, its castrated priests, its links with something lost in time but fertile, dark, and demanding, was frightening.

"I don't like her," I whispered to Antony. Seeing her made me think of secret rites, blood spilled, daughters violated and sons unmanned, all to satisfy her. But she would be insatiable, as the earth is insatiable for our bodies even as it feeds and sustains us—because it knows it will eventually devour us. This Artemis was a stern devourer.

"Don't let her hear you," said Antony, in jest.

The sightless eyes of the goddess seemed to be aimed in our direction.

We turned and left her on her pedestal, at stiff attention.

Outside, on the temple platform, I lingered to study the figures carved into the bases of the columns. A light breeze whispered, and the still-flat surface of the sea was a shining sheet reflecting the late afternoon sun.

Antony stood impatiently, shifting his weight from side to side, crossing his arms and drumming his fingers. When I am with someone who is eager to be gone, it is difficult to lose myself in art. With a sigh, I turned from the columns. I would return another day. But I was annoyed, and as soon as he spoke, I disagreed with him.

"All this," he was saying, gesturing with his hand toward the soaring columns, white as milk, "is what they do not understand."

What was he talking about? And why must he talk, instead of letting me enjoy the carvings? "Who? Who does not understand what?" I said, hoping for a short answer.

Instead he launched into a list of his misgivings about the Senate, and how they must be made to understand—and approve of—his actions here in the east.

"It is different here," he said. "These ancient kingdoms—they do not wish to become modern, to do away with their kings. Just because Rome will have no king does not mean others must follow suit."

Well, what of it? "Yes, true," I concurred.

"The Romans do not understand the territorial grants I made in Alexandria," he said.

So that was what this was about! Before I could say anything, he went on.

"But they must be made to understand—and approve. I will announce it in a letter, which the new Consuls will read to the Senate when they take office. Thanks be to all the gods that the two Consuls for next year are my men—my admirals Sosius and Ahenobarbus. I will address the Senate through them! They will take my part against Octavian!"

Why was he so obstinate, so blind? I looked longingly at the carvings; hopeless to focus on their pristine beauty now. "Curse the Senate!" I said, too loudly.

Heads of others on the platform turned, straining to hear what would follow. Even Antony was brought up short.

"I—" he began, casting about for words. "The Senate—"

"The Senate ceased to have any moral authority when it stood by and saw Caesar murdered," I snapped. "Now most of those members are gone, and have been replaced by—what? Little men who know only envy and equivocation and timidity. Forget them! Even if they supported you, it would mean nothing."

"The constitution of Rome abides with the Senate," he said quietly. "But of course, I cannot expect *you* to understand!"

"It's you who do not understand!" I shot back. "You cannot see the changes that have swept over Rome, and that they are permanent. The Senate's authority is gone, it's as cut off as—these priests' manhood!" I indicated a passing priest, hurrying down the steps. He glared at us.

"They are the only authority left," he maintained stubbornly.

"They are the only *semblance* of authority left. But it is only the shadow of authority. The Senate died along with Caesar. And it didn't even have an official funeral."

Angrily he strode down the steps. Whenever he heard something he did not fancy, he rejected it.

I followed him. "Don't run away from me when I am talking to you!" I said. If any of my subjects had dared do such a thing . . .

I caught up with him. We were still in the temple precincts, and a quarrel seemed out of place. "People are looking," I said. "Behave yourself!" Had he no thought for our reputations?

"I don't care!" He stamped away.

"You must maintain decorum!" I said. "You are not an adolescent roaming the streets of Rome with Curio now! If you would rule the world—"

He turned on me. "It's you who would have me rule the world!"

Now a large crowd was staring, and listening. I fell silent, and began walking swiftly by his side. This must be suspended until we were in private.

Alone that night, in our spacious house so graciously provided by one of the city councillors, Antony appeared to forget the tiff. He was high-spirited, drinking too much wine, eating too much, and laughing too much. I saw through it, and waited for us to resume the argument—or conversation.

This particular dining room had a mosaic featuring bits of food meticulously rendered, so it looked like droppings from a banquet—there were bones and fruit skins and shellfish littering the floor. It was much in fashion at the time, and I appreciated the artist's skill in depicting the food, although I thought it rather wasted. Why portray garbage? But Antony, as he drank more, became fascinated with it, and started dropping his own food on the floor.

"Why, I can hardly tell the difference!" he said, watching a melon rind wheel across the floor and finally lie still next to a bunch of mosaic cherries. "Look!"

He leaned on his forearms and studied it carefully.

"Even the twins have outgrown such behavior," I said, more sharply than I intended. "Now you are on a level with Philadelphos."

He cocked his head. "They say infants have great wisdom," he said. "And how many grown people wish they had time to play?"

"It seems you must be either an infant or the ruler of the world to do so. All the people in between do not have the luxury."

"Ah . . . the ruler-of-the-world business again. I knew it was bound to come up." He heaved himself up on his elbows and gave a half-smile. "Well, I am ready. Tell me of my high destiny." He reached out and took his goblet, peering into its depths. He sloshed some more wine into it and drank it down.

"Antony, you drink too much." There, I had said it.

He laid his hand over his heart. "You wound me," he said, looking stricken.

"It is true. It is not—not good for you." What I wanted to say was that when he was younger it had not affected him, but now . . .

I expected him to argue, but he did not. "I know," he said. But that did not stop him from filling his cup again. "But I like the way it sets my mind free . . . lets it roam where it will . . . and sometimes it shows me wisdom, or a new way." He swallowed it down. "And sometimes it just puts me to sleep," he admitted. He held out the goblet. "Farewell, fair friend—since Cleopatra will have it so." He put it down ceremoniously, carefully. "And to think that we are in a region with the world's best wines nearby. Lesbos and your sweet nectar, Chios with your magic grape, you must come no more!"

"Why must you go to extremes?" I asked. "You do not have to banish it from your life altogether. Just moderate it."

Now he spoke altogether seriously. "There are some of us with a temperament that precludes moderation. We must have a total embrace, or a total forsaking." He stood up. He was not unsteady, and his words were clear. "Had I not been such a man, I would not be here now, with you. I would have played with you, enjoyed our time together, but never pledged myself. That would have made Rome happy. Rome—which was all too pleased to see you as my mistress, but horrified to see you as my wife. I spit on such conventions."

"Why then, oh, why, do you then ache for their approval? If you do not approve of *them*, why should they approve of you?" Why should we wish those we do not respect to respect us?

"I do not know," he said. "In Rome, we reverence our mothers above all others. And for good or ill, Rome is my mother."

By now I had risen from the table, too, and he embraced me, folding me close to him. I leaned against him, wishing there was something I could do to lessen his pain. It was clear he must displease his mother, Mother *Roma*, at least the Rome as she now was. But mothers had a way of rejoicing in the feats of wayward sons, if they were only successful.

"You underestimate the love of a mother," I finally said. "She will never abandon you. Rome will welcome you. Rome is not the Senate, nor is she Octavian. You are as Roman as either of them. And when you prevail, and return victorious to the hills of Rome—"

"Ah, that again." he sighed. "It always comes to that."

"Yes, it comes to armies," I said. "Rome has always been about armies. The history of Rome is the story of her armies."

Arms about each other's waists, we wove our way slowly to bed, picking our steps carefully. My reluctant Imperator, my jolly Dionysus, quiet now, subdued . . . he seemed to wish only to sleep. The weight of what he must do pressed down on him, and he had sought the wine in order to be free. And I had spoiled it, ruined his escape.

But as he lay silent beside me, I felt his arm tighten underneath my head. His fingers reached out and began to play with my hair. It made my skin tingle.

"A woman's hair . . ." he began, speaking to himself. "Most beautiful of all her jewels."

I lay silent, my eyes closed. Let him do what he wished. I loved him so—I only wished the best for him. Why could he not understand that?

"My Queen," he finally said. "I have never really grown used to having a queen in my bed."

And I had never grown used to having a hearty mortal in mine.

"Then we are forever new to one another," I whispered. "May it remain so." And I kissed him in such a way that he knew how greatly I prized and desired him.

He did not disappoint me in his response.

<hr />

69

We got up the idea of an excursion to Pergamon.

"I'll present it all there," said Antony. "I'll explain my plan on the way. They will be more receptive if we are on an outing."

I was dubious. "I will enjoy the theater, but why must you pander to them in that way? You act like a father who is afraid of his children. They can listen well enough in Ephesus."

"No, I must sweeten the pill."

The pill consisted of the Donations of Alexandria, all wrapped up in his Armenian conquests. A letter to the Senate, outlining both, would be dispatched by the new year. They would rejoice in the new province, while approving the depositions of territory—so the theory went.

"Very well." I knew better than to argue with him. He seemed so dead certain that he knew his Romans.

Pergamon was over eighty miles away. The Roman commanders were only too eager to go, as if they needed a guide. I kept forgetting how unsure of themselves they were in this regard. At some deep level they were afraid of the Greek world—afraid of being seen as bumpkins, barbarians, even though they owned the territory.

Pergamon had started the fad of willing one's kingdom to the Romans. Attalus III had done so, and then my great-granduncle Ptolemy Apion in Cyrene had followed suit. At one point, even Egypt itself had been willed to Rome, by my granduncle Ptolemy X. (Luckily Rome ignored the bequest, as there was a question of his basic right to the throne.) Perhaps they were but bowing to the inevitable. But it did not make them popular with their subjects.

Pergamon had been a Roman province for a hundred years now. When Alexander's three generals—Antigonas the One-Eyed, Seleucus, and Ptolemy—had scrambled for territory, Asia had fallen to Seleucus. But he had proved unable to keep his kingdom from fragmenting, and Pergamon had broken away.

Pergamon—home of the poison garden of Attalus III, home of parchment, and home of the greatest library outside of Alexandria. She had tried, but never quite equaled, us Ptolemies in Egypt. And then, with a great sigh, like that of a camel lying down with its burdens, she had given up and bequeathed them to Rome. Now she stood, shorn of her power, awaiting our arrival.

We approached, seeing the flat plain and the elevated city from afar. What a commanding site! The acropolis reared itself a thousand feet above the plain, gleaming white from a distance. We reined our horses and looked at it.

Our rival in intellectual status, was all I could think. Once Alexandria and Pergamon had competed for the glory of being the true artistic and intellectual daughter of Athens. But politics, power, armies had had other plans for Pergamon. And what would have become of Alexandria, had not Caesar and Antony been men—and I a woman? O most fortunate, to be born in the right shape and at the right time! I silently thanked Isis. Egypt was secure, as Pergamon could never be.

"Fabled city," said Sosius. "I am always thankful to behold it."

"If you must be on land, I suppose Pergamon is good enough," snorted Ahenobarbus.

As we came to the city, we rode past the justly famous medical center of Asclepion with its sacred spring, therapeutic vaulted tunnel, and hospital for dream interpretation, and toiled our way up the long road that wound its way up the terraced side of the mountain, past the gymnasions, past the baths, past Hera's holy place, past the lower agora, and then finally past the upper agora—and to the acropolis itself. Here were the very guarded inner selves of Pergamon: her library, her theater, her altar of Zeus, her royal palaces.

The city fathers were waiting—oh, so anxiously—to escort us into the former royal palace, now a Roman government building. A feast awaited to refresh us from the three-day journey. The tables seemed to sag from the weight of the gold vessels and heaps of food, except that iron and marble do not sag. Tall silver pitchers were filled with the finest wine from the nearby island of Lesbos, ready to drown all thirst.

There were more than twenty in our party—not only Sosius and Ahenobarbus, Consuls-to-be, but Dellius and Plancus as well as city magistrates from both Ephesus and Pergamon. Their wives had joined us, which gave the occasion a lighthearted social air. Perhaps Antony had been right to wrap his serious political business in this benign cover.

From my place, several feet away, I saw him providing himself with several cups of wine in quick succession—no moderation here! He was laughing and acting his effusive best. I strained my ears to hear what he was saying, and I studied the expressions of Sosius and Ahenobarbus as well as I could.

There was talk about Sosius's Triumph in Rome; he had celebrated one just a year ago, commemorating his victory in driving the Parthians out of Jerusalem for Herod. Now he had returned to these regions, but I could not help thinking that we would have been better served by his remaining in Rome. We needed all the partisans there that we could get, and a popular war hero like Sosius was good to have, if only to balance Agrippa. But he seemed happiest here, where he had more power, like many Romans who were on the "Asia circuit." He was a man with even features and a steady temperament, in contrast to the gruff, volatile Ahenobarbus.

Now they were both leaning forward to listen intently to Antony, who (I could see plainly) had let loose his famous charm. He smiled; he gestured; he laughed, throwing his head back; he nudged them confidentially. But they remained restrained: a bad sign.

I could overhear only a few words from Antony, like "new year" and "self-evident" and "well-deserved." Ahenobarbus was frowning, and—

"So we are to see a comedy this afternoon?"

Curses! Dellius, next to me, wanted to have a conversation. Now I would have to turn away from Antony.

"Yes," I said. "It is Menander's *Girl from Samos*. The day is too fair to stain it with death and weeping, even make-believe versions."

I could just make out the words "I can rely . . ." from Antony's place when Dellius replied, "We think alike, fair Queen." He was smiling at me as if he meant something more.

"In that we both like comedies?" I said innocently. "Menander was a favorite of Caesar's." That had always surprised me, but it must have offered him escape from his burdens, just as the wine did for Antony.

"Comedy is not a thing I associate with Caesar," Dellius said.

Now I could see Sosius and Ahenobarbus helping themselves to the sliced spiced eggs and olives, smiling broadly. Perhaps it had all gone smoothly. Antony was pouring out more wine, beaming. Yes. It had obviously gone well.

"Most gracious Majesty," said the Pergamene official on my other side, "is this your first visit here?"

"Yes," I said. "Though I have always longed to see the legendary city. My physician would be particularly interested in the Asclepion, and in Attalus's garden—which probably no longer exists."

"A small part of it does, madam, and I would be honored to show it to you. It is near the . . . the library."

Ah yes. The library. This was a delicate matter. Had scrolls already been removed? Were empty places on the shelves glaring at library patrons? But if he did not mention it, neither would I. That is diplomacy at its most basic.

"I have heard of the statue of Athena there," I said. At least that was left. I did not need another Athena statue in Alexandria.

In midafternoon one party went to visit the Athena sanctuary and the Altar of Zeus, while others of us were taken to Attalus's garden and the library. The famous garden of poisonous plants was much smaller than Olympos's, and it was guarded by soldiers—as much for show as anything else, I suspected. Each bed of plants was marked and labeled, and I wondered what was unique to this particular spot. Olympos would know, of course. I wished he were here.

"Some of it, alas, has died out," my host said. "Even poison has its life span." He led us along the pathways, cautioning us not to brush against any of the stalks or leaves. "And here, on this side, are the plants used as antidotes."

"Do they work?" Dellius had remained steadfastly by my side.

"Some of them," the guide said. "Attalus used to administer the poisons to condemned criminals and then give them the presumed antidote. Some of the men lived!"

The library, a stern marble building, was much smaller than ours in Alexandria. I wondered how two hundred thousand scrolls could even be stored here. True to his word, the man took us in and showed us the reading room and the famous statue. I could see for myself that many of the scroll-sockets were empty; they looked forlornly out at the few readers in the main room.

A mighty wind was whistling as we walked around the acropolis; it was so high that it must have wind all year long, and I imagined that in the winter it must be very cold. The trees were bending and swaying, their branches whipping, and my stole streamed out behind me, pulling at me like a sail.

It was nearly time for the performance, and Antony's group met us on the grounds of the Athena temple overlooking the theater. I could hear them before they came into sight; their noise shattered the quiet and pierced the very wind.

"Hail! Hail!" Antony was marching in, holding a thyrsus made from a pine branch, whipping it about. Even from here I could see that he was exuberant—and drunk. Beside him, his party were laughing and capering—had he gotten them drunk, too, or were they just humoring him?

"The theater calls!" he said, gathering everyone about him, a merry shepherd with his flock. "Let us descend!"

As we rounded the two-story stoa surrounding the temple, with its bronze statues of defeated Gauls in the niches, I gasped to see the theater plunging down to the middle level of the city. Straight down it went, or so it looked. It was the steepest hillside I had ever seen used for seating; it looked almost perpendicular. Far below us lay the stage; it would be a free fall from the top.

Antony was teetering on the edge—was he joking or not? It looked over a hundred feet to the bottom. I hurried over to him and clutched his arm to try to steady him. But he shook me off, waving his wand at me in teasing admonition. Far below us a crowd was streaming into the theater and filling the seats. At the very bottom in the front row was the king's box, fashioned of marble, where we would sit—if we could ever reach it. Perhaps it would be best to descend on the path and approach from the bottom. But when I said so, Antony just laughed—too loudly.

"What, shall the god not descend from his heights?" And he boldly stepped down onto the uppermost tier of seats, where he stood swaying. Then he stepped down to the next level. Then he jumped, feet together, onto the next. "Come!" He turned and gestured to us, looking backward. At the same time he stepped back, caught his foot in his toga, and spun over and over down the stairs, a blur of white.

It happened so quickly it was hard to follow. The steep angle and his weight combined to accelerate his fall. Dellius was off like a bowshot after him, but nothing could match the speed of a free fall. Then, suddenly, he shot his arm out and grasped the corner of a seat, where the momentum spun him around and slammed his back against the stall. It took great strength in his arm to act as a pivot in swinging him around like that in mid-fall, sending him in the opposite direction. I heard a loud crack as he hit the stone seat—had he smashed his head? All I could see was a mound of clothes. I hurried down the stairs sideways as if they were a ladder, but Dellius had already reached him. Behind me came the others.

Then, slowly, like a turtle emerging from its shell, Antony's head stuck out of his toga and he looked around, dazed. He was still grasping the corner of the seat with his large hand, and only then let it go, leaving a bloody print on it. He shook his hand up and down as if it were numb.

Dellius was speaking to him, bending down, and then Antony got up. He seemed unhurt. The voluminous toga that had been his undoing in tripping him had also served to muffle his fall.

"A fitting beginning for a comedy!" he said heartily, to assure everyone he was all right. Nervous laughter broke out from the group.

I took his bloody hand in mine and went slowly down the steps with him until we reached the royal box. I could not trust myself to speak. I was deeply angry at him, but the fright I had felt in seeing him fall had wiped it out.

When we were seated, he said contritely, "I am sorry."

When I did not reply, he added, "It won't happen again."

My hand was slippery with blood from holding his.

Finally I said, "Perhaps on your way out you should stop by the temple of Dionysus at the far end of the stage and give him thanks for saving you."

The actors, belonging to the theatrical guild of Dionysus, came trooping out with their masks, and the comedy began. But I paid scant attention to it.

———

That night, Antony's cuts and bruises having been cleaned and treated, he said, "Togas are lethal." He laughed. "I caught my foot—"

"Antony," I said quietly, "it wasn't the toga."

We were lying side by side in the bedroom in the old palace. He had trouble finding a comfortable position.

"Everything hurts," he admitted. The wine had long since worn off, and he was dead sober. "Just when I could use it to ease the pain," he said, then quickly added, "I am just joking. I think I learned my lesson today. You were right in what you said before. More moderation is called for." He sighed. "As I said then, moderation is something that does not come easily to me."

I kept seeing that fall; it seemed to play over and over again in my head. I shuddered. "For your own sake, you must learn it," I said, hearing how I sounded like a stern tutor. Why is it so difficult to be strict with those we love, even in their own interests?

"Yes, I know. Octavian will use it against me."

"That's the least of reasons. It's dangerous—today proved that."

"Today was most successful." So now he chose to drop the embarrassing subject. He shifted his weight around and folded his arms behind his head. "Ouch." He paused. "Ahenobarbus and Sosius will read my report to the Senate as soon as they take office next month. They agree that my case must be presented to Rome. How lucky we are that the two Consuls for this year are these men—*my* men."

"So you won them over to your plan."

"There was nothing to win over. The merits of the case spoke for itself."

"Then why were you so nervous you needed to get drunk?"

There was a long silence. "A good point. I suppose because so much depends on it. I *must* win back the good graces of the Senate; our future depends on it."

I disagreed so completely that I said nothing. It distressed me to see how obsessed he was with the Senate. The Senate could not grant him anything worth having. He would have to win it in spite of the Senate. But Antony was not a revolutionary, like his rival, who cloaked his imperial ambitions behind Republican trappings.

I closed my eyes and willed myself to sleep.

Who could have foretold what happened? No astrologer predicted it, no soothsayer even hinted at it. Not that I would have believed them if they had.

In three months the Senate came to us.

Yes, the mighty Roman Senate—or part of it—came as fugitives to Ephesus, cast out of Rome by Octavian.

Ahead of them, just in time to warn us, Ahenobarbus and Sosius put in with their swift Liburnian, and came rushing to our house, where we were sitting in the atrium enjoying the fine spring weather. The sun, straight overhead, was sparkling in the little square pool with its mosaic bottom.

"Imperator," called Ahenobarbus from the doorway. "We have been driven out of Rome!"

Right behind him was Sosius, panting from the run from the harbor.

We stared at them as if they were apparitions. They were supposed to be a thousand miles away, leading the Senate—defending our interests.

"What?" Antony leapt up, dropping the letters he was reading off his lap. One of them rolled into the pool and sank with a gurgle.

"Most noble . . . most noble . . . I can no longer say 'Triumvir.' . . ." Sosius looked stricken.

Yes, the Triumvirate had officially expired with the new year, and was hardly to be renewed! Now Octavian was a private citizen, technically at least. But Antony still held his military command and his eastern title of Autocrator.

"Pray, be seated." Antony was ever the considerate host. "Refresh yourselves." He dragged over a bench himself, and bade them take the good chairs, as if this were a courtesy call.

They sank down, arranging their togas around their knees. Ahenobarbus looked fierce, his eyes flashing above his wiry beard.

"You have had no word of this?" he asked. "You did not receive my messages?"

Antony shook his head. "Tell me now."

Ahenobarbus gave a grunt. "The long version or the short?"

"First the short," I said. Now he glared at me, then turned back to Antony. But if he expected Antony to disagree, he was disappointed.

"In the first month of the new year, I was to preside over the Senate," he said. "I judged the climate completely wrong to read your dispatch."

"But how else could Rome know?" I burst out. It seemed to me he had exceeded his commission in deciding to withhold the information. That was for us to decide, not him.

Now he looked poisonously at me, then continued stiffly. "There was such hostility toward your eastern policy that I felt that to mention the Donations was to inflame them further. Octavian was absent from Rome. I hoped to fathom the feelings and then devise a strategy. But *he*"—he shot a look at Sosius—"when he took the chair the next month, decided to attack Octavian directly and call for a vote of censure against him. Then a tribune vetoed it. And before we knew what had happened, Octavian appeared in the Senate house, surrounded by armed men, and threatened us. He refused to let us read your dispatch at all, even the part about the Armenian conquest. He said he would return the next day and present all his grievances against you, with written proof, and exact punishment on Antony's 'creatures.' We didn't return on his appointed day, but left. At the same time, three hundred senators decided to come with us. 'Any other traitors who feel the call should depart now!' Octavian warned. And so they are following—about half the Senate."

Antony looked stunned. He was speechless.

"So where does the true government of Rome reside?" I asked. "In legal terms, which half of the Senate counts?"

"They can both claim legitimacy," said Sosius. "There is a tradition that if the Senate must flee elsewhere, the government resides with them. But in this case, large numbers have stayed behind. Now Rome has no government at all! The Triumvirate has expired, the Senate split—" He looked as if he were going to burst into tears. "We are adrift on a perilous sea."

"Get hold of yourself!" barked Ahenobarbus.

"I can't bear another civil war," Sosius lamented. "It has gone on and on for so long—will Rome never be at rest? Caesar, Pompey, Sextus, now you and Octavian—no, no!" He moaned. "We cannot stand another one."

"We will have to," I said briskly.

"What do you mean, 'we'?" growled Ahenobarbus. "You are not Roman."

"I am intimately involved in all these movements," I said. "Since I bore Caesar's child fifteen years ago, I am part of Roman politics, like it or not."

"I *don't* like it!" he returned.

I was taken aback—not at his sentiments, but at his honesty. "There are days I don't like it, either," I said.

Still Antony's speech had not returned. Both Consuls turned to him, waiting.

"Imperator," said Sosius, "tell us . . . what shall we do?"

"I don't know," Antony finally said. He looked perplexed. "Wherever shall we put all these senators?"

"You revered the Senate so," I reminded him. "Now you shall have them on your hands!" Perhaps it was cruel of me, but I was upset as well. Everything was so messy—and Octavian so full of surprises.

They arrived within a few days, spilling off the boats, making their way up the harbor road and into the main part of town, clutching their belongings.

How odd they looked, away from Rome! Transported to another setting, they lost all their formidable qualities and just seemed like any other foreigners.

We found lodging for them only by straining the hospitality of the Ephesians to the limit.

Octavian had promptly appointed two of his men—Valerius Messalla and Cornelius Cinna—to fill the vacant posts of Consul. The ranks had closed behind us. Our Consuls were deposed. Our entire party was in exile. There was only one way to get back—fight, defeat Octavian, and return to Rome in triumph. At last it had come to this. I had been waiting twelve years since Caesar's death to see his true heir recognized, his false one driven from the throne. For throne it was: the Roman throne, created by Caesar, destined for his son.

The forces gathered in Ephesus. Antony now had eight squadrons of sixty ships each, with forty support ships and five scouts per squadron—almost five hundred ships. He also counted another three hundred transport and supply vessels. Altogether our fleet numbered eight hundred—a staggering size. For the first time since Alexander, all the sea power in the east lay at one man's command.

Canidius had brought the sixteen legions from Armenia, and seven more were drawn from Macedonia. The client kings all over the east had pledged their troops: Archelaus of Cappadocia, Amyntas of Galatia, Tarcondimotus of the Amanus, Mithridates of Commagene, Deiotarus of Paphlagonia, Rhoemetalces and Sadalas of Thrace, Bocchus of Mauretania, Herod of Judaea, Malchus of Nabataea, and the King of Media. These totaled some twenty-five thousand men, in addition to the seventy-five thousand legionaries.

Did I neglect to mention that I was supporting all this? Yes, the treasury of Egypt was covering all the expenses of maintaining this army, as well as the navy—some twenty thousand talents in all. A great deal, considering that it cost about fifty talents to maintain a legion in the field for a year. It was also more than my father's entire original debt to Rome. So much had Egypt prospered in the years of my reign that what had been an enormous and impossible debt to him was lying at my fingertips, ready for disposal.

I was underwriting all the expense—carrying this army on my back—or, rather, on my treasury's back. And yet the Romans dared to order me to depart! The insolence of Romans never failed to stun me. Without me, there would be no army, no provisions, no housing for them, no bread and wine. . . .

Yet they tried to persuade Antony to dismiss me!

Ahenobarbus started it, muttering that "all would be well if Cleopatra would depart to Egypt." Others took up the chorus, saying that my presence was damaging Antony's cause. Just how, they did not specify! All this, while eating my bread!

Antony ignored the murmurs. Later they got louder, but during that spring they were still soft enough to be passed over.

We decided to do something Alexander had done: hold a festival of music, drama, and poetry prior to going to war. It was a very Greek thing to do; no Roman would think of it. Yet were we not fighting to preserve our different way of life?

We gave orders for everyone to assemble on the island of Samos, which lies just off the wide Bay of Ephesus.

70

The marble seats of the theater glowed violet in the twilight, like other night creatures that give off light at dawn or dusk: fireflies, will-o'-the-wisps, glow-worms, the shining wake of a ship in moonlight. They climbed up the hill—a gentle slope, this, at Samos—empty of patrons, patiently waiting for the audience they knew must come.

The flat stones of the stage, empty as well, invited me to walk upon them. I did so, in slow, measured footsteps, undergoing transformations of character every few paces. I was Medea, my hands red with blood, I was Antigone, guiding her blind father, I was the virgin prophetess Cassandra. In the moments when I pretended, I could feel something change inside me. Had there been rows of faces looking at me, I could have convinced them, too, that I was someone else.

What an odd power and freedom, I thought—to pretend to be someone else, someone who may not have ever existed at all, or is long dead. In some godlike way, it makes me—briefly, oh, so briefly—the bestower of life on the lifeless. The infuser of warm breath and blood to the shades.

And why limit myself only to other womanly incarnations? Why not be Oedipus himself, or Achilles—or anyone I fancied? The imagination in full force can know no bounds, and the biggest difference between me and these people was not in being a man or a woman but in existing at all.

Silence. No audience, and therefore no rebirth for the dead heroes. At least not tonight. I would have willed them to appear, but the only mortal disguise they could use was the body of an actor, with an audience to see him.

Acting is the only art that one cannot do alone, I realized, and still call oneself an artist. There can be secret poets, secret painters, secret musicians, but no secret, solitary actors. An actor without an audience is lacking an essential element.

"Alone?" Antony asked in a loud whisper.

I felt embarrassed. How long had he been watching? Had he guessed what I was doing? I had to smile at my own conceit: that my enactments were so good he would have immediately known which character I mimicked. And in the fading light, too.

I whirled around. I did not see him anywhere, and the seats looked as empty as ever. Now even the purple glow was fading out, ebbing away, as the night robbed everything of color.

"Rehearsing?" Now the voice seemed to come from a different place. But I was surrounded by emptiness.

"Where are you?" I whispered, and the perfect setting magnified it so it could be heard all around.

"Everywhere," came back the answer. "You cannot escape me."

"Then come and show yourself." I waited, sure a rustle or a movement would point him out to me. But in the gloom I saw nothing.

A light, warm wind was flowing down the hillside, bringing the scent of new meadow grass and thyme with it. Spring on an eastern Greek island was the nearest we could come while alive to actually wandering in the Elysian fields.

A slender crescent moon hung low in the sky, hovering over the fields. Where was Antony? We needed to walk hand-in-hand across the warm, scented expanses.

"Who would you most like to be?" Now the teasing voice seemed to come from a different place. "Answer me that, and I shall grant it, in person."

"There is no one else I would rather be all the time," I said, realizing the rare pleasure of that. "But I suppose, just for tonight, I would like to be one of the goddesses of the gentle breeze, so I could fly and stream over the island, wherever I wished."

There, now I had played the game. He must now fulfill the promise.

He emerged from behind the altar of Dionysus, which stood near the middle of the stage, peeking up over its top like a schoolboy. I was astonished—how had he hidden there without my seeing him? "Sometimes what you seek is very near to hand," he said, stepping out.

"If one cannot see it, it does little good," I said. "Now, can you teach me to fly?"

"Dionysus could, in the guise of wine," he said. "And we have invited all the members of the Dionysian actors guild to come to Samos and perform—so we shall all fly."

I laughed. "A tricky answer." The wind whispered in my ears. "Oh, Antony—this festival is most solemn and portentous. The ancient Greek way of going out to war—when war was a ritual and a contest rather than a science—holding games, drama, music, all to placate the gods . . . perhaps we shouldn't have done it." The sacred character of it—had that been lost, forgotten, so that all the world would see was revelry? We were too much associated with that as it was. Yet to forsake the old ways entirely seemed insulting to the very gods we wished to aid us. As if we cared more about what Octavian and Horace thought than Zeus himself. . . . "They will ridicule us in Rome," I said.

He shrugged. "We won't hear them." Now he walked around the stage. "Here is where our thoughts will be—with this reenactment of the mighty deeds done by gods and heroes. May we be worthy of them." Suddenly his voice took on that oratorical tone meant for more than just me. He was addressing an invisible audience—a past one, and one yet to come. "These deeds must not be forgotten. We are re-creating our ancestors in our own lives—they dream the state we are in. When we live, they live too. They dance in the sunlight once more, feel the radiance that makes life sweet."

His voice made me shiver. To call back the dead, grant them life through us . . . yes, drama was perhaps the most frightening act we could perform, and the most generous.

"Will the senators understand this?" I asked. "And the client kings, who have no part in Greek thought?"

"You concern yourself overmuch with that. At the least, they will be entertained. And they will doubtless find it more pleasant than the Roman way of opening a war—which always seems to start not with a play, but with taxes!"

I laughed. Yes, the Romans labored under that burden—money troubles. Octavian was about to launch a tax drive that was bound to make him odious. He was going to demand a quarter of a person's income to finance the army. Romans, who were used to receiving tribute from provinces to pay their government rather than doing it themselves, were in for a shock.

From somewhere in the night I heard music—drums, flutes, lyres—and voices singing a refrain.

"They are practicing," said Antony. "The Dionysian songs will fill the island."

The sweet and haunting melodies hung over us in the warm air.

"It is ghosts singing," I said.

"Ghosts sighing," he said.

We stood together listening.

Finally I took his hand. "Let us walk. There is a path here in the field. . . ."

It wound its way toward a ruin, whose roof had long since vanished and whose weathered pillars were missing their capitals. Tall weeds and shrubs bordered the path, and reached out to clutch at our clothes. But from the rise we could see the flat sea and the small distance separating Samos from the mainland. It was called the Seven Stadia Channel, which meant it was no bigger than the expanse of water between the Pharos and the mainland of Alexandria proper. Yet an island had a special feel to it, if it was properly an island.

I wondered, idly, when an island stopped feeling like an island . . . when you could walk to it in low tide? When a mole was built connecting it to the mainland? The Pharos didn't feel like an island any longer, and neither did Tyre. Once-invincible Tyre . . . joined to the mainland by Alexander in his siege.

Alexander . . . yes, he would understand what we did here on Samos. He would be present tomorrow.

For more than twenty days the island rang with celebrations, as the leaders of our forces all gathered for the blessing, drenched in wine, food, song, and drama. The client kings had brought oxen from each of their cities to be sacrificed, and in a special ceremony just for them—for the rulers of Cappadocia, Cilicia, Mauretania, Paphlagonia, Commagene, Thrace, Galatia—Antony reminded them, in his ringing voice, of the prophecy of the east's rising against Rome, shearing her hair and lowering her. "The woman who shears the hair, the Widow, stands here beside me, the Queen of Egypt. And we fight together in the name of her son's inheritance. It is not your lands or territory that will be lessened, but Rome will fall to his lot."

There was a deep murmur of approval and desire. This was their moment, the moment the east had been seeking for over a hundred years. What Mithridates had failed to do, we would: deliver the east from its stooped humiliation.

Day after day the hills resounded with our celebrations. "What will they do to celebrate the victory, when they went to such expense of festivity for its opening?" people were asking—the question we meant them to ask. Let our friends and foes know we would hold nothing back: that here we dedicated our entire beings, our treasury, our army, our navy, our creative forces to the supreme test.

In May we went to Athens, after ferrying the army over to southern Greece.

Greece. A Roman civil war was to be decided in Greece, for the third time in only seventeen years. For the third time the thin, hard Greek soil would soak up the blood of Romans fighting for dominance in their homeland.

I had been profoundly affected by each of these battles. The first had brought Caesar into my life, the second, Antony. Now it was the fate of my children that would be decided by the forthcoming clash. Would they receive their inheritance, secured by Antony's victory, or lose everything, be banished into the nameless void outside history?

There could be no mistakes in this campaign. Pompey had lost against Caesar because he had not pursued his initial rout, and his strategy was not flexible enough; Brutus and Cassius killed themselves after misreading signals from their own camp. It was not lost on me that the losers in both previous clashes had been the Romans who stood their ground in Greece; the winners had been the Romans who invaded from the west. Yes, there must be no mistakes.

We had nineteen Roman legions dedicated to the war effort. Another eleven were standing guard in Egypt, Syria, Cyrenaica, Bithynia, and Macedonia.

So Greece would be the battlefield. But what part of Greece? North, south? Middle? Where should the troops be deployed?

We had gone round and round on this vital question, in consultation with some of the senators, as well as our generals, late at night after the revelers had gone to bed. After the entertainment, that was when the real work— and the real decisions—were tackled. And it would continue in Athens.

All my life I had wanted to go to Athens. As a child I had been taught about the glorious font of all our cultural history, the mother of all Greek-speaking and Greek-educated people. Then my father had spent time there after having been driven off his throne, and I used to wish myself there with him. After that, it seemed that no matter what age I was, there was something in

Athens to appeal to it: the architecture, the art, the scholars, the schools of oratory and philosophy, the shrines, the witty salons. Athens was a place it was impossible to outgrow.

Because I was Macedonian, and Greek-educated, Athens had always been my place of spiritual pilgrimage. But then it had begun to acquire the dark coloration of association with my enemies. Brutus had pranced about there, posing under the statues of his idols, the ancient "tyrannicides." The Athenians had even hailed him as a liberator when he fled there after Caesar's assassination, and raised a statue of his own to him. Cicero had made himself at home there, where they lauded him almost as much as he lauded himself. And then—it was where Antony had passed most of his married life with Octavia.

And, oh! the Athenians had outdone themselves in honoring Octavia, giving her this title or other, putting up inscriptions. . . . Thus Athens had become *her* city, spoiling it for me. So that now, when I came to it at last, it had already been appropriated by my enemies and rivals.

Antony seemed happily oblivious of all this. As we made our way up the broad, welcoming avenue, lined with cheering crowds, our carriage passed right under a plaque honoring Octavia as "goddess of good works" and "Athena Polias." I stared at it, going rigid with the actuality of seeing it. I clutched at his arm and muttered, "Look!"

He swung his head around. "What?"

"That plaque!" I did not want to point at it, as others would see me.

"What plaque?"

By now we were past it. I let go of his arm. "Nothing." But I made up my mind that now he must formally divorce her. *Now.*

There had been gentle hints on the subject among the senators and commanders during some of our meetings—but not in the right direction. They had reminded Antony that the breach with Octavian was not irreparable; after all, Antony was still married to his sister. Ahenobarbus all but came out and said he wished Antony would go back to her, so there would not be a war. But even he had not dared to go quite that far—at least in front of me.

I couldn't bear it any longer. For five years—five years!—I had bowed to all the political arguments about the wisdom of keeping up the formal ties with Octavia. I had indulged Antony's sad excuses about her impending motherhood, her use as a weapon against him, her delicate feelings.

None of those arguments would serve any longer. They were stale and irrelevant, and all the cautionary reasons for keeping up the pretense were shattered by the pain it caused me to see the mementos of her all over the city.

We were housed in . . . not a palace, since the Greeks did not have kings, but what might as well have been one. I have observed that where there are no kings, wealthy citizens live like them, so that instead of one palace, there are dozens.

Antony looked supremely contented as he padded up and down our bedroom, as if he were trying it on for size. He was wearing what I called his "oriental potentate" gown—red silk, encrusted with gold thread and pearls, with enormous sleeves. Decorated slippers flapped on his feet.

If he did not wish to be called a degenerate oriental, I thought, he ought to abandon this costume. But I said nothing; tonight was not the night to provoke him on lesser matters when I needed to confront the biggest one.

The acropolis, crowned by the Parthenon, was visible from our window, and the just-full moon gave life to its still whiteness. Antony had stopped pacing and was staring at it.

I came and stood beside him. The legendary Parthenon at last . . . all my life I had viewed the white Lighthouse of Alexandria from my window, and now another white marble wonder was there to fill my eyes. But then, unbidden, came the picture of Antony cavorting as Bacchus on the very slopes of the acropolis in his wild celebration a few years ago. And of Antony being "betrothed" to the goddess Athena in her annual ceremony in the Parthenon. This city was his in a way it could never be mine. I was just the visitor-come-lately, the outsider.

I would not spoil this moment with mention of Octavia. Let him look at the Parthenon as long as he wished, and I would stand silently beside him. But when he turned . . .

"Antony, the time has come," I said. I hoped my voice sounded gentle and persuasive, not shrewish. But even as I blurted out the words, I berated myself for being so blunt. I should be subtle, beguiling, but my own feelings were too strong to be disguised.

He looked at me expectantly. He thought something good was coming; he imagined I had lured some exotic entertainment to the chamber, or had ordered dishes of Athenian delicacies to be sent up. "Yes?" he said eagerly.

I took his arm and leaned my head against his shoulder. "You must divorce Octavia," I whispered.

"What?" he said. Frowning, he turned me to face him. "Why do you say that?"

Because I cannot bear it anymore. I cannot bear my ambiguous position in the eyes of the world, cannot bear sharing you. And on the eve of a war, all things must be made clear and tidy, all debts settled. I dropped my eyes demurely. "Because—you have postponed it long enough. It is confusing our friends and allies. It is hindering our cause." There—was that political-sounding enough for him?

"I don't know what you mean," he said stubbornly.

This was going to be difficult, then. I hated that.

"Your marriage was a political one, meant to unite you and Octavian. It failed to do that. You are on the brink of war. The Triumvirate has expired. Marriages made for political reasons must be terminated when the politics have changed. That is the Roman way, is it not? Octavian himself has made, and discarded, many matrimonial ties. There was the Sextus connection, another connection with you—remember the Claudia marriage?—and the betrothal of little Julia to your Antyllus. All snapped in a second. Only *you*"—O dear Isis! keep that tone from my voice—"persist in your old political marriage. Now you should, as befits an honorable man, end it."

"It still serves a purpose," he said.

"What purpose?" I could hear my voice rising.

"It still provides an excuse for certain Romans to adhere to my cause. As long as I retain my formal marriage to Octavia, it gives the lie to Octavian's attempts to paint me as un-Roman."

"It gives the lie to your life with me!" I said. "That's what it does!" And now all my caution, all my restraint, dissolved, and for the first time in my life I acted entirely and completely as a woman, no other considerations clouding my mind. I grabbed his arm. "For five years I've endured it! I cannot stand it any longer!" I began weeping loudly. "You could not stand the memory of Caesar, you wouldn't even let me wear the family token he had given me—how do you think it feels to have you married to a living woman? I hate her! I hate her!"

What had I done? The three words had escaped my mouth, where they would exist in Antony's mind forever, and nothing could recall them. I wept even harder, in shame at my own loss of control.

Antony bent down and knelt in front of me, embracing me. "Well, then," he said simply, "I shall divorce her," as if there was, suddenly, no other consideration.

Was it to be that easy? I was so startled I stopped crying. "Will you?"

"Yes," he said. "Tomorrow, if that pleases you." He reached up and touched my hair. "I fear it is too late tonight to send for a scribe." He smiled.

Now all his caution entered into me. I knew this move was a provocation to Octavian and the final step before open hostilities. But it must come to this.

"Tomorrow, then." I nodded. Tomorrow—tomorrow would end it.

"And now, my dear, I think it is late," he said gently, leading me toward the bed. It was heaped with rich sheets, pillows, scented herbs, and its frame was gilded. But all that luxury was lost on me tonight. I was very, very tired, and everything here felt alien. I wanted to sleep next to him quietly and let him take away all the strangeness. It was the last time I would have Octavia as a presence between us.

The letter of divorce was dictated the next morning, and by noon it had left the "palace." That night there was to be a dinner and gathering, and Antony planned to announce it then. We had been holding these council meetings fairly regularly, but this would be the first one in Athens.

It is hard to be in exile, and I had begun to feel sorry for the senators. They had left Rome almost three months ago, fleeing with little notice, and now they must live as perpetual guests and wanderers—until that day when it was safe for them to go back to Rome. Considering all they had to endure, they had been remarkably patient. Of course, they had been well fed and housed—at my expense. But by now they were growing restless and increasingly at loose ends. I had hoped Athens might soothe and divert them, for they still had a long wait ahead of them. It was obvious that the war would not erupt this year. Octavian had made no move to gather his forces, and it was he who would have to make the journey.

In the meantime, we had had the luxury of being able to equip and deploy our forces at our own pace. We were proud of our commanders: Canidius, Titius, and Plancus by land, and Ahenobarbus and Sosius by sea. The two ousted Consuls would now take their stand on the decks of warships.

After the meal, when everyone's stomachs were stretched with the pleasure of fine food, and the wine—still flowing—was soothing their minds, Antony murmured, "Welcome to Athens, faithful friends." He raised his cup. "I trust you will find the summer days here fair. There is still much to be decided, such as where we will take up winter quarters while we—wait." For what, he did not say, nor did he need to.

"Are we settled on the middle part of Greece as the place to take our stand?" asked Plancus. "I am yet to be convinced that a more northerly position would not be better. Why surrender the Via Egnatia? It is the vital link between the Adriatic and the Aegean, between Dalmatia and Macedonia. It is the only real road there." He looked truly puzzled, and his blue eyes went from my face to Antony's.

"A good question, my friend," Antony said. "But we don't need the road. We need to be stationed farther south, where the offshore islands offer a base for our fleets. The road will not be bringing in our supplies; the sea will. We will be supplied from Egypt, and it is vital to protect the sea route. We must keep that route open, so we always have a secure place behind us."

"To retreat to?" barked Ahenobarbus.

"One always needs a retreat," Antony said firmly. "Pompey did not have one, and neither did Brutus or Cassius. I am not ashamed to admit that had it not been for my places of refuge after Mutina and Parthia—thanks be to the gods for Transalpine Gaul and Syria!—the outcome would have been total defeat, not just a temporary setback."

"So you are thinking of retreat!"

"No. But Egypt must be protected. It is, after all, the source of our wealth. And my wife's kingdom." He looked over at me.

"Perhaps she should retire there and await the outcome." It was Ahenobarbus again.

"No!" I said. "Why should I? I have supplied a quarter of the navy, have staffed many of the other ships with the finest Egyptian oarsmen, and am supporting the entire army!"

"Just because you are a wealthy patron does not mean you must be present," said Ahenobarbus.

"I must disagree," said Canidius. "She is not just a patron. The Queen has ruled the world's richest country for twenty years, has led an army herself, and is certainly more experienced than any of the male client kings we are permitting to join us. It would not be fair to exclude her."

Ahenobarbus grunted and crossed his arms.

"Besides, it is in the name of her son—and Caesar's—that this war is being fought," said Plancus.

"Is that what it's being fought for?" asked one of the senators. "I don't like it."

"Yes, it works against you in Rome," added another. "We need another name and plea to rally under."

"Indeed you do." A stranger rose from the shadows in the back of the room. He looked around, then said, "I have been sent by your friends in Rome to warn you."

Antony said, "Who are you, friend?"

"Gaius Geminius," he answered. "A senator who is your partisan, yet did not leave Rome with the others. I thought to do more good for you by remaining."

"Well, then, what have you to say?" asked Antony.

Geminius looked around at the wine cups. "It were better said with clearer heads. But this I tell you, drunk or sober: The Queen should return to Egypt, if you wish your cause to prosper."

I stood up in anger. "His cause will never prosper as long as Octavian remains!" I said. "It is not I who dooms Antony, but his implacable enemy, and mine, Octavian! Enough of these lies about me, blaming me for Octavian's enmity! He would hate Antony even if there were no Cleopatra, had never been a Cleopatra. Can you not see that?"

"But his sister, Antony's wife—" began Geminius.

"She is his wife no longer!" I said. "He has sent her papers of divorce."

A babble of voices rose, all crying, "When?" and looking to Antony for confirmation.

"Yes, it is true," he admitted. "The marriage is formally over. It actually ended a long time ago."

Everyone was staring. They looked angry, cheated.

One senator shook his head. "When this is known in Rome . . ."

"So many of the finest families were torn, not knowing whom to support," another said. "Everyone respected Octavia, and she entertained your friends and clients on your behalf. Now where will they go? You have evicted them, along with her!"

"She'll go straight to her brother's house—where else can she go? And they'll follow. Oh, folly, folly, folly!" The senator stood up in dismay, eyes bulging.

Geminius looked as if he had been struck in the face. "I see my long journey has been in vain," he said sadly. He held up a coin. "These two things together—the Queen's portrait on your coins, and now the divorce—end even the pretense of your Roman allegiance."

It was Antony's turn to look shocked. "That's ridiculous! How many times has each of you been divorced? Everyone in Rome is divorced! It was a political marriage, and—"

"And its ending has a political meaning," finished Geminius. "A grave political meaning." He paused. "And as for the coin—putting a foreign ruler's head on a Roman coin is an unforgivable effrontery! It mocks Rome!"

"Egypt is Rome's ally—" Antony began.

"Since when do you put allies' heads on coins?" Geminius countered. "Is Herod's head on them? Is Archelaus's? What about Bogud's? You see how lame that claim is!"

"I—"

"You have lost your reason," said Geminius. "But do not expect us to lose ours along with you."

"I have done nothing to deserve such a judgment," said Antony firmly. "I have governed the east well. The frontiers are in order; the region is recovering financially from the devastations of the civil wars. I have conquered Armenia and presented Rome with a new province. These were the monumental tasks assigned to me after Philippi, and I have completed them, and completed them well. Instead of looking at that, you fasten on a minor thing like whose portrait is on a coin! Is there anyone here in this room who could not be faulted for some minor mistake or miscalculation? But it's like complaining about a ten-*denarius* fine when a man has earned you a million!"

It was all very logical. But this was not about logic, it was about emotions. Their emotions were whipped up, their minds tossed about on the choppy sea.

I considered leaving the room, but decided it looked cowardly. Instead I just sat there, feeling my ears growing hot. They were probably bright red. I could feel Geminius staring at me, as if to say, *What is it about her? She looks ordinary enough from here.*

"I understand Octavian is collecting taxes," said Antony, attempting to change the subject. "And that there is unrest."

Geminius's mouth gave a jerky smile. "Unrest, and more than unrest. There have been arson, riots, murder. But the soldiers suppressed it."

So completely did Octavian have control of the army. I realized that in the ten years since Antony's men and Octavian's had fought side by side at Philippi, the armies had grown apart. There were no active soldiers left in Italy who had ever served under Antony or Caesar; they had long since retired. The new soldiers were all Octavian's, with no divided loyalty.

"Perhaps we should invade Italy now, while people are still disgruntled with Octavian and his situation is shaky," said Dellius suddenly. "Our army is ready, the ships here to serve as convoy, and it is only June."

"Only if the Queen remains behind," said Plancus. "Any attempt to invade with a foreigner would unite all Italy instantly."

"Then you will have to do without my ships, too!" I said. Did they forget who was paying and supplying the forces? The ingrates!

"It is difficult to invade Italy, anyway," said Ahenobarbus smoothly. "There are only two harbors on the east and south coasts, Brundisium and Tarentum, and landing at them is impossible if they are armed against you— just ask Antony and me, from our earlier attempts."

"So you are determined on war?" Geminius asked. "Now I see my mission was doomed before I set out. I wish I had not wasted the time!"

"No, we are not set on war," Antony assured him. "After all, how many times have Octavian and I almost fought, only to pull back at the last moment? Five years ago at Tarentum, eight years earlier at Brundisium. It seems we quarrel often, but no blows are struck."

"Are you calling it a lovers' quarrel?" asked one of the senators, and everyone burst out laughing with high, nervous titters.

"There is little love lost between them," said Titius.

At this point I excused myself. I could not bear to sit there any longer. My head was aching, and the welter of accusations and justifications was confusing even me. I needed to get out of that room.

I was not familiar with the way the house was laid out; it was the headquarters of our legate stationed in Athens. Rome always did her sons proud, and this dwelling was no exception. Little wonder that officers were reluctant to rotate back to Rome, when they could live like this abroad. I wandered down wide hallways, with arched niches filled with statuary, all copies of masterpieces. To the right, Leochares' Apollo looked down on me beneficently; to the left, Pheidias' Dionysus leaned out toward me. Just like Antony and Octavian, their patron gods stood across from each other, staring.

I stopped and lingered before the Dionysus. The workmanship was superlative. I knew that Athens had gained a new prosperity when wealthy Romans had begun requesting artworks to adorn their homes. Since the world could not order great artists to be born on demand, Athens had risen to the occasion by turning out copies of masterpieces in local workshops and shipping them out everywhere. Today the Roman governor of Syria or the corn merchant on the Esquiline could gaze possessively on identical copies of Praxiteles' Aphrodite. Athens could barely keep up with the orders, and this hallway was a good example of why.

In spite of its grand size, there was still a formal courtyard surrounded by a roofed colonnade, as in a family home. I found my way to it by following the flow of air through the hallways.

Air. I needed air. Gratefully I stepped out under the roofed shelter and leaned against one of the columns, cooling my cheeks on the smooth stone. The garden was dark; the moon, past full, would rise later tonight. I could hear a fountain in the middle of the grassy courtyard; the wind, stirring the flower beds around me, brought the delicate sound of splashing water to my ears.

I sighed; this cool, dark refuge was what I needed to regain my equilibrium. Who would have thought the divorce would have stirred up such heated emotions? But I should not have been surprised. Antony had always had the potential problem of trying to ride two horses: being a Roman magistrate with the inevitable clashes with other Romans, and claiming eastern rights and titles as well. The strain of trying to play both roles was becoming impossible; the horses were pulling him in different directions. Those who had supported the Roman Antony—that is, the senators and his partisans still in Rome—were horrified to behold this other side. They might refuse to march under his banner at all. But their demand—that he jettison the eastern side— was impossible, in military terms, if nothing else. Abandon the eastern side and he abandoned the money that supported his military machine.

I tried to think of myself as only that—a military ally who was indispensable. Even had I been a man—Geminius's Herod or Archelaus—with the wealth of Egypt, I would be crucial to his success. He could not leave me— leave Egypt.

My eyes became a little accustomed to the dark now, and I could make out the statues—more copies, undoubtedly—standing at gray attention in the garden, surrounded by box hedges emitting their characteristic strong scent. It vied with the lush, full smell of the roses nearby, in full bloom.

There was a marble bench discreetly set against the wall, and I sat down on it. I would stay here until my thoughts stopped racing, I promised myself. There was no hurry, no need to leave. I leaned my head back and closed my eyes. I could hear the fountain distinctly now. I let its silvery sounds caress my ears.

I felt trapped here in Athens, as if I could not breathe. From the moment we had landed, one unpleasant finding had followed another. Even Rome had not felt so . . . unfriendly. I was tired of the senators. I wished they would leave . . . no, I didn't. If they left, it would be bad for Antony's cause. I missed the children. I had had to hurry away from Alexandria six months ago, leaving them. June. Tomorrow was Caesarion's fifteenth birthday, and I would not be there.

Were all these—all the nineteen legions and the four hundred senators— truly gathered in the name of my fifteen-year-old son's rights? Oh, Caesar— what a task you left for me. And I am tired, tired, tired . . . of pursuing it. I may not be up to it. Your demand may be more than a mortal can bring about, even a mortal who is also a goddess.

There was no answer, of course. The fountain splashed on, and I could even hear—very faintly—a nightingale somewhere in the dark.

I must have slept, because I awoke with a start when I heard voices. Men were passing into the garden on the opposite side, their feet crunching on the gravel paths. Instinctively I held still and waited. The meeting must have broken up—or else these men had left early.

There were no other sounds, so I assumed it meant they had stolen away together, or even that they lived somewhere in the labyrinthine house. They were passing by the fountain. I could see them now, or rather, make out their light-colored tunics moving in the gloom.

"—it's impossible," one of them muttered.

"You could see that tonight," his companion answered, in a familiar voice. "We must choose."

"I'm tired of choosing. Just once I'd like to choose right."

"Well, even when you choose wrong, you've been able to correct it."

"I? What about you?"

"Sure, I have a genius for choosing the losing side. I admit it. But at least I don't stick with it."

"So much for Sextus." There was a laugh. A laugh I had heard before.

"How many times have you changed sides now?" The voice was half-admiring, half-sneering. "First Caesar, then Cicero, then Antony. Love 'em and leave 'em, that's my uncle." A slap on the shoulder.

Plancus and Titius!

"I didn't *leave* Caesar," he protested. "He left me."

"Oh, you mean when he was killed? Thoughtless of him." A laugh.

"Still, we should congratulate ourselves. We've never failed yet to scramble for the winning side," he continued.

"Better late than never," agreed Plancus.

"So you think he's going to lose?"

They were passing right before the hedge near me. I held my breath and gave thanks that my gown was dark and hard to see.

"I don't know. It isn't his love for the Queen that disturbs me, it's his dependence on her. He is not free to make the best military plans, but must always consider Egypt and its position. The gods know he's a great tactician, probably the best in the world, but he must compromise his overall strategy because of Egypt. And in war, do you know what they call generals who compromise?"

"Losers," said Titius.

They passed by, their arms about each other's shoulders, laughing. Their sandals ground the gravel underfoot.

71

"Plancus has gone," said Antony in disbelief, as he read a note just delivered to him in our rooms.

At least he had the courtesy to write a note, I thought. His mother had taught him well. *If you are going to be a turncoat, my boy, always mind your manners. Otherwise you'll reflect badly on traitors.*

"And Titius with him, no doubt," I said. I had not yet had the opportunity to tell Antony about the conversation I was privy to in the garden, and I was saddened to hear it confirmed. I had hoped it was just a passing mood with them.

"You knew about this?" He looked surprised. "How?"

"I caught part of a conversation between them, but they were only thinking aloud; you know how people rehearse many ideas, but act on few."

"What was their reason?" Antony kept rereading the note. "This says little, only that after much deliberation, he has decided to return to Rome."

"I am sorry to say that they were joking—joking about their history of switching sides."

Antony let out a long sigh. No one had ever left him before, and he, whose strong sense of loyalty was one of his main characteristics, attached great importance to it. "And Titius, you say?"

"Yes. Shall we pay a call on him? I venture to say we will not find him at home!"

Titius had been assigned a villa beside that of his uncle, beautifully situated on rising ground with a superlative view of the acropolis. Again, a private palace that any king would have been proud to claim.

We alighted from the litter and our servant knocked loudly on the door. Eventually a house servant answered, and when we identified ourselves and demanded to see the commander Marcus Titius, he blinked at us and shook his head.

"The honorable commander is not here," he said.

"And when will the honorable commander return?" I asked sweetly. "Shall we wait?"

He looked alarmed. "Oh no, Your Majesty, that would not be fitting. We have no suitable place—"

I brushed past him easily. "I am not particular," I said. "In fact, I have long wished to tour this villa—I understand that it has several fine mosaics in the dining room. I shall amuse myself for a while."

"Your Majesty, I must ask you to refrain from—"

"And I—I'd like to inspect the commander's weapons room. He has long promised to show me his collection of shields, including the copy of Ajax's. He has bragged about it for years!" said Antony heartily. He headed in the opposite direction, to the servant's dismay. He did not know which of us to follow. Finally he settled on Antony.

As soon as they had gone down a hallway, I turned around and followed them. The house was clearly empty. There were a number of telltale trunks stacked in the atrium, and the scattered debris that always seems to appear during packing lay on the floors: dust balls, scraps of paper, pins, and pieces of string.

"O Athena!" Antony's voice rose in mock surprise. "All the shields are gone!" He stuck his head out of the door and called to me. "Come and see! Someone has stolen Titius's prize collection! Why, you—" He turned to the servant. "He'll have your head for this when he returns!"

I entered the room, which was stripped and echoing. "Alas, poor Titius!" I had not thought it in me to go along with Antony's game—he, who played when others would weep—but found myself caught up in it. It made things sting less. "How grieved he'll be! Were you asleep when you should have been guarding?"

I could see the pegs in the wall where the shields had hung. Titius always kept them nearby, as if they brought him luck.

"No—yes—" He looked miserable.

"All right, my lad, you needn't pretend any longer," said Antony in consoling tones. "You needn't protect him. We know he's gone, and we know where. We just want to know when—and why."

"He left last night. As for why, I swear I don't know."

"He didn't leave letters to be delivered?"

"No, sir. In the name of all the gods, I am telling the truth."

It's the younger generation. No manners. I almost laughed at the thought. "Has he taken everything?" I asked.

"Everything that could be packed," the servant said.

We left the room and returned to the atrium. Suddenly I said, "As long as I am here, I *should* see the famous mosaics." I made my way toward the dining room. On the way I passed a bust of Octavian perched on a pedestal. "Why, look! He's forgotten his Octavian!"

Seeing the face and features of my foe again was startling. After all, I had last seen him when he was barely eighteen, before he became a man, not to mention acquiring an official portrait. This was how he wished to be regarded now. I came closer, scrutinizing it.

Well, he had changed, but I would still recognize him. He was thinner, and his neck longer, his hair longer and more disheveled. (Why did he want to be portrayed so untidily?) His head was cocked arrogantly, restlessly, his brows furrowed a bit. This was a hungry, seeking man, sizing up anything his eyes fastened on, critically. I had to admire the honesty and nerve of someone who allowed such an accurate characterization of himself to circulate. The energy seemed to burst from the stone.

"What's wrong? Didn't he want this?" I pressed the boy.

"He was afraid the marble would crack. Look, there's a fault below the ear." The servant pointed to it.

I could see the hairline fracture just beneath the little, low-set ears. "What a shame just to leave him here, all alone! I think we should adopt him!" I turned to Antony. "Don't you think we need an Octavian bust? Let's take him home. And *we* won't agonize about him cracking. Apollo will surely protect him, and if not, why, we'll just glue him back together!" Somehow capturing the statue gave me a nasty sense of triumph over Titius and Plancus.

"Whatever you wish," said Antony. "But we must find a suitable place for him."

In the war-planning room, I thought. It is best to keep your adversary before your eyes there.

That night, when the household noises had ceased and all the servants— even Eros—had finished their tasks and withdrawn, we talked seriously about the defections. Antony had a drawn look on his face that made him, for the first time, look his fifty years. He was forcing himself to review reports of his junior commanders, in search of good replacements. It was not exactly diverting reading, but it was crucial.

"There's young Dentatus," he said. "He shows promise. And Gaius Mucianus was recommended by—" He sighed and put down the papers. "Plancus and Titius will be sorely missed. Not that any commander is irreplaceable, except Caesar himself."

"I think Agrippa's loss to Octavian would be crippling," I said. "He is no Caesar, but he is the nearest thing to a successor, militarily. Except for you, of course," I hastened to add.

"No point in dreaming about that. Agrippa isn't likely to appear at our headquarters tomorrow."

I had to ask it. "Antony, why do *you* think they defected? And what does it mean to our cause?"

I watched as the thoughts marshaled themselves. His face showed the struggle he had to make sense of it. But he would answer honestly, for that was his nature. He, like Caesar, did not flinch before the truth.

"Inasmuch as he stands for anything, Plancus has always favored peace and compromise," he finally said. "He served Caesar loyally, if unremarkably, in Gaul and afterward. Later he voted for amnesty for Caesar's assassins, and tried to support the Senate. Then, when it came down to it, he lost heart for Cicero's policy, and joined me. He never has been a fervent supporter of anything. I suppose he couldn't sustain enough enthusiasm for the coming conflict."

"Does he think that Octavian will require less?"

"Perhaps he feels he will be given less responsibility there. And also, lately I caught him in some questionable financial dealings. He was a bit of a thief, as it turned out. I was going to have to take away his privilege of using my signet ring and acting as my agent. He knew what was coming."

So! He had taken his revenge this way. But would Octavian take him? Octavian (to his credit, I must admit) was reputed to like treachery, but despise traitors. Sometimes he executed them—after extracting their information.

"But the bust of Octavian—does that mean he always favored him?"

"Who knows? Maybe it was just an extra one lying around. Octavian has flooded the world with his statues, since they are to be set up alongside Caesar's in all the temples dedicated to Rome, and that's a lot of temples."

"And Titius?"

"Titius." He sighed. "I admit he had talent. Although a bit of an opportunist, and a flatterer—"

I remembered the way he used to kiss my hand, and look meltingly at me. And then I remembered, too, naming that city after him: Titiopolis. I had kept my word. Well, I would change it back again! And Plancus, painting himself blue and dancing around naked at the banquet . . .

A bit of a flatterer . . .

"Antony, how many support us only from policy, and how many because of personal loyalty? It seems that we cannot rely on the ones who have joined us for political reasons. Are they with us out of conviction, or only because they are vaguely against Octavian?"

"They make it their business to hide that from us, my love," he said. "And it is dangerous to read others' minds. We will just have to trust their better natures." He smiled and pulled me over against him. I rested my chin on the top of his head. "Distrust rots a man's soul."

I supposed he was right, but it was too noble for me.

Almost two months after Octavia had received her papers of divorce, and left Antony's house, weeping, so it was said, Antyllus, Antony's eldest son, arrived in Athens. Although the wily Octavian had long urged his sister to consider herself divorced and abandon Antony's home, rubbing it in how badly she was treated, when the actual divorce came, he made much of it. He made sure that she transferred from Antony's house to his in broad daylight, with the train of her children trailing after her. She was the wronged woman, the perfect mother, now cast out. With her into Octavian's house went Marcellus, aged ten, the two Marcellas—aged eight and sixteen—then Antony's son Iullus, aged ten, and the two Antonias, aged seven and four. Only Antyllus, at thirteen the eldest of Antony's, wanted to go to his father rather than remain in Rome. And, sensing that he was too old to be used easily, Octavian let him go.

I had been curious to see Antony's son, this boy who was his Roman heir. Antony talked of him often enough that I knew he carried him close to his heart. But he had not actually seen him in almost nine years, and he was startled by the tall boy who greeted him. He was already in that awkward, gawky stage, without the winsomeness of childhood, that causes such agonies for a youth. He had none of Antony's solidity, but was thin and weedy, with a long, narrow face, and teeth that seemed too big for his mouth. How had Antony and Fulvia ever produced such a slight creature? Still, he had a sweet disposition (which he had inherited from Antony and not from Fulvia), and he was a long way from being grown. He might fill out later.

At first he was shy around his father, but Antony soon disarmed him, and the boy provided him with his only respite from the mounting crisis of the coming war. When he was with Antyllus, he was able to suspend all the cares pressing down on him. Watching them together made me long for Caesarion, for Alexander and Selene, even for little Philadelphos. It is good to have children to take us into other worlds, even as we try to prepare the present one to hand on to them.

It was from Antyllus, surprising as that may seem, that we first heard about Plancus and Titius's doings in Rome. And he mentioned it innocently enough. He had been asking questions about Egypt and the pyramids, when he suddenly said, "Is your tomb as big as the Pharaohs'?"

I didn't know what he meant. "My tomb?" I asked.

"Yes, your tomb. I kept hearing about it in Rome. They were all talking about it. What's so special about it?"

I had to think hard. "Nothing, really. It is next to the Temple of Isis, on my palace grounds. It is just a regular mausoleum, except"—perhaps this is what he meant—"it has special doors that can't be reopened once they are closed. Why?"

"Well, everyone says the tomb must be special, since my father insists on being buried in it, instead of in Rome. I tell you, *everyone* was talking about it!"

"And how did they know that?" asked Antony, putting down the reports he was reading.

"They said it was in your will."

We looked at one another. The will. It was in the safekeeping of the Vestal Virgins, absolutely inviolate.

"How did they know what was in my will?" asked Antony. "It's supposed to be a secret—until I die, that is."

"Oh"—Antyllus shrugged, paying more attention to the toy soldiers he was arranging on a heaped-up blanket to serve as a mountainous battlefield—"they stole it from the Vestal Virgins."

"What?" Antony got down on one knee and looked sternly at his son. "No joking, now. No playing. Did they really steal it?"

Antyllus put down the soldiers. "Yes. Uncle Octavian made them. Some Romans who had come back told him about it, and he demanded to see it."

"He isn't your uncle!" I said sharply.

"He made me call him that," said Antyllus. "He would get angry if I didn't."

"Well, stop it!" I said. "You aren't closely related to him!"

"Hush." Antony frowned at me. "That isn't important. What I want to know is *who* stole the will."

"Uncle—I mean Octavian. He grabbed it by force from the Vestal Virgins. It caused a big ruckus in Rome. Everyone was carrying on about the way you wanted to be buried in Egypt. It made people mad. And, oh, let's see . . . I don't remember what else. It was the tomb part people kept talking about."

Plancus and Titius. They had witnessed the will. They had told Octavian about it, and he had used it in his uncanny way. But how had he dared to violate the sanctuary of the Vestals? He was gambling that what he found in the will would make it worthwhile. That bastard. And he had won.

That night in our chambers, I lay quietly against Antony's shoulder and talked in hushed tones. "We need to take stock of our position," I said. "Plancus and Titius have changed the equation. What is happening in Rome?"

"It sounds as if they have won a pardon from Octavian by presenting him with inside information about me—what they were privy to as the keepers of my seal, and witnesses to the will," Antony said. "They had to offer him something he wanted in order to be taken in. After all, they had been with me for ten years. That would have tainted them in his eyes."

"How damaging is this information?"

"I never thought it was damaging at all," he said. "I don't understand why it should be."

The sounds of a summer night drifted in through the windows, songs from nearby courtyards, laughter, footsteps on the paving stones below. On the streets of Athens, people were enjoying the warmth, the clear, starry skies above them.

I put my head on his chest and listened to the slow, steady sound of his heart. How calmly he lay there, how unconcerned he seemed. I put my arms around him, feeling the strong, arched ribs under my hands. He was like a sturdy, rough-barked oak that gave shelter. Just touching him made my worries and fears subside. The defections of Plancus and Titius had disturbed me deeply, but less for the loss of their persons than for what it symbolized. It might sap the morale of those still with us. Desertions could spread, like plague.

The reports that finally came from Rome were astounding. Antony was right; as price of their admission to Octavian's good graces, Plancus and Titius told him that Antony's will contained shocking information that he could put to good use.

Plancus and Titius's appearance had been timely. Octavian, freshly returned from Illyria, was only a private citizen now. The Triumvirate had officially expired, and Octavian held no public office. Furthermore, he had no constitutional reason to lead a crusade against his ex–fellow Triumvir and brother-in-law. Antony had not done anything aggressive or illegal, and Octavian had earlier declared the civil wars over. Antony still had a loyal following in Rome, plus almost half the Senate with him, and there were vast numbers of fence-sitters who kept themselves aloof from either faction. Unless Octavian could find some excuse to attack Antony and to marshal public opinion on his side, he could not proceed.

Then came the divorce. Routine enough in itself, it provided evidence that Antony was casting off his Roman ties for the Egyptian Circe. It gave fuel to the fire, fanned by Octavian, that Antony was becoming un-Roman. Then the will, with its wish that Antony be buried beside me, "proved" that Antony had repudiated Rome and planned to move the capital to Alexandria.

"While he lies embalmed like a Pharaoh in that foreign land, I—no matter where I fall in battle—I, Imperator Caesar, will lay my bones in the family tomb I am even now constructing beside the Tiber. Even my dust will not forsake or abandon you, Mother Rome!" Octavian had cried, when he revealed the contents of the will.

The response was an explosion of anger and disgust at us. Antony was called every vile name imaginable. Plancus stood up in what was left of the Senate and described Antony's servile fawning on me: Antony left a senator in mid-speech to follow my litter and place himself among my eunuchs; he stopped in the middle of council meetings to read love poems written by me on jeweled tablets; he even rubbed my feet in public, anointing them with oil and kissing them passionately.

I remembered the time in Ephesus when Titius had intruded on us in the privacy of our own house, where Antony was rubbing my feet because I felt ill. Now Plancus had exaggerated it into this slander.

Plancus entertained the Senate for days outlining one folly, evil, or mistake of Antony's after another. The catalogue of Antony's failings was as high as the pyramids.

Finally one old senator rose and remarked pointedly, "My, Antony certainly managed to do a great many evils before *you* could bring yourself to leave him."

Public fervor was one thing, but Octavian needed something more binding before he could strike. Since burial plans did not constitute disloyalty—one senator had objected that it was unfair to punish a living man for what he intended after his death—Octavian would have to invoke a "higher sanction," one above the constitution. He thought of a way: Romans would swear allegiance to him, in his own person, rather than for any office he held. Thus he would be the patron, and all the country his clients.

An oath of allegiance was hurriedly composed, and by autumn people were persuaded to take it.

I held a copy of it and read it aloud to Antony, who could barely bring himself to listen.

" 'I hearby bind myself to have the same friends and enemies as Imperator J. Caesar *Divi filius*, to fight with body and soul, by land and sea, against anyone who should threaten him, to report treason seen or heard, and to consider myself and my children less dear than the safety of the Imperator Caesar. Should I break my oath, may Jupiter visit me and my children with exile, outlawry, and ruin,' " I read. "Thorough, isn't it?"

Antony shook his head. "Bononia refused to take it," he said.

"Yes, that town is loyal to you." But the army, the veteran colonies, most of the leading citizens of the towns had taken it. Meanwhile, in Rome, the fence-sitters had finally been pushed off into Octavian's yard. The will and the divorce had done it—both personal things, pertaining to Antony's private life. How ironic. They enabled Octavian to claim that all loyal citizens, shocked and saddened at Antony's disgrace, had risen up in a spontaneous expression of their devotion to the *Divi filius*: champion of Roman fortitude, virtue, and tradition. Hence the oaths.

"We still command more resources," said Antony. "Our army is bigger, our navy superior, and our treasury deeper. When the clash comes, we will prevail. I am a better commander than Agrippa and Octavian put together. Do you remember when we talked about creativity? Mine is in warfare, and it will not fail me now."

742

"There *was* something in the will that shocked Octavian, but it was not what he shouted about," I said. "The real thing that frightened him he kept to himself."

Antony rubbed his forehead, as if he would erase the lines there, lines that had settled on him since coming to Athens. "What was that?"

"In the will you emphatically support Caesarion's inheritance. By that we deny Octavian a place in the west, as well as in the east. We give him no place to go. He knows that, and cannot submit to such a scheme."

"Yes, that is true," admitted Antony. " 'Thus we must make war, that we may live in peace,' as Aristotle said."

Golden summer days lasted into October in Athens, but we were far too busy making our military arrangements to notice the swirling leaves or stroll among the butterflies, dancing their last. Soon each contingent would depart to take up its watch in different parts of Greece. Antony and I spent many hours perfecting the plans before we were ready to unveil them.

For almost the first time, a major campaign would rely equally on sea and land power. Since neither army would be on its home ground, and Greece had scant food, that meant food supplies must be transported by sea. Theirs would come from Italy, and ours from Egypt. Obviously, whoever could manage to cut the other's lines would starve the enemy army out. So the ships were crucial, and we were proud of ours. Not only did we have more than five hundred warships with every size well represented, but our rowers were expert Greeks and Egyptians. It did little good to have fine ships if the oarsmen were inept. In addition, our admirals Ahenobarbus and Sosius were seasoned commanders.

As for the army, we still had the core of Roman legionaries, some of whom were veterans of Parthia and even Philippi, as well as newer recruits. The legionaries numbered some sixty thousand, the light infantry and client kings' soldiers another twenty-five thousand. Amyntas of Galatia had contributed two thousand of the world's best cavalry to the ten thousand we already had. That gave us land forces of almost a hundred thousand men. Antony would lead the troops, with Canidius and Dellius under him, in addition to the kings of Cappadocia, Paphlagonia, Thrace, Cilicia, and Commagene commanding their own forces.

I wished to command my squadron of Egyptian ships, but Antony was hesitant. In the first place, he did not like the idea that we would be separated in battle—one on land, one at sea—but he also worried that Ahenobarbus would balk at it. And we needed Ahenobarbus's expertise against Agrippa. I held my peace, sensing that things might well be different later. One thing I knew: I would not sit on the sidelines. I would be fighting somewhere.

I also wondered if Caesarion ought to be involved. He was old enough to begin training as a soldier. But Antony was insistent that Antyllus leave and go to the safety of Alexandria, and he urged that Caesarion remain where he was.

"Full-scale war is not the place for boys to learn soldiering," he said. "Especially if one is also the heir. The stakes are too high, the chances of an accident too great." He was so adamant that I bowed to his wishes.

"What you mean is, you don't want them in the way," I said.

"Exactly," he said. "I will have enough to worry about, without them underfoot. And what hostages they would make!"

Still, I wondered if they would not feel cheated afterward. How could a son of Caesar's sit by while a war was fought in his name?

At length, all the details having been perfected, we held a council of war in the enormous Stoa of Attalos near the agora. We needed all that space to accommodate our men, and to display the maps and make our presentations. It was the last time we would all be together under one roof.

As if to emphasize his Romanness, Antony was wearing his general's costume: buckled brass and silver cuirass with relief ornamentation, a string of military awards across his chest, a sweeping purple cloak, heavy nailed sandals.

I had been careful to avoid all ornamentation, attiring myself in a plain gown and cloak, and wearing the ancient Egyptian award for military valor, stylized golden flies, which I had earned in raising my army in Ashkelon against my usurping brother, as well as taking my fleet to sea to be used against the assassins. I wanted them to realize that one side of me was of a warrior.

Behind us a gigantic map had been fixed to a frame; Antony was standing beside it, spear in hand. Looking straight at us were the faces of all our chief officers and the ten kings. Behind them were the senators. Legates, tribunes, and centurions filled the rest of the hall.

"We have feasted and celebrated, my friends," Antony began. "Now it is time to dedicate ourselves to the coming test. May all the gods look with favor on us, and give us the victory."

He pointed at the map, tapping the peninsula of Italy to the left with his spear. "Octavian must cross the sea to get here," he said. He gave a laugh, meant to be disarming. "Depending on where he ferries his troops across, the journey may be either long or short. If he departs from here"—he thumped the site of Brundisium—"he will have only about seventy miles to sail to reach Greece. If he chooses Tarentum"—another thump—"and heads south, it will be closer to two hundred miles. What we must do is be prepared to intercept him at either end. Therefore I propose a chain of nine naval stations on sheltered islands just off the coast of Greece, stretching from Corcyra in the north to Crete in the south."

There was a slight murmur; the men were nodding, looking impressed.

"Above Corcyra the coast of Greece is difficult to land on, so we need not worry that Octavian will try that. So we will guard Corcyra, then have a major naval station south of that, at the Gulf of Ambracia. The gulf is ten miles deep and provides safe anchorage from winter storms. The main fleet will winter there."

He looked around for questions. There being none, he continued. "Just off the Gulf of Ambracia is the island of Leucas, and we will put our third naval station there. Then, proceeding south, almost in the middle of the chain, there will be another at Patrae, on the Gulf of Corinth. There the main army will winter, and I will have my headquarters. Guarding it will be two more stations, at Cephallenia and Ithaca, home of Odysseus. A little farther south, on the island of Zacynthus, Sosius will command his fleet. He has long experience at Zacynthus, having served there for seven years already."

Sosius stood up and nodded.

"A major station under the command of Bogud of Mauretania will be situated at Methone, in southern Greece. Then, the last one on Greek soil, at Cape Taenarum, will serve to protect our food supply coming from Egypt. Below lies Crete, where our ninth station will be. So you can see, it is a shield stretching down the entire western flank of Greece."

"But what about the Via Egnatia, in northern Greece?" said Dellius. "Why just abandon it? I don't like it."

"We have no need of it," said Antony. "We cannot receive supplies that way."

"But the enemy can," insisted Dellius.

"No, the enemy will find it of little use if we are south. It only goes east-west, and cannot help them transport supplies over the mountains in our direction. It is a wonderful road, but of no use at all to us in this contest." Antony looked absolutely certain of this.

"Why station the army near the Gulf of Corinth?" asked Ahenobarbus.

"If the enemy comes by sea from the west, then we will be ready, and easily deployed toward the coast. If, however, he should make the long overland march through Illyria and come down from the north, we can block him. We will be prepared no matter which direction he comes in." He added, "But I doubt very much he will make an overland march. For one thing, it is almost a thousand miles."

"Better a thousand on land than seventy on the sea!" cried Canidius, playfully.

"Landlubber!" yelled Ahenobarbus.

"Keep in mind that this will be a difficult undertaking for Octavian," said Antony. "Time, money, and supplies are on our side. All we have to do is maintain ourselves in Greece, and wait. *He* has to get here, keep his troops paid, and transport all supplies. We have had the opportunity to assemble and bring in anything we wish, at our own pace—a great advantage."

"And where will *she* be?" asked Ahenobarbus suddenly.

I rose. I certainly could speak for myself. "As commander of the Egyptian ships, I shall be with my fleet," I said.

"You own the ships, but do you command them?" Ahenobarbus said. "You must have an admiral."

"That is to be settled later," said Antony quickly. "The Queen will be in Patrae with me for the winter."

I could see this was going to be a bone of contention between us. Well, he was right—it would be settled later.

"Perhaps the Queen should return to Egypt," said Ahenobarbus.

Not this again!

Before I could answer, he offered his clever argument. "If she would allow her son to take her place, the troops would perhaps be less confused. After all, he is Caesar's son, and a king in his own right. It would remove the source of Octavian's lurid gossip and put more heart into the soldiers."

Having considered it myself, I had to admit that he raised a good point. Ahenobarbus looked surprised, and Antony glared at me.

"It will be settled later," Antony repeated. "In the meantime you will have much to do to set up your stations before winter. We must be securely positioned when the weather turns. And do not forget that I am to be Consul next year—serving along with Octavian. I look forward to January first, when I will assume the office. I do not plan to relinquish it again!"

But Octavian outmaneuvered us. He had two more tricks in his hand, and in November he pulled both out. He declared Antony's Consulship void, and stripped him of his *imperium*. Antony was no longer in his right mind, Octavian declared, and thereby not fit for public office. "He is either heedless or mad—for, indeed, I have heard and believed that he has been bewitched by that accursed woman; her slave, he undertakes a war and its self-chosen dangers on her behalf against us and against his country. Therefore let no one count him a Roman, but rather an Egyptian, nor call him Antony, but rather Serapis. Let no one think he was ever Consul or Imperator, but only gymnasiarch. For he has himself, of his own free will, chosen the latter names instead of the former, and, casting aside all the august titles of his own land, has become one of the cymbal-players from Canopus. It is impossible for one who leads a life of royal luxury, and coddles himself like a woman, to have a manly thought or do a manly deed."

But did he declare war on him? No, he was far too clever for that. There was still enough sympathy for Antony in Rome to make that too dangerous. Instead he marched to the Temple of Bellona in the Field of Mars and enacted an ancient ceremony.

Leading a solemn procession to the doors of the war goddess's shrine as *festialis* priest, followed by men in military cloaks, he dipped a lance in fresh blood and hurled it in the direction of Egypt.

"This foreign queen, who has set her sights on Rome, and wants to rule us, dispensing judgment from the Capitoline hill, as her oaths have revealed—we solemnly declare her our enemy. The Egyptian Queen, Cleopatra of the house of Ptolemy, who has trodden our general underfoot and made him her slave, this Egyptian who worships reptiles and beasts as gods, feeble in courage, must be vanquished!" he cried, brandishing the lance before throwing it. "We declare a just and righteous war—*justum bellum*—against this foreign sovereign who threatens our state. We must allow no woman to make herself equal to a man!"

All these words, written and witnessed, were delivered into our hands at Patrae. I could almost hear them, could hear Octavian's shrill voice crying them aloud to the crowds and the sky.

HERE ENDS THE SEVENTH SCROLL.

"The most blessed New Year to you." I raised my goblet and hailed Antony. Dining with us were our intimates, who followed suit. "Janus, the god who looks both ways, open this year to us and shower his blessings on us."

Antony allowed himself to be saluted, then announced that he had small gifts for everyone. Boxes were distributed; each contained thirty gold coins, the magnificent issue he had struck to honor each of his thirty legions, as well as his praetorian bodyguard and corps of scouts. Each displayed the eagle and standards on one side, and a warship of our fleet on the other. They were worth a fortune, and our friends were stunned. It seemed that Antony's generosity was something one never grew used to.

"Hail, Consul!" one said, since our Senate—the legal one—had duly declared Octavian's action in appointing Messalla Corvinus as his replacement invalid. But all this was just a game. The legality of our actions, or Octavian's, could be ratified only one way now: by arms.

While we waited in Patrae, winter storms lashed the seas. But we were secure, tucked away in the protecting Gulf of Corinth. It was an interesting part of Greece—or would be, in better weather. We were not far from Olympia, where the Games were held, and its world-famous statue of Zeus. But this was not the time for sightseeing. In the other direction lay the ruins of old Corinth and the new colony set up by Caesar. The city itself lay on the shore just beyond a fertile area of orchards and vineyards.

Antyllus had been dispatched to Alexandria, there to make himself a home with his half brothers and sister; I hoped they would welcome him warmly. It could not be easy for him to be uprooted from the only home he had ever known and sent to a new one, with neither father nor mother to ease the shock. I had written letters exhorting the twins and Caesarion to be friendly.

Before leaving Athens, the client kings had all sworn allegiance to Antony, in a pale imitation of the oaths Octavian had extracted in Italy. And Antony had in turn sworn to them that he would fight on without reconciliation. While in Athens, Herod had whispered what he thought was astute advice into Antony's ear: kill me and annex Egypt. He said it made perfect sense, and would solve the problem of the contention in our camp.

So. Herod could not be allowed to participate directly in our campaign. But he could still be used; I tied him up in his own country, fighting the Nabataean king, who had been tardy in paying his rent for the bitumen.

With our large reserves of money, and our ability to mint coins—Antony still possessed a mint in Italy itself—we distributed bribes to key people in Rome, in order to contrast ourselves against Octavian's extractions and taxes. This made us, for a time at least, very popular.

Yes, everything looked favorable. On January first, the new year, Janus seemed to be facing ahead with a boundless future for us. We had mountains of money, an enormous fleet and army, unlimited food supplies from Egypt, and the best general in the world leading us.

Was that when I was the happiest? Are we happiest when we are holding everything that is dear to us, or when we are reaching out, in all confidence and hope, to grasp it? I think for me it was when it was there, nearby, almost there, within sight, and the waiting was only a delicious sauce poured over the days, drenching them with sweet anticipation.

When I think of that winter, for some reason the color red seems to permeate the days and nights. Both our dining chamber and our sleeping quarters were painted deep, brooding red, and the floor of the council chamber was of purple-red porphyry; the chill rain and wind meant that coals were always glowing red-eyed in braziers, and torches flaming. I had several warm wool gowns dyed the most striking scarlet, and I always *felt* warmer when I had them on. Antony, too, had tunics of that shade, as well as thick mantles in a duller rust color. Even the sun—on the days that it shone—slanted into the windows in rays dipped in rubies, pooling on the floor. We had discovered an exquisite local wine, so dark its depths only gave off glints of red, but red it was nonetheless. We drank it some nights until our heads barely started to spin, and then we set the goblets carefully on the small table and retired to our bed, there to experience the heightened feelings that a small amount of wine can induce.

And, oh! how I loved to hold him, touch him, those long nights in Patrae. Since Pergamon, he had forsaken his former careless eating and drinking, and now he was again the Antony of years ago. Exercise had burned off the flesh of ease and excess, leaving his arms and shoulders hard, his belly flat, his thighs lean and strong. The young Antony had returned, the soldier who had shone bright for Caesar. This was the Antony I had first loved at Tarsus, now come back to me in glory.

Lying in bed, half-covered by the blankets, I would drowsily ask why he had come to my door that night long ago. It had become a ritual for us, as it does for all lovers: *where, when, why? remember.* . . . I understand even old people rehearse their private religion of how they first loved, most guarded of secrets. And he would answer, sleep blurring his words, "Because I had to." The question and the answer were always the same. *Why? Because I had to.*

And I would lean down and kiss his lips, holding his face in my hands, feeling his cheekbones under my fingers, tracing the round rim of his eye sockets, kissing his closed eyes. He would murmur and reach up, slowly, to put one hand in my hair, first caressing it and then clutching my head in his strong fingers. His kiss would change, and sleep would slide away, replaced by the urgency of desire and the loosening of restraints that the magic of wine conferred. Soon we would be lost in the thickets of body-madness, seeking to reach one another in a way we never had before. We never did, and it was good we did not, because then it would have become the past rather than the future.

I never grew tired of him, of the physical essence of him. We are more than our bodies, it is true; but we cannot be divorced from them. They *are* us, and the only way in which we can see one another. Perhaps the gods are above this, but in their mercy, they have given us the guide of bodies. We cannot go too far astray that way. And I loved Antony in his bodily form— Isis help me, how I loved it!

The days passed—days in waiting, in the luxury of breathing slowly, enjoying our food, our long-neglected interests, and each other. In some ways it was like regressing in time, back to when we had simpler lives. Our children were not with us, nor were our ministers and officers, and we were not in our home countries. The obligatory formal daily audiences were gone. In place of them we could read, exercise, write, daydream. All of them were necessary to nurture what we were, to make us truly Antony and Cleopatra, the selves beyond the public persons—the selves that had originally given rise to the public persons.

"I wonder," I said idly to Antony, one midnight as we lay in one another's arms, "what we would have been without one another?" My head was resting on his chest, and I was savoring the warmth of it, soothed by the barely felt heartbeat under my ear.

"You would have been the great widowed Queen of Egypt, and I a partner with Octavian, shouldering what Caesar had left behind . . . perhaps always yearning for what was lost, but knowing that it was gone. No man is his equal; no man can duplicate what he would have done. It would have been, by the world's judgment, a worthwhile life."

"But lacking."

He kissed the top of my head. "Oh yes. Very lacking. Strange how what is worthwhile can be so lacking."

"And now . . . we are trying to forge a new world. Would Caesar approve, do you think?"

He paused a long time. I wondered if he had gone to sleep. Finally he said, "Even Caesar was bound by his time. Time has now gone past him, left him behind."

How that hurt! To think of Caesar as finite, finished, over, a prisoner of time.

"He would say to us," Antony continued, " 'Pursue your dream. Only take care of the details. Dreams without details cannot come true.' Just as I cannot make love to you without a body"—he pulled me against him—"soldiers cannot march without boots. Remember the boots; remember the details."

"Yes. The boots—" But he was pressing up against me in a way that told me he was not ready for sleep. Neither was I.

"I feel guilty," I murmured, "since I am enjoying this time so much. I should be anguished and tortured with the waiting, and instead it has been a gift. A gift of time, a gift of thought, a gift of one another." I ran my hand through his hair, his hair that was still thick and felt springy and healthy.

He loosened the front of my gown, and slowly kissed the hollow of my throat and my shoulders, then the tops of my breasts. "Then open the gift," he said, "and stop talking."

The gods snatched away the respite, our little island of time. January spun away, then half of February. And in spite of the seas, reports from Rome struggled through. Octavian's forces were still being readied, and he was putting the final touches on his campaign to win the hearts and minds of the Romans.

As I said earlier, we still had many favorable to us in Rome. Antony's family, his long-standing aristocratic ties, his service to his country, had not been forgotten. Then, our monetary bribes had done much to remind people that there were powers other than Octavian and his lot. So, before he could leave the capital, Octavian still had much work to do.

One blustery day in February, Aulus Cossus arrived on a ship, bearing copies of Octavian's speeches. Protocol demanded that we receive him graciously, and that we did, although his arrival was an unwelcome jolt and return to the ugly world outside awaiting us.

We received him informally, hoping to put him at his ease. He was an old friend of Antony's mother, and had abstained from the tumult of choosing sides in Rome.

"I'm too old," he said, "and no one is interested in me. A blessing." He was a spindly man, and so dried up it was no wonder no one was interested in him. "I still miss your mother," he said simply.

"As do I," said Antony. She had died while he was in Parthia. At least she had been spared knowing—for Antony would have had to have told *her* the truth—of the disaster there. Now all Antony's family was dead: his father, two brothers, and mother. As were mine. We had only each other.

"I must tell you," he said, "that Octavian's speeches and doings have been well received. Here." He thrust a copy of the speech Octavian had given on the steps of the Senate house into our hands.

Antony took it and read it, slowly. His smile faded as he went along, and then, wordlessly, he handed it to me. He stood up, and, arm around Cossus's shoulders, walked toward the covered portico where we showed guests the artworks as a diversion.

I read it. Octavian had opened all gates in this one. He left no abuse unuttered. After reviewing his mighty military resources, he began blasting me.

> For us, Romans and lords of the greatest and best portion of the world, to be trodden underfoot by an Egyptian woman is unworthy of our fathers; it is unworthy also of ourselves. Should we not be acting most disgracefully if we should meekly bear the insults of her throng, who, oh heavens! are Alexandrians and Egyptians (what worse or what truer name could one apply to them?), who are slaves to a woman and not to a man? Who would not lament at seeing Roman soldiers acting as bodyguards of this Queen? Who would not groan at hearing that Roman knights and senators fawn upon her like eunuchs? Who would not weep when he both hears and sees Antony himself, the man twice Consul, often Imperator—when he sees this man has now abandoned all his ancestors' habits of life, has emulated all alien and barbaric customs, that he pays no honor to us or to the laws of his father's gods, but pays homage to that wench as if she were some Isis or Selene—calling her children Helios and Selene, and finally taking for himself the title of Osiris or Dionysus, and, after this, making presents of whole islands and parts of the continents, as though he were master of the whole earth and the sea?

I shut my eyes a moment. I could see it all from the Romans' point of view, knew that if only Antony were able to return and show himself to them . . . But the animosity stirred up by Octavian made that impossible. Oh, he had been so thorough in his plans and his malice!

I forced myself to continue reading. I had to see it all.

> Yet I myself was so devoted to him that I gave him a share in our command, married my sister to him, and granted him legions.

As if it were all in Octavian's gift! A share . . . granted him . . .

> After that I felt so kindly, so affectionately, toward him, that I was unwilling to wage war on him merely because he had insulted my sister, or because he neglected the children she had borne him, or because he preferred the Egyptian woman to her, or because he bestowed upon that woman's children practically all your possessions, or for any other cause. I did not think it proper to assume the same attitude toward Antony as toward Cleopatra; for I adjudged her, if

753

only on account of her foreign birth, to be an enemy by reason of her very conduct, but I believed that he, as a citizen, might still be brought to reason.

I felt the color draining from my face. So I was to be judged only as a foreigner, while Antony was exempt from blame, being a Roman?

He, however, has looked haughtily and disdainfully upon my efforts, and will neither be pardoned though we would fain pardon him, nor be pitied though we try to pity him.

Let no one fear him on the ground that he will turn the scale of the war. For even in the past he was of no account, as you who conquered him at Mutina know clearly enough.

In the past he was of no account! I trembled with the lies. Did no one remember? Did no one in Rome remember Gaul, and Pharsalus, and Philippi? Oh, the littleness of men's memories, the erosion of their deeds! Then was Caesar dead indeed, with no hope.

And even if he did at one time attain to some valor by campaigning with us—

Campaigning with *him*? When Octavian lay sick and cowering in his tent? Oh, the lies!

—be well assured that he has now spoiled it utterly by his changed manner of life. It is an inevitable law that a man assimilates himself to the practices of his daily life. A proof of this is that in the one war he has waged in all this long time, and the one campaign that he has made, he returned in utter disgrace from Phraaspa, and lost ever so many men besides in his retreat. So, then, if any one of us were called upon to execute a ridiculous dance or cut a lascivious fling, such a person would surely have to yield the honors to him, since these are the specialties he has practiced, but now that the occasion calls for arms and battle, what is there about him that anyone should dread? His physical fitness? But he has passed his prime and become effeminate. His strength of mind? But he plays the woman and has worn himself out with unnatural lust. His adherents? So long, to be sure, as they expected to get rich without danger, some were very glad to cleave to him, but they will not care to fight against us, their own countrymen, on behalf of what does not belong to them at all.

He was disgusting! I was so angry I could hardly continue reading.

Why fear him at all? Because of the number of people with him? But no number of persons can conquer valor. Because of their nationality? But they have rather practiced carrying burdens than actual warfare. Because of their experience? But they know better how to row than how to fight at sea. I, for my part, am really ashamed that we are going to contend with such creatures, by vanquishing whom we shall gain no glory, whereas if we are defeated we shall be disgraced.

Whom do we really fight against? I shall tell you! Who are Antony's generals? There is Mardian the eunuch, and Iras, Cleopatra's hairdressing girl, and Charmian, her wardrobe mistress! Those are your enemies—to such depths has once-noble Antony fallen!

As if Mardian would not be a better general than *you*! I thought. You weak, coughing invalid, as helpless as a turtle on its back without Agrippa—how dare you even compare yourself to Mardian?

Yet Octavian's audience would not know the truth. How many had come of age since Philippi? How many had passed off the stage of life since the Ides of March took Caesar? Truth could not exist like a granite outcropping all by itself; it was infinitely changeable, it was altered by what surrounded it. Octavian's speech would enter the public record and the dust of time would sanctify it. If it survived. Truth was a matter of chance survival—a scrap here, a fragment there, spared by accident.

Antony returned, without Cossus, and picked up the folded speech. "And I thought Cicero was bad," he said lightly.

"Cicero laid the foundation that Octavian has built on," I said. "Long ago he smeared you for drinking and keeping low company. He even castigated you for cowardice, just because you weren't with Caesar in Spain. Remember his vow: 'I will brand him with the truest marks of infamy, and will hand him down to the everlasting memory of man'? It's been fulfilled. We have him to thank for sowing the field that Octavian is reaping now!"

"Cicero," Antony repeated unhappily. "It looks as if Octavian will be able to leave his back secure. A few more of those speeches, and we won't have any supporters left in Rome—or none that will dare admit it. There will always be those who keep low and wait for the outcome before rearing their heads."

"Then we must assure the outcome!" It all came down to that.

In addition to his speeches, Octavian's agents began discovering "omens" that they trumpeted to the credulous. Antony's statues were selectively struck by lightning all over the Mediterranean, so it was said, or else they mysteriously began sweating blood. If it wasn't Antony's statues, it was statues of Hercules or Dionysus, his gods. Then they claimed that a group of boys had spontaneously begun playing war in Rome, calling themselves Antonians and Octavians, and lo and behold! the Octavians won. What a *sign*!

Probably the truest indication of the real feelings in Rome was the report that a man had trained two ravens, one to say, "Hail Octavian, victorious Imperator," and the other, "Hail victorious Imperator Antony." He meant to make a sale, no matter what.

I was not afraid. I felt we could not lose unless we made an overwhelming mistake, and that seemed impossible. Had we not foreseen every possibility? We had prepared to meet the enemy anywhere up and down the coast of Greece, by land or by sea. We had ships ranging from "threes"—the fastest ships afloat—to "tens," which were floating castles, bound with iron, armed with catapult towers. In the army, too, we had a mixture of the core Roman legions with cavalry and auxiliaries. No matter what the enemy came up with, we could match it. There would be no taking us by surprise.

Of course, we had some weaknesses. By far the worst was the problem of maintaining our forces in fighting readiness over the winter. The army was stationed in different areas to make the burden of feeding them a little less onerous; like locusts, an army will strip its surroundings of food. We were importing the food, but the very presence of an army is like the weight of an elephant on the ground around it. Most of the legions were concentrated near us in Patrae, and Antony visited them regularly to keep up their spirits—and his. There was the Third Legion—the Gallica—first raised by Caesar, which had fought with him at Munda and with Antony in Parthia. There was the Sixth, the Ironclad, which had fought with Caesar in Gaul, Pharsalus, Alexandria, and Munda, and with Antony at Philippi and Parthia—glorious history. Then there was the famous Fifth Legion, the Alaudae, "Crested Larks," native Gauls who had served Caesar in their home territory and in Spain, Pharsalus, Thapsus, and Munda, and Antony in Parthia. He drew strength just from walking among them.

I went out with him several times, and I was moved almost to tears by their obvious care for one another. I had heard it said that Caesar had an almost amorous bond with his men, but I had not understood it until now, because I had not seen it with my own eyes. The way they looked at one another, Antony and his soldiers, the tone beneath the hearty ring of their voices, the eagerness to please, the bond of the possible ultimate sacrifice required, all cemented them into a single unit of men and commander. It is a magic that can never be predicted, since it requires a certain type of man on both sides.

They were showing the strain of waiting, like a horse wanting to run. I could see that, too.

"When, Imperator?" they would call, pulling at his cloak.

"When the enemy is sighted," he would say. "It will not be long."

It was worse for the navy than for the army. Lying in harbor is something normally to be avoided; it rots ships and morale. True, Agrippa had maintained a winter naval station when he was training his crews, but it was for a shorter time, and they were kept busy with exercise. Ours languished at their oars.

"Antony, is it to be a sea battle or a land one?" I could only ask the question safely when we were completely alone. I did not see how it could be both, and yet we were maintaining both services at full strength.

"I don't know," he had admitted, stunning me.

"You don't know?" I could only repeat it back. "Aren't you supposed to decide? Take the initiative?"

"It will depend on how things develop. It would be fine if we could knock them out on sea and prevent their ever landing—fight a pure naval battle. But that would be difficult. Ships are not as manageable as troops. The weather plays too big a part, for one thing. And mobility is a problem. Ships cannot move except by wind or oar, unlike the tramp of feet on solid ground."

"You prefer a land battle." I had noticed the way he had said "tramp of feet on solid ground," so affectionately.

"I admit it. I have much more experience that way. Although I have had some successes at sea, I am a relative newcomer to it." He put his hands on his chin, staring down at a small map of the Gulf of Corinth.

"Ah! You Romans don't have salt water in your veins like the Phoenicians and Greeks," I said. "And *you* come from a very old Roman family." I paused. "Of course, Sextus and his father were at home on the water. And Agrippa seems to be."

"Another reason I would prefer the land. Agrippa seems like a seal— graceful in water but clumsy on land."

"Then perhaps we should allow them to arrive unmolested, just to get them on land."

"And not use the navy at all? No, we should use it at least as a barricade. The fewer men they manage to land, the better." He paused. "And if we can lure them to Actium, where our main fleet is, we can overcome their fleet by our superior numbers and smash them."

Another weakness was that our line of defense was so spread out—all the way from northern Greece to Africa. Yet it is an axiom of war that the defense must be wide, whereas the attacker is free to select one spot and concentrate all his force against it—much more efficient and economical.

Still another problem lay in our being so completely dependent on receiving supplies by sea from Egypt, eight hundred miles away.

Yet how could it be any other way? The war theaters covered gigantic portions of the earth's geography. Antony's authority stretched from the Euphrates and Armenia to the Ionian Sea and Illyria, across Africa from Cyrene to Nubia. Octavian's spread from Illyria to the westward ocean, and included Gaul, Italy, and Spain to the Pillars of Hercules. The entire world was participating in the war, allied with one side or the other. The gains for the victor would be staggering, almost incomprehensible. So would the losses for the vanquished.

Let it begin! I could bear the waiting no longer. I was afraid we would lose our edge if action did not finally commence. But it was Octavian who was to determine the pace. And so we held our breaths at Patrae, still in the grip of late winter, watching the gray, stormy seas.

73

The seas stayed rough all through March. The winter did not want to release its grip on us, as if it were deliberately holding us back from action. Then, I thought it was cruel; now I wonder if it was kind; if the gods of the winds had pity on us and said, *Let us protect them just a little longer, let them live in the glory of the untried, the yet-to-come, spare them what is written. . . .* Who knows? Or perhaps it was just a fact, unconcerned with human fate at all, and our imaginations endow them with all this feeling and plotting.

In the middle of March—yes, on the Ides of March, I must say the words, that day forever cursed, stalking me through the years—fate struck, as if he had a return appointment with me on that date alone. Regular sea travel had not yet started, but Agrippa took half his fleet, and, risking a dangerous southern course, headed for our naval station at Methone.

Effecting a quick landing, he attacked Bogud, and in the action Bogud was killed. The station was lost—one of our key outposts, guarding our food route, lost in an instant.

The reports came quickly to us—naturally, as we were less than a hundred miles north. Frightened messengers—afraid that we would take out our shock and anger on them—came trembling into our presence, the reports flapping in their hands.

It had been one of those dreary, gray days, the kind that make you drowsy. We had found it hard to attend to any real business, and were making lazy circles on the maps spread out on our worktable with our fingers. I knew it all by heart, had been over it a hundred times. This cove, this mountain, that island . . .

The appearance of the messengers sent our languor fleeing. Antony was on his feet and reaching out for the dispatches, his face already changed. He, and I, knew something bad had happened. How bad, we did not guess.

"I see," Antony finally said to one of the messengers. "And you have come from there? How long did it take you?"

"I rode two days and a night," he said. "When I left, there was still fighting going on in the harbor, but it was essentially over. Bogud was dead, his flagship captured and burnt, the fortress-town taken."

Now I did not need to read the report. I looked at Antony; what would we do?

"Taenarum and Zacynthus are still secure?" he asked.

"As far as I know," the messenger said. "I do not think there were two naval actions going on at the same time. All of Agrippa's efforts were concentrated on Methone."

"So far south," said Antony, sinking into a chair. He looked around distractedly, then, out of habit, politely offered the messengers refreshment.

"They need a meal," I said, fastening my mind on the practical, as I tend to do when a crisis occurs. "They have not eaten for days. Go with our attendants," I told them. When they were gone, I turned to Antony. "What does this mean? How could we have lost one of our most secure, and important, harbor fortresses?"

"So far south," he kept repeating. "Who would have expected him to take a long diagonal route and attack us on the southern flank? I expected a crossing in the north, where the distance is much shorter, and we could intercept them. Now . . . now . . . is this where the main army is to be landed? Well, it is good that we have stationed our army in the middle, to be deployed in any direction."

Yes, that had been the purpose of it. But it also had the disadvantage that wherever the enemy landed, we would most likely not be there. Again, the hard fact of maintaining a defensive line, trying to anticipate an enemy's every move.

"What does it mean?" he said, coming back to my question. "It is difficult to calculate exactly what it means. Our food ships will have to sail farther out to sea now, but they can still get through. No army of Octavian's is in sight yet. We are still waiting to see what ground he will choose."

But it soon became clear what it meant. Agrippa left a strong squadron on Methone, which immediately began to harass our other naval bases, drawing off ships and men to combat him, weakening our overall defenses. Octavian, with the other half of the fleet, now sailed the expected short northern route and attempted to take our northernmost station at Corcyra. Perhaps he meant to base himself there and attack our main station at Actium. But a storm prevented him from capturing the island.

His hero Agrippa solved the problem by his continuing attacks on our other stations; soon the Corcyra ships were engaged in protecting their brother stations. All the action seemed to be taking place in the south, so the north was left almost unguarded. Under cover of this activity, when all eyes were fastened on Taenarum, Zacynthus, Ithaca, and Cephallenia, Octavian ferried his army the rest of the way across and landed at Panormus, near where Caesar had landed when pursuing Pompey. It was some hundred miles north of Actium, two hundred miles north of us at Patrae.

The army moved southward swiftly, apparently hoping to fall upon Actium and take it by surprise, with Octavian's fleet attacking ours and the army unchallenged. Their speed was astounding: only four days after landing, they had reached the harbor of Glycys Limen, at the mouth of the river Acheron, the last harbor before the entrance to Actium. This is when we were first informed of his arrival. It was as if he had come down from the sky.

So. The time had come at last, and after months of waiting, we must now make a mad dash up there. Octavian had indeed seized the initiative; could we now convert our defensive position into an offensive one?

"He won't take Actium," said Antony, more confidently than I thought was justified; after all, it is easy for an army to take an unmanned area. "The entrance to the gulf is only half a mile wide, and narrowed even more by shallows just outside its entrance. On either side of the entrance we've erected guard towers that won't let anything get past; they will rain down catapult boulders and fireballs on men and ships alike."

"How soon can we reach it with the army?" I asked.

"We'll leave immediately," he said. "The bulk of the army here at Patrae will be ready to march with us; we should get there in two or three days. We have to rescue the fleet; if we don't secure the approaches to Actium on land, Octavian's forces will line the shore and prevent food supplies from reaching our ships stationed in the gulf."

"What about the rest of the army?"

"They will follow as soon as possible. I haven't had a report yet on the size of the army Octavian has landed."

"We can be certain that it is . . . adequate for the task," I said. Agrippa would have seen to that, I thought grimly.

Octavian's attack was beaten back, as Antony predicted. He had attempted to draw our fleet out into open water for a battle, suspecting (correctly) that we did not have soldiers on board, and that the ships were not manned to fight. But our commander thought quickly, and stationed oarsmen and sailors on deck with imitation arms; the oars were poised as if ready for an attack, and the ships drawn up in battle line to face the enemy. It was a good bluff, and deceived Octavian. He withdrew and took his ships around to the only anchorage available to him, the Bay of Gomaros, just above the entrance to the gulf. And it was there we found him when we arrived at Actium.

We had ridden hard to reach Actium as soon as possible, with the army covering ground on a forced march behind us. The rocky, barren landscape we traversed drove home the ugly fact that there was no food to be had here in an emergency.

What kind of an emergency? The emergency of being trapped at Actium? The thought was chilling. I must not allow myself to consider it.

I do not think Antony expected me to be able to keep up with him. Once he had set out, he was all fierce determination, pressing on without consideration for himself, his horse, or me. He rode north on his mission, tirelessly, barely stopping. But excitement and suspense gave me strength, and I did not fall behind.

In the gray dawn, from the hills behind it, we first sighted the long, flat gulf wherein lay our fleet. It was large enough to contain our three hundred–odd warships, and they rode at anchor, looking formidable. I felt proud when I saw them.

We rode toward the mouth of the gulf, but it did not take long for me to appreciate the dismal conditions. Surrounding the water, the land was low, marshy, and treeless; we could not approach the shoreline very closely, for the ground was treacherous. I caught sight of snakes in the tall grass, and clouds of insects, buzzing and stinging, rose from the swamps as we passed.

Smoke was rising from what appeared to be a camp on the southern peninsula that guarded the entrance to the gulf. This site was the promontory of

Actium, and gave its name to the entire campaign. When people say "at Actium," they mean all of it, what happened by land and sea, but correctly it was only this little site.

In proper Roman fashion there were moats, fences, guard gates. Have the Romans ever made a careless camp? Antony and I rode up to the gates, where a guard demanded the password; Antony shouted out, "By Hercules! This is Antony! What other word do you need?"

In disbelief, the guard summoned a fellow, who verified that, yes, this was indeed Antony, as he himself had once seen him. Now the gates were thrown open and we rode in, to the stunned faces of the garrison who had been holding the fortress. They looked glum, too tired and run down even to smile. The winter here had clearly been unhealthy for them.

"O fortunate soldiers!" Antony shouted as he rode down the main street of the camp. "To have been the first to sight the enemy! It is a great honor!"

Antony's purple cloak was mud-stained and his feet filthy, but he looked fresh and shining compared to the soldiers, who simply stared back at him. Finally a faint cheer or two rose from the ranks.

"The army is on its way," he assured them. "Canidius Crassus is bringing eleven legions from Patrae, including the old Ironclad. Remember the Ironclad?"

They just looked back at him, wooden-faced.

"More legions are coming from elsewhere. And cavalry as well."

The commander of the garrison, Marcus Grattius, welcomed us into his quarters, when we dismounted wearily. My legs were shaky, and the ground felt odd.

The door shut behind us, Antony clasped the commander's shoulders. "How bad is it?" he asked. "How many of them are there?"

Now it was the turn of Grattius to remember that we were probably hungry and thirsty. But before we thought of even washing our hands, Antony demanded the figures.

"It is a large army," Grattius began cautiously. "You must understand, I have not been invited to review it!" He laughed, a sad-sounding laugh. "But from what I have seen, I would estimate about eighty thousand men. I have no way of knowing how many legions, or which legions. Of course they are all Romans—no foreign allies or auxiliaries." He turned as his attendant brought ewers of fresh water and towels for us. "Ah. Here we are."

Antony held out his hands as the water was poured over them into the basin.

"And where are they?" he asked, speaking above the sound of the water.

"They have established a camp on the northern promontory, on higher ground."

Higher ground. They were smart.

"It is well sited, except that it has no water supply. For that, they must descend to either the river Louros or the springs on lower ground."

A weak spot! I was relieved to hear it.

"It cannot easily be circled from the north, and it would be difficult to attack it from the south, being uphill. And the flat ground below can serve as a battlefield."

"Or a camp for us," said Antony quickly. "We should establish ourselves there; that way we will command both sides of the mouth of the gulf."

His hands were being wiped dry, and now the attendant came to me. The water on my dirty hands felt good.

"There is another drawback to their position," Grattius told Antony. "The bay where Octavian is anchored is usable only during good weather. It offers no protection from any storm, being exposed on three sides."

"So he will be driven to seek something else," I said. "How secure is Leucas?" Leucas, a mountainous island that lay just offshore from Actium, was manned by our forces. It was a crucial possession: As long as our ships could land there, we could receive the food supply from Egypt without interruption.

"Very secure," said Grattius.

Leucas was an island in name only, because the water separating it from the mainland was so thick with reeds and sandbars that no ship could sail through it. True to the maddening nature of the terrain at Actium, no one could march across it, either. It supported neither horses nor ships, being something halfway between land and sea.

"I am relieved to hear it," said Antony. His words would have convinced anyone but me; I knew he would visit it straightway to make sure.

Now that things were resolving themselves into concrete details, Antony seemed in control once more. Details he could attend to, rearrange, plan. No more surprises, now that his hand was on the helm. It is good when the nebulous begins to take a familiar shape and become something manageable, merely life-size.

The food arrived. Although my head was spinning from hunger, I was almost beyond the point of having an appetite. But I smiled politely.

There was crane, duck, heron.

"As you can see, we have an abundance of waterfowl," Grattius said.

"Yes, I imagine they nest in the marsh," said Antony.

Along with the mosquitoes and gnats, I thought.

"The fishing is good, and we also have a specialty in the area: enormous prawns. What's a delicacy elsewhere is common fare here." Proudly he gestured toward a bowl of prawns floating in a thick stew. "I am afraid I cannot say the same for the wine," he said apologetically. " 'Army rations' says it all."

"I don't care," said Antony, "as long as it cures thirst." He drained his cup. "Forgive me. I forgot to tell you how grateful—and impressed—I am with your ploy to arm the oarsmen and put them on the decks to look like soldiers. Quick thinking. There'll be a commendation for that."

The commander smiled, pleased to be praised by his leader. "Thank you, Imperator," he said simply.

———

We were to stay in the quarters of a centurion; Grattius had offered his, but we refused. As soon as our army arrived, we would be setting up another camp, a much larger one, and would have our own headquarters, with the commander's tent, *praetorium*, and the attached headquarters, *principia*.

That night, as we prepared to retire, Antony said, "Remember how you insisted on sleeping in a tent and turning your back on Artavasdes' palace? Now you can live in one, but we must hope for a quick resolution and therefore a short stay."

I had lived in tents before; when I had been in exile, expelled from Egypt. I remembered my days outside Ashkelon, and the sandstorm there.

"I will be here, with you, in a tent, for as long as it takes," I assured him. I was well aware that others would be less than pleased with that. But I had no intention of departing; let them cry "go back to Egypt" until they were hoarse. As long as Antony did not wish me anywhere but by his side, I could endure their hostility. No, I would not budge.

"Besides, without me, the client kings will lose heart. They will not fight just to advance Rome; why should they? They feel they have already given enough to Rome."

"What?" Antony asked.

I had been thinking out loud. Was I that tired? "My mind is wandering," I said quickly. "I meant nothing. Just that I will be here with you in your tent . . . as long as you wish me here."

"I have never fought a war with a woman by my side," he said.

"You have never had a queen for a wife," I reminded him.

"Do you mean to remain in camp, or will you wish to . . ." He sighed. He was too weary tonight to fight a personal battle with me over my direct participation in the war.

Now was not the time to discuss what I would, or would not, do. I was not sure myself. "Tonight I wish to sleep, as soon as possible," I said soothingly. And I did; I hoped that after staying awake all night riding, I would not be so overtired that I could not sleep.

He smiled, relieved to put aside all business. Now this interminable day-night-day would end. He would rest. Tomorrow he could face the situation with a clear head.

The centurion had prepared his regular bed for Antony, and set up another one for me nearby. Both were folding frames with leather straps, laid with blankets. Both looked very small.

"I see the military life has already begun," I said, eyeing the bed. "I suppose it's as hard as a stone, too."

"Of course. Soldiers must be tough." He pulled back the blanket and stretched out on the creaking frame. It shuddered and settled. He draped his arm over his eyes. It was not something he normally did; was it field behavior, to shut out the light?

"With equipment like this, how did soldiers ever get their lascivious reputation?" I lay down on my bed; it felt like the ground, except that it was not damp.

"They go outside their tents for relaxation," he mumbled. "Where do you think the term 'camp followers' comes from?"

"I don't think there'll be many women who will follow this particular camp," I said. Actium was not a congenial location to practice the oldest profession.

"No," he said, "only you." Then I heard him fall asleep.

Under the stretched leather of the tent's ceiling, I heard the wind straining the seams. They creaked and moaned, an ugly sound.

So it had finally begun, and here was where we must make our stand, in this dismal place so far from Rome or Egypt.

I awoke before dawn, shaking with cold. The single blanket had been inadequate, even though I had wrapped myself in it, and was . . . was I still wearing my clothes? I ran my hands down my arms and felt sleeves. Yes. We had been so muddled and exhausted we had forgotten to undress. I lifted my head out of the blanket in the dim light and saw Antony's brown tunic still covering his shoulder.

Actium. We were at Actium, huddled in a tent. This was the morning we had waited for for so long. But I had never imagined it like this.

The pillow was cold, but I supposed I should be thankful there even *was* a pillow. I burrowed my head into it and waited for Antony to awaken. While I did so, I said one prayer after another for our army, our fortune, our allies, and our children . . . back in Alexandria. *May we leave you an inheritance of glory, not shame.* Let us not be the cause of grief to them. In trying to secure their future, let us not lose it for them.

Eros tiptoed into the tent and awakened Antony. When I saw him I knew Canidius had arrived sometime in the night with his legions, and all was well.

Antony staggered up, shaking his head.

"My lord! My lord!" said Eros. "They have come. They are waiting for you."

The water for washing was so cold it turned my face into a mask. As we left the tent and walked along the hard dirt street, the brisk morning air did nothing to warm it. Grattius joined us and we left the fortified area to meet our troops. They stretched out all around us, surrounding and engulfing the camp. Eleven legions—about forty thousand men—were a huge host. But had Grattius not said there were twice as many across the water?

Besides these newly arrived men, there were the seventy thousand oarsmen who had been stationed here all winter, plus the soldiers of the garrison. How was this unhealthy place to house and keep them all? The refuse alone would make a mountain of debris. But that was what the military engineers and diggers had to attend to; it was not all the glory of building ramps and siege machines.

"Sir!" Canidius rode up, saluting sharply. His long, lined face looked even longer and more lined. "We present ourselves and wait to make camp where you direct."

Stretching out before us was adequate space all around the existing garrison, well away from the water's edge. Antony rode around it and returned, nodding. "I think we must keep all together for now. When the other troops arrive, we can spread out on the other side of the water. Of course, the engineers have the final say."

In true Roman fashion, they busied themselves all day surveying and laying out the lines of the camp, and by nightfall our tent and the wooden structure that would serve as our headquarters had been erected in the middle. While they worked, we conferred with Canidius, Ahenobarbus, and Dellius on the general situation. Of course I was present; it did not take long for me to see how this displeased the other commanders, particularly Ahenobarbus.

We were seated around a long trestle table in the garrison headquarters, where Grattius had unrolled a gigantic scroll containing a map of the area, painstakingly sketched. He pointed out to us where the enemy was camped, and the features of the landscape—where the bogs were, where the fresh springs were located, the elevation of the camp.

Canidius pored over it, saying very little.

Ahenobarbus asked a few questions about the state of the fleet.

"We have lost a number of the oarsmen," said Grattius. "Disease has taken its toll."

Lost oarsmen! I had provided crack Egyptian and Greek rowers. How were we to replace them?

"How many?" I asked. Ahenobarbus glared at me. What, could I not ask a simple question?

"I would say a good ten thousand already," Grattius said.

Ten thousand! And what did he mean, "already"?

"In the summer, when the heat causes swarms of mosquitoes, disease increases," Grattius explained.

"But of course we won't be here in the summer," Ahenobarbus snapped.

"No, of course not," Antony agreed. "As soon as the other legions, and the kings, join us, we will give battle."

"Land battle?" asked Canidius eagerly.

"It depends on the condition of the fleet," Ahenobarbus countered. "Right now there are only five squadrons—three hundred ships—inside the harbor. The rest are stationed up and down the coast."

"We lost a number at Methone," I reminded him.

"Yes, true, but we still have seven squadrons. When they arrive, they can attack Octavian's fleet from the west, and allow the rest of ours inside the gulf to exit and join in the attack."

"Octavian has been giving signs that he will seek battle," said Grattius. "First he tried to attack our fleet—"

"And was deceived by your stratagem," said Antony proudly.

Grattius nodded. "And now we have sighted a lot of milling up on the heights. Yesterday they lobbed fireballs over at us, and fired stones into the camp. They mean to provoke us into battle."

"When they outnumber us two to one," said Canidius. "How surprising!"

"We must hold them off until we are at full strength," said Antony. "And then—!" He smashed his fist into his palm.

"Right now the enemy fleet has no very secure harbor, and it is also to its advantage to fight immediately," said Grattius.

"At least they are free to come and go as they wish," said Ahenobarbus. "We, on the other hand, are bottled up inside the gulf. We can go nowhere without fighting our way out. We can choose no other ground for combat by land or sea; the enemy has pinned us down in this spot." His deep voice was resonant, compelling.

"When our army is at full strength," said Antony, "we will drive theirs back, into submission. Then their fleet will have to withdraw."

"I have another idea," said Ahenobarbus suddenly. "Was not war declared against Cleopatra? Then why not unmask Octavian's dishonesty? You"—he looked directly at me, not even using a courtesy title—"should depart with your fleet for Egypt immediately. This will force Octavian to follow you—after all, you are his foe, so he claims—and free Antony and me to sail to Italy and invade."

"True, if the Queen acted as a decoy—" Antony nodded, joined by Canidius.

How naive could they be? But I knew Ahenobarbus was not naive; he just wanted me gone. "If it does not work," I countered, "then we will have split our forces. Have you sage commanders never heard the tired old phrase 'divide and conquer'? No. It is a bad idea." I looked straight at Ahenobarbus, who scowled.

"We should attempt to send spies into their camp," said Dellius, to change the subject before tempers flared.

"I have tried, but it hasn't worked," said Grattius. "We can try again."

Men kept pouring into the camp, and it felt odder and odder to be the only woman among thousands of men. The only woman! When I was with Antony and his commanders, it was not so glaring—I was used to being the only woman in council meetings—but when I rode out in the mass of soldiers, all staring at me, I felt it acutely. There must have been women present, somewhere—smuggled in, or serving as cooks and laundresses—but I never saw them. Instead I was drowning in this sea of maleness.

It should have been a woman's delight, but I found it disturbing. It made me ponder the question: What is it that differentiates us? Why should I *feel* so different from them? What made me so aware of it? The way they looked? The way they looked at *me*? Or was it the way I looked at *them*? And yet I begrudged Ahenobarbus his objection to my presence at the council table, just because I was a woman.

They were all here: the rest of the legions, the eight kings attending us in person, bringing with them their troops and those of the kings who could not be here but contributed men and arms. The senators, all three hundred of them, had arrived from Patrae and Athens. The extended camp had been set up, with spacious headquarters and dining pavilion. Even Antony's and my tent was moderately comfortable. Or perhaps it was just that I was growing used to conditions in the field.

With the arrival at last of Charmian and Iras from Patrae, I was rescued from my position as the sole woman at Actium; along with them came a contingent of other women who would serve at headquarters as musicians, cooks, seamstresses, weavers, and providers of the long hair needed for the torsion springs of crossbows and ballistas. Nor were they here to relieve the lusts of the soldiers; intrepid camp followers had managed to find their way here after all, arriving shortly thereafter. Tempers in the camp improved mightily, and the number of spats and fistfights among the men fell quickly.

"Why, we are becoming halfway civilized," I told Antony. There were now coverlets as well as blankets on our bed—which was large enough to share— and braziers kept the chill away. We even had heated bathwater—sometimes.

He was pleased, having just reviewed the troops. We were now at full strength; nineteen Roman legions, with the Asian light infantry and cavalry, brought our total forces to about a hundred thousand men. We outnumbered Octavian. Our only possible weakness was that about a third of the legionaries had no battle experience, having been recruited after the conquest of Armenia.

Our attempt to place spies in Octavian's camp had been unsuccessful. Theirs was a close-knit and loyal bastion.

Now, in the lull before we joined battle, we would gather in the dining pavilion for a feast with our commanders and allies. It was an ancient tradition in the east, and seemed fitting.

Charmian had brought some of my ceremonial clothes in the trunks from Patrae, and she proceeded to dress me, choosing a modest gown of the richest material—embroidered brocade trimmed with pearls. I had wanted to wear what I referred to as my commander's uniform—it had a silver breastplate with a red cape fastened to the shoulders, and a silver helmet in the shape of a vulture's wings—but she emphatically pronounced it unsuitable.

"The Romans will be wearing their ceremonial uniforms, but that is because they have nothing else. The eastern kings will be attired sumptuously; wait and see."

She was right, of course. As Antony and I took our stand on the dais, before the standards of the legions and the emblems of the other contingents, and watched the monarchs and admirals and generals parade past us before taking their places, it was appropriate that Antony, as supreme commander, be in his most glorious military attire and that I be less conspicuous. His gold breastplate, richly ornamented with symbolic scenes and figures, enhanced his heroic proportions and made him seem to tower above the others, to differ in his very substance.

Each man was announced. There was Prince Amyntas of Galatia, the man Antony had elevated to his present position, tall and graceful, his robes flowing. "I present my two thousand cavalrymen," he said proudly. He was right to be proud of them, for they were reputed the best to be had.

Archelaus of Cappadocia followed, a short man going bald, a distant cousin of my suitor from long ago. He described his contribution and then passed by to take his seat below us. There was Deiotarus of Paphlagonia, as bulky as a Cretan bull, bowing and declaring his loyalty. Next came Tarcondimotus of upper Cilicia, a dark, nervous man, who pledged his utmost support and slid away. There was something snakelike about him.

Following him was Mithridates of Commagene, a jolly, round man with billowing robes that hung in folds from his ample girth, whose men were said to be fierce fighters. Then Rhoemetalces of Thrace, with a lumpy nose but beautiful earrings, and another Thracian prince, Sadalas, slick as a sacred cat of Bast. Behind them was Iamblichus of Emesa, stately and staid.

In addition, representatives of Malchus of Arabia, Polemo of Pontus, and the King of Media passed before us and recited their countries' contributions.

Our generals presented themselves—Canidius Crassus and Quintus Dellius and their tribunes—followed by the admirals: Gellius Publicola, Marcus Insteius, Ahenobarbus, Gaius Sosius, Quintus Nasidius, and Decimus Turullius. Sosius was still in command at Zacynthus, and Nasidius at Corinth. Turullius had incurred our displeasure when, in his zeal to help our shipbuilding efforts, he had cut down the sacred grove of Asclepius in Cos. It gave a bad name to our cause and was impious besides. We did not need any gods to be out of sorts with us just now.

The senators filed in, walking with slow dignity, and took their places. Somehow they had managed to have fresh white togas on hand for the occasion, lending an air of Roman *gravitas* to balance the gaudy eastern costumes.

It was now mid-April, and the nights had lost their deep midnight cold. The flimsy wooden pavilion, with its low roof, was more than warm enough with all these people crowded in. The industry of the junior officers had fashioned temporary dining couches, tables, and serving stands, draped with blankets and colorful spreads for the kings, generals, admirals, and leading senators. The rest had to make do with saddle blankets and military cloaks hung over the wood. Antony had, as a roguish prank, set out a place for his fellow Consul Octavian, which would remain empty.

"After all, are we not serving together?" he had joked to me.

"Not to his knowledge," I replied. But I was glad Antony boldly claimed the position from which Octavian had tried to dislodge him. Show, it was all show . . . but legality, constitution, all did not matter now. What mattered were the army and the ships.

The field conditions meant that the normal Roman seating arrangements of three-person couches had to be replaced by the eastern expedient of longer tables and couches; many more people were crowded close together. Antony and I were at the head of one very long table, with "Octavian's" place between us, and Canidius Crassus and Amyntas of Galatia on either side.

After the silver trumpet sounded and before the procession of dishes began, Antony stood and cried, "Welcome all! We expect you to eat full and drink deep, and not stand on ceremony, since we are in the field. When you want something, reach! When you wish to speak to someone far down the table, yell! And anyone having anything to say to me—why, just come right up! My heart swells to look out and see you, and before we part I shall speak of our campaign. But until then—I am pleased to tell you that there is Chian wine for all, as the ship just landed here at Leucas this afternoon." Feet stamped and people applauded. "The nets have hauled in fish and prawns all day, so you can eat till bursting. Neptune has seen to it!" He flourished his cup and took a swallow. "Let us enjoy his bounty!"

He sat back down and nodded to Octavian's place. "Pity you cannot join us," he said.

"If he did, we could stab him," said Amyntas eagerly. He brandished his dagger, which appeared gleamingly out of nowhere. It was curved and had some sort of engraving on its blade.

Antony looked appalled. "No," he said. "I swear that if my brother Triumvir were to walk in and take his place here tonight, I would welcome him and treat him courteously."

Yes, he probably would. That was both his flaw and his nobility.

"I don't think he's likely to show up," said Canidius. "For one thing, we didn't invite him, and I don't think he's succeeded in placing any spies in our camp to tell him."

The first of the dishes, bass cooked in wine and thyme, began making its way around. In my treasure brought from Egypt were gold platters, enough to serve the highest-ranking, and the fish was ladled out onto them. There were also gold knives and spoons, as well as cups. Always carry a limited gold service with you, was my motto.

Ahenobarbus, seated beside Amyntas, eyed the dagger. "You may sheath that now," he said coldly. Ahenobarbus did not care for most of our allies, and did not bother to hide it. "I trust your horses all made the journey safely," he said, tasting his wine. "It is a long way from Galatia, especially with two thousand horses."

"It was difficult," said Amyntas. "But now they are here. I trust they will be able to eat well enough. Little grows here, even for horses. Only goats can find anything tasty on the hillsides."

Amyntas was reported a most skillful horseman.

"I hope you will show me your favorite horse," I told him. "I would like to see you ride." I always liked seeing the best, whether it was a money-changer or an orator.

"Indeed." He nodded and gave a thin-lipped smile.

Beside Canidius, the blocky Deiotarus had heaped his platter so full there was no room for the next dish, boiled prawns with figs. The server sighed and passed him by. No wonder the man was so muscle-bound. He kept eating, silently.

"Do you have the same type of fish in the Black Sea?" I asked. His kingdom of Paphlagonia lay along the southern coast of the Black Sea.

"Eh?" He looked up sharply, his mouth full.

I realized his Greek was probably shaky. So I switched to Syriac instead, but he did not understand that. I had better luck with Aramaic when I repeated the question.

"Oh yes," he said. "And many more besides; we have the best fish in the world." He chewed. "Turbot, bluefish, tuna!" His eyes lit up. "Mackerel, and—anchovy!"

He had also contributed cavalry, but not many.

Sosius beside him was eating sparingly, and there was ample room on his platter for the honey-roasted duck that followed the prawns. He indulged in a bit more wine, tasting it appreciatively. "An impressive gathering of forces," he said. "I salute you. I feel remiss, remaining at the outpost of Zacynthus when the action will be here."

"But it is of vital importance that we keep Zacynthus and its channel in our hands, after having lost Methone," I assured him. And it was.

The kindly admiral smiled and said, "We will keep it."

Across from him, Tarcondimotus of upper Cilicia was nibbling nervously at the pieces of duck, holding the crisp shreds in his long, bony fingers. The way his wrists stuck out of his shiny bejeweled sleeves like serpents emerging from a dark cave, and his eyes, so close-set in his narrow face that they looked slightly crossed, all strengthened my first impression of him as a snake. I half expected to see a forked tongue dart out of his mouth as he savored the duck. Even his robe was banded and mottled, albeit in silk and jewels.

"How many men have you brought?" I asked.

"Ships," he said. "I have brought ships. Twenty of them."

Yes, of course. His country had tall timbers. But it was not on the sea, and had no history of sailing. The famous pirates were from a different part of Cilicia. I wondered how competent his ships could be.

"Wonderful," I said.

Next to him was the familiar Dellius, making the polite conversation at which he excelled. I watched him, remembering the first time I had met him, when Antony had sent him to summon me to Tarsus. His famous charm had failed him then, but never since. Antony employed him on delicate diplomatic missions, and had relied increasingly on him since Parthia, where he had written a flattering history of the campaign. (As flattering as facts would permit.) Time had done little to improve his looks, but I had got used to them now.

He lifted his cup and drank to "the Consuls," nodding toward the Octavian seat. Antony laughed and drank with him.

Across from Dellius sat Iamblichus, a prince from the remote Arabian peninsula. He looked lost. I wondered if he had brought a corps of camels. But they would be of little use here.

"So it is to be a land war," Canidius said smugly to Ahenobarbus. "In a few days we will be ready for our attack."

"It's foolish not to wait for the other squadrons and use the fleet," insisted Ahenobarbus. "And we might ask ourselves what will happen to the Republic when all this is over. Haven't we waited long enough for its restoration?"

Not this Republic talk again! Antony had made noises about promising to restore the Republic, and Octavian was claiming to represent the Republic. Enough about the Republic—it was beside the point!

"Antony will restore the Republic," said Canidius.

"Not with *her* by his side," said Ahenobarbus. Yes, he actually said that out loud. "She makes his position impossible."

Canidius shrugged. "I am a commander, and my job is to win battles with the men I lead. I don't worry about anything else." He looked hard at Ahenobarbus. "I suggest you concentrate on your ships and let the rest sort itself out later. It always does."

Ahenobarbus looked shocked. "What, don't you care? Don't you care what sort of government you live under? Have you become a slave, a slave like— like—"

"Stop before you say anything further," said Canidius. "I must protect you from the folly of your own tongue."

Grumbling, Ahenobarbus took an enormous swallow of wine, as if to drown his own words. He saw me looking, and frowned.

Hanging a few feet back was a server, little more than a boy, who looked hungry, and kept snatching pieces of food from the serving platters when he thought no one saw him. Then he would lick his fingers, smile, and graciously proffer the platter to the next guest. He must belong to one of the women who had just arrived. I found him amusing as well as resourceful.

That's right, I thought, grab what's passing and take it for yourself if you need it. Perhaps I would employ him; he had promise.

Now Antony had risen to address the gathering. He held up his hands, and silence fell instantly over the company. Above his purple cloak his well-muscled arms made a striking V.

"My friends, allies, comrades-in-arms, in the quiet before the unleashing of our might, I must tell you what I would have you know." He looked around at the throng, gathered from Italy in the west to Arabia in the east. "All is prepared, all is in readiness!" he cried, and a cheer went up. "And in such a varied army, you have each brought the war skills of your own country, making the whole mightier than each of its parts. We have hoplites, cavalry, slingers, archers, mounted archers, catapults, most of which are not to be found in the enemy army."

He lowered his arms and picked up a heavy gold pitcher, brandishing it to show our wealth. "Our enemy is poor and out of funds. He had to extort money from his unwilling people, which had the effect of making them prefer us! We, on the other hand, have each contributed so that no one land feels the burden."

Well, that was misleading. Egypt was providing the funds to support the army and the fleet. I suppose he felt his wife didn't count.

"And then we must consider another factor. I do not wish to speak of myself, but in this case the discrepancy between myself and their leader is glaring. Now I realize that you are the sort of soldiers that can win even without a good leader, but how much better to have a good one! And I may say, I could prevail even with poor soldiers. But with you I can do more than just prevail. Together we can triumph spectacularly. For I am at the age when commanders are at their very prime, both in body and mind, being hampered neither by the rashness of youth nor by the slackness of old age."

The company gave a cheer of approval. Antony acknowledged it and continued. "I have spent my whole life acquiring military experience. I know everything, from the tasks of the lowest soldier to the demands of the highest Imperator. I have known fear, and I have known confidence; thereby I have schooled myself, through the one, not to be afraid of anything too readily, and through the other, not to venture on any hazard too heedlessly. I have known good fortune, I have known failure; consequently I am able to avoid both despair and excess of pride."

Now the cheers broke out in earnest. As a soldier, Antony had no living equal.

"I stress this not to boast, but because you should realize how much better we stand in that quarter than the enemy. Their greatest lack—greater even than their lack of funds, their lack of diversity of equipment, their lack of numbers—is in their leader."

He paused and indicated the empty seat. "About his deficiencies in general I do not need to speak, but I can sum it all up in saying what you already know: he is a veritable weakling in body and has never by himself been the victor in any important battle either on the land or on sea."

A hush descended on the room. "Indeed, at Philippi, in the very same campaign against the very same people, he managed to be defeated while I conquered. As he was my ally, I graciously permitted him to share my victory."

That was true. But then, once Agrippa had entered the picture, it had changed. Even Octavian had realized he could not win alone, and so he had remedied the situation in his practical manner.

"Now, as to the two forces: Our navy is impervious to theirs, because there is no way they can inflict damage on us; our ships are too thick-timbered and high, and will carry archers and slingers to sink any who dare come near. And forget about Agrippa! Yes, he won against Sextus, but it was slaves and pirates with poor equipment he really fought against. And even then, Sextus beat Octavian soundly first. So remember that."

More wine was poured into my cup, but I barely noticed. One of the other servers dipped a red-petaled flower into the cup. I did not see who.

"As for our army, it is not only larger, but better equipped and led by a superior commander. So let us take courage! We fight not for small or insignificant goals, but in a contest for the very world."

I did not want the wine; my head told me I had had enough. I motioned to the boy in the shadows. He darted forward, not even embarrassed that I had observed him earlier, and took the cup, tasting it immediately.

Antony's voice had risen to that rich timbre that carried long distances. "And so, my comrades, if we are zealous, we shall obtain the greatest rewards; if we are careless, we shall suffer the most grievous misfortunes!"

He looked around. "Yes, misfortunes! For who would fall under Octavian's mercy? He has none. Where was his mercy to Lepidus, to the freedmen from whom he extorted money, to the landowners whom he turned off their property? To me, his own partner and a colleague of Caesar's, whom he has attempted to turn into a private citizen, deprived of his *imperium*? And by his own word, not by the consent of these senators here, who dared to oppose him and were banished from Rome! If he attempted such against me, in the fullness of my power, having just conquered Armenia, imagine what he would do to someone kneeling at his feet. And yet—here's the joke—he maintains he isn't at war with me at all! It is you he's declared his enemy. So he will treat you even worse!"

That was not strictly true, either. It was Egypt, and only Egypt, against which he had declared war. I bore the brunt of everything—the cost of the war, the opprobrium of Octavian's Rome.

"It is in our power to preserve our own liberty and to do something even more heroic: to restore liberty to the Roman people, now slaves to Octavian and his faction. Therefore let us strive to prevail at this present moment and gain happiness, for ourselves and the Romans as well, for all time!"

A frenzy of cheering broke out. Once again the master of oratory had hit his target, the most crucial audience he had ever faced.

People jumped to their feet and stamped. Just behind me I saw someone going in the opposite direction. Someone pitched, headfirst, onto the ground.

It was the serving boy, and he was rolling around and clutching his sides.

"Canidius!" I grabbed his arm. "Look!" I pulled him away from his place next to me, toward the boy. I thought he could help pick him up. But instead he held me back and knelt down beside the writhing boy.

He was jerking his head back and forth and baring his teeth, while his legs splayed and his back arched.

"Poison!" said Canidius. He took a spoon and tried to stick it between the boy's teeth so he wouldn't bite his tongue, but they were clenched too tightly. "Be careful." He wanted to avoid being bitten or scratched, having no idea what kind of poison it was. He searched the ground for any nails or glass. There was nothing but the gold cup, now lying on its side, a puddle of liquid around it.

"Don't touch it!" I said, suddenly knowing. It was the wine; it had been poisoned.

I turned and looked at the others at our table, dreading to see them fall stiffly backward. But no one did.

It was my wine alone that had been poisoned.

The flower. The flower that was dipped into it—by whom?

In the shouts for Antony, no one noticed the sprawled figure of the boy in the shadows, with Canidius and me beside him.

Someone in here had tried to poison me. Or was it someone from Octavian's camp? *I don't think he's succeeded in placing any spies in our camp.* Had Canidius been wrong?

I felt weak with shock. Right before our eyes, the boy went limp and died. It was a very fast-acting poison.

Now Antony had looked around for me, and was frowning. I would have to return to my place and act as if nothing had happened. It was especially important for the enemy to know he—or she?—had failed.

Antony was holding out his hand, waiting for me. Shakily, I took it and smiled at him and the guests. I was warmly cheered; no hint of opposition anywhere.

Now we would have entertainment, meager, but such as the camp could provide. There would be jugglers and singers, a few acrobats, and a camel trained to dance. The musicians struck up, playing their rattles and cymbals at full volume. My heart kept time to them, and sounded almost as loud to me.

The night was not finished with its surprises. As the camel was attempting to cross one padded foot over another to the rhythm of a drum, a sailor came running into the room.

"Imperator, where's the Imperator?" he cried wildly.

"I am here," said Antony, rising. "What is it?"

The man's clothing was stained and torn, his shoes soaked. He grasped Antony's shoulder and whispered something in his ear.

The camel was spinning around with decorated tassels flying off his saddle, and people were applauding, throwing pieces of dates at him. No one noticed the sailor but those of us at the first table.

I saw a dark curtain fall over Antony's face. He questioned the man quietly. "And how long ago? . . . When did you come? . . . Any survivors? . . . What is left? . . ."

The answers were given, and at length Antony bade him seat himself. Then Antony leaned over and told me, Canidius, Ahenobarbus, and Sosius, "Leucas has been surprised and taken."

Leucas. Our guarding island, where our supply boats landed.

"Agrippa?" asked Canidius.

The sailor nodded.

"By all the gods and goddesses, that man—!" Ahenobarbus exploded. "But the squadron there—"

"Sunk, or burnt," the sailor told him. "He struck at sunset. No one expected—"

"By Zeus, it's your job to expect it!" yelled Ahenobarbus.

"Not his job," said Antony. "The admiral's. Is he—?"

"His ship was sunk," said the sailor. "I presume he is drowned."

Antony gave a cry of pain.

"So now we are down to six squadrons, total," said Sosius.

"And some of them undermanned," said Ahenobarbus. "The oarsmen have been ravaged by disease."

"Now where will we land our food, clothing, weapons?" asked Canidius.

"It will have to come overland," said Antony. "The ships will have to land at one of the southern ports and unload the grain there, and then carry it here by pack animal."

"No, that's too difficult," said Sosius. "You can sail farther out, as I still hold Zacynthus, and then make a dash into the gulf from due west."

"Neither of these is satisfactory for long. Well, we will have to force the battle right away, before our food runs low," said Antony. "Yes! Battle within two days. This decides it."

The camel was finishing his dance, and his proud trainer was bowing to cheers. The camel stopped, then snorted and spat.

74

"Tighter, Eros." Antony was testing his breastplate, pulling on the straps.

"Yes, my lord," he said obediently. "It has been a long time since I have performed this duty." He yanked on one shoulder strap.

"I know. Three years since Armenia." He felt along his neck, adjusting the scarf that protected it from the edge of the armor. "By Hercules, it feels good to buckle on fighting gear again!"

I stood in the room, watching silently, seeing the beauty in the ceremony of attiring a warrior, while my heart hated the danger in it. I would rather have been going forth myself. But Antony had begged me not to, not even to ride in the rearguard. We find it easier to hazard ourselves than those we love.

He was holding his helmet, heavy ornamented bronze with a beak in front to protect the eyes, and cheekplates to shield the sides. Eros had lovingly polished it last night, and now it gleamed, topped by the distinctive crest that served to identify the commander-in-chief.

From his decorated breastplate, depicting scenes of his ancestor Hercules, hung a kilt of leather strips, augmented by metal ones signifying his rank. Beneath the strips I could see the purple of his tunic, which showed when he moved.

His arms and legs were bare, but his heavy nailed sandals laced halfway up his calves. He was holding his sword, turning it over lovingly in his hands. It was about two feet long, double-edged.

"My friend," he addressed it, "we have work to do today." The sword had been his companion on many other campaigns; if only it could write a book.

Eros fastened it, in its scabbard, on the right side of his belt, then stepped back. "There, lord. It is done."

Antony tucked his dagger in place on his left side. "The shield," he asked Eros.

Eros handed him the curved rectangle, with its brightly colored emblems designating the rank of the highest general.

I suddenly had a sickening vision of Alexander inheriting them; and it was sickening not because in time it would be fitting, but because Alexander was still young in the picture that flashed into my mind.

"I am ready," said Antony. "Come and kiss me."

My heart felt as heavy as a stone. What if this was the last time? I walked over to him and kissed his cheek.

"No, not that way!" He clasped me against him, against the heavy metal breastplate, and bent his head to kiss my lips. But he did not linger on them, as it would be unseemly.

"We'll beat them back to their ships!" he exclaimed, striding to the door to mount his horse waiting outside. And then he was gone.

Eros grabbed up his own much less elaborate armor and followed.

True to his promise, it was only two days since the fall of Leucas. It was of utmost importance to strike as soon as possible, before the deprivations that would inevitably follow. Earlier, it was Octavian who had sought a quick resolution, while we delayed. Now the tables were turned.

His capture of Leucas had solved Octavian's fleet anchorage problem. Now he had a protected place for his ships as long as he liked; he need not fear storms. His fleet was secure, and his food supply ensured for his army. And we—we were blockaded. Trapped at Actium, both the army and the navy. With astonishing swiftness we had lost our strategic advantage; our lifeline to Egypt had been cut. We had to break out, or perish.

And as for perishing . . . that night when we lay in bed together, I had told Antony about the poisoned cup meant for me. He had been practical about it.

"From now on, make sure everything is tasted first," he said.

"Is that all you have to say? I know that!"

"And you have no idea who held the poisoned flower?"

"No, I paid no attention. Someone who thinks his troubles could be solved by eliminating me. That means they think you will abandon this course without me—someone who does not want to sever ties with Octavian's Rome. It must have been a senator. Or even Ahenobarbus." The latter's disapproval of me was patent.

Antony had yawned. "No, it must have been an easterner. Poison is not the Roman way."

"Romans are notable for their willingness to adapt foreign customs."

"Not this one," he insisted. "Just be sure to take precautions. . . ." He had sighed wearily and fallen asleep.

Now he had ridden out to lead the army into battle, and I must wait at headquarters. Wait, wait, wait. Truly it would have been easier to have ridden out with him. Charmian and Iras stood by to keep me company as they had done so many other times. But there was no amusement or diversion that could fill my mind and heart.

Antony did not return at sunset. Not until near midnight did he rush back into headquarters. One look at him, with his clothing as it was when he departed, told me there had been no fighting. He yanked off his helmet and tossed it on the bed; his sword followed suit.

"He won't come out!" he yelled. "He won't face us!"

"Here." I helped him undo the breastplate. Underneath, his tunic was soaked with sweat, the sweat of anger, not exertion. I removed the heavy armor and put it safely on the floor, then smoothed out his wrinkled tunic.

"We issued a challenge. We fired stones and arrows into his camp. They are shut up in there like a turtle in its shell. He has built defensive walls down to the sea; that kept us from getting close enough to overrun them. Well, tomorrow we'll destroy them. We'll build machines that can flatten them. We'll—" He untied his sandals and peeled them off, kicking them across the room.

"You yourself have said that there's no way to force a dug-in army to fight, except by siege or subterfuge. I would think subterfuge would work better here than trying a siege. Remember, we are the ones blockaded. In effect, we are already under siege. To maintain a siege when you are already besieged— now there's a trick!"

"What, are you telling me how to conduct a war?" he yelled.

"No, I am merely reminding you of what you—in calmer hours—have pointed out to me."

He flopped down in a chair. "The weakness in his position is the lack of water. We'll cut off his water supply. The springs down on the flat ground— he's run his walls around them. But we'll ride around the head of the gulf and get inside them. . . . Yes, that's what we'll do. At dawn tomorrow—"

"Then you must rest." I rubbed his shoulders, hoping to calm him. "That is only a few hours away."

Before it was fully light, Antony and a cavalry force set out to ride around the gulf and come at Octavian from the east, sneaking up inside the walls and taking the springs. With him rode the eastern princes who had supplied cavalry: Amyntas, Deiotarus, Rhoemetalces. The Roman legions, led by Canidius, stood at the ready to swarm over the walls from the other side once the signal was given.

―――――

This time when he returned, his clothes were dirty, his shield scarred, its bright paint scored by arrows and sword cuts. But he was walking stiffly, and when he removed his helmet, his face was oddly expressionless.

Was he hurt? I flew to him and begged him to tell me.

"Hurt? In the body, you mean?" He sounded confused.

What was wrong with him? "Yes, of course that's what I mean! Is it your head?" Had he suffered a blow there that had dazed him?

"No. No, it's my—it's my—it's not a wound. No."

"What has happened? Did you take the springs?"

"Yes, indeed we did. The fighting was fierce. When their precious water was attacked, that got them out fast enough. They won't be drinking *there* anymore!"

There was more to it than this. "Then what?"

"We were to follow up by attacking the camp directly, since we were now inside the walls. But then, our faithful Deiotarus of Paphlagonia suddenly deserted. Yes, just deserted, with all his horsemen!"

"Deserted? You mean he ran away?"

"Yes, straight toward Octavian." He sounded both stunned and furious.

"No! He has joined him?"

Antony nodded. "Gone to ally himself with the enemy."

"But—" What possible gain could he expect from Octavian? I stopped. I had nothing to say.

The bull-man who had stuffed himself at the banquet and talked about his favorite fish! A curse on him!

"So now I know what easterner might have wanted to poison me," I said, just to say something.

"Well, we attacked anyway," said Antony. "And they came galloping out of their camp to meet us. And guess who led the cavalry charge?"

"Not Octavian," I said. Of that I could be sure.

Antony gave a brittle laugh. "A familiar face. Marcus Titius, late of our company."

"I hope you killed him," was my first, honest, response.

"No, he got away. He needs to live to continue changing sides. After all, he is young, he has a long life ahead—a long life of betrayal! Why, he may even come back to us someday!"

I hated the bitterness in his voice; it was a new note for him.

"The legions did their job," continued Antony. "The walls are down, and we are now encamped around their springs. So we are holding both sides of the entrance to the gulf."

"Are they now completely without water? What about the river Louros?"

"Yes, they still have that. It's farther from their camp. Next we can try to cut that off as well."

He slumped over and buried his face in his hands. I stood behind him and rested my head against his.

"It's only one man," I told him. "An insignificant ally. You have lost little, if it does not cause you to lose heart. Often such trifles cause us grief all out of proportion."

He reached his large hand up and grasped mine. "You are high-spirited, and such spirits are not easily cast down."

I squeezed his hand to reassure him. "The difference between victory and defeat lies in knowing which things to overlook. Think no more about Deiotarus, only think about the river Louros!"

The situation worsened. Agrippa continued his attacks on our naval stations; next Patrae and Ithaca fell. We had lost the Corinthian Gulf completely, as well as the last open passage that ships could make directly into Actium. Now everything must go by land, being dragged over narrow roads and craggy cliff passes from far to the south. We soon began to feel the pinch as food stores dwindled; it does not take long for almost two hundred thousand people to deplete their reserves. I remembered hearing that Caesar's men had been in like state in Greece just before the battle with Pompey, and were reduced to eating grass. Unfortunately, we did not have even grass to hand.

Mid-June, and I sat under an awning before our headquarters. It was stifling both inside and out; only this little shaded stretch of outdoors offered any relief. The fresh air that blew down from the mountains during the night had ceased. I leaned my head back against the side of the building, feeling the sweat—even at this early hour—starting to course in a leisurely way down my neck and trickle between my breasts. I fanned myself with a small fan, but all it did was move the fetid air across my nose. The stench of the marshes with their foul vapors, blended with the reek of the refuse from an entire army, smelled like a corpse on the third day. Any hope we had had that the tides would scour the area were disappointed; they were not strong enough, and merely sloshed back and forth listlessly, moving the filth but not removing it. If anything, they made it worse by stirring it up.

A meeting had been called, but no one had yet appeared. Many people were ailing. It was worst among the oarsmen; they were falling ill at an alarming rate, and deaths were reported. Antony had gone out to inspect the ships for himself, with Ahenobarbus and Sosius, who had left Zacynthus in a junior commander's hands. Once Patrae, Cephallenia, and Leucas were gone, Zacynthus had ceased to have much strategic importance.

I wiped my forehead with a scented handkerchief, as if that would counteract the swamp-smells around me. Flowers seemed from another world, a lost world.

Through the wavering, heavy air I saw Canidius and Dellius approaching, or rather trudging. In the heat, they had abandoned all their uniform except

the obligatory underlying tunic, and that was grimy and sweat-soaked. Canidius's was a faded yellow, and Dellius's had once been blue.

"Greetings on this fair day," said Dellius, his voice dripping sarcasm as
much as his forehead dripped sweat.

"And where is our Imperator?" asked Canidius.

"With the fleet," I told them. "But he will return shortly."

"The fleet is in a sorry way," said Canidius. "I think it will have to be
abandoned."

"Let them decide that," I said, more sharply than I meant. The heat had
stripped away our outer courtesy as well as our outer clothing.

"Have some wine while you wait," I offered them as a distraction. A pitcher
and cups stood on a small table we had set up outside.

Dellius poured himself a cup, tasted it, and made a face. "One thing we're
not short of here is vinegar."

The stocks of decent wine had long since run out, and what we drank now
was more medicinal than anything else. At least it did not make us sick.

"Be thankful we are spared the local water." Dellius had gone sour along
with the wine. "Ah. Here they come." I was relieved to see Antony and the
other two approaching.

"Greetings!" It never failed to amaze me how Antony could keep his essential sweetness of nature in the most bitter situations. Now he was actually
smiling. He raised his arm in salute. "Ah! My captains!"

"Help yourself to the swill," said Dellius, indicating the pitcher.

Antony did, and cocked his head. "I've had worse. In the retreat from
Mutina, we had to drink—well, never mind. Just remember the donkeys
stand ready to supply our lack." He touched my shoulder. "And how are you
bearing up?"

"I am used to heat," I said, to chastise Dellius. "Egypt is not exactly cold."

"True. Well, shall we begin?" Antony pulled up a stool and the others did
likewise. So we huddled, the six of us, supreme commanders, under a makeshift awning and a shrinking shadow.

"What did you find?" I asked Antony.

He shook his head. "It is bad," he admitted.

"Bad, and worse than bad," said Sosius. "Both ships and men have been
attacked. The men by disease, the ships by the rot-worm."

My spirits sank. The warm waters had bred the worms, a ship's worst enemy. We had not been able to haul the ships out over the winter and tar
their timbers, whereas Agrippa's had spent that time in drydock.

"I fear there will not be enough oarsmen to power them," said Ahenobarbus. "Even triremes require a hundred and seventy rowers, whereas the larger
ships, well—" He coughed and reached for a cup of wine, or what passed for
wine. "Pardon me." He hacked loudly, embarrassed.

"What will we do about the oarsmen?" I asked.

"We have already taken action," said Antony. "In this emergency, we have
had to—recruit locally."

"What do you mean, recruit?" There were no people in the area, and certainly none likely to volunteer for service.

"What he means," said Ahenobarbus roughly, "is that we are grabbing men. Kidnapping them—pulling farmers out of their fields, yanking mule drivers off their mules, snatching grinders from their mills."

Had it come to this? I was ashamed. "No!"

"War is not a pretty occupation," said Antony, and the soldier now showed, granitelike, through the politician. "But we must not lose sight of our essential objective: to win. Everything else must pale beside that."

Yes. Always the winning. There are those of us who understand that. As for the rest—let them go. They do not know how to bleed, how to sacrifice. "Can they row?" was all I asked.

"No," said Ahenobarbus bluntly. "Oh, they can move a ship. Muscle power alone can do that. But maneuver it, execute any real naval tactics, no—it is beyond them."

"But it is essential that we at least be able to move them. Otherwise we must burn the empty ships," said Sosius. "This way they can follow any breakout to safety."

"So that is what you are thinking of." Now I realized their aim.

"Yes," said Antony. "We have decided." He nodded to Sosius and Ahenobarbus. "They will lead a dash out of the gulf, while we"—he nodded to Dellius—"act as decoys by riding northward, as if we are seeking aid from Macedonia and our ally, King Dicomes. That will draw Octavian's attention. Then, when the ships have escaped, we will meet on the farther side of Greece, beyond Agrippa's reach."

It was a daring plan, and reflected Antony's creativity in battle.

"What of the army?" asked Canidius.

"I will take six or seven legions on board the ships," said Antony. "The rest will remain here, under your command."

Canidius looked unconvinced. "And what will I do? Wait to be attacked?"

"You won't be attacked," said Antony confidently. "Octavian will be thrown into confusion. Remember, he fights only under Agrippa's banner, and Agrippa is not here."

"Yes, I believe he is still occupied in the Gulf of Corinth," said Sosius. "He has now made after Corinth itself, and the naval station under Quintus Nasidius there."

"Good," said Antony. "Let him spend himself there."

"And I?" I asked. "Where will you have me be?"

"On board your flagship," said Antony. "You must extricate yourself from this place."

Ahenobarbus put down his cup and was taken with a coughing fit. Again he excused himself, saying it was nothing.

The awning began to rustle, a tiny little movement. It was nearly noon, and the scorching sun stood directly overhead. Antony stepped out and, shading his eyes, looked at the horizon.

"It begins," he said. "Soon the offshore breeze will start blowing, and you can expect relief, my friends."

Dellius snorted. He sounded like a disgruntled pack animal. "Relief? What's that?"

"When you are becalmed, even a puff of a breeze feels like paradise," I said.

"We are fortunate that we can count on the wind every afternoon," Antony said. "And every night. It blows down from the mountains all night, and in the afternoon reverses itself, so it comes across the waters and seeks us here." He smiled. "The god of the winds is doing what he can to ease our situation."

"Bah," said Ahenobarbus. "If he cared about our situation, he would blow so we could round the island of Leucas more easily. As it is, we will have to sail far out into open ocean to get clear of it when we try to break away."

Antony clapped him on the back. "Why, an expert sailor like you can manage well enough."

He grunted. "Yes, but can anyone follow me?"

That night, alone with Antony—our tent cooled by the mountain air, for all that it wafted the marsh odors toward us—I asked him more specifically what the true situation was. The doors stood open, the windows begged for the east breeze to enter.

He spoke soberly of what he had seen that morning. "The fleet is severely compromised," he began. "Both the men and the ships suffer." He paused, then poured himself some of the equally compromised wine. He kept no secret store of good wine for himself; he drank what his men drank. "I fear they are no longer battleworthy."

I stifled a cry. All my glorious ships! My men!

He came over to me and took both my hands. "Do not despair," he said. He lifted my left one and, holding it up, looked at it. He was staring at his own seal ring, with which we had joined our fortunes in Antioch all those years ago. "My dearest wife, when we bound ourselves to one another . . ." He dropped my hand. "Perhaps this was not what you envisioned."

"What do you mean?" I said.

"I mean you did not promise to endure . . . this." He jerked his head around to indicate not only the quarters we shared together, but all of Actium. "You thought to join two empires."

Yes, I had thought that. But in the passing years I had come to bind myself completely to Antony the man—not the Triumvir. "I will never abandon you," I said simply, "nor wish myself elsewhere than at your side."

"Ah," he said, "but the plan calls for us to part."

"And reunite," I said. "Does it not?"

"Yes. But first—" He dropped my hands and outlined the plan.

Sosius would lead the ships out of the gulf while Agrippa was still occupied in the south. Some fighting would ensue with the small blockading fleet, but

Sosius should be able to defeat the enemy handily. I would follow the first squadron of Roman ships, and we would later sail around the Peloponnese to a safe spot in Greece on the east coast.

"And you?" I asked.

"I will distract their attention by riding north with a large detachment, drawing off a legion or two," he said.

"I do not like being parted, and unable to reach one another," I said. I had grave misgivings, but I would not dishearten him.

"It is our only chance." The gravity of the situation revealed itself in his voice. "We have no choice."

I attempted to smile. "Why, then, when fate offers you no choice," I said, "you must appear to relish it."

He embraced me. "There's my brave captain," he said. He bent down to kiss me, and I welcomed it. It had been a long time since we had lain in one another's arms, and I felt distanced from him.

I reached up and touched his thick, sweat-dampened hair. "I will follow you and your fortunes throughout all the earth," I said. I had never thought to say that to another person, with no reservations. Even with Caesar, there had been conditions.

"May they ride a flood tide of victory," he said. Now he wrapped his arms around me. "I would be grieved to ask you to share anything else."

"Then you do not trust me," I said. "If you expect me to share only your fairer hours, then I am not a true wife, but merely a political ally."

"No, you are not that," he assured me.

He kissed me as if to prove that it was more. I held him to me, reveling in the feel of his body against mine. I felt that I loved him in his entirety, the solid flesh that stood on this ground, as well as the mind that made plans for far away.

We retired to our bed. I held him, whispering how I loved him. And I did; this time at Actium had showed another side of him. The more that was revealed of him, the more I found to love. There were no disappointments or lacks in this man; he *was* all he outwardly appeared to be.

Through the open window the mountain breeze entered and spread itself out in the room, as if to soothe us. I welcomed its coolness, which came as a ministering spirit to us, hovering over our heated bodies.

"Is this a fitting place to make love?" he whispered.

In truth, it had not been. Actium was the enemy of eros, skewering desire and turning it inside out. But tonight we would defeat it.

"The fitting place to make love is wherever I find you," I said. And it was true.

He sighed, and I could tell he had hated the long abstinence.

"Here," I said, "render yourself into my hands." I pressed on his shoulders and turned him over. He lay motionless on his back, mine to do with as I liked. "Oh, if an enemy should find you so," I murmured.

"They never will," he vowed. "Only you."

Standing on the deck of the flagship *Antonia* in the early morning hours, I touched my helmet to make sure it was securely in place. This time there had been no argument about whether I should wear protective clothing; both Antony and Sosius were only too glad that I had a helmet and breastplate, and fitted me with sturdy boots as well, and a thick fireproof cape.

"There may be fire thrown on deck, and most likely arrows and stones as well," said Antony. "Keep the shield with you at all times." He had handed me a small round one. He looked distressed to be leaving me, but he was no more distressed than I at having him gallop off over the mountains. "Do whatever Sosius tells you."

Yes, I would be up on deck. Belowdecks, with the rowers, I would not be able to see if the ship was rammed, and might be trapped. If we should be hit, there was a small rescue boat we could launch to escape from the deck. Besides, cowering away from action did not suit me.

"Yes," was all I could answer. I took his hand and looked at him. This was too public a place for private farewells. I had to believe it was not a farewell at all. And what we had to say had already been well said the night before.

The plan was for us to sail around to Iolcus—the port from which Jason had embarked to search for the golden fleece—and meet with Antony there.

We had loaded the flagship with our treasury, which weighed it down. But it was the ship most likely to withstand a battering, as it was the largest of the fleet, a "ten," and the safest place for our treasure, which is always risky to move.

Now we waited for the tide to turn to help us in our efforts to get clear of the narrow mouth of the gulf. Our makeshift oarsmen needed all the assistance they could get. We would row as far out as possible before raising sail so that the afternoon breeze (Isis! Let it not fail today!) coming from the west-northwest would carry us past the mountainous bulk of Leucas and out to open sea.

As for Octavian's fleet, it rode at anchor near the entrance of the gulf, blockading it. But the best fighting ships were away with Agrippa, and these leftovers were commanded by Tarius Rufus, no one to worry about.

Antony clasped my forearm, and looked up at the sun. "I must leave," he said apologetically. "It grows later and later." He was rowed back to shore, and I saw him disappear into the ranks of his men.

Noon, and the wind was still. The fiery sun reflected off the water, which was as flat as a table, no ripples anywhere. The far horizon melted into the sky.

Everything was ready. We had taken six legions on board the vessels, armed and ready for fighting. We hoped to surprise Rufus and slip away rather than engage in combat, but that was probably too optimistic.

My helmet was hot, and I felt stifled inside the cloak. I opened its front; no need to be bundled up now. On deck, the archers with their store of arrows, the slingers and javelineers stationed in the towers, were eager to set off. At both prow and stern were mounted catapults to fling stones and shoot arrows. Oh, we were a proud sight. But it would be better not to have to use any of it.

At the signal from Sosius, the squadrons began to move in file toward the opening. We had close to three hundred ships, and keeping them in formation was a task in itself. The first lot emerged safely, and from what I could see, Rufus's fleet was anchored to the north, not near the entrance at all. Then, as we streamed out and as my ship approached the mouth of the gulf, there was movement to our right; Rufus had been startled into action. The oars on his "six" were digging frantically and the ship was moving fast toward our lead ships. Trailing in his wake were two others, hoisting their collapsible towers and preparing to pelt us with rocks and arrows. And behind them a host of triremes and quadriremes stirred themselves into action.

Our oarsmen speeded up so we could escape the confined waters. We shot out past the two guard towers at the entrance to the gulf, but Rufus and his ships were closing in on us.

"Down!" yelled Sosius, just in time for us to duck and avoid a volley of stones. He then stood up and signaled to his own men to fire back. Fireballs followed, but rolled harmlessly off our deck and into the water.

Making quickly for our sides were two smaller ships, perhaps triremes. Their crews were propelling them through the water at high speed, and their gleaming rams, riding high out of the water, were aimed at our sides. One of them thudded against us, but was thrown back by our reinforced timbers. The other poised itself for an attack below our waterline. But a stone from our catapult almost swamped it, knocking it spinning. A cheer went up from our decks.

Several ships farther out had now engaged and were fighting. This was not going to be easy. "Faster!" Sosius ordered, to move us out into open water. We could not help our brother ships other than to fire on their enemies, and that we did, hoping to sink them.

Suddenly our ships broke free; Rufus's vessel had been injured, and all was thrown into confusion. We had a clear shot to escape. I felt immense relief and jubilation. Free! Free! We had got away!

But still no wind, and we could not raise our sails. Where was the wind? Why today, of all days, must it be late? The rowers could not keep up their speed for long. Behind us there were many more ships waiting to come out into the open water. And then . . . then . . . a heavy mist seemed to originate from the far side of Leucas, white and impenetrable. Like a malevolent blanket it spread out, creeping around the island, to the gulf entrance and, with astonishing speed, over both fleets. We could not steer, except blindly.

On faith we had to keep rowing forward, not at all sure we were going straight. We had to slow our speed for safety. I clung on to the rail, trying to see something besides whiteness to the south. And swimming through the mist I saw what I must dismiss as an evil vision, brought about by the confusion. It looked like . . . it looked like . . . it could not be . . . enemy ships!

Oars lifted out of the waves in perfect rhythm, flinging arcs of water to each side, and the prow of Agrippa's "six" reared itself not three hundred feet away. And dimly, farther back, were the shapes of others, like a running pack of lions.

"Back water!" yelled Sosius, seeing it at the same time as I. "Change course!" We must change direction and try to ram him head-on, rather than present our side to him. "Prepare to fire!" Soldiers climbed up on the towers, and the rest lined the rails, bows at the ready.

But the size of our ship meant that we could not change course quickly. We were in the process of turning when Agrippa was upon us, and the ship shuddered with the impact. I was thrown to my knees, and clutched at a pile of rope to keep from sliding across the deck. Crawling to the rail, I saw Agrippa's ship below, reeling from his assault on ours. Our stout reinforcements had saved us; his ram had not been able to pierce our sides. Our soldiers were now unleashing a hail of arrows at him, and managed to start a fire on his deck. A swarm of men ran out with hides to smother it.

"Let the Queen surrender!" I heard someone yelling; was it Agrippa himself? I pulled myself up to my feet and looked down. Could that be he, the tall, wide-shouldered man calling up to us, brandishing his spear? But in the melee it was impossible to tell, and it had been years since I had seen him, just a boy, in Rome.

The enemy had now formed a barrier out to sea that we could not cross; their numbers were so great they could afford to form a double line.

"Back!" ordered Sosius, and he signaled to the others to change course.

"Back?" I cried. After all this, we would have to return? I ran up to him and grabbed his arm. "No, no!"

Roughly he yanked it off. "We must!" he said. "We are outnumbered and surprised. Would you lose the entire fleet?"

"We couldn't—some would escape—"

"Not enough," he said. "We cannot risk it."

I had the authority, but not the naval experience, to countermand his orders. I had to meekly stand by while we—oh, the shame of it!—turned back into the gulf, rejoining those ships which had never managed to leave in the first place. I wept with anger and frustration.

I reentered the headquarters which I had thought never to see again. How different it looked now, what a hated prison! It looked—it ought to have been—deserted! Is there anything more humiliating than to return like that?

And Antony was gone, already crossing the mountains with Dellius and Amyntas and the Galatian cavalry and the three legions. When he got to Iolcus, and we weren't there—

I flung myself down on the abandoned bed and beat it with my fists. The bed, not meant for such an attack, collapsed in a welter of legs and straps.

Antony returned when he heard of our disaster. It wasn't only for me; he was unwilling to abandon his fleet and half his army. Now we were all back where we had started, except for the unfortunate ships lost in the attempted escape.

"A fog that late in the day"—he shook his head—"and Agrippa coming to the rescue in his timely fashion. It's hard to believe."

"Don't forget that the wind failed, as well." One would almost think that the gods had deserted us, that our cause was doomed. But I must not allow myself to think like that. What if Caesar had thought that way at Alesia? That was no way to win battles.

"Uncanny." Antony was sitting, his arms resting on his knees, hands hanging limply. "I would say—no, never."

He had been thinking the same thing as I. But we must not give in to that mood. The gods enjoyed testing us to see what we were made of, that was all. This was not final.

"It is time for another attack on the river Louros," he said. "I think we will have conviction behind our assault this time."

The day stood fair, the wind—obedient now, perfect for an escape, as if mocking us—blowing early. Antony would lead the attack in person, commanding the Roman cavalry and supported by Amyntas and his Galatian horsemen; Dellius would provide the muscle of two legions behind them. In case they were successful in forcing a wider battle, Canidius and the other legions were ready for the signal to swarm up the hill.

As before, they would ride around the head of the ten-mile gulf and approach the river from the east. If they could succeed in surprising or overpowering them quickly, Octavian's forces would be without a water supply. Let them drink seawater, then, and go mad!

Mounted and wearing my protective helmet and shield, I waited with Canidius. No, I did not expect to fight; I was not trained with swords or spears. But I could not bear to wait out of eyesight, not knowing what had happened until it was long over. And so, properly prepared, I sat my horse and watched, my eyes trained to the east, searching for any betraying movement.

Canidius rode over beside me. His horse looked thinner than was ideal, but that was not surprising.

"Hail," he said, reining up. His helmet gleamed in the fierce sun, making an intense spot of light that moved as he moved his head. He gestured toward the east, jerking his horse that way. "Today, the gods willing, the tide will turn in our favor."

Yes. *The gods willing* . . . They had been stubbornly against us so far. But their most outstanding characteristic was capriciousness. A shove here from Apollo, and Patroclus stumbles, a whisper from Athena and a mortal blow is averted. . . . Let this work in our favor today! Let them embrace us!

"What must be, will be." I was surprised to hear these words come from my lips. They were not exactly what I meant. "And what we wish, will be," I assured him.

Behind me the massed legions were waiting, standing patiently, as they had been trained to do. I could smell the leather of their gear and hear the low murmurs of their voices.

"How are their spirits?" I asked Canidius quietly.

"Were they higher, I would be well content," he replied tartly. "The conditions day after day wear away at them. And then there are the taunts from the other camp, the arrows and stones carrying messages, fired right into our midst."

"Saying what?"

Silently he handed me a paper, which he had kept folded inside his glove. "I picked this one up this morning."

I opened it. "ANTONY IS NO LONGER HIMSELF. YOU FOLLOW A MADMAN. HE CANNOT PROVIDE FOR YOU."

"Tired old lies," I said lightly.

"They are taking their toll," said Canidius. "I am hard put to counteract them."

"But they have seen him, they hear him speak!" I gathered the reins into my hands, wrapping them around my palms.

"Yes," he admitted. "But the lies wear away at them like drops of acid, corroding everything they touch. They wonder, in their hearts, how Antony can give them their plot of land when it is all over. He has no rights in Italy now. And that is what they really want."

"But the purpose of war is to *win!* Just as Octavian will seize Egypt if he wins"—horrible thought! insupportable outcome!—"Antony's rights in Italy will be restored." It was all so simple.

"Their hearts have grown faint," said Canidius bluntly. "Perhaps there have been too many years of civil war, and it is hard for them to believe in anything anymore. They are just tired, and want an end."

"Then they must fight to achieve it!" But I was not addressing the men; my exhortation fell only on Canidius's ears. His words were chilling, ominous. Had Antony lost his power to inspire and lead them? Had his fortunes run aground, mired in the faintheartedness of his men? What a fall that would be, what an unexpected thing to topple an empire!

"Yes, I know," he said. He turned his head abruptly to the east, his attention instantly riveted in that direction.

Now I could see the sun glinting on something moving; far across the gulf, many points of light danced as riders approached the swamps guarding the approach to the precious river.

"There!" I said, almost under my breath. But Canidius's eyes were focused on his legions; he had forgotten me, as well he should. The only thing that mattered now was the fight that would unfold at the river, and how we could win it.

He trotted off to take his position, and I was left to stare at the tiny moving figures on the far side of the gulf. No sound carried across the water; all I heard were the cries of gulls swooping and diving.

I clutched the reins and waited. If there was a charge up the hill, I meant to follow with the rearguard. I would not grieve Antony by placing myself in too much danger, but I must be there, must be a part of our battles.

I was trembling. I was surprised; I had not thought myself so tightly wound with anticipation. The troops were drawing themselves up, fastening their helmets, adjusting the hand-straps on their shields.

Then, from far away, a rise of voices—cries and shouts. The faint sounds of a tumult reached us.

"Ready!" Canidius ordered, his horse nervously prancing before the lines.

A horn sounded from the river, blowing notes we were to follow.

"Signa inferre!" It was not the command for a charge, but only an order to advance. The troops marched briskly in formation, aimed toward the hill, Canidius at the fore.

O Zeus! O Hercules! Be with your son today, give him strength and glory! I prayed. *Let Antony ride, resplendent, into the enemy lines, scattering them into confusion.*

A lone, wavering note sounded from the attackers, the music suddenly choked off in midnote. What had happened? I was halfway up the hill, but through the lines of troops and the distance, I could see little.

I saw some movement from the west side, but truly, it meant nothing. Canidius and his legions were still marching smartly uphill, but then the vanguard seemed to halt.

And then I heard the wild whoops, the cheers; something momentous had happened, but I was still ignorant of what. I saw horses galloping westward, but whose? Was it Antony leading the attack? They were moving swiftly.

The unmistakable din of fighting now reached my ears. Even if one had never heard it before, it was identifiable. The most sequestered scholar, who had only read Plato, would have recognized it instantly.

The moment had come! I drew myself up in the saddle, ready to gallop forward. Waiting was agony, but it would only last a little longer. And then—and then—!

My heart had leapt, utter relief buoying it up. The moment that would decide all had come at last. And it was as welcome as a lover, although I had dreaded it as I would an emissary of death. How surprising we are, even to ourselves. Our ranks bristled with swords drawn, horses trembling at the ready. And then, Antony's lines far away seemed to split in half—one side kept galloping west; the rest milled and then headed downhill, in our direction.

"Canidius!" I cried, searching for him. What had happened? I must know; he must tell me. But I could not find him.

The legionaries stood their ground, proceeding no farther. A horn sounded. Retreat!

Retreat? Why must we retreat? The troops around me began falling back, but I moved off to one side and let them pass. Soon Canidius and the front ranks were marching past, but still I stood aside, waiting.

I recognized Antony's bay warhorse, flashing with all his trappings, heading down the hill, followed by his mounted troops. He was not running away, but he was moving fast. I signaled to him as he approached; he motioned to me to fall in with him, and I did. His face was set grimly ahead, and he barely looked at me.

"Antony, what is it?" I cried, hoping he would hear me and be able to respond.

He did not answer, just leaned forward, urging his horse.

"What has happened?" I called again, leaning sideways toward him.

"Amyntas has deserted," he shouted, "taking his cavalry with him."

Amyntas and the Galatian riders! The backbone of the cavalry!

I almost fell off my own horse, so shocked I forgot to grip with my knees. This was a body blow!

"No attack," he said. "We were betrayed by our own forces."

So the river was still secure! Octavian could drink all he wished, in safety.

We galloped back into our camp, with only the remaining Roman cavalry to accompany us. Canidius and Dellius were left to deal with the untried legions, who would tramp back into camp behind us.

Antony retreated into his wooden headquarters, brusquely fending off questions and entreaties. Eros went in after him, and was turned out. He emerged looking distressed. Outside the headquarters a crowd of soldiers gathered; they were bewildered and wanted their Imperator to explain what had happened. Even Sosius was not admitted, and stood angrily by the door, insulted.

Antony had to come out and face them. I must see to it. I strode through the crowd, my helmet tucked under my arm, using my shield to push the men aside. I tried the door and found it bolted from inside.

"Open this door!" I said, loudly enough to carry through all the rooms, to reach him wherever he was.

There was no answer.

"Open this door, in the name of the Queen of Egypt!" I commanded.

Still silence. I hammered on the door, and finally I heard a sound inside.

"The Queen of Egypt demands to enter these headquarters," I repeated.

"The request of the Queen must be deferred for now." Antony's voice was muffled and sounded far away.

How dare he? In front of all these men, to deny me entrance! Maybe the slogans were right; maybe he *was* losing his mind!

"The Queen will enter!" I insisted, loudly.

"Who?" he asked. "Who will enter?"

"Your wife," I finally said. "Your wife asks leave to enter."

Only then did he unfasten the door and admit me. The crowd cheered; I was too surprised to be angry.

Once inside, Antony sat stonelike on a chair, grasping its arms and staring straight ahead. I stood in front of him and waited for him to raise his head and look at me. Instead he stubbornly kept it at the same level.

"Antony!" I said. "This is not seemly. You cannot hide in here."

Finally he spoke. "Can I not have a moment's privacy? I must have a few moments to myself."

"Not *these* moments," I said. "Not immediately after the—"

"The battle? What battle? The Battle That Never Was. Or perhaps you mean the desertion! Is that what you mean?" His voice was as bitter as the waters of the Dead Sea I had tasted long ago.

"Whatever it is, you must say some words to your men. They need it; they are depending on you."

"What, to make sense of it for them? Shall I tell them what it means? The best horsemen, gone to Octavian? And that it was Amyntas—Amyntas, the prince I chose, and elevated, and made what he was!" Now the pain beneath the anger began to emerge. "Perhaps I cannot choose; perhaps I lack the ability to discern a man's character. I trusted Artavasdes—and I trusted Amyntas."

"When someone wishes to deceive, it is hard to penetrate his screen." I remembered Amyntas's little show of pulling out his dagger and demonstrating how eager he was to stab Octavian. I tried to be soothing, but Antony's words had a ring of truth to them. It had taken him a long time to finally see through Octavian, and only because Octavian had obligingly dropped his mask. And then there were Plancus and Titius.

He lifted his chin and looked at me, but I did not like the expression in his eyes.

"They say I was a fool to trust *you*," he said. "That all you have ever wanted me for was my power to bestow territory on you." He laughed, but not in mirth. "And I have done that, indeed. The Donations—now even this war—"

First I had had to humble myself in public and address him only as his wife before the troops—and now this. I tried to remember that he was in shock from what had just happened, and in his pain was lashing out at anything near. Still, it hurt that he could think it even for a moment.

Oh, he was just angry, we tell ourselves when someone blurts out something he later apologizes for. But a word, once spoken, lingers forever; to keep peace we pretend to forget, but we never do. Strange that a spoken word can have such lasting power when words carved on stone monuments vanish in spite of all our efforts to preserve them. What we would lose persists, lodged in our minds, and what we would keep is lost to water, moths, moss.

"It grieves me that you would think that," I finally said, stiffly. "I think I have lost more in this association than you!" There, now I had attacked back, when I had meant to hold my tongue. "I have spent a fortune, and my entire country is at risk!"

"Always your country! Do you think of nothing else?"

Outside I could hear the sounds of the crowd. He would have to address them soon.

"I am a queen," I said. "And that is what queens must do."

Now he stood up, and grabbed my shoulders, twisting his fingers against the bone. "And I thought you were my wife, and held that office highest of all things."

"Is that why you would open the door to the wife, but not to the Queen? Why must you make it a contest between the two? They are the same person." I wished he would let go of my shoulders. "And you are the Imperator, and must go back to your men! What we as husband and wife have to say must wait."

"Ah yes." He kept squeezing my shoulders. "This defeat is decisive for the land operations," he said. "I do not—I do not—" He looked close to tears. "I do not know the next step. I cannot see ahead of me."

"They don't need to know the next step!" I told him. "They only need to know that their leader is himself, and that they may have confidence in him. Antony, if your men lose confidence in you, then the battle is lost in advance."

"What battle? What battle?" he kept saying. "There can be no battle."

"You do not know that. Wait. Sleep. Think. But, for the love of Hercules, go out and speak to them!"

Now he dropped his hands from my aching shoulders. "Yes. I will."

As if some spirit had entered him, he went outside and talked to his men. I heard his voice, loud and sure, heard the cheers and laughter. He was convincing, then. I felt relief flow over me like a mountain stream, cool and refreshing. There might still be hope.

That night, desolation settled on him. He had asked Sosius and Ahenobarbus to attend us after supper to discuss the state of the fleet, now that the land operations were suspended. We had lost several ships in the attempted escape, and poor Tarcondimotus of upper Cilicia had been killed in the action.

"You see," I said, "not all the client kings are disloyal. He gave up his life. And so far from home." It seemed sad that he had met his end on the sea, since his country was landlocked. I also regretted comparing him to a snake, if only in my own mind.

Antony shook his head. "Poor devil."

"If we give up now, it will have been in vain." I feared that Antony was close to despair.

"So there must be more deaths to redeem his?" He looked around. "Where *are* they? It grows late. And I am—tired." He poured out a big cup of wine.

We waited silently, and then after what seemed forever, and a second cup of wine for Antony, Sosius appeared. His usually calm face was strained.

"Welcome," said Antony. "I will try not to keep you very late. As soon as Ahenobarbus appears, we—"

"He won't appear, sir," said Sosius, his voice shaking. "He's gone."

"To Octavian?" Antony did not sound surprised, but resigned. That was more alarming to me than Ahenobarbus's departure. "He left a note?" He sounded as if it were a courtesy note for a dinner party.

"Yes, sir. Here it is." He held it out with hands that trembled slightly.

"Hmm." Antony broke the seal and read. "Like a true sailor, he has embarked before the tide has completely ebbed." He tossed the letter on his table. "Read."

I let Sosius look first, then I took it. Ahenobarbus had had himself rowed across as soon as darkness fell. But there was something odd about the letter; it had a note beyond political leave-taking.

"Had his cough worsened?" I asked.

Sosius had to think. "Why—yes. He was in bed early last night, and at dinner he ate little because of the cough."

Perhaps he had crawled away to die. Perhaps he thought Octavian would be more merciful to his heirs in Rome if he made peace with him. Perhaps—

"His possessions are still in his quarters?" Antony asked suddenly.

"Yes, everything," said Sosius. "Even his favorite brass-bound trunk."

Only a dying man would do that.

"I will send them all after him," said Antony.

"Sir!" protested Sosius. "A man should pay some price for desertion!"

Antony shrugged. "But not his brass-bound trunk." He laughed thinly. Then he poured more wine.

"Sosius, if you wish to follow"—he nodded solemnly—"do so now."

"Sir!" Sosius was shocked.

"Because, henceforth, if I catch any deserters, I am going to execute them as a warning. This is becoming a dangerous hemorrhage, and I will have to take drastic measures to stanch it." He lifted his cup. "But you, friend, I will give safe passage."

"Sir!"

"Very well. But this is your last chance." Antony took a long swallow.

The wine . . . oh, dear gods! Let us not have another episode like Pergamon! I watched him carefully.

But he seemed dead sober, as if the shocks of the day had cut him so deep even the wine could not numb him further.

"I think we must turn our attention back to the ships," Antony said. "After the attempted escape, what is their state?"

Sosius gave a quick tally: There were more ships than able oarsmen to man them, and the remaining rowers were in a bad way, both in body and spirit. Their bodies suffered from the food shortage—our only source of grain was bags hauled by Greek villagers over the mountains—and their spirits from the inactivity, inexperience, illness, and failed escape.

"A deadly combination, sir," said Sosius.

"By the gods, man, can they still sit and row?"

"Yes," he answered.

"Then row they shall," said Antony grimly. "And soon."

At last we could retire to sleep, the faithful Eros and Charmian silently preparing us. Once we were alone, we still did not speak. Words seemed futile. Antony lay on his side, turning away from me.

793

Just when my weary mind finally began to release its grip on this day, and the pinpricks of light from the hanging lantern were starting to blur, another message arrived. Antony sat up and read it in the faint light.

Rhoemetalces of Thrace and Marcus Junius Silanus, a commander, had slipped away under cover of darkness to join Octavian.

(75)

"You have only seen him win. You don't know a man until you see him lose." Olympos had once said those words, casually, about a chariot racer I had wished to reward by appointing him overseer of the royal stables. Now they haunted me.

You don't know a man until you see him lose.

Antony's despair, his fits and starts, his irresolution after the second cavalry attack failed, were worse than the defeat itself. I watched in disbelief as this man, whom I thought I had known down to the bone, seemed to break up like a ship caught on the rocks.

Prince Iamblichus of Emesa and Quintus Postumius, a senator, tried to sneak away, but were caught, and executed by Antony as a warning. That stopped the desertions among the higher ranks, but how much longer would it be until the common soldiers aped their officers and began deserting themselves?

We were constantly tormented by the messages and slogans fired into our camp, all of them insulting and most urging our men to desert. Someone—Octavian himself?—was thoughtful enough to send a copy of a poem written by Horace celebrating our ignominious sea retreat and Amyntas's desertion. It must have been Octavian, since the poem was written to his intimate, M aecenas. Who else would have had a copy of it?

It seemed they were rejoicing in Rome, bringing out their best wine.

> *When, blest Maecenas, shall we twain*
> *Beneath your stately roof a bowl*
> *Of Caecuban long-hoarded drain,*
> *In gladsomeness of soul,*
> *For our great Caesar's victories,*
> *Whilst, as our cups are crowned,*
> *Lyres blend their Doric melodies*
> *With flute's barbaric sound?*

A Roman soldier (ne'er, oh, ne'er,
Posterity, the shame avow!)
A woman's slave, her arms doth bear,
And palisadoes now;
To wrinkled eunuchs crooks the knee,
And now the sun beholds
'Midst warriors' standards flaunting free
The vile pavilion's folds!

Maddened to view this sight of shame,
Two thousand Gauls their horses wheeled,
And wildly shouting Caesar's name,
Deserted on the field;
Whilst steering leftwise o'er the sea
The foemen's broken fleet
Into the sheltering haven flee,
In pitiful retreat,

Vanquished by land and sea, the foe
His regal robes of purple shifts
For miserable weeds of woe,
And o'er the wild waves drifts. . . .

Come, boy, and ampler goblets crown
With Chian or with Lesbian wine
Or else our squeamish sickness drown
In Caecuban divine!

Thus let us lull our cares and sighs,
Our fears that will not sleep,
For Caesar and his great emprise,
In goblets broad and deep!

Both the truths and the untruths made me sick. Amyntas had not deserted because he was disgusted by the sight of my pavilion (what pavilion?) or my eunuchs (what eunuchs?); nor was Antony my slave. But we *had* been forced to effect a "pitiful retreat" back into the gulf, and . . .

Should I show it to Antony? It would have fired the old Antony; first he would have laughed, then he would have set out to punish the taunters. But this new Antony—this stranger, *vanquished by land and sea, his regal robes of purple shifts for miserable weeds of woe*—would it break him completely? I folded up the offensive poem and hid it. I was afraid to take the chance.

Swelter: to be faint from heat. To be oppressed by heat. To sweat profusely. That is what we did, at Actium in July. July. The month of Julius. On Caesar's birthday, the twelfth of that month, we held a sweltering dinner of commemoration, in which sweltering guests ate meager food, served by sweltering servants under a moon that even seemed to emit heat. Yes, a hot moon, its beams burning, searing the scum-rimmed waters of the gulf, making their stink rise.

The food on our plates was scant enough. There were some boiled beans, some toasted cattails (I had remembered the toasted papyrus stalks in Egypt and tried a substitute), moldy bread, and the ever-sustaining fish. And wine so sour it made the mouth pucker.

I thought of Maecenas and Horace drinking their delicate amber Caecuban, somewhere in Rome.

"Why, I wager even Octavian's pretty little pages are drinking Falernian," said Dellius, echoing my own thoughts. He was frowning into his cup. "If he brought them with him, that is."

"He probably never travels without them," I said. Octavian, like many Romans, evidently kept what were called *deliciae* for his pleasures. But of course he felt free to insult Mardian as a eunuch!

Dellius took another swallow of the wine, making unpleasant noises with his mouth to indicate his suffering. I tried not to dwell on the enemy camp, with its ample supplies for the men and dainties for the officers.

The last of Antony to change was his public self, and he was able to preside over the gathering in his old manner. The moonlight falling on his tousled hair showed a head still held high, dark eyes alert to all that passed, white teeth ready to flash in laughter. Sweat gleamed on the cords of his thick neck, and on the sinews of his forearms as he held his cup, but the heat did not wilt him.

"To the god Caesar," he said, raising his goblet.

Everyone drank.

But the unspoken thought must have hovered in everyone's mind: What would Caesar do in this position? It was unthinkable that he would not be able to extricate himself and force a victory. But how? How?

"And to his true son, Ptolemy Caesar," Antony continued. He raised his cup again. The others followed.

We must not lose sight of that; it was Caesar's son's heritage we were defending. Surely Caesar himself would lend us aid! I thought.

I felt unwell, unsteady and weak. I kept telling myself that it was merely from the near-starvation rations we were on. I prayed it was nothing more. Ahenobarbus had indeed died only a few days after his departure. Even the highest-ranking were not immune from the diseases sweeping through the troops.

Gathered about us were our officers and about twenty senators, none of them looking robust. I heard a cough here and there, discreetly muffled. In the general discomfort of the camp, togas had long since been laid aside, and the senators were wearing only tunics, as were the military officers. Without their distinctive dress, they were hard to tell apart.

I picked at my food; starved as I was, I had no appetite. The moon seemed to be glaring down at me malevolently.

"When do we leave?" asked a senator suddenly. "It seems that we must move, do *something*."

"And what do you suggest, Senator?" Antony asked blandly.

"Run the entire army over them. Send all nineteen legions against them—overrun their camp."

"Ah! If only we could. But they are surrounded by stout defenses."

"Then batter them down!"

"I am afraid I did not bring siege machines."

"Wouldn't have mattered if you did," I heard someone muttering from the back. "They didn't last long in Parthia."

"We will indeed do something," Antony assured them. "But we must be sure it is the right thing. We cannot afford a mistake—now."

Men were shaking their heads, as if they were thinking, *Yes, you've made enough already*. But most likely they were all in their own dream worlds, making perfect military plans—even the non-soldiers. Especially the non-soldiers. It is impossible to get a consensus from so many people, which is why great commanders have to act alone, trusting to their lonely inspiration.

"Pity about Marcus Licinius Crassus," someone dared to say.

Crassus, commander of our garrison in Crete and of the four legions guarding Cyrenaica, had gone over to Octavian.

Antony handled it well. "Crassus changed for political reasons, but—what a tribute for us!—his troops did not follow suit. Yes, they refused to be disloyal, and thus Cyrenaica is still secure. I have appointed Lucius Pinarius Scarpus, a relative of the great Caesar's, in his place there." He lifted his goblet again. "Caesar, you are with us still!"

"Where was he in Corinth?" someone asked. Agrippa had succeeded in ousting Nasidius from his command there; we had now lost the entire region.

Still Antony would not be provoked. "Everyone knows Caesar was not a naval man," he said, with a smile.

"General Atratinus in Sparta has gone over," someone else said, "and I have been informed that Berytus has thrown off the Ptolemaic yoke." He turned to me accusingly.

I felt a flash of anger at his taunt, but I did not show it. "Berytus was always a troubled spot," I finally said. "Such places take advantage of unsettled conditions. But it is temporary." I paused. "Quintus Didius in Syria, with his three legions, is still our loyal governor, and will address the problem."

Forcing myself to smile as I sipped the wretched wine, I knew the real difference between our camp and Octavian's was not the quality of the wine but the bickering, questioning, and rivalry between our leaders. Our lack of consensus was glaring, whereas in Octavian's headquarters they were probably all of one mind. This put us at a grave disadvantage. *There is a strength in the union even of very sorry men*, Homer had said. By the same token, even the strongest men are undone by quarrels.

"Have you noticed," someone asked snidely, "that no one seems to be crossing the lines to come over here?"

A swarm of insects flew overhead, buzzing and circling our torches. Some were burnt, making crackling noises. I nodded to our attendants to start fanning to waft them away. It was that still time of evening, before the nightly breeze came down from the mountains.

The dinner ended early, to my relief. I was pleased that we had managed to honor Caesar even here, but any gathering was now unpleasant. The guests wandered away, back to their tents; no one wanted to linger by the water's edge.

But Antony and I did, turning to see our fleet waiting, like chained animals, on the moonlit waters. We stood side by side on the banks and watched.

"You answered them well tonight," I finally ventured to say. "It is unfortunate that we must have these gatherings."

He sighed, discarding the mask of the hearty man he had just played. "If we did not, worse rumors would arise. They would say—oh, the gods know what! I must show my face on a regular basis, attempt to placate them."

"And listen to them."

"Yes, listen to them. Both what they say and what they do not say."

"I think the latter was louder tonight."

"Oh yes, I sense their mood. General discontent, fear, panic—nothing good!" He gave a quiet laugh, and tightened his arm about my waist. "You are so thin. Are you feeling well?"

"Yes," I lied. No need to add to his worries. "It has been a long time since you put your arm there; you have just forgotten." He had kept away from me, living in an abstinence that would have shocked Octavian. But when the spirits are crushed, the appetites flee.

"I would never forget," he said. "Do not take my absence for something willful."

I leaned my head back against his arm to show him I meant nothing by my remark. "I know," I finally said.

The sacred month of July dragged past, and then we were in Sextilis, still sitting, still sweltering. Food stores had fallen further and were now failing in earnest; every day more dead men were carried from the ships and camp, and the dull *thump-thump* of dirty water against the hulls of the ships beat an ominous rhythm. It was dirty because of the human refuse continually dumped overboard. Moss and slime grew on the timbers, birds nested under the inactive oars, and we feared that if we did not move soon, the ships would be completely unseaworthy.

Antony spent many hours staring at his maps and reading reports, breaking off to stare glumly into space. We spoke little; people confined together in inactivity have a tendency to lapse into silence.

I never regained my sense of well-being. Perhaps I had a touch of the illness attacking the men; but I kept it from Antony as well as I could. Only when he was gone from headquarters did I allow myself to lie on my cot, wrapped in a sheet, sometimes feeling a chill pass over me even in this ovenlike heat.

Charmian would kneel near me and smooth my hair, wipe my face with damp cloths.

"We will not tell the Imperator," she would say, with a wink.

"No," I said. "We will not tell him." The gods forbid that he should know!

Toward the end of Sextilis, with the break in the weather, something seemed to change in Antony. He flung off the black clouds that had shrouded him like those of Strongyle, and reclaimed his old self, wrenching it by sheer self-will out of the mire of despondence.

"It is time," he said grimly one night.

Everything else was the same: the same guttering lamplight, the same grumbling and aching stomachs, the same lines of defense. Why now?

"I will call a council of war. The situation cannot continue."

At last! At last! The stalemate would be broken. Antony had determined on his course. Now, by all the gods, let it be a wise one!

"Yes," I said softly, rising and coming to his side. I put my hand on his shoulder; he almost jumped. We had touched each other so seldom of late. Finally he reached up and took my hand in his; his felt so unfamiliar. But I squeezed it nonetheless.

"I think it must be by sea," he said simply. "All our land routes are too dangerous."

"By sea?" For so long the two had weighed equally.

"We can escape by sea," he said. "We cannot escape by land."

"Escape?" It had come to this? We were thinking only of escape? My voice betrayed my disappointment.

"Retreat, if you prefer that term," he snapped.

"To have gathered a fleet and an army like this, and not to use them!" I lamented the loss. It seemed—profligate.

"Neither the army nor the fleet is what it was," he reminded me. "If we could have used them in the beginning . . ." He sighed. "Now everything is changed. The worst crime a commander can commit is to fight today's battle with the troops of yesterday."

"Of course." I must defer to his experience. Let us not compound one error with another.

"If we can extricate most of our fleet, retreat to Egypt, and regroup there . . ." He was thinking out loud. "The followers of Pompey were able to do this time and again."

But that army had ultimately lost. Once someone is on the run, he has lost his initiative and is the hunted rather than the hunter. I refrained from pointing this out.

"So Egypt is to be the arena," I said faintly. I did not like it. What if Octavian pursued us to our own shores? I did not want fighting there. That was why Pothinus had killed Pompey—to forestall exactly that.

"No, no," he reassured me. "We will merely recover there, and gather our forces again."

"Perhaps it would be better to fight it out here, in Greece, now." Spare Egypt! "Your army is still intact, and Canidius is a fine general."

"If they won't fight, we can't," Antony insisted. "All we can do is leave."

"But why would Octavian bring an enormous army here and then refuse to fight? It makes no sense!"

"Stranger things have happened." He rose and took my hands in his, looking at me in a way I had almost forgotten.

It had been late already when he had hunched over his maps. Now it must be midnight. The camp was utterly quiet, like a hibernating beast. He blew out the lamps and plunged the tent into darkness, then pulled me over toward the sleeping area. Beside the bed, he took my head in both his hands and whispered, "Forgive me for neglecting you, my most precious—"

"Ally?" I could not help joking. "At least *I* have not deserted."

He bent his head and kissed me. "That is not funny," he said.

I tightened my arms around him. "No, it is not," I said. "Forgive me."

"It seems we both have something to forgive," he said, falling on the bed and taking me with him.

Speech after long silence, touching after long abstinence, has a headiness all its own. It was as if he were a new person, and I must learn him all over again.

At last it had come: the council of war, where we would meet in unison one last time before manning our posts. Everyone had to be certain of his duties, and of our supreme strategy: not as simple as one would suppose.

The leaders were still deeply divided on what we should do. The only agreement was that we must do something, or perish at this wretched site. Both army and fleet had become a liability, too large to be abandoned, too weakened to be reliable. The only question was, which one was in worse condition?

Seated around the trestle table were our four admirals—the experienced Sosius and Publicola, and the less-trained Insteius and Octavius (unfortunate name in our camp)—and our leading general, Canidius, as well as Dellius.

The heat had continued unabated, as had the disease and debilitation, and as we talked, flies buzzed around the stifling chamber, boldly landing on the maps Antony had unrolled. They crawled excitedly, and I wondered if they were anticipating all the corpses that would litter the area depicted on the map and give them joy. Antony swatted one, and its iridescent blob smeared the area of Athens.

"My friends," he said, leaning forward on his knuckles, "we must now cast our final plans."

Now that the moment had come, everyone suddenly seemed reluctant to settle on a strategy.

"Canidius, the state of the legions?" asked Antony, to fill the hesitant silence.

Canidius rose. "Of our original hundred thousand men, we have about seventy thousand still here—and fit to fight."

Now a groan or two escaped around the table. To have lost thirty thousand men, and no real battle fought! Truly disease is a worse enemy than catapults and swords.

"Our biggest loss is in the client kings who deserted; the remaining soldiers are Roman legionaries, many of them veterans."

"Just as well," snorted Publicola. "Octavian never had any of those worthless foreigners to begin with. He was smart."

I wondered whether he considered me a "foreigner," or was past caring what I thought.

"True, now the numbers are almost equal," said Canidius.

"Minus the riffraff," Publicola emphasized.

"In any case," said Antony, "with equal numbers, and Romans versus Romans, would you say we are evenly matched?"

Canidius thought for a moment. "Yes, except for morale. Spirits are always higher on the side that can claim recent victories, even if they are small ones. However, the men are eager to move, eager for action. I would recommend that we abandon the fleet, and effect an ordered retreat east to Macedonia to link up with our forces there. We can call on help from King Dicomes nearby. Octavian will follow us, and we can draw him into the land battle we have sought for so long." He looked at me. "The Queen and her retinue can depart for Egypt by land, there to await the outcome."

I was taken by surprise. "But, Canidius," I said, "you supported my presence here!" I felt betrayed.

"That was before Agrippa rendered your fleet helpless," he said. "Now you are only a liability—a target for Octavian's abuse. You are harming Antony's cause to remain."

What he said was true, but there was no help for it. If Egypt did not participate in this war as a sovereign state, we became like the other client kingdoms—worthless allies. The shame would be unendurable. We would deserve the censure that Rome already heaped on us.

"It seems to me that if you retreat, the troops will misunderstand and think we are conceding defeat," I argued. "Then they will desert in droves, and there will be no army left to stand and fight the pursuing Octavian."

"The alternative plan is to escape from the naval blockade and save as many ships as possible," said Antony. "After all, if we lose our entire navy, the land army will be trapped in Greece, unable to cross into Asia because we will have no transport, while the enemy rules the waves unchallenged."

"Bah!" said Dellius. "Forget the fleet!"

"What is the state of the fleet?" Antony asked calmly.

"We are badly undermanned in rowers, and the ships suffer from disrepair," said Sosius.

"How many ships would you estimate could be manned with our oarsmen?" asked Antony.

"No more than three hundred," he said, "counting the Egyptian ones."

Now more groans sounded around the table. This time last year, we had had five hundred warships and three hundred supporting merchant ships, plus scouts. What a decline!

"We must burn the extra ships, then," said Antony. "No sense in making a gift of them to Octavian."

Burn my ships! No, not my hard-won ships! "The Egyptian ones are manned by my own mercenaries, and are entirely reliable!" I said quickly.

"The few that are left," said Publicola. "They had no magic to survive the fevers and dysentery any better than the rest."

"Forget the sea!" Canidius burst out. "The fleet is emasculated. Antony is not a naval commander, but a land general. The Roman veterans are still battleworthy. Agrippa is not much on land, and Octavian is nothing anywhere. Seek your victory where you are strongest, not where you are weakest!"

Antony shut his eyes as if to shut out all the conflicting noise. He was fighting within himself. His instinct was to fight by land, but as supreme commander he had to keep all the issues in mind, and think of the overall strategy, not just one battle. Clearly the sea offered him the best chance to husband his remaining resources and preserve a long-term goal of victory.

What would Caesar have done? But whatever it would have been, it would have needed Caesar himself to carry it out.

"I think . . ." Antony finally raised his head. "It must be by sea."

"No!" cried Dellius. "That's a mistake!"

"Listen," said Antony slowly, "Queen Cleopatra is right. Taking a weakened army in a retreat over mountain passes is disastrous—well I know. And so should you, after Parthia. We have no commitment from Dicomes, and if the other client kings are any indication, it is best not to rely on him. Once the army withdraws, the fleet is lost, trapped here with no soldiers on board to fight its way out of the gulf, and can provide no protection for the crossing into Asia. We would then lose both fleet and army, and stand naked before the enemy, surrounded, embayed, begging for terms."

"Aren't you leaving out the possibility that there will be a land battle and you can defeat him?" sneered Dellius.

"It is unlikely he will be drawn into battle to fight for something he can win while doing nothing. If there is any consistent behavior in Octavian over the years, it is that he follows his own motto: *Festina lente*, hasten slowly. He inches along, but inexorably. And he never does for himself what time, or fate, or another man's mistake, can do for him. No, he won't fight. He'll watch us go, and catch us easily with Agrippa's ships when we try to cross the Hellespont."

"We might as well fight by sea and send as many of the enemy to the bottom as possible when we make our escape," said Sosius.

"To break the blockade is no riskier than to withdraw the army, and we stand to save more," I said. "We can take four or five of the best legions on board as fighters, and increase our chances of winning, and spirit some of the army away as well."

"By Hercules!" cried Dellius. "Is Octavian right? Is Cleopatra running this war?"

"Why should I not speak?" I said. "I can read the map as well as any of you—yes, and the numbers too!"

"I hate retreat as much as any man," said Antony. "It is a bitter fruit, as I know, having chewed it both in Mutina and in Parthia. But there are some retreats that are nothing more than a regrouping. I put this in that category."

"But—" Canidius looked bewildered. "What am I to do? Just wait to surrender?"

"No, you will effect the withdrawal, but only after the sea battle is over. We can then provide ships to transport you into Asia."

The flies were buzzing around his head, as if they, too, were protesting. *Not enough casualties!* they were saying. *We don't like your plan!*

"So we have decided," said Antony. "We break the blockade and take our treasure and as many ships and soldiers as possible to Egypt. The army will wait, and then make an orderly withdrawal into Asia. We will burn the surplus ships. All this will take place within the next few days."

"*You* have decided," said Canidius.

"I am the commander! Who else should decide?" Antony cried. "It is I who command and you who must obey!" He softened. "But I value your judgment."

"Even though you ignore it?"

"Because I do not follow it in all particulars does not mean I ignore it."

"I just pray to all the gods that you are right," said Canidius.

"Why, so do we all," said Sosius.

The meeting broke up in near confusion. The naval commanders were delighted with the decision, but clearly there was little to choose from between two unpalatable plans. Both involved a high degree of loss, and a high degree of risk. I was unhappy with the prospect of using Egypt as a staging ground, but like everyone else, I had had to compromise. When I had provoked Octavian, I had gambled with Egypt and losing even that which I had.

Perhaps I should never have . . . I shook my head. What was done was done. The next generation would have had to fight the same battle. It was inevitable. And that it came in my day—well, fate had chosen and fitted me for it. All I could do now was buckle on the breastplate and hold tight to the shield.

It was heartbreaking to watch. Yet I forced myself to stand on the shore and ache as the ships marked for destruction were torched. They huddled together like people trying to stave off a collapsing roof or an earthquake, but they were doomed, forced to stay, chained fast by their anchors.

Also like innocent people caught in a fire, they were of all types—triremes, quinqueremes, even "eights" and "nines." They had been smeared with pitch and oil to make them burn better, sacrifices to our mistakes. From the shore, men threw flaming torches onto the decks, and the fire caught quickly.

"Oh, Antony," I said, taking his hand. It actually hurt to watch. I remembered walking through the boatyard when they were just being built, all new and proud. My children! If the sight of the perishing ships caused me such pain, how did any mother ever endure the loss of a real child?

"It has to be," he said.

"They pay the price of our miscalculations," I said. "It seems we have made one mistake after another."

"All war is a series of calculations," he said. "Building them at all was just another calculation. That is what makes war so expensive—all the guesses we must make, each one costing gold."

"But to see gold burning like that!"

"Think of all the gold resting on sea bottoms, lost in shipwrecks. When we break out, we can only pray that our treasure on board will survive intact. But you will be with it, on the flagship, our largest and strongest."

I always hated taking treasure on board ships. But what were we to do? Leave it for Octavian? Better the sea bottom!

The fire had truly caught now, passing from ship to ship, making a garish necklace of flame. The yellow pyres, reflected in the calm water, appeared twice as grand. All the smells of different types of burning wood—from the pungent scent of dry cedar to the mushroomlike odor of old, wet planks—drifted toward us, enveloping us in a mantle of smoke. It stung my eyes, but I could not leave. It was a funeral, and I must stay. I owed them that, my ships.

Antony put his arm around me. "Come," he said. "No need to torture ourselves."

Mistakes . . . miscalculations . . . misinformation . . . The remembrance of them smothered me like the smoke, the tangible proof of them. Oh, torment of remorse! Is there anything more fiendish, more unmanning? It made me doubt all that we now planned.

Fire even has a voice, a voice very like that of remorse: high, keening, evocative. It rose now from the company of ships, dying, almost a whistle.

There were others gathered, watching, and I had no doubt that from his heights Octavian could see the red-stained waters, could smell the ashes. People passed shuffling behind us, but no one would intrude on us. But gradually I became aware of someone standing off to one side, watching us rather than the ships. He was hooded, and I could not make out his features.

"Antony," I finally said, "who is that? He is staring at us most rudely. Do you know him?"

Antony peered into the gloom, as if his eyes could somehow pierce the dark. He shook his head. "There is something familiar about him, but no." He raised his arm. "Sir! Come here!"

804

The man stood unmoving for a long moment, then came toward us as if he were the summoner, not the summoned. As he approached, he threw back his hood.

"Why, it is—" Antony struggled for the name.

"Hunefer," the man finished. "It is a long way from Rome, my lord."

Now I recognized him, too: the Egyptian astrologer I had sent to Rome with Olympos so long ago to attach himself to Antony's household and spy. He had better not betray me, even after all this time!

"I am pleased to meet you," I said pointedly.

Hunefer nodded. "And I, you." He indicated the ships. "A sad day for us."

"What are you doing here?" Antony insisted on knowing.

"I have long followed your fortunes, my lord; I came here to share them."

"Well, then, they must look favorable, or you would have stayed away!" Antony sounded pleased, as if the man's very presence was a good omen.

"Perhaps he's just loyal," I said quickly. I could not bear to hear a fortune right now. Even if it were good. *Mistakes. Miscalculations. Misinformation* . . . Misfortune. No fortune.

"Even loyal servants don't go rushing into a burning house," said Antony. "Or board a burning ship."

"Perhaps he was just trapped here, like all the rest," I said.

"Madam," said Hunefer, "sometimes the future unmasks herself like a guest at a revel. Then we come close to touching time herself. We cannot turn away from what she would reveal."

"He told me that my fate-spirit, my daimon, was overshadowed when Octavian's was near," Antony remembered. Of course Olympos had reported it to me. "Well, you were right, old friend. Ever since Octavian landed in Greece . . ." His voice faded. "But for the six years before that, all was well. So, once we remove ourselves from here . . . ?"

It had turned into a question.

Hunefer was silent so long that Antony finally said, "We *will* escape from here, won't we?" The pity of it!—reducing his wish for victory to mere escape.

"Part of you, yes," Hunefer said slowly. "Another part of you, you will leave here."

"Part of the army? Part of the navy?"

"The stars only say 'part of you,'" said Hunefer. "It is not clear."

"Part of—me?" he asked. "My body? My troops? Surely you can discern that!"

"He means the ships," I said quickly. "The burnt ships! That's a large part. And the oarsmen and soldiers who have died—they will remain here forever." I glared at Hunefer. Stupid old man! Whatever he saw, he should keep it to himself. It was too late now to do anything but harm.

"No, madam," he insisted. "That has already come to pass, and is done. This—"

Suddenly a great realization settled on me, of the way the gods tease us with partial revelations and veiled hints, knowing we will follow them to our doom. Then when we come to grief, they laugh. Such is their amusement. If we fail by following our own ideas, we can take some pride in that; we are not another's plaything. Even *mistakes . . . miscalculations . . . misinformation* have an innate human bravery lacking in merely following supernatural direction. Let us win, or let us fail, but let it be all ours! I turned on him.

"Enough. We will not hear." I linked my arm through Antony's. "Come. To our tent." I steered him away.

The heavy air in the tent oppressed like bondage. Flies were everywhere now; they must breed and double every night. Ugly black buzzing things, they plagued us, forcing us to sleep under nets. Even so, they woke us by diving against the cloth, as if they were arrows intent on piercing it.

The lurid red of the burning ships making the tent walls glow, the attacking flies . . . all seemed a foretaste of Hades.

"I remember a temple we came across in Parthia," Antony mumbled sleepily. "There's a god there, a god who commands legions of flies, I forget his name. . . . He's evil, causes swarms of flies to attack. . . ."

"You must have angered him, then," I said. "He must have followed you all the way from Parthia. You and your men."

I meant it to be funny, but what if it was true? There were veterans of Parthia here; were the flies particularly bad around them? I did feel plagued, pursued . . . there was something unnaturally hellish in this place.

"Did you destroy his temple?" I asked.

"I . . . I remember looking at the carvings. On our way back, perhaps . . . yes, I think we did, because archers were hiding in it, attacking us."

They had destroyed the fly-god's temple? I wished the answer had been otherwise.

"What was his name? Try to remember!" We could placate him, promise to build him a new temple, one in Alexandria. . . .

"I don't know," said Antony. "I never knew it would be important." He sat up on his elbows. "I don't think it's important now. Your imagination is playing tricks on you. There are always flies in summer wherever an army camps. Forget this god, this . . ." He laughed. "Asmodeus. That was his name."

Asmodeus. I had heard the name; one of those gods from farther east, where they seemed to breed vicious ones like the Ma and Kali. I would see to it that amends were made—after we escaped.

Antony turned over, and from his breathing I knew he slept. But I lay there, imagining I could feel the heat from the flames, tormented by the flies waiting outside, crawling on the curtain. I shuddered.

While Antony slept, I felt all the gods fighting overhead. I wished Caesar would appear and scatter them, give us some sign on the eve of this battle, as he had at Philippi. But I felt abandoned by him, as if he had lost interest in our affairs. Perhaps that meant he was a true god now; nothing left of the mortal, not even affections.

And Antony, all too mortal, slept on.

Early in the morning Canidius came to our tent and told us: Dellius had deserted to Octavian.

Still groggy from the night, Antony shook his head. His eyes were dull. "Gone, then," was all he said. He sighed as if an extra sack had just been loaded on his bent back. "And he knows all our plans."

I was charged with anger, sizzling as if I had been hit by a spark of lightning. He had meant to leave, but had waited until after the council of war, so he could bring valuable information to Octavian. I knew it as certainly as if he had left a confession. "The perfidious traitor!" I cried.

"Now Octavian knows everything," Antony said. "Even my secret councils of war are exposed to him." He paused. "Dellius. My helper, my companion . . ." He turned to me. "I even sent him to bring you to me. Long ago."

I was afraid he was going to break down in front of Canidius. "Don't remember! Don't remember!" I cried. "Blank him out, tear him out of your memories, never think of him, or recall a single word. He must cease to exist—no, never *have* existed."

"And when he returned, and told me what you had said, that you wouldn't come to Tarsus, why, then I—"

"I said don't think about him!" I shouted, ignoring Canidius. "And don't soil your memories of me by attaching him to them!"

"Canidius," said Antony, with no emotion at all, "you may announce that I will replace his command with one of the tribunes." He gave a wavering smile. "It is of no matter. No matter. Now he can write an account of the war for his new master. I wanted no accounts. No, no accounts." He clapped his arm around Canidius's shoulder and walked to the door of the tent with him.

Bright light streamed in as they pulled open the flap. I could see the smoke still rising from the dead ships, inky smudges against the bright blue sky.

"My friend," Antony said, dropping the flap back, and turning around. "My friend is gone." He paused. "I do not think I will send his trunks after him."

76

"Is even Zeus against us?" Antony cried as he saw the flash that signaled lightning from the west. A black bank of clouds had appeared on the usually clear horizon, and even as we watched it grew higher, spreading out like a stain.

The remaining ships—some two hundred thirty of them, including sixty of Egypt's pride—were in the process of being loaded with legionaries, armed and ready for fighting. We had ordered sails taken aboard, which had caused alarm and confusion among the men as well as the commanders. Sails are never used in fighting; they hinder movement and take up valuable room. So, late the night before, Antony had gathered a few officers together for the last time, and revealed our plan. Even Dellius had not been privy to it; had he suspected there would be further discussions, he would doubtless have delayed his departure.

The plan was this: We wished to escape with as many ships as possible and sail for Egypt, using the afternoon breeze to push us south. It was simple but not easy—a frustrating combination. In order to round the huge bulk of Leucas safely, we would have to be far out to sea before the wind could fill our sails from astern and take us on our way. And in order to get there, we would have to fight our way out past Agrippa's blockade.

The worst thing that could happen was if Agrippa insisted on fighting midway out to sea, where he could attack us before we could make use of the breeze; the best, if we could trick him into thinking he was luring *us* far out to sea, letting us choose the battle site. His numerical superiority meant that he would naturally favor plenty of room in which to maneuver, which meant going a long way out to sea. But as soon as we got far enough out, we could raise our sails and make away. Without sails, they could never catch us. Oarsmen alone could not keep up for long.

Unfortunately it was impossible to hide the fact that we were taking the sails on board. Agrippa would probably suspect, and try to disable us before we could get away.

"We'll divide into four squadrons," said Antony. "A line of three in front, with the Egyptian ships behind them. Publicola and I will command the right wing, Sosius the left. The center will be commanded by Insteius and Octavius, and I expect it to thin out and open a gap in the middle as the action progresses, allowing the Egyptian ships to sail through into open water. Once they are clear, the rest of us should disengage and follow as soon as possible."

"We can assume Agrippa will command his left wing?" asked Octavius.

"We can assume nothing," said Antony, "but it is a logical guess. Now our left wing, under Sosius, is the one that will have to get farthest out before it can turn south, because it starts off nearest to Leucas. Therefore, I must admit here and now, it has the least chance of escape. So it must prepare for the heaviest fighting."

"On the other hand, if we could lure Agrippa's ships into the very constricted waters of the gulf, that's where we could prevail. His ability to maneuver would be completely lost there," said Sosius.

"Another battle of Salamis, with Agrippa playing Xerxes? Wishful thinking," said Antony. "Agrippa knows his naval history all too well. No, he'll stand out to sea and wait. But we mustn't issue out until almost noon, because if we arrive before the breeze, we are utterly lost."

"If the battle took place in an area closer to shore, where Agrippa could not separate our ships, we might beat them," said Sosius. "Our ships are bigger, after all."

"But there are fewer of them," Antony pointed out. "I estimate he has more than four hundred fighting ships to our two hundred."

"And the soldiers to man the ships?" asked Insteius.

"We will take twenty thousand," said Antony. "Five legions. Plus two thousand slingers and archers. That means about a hundred men per ship—a good fighting ratio. That leaves fifty thousand men under Canidius still on land."

It had seemed a good, rational plan, with the best chance of extricating us from the prison of Actium. We could not expect to deliver all the ships, but a goodly number was better than nothing. The Egyptian ships, along with the remaining merchant vessels, would avoid the fighting if possible, keeping well behind the rest.

It was dark when we carried the treasure chests aboard the flagship, so Octavian could not see. I had packed the jewels, the gold plate, carefully, wondering why I had brought them in the first place. Once I had thought them important to have on hand, for gold, emeralds, lapis, and pearls were always negotiable, but that supposed there was a market for them. As it turned out, the flies did not care, the rot-worm could not be bought off.

And now this—a violent storm on the very day we had planned to embark.

Antony stood staring at it, as it galloped toward us. "No rain for weeks! Truly, Zeus hates us!"

The men had halted on the gangplanks. On board, the sailors and soldiers gripped the rails and waited.

"Perhaps it's a stroke of luck for us," I said. "Can we make a dash for it, using the storm to keep Agrippa in place? Didn't you use a storm to slip past Pompey's blockade once?"

"Ah yes. But this is the one direction where we are helpless—the storm will blow right in our faces, from exactly the quarter where we wish to go. No, we must wait."

He began signaling to the men.

Once more to wait.

The storm broke, as if it had stored up rain and wind all summer, sucking it up from the fetid marshes and holding it in reserve somewhere. Torrents of rain poured down, flooding the tents and paths, and a fierce west wind tried to force the ships back to the very head of the gulf.

It kept on for four days and nights. Through the gray curtain of rain I could see Agrippa's ships being continually rowed in place to keep them from being blown in against the shore. Did they never tire? But after four days, surely they would be exhausted, whereas our oarsmen were spared that, given the protection of the gulf. We should start out with an advantage. I pointed this out to Antony, who seemed so determined that the gods were against us.

"Perhaps Zeus sent this just to tire Octavian out," I said.

"Perhaps," was all he replied.

"Look! Look!"

On the second of September, Antony stood at the door of the tent, pointing to the clear sky.

"Today is the day." He turned to me and held out his hand. "Today."

As we watched in the dawn, streams of soldiers filed past on their way to the gangplanks. They seemed cheerful, glad to be moving at last. Some looked younger and healthier than others; I suspected that some ailing ones had begged to be allowed to go on the ships, and been yielded a place by stronger men.

One older veteran stopped in his tracks and broke out of line.

"Come back here!" ordered the officer, but the man ignored him and strode toward Antony.

He trotted up to us and grabbed Antony's arm. "Imperator!" he said. "Think again! Don't do this!"

Although Antony was used to considerable familiarity from his men, this annoyed him. It was neither the time nor the place.

"Back in line, soldier," he said shortly, trying to detach the man's fingers.

"Don't you remember me, Imperator?" the man said. He had lost one eye.

Antony stared at him. "No," he said frankly.

"I was with you in Parthia. You came to me at the field hospital, with the Queen. Remember? Remember?"

He had been one of a hundred that Antony had visited; how could he possibly remember him? Yet such had been Antony's concern at the time that the man imagined he had stood out from all the rest.

"I told you then that I had ten years left of service"—the man was determined that Antony would remember that very brief conversation—"and that I had served two years with Caesar himself. I am from Campania."

"Yes . . . good soldiers there," Antony agreed, still trying to remove the hand.

"Now it's only five years I have left. But I have seen many campaigns, and all on land. Don't do it! Don't fight by sea!"

Antony seemed actually to remember the man, at last. "Oh yes . . . you were with Gallus. In the retreat, that's where you lost your eye."

"Yes! Yes!" He pointed to his eye. "Don't disdain this wound of mine! I got it fighting on land. And that's where we should be fighting today! Sir, please!"

Antony succeeded in detaching his gripping hand. "Good soldier, I appreciate your concern," he finally said. "But you must obey orders." He pointed to the line of soldiers boarding the ship. "Return to your company."

For a moment I thought the man was going to throw himself at Antony's feet and refuse to move. But he just squared his shoulders, looked sadly at us with his one remaining eye, and obeyed.

For safety, the senators were boarded on the Egyptian ships, which were not expected to see action. Antony was rowed in a small boat around the fleet, where he addressed his men for the last time, exhorting them to be brave and follow the plan to the best of their ability.

"And this shall be for your glory," he cried, "that you can tell your sons you were with Antony at Actium." His golden voice seemed magnified in richness by the water, as he stood in the rocking little boat, his helmet off. The sun touched his hair and made him seem, just for that moment, to be the very young Antony who had first ridden into Alexandria.

Last he was rowed alongside my flagship and came on board. I wished I could have had a moment alone with him to say farewell. But the time for that was past.

In my eyes his oddly youthful appearance remained, even as he approached and laid his hands on my shoulders, in full view of the crew and soldiers and senators.

"Keep yourself safe, until we meet at Taenarum," he said. That was where we had agreed all the escaping ships should gather, on the southernmost point of Greece. "May all the gods protect you."

"And you," I said.

It seemed so little to say, but what else was there? Aside from my moving my hands up to cover his, we did not touch. No embrace, no kiss, almost as if we were afraid to. And perhaps we were; it would cause too much anguish.

Then our hands fell away, and we parted. He would board his own flagship, already waiting on the right wing, and it would begin.

The battle of Actium, the battle for Actium, the battle to escape Actium, call it what you will, it must begin. And if the right wing took too much battering, it might well be sent to the bottom, while we looked on helplessly from behind.

I wanted to hurry after him, be rowed to his ship and face whatever awaited him. The separation was agony; had I not been a queen, it would not be necessary. But I had my own duties, my own obligations, and could not desert my post. I owed it to Egypt to survive and return, to build bulwarks against Octavian's hunger to annex us for as long as possible, in case Antony, my true bulwark, fell. . . .

No. It was too dreadful. I would not think on it, or allow myself to picture it. He needed to know I was strong behind him, not whimpering and cowering.

"Make ready!" I ordered the crew briskly, then turned the command over to the captain.

Ahead of us the line of almost two hundred ships was being rowed toward the narrow mouth of the gulf, for the first time in months. Beyond that, the land widened out for another two miles until it fell away entirely and the open sea was reached. From where I stood, I could see the faint line of Agrippa's confronting ships beyond the mouth of the gulf.

Now our ships halted, and Antony's first plan—for them to form a double line and sit on their oars, inviting battle from Agrippa in the constricted waters—was put into effect.

It was midmorning, and the sun was just clearing the mountains to the east, making the water glitter and outlining the shapes of the ships dotting the surface. No one moved. Agrippa held his line steady and advanced no farther. He was not to be drawn in closer to shore. But we had anticipated that, though it was a pity. We would have welcomed the opportunity to try to thrash the great Agrippa, to inflict grievous damage on the architect of our misfortune. For it was his sword arm that had given Octavian the power he now wielded, and caused us such woe.

The wind had died and the surface of the water was glassy. The first—always wishful—plan for battle must now be discarded, to be replaced by the second. Now Antony must wait another hour or so until the breeze would rise.

O dear Isis! Let it rise today, of all days! Do not fail us! Even prayer seemed an affront, as if I lacked faith. She would know I had failed the test—and punish me.

I paced the deck, trembling with worry, aware that the senators were watching with their little bird eyes. I did not care. *Let it come! Let it blow!* There were only Isis and me now, no senators, no soldiers, no oarsmen. Only Isis and me, her daughter.

Let it come! Open the skies and let the wind free!

Utter stillness, and the sun burned on the flat water.

I tore off my protective helmet and shook my hair out, letting it fall over my shoulders, as if the shaking and flinging could actually stir up a wind by magic.

And I saw the very ends of the hair settle against my arms—then, ever so faintly . . . move, as if the breath of a baby blew against the strands. Barely perceptible. Then again.

I thank you, Isis! I cried in my mind, giving thanks in advance, to show my good faith. But there must be more than this.

"I thank you, Isis, for the wind you send!" I cried aloud, startling the senators, who perceived nothing. There, I had committed myself, and Isis rewarded my declaration.

The wind roused itself and started to give gentle puffs. Tiny ripples rose on the water, like fingers pushing against a fabric, and grew bigger. A shout rose from the men.

"Now fall to it!" cried the captain.

Ahead of us the oars flashed, moving the line of Antony's ships out into open water. Our left wing, under Sosius, being the closest inshore to Leucas and farthest south, needing most to get out to sea, moved first and fastest. Agrippa's forces backed water, retreating farther out, and the two lines of ships advanced, always keeping a mile or so apart.

Not enough wind yet, nor had it swung around to the best direction for us. There would have to be more waiting. The rowers slowed, but continued moving the ships out. Our own squadron, far to the rear, now passed out of the gulf, past the hateful promontory of Actium, which I cast off like a bad dream. All these months spent there, in misery—let me never behold it again! Just beyond the two points were sandy shallows that we had to steer around.

In my last backward glance, I saw the huge armies on both sides, passive onlookers to the action. They were drawn up and waiting, but did nothing. Then we were out of sight.

Farther and farther out the ships ventured, and all the while the breeze was increasing, turning into a wind. At first it had blown from the southwest, but then it began to shift, as it always did, turning in a circle and originating from the northwest—what we needed to fill our sails and carry us south.

I breathed it in. This wind, blowing from the direction of Rome, should be foul and deceitful, like everything else from there. Instead it was clean and strong, our salvation. Perhaps Caesar, the one good thing from Rome, was embodied in it. Perhaps it blew from his tomb to help his living heirs, his son.

How far was Agrippa going to allow us to advance? The farther, the better. Could he possibly have no idea of our plan? That would seem too good to be believed.

And it was. Finally he stopped backing up and his ships held their line, halting our progress. He refused to cooperate. Battle must be joined.

A hail of missiles—stones, spears, and fire—were launched on one another, a deadly arc between the two lines. Then the air was blackened by the rush of arrows and lead pellets shot from the slingers and archers in the towers guarding the larger warships; noise rose, and the ships began to fall on one another.

Agrippa, determined to keep us from breaking through, doubled his lines, and set his numerous smaller ships to harry us, surrounding the Antonian warships like so many besieged castles. Agrippa's little ships would dart in, trying to ram a hole in a big ship and escape before the besieged could dump stones and hurl javelins down on them. They attacked the lower parts of the ships, crushing the oars, shattering their blades, snapping off the rudders, while trying to clamber on board. On our side, we pushed them off with boathooks, cut them down with stones, and crushed them with heavy missiles.

The fighting turned into confusion, ship against ship, sometimes two or three smaller ships tearing at the larger ones, like dogs in a pack attacking elephants. The first ship sank: one of ours, a smaller one. Then screams reached my ears from across the water as one entire shipload of Octavian's was sunk by a well-aimed catapult stone, all hands aboard. Then all the fighting, all the screams, blended together and became indistinguishable. Ours or theirs? In death agonies, everyone has the same voice.

The lines were dissolving into a melee. I could no longer even see Antony's flagship, it was so engulfed by the swirling fight. Smoke was rising. Some ships were afire, and now grapnels and boarding-bridges were put into play, the armed soldiers swarming onto enemy decks, swords drawn.

The waters were churned by more than the rising wind, they were whipped up by falling timbers and flailing men; the salt spray that blew into my face was blood-tinged, flecked with red foam.

The groans of the disintegrating ships as their timbers tore apart were so mixed with human screams that they made one long animal howl, punctuated by the thuds as ships were rammed or collided. I could see tiny figures turning, rolling, falling from decks into the water, hitting oars and breaking them off with a sharp crack.

The rising wind created whitecaps that flashed red with blood and the reflection of flames from burning ships, rising from stricken decks like flapping curtains. Burning oil from the fire-missiles spilled off the decks and into the sea, spreading out into a carpet of flames. Smoke, harsh and black, billowed from the thick of the fighting, obscuring the ships themselves.

Then I saw a gap appear in the center. The left and right wings had succeeded in pulling the fabric open so we could sail through the rent, if we moved quickly. And we were far out enough to do it; we could catch the wind properly.

"Sails! Hoist the sails!" the captain commanded, and the purple linen sails were unfurled and spread. Like a fist hitting a palm, the wind smacked them, stretching them taut. On all sides, at the sight of the royal sails aloft, the rest of the squadron followed suit. The oarsmen kept at their task, and the power of wind and oar together made us fly through the center, past the grisly sight of hundreds of floating men—the dead ones bobbing, the live ones screaming and waving—and out into the open sea. Huge spars from ripped ships spun and turned on the water like spokes.

The sails creaked as the wind strained them, and the acrid smoke made me choke as we passed through the clouds of it, where I could see nothing, could not discern Antony's ship. On all sides, like falling stars, the fiery missiles continued to rain down, and one or two landed on our deck, where they were quickly smothered by wet hides.

Then we were out in the open sea, the ship flying southward, the mountains of Leucas off to our left. Good-bye to Actium—I could see the last of it far over my shoulder. In our wake the other ships were following, as our purple sails had signaled them to do. The fighting was still fierce along the engaged lines, and I prayed they would not close up before the last of our squadron had sailed through. Plumes of smoke rose in columns, marking the line of conflict.

Now, if only the rest of the force could disengage and follow!

We flew down the coast, past Leucas, past the open channel (now guarded by Agrippa's forces) of Cephallenia, past all the places now lost to us, but rejoicing in our freedom nonetheless. The wind rose higher, and behind us the sky was now as black as the smoke; a squall was coming.

Welcome! The harder the winds blew, the better for us, speeding us on our way.

Oh, let the others follow! Let the others break away! It was a desperate plea, for I had seen how closely grappled all the ships were.

Far, far to our rear I thought I saw some warships; they must have come from the extreme left wing under Sosius, which I thought had evaded the general fighting. And behind them, what?

I clung to the rail, bouncing with each slap as the ship hit the troughs between waves. The wind was tearing at my cloak, but I felt that if I just stayed there, staring, I could will Antony's ship to appear.

Eventually I did see a quinquereme approaching, its lightness and speed catching it up to us. It gained steadily. But I did not recognize it. Could it be the enemy's?

It drew alongside us, and then I saw him: I saw Antony standing on the deck, smoke-begrimed, his arms bloody. But he was signaling, and seemed unhurt.

He was safe. He was here. I shouted for the men to lower a rope ladder and take him on board, and the rails were lined with our senators and soldiers, cheering. Antony climbed up and mounted wearily over the rail, his face strangely blank.

To the cries and welcome of the people on board, he had no response other than a halfhearted wave of the hand. I pushed my way through and embraced him. He brought up one arm and held me to him. The other hung limp at his side.

"My eternal thanks to all the gods," I whispered in his ear. "We are safe."

Still he did not respond, as if he were stunned. "Not all," he said. "Not all."

"How many followed you? And"—I suddenly thought of this—"where is your flagship?"

"I could not break free, so I had to abandon it. The plan has gone awry. We were so closely grappled and surrounded that most of the ships could not follow. The entire center and left wing were held in place. Only the right wing—where, ironically, Agrippa faced us—had any ships able to escape. They are following. I am not sure how many."

All around us people were pressing, waiting for him to address them.

"Antony, you must speak to them," I urged him, as I had once before.

But his self-command had deserted him. He shook his head, taking off his helmet and holding it like an empty bucket. "No. I cannot," he mumbled, and bolted away to the prow of the ship.

I made excuses for him, but now I had to speak in his stead and invent something.

Fast Liburnians appeared, giving chase. Agrippa had sent them after us, and Antony, seeing them, seemed to rally and commanded his other ships—for some had now followed and caught up with us—to turn and face the galleys. One was manned by Eurycles of Sparta, who bore a vicious personal grudge against Antony. They challenged each other to fight, then Eurycles turned and managed to ram and capture a sizable ship of Antony's, as well as one of mine, which unfortunately was carrying some valuable royal stores. Satisfied, he turned back and we sailed on.

For the few moments of the fight, Antony seemed charged with high spirits, but as soon as it was over, he fell back into silence and stood watching the setting sun, refusing to move even after darkness fell.

"It doesn't matter about the stores," I assured him. My words were snatched up by the wind.

He turned his head to me. "Do you think that is my concern?" he asked. "I thought I was prepared to lose ships in the escape. But actually seeing it ... that proved quite different. I feel wounded, although I am not." He paused. "I fear I can lead no more."

What nonsense was this? He had expected to lose ships.

"But we have managed to escape with our treasure, ourselves, and a third of our ships," I told him. "Will not Octavian curse when he realizes it? Think of what you have snatched away right under his nose. You were blockaded, and you slipped away with the prize."

"My reputation . . ." His voice trailed off. "My reputation is gone. My credibility as a leader of Romans has collapsed."

"This is absurd!" I said. "You have cheated Octavian of the very prey in his nets."

"I can't expect you to understand!" he snapped. "What I mean is—it is your nature to always see victory in the face of defeat. I don't think you even know what defeat is. But is that bravery or naiveté?" He turned away and disappeared in the darkness, leaving me alone at the rail.

Far to the north, a tiny glow marking the site of the battle was still visible.

77

The wind and sea bore us onward, past the luxuriant island of Zacynthus, where of late Sosius had had his command; the dawn showed the peaks of her mountains a tender pink.

Antony had not come to my quarters, which were close to the size of regular land rooms—a "ten" is a very large ship indeed. Where had he passed the night? I was almost afraid to find out. Then word was brought to me that he was sitting, like a statue, at the forefront of the ship. He had spent the hours of darkness there, and showed no inclination to move, nor to eat or drink anything.

"You must go to him," Charmian urged me. "Bring him back here, let him lie down and restore himself."

I knew that would not do. Antony, that most public of men, had chosen to be alone, and I must not trespass on it. But I did steal to the bow of the ship, where I saw him sitting cross-legged, his hands on his knees, his head lifted and staring out to sea. In his solitude, he looked stony and bereaved. It was all I could do not to rush over to him, bend down, beg him to let me comfort him.

There had been a serving-woman in the palace once whose son was killed by crocodiles when bathing in the Nile, and she had worn a mantle of sorrow ever after, her face so changed that even when she smiled, it was no smile. Now Antony had that look.

But he had known the probable outcome before we even embarked! He had spoken of it most logically, arguing that we would salvage what we could from a near-hopeless situation. The truth was that Actium was lost when Agrippa took Methone—four months ago.

All this was no reflection on Antony or his generalship. How could it be, when no battle was fought on land? He had suffered defeats and reversals before. Who had not, save Alexander? The important thing was not the defeat, but what he did afterward.

You've only seen him win. You don't know a man until you see him lose. He must not take this as final. There was still Canidius with his army, there was still Egypt, there was still . . .

I watched as a big wave sent cold salt spray into his face and he sat, unflinching, almost as if he were being flogged and relished it.

I could not stop myself. I ran over to him. "Antony, Antony," I said, wiping off his chilled face. "Stand up, and be a man!" My words sounded harsher than I meant. But he must, or lose everything, including himself. Especially himself.

"I can no longer be called a man," he said. "I have dishonored the name."

"What are you, then? A boy? A eunuch? Are only generals men? No, a man is anyone who bears on his shoulders whatever fate is pleased to lay there, and holds his head up all the while."

"A lot of pretty words from someone who has never tasted defeat," he said. Still he refused to get up.

"When I was exiled from my throne, that was no defeat?" I answered. How easy it is to forget the tribulations others have endured! We always think we are the only ones. "When Caesar was murdered, and his son unprovided for, and Octavian named his heir, that was no defeat? When *you* married Octavia, branding our children bastards, that was no defeat? The entire world mocked me."

"You never lost hundreds—no, *thousands*—of men, dead, dead for nothing . . . no, not nothing, dead because they trusted you, followed you, and paid everything for it, and there was no way you could ever undo it!" he yelled. "Dead, dead, all dead, at the bottom of the sea, and rotting in Parthia, and—"

"So now it's all of them rolled up into one? Parthia was five years ago, and a different war. War kills people. If you didn't want to take responsibility for that, then you shouldn't have become a soldier!" I shouted over the wind, right into his ear. His face was still turned resolutely away.

"They're all dead!" he cried. "Dead, dead, lost . . ." Now he put his hands up to his face and wept.

What if someone saw him? What a disgrace!

"Hush, stop it!" I said, shaking his shoulders to jolt him out of it. He should at least wait until he was shut away in privacy. At this very instant, deckhands could see him.

But he wouldn't stop, and instead sat hunched over and weeping loudly. Like a child! "I . . . have . . . lost . . . everything . . . lost . . . my way. . . ." He forced the words out between sobs.

"You have lost nothing that you cannot recover," I told him stoutly.

"My reputation . . . my faith . . . I cannot recover. Others must grant the first, I must grant myself the second, and I . . . I cannot."

"Yes, you will," I assured him. "In time—"

"No, never. It is gone forever. Lost in the water. I am unarmed—no longer a leader, a general, even a soldier."

The buoyant Antony, his quick glad spirits drained away . . . forever? Why is it that one thing will destroy us when other—and equally hard—blows do not? Perhaps we can only absorb so many, and Parthia had been his limit. My dream of his death might have been true in a way I had not known.

"No," I said, cradling his head, for the first time afraid that he was speaking the truth. "No, you must go on. You must shoulder this; you are strong enough. Else Hercules was not truly your ancestor!" I tried to appeal to his old self; he had always prided himself on his descent from Hercules. It had carried him through many another discouraging moment.

"Hercules would disown me," he said. "Hercules would be ashamed."

The ship dipped and sent another stinging arc of sea spray onto us. It dripped off Antony's hair but did nothing to interrupt his weeping.

"He would not be ashamed of you for losing Actium, but for what you are doing afterward." Surely he could understand that?

You don't know a man until you see him lose.

"I should have died; I should have gone down with my ship. At least then my men would not feel their commander deserted them." I could barely make out his words.

"You didn't desert them," I said. "Is surviving a battle desertion? Some will walk off a battlefield and others won't. That is not the same as desertion, unless you think it's everyone's obligation to die. *That* would please the enemy."

Now he threw his head back and cried out mockingly, " 'And this shall be for your glory! That you can tell your sons you were with Antony at Actium.' Oh, the shame of it! The shame!"

"Antony—" He was torturing himself more cruelly than any flogger could.

"Go away!" he said, shoving me so hard I stumbled against the coiled ropes on deck. "Leave me!"

I did so, but not before assigning someone to watch him carefully from behind, and stop him if he tried to leap overboard or stab himself in his despair.

I was shocked; I could not believe he had come to this.

It took three days to sail around the Peloponnese and reach Cape Taenarum, where there was a small harbor and roadstead. The entire time Antony remained where he was, brooding, weeping, making atonement to his lost men, his lost dreams. He was shattered, as a man and as a general, overwhelmed by his losses. But when we sailed into the harbor, he left his post, went below and cleaned himself up. His first wild grief had subsided, and now it was time for the funeral. He must attend the obsequies, and comport himself bravely.

Once anchored, we awaited the arrival of whatever stragglers might have managed to break away and follow us, as well as the heavier transports and the ships from the few ports we still held, while we counted the accompanying vessels and refitted them for the long voyage back to Egypt. Some hundred ships, all told, had escaped. The senators were all safe, and poured off the ships onto the docks; about sixty-five hundred legionaries survived and were with us. Mithridates of Commagene and Archelaus of Cappadocia were still loyal and with us, and King Polemo of Pontus was still ours. Antony forced himself to greet them heartily and thank them for their steadfastness. I watched him, and only I could see the despair that lay behind the good manners. Good manners are the last thing to desert us, so it seems. They remain behind to mock us with their hollow sound when all else has fled.

On the sixth day, in a hastily erected banqueting pavilion on shore, Antony gave a farewell feast for his friends. First we had tramped up to the acropolis to stand at the temple of Poseidon and give thanks to him for our miraculous escape. (At least that was what the official prayers said.) Standing looking out over the wide expanse of water below us, I felt an acute longing to be on the shores that awaited us far to the south: Egypt.

I was ready to return to Egypt, be restored by Egypt, have solutions to our dilemma whispered to me by the sands of Egypt. Egypt would not fail me. And I would not fail it.

At this very tip of land, which protruded like a finger from the mountainous spine of Greece, I felt all of Europe at my back. It was time to leave, to go home.

We trailed down the steep slope and then into the makeshift banqueting hall. But Antony had provided well, and Poseidon had yielded up a bountiful catch for us, along with wild goat meat from the mountains.

Antony had still not confided in me, and so I was as much a guest as anyone else. I had no idea what he had planned. After everyone had eaten (I noted that he himself ate little), he rose and addressed them. After thanking them for their loyalty, he then announced that he was releasing them from their pledges.

"We have fought a good fight, my friends," he said, lifting his cup to them. "But where I go, you cannot follow."

Did he mean . . . ? Oh, surely not! But it was the Roman way. Commanders in his position often . . . and before a public audience, too.

The thought must have occurred to the others, too, for they rose in protest. "Good Imperator, no!" they cried.

Now Antony looked close to tears, as he was touched by their horror at the threat of his loss. "No, no, good friends," he assured them. "I withdraw to Egypt. You cannot accompany me; there is no purpose in it. You must make your peace with Octavian."

Again a cry of protest.

Antony held up his hands. "Hear me. It is not necessary to follow me further. It will only be to your harm. You must accept what has happened, and see to your own safety. I can offer you a safe conduct to Corinth, and protection and hiding with my steward Theophilus until you can make arrangements with Octavian."

The buzz in the tent grew louder.

"Do not fear. Caesar made clemency fashionable," he said with a disarming smile. "I am sure Octavian will follow his example." He looked around. "He will reserve his wrath for the Queen and me, no others."

In his present mood, he would probably welcome that wrath, as some sort of deserved punishment.

"And now"—he gestured toward two of his attendants, who dragged a chest across the ground and flung open the lid—"I have raided one of our treasure ships to provide for you. Take the money, take the gold and silver, as payment for your services and as protection for your future."

He had helped himself to the treasure ship? Without consulting me? I stared at him.

The men were shaking their heads, refusing the gift. Antony kept urging them, and they finally filed up—does any sane man refuse gold for long? Some of them were weeping, and for that I did not begrudge them the money. Surely Antony would be touched by seeing that in the eyes of others he still held his honor.

That night he finally came to my—our—chamber. He had discharged his duty, had said honorable good-byes, and must now strip himself of all that remained, and prepare for the long journey ahead.

He had laid aside his mask when the guests departed, and now was solemn and subdued. "I am a man in exile," he said. "I have no place to go, except to hide in my wife's country, and beg for shelter." He sank down on the edge of our bed, and it creaked under his weight. "I am a Roman driven from Roman shores."

I was weary of this; I had no more words to dissuade him. "Come to bed," was all I said.

"I am no longer a leader of Romans; now I have truly become what they called me: an easterner, a foreigner. Rome has cast me out." As he spoke he untied his sandals, bending over so low I could hardly hear him. Slowly he removed his formal clothes by himself; since his defeat he had not even allowed Eros in his presence. Then he lay down and stared up at the ceiling.

I rose to the bait. "Aren't you forgetting Canidius and his fifty thousand men?" It was reported that, as arranged, Canidius had begun withdrawing the army to make the trek into Asia. "And the five legions in Cyrenaica, and the three in Syria? You are hardly a Roman without followers."

"Ahhh." His voice was a long sigh.

He was clearly exhausted, for he fell deeply asleep in an instant. I was relieved; it was the first time I could relax my vigil over him. I was still worried that he might try to emulate Cato, or Brutus, or Cassius. His polite performance tonight had not fooled me.

It would have been good if he could have been allowed to sleep, to repair his torn spirits. It would have been kind of the gods to grant us that. But in the darkest hour of night, we were awakened by a messenger with urgent news.

Canidius was here.

"Send him in." I pulled on a decent covering gown and helped Antony to throw on a robe. The news must be terrible. Canidius was supposed to be far away with the army.

Well, let us hear it. Let all the blows rain down on us. Let every disaster empty itself on our heads.

Antony had pulled himself to his feet, leaning on a tent pole. He was groggy after being fetched from the depths of sleep so soon.

Canidius came in, holding a lantern. His hair was wild, his face sweaty, his garments stained. "Forgive me, Imperator," he said, kneeling.

Antony touched the top of his head. "Yes. I do. Whatever it is. It doesn't matter." He reached out his hand and made Canidius rise.

"The army has surrendered to Octavian," he said. "I fled for my life."

"Many deaths?" asked Antony, as if he wanted there to be: more men to heap on his pile of remorse for his failures.

Canidius shook his head. "None."

Now Antony was brought up short. "What?"

"No deaths. There was no fighting. We had marched a little way toward Thrace when Octavian sent a column to negotiate a surrender. The men—the centurions—knew they could hold out for good terms, that Octavian would be anxious to avoid fighting. And so they bargained, with a skill that would make a rug merchant proud. In the end the centurions were able to extract a promise from Octavian to preserve the six historic legions, like the Fifth, the *Alaudae*, and the Sixth, *Ferrata*, the Ironclad, and—"

At the sound of the precious names, Antony gave a piercing cry like a wounded animal. "No! No!"

"The rest will be absorbed into other legions in the usual way," Canidius finished. "And they will get their settlement, and their land in Italy—"

Antony turned to me, ignoring Canidius. "Yes, that's what they want," he said. "Remember the old soldier, the one after Parthia, the one who said, when we visited him, that he wanted his plot of land in Italy, not a foreign place? The old veteran—O gods, did he die at Actium? I shouldn't have taken him on board the ship! If he'd remained, he'd be going back to Italy!" With that, he threw himself on the bed and beat his chest.

Canidius looked at me, his eyes wide.

"He has been this way since the battle," I said. "Do not be alarmed."

But Canidius was. "Madam," he said, "this is the saddest spectacle I have witnessed in all the war."

Finally Antony sat up, brushing the tears from his eyes. "Forgive me," he said. "But the old man—" He shook his head.

"I had to flee," said Canidius. "I could not expect Octavian to show mercy to *me*." He paused. "But you should know the truth. I stayed with them until the terms were complete. Octavian's version, which is part of his agreement to flatter the troops, is that they went on bravely fighting until they were deserted by their cowardly commander."

That was a bad choice of words—but how was he to know?

Antony gave a sigh, but said nothing.

"But there was no fighting. And the troops made peace only because they knew there was now no way for you to pay them. They were forced into it."

"Because I had deserted them, you mean?" Antony yelled. "Run off with the treasury?"

"I didn't say that. It was just a fact. Their paymaster was gone. Octavian was near."

Now Antony glared at me. "What was that you said, about Canidius and his troops? You'll have to change that." He shrugged. "It's all over. It's all over. Come, my last companions, we have a sea voyage to make tomorrow."

After Canidius had been shown out, Antony flung himself facedown on the bed and did not stir, lying like a dead man.

It took nine days to sail from Taenarum to the shores of North Africa. We had to give a wide birth to Crete because it now belonged to Octavian, and we could not put in there. Canidius went with us, as did several of Antony's die-hard friends (he still had them, in spite of his contentions), including one who had once served Brutus, offering to die in his stead, and then clinging loyally to Antony after being spared. I hoped he did not mention Brutus and his "noble" end, which might spur Antony on to imitate it.

Antony had quelled his outbursts and now entered into a phase that was even more disturbing: a stony, stoic, disinterested manner. He was alert, pleasant, attentive, but all with a deadly detachment that was chilling. Halfway into the voyage he had suddenly demanded to be taken to Paraetonium, at the westernmost edge of Egypt, where there was a small military outpost. He claimed he needed to "inspect" it—but what was there to inspect? It was nothing but a cluster of mud buildings, a small landing, and a lot of sand, heat, and scorpions. In nearby Cyrenaica, we still had five legions. I knew he wished to hide there, out of sight of mankind, and lick his wounds. Or inflict the wound that would end all wounds.

But what could I do? Forbid him? Had I not been the one reminding him he was still a general who commanded legions? Now he claimed he wished to visit a military post. Stay with him, guard him? It was demeaning for both of us, and it was crucial for me to return to Alexandria before the dreadful news of Actium had reached it. I dared not delay.

We made landfall just a short way from Paraetonium; the blinding white rocks and sand seemed to radiate heat. Baking in the sun were the low, brown buildings, with a drooping palm or two providing no shade at all at noon. Motley, shedding camels dozed around what passed for a well.

Antony silently gathered up his belongings and put on his uniform, as if he were going to a grand ceremony. Attired thus, he looked like his old self— if you did not look into his eyes. And the beak on his helmet prevented it.

Alone in the cabin, we faced one another.

"Antony, inspect your post here, then come back aboard," I said. "We will wait." It would hardly take very long for him to see what there was to see.

"No," he said. "I need to stay. I will follow. I promise."

"When?"

"That I cannot say."

"Please don't delay! You are needed in Alexandria. The children—"

"Give them this." He stripped off his silver military awards carelessly and dropped them into my hand. "Tell them what they were for." He paused. "Now I must go."

"No good-bye?" I could not believe we could part like this, stiff strangers.

"It is only for a little while," he said cryptically. Then he bent and kissed me, a formal kiss that turned into a real one.

As he and his two friends descended onto the shore, I saw that he still had his sword, as well as his dagger. He had not given those to me for the children's remembrance. Obviously he thought he still had need of them.

We were two days' sail west of Alexandria, and I needed that time to decide what to do. With Antony gone, my anxious watching could stop, and I felt an immense, sad relief as we sailed away from Paraetonium. I stood watching it recede, although the dazzling light made my eyes ache and finally the site vanished in a blaze of white. I knew he would be wrestling with his own fate in that lonely outpost, but he would have to do it alone, as ultimately we all do. Others become superfluous annoyances when our supreme hour of decision comes.

From the time I was very young, I felt I had a sort of power to predict things. Often I would get a nudging feeling that *this* would happen rather than *that*, and when it turned out that way, I would tell myself that the gods had granted me the power of prophesy. But now I knew that what I possessed instead was an acute ability to weigh factors and make informed guesses—

perhaps a more valuable trait for a ruler. At this moment, however, I did not know, I could not guess, which way Antony would go. All the factors seemed to weigh evenly, would tear and pull at him equally on both sides. Selfishly, I wished that he would ignore the beguiling sword and the Roman way, and decide to live, taking his stand with me. But not if it would utterly destroy him as a man.

And so I gave him to the gods; I mourned him in my heart as if he had already taken the Roman course. He must be dead to me now if I was to do what I must.

I knew with a certainty (not prophesy, but shrewd guess) that Octavian had sympathizers even in Alexandria. There always are people who wish for change, who are dissatisfied with the king. I had once been told a very hard truth: There is no one whose death is not a relief to *someone*. That is triply so for a monarch. Well, I must strike at them before they struck at me, which they would feel free to do as soon as the news of Actium reached them. I still had a little time.

I must sail into Alexandria alone; the rest of the bedraggled ships should lag behind, lest their condition shout the truth. And I would sail into the harbor with the ship garlanded as if we had been victorious. Yes! I would not betray, by so much as a flicker, what had really happened. Then I would speed into the palace and have my enemies—who had doubtless gained strength in my absence—rounded up and dispatched.

And Artavasdes, our enemy. Even before his capture, he had been in league with Octavian. His master would doubtless restore him to his throne in Armenia, and thus our clemency in sparing him would be thrown back into our faces.

Well, I could prevent that. He would never live to laugh as he ascended the steps of his throne again, as he had smirked in ascending the steps to us at the triumph. It was good Antony was not here to stop me.

HERE ENDS THE EIGHTH SCROLL.

824

THE NINTH SCROLL

78

The *Antonia*, her gilded stern scrubbed to shining once more, her purple sails brushed free of salt, her bow garlanded, sailed triumphantly into the harbor of Alexandria. I had stationed my attendants on deck in colorful attire, and threatened them with dire punishment if they did not wave and sing joyfully. For myself, I put on my royal robes and headdress, and stood under the mast where I could be seen by all.

Never has the sight of the white, pure Lighthouse been more beautiful to me, calling me home after what had been a very long and perilous journey. My limbs ached with the weariness of it, but I must appear fresh. And the tall serenity of the Lighthouse, unmoving in spite of the waves dashing across its base, gave me strength.

The shores were lined with crowds, cheering wildly and throwing flowers that floated out on the water, little dots of red, yellow, purple, blue. The palace, on its grassy peninsula, beckoned coolly. Behind the shore rose the cubes of the buildings, as white as salt. I closed my eyes and made a vow.

I must keep it, must keep Egypt; the Ptolemies could not forfeit it as pun- ishment for Roman failures in the field. I must do whatever it took to keep it for my children: humble myself to Octavian, abdicate in favor of my son, make other alliances that would keep Rome from swallowing us, kill my enemies. I must even, if necessary, kill myself. *Anything.* No price was too high. I could not let nine generations of Ptolemies end with me, let the last of Alexander's heirs be vanquished and vanish from living history. *Anything.* And I must not flinch.

We docked at the royal landing stage; I sent messengers out immediately to post proclamations of the victory (which I had hurriedly composed in my cabin) all over the city. After waving, greeting the crowd, we were whisked into the palace and out of sight.

Now the real work could begin.

I climbed the wide steps up to the inner hall of the palace, where Mardian, Olympos, and the children were lined up waiting. I threw protocol aside just as Antony had stripped off his medals and threw my arms around them, seized with joy at seeing them. Getting my arms all the way around Mardian was proving more and more difficult; in his excitement, Olympos forgot to be unemotional, and even kissed me; Alexander almost knocked me down in his effusiveness. Little Philadelphos clung to my legs, and Antyllus bowed smartly.

Standing a little aloof was Selene, who gave a shy smile. And behind her— my heart stopped when I saw Caesarion.

While I was gone, he had turned into a man. Somewhere between being fourteen and now months past sixteen, he had passed into adulthood.

Now—and even his movements were different—he came toward me. I had to look up at him. He took my hand in his, and it was a big hand, which utterly covered mine.

"Welcome, Mother," he said. His voice had changed, too.

Now I knew it more than ever. I must do anything to preserve his rights, his throne. Literally anything. My son, Egypt's new king.

"Why, Caesarion!" I said, so stunned by this new self I was at a loss for words. "I—have missed you," I finally said. I would never stoop to saying, My, *how you have grown*.

"And I, you. I am so happy it is over, and you are back. Tell us, what happened? The victory—how grand was it? How many ships sunk? Where is Octavian? Is he dead? I hope so!" He grinned.

"Don't tire your mother with all these questions," Olympos said sharply. I knew then that he had guessed. Well, soon he would know.

"That's all right," I assured Caesarion. "Let us retire into our private quarters, and there I will tell you all. All . . ."

Safely inside our most private withdrawing rooms, the doors bolted, all attendants dismissed, I told them the dreadful truth. They took it silently and unresisting. Only Caesarion looked dismayed, and kept asking for diagrams to illustrate what had happened, which squadron went where, which legion was deployed where. . . .

Finally Mardian asked, "Where is Antony?" From the way he asked it, I knew he thought Antony was dead. But surely he did not think I was so self-controlled I could have concealed it this long!

"He is . . ." How to describe it without adding to his dishonor? ". . . at Paraetonium. He wishes to inspect the legions to the west at Cyrenaica."

"Oh no!" said Mardian.

"What is it?"

"The legions deserted to Octavian. Right out from under their commander! Poor Scarpus had to leave; he is probably sheltering at Paraetonium.

We had heard that Octavian had appointed Cornelius Gallus to take over the legions, and he was on his way."

"The poem-writing soldier?" I asked. Now he could sit on the sandy coast and compose poems about his glorious master and the fall of Antony.

"The same," said Mardian. "So Scarpus and Antony must be together."

Just what Antony needed. Two deserted generals together, sharing wine and misery in a mud hovel. Now my fear leapt back upon me. I remembered King Juba and Petreius, in their lurid double suicide—and in the same setting, too.

"He will be in Alexandria shortly," I said, with conviction. My anguish about him must be kept for myself alone. "But before the news leaks out, there are things we must do. The legions stationed here are still loyal?"

"Yes," said Mardian.

"Then . . ."

My commands were carried out. The "Octavians" had been conveniently vocal in their cheers for him and their mutterings against us; it made it easy to identify and arrest them. We discovered quite a storehouse of weapons and piles of incriminating correspondence. The leaders were executed, their properties seized. There had been a sizable number of Octavians, and it disturbed me more than I liked to admit. In my very own city . . . I knew everyone had enemies, but still! . . . The ingrates!

I ordered the remaining warships to sail to the spot where the neck of land separating the Mediterranean from the Red Sea is at its narrowest, some twenty miles. There, after devices were built for hoisting them from the water, they were to be hauled across the sands on frames mounted on log-rollers, to be relaunched in the Red Sea. There my fleet would be safe from Octavian, and I could have it ready for eastern voyages. I was thinking more and more that the safety of my children could only be guaranteed in the east, somewhere beyond Rome's reach.

At the same time I ordered more ships to be built to replace the ones lost at Actium. When Octavian arrived, we would fight again, and this time my fleet would not have been held captive in a hellhole first.

It was one thing to be busy all day, attending to these vital matters. It was another at night, alone in my chamber. Then the dark would close over me like a fist, shutting out all hope and comfort. Antony's quarters stood empty, awaiting a master I feared would never return. Sometimes I would go there, lie down on his bed, as if by so doing I could will him back. How forlorn are rooms forsaken—spurned, as it were. I was sure he gave no thought to them anymore. Instead he paced out his time in exile at Paraetonium. Was it a struggle for him to live through each day? When the sun came up, did he steel himself to make it his last sunrise? And at sunset, the same? What is it about one particular day that whispers persuasively, *Today is the day you seek?* Every morning I awoke in dread that it was his last, and that a black-sailed ship would soon land in Alexandria, carrying a mournful cargo.

And then what would I do? It would be like Caesar's funeral, only worse, because there would be no Antony to speak this time. That voice would be stilled.

Should I send a ship and soldiers to bring him back? No. Of all the indignities he had suffered, this would be one of the worst: to be fetched home under armed guard, protected from himself like a lunatic who might inadvertently come to harm. It would mean I felt he did not know himself, did not know what was best for himself, was not in his right mind. How could I inflict that on him?

I must see to it that another tomb vault was constructed next to mine in the mausoleum. Now there was only one; strange that when I was very young I had first set about fashioning my tomb, when I had thought I had no need of it. Then it had been almost a game. But I had thought no more about it as I acquired a family: my four children and my husband.

Antony would lie in Alexandria after all. The request in the will that had caused him such problems in Rome would now be fulfilled, partly because of the very animosity it had aroused. Well, then. It must be worthy of the sacrifice he had made to achieve it.

These horrible thoughts kept me awake night after night. During the day I was exhausted, my head spinning, and each day I would think, *Tonight I will sleep soundly*, only to be cheated again.

The days belonged to my duties as a queen, the nights to my loss as a woman. The hardest truth for me was that Antony's and my destinies now had split. He had come to the end of his, whereas I still had mine to traverse.

He had been called to a high place—to be Caesar's successor, to rule Rome—had pursued it to the best of his ability, and had failed. He was right. It was over. I had been called to preserve and protect Egypt. That, too, I had done my utmost to achieve. But it was not finished yet. There was still a chance to fulfill my mission. Not a big chance, but a chance nonetheless. And that was all I asked: just the tiniest chance.

So much depended on Octavian now. What would he do? Would he pursue me to the gates of Egypt? Or would he turn back, like a dog that gives up chasing a cart? He had much to do in Rome; and what would he do with Egypt if he took it? A wise Roman had once noted that Egypt would be "a loss if destroyed, a problem to govern, a risk to annex." All this had given Rome pause before. Perhaps it would again.

And if Octavian arrived, would the Roman legions stationed here obey me, with Antony dead? Or would they go and surrender straightway? I could count on my fleet, and on my Egyptian soldiers, but perhaps on no one else.

There was a garrison at Pelusium guarding the eastern approach, just as Paraetonium guarded the west. But enemies would approach on three sides, from the sea and from both directions on land. All would converge on me here at Alexandria. I would have to meet them alone. No Caesar, no Antony. My male protectors, once so mighty with their Roman power, had fallen, leaving me standing on the battlefield by myself, as I had begun, almost twenty years ago. Then it had been Pothinus and the Regency Council I faced. Now it was the entire Roman army, of some . . . how many legions? With Antony's added to Octavian's, some thirty-five or so.

I almost laughed to imagine thirty-five legions bearing down on me, a hundred fifty thousand men with javelins and swords, come out to take one woman. . . . It was a compliment. I hoped they would not be disappointed when they finally confronted their quarry in person. Even standing as tall as possible, I was not very big.

And then what would they do? Take me back to Rome, to march in Octavian's Triumph, as Caesar had taken Arsinoe? To wear silver chains and trudge behind the chariot, to be spat on, then taken to the underground prison, strangled, and thrown into the sewer? No, I knew I would never allow that. And that lay in my hands to prevent. It must be prevented, not only for my own pride as a queen, but out of respect for Caesar. Never should his chosen love, and the mother of his son, meet such a fate. It was not a fitting end for the mate of a god. There would be those in the crowd who would remember when I walked beside him, honored and sharing in his glories.

No, Rome, I will never see you with these eyes again, I vowed.

For several weeks there was no news at all. Mardian dutifully kept me informed of every scrap of gossip, every whisper on the wind. My head aching, I would sit with him at the work table in my quarters, hearing reports about our crops, our tax-collecting, the progress of the ships . . . until at last one day there was something.

"Octavian is in Athens," he said, reading the letter. "All of Greece has pledged allegiance to him, except for Corinth." He laughed. "He has been inducted into the Eleusinian mysteries."

That made me laugh, too. I could not imagine Octavian believing in it; it was far too emotional and otherworldly for his like. But I supposed he did it to seem properly Grecian.

"He has disbanded large numbers of the soldiers and sent them back to Italy," Mardian read on.

So now there might be only seventy-five thousand men after me. What a comfort!

"How he will pay them . . . now there's the problem," Mardian mused.

"He'll pay them by taking Egypt," I said. And suddenly I knew that was true. It was essential that he get his hands on my treasury, against which all the problems of governing or annexing Egypt were nothing. He had financed his entire career on promises; now he would have to render payment. And it must come from me.

I must pay for my own defeat!

No, I would never let him have it! I would destroy it first!

How quickly all the issues were resolving themselves, I thought. The choices grew fewer and fewer.

Ten days later Mardian was reading another dispatch. Now Octavian had removed himself to Samos and was establishing winter quarters there.

"That means he plans to march on us in the spring," I said. "Unless he makes it sooner." So little time! So little time left!

"Hmmm—" Mardian looked pained, and kept fidgeting with the brooch fastening his cloak. "Hmmm—"

"If it's too painful for you to read, let me have it!" I said.

"Very well." He handed it to me.

Octavian had been receiving the client kings and reordering the appointments. The ones who convinced him their conversion was genuine were allowed to stay on. Thus Amyntas of Galatia was confirmed, as were the newly loyal Polemo of Pontus and Archelaus of Cappadocia. I could not blame them; Antony had disappeared. What else could they do?

It had not been the sea battle of Actium that was decisive, but the surrender of the land army. It had stripped Antony of his position as leader of a Roman party, as he had realized.

And then I read about Armenia. Although I had taken care of Artavasdes—he was executed—his son Artaxes had seized the throne the moment Actium was over, and gleefully massacred all the Romans in the area. The Roman province of Armenia was no longer Roman. Antony's gift to Rome, the trophy of his wars, had been snatched back.

"Is he to have no lasting monument at all?" I cried.

Only the monument in my mausoleum? For a man who had owned half the world, rearranging kingdoms and principalities as a housewife rearranges furniture? Was nothing of his to endure? That seemed the cruelest punishment of all, extending far beyond a lifetime.

"It is the fate of the vanquished," said Mardian slowly. "The victors appropriate what they like, and rescind what they don't." He sighed. "You know in our own country one Pharaoh erased the name of his predecessor often enough. Some names have vanished completely, so that we don't even know they ever existed."

Yes, but for it to happen to *us*!

The Nile had swelled to his greatest extent, flooding the fields, and now began to recede. Mardian proudly presented me with the projections of the harvest to come.

"It will be the most bountiful in recent memory," he assured me. "That is, if nothing interferes, such as locusts." He had brought some cakes flavored with honey, dark and runny, from the islands off Spain.

"Just in time to enrich Octavian," I said. I nibbled on a cake, which was very messy. There was no way to avoid having sticky fingers and a smeared face.

There had been new reports on his whereabouts. It seemed that the veterans he had recently sent back to Italy were rioting, demanding their payment and plots of land immediately. Even Agrippa had lost control of them, and so Octavian had had to rush back there, though it was winter, and risky sailing. I felt great relief knowing he had left our corner of the world. Perhaps he would find himself so embroiled in trouble he would tarry there a long while, giving us time to rally. . . .

But it also meant his eventual arrival was now a certainty. His time of promises had run out, and only gold could keep him in power. My gold. He would have to come and get it.

It is the fate of the vanquished . . . names erased . . . no existence . . . nothing to endure. . . . There had to be a way to outsmart Octavian, to cheat him of his final victory over our memories, our very existence. Already I had seen how he created his own version of events to flatter himself and to blacken us—as in his pretense that the soldiers had fought on bravely until Canidius deserted them. And as in another story now circulating: that I had fled Actium in cowardice, with Antony following because he was blinded with love. And after it was all over, Octavian would compose his own history of our struggle, while ours would be obliterated.

So it was then, in those bleak days of late autumn, with the sea rising in storms and sealing Alexandria shut, that I began this history of myself and my purposes. I was determined to record it, so that there would exist a record of what had truly happened, to refute the later lies. And I would not be so stupid as to deposit it in some public place, as Antony had done with his will! What is easier than to seize and search the official archives? No, this story, this statement, this confession would be put in a very safe place, where Octavian would not seek it. I would have it conveyed to Philae, there to be committed to Isis in her sanctuary; and another copy would be taken even farther south, to my sister ruler, the Kandake. It would lie beyond the reach of Rome, waiting until its day came, when there would be ears to hear and believe our side. For in time, they would come, and listen. Isis would know the moment to reveal it.

The Kandake . . . she had warned me about the Romans, long ago. Now she would be the final refuge of my truth.

And so I took two trusted scribes, and told the story you have read, beginning with "To Isis, my mother, my refuge . . ." and coming at last to . . . this.

I found it filled my days in strange ways, reliving my own past, threading events together like beads on a necklace, hoping they made a pattern. For we imagine they must make a pattern, which must be comprehensible from a great distance. Perhaps that great distance can only be time, which means it is impossible for me to grasp the meaning of my own life while I am still living it. I have tried to be honest, to record exactly what happened. It will not be contemporaries who read it, after all, but others who may be ignorant of the surrounding events, and therefore bring an open mind to them.

There were more things to be attended to; there was the future as well as the past. I must impart to Caesarion what it was essential he know in the days to follow. Rather than call him for a formal meeting, I waited until the moment arose naturally, although there was nothing natural in my careful compilation of ideas. I needed to study him carefully, assess what he would be capable of. I must not assume he was a replica of either me or Caesar—that was sentimental thinking, and it could prove costly.

I knew he had a keen interest in weaponry and mechanics—I remembered the miniature trireme he had played with—and under the pretext of wishing a demonstration of the bending properties of the spearheads in the newest javelins (which were tempered in only two crucial places, making them hang at awkward angles when they struck), I was able to spend several mornings with him. He observed the javelins and I observed him, while pretending to be utterly fascinated with the weapons.

Well, he had a good head for mathematics; he was able to do calculations easily, and he had no trouble figuring the trajectories of missiles or the volume of water displaced by boats. Strange how we can love our children and know so little about their actual talents and weaknesses. I had never known this about him.

I mentioned certain military records, which were in other tongues. Together we read them, and I was pleased with his grasp of Syriac, native Egyptian, and Hebrew. Of course his Latin was better than mine. He had practically memorized all of Caesar's writings.

"His writing is so fine," he said with a sigh, lying on the floor, propped up on his elbows, staring at Caesar's *Treatise on Analogy*. "Better than Cicero's, I think. Even Cicero admitted Caesar's vocabulary was 'so varied and yet so exact.' I wish I had inherited that. I have to use three words to hit the target, where he could select one."

"Still, as long as you hit it . . ." I made him laugh.

He laughed easily; he was naturally friendly, which was essential in a ruler. It is something that cannot be learned, or forced.

How odd to sit there, analyzing my successor. *This is good, this needs help, this won't work at all*. Had my father done the same with me? The lighthearted excursions we had made together might not have been so lighthearted on his part, after all.

He lay full-length, cradling his head on his arms. He had grace of person, a pleasing spontaneity, and lack of self-consciousness. His fair hair flopped over his brow, almost in his eyes. Perhaps Caesar's had been like that at that age. How we search for traits that might linger on in our offspring.

While his earlier resemblance to his father had not faded, and would recall Caesar to anyone who saw him, he was not a duplicate. No one is, in spite of parents' fond wishes. Each of us has only one lifetime.

I enjoyed the hours with him, for they are never enough when you must carry high duties of state. I had been separated from him too often.

The wind had risen, and the door leading out to the rooftop terrace blew open. He sprang up to close it, and as he pulled the door shut, at once the image of Caesar doing exactly that—the same gesture, the same door, the same half-turn of the body—came back to me. It was the day we had first talked about our child, and now that child—a man—stood in his father's place. How the days melt down, when seen over the years; how quickly we spring up and vanish. How young I had been then, not much older than Caesarion now. How adult I had felt! My heart grieved for that eager, naive young woman, happy in her ignorance.

Yet I was not old now. I had not even passed the age of childbearing. But feeling my life needed a summary, making provisions for death, for my successor—that killed youth, regardless of the actual years I counted.

"Nasty weather," he said. To him the door was just a door that needed to be closed, not a symbol.

"It keeps Octavian away," I said. The moment had come. I got up and went over to him. "You must know that he will eventually come. And when he approaches, I intend to surrender my crown and scepter to him, as is traditional with client kings."

His mouth fell open. He must learn to hide his feelings better, the judge in me thought. "No!"

"I will ask him to confirm you in my place. It is a time-honored custom. He is likely to do it. I know him; he wants proper respect paid, but he may prefer to take the easy way out and leave a Ptolemy on the throne." I looked directly at him. "Now I need you to tell me, and tell me truthfully: Do you feel ready to take this on? You will be seventeen, only a year younger than I was when I became Queen."

He looked uncomfortable; a frown crossed his face, and he chewed on his lip. Another mannerism he would have to conquer. But we would work on that later. Finally he said, "But . . . where will you be?"

How astute of him to ask that crucial question. And I must answer it. "I am afraid that as long as I live, he will prove . . . intransigent."

"You mustn't think of such a thing! No, I won't allow it!" He looked horrified, and I realized that my death would leave him an orphan. Even Antony would be gone. Seventeen is young to be all alone, too early to have started a family of his own to comfort him.

"Please don't make this any more difficult!" I cried, feeling cruel.

"I don't want the throne, if you have first to grovel to Octavian and then kill yourself. What do you think I am made of?"

"Whether you want it or not, you have to take it. If you do not, then Egypt is lost, and Caesar's line dies." I yanked on his tunic. "What do you think I have done it all for? Why have I lived my life as I have? For Egypt, and then for you and your inheritance. Don't make it all a useless sacrifice!" I had not reckoned on the object of all my efforts being recalcitrant. But I should have. People are unpredictable. What an irony, if he didn't want it, or refused to take it! "I think you are made of stern stuff," I finally answered. "I think you are the son of Caesar and Cleopatra."

"I wish I weren't!" he cried. "It requires too much of me! I can never fulfill your ambitions or your sacrifices. And as for my father—I'd rather be the son of a mortal! Someone who made mistakes, who lost a battle or two, who used the wrong word occasionally!"

"Someone like Antony," I said. "But you have had him for a father, the only father you've ever known. The gods were kind."

"And now he's gone, too! Why does everyone desert me?" He burst into tears. "Don't leave me!" He grabbed me and held me so tightly I could hardly breathe. His sobs may have been a child's, but he had the strength of a man in his arms.

This was horrible, worse than I could have imagined. I shouldn't have told him now. There is never any affair of state that justifies a mother deciding to kill herself, not in a child's eyes. When the events forced it, that was another matter. . . .

"Very well," I managed to get out. "I will do nothing violent. But I will then insist that you leave Egypt as the time approaches. Seek safety elsewhere, while I take my stand against him. Will you do that?"

He finally dropped his arms and let me go. "Leave Egypt?" he said.

"We cannot both be here," I said. "Surely you understand that. I will face him, but only if I know he cannot harm you. And before you depart, I will proclaim that you have come of age and that the Egyptians now have a man to lead them. That will make it easier for Octavian to recognize you. Will you agree to that?"

"In exchange for your life, yes."

"Alexandria will resound to one last celebration, then," I said. "It will be like days gone by."

He clasped me to him again, still trembling. "Don't leave," he kept saying. "Don't leave me."

Finally he let me go. Shaking myself free, I decided another moment had come, although I had not planned it. I placed in his hands the special box I had kept for Caesar's letters to me. No one but I had ever read them. But he needed them.

"These are your father's letters to me," I said. "No other eyes have ever looked upon them. But you should read them; you are included in them. And I think you will find that he made mistakes. There are even some words crossed out. He chose the wrong ones sometimes."

"That's only because he was writing in Greek," said Caesarion, half smiling.

Surrendering the letters was like opening a door into my soul. But he needed them more than I did.

"I love you, Mother," he said. "Forgive me if I would rather have you than your throne."

I forced myself to laugh and make a joke. "Then you are not a true easterner, for we are renowned for killing our parents to get their crowns." But I had been proud of the fact that my children were not like the other Ptolemies in that regard. "It must be your Roman blood."

The next step in my plan likewise went awry. I wanted Olympos to recommend and procure the best poison for me. He, too, was horrified.

We had been talking of other things; he had been most insistent that I needed to eat cucumbers and lettuce and melons to offset the privations of Actium, where there had been nothing fresh.

"I could tell just by looking at you that you were practically starving," he said, settling down on one of my couches and putting his hands behind his head.

"Why, because I could wear some gowns that had been too tight?" I asked. "I was pleased about it."

"Women! Vanity! Would it interest you to know that starving doesn't improve anyone's looks, no matter what gown they can fit into? Your skin had lost its color, your hair was dull, and your face had a pinched look."

"Well, I'm better now," I said. "There's plenty of food here." All the food that had been held up in Egypt, never reaching us.

"Better, but not well." He cocked his head. "We have to get you back to your fighting form, the better to seduce Octavian when he arrives."

"Very funny."

"Well, it's worth a try. He must be tired of Livia by now. Another married Roman strays into your orbit. . . ." He rolled his eyes. "They say he's partial to Corinthian vessels. Perhaps you can hide in one, and pop out."

What would I ever do without Olympos? "You know what they say," I said. "Never play the same trick twice. That's too much like the rug." I paused. "No, I have a new scene in mind. But I need your help. I want the best poison you can procure."

The smile faded from his face. "You want to poison him?"

"No. Not him."

I had never seen Olympos taken entirely by surprise, naked emotions playing on his face. I saw it now. "No!" he said. "No, I can't believe you would ask that of me." He jumped to his feet.

"Dear friend—" I rose, too.

"No! I said no!" Horror and anger were fighting within him. "I cannot!"

"If you cannot, who will?" I asked. "I am afraid it may prove necessary, and then I will be driven to—to ugly measures, unless you help me."

"I cannot use my skills that way," he said. "And even if I could, I could never aid you in—You are my friend, my lifetime companion, dearer to me than—than—"

"All the more reason why you should spare me suffering! Or do you want me tortured? Taken to Rome and killed there? Or forced to use knives or swords? Oh, pity my situation!" Now I felt trapped. I had betrayed my intentions to him without obtaining any help with them.

"The Cleopatra I know would face her enemies, not avoid them."

"Oh, that I intend to do," I assured him, for it was true. "All that diplomacy, charm, sacrifice may win for me, I will venture. But if they fail, I need to know that I will not be humiliated or tortured. I need to know I control my own last fate."

"This is premature. After all, Octavian is in Rome. Everything is quiet. Wait and see."

Why could he not understand? "We know what is coming," I said. "We must prepare."

He looked at me acutely. "You said diplomacy, charm, sacrifice. Just what do you have in mind?"

"I will flatter Octavian, surrender my crown to him, ask him only to pass the throne on to my son. That's diplomacy. I will hide my treasures, threaten to destroy them unless he agrees. Already I am gathering them into one spot, where I can set fire to them. That's sacrifice. And then, when I finally see him, I will remind him of Caesar's love for me, his respect. He will not dare to insult his 'father's wife.' That's charm." That was my tentative plan. I had no wish to die. But I was ready to. That was the difference.

"What if, when he sees you, he responds to your . . . charm in some other way, and demands some demonstration of it?"

I had thought of that. It was unlikely; enemies do not usually arouse lust. But conquerors routinely took women as part of their victory. And to take Antony's woman would be the final triumph over his foe, the greatest insult he could tender.

The thought was repugnant; I did not know if I could bear it, not even for Egypt, not even for Caesarion. The poison would be far better. But that might have to be afterwards; in fact, it would be obligatory afterward.

"I would get drunk first," I said. "And I assume you would have no scruples about providing me something to add to the wine to wipe out all my memory afterward."

I suppose that was the answer he wanted. It showed I wanted to live. Let him think it—as long as he got the poison!

"You stop at nothing," he said, with grudging admiration.

"I am desperate," I told him. "Don't fail me!"

"I didn't save you when the twins were born, only to murder you ten years later." He shook his head. "I won't get poison."

"Then you are crueler than Octavian!" Well, I would manage without him. I would think of a way. But I still needed some other assurances from him. "I want you to promise something else, then."

"Not until I hear it first." He crossed his arms across his chest.

"I want you to take the two copies of my life story out of Alexandria. Put one in the base of the great statue of Isis in her temple at Philae; take the other to Meroe, and the Kandake."

"Meroe! You want me to go all the way to Meroe?" His voice rose in protest.

"I think, after Octavian arrives, you will feel the need to travel." I smiled at him. "Do you promise? It is all I ask."

"All? Do you know how *far* it is?"

"Yes. I have been there, remember? You will be glad enough to leave Alexandria for a year or so. And when you return, Octavian will be gone."

"And you? Where will you be?" He was still suspicious.

"Taken off to Rome, since you will have it so," I said. No use to discuss it further now. "Do you promise to take the scrolls?"

He sighed. "Yes. I suppose so."

"No, do you *promise?* Do I have your word?"

"Yes."

"Then I can trust it, I know."

The year rolled relentlessly on, sliding into the darkest time. It was no darker outside than in my mind, where hate, fear, worry battered my heart. I continued training Caesarion, showing him the archives, the inventories, and trying to teach him the valuable arts of ruling: how to select administrators, how to compose correspondence that achieved one's aims, how to reward good servants and discern cheating ones. I spent hours with Alexander and Selene, telling them stories of Antony, lest they forget their father. I gave them the medals, recounting the battles where they were earned. I included Antyllus, in some ways the neediest of them all. He had come alone to Alexandria, a stranger, to take his place with unknown half-siblings. He had no mother, and had been taken from the house of his stepmother. I ached for him, the ache made worse by picturing Caesarion soon in his place. No father, no mother, no stepfather . . . well, at least Antyllus knew Octavian, I thought grimly. Surely Octavian would take him in and treat him kindly. My littlest, my last baby, now five years old, I played games with, enjoying his quick laughter, his chubby hands, his lack of questions that I found too painful to answer.

Mardian appeared one day, looking unusually glum. He had received a message.

I sighed. "What is it?" One bad thing followed another, like the waves rolling in relentlessly, smashing against the breakwaters. There was now no news that could be good; there was only bad and worse. And the worst: that Antony had . . .

"The ships," he said, handing me the letter. "Malchus."

I had thought I was past disappointment, but reading that Malchus had ordered my ships burnt was crushing. And he had waited until they had been laboriously hauled across the sands and safely launched in the Red Sea before descending on them and torching them.

"O ye gods!" I cried. "Now all my enemies rise up!" Malchus had harbored a grudge against me ever since I had taken his bitumen rights.

"Now that Didius is . . . has . . ." Mardian coughed delicately.

Quintus Didius, the Syrian governor, had gone over to Octavian a month ago, with his three legions.

"What about him?" I asked.

"To prove his new loyalty, he has unleashed Malchus on you. Malchus could not have struck without his permission."

"Of course not." So the ships were gone. No escape by way of that route. I was inured to it now, to all these losses and setbacks. My only goal was to keep going, and hope for a miracle to reverse the incoming tide. Octavian *was* mortal. There were still shipwrecks, fevers, accidents. . . . All it would take was one. And that was in the hands of the gods, and they were more likely to grant it if they applauded our resolute efforts here below. No one, man or god, likes a quitter. And so I soldiered on, alone.

79

There was only one place left that promised me solace. Antony's vacant rooms were a palace of torment; the children's quarters, with their high, resounding noises of life, were only a spur reminding me of the solemn charge with which I was entrusted; Mardian's reports of Egypt's prosperity were almost galling; and Olympos and I now played a game of cat-and-mouse about my intentions.

As I went out into the city, I could not help assessing what the Alexandrians—volatile, pleasure-loving, and yes, superficial—would be capable of withstanding. A siege? Doubtful. Bombardment? No. And certainly not for the sake of a disgraced Roman general. For me? Perhaps. They watched me carefully as I was carried through the streets in my litter, their dark eyes glittering. They were assessing me as I was them.

Octavian made deals. He would offer them terms to preserve their glorious city; and there was part of me that was grateful, knowing my city would live on somehow, surviving me.

The white tomb of Alexander beckoned, as it had to me all those years ago. In the glistening building that housed his remains—cool in its passageway under the dome—sounds were hushed and the light that penetrated was scattered and gentle. The utter stillness was what struck me now, whereas when I was a child it was the gleaming gold, the sword, the breastplate. Now I realized that I could never grasp what death truly meant, how it could change movement into absolute stillness and rigidity, but that if Alexander, that most restless of men, could lie so still . . .

Instead of comfort, it was horror. I would never go there again, and I emerged blinking into the sunlight, craving any movement I saw—the scurrying of a lizard, which now had power Alexander had lost forever; the waving of a workman's hand; the stumbling of a donkey on the pavement. I entered my litter, and felt the thudding of the footfalls of my bearers, alive, moving. . . .

Only in the Temple of Isis, on the eastern side of the palace promontory, where the sound of the sea echoes through the hall like the noise inside a fragile seashell held up to the ear, was there any peace for me. From the portico I could see the shining aquamarine water with its decorative white froth trimming the waves like lace. The crying of the wind, imitated by the seagulls, seemed to be calling to me. Inside the shaded hall, the statue of Isis, as white as new-cut ivory, stood inviting me to draw near.

There, at the feet of the goddess, the only mother I had ever really known, I could rest my head and lay aside my pretense. She saw everything, she knew everything, and I could trust her: things we long for in our earthly companions.

O Isis! My mother! I feel myself to be a child, lost and alone. . . .

Long ago my mother had vanished into that beguiling tender blue of the harbor, resigning me to Isis's care.

I am small, very small. I only come up to the statue's base, and I reach out and touch it, my fat little hands curling with sorrow, offering a sad bunch of wildflowers to the goddess, terrified of her. "This is your mother now," the old nurse says, but she is white and remote, and I can barely see her face. I want my own mother's face back, her high coloring, her red lips, her greenish eyes. I put out my hand again and see, overlaying it, my mother's hand, her slender fingers flailing in the water and disappearing.

I cry to the goddess, *I am yours—take me, too, I want to go with her.* But the goddess draws me up, takes my chin, whispers, *Child, my child, death is not for you. You are mine, and will be my hands and eyes, my executor, my incarnation—forever and ever.*

I had forgotten, my memories perhaps sealed by her power—until now. As I stand in her shadow, it all returns, only now I am taller, my hands—slender and ringed now, like my mother's—reaching to the goddess's knees, my mother's face faded beyond recall, Isis and her serene beauty the only mother I know.

What would you have me do? I ask her. Only you can guide me. Shall I resist? Am I to die soon? What of my children? Where will they go, what will you do with them?

O Isis—you who control fate, you who open and close the doors of our journey, tell me whence I go, where and why. Tell me. I am ready to hear.

And, faint as the sea-whisper, the murmur of the tides lapping at the base of the temple, I hear the sound of doom: *Only a little while more, a little distance yet to go, and bravely borne, and you may lie down beside me.*

Beside her. My mausoleum was beside the Temple of Isis, with an adjoining passageway. So.

As long as men come to worship me, as long as women come to pay homage, to lay flowers and wash with the sacred water, so long will they pass your earthly remains and honor you, too. You, my true daughter, will be part of me and those who love me, until the crack at the end of the world—the end of our world. . . .

It is over, then? It does not seem possible, but it is only the statues who abide forever. Even Alexander lies as still as dust under his canopy, and he was younger than I.

But only six years younger! I am thirty-nine! Too young; it has gone too fast, far too fast to be over!

Octavian—Octavian is also six years younger than I, exactly Alexander's age; no, not quite yet, not until next September will he attain Alexander's age. And then . . .

Is it to be then? I asked Isis. Is it to be then, but not before?

And she told me, *Yes. Then.*

But I wanted to change it, *would* change it. Was it truly written, or could it be rescinded? If the gods admired or applauded our efforts, did they not have the power to change even what is written? They had pitied Psyche, and her great struggle earned her a place on Mount Olympus, a drink of ambrosia converting her with a sip from mortal to immortal. And Hercules . . . his labors had made him a god after all.

Only those who struggle are worthy of a reprieve. And so I had learned nothing, except what was waiting to be changed by my own determination. How easy to submit, how great the reward for resisting! Thus the gods encourage us to rebel, by their own inconsistency and approval of our daring.

"They told me I would find you here."

I barely heard the voice; it was low and came from the portico. I turned to see a black outline, someone standing, leaning an arm against the column, black against white.

"Who intrudes upon me?" I demanded. I wanted no human beings in this sacred space.

He removed his hand from the column and walked toward me, still just a black bulk, moving deliberately, slowly. . . .

"You do not recognize me?" Antony's voice framed the words in sorrow and disappointment.

He was alive! He was here, refuting death itself! I ran to him and flung my arms around his neck, which I had thought never to do again.

The black-sailed ship . . . the sarcophagus . . . the speechless funeral . . . all the tormenting images I had wrestled with gone, shriveled like the wraiths of imagination they were. His breath was warm, his flesh solid—this was no ghost.

"O thanks! Thanks be to all the gods!" I cried. He, too, had defied their orders, and now he lived and was here. He had turned his back on the Roman dictum.

"I had to see you again," he said. "I could not leave with our parting as it was."

He bent down and kissed me, holding me to him fiercely. My soul sang at his touch, at his restoration.

"I cannot hold you close enough," I said. Above us Isis looked down, her face expressionless.

We would return to the palace. He would see the children. How happy he would make them! They would not face the loss I had, that hot, still day in the harbor. I would tell him of all the preparations, the news.

"And now I can bear it," he said, pulling away from me. "To have parted properly is fitting."

"I do not understand." Surely he had not come all this way to . . . I turned and looked at Isis. Was all this her will, a cruel trick?

"I will live here, but not with you," he said. "I am no fit company, no longer worthy to reside in the palace. I will dwell in solitude, in a small house—the meaner the better—on the harbor, awaiting the inevitable approach of . . . the victor."

"But—" I searched for words. This fit no pattern. It made no sense, answered no requirement of honor. "Surely you have some other purpose! Why did you return, then?"

"I told you—to see you."

"But you will cause me great pain. How can I live in the palace, alone, knowing you are in the city, refusing to come to me? And the children! How can you explain—how can I explain—to Alexander and Selene that their father is here, but will not see them? They are frightened, confused! They need you!" What madness had entered him?

"I am no longer Antony," he said. "It is better that they do not see me. Let them remember me as I was. Let them cherish the medals—mementos of a great soldier! Not this man—not this man!" He extended his arms, brushing them down over his chest, then holding them out in resignation.

"You are their father!" I said sternly. "Children care less about medals and honor than you imagine. They crave only the life and presence of their father or mother." My mother, sinking beneath the waves, abandoning me . . . but she had not done it on purpose. "You are cruel!" When he still stood unmoving, I cried, "The gods will punish you for this! Deliberate cruelty is unforgivable! You couldn't help Actium, but this is your own doing! And you will pay for it!"

He was not to return to the palace, but turn his back on it and on us, letting his quarters remain empty . . . never to act as husband and father again.

"Antony died at Actium." His voice was low.

"What is standing here, then?" He looked real enough to me.

"A shadow, a dark double."

"Then let it come to us."

"It is not worth the having," he said.

"If this unfeeling man is the remnant of Antony, then you have spoken true!" I cried. "This is not Antony, who was above all kind and generous! This is more like Octavian! Has he taken you over? Hardened you into a version of himself?"

"Let me depart in peace!" he said. "Remember me as I was!"

"It is impossible. Whatever our last glimpse of someone, that remains with us. Oh, Antony—" I held out my arms to him. "Come back with me. Let us stand together, wring some last pleasure and victory from our days—"

But he had turned away, his cape trailing out behind him, descending the temple steps.

I bent my head over the base of Isis's statue and wept. He had invaded my interview with the goddess, returned from the dead, teasingly, only to depart.

What shall I do? What shall I do? I implored her.

Let him go, she answered. *Now there is only you. You, and I. I will not flee, or fail to uphold you in your need. Give yourself to me. Your need of mortals is over.*

It was sunset before I left the temple; the rose reflection of the red glow on the horizon coated the columns, threw slanting rays across the floor, bathed Isis's face in living hues. The tide had receded, and ugly black rocks revealed themselves, nibbled by the waves.

I was exhausted, as if I had fought a mighty battle. I dreaded returning to the palace, to all the questions and scrutiny, but unlike Antony, I would make myself face them.

My arms ached from the brief embrace, bringing forgotten sensations back to me. The feel of his lips on mine—now I must forget them again, and forget them in anger and disappointment. Better for me was the parting in Paraetonium! I hated him for this surprise, this titillation. And I could never forgive him for wounding his children so. Even the Roman way would have left me with more respect for him! Then I would have been sorrowed; now I was shocked and betrayed.

Heart, we must forget him utterly! I told myself sternly as I marched back to the palace. How to face Mardian and tell him . . . ?

I need not have worried. It was Mardian who had spoken to him, had told him where to find me. He was waiting anxiously.

"Did he . . . ?"

"Yes!" I cried, anger and sorrow struggling like gladiators within me.

"And where . . . ?"

"He has gone off to—I know not where! He says he will live alone—not coming to the palace. Oh, Mardian!" I embraced his comforting bulk. Dear Mardian, my stalwart, ever-constant friend.

"He is a broken man," he said. "Don't judge him too harshly."

"But the children! How can he—?"

"He is ashamed to face them." He guided me back into his most private room. "He has had another blow."

"What?"

"He did not tell you?"

"No. He said nothing, just a sort of formal farewell."

"Ah." Mardian gestured for me to seat myself on one of his soft couches.

As I did so, sinking into the welter of pillows, I felt profound relief. I had been standing for hours. "What has happened to him?" I cared terribly. I wanted to protect him against any more lashes.

842

Mardian picked up a slender glass pitcher and, without asking, poured out a sweet drink of honey and fresh-pressed grape juice for us. He handed me a goblet, and I took it gladly. "Scarpus arrived a few hours ago," he said. "It seems that Gallus and his men finally reached Cyrenaica, where Scarpus's former legions were waiting for them. They joined forces, and Antony decided to go to the camp and make a personal appeal to his former soldiers there. He would stand outside the gates and address them."

No! What a humiliation! But that he would undertake it showed he was not beaten yet.

"But what happened?"

"Scarpus was standing with him, and as he told it—it was pitiful. Every time Antony raised his voice to speak—and you know how he has trained it to carry great distances—Gallus gave the order for the trumpets to sound and drown him out. It went on and on like that for hours. Finally the day ended, and Antony had to depart unheard."

An actual shaft of pain shot through me. Enough, enough! I begged Isis. Lay no more upon him!

"And then he came here," I said.

"Apparently so."

This last blow must have unhinged him. He could only crawl here in shame—like a dog seeking a safe place to lie down and die. Oh, if only I had known this when he was standing before me!

"He did not relate this to you?" said Mardian.

"No." He had probably felt there was nothing to relate. O Antony! "No, he said nothing."

"What did he do, then?"

He looked at me. He kissed me. He said farewell.

I shrugged. "Muttered a lot of nonsense about living alone, watching for Octavian—" Now I felt tired, defeated. I, too, sought a safe place to lie down. I did not want to return to my rooms, where the children would come in, where Iras and Charmian would be. I understood how Antony felt, if only fleetingly. "Mardian—may I be your guest tonight?" I did not have to explain it to him.

"I would be honored," he said. "It has long been prepared."

As my chief state minister, his quarters rivaled mine in size and, I daresay, surpassed them in sumptuous appointments. He had an eye for beauty and the means to indulge it; the customs officials were well versed in his tastes, and whenever a cargo of Syrian pearl-inlaid tables, Indian camphorwood chests, or Coan silk bed-hangings put in, they invariably set aside a sample for him. The result was a series of rooms dripping with decoration, with no empty spot on wall, floor, or table. The only exception to this was his workroom, which was as spare as a hermit's cell.

A hermit's . . . as spare as Antony's, now?

"I believe in keeping only the pertinent papers to hand," he explained once. "All the rest of the clutter just confuses the mind."

"How, then, do you live in all this?" I would have found it stifling. I must have space to breathe, and to rest my eyes.

"Ah, once outside the workroom, I find my senses need caressing," he said.

He led me down a corridor, past rooms glittering with treasure like a merchant's den, and to the very last chamber, a corner one that overlooked both the sea and the palace gardens. I could see my mausoleum from the window, and Isis's temple, too, violet against dark blue in the deepening night. They made me shiver. There were the steps where Antony had walked away. Where was he now? I looked in vain for any movement in the shadows beneath the portico.

"Here, my dear, you may stay as long as you wish." He indicated the chamber, its cushioned benches overflowing with embroidered throws, the enormous bed enveloped in filmy curtains.

"You know you are safe saying that, for I must be back in the audience chamber by morning," I said. I reached up and touched his smooth cheek.

He laughed. I had always liked his laugh, and now found it as familiar a friend as he himself. "But you need not, if you do not wish to. I can attend to it."

"I know that." He had turned out to be that rarest of things, a cherished friend who was also the best person for a high position. "But I will be there, you know. I do not shirk." I turned toward the bed. "You have provided so much here, I feel negligent in planning only to sleep." My eye had caught the piles of scrolls, the paintings, the game boards of inlaid ebony, the musical instruments, all waiting for the guest.

"I can send a singer in to lull you to sleep," he said. "I have a very fine one, from Lycia—"

"No. Silence will be sweeter," I assured him. I waited a moment. "I went to Alexander's tomb today," I finally said. "Do you remember—?"

"When we first met there? Yes. You thought I was hogging him!" He laughed, that lovely laugh.

"Mardian, it was different today. He wasn't different, but I was, the world was—never go back there!"

"Well, I haven't been in many years. You know how it is—when you *live* someplace, you never see the famous sights, except when you're a child and get taken there. I daresay—"

"No, I mean it! It was oppressive, frightening." I wanted to explain it to him—or perhaps to myself.

"You've never been frightened of anything, as long as I've known you," he said stoutly. "And now you say a tomb has unnerved you?"

"No, not the tomb itself, just . . . the end of things." It was more difficult to put into words than I expected. "Don't return there, I beg you."

He shrugged. "I was not planning to." His hand swept around the room. "Now, here, I have provided pillows stuffed with the down from baby swans' necks. . . ."

———

I lay on the bed, my head sinking into the plump pillows—sacrifice of the young swans—my view of the chamber misted by the thin blue silk curtains drawn around the bed. How secure I felt here, how protected by the layers and layers of luxury. Perhaps that was what they were for, to cushion Mardian against the outside world. Perhaps that is all money ultimately does—cushion us against the world, smooth out its rough texture for us.

To have a friend like Mardian at a time like this was a healing balm. I, like Antony, needed a restorative place of withdrawal, but I would not linger here. Just for tonight . . . just for tonight . . . Dear Mardian. He never failed me.

The shadows thrown by the three suspended oil lamps made patterns on the walls, and it was easy to see people in them, profiles, stories. The shades . . . the shades of Hades . . . how alive were they, what did they remember, what did they feel? I would soon know. Even to be a shadow on a wall, like these, was better than to be nothing. I did not want to be extinguished, did not want to die. Thinking about it so carefully ahead of time made it worse, but to be struck down suddenly was no better. As men we think, and garland our deaths with thoughts, like flowers bedecking a tomb. To be robbed of that opportunity is to die like a beast. Still . . . the beasts do not poison their last hours with morbid thoughts, so which is preferable?

Sleep was now lapping around me. I could feel the edges of my thoughts blurring; this long day was finally ending. Antony. My children. There was still so much to be done. But that was tomorrow. Tomorrow . . .

Sometime in the middle of the night, the wind rose and pushed past the fastened windows, stealing even into the corners and warmth of the bed. A winter storm—one of the last, for winter was waning. Hearing the sound of waves stirred to madness outside, I was again at Actium, again a prisoner of the water. I sat up, brushing aside the the curtains and letting the cold touch my skin.

The water. The water. That sound, the same inimitable sloshing that had surrounded me at all the crucial times of my life. The Alexandrian harbor, the muffled boat ride west to Caesar, the journeys to Tarsus and Antioch, and then Actium—all turning points, all somehow connected with water, with boats. How many more boats were waiting to decide my future? There was the boat on which I planned to send Caesarion to India, the last-stand battle against Octavian in the harbor, a riverboat to take my story south to Philae and Meroe . . . and possibly a boat to flee to safety, with Antony. More boats. More water. But there was one boat I would never board: a boat to Rome, as a prisoner. No, rather than board that boat, I would be on the one ferried by Charon, across the river Styx.

Fate by water. Death by water. How odd, for the Queen of Egypt, a desert country, to have her destiny decided, over and over again, by water.

I told the children that Antony was in Alexandria, but was "unwell"—a truthful enough statement. I had been told where he had located himself, in a small house on the west side of the harbor, and I knew that from his window he could see the lights of the palace, could see the royal harbor with the gilded ships riding at anchor. He apparently shuffled around during the day, keeping to himself, barely eating, spending long hours at the window, staring out to sea. He kept his sword always about him, and once again I had to awaken each day wondering if a sad-faced servant would approach the palace, saying, *I bear sad tidings.* . . .

His sarcophagus stood ready in the mausoleum; of pink Aswan granite, it matched mine. That is less portentous than it sounds, for mine had been waiting for years. More immediate than that was the growing pile of treasure heaped in the largest chamber of the marble-and-porphyry building. A large area had been smeared with pitch and carpeted with tinder, and on that a pyramid of cinnamon, pearls, lapis, and emeralds rose from a base of ivory tusks, gold ingots, and ebony bars. I had carefully overseen it, making sure that the treasures were ordered in such a way that the greatest number could be packed into the smallest space. They would burn, burst, melt, once the pitch was torched, and Octavian would be deprived of money equal to all his legions' debt. I would use it to bargain for Caesarion's throne, and, failing that, for the joy of seeing it elude Octavian's grasping hands. It was not all of my treasure, but enough of it to give Octavian pause. Only a madman would not try to prevent its loss. And Octavian was no madman; he was a deal-making businessman.

In order to gain concessions, one has to have something to bargain with. It never failed to amaze me how many people—otherwise intelligent—fail to grasp this simple fact. They rely on sentiment, mercy, decency, when nothing but money or force will carry any weight. Well, we had lost the force at Actium, but we still commanded money.

"Now, pack those pearls tighter!" I ordered the workmen, who were pushing the pearls into bejeweled sacks and stacking the sacks onto the pyramid—a misshapen replica of the ones standing in the desert. "We want as many as possible!" This depleted almost my entire store of pearls: the prize ones from the Red Sea, the small ones from Britain, the oddly swollen and outsized ones from the seas beyond even India. They were vulnerable to heat, and would explode in a fire, sending slivers of iridescence all over the room. Once before I had invested my pearls in a desperate venture for Egypt—I smiled as I remembered the wager with Antony—and now they would serve again.

"Good!" I rubbed my hands together in approval. There was something fascinating in this projected, profligate destruction. Something grand. "And the emeralds?"

They indicated some sacks lying lower in the pile.

"Oh, we need more than that!" I said. Was that all? "Perhaps you will have to add turquoise to them to swell their ranks." Yes, why not? Blue and green together. Earth and sky. Are we imitating nature? I laughed giddily.

Was this right? Was I becoming as unhinged as Antony, unstable in this high wind of misfortune and desperate stakes? Why was I taking such mad delight in this? It was more than just the contemplated thwarting of Octavian. Destruction, sacrifice, extravagant offerings to the gods who would doom us—it was a dizzying, intoxicating brew.

"Yes, add the turquoise!" I said. "And if that is not enough, put lapis in as well." Lapis, with its glistening gold veins, its royal hue . . . never would it bedeck the First Citizen, *Princeps*, Octavian, to make a Republican crown! "Lapis on the heap!" I heard high, shrill laughter: mine. The workers bent and unloaded their precious burdens, a solemn stream coming from the palace, ants preparing the great nest of treasure.

"Octavian has landed in our part of the world." The news we had waited for—here at last.

Mardian, a rustle of red, handed me the dispatch.

I read it carefully. He had left Rome at the very earliest opportunity, and sailed back to Samos. "He does not disappoint," I said.

Mardian nodded. "Never."

"From here on I fear he will be quite predictable in his movements." He would come for us, advancing slowly—*festina lente*, hasten slowly—through Syria, then Judaea, then to the eastern gates of Egypt. "We are the ones who must be unpredictable." Let him not count on an easy victory, nor on no surprises. There was the Egyptian fleet, there were four Roman legions here, and there was the treasure-pile in the mausoleum . . . and there was Caesarion, almost a grown man. In fact, I realized with a start, the exact same age Octavian himself had been the last time I had seen him. Would he remember what he himself had been at seventeen? He never forgot anything.

"More of the client kings have gathered to kiss his hand," said Mardian.

"I did not think there were any left!" I said, fighting hard to keep my voice light and free of bitterness. "Who else could there be?"

"Yes, you are right, most of the kings have already bent the knee. Now it's mostly small territories, or cities, like Tarsus—"

Not Tarsus! Not the place where I had gone to Antony, where we had first loved—trampled under Octavian's heel, soiled! It hurt like a swift blow in the stomach.

"Antioch, too, I suppose," I said. He would besmirch both places.

"Not yet," said Mardian.

"Then I will have a little while to remember it as it was," I said. "Is there no one left loyal to us?" I could not help this cry.

"Indeed, yes," Mardian replied. "And from a most unexpected quarter—a school of gladiators at Cyzicus in Bithynia, that Antony was having trained to perform in his victory games. They have defied the governor there and set out for Egypt, to fight for us."

So there were still some . . . how surprising. How heartening.

Next Octavian went to Rhodes, where Herod came to him and surrendered his royal insignia. Herod, who always had a winning way with words, said that he had been stalwartly loyal to Antony, and that if Octavian would accept his vow of fealty, he would be equally loyal to him. Octavian accepted, but most likely because he had no one to put in Herod's place, since Herod had taken the precaution of executing his only possible rival. Along with Herod had come his creature, Alexas of Laodicea, wagging his tail and slobbering on Octavian's hand. It was Alexas, once a friend of Antony's, whom Antony had sent to Herod to beg him to remain loyal. Instead they had both run to Octavian. I was most pleased when I heard that Octavian had executed Alexas. He felt that Alexas had urged Antony to make the final break and divorce Octavia, and that was unforgivable.

That meant—as if I had not known it—that Octavian would pour every drop of his acid hatred onto my head. For if the bystander Alexas had had to be executed for his part in the divorce, what must become of the woman who had caused it all?

"Put them here." I indicated the sandalwood box, covered with gold sheet and lined with ten layers of tissue-thin silk, in every color: a rainbow in a box. The outermost layer was midnight-blue, the next purple, and so on, lighter and lighter, until the final one was shimmering white. A fitting background for the gold diadem and scepter.

Charmian and Iras, each carrying one in their graceful hands, set them on the silk, looking longingly at them. They remembered when I had worn them, at the Donations.

Of course I had others, but these were among my finest. And they were going to Octavian.

Would he be tempted to try them on? Late at night, would he leave the box carelessly in his room, and then, when no one was looking, lift the diadem out and set it on his high forehead? I imagined that he would find the gold chilly at first, but be amazed at how fast it warms, next to the skin. It is easy to become accustomed to. Oh, very easy, even for a dedicated Republican.

How ironic, what a joke of the gods, if he should end up going the way of Antony after all. The best way to conquer an enemy is not to crush him but to corrupt him.

"But too late for us," I said to myself, stroking the diadem. Even if Octavian turned into a replica of Antony, and came at last to understand what had happened here in the east and how it had happened, it did us no good.

"Madam?" asked Charmian.

"Nothing. I was only bidding these farewell." I touched them again. "I was trying to imagine what it would be like to receive them." I hoped they would have the intended—though unlikely—effect. They gleamed conspiratorially, like winking eyes.

Reluctantly I folded the silk over them, covering their beauty. I drew the lid down, then locked it with the gold-and-emerald lock, with a Hercules knot design, that my goldsmith had made to fit the latch. "A knot he must untie," I said. I thought his self-importance would cause him to compare it to the Gordian one that Alexander had severed to obtain his eastern realms. But perhaps I gave him too much credit. Imagination was not his leading trait.

There was a formal letter to go along with it, resigning my throne and its insignia into his hands, if he would please to bestow them on my son as King of Egypt—"a title you have already granted him," I reminded him. I said that I came from a long and honorable line of kings, related to Alexander himself, and that we knew Egypt and had ruled it well, and he could find no abler governors to continue in this line. I pledged my son's loyalty, and pointed out that he had taken no part in the fighting at Actium.

"Although you have declared war on me and pronounced me your enemy, my son has remained aloof from our quarrels, and will serve you faithfully," I assured him. "From his earliest days I have trained him for ruling, and you can find no better or more dedicated"—my hand had almost rebelled against writing—"servant to your wishes." But it had to be. I had to say it. "Remember his youth, and your own in the day when Caesar fell. Just as Caesar knew your promise, so you should be able to discern it in this worthy young man. Do not punish him for my own deeds, for they are a thing apart." There was more in this vein. I never apologized for my own actions, but emphasized that they were mine and mine alone. I hated people who pretended they had not done what everyone knew they had, or that it was somehow not their fault, or that they had been forced to it. I knew Octavian would, too. Hence no apology. I thought the letter struck a good middle ground between pride and submission.

"Thank you, Charmian and Iras," I told them. "Would you be so kind as to send for Caesarion?"

I wanted him to see the treasure, and read the letter before it was sent. He must know everything.

He was not interested in opening the box, but read the letter carefully. He rolled it up again and put it in the ivory tube that would serve as its envelope. "Are you sure you wish to do this?" he asked. "This is so—unlike you."

"What do you mean?"

"Just to surrender them, and sound so final about it."

"Ah. It is the only way to avoid its being truly final," I said. "If I wait until he demands them, then—if he takes them himself, he will never release his grasp on them."

He frowned, wrinkling his brow in a way that was most endearing. "Do you honestly think these will ever be bestowed on me by *his* hands?"

"It may be possible," I said. "It depends entirely on how he achieves his goal of conquering Egypt. If it is too difficult, it may put him in a bad mood!" I laughed. "Or, on the other hand, it may give him pause and impress on him the wisdom of keeping a native dynasty on the throne. There are too many unknowns now. But one thing I do know: You must prepare to leave Egypt." When he opened his mouth to protest, I said, "You promised! When I promised not to—" I would remind him sternly of our bargain.

"Yes, yes," he said. "But later. Not yet—"

I shook my head. "It must be soon. You will have to travel down the Nile as far as Coptos, a ten-day journey. Then make the desert crossing to Berenice, on the Red Sea—"

"What, in the heat of summer? You are joking!"

"No, it is necessary. You must be in Berenice by early July in order to take a ship to India during the monsoon, the only time ships can sail east. There you will wait, in safety, until all this is—over. If Octavian confirms you, then you can return. If not, then I will have the consolation of knowing that you have slipped from his grasp. No matter what he does to the rest of us, he cannot touch you!"

"Do you honestly think I can ever draw a happy breath, knowing my whole family has perished, and I survive, a miserable exile?" He looked insulted.

"You will not be a 'miserable exile,' but the son of the great Julius Caesar and Cleopatra, Queen of Egypt. Wherever you go, you will be honored. I am making arrangements even now with the ruler of Bharukaccha in India to receive you. Not such a bad life. Remember, Octavian is sixteen years older than you, and his health has always been poor. A bone sliver caught in the throat, a slight cold that settles on his lungs, a small riding accident, can change things in the twinkling of an eye. And he has no son, nor is likely to have one—his marriage to Livia is as barren as an Aegean rock. Live, and wait." I patted his cheek. "They say India is a pleasant land of colors and scents. I have always wished to see it myself."

He crossed his arms sulkily. "I don't imagine I will be paying much attention to the colors and scents," he said stubbornly.

"They are supposed to be overwhelming," I said. "And if a seventeen-year-old does not respond to the calling of his eyes and nose, then he is a poor creature! I will tell you what I have learned: The young are meant to bear sorrow lightly, and all their senses conspire to help them." I took his hand. "You must never forget us—not me, not Antony, not Alexander or Selene or Philadelphos—but if you can sing, savor fine food, and feel your heart stop at the sight of an exquisite work of art, we will live on in you. That is all I ask."

"I do not understand."

"You will." Now I touched his fine, silky hair. "That I promise you."

Abruptly I turned away, acting very busy, picking up the letter. "So? You will be ready. Next month it must be." It was already April. "Before that, we will have a final, important ceremony. But more of that later." I could not continue the conversation; he had to leave before I betrayed how hard it was for me. "Perhaps you should compose a letter of your own to Octavian." Let him leave, now. "Go."

He bent over and kissed my cheek. "Very well, Mother."

After I heard his footsteps fading away, I bent over the box and wept; tears fell into the intricate workmanship. But gold was impervious to salt, and it would never show.

Sending him away was going to be the hardest part of it all, knowing I would never see him again—and that I would break my promise to him, making him keep his side of our bargain while I did not. But it was a duty of queenship, and someday he would understand. I had spoken the truth just now.

The wide harbor now wore its tenderest colors—its frothy blues and its shadowy greens, its milky-white foam. No wonder we think that Venus was born of seafoam, for it is so ethereal it is hard to believe we can actually wade into it and dip our hands in it. With the children I often came down the wide palace steps leading into the water, at our private place where the sandy bottom was shallow, and they could collect starfish and anemones. The dolphins were back with the spring, sporting themselves, showing their sleek backs.

As a child I had spent hours here, but like many things of childhood—tiny coral bracelets, illustrated stories, baby-sized pillows—I had set it aside in my mind and forgotten it. Also like many of those things, it did not deserve to be forgotten. I found my hours here with my own children to be deeply restorative, a refuge where time suspended itself and was measured only by the height of the sun. We wore floppy-brimmed hats to protect us from sunburn, and built miniature forts out of sand and shells. Their most ambitious creation was a model of the Lighthouse; Alexander wanted it to be as tall as he, but it crumbled every time it got shoulder-high.

"The amount of water in the sand must be perfect," Caesarion would say, sometimes coming to watch the progress but never participating; he considered himself much too dignified. "If it is too much, the sand can't bear weight. But if it is too little, the sun will dry the bottom out before the top is finished, and it will collapse."

The impatient Alexander would smack it and knock it flat in frustration. "If you know so much, why don't you make one yourself?" he would insist.

"He doesn't want to get his fine tunic mussed," Selene said. "He is much too grown-up for playing in the sand." She cocked her head and looked at him, squinting. "Isn't that right?"

The twins were almost ten now, just on the brink of leaving childhood themselves. Perhaps that was why they enjoyed it so.

"He hasn't time." I defended him. "He is learning many tasks." And my heart was heavy with it. In addition to his usual lessons with his tutor, Rhodon, he was having to master all the things I would have him take away inside his head—things to learn that normally would have been spread out over several years.

"Yes, that's right," Caesarion agreed. "In fact, I must get back to Rhodon now. He let me wander away in the midst of Xerxes' account." He turned and walked back up the steps—poor child. Poor man.

Philadelphos was playing with the beached trireme, putting sand crabs on its deck and trying to make them sit at oars. He still tried to get Alexander and Selene to board it; sometimes they humored him and did it. They would sit at the oar-bench and try pulling in unison; the boat usually sank with the unbalanced weight, gurgling to the shallow bottom.

I clung to those precious, private hours, knowing they were numbered.

Some mornings I would come to this spot very early, long before sunrise. My sleep was disturbed now, and I seldom slept the night through. I found that sitting quietly on the steps, watching the light gradually fill the sky and turn the harbor from a dark void into a pearly plate, was balm for my soul. Sometimes I would relive parts of my life, as I wished to recount them in my story that day.

The marble steps, slippery with night mist, would grow warm under me as the dawn came up. Sitting there, seeing the Lighthouse glowing red at the top, as it always had, with an empty horizon beyond it, it was hard to imagine that there was any threat to us. Everything was calm, ordered, functioning smoothly. Thus it had always been, thus it would continue—so it seemed. But preparations had to be made on faith, faith in the end of things as we knew them.

As the first rays of sunlight broke through the soft blanket of clouds in the east, I would go to the Temple of Isis and perform the ancient ritual with her sacred water, opening my day. Then I would linger there with her until I sensed that it was time to begin the demanding round of decisions and duties that would occupy me until Iras drew my curtains at night, when I would supposedly sleep.

I was thus savoring my private hour when I saw a figure walking in the darkness along the sand. Because the eastern harbor is a great arc sweeping from the Lighthouse to the farthest tip of the royal promontory, it is possible at low tide to walk the shoreline all the way from one end to the other. But few ever do, oddly enough.

I looked closer. Then rose, startled. It was Antony. Alive, away from his hermitage! For so long I had steeled myself for the messenger, expecting him at high noon, when the sun beat down pitilessly, or sunset, when things come to their natural close. I had even rehearsed what I would say. And the tomb was ready.

But this—this I had not expected, not rehearsed. "Antony?"

He bounded up the stairs and embraced me. His arms were tight and hard around me.

"My dearest, dearest wife—" The words were rushed, whispered against my ear. He was kissing the side of my face, my neck, as if he dared not kiss my lips.

He was here, alive, whole, warm. But it was frightening; in my determination to be strong, I had already buried him and mourned him. His touch on me seemed unnatural—yet it was only in my imagination that he had ever ceased to live.

"Antony?" I drew away and clutched myself, to escape his embrace. "You are—" I touched the side of my face, where his kiss lingered on the skin. "You are—I thought you had—"

Now he dropped his arms and backed away. "Of course. Forgive me. But I did not ever think to find you here, sitting, waiting—it made me bold. I meant to write, send a proper messenger, but—"

"This is better," I said. How lucky we were, to have it come about like this. But my head was reeling. "But you must give me time, explain . . . you said you would never come back. And I had feared, and in my fear—"

"Yes. I know. I understand." He sat down on the stairs, letting his arms dangle over his knees in that way I remembered so well. Cautiously I sat down beside him.

Silence blanketed us. The only sound was the lapping of the tamed waves within the harbor.

My heart was hammering. I was deliriously happy that he lived, and was sitting here beside me, but now all was in turmoil. Wherever Antony was, turmoil reigned, not the least of it in my heart. Shakily I extended my hand and took his.

"Are you recovered?" I said in a low voice.

"Yes. It just took time. Time, silence, solitude."

Well I knew what he meant. But silence and solitude were normally things he shunned. He must have been greatly changed by Actium.

"Thanks be to the gods." I leaned over and kissed his cheek—again, hesitantly. He could feel it, I knew. But I could not help my wariness.

He tightened his hand on mine. "May I return?"

"Your quarters have long been waiting." I did not see fit to mention the sarcophagus, also waiting. "The children will welcome you warmly."

"And you? Do you welcome me?"

"What an odd choice of words—much too pale. I have been—bereft without you." I paused. "I was missing the spirit of my life," I finally said. It was impossible to put into words. Without him, vitality had fled. I leaned over and kissed him, allowing myself to feel it at last.

"There is no point in dying before one's time," he said. "And that is what I have done. Now I lament the lost months!"

"You could not help it." When we are felled, we are felled. But if we rise to our feet in a little while, we can count ourselves lucky.

"May we go inside?" he asked politely. "I would like to return before the palace starts bustling."

I stood up, drawing him with me. "Of course."

Together we climbed the steps to the still-sleeping palace. The corridors were empty, the wall torches still sputtered in their sockets, doors stood shut.

Antony stole into his quarters and then looked at them in surprise. "Like an old friend, they look different to me now," he said. He had not been here since Actium.

I drew back the curtains to his inner room, revealing the couches, the table, the bed where I had passed long, yearning hours thinking of him—hours that I would never tell him about. "I think you will find it all in order," I said crisply, as if I had not seen it, either.

He walked around wonderstruck, touching this surface and that. Finally he turned to me and said, "O my heart!" and held out his arms.

I flung myself into them, treasuring their embrace. All my mourning, all my acceptance, must now be flung to the winds, unneeded. He had come back, and come back as he had once been.

"My lost friend," I whispered.

"Why 'friend'? Are we not still husband and wife?" He shook his head. "Or have you divorced me?" From the plaintive tone, I realized he feared it had happened. He kissed me fervently as if to convince me to stay with him.

I tried to assure him. "I'm not a Roman," I said. "I don't divorce with every whim or change in fortune. It's just that . . . I feared I was a widow, not a wife."

He gave a shuddering sigh of relief. "You are still—we are still—"

"But you must give me time—" My words were muffled by an onslaught of frenzied kissing. He was like a starving man, and I could hardly fend him off. The celibate life in his hermitage had not agreed with his nature, that was evident.

"Antony, please stop!" I was insistent. What I meant—but could not say— was that I was almost afraid for him to touch me, as if I did not want to open all those feelings again. For I had conquered them, and if this was just a brief interlude, then . . . I could not bear to go through it all again.

He let go of me. "Forgive me," he said. "I seem to have forgotten my manners; living alone has that effect." He was trying to make light of it, but I could tell that he was hurt.

He could not expect me to adjust instantly to every whirl in his behavior— first the withdrawal, then the two unannounced returns, next . . . another disappearance? It was too painful; I must protect myself in some way, at least at this moment.

"It's not a matter of forgiving you," I finally said. I must choose my words carefully. He would be vulnerable to misinterpreting them. "There is nothing to forgive. I was so grieved when you were gone from me; I was so afraid that you would never return. All I prayed for was that one day you would be standing here again, in your rooms, with me. But . . . in some ways you seem more like a stranger to me now than you did at Tarsus! What I have gone through in these last few months, what you have gone through . . . it separates us. We will have to hear one another's stories, learn what has happened to each other. . . ."

"Don't you want me back?" he cried.

Was he going to rush off again? Zeus forbid! "Yes! Yes!" I assured him. I could sense that he was confused about where he belonged. But surely he had not expected to walk back into the world he had fled from? It had changed mightily in those months; while he had brooded, Egypt and I had been busy dealing with Octavian and the aftermath of Actium.

But now was a quiet time, a good time for his return. And for our reunion.

"Yes, yes," I repeated. "I want you back more than anything in the world." And it was true.

My mother had been taken from me, and never returned. Caesar, too. It is not often that the dead come back to us, and I rejoiced. I must never let him know that I had counted him so completely among the lost.

80

As in a dream, when we revisit places we thought never to see again, Antony and I sat high on silvered chairs of state, the waves of people spread out as far as we could see on all sides, until they merged into the very sea itself. Overhead the sky was a deep, ringing blue, and the stately buildings of Alexandria as white as the clouds floating benevolently over them.

I am five, watching the state procession of my father, the Dionysus-cart creaking along past the Library . . . I am eighteen, celebrating my own accession, riding through the white streets, crowds lining it, wild, curious eyes staring . . . I am twenty-five, following the bier bearing Ptolemy with the high, wailing cries of mourners . . . I am thirty-five, watching Antony parade through the streets with his mock Triumph, Armenian prisoners walking behind, and again, another celebration, Alexandria festooned and scrubbed, when Antony decorated me and our heirs with all the realms of the east.

Alexandria, handmaiden of all this, now stands by once more to watch and applaud as we enact the last ritual, the coming-of-age of both Caesarion and Antyllus. Caesarion is to be enrolled in the Greek Ephebic College for military and civic training, and proclaimed a man, while Antyllus is to assume the *toga virilis*, the mark of a Roman adult.

No expense was spared. After all, what was the one thing we still had in abundance? Hope might have fled, soldiers might have deserted, ships might have burnt, but money, courage, and defiance—those we still had. Antony and I had agonized over whether it was wise to elevate the boys to adulthood. Which would assure their survival best? Antony felt that Octavian was more likely to spare minors, but I pointed out that it was too late for that. We had taken up arms in the name of Caesarion's rights, and Octavian would never overlook that. As for Antyllus, the notorious will had named him Antony's personal heir, and now he would suffer all the punishments for it. At least as adults they would command the respect and attention they were due, rather than "disappearing" as children often did.

"They will have to be formally charged and dealt with," I said. "There must be a record of the doings. But Caesarion will be safe and out of Egypt, and Antyllus will have committed no crime beyond being your heir. And since Octavian actually knows Antyllus, he will most likely spare him. Proclaiming them adults offers them the best chance, and also offers partisans the opportunity to champion them." It all sounded very sensible, but it could so easily go the other way. Were we dooming them instead of saving them?

"Perhaps it will be Alexander who is made King," Antony said. "That would get around all the difficulties of the older boys."

I laughed. His optimism was touching. "Do you honestly think Octavian would place your son on the throne of Egypt? Reward you, in effect? You must be dreaming. He is not known for his bigheartedness." I shook my head. "If my children were pure Ptolemies, it might be different. As it is, it is their Roman blood that causes the trouble."

Antony nodded. "And to think they are all cousins—and cousins to Octavian."

"That is what makes them dangerous to one another," I said.

So we had arranged the ceremonies, the day when Caesarion would ride in his chariot through the streets of the city, wearing his royal robes, clutching the scroll and medals admitting him to the Ephebic College, and then present himself to me for a public declaration. Antyllus, though only fourteen, qualified for elevation into adulthood as well.

I was proud to show myself to the city and put an end to wild rumors about my health, my appearance, my state of mind. And I was grateful for Antony to have the chance to do likewise.

He seemed to have recovered from the nadir of Actium and the humiliation by Gallus and the trumpets. It told me that perhaps the cruelest thing about a very high, visible position was that one could never withdraw to let nature perform her healing, but must remain chained and hoisted up to public view. If only Caesar, after Spain, had had the luxury of those months of Antony's! He, too, might have regained his balance and peace of mind. But enough of that, I told myself sternly.

Now Antony and I sat side by side, wearing our best ceremonial attire, watching our eldest children—by other mates—come into their own. The children we had made together were seated behind us. I wondered what future awaited them. Perhaps Antony was right, and they would win out in the end. They would have the magic of our names but not the stink of our opprobrium, and their very youth and innocence could preserve them. I had thought of sending Alexander and Selene to Media, where Alexander's betrothed waited. But I did not know. I just did not know. . . .

A blare of trumpets told us that the procession was drawing near. We sat up straighter and prepared to welcome our sons to the platform. Around the side of the Gymnasion the glittering chariots wheeled, and a burst of cheers exploded on the air.

How tall they stood! How proud, how impervious to any blows! Flowers flew through the air, pelting them with approval and admiration.

Remember it always, my son, I prayed silently. *Hear those cries, see the faces, taste the joy of total acceptance, most intoxicating of wine. It does not stay.*

The chariots approached, and at the foot of the platform they drew up abreast, then stopped. The boys—men now—stepped out and mounted the platform where we awaited them, as proud parents as any farmer or fisherman whose son first takes the plow or the net.

Caesarion stood beside me, taller than I, infinitely lovely and promising, at the very brink and threshold of his own life apart from mine. What he would be, he himself must now unfold.

I took his hand and held it high, aloft. I felt the weight of my crown and headdress, bearing down upon me. Before me the multitude spread out.

"My people," I said, and my voice, trained as well as Antony's, rang out. "Today you have a man, a King in Egypt, to lead you. Hearken to him!"

Then I turned to look at Caesarion, my firstborn, my pride, seeing on his face all the high solemnity and mystery of this day. My own life fell away like the lighthouse the children had made, and it seemed but so much sand. Here was my achievement, here was my legacy. And Caesar's.

Afterward we retired to the palace for a banquet. Always there must be a banquet, although I do not know why. I suppose our mortal natures need to feast and raise cups in jubilation.

Now we were seated at a long table—no Roman reclining today—and Caesarion took the place of honor, while Antony and I flanked him, Antyllus beside Antony.

Caesarion was still wearing his celebratory crown, his fine features flattered by it. What a king he would make. I was not being sentimental, but my eyes were keen discerners of what really was. Somehow, in the dim hours between dusk and dawn in the palace as it then was, Caesar and I had created a rare creature, and all by accident, all unknowing. Such is fate.

My voice would tremble; I could not trust it. And so I silently raised my cup and drank to him, to my jewel, my achievement.

"My boys, you acquitted yourselves well today," said Antony loudly. "Mark you, I do not expect to lose games to you anytime soon, regardless of your new status."

I was drinking from an agate cup, one that had been in our family for generations. I let my lips linger over its rim, which seemed to impart a very smoothness to the wine. Still I could not trust myself to speak, but I hoped that would soon pass. I did not like being mute.

The feast continued. I could report every dish, every comment. But time is becoming a very short commodity with me now. I still have gold, but time . . . no time. Octavian has snatched that from me. And so I must leave the dinner, which was set such a short time ago. A short time . . . a lifetime.

The sea was calm, that peculiar Alexandrian blue-green, the one hue not captured in any gem; turquoise is too opaque, aquamarine too pallid, lapis too thick and stubbornly dark. But the reply did not come by sea. As befitted its message, the letter from Octavian slithered in unobtrusively by land. I received it, delivered by a regular messenger: a high insult.

> *To the Queen Cleopatra, intransigent enemy of Rome:*
>
> *Salutations. I have received your tokens of submission, and am grat-ified thereby. As to your requests, I cannot answer at present. Too much stands between us. How can I consider the deposition of the crown when you have shown me no goodwill? I need assurance that you are a thinking being—which you always were before your alliance with the unfortunate Marcus Antonius—and are stable and dependable. Therefore I require some reasonable proof. What should serve? The head of said Antonius, or else to drive him from your domains into our hands. He is a spent force, and an impediment between heads of state such as ourselves.*
>
> *Do it, and you shall find us most reasonable. But first, do it. Oth-erwise we shall determine that you are not trustworthy.*
>
> *Imperator G. Caesar*

I kept rereading it. His boldness was head-spinning. So I was to sacrifice Antony . . . and for what? He had not specified. "You shall find us most rea-sonable." It meant nothing. And he was astute enough never to commit anything to paper that could come back to haunt him or nip at his heels.

I noted that he had not returned the crown and scepter. He was probably stroking them this very minute, cooing to them! And the "we"! He was royal already, I noted.

Antony's head. Did he think I would station a servant behind the curtains, drawing his breath slowly, ready to strike after we had finished making love, ending Antony's life as he drowsed off? Did he think I would kiss him, caress his hair, welcome him, planning his murder immediately thereafter?

Oh, Octavian, I thought, you have believed all the evil you have put *abroad about me! The evil Queen, slave to her ambition: Cleopatra! Cleopatra, most vile!*

When Antony came into my room that night, I could not help thinking: that head. To strike off that head . . . what an ugly, squalid offer Octavian had made, treating that noble head like meat in a market stall. Had all the glory melted down to such vulgarity?

The end was here, and nothing remained to us but to meet it with honor. How does one throw open the doors to the enemy, with honor? I did not know. It was not written. I must discover it.

That dear head, more precious than all kingdoms; that head which had given me freedom and bliss—I would fight to my last breath to preserve it. Octavian was dead wrong in his supposition. Perhaps he was equally wrong in his other suppositions. I could only pray so.

The days crept by, each one perfect and bracing. Every morning was a shining bead of dew, clear and pure and untroubled; the white noons were filled with purpose and motion; the evenings, with dark, wine-colored clouds playing in the fading sky, as the stars behind them came out, as always. As always . . . it went on as always, and only by the sheerest act of imagination could we force ourselves to believe a threat hovered somewhere just over the horizon, beyond our sight.

The end was supposed to be accompanied by the flash and smoke of battle, or the rattling cough of old age, or even the spots of plague. It was not supposed to come into a perfect world, a world so beguiling, so sweet, so quiet. Perhaps this was the final enemy to be confronted: this false sense of safety.

I could delay no longer. It was already late May. Caesarion would have to leave. We had heard that Octavian had now transferred his legions from Asia into Syria. He had gone to Antioch, sitting himself down in our palace, that drafty relic which had served our hours of joy so well. Then he had passed on, going south. He was less than five hundred miles from our eastern border fortress, while Gallus was sitting less than two hundred miles to our west, having already captured our stronghold there. They would close in on us; although the southern desert would remain open, Caesarion had to reach Coptos by mid-June. He must go.

But, O! the world of woe in those three words! I had to cast him adrift at the mercy of fate for the rest of his life. I knew that when he sailed away, I would never see him again.

I would go with him until he reached the main channel of the Nile, and then I must turn back. And so we set out, in a small boat from the steps of the lake harbor, and retraced the journey I had made so many years ago with Mardian, Olympos, and Nebamun, when we ran away from the palace. Now my son was also running away from the palace.

The tall lake reeds had grown thicker than ever, and the boatmen had to work hard to push them aside. They showered us with golden pollen and stirred up pairs of white dancing butterflies to circle our heads. Then we were entering the canal that would bring us to the Canopic branch of the Nile, and from thence into the Nile proper. I almost hated the smoothness of our progress. I had seen to it that the canal was dredged and the weeds cut back, so it was faster going these days.

Once we reached the Canopic branch, we hoisted our sail to catch the north breeze, and made steady progress, past the green fields, the towering palms, the donkeys and their waterwheels.

"The Nile will just be starting to rise down near the first cataract," I told him. "But you should reach Coptos before the full extent of it."

"I know." We were standing by the railing, watching the land slide past, and he covered one of my hands with his. "I have studied all of it extensively." He gave one of his winning smiles.

Another journey, up the Nile, with Caesar, when this boy was still in my womb—yes, he was retracing that unremembered journey now. "But you have only made the journey once or twice," I said. I remembered our excursion to Dendera, to show him his portrait as a Pharaoh on the temple walls. "It always looks different when one really sees it, after studying it in books." I saw how clean and firm his jaw was, tilted up in confidence. He wore Caesar's mother's pendant around his neck, the one Caesar had given me when—

Perhaps the worst thing about the end of something is the compulsion to remember and recount all that has come before. The memories were strangling me like the tangle of waterlilies fouling boats' oars. No more, no more . . . I ordered my mind to stop, to shut the vivid memories down.

Let me just stand here, on the deck with my son, and be only here, only with him, and only now, I begged.

And it was granted to me, so that all the rest of it fell away like tattered wrappings, and those days were ours alone.

When we reached the Nile proper, a stoutly fitted barge awaited us at the landing just downstream from Memphis. It was not identified as a royal vessel, for I did not want to make Caesarion a target of attention. This one was owned by a grain merchant who was utterly trustworthy. The soldiers and guides who were to accompany him across the desert track to Berenice, and serve as his bodyguard all the way to India, were on board. His tutor, Rhodon, would also make the journey, and had packed two trunks of books.

Now it could be delayed no longer. We must part.

"Can you not come with us as far as the pyramids?" he asked, his eyes searching. "We could stop and have an excursion—"

And see nothing, I thought, because our eyes would be too full of tears.

"No. It is better thus. We will come again, together, in happier days," I said, letting myself look at his face as if this one last time would somehow give me something different.

He bent and embraced me, his words in my ear. "Oh, Mother," was all he said.

"May all the gods go with you," I whispered. "And may your father protect you." Yes, let the god preserve his son! I held him as close as I could for as long as I could. Then I forced myself to let go, to drop my arms away and step back.

This little space between us, only two feet or so, must grow to enormous lengths, must stretch to almost the width of the world. It was too much to bear to understand it truly.

"Farewell, my son."

I let him be the one to turn and mount the gangplank to the waiting barge. Against his back I hurled prayer after prayer, beseeching Caesar to come to the aid of his only earthly son and heir.

Do not fail us! I cried from the depths of my soul. Do not fail us now!

The sober return trip was made without sails, as we rode downstream on the Nile current. Caesarion's barge grew smaller and finally vanished. Just before we steered toward the Canopic branch, we took a connecting canal to halt at the landing for the temple at Heliopolis. I would not go ashore, but I wanted to send greetings to Nakht. He surprised me by hurrying down to the landing stage with two white-robed priests in tow, and then, with my permission, coming aboard.

"Most divine Majesty," he said, bending low. "I am so thankful you are here. It is in answer to my devout prayers, for there is important news that I could not trust to a messenger." He indicated the other two priests. "These, my brothers in service to the gods, are from the temples at Philae and at Abydos."

I was startled; I had not even prayed about this, and yet here they were, the answers. "My heart rejoices to see you," I said. Both the highest pilgrimage temples of Isis and Osiris had come to me in the persons of these priests.

"We bring you important news," the taller one—from Philae—said. "The people of Upper Egypt stand ready to rise and fight for you."

I was deeply touched. This meant that they considered me—a Ptolemy—to be a true Egyptian as well. And offering to do battle was the ultimate proof and sacrifice. But I did not even have to think about it.

"Tell the people I accept their loyalty and pledges, and that I am moved to the depths of my heart to know that they love me as a queen and as one of their own countrymen. But I will not inflict needless suffering on my people." It was pointless for them to rise against the twenty or more Roman legions. And if even Antony could not bring himself to draw up his forces for battle, trying to hold the line of the Nile, then why should they?

"But—" The priest of Abydos looked dashed.

I held up my hands. "Do not think we belittle the offer. But it would be in vain, and I will spare them any hopeless efforts, which would only lead to harsh punishment."

They had to accept it. "Very well."

"But there are two great services you, and only you, can do for me." I ushered them belowdecks to my private quarters, and there I made the arrangements: with the priest at Philae for the testament I would send him by Olympos; with Nakht of Heliopolis for instructions for him to obey when the time came. Thus I secured both the continuance of my life and the ending of it, through the mercy of Isis.

81

"Put a few more in this corner." Antony was directing a servant to upend a basket of rose petals where he stood pointing.

The servant shook the container, and a flood of red and white petals gushed onto the floor. The inimitable smell of roses filled the air.

"Isn't it something?" Antony asked, his voice betraying nothing but light curiosity. "Why is it that luxury goods always get through a blockade? Cyrenaica may be occupied by hostile forces, Paraetonium in the hands of Gallus, but somehow cargoes of fresh roses continue to reach us."

"I suppose it's because they are so unimportant in the eyes of Octavian." Beauty got through the filter when all else failed, because it was so insubstantial. Yet it can feed us better than food sometimes.

"We must be the most well-fed, pampered siege victims in the history of the world. What they've done is to seal us in with all our riches." He picked up a heavy gold goblet and poured it full. Carefully he looked in it, widening his eyes at the sight within. "Laodicean." He sipped carefully. "And just think, warehouses full of it, just waiting for us. Ah, what a way to go!"

I imitated him; why not? I might as well drink it as let it turn to vinegar after Octavian took over. The liquid was heady and full of the memories of autumn sun. It caressed my mouth and slicked my lips with sweetness.

"Do you think twenty amphorae are enough for tonight?" he asked, gesturing to the vessels already lined up and waiting.

"That's almost enough for a legion," I said. "Surely you don't expect—"

"Only joking. It's just for show. Tonight we must be as lavish and overabundant as the Nile Valley after flood time, our bounty bursting from every seam like overripe melons."

"As overripe as your similes?" I said, smoothing the hair at the back of his head.

That head... the one Octavian wanted. Now we had each had offers to kill the other; Herod had advised Antony to do away with me, and Octavian had suggested I do the same with Antony. Yet here we were, planning a banquet together in defiance of them both.

"I thought you liked my extravagances," he said. "In every part of my life. I, who do not withhold rewards, or impulses, or food and drink, am not likely to stint with mere words!" He turned and kissed me. "Nor kisses."

The wine made a sticky seal of our lips.

"Indeed, no," I agreed. But this banquet... I could not believe he had wanted to do it.

"Good." He picked up the goblet again. "Now, as to our guests—amazing how many of the old Incomparables are still about. And of course we've got new candidates for the order." He took a deep swallow of the wine.

"The... order? Antony, what are you thinking of?"

"My secret. My surprise! Just wait and see."

"Don't be mysterious. It's tiresome." What I meant was that his surprise might be so inappropriate I should know about it in advance, in order that I might be able to stop it.

"Ah, ah!" he wagged his finger at me. "No, you'll just have to wait, like all the rest!"

"Antony—"

He stepped back. "No! No persuasion! I am a rock, not to be moved!"

"Well, that's something new," I said. Why were his surprises always something one had to brace oneself for? "I thought that was Octavian. They say sometimes longtime enemies take on each other's traits."

He shrugged. "Then we'd best deplete all the wine in Alexandria in case he wants to drown himself in it, in imitation of me!" He poured more out. "And the best time to start is now."

I returned to my quarters and let him finish preparing for his... what? I had encouraged his high spirits, I was so fearful of a return of his despair, but I realized this was just its mirror image. At any moment it might turn itself inside out, and the sunny mood show its other side—black opaqueness.

Since Caesarion had left, I had felt some relief. He should be almost to Coptos by now. I had completed most of my other preparations. The treasure-pyramid stood ready for torching in the mausoleum, the sarcophagi were lined and finished, letters had gone out to Media about sheltering Alexander and Selene—but no reply had been received yet. Writing the account of my life absorbed me, gave me solace in the brilliant sunlit days as we waited. I had almost reached the present time in it, and was determined to press on until the very last instant. Then I would trust Mardian and Olympos to write the final chapter. This they could do at their leisure, at as long a perspective as they wished. There was certainly no hurry. I did not expect Isis to reveal it to any eyes until a long time hence. In fact, the further removed it was from this era, the fairer a hearing I was likely to get. But of course that decision lay in her wisdom. It was my task only to write it.

Charmian and Iras had been both sad and solicitous, and I regretted that they were bound up with me. They did not have the choice of leaving, as did lesser people like Plancus and Dellius. What a bitter jest, that bad people are given more freedoms than good ones.

We still had four legions here in Egypt, as well as the Egyptian troops and my Macedonian Household Guard. The fortress at Pelusium was garrisoned with Egyptians to block Octavian's way. We also had a fleet of some hundred ships—survivors of Actium as well as newly built ones. Attached to the Roman legions was a small but well-trained cavalry force. Also, word had come that the Cyzicus gladiators were still on their way to us, having successfully fought past both Amyntas and the Cilicians. We certainly had enough manpower at our command to put up a fierce defense. But Antony refused to consider deploying the legions or mapping out any strategy at all. He seemed to regard any resistance as futile.

"We are hopelessly outnumbered," he said. "Why slaughter people needlessly?" I could not object; had I not said exactly the same thing about my supporters in Upper Egypt? But Egyptians far up the Nile could escape any participation, whereas the legions and fleet were already drawn up. It was useless, however, without a leader who wished to lead. And Antony would never lead again.

Admitting it had caused me deep pain. But the price of having him back at all was to watch him step aside from that command he had held for so long, stop exercising its power.

The city now knew all too well what had happened at Actium, and I could feel it holding its breath, waiting to see what would come next. Alexandria had never bent the knee to anyone but Caesar, and that was a fight the Alexandrians themselves had provoked. But this . . .

Would there be a siege? Would there be fighting in the streets? If people tried to flee, where would they go? They prepared themselves as a city of traders and sophisticates would: they took inventory, kept buying and selling, and tried to figure out ways of escape or bribe or barter. Oh, I knew them, and I knew what they were about. Not for them the heroics of the city of Xanthus, which burnt itself to the ground rather than be taken, nor the weeping and wailing of the Trojans. They gave elegant dinner parties and argued the fine points of philosophical schools of thought in regard to suffering. They downed expensive wine at a ferocious rate, doused themselves in long-hoarded perfume, and draped themselves in jewelry, as if to use it all up this side of the tomb. They would expire wrapped in all the good things of life.

At dusk I began readying myself for Antony's banquet. Was I not the most Alexandrian of Alexandrians? Should I not therefore enjoy my own royal version of what was taking place in mansions all over the city? Yes, let me put on my best. Let Charmian bring out the red Grecian gown with the pearl border and gold fringe. And let there be the brooch given me by the King of Pontus, mounded with gems from beyond the Black Sea, to pin the shoulder folds. Around my neck must lie the glittering wedding necklace. And yes—where was the gold bracelet the Kandake had presented me? I wanted it weighing heavy on my arm.

And as for perfume—I had more than any merchant. Aromatic oils lay waiting in their stoppered alabaster bottles: lily, rose, narcissus, hyacinth. Tonight I would not choose rose; I wanted to smell different from the rest of the room. Narcissus, that would do. Its rainy dark scent was perfect for this gathering of the doomed.

Iras spread delicate oil on my cheeks, making tiny circles. She dabbed reddened ointment on my lips, rubbing it in carefully.

"Your skin was always your beauty," she said. "And it looks no different now from when you were twenty."

"Well, I am almost twice that," I said. But most likely I was never to reach forty.

She took a comb and began to dress my hair. Usually Iras did it, but tonight I preferred Charmian. The feel of her hands, drawing my hair into a thick rope, pulling it out to its full length, was very soothing.

"Shall I braid it?" she asked. "Small braids to frame the rest?"

"As you like," I said. In the heat of the evening, I wanted it up off my neck.

My hair, always my vanity. I had tended it carefully all the years, and it had certainly rewarded me, giving me the illusion of beauty. I had indeed been blessed in the hair the gods saw fit to give me.

"There's so much of it," Charmian complained. "I do not think I can gather it all up in this fillet."

"Then let some of it escape over the sides." Just as long as it did not lie damp on my neck.

"There." She handed me a polished mirror and let me stare at myself.

The face looking back did not show all it had been through. It was as if I had willed my body not to absorb the blows of my experiences, and it had obeyed. There was nothing written on the clear eyes, the arched brows, the smooth and unlined skin—nothing of childbirth, field conditions, trial, or pain. I looked like a virgin of the world. I laughed out loud, seeing it.

"My lady?" Charmian frowned. "Don't you like it? I can redo—"

"The hair is fine," I assured her. "I was just marveling at how heavy blows don't always imprint themselves on our flesh."

"I think it must be either the flesh or the soul," said Charmian quietly.

"Then I am sure it is my soul and spirit that have taken the brunt of it," I said. I wondered what they would look like, in a mirror. Better not to see.

I rose. Time to be going, time to be mirthful.

The chamber was filled with people—where had Antony rounded them all up? They were jolly, wearing bright colors and flashing jewelry. They were mainly Romans, doubtless from the legions, but there were also Alexandrians from the Gymnasion, the Library, the Museion, and Zeus only knew where else. They had the flushed and expensive look of aristocrats, except for the token philosophers there. And even they were well-to-do, mostly adherents of the school of Epicurus.

The delicate scent of the roses, their perfume released by feet treading upon them, filled the room. I breathed deeply, trying to pretend, for one brief moment, that I was in a garden rather than here. But the buzz of voices, the heat from so many bodies, and the tinkling music from harpists made that impossible.

"A crown, most gracious Queen," one of the servants said, coming toward me holding an elaborate chaplet of willow leaves, berries of nightshade, and poppies. I allowed myself to be crowned, although the plants were associated with the underworld.

Antony saw me and immediately rushed over. "Welcome, my heart!" he said, offering me a brimming goblet of what proved to be rose-flavored wine. "Drink, drink of Lethe, and remember nothing!"

If only that were possible! But this wine could not do it.

"Who would have thought there were so many?" he asked, looking around. The milling company filled the room, making colorful eddies around one speaker or another.

"So many what?" I asked. "So many high-spirited Alexandrians?"

"You will see," he said.

I saw stands holding bowls filled with gold coins, into which people dipped their hands, helping themselves as they passed. I also saw some familiar objects: actors' masks, the bust of Octavian, some gold vessels and plate on a display table.

I saw no dining couches or tables anywhere. "When do we dine?" I asked.

He shrugged. "When it seems right. I cannot predict."

"But the food—"

"Oh, that's no problem," he said airily. "The food will always be done to perfection. I have the kitchens preparing a dozen oxen, all roasting at different rates, so one of them will be exactly right whenever we choose to eat."

My mouth fell open. The waste! Was he mad?

"What are we saving it for?" he said, answering my thoughts. "Let us leave the pastures empty, the kitchens bare, to greet Octavian." He drank some more Lethe. "Let us strip ourselves bare before Death does it."

He was always theatrical—was this only a performance? Or was he *pretending* to give a performance to mask his real intentions?

"Ah—and here is our true host," he said, greeting someone costumed as Hades, lord of the underworld. His black cloak dragged on the ground, and he had a circlet depicting flickering flames around his head.

Silently he bowed. Behind his eye-mask I could see dark irises.

"Are you prepared to welcome such a large company?" Antony asked. "They are here to be initiated."

Hades turned his head slowly. "The company may not be as large as you suppose," he said, with a voice that suggested hollows, wells, caves: hints of ripples, drips, echoes. "Do not be disappointed if they do not all wish to set their feet upon the sill of night." He gave a smooth, but infinitely unpleasant, little laugh. "It is, after all, still high summer here. But doubtless there will be enough to have made my journey worthwhile." He bowed supply and insinuated himself in the crowd, disappearing.

"Who was *that*?" I asked. He was too realistic.

"Isn't he marvelous?" said Antony. "He's a well-known actor here in Greek comedies."

"Comedies? Clearly he's missed his calling."

Antony steered me past a knot of men and women encircling someone holding forth on the meaning of life.

"Young, young, he's very young," said Antony. "All the young philosophers like to declaim on *that* topic."

Behind me I could hear him droning, "Whether one is or is not, one and the others in relation to themselves and one another, all of them, in every way, are and are not, and appear to be and appear not to be."

"Plato," I said, more to myself than to Antony.

His brows went up in surprise. "My little Alexandrian," he said fondly. "Perhaps you'd like to declaim?"

"No," I said. "What I have learned in life would not help many others." There were few general rules to be gleaned from me.

We strolled about for some time, greeting the guests, listening to their conversations. Remarkably, there was no mention of Octavian or the political situation. Instead the talk was all of fashions, food, entertainments, and excursions.

Finally Antony strode to the front of the chamber and clapped his hands for attention. "My good friends—going all the way back to that first winter I came to Alexandria—welcome! Ah, what times we had then! Remember the fishing? Remember the visits to Canopus? Remember the banquets, the races? Ten years ago—how can that be? Now it is time to embark on a new adventure together. First I will auction off some items from those former days. You may use the gold I have placed in the bowls for you, to bid on them if you wish."

He flicked his hand over toward the objects I had noticed earlier, and a servant held the first one up.

"What am I bid for this fine mask of comedy, with its mate, tragedy? You might well have need of them in the days to come, when you play a part. . . .

"What am I bid for this bust of Gaius Octavianus? It lately graced the hall of Marcus Titius. This will help you recognize him. . . .

"And this! An outstanding specimen of its type, a solid gold chamber pot? Its fame has spread as far as Rome. It has other uses as well . . . perhaps for flowers?"

I had never seen such a thing in my life. He must have commissioned it especially for the auction!

He conducted the rest of the auction briskly, finally saying, "And thus do I bid my former life farewell."

He motioned to the harpists, and they plucked the strings of their instruments.

"Listen!" said Antony, as a slender singer appeared beside them. "Heed the words."

She sang in a hushed, sweet voice that caused the company to cease talking and strain to hear. "Follow thy heart's desire while still thou remainest in life! Pour perfume on thy head; let thy garment be of finest linen, anointed with the true most wondrous substances."

She moved her graceful hand, barely lifting a fold of her sheer linen gown. I could see all the fingers through it.

"Do that which is pleasing to thee more than thou didst aforetime; let not thy heart be weary. Follow thy heart's desire and that which is well pleasing in thine eyes. Arrange thine affairs on earth after the will of thy heart."

Now her voice was plain to hear in the quiet of the chamber.

"Weeping obtains not the heart of a man who dwelleth in the grave. On! live out a joyful day; rest not therein. Lo! it hath not been granted to man to take away with him his belongings. Lo! there is none who hath gone hence and returned hither." Those words . . . I had heard them in Rome, long ago. . . .

"Thank you," said Antony. He turned to the company. "Friends, long ago we had a brotherhood, a society, we called it *Amimetobioi*, the Incomparable Livers. Now I propose we form another, suitable for today, and call it *Synapothanoumenoi*, We Who Will Die Together. Yes. Let those who will join hands with us, and we will seal the pact by dancing once around the chamber to the sound of the harp. A dance of death. And Hades will lead us."

The actor appeared at Antony's side, and extended his gloved hand. He spoke no word.

The stunned guests just stared at him, and then, to my astonishment, the first man stepped forward and took my hand. Another followed him, until almost everyone had joined hands and formed a chain stretching around all the walls.

"Now!" Antony signaled to the harpists, who began playing softly, and the line of dancers moved slowly around the room, crossing their steps, bowing their heads. The flowers on their heads trembled with the motion. The high solemnity made a funeral procession.

Then one of the women took off her bracelets and held them up to make a rattle, and the jangle livened the parade; others turned their jewelry into cymbals, clappers, and bells. The pace speeded up, until we were running, our feet thumping the marble floor, making it resound. The cortege had turned raucous. Life burst defiantly through the mourning.

"Wine, wine!" yelled one man, holding out his hand for a quick servant to press a cup in it.

"More here!" yelled another, and finally the line fell apart, as panting people grabbed cups of wine.

"And now the food!" cried Antony, and at his word a team of slaves dashed in from all the entrances, bearing couches and tables. Superbly well rehearsed, they managed to set up a dining room for over a hundred people in an instant.

People dived and flopped onto the couches, squealing with glee. Before they were served, Antony spoke again.

"Feast well! The best of Alexandria is here for your pleasure. Eat, drink, play, come hither!" He paused. "For as long as we still have, we will gather to do thus. And let us not grieve at what is to come, but remember the epitaph of an Epicurean: 'I was not, I was, I am not, I do not care.' Thus are summarized all the states a soul passes through on its way to eternity."

After he took his place near me, I leaned over and said, "That is too cynical."

He was chewing vigorously on a fig. "Why, do you think otherwise?"

"Yes," I said. "What you quoted was ignoble. It sounds like a beast of the field."

He made a wry face. "I envy them."

"No, you don't. They have no memories." I motioned to one of the servers to find my agate cup and bring it to me. When it arrived, I turned it around in my hands. "I am not ready to auction this off. It belonged to my father. Yet it seems fitting to drink from it tonight." He had met many crises with courage.

"Sir, how do you like this maxim?" a youth on Antony's other side was saying. " 'Why dost thou not retire like a guest sated with the banquet of life, and with calm mind embrace, thou fool, a rest that knows no care?' Is that what our club is about?"

Antony clapped his shoulder. "Yes, my lad, yes."

He was clearly enjoying his game—who was I to spoil it? It was better than the hermitage. But that it was merely a game I had no doubt; it did not reveal anything of his true state of mind. He was theatrical to the marrow of his bones, always taking refuge behind costumes. He might have auctioned off the masks of tragedy and comedy tonight, but he had others waiting in reserve.

From every couch, so it seemed, people were declaiming their philosophies, seeing who had the greatest command of quotes. It was all very clever, like anything Alexandrian. I sipped my wine from the agate cup and said little. The delicacies of orchard, sea, and field passed my palate unnoticed.

Hades ate heartily; he was quite robust for a shade.

Late that night, preparing for bed, I heaped my jewelry in a pile by my forest of perfume bottles. Iras could put it away in the morning. I pulled off the wilted crown of flowers and placed it alongside.

"You outdid yourself," I finally said to Antony. "I must say, I could never have predicted any of it." Because it was so bizarre, I added to myself. I hoped people did not think he was deranged, but then, they had joined in with gusto. Perhaps they were all deranged. It was said that in the last days, people in a group could behave very strangely.

But I did not feel a part of that confusion and despair. That my life might end, and be ended by me, I accepted. But it was a political fact, not a philosophical one. I would not glorify a political necessity by trapping it in all sorts of nonsense.

I had no innate wish to die, I was not eager to die; I would far prefer to live, unless it was incompatible with honor—mine or my country's. Death, like life, should serve a purpose.

"What are you thinking?" Antony asked quietly. He was already lying down, his arms behind his head. "I wish to know your thoughts."

I was thinking I am not in love with death, as you are. I looked down at him. He looked oddly happy, as if he had crossed some barrier tonight.

"I was thinking . . . I was trying to remember an old Egyptian poem. All that quoting tonight put me to shame." It was looking down at him that had brought it to mind. I sat down beside him. "It went: 'The voice of the dove is calling; it sayeth: "The earth is bright, where is my way?" Thou bird, thou art calling to me.' "

He looked puzzled. I had to think hard to recall the lost words, once known so well, of the rest of it.

"Then . . . it went . . . let's see . . ." I willed the words to return, and they obeyed. " 'But I, I found my beloved on his couch. My heart is rejoiced above all measure, and each of us sayeth: "I will not part from thee." ' "

I felt for his hand and found it. " ' "My hand is in thy hand. I walk and am with thee in each beautiful place, thou madest me the first of the fair maidens, thou hast not grieved my heart." ' "

It was true. I leaned over and kissed him.

"That is not in the mood of the evening," he said quietly.

"No," I admitted. "We are still too much alive to embrace that mood."

He sighed. "You are banishing it, I fear." He reached his arms up to embrace me. "Do you really feel that way about me?"

"Yes," I said. "From the very beginning until this moment."

"Moments," he mused. "I wonder how many of them we have left?"

"You should stop this now," I said briskly. "It's tiresome with the guests gone."

He rolled over, with me in his arms. "You are so determinedly down-to-earth," he teased.

"And you should know," I told him, before enjoying some earthly pleasures, "that I know the name of the new society is stolen from the title of an obscure Greek comedy. It isn't original. Shame on you."

He groaned. "Oh, I should never try to put anything over on an Alexandrian. I hope no one else knew!"

"They probably did," I said. "After all, they are Alexandrians, too."

When I awoke in the early dawn, it was utterly still in the chamber. No wind stirred the hangings; Kasu the monkey—quite elderly now—slept peacefully in her basket under a table. Antony was deeply asleep on his back, the rise and fall of his chest pulling soundlessly on the linens. He sighed and turned onto his side. In the growing light I could see his eyes moving under the lids; he must be having a dream in which people were running. He had dark, thick eyelashes that locked together when his eyes closed, and I used to tease him and call them "camel's lashes," because camels have surprisingly long lashes to keep the sand out of their eyes. I had said only camels and dancing girls were supposed to have such lashes, not Roman generals. Behind my teasing lay the fact that I envied them. I was pleased that the twins had inherited them.

My mind was fully awake now, but I did not wish to arise yet. I would lie pretending to be asleep; sometimes I thought best that way, with just a touch of dream still clinging to me. The warmth of the body close beside me cosseted me, making me feel safe. Safe forever and ever. But not so. . . .

Octavian was coming closer. What if I managed to see him in person? A face-to-face interview could accomplish much that formal letters did not. I seldom failed in a direct meeting; it was my greatest strength. If I saw him, looked him in the eye . . .

I turned over, suppressing a slight shudder. Those eyes . . . what had Olympos called them? *Clear, grayish blue, utterly emotionless . . . a flatness with life yet behind it.* I remembered those eyes. I did not really care to look into them. But if I could . . . perhaps . . .

Antony twitched and jerked, starting to wake up. He would never want me to do it; he would object. But months ago I had decided to do anything. There was no line I would not cross, unlike the proud and noble Antony. In that way Octavian and I were alike. Years ago I had said, *May the best man win*, between the two of us. The contest was not over yet. An interview with him, alone, could work in my favor.

Antony's arms tightened around me. If he had known my thoughts, he probably would have recoiled rather than embracing me. He started rubbing his head against mine affectionately.

At the movement, the monkey made her arthritic way across the floor and jumped stiffly up onto the bed to join us.

Antyllus stood before us, seeming taller since he had qualified for the *toga virilis*. He was wearing it now, its natural white as pure as the marble of the Lighthouse.

"You will greet your cousin respectfully," Antony was instructing him. "After all, you have grown up in his sister's home, and known him all your life. You were once betrothed to his daughter."

"I didn't know him *well*," he protested.

"No one knows Octavian well," said Antony, "probably not even his own daughter. That does not matter. I am sending you as my emissary to salute him and present these gifts of gold to him. Give him the letter in which I remind him of our years of friendship, of joint rulership, of ties of kinship. I ask him to let me retire into private life and live in Athens. After all, Lepidus did so. If he refuses, give him this personal letter."

"Is it wise for him to go all the way to Ptolemais Ace?" I asked. I did not like sending Antyllus directly into the enemy camp. Had Antony never considered that Octavian might take him as a hostage? It seemed rash to me.

"He'll do well enough," said Antony. "It is only three hundred miles by sea."

"Don't remind me how close Octavian is!" Luckily he would have to march by land, much farther, and through the Sinai, too. "And that's not what I meant. I meant, why put your son in his hands?"

"I have to send the highest-ranking emissary I can, and that is my eldest son and heir. Octavian will not respond to anything less."

"He may respond in a way you won't like," I said. "I think it's a dangerous risk."

Antony sighed. "We must hope for the best. Now, Antyllus, no one must see the contents of the second letter but Octavian, in privacy. Make sure of it."

"What's in it?" I was suddenly suspicious.

"I said no one but Octavian," Antony said firmly. "Not even you." He put his hands on his son's shoulders. "I have the utmost confidence in you," he said. "I will be awaiting the answer you bring back."

The boy—young man now—squared his shoulders, proud of his mission. "Yes, Father. I am honored to do it."

While we waited, Antony and his *Synapothanoumenoi* held many banquets, rotating around to each mansion throughout the city. Each tried to outdo the last in abandoned profligacy, as if determined to waste all earthly possessions in a blaze of glory, like a funeral pyre. I found them boring, not even a good distraction. Why has no one ever written on the fact that impersonal debauches or extravaganzas leave as much space for brooding as does complete privacy? One is equally alone in both.

Mardian brought the two muscular men in tattered clothes before us.

"Here are those you seek," he told them. To us he said, "Your champions are here."

They were utterly unfamiliar. "Good sirs, who are you?" I had to ask.

"We are gladiators from the school at Cyzicus—trained to fight in your victory games. Which still might be held someday, the gods willing! We have not gone over to him." The man who was speaking was stout and had a shaved head. I wondered what his weapons of choice were. Thracian? Samnite? He would not do well with the net; his arms were too short.

"But we were halted by King Herod once we reached Judaea. The rest of our party is detained there; we escaped to come to you." His companion had the long legs and dark skin of a Nubian. Good gladiators came from all over the world.

"And you are all that got away?" asked Antony.

"Yes, lord. I am afraid so."

"You and your company have proved more loyal than all the client kings with their effusive vows of allegiance," said Antony. Was his voice trembling, just a little? "For that I am deeply grateful. You are the heroes among heroes." He turned to Mardian. "Give them the gold of their deserving, and let them be housed in the palace."

"You will have to be retrained," I told them. "The games we normally have here are Greek. No killing. Still, I imagine you can adapt."

They bowed in a most professional manner.

Hard on their heels, Antyllus returned. I was deeply relieved that Octavian had not "detained" him as Herod had the gladiators, but Antony was disappointed in the reply.

Alone with us after the dinner welcoming him home, Antyllus recounted his experience.

"He treated me courteously enough," he said, "but it was as if I were a stranger! He did not betray any familiarity with me, let alone warmth."

"He spoke with you in private?" Antony asked.

"Yes, in the old Phoenician palace he was using for headquarters," Antyllus said. "It overlooks the sea, so close that breaking waves send spray in the windows. It made quiet conversation difficult. But I was alone with him, except for his guards, of course. He was seated casually—he even crossed his legs! He told me to pull up a chair, then chatted away."

"Well, what did he say?" Antony pressed.

"His chatting was nothing. I don't remember. He kept staring at me, while pretending not to."

"Yes, that's his way," I remembered.

"He examined the gifts carefully, running his hands over the rim of the gold plate. He said he must refuse your request to retire into private life in Athens. He said the city was too fervently pledged to him now for it to be safe for you."

Antony was fidgeting with his hands, most unlike him. "Did you present the second letter?" he finally burst out.

"Yes." He rummaged around in a carrying case, and handed the letter back to Antony. The original seal had been broken, but another had been affixed. "He said for you to read it in private. He wrote an answer on it, very quickly. Just a word or two."

"Well, what was it?" Antony asked, taking the letter.

"I don't know, sir. Truly I don't. He didn't say."

"Oh." Antony turned the letter over in his hands. We were all watching him. Slowly he broke the seal and unrolled the letter, his eyes darting down to the end of the scroll. Whatever he read there caused a look of consternation to cross his face. "Oh." He rolled it up again, then tucked it in his belt.

"Well, perhaps we will have better luck sometime later," he said, an unconvincing smile spreading across his face. "I am proud of you, my son. You have executed a most difficult mission, and done it well." He raised a cup to him, and asked us all to drink to Antyllus.

The evening passed in congenial conversation, while sipping good Falernian wine. I urged Antony to refill his cup regularly. I wanted his head swimming, so he would be careless of his clothes when he undressed. But to my frustration, he was unusually restrained tonight. And at the end of the evening, he made off for his own quarters, announcing that he intended to sleep there.

"I have an aching head and would do better by myself," he said. "The palace noises are farther removed there." And he sauntered off, calling for Eros.

I waited until I thought enough time had passed, then I stole over to his apartments. The startled Eros let me in, and I slid past him into the bedchamber. If I was lucky, Antony would be asleep. But no! He was sitting up, the lamps still lit, reading. He looked surprised to see me.

"I did not wish to be alone tonight," I said apologetically. "But I will stay on this couch, and not disturb you if your head cannot stand jostling."

"Oh," he said, his polite smile unfailing, while he touched his forehead, "it is not as bad as all that. I would not banish you to a couch."

Then followed a set of steps in which we each assured the other. At length we retired to bed together. (I would rather have been on the couch, the better to get up unobserved.) He had put out all the lamps, but I was fortunate in that the moon was nearly full and by midnight cast a shaft of bright light across the floor. His even breathing told me he was asleep by that time.

As carefully as possible I climbed from the bed and inched my way across the floor to where he had left his clothes when he undressed. The letter was still with the belt; he had covered them up with his discarded outer garment. I stuck my hand under it and felt for the leather case. I found it without difficulty. I crawled across the floor and unrolled the letter as quietly as possible, just outside the rectangle of moonlight.

Antony suddenly turned over and I froze. What if he was awake enough to notice I had gone? He seemed roused, and I did not dare move. But then his sleepy coughing told me he was still safely unaware, and ready to drop back into slumber. I waited another few minutes and then edged the letter out into the light where I could read it.

> My dear brother, I come to you now as that. Between brothers, I hereby declare to you that I am willing to do that which honor allows me. Death will be my friend and our bond if thereby I can guarantee the life of the Queen. I gladly exchange my life for hers, and I trust that you will honor your word, once given. Let her live, I ask you. No, I beg you. Your word then given, I will straightway fulfill my promise. I salute you in death, a death I gladly offer.
>
> —Marcus Antonius, Imperator

And scrawled right beneath it, under Antony's signature and seal, were the stark words: "Do as you will. Nothing can save her.—Imperator G. Caesar, *Divi Filius*."

I felt cold all over. My nose, my fingers . . . Antony had offered this, without telling me? And the thing that Octavian had demanded of me, he now refused, when Antony himself offered it. It seemed that Antony's head was not what he had wanted after all, but only to prove he could make me betray him. He was a fiend.

Shaking, I rolled the letter up again, replaced it, and got back into bed beside Antony, wanting to wake him up and hold him more tightly than I ever had. But better to let him sleep.

82

The summer continued to unfold, the high-riding sun mounting to his farthest reach in the sky. The month of Julius arrived, and on its first day we gathered around his statue in Caesarion's old quarters and offered up prayers and requests. Our son must be at the shores of the Red Sea by now, awaiting the ship to take him to India by mid-July. I had heard nothing since he departed. A few days earlier his seventeenth birthday had come around, and I had thanked Isis for him and beseeched her to protect him. One can never ask too many gods, and since Caesar was a new one, it seemed prudent to go to Isis as well.

Reports were that Octavian had left Ptolemais Ace and was proceeding south; he was expected to reach Joppa before long. Herod was providing him with not only a hero's welcome but with troops, supplies, and guides. Behind him streamed all his legions; Octavian was finally granted the chance to march along at the head of a mighty army, like a genuine general—instead of the imitation one he was.

It was time for another mission to him. There still might be a chance to buy him off. He must be told about the treasure I stood ready to torch. We must exaggerate the size of the force and resistance waiting to meet him; perhaps he would take the easier way and negotiate. The best we could hope for was abdication and banishment for me, banishment for Antony, in exchange for Caesarion—or even Alexander and Selene—being made ruler in my place. He could have the treasure in return, pay off his soldiers. That way we would both get what we wanted without bloodshed: he the treasury, I the continued independence—nominal, of course—of Egypt under the Ptolemies. Egypt's strength would be gone, but at least she would still be in existence. It was not altogether impossible that I could bring this about.

This would be my mission, and I would send Euphronius, the children's tutor, as ambassador.

"Send a schoolmaster?" Antony was incredulous.

"Yes, why not?"

"But wouldn't Mardian, or even Epaphroditus, be more respectful?"

"I am not trying to be respectful. Sending Antyllus did not seem to carry much weight. Perhaps it's better to do the opposite, and send a menial. *That* will catch his attention." I had decided this would be my last appeal to him; as he approached closer, there would be nothing but silence to greet him.

There was gold to go along with the letter, in which I repeated my request that he put my heir in my place. I said I would surrender the throne into his hands on this assurance. I also said that I had secured a large portion of the Ptolemaic treasure in a place where it could be destroyed in the twinkling of an eye, if I saw fit. His refusal to accede to my wishes would cost him, literally, a fortune. He did not wish that, did he? Then let us be reasonable, and come to an agreement.

I sealed the letter, pleased with its wording, but, above all, pleased with my foresight in assuring that I still had something to offer him. As I said earlier, in order to negotiate, one has to have something to bargain with— something the other person wants, and wants badly. Antony's life did not fall into that category, so Octavian had no incentive to consider his desperate request.

It seems that in this miserable life, it is not the despair of the supplicant that moves the hearer, but his own selfish desires. If he needs a footstool, and the bent back can serve, then . . . Otherwise, a kick sends him on his way.

Just as Euphronius was ready to depart, Antony suddenly decided he wished to add a letter of his own. This time I insisted on reading it, as I wanted no repeat of the previous one. What if, on a whim, Octavian said yes? He was just cruel enough to say it offhandedly.

"Single combat?" This was not at all what I had expected the letter to say. "What do you mean?"

"Only that if he would agree to meet me, man to man, and we could fight, and thereby determine the outcome, it would save so many lives."

Was he mad? Was he never fully to regain the hearty common sense he had had before Actium, but continue to have relapses into odd thinking and behavior?

"You know Octavian would never agree to that," I said slowly. "He has nothing to gain by it and everything to lose. Why would a man with twenty legions, who is a poor fighter, agree to personal combat with his superior, who has no army left? He will laugh at you. Don't send this!"

"What else can I do?" said Antony. "I must propose something!"

"It makes no sense to make proposals you know won't be accepted. And we aren't Greeks from the age of heroes; great issues aren't decided by personal combat anymore. You can't play Hector. I know the part suits you, but it can't be."

"I must send it anyway," he insisted. "The gesture must be made."

The days stretched out. An eerie waiting seemed to grip all Alexandria, although the city seemingly went about its business. But in every house, supplies were being gathered, books balanced, quarrels either mended or pursued to the end, postponed letters written. Fathers gave sons the advice they imagined they would be remiss to withhold, and wills were drawn up. But the expected event was so ill-defined that more specific actions could not be undertaken. There might be fighting, there might not. Only the name of the ruling Ptolemy might change, or the whole government might undergo a massive upheaval, ending with Egypt a Roman province.

Epaphroditus kept me apprised of the changing moods of the city. He was attending me more often now, presenting the financial picture as a flooding Nile promised another bountiful harvest. Sadly, he also said he feared the Jews of Alexandria might welcome Octavian because he came in company with Herod.

"Not that Octavian is our friend, as Caesar was," he said. "But Herod is their hero, and they think of Judaea as their homeland."

I looked at my minister, older now but no less handsome than when I had first persuaded him to work with me. "First you say 'our,' then you change to 'their,' " I pointed out. "Why?"

He rubbed his forehead. "I am caught between merely observing what my people do and joining them. I hold myself apart from the common thinking. Certainly I don't look on Judaea as my homeland, and I think it's foolish of anyone who has lived away from a place for generations to call it home. It's a sentimental corruption of their thinking, and can be dangerous." He laughed. "Why, we could no longer read our holy writings in the Judaean tongue, and had to have it translated into Greek, and *that* was two hundred years ago! We have been gone from that land a long time."

He looked so fierce in asserting his disapproval that I had to smile. "Well, the Ptolemies have been gone from Macedonia for just as long, but we still call our palace guards the Macedonian Guard," I said.

He snorted, as if to say, *Then you are foolish, too.*

"It is hard to let go of a cherished identity," I said. That was why being declared un-Roman was such a blow for Antony. After all, if he was not Roman, what was he? "I shall be disappointed if the Jews—who are, after all, two-fifths of the city—turn from me to Octavian." It was one thing for client kings, whose loyalty did not go back very far, to desert. It was another for one's own citizens. "Is there anything more painful than desertion?" I blurted out.

"Probably not," said Epaphroditus. "It robs us of even our memories, since they must always be viewed through the smudge of betrayal."

"Well, enough of this." My spirits were low. I straightened my back. "Let us discuss the import taxes. After all, ships are still docking. We are not blockaded by sea. . . ."

It was a day like all the rest—as fine and light as the lines on a painted Greek vase—when the messenger was announced. As day after day strove to outdo the last in perfection, I had conceived a fancy that each one knew this might well be my last summer, and wanted both to console and torment me. *Savor us; bid farewell to that which you are losing.* So there was no other sort of day on which the messenger could have arrived, save one wreathed in warmth and sun and cool breezes.

Mardian announced him with a sniff. "A fellow who calls himself Thyrsus has come from Octavian." He tilted his head to convey disdain. "I suppose you will wish to receive him?"

So the answer had come! I gripped the arms of the chair where I sat. "Of course. But not here. I will receive him in the audience chamber." I rose. "Tell him it will not be until late afternoon." Let him wait, and wonder.

I hurried away to change into formal clothes. So quick an answer. My threats must have stirred Octavian's attention. Should Antony also be present? Surely there was an answer for him as well. But no . . . better that I speak to the man alone. Octavian was not going to agree to Antony's suggestion, so there was no point in giving him an opening for insult.

"Charmian, my audience clothes!" I demanded when I entered my chamber. "They must themselves suggest the richness of the treasure I withhold from Octavian's grasp." I must look as fabulously wealthy as Roman imagination had painted me all these years. This was the first enemy who had approached the throne, and he must be dazzled—especially as Dellius, Plancus, and Titius had undoubtedly spread lies to Octavian. This one must return goggle-eyed to his master.

The neatly folded stacks of glittering material looked like an artificial field of wildflowers, available in every hue and texture. Should I wear gold? Too obvious. Silver? Not at its best during the day. Red? Too blaring. Blue? Too retiring. White?

I fingered the material of a favorite white silk gown that floated around my ankles as if a whisper of a breeze were always blowing across the floor. But no. That was a gown for private moments.

Black? Too severe, and suggestive of mourning. Odd how I could have hundreds of gowns, and yet so few would do for any particular occasion.

From between a black gown and a yellow I saw a fold of purple barely protruding. A purple that had been twice-dyed, giving it a deep, inimitable color . . . yes. "That one," I told Charmian. As she pulled it out, I remembered that the style was perfect: discreet banding of gold threads at the hem and the shoulders, neck shown to advantage, arms covered. Under its ample folds, only the slightest hint of legs and body showed, revealed fleetingly whenever I stepped forward or stirred on my throne. Gold sandals must clasp my feet and kiss the hem of the garment.

The wedding necklace would form a riveting collar of gold around my neck, and of course there would be a gold circlet with the royal cobra on my brow. Let the Republican Roman gaze on pure queenship, and shield his eyes! Octavian and his consciously frugal homespun togas would fade into invisibility.

"Who is this man, my lady?" Iras asked as she arranged my hair around the circlet.

"Octavian's messenger," I said. "No one of any note: I have never heard his name before—Thyrsus."

She said in her soothing manner, "Octavian had doubtless never heard of Euphronius either. Whatever you do, he mimics." She pointed over to Kasu, who was combing her fingers through her wiry crown of head-fur, copying Iras at work. "Like our monkey."

I appreciated her loyalty and sense of humor. But the truth was that Octavian probably knew the name of everyone in my palace, and what he or she did. I did not doubt his spies eavesdropped even on my most intimate moments whenever possible.

The sun was halfway down to its setting place. I had made this Thyrsus wait long enough. Time for our meeting. I arose, liking the way the purple gown rustled against my legs.

He was announced while I sat on my throne, and he waited, invisible, in an outer room. The air, which perfumed itself from the flowers in the gardens surrounding the palace, was rolling voluptuously through the open windows, enveloping me in soft fragrance.

In writing this, I realize that this was my last formal audience. My first had taken place in this chamber by my father's side when he had started training me to be his heir. It seemed, in the worn phrase, only yesterday. We always know when something is our first, but we seldom—through the kindness of the gods—know when we do it for the last time. Had I known . . . But what would I have done differently? Nothing. Nothing except pay closer attention to all the details, the better to remember them.

"Thyrsus, envoy from Octavian Caesar's camp," my attendant announced. That neatly satisfied both sides—the pointed "Octavian" for me, the "Caesar" for him.

A tall young man strode in, with the proud carriage of an eagle. I sat as impassive as possible, so that no human element would detract from all the trappings of splendor around me. I saw him staring at me, looking as travelers do who first stumble toward the pyramids or the great Temple of Artemis, primed to see a wonder.

He fell to his knees, only a few feet from me. "Oh, madam!" he said, using one hand to shield his eyes, as if the sight were too much for a mortal. But the gesture was too smooth; it had been rehearsed.

"Rise," I said. I held out my scepter to indicate my wish.

"My knees will not obey," he said. "They are made weak by your splendor."

"Order them," I said. The flattery was too thick.

He forced himself up, never taking his eyes from mine. "Whatever you order, I shall do my best to obey."

"You are Octavian's aide? What is the rest of your name—Thyrsus?"

"Julius Caesar Thyrsus," he replied, proudly.

"You are a freedman?" I was incredulous. He had sent a freedman to address me? So this was his answer to my tutor! He was determined to find someone lower on the social scale. Next he would send a slave.

"Yes, madam. I was freed by the generosity of my former master, now my patron, Imperator Caesar, *divi filius*."

"You mean Octavian." Let the contest begin.

"As you wish, madam." He smiled, a hesitant, winning smile. His eyes were very blue.

"Your master would not be pleased to hear you capitulate on his titles so easily," I said.

Again the man smiled. "My master is not here, lady, and you are. I wish to please you, and say nothing that would roil your spirits. If 'Octavian' sounds sweet to your ears, so be it."

How accommodating of him. I wondered what his true instructions were. Was this all done in accordance with Octavian's plan? "What would sound sweetest to my ears would be to hear that Octavian had departed for Rome, to let me and my kingdom continue in peace. But such words I will never hear. Where is he now?"

"In Ashkelon."

Ashkelon! My city, so precious to me at crucial times of my life. He sat there now. The thought was painful.

"He is making the final preparations for the march down the desert highway through the Sinai." His tone was kind, not haughty.

"And then to assault Pelusium," I said. Pelusium was the key to Egypt, its eastern gateway. If it fell, the road to Alexandria was clear.

"That is the plan, madam. I tell you nothing you do not know."

"This time of year the desert road shimmers with unbearable heat, and you must march two days without water," I warned him. "Between Rhinokolura and Pelusium there are no wells."

"We have camels."

"You cannot drink from their humps."

"They can carry many waterskins."

"Not enough for twenty legions."

"Each soldier also carries water."

"Enough of this sparring," I said. "I say it will be difficult, and you say you know that. Let it rest. No battle is without its challenges. That is why it would be best if we could avoid battle altogether, which both Antony and I have proposed. I await Octavian's reply to our offers, which I assume you carry with you." I found his manner so likable that I could take no offense at his half-playful arguing.

"Yes, I do." He gave a short, musical laugh. "But they are not written down. I am to speak them."

"Well?"

"As for Antony's request—surely it was a jest?" He looked genuinely puzzled. "Single combat? My commander dismissed it, saying only that if Antony wished to die, there were many methods he could choose."

I winced inwardly. What other answer could Octavian give? It both shamed and insulted Antony for his foolish offer. "I see," I said. The less said about it, the better. "And mine?"

"Ah. Yours. That you will yield Egypt to him without a fight if he promises to put your children on the throne to succeed you, and not make Egypt a Roman province. Now that . . . has many considerations."

"I should have reminded him that once before, Rome captured Egypt, when his . . . adopted . . . father Caesar fought the Alexandrian War. But he wisely did not annex it to Rome then. Caesar judged it better to leave Egypt as it was. Can his political heir be less wise than Caesar the god?" I was anxious to know Octavian's mind; why did this fellow not speak it out?

"Caesar did not take Egypt because he was a captive himself—captive to your charm. It was in deference to you that he held back." He paused, as if he were debating whether to speak further. "And his glorious successor, the young general Octavian, is not as proof against them as he appears."

I had not expected this. What a clever trap. But . . . long ago Antony had muttered, *I know he has a lust for you.* "Is it so?" I replied cautiously.

"Yes, although I hesitate to reveal it," he said. He seemed so sincere. "He is most eager to have the opportunity to prove himself your friend."

Now I had to laugh. My friend! "Is that why he has declared war on me and called me a whore?"

"Sometimes the stronger our feelings, the crueler our words, to mask them," he said gallantly.

"Oh, I am sure his feelings toward me are quite strong. But strong in hatred, not in friendship."

"You are wrong. But give him the opportunity to prove his good intentions. Lay down your arms and welcome him to Egypt, as you did Caesar. Then he will prove a kind lord to you and yours."

"Is this before or after I present him with Antony?"

"Forget about Antony," he said. "He is negligible, inconsequential between great rulers of your stature."

"I see." And I did, to my sorrow. But Octavian's desire to lull me into submission might be turned against him, if I could somehow manage an interview while I still held my treasure safe. "Now let me reiterate my situation. I know that what Octavian desires is not me, but my treasure. He needs it to pay his soldiers, who have been living on promises for years. But he will never get it until he has met my conditions. Otherwise I will destroy it. Let me show you how." I rose from the throne and came down to stand beside him. "Come with me."

"If you would only welcome him as you did Caesar, you would find him most agreeable."

Why did he keep using that phrase? Did he mean welcome him into my bed?

"If he would be straightforward in his dealings, as Caesar was, we could come to an understanding," I answered.

"You are young," Thyrsus said, sighing. "Is it not time you left old men behind? Youth has charms that age knows not."

"Then Octavian would not find me charming, as I am older than he."

He pretended to be surprised. "Is it even so? But you look so young."

"It must be the magic arts that Octavian swears I practice that have preserved me," I said. "But he himself seems a child to me."

"Oh no, my lady, he is now thirty-two. The same age as Alexander when he died. Was Alexander a child?"

"A glorious and eternal god-child," I said. "Come." I would lead him to the mausoleum and show him my ransom.

We passed through the connecting rooms of the palace, and the bright sunlight hurt my eyes when we stepped outside. The summer sun, magnified by the white marble of the city and the flat mirror of the sea, was so intense it bleached colors from whatever it touched.

"Where are we going?" he asked, shading his eyes.

"To a place where the sun never penetrates," I said, pointing across the grounds to the mausoleum, next to the open Temple of Isis. "To my tomb."

"So, even though you are Greek, you have succumbed to the Egyptian fascination with death?" He asked it curiously. "Even in this city of high noon, the shadow of the tomb falls across our path."

We were approaching the building. It loomed bigger and bigger before us, its portals beckoning. "To grow up in Egypt is to rub shoulders with the dead. It is inescapable; the monuments are part of the landscape. We do not believe that a body should burn like a candle and then be emptied unceremoniously into an urn." I paused. "But all this is not for many years," I assured him, "if Octavian will listen to reason. After all, why should any of us die prematurely?"

Let us live, I wished fiercely. Let us spend as many years as natural life allows us, here beneath the sun. It might be possible. If . . .

I led the way up the steps surrounding the mausoleum and through the open doors. Beside me, his heavy nailed sandals grated on the stone.

Inside, the shadows engulfed us. It took a moment for our eyes to adjust.

"This is all for you? And Antony?" he asked, His voice hushed.

"Yes. We will lie apart from the rest of the Ptolemies." I was waiting for the stinging darkness to recede so I could show him my creation—my treasure-hostage. It was cool in here, cool in a suspended, seasonless way.

"Why have you brought me here? I don't like tombs."

"Ah, but this is a very special tomb. For one thing, these doors." I extended my arm and pointed at them.

"What about them?"

"They remain open now, but are engineered so they can be closed only once. When they descend down the tracks of their posts, they seal themselves shut forever. After the last funeral—mine or Antony's—when the mourners depart, the doors will enclose us in solitude for all eternity." I paused. "It is an old Egyptian idea, grafted onto a Greek-style temple. We will not be disturbed by tomb robbers, for no valuables will be buried with us."

I sensed, rather than saw, his shudder. "Let us leave."

I ignored his request. "The valuables I am going to show you will have all been given to Octavian, and the mausoleum will be empty of treasure. That is, if he agrees to my request."

Now at last we could see. I led him past the two sarcophagi and around the polished black pillars to the mountain of treasure. He stood staring at it, taken by surprise at last. He had not been prepared for this.

I walked around the pile. "Here it is—gold, silver, pearls, lapis, emeralds—enough to pay any debts Octavian has, no matter how large. This represents many times the annual income and treasury of Rome. It was accumulated by my ancestors—the last unplundered source of wealth in the world, save that of the Parthians. Think what your master can do with it! And it is all his, without a drop of bloodshed, without the loss of a single life, if he just agrees that either Caesarion or Alexander and Selene can be crowned ruler of Egypt. As for my person, I will remove myself. As you can see, I have prepared a place to go." I nodded toward the sarcophagi.

"By all the gods . . ." His voice was faint.

"And this is not all," I assured him. "Of course Rome would have the grain of Egypt at her disposal, year after year. That would be part of the bargain."

"I do not think Octavian pictured this," he finally said. "But, fair lady, this could never make him happy if it were got in exchange for your life."

"Oh, I imagine he could force himself to appreciate it," I said. "So. What will be his answer?"

He reached out and stroked a bar of gold. "It isn't even cold," he said wonderingly.

"That's right," I said. "Whoever describes gold as being hard and cold has never had the privilege of touching large pieces of it in pure form. As a metal it is very soft, forgiving, and eager to shape itself to you; and it never feels frigidly cold like iron. A mysterious substance, gold." I touched it fondly. "Bring me your master's answer as soon as possible. For you can see that I have the means of destroying it all if his answer does not please me." I indicated the wood and pitch at the bottom of the pile.

"He desires to please you." Thyrsus took my hand and kissed it. "It is his deepest wish." He stepped closer, and did not let go of my hand. "Trust him, and trust the power you already wield over his . . . his feelings." He kissed my hand again, lingering.

"Then let him stop disguising them, and allow them to shine forth," I said. "Things hidden cannot be responded to."

He kept kissing my hand, and his thick hair fell forward, touching my wrist.

"So!" A harsh voice rang out from the doorway: Antony's.

Thyrsus sprang away guiltily.

Antony almost leapt across the space and grabbed Thyrsus. "So! This is what Octavian sends! A fawning, silly boy! And you!" He rounded on me. "How can you stand there, allowing him to slobber all over your hand, encouraging him, leading him on?"

He almost lifted Thyrsus off his feet, hauling him up by one shoulder. "Betraying me!"

"No," I said. He had misunderstood everything, and spoiled my carefully constructed plan. "Stop it. Let him go!"

"Don't take up for him! How dare he take such liberties?" He stuck his face up into Thyrsus's. "Who are you?"

"Octavian's friend and freedman, Thyrsus," he squeaked out.

"A freedman! He sends a *freedman* here as his messenger? And a freedman approaches the Queen of Egypt, sidles up, like a confidant? Oh, the insolence!"

"Sir," said Thyrsus, "I have done no wrong, nor acted disrespectfully. The Queen brought me here for her own reasons."

"Is that so?" yelled Antony. "And I suppose she invited you to take her hand? You need to learn manners, young man! Guards!"

The two soldiers guarding the entrance to the mausoleum came to his call. "Sir?"

"Whip this man!" he ordered. "Take him out and whip him thoroughly!"

"I am Octavian's official envoy!" he protested. "You dare not—"

He should not have used those words, *dare not*. I attempted to placate Antony.

"Please!" I said. "This violates protocol. It is unworthy of you!"

"So now you take his part? I should have known!"

"I only seek to prevent you from rash action that will harm your reputation."

"Tell your master Octavian that if he wishes to get even, he can whip Hipparchus, my old freedman, who deserted me for him!" he shouted at Thyrsus. "Thus I will be doubly satisfied!" He laughed harshly as the soldiers dragged Thyrsus away.

"You fool!" I cried. "You've ruined everything!"

"What have I ruined? Your double-dealing with Octavian?" he sneered.

"I am trying to save Egypt for my children! It is all we can hope for!"

"So you simper and entertain whomever Octavian sends?" he cried. "I am disappointed in you."

"I am bargaining, the most desperate bargain of my life. This treasure"— I pointed at it—"for Egypt's freedom."

"I notice you say nothing about *our* freedom."

"I am afraid that is not likely," I said. "I have limited hopes, not impossible ones."

"What did he say?"

"To my offer, he made no reply yet. *That* was why I was showing Thyrsus the treasure, so he could comprehend what the offer really meant. As for yours . . . Octavian has rejected it, as I knew he would."

"What exactly did he say?"

"That you could find other means of doing away with yourself."

"Perhaps I shall, then!"

"We both shall, when the time comes. Now calm yourself." I sought to soothe him.

But my spirits were dashed. Octavian would not forgive the insult to him in whipping his envoy, and it would harden his heart against my offer. He would not consider it now.

Oh, why did Antony have to come in when he did?

Hurrying away to my own apartments under the pretext of a meeting with Mardian, I withdrew to think. Perhaps I could fix it. But Antony must not know. I must see Thyrsus before he returned to Octavian's camp. I would have to—to tell him something. Do something. Something strong enough to overcome his mistreatment. But what? What?

I told one of my guards to go immediately to the punishment grounds and order the whipping stopped, if it was still going on, and to detain the man. Then notify him to wait for me. As soon as he left, his sword slapping smartly against his side, I summoned Olympos, who was none too pleased to be hauled from his supper.

"Make me the best ointment you know for healing wounds!" I ordered.

He got that superior look on his face. "What kind of wound?" he asked. "They are not all the same. A puncture wound? A dog bite? A sword thrust?"

"The stripes from whipping," I said.

He looked surprised. "Why, who has been whipped?"

"Someone who shouldn't have been!" I said. "Antony has violated every rule of protocol and had Octavian's messenger whipped!"

Even Olympos looked shocked. "No!" Then, "What did he do to deserve it?"

"Nothing," I said. "Nothing, but . . . be young and on the stronger side, and carry himself accordingly." That was the truth of it.

"Ah." Olympos shook his head. "It is most unlike Antony. These are dark days for him." Then he said briskly, "I'll make it up right away. I think for raw skin like that, a compound of roasted natron, vinegar, honey, and bile . . ."

While he was gone, I busied myself composing some nonsense of a note for Thyrsus to take to Octavian, something I could sign with my royal seal. It did not matter what it said, as long as it promised nothing, but gave him something to open.

"Most noble Oct—" No, not that name . . . "Young Caesar, I long to lay all my treasure at your feet in exchange for your solemn promise that you will confirm my son on the throne of Egypt. . . ." Nothing new, but it was words.

———

Holding the precious jar of ointment in my hands and hidden under the shadow of a voluminous hooded mantle, I passed silently down into the military quarters adjoining the palace, where Thyrsus was being held.

He was slumped on a bench, his thick hair matted with sweat, his head down between his knees. In the torchlight I could see the welts on his back, red ruts like miniature cart tracks. Little scraps of skin were torn and hanging on each side. He was groaning and shivering—no longer the proud young envoy.

I stood before him and pulled back my hood. His eyes had traveled up from the sandals that were no soldier's, all the way to my face, and his shock at seeing me was evident. But he did not rise; perhaps he felt that all rules had gone by the board now.

"I cannot erase the stripes from your back," I said, "although I wish I had that power. But I can give you this—to help heal them." If only it had the power to make them disappear, so Octavian wouldn't see them. But that was beyond even Olympos's skill.

Before he could respond, I went behind him and began spreading the ointment on his wounds, touching them as lightly as possible. Still he flinched at it, because they were deep and raw.

How many were there? I counted some eight or so—how many would there have been if I had not stopped it?

"We must ask your pardon," I said quietly.

Now at last he spoke. "A queen ask pardon of a freedman?" He was boiling angry.

"When the freedman has been wronged, yes," I said. "This should not have happened. If it lies within your gift, please sponge it from your memory. Not everyone has the greatness of mind to do so, however, and I cannot expect it." I continued smoothing the ointment on his back. He *had* been cruelly treated. "We do not deserve it."

Those last words seemed to melt him. He turned his head and said, "*He* does not, but I would forgive you anything." Then he laughed, a very small laugh. "They told me that you are both dangerous to know and able to make the knowing worth the danger." He winced as I touched a deep cut. "Now I see what they meant."

"Who said that?" I must know.

"Almost everyone in my camp. And—Octavian himself."

"Tell him, then, that I have taught him the truth of the first part of the sentence, and would be willing to proceed to the second. If . . . well, he can read it in this note I have brought for him."

O Isis! Was I really doing this? Spreading salve on the wounds of a freedman, giving coy hints to my utmost enemy? But I had promised to do anything for Egypt. . . .

"What is in it?" he asked.

"Ah. That is for the eyes of Octav—for the Imperator alone." I paused. "I have brought you a cloak to replace the one ripped from your back. Take it, and when you see it, try to remember not what the soldiers gave you but what I did." I pulled it out of its bag and spread it out across his shoulders. It was of the finest, softest wool of Miletus, and his bleeding back would stain it, but he needed some covering to make the journey and protect him from road dust. I also hoped it would serve as some visible reminder of my secret visit to him. I would not be so obvious as to give him jewels.

83

It was time to take them out and reread them—the letters from Caesar. After my son had read them, we had divided them. He was to take half with him wherever he went, as his talisman and keepsake. I was to keep the rest, to sustain me and perhaps soften Octavian's revenge by reminding him of the esteem in which his "father" had held me.

I made sure I was alone, and unlikely to be disturbed. In a way I dreaded opening them and reading them, because words written by the departed take on entirely different meanings. They seem to whisper secret messages or exhortations that the living person might not have meant. I knew that, in my present circumstances, the words of Caesar would loom portentously.

I sought my most padded and luxurious couch before placing the small box to one side of me and opening the lid. Inside lay the letters—so few, really. Caesar had had so much official correspondence, not to mention his war reports, that he could spare little time for personal letters. And he had been cautious about committing much in writing. I remembered how eagerly I had awaited his letters after he first left Egypt, how deserted and bereft I had felt. And then the first one—I opened it slowly—had been so impersonal.

The paper was brittle now and little flakes fell off when I spread it out. The ink was faded; it was almost twenty years since it had been written. The smell of time rose from the surface.

> Greetings to the most exalted Majesty Queen Cleopatra. I am pleased to receive news of your son's birth. May he live and prosper and have a reign of blessed memory. May his name be great in the annals of your history.
>
> I find myself beset with problems here in Rome to be taken in hand. I allow myself only a few days in order to do so, for I am bound to set sail for Carthage to carry on the last battle against the rebel forces of Pompey. They have gathered in North Africa and I must pursue them.

When all is done, I will send for you, and I pray your duties in Egypt
will permit you to leave for a little while and come to Rome.
                                    Your—Gaius Julius Caesar.

That was all. But yes, the words did mean something different now. In order for my son to have a "name great in the annals of history" he would have to survive Octavian, which I was now bending all efforts to assure.

And the problems with which Caesar was beset in Rome—they were never solved, and caused his death. He was always hedged about with crises, as I was now. Even the greatest can be brought down by them, no matter how clever or how hard he struggles. There is not always a triumphant ending for the bravest. How could I succeed where Caesar had failed?

And the invitation to Rome—"leave for a little while and come to Rome." Soon Octavian would issue an similar invitation, but it was one I would not accept.

I put it aside and opened another.

To the most Divine and Mighty Queen of Egypt, Cleopatra, Greetings:
    The war is finished, and I have been victorious. It was a difficult campaign. I cannot say veni, vidi, vici—*I came, I saw, I conquered—this time. I would have to say, I came, I saw, I waited, I planned, I overcame—the opposite of succinct, both the statement and the war. But it is the final outcome, the* vici, *that matters.*

Now that also meant something beyond what he had written in that time and place. The final outcome was all that mattered. In this hour of last reckoning, he was reminding me of that.

But even when you win, final victory may not be yours. Caesar had won all those land battles, only to yield up his life at the hands of his own countrymen. And then, later, others of his countrymen had elevated him to godhood. First victory, then defeat, then greater victory . . . the wheel keeps turning, and we cannot always live to see where it will finally come to rest.

Caesar, you have gone before me, I spoke silently to him. I will try to follow as best I can, unconquered to the last. And as you have shown, there is a way to triumph beyond the immediate circumstances of one's death. Even the death itself can be used to further one's life.

But we have to go into it unknowing the final accounting. . . .

I returned the letters to the box, on top of the few others still there. Perhaps I would read them later. I rested my hand on them, drawing strength just from their stubborn physical survival. Those private little works of his hand had not been destroyed in the great funeral pyre. What remains behind to testify for us can be surprising.

"Madam." There was a gentle knock, and the sound of Charmian's voice.

I had thought to be undisturbed. But I had finished with the reading. "Yes?"

"It is Epaphroditus, madam. Shall I admit him?"

"Let him enter."

Back I must come to the particulars of life.

Epaphroditus swept in, two pouches under his arms. "Your Majesty." He bowed quickly, to get it over with. "I have here the inventories you asked me to make, along with the treasury figures." He held up one pouch.

I needed to know exactly what we would be handing over to Octavian—or trying to save. "Thank you." I reached in for the papers, but I could feel how thick they were. "Summarize them for me," I said. I swung my legs down from the couch and indicated seats for us at the work table. I placed the pouch there and withdrew its contents.

He unrolled one scroll and said, "Here are the final tallies." He stabbed a finger at a column of figures. "I regret to say that Egypt's finances are very healthy. We have had the best harvest in years, with this year's Nile rise promising to repeat the bounty. The losses of Actium have been recouped, and even the destruction of the fleet en route to the Red Sea has been covered."

"I regret it, too. I wish Octavian would stumble upon empty granaries and a depleted treasury." I looked at him. "You have done well, old friend. You have served me faithfully, against your own inclination, all these years. After today you must resign and lose yourself among your people again. Be nowhere near the palace when the end comes. Leave your reports here, and take my thanks as your farewell."

He looked deeply unhappy. "It seems an ungrateful thing to do."

"Not if I command it," I said. "I want as few to perish with this doomed regime as possible. In that way we triumph over the Romans. There is only one thing more: I would like a falsified report that I can submit to Octavian that leaves out portions of the wealth. I will hide some assets so that they may be available later to my children. I think"—I looked at the rows of figures—"there will be enough left to satisfy Octavian. He will not suspect the missing portions."

Epaphroditus reached out and covered my hand with one of his. "I cannot bear to hear you talk that way. So resigned to the worst. So *accepting* that it is all over."

"We must hope for the best, while preparing for the worst. I never forget, not even for an instant, that if Octavian were to die in battle—and it does not have to be a big battle, for arrows fly equally fast in a minor skirmish—everything would change in that moment. Rome would be leaderless. Antony would suddenly be the man of the hour. All these preparations would be a mockery. But . . ." I knew it *could* happen, but I could not rely on it.

"I have brought something else, which I will leave with you," he said, putting the second pouch down. "Some writings from my people which you have professed to find comforting."

"So they have writings covering even this situation?" I said with a slight laugh. "You come from a remarkable people."

"I have marked out the passages I think will speak to you," he said.

"Thank you, dear friend." I stood up and took his hands. I wondered if I would ever see him again. This long, slow withdrawal of the tide was painful. More and more of the shore was left behind, forcibly abandoned.

In the late afternoon I opened his second pouch, curious to see what it was he had collected for me. Koheleth, or Ecclesiastes, it was called. It looked like verses of poetry, and certain passages had been selected for my attention. Nonetheless I began at the beginning, for it told a story.

> I the Preacher was King over Israel in Jerusalem. And I gave
> my heart to seek and search out by wisdom concerning all
> things that are done under heaven. . . .

The writer had pursued knowledge, riches, pleasures, and great works, and found them all wanting, all vanities.

> Better is the end of a thing than the beginning thereof:
> and the patient in spirit is better than the proud in spirit.

> I returned, and saw under the sun, that the race is not
> to the swift, nor the battle to the strong, neither yet bread
> to the wise, nor yet riches to men of understanding, nor
> yet favor to men of skill; but time and chance happeneth
> to them all.

> For man also knoweth not his time: as the fishes that
> are taken in an evil net, and as the birds that are caught
> in the snare: so are the sons of men snared in an evil time,
> when it falleth suddenly upon them.

Like Caesar in the Senate, like us waiting now in Alexandria. *Time and chance happeneth to them all.*

Yet what could I do besides wait, and arm myself?

The late afternoon sun was slanting in the windows, making long diagonal bars of light in the air. I suddenly felt very alone, manning the ramparts by myself. Caesar dead, Caesarion gone, my supporters sent away to safety, Antony to fight no more. And here I stood, peering out over the walls and bracing myself for the assault.

> Remember now thy Creator in the days of thy youth,
> while the evil days come not, nor the years draw nigh,
> when thou shalt say, I have no pleasure in them;

> While the sun, or the light, or the moon, or the stars, be
> not darkened, nor the clouds return after the rain:

> In the day when the keepers of the house shall tremble,
> and the strong men shall bow themselves, and the grinders

cease because they are few, and those that look out
the windows be darkened,

And the doors shall be shut in the streets, when the
sound of the grinding is low, and all the daughters of
music shall be brought low;

Also when they shall be afraid of that which is high, and
fears shall be in the way, and desire shall fail: because
man goeth to his long home, and the mourners go about
in the streets.

Or ever the silver cord be loosed, or the golden bowl be
broken, or the pitcher be broken at the fountain, or the
wheel broken at the cistern.

Then shall the dust return to the earth as it was: and the
spirit shall return unto God who gave it.

Vanity of vanities, saith the Preacher. All is vanity.

The end of the day. The sun sloping down, Octavian on his way. With the luxury of privacy, I wept for all that the sun was setting on.

Better is the end of a thing than the beginning thereof. No, never. The Preacher was wrong.

Antony found me sitting alone in the room, grown quite dark now. The sun had sunk, the purple twilight had come and gone, and now night enveloped me.

"What's this?" he cried. "No lamps? What's the matter?" He rushed off to light one and bring it. He waved it in front of my face.

"Are you all right?" He looked anxiously into my eyes.

"Yes," I said. "I was just sitting here and—thinking."

"Deep thoughts, that kept you from lighting a lamp."

"It was peaceful." And it had been. Acceptance always brings peace—after the first wild mourning.

"What's this?" He reached out and took the scroll, unrolled around me like a long ribbon.

"Something Ephaphroditus brought, along with his reports."

"Hmm." Antony lit more lamps, until the chamber was bright. Then he held up the scroll and started reading. "Poetry in one hand, figures in the other. Strange man, Epaphroditus." His eyes scanned the verses rapidly. "Whoever wrote this was in a bad way," he said, shaking his head. "Poor devil."

The poor devil is us, I wanted to say. Don't you recognize us there?

"Hmm. Hmm. Well, he's right about *this*," said Antony.

"About what?"

"Listen to this. The poet says,

"Go thy way, eat thy bread with joy, and drink thy wine
with a merry heart; for God now accepteth thy works.

"Let thy garments be always white; and let thy head lack
no ointment.

"Live joyfully with the wife whom thou lovest all the days
of thy life, which he hath given thee under the sun:
for that is thy portion in this life, and in thy labor which
thou takest under the sun.

"Whatsoever thy hand findeth to do, do it with thy might.

"He speaks true in that. It's all we can do." He had found those happy verses in the writing, while I had overlooked them. How like him. He put the scroll down and reached out for my hands, pulling me up to my feet, holding me against him. He fell silent, just letting us lean together.

There were two of us on the ramparts after all, one to arm, the other to comfort, taking turns. That was the depth and surety of love, a love that does not desert.

"Now, my dearest, I think we need a little wine—as the Preacher recommends," he finally said, leaving me to locate a pitcher and cups.

"For a merry heart?" I asked.

"Indeed so," he said, flourishing the cups.

Antony: always able to seize joy across the ordinary, across suffering. That was his magic, still undimmed.

"A messenger from Octavian, madam," said Mardian, peering around the ivory screen into my work chamber. He said it so matter-of-factly that no one would have suspected we had been waiting anxiously for news, any news, of his whereabouts.

I rose. "Just arrived?"

"The travel dust is still on his cloak," Mardian said.

The young soldier was indeed dirty from his journey, but I noted that he was a military tribune, not a common foot soldier. Evidently Octavian had decided to send an envoy of higher grade than the previous one.

"We welcome you," I told him. "What has Octavian to say to us?"

He stood straight and tried not to look as if he was observing everything to report back. "Madam, Imperator Caesar wishes to inform you that he is approaching the very border of Egypt. He rests now at Raphia."

"Ah yes, Raphia. An important landmark. It was at the battle of Raphia long ago that Ptolemy the Fourth first employed native Egyptian soldiers to defeat his enemy from Syria. A turning point." I looked at the young man. "And I suppose Octavian hopes it will prove so again."

"It would be a great blessing to us all if it was," he said. "My commander asks that you send word to Pelusium to surrender."

"And why does he think I would?"

"Because, he says, you have made him an offer based on no bloodshed."

"But he has not replied to my offer, and therefore I assume he does not wish to accept it." No word from him meant no agreement. And after the treatment of Thyrsus, what else could he do?

"Quite the contrary. But the only way to show *your* good faith is to let us pass unhindered through Pelusium."

I laughed. "His discourtesy in not replying has made that impossible. It has aroused certain . . . suspicions of his intentions. Now I cannot trust him." As if I ever could!

"It is the other way around. You must demonstrate that your offer was made in good faith, and that you wish absolutely to avoid bloodshed, even at some sacrifice to yourself."

"Young man, are you aware of what my offer to him *was*?"

"No, he has not told anyone."

"I thought not." I decided not to reveal it, either. Then it was only between the two of us. "He has sent no instructions about it, nor any message for me?"

"He sent you this," he said, opening a leather pouch and producing a small box.

I opened it and found two things inside: a coin that had both a sibyl and a sphinx on it, and a jasper seal with a sphinx. "If he means to be baffling, he has succeeded," I finally said. I took out the seal and turned it around between my fingers, examining it.

"He said to tell you that the coin dates from Caesar's time, while the seal is his own. He gives you a riddle to solve, as the sphinx—which is yours in Egypt as well as his, as his personal emblem—gave riddles. He says, 'There is room in the mystery for two.'"

I could not imagine what he meant. That we both could share in Caesar's legacy? That there had been prophecies about us in the Sibylline books? That he was coming to take the Egyptian sphinx, which he regarded as his symbol? That only two out of the three of us—he, Antony, and I—could survive? That there was room in the mausoleum—the mystery of death—for two of us? Or that two could share the treasure heaped up in it?

"And what am I to do with these?" I held out my hand with the coin and seal.

"If you have any message for him, at any time, affix the sphinx seal, and he will act on it immediately." I could tell that the soldier knew nothing more than that.

"Well, I have no message for him now, other than one you can convey in person: I can make no concessions without a formal request and agreement between us, and I still intend to destroy the treasure. That is all."

"What treasure?" So Octavian had not told him even about that.

"He knows what I mean." I smiled. "Tell him I applaud his murkiness, and I will attempt to fathom the riddle at my leisure."

"So . . . we are to proceed to Pelusium?" He looked disappointed; clearly they hoped that we would just capitulate.

"As best you can," I said. "And we shall defend it, as best we can."

We gathered together to have a family meal in the dining chamber of Antony's quarters. All the children, even the youngest, were to partake. Everything was still and frighteningly normal. There was no exodus out of the city, because where could people go? Alexandrians had always been apart from Egypt, and her citizens were not likely to find the flat farm fields of the Delta compatible, or live in tents in the desert. If they sailed away, there was no beckoning destination. And so things continued in their daily fashion.

Young Antyllus had requested a Roman dish he was homesick for: stuffed cuttlefish and baked gladiolus bulbs. He had apologized, saying he realized it was homely fare, but he missed it. I told him I would have the dock warehouses searched for those bulbs, but if we had none, then onions would have to be substituted. But I had managed to find some. You can find anything in Alexandria.

Alexander and Selene had sophisticated tastes, which was not surprising, as they had grown up in the most sophisticated court in the world. They asked for such things as gilded prawns and squill patties, and specified that they did not want any olive oil from a second pressing.

"Snobs," said Antony. "To think my children are snobs."

"I'm not," said Antyllus.

"I know," his father said. "That's because you didn't come here until your tastes were formed."

"Neither did you," I reminded him. "But you converted quickly enough."

"No, merely broadened my tastes. I still like plain fare well enough." He stretched himself out on the dining couch and rested on one elbow. "It pleases me to have you all gathered around me," he said. "What more could any man want? Three fine sons, a beautiful daughter, and an indescribable wife." He raised his goblet and drank solemnly to us all. "I am satisfied with my epitaph."

"Let us not talk of epitaphs!" I said quickly. "We can never be sure what is to be written of us afterward."

"Nonetheless, I have not done badly," Antony insisted.

"Where's the duck?" asked Philadelphos, little Hedgehog. Ever since he had been taken hunting in the marshes, he had claimed duck as his favorite food, but it was really only the memory of the boats, the water, and the rustling of the reeds that he loved. I noticed he always left most of the duck on his platter. At five, duck was still too greasy for him to digest easily.

"It is coming," I assured him.

I looked around at my brood, keenly missing Caesarion. I prayed all the gods kept him safe. How different my four were from me and my siblings. My children actually seemed to care for one another, and there was not a monster among them. The Ptolemies seemed to produce fiends in each litter, but I had escaped that. There were no Arsinoes here, no Berenices. Perhaps it was the admixture of Roman blood that sidestepped the bad results of generations of inbreeding.

Alexander and Selene . . . I had not received any reply from Media about them, and it was now too late to send them away. They must stay here in Alexandria with me, ready for whatever came. Perhaps it was for the best. They were young and disarming enough that they would be persuasive on their own behalf. When Octavian saw them, he might be moved.

Alexander was a strapping boy, hearty and open; his twin sister was soft-spoken and poised. Both of them possessed the beauty of person that goes far to soften the hearts of enemies.

I would ask for the throne for them, and since they were here, it would be easier to confer the crown on them than on Caesarion, so far away. They would make—I hated to use the words—harmless figureheads for Octavian. He would not be adverse to elevating cooperative children, so I reasoned, even though they were Antony's. They were also of his own Julian family.

"So if it chance that you meet Octavian alone," I told them, "treat him with all courtesy. Be sure to call him . . . Imperator Caesar." It was all I could do not to choke on the words. " 'Octavian' antagonizes him."

"Why?" asked Alexander. "It's his name!"

"Well, it is one of his names. It is the name he had when he was your age. But as he grew older, he acquired others, ones he liked better. Just as you are both 'Alexander' and 'Helios,' so he has four names. Someday you may prefer to call yourself 'Helios.' Then you will understand."

"I don't think so!" he said. "It would make me seem very pompous."

"Some people do not mind being pompous," I said.

"I am pleased that my children aren't among them," said Antony.

"Aren't we cousins to Octavian?" asked Selene.

"Distant," said Antony. "He is Caesar's great-nephew, and I am Caesar's third cousin, once removed. You figure it out!"

"Hmmm." Alexander knitted his brow. I could see him trying to sort it all out in his head. He was quite good at mathematics. "I would need a paper for that," he finally admitted.

"I wish you to indulge me in a fancy," I told them. I held the stem of the agate cup in my right hand. "This was my father's drinking cup," I said. "I remember him filling it, lifting it to his lips. Drink from it with me." I motioned, and a servant filled the vessel. "I think he told me once it had come from Macedon, but I honestly cannot remember. In any case, I always associate it with him, and now I would like to see it in your hands." I sipped from it and then handed it to Alexander.

He dutifully tilted his head back and drank from it, then passed it to Selene. She closed her eyes and lifted the cup daintily.

"Philadelphos, too?" she asked.

"All of you," I said.

My youngest took a big swig from it, then handed it to Antyllus.

What would become of Antyllus? I wondered. Antony had made no provision for him, as if he could not bear to. He trusted that Octavian would carry him back to Rome and preserve him. There was no place to send him, no shore of refuge; Egypt and India were not part of his heritage. Poor Antony, the displaced Roman. My heart ached for him.

"My children, in only a few days Alexandria may be attacked," I told them. "You are to follow the instructions my captain of the Household Guard gives you for your safety. We have prepared hiding places for you in the tunnels beneath the palace. They are stocked with food, lamps, water. When you are given the signal, you must take shelter there. We have no way of knowing what will happen after that." I paused. "Whatever you do, whatever you feel, remember your blood. It is precious, and will be honored even by the enemy. Do not be afraid."

"Aren't we going to fight?" asked Alexander.

"Indeed yes!" Antony said in his old voice. "We have four legions at our service, as well as the formidable Macedonian Household Guard, and the Egyptian soldiers. And our cavalry is well trained. I shall lead them myself."

"Not to mention our fleet," I reminded him. "We still have some survivors from Actium, as well as the new-built ships, at the ready."

"We will draw up the battle lines around the city," said Antony. It was as if, knowing the efforts to be last-ditch and doomed, he was now ready to throw all his might behind them. But he should have gathered his far-flung legions earlier, fortified the Nile, strengthened Pelusium and its garrison of Egyptian soldiers. Too late, the flame of resistance burned brightly in Antony, his heroism flaring now like a funeral pyre.

"Octavian is marching toward Pelusium," I told the children. "He has to traverse the desert highway to do so, a wavering, waterless stretch in these days of high summer."

"Pelusium," said Antony. "I took Pelusium . . . long ago."

"Yes, you are familiar with it," I said.

"When I was a young cavalry officer, and Gabinius had decided to restore your grandfather Auletes to the throne"—he leaned forward, speaking to Alexander and Selene—"for ten thousand talents, he sent me on ahead to take the fortress, while he waited in comfort back in Judaea. I took it by storm . . . yes . . ." He had retreated back far in time, the years rolling off him. His voice changed. "It's a difficult place to capture, but I led a massive assault on it, and it fell. Then, the way having been cleared for them, Gabinius and the King followed. They wanted to kill the Egyptian prisoners of war, but I absolutely refused. They had fought bravely, I said, and should be spared. Oh, were they angry with me!" He took a deep drink of his wine.

"And you became wildly popular with the Egyptians as a result," I said. "They were touched, one and all, by your mercy."

"Yes, it was the beginning of a mutual love affair with Egypt," said Antony.

"From that moment onward, we were as one." He paused dramatically "And then I met your mother," he said to the children, leaning over conspiratorially. "When she was only a little older than you." He touched Selene's chin.

"I cannot imagine her ever that way," she said, with all the ferocious ignorance of the very young.

"Oh, she was, she was," said Antony. "She was young as Persephone, before Pluto grabbed her. As young as the flowers she gathered. And I loved her from the first instant I glimpsed her."

"He embellishes," I assured the children. "His memory gilds the past."

"No, it is true!" averred Antony.

"Ever gallant," I said. Perhaps I was embarrassed because I had not loved him then, or even realized I would ever see him again. It seemed so blind of me—how could I not have known? My only strong memory of him was standing beside him at the Dionysus festival. He had spoken knowledgeably of wine, and had been kind about my father's indulgence. For that I had been grateful.

"Pelusium may hold fast," said Antony. "Octavian may never breach its defenses. But whatever happens, remember that you will be safe," he told the children. "There is etiquette in war, and the children of the high-ranking are always treated courteously. Alexander started that, with the wife and children of Darius. They expected to be murdered or sold into slavery, but he treated them honorably. He even married Darius's daughter."

"Well, I shall never marry Octavian!" said Selene, with a toss of her head.

"I told you they were snobs," said Antony, turning to me, laughing. Then he looked at them. "Listen, my dearests. You must do whatever seems expedient at the time."

I suddenly remembered a verse from Epaphroditus's poetry. "Yes. 'For a living dog is better than a dead lion.' "

Because as long as there is life, the wheel of fortune can turn and elevate you.

The sweetness of the luscious figs and dates in honey custard we ate to finish the meal did little to help our spirits. I watched the children eating, and they all seemed winsome to me; only a monster would think of harming them. But the young of all species are appealing, even baby crocodiles and cobras. Hard-hearted hunters kill them without a thought, condemning them not for what they are, but for what they might become. My heart ached for it. I could only pray that a combination of political hesitation, pragmatism, and family sentiment might stay the hand of Octavian, who was no high-minded Alexander. But he was known to be oddly reverent toward his own relatives—the Roman family was his only real god, in spite of his shrines to Apollo—and these children shared his Julian blood. Since he believed it was sacred and inherently better than any other, he might wish to conserve it.

O Isis, let it be so!

I stood and held out my arms after the last platters had been removed. "Come here, all of you," I said. I wished to embrace them, for us all to embrace one another. The four of them obeyed, and Alexander and Selene hugged my sides, their heads just under my shoulders; Philadelphos encircled my knees, and Antyllus and Antony made an outer protective shell around us all.

Quite unbidden, the thought *Never leave me!* flashed through my mind. But all I said was, "Let all of us always remember one another, and this moment."

"Pelusium has fallen." Antony pushed aside the curtains into the room where I was working and blurted it out.

"No!" I rose. "So quickly!" It had not been more than seven days since our last word that Octavian was on his way from Raphia.

"There was little or no resistance," he said. "It fell so easily that there is suspicion of collusion. The garrison commander, Seleucus . . . was he bought?"

I guessed what he was thinking. *Unreliable, cowardly Egyptian troops!* But it was not so. "What exactly happened?" My heart was racing. Pelusium gone. The way to Alexandria open.

"The invaders were allowed to come close to the walls, and immediately both sides started bargaining. Shameful!" He shook his head. "Pelusium is hard to take, since there is no water anywhere outside the walls. Attackers are at a serious disadvantage, because they arrive already thirsty. The fort has all the advantages. To surrender like that!" He clenched his fists.

I should not have said it, but I did. "If you felt it was so strategic, why did you not invest it with one of your legions? Why did you leave Seleucus to come to the obvious conclusion that you didn't consider them important?"

"I trusted them to hold it themselves!"

"The message you gave was the opposite, that you didn't have any trust in them at all, and had sacrificed them in advance."

"How dare you say that?" he yelled. "And if you thought it, why didn't you speak up then?"

"Because you were sunk in your hopelessness. You had given up, and could not be roused to action."

"I hadn't!" His face grew red.

"What else could forming a club dedicated to dying together signal? Even if you didn't mean it, the rest of the world took you at your word. Everyone heard about it, you can be sure of that. If you were Seleucus, and heard that your commander-in-chief had banded together with friends pledged to die, what would you think?"

"It was just a jest."

"No, it wasn't. Not to those watching you. I am sure Octavian has heard about it as well; doubtless he feels it will make his task easier."

"You should have stopped me!"

"I tried. But you ignored me." I spread my hands. "Enough of this blaming.

What will we do now? He will be here soon—here in Alexandria!" The thought was horrible.

"Talk to the messenger yourself," said Antony sulkily. He called him in, a young Egyptian cavalryman.

He had ridden fast to get here in only a few days, racing across fields and jumping canals in the Delta. The Nile had not started to rise yet, so there were no flooded fields to block him. He had not dared to sail, because Octavian's fleet already controlled the sea between us and Pelusium.

"Your Majesty," he said, falling to one knee and staring at me.

No, not now! I thought irritably. Don't let him gawk because he sees me close-up. "What is your name?" I asked briskly.

"Sennufer, Your Majesty."

"Rise, Sennufer," I said. "A name from Upper Egypt, I see." And he had the sinewy strength and fine bearing of those people. "What exactly did you see at Pelusium?"

"From the walls we saw the host of Romans approaching from the desert road; they were moving surprisingly fast for their second day of a forced, waterless march. They kept their formations well, too. They surrounded the fortress—"

"How many of them were there?"

"Not as many as we had expected. Not more than seven legions."

I turned to Antony. "Then he must have left the rest behind in Syria and Judaea." Hope sprang up inside me. If he had only seven legions, and we had four, plus the Egyptians, then . . .

"Octavian is not nearly as sure of his new-pledged allies as he pretends, then," said Antony.

"We have a chance against him," I said. "Now tell me, how did the troops behave? What happened as they approached the walls . . . ?"

After he was shown out, I felt a giddy sense of hope. Pelusium was gone, but our numbers were more evenly matched than we had realized. And all our forces were concentrated in Alexandria, where we could take a stand, fighting with the advantage of defending our home territory. Antony had finally awakened and would lead as only he could. The men would follow him; he had the inborn ability to inspire his troops. They would cry out in gratitude and relief that their leader had finally come back to himself.

When Octavian came calling, he would get a bloody surprise. And if the gods were truly on our side, he might find himself in his beloved Roman mausoleum sooner than he had anticipated. What a good thing he had readied it before his departure.

HERE ENDS THE NINTH SCROLL.

THE TENTH SCROLL

84

The sea was still. The whole world was holding its breath. Through the streets, deserted at high noon, the wind had failed, leaving the walls of the buildings to radiate blinding light and heat. From my high vantage point on the palace walls, I could see nothing stirring in my whole city. *And the doors shall be shut in the streets. . . .*

I leaned over the ramparts of the tower on the side that faced the harbor; below were the broad marble steps descending into the water, visible as wavering lines below the surface. This was where servants gathered, where children splashed and played, where the little trireme was tied up. But today no one but soldiers were there, deployed around the grounds: my Macedonian Guard, the last bastion an invader would have to dispatch before storming the palace itself.

The stone under my arm was sizzling hot, almost hot enough to burn my flesh. The last day of the month of Julius; already we were in the Egyptian month of Mesore. And still no Octavian.

I pulled back from the edge of the wall, its dazzling light making my eyes ache. Against the whiteness the sea's blue was pure as the soul of an unborn child. Out past the Lighthouse, beyond the breakwaters, the blue was unbroken. No ships on the horizon—yet.

My own fleet was drawn up in the harbor, waiting. As at Actium. There were some hundred battleships, both Egyptian and Roman.

The messages from Octavian had ceased. I had never made use of the sphinx seal, for I had nothing to say to him beyond what had already been said. Evidently he was prepared to call my bluff—if he judged it to be so—

and proceed to Alexandria and take his chances on seizing the treasure before I could destroy it.

The intensity of the light and the radiation of the heat made me dizzy. But I forced myself to stay where I was.

It will be dark and quiet enough in the mausoleum, I reminded myself. *Get your fill of the sun now.*

We had had reports of his progress, of course. Lookouts had galloped to us, reporting, *Now he's at Daphnae . . . now crossing the Necho canal from the Bitter Lakes . . . now at Pithom . . . now at Heliopolis. . . .*

Heliopolis. Once he passed that, and crossed over the Nile proper, then little distance was left between us.

He had seven legions, and Agrippa was not with him. He marched without his right arm, coming to believe in his own superior luck. In a hideous reversal, he marched along the same route Caesar had taken to defend me and save Alexandria. Caesar had proceeded stealthily and caught the enemy off guard, but we were only too well apprised of Octavian's whereabouts.

Then, four days ago, he was sighted at Terenuthis, on the Canopic branch of the Nile, and yesterday at Canopus itself, fifteen miles away.

It had been a fast march. Would he rest his troops before the final push? They would be tired from the unbroken exertion from Raphia onward. And he surely knew that the struggle for Alexandria would be fierce.

We had four Roman legions, with enough Egyptian troops to constitute a fifth, as well as a respectable arm of cavalry. Antony had stationed the Egyptians at strategic places in the city and drawn up the Romans just outside the Gate of the Sun on the east, ready to face Octavian.

Now, at such a late hour, Antony's fighting spirit had returned, as if Mars had been slumbering and belatedly awakened to anoint him with war blood. He had been exercising the troops and readying them ever since Octavian had taken Pelusium.

Something on the horizon . . . ships? I shielded my eyes and looked as hard as I could, but it faded. Perhaps it was only a gull, seen out of the corner of my vision. Toward the other direction, the east, I could not see over the walls of the city from where I stood.

All was in readiness. The children were practiced in what to do, places of refuge for them waited in the depths of the palace, Mardian and Olympos and Charmian and Iras had their final instructions. I had, in my thorough way, tried to provide for everything, down to the last detail. Especially the last detail.

But I believed we still had a reasonable chance, not only of survival but even of victory. Octavian would be fighting with severe disadvantages—tired, unpaid soldiers on unfamiliar ground, with himself as their commander. He was no match for Antony at his best, or for our rested troops fighting for their home city.

I had been holding a bouquet of summer flowers, and they were wilting in the glare. So I pulled the flowers out one by one and dropped them down into the waiting water, seeing them fall through the air and land lightly. Little spots of color floated bravely, making a mosaic of sorts.

Footsteps—heavy ones. Antony bounded around the corner, having taken the steps two at a time in spite of his heavy armor and sword.

"He's here!" he said. "Just sighted, down the road to Canopus. He's rushing, pushing the men at double march. He must mean to get here and pitch camp before sundown."

The plumes on his helmet swayed, and its beak prevented me from seeing his eyes. But his voice sounded young, eager.

"I see nothing," I said.

"The dust cloud should be visible soon," he said. "He is kicking up quite a storm. The cavalry is leading by a mile or so; he's using them as scouts. We'll attack them before they can find a resting place."

"What, now?" It could not be now; it was already afternoon and . . . I had had it so firmly in my mind that the confrontation would be a massive battle.

"Catch him by surprise," said Antony. "Destroy his advance guard." He patted his sword. "Ah, to do a man's work again!" He caressed it like a neglected pet.

"What shall we do here?" I asked. I would have to ready the mausoleum, gather the children. . . . O gods! Was it all to be set in motion now—now, on this cloudless, still day? Deeds set in motion, to slide along of their own accord, unstoppable like the tomb doors on their tracks?

"Pray to all the gods for our success," he said, taking both my hands in his and enclosing them. "They will hear you."

I looked at his sunburnt face, his eyes still invisible under the helmet's shadow. "Kiss me," I suddenly said. It seemed very bad luck for him to venture forth without it.

Quickly he bent and kissed me, his mind already far away. "Farewell, then," he said.

Was this all? I knew it was all it could be, but it seemed a very meager leave-taking. "Farewell," I echoed, seeing him turn and disappear down the steps, a swirl of cloak.

I clung to the sharp edge of marble at the rampart, feeling unable to move, to leave, to begin to do what I must. To set things in motion . . .

Now I could see the smudge on the horizon. The ships were coming. Octavian's fleet was on its way, under oars rather than sail.

So this, my tenth scroll, is to be the last. I have just begun it. And it is fitting. Ten is a number with its own mystique; not as magic, perhaps, as seven or three or twelve, but it will do well enough to contain my life. There are ten fingers, there are ten lunar months in the forming of a child, and ten days in the Egyptian week. Isis at Philae visits Osiris on his island every ten days. And all men revere the number one hundred, which is ten tens.

Along with everything else, provision is made for thee, scroll, and all thy brothers. I will fill thee up until my hand can write no more. And if it chance that all this is silly and premature, why, then there may be twenty scrolls someday, as my life continues to unfold—not stopped on a hot, still day.

The hours crept by. The water clock dripped. The shadowlessness of noon gave way to the slanting pools of darkness that grow out of buildings, stones, trees. And I sat, waiting, alternately writing this and gripping the arms of my chair.

Mardian joined me. It is not true that another person can distract you. Waiting together made it worse. At one point he reached over and took my hand in his. It felt different.

"Why, Mardian," I said, "you have taken off your rings." He was never without them, his emerald and lapis beauties.

"Perhaps it is my own way of going out to battle," he said. "Stripping away all that which cannot help me now, and I'll be cursed if I allow it to help another!"

Mardian had no family, no one to leave it to. And no one to mourn him afterward. I had thought of everything but that, imagining that he would be left behind to oversee things—whatever those things would be. But they would never let him do so, and he would suffer punishment as if he were of my own family.

"Mardian," I finally said, "we have talked of many things, and I foolishly gave you instructions to carry out—afterward. I see now how unthinking that was. Not because you are unreliable, but because I provided a refuge for everyone but you. Forget about the instructions and come with me when I give you the signal."

"Come—where?"

"With me, Charmian, and Iras. We are resolved upon our course of action. I need not describe it; I am sure you know it. What is left unsaid cannot be argued against. You are welcome to join our circle. I am afraid it is the only safe, secure refuge I can offer. The only one that is unanswerable to Octavian."

"I see." His voice was sad. Had he expected that I had come up with some other, miraculous solution? Or surely he had not believed that I had just meekly accepted Olympos's dictates? "It cannot be otherwise." He nodded gravely.

"No," I said. "Olympos does not control all the keys that can unlock the secret house of death. Although he would like to!"

Olympos they would let alone. He would be free to come and go and carry out my mission. If he liked, he could even go to Rome and observe the Triumph! Yes, he would have entire freedom.

"Thank you for your invitation," Mardian said, as if I had invited him to a fine banquet. And, in a way, I had. "If necessary, I will accept. But perhaps it will not be necessary. The city is well prepared, and the troops fairly evenly matched. Lord Antony seemed in his old form, and—"

"Yes. He has come back to himself." But even his old self had lost battles.

———

Dusk had come, a deep, rich purple one—as intense as the noon it followed. The tender violet seemed to well up from the sea itself and spread out over the city. It was a night the Alexandrians would have reveled in, holding dinners and lectures and debates, all flavored with imported sweet wines and delicacies. But in the lengthening evening there was no stirring in the streets.

Servants came in to light the lamps—the few servants remaining. I had dismissed the freedmen and sent them home. Now only slaves and very loyal attendants stayed on. Gone were the hordes of attendants who made the palace a colorful, noisy place. The glow of the lit oil made yellow halos in the chamber.

Then we heard it—a clatter at the gates. We both stood and clasped hands. Whatever it was, the moment had come. I shut my eyes and took deep, long breaths.

More noise, the sound of horses and armed men. I flew to the window and looked down. The flaring torches in their hands showed the riders to be—Romans. But which Romans? They were laughing and flushed, jumping with energy.

Then I saw, bareheaded, Eros. He was wheeling his horse in circles, drawing arcs with his torch.

"Eros!" I cried, and then I saw Antony behind him.

He looked up, and his face was exultant. Without waiting, I grabbed Mardian's hand and together we rushed down the steps and out into the courtyard, into the milling horsemen.

"My Queen!" cried Antony, as we reached him. He leaned over and scooped me up onto the saddle, kissing me all the while. I was suspended in the air while his lips clamped down on mine and barely let me breathe.

"We've done it!" he cried, as he helped me into the saddle in front of him. "We fell on them so quickly they could barely get onto their horses—routed them—killed a hundred or so, and sent the rest scurrying back to Octavian!" He laughed, and kissed me again. "You should have heard them yell! Like scalded cats!"

Canidius had pulled Mardian up onto his horse, and now we smiled at each other, relief flooding us and making us limp. The death instructions receded, seemed an obscene dream.

"Come! A feast! A feast!" Antony cried to his men. "Can that be arranged, my love?"

"The kitchens are as ready as need be," I assured him. We would manage.

"And wine, wine, enough to rejoice us but not impair us for the morrow," he said. "And music—"

"Yes," I said. "Tonight, anything."

Details followed. Of how they had streamed out the gate, galloped down the road some five miles, past the grove of Nemesis where Pompey's memorial was, and found the beginnings of a camp being set up. The trenches had been started and the streets outlined, but nothing else. The men were resting with their horses, and scarcely had time to mount after they saw Antony's forces bearing down on them. They were tired, and had little fighting strength to counter the attack. A number were slain outright, and the rest scattered, disappearing in all directions.

"Some of them even rode out into the sea!" said Antony. "As if they expected Poseidon to rescue them!" His big hands were curled around a gold drinking cup, and he swallowed a draught of wine. "Ah. And here is the bravest soldier of all—my lieutenant Aulus Celsus. He rode right into their midst, wreaking havoc, endangering his own person."

I looked up to see a burly young man still wearing his armor—stained leather cuirass and battered helmet tucked under his arm. Antony had swept everyone in for the feast dressed as they were.

Celsus bowed stiffly. "It was my pleasure and duty."

"He is too modest," said Antony. "The truth is, he was the very hand of Mars. I would be content—no, proud—if any of my sons made such a soldier."

"It seems you are in need of better fighting gear," I said. "We will make your reward useful as well as profitable." I nodded to one of my attendants. "The gold armor that was old Polemo's—it shall be yours." The storehouse of military treasure was not heaped in the mausoleum, as weapons and armor do not pile tightly.

"Oh no, I could not—" He started to demur, but Antony stopped him.

"And I say you shall," he insisted. Then, after Celsus had taken his leave, Antony whispered to me, "That was as profligate as me."

I did not care. Riches meant little at the moment; they had become just more items to be disposed of. I shrugged.

The noise in the room was rising, aided by the wine and the soaring relief. It was almost like days gone by—but the tension was still there. The men were eating heartily and drinking deeply, but not to lose themselves. At length Antony rose from his couch and held up his hands for silence. It fell quickly—too quickly, showing it had been lurking all the while.

"My friends," he said, "for your bravery today, I commend you. For our fighting tomorrow, I exhort you to slack not! For tomorrow . . . tomorrow we shall meet the foe in our full force, and his. Not just a vanguard, but the whole army. All our fortunes ride on this battle."

The men all stood attentively, but their faces were blank. I could not guess their feelings.

"I challenged Octavian to single combat," he suddenly said. "Yes! I invited him to meet me, man to man, sword in hand."

I had not thought it was possible for them to become stiller and more blank-faced, but they did. The roomful of soldiers stared at him, not even moving their eyes.

"And he refused. But rather than refuse outright, he said flippantly, 'If he wishes to die, there are many other ways open to him.' How clever. How cutting. But you see, he was right. I have thought much on it." He held out his cup for it to be refilled. A servant came forward, and Antony waited for him to finish pouring before he resumed his words. "And I have concluded that tomorrow I shall seek either to live or to die in honor. To defeat the enemy would be honor, and to die in battle would be equal honor. Either way, I conquer." Now he took a long, deliberate sip of the wine. "So drink with me, and pour the wine freely in my cups, for tomorrow you may serve a new master, and I lie dead."

Now at last they stirred, and words poured forth like the wine.

"No, sir, you cannot—"

"Never, I will die with you—"

"Why go into battle, then?"

The page pouring the wine had clasped his arm and begun crying.

"Nay, stop," Antony said. "I did not mean to make you weep. Nor do I mean to lead you into a battle where I do not expect victory. I only meant that, should the gods see otherwise, they cannot bereave me of my honor, even though I fall."

His words were disheartening them. For a commander to speak so matter-of-factly of his death was hardly inspiring. Some of the younger ones were shiny-eyed, and the more seasoned ones were shifting on their feet.

"Just fight as you fought today, and tomorrow we will gather in this same hall, to feast and shout until the fretted ceiling overhead shakes as with an earthquake!" I cried. "The wind sits fair for victory!" I stepped forward. "I have spoken to the gods. Isis will not desert, no, she will protect us! And Hercules, your ancestor"—I took Antony's hand and held it aloft—"will wield the club for us." I looked around at the men. "Do not your officers wear the ring engraved with the likeness of Hercules?" I knew Antony gave such rings to his men. "He will strengthen your arms!"

Antony's staunch followers now crowded around him to assure him of their devotion. The musicians struck up again. The wine flowed. Outside, the streets were still deserted.

Waiting in the chamber. All dark except for one lamp. Charmian has removed my gown, folding it and storing it as she has a hundred—a thousand—times. My sleeping garments slide over my head, as if I truly plan to sleep. I hold my metal mirror up to my face, and in the dim light I see only wide eyes, devoid now of the kohl lining them, the powdered malachite on the lids. Just ordinary eyes, not even weary or lined. Nothing shows in them, neither joy nor fear. Only a slight curiosity.

Yes, I am curious. It has been reduced to that, now. The unanswered questions will surely be answered tomorrow.

Antony is here . . . I must stop.

He stepped into the room, bringing light with him.

"What? So dark?" he said, taking his lamp and using it to light the others, including the many-branched one standing in the corner. While he did so, I left the writing desk and stole over to the bed, then climbed on and covered myself.

I watched him as he moved about the room. Still so unbowed, so full of strength.

"Ah. Time to rest," he said, turning to strip himself of his armor and tunic. He did it himself in easy movements, not wanting to call Eros. "In only a few hours I will put you on again," he said to the garments. He laid his sword and dagger on top of the pile.

"Leave those things," I told him, holding out my arms to him.

He came to me as he had, also, a hundred, a thousand times, and embraced me. Everything we were doing was only a repeat of a thousand prior actions— undressing, holding each other, lying down. Nothing singular in anything. The very ordinariness of it was lulling.

"You have spoken to the children?" Only in that did I betray the difference between tonight and any other.

"Yes. Just now. It was hard."

Tomorrow they would leave their quarters and go into the special rooms prepared for them. "For them as well," I said.

"I think to them it is something of a game," he said. "Children love secret passages, locks, hiding."

I held him against me. "Why did you light all those lamps when we must try to sleep?" I asked him. I did not want to have to get up and extinguish them. He pulled back a little. "Because I wanted to look at you." He did not say *one last time*.

I was touched. "Then look," I said quietly.

He studied my face as intently as if he were inspecting a text. "For years this has filled my vision," he said. "It has been all I have seen."

I could not help smiling. "Then all of Octavian's rantings are true," I said. "The Triumvir had no eyes for anything but the Queen, his world had shrunk to her bedroom—"

"No, that is twisting it. I only meant that you have filled my world, but not obscured it. If anything, you have enhanced it, clarified my vision."

He did not need to say all the things he had done for me, in my name. Now the reckoning was at hand. He stopped looking, closed his eyes, bent forward, and kissed me.

We embraced for a long time, a lingering clasp. Beyond passion. Finally, lying quietly side by side, I had to say it.

"Tomorrow, when you leave, I will ready myself to go to the mausoleum. Charmian, Iras, and Mardian will be with me. But we will wait to shut ourselves in until we have word of what has happened. Should it be Octavian who rides up to the palace, he will never take us alive. Nor lay his hand on the treasure. But there can be no mistake. You and I must have a clear signal for what has happened. If I do not hear the trumpet sound two notes, and you cry, 'Anubis!' I will flee to the monument and there proceed to the rest."

"Why 'Anubis'?"

"Because anything else—my name, or your name, or 'Isis!' or 'Victory!'— could be shouted by anyone. But no one will think to shout 'Anubis.' That way there can be no mistake."

"Then we are resolved that unless Octavian is beaten, we will die?"

I hated that word, die. "If he is not beaten, we will die anyway, only the time and place will be of his choosing."

Antony bent his head. "Yes."

"Let us talk no more about it," I said.

"Strange how many times I have made final arrangements," he said. "In Parthia, at Paraetonium . . . then my friends refused to let me, and now you, my wife, urge it."

It struck me to the quick that he would see me as a minister of death, more unfeeling than Eros or Lucilius. "It was not the time then," was all I could say. "To do things prematurely angers the gods, but to delay at the proper time thwarts their will for us." I kissed the side of his face, the very borders of his hair, where it curled over his forehead, his ears. "I would keep you forever," I whispered. "And I will, but not here. We will have to continue in Elysium."

Did I really believe in it? Were there Elysian fields, meadows with butterflies and wildflowers waiting for us? I wanted to believe it. I want to, now. Now . . .

"Can we not die together?" he said plaintively. "To die apart is the cruelest blow."

"There is no way," I said stoutly. "For I would stop you, and you stop me. Neither of us could let the other go first, and stand by. While we delayed, Octavian would come upon us. No, this is the only way." Yet I held him tighter, as if that would prevent it.

I could not go into battle with him; I had to stand to the last in my city. He could not shirk the task of leading his army. At dawn we would part, and each meet the death fashioned for him. It would be foolish for me to be slain on horseback, pitiful for him to hide in the mausoleum and take my method of death, since it was uniquely royal and Pharaonic. He must die as a Roman, I as an Egyptian.

"If you would keep me," I said, "then fight tomorrow as you have never fought before. Think you not that at this very moment Octavian is also making death preparations? It may be he who lies low tomorrow, not even attaining the age of Alexander. It lies in your power!"

"Whatever lies in my bodily power, you can rely on me to perform," he said. "But the gods—"

Damn the gods! came the impious thought. We will defy them!

Antony closed his eyes and lay still, his arm draped over one of my shoulders, the hand dangling. In the dim light I could see all the fingers curled the way they are at rest, a graceful half-circle. His breathing was not as deep as true sleep, but he was drowsing lightly.

As I lay there I heard faint strains of music. Was someone in the silent city awake and celebrating? The pall of unnatural quiet, so un-Alexandrian, had persisted until now.

As I listened, I heard it again, more distinctly now. There were pipes and tambourines. It sounded like a distant procession. But who would parade through the streets tonight?

I slipped out from under Antony's arm and stole across the cool marble floor to the window. The friendly lamplight in the room masked the deep night outside. I could see nothing. The city lay still and waiting in all directions; few torches were burning anywhere, and only the whiteness of the stone served to light the whole.

The sea shone back, reflecting the starlight and empty sky, and I could see Octavian's fleet, hovering just beyond the breakwaters. From the east, was it my imagination that the sky was faintly red from the enemy campfires?

The music, again. Louder now, distinct, coming from just outside the palace, just at the Canopic Way. A huge company of revelers, singing, crying out, playing the pipes, the drums, the cymbals. At any moment they would emerge on the other side, going eastward, and I would see them.

The sound rose, swelling as if it were directly underground, passing under the palace itself, a noisy company, an enormous band. . . . But even though the sound passed by, and now was on the other side of the Canopic Way, I still could see nothing. I opened the doors of the terrace and stepped out, straining to see down the wide marble street, which was . . . empty. Yet filled with sound, a sound suddenly, horribly, familiar. I had heard it before, heard it the night my father died.

It was Dionysus, Dionysus accompanied by his band of bacchantes, his worshipers, leaving us. Leaving Antony!

The noise was growing fainter now, and it was passing out of the city gate, out of the Gate of Canopus, toward the east.

Antony's god had deserted him, as he had deserted my father.

It was unmistakable, a deadly, ugly leave-taking.

My heart was pounding, and I clung to the rail. Without his god, without Dionysus, he was lost.

That coward of a god! I hated him. What good is a god who deserts you in your last hour? He does not deserve to be a god, he is lower than Plancus, than Titius, than Dellius!

O, would that the house of Ptolemy had never trafficked with Dionysus!

Had Antony heard it? I rushed back to the bed and climbed in. He seemed to be still asleep. That was merciful. I lay down beside him and watched as the room slowly grew light.

But you, Isis, will never desert your daughter. You are the supreme goddess, able to deliver. I must trust in you. Even now. Especially now.

85

He came awake easily—if he had ever been asleep. It was still almost dark in the room, but this day—this day that would go on forever, end forever—must start well before the sun.

He swung his feet down over the bed and shook his head. "I had strange dreams—such dreams as it were better I had stayed awake. I dreamed . . . odd music. . . ." He shook his head as if to clear it.

"Think no more on it," I said briskly.

He was eyeing his clothes, and he clapped for Eros, who appeared in only a moment. He must have been sleeping just outside the door—or rather, staying. For it was doubtful any of us had slept.

Had Eros heard it, the leave-taking? I could not ask, but from his white, drained face, I guessed that he had.

Holding the bowl of heated water, Eros let Antony splash his own face and neck. Then, very gently, he wiped the water away from his master's face.

The clothes went back on: the undertunic of red wool, the heavy cuirass, the scarf to protect the sunburnt neck, the high-strapped sandals. He fastened the sword on his right side, tucked the dagger in its proper place on his left. The hot helmet would not be put on until he actually rode forth.

Light had stolen bit by bit into the chamber, and now I drew back the curtains to admit the day. Outside the sea was gleaming, the two fleets riding on its bosom, facing each other.

He stood there and we looked at one another across the expanse of floor. Eros slipped out, disappearing into an adjoining chamber.

Antony looked like a statue of Mars, standing motionless in his armor. The proud head, head that had carried my heart with it through many toils and dangers, stared mournfully at me. I could not bear that look in his eyes, a look that said, *Farewell, farewell, now all unwilling we must part.*

I flew into his arms and held him, pressing my face up against the hard metal of his armor. Already he was beyond me, encased.

Then I felt him pulling on my hair, drawing my head back to kiss me. I lifted my face to meet his and receive the kiss.

"Good-bye, my love," was all I could say.

I knew I would never see him again.

Quickly he turned and left the chamber, clutching his helmet, without a backward glance.

And so it was over. Is over. I wait now, midmorning, for the news I do not want to receive. After he left, I dressed myself, called the children, hugged and played with them. Mardian is here, and the others. Olympos came. I showed him the scrolls, where I had stored them. He promised. Then he kissed my cheek and left, to hide in his house until the danger had passed. I told him there would be just this one scroll to add to the rest; I would have that with me, wherever I was. He seemed to accept it; at least he asked no questions.

One by one they leave. I am stripped bare like an athlete before a contest.

Mardian touches my shoulder. "What is their battle plan?" he asks.

"Publicola will command the ships," I say. "Antony will lead the cavalry, Canidius the infantry. This time there is no question of the enemy refusing to give battle. They have been encamped only a few hours; they have not had time to dig in well enough to resist an attack." No second Actium.

He shakes his head. "And we shall know . . . how?"

"By the sound of the returning soldiers. If the day is ours, the shout will be 'Anubis!' "

"How fitting," he says.

High noon, but not as hot as yesterday. The slight breeze cools us. I am again on the ramparts, and I see the motionless fleets, still drawn up in battle lines. Why does no one move? What are they waiting for?

Clutching the marble edge, I see at last the oars flash, see them plunge down into the water, rise, shoot the ships forward. Our fleet is on its way out of the harbor, heading toward the breakwater, to confront Octavian's.

The enemy ships now move a little, drawing back. They will lie in wait like a panther, let us come to them.

Now . . . now we are close enough to start firing stones and fireballs at them. Why don't we? Fire! Loose a volley on them!

But they stream on, harmlessly. Instead . . . I cannot believe my own eyes . . . they turn themselves broadside and salute Octavian's ships! They raise their oars to signal nonaggression. And now . . . a shout of camaraderie!

Caps fly through the air . . . rejoicing . . . reunion! The two fleets join in brotherhood. Our navy, the survivors of Actium, and the new-built ships, have joined the enemy.

That was several hours ago. I knew then that the day was lost. Dionysus had laid us low. Calmly (for what was there to be wild about? it was over), I ordered the children to their hiding place, took my mantle and this scroll, and walked slowly to the mausoleum. Its wide doors were open, bidding me welcome.

Following behind us were two slaves carrying a trunk, in which my royal robes and crown and scepter were laid. This crown was finer than the one I had sent Octavian, as he would doubtless note when he beheld it. Another slave walked behind the trunk, carrying a large basket with a tightly fitting lid. Now these had been deposited on the floor of the monument, and the slaves departed.

There is no natural light here except what enters from the second story. And yet I hesitated, unwilling to proceed, in case I heard the miraculous word *Anubis*. The story of the army was yet to tell, regardless of what happened at sea.

In the quiet heat of noon I made my way to the adjoining Temple of Isis in order to offer final prayers. It was a formality only, as I had no words left to use. I stood before the milky-white statue of the goddess and silently pleaded with her to soften Octavian's heart and spare my children and Egypt. Look on them with mercy, I asked. Impart some of that mercy to him.

Outside the sea was washing against the base of the temple. The harbor was filling with returning ships. Not much time left.

I descended from the high platform of the temple and returned to the monument. I could hear shouts now, a din of riders. Something had happened beyond the city wall. Something decisive.

I cried to one of the passing servant boys to run out into the Canopic Way and tell me what he saw. He obeyed and sprinted away.

There was noise, lots of noise, but no trumpet blasts of victory. Just cries and screams, and the thudding of hooves and tramping of feet.

I stood in the door of the mausoleum. I would not move until I knew; it would not be much longer now. . . .

The boy came running, his long tunic streaming out behind him. He skidded to a stop beside me and stood panting. "It's . . ." He gasped for breath. "The legions are defeated, and the cavalry deserted to Octavian." He bent over in pain from a cramp in his side.

"The legions fought? And were beaten?"

He nodded, still doubled over.

"And Lord Antony—he led them? Is he—did he—?"

He shook his head. "I know not."

"Has he entered the city?"

"I know not. I think not. There seemed to be no officers, only common foot soldiers in the returning men." His breath was still harsh.

So Antony had perished on the battlefield. It was as he had wanted it.

"Thank you," I told the boy. I wanted to reward him, but had nothing but my jewelry. I took off the pearl earrings and put them in his hand.

Before I could move at all, I shut my eyes to stop the fierce wheeling of the ground all around me. So this is what is feels like, this is how you are told. Not even the solemn, final words that impart some dignity. Instead, a guess, a surmise, a confusion.

Is he? Did he? I know not. I think not.

O Antony, you deserve a higher announcement than that, and I deserve to know for a certainty. Else how can I have the courage I need in this hour?

Lying dead on a field? Would he be recognized? Yes, of course, from his marks of rank. But he would be tended by enemies. Oh, it was too much to be borne.

And now he lay far from me. I was stunned, as stunned as if we had not prepared, had not expected it. Now the cruelty of it robbed me of speech and movement. I stood unmoving, rooted, while all around me people were running, panic-stricken.

The mausoleum. I had to get back inside it. To safety. To Mardian and

Iras and Charmian. I forced myself to turn, leave the sunlit grounds, and reenter the tomb.

I ordered the inner doors closed. They are not the permanent ones, for those can be sealed only once, and we have funerals to conduct first. But they are strong enough, locked in all the conventional ways, fitted with iron bands and oak bolts. An enemy would need a battering ram to enter.

Here we have huddled for hours, waiting to know for an absolute certainty what has happened. My right to know must be satisfied, I tell myself; it is only that, not cowardice or second thoughts, that keeps me from lifting the lid on the basket. . . .

How long can they live in that basket? Many days, I have been told. The silent creatures just lie motionless, barely breathing. Nakht had done well, obeying my orders. He said they were prize ones, two of Ipuwer's favorites. But could they be the same? How long did the creatures live?

There was so much I would know, so much I would learn! my healthy mind cried out in protest. I am still young—I don't want to die this afternoon. Not this afternoon . . . perhaps tomorrow afternoon, or the next night, but, sweet Isis, not this afternoon!

But that was a momentary lapse and rebellion of my desire against the sternness of my will. It must not happen again. I bent and listened for any sound from within the basket, to assure myself that deliverance was at hand, and all I had to do was lift a light woven lid of straw.

Through the grille on the doors I could see, and hear, that the city was boiling with troops. Had Octavian arrived? Were these his soldiers? We climbed the stairs to the second story, which had a sort of inner balcony and windows that looked out over all the grounds. It was the one part of the building that was incomplete, and two of the windows were lacking bars.

With sadness I saw the tumult in my beloved city, lying helpless now before an invader, its gates thrown open, its citizens running in panic. And I was powerless to help it; all my life, dedicated to keeping it safe, has been spent laboring in vain to prevent this hour. My alliances, my plans, my stratagems, my sacrifices had staved it off but not stopped it.

Why delay any longer? Why behold this grisly spectacle of failure any longer? I was resolved to do it now; suddenly death was welcome. I spun away from the window and motioned to Charmian and Iras. But Charmian was pointing to something outside, and her face was rigid.

"Yes, it is pitiful," I told her. "But do not torture yourself by watching any longer." I took her hand.

"Madam, it is—see where they are bringing him," she whispered, pointing our hands together in the direction of an odd little procession.

Far to the right, on the path from the palace, men were carrying a litter with a sprawled body on it, and a knot of attendants clustered on both sides.

Even from this distance, I could see that the man—it was a man—was covered in blood, but lived. He did not have that limpness that betokens death.

"O my friend, it is—it is Antony," said Mardian, his voice strained.

Yes, it was. Had he been carried from the battlefield? Had he wished to lie here with me, today? In a hot gush of relief, I poured out my thanks to Isis that I yet lived. I would have missed him, had I steeled myself only a few minutes earlier.

He was trying to sit up, but did not have the strength. The whole front of his tunic was bathed in blood, and it was dripping off the litter and staining the ground. The armor was gone.

One of his attendants banged on the door, but I cried from the window, "We cannot open it now, lest Octavian storm inside and take the treasure. But the window—can we not use that?"

There were ropes still dangling from the unfinished upper masonry, and we lowered them to fasten to the litter. It was a long way to the ground, and I wondered if we would have the strength to haul him all the way up. He was a heavy man, his body now was almost dead weight, since he could not haul or help us pull.

He looked so weak, lying there, the blood bubbling up from wherever the wound was, his face pale and his words coming only with difficulty.

"Courage! Courage!" I cried, to strengthen him, as we four strained to pull the ropes and hoist him. None of us had enough strength, and it was grueling. Inadvertently we banged the litter against the wall over and over again, and each time I could see the pain chase across his face as he was jolted on the stone.

"Oh, hurry," he begged in so low a voice I could barely hear it. The sun was beating down on his blood-smeared face and cracked lips, and flies, attracted to the blood, were plaguing him. He was too weak to lift his hand and ward them off.

That hand, which had always been so strong . . . too weak now to wave away flies.

With a surge of determination, the four of us together yanked the ropes up and got the litter to the windowsill, where we lifted it over and set it on the floor.

"Oh, my dear—do not die without me!" I heard myself saying, as I threw myself on his chest, which was sleek with blood. Now I was covered in it, too, but I wanted to be. I took the palms of my hands and smeared my face, my neck, with his blood. Then, without even knowing it, I tore the top of my gown open and stripped myself of it, covering his chest with it. The blood soaked right through it.

"My lord, my husband, my emperor," I whispered by his ear. "Wait for me!"

I knew nothing could save him; the wound was mortal. He could barely speak.

"How did you get this?" I asked, laying my hand over the wound. "How did it get through your armor?"

"I—I myself," he said. "No enemy but Antony. Antony only conquers Antony."

"My brave Imperator," I said, and only he could hear me. I bent to kiss him. His lips were already cold.

"Eros—" he whispered. "Eros—"

"What of Eros?" I only now noticed his absence.

"He failed me." Antony attempted to laugh, but it was so painful he could not. "He—disobeyed his instructions. When he was to have killed me, and I turned away, he killed himself instead."

How horrible! And left Antony to dispatch himself.

"Oh, my dear—" I cradled his head in my arms. This was not the noble end we had planned, but messy and painful and inelegant.

"Some wine—" he asked faintly.

A cup was brought to him, and he managed, with our help, to raise himself a little to drink. "Octavian comes," he said. I had to strain to hear him. "You must not trust anyone about him, but an officer named Proculeius. Deal with him."

"Deal with him! There will be no dealing; I will not linger on in this world."

So he thought I might survive after all? His hopefulness was touching. He had kept it to the end.

He grasped my hand in his. With my other hand I beat and tore at my breasts in grief. He tried to take it, too, and stop me. But he did not have the strength. "Please," he whispered. "Do not pity me for this last turn of fate. Remember all the good fortune I had, for many years, and that I was the most powerful and illustrious man in the world. And even now I have not fallen ignobly."

"Yes," I said, through my tears. They were blurring my vision of his face, while he still lived and his lips moved. "No. You have been given an honorable death. The gods granted you that one last gift."

I could feel the grip in his hand slackening, and he gradually, reluctantly, released mine. His eyes closed and he seemed to concentrate all his strength on a series of gasping, heaving breaths—each causing more blood to spill out of the chest wound. Then they shuddered to a stop, and he ceased breathing.

"No! No!" I cried, willing the chest to move again. But it did not, and the hand fell away and slid down to lie upturned at his side. The fingers, curling in that half-circle, just as they had when he slept. . . .

His lids were shut, and the long eyelashes locked together: the beautiful long lashes that I had teased him about, now holding the lids down to cover the starkness of death, to veil its indecency.

Antony was dead. The whole world rolled away.

"Madam—madam—" I felt someone pulling on me, trying to separate us. I was almost stuck to him by the blood. I did not want to leave, be taken away. I clung tighter.

"Dear friend," said Mardian. "You must. He is gone."

916

I refused to let go, and they had to pry me away, and Mardian carry me in his arms down the steps, leaving Antony on his litter, alone.

"No—" I said feebly, reaching back.

"He can have a proper funeral," Mardian said. "But that must wait. Have you forgotten Octavian? He must be nearly here!"

Octavian. What did I care for Octavian? I cared for nothing now, just to lie in the sheltering arms of Mardian, my oldest, truest friend, and cease to think. The world had shrunk down into a dried black husk, and Antony was lying dead, alone, up there. . . .

I clutched his arm, wordlessly. Or did I speak? I do not know. Only that in the swirl where I almost felt my spirit leaving my body, floating silently and secretly up the steps and back to Antony, there to join with him and flee from all the blood and foulness of this hour, I was suddenly dumped onto the floor. Mardian had flung me down before the great doors.

He pushed me toward them, his hands on my shoulders. "Look out there!" he demanded.

No. I cannot face all this now. Not in such immediate succession. But he is relentless, guiding me toward the grille.

Swarms of people. What people? What matter? I feel so weak, I grab the bars to enable me to stand. There are shadows across the grass. Hours have passed, hours when Antony took his slow, painful leave of this world. It was a time beyond time; how odd that real time stole past, outside. I do not want to reenter it. I want to stay in this timeless, seasonless, unchanging place of stone and sealed doors.

"Madam," said Charmian, by my side. She wiped my face with a scarf, and it came away red with blood. "Courage!"

Now time snaps into place again, like a band on a pulley, connecting everything. Now I see people outside. Roman soldiers. Not ours. Others. Octavian's.

There are hordes of them, striding across the grass, across my palace grounds, lounging on the steps of Isis's temple. They are drinking from their water bags, peeling fruit, laughing. It is a holiday for them: the obscene holiday of victory, now beheld by the vanquished. Is any taste so bitter in all the world?

"Look where they come," Mardian whispered. And I could see a company of officers striding purposefully toward us. Was Octavian among them?

No. I would recognize him anywhere, even across all the years. He was not there. One of them separated himself and approached our doors. He was a tall man, dressed as a staff officer; not even a general.

He came closer and closer, until the vision of him was distorted by the grate and the nearness. I saw a big, sunburnt nose, saw the beads of sweat on his face. A banging. He was hammering with a sword handle on the door.

"Queen Cleopatra!" he yelled, only a hand's breadth from my ear. The loudness was painful. "Come out, and yield yourself to us!"

The volume of the voice and its very nearness were startling. I could not answer, could not find my own voice. Must I speak to the outside world?

"We know he is dead! We have his sword, taken from his side by his guard, Dercetaeus. This, the very one he used to kill himself!" I could see the flash of the sword, recognized it. Its blade was coated with blood.

Anger swept through me; good clean anger. That sword—it belonged to Antyllus, or Alexander—not to this gloating enemy.

"Give me that sword!" I demanded. "Do not befoul it with your touch!"

He stepped back, startled. It was not the response he had expected.

"And so I shall, when you open the doors," he said.

"Never! I will die in here, and my treasure along with me. Your master knows well enough what I have promised. I gave him the opportunity to forestall it, but he chose not to. Now he shall pay the price—the treasure of the Ptolemies will go up in smoke, an offering to the gods," I yelled through the door. I was surprised I had such strength left in me, at this hour.

"You wrong my master," he said. "You must not impute such cruelty to him. Harm yourself? No, he will not have that!"

"Yes, he would pamper and preserve me to parade me through the streets of Rome in his Triumph. His trophy. Never!" He would keep me like a sacrificial animal, until time for the offering.

"No, no! He only wishes you well. Do not deny him the opportunity to show what he is made of."

"Who are you?" I demanded.

"My name is Gaius Proculeius."

Proculeius. Antony had said to trust him. But why?

"I have heard you spoken of," I said cautiously.

"In what manner?"

"That you are trustworthy." But I was not sure of that; Antony often trusted where he should not.

"For that, I thank you."

"If you are trustworthy, then relay to your master, for one last time, my absolute condition: that he bestow the kingdom of Egypt on my children—Caesarion or Alexander as it pleases him—and spare the others as well. That being done, the treasure is his, yes, and my person, too, to transport where he will."

I did not mean this, for I would never walk in Arsinoe's footsteps. But the treasure—ah! the treasure—he could have in exchange for my children's lives and inheritance. He could make do with a statue of my person for his procession.

"He only wishes you well," Proculeius insisted.

"He wishes my treasure well, that is all," I said. "Tell him what he must do to obtain it, and that I will not be dissuaded."

"Trust him," said Proculeius. "You cannot imagine how generous and kind he can be. Only grant him the opportunity to show it!"

"The day grows late," I said. "Take my message. Or, by all that's holy, such a fire will fill the night skies from my burning treasure that Octavian will not need a lamp to read by!"

918

He bowed quickly and left, clutching the sword. The sword that I longed to open the doors for, reach out and grab.

"Well," said Mardian. "That was quite a performance."

I sank down on the cool floor. "Oh, Mardian. It is hopeless. Whatever assurances he gives me, I can never believe them. I am a prisoner in here for the few days I have left. Regardless of any message from Octavian, I am bound to destroy all this, and myself as well."

I had failed; failed to secure even the promise of the throne for my children, and all I could do now was destroy the treasure in spite. I longed to do it; end it all now. My misgivings had flown. I had no desire to live on, to see even another sunrise over this soiled world.

"But if Octavian came in person, would you believe him?" Mardian asked.

"No. All this is just playacting. He would say what is necessary to lay hands on the treasure. I would do the same myself. I understand him, as he understands me." As the noble Antony had never really understood either of us, being made of different, and finer, material. "No, there is no remedy but death; death to shut out the failure that is ringing in my ears, deafening me."

It began to grow dark outside. We lit lamps, which we had had the foresight to bring in with us, along with fruit and wine. We could hold out in here a long time. In the flickering shadows, I looked up the steps, half hoping, expecting, to see Antony lurch down them. Himself, or his shade?

Mardian saw me, and reached out for my hand. "You must not. You must not go up there."

"Only for a moment—"

"Not in the darkness. Not now."

A commotion outside. More banging on the door. I rose and went to it. A new face was pressed against the grille. Flaring torches illuminated it.

"I would speak to the Queen!" he cried.

"Who would?" I demanded.

"Cornelius Gallus," he replied.

Gallus. The poetry-writing commander who had taken over in Cyrenaica, after Scarpus's troops had deserted. So they had sent a general this time.

"The famous General Gallus," I said. "Have you brought your verses? Have you written something celebrating the fall of Alexandria?"

"Put up your spite, lady," he said. "I come in peace—Octavian, my gentle friend and yours, offers his hand in bond of brotherhood."

"He may be your friend, but he is not mine," I said.

"You wrong him. . . ." And more in this vein; on and on. Nothing was said, nothing offered. Just words. Words to lull and delude me.

And then . . . and now . . . How it happened, and happened so fast, I cannot reconstruct. I was talking, speaking through the grille. . . . I heard the honeyed words, detected the poison beneath them. . . .

I am weary of him. Let him go away. My feet ache. And then, a clatter from above. From where Antony is . . .

Crazy with excitement, I turn, cry, *I knew you would come back.* . . .

Did I really? Had I been waiting for him to stand once again, come back to life, seek me out by the force of will and desire, stronger even than death itself? Or is it just the madness that grips us in the wake of final, absolute death?

Someone is bounding down the stairs, his face and form in shadow, and even as I turn to face him, he grabs one of my arms.

This is not Antony's touch. So—I must end it. I pull my dagger from my waist, and odd the thought that floats through my mind: *Pity it cannot be the snakes, no time for the snakes, only the knife.* And I am sad about it. *I have failed here, too.*

A hard hand wrenches it away from me, twists my wrist so hard it stings. I hear the dagger clatter on the floor, hear a harsh intake of breath.

Then, "What else is there?" And I am being shaken so hard my teeth rattle, and what is left of my gown smacked and felt. "No poison, then."

Never has anyone laid such rough hands on me, treated me so.

"I have her!" he shouts. "It is safe now!"

Two men follow down the steps and rush to the door, pulling back the bolts, sliding them out. They fling the door open, where Gallus is standing, smiling.

"Good work, Proculeius," he says, stepping inside.

Proculeius. The one Antony told me to trust. Thus he was betrayed, again.

"Yes, very clever, Proculeius," I said. He continued to hold me, and Gallus stared, wide-eyed.

Only then was I aware that I was still half naked; the whole upper part of my garment I had torn off to cover Antony. And my skin was all smeared with dried blood, Antony's lifeblood.

"O piteous sight!" Gallus said. "So this is the *fatale monstrum*, before whom Rome quaked?"

"She still has plenty of fight in her, sir, do not be deceived. I disarmed her of her dagger just in time, and shook her to be assured there is no poison on her person."

"Well done," Gallus said. He removed his cloak and draped it around me, but I shrugged it off. I did not want anything of his to touch me.

"It must be so," he said. "I was but following my orders." He did not sound joyous. "Unhand her, Proculeius."

I felt him release me. "So you deceived me with words at one door while you stole in upstairs?" They must have seen where Antony had been taken in. Perhaps there were even telltale smears of blood on the wall. Now they had besmirched even that, by following in his wake.

"We only sought to prevent you harming yourself, in your present state of mind," Proculeius said. "It was Octavian's concern for you."

"Concern for the treasure, you mean." I glared at them. "You might as well see it," I said. "Come, look."

I led them around to where it was heaped. They followed close on my heels, expecting that I was leading them into a trap. They gave me great credit for wiliness.

"Here." I flung out my arm and pointed to it. Let them look. The pile was high, and from their hushed breathing, I knew it was more than they had imagined. "It is yours."

Like children—why does gold unman us so?—they approached it, gaping. Proculeius dropped to his knees, as if in worship. He stretched out one hand and grasped the corner of a small statue of Bast.

"Take it," I said. "Octavian will never miss it. Besides, have you not earned it for tonight's work?"

He snatched it out, causing a few other objects to be dislodged—a box of sapphires, and an ivory bowl.

"Oh, take them, too," I told him.

"Wait," ordered Gallus. He suspected me of something bad, and he was right. Perhaps I could get Proculeius and Gallus to dishonor themselves by fighting over the gold, and stealing from Octavian. A small victory, but it would be of some consolation. "Leave it." He turned to me. "You and your servants must come with us," he said. "It is time to rest."

At swordpoint we were led away, through the drinking soldiers sporting themselves on the grounds. They all stared as I passed, undressed and bloody, and fell silent.

86

A prisoner in my own palace. Marched past the majestic portals, the marble rooms, the polished, shining hallways. My own quarters barred to me. Mardian deprived of his. I turn my head toward the passage leading to my apartments, am told roughly, "Not that way!"—as if they know my home better than I, these strangers.

We are steered down a vaulted passage, toward the lesser guests' quarters, but not before a swinging litter passes, its occupant unmoving, face discreetly covered. There are two stiff, sandaled feet protruding.

The litter has come from the direction of Antony's apartments.

"Is that the last of it?" one of my guards asks.

"Yes. All clean now." And they move briskly off.

"Eros?" I ask. I know the answer. They have removed him from where he fell in Antony's room.

"Yes," my guard snaps.

Poor Eros. If I had been capable of feeling anything more, my heart would have ached. But after so many horrors, another cannot increase the depth of pain.

They would reuse Antony's apartments, lodge his enemies there. And mine? For whom was mine reserved?

"Who has the honor of staying in the Queen's apartments?" I ask.

"He is already there. Imperator Caesar."

So Octavian had entered Alexandria already, seized possession of it all.

"When did he arrive?" I keep turning my head to ask, as we are shoved along.

"He entered the city late this afternoon," the soldier says. "He rode in in a chariot, with the philosopher Areius by his side. He called all the officials to gather in the Gymnasion, and there he assured them he would spare the city, out of respect for Alexander, its founder, and also for the sake of the beauty of the city itself; and finally to gratify his friend Areius."

"How noble," I say. Now he was posing as the philosopher-king. "How Alexandrian."

"He addressed the assembly in Greek," the man says.

"That must have been a feat," I scoff. Everyone knew his Greek was painfully poor. More playacting, from the master masquerader.

"Here." They stop abruptly, and indicate a door. The room inside waits.

It is a lowly thing, something I would only assign an envoy's secretary. But Octavian must needs spread himself out in mine.

"Inside."

Charmian, Iras, Mardian, and I are all herded in.

"Clothes and food will be sent," they say. The door clangs shut.

The room had four small beds—cots, really. There was a washstand, one lamp stand, a window so newly fitted with bars that the smell of ground stone and hot metal still lingered. From it I could see the wing of the palace that this morning—this morning!—had been mine.

Charmian had grabbed up the writing materials, but when I asked her what of the fateful basket, she shook her head. "I forgot, my lady, I am sorry. That, and the trunk, remain behind."

Another blow! Even that taken away from me.

In a few minutes a box of clothes and blankets was delivered, as well as some bread and fruit. In stubbornness I wished to refuse both, but the truth was I had to remove what was left of my torn, bloody gown. I let Iras take it off, and Charmian sponge away the blood with a wet cloth. The water in the bowl grew rosy, as Antony's blood dyed it. She emptied it out the window, which grieved me.

"Now . . ." She wrapped one of the coarse common gowns around me. "Rest." I lay down, but knew I would never sleep. Outside I could still hear the soldiers carousing on the grounds. It went on all night.

———

Early in the morning a soldier entered, without knocking or asking leave.

I sat bolt upright. It was time to end this. "I demand to see the Imperator," I said. "Immediately."

He looked puzzled. "The Imperator has a full day," he said. "He intends to visit the tomb of Alexander, and then to meet with the treasury officials—"

So he would ignore me! How much lower could he grind me? How much pain inflict on me? "Tell him to postpone Alexander," I said. "He won't leave his tomb. Like all the rest of the world, he will await the Imperator. But I must speak to him now about the funeral of Antony. Please!"

Mardian and the women were now watching, listening.

"Already he is besieged with requests to bury Antony," said the soldier. "Some of the eastern kings, and his Roman kinsmen—they are competing for the honor."

Would that they had competed for the honor of serving him when he needed them! "It should be I, and only I, who buries him with my own hands," I insisted. "Am I not his wife, and a queen?"

"I will tell the Imperator of your request," the man said, as if it were something minor.

"And my children! Where are my children?"

"Under a trusted guard," he said.

"They live? And are unharmed?"

"Yes," he said.

"Do you swear it?"

"By the honor of the Imperator," he said. "Not a hair on their heads has been touched."

"May I see them?"

"I will have to ask."

I was reduced to a menial, a mother who wished to see her children, a wife to bury her husband, denied even asking for it except through a messenger.

"What is the Imperator doing that he cannot see me within the next hour?"

"He is overseeing the treasure being taken from the mausoleum. It must be inventoried."

"Of course." There would be no tearing Octavian away from counting his booty. "But there is something more precious there—the body of my husband."

"It will be removed, and treated with honor," he said. "I can assure you of that."

The day passed slowly, my first day of captivity. In its own way it was a blessing to be held in such strict confinement, for I was so stunned and weak all I could do was lie on the bed, or sit looking out the window. With my three faithful friends, I could unburden myself, weep and sleep, as the moods took me.

There was no word from Octavian, just a supper tray shoved in the door after dark.

My keepers delighted in stepping into the room unannounced, at odd hours. Before it had grown light, the same officer appeared, opening the door loudly.

"Madam!" he said, bending over my bed.

"You need not shout," I said. "I am quite awake. But please light my lamp." He was carrying a torch.

"Certainly." He turned obligingly to do it. He was not unkind, this loud soldier.

"What is your name?" I asked.

"Cornelius Dolabella," he said. "I have known the Imperator many years, and served him since the last campaign." He hung the lamp on its stand. "I wish to tell you that my commander has graciously granted your wish. You may make all the funeral arrangements for Antony, conduct it however you please. And you are to be moved into more comfortable quarters. He has also assigned one of his most trusted and esteemed freedmen, Epaphroditus, to you."

Epaphroditus! What a strange thing, that he should also have a favorite companion with that name. It had always been a fortunate name for me; might it prove so again?

"I thank the Imperator," I said.

"He says you may spare no expense," said Dolabella.

"The Imperator is generous." He could afford to be, now that he had my treasury.

Antony's funeral . . . how shall I write of it? That it was magnificent, befitting a king? No earthly tokens and salutes were withheld; and the glittering trappings of majesty that had so offended Rome in advance—in his will—surrounded him. He was borne in a golden coffin, on a heavy, gilded hearse. The funeral cortege was thronged, with the chief mourners keeping pace behind the hearse, solemn dirges playing—like a very slow, drawn-out repetition of the Dionysus procession that had played its way out of the city three nights earlier. The same pipes, the same drums, the same cymbals, now wailing a sad melody. It began in the palace grounds, then wound its way through the city, past scenes where we had been so happy, had had our glorious moments. The Museion . . . the Gymnasion . . . the Temple of Serapis . . . the wide Canopic Way . . . Alexander's tomb . . . and ended back at the palace, once our place of joy.

Then into the mausoleum, where the granite sarcophagus was waiting, its lid off. The great coffin lifted, placed within it, the lid slid over it, the sad, melancholy thud as the two pieces locked together, sealing him in. I knelt and laid a necklace of flowers on it, like those placed on the Pharaohs; leaned across the cool stone and whispered, "Anubis. Anubis at last, my dearest." My farewell.

That was what the people saw.

But I . . . I saw other things. Before the coffin had been closed, I had come to the chamber where it rested on its bier. The best funeral directors in the world had taken charge of my beloved Antony, doing everything in their earthly power to prepare him for this journey. Four great torches flared at each corner of the bier, fixed in iron sockets. I stood beside the coffin and looked in, dreading what I would see.

He looked different, smaller, all the robust joy of him having fled with his spirit. And so still. He lay so still, more still somehow than a stone statue, because it is not in the nature of flesh to be so utterly without movement.

I could stand it. This was not him. This need not be my last memory of him, the picture I would carry with me. I clutched the side of the coffin, leaning over to give him a formal farewell kiss. And then I saw it.

His hands, still exactly his hands, looking so alive. The scar on his right hand, where Olympos had treated it, that I knew so well, that *was* Antony. All of him seemed to be there in his hands, clasped quietly. It was the hands that undid me.

I remember little of what happened next, although some snatches of scenes remain, oddly clear like a painting, that allowed me to recount the details above. But such a frenzy of grief overtook me that it was all I could do to stumble behind the hearse and make the journey through the streets. There were crowds, all staring, but I saw them not, saw nothing but the slow, groaning hearse, felt nothing but the pain of loss. I knew now what I had lost, Antony gone, Egypt taken, the dregs of defeat. The waves of heat rising from the white marble streets and buildings blinded me, overcame me. I ripped my clothes like any village widow whose life is ruined, beat on myself without even knowing it, tore at my hair. They say I wailed, too, like a common woman, and cried out in pain to the gods. But all I remember is the pain itself, blurring everything else, not what I said or did. I had ceased to exist, obliterated under a crushing mound of anguish.

Upon returning, I collapsed into my bed. There was one other thing . . . something I had not noticed at the time, but that now nagged at me, an ugly question.

Dolabella was on duty. I saw him standing by the door, keeping a discreet distance. But I called for him, knowing he would tell me.

"Madam?" He was leaning over my bed, where I was lying shivering, even in the heat of this day.

"Antyllus," I said. "Antony's son. Where was he? Should he not have been among the mourners?"

His face clouded. "The young Marcus Antonius is dead," he finally said. "He was killed by soldiers as he took sanctuary in the shrine of the deified Caesar."

"No! How could he have been? How could such a mistake have happened?" But in the confusion of an invading army, anything is possible. Antyllus!

"It was—it was not a mistake, my lady," the honest Dolabella said. "The Imperator ordered it."

"O sweet Isis!" I breathed. He would slay my children, then, too. We

Ptolemies were doomed. If he was pitiless to Antyllus—Antyllus, who was no threat to him, who claimed nothing that Octavian wanted, whose only crime was being Antony's son—how could mine, doubly damned by being Cleopatra's as well, escape?

That is when the fever took hold of me and I entered the delirium.

They said it was because I had lacerated my breasts and they had become inflamed and caused the fever. But no, it was all that I had beheld in the last three days, and all I knew. All was over, gone, and I was determined to die. The sacred serpents, my weapons of deliverance and seal of my daughterhood of Re, had slipped from my possession, but there still remained a way open to me. I would refuse food, give in to the fever, waste away. When we want to die, our bodies will oblige. They cannot hold our spirit captive for long. Our wills are stronger than our flesh, and can drive it to shrivel up and cease to live. No food, no water, I would take nothing, but lay tossing and thrashing on the bed, bathed in sweat, and tortured by such dreams as would make the blackness of death a gentle friend.

Mardian floated in and out of my sight, hovering. Iras was always there, dabbing with a scented cloth. Then one day I saw Olympos. They had let him in. That meant I was sinking. I was thankful. He attempted to dress my wounds. I pushed him away, tore off the bandages. He tried holding my mouth open to pour soup down it, but I bit him. He let out a howl and jumped away, shaking his hand.

"For a dying woman, you have strong jaws," he said.

Inwardly I laughed, but I would not respond outwardly. I turned my face to the wall.

Olympos sat down on the bed beside me. He gently brushed my hair away from my ear, where it was matted by sweat, and whispered, "Whether you want to hear or not, listen."

I gave no sign that I heard him.

"Octavian has sent a message." I could hear a rattling of paper by my ear. But still I did not move. "Mardian will read it to you."

The creak of the bed told me he had gotten up.

"Madam," said Mardian in his gentle voice, "it is imperative you listen." When he got no response, he bent closer. "Octavian says that unless you cease harming yourself, he will execute your children. He knows you are trying to kill yourself, and he will put a stop to it. Die, and your children will die also."

So they still lived. He had spared them—so far. Why? What was his purpose?

"Do you hear me?" Mardian asked insistently.

Slowly I nodded. Then I said, "I hear."

There was no doubt that Octavian would carry out his threat. But why did he want me alive? Surely his much-vaunted "clemency" would not be stained because a stubborn woman had starved herself. I did not delude myself it was because he wanted to keep me on the throne. Alive . . . there was only one thing where it was essential that I be presented alive: his Triumph. He wanted to exhibit me. And he would not be balked of his prey.

But if there was something he wanted, even something as repulsive and degrading as that, then I still had something to bargain with. The treasure was gone, but my person remained. It was worth the chance to secure my children's lives, if not their throne.

I submitted to the ministrations. I let Olympos spoon soup into my mouth, let him sponge my body with a cooling lotion that helped bring the fever down. My protests died away, but still I did not wish to respond to their fussing.

Eat this . . . drink this . . . a pillow? Your wishes, my lady?

My wishes were that somehow I might secure the survival of my children, then die and be entombed beside Antony. How to ensure this? My thoughts were racing, trying desperately to form a plan. But I was so tired, so depleted, so confused. I had tried so many plans, staked myself so many times, gambling on this action, or that . . . I did not know if I could do it even one last time.

But you must. Or all the rest will have been for nothing.

I knew that, but I had little faith in my schemes now. I had concocted so many, and so few had come to fruition. Fate—it was fate, Tyche, Fortune, who held the outcome in her hand. Prevailing against her might not be in my destiny.

But you must try, must try. . . . I am so weary of trying.

Octavian. If you can only see Octavian, have an interview with him . . . you excel at interviews. Remember, a personal meeting has rarely failed you. He will be smug, satisfied with his victory, probably gloating. If you fall abjectly at his feet, he will swell with pride.

Or . . . what about Caesar? Can you not appeal to his love of Caesar? Take refuge behind Caesar's shield? How can he dishonor you, whom Caesar honored? The letters . . . the Caesar letters . . . *They are still in my apartments . . . where Octavian is. How to get them?*

Or should I pretend I expect to live and am concerned about my diplomatic relationships in Rome?

Oh, what tack to take? If only I knew him better! I cannot guess his thoughts, and yet I must guess correctly. I will have only this one chance.

I must recover, so I can face him as an equal. Let him think I have been neither crushed nor broken by this, but am still a formidable statesman with whom he must negotiate—or at least respect.

I need a few days to regain my strength.

"How long have I been ill?" I asked Olympos. My voice was much weaker than I realized; it was just a whisper.

He was instantly beside me. "This is the fifth day since the funeral," he said.

Five days. I had dreamed away five days. Octavian had been in Alexandria for eight, then. Antony dead for eight. I shuddered, and Olympos drew a covering over my shoulder.

"Go to Octavian," I said. "Or tell Dolabella to do so. Tell him I am recovering, but that I wish to have a box I left behind in the apartments, which I will let him inspect. And my papers—the ones in the workroom. I need them, too. Let him see them, so he knows it is no trick. But I need them."

Mardian rustled over. "You don't need papers! You mustn't trouble yourself with—"

"I think it is a good sign she asks for them," said Olympos dryly. "It means she is scheming again."

I had not got that far; I was not sure I could scheme, or that I had the means at hand to do so. But the papers would help me decide.

"The ivory box with the lock," I said. "And the papers—in the wooden container in the workroom, by the stool."

"More soup first," said Olympos firmly. "Here we have some delicious soup of goat's milk and barley. . . ."

It warmed my stomach, helped push the dizziness away. I struggled to sit up and see where I was. The quarters where we had been transferred . . . the sun was coming in, and that meant we were facing south. There were no bars on the windows; they were pretending we were not strict prisoners.

"Outside—who is stationed outside the door?" I asked.

"There's that Epaphroditus in the outer chamber," said Mardian, "and then, outside that, two or three guards."

From the way he said "that Epaphroditus," I could tell he did not like him.

The afternoon passed; I saw the slant of the light change as the sun moved across the windows.

I was still shivering and weak, as I discovered when I tried to sit up. My bones felt like jelly. It would take as many more days for me to recover as I had been ill.

Mardian ceremoniously brought in the two boxes, and placed them on a table. "He made no trouble about it," he said. "Or so Epaphroditus claimed."

Now I must look through them. But later. I had not the strength now.

"Draw the curtains," I said. "Shut out the light. I must sleep."

I dreamed, a deep, sweet dream of being on the seas, riding over the wave troughs, a western wind filling the sails. I knew it was a western wind, as one does in dreams, and that it was bringing me home, back to Egypt, with Rome at my back. Caesarion was with me, still a small child, holding my hand. I could taste the salt spray in my mouth, could feel the jolts as the ship rode the waves . . . exhilarating, fast. . . .

"Madam!" An urgent voice filled my ear, a hand shook my shoulder. "Madam! It is Octavian!"

The words twined themselves around my dream, so somehow it was the ropes of the ship singing "Octavian, Octavian!" But the shaking continued, and I had the horror of hearing the words, loud now, no dream.

"The most glorious Imperator Caesar," barked a stranger's voice.

I opened my eyes to see him standing there, stiffly, staring at me from the door of the room. Octavian himself.

Although a cold recognition ran through me, it still seemed like a dream. The man himself, in the flesh, after a hundred statues, coins, imaginings.

And to have swooped down on me like this. He had won the day; I had not even the vestige of a plan of how to address him, had not looked at the papers, had not even stood up or dressed myself—

I was lying in a sweat-soaked sickbed, dirty, undressed, weak. He had all the advantages; I could not face him like this.

He was staring at me in frank distaste, colored by suspicion at what his eyes beheld. Finding some hidden store of strength in my legs, I left the bed and walked across the floor to him. Then weakness caused me to sink to my knees in front of him and grasp his feet. I shivered as I touched them; all this still seemed part of the fever-dream. I was too aware that I was wearing only a thin sleep-garment, that my hair was wild and matted.

"Up, up," he said, in that voice that I would recognize anywhere. Flat, quiet, a deadly monotone.

In truth, I did not have the power to rise. I just huddled there, shaking.

"Up, up, I say." An emotion at last: a hint of impatience, annoyance. He reached down and touched my shoulder, then offered his hand. It was dry, like a lizard. He drew me up.

"Imperator," I said in so small a voice it was almost a whisper, "the day is yours. Hail, master—for heaven has granted you the mastery and taken it from me."

He motioned to Epaphroditus—a burly, plain man, nothing like my Epaphroditus—to help me back to the bed. I did not argue; I was at a loss as to what to do. Then, to my horror, Octavian sat down on it beside me.

We looked at one another. I tried to concentrate on what I saw and forget what he was seeing. Strange how little he had changed, but how age puts a new stamp on our features. The triangular face, the wide-set eyes, the little ears, the prim mouth, all the same, but the expression in the eyes, the hard-set clamping of the mouth, had cast the old sweetness away and replaced it with an implacable wariness. *The Roman boy*, Antony had called him, but he was no boy, and had not a shred of youthfulness.

His gray-blue eyes, with that darker rim around them . . . they were looking directly into mine, no deference or shielding. This was a man who was not afraid to stare, where the boy had veiled his looks.

How hard you have grown, I wanted to murmur. *And how old you have grown*, he would answer.

Now his eyes moved to my neck and farther down. He was inspecting the wounds on my upper body, as if to convince himself they were real. Satisfied, he took his eyes away and attempted a stiff smile.

"I trust the Queen is recovering?" he asked politely.

"Little by little, I mend." It was hard to get the words out.

"You must take care of yourself," he said. "Your health is important to us."

I must think. This was my interview, whether I wanted it now or not. I must use it as best I could. "For that, I thank you," I said.

He kept staring at me. Finally he said, "For years you have filled my vision. Wherever I looked, you blocked my way." He shifted his weight a little. He was about to take his leave!

"Sir, may we speak in private?" I asked him. "May I send these attendants away?"

He looked startled. "The guards—" he said.

"Of course you must leave the guards at the door," I said. "But the others?"

He gave a curt nod; with so small a motion may the master of the world dismiss all those around him. Charmian, Iras, Mardian, Olympos, and Epaphroditus all filed out.

Octavian and I faced one another, less than an arm's length away.

I tried to smile. I knew my smile was a good spokesman. I lifted my chin as if I felt better than I did. I would have to forget about the dirty, transparent clothes, and my uncombed hair. I would have to make him forget them, too. "Sir," I said, "what can I do but ask you to remember that night so long ago, when we first met at the home of Caesar? We were both dear to him, and it would grieve him if we continued to hate one another. Under his shadow we must reconcile."

"I do not hate you," he said, and in his cold voice I heard something worse than hate.

"You have ample reason to, and would be as godlike as Caesar himself if you did not."

He grunted, and crossed his arms, as if to protect himself.

"But I ask you to consider, and respect the trust I was held in by the man whom you love and honor more than anyone who ever lived," I said. "I wish you to read these letters, letters he wrote me in his own hand, so you can learn something of me from him, see me through his eyes." I got up and took the box from the table, and handed it to him.

I was deeply thankful that I had retained some of the letters. Let them plead for me now!

Octavian unlatched the box and drew out a letter. Wordlessly, he read it. Very fast—too fast.

"Of what avail to me are these letters now?" I murmured, as if to Caesar himself, embodied in the letters. "Would that I had died before you. But in this young man, perhaps in some way you may still live for me."

Octavian just grunted again, and took up another letter. His eyes skimmed it, and he folded it up.

Surely he would read them all, and more thoroughly!

"Very interesting," is all he said. He closed the box. Now he shifted again, ready to take his leave.

I must think of something else to delay him, sway him.

"I regret my actions that have caused Rome grief," I finally said. "We are not always free to choose our course of action."

"On the contrary," he said, "we are always responsible for what we do—and for what we cause others to do, leading them into error and treason."

He meant Antony. He meant I had led him astray.

"Lord Antony and I were not always in agreement in everything," I said. True enough. "Sometimes he pursued actions, and I was punished for them. I am well aware that Rome declared me, not Antony, the enemy. And yet, forget not, it was Caesar who placed me on my throne, Caesar who declared me an ally of the Roman people. He was wise, for I have been a devoted ruler of my country, and I have never been Rome's enemy." I paused. Was he listening? "Like you, I pursued the murderers of Caesar, and would not rest until they were punished."

"Yes, well, they are all dead now," he said with satisfaction. "They have paid the price."

"We are not so far apart, you and I, in what we want."

"And what is it you want?" he asked bluntly.

"To have the throne continue with the Ptolemaic line. To be Rome's ally. And to live a quiet and honorable life, in exile if necessary."

He did not answer immediately, but turned the words over in his mind.

"That is for the Senate to decide," he finally said. "Now that the Republic will be restored . . . but you may rest assured that I will safeguard all your interests."

"I am entirely yours, Imperator," I said. "I throw myself on your mercy. Only give me some assurance that my children will wear the crown!"

He sighed, as if he found this embarrassing. "I will do what I can," he said. "Certainly a house that has ruled for three hundred years . . ." He let the sentence trail off, teasingly.

"When I sent messages to you, I promised all my treasure in exchange for that. I now yield up that treasure to you, more than just what was in the mausoleum. Here it is, a thorough accounting." Now I rose and placed the big wooden box in his hands. "I had it all drawn up for you, long before you arrived. See the date, see the seal?"

He was immediately interested. The list of property excited him as the letters from Caesar had failed to. He was a man of the here and now, and cared little for sentiment.

"Hmm." He unrolled one scroll and held it out. His arms were surprisingly muscular. Perhaps the campaigns had done him some good after all. And he wasn't coughing, either. "And this is everything, you say?"

"Yes, everything I own. In exchange for my children's lives, their right to the crown of Egypt."

"Hmmm." He was studying it carefully. Suddenly he bellowed, "You! Mardian!"

What was he doing?

Mardian appeared, puzzled and on guard. "Yes, Imperator?"

"This list," Octavian said. "Look it over! Is it a complete list?"

931

Mardian looked at me for directions, but Octavian was watching my face to make sure I signaled nothing. I just smiled.

"Uhh—" Mardian was sweating; I could see the beads forming on his forehead, like seed pearls. "I—no, most noble Imperator, there seem to be some omissions." He shot a miserable look at me. But, in doubt, he had just decided to tell the truth.

"Aha!" said Octavian, a wicked smile on his face. "What sort of omissions?"

"There seems to be—there is some property withheld."

"What sort of property?"

And in that instant, Isis granted me the power I needed. I saw directly into Octavian's mind; it was as if I could read his thoughts as easily as he read the scroll.

He plans to take you back to Rome for his Triumph, mocking you and then killing you. He will grant you no mercy at all. Your only hope of outwitting him and escaping is to convince him you are eager to live, and are still plotting earthly schemes. He will try to counteract them—and while he is standing guard in one direction, you are free to go in another.

Use the false accounting to prove it to him. . . .

"Shut up, Mardian!" I screamed, and leapt at him. The gods that had given me the insight had also given me the strength to spring half across the room. I started pelting Mardian on the shoulders, the arms, and trying to smack his face. "You miserable traitor! How dare you betray me?"

Then I turned to Octavian and started crying. "Oh, this is more than I can bear! To have had to receive you in such a fashion, when you have honored me by a visit, and then to be insulted by my own servant!" I cast my eyes down. "Yes, it is true. I have held back some jewels, some art, but only because I needed something to try to placate your wife and your sister in Rome. Yes, I hoped to buy some mercy from the women in your family, praying that they would pity me, woman to woman. I did not know what else to do."

He laughed condescendingly. "Of course you may keep your baubles. Do not worry about such things. Keep anything you like."

"But they are not for me, they are for Livia and Octavia."

He smiled. "Yes, indeed."

And again, I could see into his mind. He believed that I fiercely wished to live, and was scheming to better my lot. I had won.

"Now, most gracious Queen," he was saying smoothly, "you may be well assured, your treatment will be far beyond your expectations. You may trust me."

He smiled, the first genuine smile of the entire interview. There was even something else in his eyes: the lechery that Thyrsus had hinted at. "And now I must take my leave. I would not overtire you." He bent his head and kissed my hand. His hair flopped forward, and when he straightened, he smoothed it back, as if he would look his best for me.

I rose to see him to the door. "You are too kind, Imperator," I said.

When the tramp of feet assured me he was gone, I fell into Mardian's arms.

"Are you mad?" he said. "What is all this? What have you done?" And then, plaintively, "Why did you hit me?"

"Quickly, before Olympos returns—I must tell you that I have seen through Octavian. I know what he means to do. But we will still be able to carry out our original plan, if he is deceived into thinking we have put all such thoughts far from us. I had to pretend you had exposed my scheming. Be on guard! We will find a way, now!"

A feeling akin to happiness now rose in me. I did not know what it was. But I know now. It was completion, triumph, grasping the Olympic crown in my hands and lowering it onto my head.

⟨ 87 ⟩

Octavian outdid himself in lavish attentions. Within an hour, platters heaped high with melons, pomegranates, dates, and green figs arrived, followed by an amphora of Laodicean wine (Antony had not succeeded in depleting all the palace supplies, in spite of his strenuous efforts). He even sent his own physician in to "help" Olympos, who listened disdainfully to his advice.

The fresh figs were good. "He means to fatten me up," I said. He wanted me well enough to walk those miles behind his chariot, through the city of Rome and the Forum. And of course I would need the strength to drag chains along with me. Yes, it would take a lot of nursing and good food. Sweet Octavian.

He cloaked his dagger in unctuous compliments that he sent along with his gifts. His heart was gladdened to see that I was out of danger. He was honored that I would trust him to carry out my wishes. I must think no more about the gifts for Livia and Octavia, but bedeck myself instead. And so on.

I lay back on the bed—spread now with the finest palace linens, sent posthaste by Octavian—and willed myself to regain my strength. Already the excitement and danger had wrought a change in me. My appetite surged back, and soon we had depleted all of Octavian's offerings.

"Ask for roast ox," I told Mardian. "He will send it within an hour."

And he did. Oh, he was most solicitous.

I slept a true sleep that night for the first time since Alexandria had fallen.

Since Octavian was eager to be so accommodating, there was one request I must make in earnest: to see the children. I sent a properly cringing, cloying letter to him and waited. Soon Dolabella was knocking, answer in hand. My request was granted. The children would be brought to my quarters.

Oh, now my heart truly rose! I hungered for the sight of them, as only another mother can understand. I needed badly to see them, hold them, feel their sturdy shoulders and arms. I needed to know how they fared, what had happened to them in the nine days since we had been parted.

Octavian had yielded up my robes and gowns from the wardrobe room, and so I was able to lay aside the soiled sleeping-garment and dress myself. It was important that they should see me as I wished to be seen, so they could remember.

My own mother . . . what did I remember of her? My children were all older than I had been when my mother vanished, and would carry a clearer picture of me. Alexander and Selene were almost as old as I had been when Father lost his throne and fled, and I remembered that acutely. Yes, they would remember. . . .

"Mother!" The three of them were ushered into the room, and the high-pitched relief in their voices was impossible to miss.

"My dearests!" I bent a little to embrace all three of them, holding them to me as tightly as possible. They were here, they lived, they would survive. With or without a crown, it did not matter anymore, if they would just survive!

"You've hurt yourself," said Selene, looking at the marks on my arms and chest.

"It was an accident," I said. "And they are greatly improved."

"But how did it happen?" asked Philadelphos. "Did you run into something? A door full of nails?" He wrinkled his nose and strained himself imagining it.

"They are the marks of grief," I said. They must be told. Did they know about Antony? I led them over to a wide bench by the window and we sat down. "Your father has died," I said.

Alexander let out a cry. "Why?" he asked.

"When the city fell—you know we lost the battle. . . ."

"Did he get killed in the fighting?"

How could I explain it so they would understand?

"No, not in the fighting itself, but afterward."

"But how? How?" He was insistent.

I shook my head. "There was confusion," I finally said. "He had to do what a brave man must. It would not have been right for him to be taken prisoner. It would have been—dishonorable."

Selene broke into tears. "Do you mean he killed himself?"

I must tell the truth. "Yes. But he had no choice. It does not mean he wished to leave you." *Rulers are different. We have to do things ordinary people are spared.*

"Why didn't he have a choice?" asked Alexander. "What was so bad about being a prisoner? We are prisoners, aren't we?"

"Yes, but only for a little while. He would have been a prisoner forever."

"What about you?" asked Selene. She was looking directly at me. She always asked the most acute questions, as if she saw more than the others. "If he could not bear it, how can you?"

Oh, why must she ask that? Olympos and Caesarion had taught me well that I could not answer honestly. I could not risk it. And it was too hurtful to confess, anyway. I had already prepared my answer. "I am too well guarded to do what Antony did," I said. "Octavian would prevent it. So you need not worry. I imagine we will all be going to Rome—although separately. Or perhaps you will stay here while I go to Rome. I do not know yet whether it is you or Caesarion who will rule after me. The most sublime Octavian will decide."

"Octavian!" said Selene. "He has already visited us, and had us to his quarters. Your old rooms! He seemed very interested in us. He asked a lot of questions."

"Like what?"

"Oh, our favorite foods, how many languages we spoke, our patron gods. You know, polite things."

Yes. Polite things. "And what did you think of him?" I asked.

"He's scary!" said Philadelphos. "He just stares, that funny stare, even when he's acting friendly."

I laughed. An accurate description.

"You mustn't be afraid of him," I said. "Now that he's got what he wants, he will most likely be pleasant enough. You must pretend to like him, though. He is very sensitive about that."

"I suppose I should hug him and call him uncle!" said Alexander in a huff. "I don't want to! He killed my father!" Then, abruptly, "When is Father's funeral?"

"It already was," I said. And my heart ached that I did not even have Antony's sword to give him. Octavian had it. But perhaps it was just as well. What son would cherish the sword that had deprived him of a living father? "And it was not Octavian who killed your father. It was just . . . the fortunes of a lost war." And a lost empire, a lost world. The losses were all-encompassing, stretching out into eternity.

"Why wouldn't they let us see it?" asked Selene.

"Perhaps they felt it would be too painful," I said. Please don't let her ask about Antyllus! Don't ask if he was there!

Mercifully, she asked instead, "Do you think Octavian will make us live in Rome?"

"Not if you are ruling here. But he may take you for a visit. Would that be so bad?"

She shrugged. "I suppose not. But I'd rather go to India."

Now I was watching them carefully—more closely than Octavian, probably—trying to imprint their images on my heart forever. My three beautiful young children, all I had left of Antony. I tried to disguise it, hoping I was subtler than Octavian. Watching is difficult to hide. And the reason for my looking . . . that I would never see them again. I had to will my eyes to remain clear, not well up with tears, else they would suspect.

"My loves," I said, embracing them one by one, "we will endure this, and remember it only as a bad dream, look back on it and smile at our own bravery."

Letting them go was hard—one of the hardest things I have ever done. Now I had only one more thing to let go. All else was gone.

I wished I had something wise to say to them, some fitting words of parting. But nothing came to me. There were no words grand enough, or kind enough.

They were gone, taken chattering back to their rooms, their guards ever vigilant. Their every movement would be watched. Octavian would keep them tightly in his grasp. As he meant to keep me.

After they were gone, a void opened around me, in spite of the company still in the room. Iras was standing looking out to sea, Charmian tending the clothes, more from habit than from need. Her slender fingers smoothed the silks, folding them so precisely that they could be stacked ten or fifteen high. It was as if she thought I would wear all of them. Her silent, graceful, familiar motions were lulling to watch.

Mardian was reading, something he usually had little time for. Olympos was sitting glumly, his arms crossed. He looked tired and defeated. We were all trapped, only passing time in our cage.

Olympos, my dear, fierce friend, I think—if you should read this, although you respect privacy so much I doubt you will—keeping the secret from you was one of the greatest sorrows of those last days. You gave me no choice (*he had no choice; it does not mean he wished to leave you*), but it made what was already difficult even more painful. To be unable to say good-bye—that is a special punishment, worse the more we care. So, now I say it, say that good-bye I could not, then. Good-bye, may all the gods keep you. And do not forget, do not forget, all you know.

Outside the day was fresh and bright. I could see the sparkling sea, the waves tossing foam like pretty girls tossing their hair, beckoning to Alexandria, come and sport with me. . . .

Alexandria. It had been spared. It would escape the flames, the looting, the destruction that usually followed in the wake of defeat. My city would live, and my children. I had had all I could ask for.

The wind was singing, a lighthearted song. But inside we were prisoners and could only watch from the windows. It was the half-life of an invalid.

Invalid. Not valid. To render null. To weaken or destroy the force of. To dismiss from duty. To deprive of effective or continued existence. A world of woe in that one word, *invalid.*

I was now *invalid.* I could regain validity only through death.

Heads bent over our tasks, we drifted on our thoughts, until a knock on the door stirred us. Dolabella stepped in, smartly dressed like the rising young aristocrat he was. I thought idly what a winsome man he was. He would go far in Rome.

"Your Majesty," he said, "may I speak to you alone?"

I nodded, and the others rose silently and went into an adjoining room.

"Now," I said, smiling, "will you take some refreshments?" Octavian had left us so well provided for that I could almost entertain a cohort.

He just shook his head, glumly.

"Why, Dolabella," I said. "What is it?" His manner was alarming.

He came across the floor in jerky steps and then fell to one knee before me. He took one of my hands and looked at me imploringly. "Madam, dearest Queen, I hope you will believe me when I tell you that in the few days I have served as your guard, I have developed . . . a great respect and sympathy for you."

What was this about? "What are you trying to tell me?" I asked. I had a great dread of knowing. He had such a look of anguish that I knew it was something serious—and that he spoke the truth.

He said in a low voice, "I have just overheard the Imperator settling his plans. In three days he will leave Alexandria and return to Rome by way of Syria."

"And—what of us? What of us, here?"

Now his voice sank even lower. He did not want anyone to report that he had told me. "You are to be put on board ship and transferred to Rome."

So soon! Three days!

"And once I am there . . . what will he do with me?"

Dolabella looked away, and took a deep breath as if steeling himself.

"He'll lead me in his Triumph," I finished for him. "Do not be afraid to speak it, for I have always known it. Are you certain?"

"Entirely. He was planning the festivities. There will be three Triumphs, one for Illyria, one for Actium, and the last for Egypt. You are to be its chief ornament."

"Why, I can do double duty, appearing in two! For, after all, since he claims these were not civil wars, it follows that Roman did not fight Roman at Actium, but fought only Egyptians." It was a bitter joke.

"It is possible you would appear in both," he agreed, miserably.

"I thank you for warning me," I said.

Three days!

"I am grieved to have to do so, but it seemed crueler for you not to know."

"Yes. I am grateful that you understood that."

Three days!

"If there is anything—"

"Yes. Yes, there is," I said. "Let me write this request to Octavian, and you can take it to him. Please do your best to persuade him to allow it. It would mean so much to me, especially in the circumstances."

With an odd calmness, I went to my writing desk, pulled out paper, sought the words for the simple request. I had so little time. The guards must be misled like Octavian, made to relax their grip on me, grow careless.

Hail, great Imperator Caesar, I beg your divine mercy in allowing me to pour offerings and libations on the tomb of my husband, and to observe the ancient custom of Egypt in serving a funerary feast there. Without it, his spirit cannot rest.

I handed the note to Dolabella, who read it carefully. He nodded. "I shall do all that I can, my lady."

"It is important to me. I cannot leave without it. Surely he will not be so hard-hearted as to deny me. The soldiers can guard me all the while."

But not in the mausoleum. They would avoid going in there, contenting themselves with watching the doors and inspecting the food going in. They would not suspect the danger already inside, waiting.

Let the basket still be there, in the shadows where it had been hidden!

"I will do my best," he said. "This is a mournful task."

"Do not grieve yourself over it. It is I who have brought myself to this. It is not your doing. Your kindness only makes it easier to bear." I reached out and touched his arm. "Now go. Do what I ask."

He nodded, then turned quickly and left.

So little time. I called my friends—for so they were, rather than mere attendants—back into the room. There could be no hiding what was to come—except from Olympos. I would have to manage him cleverly. (Forgive me, friend!)

"What was it?" asked Mardian, his normally pleasing voice agitated. Behind him came the others.

"Dolabella has been kind enough to inform me that Octavian is shipping me back to Rome for his Triumph."

Do not let them start wailing and protesting! I begged the gods. And my prayer was granted. My companions, levelheaded and strong, just nodded.

"We will make you ready," said Charmian, and we all knew what she meant—all but Olympos.

"Octavian is going by land, as he does not like the sea," I said. But I did. Another sea journey for me, to another destiny. This one I declined to take. "I may well arrive in Rome before him." If news truly traveled on the wind, then it was a certainty.

"When is this to be?" asked Iras.

"In three days' time," I said. I turned to Olympos. "I wish you to return to your wife now. You are the only one of us with a family outside the palace. Please go there. You have done all you can for me—see how I mend?"

"No, I must stay until that ship sets sail!" he insisted.

"No," I said. "Remember your task? It is imperative that you depart now. Distance yourself from us while you can. You already have the completed scrolls—all except this last, which I am finishing, and will finish, before I am taken away. Be sure to come and collect it; it will be with my other things. I will write instructions allowing it, which they will honor. Then fulfill your promise. To Philae, and Meroe. In your own time. You will know the hour."

He grasped my hands in such a tight grip it hurt the bones. "I cannot just walk away, out of the palace, back to the Museion."

I looked deeply into his eyes, and tried to make my command clear. "You must." I paused. "It is over. Do not fail me now."

"Is an ending so simple?" he asked. His voice had faded almost to nothing.

"We must make it so," I said. "Let us not torture ourselves by drawing it out."

He let go of my hands but continued looking, hawklike, at me. Then something in him gave up, yielded, and he leaned forward and embraced me. He kissed my cheek. I felt his to be wet.

"Farewell, my dearest," he said. "I have preserved you safely to this hour. Now—I must give you to the gods."

He pulled away and walked resolutely to the door, his back to me.

"You have done well," I said. "For I have long been moving toward this hour."

He lurched out of the room, as if he was in pain. I heard low arguing between him and the Roman guards, but they had no orders to hold him, and had to let him pass.

When I was absolutely sure that he was gone—forlorn feeling!—I gathered the remaining three around me.

"Listen," I whispered, to thwart any eavesdroppers. "We will carry out our plan tomorrow. I have asked Octavian for permission to visit the mausoleum and perform final rites for Antony. We will dress in our finest garments, and partake of a funeral banquet, in privacy. Do you understand? I will send for my crown and jewels, ask Octavian to lend them. He will not refuse. Then we will be ready to depart and make our journey."

"To Rome?" asked Mardian, an ironic twist to his mouth. He spoke loudly enough to be heard, should anyone be listening.

"Yes, we will go meekly to Rome," I said, smiling. "We will all go together."

"Then let us begin our preparations," said Iras.

"Yes, you must help me select my clothes. For the most important occasion of all."

Now I was thankful that Octavian had sent so many gowns to these rooms. I would have a wide choice. Something to occupy me for the passing hours.

Silently Charmian held up each gown, shaking out its folds and letting it hang free. She had just finished folding all of them; the labor to be undone so soon. The sorrow of it, part of the larger sorrow.

How many times had I done this? How many audiences and meetings had I draped myself for? Each of them had seemed pivotal at the time, each of them indeed important, but none had approached this.

Rustles of silk, whispering in all the colors of the sun and the fields: white, primrose, fern, poppy, the blue of the sea around the Lighthouse. Each had brought joy to my heart in its time. But none was right for—this. I needed a singular gown in which to meet Isis at last.

"There." There it was, never yet worn. A green so pure that beside it emeralds were dirty and grass dull. The green of Egypt's fields, the fierce green of her crops under the sun, glowing under the eye of Re. Green seemed the most Egyptian of all colors: her Nile, her crocodiles, her papyrus. And Wadjyt, the cobra goddess of Lower Egypt, whose very name means "the green one."

"I shall wear this one." I reached out and took it from Charmian.

The fine silk was soft in my hands. The neckline was low, square. Perfect. That would allow for a wide gold collar, as in an old tomb painting.

"And your hair, my lady?" asked Iras.

"It will need to go under my royal headdress," I said. "It must be simple."

"Simple is best," she agreed.

"We must send for the finest bathing oils and perfumes," said Charmian. "For your hair must be perfect. Everything must be perfect."

"Octavian will grant whatever we ask," I said. "Let us make the request now, so he has time to send it by tomorrow morning."

As it was growing dark, and the enemy Epaphroditus stepped in to see to the lamps, we greeted him pleasantly. He gave an embarrassed smile and wished us a good evening.

"The supper is on its way," he said. "I trust you will find it tasty."

"There is little I do not find agreeable," I said. "My appetite is not finicky."

He waved the burning stick he used to light the lamps. "That makes it easy," he said. He paused. "As to your requests—I expect an answer soon."

"I realize the Imperator has much to attend to," I assured him.

"He will not neglect this," said Epaphroditus.

The supper finished, the dishes removed, we sat waiting, silent. In the last hours, there is no busywork to make time pass. It was quite dark outside, and a brisk breeze coming in the windows made the lamp flames dance. I could hear the slapping of the water against the seawall. The harbor was playing tonight, saying, *Listen! I am calling! Take your boats, ride upon me!* And perhaps the lovers, the friends, the children, all the free citizens of the city, would accept the invitation.

Yes, the city was free. It would endure. And my children would take up the trust I left them, as I had taken my father's. I had done all I could to ensure that. Caesarion . . . where was he? On his way to India?

I had done all I could. Nothing more remained. One son sent away, the others left to obey and appease the victor. Those were the only two routes open to them. Surely one would avail.

We lie down in the darkness, stretching out as if to sleep. Stretching like Nut, the sky goddess, who swallows the sun every night and gives birth to him each morning. I feel the smooth sheet beneath me, for the whole length of the bed.

How close Old Egypt is tonight. Hovering over me like Nut, surrounding me protectively. On our last night, the gods bend down, touch us.

Dawn. Dawn on the tenth day, the last day. So ten is to be my sacred number, the one reserved for me. The ten scrolls were emblematic. I still have this tenth, and I mean to keep it with me until the end. I yet have things to impart.

"Permission granted!" Epaphroditus steps into the room, beaming. "I am pleased to tell you that the Imperator has graciously consented that you may leave the palace and attend the tomb of the lord Antony as you have requested. He himself will provide the traditional food for the banquet, and the guards to attend you. He regrets that he cannot attend in person, but his thoughts will be with you."

I incline my head. "My thanks to the Imperator."

"In addition, he is sending your crown, jewels, and other insignia. You may keep whatever you like; he had already assured you of that. They are on their way even now." Epaphroditus bows smartly.

"And the special oils?" asks Charmian.

"Oh yes. Of course."

So it is all to be permitted. Still, the "gracious" Imperator has not seen fit to inform me that I am being taken to Rome. An oversight, no doubt.

And now it is time. The bath is drawn, the precious oil of lotus is poured from its slender stoppered bottle and mingles with the warm water. I float in the fragrant pool, lying motionless. My hair is washed in rainwater, rinsed with scented water brought all the way from the sacred well at Heliopolis. Iras combs it out, lets it fall straight where it will dry.

We open the coffer of jewels. They are all there; Octavian has removed nothing. There is the magnificent collar with its layers of carnelian, lapis, gold, turquoise. It covers from the neck to below the shoulders. There is the wedding necklace, the fantasy of gold leaves.

"Both of them," I say. "Why not both?" Why not, indeed?

The headdress is shaped like a vulture, the protective goddess of Upper Egypt, and the feathers spread out over my head, encasing it. The wings make shields around my cheeks. On my brow is a wide *uraeus*, the sacred cobra of Lower Egypt, hood spread, ready to strike.

Already I feel remote, removed from Charmian, Iras, Mardian. The gradual layering of costume, heavy with symbol and power, has changed me into something else, even though they were the ones to bedeck me and effect the transformation. Now it is done, and I am another creature.

Even if my children were to burst into the room, even if I were told I could return to my old life, I could not. The change is basic, and irreversible. Just so can death anticipate itself.

The soldiers arrive. We leave the room, through the passage, step outside into the open air. The day is bright and clear, the air pure. A day at its height, as if it wanted to leave an impression to carry into the darkness, to linger in our hearts. There are six soldiers, large men, and the faithful, spying Epaphroditus. His master must be informed, know all that passes.

Across the grounds of the palace. Green grass, shaded paths. The soldiers all gone, no one watching. The day sings, rejoices.

Our little procession keeps a stately pace. It is hard to move beneath all my regalia; the collars, the headdress press on me, weigh me down. Under all this my body is small and light, but it is smothered, shackled.

The yawning doors of the mausoleum. I dread to enter, but only because beholding Antony's tomb causes me such pain. Seeing my own, ready, gives me joy.

The tramp of their feet: The soldiers are following us into the tomb itself. Very well, then, let them listen!

I approach the granite sarcophagus, so neatly sealed, so finished, so final. Antony dead for ten days. Ten days, ten portentous days. How have I lived without him all this time?

I hold the wreaths of flowers, the Pharaonic garlands of cornflowers, willow, olive, poppies, yellow ox-tongue. I kneel and drape them over the cold stone. Then the sacred oil, poured onto the surface and spread by my fingers until the granite gleams higher than ever.

"O Antony," I say. I believe that he can hear me. At the same time I know the soldiers are listening intently.

"Beloved husband . . . with these hands I buried you. Then they were free. Now I am bound as a captive, and pay even these last duties with a guard upon me. They watch me to keep me whole for the celebration of our defeat. I am to help them rejoice in our downfall." I keep rubbing the oil into the stone, with circling movements. The soldiers bend close, the better to listen, catch each word.

"Expect no further offerings from me; these are the last honors that your Cleopatra can pay your memory. I am being hurried away from you. Nothing could divide us while we lived, but now, in death . . ." Were the soldiers listening? Did they hear clearly?

I speak louder. ". . . in death, we are threatened with separation. You, a Roman born, have found your grave in Egypt; I, an Egyptian, am to seek that favor, and none but that, in your country."

Then the soldiers vanish from my consciousness; there is only Antony, and me. Now I speak only to him, in a whisper. "But if the gods below, with whom you now are, either can or will do anything—since those above have betrayed us!—suffer not your living wife to be abandoned; let me not be led in triumph to your shame, but hide me and bury me here with you . . . since, among my bitter misfortunes, nothing has afflicted me like this brief time I have lived away from you." I am crying—I, who thought myself to be lifted past all feeling.

Life apart from him . . . had there been any?

The soldiers lean forward to hear. I rise and, lying across the sarcophagus, kiss it. The hard, cold stone is my bed. There are no more words. I wait for the constriction in my throat to release its grip.

They also wait, stiffly. Charmian, Iras, and Mardian do not dare to move, and no one touches me. Finally I pull myself from the sarcophagus.

"And now we will have the funeral meal," I say.

The chief soldier gives the order, and—so soon it feels like an instant—a procession of dishes is brought in and set before us on a ceremonial table.

In ancient days, Egyptian tombs had chambers where the family of the dead man could feast before his statue. His spirit would come and join them.

"I thank you," I say. "Now, since you are not Egyptian, nor of this family, I would ask you to withdraw and keep watch at the door. And please take this message to the Imperator, expressing my thanks." I hand the note to the head soldier.

Politely they withdraw.

"Pray close the doors," I say.

"Shall we see?" whispers Charmian.

"In time, in time," I say. Now there is no hurry. Let everything be done in order, as it is meant to be. "Spread the feast."

A repast worthy of the gods is ours. There is the traditional mortuary offering of beer, bread, ox, and geese: *every good and pure thing upon which the god lives, for the ka of Marcus Antonius, deceased.* There is also Roman bread, and Antony's favorite wine. Pity we have no appetite. But so that the ritual be observed, we taste everything once. We would not have the cooks labor in vain.

"Give me the scroll," I ask Mardian, who takes it from his carrying pouch, along with writing implements.

"Please allow me a few minutes to write," I ask them. In the dimness I spread the paper out and record what has passed since we have left the palace. It is brief, hurried. Forgive me. Neither the right words nor the right conditions are at my command. But they must serve for you, Caesarion, Olympos, and anyone who needs to know of these last hours. Now I leave it, to await the last.

"Now," I say to Iras. "You may see if all is as I have prayed."

With her grace of movement—ah! I will miss it!—she slips around to the dark part of the mausoleum. We wait. Isis will not fail me. She awaits me. She has stayed the hand of any soldiers, has blindfolded any searchers, so that I may come to her now, in my own time.

Iras glides back out into the light, holding the basket aloft. "It was over-looked," she says. "But the trunk, with the clothes and crown, is gone."

The trunk had been large, and held a treasure. A dusty basket is easy to overlook. Particularly one with old figs in it—dark figs, bulbous and musty. Masking the characteristic scent of the serpents—a smell not unlike cucumbers in the field, lying under the sun. Nakht had done well.

"Give it to me," I say. It is heavy. I had not expected it to be so heavy.

I put the basket on the funeral table, lift the lid. A slight stirring inside. A gentle sliding. Then something rears up.

I take the serpent in my hand. It is thick, cool, mostly dark with a lighter underside. Its tongue flicks out. It seems very docile.

I draw it slowly out of its basket. It is longer than I had guessed; as long as the span of both my arms. And as it flops out, I see more movement in the basket. Nakht has sent two. That was foresighted of him.

"So here it is," I say, staring at the serpent. Its dark eyes look into mine. Its tongue wavers, testing. I hold it up.

Mardian, Iras, and Charmian flinch. They cannot help it.

"Madam—" says Charmian, but her protest dies on her lips.

The creature seems sluggish. He lies upon my hand as if he were a pet, as tame as my dear monkey. But we have not all the time in the world. Octavian will get the note soon. He will know.

I smack its head, and it draws back, hissing. Then the hood—familiar from a thousand representations, reflected on my own crown—spreads itself.

So quickly that I cannot follow it with my eyes, it strikes. It bites my arm, sinking its fangs in. They feel like needles, tiny little pins.

Now I wait. With great joy I know I am delivered. I can only write a little more. It was my other arm it struck, but I yet have things to do before I sleep. My arm tingles; the fingers grow cold, as if they do not belong to me. The loss of sensation is creeping upward, but there is no real pain. At the same time it is affecting my mind; I feel a carelessness—more deadly than pain—taking possession of me. It is a fuzzy lightheartedness . . . why be concerned? Why take pains to finish the task?

Because I am the Queen. And my will is stronger than the poison. I will do what I must, until the last moment.

So I close you, and entrust you to Olympos. May my story be preserved, and the truth survive. The world is a hard place to leave. I have done my best by it, served it and loved it with all my being.

Isis, your daughter comes. Please spread your robe, and welcome her. She has journeyed long to reach you.

I feel a tugging, pulling me downward. Now I must close you, scroll. Farewell. *Vale*, as the Romans say. We part now. Remember me. May you live a thousand—ten thousand—years, so that I may live also.

Peace, my heart. Obey me and stand still. For I have done.

HERE ENDS THE TENTH SCROLL.

THE SCROLL OF OLYMPOS

1

Fool! Fool that I am! I suspected nothing, all these months—I cannot believe I was so taken in. But was not your way better than mine? What could my way offer you? I am ashamed that evidently I knew you so much less well than I thought. Puffed up with my own sense of responsibility, I thought I could control events—or rather (see, even here I flatter myself) I was afraid to help move them. Instead I sat like a rock, thinking I was wise and strong, when all I truly was was a hindrance and a wedge between us.

The sun was setting and I was just finishing my own supper when the soldiers stormed in. (Why am I writing this as if you do not know it all, as if you did not, somehow, behold it? I am frantic, trying to calm myself. Talking wildly.) There were three of them, enormous fellows, made even more enormous by their thick breastplates and high helmets. One of them grabbed me by the shoulder and shook me. I thought my teeth would fly out.

"Filthy Greek!" he shouted. "Filthy, lying, treacherous Greek!" Then he threw me against the wall. I hit it so hard I actually bounced off and fell onto my face on the floor.

Then I was hauled up again, and there was more yelling in my ear. All the shaking, throwing, and bouncing made me feel nauseated. I was afraid I would vomit right onto the soldier's sandals, which were wavering dangerously before my eyes.

"You did it, you can undo it!"

"Let him loose, Appius," one of the others said. "It won't do any good to have him dead, too."

"If he can't fix it, he *will* be dead," my tormentor said.

As soon as I heard "dead," I knew. And, oddly, what I felt was relief.

(Then why had I tried to prevent it? Why had I driven you to resort to the bizarre?)

"The Queen is—you have to save her!" bellowed Appius, the leader.

"Where is she? What has happened?" I asked. A fair question, would you not agree?

"You know well enough," he snapped. "Since you arranged it!"

He jerked my arm and started pulling me toward the door. For good measure another soldier stuck a dagger at my back—as if I needed prodding.

When we reached the mausoleum, a huge crowd was gathered outside, but the door was strictly guarded. People were trying to peep inside, but the soldiers shoved them back at spearpoint. However, they fell away in exaggerated respect as I was escorted in.

In the dim light I could see yet more people gathered inside. But I had no eyes for them. All I could see was you.

Oh, I congratulate you. You had arranged it so well, as well as anything you had ever undertaken. Perhaps everything else had been just a preparation for this, your coup and masterpiece.

You were lying there on the wide lid of your sarcophagus, as still as stone, wearing your royal robes and crown, your arms crossed, with the crook and flail folded over your breast. That you were completely dead was certain. There would be no rescue, no reversal.

Nonetheless I approached, while my captors watched eagerly—as if I had some secret of life and death, when all I was was a poor mechanic who could tug at the doors of the underworld occasionally, when the gods permitted me.

I should tell you (if this is still important to you) that you were utterly beautiful. Whatever means you had chosen had left no mark on you, indeed seemed to have enhanced your appearance. Or perhaps it was just the joy of departure. You were so very happy to escape.

It was not until I took my eyes off your face that I saw the crumpled bodies of Iras and Charmian lying beside the sarcophagus. I bent down and touched them. They were dead, too.

Only then did I take your hand, just to be sure, before I spoke. Some trace of warmth yet lingered.

"They are all beyond saving," I said.

"The Psylli can work miracles," said one of the soldiers. "The Imperator has already sent for them."

Now I was astounded. "It was snakes?" I asked.

"We think so," said one man. "We found a trail outside, and this basket—" He held up a wide-mouthed basket that had figs in it.

I looked at you carefully. There seemed to be two tiny marks on one of your arms, but I could not be sure.

Snakes. How fitting. Not only are they sacred to Egypt, but associated with the power of the underworld and with fertility. Perhaps I did you a favor by refusing more conventional poisons.

The Psylli arrived, with much ado. These tribesmen are renowned for supposedly being immune to snake poison, and able to suck the venom from a victim's wound and revive him. But they were far too late, in spite of making a fuss and lingering over your arm.

However, they soon found a target for their attentions, because a moaning from the back of the mausoleum revealed Mardian, doubled up and unconscious. They hovered around him, locating the bite in his leg and treating it vigorously.

In the meantime, Octavian arrived, angry and white-faced. He marched directly over to the sarcophagus and stared down at you. I thought he would never stop; his face was unreadable. Finally he stepped back and said, but only to himself, "Very well, then. Indeed I shall grant the request."

He shook his head and only then looked around. "All dead?" he asked.

"Sir, the Queen was already dead when we got in," said the head guard. "The women were in the process of dying. One was lying here"—he pointed to the limp Iras—"and the other one was straightening the Queen's crown. I seized her and said, 'Mistress, is this well done of your lady?' and she answered, 'Extremely well, and as becomes the descendant of so many kings.' Then she fell dead, too."

"She spoke the truth," said Octavian. He had an odd smile on his face, it was a smile of—yes, admiration. You had impressed him. Outsmarting him had won his highest respect.

"Prepare them all for the burial the Queen requested." He handed the guard a note.

He looked at you almost fondly. "The note spoke well for you." He glanced over at the other sarcophagus. "You and your Antony will lie here together. No, death will not separate you." Then he turned smartly on his heel.

"Sir," said one of the guards, "there is this one fellow here who survives." And they carried Mardian around to Octavian, and laid him at his feet.

Octavian laughed. "So this is all the efforts of the Psylli have achieved? He is of no use to me. Nor to anyone, now. Retire from public life, if you recover," he said, dismissing him. "Come." He motioned to his guards. Then, abruptly, he turned to me. I thought he had not even seen me, let alone remembered me.

"I will forget the words you spoke to me in Rome about the false claims of the Queen's son," he said. "I suggest you forget them, too."

Then he was gone.

The Psylli left, and all the extra guards. Morticians came in to ready the dead for burial, and I looked my last at you.

No matter how long we look, eventually we must stop looking, and go away. It is what the living are forced to do. No amount of looking ever makes us ready to leave.

But I could not live here, in the mausoleum. You had given me a task. My work was yet to be done.

Yes, it was well done, and fitting for the descendant of so many kings. I salute you, even as I grieve.

Friend of my childhood, I had hoped to share old age with you as well. But goddesses do not grow old.

2

From Olympos, to Olympos:

As I have always kept the most meticulous medical notes (those who think I have a prodigious memory are wrong; I merely have a prodigious system for recording and organizing what I have found), so I will record briefly what happened in the tumultuous days following the death of Octavian's last enemy, the Queen of Egypt, Cleopatra the Great. For she was truly the greatest of Egypt's rulers, a political genius who turned the weak country she inherited into something before which even Rome trembled. Who else but a political genius of the first order would have thought of using Romans to threaten Rome? And she was the last to reign over Egypt as a free country. Yes, these notes may be necessary someday, if only to offset the official version of events, preserve a different viewpoint.

I secured the Queen's last scroll from where it rested near the tomb, neatly rolled up (how like her!), and took it home, where I read it, to my woe and wonder. Mardian was transported to my house, where Dorcas and I nursed him. His recovery was slow, but as I pointed out to him, it was his fat that saved him. That, and the fact that he was bitten low on his leg, below the knee, and that the snake had already bitten three other people before him, and evidently was running low on venom! I have observed that fat people survive poisonous bites better than thin ones . . . possibly the fat traps the poisons?

He was feverish and delirious for days, muttering and moaning, while his leg swelled and the skin stretched so taut it shone. But at length it subsided, and he was able to recount those last hours in the mausoleum. How the funeral feast was held, how the serpents had been sent from Heliopolis by an arrangement made months before, and how they were waiting inside the building. There were two of them, but only one was used. Where had the other gone? A mystery—both had vanished in the sands outside. How they had planned it all, and how smoothly it had gone. The note sent to Octavian was a request for burial rites. Of course, as soon as he opened it, he knew. Then he sent soldiers running to try to prevent it.

The poison must have been very swift, since they had not allowed themselves much time to carry out the plan. Mardian told me the asps were prize ones from Heliopolis, bred for their fast, fatal bites. Even normal asps are used in Alexandria as the most humane and painless means of execution, so these must have been a step beyond even that.

The funeral was royal and magnificent, but only an echo of other celebrations in Alexandria's history. The city was mourning, having fallen at last to Rome, and having lost its proud Queen. Silently its citizens stood watching the cortege, bidding farewell not only to Cleopatra but to their freedom and their glory among cities. Mardian and I stood with the rest, he leaning on crutches.

Both Iras and Charmian were entombed beside their mistress, and Octavian erected a memorial tablet to them. As I have said, he seemed quite taken with the courage and grace of the death scene in the mausoleum.

As soon as the funeral was decently over, Octavian went sightseeing. He visited Alexander's tomb, but, not content with merely looking at the conqueror, he insisted that the crystal cover be removed so he could touch him. Evidently he was imbued with the idea that some power would pass from Alexander to him; after all, were they not the same age, and both possessed of an enormous empire? And, truly, Octavian now controlled almost as great an area as Alexander had. He must, then, be Alexander's true successor. Then something untoward happened: a piece of Alexander's nose came off in Octavian's hand. Was the great one rejecting Octavian, or giving him a precious relic? Like most symbolic events, this one was open to wildly differing interpretations.

Shortly thereafter Octavian ordered all of Antony's statues to be overthrown, but a timely bribe of two thousand talents by a loyal friend of Cleopatra's prevented hers from being likewise destroyed, and thus they remain standing throughout the land.

Enemies must be punished: Canidius was executed, as were some senators who had adhered too closely to Antony's cause.

Making a show of his restraint, Octavian was reputed to have taken nothing from the palace except an agate drinking cup, an old possession of the Ptolemies. It was one I knew Cleopatra to have set great store by. But the victor can take his pick of whatever excites his fancy, large or small.

Behind his smiling face, Octavian proceeded to his heinous deed, the one he had planned all along, as his words to me in the mausoleum revealed. I must record it in the briefest manner, because to linger over it is to ache with helpless fury and sorrow.

Using the swiftest messengers, Octavian was able to reach Caesarion and Rhodon before they boarded the ship for India. Money persuaded Rhodon in turn to persuade Caesarion that they must return to Alexandria, where Octavian wished to make him King. Once they were there, acting on the practical advice of his philosopher friend Areius, who paraphrased Homer in saying, "Too many Caesars is not a good thing," Octavian had Caesarion killed.

Of all the lost things in all the world, the things we will never know, this lost son of Caesar and Cleopatra's must stand as the most tantalizing. What would he have been, what being would he have grown into, with the gifts he had from both of his remarkable parents? Octavian did not wish to find out—and so we never shall, either.

Only one small glint of mercy here: Cleopatra never knew of his fate; she closed her eyes and went into the dark believing that he was safe. Isis had protected her to the last from that which would hinder her passage into the other world by grieving her spirit.

Where was Caesarion buried? No one knows; I like to think it was beside Antyllus, wherever that was, and that the two boys are together, consoling each other over the fateful downfall of their parents. Both were heirs whose potential challenge Octavian could not brook.

Such matters having been taken care of, Octavian took his leave of Egypt, carrying his agate cup, his victory, and Cleopatra's three remaining children. If their mother had refused to grace his Triumph, he must make do with them.

3

My duties were not over. I had thought they were, with the departure of the Romans. But no. Those of us who are living do not have our obligations and involvements end as neatly as those who have chosen death. Life drags out, drags on, and continues making intermittent, unexpected demands on our loyalties.

Human decency and respect constrained me to follow the royal children and watch over them in Rome, if only from a distance. I seemed doomed to continue ministering to the Queen long beyond what I had imagined when I gave my promise.

I followed them to Rome, arriving in the heat of the summer. The children were all lodged together with the long-suffering Octavia. I could see them when I walked on the Palatine at sunset. They looked content enough as they played games on the grounds with their half-siblings, Antony's other children. Octavia presided over a household of some nine children now, including hers and Fulvia's as well as the Egyptian ones. Octavian's only child, Julia, must have been there often as well, meaning the ages ranged from the nineteen-year-old Marcella to little Philadelphos, age six. I did not make myself known to them, thinking it was better that way, but I hovered on the edges of their lives, spying from the path outside their house.

Octavian had dallied, making his way slowly overland. It was not until March that he returned, and then he set about planning the details of his Triumph—or, rather, Triumphs, for there were to be three of them, on three successive days. He chose the month that was called Sextilis, the month that Alexandria had fallen. He would parade through the streets on the very day that the Queen's funeral procession had wound through Alexandria. He liked things to be neat like that.

In the meantime, while awaiting his arrival, the city busied itself thinking of honors for their master, and deeds to please him. The Senate passed a resolution condemning Antony, declaring the day he had been born to be cursed, and forbade anyone to use the names *Marcus* and *Antonius* together. His name on all monuments was to be erased, as if he had not existed. They declared the day that Alexandria had fallen to be a supremely lucky day in the calendar, and even proposed that henceforth all Alexandrians must celebrate it as the start of a new era, the first day of a refigured calendar. They proposed that Octavian be granted tribunician power for life, and that he was to be prayed for at all banquets, public and private, and have libations poured to him.

Then our old friend Plancus, he of the blue body-paint and timely desertion, created a new name and title for G. Julius Caesar Octavianus, *divi filius*: Augustus, the Revered One. It hinted at godhood, but not so blatantly that it would offend old-line Republicans. It was satisfyingly vague but majestical nonetheless. Octavian was most pleased, and allowed it to be bestowed upon his laureled head. He had now been transformed into Imperator Caesar Augustus, leaving any common-sounding names, which might betray his origins, behind him.

Like Caesar, he must have a month named after him. It was assumed that—like Caesar—he would choose his birth month, which in his case was September. But no. He chose Sextilis, his great victory month, for his memorial. Henceforth it was to be known as August.

And so, on the thirteenth, fourteenth, and fifteenth of August, the Triumphal processions would rumble through the streets. They were rumored to be even more lavish than Caesar's. Horace and Vergil had both written laudatory verses in commemoration. Bizarre African animals were to be shown for the first time to Rome. No one living must ever forget these celebrations.

How to describe them? As briefly and plainly as possible—I am not here to laud Octavian. It is true that I will never forget them, but for personal reasons.

The first, commemorating the victory over the Illyrians, was a modest affair. There was a parade of prisoners, with three chieftains as figurehead enemies, and the recaptured standards lost by Gabinius years earlier, and banners proclaiming the defeat of the Pannonians, Dalmations, Iapydes, and some Germanic and Gallic tribes. The Vestal Virgins came out of the city to meet the Triumphal chariot and escort it into Rome, and the senators walked alongside the soldiers behind the chariot.

The second, celebrating the naval victory of Actium, was more lavish. Adroitly, no Romans were featured, but only the client kings—half of whom had deserted before the battle was even fought! Ah, the genius of rewriting history! Poor Adiatorix of Galatia and Alexander of Emesa were marched out, men who had barely figured in the fighting. Agrippa was awarded a blue banner for his achievement, and it was announced that henceforth the victory of Actium would be celebrated with sacred games every four years, a sort of rival Olympics. Beaks of the captured ships, from "fours" to "tens," would be mounted on a platform as a memorial in the Forum.

And now we come to the Alexandrian Triumph, the last and the grandest. The same array of Vestal Virgins and senators and soldiers made up the parade, but they were dwarfed by the prizes exhibited. A hippopotamus and a rhinoceros plodded along the Via Sacra. Lines of Nubians embellished the Forum, providing exotic prisoners. Carts groaning with booty swayed along the stones. I said that Octavian did not take anything from Alexandria, but of course he had helped himself to the treasury, which he had come so far to get. The amount of gold transferred to Rome had the effect of immediately lowering interest rates there from twelve percent to four.

A representation of the Nile itself, complete with all seven mouths, rolled past, followed by flat wagons displaying Egyptian statues, snatched from the temples.

At last Octavian himself appeared in his chariot, being saluted as the conqueror of the world, wearing the crown, rather than having it merely held over his head by a slave. And then . . . O shame! Walking behind the chariot, in chains, were Selene and Alexander, with little Philadelphos between them, followed by a lurid, huge depiction of their mother, snakes twined around her arms.

She looked fierce, her eyes blazing, her fists clenched. Was she supposed to be dying? She was stretched on her couch, but not limply. She radiated power and purpose. Was it to depict her as the rapacious enemy who had posed such a threat to Rome? Whatever it was, it caused the crowd to cry out, to cheer. Were they applauding her or rejoicing? Possibly both. The snakes suggested Isis as well as her death. It was not unworthy of her. So she had eluded Octavian's victory parade, and this was his way of saluting her for it: the enemy larger than life.

Beside the picture an actor walked, reciting some of Horace's poem about Actium:

> She preferred a finer style of dying:
>   She did not, like a woman, shirk the dagger
>   Or seek by speed at sea
>   To change her Egypt for obscurer shores,

> But gazing on her desolated palace
> With a calm smile, unflinchingly she laid hands on
>   The angry asps until
> Her veins had drunk the deadly poison deep:
>
> And, death-determined, fiercer now than ever,
> Perished. Was she to grace a haughty triumph,
>   Dethroned, paraded by
> The rude Liburnians? Not Cleopatra.

As the parade concluded, Octavian dismounted from the chariot and mo-tioned to the children. Now was when prisoners were taken off to a prison cell to be strangled while the victor gave solemn thanks at the Temple of Jupiter Capitolinus. But Octavian took Antony and Cleopatra's children with him to mount the steps up to the Temple. Thereafter they vanished back into his household.

There were yet two ceremonies to be observed, tacked onto the end of the Triumph. The doors to the Temple of Janus were formally closed, pronounc-ing an end to war. And Octavian made his way to Caesar's temple, there to dedicate a statue of Victory and present Egyptian spoils.

Then it was over, and the general celebrations could begin—the eating, drinking, dancing. I shall not describe it; all crowd celebrations are the same. But I pushed my way through the mob to reach Caesar's Temple of Venus Genetrix in his Forum. I had to see if . . . it would be surprising if . . . but Octavian was a surprising man, I grant him that.

And he surprised me now—pleasantly. For standing where Caesar had placed it seventeen years ago was the gold statue of Cleopatra as goddess and consort. The enemy in the Forum still reigned supreme and honored in this house of Caesar; so revered was Caesar that no one dared attack the statue. Or perhaps it was more than that; perhaps the Romans, who admire courage and a resolute foe above everything else, secretly wished to honor their greatest adversary and keep her where, over the years, they could pay her homage.

4

And now I address you again, my friend, my Queen. Strange how death does not stop us from talking to our departed ones. Or, rather, there are stages we go through: At first, when the gulf is recent and therefore not so wide, we chatter freely, feeling them to be just behind us. Then something happens— grief, gazing on the tomb, seeing the empty seat—that creates a thick wall between us. Then time itself, such a fluid thing, dissolves the barrier and we are back where we started, close again.

Such has happened to me, in regards to you. And once that separation had vanished, I was able to set out to complete the journey that you entrusted to me.

Oh yes, the scrolls are bulky and heavy. They require a stout trunk to house them. I have all ten of them—twenty, actually, since you insisted on copies going to the Kandake. You always knew that we must help chance to triumph, hence an extra set is prudent.

It was good to leave Alexandria; you were right about that. My medical practice has exploded beyond what I can manage, as I have become monstrously famous—or notorious—as the Queen's physician. They credit me with the asps, with which, of course, I had nothing to do, and with miraculously saving Mardian, which also was not my doing but his luck in being bitten last, and being so bulky. The notoriety is a nuisance, and keeps me from the anonymity I prize. So a lengthy excursion to Meroe is most welcome, and refreshing.

Passing through the canal, then down the Nile, I am retracing our childhood excursion of so long ago. Egypt never changes: the same palms, the same mud-brick houses, the same pyramids. It is good to remind myself of that. Here, beyond Memphis, I question whether they even know that Octavian is the new "Pharaoh."

Yes, he has embraced this identity. He is posing as your heir—isn't that amusing? By taking in Alexander, Selene, and Philadelphos, and rearing them in his Roman household, he pretends to continuity of the line. I understand carvers are busy in temples depicting him in Pharaonic crown, sacrificing to Osiris and Horus. But I do not plan to stop and look at them.

Egypt, Egypt, eternal Egypt . . . always unique. The new "Pharaoh" has declared it a special province, one that no prominent Roman may even visit without express permission. It is to be maintained as a gigantic park, Octavian's own playground. Cornelius Gallus will oversee it, but he is not its governor. It has no governor.

Timeless eddies on the river, sandbanks with crocodiles, temples, sand, papyrus reeds, and the wide bosom of the Nile reaching down into Africa. It is easy to forget everything else, and let time swirl away.

I will push on past Philae, going all the way to Meroe. There has lately been some trouble around the First Cataract between the Nubians and the Romans, and I think it safer to make my way south first. I must confess that I plan to question the physicians of Meroe and take back samples of any medicinal plants they may have, and thus I am anxious to get there.

I have arrived. It has taken me four months! Months in which to read your account of your own journey here, past all the cataracts. It is not something lightly undertaken. Now the city looms before me, and the banks are lined with the curious. I can only hope that the Kandake is still well, and reigns. Odd how we think distance can confer longevity as well.

She has received me. She lives, although arthritically, and moves her bulk in great majesty through her palace. She was rhapsodical about you, recalling your visit to her so many years ago.

"But I warned her about the Romans," she said, wagging her finger. "I told her to stay away from them, and to make an alliance with me instead." She was seated on a wide-legged bench, with the proffered chest of scrolls at her feet.

"I think it was they who could not stay away from her," I said. And it was true.

"I told her I would avenge her when the Romans—whom she insisted on trafficking with!—let her down. And I have." She nodded solemnly. "I have." She pointed to her left eye, which was blind. "I have surrendered my eye to the Romans."

When I looked puzzled, she continued, "They thought to take Philae along with the rest of Egypt! Our holy precinct, and the estates south of the cataract! They declared it a protectorate, and even put their filthy statues of Octavian in the temples! I could not allow it. No, I could not. It was not to be borne." She rose, slowly, like a mountain coming to its feet. "I will show you what we did!"

Like an island that miraculously moves through the sea, the Kandake floated through the vast halls of her palace and led me to the forecourt of a temple in the royal enclosure. She gave some commands in Meroitic to her attendants, who scurried away and then returned with shovels to start digging.

"I led my own bowmen on a raid to the temple, while the rest of my army attacked Philae itself, Aswan, and the Elephantine Island, and routed the Romans there. In the fighting my eye was injured, and later I lost the sight in it." She seemed to accept it as a badge of honor. "But I can see well enough with the remaining one!" She turned it fiercely on me.

"Oh, we scattered them and ran them off," she continued. "But that was not enough. No. We needed to do *this*." She pointed to the hole that was being dug before the temple, and to a roundish green object just coming into view deep in it.

As the men continued to dig, the object revealed itself to be a bronze head, which emerged from the sand like a waterlogged body floating to the surface. The workmen pulled it out and held it up, where it stared balefully at us, sand streaming off it.

It was a huge head of Octavian, the eyes looking sadly at us, starkly white against the green tarnish of the bronze. They must have been made of alabaster, but the effect was startling.

"We decapitated his statue, the one he had boldly set up inside the holy quarters. Then we brought it back here and did a ritual desecration on it, burying it in front of the temple to our victory."

The primitive fierceness of the gesture was unnerving. I felt myself to be in a very alien place indeed. Octavian's severed head kept looking at me.

"Now your Queen can rest in peace," she said. "She has been avenged." The Kandake lifted her chin proudly.

"Yes, indeed," I agreed. It seemed imprudent not to.

I have no doubt that your scrolls will be safe in her keeping.

And now to Philae, the final leg of the journey, where I shall discharge my solemn promise and complete my last duty to you. Then indeed you may rest, knowing all things are finished according to your wishes.

The Romans are still smarting from their thrashing at the hands of the Nubians, and are planning reprisals. But for now they are busy repairing the damage. I see the toppled statue of Octavian, its neck sawed through, lying on its side near the forecourt of the great Temple of Isis.

But I wish to think no more of Octavian or anything beyond this little island, with its exquisite temple, its sanctuary to Isis. White, small enough to be perfect, lying before me, I want to take possession of it. This is a Ptolemaic achievement, the marriage between Egypt and a great dynasty that became the country it conquered. Your ancestor Ptolemy V is carved on the walls, your father Ptolemy XII adorns the pylons guarding the inner sanctuary. And inside, in the sheltering dark, is the great statue of your goddess-mother, Isis. There I will leave the legacy you entrusted to me, to entrust to her. I will also leave my own, the pitiful addendum. This is where it belongs, the story drawn out to its conclusion.

All this temple is yours. In some recess, invisible to me, is the chamber where you stood when you united yourself with Caesar. You linger here, remaining just beyond the annihilating grip of Rome.

The old priest has accepted the scrolls without question. He showed me the hollow in the pedestal of the great statue of Isis, where sacred relics are kept. Reverently he has placed the ten scrolls there. He awaits this final one, but he is patient. Oh, very, very patient. I can well believe he has been here since the first Ptolemy.

Then he shows me his treasure: a statue of you, carved of tamarisk. It is life-size, and the voluptuous curves and colors of the wood give it such warmth that for a moment I can believe it is you, there, before me. It gives me both joy and pain to behold it.

He tells me he is covering it with sheets of gold, so that it may last for centuries, and you may be worshiped alongside Isis. Already you have many devotees who come here to pay homage.

It seems wrong, somehow, to cover the vitality of the wood, a living thing, with the stern eternity of gold. But just so are you transformed into a goddess, and only in that form can you endure, to soar into man's imagination and reign forever.

He tells me that Philae is a Greek corruption of the ancient Egyptian *pilak*, meaning "the end." The island was once the end of Egypt, the end of our comprehension of ourselves. So it is your end, the final resting place of your thoughts and deeds and life, guarded by gods, saved from destruction. You will never die, folded here in the embrace of Isis.

At last I believe that, and surrender you with joy.

FINIS

When I set out to write a biographical novel of Cleopatra, I kept encountering two contradictory reactions, both based on misconceptions.

The first was: Why a book about Cleopatra? Everyone already knows everything about her, don't they?—her perfumes, her snakes, her wiles, her lovers.

Indeed, no. Much of what the general public "knows" about Cleopatra comes directly from the invective of her enemies. The fact that some of her enemies were writers and poets of the caliber of Cicero, Vergil, and Horace assured that their version of events would survive and become widely known, whereas her side of the story would be officially suppressed.

The second, opposite idea: So little is known about Cleopatra and those times that it would be impossible to write meaningfully about her. Again, not so. A great deal is known about her, from the list of languages she spoke, to the names of her servants, to the timbre of her voice, to her preference for colored pottery from Rhosus in Syria. Other aspects can be deduced; for example, she must have been small and slim to have fitted undetected inside the rug. And yes, she was smuggled into Caesar's quarters inside a carpet or bedroll.

After any battle, one of the prerogatives of the winners has always been to preserve an official account of their doings and to destroy or suppress other versions. Prior to the final battle recounted in this book, both sides had their vocal partisans; after Octavian's victory, those of Antony and Cleopatra were silenced.

Nevertheless, enough unofficial material survives through secondhand sources for Cleopatra's side of the story to be pieced together. And in telling

Octavian's tale, three ancient historians writing 150 to 250 years afterward—Suetonius, Plutarch, and Dio Cassius—inadvertently preserved much of the other side's as well. Plutarch is especially helpful, as he relies on the memoirs of Cleopatra's physician, Olympos, for the famous story of her final days and death. At this point Plutarch's account switches from being hostile (Octavian's version) to showing some sympathy toward Cleopatra, an abrupt change that is preserved in Shakespeare. (That is why the Cleopatra of Act V is markedly different from the one in the rest of the play.)

As with all characters who belong as much to legend as to history—and here we have four: Cleopatra, Caesar, Octavian, and Antony—it is important to know what is real and what is not.

Many things I have described here could pass for dramatic inventions but are in fact well documented. After hiding in the rug, Cleopatra did meet Caesar, and they did become lovers the same night; her brother and his councillors did find them together the next morning. She did bear him a son whom he allowed to carry his name.

Caesarion was said to bear a striking resemblance to his father, especially in his movements and walk. And Caesar is known to have had epilepsy in his last years.

Cicero did meet Cleopatra in Rome and, judging from his comments about her in letters, had a personal grudge against her.

Antony's famous speech at Caesar's funeral ("Friends, Romans, countrymen . . .") is Shakespeare's creation; the historical one, taken from Dio Cassius, is reproduced here.

The battlefield scenes are likewise historical, as are Octavian's juicy personal attacks against Antony and Cleopatra, and vice versa. It is one of the ironies of history that the only letter of Antony's to survive (because it was quoted by Suetonius) is the angry one he dashed off to Octavian accusing him of having multiple affairs. And yes, Octavian was an active adulterer and did wear "elevator" sandals.

Mardian, Olympos, Iras, and Charmian are all historical figures, but their appearances and personalities have been imagined by me. Epaphroditus is fictional, but we must assume that Cleopatra had an astute minister of finances. Most of the other characters are real; I have not needed to invent many, and only minor ones.

The famous scene where Cleopatra met Antony costumed as Venus actually took place—although she was not on a barge, as popular mythology has it. Barges were not seaworthy and did not leave the Nile, hence she must have used a regular ship, specially equipped. Cleopatra really did give a dinner for Antony with rose petals a foot deep for the carpet, did make a wager with him on the cost, and did pretend to drink a dissolved pearl. On another night Antony really did invite her to a rough "soldiers' dinner."

The meetings and relationship I have described between Cleopatra and Herod are all historical.

Antony's personal servant really was named Eros, and he did kill himself rather than kill Antony. Octavian did have Caesarion and Antyllus killed, and it is true that one of the only things he removed from the palace in Alexandria was an agate cup that belonged to the Ptolemies.

The coinage issues are as I described them, and they were all meant to make important political statements.

The Kandake of Meroe did raid Philae, and a bronze head of Octavian was taken away to Meroe and buried to designate desecration.

And it is true that Cleopatra ended her life by the bite of the Egyptian cobra, which, according to ancient Egyptian belief, conferred a symbolic meaning to death. She probably selected it as much for this reason as for its quick, painless action.

But this is a novel, and there are also fictional creations in these pages. One of the most important is Cleopatra's mother, and her death. Surprisingly, given Cleopatra's fame, the identity of her mother is unknown. It is assumed that she was a half sister of Ptolemy XII and that she died when Cleopatra was quite young. More than that we do not know. It is also assumed that the younger children had a different mother, but again, we do not know.

Cleopatra's visit to the Kandake is fictional, although such a visit would certainly have been in character for both of them.

I have not followed the convention that Cleopatra sent false word of her death to Antony, and that Antony felt she had betrayed him. These come from hostile traditions and seem, to modern historians, unlikely. I also omitted the traditional old man with his basket of figs being the bearer of the snakes. Exactly how she arranged for the snakes is a mystery, but we know the basket of figs—minus the snakes—was found inside the mausoleum.

Since the correspondence of Caesar, Antony, and Cleopatra to one another does not survive, I have had to re-create it.

What did Cleopatra look like? The modern idea that she was actually unattractive is not borne out by the ancient historians. Dio Cassius says, "For she was a woman of surpassing beauty, and at that time, when she was in the prime of her youth, she was most striking; she also possessed a most charming voice and a knowledge of how to make herself agreeable to everyone. Being brilliant to look upon and to listen to, with the power to subjugate everyone, even a love-sated man already past his prime, she thought that it would be in keeping with her role to meet Caesar, and she reposed in her beauty all her claims to the throne."

Florus (A.D. 75–140) says that when she threw herself at Caesar's feet, "He was moved by the beauty of the damsel, which was enhanced by the fact that, being so fair, she seemed to have been wronged"; he also says later that she appealed to Octavian "in vain, for her beauty was unable to prevail over his self-control."

According to Appian (A.D. 90–165), "Antony was amazed at her wit as well as her good looks," and that "it is said . . . that he had fallen in love with her at first sight long ago when she was still a girl and he was serving as master of the horse under Gabinius at Alexandria."

Plutarch's familiar comment that "her actual beauty, it is said, was not in itself so remarkable that none could be compared with her," does not imply (as some would have it) that she was plain. All these observations seem to affirm that she was quite attractive, if not a conventional beauty. No known statues of Cleopatra survive, though some are identified as such based on the resemblance to her portrait on coins. These coins are of two types, puzzlingly unalike in looks: an attractive one in the Hellenistic style, and an idol-like one on coins she shares with Antony. The carving of her on the Temple of Hathor at Dendera, which I describe her visiting, is not an individualized portrait but a generalized representation of a queen.

What was her coloring likely to have been? The Ptolemies were Macedonian Greeks and these people exhibit a range of hair and eye shades from light (blond, blue-eyed) to dark (black hair, brown eyes). Skin tone, too, can vary from quite light to the Mediterranean "olive-skinned." I have given her dark hair because her grandmother (her one non-Ptolemaic ancestor) was half-Syrian, half-Greek. There is no evidence for Egyptian ancestry; however, she did find a spiritual affinity with her Egyptian subjects, speaking their language and honoring their ancient religion.

What became of the surviving children? All were brought up in Octavian's household. Cleopatra Selene was later married to Juba II of Mauretania, the little boy who had marched in Caesar's African Triumph; she reigned as his Queen of Mauretania from 20 B.C. to A.D. 17, and had two children, Ptolemy of Mauretania and Drusilla. One source says that Alexander Helios and Ptolemy Philadelphos went to Mauretania with them.

Ptolemy of Mauretania reigned as King from A.D. 23 to A.D. 40 but made the mistake of going to Rome to visit his cousin Caligula, who had him murdered. Some sources say Drusilla was the first wife of Marcus Antonius Felix, the Roman procurator of Judaea (he is mentioned in Acts 24:1–23), but after that she vanishes. So there are no known descendants of Cleopatra beyond the second generation.

Antony fared better. Through his oldest daughter, Antonia, who married Pythodorus of Tralles, he became the ancestor of kings and queens of Lesser Armenia, parts of Arabia, Pontus, and East Thrace. And through his two daughters by Octavia, he became the ancestor of the emperors Caligula, Claudius, and Nero.

By that time, Rome was embracing the very customs it had found so abhorrent in Antony and Cleopatra—divine monarchy and eastern extravagance. So, in spite of Octavian, their way triumphed in the end.

I must confess a fascination and commitment to Cleopatra that goes back to my own childhood; in many ways I have waited forty years to write this book. I made the first of my trips to Egypt in 1952, wrote my first school-project version of her story in 1956, and since actively working on this book I have returned to Egypt four times, have traveled to Rome, Israel, and Jordan, and have haunted the British Museum on a regular basis. It has been my privilege to spend the last four years almost exclusively in Cleopatra's presence, and I leave her side reluctantly.

For those interested in some of my sources, I include them here.

Ancient sources: Caesar's *Civil Wars, Book III; The Alexandrian War* (Cambridge: Loeb Classical Library, numbers 39, 402); Vergil, *The Aeneid,* Book VIII; Horace, Ninth Epode, Book I, Ode 37; Lucan, *Civil War,* Book Ten—a florid, lascivious, and imaginative account of Caesar and Cleopatra's time in Alexandria. Lucan fills in all the blanks the discreet Caesar left in his account of the same events.

Appian of Alexandria, in *Roman History: The Civil Wars,* Books II–V, written around A.D. 140, gives a relatively fair account of Antony's story, although he lays the blame for his ruin on Cleopatra, as does Velleius Paterculus, writing around A.D. 30, in *History of Rome,* Book II, which is anti-Antony as well as anti-Cleopatra. Cicero provides much contemporary material in his letters to Atticus, and in his Philippics against Antony.

The three main sources for a personal feeling about the characters, though, are Suetonius's *The Twelve Caesars,* written about A.D. 110 (he has a life of Caesar and a life of Augustus); Plutarch's *Lives,* written about A.D. 120 (he has lives of Caesar, Brutus, and Antony, and is our most important single source on Cleopatra, drawing on material from Olympos as well as family knowledge), and Dio Cassius, *Roman History,* written around A.D. 220. Dio provides a helpful chronological framework for the episodes in Suetonius and Plutarch.

Shakespeare, of course, must be included for his *Julius Caesar* and *Antony and Cleopatra,* both inspired by Plutarch.

A basic modern work is *Cambridge Ancient History* (London: Cambridge University Press, 1934, volumes IX and X; second edition of volume IX, 1994).

Modern biographies of Cleopatra include Michael Grant, *Cleopatra* (New York: Dorset Press, 1992 [reprint of 1972 edition]), a balanced, thorough, and readable life; Ernle Bradford, *Cleopatra* (London: Hodder and Stoughton Ltd., 1971), a beautifully illustrated and well-written popular history of the queen; Arthur Weigall, *The Life and Times of Cleopatra* (London: Thornton Butterworth Ltd., 1914), an early but engaging recounting by the Inspector General of Antiquities in Egypt; Jack Lindsay, *Cleopatra* (London: Cox & Wyman Ltd., 1971), especially good with the prophecies and symbolism; Hans Volkmann, *Cleopatra: A Study in Politics and Propaganda* (New York: Sagamore Press, 1958), one of the first to examine her legend from this viewpoint, paying particular attention to Octavian's propaganda machine; Lucy Hughes-Hallett, *Cleopatra: Histories, Dreams and Distortions* (New York: Harper & Row, 1990), a fascinating look at all the ways Cleopatra has been seen through the ages, which reveals as much about us as about her.

As for the other main characters, there are many biographies about Caesar. I can recommend Michael Grant's *Julius Caesar* (New York: M. Evans & Co., 1992 [reprint of 1969 edition]); Ernle Bradford, *Julius Caesar: The Pursuit of Power* (London: Hamish Hamilton Ltd., 1984); Matthias Gelzer, *Caesar: Politician and Statesman* (Oxford: Basil Blackwell, 1968); Christian Meier, *Caesar* (London: HarperCollins, 1995 [original German edition, 1982]); J. A.

Froude, *Caesar, A Sketch* (New York: Scribner's, 1914), an early "psychobiography."

Marc Antony has not been blessed with so many biographies to choose from. The most recent, Eleanor Goltz Huzar's *Mark Antony* (Minneapolis: University of Minnesota Press, 1978), is difficult to find but worth the search; Jack Lindsay's *Marc Antony: His World and His Contemporaries* (London: Routledge & Sons, Ltd., 1936) is well written; and Arthur Weigall's readable *The Life and Times of Marc Antony* (New York: G. P. Putnam's Sons, 1931) completes the trio.

Biographies aside, I can recommend a number of books about the period in general and other specific topics. Peter Green's *Alexander to Actium* (Los Angeles: University of California Press, 1990) is a huge, sweeping, brilliantly written panorama of the three-hundred-year Hellenistic Age; Paul Zanker, *The Power of Images in the Age of Augustus* (Ann Arbor: University of Michigan Press, 1988), is a careful and interesting study of the ways Octavian used visual images to create his own myth; Robert Alan Gurval, *Actium and Augustus* (Ann Arbor: University of Michigan Press, 1995), is a close look at the symbols used by Octavian after he vanquished Antony. John M. Carter, *The Battle of Actium: The Rise and Triumph of Augustus Caesar* (New York: Weybright and Talley, 1970), is an invaluable study of the situation, and actually quite favorable toward Antony; Ronald Syme, *The Roman Revolution* (Oxford: Oxford University Press, 1939), is the classic study of the period, and has no illusions about Octavian.

On more general topics, Roland Auguet, *Cruelty and Civilization: The Roman Games* (London: George Allen & Unwin Ltd., 1972), tells about the games and spectacles in gory detail; Guido Majno, *The Healing Hand: Man and Wound in the Ancient World* (Cambridge: Harvard University Press, 1975), offers a compulsively readable account of ancient medicine by an eminent modern scientist/physician; Ilaria Gozzini Giacosa, *A Taste of Ancient Rome* (Chicago: University of Chicago Press, 1992), reveals everything you always wanted to know about Roman dinner parties, and how to give one.

There is also Michael Grant's *The Army of the Caesars* (New York: Scribner, 1974), covering equipment and tactics; Judith Swaddling, *The Ancient Olympic Games* (London: British Museum Press, 1980); and Lionel Casson, *Ships and Seafaring in Ancient Times* (London: British Museum Press, 1994), a fascinating guide as to what went on on the seas long ago.